Bolan barely had time to reach out

In the same motion, he instinctively lashed out with his other hand, striking his attacker with a karate chop to the shoulder.

The blow was slight but still strong enough to throw the youth off balance. He lost his grip on Bolan's shirt as he flailed his arms, trying to keep himself from reeling backward. His reactions were too slow, however. One second Bolan was staring into the youth's horror-stricken eyes; the next he was gone.

Thirty yards below, the youth was splayed across the boulders, skull cracked open, his lifeblood spilling over the rocks. Bolan felt a grim weariness come over him. Young men who were supposed to be a part of America's bright future had chosen to die trying to bring their country down.

"What a waste," Bolan whispered into the night.

D1115244

MACK BOLAN ®
The Executioner

The Executioner
Don Pendleton's®

HOMELAND TERROR

A GOLD EAGLE BOOK FROM
WORLDWIDE®

TORONTO • NEW YORK • LONDON
AMSTERDAM • PARIS • SYDNEY • HAMBURG
STOCKHOLM • ATHENS • TOKYO • MILAN
MADRID • WARSAW • BUDAPEST • AUCKLAND

First edition November 2006
ISBN-13: 978-0-373-64336-3
ISBN-10:   0-373-64336-5

Special thanks and acknowledgment to
Ron Renauld for his contribution to this work.

HOMELAND TERROR

It is easy to be brave behind a castle wall.
—*Welsh Proverb*

Rich and powerful men manipulate the weak and poor to do their evil bidding. I will make sure that justice is served to those cowards.
—Mack Bolan

THE
MACK BOLAN
LEGEND

Nothing less than a war could have fashioned the destiny of the man called Mack Bolan. Bolan earned the Executioner title in the jungle hell of Vietnam.

But this soldier also wore another name—Sergeant Mercy. He was so tagged because of the compassion he showed to wounded comrades-in-arms and Vietnamese civilians.

Mack Bolan's second tour of duty ended prematurely when he was given emergency leave to return home and bury his family, victims of the Mob. Then he declared a one-man war against the Mafia.

He confronted the Families head-on from coast to coast, and soon a hope of victory began to appear. But Bolan had broken society's every rule. That same society started gunning for this elusive warrior—to no avail.

So Bolan was offered amnesty to work within the system against terrorism. This time, as an employee of Uncle Sam, Bolan became Colonel John Phoenix. With a command center at Stony Man Farm in Virginia, he and his new allies—Able Team and Phoenix Force—waged relentless war on a new adversary: the KGB.

But when his one true love, April Rose, died at the hands of the Soviet terror machine, Bolan severed all ties with Establishment authority.

Now, after a lengthy lone-wolf struggle and much soul-searching, the Executioner has agreed to enter an "arm's-length" alliance with his government once more, reserving the right to pursue personal missions in his Everlasting War.

Prologue

Sykesville, Maryland

It was Mack Bolan's second day at the Wildest Dreams Covert Ops Fantasy Camp. So far he'd been impressed by the camp's regimen, which approximated the Stony Man blacksuit trainee program back at his own base of operations in Virginia. Already he'd undergone rigorous exercise workouts, field drills, martial-arts seminars, and an afternoon devoted to countersurveillance techniques and evasive driving maneuvers.

For the blacksuits, tests of this sort were more of a review, as most were culled from law enforcement or the military and had already proved themselves fit, as well as competent to engage the enemy. In sharp contrast, the two dozen initiates at the fantasy camp were, with few exceptions, unprepared for the physical challenges they'd coughed up nearly four grand apiece to take part in at the former Fort Hadley Army base. Most of Bolan's bunkmates were a motley crew of Walter Mittys, overweight desk jockeys and delusional Rambo wanna-bes who, by the end of the week, would no doubt welcome a return to the humdrum of their nine-to-five jobs. Not surprisingly, within five minutes of lights-out, everyone in the barracks—including the few campers who'd weathered the day's challenges without collaps-ing—had surrendered to exhaustion and was fast asleep.

Everyone, that was, except for Mack Bolan a.k.a. the Execu-tioner.

He lay still a few minutes longer, then quietly slipped out of his sleeping bag and threw on the camou fatigues he'd been issued shortly after arriving at the camp the previous day before under the name Mel Schiraldi. With his dark hair trimmed to a buzz cut and his cobalt-blue eyes cloaked by a pair of brown contact lenses, Bolan bore a passing resemblance to the real Mr. Schiraldi, a Baltimore fitness instructor who'd made his reservations with Wildest Dreams more than three months earlier. Schiraldi had been convinced to let Bolan take his place in exchange for an all-expenses-paid Caribbean cruise and five thousand dollars in spending money, all courtesy of the Sensitive Operation Group's discretionary fund. A small price to pay, SOG director Hal Brognola had reasoned, to allow Bolan to infiltrate the fantasy camp without drawing the suspicion he would have received as a last-minute walk-in.

Once he'd dressed, Bolan quietly carried his boots past the other bunks. Moonlight shone through the barracks windows, illuminating the wooden floorboards. Bolan took care to step on the joints where the wood was hammered down tight and less inclined to creak under the weight of his hard-toned, two-hundred-plus-pound frame. It was a trick Bolan had picked up through his years of stalking the omnipresent beast he called Animal Man, a beast that at various times had taken the shape of everything from Mafia hit man to al Qaeda terrorist. This night, Bolan was out to stalk yet another manifestation of that beast.

The rear doorway of the barracks opened onto a crushed-gravel path that wound through thickets of overgrown bramble to the latrines. It was late spring, and the small stones were cold against the Executioner's bare feet. Once he came to a break in the shrubbery, Bolan abandoned the path and headed through tall grass to a knoll canopied by the branches of an ancient magnolia grove. Bolan paused at the base of one of the trees and donned his socks, then pried loose the thick heels of his customized boots.

Each of the heels was hollowed out to form a storage cavity. One heel contained a set of foldaway lock picks and a miniature earbud transceiver. Wedged into the other cavity was the closest thing to a weapon that Bolan had at his immediate disposal: a palm-sized neoprene plastic box that contained a high-powered flashlight, GPS transmitter and a firing tube loaded with a single .22-caliber round. Bolan hoped to complete his mission without being drawn into a firefight, but if it came to that, the minigun would at least be a step up, however small, from taking on the enemy unarmed.

Bolan extended the transceiver's retractable flex mike and clicked it on before planting it in his ear. Within seconds he was in contact with Stony Man pilot Jack Grimaldi.

"I'm on the prowl," Bolan whispered.

"Gotcha," came the tinny reply through his earbud. "GPS signal's coming in strong."

"Stand by, then. I'm going in."

Bolan tapped the earbud, shutting down the transmission. He quickly snapped the heels back into place, then slipped on his boots and made his way to the last of the magnolias.

Downhill from his position was a cinder-block storage building no larger than a one-car garage. Earlier in the day, while driving a BMW Z3 on an obstacle course through the surrounding foothills, Bolan had glimpsed a Ford pickup truck pull up to the shed. The road had quickly led him beyond view of the vehicle, but once he'd finished his road test—deliberately nudging a few pylons so as to not advertise his expertise behind the wheel—Bolan had passed the compound just as two men transferred a heavy crate from the truck to the outbuilding. Judging from the crate's apparent weight and coffinlike dimensions, the Executioner had felt certain that he'd confirmed that the fantasy camp served as a cache for stolen arms reported missing three days earlier from the U.S. Army's proving grounds in nearby Aberdeen.

Such thefts were disturbing enough when they involved firearms and conventional ammunition. But in this case, along with an assortment of M-16s and government-issue autopistols, the thieves had gotten their hands on an even more worrisome weapons trove. The implications of the heist were grave enough to earn mention in the daily intelligence brief that had crossed the President's White House desk the morning after the incident.

The President, in turn, had placed a priority call to Stony Man Farm, putting into motion the plan that now saw Mack Bolan roaming the fantasy camp grounds in the guise of fitness guru Mel Schiraldi.

The Executioner lingered a moment at the top of the hill, waiting for the moon to disappear behind an incoming bank of clouds. Drifting on the faint breeze was the smell of barbecued chicken. Bolan shifted his gaze to a two-story clapboard building nestled between the foothills a hundred yards away, near the same mountain road where he and the other campers had earlier tested their driving skills. Smoke trailed up from behind the building, which had once served as the Army base's administrative headquarters and now housed the Wildest Dreams "faculty." Bolan assumed there had to be some sort of patio behind the building with an outdoor grill. He also figured the camp staff was likely having a late dinner.

Like him, they'd barely broken a sweat during the day's activities, and he knew it would be awhile before they all turned in. Their rooms were in the same building, though, and the previous night when Bolan had staked out the quarters, no one had ventured out once the lights had been dimmed. The only other personnel to be concerned about were guards posted out near the main entrance to the complex, but the gate was nearly a quarter mile away, hidden from view behind the bramble and magnolia trees.

The lax security led Bolan to believe that the camp organizers were confident their fantasy enterprise allowed them a means by which to hide in plain sight and pursue their ulterior business without drawing scrutiny. Clearly, the founders of Wildest Dreams—retired Marine Sergeant Jason Cummings and longtime *Mercenary Quarterly* editor Mitch Brower—were unaware that the Bureau of Alcohol, Tobacco and Firearms had recently linked them to trafficking in black market arms, not only with overseas soldiers-of-fortune, but also a number of U.S.-based militia outfits, including several fringe groups advocating an overthrow of the federal government. Bolan, like his SOG counterparts and the President himself, was concerned that the

Aberdeen weapons heist signaled the approach of that day when the militias crossed the line from mere propagandizing to carrying out their threats of armed insurrection.

Once the clouds fully obscured the moon, Bolan broke from the trees and started downhill. Halfway to the storage building, he froze. Behind him, he heard the sound of an approaching car. He was near the camp's outdoor workout area and quickly took cover behind a stack of old tires used for agility drills. Moments later, the twin beams of the BMW Z3's headlights swept across the grounds. The sports car was heading down the road that led to the main building. The Executioner ducked still lower as the lights passed over him. Clutching his paltry minigun, Bolan held his breath and listened intently for any sign the car was slowing.

The BMW purred steadily as it drew closer. Bolan was on the driver's side of the road and, as the Z3 rolled past, maintaining its speed, he peered out and caught a glimpse of the man behind the wheel. It was Mitch Brower, the *Mercenary Quarterly* editor, a square-jawed, middle-aged man with close-cropped gray hair and sideburns. In the passenger seat was a woman. Bolan's view was too obstructed for him to get a good look at her other than to note that she had long, straight hair and lean features. She and Brower were talking to each other, clearly unaware they were being watched.

Bolan waited for the car to pass, then crawled to the cover of a chest-high length of concrete sewer pipe half-submerged in a shallow, man-made pond. As part of their training the day before, he and the other campers had been forced to slog into the pond's icy water and then crawl through the pipe wearing a full backpack. The Executioner had aced the test and then gone back in the water a second time when one of the campers had been overcome with claustrophobia halfway through the pipe.

Staring past the pipe, Bolan watched Brower pull around to the side of the building and ease into a parking space between a Chevy Suburban and Jason Cummings's Hummer H2. Also parked in the lot were an open-topped Jeep and a handful of older cars whose crumpled frames were a testimony to their use in demonstrations on how to bypass roadblocks and crash through gates and fences.

The woman let herself out of the car and walked at arm's length from Brower as they headed toward the front walk. From the way she carried herself, the Executioner sensed that she was younger than Brower, but there was no suggestion of intimacy between them. She was more likely a colleague than Brower's mistress Bolan figured. He wondered what role, if any, she might have played in the Aberdeen heist. There was no point dwelling on it now, however, he realized.

There was work to be done....

"SO, WHAT'S THE VERDICT?" Joan VanderMeer asked as she and Mitch Brower entered the converted administration building. The quarters were sparsely furnished, and there was little in the paneled front entryway other than a framed movie photograph of George C. Scott portraying General Patton and a bulletin board festooned with business cards and flyers posted by previous participants in the fantasy camp.

"That chicken smells good," Brower responded evasively as he closed the door behind him. "I hope there's some left."

"We just ate, remember?" VanderMeer teased as she swept a strand of reddish hair from her forehead. The woman was in her early thirties, with pale blue eyes and a slowly fading spray of freckles across her upper cheeks. She looked like a genteel elementary schoolteacher, but the tone of authority in her voice suggested she didn't need to be around children to show that she was in charge. In truth, there were few figures more influential in the militia movement.

"And don't change the subject," she added, engaging Brower with a smile that was as direct as it was disarming.

Brower grinned back at the woman. Over dinner down the road at a Sykesville diner, Brower had listened patiently as VanderMeer lobbied him on the merits of starting up a Web site to supplement the editorial content of his soldier-of-fortune magazine. She'd put forth a convincing argument—citing increased revenue from merchandising and a wider advertising base—and had offered to not only personally help set up the site but to also bring in someone who could maintain the site. Brower was old school when it came to favoring the printed page as the best means of getting his message across, but he knew there was a ring of truth to VanderMeer's sales pitch. Furthermore, a part of him was resigned to the fact that his dwindling subscription base was due largely to the growth of the Internet. If he didn't change with the times, Brower suspected that he would eventually find himself obsolete, along with the magazine he'd spent more than twenty years running.

"You're as headstrong as your father used to be, you know that?" Brower told the woman as he led her down a long corridor to the dining room.

"I'll take that as a compliment," VanderMeer said. "But you're still not answering my question."

"All right, all right, I give up!" Brower said with mock exasperation. "My God, woman, you're more persistent than my athlete's feet."

"Just don't get any ideas about rubbing some kind of ointment on me." VanderMeer smiled back at him. "Unless I ask first, of course."

The pair shared a laugh as they entered the dining room. Jason Cummings and the rest of the fantasy staff were finishing their chicken dinners. Cummings was Brower's age, a bald man with an antiquated handlebar mustache and nearly the same physique he'd had more than thirty years earlier when he'd played nose tackle in the Rose Bowl for Army. His eyesight hadn't fared quite as well, but he was too vain for glasses; the crow's-feet at the corners of his eyes elongated as he looked up from his plate and squinted at Brower and VanderMeer.

"Sounds like you got yourself another convert, there, Joanie," he said, smirking at the woman. Cummings had succumbed to VanderMeer's sales pitch more than a year earlier, bringing her in to upgrade the fantasy camp's Web site.

"Something like that," Brower conceded.

Cummings was seated at the end of an elongated dining table. The four other men at the table, all in their mid-forties, were all absorbed with attacking the food heaped on their plates. Louie Paxton, a long-haired, potbellied veteran of the NASCAR circuit, oversaw most of the camp's road tests. The man seated next to him, Xavier Manuel, had served four stints as a Marine drill sergeant, making him the natural choice to lord over the workout area. Similarly, Ed "Charlie" Chang's years as a stunt double in Japanese kung-fu movies had given him the experience to run campers through a rudimentary course in the martial arts.

Paxton, Manuel and Chang had been hired solely to keep up the pretense that Cummings and Brower ran nothing more than a bona fide fantasy camp. They were well-compensated for their work, and even if they had reason to suspect Wildest Dreams was a front for other activities, their weekly paychecks left them disinclined to ask questions.

The fourth staff member, Marcus Yarborough, was another matter. Hired based on a referral by Joan VanderMeer, Yarborough was in charge of the camp's shooting range, trading in on his purported experience as a Navy SEAL marksman. Cummings and Brower had been told the man had done some trigger work outside the Armed Forces, as well, and twice over the past three years Yarborough had been contracted to kill fantasy camp participants who'd unwittingly stumbled upon evidence of clandestine activity. In both cases, the murders had been carried out after the victims had been lured from the premises: one wound up dead in a supposed hunting accident while the other's death went down in the books as a suicide. Yarborough had carried out the hits without being told what evidence his victims had come across. He'd convinced Cummings and Brower that the less he knew about their illegal activities, the better. In return, he demanded the same discretion with regards to his past, about which he was resolutely tight-lipped.

Thin and clean-shaved, the sharpshooter rarely smiled and always seemed preoccupied with some grave matter that took precedence, at least in his mind, over what was going on around him. When introducing him to campers, Brower and Cummings took a good-natured swipe at Yarborough's brooding nature and invariably referred to him as the Grim Reaper. The campers lapped it up, and the ex-SEAL commando was almost always mentioned whenever people wrote back to say what a good time they'd had at the camp. Yarborough was, after all, the embodiment of the cold, detached assassin they'd seen in countless spy thrillers.

By the time Yarborough finished eating, Cummings and Brower had left the dining room to confer down the hall at the camp's administrative office. Joan VanderMeer had remained behind and was flirting with Louie Paxton and Eddie Chang, but when she finally caught the sharpshooter's gaze, she twitched her head slightly, indicating the door that led out to the back patio.

Yarborough nodded faintly, then took care of his dishes and fished through his shirt pocket for a pack of cigarillos. There was no smoking allowed in the building, so Yarborough headed for the patio.

"Got a spare one of those I could try?" Joan called out to him, giving herself a reason to follow Yarborough outside.

"Suit yourself," the marksman told her.

VanderMeer finished the joke she was telling the other men, then excused herself and followed Yarborough outside. The patio was little more than a small, square slab of concrete crowded with a couple of warped Adirondack chairs and a propane-fueled barbecue. Yarborough offered Joan one of his cigarillos, but she waved him off.

"You know I hate those things," she told him.

Yarborough shrugged and lit up, then spoke through a cloud of smoke. "You wanted to see me?"

VanderMeer nodded. "You know about the heist at Aberdeen the other night, right?" she said.

"Maybe," Yarborough replied. "It's none of my business."

"You helped unload the crates this afternoon," VanderMeer said.

"Doesn't make it my business," Yarborough countered. A sudden cough rumbled up through his chest. The sharpshooter doubled over, as if trying to force the cough down. It didn't work. He hacked violently, then spit into the gravel at the base of the barbecue.

VanderMeer couldn't be certain, but it looked as if he was coughing up blood.

"Jesus, are you okay?" she asked.

Yarborough shrugged. "Down the wrong pipe," he said. "Don't sweat it."

VanderMeer stared at Yarborough, then went on, "Look, there's something you should know. Not everything from that heist was stashed away in the shed here. There was one piece that—"

The woman was interrupted as the door to the patio swung open and Jason Cummings poked his head out, a 9 mm Uzi submachine gun clutched in his right hand.

"There you are," he told Yarborough. "Grab a gun, quick!"

"Problem?" Yarborough asked, grinding his cigarillo into the gravel. His coughing jag had passed as quickly as it had overtaken him.

"Somebody tripped an alarm out on the grounds," Cummings said. "They've broken into that storage shed near the pond."

THE ALARM WAS SILENT, but Bolan spotted the separated sensor pads above the door the moment he entered the storage shed. The entire system was rigged from the inside, and there was no way he could have spotted it prior to picking the lock, but still the Executioner chided himself for the oversight. *I should have known,* he thought to himself angrily.

Bolan fought off the urge to flee. Instead he tapped his earbud transceiver as he moved deeper into the enclosure, directing the beam of his palm-sized flashlight onto the crates stored against the far wall. There were more of them than he was anticipating— nearly a dozen in all—but only a few bore stenciling that linked them back to the Aberdeen proving grounds. By the time Jack Grimaldi's voice crackled in his ear, Bolan had honed in on one of the stenciled crates and pried the wooden lid open.

"What's up?" Grimaldi asked.

"I tripped an alarm," Bolan reported, even as he was staring down at the cache of missing weapons he'd come to the fantasy camp looking for. "The good news is I found the rocket launchers. All but one, that is."

Secured within custom-cut, foam-lined compartments inside the crate Bolan had just opened were three Army-issue M-136

AT-4 rocket launchers, each loaded with an 84 mm warhead capable of piercing nearly 400 mm of rolled homogenous armor, a thickness surpassing that found on most tanks and concrete bunkers. There was a conspicuous cavity in the molded foam where a fourth launcher had once rested.

"Forget the damn launchers," Grimaldi snapped. "I'm coming in. Get your ass out where I can see it!"

"Will do," Bolan said, "once I find something better than Cowboy's popgun to defend myself with."

Bolan clicked off the earbud and hurriedly inspected the contraband stored in the other crates. By the time the first glimmer of Jason Cummings's headlights shone through the open doorway of the shed, Bolan had found what he was looking for.

"I KNEW IT WAS A MISTAKE to move that stuff here and sit on it!" Jason Cummings seethed as he gave the Hummer more gas. "We should've stashed it all off-site somewhere!"

"Hind-fucking sight doesn't help us!" Mitch Brower snapped in response. He knew Cummings was right, though, and was furious with himself for having insisted they keep their cache of stolen weapons close by until they'd brokered deals to sell them. There was still a chance this would prove to be a false alarm—something as benign as rats tripping the sensors or one of the campers out snooping around—but in his gut Brower knew better. They were in trouble.

The Hummer's front tires squealed in protest as the retired sergeant rounded the curve leading to the workout area. The Uzi was cradled in his lap. Brower sat next to him with a slightly larger 9 mm L-34 A-1 Sterling, the mainstay subgun of Britain's Royal Marines. Glowing in the rearview mirror were the headlights of the Jeep that Marcus Yarborough was driving.

Eddie Chang was riding shotgun alongside Yarborough in the rear vehicle, having ignored Cummings's orders to stay behind with Joan VanderMeer, Louie Paxton and Xavier Manuel. Having no idea what was at stake, the martial-arts expert was treating the whole affair as a lark. He was unarmed and assumed that Yarborough's Uzi was loaded with blanks.

"C'mon, admit it," Chang shouted over the roar of the Jeep's engine. "This is one of those improv exercises, right? Like that time the sergeant hired those Green Berets to barge in pretending they were armed robbers fleeing a bank job."

"Zip it!" Yarborough yelled back, eyes fixed on the road ahead. He took the next turn sharply, staying close behind the Hummer. Up ahead, he thought he could see a figure charging out of the storage shed. Yarborough thought back to earlier in the day when he'd grudgingly helped Mitch Brower haul several weapons crates into the shed from the back of a Ford pickup. He wondered if he'd gotten himself caught up in some kind of government sting operation, and as he quickly scanned the surrounding grounds, he half expected to see a SWAT force materialize out of the shadows. What he got instead was the sudden, blinding glare of a flash grenade that had just detonated on the road in front of the Hummer.

"What the hell?" Eddie Chang raised a hand before his face, but the grenade had already left him temporarily blinded.

Yarborough was similarly stricken, and he feared Cummings and Brower had probably been blinded in the Hummer directly ahead of him. He figured Cummings would go for his brakes and did likewise.

The Jeep's tires screeched, and Yarborough felt the vehicle go into a skid. Any second he expected to slam into the rear of the larger vehicle.

"We're dead," he muttered.

BOLAN KNEW the incendiary flash was coming. Before the grenade burst forth with its blinding light, the Executioner turned his back to the explosion and cast his eyes downward, locking them on the 7.62 mm Belgian FN FAL carbine he'd wrested from one of the crates inside the storage shed. He'd already fed a 20-round cartridge into the breech and cleared the weapon for firing. The grenade had tipped the balance in his favor, but only for a moment. Bolan knew he was outnumbered. If he didn't act fast, any second he would be outgunned, as well.

Once he heard the crunch of colliding metal, Bolan turned

back toward the road and drew a bead on the Hummer, which had slewed sideways and skidded halfway off the road. The vehicle was so large it was difficult to even see the Jeep that had rear-ended it. Not that it mattered. Bolan's focus was on the men in the front seat of the Hummer. He could tell that Brower and Cummings were still half-blinded, but they both had their subguns in view and would likely start firing once they could see their target.

Bolan wasn't about to let it come to that. Finger on the trigger, he cut loose with the assault rifle, raking the Hummer's front windshield with a concentrated autoburst. The glass shattered and the men inside the vehicle shuddered as the rounds slammed into them, killing them both before either could get off a shot.

By now the afterglow of the flash grenade had dissipated, leaving the grounds even darker to the eye than before the explosion. Far behind Bolan, past the tree-lined knoll, the Executioner could hear the first cries of the fantasy campers as they rushed from their barracks, drawn by the blast. Bolan suspected guards from the main gate would also be racing to the scene any second, joined perhaps by more men from the main building. No one had yet emerged from the Jeep that had crashed into the rear of the Hummer, but Bolan wasn't about to waste precious seconds moving forward to engage them. He wasn't about to stand around waiting on the arrival of Jack Grimaldi, either.

Bolan had taken a second grenade with him when he'd left the storage shed, this one an avacado-sized M-61 fragger. Once he'd stepped several yards to the edge of the man-made pond, he thumbed free the safety pin, then lobbed the projectile back toward the shed. He'd left the door wide open, and the grenade sailed clearly through the opening. Bolan couldn't recall exactly how much of a delay the grenade was equipped with, but he took advantage of what little time he had, casting aside the carbine and diving into cold, murky depths of the training pond. By the time the grenade detonated, he'd clawed his way inside the half-submerged sewer pipe.

THE INITIAL BLAST of the frag grenade was fierce enough. But when shock waves and incendiary bursts ripped through the weapons carts and triggered secondary explosions, the shed was turned into the equivalent of one large bomb. For a second it looked as if the sun had briefly awakened from a nightmare, as the shed gave off a glow far more baleful than that of the flash grenade.

Off in the distance, the campers who'd rushed from the barracks clutched at the nearby magnolias to keep from being thrown to the ground by the earthquakelike trembling beneath their feet. Downhill, the shock waves were even more intense, rocking the Hummer sideways and sending it tumbling on top of the Jeep, which had already been rendered inoperable after rear-ending the larger vehicle.

Eddie Chang, dazed and still half-blind in the front seat of the Jeep, opened his mouth to scream when the Hummer loomed above him like some pouncing beast. The scream died in his throat, however, as he was crushed by the three-ton juggernaut. Marcus Yarborough was spared a similar fate, as he'd been thrown sideways out of the Jeep during the initial impact. He'd landed hard on one knee, then passed out when his head struck the asphalt.

When he came to moments later, roused by the trembling of the road beneath him, Yarborough's first impression had been that someone was shaking him awake. Disoriented, a din in his ears and his field of vision swarming with blips of light that zoomed about like errant spaceships, Yarborough groaned and slowly sat up. A shiver of pain radiated from his bruised knee. The Hummer had come to a rest on its side only a few feet away, and he could see Mitch Brower's bloody corpse dangling halfway out the shattered windshield. The nearby Jeep had been left half-flattened, its tires blown out, Eddie Chang crushed nearly beyond recognition.

By the time Yarborough had fully regained his wits, a handful of fantasy campers were on their way down the slope leading to the workout area. Their eyes were not on the sharpshooter, however, so much as on the fiery crater where the storage shed had once stood. Nothing remained of the structure but a few chunks of foundation and smoldering bits of cinder block lying in the surrounding grass. Recalling the weapons crates he'd helped transfer into the shed earlier in the day, the sharpshooter began to realize what had just happened.

Before the campers could reach him, Yarborough heard the bleat of a car horn. Turning to his right, he saw the BMW Z3 pull up alongside him. Its lights were off, and he couldn't see who was behind the wheel until Joan VanderMeer leaned over and swung open the passenger door.

"Hurry!" she urged. "Get in!"

Yarborough grabbed hold of the door and stood up, then tumbled into the front seat next to VanderMeer. He barely had time to close the door before the woman had shifted the car back into gear. She drove off the road long enough to circle around the other two vehicles, then returned to the asphalt and accelerated as she headed back toward the camp headquarters and the mountains that loomed behind it. As she switched on the headlights and gave the sports car more gas, VanderMeer told Yarborough, "We're outta here!"

THE HALF-SUNKEN SEWER PIPE Bolan had crawled inside withstood the concussive force of the blasts that had neutralized the storage shed, but the pond had been showered with debris. When he emerged from the concrete tube and stood, drenched and shivering in the waist-deep pond, the Executioner was surrounded by floating bits of shrapnel, some of it giving off wisps of smoke. He'd lost his earbud somewhere in the pipe and wasn't about to go back searching for it. Instead, he slogged his way to the steep embankment and pulled himself up to level ground.

Bolan quickly surveyed the aftermath of the mayhem he'd unleashed, then glanced skyward, alerted by the sound of an approaching helicopter. Soon he could see the aircraft sweeping past the magnolia treetops. He wasn't sure if he was still giving off a GPS signal, so he made a point to wave his arms. If Grimaldi was looking his way, Bolan figured the pilot would be able pick up his silhouette backlit by the still-blazing crater.

One of the campers thought Bolan was signaling to him and

waved back, shouting, "I see you, man! What the hell happened?"

"Is this for real?" another of the campers said, eyes fixed on the bodies ensnarled in the overturned Hummer and the half-crushed Jeep. "Hell, those guys look like they're fucking dead!"

Bolan paid no heed to the questions. He'd shifted his gaze back toward the administration building and the hills behind it. He could see taillights up on the mountain road, and once he checked the parking lot next to the building, he knew that someone was fleeing in the BMW. He also knew that by the time Grimaldi picked him up, it would likely be too late for them to give chase. Just on the other side of the mountain was the main highway, as well as the residential sprawl of Sykesville. Too many escape routes, too many places to hide.

As he waited for Grimaldi to land the chopper, Bolan glanced back at the crater. At least he had the satisfaction of having destroyed the weapons cache before it could be put to use by enemies of the state. Even that realization was tempered somewhat, however, as Bolan couldn't help wonder what had happened to the one rocket launcher left unaccounted for. It was still out there, he realized, like a proverbial loose cannon.

McLean, Virginia

Edgar Byrnes's breath clouded in the chilled March air as he brushed snow off the woodpile and gathered a few logs for his evening fire. It was dusk. The moon was out, a thin, waxing sliver poised like a scythe above the dark storm clouds rolling in from the Atlantic. A faint breeze stirred through the forest of elms and sycamores surrounding the four-acre farm Byrnes called home. Leaves were budding on the trees despite the late frost, but through the branches Byrnes was still able to glimpse the outline of a monolithic building located a quarter mile away on the other side of the woods. It was the only visible trace of modern civilization, and in another week or two Byrnes knew the trees would fill in, obscuring the structure from view entirely.

We can't wait much longer, Byrnes thought to himself as he carried the logs past a weathered lean-to shared by three cows, two horses and menagerie of pigs, chickens and sheep. One of the horses, a sturdy roan with a jet-black mane and tail, was out in the corral, snorting as it paced back and forth through the mud.

"Sorry, Jefferson," Byrnes called out. "Too cold to go riding tonight."

Once he reached his small one-room cabin, Byrnes freed one hand to let himself in, then kicked the door shut behind him. Last month, shortly after he'd been hired to work the farm, his first job had been to patch cracks in the mortar between the hand-hewn logs that formed the cabin's four walls. He'd done a good job but such crude insulation could only keep out so much of the cold; inside it was still freezing.

After setting the logs onto a bed of kindling in the large stone fireplace, Byrnes blew on his hands and rubbed them over the lone flame of an oil lamp he'd left burning on a nearby table. Once the feeling came back to his fingers, he plucked a few hay straws off the dirt floor and used the lamp to light them, then crouched before the stacked wood. The straws' flames crackled as they took hold of the kindling and began to spread. Soon the logs had caught fire as well, sending smoke up the chimney.

Byrnes pulled a wooden rocker close to the hearth and sat down. His workday, which had begun nearly twelve hours ago at the crack of dawn, was finally over. He smiled tiredly, filled with a sense of accomplishment.

It would soon be a full eight weeks that Byrnes, a thirty-two-year-old Gulf War veteran, had been working at the Michael Conlon Farm, a state-owned Colonial homestead painstakingly maintained to reflect what ordinary farm life had been like back in the days of the country's founding fathers. For Byrnes the experience had been a joyful revelation, so much so that there had been times when, for days on end, he had forgotten the true reason he'd come to work here. He'd learned so much in that time: how to make soap from tallow; how to tan animal hides and use the leather to make shoes and clothes; how to spin wool from sheep; the best way to fetch water from nearby streams and boil it with fresh vegetables from the garden to make a nourishing stew.

The past few weeks in particular, when he'd come to be the sole caretaker living on the premises, had been like heaven. Having the place to himself most days, he exulted in the solitude and isolation, the sense that he had indeed been transported back to a time when America was the home of those who were self-reliant and bound by high ideals—a time before values had eroded in the face of complacency and the government had grown into what Byrnes felt was a festering cancer eating away at the foundation upon which the nation had been built.

Staring into the fire, stroking the thick brown beard he'd grown to cover chemical burns sustained during his time in the Gulf,

Byrnes found himself wondering, as he had so many nights before, what it had to have been like to have been a part of that simpler and nobler past. Of one thing he was certain: back then the men who'd put their lives on the line to fight the Revolution had been treated as heroes and looked after once the war had been won. Nothing like today. No being shuttled through some uncaring bureaucratic maze; no denial of hard-earned benefits; no shameless attempts to dismiss claims of illness stemming from exposure to carcinogens and other toxins while in the line of duty. And all those years ago, Byrnes knew there had been no insidious attempts to silence those who might dare to band together to give their grievances a stronger voice. Back then, the notion of a citizens' militia had been applauded and championed, not spit upon by self-serving federal agents and the brainwashed masses.

Byrnes felt he'd been born in the wrong century. And the penalty for his bad luck? Instead of being honored as a returned warrior, he saw himself viewed as a pariah. An outcast and fringe lunatic. Little wonder it had taken the isolation of the farm for him to find even the faintest glimmer of inner peace. And he knew that peace was as illusory as it was temporary. Soon he would be called upon to carry out his mission, and when that happened, all his memories of the past months would be just that: memories. The realization darkened Byrnes's mood as surely as nightfall had begun to press its inky blackness on the cabin windows. Byrnes could feel himself tensing in the chair as his rage, like some roused beast, began to once again overtake him.

By now the fire in the hearth was blazing. Agitated, Byrnes began to fumble with the buttons of his coat. The buttons were made of bone, and it was no easy task to work them through the hand-sewn loops. He was struggling with the task when an overheated strip of bark was launched out of the fire at him. Startled, Byrnes let out a cry and recoiled, overturning the rocker in his haste to throw himself to the dirt floor. Panic seized him as he crawled away from the fire and curled into a fetal position, clutching his head protectively. Sweat beaded his face and his heart convulsed inside his chest. He was overwhelmed by a mad rush of flashbacks taking him back to the hell that had been Khamisiyah. The rattle of gunfire, the stench of diesel, men howling in pain, the splash of something hot as molten lava against his face—the sensory overload was as intense as it was sudden. Within seconds the beleaguered veteran gave in to the recurring nightmare and blacked out.

Moments later he came to, cold earth pressing against his bearded face. The ember that had triggered his blackout lay a few inches away, still glowing faintly. Byrnes watched the ember burn itself out with cold detachment, waiting for his mind to clear and for his pulse to return to normal. Finally he was able to struggle to his feet and right the toppled rocker. He sat back down again, drained, trembling, eyes trained on the fire. A racked sob shook through him. He clenched his fingers around the arms of the chair, determined not to give in to his sorrow and feeling of helplessness.

"No more," he murmured aloud, his voice hoarse. "No more."

For the next hour, Byrnes remained in the chair, rocking gently, transfixed by the fire, watching it slowly burn itself out. The lamp on the table beside him went out as well, and as the cabin grew dark, several more embers snapped out onto the floor.

Finally, as the last few flames licked at what remained of the charred logs in the fireplace, the evening chill crept back into the darkened cabin. Even colder and darker now, however, was the expression in Byrnes's eyes. He had the look of a man at the end of his tether, a man who'd reached a point where he saw but one course of action and was steeling himself for the demands that course would entail. Byrnes was through waiting for the call from his superiors. He'd decided it was time to take matters into his own hands, to renounce his inner demons and seize control of his own fate.

Rising from the chair, the veteran relit the oil lamp, then crossed the room and stood on a small wooden bench set in the corner. He reached up and gently worked free two loose boards straddling the rafters that made up the cabin's ceiling. There was a small cavity between the slats and the roof. Byrnes used the space to store several of his concessions to modern-day technology. He made frequent use of his cell phone and notebook computer, but this night it was a third item—which he'd been given just two days earlier—that commanded his attention. He reached deep into the cavity and carefully pulled out a forty-inch-long M-136 AT-4 rocket launcher.

The fifteen-pound weapon—a high-tech fiberglass-wrapped tube housing an 84 mm warhead—was equipped with a night-vision sight and had an effective firing range of nearly a quarter mile, roughly the same distance between the farm and the building located on the other side of the woods.

Byrnes stepped down from the bench and set aside the stolen launcher long enough to place his cell phone and computer into a backpack, then added a few more items before carrying both the pack and weapon outside. A light snow had begun to fall. The large, almost weightless flakes reminded Byrnes of the ashes that had once rained down on him from the fiery skies of Khamisiyah. He did his best to shrug off the comparison. Now was not the time to give in to the memories. He needed to keep his focus on the present, on the task at hand.

As he passed the lean-to, Byrnes could see lights through the woods, illuminating the outline of the building that would be his target. The wind had died, increasing the chances of his getting off a good shot. He'd fired AT-4s during his tour of duty in the Gulf, and prior to coming here he'd taken a few refresher courses with similar weapons at the American Freedom Movement compound fifty miles away in the heart of the Blue Ridge Mountains. He was confident he could hit his mark. After that? Byrnes had no set plan, but he knew that this would be his last night at the Michael Conlon Farm.

The roan horse was still out in the corral.

"Change of plans, Jefferson," Byrnes called out as he hung his backpack on the corral's gate latch. Clutching the rocket launcher in both hands, he told the horse, "It looks like we're going to go riding tonight after all."

2

Washington, D.C.

The Fourteenth Capitol Partners Spring Gun Show, one of the largest such annual gatherings held east of the Mississippi, had ended a little over an hour ago. The three-day event had been a rousing success, with sales running into the tens of millions of dollars, but there was still plenty of stock left over. A handful of larger suppliers had just finished taking down their stalls and were transferring leftover inventory into trucks parked behind the building, a one-time appliance superstore located in an isolated industrial park fourteen blocks from Georgetown University. The parking lot, like the surrounding neighborhood and the handful of other vehicles parked along the street, was lightly dusted with freshly fallen snow.

Inside a nondescript panel truck with tinted windows, Mack Bolan watched the activity taking place around the loading docks. Earlier, the Stony Man warrior had roamed the aisles inside the hall without spotting anything suspicious. Now, hours later, the crowds had dispersed along with most of the vendors, but he was still on the lookout.

The surveillance mission was a consequence of Bolan's visit to the Wildest Dreams fantasy camp. As Bolan had feared, those who'd fled the camp in the BMW had eluded capture, and neither Louie Paxton nor Xavier Manuel had claimed to know who had been driving the vehicle. Since Marcus Yarborough was missing, along with the woman Bolan had seen with

Mitch Brower, he suspected they'd ridden off together in the sports car.

Bolan had been on the lookout for Yarborough inside the exhibition hall, but he'd been even more intent on finding the missing AT-4 rocket launcher. According to evidence found in the fantasy camp's administrative office, the launcher had been sold to a Viriginia-based militia called the American Freedom Movement. The AFM was already under investigation by the Bureau of Alcohol, Tobacco and Firearms, and one of BATF's informants had confirmed the launcher transaction. He'd also claimed the militia outfit had been dragging its feet on a deal to purchase the remaining weapons Jason Cummings and Mitch Brower had stored at their Sykesville facility. According to the informant, if Brower and Cummings didn't drop their asking price, the AFM had already concocted a backup plan: to bolster its arsenal instead by stealing wares from the Capitol Partners Gun Show. The militia had already been linked to several similar thefts over the past two years. While casing the exhibit booths, Bolan had seen enough collective firepower to sustain a small army. He wanted to make sure the AFM didn't wind up being that army.

Bolan wasn't alone inside the panel truck. His longtime colleague Jack Grimaldi sat up front behind the steering wheel, his ball cap pushed back on his head. True, the wiry-haired pilot was more at home in an aircraft cockpit, but when the occasion demanded it, Grimaldi had proved he could handle ground vehicles with as much finesse as the most seasoned wheelman.

Crouched beside Bolan in the rear of the truck was John "Cowboy" Kissinger, a master weaponsmith familiar with nearly every handgun and rifle that had been on display at the exhibition. Kissinger had designed a few handguns of his own, including the multifunction palm gun Bolan had concealed in his boot during his short-lived assignment at the fantasy camp.

"My money says they'll try a hijack instead of bringing their own truck," Kissinger speculated aloud, blowing on his hands to keep them warm. The men had been on stakeout for nearly three hours, during which time the sun had gone down and the temperature outside the truck had dropped more than twenty degrees. Although Bolan seemed unfazed by the extended wait, Kissinger's anticipation was almost palpable. He was like a coiled spring.

"No bet," Grimaldi responded, cracking his knuckles to pass the time. "They pull a heist, they get what they're looking for without having to waste time moving stuff from one truck to another. And judging from the intel we've got on these guys, their MO is 'hit and run' all the way."

"We're all on the same page, then," Bolan said. He had out his Beretta 92-FS, safety thumbed off, firing selector set for 3-round bursts. Kissinger and Grimaldi were armed with standard-issue Colt Government Model 1911A automatic pistols. Also in the truck was a pair of M-16 A-2 assault rifles, one equipped with an M-203 grenade launcher. The hope was they could nab the would-be hijackers without having to resort to heavy artillery.

The Stony Man crew watched as two trucks—one a converted postal carrier, the other a twenty-foot bed rental—groaned their way out of the parking lot through the light snow and headed down the access road leading to MacArthur Boulevard and the Georgetown Reservoir. That left two semis, both backed up to the loading dock at the rear of the exhibition hall. Four uniformed rent-a-cops stood by watching as vendors wheeled dollies stacked with crated weapons to the dock. There, coworkers helped move the stock into the trucks. The whole operation had a look of practiced efficiency. Nothing seemed amiss.

"Could be we're on a wild-goose chase," Grimaldi ventured. "I mean, all we're going on is a tip from some scumbag informant. Who's to say he didn't pull this whole thing out of a hat—"

"Hold it," Bolan interrupted, signaling Grimaldi to be quiet. He cracked open the window closest to him, letting a cold draft whisper into the truck. Soon Grimaldi and Kissinger could hear it, too: the faint, high-pitched drone of single-cylinder engines. There were at least two of them, approaching from different directions.

"A little cold to be out on a motorcycle," Kissinger murmured, reaching for the Colt tucked in his web holster.

"Not to mention the snow," Grimaldi said.

The Stony Man trio wasn't alone in suspecting the heist was about to go down. A walkie-talkie on the seat next to Grimaldi suddenly squawked to life. It was Mort Kiley, point man for a BATF field team positioned just around the corner inside an unmarked utility van. Kiley had originally intended to have his crew take the point position, but Bolan had pulled rank, using doctored credentials identifying him and his colleagues as special agents with the Justice Department. Kiley and his four-man BATF crew were playing backup.

"Got ourselves a party crasher," Kiley's voice crackled over the two-way's minispeaker. "Guy on a dirt bike approaching at… Wait, he's slowing down."

As Bolan and the others listened, they suddenly heard—both over the walkie-talkie and out on the street behind them—the sounds of gunshots and breaking glass. Kiley shouted something unintelligible before being silenced by yet another round of gunfire.

"Not good." Grimaldi cranked the panel truck's engine to life.

"Go check it out," Bolan told him as he threw open his door. "We'll handle things here."

The Executioner slipped out of the truck and hit the asphalt running. He'd exchanged the boots he'd worn at the fantasy camp for lightweight hiking shoes. The crepe soles muffled his steps. Kissinger was right behind him, the Colt pistol freed from his holster and held out before him, ready to fire.

Grimaldi, meanwhile, swung the truck around and fishtailed past the men, raising a fantail of road slush in his wake. By then, Bolan and Kissinger had crossed the street. The Executioner took cover behind a mailbox anchored to the sidewalk near a row of parked cars. Kissinger split off and raced toward a large sign propped on stanchions rising up through a planter box situated near the parking lot entrance.

From his position, Bolan could see most of the lot, as well as the road. In the distance a thick stand of elm trees separated the industrial park from a nearby housing development. It sounded to him as if one of the motorcycles was approaching from the direction of the trees. Those gathered behind the exhibition hall had heard the commotion, as well. The rent-a-cops and several of the vendors had drawn their guns and were looking out into the night, tracking the sound. Bolan and Kissinger both did their best to conceal themselves, not wanting to be mistaken for hijackers.

Moments later, a mud-encrusted Husqvarna 250 Motocross emerged from between the elm trees, lights off, knobbed tires churning up snow and dirt as it raced up a footpath leading to the street. The rider was dressed head-to-toe in black leather, wearing goggles and a stocking cap, but no helmet. He had both hands on the handlebar controls, but visible in a shoulder holster was an Uzi Eagle autopistol. Once he reached the street, he cut across both lanes, clearly bound for the parking lot.

Before Bolan could fix him in his sights, however, the biker suddenly veered to his right and yanked on his handlebars. Goosing the bike's throttle, he brought up the front wheel and bounded cleanly over the curb. Bolan tracked the biker and was about to cut loose with his Beretta when someone fired at him from behind, creasing the mailbox just inches from his face.

Holding his fire, the Executioner instinctively dropped to the snow-covered sidewalk.

"Sniper on the roof!" Kissinger called out.

Bolan barely heard the warning; he was too busy scrambling clear of the mailbox. He took cover behind a pickup truck parked on the street. From his new position, he could see the biker clear the sidewalk and power through the sparse shrubbery that ringed the parking lot. By the time Bolan got off a shot, the biker had entered the lot and was speeding toward the loading dock.

When one of the vendors raised his gun, the biker slammed on his brakes, throwing the Husky into a sidelong skid. Once he'd laid the bike down, the rider jumped clear, avoiding the gunshot fired his way. The motorcycle's momentum, meanwhile, sent it clattering across the asphalt.

The vendor let out a howl as the bike knocked his legs out from under him. His gun flew from his hand as he fell, sprawling, to one side. Before the vendor could react, the biker bounded to his feet, unleathered his Uzi and fired into the vendor's face.

Kissinger caught only a glimpse of the execution; his view was obstructed by the signposts and shrubs in the planter. By the time he changed positions, the leather-clad intruder had already disappeared between the two semis. Worse yet, Kissinger had placed himself in view of the rooftop sniper. When a 7.62 mm rifle round tore through the shrubs, the Stony Man weaponsmith quickly drew back and dropped behind the planter. More gunfire soon came chattering his way, not from the roof but rather from the rear of the exhibition hall.

"You've got the wrong guy!" Kissinger shouted.

His warning went unheeded. More rounds hammered at the planter and the sign stanchions, seeking him out.

Bolan, meanwhile, switched to firing single rounds, hoping to conserve ammo as he traded shots with the rooftop sniper. He plinked a shot off the condenser unit his foe was crouched behind, then ducked when a return round shattered the pickup's windshield. Bolan scrambled to the rear of the truck and dropped the Beretta's foregrip so he could grasp it with both hands and improve his aim. Up on the roof, the sniper swung around and was ready to fire when Bolan beat him to the trigger. Nailed in the chest, the sniper dropped his rifle and staggered clear of the condenser unit, then teetered lifelessly over the edge of the roof.

The Executioner tracked the man's fall, then shifted his focus to the activity around the loading dock. Given all the gunfire, Bolan assumed the biker had been cornered and was making a last stand. It quickly became clear, however, that he'd gotten it wrong. Instead of going after the biker, the rental cops—all four of them—had turned their guns on the surviving vendors. Taken by surprise, the vendors were easy targets and fell quickly.

"Inside job," Bolan murmured, incredulous. Raising his voice, he cried out to Kissinger, "The guards are in on it!"

As SOON AS Jack Grimaldi steered his panel truck around the corner, he saw that he was too late to come to the aid of Mort Kiley or his BATF cohorts.

Another biker, astride a second Husqvarna, had just put a bullet into the head of a federal agent lying on the road next to the ambushed BATF utility van. Kiley had never made it out of the vehicle; he was slumped on the back floor, his left forearm dangling from the half-opened side door. The driver was slumped behind the steering wheel at an unnatural angle, his blood streaking the window beside him, clearly another victim of the biker's surprise attack.

"Bastard!" Grimaldi growled, flooring the accelerator. He flashed on his high beams and bore down on the biker, gambling that the other man was out of ammunition.

The gamble paid off.

The biker, helmetless and dressed like his counterpart in black leather, instinctively raised his gun at the approaching truck. He had a clear shot at Grimaldi but pulled the trigger on an empty chamber. He cast the useless gun aside and put his bike in gear.

"You aren't going anywhere," Grimaldi seethed, focusing on the biker's hands as he drew closer. When he saw the gunman turn his handlebars to the right, Grimaldi countered, jerking his steering wheel to the left. The biker lurched forward, hoping to veer around the oncoming truck. Grimaldi anticipated the maneuver and swerved into the assailant's path. His fender clipped the bike's front wheel squarely and sent the rider vaulting headfirst over the handlebars. The assailant caromed off the truck's grillework and fell limply to the ground.

Grimaldi slammed on his brakes. The truck brodied across the snow-slicked street and came to a stop mere inches from the slain BATF agent lying on the road. Yanking his Colt from his web holster, the Stony Man operative bounded out into the street and took aim at the biker, who was slowly struggling to his feet.

"Freeze!" he ordered.

The biker was crouched over, his back turned to Grimaldi. He stayed put, but Grimaldi could see his right hand drifting toward the loose vest he wore over his leather jacket.

"Hands out where I can see them!" Grimaldi barked.

The biker stretched his left arm outward and began to slowly turn. He let his right arm drop for a moment, then suddenly reached inside his vest. He was pulling a backup pistol from the waistband of his riding pants when Grimaldi fired.

The biker let out a cry and staggered backward, but managed to stay on his feet despite having taken a close-range shot to the chest. When he turned to Grimaldi, gun raised, the Stony Man pilot figured the guy was wearing body armor, so he aimed higher, putting his next shot through the assailant's forehead. The biker dropped his gun and sagged to his knees, then collapsed.

Grimaldi slowly moved closer, Colt trained on the biker. The other man was in his early thirties, clean-shaved, with short blond hair. The killshot hadn't completely disfigured him, and when Grimaldi took off the man's visor he recognized him from a series of mug shots he and his colleagues had been shown a few hours ago back at BATF's Georgetown field office. The guy's name was Byrnes. Grimaldi couldn't remember his first name, but he knew the guy had two other brothers, linked, like him, to the American Freedom Movement.

Grimaldi glanced back at the BATF surveillance vehicle, then once again eyed the slain biker. The man was beyond being interrogated, but Grimaldi still found himself asking the foremost question on his mind in the wake of the ambush.

"No way you just stumbled across them," he thought aloud. "You knew they were on stakeout. Who tipped you off?"

WALLACE "DUBBY" BYRNES, youngest of the three brothers who had followed their late father's footsteps into the ranks of the American Freedom Movement, had banged up his knee when he'd skid-dropped his Husqvarna in the parking lot, but he ignored the pain as he clambered into the cab of the nearest of the two semis backed up to the loading dock. The keys were in the ignition, and he let out a joyous whoop as he started the engine.

"Hot damn!" he hollered triumphantly.

He'd done it! He'd helped steal a semi filled with enough guns and ammunition to handle a year's worth of AFM recruits. Not only that—he'd been the one who'd taken it upon himself a few weeks ago to start dating a BATF dispatcher, figuring it would help determine the extent to which the Feds were on their trail.

His brother Harlan and all the others back at the compound had thought he was nuts and mocked him for coming up with such a hare-brained scheme. This afternoon, though, that scheme had paid off when the dispatcher—who had no idea Dubby was with the AFM—had mentioned something about a pending militia bust in Georgetown. Dubby had convinced his brother they should hop on their bikes and rush over to check on things. Now here they were, riding to the rescue, and they'd done it!

Dubby couldn't wait to see the look on his brothers' faces when he told them the news. There'd be no more calling him Squirt. Not after this. From now on, they'd call him Dubby like everyone else.

The twenty-three-year-old biker's euphoria was a bit premature. He may have taken over the wheel of the Mack truck, but there was still the matter of escaping from the parking lot and making it all the way back to the AFM's mountain compound without getting caught. Dubby got his first reality check when the driver's-side window shattered while he wrestled with the truck's gearshift. The bullet whizzed past his face and lodged in the cab ceiling, but not before he'd been struck by a few shards of glass. Blood began to seep from gashes in his neck and cheek.

Neither wound was severe enough to take Dubby out of the fight, and he swore as he grabbed for the Uzi Eagle he'd used earlier to gun down the truck's owner. He knocked loose the remaining glass in the window frame with the Eagle's squat polymer butt, then shouted out into the night, "All right, who's asking for it?"

JOHN KISSINGER COULD SEE that he'd missed the biker attempting to steal the Mack truck. The biker was leaning out of the line of fire, and Cowboy didn't want to waste any more ammunition, so he turned his attention to the other truck. Bolan had neutralized the first guard trying to get inside the vehicle, but a second guard had yanked the body aside and climbed behind the wheel. Now the semi was pulling away from the loading dock, headed Kissinger's way.

Kissinger propped his gun hand on the planter to steady his

aim as he squinted past the glare of the headlights, keeping the driver in his sights. Once the truck had reached the exit, Kissinger pulled the trigger.

The windshield spiderwebbed as the round punched through the glass, striking the driver in the upper chest. The dead man's foot slid off the accelerator, and the truck slowed to a stop halfway into the street, blocking the only exit from the lot.

"Whaddya know, something went right for a change," Kissinger muttered.

The disabled truck blocked his view of the gunfight taking place between Bolan and the other guards, so Kissinger backtracked along the planter to his original position, hoping the biker would realized he'd been hemmed in and bail from the other truck. Before he could confirm whether or not the ploy had worked, Kissinger was distracted by the metallic plink of something bounding off the asphalt on the other side of the planter. Kissinger had been in enough firefights to know the sound.

Grenade.

Kissinger had no time to react before the projectile detonated. Half the planter disintegrated, as did a good portion of the stanchions holding up the massive sign he had taken cover beneath. With a cracking sound nearly as loud as that made by the grenade, the weakened posts collapsed under the weight of the sign.

Kissinger tried to roll clear as the marquee plummeted toward him, but the bottom edge caught him on the right arm and shoulder, knocking the gun from his hand. The next thing he knew, the Stony Man armorer was pinned to the ground. The air had been knocked from his lungs and a stabbing pain coursed through him. A blur of light crowded his field of vision, then Kissinger's world was plunged into sudden darkness.

WHEN HE SAW that his colleague was in trouble, Bolan broke from cover and started toward the fallen sign, only to be driven back by gunfire from the two rogue guards still prowling the loading dock area. The Executioner crouched behind a late-model Lexus illuminated by a nearby streetlight. Bolan shot the light out, emptying the last round in his Beretta. He fished a spare 10-round clip from his pocket and quickly swapped magazines, then peered over the hood of the Lexus. He fired at one of the guards and sent him sprawling across the body of a vendor who already lay dead on the loading dock next to an overturned crateful of MAT 40 subguns.

The remaining guard had fled to the rear of the second semi, which was trying to squeeze past the first truck, stalled at the parking lot exit. The engine rumbled as Byrnes drove forward, and seconds later Bolan heard a screech of metal on metal as Byrnes brushed against the other truck. Undeterred, the militia-man drove on, taking out another section of the planter as he forged a new path to the street. From where he was standing, Bolan couldn't see if Kissinger had been in the truck's path.

Dubby Byrnes turned sharply once he reached the street, then gave the semi more gas. When he spotted Bolan, he veered the truck toward the Lexus. Bolan had no time to fire. He dived headlong to his right, landing hard on the sidewalk just as Byrnes's semi clipped the front end of the Lexus and sent it caroming backward into the Volkswagen Passat parked behind it. Bolan's instincts had just saved him from being crushed between the two vehicles. Still, he'd scraped his right elbow landing on the sidewalk, and the entire arm throbbed as he scrambled back to his feet.

Much as he wanted to check on Kissinger, Bolan knew that trying to stop the truck was his top priority. Dropping the Beretta's foregrip, he clutched the pistol with both hands and circled the crumpled Lexus. He was immediately spotted by the security guard who'd climbed up into the back of the fleeing truck. The guard fished through the shipping crate nearest to him and came up with an M-68 frag grenade similar to the one that had taken Kissinger out of the battle earlier. He slipped his thumb through the release pin and was about to heave the pro-jectile when Bolan stitched him across the chest with a 3-round volley of 9 mm Parabellum bullets. The guard dropped the grenade and keeled over backward, his heart shredded. Bolan wasn't sure if the pin had been pulled on the grenade, but he once again went with his instincts and dived back behind the Lexus.

Once the grenade detonated, shrapnel ripped through the truck's cargo much the same way Bolan's M-61 had stirred things up back at the storage shed in Sykesville. The chain-reaction blasts were equally devastating. The truck's walls turned into razor-sharp shards, and flaming chunks flew out in all directions, pelting everything within a fifty-yard radius. A flash fire quickly consumed the crated weapons and ammunition, triggering still more explosions. The Lexus Bolan was crouched behind rocked in place for a moment, then came to a rest. By the time he rose to his feet to survey the damage, the truck had been turned into a rolling inferno.

DUBBY BYRNES WAS THROWN forward by the first blasts, breaking ribs on the steering wheel before he smashed into the windshield, cracking the glass along with his skull. By the time he'd rebounded back into the driver's seat, shrapnel had ripped through the backrest and pierced his leather jacket, nicking his spine and puncturing his right lung. Miraculously, he was still conscious, but the spinal trauma had left him paralyzed from the waist down, and when flames surged through the cab, he was unable to escape. His shrill scream was abruptly silenced when the fire roared up into the engine compartment and made contact with the fuel line. A final explosion—every bit as loud and powerful as that made by the grenade—obliterated the cab, putting Byrnes out of his misery.

THE STREET HAD FALLEN SILENT, but the din from the chain-reaction blasts still reverberated through Bolan's skull. Half-deaf, he cautiously approached the ravaged truck. Flames still licked at the charred shell, sending thick clouds of smoke up into the night. An eerie haze filled the street, almost like a fog, mingling with the light snowfall. Bolan knew the driver could not have survived the explosion.

As the Executioner turned to make his way back to Kissinger, another vehicle slowly rolled into view through the haze, passing the ruined semi. Bolan raised his pistol but held his fire. It was Grimaldi in the panel truck.

Bolan slowly slid his gun back into his web holster and waved to get Grimaldi's attention. The panel truck picked up speed, then slowed to a stop alongside him.

"The grenade launcher's still in back here," the Stony Man pilot called out to Bolan as he leaned across the front seat and threw open the passenger door. "How the hell did you turn that truck into toast?"

"I had their help," Bolan conceded. He had to raise his voice, as the night had come alive with the screaming of sirens. He got in the truck and explained what had happened, then told Grimaldi, "Let's get back to the hall. Cowboy's down."

Once they were within view of the fallen sign, Grimaldi pulled to a stop in front of the stalled semi. He and Bolan scrambled to the planter and carefully lifted the toppled marquee, then shoved it to one side so they could get to Kissinger. The armorer wasn't moving, but he had a pulse and was breathing, however faintly. Bolan and Grimaldi both saw a thin crimson rivulet seeping from the corner of the man's mouth.

"Internal bleeding," Grimaldi murmured.

Bolan nodded. Glancing over his shoulder, he saw the flashing rooflights of several approaching vehicles.

"Let's hope one of those is an ambulance," he said, turning his attention back to Kissinger. "He's hanging on by a thread."

3

McLean, Virginia

Three hundred yards from the lean-to rooftop where Edgar Byrnes lay peering through the night-vision scope of his M-136 AT-4 rocket launcher, Roberta Williamson was finishing another routine workday on the sixth floor of CIA headquarters. Yes, she'd put in overtime, but that was the norm for her these days. She'd only been at the Langley facility ten months, and she still felt the need to do extra work to prove herself worthy of the promotion she'd received after five years of field work with the Agency's Paris bureau. She was now an intercept analyst for the Company's counterterrorism division, part of a thirteen-person team charged with ferreting out communication links between al Qaeda sleeper cells in the States and their overseas contacts. It was demanding work, but Williamson loved the challenge.

For Williamson, the biggest downside to her job was its sedentary nature. She'd put on twelve pounds since reporting to Langley, and long hours at the desk had given her lower-back problems, as well. She knew more exercise would help on both fronts and she tried, whenever possible, to leave time at the end of the day to do some stretches and then jog around some portion of the facility's 130-acre grounds. This night it was snowing outside, so Williamson figured she had an easy excuse to skip the workout. When her phone rang, however, she suspected her boss had other ideas. She smiled ruefully as she picked up the receiver. "Williamson here."

"Hey, Robbi. It's your conscience."

"I figured as much," Williamson replied.

"So, whaddya say? Up for a jog?"

She chuckled, "Do I have a choice?"

"Be right there."

"Bastard," Williamson teased before hanging up the phone. She was still smiling as she pushed away from her desk and kicked off her pumps.

Her "conscience" was former Army Colonel Felix Garber, the fifty-seven-year-old California native who'd recommended her for the job with counterterrorism and had served as her mentor these past ten months. Before joining the Company, Garber had put in twenty years with the XVIII Airborne Corps, concluding his service as the officer in charge of demolition operations in Khamisiyah following the Gulf War. He was now deputy director of the CIA's counterterrorism division, and Williamson suspected it was only a matter of time before he took over the top position. She and Garber had worked alongside each other several times when the colonel had come to Paris on assignment, and they'd struck up a friendship based on their mutual passion for country music, haute cuisine and the Los Angeles Lakers. Working in adjacent offices now, they'd drawn even closer the past few months, and another incentive Williamson had for losing weight was her anticipation of the day when their relationship led to the bedroom and Garber would have his first look at her without her clothes on.

She had changed into her jogging sweats and was tying her running shoes when Garber appeared in her doorway, wearing rubberized biker shorts and a sleeveless ski vest. He was in good shape and had a better physique than most men half his age.

"You want to go running dressed like that?" Williamson said. "You'll freeze!"

"Wimp," Garber said with a grin. "It's not cold out—it's brisk."

"Yeah, right." She laughed.

As they left the office and headed down the hall, Garber floated the idea of having dinner together after their run. He mentioned a new sports bar that had just opened up across the river in D.C. They'd have the Lakers game on, he told her, and their crab cakes had just gotten a good write-up in the *Post*.

"Can't say no to a good crab cake," Williamson said.

They were waiting for the elevator when Garber snapped his fingers.

"Damn!" he groaned. "I forgot to update Tangiers on that cable intercept we just cracked."

"Go ahead and fax them," Williamson told him. "I'll hold the elevator and get in a few stretches."

"Be right back," Garber said.

Williamson watched Garber head back down the hallway, admiring his legs. And that ass, she thought to herself, smiling.

The colonel had unlocked his office door and was heading into his office when a sudden explosion shook the building. The floor beneath Williamson's feet shuddered with so much force she lost her balance and bounced off the elevator doors, then fell as if struck by an invisible force. By the time she'd landed, the floor had stabilized, but a deafening alarm had gone off in the hallway and the ceiling-mounted safety sprinklers had been activated. Water showered down on Williamson as she slowly sat up, mind racing, trying to make sense of what had just happened.

Like Garber, Williamson was a California native and her first thought was that there'd been an earthquake. But then she smelled smoke and heard the unmistakable crackling sound of racing flames. Alarmed, she glanced down the hallway leading back to her office.

"No!" she gasped.

The inner walls of her office, as well as Garber's and the office next to hers, had all but disintegrated, and a portion of the ceiling had collapsed into the flames engulfing the corridor. A woman's body hung eerily out over the edge of the overhead cavity, then tumbled down to the hallway floor, joining three other corpses strewed about like discarded dolls. The fire had begun to devour the victims, and Williamson's stomach clenched at her first whiff of burning flesh.

"Felix!" she called out, staggering to her feet.

She cried out Garber's name again as she tore off her sweatshirt and soaked it beneath the ceiling sprinklers. Pressing the makeshift mask to her face, she headed down the hall. Smoke stung her eyes as she leaned over the first body she came to— Roger Olsen, a colleague she'd shared coffee with in the cafeteria just a few hours ago. The man's clothes were torn, and he was bleeding from deep cuts sustained when he'd crashed through the office wall that now lay smoldering in broken chunks on the floor around him. His jaw had been dislocated and his mouth hung open, slack and off-center. His eyes were open but there was no life in them.

"No," Williamson repeated, her voice reduced to a hoarse whisper.

The next two bodies she passed were in even worse condition, but neither they nor Olsen's corpse adequately prepared her for the horror that awaited her when she came upon the remains of her mentor.

Felix Garber's office had taken the brunt of the 84 mm warhead fired from Edgar Byrnes's AT-4 rocket launcher. When he'd returned to his office to send his fax, Garber had walked directly into the spalling effect achieved after the rocket had penetrated the outer wall of the building. Garber had been killed instantly and then cast back out into the hallway by an incendiary barrage of projectile fragments that had left his body charred and mutilated. His right arm was missing along with half his left leg, and his torso had been rent open and seared beyond recognition. His nearly severed head hung twisted from his shoulders in such a way that even though he lay on his back his face was turned to the floor.

Williamson's legs weakened and she dropped to her knees, unable to take her eyes off the grisly remains. She lowered the dampened sweatshirt and opened her mouth as if to scream, but all that came forth was a strained mewling. She became oblivious to the rank stench of burning flesh and the ominous approach of flames consuming those areas in the hall where the safety sprinklers had been rendered inoperable.

Someone appeared at the far end of the hallway and called out to Williamson, but she remained transfixed, overwhelmed by the horror around her. Two co-workers—men who'd rushed up to the sixth floor after feeling the explosion—scrambled down the corridor and pulled Williamson to her feet. She numbly allowed them to lead her beyond range of the flames. It was only when they'd reached the elevators that she found her voice. When she spoke, however, it seemed to her as her words were coming from somewhere far away, being mouthed by someone else.

"Who?" she moaned. "Who did this?"

"EASY, BOY," Edgar Byrnes called out as he slipped on his backpack and opened the corral gate at Conlon Farm. "Easy, Jefferson."

The roan horse had been spooked by the rocket launcher and neighed loudly as it clomped in circles around the corral. Other animals were making a racket inside the lean-to, and several chickens had squawked their way outside and were scurrying in all directions. Byrnes strode toward Jefferson, holding his arms out before him. In one hand he held a salt lick, in the other a carrot.

"Come on, Jefferson," he pleaded. "We don't have time for this."

The horse charged blindly past. Byrnes turned and jogged counterclockwise in hopes he could intercept Jefferson during the horse's next lap around the corral. He continued to call out, trying to calm the beast. Finally Jefferson slowed to a trot and then came to a stop in front of Byrnes, choosing the carrot.

"Good boy."

As he waited for Jefferson to consume the snack, Byrnes glanced through the woods. It had stopped snowing, and he could clearly see flames spewing from the sixth floor of CIA headquarters. A trio of helicopters hovered above the carnage, searchlights raking the surrounding grounds. Byrnes knew it would only be a matter of time before the search widened to include the farm.

"Okay, boy," Byrnes said once Jefferson had finished the carrot. "It's time."

Byrnes had already saddled the horse and strapped on the reins. He slid one foot into the nearest stirrup and hoisted himself up onto Jefferson's back, then slapped the beast's flank with the flat of his palm.

"Let's go!"

Jefferson bolted from the corral and carried Byrnes deep into the woods leading away from the CIA facilities. Byrnes had ridden this stretch countless times over the past few weeks, including the previous night, when he'd gone to pick up the weapon from his AFM contacts. The route was ingrained in Jefferson's mind and the horse retraced it at full gallop, threading between trees with relative ease. The woods were dark, but the horse forged on unerringly.

Once they reached the cloverleaf ramp leading under the George Washington Expressway to Turkey Run Park, Byrnes slowed Jefferson to a trot. There were a few other riders out, as well. The militiaman composed himself, then joined them, expressing puzzlement.

"I heard some kind of crash," he told the others.

"Something going down at Langley," one of the other riders explained, pointing out the helicopters in the distance.

"Sounded like a bomb," another rider said with a trace of anxiety. "I hope it's not terrorists."

"It's probably nothing," Byrnes reassured the other man. "That place is like a fortress. No way is anybody going to be able to attack it."

"I hope you're right."

"Me, too," Byrnes said. "Hell, if somebody can attack CIA in their own backyard, nobody's safe."

4

Philadelphia, Pennsylvania

Senator Gregory Walden had just nodded off to sleep when the phone rang on the nightstand beside him. The vice chairman of the Joint House-Senate Intelligence Committee groaned and opened one eye, inspecting the luminous readout on the digital clock next to the phone. It was nearly midnight.

"What now?" Walden groaned. The senator had already been interrupted twice tonight, once by a *Post* reporter looking for the inside scoop on confirmation hearings for the President's latest Homeland Security nominee, the other time by an aide who was having trouble transcribing some notes Walden had barked into his Dictaphone before leaving the office. He reached for the phone as it continued to ring. Beside him, Nikki, his wife for the past seven years, stirred beneath the sheets.

"Gregory, would you please get that already, for crying out—"

"I just did!" Walden snapped at her. He sat up in bed and vented further into the phone, yelling, "This better be goddamn important!"

There was a pause on the line, then a woman replied to him in a soft voice void of emotion. It was Joan VanderMeer. "Greg, it's me. I know it's late, but—"

"I'll call you right back," Walden interrupted. He hung up the phone and swung his feet to the floor and rubbed his fists against his temples.

Nikki turned to him, her peroxide hair matted flat on the side she'd been sleeping on. The covers clung as tightly to her silicone breasts as the skin did to her cheeks after her most recent facelift.

"What is it?" she asked.

"The world's coming to an end," Walden deadpanned as he stabbed his feet into his bedroom slippers. "Go back to sleep."

"Always with the sarcasm," Nikki complained.

"I love you, too, honeybunch," Walden said flatly. He grabbed his robe from the overstuffed chair next to the bed and put it on as he headed out of the room. The November elections were eight long months away. Walden wondered how the hell he was going to keep the divorce on hold that long. He'd come to hate his wife with a passion, but he knew this year's campaign would be a tight one, and he couldn't afford to lose votes by presenting himself as anything other than happily married.

The Waldens lived on the eighth floor of an upscale high-rise located just off the river between Drexel University and the train station the senator had made heavy use of years ago when he was new to Capitol Hill and needed a cheap way to commute between Philadelphia and his office in Washington. Nowadays he could afford a chauffeur. He could also afford the two million dollars' worth of professional redecoration the apartment had just undergone. The completed results would be featured in the November issue of *Architectural Digest*, just in time for the election. The photo shoot had already taken place, and Nikki, who'd made most of the decorating choices, had made sure to worm her way into a few of the shots, another reason Walden felt the need to keep up pretenses. Of course, since the photo shoot, Nikki had changed her mind about a few things and had brought the decorators back in for a hundred thousand dollars' worth of "tweaking." And she wasn't done yet. The interior decorator was due back in the morning with swatches for the dining room's third paint job in as many months.

As he dialed a number on one of his never-ending supply of prepaid cell phones, Walden stared at an obscure Jackson Pollock painting that hung over the den fireplace. Walden hated the piece; to him it looked like something a second-grader had painted. Nikki, of course, thought it was a masterpiece. Which was good for her, Walden thought, because it was probably the most valuable thing she'd be taking away from the marriage when he threw her out after the election.

"Okay, which is it?" Walden said once VanderMeer had picked up. "The Feds are on to you or there was a problem with the gun heist."

"The gun show," VanderMeer told him. "They got hold of both semis but ran into a buzz saw trying to get away."

"You want to translate that for me?" Walden said. He could already feel his blood pressure rising. First that business at the fantasy camp in Sykesville, and now this. This bungling not only jeopardized his master plan, but it also increased the chance that his cover would be blown. If that happened, he would be as good as dead.

"I don't have all the details yet," VanderMeer confessed, "but apparently BATF showed up along with some other Feds. Our people were stopped cold, and from what I've heard, it was pretty ugly. One of the trucks was blown up, so the place is crawling with media and lookie-loos."

"Shit," Walden murmured. The Bureau of Alcohol, Tobacco and Firearms was one of the few investigatory agencies he hadn't yet managed to infiltrate with his own people.

"Who were these other Feds?" Walden said as he made his way to the wet bar and poured himself a drink.

"I think they were from Justice," VanderMeer said. "Special agents."

"Figures."

Walden had used his connections to try to find out who'd blown up the weapons cache at the Wildest Dreams Fantasy Camp but had run into a dead end once the trail led to the Justice Department. It turned out that there were some levels of confidentiality even he could not bypass. And now it looked as if the same operative who'd brought down Jason Cummings and Mitch Brower had played a hand in thwarting the AFM's attempt to replace the arms that had gone up in smoke back in Sykesville. Not knowing who he was up against left Walden feeling vulnerable. But, as with the incident at Wildest Dreams, his foremost concern was that he remain above suspicion.

"Did they take anyone into custody?" the senator asked.

"I don't think so," VanderMeer reported. "I think everyone was killed."

Walden drained his drink and quickly poured another as he assessed the situation. He'd been lucky in the case of Sykesville, since neither Louie Paxton nor Xavier Manuel had known anything about the weapons stolen from Aberdeen, much less Walden's role in enabling the theft. Both men had protected VanderMeer's identity, as well, but he knew there was a chance their tongues could be loosened in the interrogation room. In Georgetown, at least, it appeared there were no survivors capable of ratting him out. Some consolation, he thought to himself.

"There'd better not be a trail leading back to us," he warned.

"We should be okay," VanderMeer assured him. "I'm on my way to the compound as we speak. I'll make sure our tracks are covered."

"Good. Once that's settled, we need to come up with a way to spin this whole mess in our favor," Walden advised. Already his mind was sorting through options. Making snap decisions while under duress was a skill he'd mastered over the years; it had helped him immeasurably in his rise through the ranks on Capitol Hill.

"Greg, listen to me," VanderMeer said. "Bad as the news from Georgetown is, I'm afraid that's not the worst of it. It's not the reason I called."

"What?" Walden was taken aback. "What are you talking about?"

There was a pause on the line, then Joan VanderMeer dropped the bombshell.

"It has to do with Edgar Byrnes," she said. "You remember him. He's the older brother of Wallace and Harlan—"

"I know who he is," Walden interrupted. "We've got him planted at that goddamn farm next to Langley with that rocket launcher from Aberdeen. Once we get all our pieces in place, he'll—"

"He's not at the farm anymore," VanderMeer interrupted. "Apparently he snapped tonight."

"Snapped? What do you mean? He offed himself?"

"Worse," she said. "He went ahead with the plan. On his own."

Walden let out a deep breath and sank into chair behind him. This couldn't be happening. "He fired at Langley?"

"Afraid so. Last I heard, there are eight confirmed dead. They're still fighting the fire."

Walden finished his drink, then hurled the shot glass across the room, shattering it against the flagstone hearth. He already had his hands full trying to figure out a way to put a spin on Sykesville and the gun-show fiasco in Georgetown. Now this.

"Please tell me he put a bullet through his head afterward," he muttered into the cell phone. "Please tell me he's in no position to talk."

Once again, there was a moment's silence on the line. Then VanderMeer warily confirmed Walden's worst fears.

"I'm sorry, Greg, but he's still out there somewhere."

5

Washington, D.C.

News of the attack on CIA headquarters reached Mack Bolan while he was speaking with D.C. Homicide Detective Bill Darwin in the ER waiting room at Georgetown University Hospital. They were less than a mile from where EMTs had first begun emergency treatment on John Kissinger after arriving at the blood-drenched battleground where the armorer had gone down. A surgical team was working on Kissinger in the OR, trying to pinpoint the source of his internal bleeding. X-rays had already determined that the man had sustained a concussion, as well as four broken ribs and a punctured lung, all courtesy of the fallen sign. For the moment at least, his condition was listed as critical.

When he heard about the rocket attack, Bolan's first reaction was the same as that of Darwin, a twelve-year veteran of the Washington, D.C. police force. Both men were convinced there had to be a connection with the aborted heist in Georgetown.

"Makes sense," Darwin said after Bolan had voiced his theory. "I mean, we know the guys here were part of this militia outfit. Going after federal buildings is just the kind of stunt they'd pull."

"I wonder about the timing," Bolan said. "CIA got hit right after we shut down the heist."

Darwin checked his notes. "Yeah. Less than five minutes apart. You think whoever fired that rocket was retaliating for what happened here?"

"Could be," Bolan replied. A part of him, however, couldn't help wondering if the attack might have been more in response to what had gone down at the fantasy camp in Sykesville. True, the CIA hadn't played a role in Bolan's mission there, but he knew the militia fringe tended to see the federal government as some unified force when it came to encroaching on their rights. As such, it wouldn't be unlike them to strike out indiscriminately looking to avenge the deaths of Jason Cummings and Mitch Brower. Bolan had already caught wind of some Web site eulogies in which the fantasy camp founders had been declared martyrs killed by the Feds because of Brower's recent editorial campaign against calls for a national identity card.

"It's ugly any way you slice it," Darwin said. "We've got ten dead here, not counting their guys, and last I heard they've pulled eight bodies out of Langley. Lucky it was after hours there or it would've been a whole lot worse."

"Night probably worked better for them in terms of a getaway," Bolan said.

"If that's the case, they got what they wanted," Darwin said. He skimmed his notes again, then reported, "They say the rocket was fired from a small farm about a quarter mile away. There are some fresh hoofprints in the snow leading off into the nearby woods."

"The guy rode off on a horse?"

Darwin nodded again. "There's just the one set of hooves leading to a place called Turkey Run Park, between the expressway and the Potomac. The park has riding paths and the prints are mixed in with those from at least a dozen other horses. They're combing the area, but the feeling is this guy, whoever he is, had an escape route planned out. Throw in a head start, and he'll be tough to catch."

Jack Grimaldi entered the waiting room in time to catch the tail end of Darwin's explanation.

"If you're talking about the shooter, we've got a make on him," he told Darwin and Bolan. "Name's Edgar Byrnes."

Bolan glanced at Darwin, who, in turn, went back to his notes, then nodded gravely.

"Bikers in your shootout were both named Byrnes," he confirmed.

"They're brothers," Grimaldi said. "All three are AFM. Followed their old man's footsteps, apparently."

"So we've got their father to worry about, too?" Darwin said.

Grimaldi shook his head. "Guy's dead. He worked at their training camp up in Virginia and ran guns along the coast until the Coast Guard caught up with him. He went down with his boat near Hatteras after a firefight."

Darwin stared at Grimaldi. "How the hell did you come up with all that so fast?"

Bolan answered for his colleague. "We have connections."

Stony Man Farm, Virginia

HUNTINGTON WETHERS took less than thirty seconds to cull through data from fourteen search engines and confirm Edgar Byrnes was interim caretaker at the Michael Conlon Farm. By the time Akira Tokaido had returned to the Annex Computer Room two minutes later with snacks from the rec room down the hall, Wethers had also pulled up Byrnes's military record, as well as intel linking his brothers and late father to the American Freedom Movement. He'd already passed the information along to Grimaldi and Stony Man's director, Hal Brognola, who was on his way in from the nation's capital.

"Nice work, Hunt," Tokaido told the bespectacled African American, handing his colleague a bag of trail mix and a bottle of mineral water. "You da man."

"If you say so," Wethers responded dryly. The one-time Berkeley cybernetics professor was not known for his sense of humor, and given the gravity of the situation playing out less than an hour's drive south of the Sensitive Operation Group's Shenandoah Valley headquarters, he was in no mood for levity.

Wethers and Tokaido were alone in the Computer Room, part of an Annex addition to the two-hundred-acre complex at Stony Man Farm. Carmen Delahunt had the night off, and Aaron Kurtzman was out of town at a conference with mission controller Barbara Price.

Tokaido, a young Japanese American, plopped into the chair

at his computer station. Wethers had forwarded him the pertinent information on both the gun-show incident and the rocket assault on Langley. As he waited for the data to upload, Tokaido finished off his cheese sticks and washed them down with the last few swallows from a can of soar.

"All right," he said, rubbing his hands together, "let's get digging. I'll bet you there's some kind of link to Sykesville and that depot heist in Aberdeen."

"Let's not overextend ourselves," Wethers advised, shifting between the various windows on his monitor. "For now, let's stick with Edgar Byrnes. He's got a laundry list of grievances with the VA stemming from his military service in the Persian Gulf. I'm looking for some CIA connection that might have motivated the rocket attack."

"I'll keep running the AFM angle," Tokaido said. "If something from Sykesville or Aberdeen pops up, so much the better."

The two men fell silent, and for the next few minutes the only sound in the subterranean chamber was the staccato clatter of their fingertips racing across their respective keyboards. In fact, Tokaido and Wethers were so engrossed in their work they failed to realize they had been joined until the Farm's security chief, Buck Greene, cleared his throat to get their attention.

"Good thing I'm not Osama bin Laden, or you guys would be dead meat," Greene quipped. He was a barrel-chested man in his early fifties with a square jaw and ever present scowl. In addition to overseeing security at the Farm, he was in charge of the blacksuit commandos who routinely roamed the grounds disguised as farmhands or workers at the wood chip mill that took up most of the Annex building's ground floor.

"Hey, Bucko," Tokaido called out, glancing up from his screen. "Sorry. We're on overdrive."

"I can imagine," Greene said. "I just heard. How's Cowboy?"

"Too soon to say," Tokaido reported, "but you know Cowboy. They don't make them much tougher."

"Here we go," Wethers interrupted. "Byrnes may have fired that rocket as part of some militia plot, but it was personal, too."

"How so?" Tokaido asked.

"The office at the CIA he targeted belongs to a Colonel Feli
Garber," Wethers explained. "I've got him listed here as poir
man for Army operations in Khamisiyah after the Gulf Wa
Byrnes worked under him there, clearing out Iraqi ammo depots
Byrnes has been claiming he was exposed to chemical-warfar
agents during the demolition work but was never told about i
He says he got splashed in the face with something at some poin
too, but the VA has dodged most of his medical claims, especiall
any that deal with chem agents."

"Uh-oh," Greene interjected. "Look, I hate siding with the ba
guy here, but you guys know as well as I do that there's bee
some covering up on that whole Gulf War front. We've got sicl
vets snapping right and left because they get fed up with peopl
calling them whiners."

"Well, this one here's just killed a handful of people wh
never knew what hit them," Wethers responded. "I'm not sur
how you justify something like that."

"Not to mention the fact this bombing's gonna trigger th
most paranoia since 9/11," Tokaido added. "I don't even wan
to think about the headlines tomorrow."

"I hear you," Greene said. "Panic in the streets, here w
come."

"And if this AFM outfit strikes again somewhere else,"
Wethers said, "things will only get worse."

"Hang on," Greene interjected. "Did you just say this wa
done by the AFM?"

"That's right," Wethers told him. "American Freedon
Movement. You've heard of them?"

"Sure as hell have," Greene said. He pointed at the comput
ers Wethers and Tokaido were working at. "Are you guys telling
me you haven't coughed up anything about their training cam
around here?"

"What are you talking about?" Tokaido said.

"I don't have an exact address or anything," Greene said
"but it's a couple mountain ranges over, probably aroun
Meredith Valley."

"How do you know this?" Wethers asked.

"A few of their recruits got lost doing some kind of night-training exercise awhile back and wound up stumbling across our perimeter," Greene explained. "Nearly got their asses shot to kingdom come by my blacksuits."

"When was this again?" Wethers asked. "Can you be more specific?"

"I can check the logbooks," Greene said, "but offhand I'd say a month and half, maybe two months ago."

"Well, if they're still holed up there, it might be worth checking out," Tokaido suggested.

"And the sooner the better," Wethers said. "If this camp figures into what just happened, they're going to be scrambling to destroy evidence."

"Who's trying to destroy what kind of evidence?"

The three men glanced to the doorway leading into the Computer Room. Hal Brognola had just entered, looking haggard from the White House meeting he'd just returned from.

"I'll let them fill you in," Greene told Brognola as he headed for the door. "I'm off to round up a few guys. I think we're about to play posse."

6

Washington, D.C.

"The internal bleeding was significant," Dr. Steven Thomas explained to Mack Bolan and Jack Grimaldi as the three men stood in the OR waiting room. "But it's stopped now after the surgery."

"He'll be okay, though, right?" Jack Grimaldi asked.

"We'll keep him in for observation," Thomas said.

"What about the lung puncture?" Mack Bolan asked.

"Easy fix, same as the ribs," the surgeon said. "Barring complications, he should be back in fighting shape in a couple months, three tops."

"Knowing Cowboy, we'll be lucky to keep him strapped down for a few weeks," Grimaldi said.

"It's probably best to wait until morning to see him," Thomas said. "He's been through the wringer."

"Understood," Bolan said.

Dr. Thomas excused himself and headed back out toward the hallway, crossing paths with Detective Darwin, who'd just finished making a few calls related to the gun-show altercation. Once Bolan had filled him in on Kissinger's prognosis, the detective reported the latest development on his end.

"Those security guards who turned on the vendors?" Darwin said. "Turns out the firm they work for is a front for this American Freedom Movement. We have their office cordoned off and are waiting on a search warrant, but my guess is we'll find out this isn't the first time they've used rent-a-cops as a goon squad."

"I just spoke with our people, too," Bolan said. "They say the FBI's got another warrant for an AFM compound in Virginia. They're on the way, and we've got a team of our own moving in as backup."

"Let's hope they're quick about it," Darwin said. "I don't see these militia guys staying put for long."

"Or giving up without a fight," Grimaldi added grimly. "If they think we've got 'em cornered, you can bet they'll come out firing both barrels."

"Back to the little mess here," Darwin said. "I still can't figure why they bothered with those two bikers. The way they had things blocked out, they probably would've been able to pull the thing off if you guys hadn't shown up."

"That's just it," countered Bolan, who'd given the matter some thought. "I think the bikers were thrown in at the last second when they found out the place was under surveillance."

"Which brings up the whole matter of them having someone on the inside," Grimaldi said.

"That's gonna take some digging," Darwin said. "We've got IA sniffing around the department, and the guy I talked to at BATF says they're prowling for moles, too, especially at the building where they grilled that informant who sprang the tip-off."

Grimaldi's cell phone chirped. As he flipped it open and moved off to answer it, Bolan asked Darwin, "How big of a dragnet do we have between here and Langley?"

"Twenty-mile radius last I checked," Darwin reported. "They've got ground units screening the highway exits and choppers in the air."

"Speaking of choppers," Grimaldi said, rejoining the two men, "is there a bird around here we can get our hands on?"

"There's probably a medevac on the roof," Darwin responded. "I can pull some strings."

"Give it a shot," Grimaldi suggested. "That AFM compound is up in the mountains about an hour north of here. I figure if we go by air we can get there before they expert any visitors."

McLean, Virginia

EDGAR BYRNES DISMOUNTED once he reached the Capitol Beltway underpass.

"Good job, Jefferson," he told his horse as he tethered it to a bent length of rebar poking out from the bridge's concrete foundation. Behind him, Byrnes could hear the Potomac's sluggish current wash over boulders and a snagged clot of driftwood. Overhead was the muted sound of passing traffic. To the south, he could see a helicopter hovering above the wooded grounds of Turkey Run Park. He knew he didn't have much time.

Fishing through his backpack, Byrnes withdrew one of the last items he'd packed back at the Conlon Farm, a hard plastic pencil case. Inside was a large veterinarian's syringe. He tested the plunger, squirting out a yellowish-green stream of liquid. Then he injected the rest of the tranquilizer into the horse's flank. The horse neighed and backed up, straining at the reins.

"It's just a tranquilizer, boy," Byrnes whispered. "You'll be okay."

The sedative quickly took effect. Jefferson fidgeted a few seconds, then folded its front legs. Byrnes eased the horse the rest of the way down onto the cold ground, stroking its mane. Byrnes knew no one would be able to see the horse from the air, and there was a good chance the shadows of the underpass would conceal Jefferson from view of anyone out on the water.

Byrnes stayed with the horse until it had passed out completely, then he moved out from beneath the bridge and skulked through a dense patch of shrubs leading to a small two-bedroom house set thirty yards inland from the banks of the Potomac. The house was owned by one of the American Freedom Movement's shell companies, and it was here that Byrnes had come whenever he needed to recharge the batteries on his cell phone and computer. It was also here that he occasionally met with Lance Iovine, the AFM leader who'd seen to it that he got the job at the Michael Conlon Farm and who, the night before last, had delivered to Edgar the AT-4 rocket launcher stolen from the Aberdeen proving grounds. There had been a few times, too, that Byrnes had ignored orders and arranged to meet at the house with his brothers, Harlan and Wallace, not for militia business but just to spend some time together.

It looked as if house was deserted, so Byrnes retrieved a key hidden under a rock on the back patio and let himself in the back door. The stale smell of cigarette smoke hung in the air and, two steps into the rear den, Byrnes noticed some empty soda cans and remnants of a few take-out meals on the coffee table. Edgar realized his brothers had been by again.

"Dubby?" Byrnes called out. "Harlan?"

Byrnes quickly checked through the house. His brothers weren't there. When he looked in the garage, he saw that their motorcycles were missing. Dubby and Harlan had been told they could store their Husqvarnas at the safehouse for the winter. Brynes couldn't understand why they'd picked a night like this to go out riding. He didn't give the matter much thought, however. He had more pressing things on his mind.

The Gulf vet knew there was a chance the authorities had spoken to the riders he'd encountered at Turkey Run Park. If he'd been pegged as a suspect in the rocket attack, it was important that he change his appearance. He yanked off his coat and went to the bathroom. He plucked a bottle of peroxide from the medicine cabinet and emptied it into the sink. Leaning over the basin, eyes shut tightly, he splashed his beard repeatedly, grimacing when the peroxide came in contact with the scar tissue on his cheeks. By the time he'd finished and patted the beard dry, it had turned several shades lighter and was streaked with shades of white. It was a sloppy job, but it would have to do. Byrnes lingered a moment before the mirror, staring at his reflection. For perhaps the first time in his life, he noticed how much he looked like his father, whose own ever present beard had begun to turn prematurely gray when Edgar was a teenager. The thought of the old man filled Byrnes with a sudden rush of anger. He fought it back.

Once he'd changed into fresh clothes, Byrnes donned a ski parka and stocking cap, then carried his backpack outside to the garage, where a nondescript Chevy Cavalier was parked next to where his brothers had kept their motorcycles. There was ski gear strapped to the roof and decals from half a dozen ski lodges plastered to the front and rear bumpers. Edgar knew that once he was out on the road he would easily pass for a diehard skier out looking to take advantage of the late-season snowfall. Still, to be safe, before ditching his backpack in the trunk, he removed a Walther P-99-QA semiautomatic pistol along with his cell phone. He stuffed both items into the pockets of his parka, then opened the garage door.

The Cavalier started easily. Byrnes backed out of the driveway and, less than two minutes later, he was on the Beltway, heading west, away from the nation's capital. A chopper hovered above the flow of traffic, and Byrnes tensed for a moment as it passed overhead. Once it moved past, heading toward the George Washington Parkway, he relaxed somewhat. He noticed that it was the top of the hour and switched on the radio. It didn't take him long to find a news station. As he'd expected, the lead story was the bombing of CIA headquarters. Byrnes smiled faintly as he listened. The media was milking the story for all it was worth, sensationalizing the details and trumpeting the incident as the deadliest attack on American soil since 9/11. The veteran's grin widened still further when the announcer divulged that among the fatalities were several high-ranking CIA officials.

"…the only confirmed name we have so far is former Army Colonel Felix Garber," the newsman intoned gravely. "Prior to joining the CIA, Garber served with distinction during the Gulf War and was decorated with the Medal of Freedom for his part in—"

"You've just been decorated again, you prick!" Byrnes howled.

Byrnes had no real idea where he was headed, and he knew full well that by taking matters into his own hands he'd likely estranged himself from the AFM and any support they might have to offer. But for the moment none of that mattered. At long last—more than twelve years after being condemned to his own private hell in the aftermath of Khamisiyah—Edgar Byrnes felt avenged.

7

Philadelphia, Pennsylvania

"I'm on my way, Senator," Gregory Walden told Huell Kostigan, the seventy-two-year-old Chairman of the House-Senate Intelligence Committee. Kostigan, the man Walden most frequently answered to on Capitol Hill, had just called him from his Washington office, distraught over the possible implications of the CIA bombing.

"This is a crisis situation, Walden," the New Hampshire senator insisted. "I could use your input on a game plan before I meet with the Joint Chiefs."

Walden had worked alongside Kostigan long enough to detect the faint hint of despair in the other man's normally stentorian voice. It was the same strained tone Walden had heard in the immediate aftermath of 9/11, when Kostigan had talked to him about colleagues reported missing in the jet-torn rubble of the Pentagon. Kostigan had never been the same since those fateful days, and Walden felt there was a chance the elder senator would crack once he realized the Langley bombing was merely the tip of a far more menacing iceberg. With any luck, the old man would have a coronary and die on the spot, allowing Walden to move in and fill the void, hastening along his master plan. For now, though, he thought it best to allay his colleague's fears.

"I'm sure we'll get through this in one piece, Huell," he told his superior. "Hang tight. I'll be there as soon as I can."

"Thanks, Greg." It sounded to Walden as if Kostigan was fighting back tears. "I knew I could count on you."

Walden had another call coming in. He quickly wrapped up his conversation with Kostigan, then switched lines.

It was Marcus Yarborough, the Wildest Dreams Fantasy Camp shooting instructor.

"It's about time," Walden told the sharpshooter. "I was beginning to wonder."

"Now you can stop," Yarborough responded evenly.

Part of Walden's planned response to the events in Langley and Georgetown required the services of a sniper. Joan VanderMeer had told him she would try to enlist Yarborough's aid before proceeding to the AFM's Meredith Valley compound. Walden was waiting for confirmation that the marksman had agreed to the assignment. Now he had his answer.

"We're on our way," Yarborough reported. "We should be in and out in less than an hour."

Something about the sniper's nonchalance concerned Walden. He asked Yarborough, "Has Joan told you everything that happened tonight?"

"Yeah, she told me," Yarborough responded. "What's done is done."

"That's it?"

"We need to move on," Yarborough said.

"And you're sure that you can?" Walden asked.

"If I wasn't sure, I'd say so," Yarborough snapped, his temper flaring.

"Fine, then," Walden said. "The faster we can move on things now, the better."

"Agreed."

"It's not enough to just take out Iovine," the senator cautioned. "There's evidence that needs to be secured. Paper trails that need to be erased."

"Not my department," Yarborough said. "Joanie says she's got that end covered. You need to talk to her again?"

"No," Walden said. "I just want it clear you both know how much is at stake here."

"We've got it covered," Yarborough said. "Like I said, we'll be done in an hour. Where do you want me after that?"

Walden had already given the matter some thought. He was issuing Yarborough's follow-up instructions when his disposable cell phone signaled that it was losing power. Walden quickly concluded the call, then deposited the cell phone in the front pocket of his winter jacket along with two others he'd used during the past hour while dealing with the curve ball Edgar Byrnes had just tossed him. He'd already dressed to go out and was putting on his coat on when Nikki padded into the den, her hair still askew, a satin robe pulled loosely around her.

"Where do you think you're going?" she demanded. "And what was that throwing a glass earlier all about?"

Walden was in no mood to be interrogated. "Go back to bed," he said gruffly. "I need to go out."

"Where?"

"Commissioner Gordon just flashed the bat signal," he told his wife. "I need to fetch Robin, then hop in the Batmobile so we can go fight the Penguin."

"I don't know why I bother asking," Nikki huffed. "I never get a straight answer out of you."

"It's my job, Nikki, all right?" Walden snapped. "There's an emergency. I have to go. I probably won't be back tonight."

"There's always some kind of emergency with you these days."

Walden stared at Nikki as if he hoped his gaze would vaporize her. "What part of 'national security' don't you understand?" he retorted.

"Oh, is that her name now?" Nikki shot back. "I heard that voice on the phone. It was a woman!"

"All right, I confess." Walden sighed with contempt. "I'm off to get a little something on the side. Can I go now?"

Nikki glared back at Walden. "Why did I ever marry you?"

"Gee, I don't know," Walden said. "Status? Money? You tell me."

"Bastard!" When Walden turned his back to her and stormed out, she shouted after him, "One of these days you'll regret the way you treat me!"

Walden slammed the door behind him and fumed his way to

the elevators. His teeth were clenched so tightly that by the time he reached the ground floor and headed out of the building, his entire jaw was throbbing.

"Having the car brought around, Mr. Walden?" the doorman asked, holding the door open as he grabbed for the ringing house phone.

"I just need a little fresh air," Walden said.

The doorman nodded as he picked up the phone.

"Your wife, sir," he told Walden.

"Tell her you just missed me," Walden said, turning up the collar of his jacket. He headed outside without waiting for the doorman's response.

The snowfall presently coating Virginia and parts of Maryland had yet to reach Philadelphia, but there was a strong breeze in the air and Walden could see dark clouds approaching the city. The observation barely registered with him, however. His mind was elsewhere. Screw election strategy, he thought to himself as he marched down the sidewalk. He had important business—vital business—to attend to, and yet here he was, preoccupied with yet another episode in an endless series of petty marital arguments. It was making him crazy.

Give it a rest, he told himself, lengthening his stride as if his wife's influence were a radio signal he would walk beyond range of. Once he'd turned the corner, he donned a bulky cap and wrapped a scarf around his lower face to obscure his features. There was a cab idling at a taxi stand in front of the Hotel Drexler. He got in and asked to be driven across the river to a nightclub on Kingery Avenue, a few blocks south of Liberty Square.

Halfway across the Market Street bridge, Walden's personal cell phone began to bleat; it was Nikki's ring. The senator didn't answer; he let the answering service take the call. Nikki could vent all she wanted and Walden would then erase the message without listening to it. He tried to turn his thoughts back to more pressing concerns, but less than a minute later, Nikki was calling back. Walden again refused to answer. When Nikki rang yet again, he finally shut off the phone. He was expecting other calls, but he couldn't take any more of his wife's intrusions.

As the cab maneuvered through the late-night downtown traffic, Walden used a penknife to disassemble the other cell phones he'd used back at the apartment. As he did so, his focus wavered. One moment he would be pondering his next political move, the next he would find himself fuming over the situation with his wife all over again. He knew it had to stop. There was too much at stake for him to be caught up in this constant juggling act. There seemed only one solution.

"You're toast, bitch!" Walden whispered as he stared out into the night.

Two minutes later, the senator's cab pulled to a stop at his destination, a retro dance club on South Federal called Rizzoteque.

Walden got out and paid the driver, then paused on the sidewalk near the end of a long queue of patrons waiting to get inside the club. He turned his back to the crowd, not wanting to be recognized. Once the cab rounded the corner, he turned and strode away. He walked two blocks south, then one east, putting the nightlife behind him. Whenever he came to a waste bin he discarded a piece from one of his disassembled cell phones. At the next corner, Walden turned south again and kept walking until he came to a quiet neighborhood of rundown, century-old brownstones that had once housed Philadelphia's upper crust but were now rented out to small businesses. None of the shops were open at that hour, and there were only a few lights on in the second-story apartments located directly above them.

Halfway down the block, Walden glanced around casually, making certain no one had followed him, then passed down a dark alleyway separating a hair salon from a travel agency. The alley led to a small, empty parking lot. There, the senator proceeded past the fanciful rear entrance to the hair salon. Next door, the rear facade of the building was nondescript, as was the back entryway. An old, weathered sign on the wall read Zernial Machine Shop, and taped to the door was a weathered strip of cardboard with the hastily scrawled message, Doorbell broken. Knock LOUD!

As soon as Walden ventured within range of the door's peephole, the door swung open. Walden found himself staring down the bore of a 9 mm Ruger pistol.

"Nice to see you, too, Henry," Walden said. He took off his hat and nonchalantly unwound the scarf from around his neck. "Do me a favor and point that thing elsewhere."

Hank Talbot lowered his gun and took a step back, letting Walden into the rear corridor of the machine shop. Talbot was a slight man, five foot seven and barely 150 pounds, with a scraggly mustache, sparse goatee and pale eyes the color of dishwater. Looking at him, few would have guessed the man made his living as a professional hit man. Even fewer would have been able to venture how good he was at his work. Last time he'd tried to add up his kills, Talbot had lost track at twenty-three.

"Is Benny here?" Walden asked.

"All he had to do was walk downstairs," Talbot drawled sarcastically as the two men headed down the short hallway. "What do you think?"

Benjamim Zernial, the shop's proprietor, was waiting for the other men in the dim lit back workroom. He was the same age as Walden, a portly man with thick, tattooed arms and a bald head adorned with a birthmark the shape and color of a squashed cherry. He lived alone above the shop and he'd only half-dressed for the meeting, wearing jeans, bedroom slippers and a stained, well-worn Phillies T-shirt that doubled as his pajama top. As with Talbot, nothing about Zernial's appearance or demeanor would have suggested that he was about to become a key player in the master plan that Gregory Walden had begun to set into motion.

The senator exchanged a quick greeting with the burly machinist, then motioned for Talbot to have a seat. He remained standing, pacing before a large, ancient industrial lathe.

"I need to get to Washington," he told them, "so let's make this quick."

"What about Yarborough?" Zernial asked. "I thought he was going to be in on this."

"Yarborough's taking care of Iovine," Walden responded, glancing at his watch. "Even as we speak."

Lance Iovine was President of the American Freedom Movement. Ben Zernial was Iovine's third in command. The militia's vice president, Chaz Prince, had died on the rooftop of the exhibition hall back in Georgetown during the failed gun-show heist. When Zernial had spoken with Walden on the phone earlier, the machinist had been assured that by morning Iovine would also be out of the picture, leaving him in charge. This, however, was the first Zernial had heard about Yarborough being the triggerman. The notion didn't sit well with him.

"You sure he's the right guy for this?" he asked Walden. "I mean, any other time, yeah. But with everything's that's gone down…"

"Yarborough's a professional," Walden insisted. He saw no point in bringing up his own similar misgivings. "He'll come through. And the less you know about the details, the better."

"Of course," Zernial said. "I understand. Go on."

Walden quickly recapped what he knew about recent events. The important thing was for them to understand the extent to which the big picture had changed.

"Bottom line," he concluded, "is that between what happened in Sykesville and these two shitstorms that went down tonight, we need to move up the timetable on Operation Clean Sweep. It won't be easy, but if we do things right, maybe we can spin this mess in our favor."

"Tall order," Zernial said, "but it's worth a shot."

"Or two," Talbot deadpanned. "Pardon the pun."

Walden ignored the wisecrack and eyed Talbot, laying out the plan he'd been formulating since Joan VanderMeer's initial phone call about Edgar Byrnes's attack on CIA headquarters. The original scenario had been for Langley to be bombed on the eve of the fourth of July, by which time Walden had hoped he would be ready to launch a coordinated series of attacks throughout the country. Now, thanks to Byrnes, that plan was out the window and Walden had been left to improvise.

"You and Yarborough both have surveillance intel on your targets," he told Talbot, "so I assume you know their routines well enough to move in and take care of business ahead of schedule."

Talbot shrugged. "No problem," he said, "but I kinda figured you'd want me to whack Byrnes first."

"I'd love that bastard's head on a platter," Walden confessed, "but we don't know where he is and we can't afford to waste time chasing him down."

"Gotcha," Talbot said. "You want me to take down Zeke Ambrose, then?"

Walden shook his head. "Leave him for Yarborough. I'd rather you go after Harville. If you head out now, you can probably reach Kentucky by morning."

Talbot glanced at his watch and nodded. "It's doable."

"Good," Walden said. "Take care of him, then move on to Birmingham and do that jerk Manley. I'd like it if he died slow, the more painful the better."

"I'll see what I can do," Talbot said. "Anything else?"

"That'll keep you busy for now," Walden said. He reached into his coat for an envelope crammed with ten thousand dollars in unmarked C-notes taken from his den safe. He handed the money to Talbot. "You'll get the usual bumps on confirmation of each kill."

"Works for me," Talbot said, pocketing the envelope. "But just out of curiosity—say we pull this off. Say Yarborough and I go down the list and you replace the guys we take out with your own people. Where would that put us, number-wise?"

"Ballpark figure?" Walden said. "If we gain control of the eight biggest militias in this country, I figure we'll have a hundred thousand guys at our disposal, minimum."

"You ask me," Zernial piped in, "I think it'll be closer to double that."

Talbot whistled. "Not a bad-sized army."

"Granted, not everyone'll goose-step to the same beat," Walden conceded. "Still, we're talking a solid core group to work with."

"And if we control the leadership," Zernial interjected, "we cut down on all the usual infighting."

"A united front," Talbot said.

"Exactly," Walden said.

"A united front armed to the teeth and ready to kick some ass," Zernial added pointedly.

Walden nodded, allowing a faint smile to crease his face.

"Throw in a little well-timed anarchy, and who knows? By the time the dust settles, we just might wind up in charge of the whole shebang."

"Well, for that to happen, Yarborough and I gotta start tipping the dominoes," Talbot declared, rising to his feet. "If we're done here, I've got a long drive ahead of me."

Walden nodded. "Go ahead. I need to go over a few things with Benny."

Talbot exchanged a glance with Zernial, then headed out the rear corridor, leaving Walden alone with the machinist.

For all his seeming bravado, Zernial was visibly uneasy, biting his lower lip and tugging absently at the hem of his Phillies shirt. Walden had always had his doubts about Zernial's leadership ability, and this latest display did little to change his opinion, but he knew the machinist was popular within the movement. More importantly, as Walden's plan unfolded, Zernial could be relied upon for unyielding loyalty and obedience, which had not been the case with Lance Iovine and Chaz Prince.

"Relax, Benny," Walden told the other man. "Yarborough will come through. You're as good as in."

"You're probably right," Zernial replied. "I guess I'm still just getting used to the idea. You know, finally being in charge. I mean, I've been stuck playing third banana for, what, two years now?"

"Some chess moves take longer than others," Walden responded. "Look at me. Eight years I've been stuck behind Huell Kostigan on the Intelligence Committee."

"Yeah, but that's how you want it, right?" Zernial replied. "You're always saying you want a low profile so you can make your moves without drawing attention."

"Touché," Walden conceded. "Right now, though, you're the one who's got a move to make. We need to figure out what you say once word comes down that Iovine's been shot. We need to put the right spin on it."

"That's easy," Zernial said. "We play up the conspiracy angle, right?"

Walden nodded, impressed. He thought he might have trouble spelling it out for Zernial.

"Whatever the media puts out," he told the machinist, "we need to say it's a lie and that people are being duped as part of a government cover-up. We need to plant the seed that militia heads are being executed right and left on orders from Washington as a way to shut them up."

"Waco all over again."

"Waco, Ruby Ridge, take your pick," Walden said. "Only in this case, we need to sell it as a broader conspiracy, not just some isolated incident."

"Well, if Talbot and Yarborough come through, we'll be set on that front," Zernial said.

"They'll come through," Walden reiterated.

"And I'll cover my end," the machinist said. "Hell, once we're through here, I'll go online and post something on the Web site. You know, sound the alarm."

"Good," Walden said, "but when you do, make it sound like it's coming from Iovine. Understand?"

Zernial nodded. "So it'll look like he got whacked on account of what he said."

"By the Feds," Walden amended.

"I can handle it," Zernial assured the senator. "And once I get the first post out, I'll blog out some rumors and see if we can get things stirred up with some of the other organizations. I know that if we plant a bug up Stanton's ass, he'll run with whatever we feed him."

Jack Foster Stanton was the outspoken head of Citizens for Armed Vigilance, a fanatic paramilitary sect so entrenched under his sole command that Walden had refrained from even attempting to bring it into his sphere of influence. Stanton, a former Green Beret, had turned on the government after being dishonorably discharged for insubordination during the Gulf War. He was also a media hound known to lunge at every chance for an interview. He usually got the airtime he wanted, too, since news producers knew he was always good for an inflammatory sound bite.

The mention of Stanton was like an epiphany for Walden; hearing the man's name, he stared at Zernial with the look of someone who'd just been told the answer to a baffling riddle.

The whole time Walden had been conferring with Zernial and Talbot about Operation Clean Sweep, the senator had been simultaneously trying to figure out a way to get rid of his wife without drawing suspicion on himself. Now, thanks to Zernial, he had not only the kernel of a plan but also a ready fall guy.

"Senator?" Zernial said, staring back at Walden, concerned by the other man's sudden silence.

Walden snapped out of his reverie.

"Stanton lives near here, doesn't he?" he asked Zernial.

"Yeah, across the river," the machinist said. "In Camden. Why?"

"That's what I thought," Walden said, still formulating the plan in his head. "Listen, once you've gone online and put out those postings, I want you to go pay a little visit to Stanton's place."

"His house?"

Walden nodded. "I'll see to it he's not around. There's something of his I want you to borrow."

8

Meredith Valley, Virginia

There had been a time, during her freewheeling college years at Idaho State University, that Joan VanderMeer had dismissed her father's conspiracy theories as sheer lunacy. She'd skimmed through a few of the periodicals Jonathan VanderMeer printed and distributed on behalf of outfits like the Montana Militia and had found the ranting to be as delusional as it was pedantic and simpleminded. She'd had faith in the American government and was certain that, whatever its shortcomings, the powers-that-be in Washington were not out to undermine the Bill of Rights or the first two amendments to the U.S. Constitution. She'd assumed, like millions of other Americans, that the government had its citizens' best interests at heart and would never stoop to totalitarian means when it came to dealing with those who might question, however harshly, the way it went about its business.

All that had changed in 1992, when VanderMeer, fresh out of college and interning as a cub reporter for the *Sioux City Clarion,* had unwittingly found herself among the first members of the media to arrive at the scene of the ill-fated Ruby Ridge shootout between FBI snipers and the family of white separatist Randy Weaver. She'd been stunned when Weaver's wife had taken a rifle shot through the head while holding her infant child the morning after the initial confrontation. Something about the FBI's handling of the incident and the subsequent justification for their actions hadn't set right with her. Her suspicions roused, she'd asked her editor to let her dig further into the story. Not only was her request turned down, but also the original story she'd filed had been killed and she was transferred to desk work as a proofreader and layout assistant. When she protested, VanderMeer was fired.

Jonathan VanderMeer had already come forward with an editorial claiming that Ruby Ridge was merely another warm-up exercise in a plot for world domination by the New World Order, a supposedly tight-knit cadre of media moguls, Jews, left-wing power brokers and other elitist factions responsible—according to the elder VanderMeer—for everything from the 1970s oil crisis to the assassination of John F. Kennedy.

Joan had found it more difficult than usual to dismiss her father's take on things. A seed of doubt had been planted in her mind. And when she learned that a plainclothes FBI agent had visited the *Clarion* offices the day she'd lost her reporting job, the seed of paranoia had begun to grow. She began to suspect that her phone was being tapped and that she was being followed whenever she left her apartment. When she found herself unable to land another reporting job, she became convinced that the government had somehow blackballed her. After six months of having doors slammed in her face, Joan warily accepted her father's offer to work for him, helping to design Web sites for his militia clients.

Jonathan played on his daughter's lingering suspicions about why she'd been fired from the *Clarion* and, in time, he wore down her resistance to the point where, to her own amazement, Joan found herself secretly beginning to side with her father's views. Pride, however, prevented her from admitting as much and the two of them continued to argue regularly.

A few months later, during the eleven-day standoff in Waco, Texas, between government officials and members of David Koresh's Branch Davidian collective, Jonathan VanderMeer had flown down from Idaho, determined to gather some firsthand evidence that would convince his daughter once and for all that the government was out to subvert personal liberties. Less than an hour after flames began to devour the Mt. Carmel compound, Joan received a call from her father saying he had proof the FBI had deliberately fired incendiary flash grenades to start the fire, which, by the end of the day, had killed nearly eighty of Koresh's followers, including more than twenty children.

The phone call had been Joan's last conversation with her father. The following morning Jonathan VanderMeer's body was found inside his crumpled rental car at the bottom of a ravine two miles from the airport where he had reservations for a flight back to Idaho. The authorities had ruled that he'd apparently lost control of the vehicle and crashed through a guardrail before plummeting to his death.

Joan wasn't buying it. She'd taken the next available flight to Texas, not only to retrieve her father's body, but also to search his rental car. When she was unable to find the evidence her father had alluded to, Joan became convinced that he'd been killed and that the proof had been seized by the FBI as part of a cover-up. She was equally certain that the government would next be coming after her.

After Jonathan VanderMeer's funeral—which was attended by a handful of strangers Joan assumed to be federal agents—she abruptly sold her father's business, liquidated the family assets and went into hiding. Befriended by some of Jonathan's friends and long-standing clients, Joan had continued to manage many of the militia Web sites she'd been working on prior to her father's death. She did the work anonymously and with increasing dedication, now a full-fledged believer in Jonathan VanderMeer's worldview. She was determined not only to carry the torch passed on to her, but also to one day use it to avenge her father's death.

VanderMeer managed to fly under the government's radar for nearly ten years, in the process helping to fuel fringe theories about the Oklahoma City bombing and the hanging-chad fiasco in 2000 that had put George W. Bush in the White House. In the aftermath of 9/11, however, a government informant linked her to postings on a Web site called EndFascismNow.com that claimed the so-called New World Order had masterminded the collapse of the World Trade Towers, as well as the subsequent attack on the Pentagon. Because her posting included a call to overthrow the government, VanderMeer was placed under surveillance in compliance with the newly implemented *Patriot Act*.

EndFascismNow.com had been infiltrated and shut down by the FBI, but VanderMeer managed to elude the sweep that put the Web site's founders behind bars. By then, however, her dossier had found its way to Senator Gregory Walden's desk. Once he'd read the file, which detailed VanderMeer's well-placed connections within the militia community, Walden knew he'd come upon a priority matter deserving his immediate attention.

Less than a week later, VanderMeer was tracked down and apprehended by undercover agents after leaving an AFM safehouse in Albany, New York. When she resisted, VanderMeer was injected with tranquilizers, trundled into the back seat of a waiting sedan and driven to a remote location in the mountains near Snyder's Lake. When she came to, VanderMeer found herself face-to-face with Senator Walden, a man she'd branded a lackey for the New World Order. Walden told her she'd gotten it wrong, that he was on her side.

VanderMeer didn't believe it at first, but then Walden presented her with proof that her father had indeed been killed back in Texas by FBI agents intent on stealing the video camera he'd used to film them starting the Davidian compound fire. Though the evidence was manufactured, VanderMeer took the bait. After talking with Walden over the next five hours, she became convinced not only that he was on the level, but that he might also be the movement's highest-ranking infiltrator inside the American government. Conversely, Walden saw in Joan VanderMeer the ideal person to help him with his plan to unite America's network of militia factions under one rule: his.

In the years following that fateful meeting, Walden and VanderMeer had worked as closely together as Joan had with her father. On Walden's instructions, VanderMeer had insinuated herself deeper into the militia ranks. She always made a point to avoid any internal rifts, instead focusing her energy of making herself indispensable by virtue of her Web site prowess. The ploy worked. By controlling the flow of information that fueled the militia cause, she was able to quietly steer her clients in a way that best served Walden's agenda.

Thus far theirs had been an ideal partnership, marked by common goals and a mutual respect. But now, in the aftermath of one night's turbulent events, VanderMeer felt everything had suddenly changed. When the senator called her back shortly after their initial conversation, he was even colder and testier than when she'd first given him the news about what had happened in Georgetown and Langley. He held her responsible for not talking Lance Iovine out of planting someone as unstable as Edgar Byrnes at the Conlon Farm, and he vowed to hold her personally responsible if the miscalculation led to them having to scrap the master plan they'd spent the past few years concocting. VanderMeer told Walden he was being unreasonable, which only strained matters further between them. Like it or not, it was now up to her to salvage things.

VanderMeer was still stewing with resentment as she pulled up to the gate leading to the AFM's isolated Meredith Valley compound in the Blue Ridge Mountains. The gate was closed, but she had called ahead, and after sounding her horn three times to signal her arrival, two shadowy figures emerged from the snow-covered brush inside the compound. One went straight to the gate, keying the padlock, while the other stood in the roadway, a submachine in one hand, a long, high-powered flashlight in the other.

Seconds later, the light's harsh beam half blinded VanderMeer. She cursed as she averted her gaze, blinking away the afterglow. By the time her vision came back to her, the man with the flashlight was standing alongside the nondescript Pontiac she had rented after abandoning Mitch Brower's BMW on the outskirts of Sykesville. The guard shone his light through the windows again, inspecting the car's interior to make sure VanderMeer was alone.

"Next time, point that damn thing away from my eyes!" she snapped once she'd rolled down her window.

"Sorry," the man with the flashlight apologized. He was in his late thirties with boyish features and ruddy cheeks. "Standard procedure."

VanderMeer was about to harangue the man further when she checked herself. There were more pressing concerns to deal with.

"Just let me through," she told the man, holding her temper in check. "I'm running late."

"Sure thing," the man told her. "Just pop the trunk so I can take a quick look."

VanderMeer glared at the man. "I just told you I'm running late! Didn't Iovine call you to give me clearance?"

"Yes, but I'm supposed to check every—"

"Look, keep stringing me along and instead of guard duty I'll have you scrubbing latrines with a toothbrush," she snapped. "The same one you use after meals! Do you have any idea who I am?"

The guard held his ground but shifted his gaze, looking for his colleague's support. By now the gate was open and the other man had stepped clear of the dirt road leading into the compound. Moments later both VanderMeer and the guard were fending off the harsh glare of headlights from two trucks rumbling uphill toward the gateway. Her Pontiac was blocking their way out of the compound. The second guard jogged over and waved away the man with the flashlight, then turned to VanderMeer. She didn't know his name, but she recognized him, and from the apologetic look on his face she knew that she wasn't going to be asked again to open the trunk.

"Sorry," the man told her, leaning close and lowering his voice slightly. Indicating his cohort, he added, "He's new. Real control freak."

"I noticed," she replied.

The guard smiled faintly. "Just pull over and let the trucks by, then you're good to go, okay?"

VanderMeer nodded gratefully. "Evacuation?" she asked.

"Yeah," the guard told her. "Iovine's worried about the Feds showing up with a warrant."

"He's probably right," she said. "What's he moving out?"

"Personnel and unregistered weapons," the guard explained. "Assault rifles mostly, but a few other things, too."

"What about Iovine?" VanderMeer said. "He's still here, right? I need to see him."

The other man nodded. "I think he's in his office shredding evidence. Now, can you pull over?"

VanderMeer eased the Pontiac to one side and watched as two trucks rumbled past. Their cargo bays were enclosed, so she couldn't see how many militia recruits were being evacuated along with the AFM's meager weapons arsenal. Judging from the size of the trucks, she figured twenty men, tops. By her estimation, that left at least two dozen recruits still at the compound.

Once the trucks had passed, she entered the compound and drove down the dirt road. Snow had begun to fall, dusting the trees that loomed on either side of her. The road dipped, then leveled off for another hundred yards. She slowed as she neared a steep incline leading down to a cluster of bungalows surrounding what, years ago, had been the Meredith Valley Ski Lodge. Deep, layered swaths of snow marked the old ski runs, and VanderMeer knew that sentries were posted near the top of the ski lifts. She traveled a few yards farther, then slowed to a stop on a stretch of road flanked tightly by old pines.

VanderMeer left the engine running and reached under the dashboard, tugging the trunk release. The truck lid slowly swung open. When she glanced in her side-view mirror, she could see Marcus Yarborough climbing out of the trunk. Once he had both feet on the road, he strode forward, limping slightly. He was carrying a 7.62 mm M-40 A-1 sniper rifle mounted with a 10-power Unertl scope. Except for the limp, the sharpshooter seemed to have emerged unscathed after rear-ending Jason Cummings's Hummer at the fantasy camp in Sykesville.

"Close call," Yarborough murmured, glancing back down the road. "I thought I was going to have to cap that moron."

"Lucky for him those trucks showed up," VanderMeer replied. She eyed the trees that flanked the east side of the road, then turned back to Yarborough "You know the way?"

Yarborough nodded. "Not a problem."

"And you're sure you're okay?" she asked.

"I wish people would quit asking me that," Yarborough said. "I've got that cough under control."

"That's not what I'm talking about," she said.

"Let's just do this, all right?" Yarborough said.

"All right. Give me fifteen, maybe twenty minutes to get Iovine where we want him. You know the signal."

Yarborough nodded. "Just get him in my sights," he said with cold finality. "I'll do the rest."

9

"Hit the wipers already!" Federal Marshal Antonio Vega grumbled from the front seat of the Dodge Ram. He was leading a three-vehicle caravan up the winding mountain highway that led to Meredith Valley.

Officer Colin Phipps, the van's driver, nodded at Vega and toggled a switch on the steering column. The wipers squeaked as they swept across the windshield, clearing snowflakes from the glass.

"Better?" Phipps said, keeping his eyes on the road.

"Much," Vega said. The portly marshal fingered the search warrant resting on his lap, fighting back the sense of dread that had his stomach in knots. His orders had been made clear before he'd set out with his nine-man crew to descend upon the American Freedom Movement's mountain enclave. He was to enter the compound, search for evidence and make sure everything was done by the book. His superiors had impressed upon him the need to avoid any missteps the AFM might seize upon to cry foul. As the attorney general had put it, "Last thing we need is these assholes claiming we trampled on their goddamn rights."

And what about our rights? Vega thought to himself angrily as the convoy made its way through the falling snow. He'd done his homework on the AFM and knew they were big on playing "pick and choose" when it came to observing legal statutes and procedures. There was no guarantee that waving a search warrant would allow the Feds into the compound without encountering resistance. Never mind the fact one of the militia's own men had just fired a rocket at CIA headquarters. Never mind the fact they'd just turned a Georgetown parking lot into a slaughterhouse trying to expand their weapons arsenal. Vega knew all about these fanatics and their persecution complex. Look at them the wrong way, and they'd complain to anyone who would listen.

Vega's internal grousing was interrupted by a crackling over the speakers of a transceiver mounted beneath the dashboard near his left knee.

"Marshal Vega, can you read me?"

Vega frowned and glanced at Phipps. The driver shrugged. Vega unclipped the microphone and brought it to his face.

"Vega here," he said. "Who the hell is this?"

"Special agents with the Justice Department," Jack Grimaldi explained. "There's no time to spell it all out, but we're in a chopper overhead and you're coming up on a pair of trucks that just left the AFM's little mountain playground."

"They're making a run for it," Vega guessed.

"Can't say for sure," Grimaldi replied, "but I'd put money on it."

"Great," Vega murmured. The knots in his stomach were tightening. He had no idea why the Justice Department agents had just invited themselves to the dance, but if they were about to run into trouble, he'd take all the help he could get.

"Look," he told Grimaldi, glancing out his window for a look at the approaching chopper, "this search warrant I've got is only good for their premises. I don't think there's anything in the fine print about engaging these half-wits once they've left the corral."

"You're probably right," Grimaldi responded, "but you're about thirty seconds away from staring down their headlights, so you've got a tough call to make. Between you and me, I wouldn't sweat the fine print at this point."

Vega drew in a deep breath and let it out slowly.

"Maybe I should've followed the old man's advice about being an accountant," he murmured bleakly.

"I didn't get that," Grimaldi said.

"I said if you've got any firepower on that bird of yours, feel free to share the wealth."

Vega signed off and clipped the mike back on the transceiver cradle, then tossed aside his search warrant and unsnapped the catch on his web holster, allowing easy access to his 9 mm service pistol. There was a portable flasher on the floor of the van. He grabbed it, then rolled down his window and reached out, using the lamp's magnetized base to secure it to the roof. He turned on the flasher and told Phipps, "Barricade the road. The party's coming to us."

GUS HOLLANDER SAW the flashing lights as he rounded the mountain bend in the first of the two AFM trucks. He swore as he tapped the brakes, slowing his vehicle. A few seconds later the Feds' vans came into view, blocking the road ahead.

"Sumbitches are onto us," he announced.

"No shit," replied Pete Robitelle, the barrel-chested man riding in the front seat next to him. He was already rolling his window down. "Turn this piece of crap around!"

Robitelle grabbed the sawed-off shotgun lying on the bench seat next to him, then leaned out his window and signaled to the truck behind them. The other driver was already slowing. Robitelle made a circling gesture with his hand and shouted out into the night, "Turn around!"

Hollander wrestled with the steering wheel, crossing lanes and continuing to pump the brakes as he neared the guardrail.

"Gonna be a tight squeeze," he said.

Hollander was right: the road was too narrow for him to make a complete U-turn. Once he was within a few inches of the rail, he had to put the truck into reverse and back up, cranking the wheels the other way. The second truck was bogged down attempting the same maneuver.

"Shit!" Robitelle howled, glancing over his shoulder. Several federal agents had scrambled past the van barricading the road and were rushing uphill toward the trucks, armed with M-16s.

Behind them, Vega huddled behind the Dodge Ram he'd arrived in, calling out through a bullhorn, "Step out of your vehicles with your hands up!"

"Yeah, right," Robitelle grumbled. He pumped the shotgun and yelled at Hollander, "Speed it up!"

"I'm going as fast as I can!" Hollander countered, still pulling away from the guardrail.

Robitelle peered back through the falling snow and saw the Feds fan out as they drew closer. There was no cover for them; between the guardrail and the steep rise of the mountain, there was nothing around them but asphalt and gravel.

"Screw it."

Robitelle raised his shotgun and leaned back out the window, drawing a bead on the agents closest to him. When the Feds dropped to a crouch and raised their carbines, he pulled the trigger. The shotgun's stock slammed into his shoulder as his round peppered one of the agents, dropping him in his tracks.

The battle was on.

"ONLY ONE WAY to play this out," Jack Grimaldi said, tilting the GUH medevac helicopter slightly as he changed course and began his descent through the falling snow to the mountain road below.

Mack Bolan was riding alongside Grimaldi in the chopper cockpit, double-checking the 40 mm charge he'd just loaded into the submounted grenade launcher on his M-16. The weapon hadn't come into play back in Georgetown, but as they closed in on the firefight being waged below, Bolan had a feeling the carbine would see action this time around.

Both militia trucks had turned and were facing away from the roadblock set up by Federal Marshal Antonio Vega. A half-dozen AFM gunners had bounded out of the vehicles and were trading shots with federal agents. By Bolan's count, three Feds were down and at least two militiamen had been hit. Despite the relentless exchange of gunfire, however, the Executioner doubted the militia was intent on making a final stand on the road.

He was right.

As Bolan watched from the air, the trucks began to pull away from the carnage, heading back uphill toward the compound they'd just evacuated. Meanwhile, one of the militiamen left behind thumbed the pin from a hand grenade and heaved it at the vans barricading the road.

"Pineapple!" Bolan warned Grimaldi.

"On it," Grimaldi said. Already he was changing course.

Bolan could only watch as the grenade disappeared beneath one of the vans, then detonated with so much force the vehicle was lifted off the ground and transformed into a three-ton fireball. Several Feds were struck by flying shrapnel, as were the other two vehicles. Even if someone had been left unscathed enough to drive, Bolan doubted either of the remaining vans was capable of giving chase to the fleeing trucks. It was up to him and Grimaldi to head off the enemy and block their retreat.

"Any way you can land this thing sideways?" Bolan asked as Grimaldi swung the chopper back on course toward the road. They'd pulled a good fifty yards ahead of the retreating militia trucks. "I want to get a round off with the launcher."

"Not sure," Grimaldi said. "I'm gonna have the same problem as the trucks. Not a lot of wiggle room down there."

"Do what you can," Bolan said. He held the carbine with one hand, using the other to maneuver the chopper's searchlight. He switched the beam on and aimed it at the front windshield of what was now the lead militia truck. As he'd hoped, the glare forced the driver to slow, buying Grimaldi more time to make his landing.

By now most of the AFM gunners had scrambled back into the trucks. One of the men out on the road loosed a round at the Feds left standing near the fiery roadblock, then turned his assault rifle on the chopper.

"Incoming!" Bolan warned, ducking to one side.

Grimaldi did the same. Bullets drummed off the chopper's outer skin. One round glanced off the windshield, cracking the glass. Grimaldi kept the aircraft under control throughout the onslaught, adjusting his course slightly as he drew closer to the road. As he'd suspected, there wasn't enough clearance between the road and the steep rise of the cliff to land at an angle. Instead, he centered the bird's nose over the median strip and brought the chopper to a rest on the asphalt. He kept the engine running. The rotorwash sent snow flying up off the road in all directions, creating a temporary screen. Bolan had tilted the searchlight so that it was aimed straight ahead, making it even more difficult for the enemy to target them.

"Lay low," Bolan told Grimaldi as he threw open his door.

Scrambling out of the chopper, Bolan dropped to an immediate crouch, the thunder of the rotors pounding in his ears. He stared down the road and saw militiamen piling out of the second truck. The driver in the lead vehicle, however, had one hand held before his face to screen the searchlight's glare. It looked as if he'd decided he was going to try to make his way past the chopper. When the truck began to groan forward, picking up speed, Bolan took aim, finger on the trigger of the grenade launcher.

"You had your chance," he murmured, unleashing the M-203's 40 mm grenade.

The warhead whooshed into the truck's grillework, then detonated, setting off an explosion that ripped through the engine compartment. The vehicle stopped in its tracks as a flame-backed shock wave rent the cab, incinerating the two men in the front seat. Another two militiamen standing on the road nearby howled as they were fragged with shrapnel. Bolan finished them off with his M-16.

Their escape route suddenly blocked, Gus Hollander and Pete Robitelle abandoned the second truck, as did the men riding in back. They were quickly confronted by a half-dozen federal agents charging up the road toward them. When Hollander and Robitelle took cover in front of their truck, Bolan fired a warning burst into the asphalt at their feet.

"Give it up!" he shouted.

The two militiamen turned and drew a bead on Bolan, Robitelle with his shotgun, Hollander with a 10-round .40-caliber Browning Pro-9. Bolan had them beat, however, and dropped both men with a volley from his M-16.

The Feds, meanwhile, had taken another five militiamen out of the fight. That left only three AFM gunners standing. Two threw up their hands in surrender. The third started to do the same, then suddenly broke into a run and vaulted over the guardrail to his immediate right.

Bolan bolted from the chopper and ran alongside the railing until he reached the spot where the fugitive had gone over. The militiaman had landed on a steep embankment and was sliding downhill feetfirst, loose snow and gravel flying out in front of him. It was a precarious drop, but Bolan could see that if the man could reach a ledge some fifty yards downhill, he'd have a chance to get away.

Discarding his carbine, Bolan straddled the guardrail, then let himself drop down onto the path made by the fleeing gunman. He grimaced as gravity pulled him down the jagged rock facing. He had little control over his descent and, much as he clawed at the rocks, he was unable to slow himself. Because the way had been cleared for him, however, he found himself gaining ground on the fleeing militiaman.

The militiaman slid another ten yards downhill, then slammed into a boulder and tumbled over it to the ledge below. Dazed, he rolled to his right. He was about to plummet over the side when Bolan caught up to him. Grabbing hold of a thick shrub, Bolan anchored himself as best he could and reached out, closing his fingers around the other man's wrist. The man went over the side, but Bolan held on and kept him from falling any farther. As the militiaman dangled in the air, gravel rattled past him, falling more than thirty yards straight down before clattering off jagged boulders at the base of the crevasse.

"I've got you," Bolan told the man, shifting his weight to give himself more leverage. "I'm going to try to pull you up."

The militiaman stared down at the rocks below, then looked up at Bolan, pleading, "Don't let me fall, man. Don't let me fall!"

"Quit squirming!" Bolan told him. "Keep still until you can grab at the ledge with your other hand."

"Okay, okay," the other man gasped.

Bolan felt as if his arm were about to pop from its socket under the weight of the man he was trying to lift. Clenching his teeth, he pulled harder, hoping the shrub would support their combined weight.

By now Grimaldi had taken the chopper aloft again and banked out over the ravine, shining his searchlight down on

Bolan and the man he was trying to rescue. It was only then that Bolan got his first good look at the militiaman.

"You're just a kid," Bolan said.

"I'm seventeen," the youth snarled, blood streaking his rock-scraped chin. "What of it?"

Bolan didn't answer. There would be plenty of time to question the youth later.

Grimaldi kept the chopper in place, holding the searchlight steady on Bolan as he hauled his prisoner up closer to the ledge. Finally the youth reached a point where he could lean forward on his own and grab at a scalloped cleft just to Bolan's right. The Executioner drew in a breath, then gave a final tug, bringing the young man to safety.

Exhausted, Bolan dropped to a squat, grabbing at his strained shoulder. His clothes had been torn in several places, and blood was seeping down his leg and right side from gashes left by the embankment he'd just slid down. He knew there was no way he'd be able climb back up to the road.

"We'll have to wait for them to get a rope down to us," he told the young man. "Then we'll—"

Bolan stopped in midsentence as the teenager suddenly rose to his feet and lunged forward, grabbing the Executioner's tattered sleeve. Had Bolan been as unprepared as the youth hoped, he might have easily found himself flung over the ledge to the rocks below. As it was, Bolan barely had time to reach out for the shrub he'd relied on earlier. In the same motion, he instinctively lashed out with his other hand, striking his attacker with a karate chop to the shoulder.

The blow was slight but still strong enough to throw the youth off balance. He lost his grip on Bolan's shirt as he flailed his arms, trying to keep himself from reeling backward. His reactions were too slow, however. One second Bolan was staring into the youth's horror-stricken eyes; the next he was gone.

Grimaldi shifted the searchlight and Bolan warily stepped forward and peered over the ledge. Thirty yards below, the youth was splayed across the boulders, skull cracked open, his life-blood spilling over the rocks.

Bolan felt a grim weariness come over him. One of the bikers back in Georgetown hadn't been much older than the man who now lay dead on the rocks below. Two young men who were supposed to be a part of America's bright future, and yet they'd chosen to die trying to bring their country down.

"What a waste," Bolan whispered into the cold night.

10

Buck Greene paused to catch his breath halfway up the mountain leading to the northern perimeter of the American Freedom Movement's camp in Meredith Valley.

"I gotta quit skipping our exercise drills," he groaned to Matt Roenicke, one of the twenty blacksuits the security chief had brought with him from Stony Man Farm. They'd driven back roads to a fire trail at the base of the snow-tipped mountain, then abandoned their trucks and split off into seven three-man units before tackling the steep slope. From his vantage point, Greene could see half the men spread out across the mountainside, making slow upward progress. He assumed the others were out there somewhere, using scattered pines and boulders for cover.

Rounding out Greene's team was Jeff Santana, a one-time Olympic decathlon champion currently on leave from the U.S. Marine Corps. Unlike Greene, Santana had barely broken a sweat despite the arduous climb.

"Want a piggyback ride, Chief?" the younger man teased.

"Want me to drop-kick your sorry ass back down to our trucks?" Greene taunted back.

Roenicke was about to get in his two cents' worth when the men were distracted by the distant sound of gunfire and muffled explosions.

"Sounds like it's out on the main road," Santana said.

Greene nodded. "To the south," he said. "The marshals were coming up that way. They must've run into a reception committee."

"That's gonna change our game plan," Roenicke guessed.

"You got that right," Greene said. "Odds are we're not just backup anymore."

The security chief tapped the earbud transceiver linking him with the other team leaders, then spoke in the general direction of the mike line trailing down the side of his neck.

"Ball's in our court, gang," he whispered. "Pick up the pace. Anybody with night peepers, slap 'em on."

Greene had night-vision goggles propped up on his forehead. He lowered them over his eyes, then led his men farther up the hill, forging a trail as best he could in the ankle-deep snow. They'd come to within fifty yards of the mountain ridge when they first met resistance. A single rifle shot cut through the night air, bringing Santana to his knees.

"That smarts," Santana moaned, clutching his chest. He said it matter-of-factly, his voice eerily calm. When he exchanged a glance with Greene, however, the security chief felt a strange shiver run down his spine. He'd seen that look only a few times in his life, and in each case it had always meant the same thing: he was looking at someone who knew that Death had just tapped him on the shoulder.

Greene crouched low and moved to the other man's side, but Santana went limp and fell away from him. His carbine dropped into the snow, which had already begun to turn red with the Olympian's blood.

Roenicke, meanwhile, took cover behind a nearby boulder and peered up toward the ridgeline, trying to pinpoint where the shot had come from.

"How is he?" he called out to Greene.

The security chief removed his fingertips from Santana's wrist and peered up at Roenicke through his night goggles. "He's gone."

Another rifle shot echoed down the mountainside. Santana's body jerked slightly as the round thumped into him. Greene lunged clear and rolled to one side, then crawled behind a pine tree several yards from Roenicke.

"They've got sentries up there somewhere," Greene warned the others over his transceiver. "Watch your step!"

The security chief adjusted his goggles, then peered uphill, scanning the tree-dotted ridgeline.

"There," he whispered to Roenicke, gesturing with his head. "Straight up and twenty, maybe twenty-five yards to the right. Looks like some kind of shed."

"I see it," the other man said.

"Keep the bastard busy," Greene told him. "I want to get closer."

"Will do."

Roenicke raised his carbine into firing position and took aim at the silhouetted structure.

"Now!" Greene whispered, breaking from cover.

Roenicke's M-16 barked to life as Greene bolted uphill, hunched over, zigzagging between trees and rocks to make himself an elusive target. A shot caromed off one of the boulders, but the security chief managed to reach the peak unscathed. There, he dropped to the ground and began to crawl toward the shed, carbine in his right hand. When he saw a length of cable feeding out from the far side of the structure, he realized it was a ski lift. The sniper was inside, preoccupied with the steady stream of fire Roenicke was directing his way. Greene circled around to his left until he had a clear view of the gunner's upper torso.

"This one's for you, Sanny," Greene muttered, lining up the sentry's head in his sights. He squeezed the trigger and watched the sniper drop from view.

Jumping to his feet, Greene rushed the shed, his carbine held at the ready. The enemy gunner was sprawled out on the ski lift's unloading platform, dead, rifle at his side. Behind him, leaning against a wall, were skis and poles.

Greene grabbed the dead man's weapon and held it aloft so that Roenicke could see it, then turned and glanced down the ski run toward the AFM compound. He noted activity around some of the bungalows, as well as inside the main lodge. For the moment, at least, it didn't appear that anyone was aware the camp's northern perimeter had been compromised. That would change soon enough, given the crackle of gunfire along the entire ridgeline.

Greene remained inside the lift unloading shed and quickly conferred with the other team leaders over his earbud. By the time Roenicke had caught up with him, he'd heard from everyone. They'd lost another man, but the remaining AFM sentries had been taken out and the blacksuits had secured the perimeter. But, given the battle sounds they'd heard earlier, Greene suspected it was no longer enough. He knew it was up to the blacksuits to engage the enemy until reinforcements showed up. Charging downhill on unfamiliar turf to confront a waiting enemy was a recipe for disaster, however. There had to be a better way to carry out their amended mission.

Surveying the southern slope through his night goggles, Greene's gaze lingered on the ski runs. The snowpack was slight, but he thought it might be able to support limited traffic.

"If there's enough ski gear," he told the other team leaders, hatching the plan as quickly as it had come to him, "I want as many guys as possible to strap up and lead the charge downhill."

AFM PRESIDENT LANCE Iovine was oblivious to the mayhem unfolding outside the converted ski lodge that now served as his base of operations. Holed away in the upstairs cocktail lounge he'd appropriated for his private office, the only sound he could hear was that of incriminating militia documents being turned into confetti as fast as he could feed them into his portable shredder.

The one-time Gary, Indiana, metal forger wasn't alone. Two young recruits were filling cardboard boxes with items Iovine planned to take on the run with him, and a third man was busy deleting files from a laptop on the desk next to where Iovine was working the shredder.

"Where are we going to take all this stuff?" one of the recruits asked as he sealed a box with packing tape.

"You'll know when we get there," Iovine snapped. "Just keep working."

The recruit exchanged a glance with his colleague, who rolled his eyes as he filled another of the boxes with a Rolodex and clipboards filled with mailing addresses. Iovine fed the shredder until it had filled to capacity, at which point it jammed. The older man cursed as he wrestled with the mechanism, prying off the lid and dumping ribboned strips of paper out onto the floor. He was slamming the lid back in place when the man at the desk turned to him.

"Sorry, sir," he said timidly, "but I think there's something here you should see."

"What now?" Iovine bellowed.

"This just popped up on our Web site." The recruit pointed at the laptop's screen. "There must be some sort of mistake."

Iovine lit a cigarette, then blew smoke across the desk as he leaned over to read the message on the computer screen. It was purportedly an official communiqué from AFM, distancing the organization from both the attack on CIA headquarters and the botched gun show robbery in Georgetown. According to the dispatch, both events had been carried out by rogue AFM malcontents who'd been recruited by the FBI to discredit the outfit's current leadership.

"What the hell?" Iovine railed. "I didn't authorize this!"

"That's the problem, sir." The recruit warily scrolled down the screen, bringing up the bottom of the web document, which bore Iovine's electronic signature.

"Someone forged my name!" Iovine was incredulous. "Someone put my name on this piece of crap! What the hell's going around on here?"

"I think I know, Lance."

Iovine whirled, tracking the voice to the doorway. There stood Joan VanderMeer.

"Some federal agents are trying to storm the compound," she told the men surrounding Iovine. "We need more help out there."

The man who'd been deleting the computer files joined the other two recruits, who'd moved to a gun rack on the south wall. Iovine's personal trove of assault rifles had already been loaded up and shipped out on the trucks that were now under federal control out on the road leading from the compound. The recruits had to make do with registered shotguns and hunting rifles. Once armed, they charged past VandeerMeer out the doorway. Iovine stayed put behind the desk, his eyes now filled with bewilderment as much as rage.

"The Feds are here already?" he cried out.

VanderMeer nodded calmly and moved toward the large picture window overlooking the grounds. The drapes were closed. She slowly pulled them open and peered out a moment, then turned back to Iovine.

"We knew they'd be coming," she said calmly, letting her gaze drift to the tumble of shredded documents spread out across the floor. "I trust you've gotten rid of any paper trails."

"I was working on it until I found out about this," Iovine retorted, stabbing a finger at the laptop's screen. "Was this your doing? Or was it Walden?"

VandeerMeer didn't answer. She glanced back out the window, then took a step back. For the first time, her composure broke.

"Oh, my God!" she gasped.

"What?" Iovine yelled, moving away from the desk.

She fell silent and continued to gaze out the window. Iovine strode past her and stood before the glass, trying to see past his own reflection and figure out what had startled the woman. Behind him, VandeerMeer discreetly took a step back and turned away from the window.

"I don't see any—"

Iovine was cut off in midsentence as a sniper round shattered the plate glass and caught him squarely in the face. The impact knocked the leader backward, and he fell to the floor at Vander-Meer's feet. She crouched beside him long enough to make sure he was dead, then looked back toward the window, where a gust of wind blew in, stirring the curtains.

"Well done, Marcus," she murmured.

11

While awaiting his chance to take out Lance Iovine, Marcus Yarborough had heard an explosion out on the mountain road just south of the AFM compound, followed by sporadic gunfire on the ridgeline directly behind him. Wary the compound was about to come under siege, the sharpshooter retreated from his favored sniper position atop an exposed rock escarpment halfway up the mountainside overlooking Iovine's headquarters. He shifted to a position amid a sprawl of dense, low-growing shrubs twenty yards farther uphill, where his view of the lodge had been partially obstructed by low-hanging branches of the nearby trees. He'd barely had time to line up Iovine's office window in his sights before VandeerMeer had opened the drapes and lured the AFM leader before the glass. It had turned into a rush job, with Yarborough's margin for error whittled to nothing. He wasn't used to working under such conditions, but it wasn't as if he'd been left with much choice.

Now, as he slowly lowered his M-40 A-1 sniper rifle, Yarborough stared impassively at the shattered window of the distant lodge, awaiting the verdict. A moment passed, then, just as the sniper was beginning to doubt he'd killed Iovine, Joan VanderMeer moved into view and cupped her hands on either side of her head, giving the prearranged signal that the AFM leader was indeed dead. She held the pose for only a fleeting second, then disappeared from view.

Yarborough was relieved, but his expression remained unchanged. Yes, he'd just carried out his mission and, yes, he'd settled a personal score with Iovine. But like most of the men in his trade, Yarborough was emotionally gutted; he'd learned long ago that feelings were an impediment that could only hinder his performance. And so there was no exultation for Yarborough. He'd done his job; that was it. Besides, he now had some unexpected complications to deal with.

Within the past few minutes, virtually the entire AFM compound had turned into a war zone, dashing Yarborough's hopes that he could merely jog undetected through the woods back to the mountain road. And even he did manage it, there was no guarantee that VandeerMeer would be able to make it back to her car, much less meet him at their arranged rendezvous point on the road. Like it or not, the sniper knew he was likely on his own.

Inching cautiously from his position, Yarborough peered downhill through the shrubs. Recruits were fanning out from the compound bungalows and firing up into the hills around him. They seemed unaware that their leader had just been claimed by sniper fire, however. Instead of looking Yarborough's way, they were directing their fire at the ski runs, where men in unfamiliar black mesh outfits were slaloming down the hill with carbines slung across their shoulders. Back up near the ridgeline, other infiltrators pelted the compound with a steady torrent of rifle-fire.

Yarborough realized he was trapped. Any direction he took was likely to place him in the line of fire. Yet if he stayed put, Iovine's body would eventually be discovered and a search party would scour the hills for the sniper. Even with a 9 mm S&W semiautomatic pistol to back up his sniper rifle, Yarborough had little faith he could survive a shootout. Flustered, he tried to shut out the din of gunfire and focus on other options. None presented themselves.

Then, in a flash, it came to him.

"The mines," Yarborough whispered to himself. Of course. He couldn't believe he hadn't thought about them from the onset.

Before he'd signed on with Jason Cummings and Mitch Brower at the Wildest Dreams Fantasy Camp, Marcus Yarborough had put in nearly ten years with the American Freedom

Movement. When not out running guns along the coast, he'd spent time at Meredith Valley as a shooting instructor for new recruits. As such, he knew firsthand the camp's layout: it had been one of the reasons Joan VanderMeer had turned to him as the man best able to carry out Lance Iovine's execution. Now he hoped that same familiarity would allow him to escape both the militia and government agents closing in on them.

Yarborough slung his rifle, then unsnapped his holster and drew his Smith & Wesson and quickly attached its extended sound suppressor. Rising from a crouch, he retreated deeper into the pines, treading lightly on the scattered twigs that lay amid the carpet of pine needles and powdered snow beneath his feet.

The assassin had zigzagged his way fifty yards up the side of the mountain when he suddenly stopped. Up ahead, he could hear the faint approach of someone making his way downhill toward him. Yarborough slipped behind the nearest conifer and tensed, straining to hear the other man's footsteps.

Moments later, Matt Roenicke wandered into view, stagger-stepping his way down the snow-covered slope, M-16 clutched in both hands. The Stony Man blacksuit clearly seemed more concerned with the recruits milling about the bottom of the hill than anyone he might have spotted in the nearby brush.

Yarborough waited until the other man had passed within five yards of him, then slowly raised his pistol. Roenicke apparently heard him and veered to one side. His reaction was too late, however. Before the blacksuit could pivot to face his assailant, Yarborough triggered a silenced round from his S&W into Roenicke's right temple. The blacksuit's carbine dropped from his lifeless fingers as he pitched to the ground.

Yarborough stayed put a few seconds, on the alert for anyone who might have been coming down the hill with Roenicke. Seconds passed. No one else came forward. Gunfire between the militia and the slain man's colleagues continued to echo throughout the valley, and soon, above the explosive chatter, Yarborough could hear the pulsing warble of an approaching helicopter. He finally broke from cover, stepped over Roenicke's body, then quickly made his way uphill, seeking a path that ran parallel to the valley floor. Once he came upon it, he followed the trail a dozen yards or so, carefully scanning the surrounding terrain. Soon he reached the landmark he'd been looking for, a spot where the trail doglegged around a cluster of large, lichen-encrusted boulders poking up through the thick brush.

Yarborough left the trail and wormed his way through the shrubbery, grimacing when the sturdy branches scraped his face and arms. Once he'd circled up behind the boulders, he dropped to his knees and put his shoulder to one of the larger rocks. He leaned into it, straining until the boulder began to roll free. Then he quickly shifted his grip and held on to the rock to keep it from tumbling downhill.

Where the boulder had once rested, there was a narrow cavity. Yarborough eased himself into the opening, keeping one hand on the boulder. Once inside, he eased the boulder back into place, immersing himself in total darkness.

Yarborough doubted that any of the recruits down at the camp were aware that years before its use as a ski facility, Meredith Valley had been a center for mining operations. Veins once rich with iron, coal and manganese had been long played out and the main shafts had been sealed off, but a series of interconnecting smaller tunnels had remained intact and even been extended so that they formed a subterranean network that Lance Iovine hoped would serve as an avenue of escape should the compound ever come under attack. During his stay at the compound, Yarborough had been shown the various entryways and had even helped dig one of the connecting passageways. At the time, he'd doubted the need for such tunnels, and both he and VanderMeer had even taunted Iovine about them, wondering if in a former life the AFM leader been a gopher. Now Yarborough was thankful for the man's foresight and almost felt a tug of regret for having just killed him.

Almost...

"SET US DOWN over there," Bolan shouted above the droning rotors of the medevac chopper Jack Grimaldi was guiding down toward the clustered AFM barracks. The Executioner was pointing to an asphalt rectangle fifty yards from the nearest building. In better weather, the strip was no doubt used as a tennis court, but for now it offered an ideal pad upon which to land the converted GHU-1 helicopter.

Grimaldi shifted course slightly, then carefully set the bird down, raising a cloud of freshly fallen snow. Bolan scanned the surrounding terrain and fired the last rounds in his M-16 at a trio of enemy gunners hunched behind a rusting equipment chest situated next to one of the barracks. As he replaced the carbine's ammo clip, he noted the progress Buck Greene's blacksuits were making against the other militiamen. Having skied their way down to level ground, the Stony Man security force had felled at least ten of the enemy and convinced another five men to surrender. Still more Stony Man soldiers could be seen charging down the various ski runs on foot, further turning the battle's tide.

"Let's wrap this up," Bolan told Grimaldi, arming the carbine's submounted M-203 launcher with one of his two remaining grenades.

"Right behind you," Grimaldi said, drawing his 9 mm Government Model.

Bolting from the chopper, Bolan sidestepped a spray of return fire from the men behind the equipment chest. Once he'd cleared the tennis court, Bolan dropped behind a concrete bench and took aim at his attackers. The grenade launcher shuddered in his hands when he fired, and seconds later the metal equipment chest erupted under the explosive force of a 40 mm warhead. The men behind the chest were flattened by the blast, riddled with frag shrapnel. None of them were alive when Bolan and Grimaldi caught up with them. Only one of the men looked to be over thirty.

"More kids," Bolan murmured.

"When they're trying to put a slug through your heart you can't think of them as kids," Grimaldi assured Bolan. "It was them or us."

Bolan knew Grimaldi was right. Still, it disheartened him to see yet more proof that the militia movement had become a magnet for the country's disaffected youth. It wasn't right.

The two Stony Man operatives grimly moved on, trading shots with another two recruits who'd just raced out of the rear doorway of the main lodge. They'd killed one when the other threw down his shotgun and raised his hands in surrender.

"Anyone else in there?" Bolan shouted as he stormed toward the entryway.

The prisoner bobbed his head and muttered, "Man and a woman."

"A woman?" Bolan glanced quickly at the parking lot adjacent to the building. There was no sign of the BMW driven by the woman who'd fled from the Wildest Dreams Camp back in Sykesville, but in light of all that had happened the past two days, the Executioner couldn't help thinking that fate had put him back on the trail of Mitch Brower's colleague.

"Go ahead," Grimaldi told Bolan as he motioned for the recruit to spread-eagle against the lodge wall. "I've got him."

As Grimaldi frisked his prisoner, Bolan set aside the M-16 and drew his Beretta. He inched toward the rear door, then yanked it open and charged in. The rear vestibule was deserted, and Bolan stepped over a few overturned boxes and entered a long hallway lined with doorways, most of them open. He moved cautiously from room to room, braced for any sign of activity. Outside, there was a lull in the gunfire. Bolan could hear voices in the distance. The blacksuits had won the skirmish and were rounding up survivors.

The Executioner finished searching the ground floor and was starting up a wide, steep wooden staircase just off the main room when he heard footsteps behind him. Bolan whirled but held his fire when he heard a familiar voice.

"It's just me!" Buck Greene called out.

"In here," Bolan said, keeping one eye on the second-floor landing. The Stony Man security chief soon appeared, limping slightly.

"Wrenched my knee coming downhill," Greene muttered.

"Things under control out there?" Bolan asked.

"Pretty much," Greene reported. "We lost a few guys, but they took the worst of it."

"Two left in here," Bolan said. Raising his voice, he called upstairs, "It's over! Come out with your hands up!"

Again, Bolan was answered by silence. Cautiously, he started back up the steps, Greene following close behind.

The two warriors slowly made their way up to the second floor, then split off. As he neared the first doorway to his right, Bolan could hear a faint rustling. He hesitated a moment, then charged into the room, pointing his Beretta in the direction of the sound. The curtains in Lance Iovine's office were stirring in the cold breeze that blew in through the shattered window. A few feet away, near the toppled shredder, Iovine lay dead on the wooden floor, blood seeping from his ravaged skull. Strips of shredded paper curled faintly as they soaked up the blood. Judging from the broken window and the way Iovine had landed, Bolan guessed that the slain leader had just been shot by someone out on the mountain.

That left just the woman unaccounted for.

Bolan glanced around the office, Beretta still at the ready. There was no sign of Joan VanderMeer.

There was a stack of sealed cardboard boxes near Iovine's desk. Bolan went over and was about to pry at the packing tape when his eyes fell on the desk, where a disconnected computer cable lay across the ink blotter like a resting snake. On a hunch, Bolan pressed his hand against the blotter; it was still warm. He was mulling the implications when Greene appeared in the doorway, looking agitated.

"There's a dumbwaiter at the end of the hall," he told Bolan, "Somebody just took it down to the basement!"

"Let's go!" Bolan snapped, heading for the doorway. "She's got a laptop with her, and it's probably filled with evidence."

ONCE THE DUMBWAITER delivered Joan VanderMeer to the basement, she scrambled out, clutching Lance Iovine's laptop tightly under one arm. Overhead, she could hear her pursuers thumping their way downstairs from the slain leader's second-story office. Once they reached the ground floor, it would take them only a few seconds to reach the basement. VanderMeer knew she didn't have much time.

She did, however, have a plan.

Like Marcus Yarborough, in her moment of need VanderMeer had recalled the underground escape routes Lance Iovine had burrowed throughout the compound. She knew there was an entrance to one of the tunnels inside the basement; Iovine had once shown it to her. Unfortunately, at the time she hadn't paid much attention to how Iovine had triggered open the sliding wall that led to the passageway. Now, as she rushed across the basement, she thought back and replayed the encounter in her mind, trying to recall the necessary details.

"Think!" she told herself once she'd reached the mortared cinder-block wall, which was partially concealed behind a leaning stack of tall storm windows. "Think, damn it!"

Finally it came to her.

VanderMeer set down the laptop, freeing both hands so that she could quietly move the storm windows, revealing an ordinary-looking light switch built into the wall. Instead of flipping the switch all the way up, she moved it halfway so that it stuck out perpendicular to the wall. She then toggled the switch sideways while simultaneously extending one finger and applying pressure to the lower screw securing the switchplate to the wall.

It worked. First there was a dull thunking sound within the wall, then the wall itself groaned faintly.

"Yes!" she said. She leaned her weight into the wall and pressed both hands against the brickwork, then strained to one side, slowly easing the wall open along its unseen runners. Once the gap seemed wide enough, she grabbed the laptop and squeezed her way through, then slid the wall back into place. By the time the inner catch had clicked shut, VanderMeer could hear her pursuers making their way down the basement steps. She'd made it, just barely.

Much as she wanted to break into a run and flee, it was dark inside the tunnel and she was afraid to move for fear of making a noise that would give herself away. As it was, she could only hope the men pursuing her hadn't heard her close the wall behind her.

Holding her breath, laptop tucked back beneath her arm, Van-

derMeer slowly withdrew a palm-sized Kahr MK-40 semiautomatic pistol from her coat pocket. She knew how to use the
22-ounce gun, but she hoped it wouldn't be necessary. If she
stayed motionless, she felt there was still a chance her pursuers
would give up the search and leave the basement without stumbling upon her escape route. Once that happened, she would feel
more confident venturing into the darkened reaches behind her.

And so she waited, listening to the men's muffled voices as
they moved around the basement, seeking her out. Soon her
eyes began to accustom themselves to the darkness. Glancing
down, she saw a faint sliver of light creep out from the base of
the wall. As the seconds dragged on, the illumination seemed to
expand and spread past her. Glancing over her shoulder, VanderMeer could begin to make out the chiseled walls of the tunnel
behind her. Still, she stayed put, clutching the computer close,
her right palm sweating around the rubberized grip of the
MK-40.

VanderMeer's resolve lasted a moment or two longer, roughly
the time it took for Mack Bolan to come across the displaced
storm screens and turn his attention to the wall they'd been
leaning against moments before. When the wall trembled faintly
under Bolan's touch, she recoiled. The Executioner was now
close enough that she could make out what he was saying.

"This wall has some give," he told his colleague. "Give me a
hand."

VanderMeer took a step backward. When Bolan suddenly
kicked at the wall, she panicked and began to flee into the tunnel.
The tunnel was still dark so she reached out with her gun hand,
feeling her way along the cold, scalloped walls. Lance Iovine
may have shown her how to access the tunnel, but she had never
actually been inside the passageway. She had no idea how long
it extended before coming to its first bend. She wasn't aware
Iovine had installed lights in the passageway, either, and when
her hand brushed against a switchbox imbedded in the stone
wall, she was reluctant at first to try the switches. But when
Bolan and Buck Greene put their combined weight against the
wall behind her, hoping to spring the lock and slide open the

door, VanderMeer threw caution to the wind and flicked the entire bank of switches.

Rows of recessed lights suddenly blinked to life in both directions, basking the tunnel with a dim, incandescent light. VanderMeer turned one of the switches off, dousing the row of recessed bulbs stretching back to the basement wall. The way before her—a thirty-foot-long straightaway—remained clearly lit.

As she continued along the tunnel, lengthening her stride, VanderMeer tried to orient herself. It seemed that she was passing beneath the tennis court and would soon be nearing the base of the mountain near the ski runs. Once there, she knew she would merge with the original mine shafts, some of which led away from the valley.

VanderMeer was beginning to think she might actually have a chance of escaping when she came to a fork in the tunnel and turned right. There, she stopped in her tracks, gasping. Less than two feet away from her stood a man holding a pistol and rifle. In the dim light she couldn't make out the man's features, and she instinctively raised her Kahr MK-40 to fire.

The man quickly reached out, however, and grabbed her by the wrist before she could get a shot off.

"Easy," Marcus Yarborough told her.

"Marcus!" VanderMeer whispered with disbelief. "How did you know I'd wind up—?"

"I didn't," Yarborough interrupted. "I'm just trying to get the hell out of here."

"Join the club," VanderMeer said, slowly regaining her wits. "Do you know where you're going?"

Yarborough nodded. There was a switchbox near the junction. The sniper unclipped a flashlight from his belt and turned it on, then flicked off the recessed lights stretching down the tunnel. He moved past Joan and started down the other fork.

"Follow me," he directed.

"THERE HAS TO BE a button or latch around here somewhere," Mack Bolan told Buck Greene as he ran his fingers along the wall both men now felt sure the woman had disappeared behind. In addition to kicking and shaking the wall in hopes of budging it, both men had already tried the telltale light switch, but for them it had done nothing more than turn on a bulb in the corner.

"Yeah, whatever it is," Greene ventured, "it's either well hidden or she disabled it from the other side."

The security chief hobbled on his bad knee over to a nearby workbench piled high with a haphazard array of tools and several small wooden crates. He started looking through the boxes, then stopped briefly when Jack Grimaldi announced himself and bounded down the steps, carrying the M-16/M-203 combo Bolan had left back near the rear entrance.

"Things are under control outside," he reported. "What about here?"

"We ran into a brick wall, so to speak," Bolan said. He spelled out the situation, then, his gaze on the weapon Grimaldi had brought with him, he added, "Maybe there's a quick way to pick the lock."

"Grenade?" Greene said.

Bolan nodded, retrieving the final warhead clipped to his ammo belt. "It's worth a shot."

"Provided we don't bring this whole dump crashing down on our heads," Grimaldi said.

"I say we take our chances." Bolan reached out for the carbine and told Grimaldi, "Go take the bird back up and keep an eye open in case she makes it out before we get to her."

"Will do."

Grimaldi retreated back upstairs. Bolan, meanwhile, led Greene to an area beside the staircase. There, the Executioner quickly loaded the grenade launcher. Greene grabbed a handful of foam packing pellets from a half-opened box and held them out to Bolan.

"Earplugs," he explained. "No sense going deaf."

Bolan took two of the pellets and grinned at his colleague. "You've been watching too many *MacGyver* reruns."

Greene smirked back as he stuffed a pellet in each ear. "No shit," he wisecracked. "Too bad I missed the episode where he opened a trapdoor with a potato peeler."

Once he'd padded his ears, Bolan steadied the M-203 and

drew a bead on the seam where the far wall joined the basement floor. When he pulled the trigger, Bolan barely heard the whoosh of the 40 mm warhead, but even the foam pellets did little to blunt the sound of the grenade impacting with the far wall. The entire basement quaked as the explosion resounded throughout the enclosed space. Bolan and Greene were knocked to the floor and showered with dust and acoustic tiles dislodged from the ceiling. The ceiling itself held up, however. Elsewhere in the basement, the workbench near the far wall had tipped over, spilling tools and supplies across the floor.

As for the intended target, there was a gaping hole in the far wall, which had also buckled inward, raised slightly off its runners. On the other side of the opening, Bolan and Greene could see the black maw of the tunnel down which Joan VanderMeer had fled.

"Bingo," the security chief muttered as he and Bolan yanked the pellets from their ears and scrambled to their feet. "We're in."

12

"They're through," Joan VanderMeer announced as the echoes of the explosion reverberated through the darkened tunnels.

"We're fine," Marcus Yarborough assured her, his breath frosting in the cold air around them. They'd made their way deep beneath the mountain to a stretch of tunnel still lined with rail tracks from the days when carts were used to shuttle ore from the mineshafts. "They're way behind us and they don't know where they're going. C'mon."

There was no room to walk on either side of the tracks; Yarborough and VanderMeer had to pace themselves, taking careful, measured steps from tie to tie. Yarborough kept the flashlight aimed straight down so they could clearly see the ties. Behind them, far in the distance, they could occasionally hear their pursuers, who sounded as if they were slowly gaining ground. VanderMeer felt anxious but kept it to herself. Finally, they came upon a break in the wall where an even narrower passageway branched off from the tunnel at a ninety-degree angle.

"Here we go," Yarborough said, stepping off the rails.

For a fleeting second, he shifted the flashlight's beam into the passageway before him, making certain it was traversable. Behind him, cast into sudden darkness, VanderMeer misjudged her final step on the rail ties and lost her balance. The laptop fell from her grasp as she flung her hands out to keep from falling. There was a sound of splintering plastic as the computer struck the steel rail below her and flipped open. One of the screen mounts snapped and the LCD monitor hung to one side like a broken jaw.

VanderMeer bounded off the tunnel wall and twisted her left ankle. When Yarborough reached out she angrily pushed him away.

"Look at this!" VanderMeer seethed as she crouched and scooped up the computer. The second screen hinge gave way, and the monitor now dangled by a thin pair of wires.

"Leave it," Yarborough told her.

"No way," VanderMeer countered. She pieced the laptop together and hugged it to her chest, then stood. "Yeow!" she gasped as she tried to put her weight on her bad ankle.

"You can't walk on that," Yarborough said. "Forget the damn computer! I'm going to have to carry you!"

VanderMeer looked around and spotted a chiseled ledge up near where a sconce had been inserted into the tunnel wall. She shoved the computer into the cavity, then turned to Yarborough.

"How much farther?"

"Fifty, maybe sixty yards," Yarborough told her. "Let's go!"

VanderMeer warily allowed Yarborough to gather her up in his arms and carry her into the smaller tunnel. There was barely room for the two of them. VanderMeer wriggled slightly, shifting position so that she could extend one arm over Yarborough's shoulder and aim her minigun back toward the main tunnel. It was hard to tell over Yarborough's labored breathing, but she thought she could hear their pursuers closing in. By the time they'd reached a point where the way before them was barred by a steel door, she could see the flickering of another flashlight back in the main tunnel.

"Damn!" she whispered in Yarborough's ear. "They're practically on top of us!"

"Hang in there," Yarborough whispered back. He scanned the chiseled wall before him and found the control panel, then turned off his flashlight and toggled a switch rigged the same way as the one back in the lodge basement. With a faint hiss, the steel door groaned open, letting in a rush of cold air.

Yarborough was removing his hand from the light switch when Buck Greene's flashlight shone down the tunnel.

"Freeze!"

VanderMeer ignored Greene's command. Instead, she

squinted into the glare and fired her Kahr MK-40. The shot boomed loudly in the cramped confines. She couldn't tell if she'd hit anyone, but the flashlight's beam wavered slightly and there was no return fire.

Yarborough quickly carried VanderMeer past the retracted door, then triggered the steel plate so that it rolled back into place just in time to deflect a volley of return fire from their pursuers.

"That was close," VanderMeer murmured.

Ahead of them, the tunnel extended another ten yards before leading them back out in the open night air. They were now on the opposite side of the mountain from the militia camp. It was nearly as dark outside as in the tunnels, but VanderMeer could see that they were surrounded by tall drifts of snow. She was relieved they'd made it this far, but she still had her worries.

"They got past one door already," VanderMeer said as Yarborough set her down and doubled over to catch his breath. "They could still get through and—"

"I know, I know," Yarborough interrupted. "Don't worry. We've still got Mr. Paranoid on our side."

"What's that supposed to mean?"

"You'll see." Yarborough stood up and held his arms out. "C'mon."

"I'm okay now," the woman insisted.

"You sure?"

"Let's go," she said, "wherever the hell it is we're going."

Yarborough unslung his M-40 A-1 rifle and led VanderMeer through the snow to a metal post rising up from the ground some fifty yards from the mouth of the tunnel. There, the sniper knelt and scooped snow away until he'd uncovered a utility box. He pried the lid open, revealing yet another of the trick switchboxes Lance Iovine had had installed to operate his seemingly endless array of security measures.

"My God, another one?" VanderMeer exclaimed.

"This one takes the cake," Yarborough said as he prepared to trigger the switch. Gesturing back at the mountainside, he told her, "Check it out."

MACK BOLAN HAD SEEN Marcus Yarborough's hand on the light switch when the steel door opened. Still, it took a number of tries before he was able to manipulate the switch and get the door to hiss open. Buck Greene was standing alongside him, gun trained on the tunnel ahead of them. By then, however, Yarborough and VanderMeer had vanished.

"Let's go," Greene said, bolting forward, despite the throbbing in his knee. "We can probably still catch them."

Bolan followed the security chief. "I got a look at the guy carrying her," he said. "He's from the fantasy camp. A sharpsh—"

The Executioner's voice was suddenly drowned out by a loud thundering. The ground beneath them began to tremble. Both men stopped in their tracks, tracing the sound. It seemed to be coming from above them and from outside the tunnel.

"Landslide," Bolan muttered, even as the first wave of dislodged rock and boulders slid down the mountainside and fell across tunnel entrance. In a matter of seconds the opening had been sealed off. The rumbling continued and debris began spill into the tunnel, forcing the two Stony Man warriors to step back.

"No way is this some freaking coincidence," Greene ventured.

Bolan nodded. "They must've triggered it somehow," he said. "We were probably supposed to be caught underneath it."

"We might as well be, as far as catching up with them goes," Greene said. "No way are we getting through that."

Bolan knew Greene was right. The avalanche had lasted fewer than thirty seconds, but the tunnel entrance had been sealed off completely; it would take them hours to claw their way through the debris.

"I can't get anybody on this, either," Greene said, tapping his earbud transceiver. "We're screwed. All we can do is head back the way we came."

Bolan nodded, fighting back his frustration.

To add to their woes, halfway back to the main tunnel the beam on Greene's flashlight began to dim.

"Great," Greene said. "Just what we need. Stuck in the goddamn dark."

"Maybe not," Bolan said. "There was some kind of lighting when we first came in here. There've gotta be some switches somewhere around here."

"Let's go for it," Greene said.

Once they reached the main tunnel, Greene swept the surrounding walls with the flashlight's dying beam. Both men were looking for some kind of control box when Bolan spotted something on the ground.

"Shine that light over here," he told Greene as he dropped to a crouch.

Greene shifted the flashlight, directing its beam to the broken laptop, which had been dislodged from its makeshift hiding place during the avalanche. The flip screen had broken free and the computer's casing had cracked open, revealing the inner workings.

"I'm no cyberwhiz," Greene said, "but something tells me we're not going to be able to just plug this in and start playing Minesweeper."

"Maybe not," Bolan conceded, "but if the hard drive's still intact there might be a way to access the data on it."

"Sounds like a job for the boys back at the Farm," Greene said. "Let's get our asses out of here and look into it."

"UNBELIEVABLE," Joan VanderMeer said, watching the last few clots of loose debris fall down the mountainside. She was pacing back and forth, not only to keep warm, but also to test her sore ankle. "I mean, how could Iovine have been so sure that switch could trigger an avalanche, much less get it to fall directly over the tunnel?"

"He brought in a seismic geologist," Marcus Yarborough explained. "Guy figured out the likeliest slide risk area, then had some boulders hauled into place and rigged with plastique so they'd start rolling at the flick of a switch. Voilà! Man knew what he was doing."

"Amazing," VanderMeer said.

"How's the ankle?" Yarborough asked her.

She took a few tentative steps. "I just turned it, I think. I'll be fine." She stared past Yarborough and said, "I see where we are now. We don't have that far to go."

There was nothing but snow-covered wilderness for another thirty yards, then Yarborough and VanderMeer came upon a cul-de-sac marking the end of an isolated two-lane road. Up the road was a small housing development. Just as Lance Iovine had set up the Potomac River safehouse Edgar Byrnes had fled to after firing at CIA headquarters, the AFM leader had used militia funds to lease one of the homes in the subdivision. If VanderMeer and Yarborough could reach the house before their pursuers caught up with them, they would be in good shape.

As they started up the road, they saw lights wink on in some of the houses.

"Just what we need," VanderMeer muttered. "People coming to check things out."

Moments later, as they heard the drone of an approaching helicopter. Glancing over her shoulder, VanderMeer spotted the chopper Jack Grimaldi was using to scour the mountainside. He'd just cleared the highest peak and was drifting down toward the slide area.

"This could be a problem," Yarborough confessed.

VanderMeer glanced down at the footprints they'd left on the snow-covered road. "Anywhere we go, they're going to be able to follow our tracks."

"Maybe not," Yarborough said, gesturing up the road. A handful of residents from the subdivision was headed toward them, some of them carrying flashlights. They were clearly on their way to investigate the landslide. Yarborough guided VanderMeer off the road and into the cover of a thicket. Moments later, the residents hurried past, preoccupied with their first glimpse of the landslide. As they made their way to the cul-de-sac, they trampled over Yarborough and VanderMeer's tracks.

"One problem solved," Yarborough said. "If they can keep the chopper busy, we just might get out of this mess."

JACK GRIMALDI HAD set out from the AFM compound intent on intercepting anyone emerging from the mountain tunnels ahead of Bolan and Greene, but even though he was now heading toward the cul-de-sac near where Joan VanderMeer and Marcus Yarborough were hiding, he hadn't spotted them. At this point he wasn't even looking for them. He had a more pressing dilemma to deal with.

At some point while encountering the enemy back on the other side of the mountain, the medevac's fuel line had apparently been creased by gunfire. The initial seepage at first had been too slight to register on the instrument panel. Pressure from the fuel pump had steadily widened the crack, however, and as Grimaldi was guiding the chopper over the mountaintop, the line suddenly ruptured, triggering a warning light on the instrument panel. When Grimaldi saw how fast the fuel needle was sinking toward

Empty, he'd quickly realized the urgency and started looking for a place to land. Quick. The cul-de-sac was his best bet, or least it had been until a dozen residents wandered into view, placing themselves directly on the spot where he'd hoped to set the chopper down.

"Out of my way!" he shouted at the onlookers who, in turn, stared back up at the approaching chopper, more puzzled than concerned that it was bearing down on them. "Move, damn it!"

Grimaldi's unheard cries went unheeded. Even though he had his hands full trying to keep the chopper stable, Grimaldi finally resorted to pulling out his Colt pistol and aiming it out the open cockpit doorway. He rattled off an autoburst, aiming high over the heads of those gathered below him. They finally got the message and began scrambling in all directions, giving Grimaldi the wide berth he needed.

It almost worked.

Grimaldi was still ten yards up in the air when the chopper ran out of fuel. The engine died and the chopper landed hard, shattering the windshield and buckling the landing skids.

Grimaldi was thrown back, then forward. He yelped as the shoulder restraints bit into his chest and shoulder, then fell silent, the wind knocked from his lungs. He gasped for air as a flutter of small, swirling lights danced across his field of vision. A cold, clammy sweat broke out across his forehead, and suddenly the lights were blotted out by darkness and an eerie sense that he was falling into a black void. And falling. And falling.

Grimaldi couldn't say how long he was out. The next thing he knew, two sets of hands were clawing at him. He heard voices, too, but he couldn't make out what was being said. Disoriented, he struggled at first, fighting off whoever it was trying to grab hold of him. Then he heard the unfastening of his shoulder restraint and realized what was happening. He stopped throwing punches at his rescuers.

"That's better," one of them told him. "We're just trying to help."

Grimaldi allowed himself to be pulled out of the cockpit, then walked unsteadily as he was led to the nearby guardrail. He leaned against the cold metal and crouched over, taking in a few deep breaths. Once his head was clear, Grimaldi slowly stood up and stared at the residents circled around him.

"You just about bought the farm there, buddy," one of them said.

Grimaldi nodded feebly, staring past the crowd at the disabled chopper. In addition to the flattened skids and broken windshield, the rotors had been bent downward by the force of the landing and there was a visible crack in the tail section. Grimaldi could see that if the chopper had conked out on him a second or two earlier he would likely have been crushed when it plowed into the cul-de-sac. As it was, he was alive, more or less. He found himself wondering if the same could be said for his colleagues.

Grimaldi stared at the residents, then looked past them at the debris heaped at the base of the mountain.

"Has anyone checked the landslide?" he asked the group. "There were two men. Maybe a woman and—"

"I was just there," one of the residents told Grimaldi. "No sign of life that I could see."

Grimaldi moved away from the railing and staggered back toward the chopper. One of the residents reached out and tried to hold him back.

"Wait," he warned, "the thing might explode or—"

"It'd need fuel to explode!" Grimaldi snapped impatiently,

cutting off the other man. "If it had fuel, I wouldn't have had to land like a dropped egg!"

Once he reached the cockpit, Grimaldi leaned in and checked the radio. It had been jarred halfway out of its mounting brackets but was still operational. He slapped on the headset and worked the controls until he'd hooked up with the same frequency as Buck Greene's earbud transceiver.

"Bucko!" he barked into the radio microphone. There was no response at first, so he tried again. Still nothing. Finally, on the third try, he got a reply.

"Jacko! That you? Over."

"Screw the 'over' shit!" Grimaldi said. "I take it you and Striker are clear of that avalanche."

"Yeah, we're fine," Greene reported. "We just backtracked to the main lodge. Those perps we were chasing got out ahead of us, though. You see 'em by any chance?"

"Afraid not," Grimaldi said, his voice tinged with disappointment. "Long story, but I'm out of the air-search business for the time being."

"WE STILL RUN A RISK doing this," Marcus Yarborough said, backing a nondescript 2005 Ford Focus out of the safehouse driveway. "They might've set up roadblocks already."

"If they do, hopefully we'll know where they're set and can work around them," Joan VanderMeer said, indicating the police radio mounted beneath the car's dashboard near her left knee. Right above the scanner, the glove compartment was filled with other amenities: a few thousand dollars in cash, two prepaid cell phones, a half-inch stack of forged credit cards and a 9 mm Luger automatic pistol, all yet another tribute to the late Lance Iovine's obsession with being prepared for all contingencies. As if she thought Yarborough might still need more assurance that driving off was their best option, she quickly added, "We can't stay here and wait for them to start going door-to-door."

Yarborough knew she was right. He also knew there was still work to do. Lance Iovine was dead, but by morning Yarborough was supposed to be ready for his next target, Zeke Ambrose.

VanderMeer was thinking along the same lines. As Yarborough backed the car out into the street, she told him, "Once we know we're in the clear, I can talk to Walden about getting someone else to take over for you. You probably want some time to—"

"Let's just stick with the plan, all right?" Yarborough snapped, cutting off VanderMeer. "End of subject!"

She looked at Yarborough, startled by his sudden show of emotion. She was about to say something, but thought better of it. Instead, she nodded and fell silent. She glanced down the road toward the cul-de-sac, where a crowd was still gathered around the downed medevac chopper. She felt certain they would get away undetected, but a vague sense of dread and foreboding had begun to settle over her. Over the past months, even years, while she and Walden had painstakingly laid the groundwork for Operation Clean Sweep, she'd always had a sense of being in control. She'd always felt that she would be able to contend with anything that came up once the plan began to take effect.

But now that a series of unexpected events had thrown those plans into disarray, VanderMeer realized her confidence had been illusory. There was no way to control things at this stage—at least not in the way she'd imagined. From here on in, the situation had taken on a life of its own, like some rampaging bull set loose from a rodeo stall. VanderMeer figured all she and the others around her could do now was ride the bull and hope they wouldn't be thrown and trampled beneath its pounding hooves.

YARBOROUGH AND VANDERMEER were so preoccupied with making their getaway they paid little heed to the late-model Chevy Cavalier parked around the corner, only its rear trunk illuminated by the overhead streetlight. No one appeared to be inside the vehicle, one of several dozen parked along the streets of the subdivision. They drove past and were soon on their way to Route 43, a two-lane thoroughfare that would allow them to bypass the mountain road where federal agents had intercepted the two trucks carrying recruits and ordnance from the AFM compound.

There *was* someone inside the Cavalier, however. Edgar

Byrnes was crouched low in the front seat, trembling as much with fear as from the cold. He still wasn't sure what had possessed him to drive from the Potomac safehouse to the one here—in effect jumping from the frying pan into the fire. He'd stopped short of pulling into the driveway when he'd seen the medevac chopper come in for its crash landing, and he'd stayed out alongside the curb ever since, at a loss as to what to do next. Byrnes had thought he'd recognized VanderMeer and Yarbrough when they'd first wandered out of the brush and made their way to the safehouse, but he'd been wary of revealing himself to them, fearing reprisal. Now, minutes later, as he watched the Focus roll past and disappear down the road, the beleaguered veteran was still paralyzed with indecision.

The fact that the safehouse had been so quickly abandoned led Byrnes to believe its security had been somehow compromised. If that was the case, he knew it was in his best interests to move on, as well, the sooner the better. But he was drained, overcome by a sense of helplessness that had steadily increased from the moment he'd first taken to the road more than an hour and a half ago. He'd spent most of that time switching from station to station on the radio, trying to piece together the deluge of breaking news. He'd been stunned by reports of two motorcyclists killed in a militia-involved shootout at a Georgetown gun show. No names had been released, but given the fact that his brothers' Husqvarnas had been missing from the Potomac safehouse, Edgar had a sick feeling that Harlan and Wallace were now dead.

And the AFM compound on the other side of the mountain had apparently been raided by the authorities, as well. There were reports of multiple fatalities, and one broadcast had gone so far as to say that it appeared the entire American Freedom Movement had been shut down in its tracks. Edgar doubted that was the case, but still, the organization had taken a serious hit, and he couldn't help thinking that all of it might have been avoided had he not taken matters into his own hands with the AT-4 rocket launcher.

The emotional maelstrom churning through Edgar's head

began to get the better of him, and soon he felt the onset of an anxiety attack. He'd already fought back one such attack while waiting in the car. "No!" he railed at himself, frantic. "No more!"

The sensation refused to abate. If anything, it intensified. Beside himself, for the second time in the past ten minutes Byrnes yanked the Walther pistol from his ski parka and slid the barrel into his mouth. He closed his eyes as he had the time before, fighting back a wave of nausea at the oily, metallic taste of the barrel. His finger was on the trigger, but, try as he may, he couldn't summon the willpower to pull it. He wept and convulsed, then finally pulled the gun from his mouth and gave into the attack, curling himself into a fetal position as best he could while still strapped into his seat belt. Soon his racked sobs gave way to a spent, pathetic whimpering.

Minutes passed before the attack subsided. Byrnes slowly sat back up, wiping the cold tears from his face with the back of his hand. He glanced down the street and saw a few residents heading back toward their homes from the cul-de-sac. He didn't want to face them. Instinctively, his hand went to the car's ignition. He started the engine, then pulled from the curb and drove away.

By the time he'd reached the main road, Edgar Byrnes had made a decision.

There was only one place left for him to go.

13

Washington, D.C.

Gregory Walden stepped out of the Hart Senate office building and yawned as he squinted against the glare of the rising sun. He'd been up all night, working alongside Huell Kostigan as they monitored developments in the CIA bombing incident and other related news involving the American Freedom Movement. It had been an exhausting vigil, but Walden knew the time had been well-spent, as it had allowed him a chance to help mold what he hoped would become Washington's official response to the situation.

Walden had convinced the Intelligence Committee chairman that both the gun-show heist and Langley bombing had been masterminded by the three Byrnes brothers, and that during the subsequent raid on the AFM compound in Meredith Valley, Lance Iovine had most likely been slain by a colleague of the brothers as part of some internal power struggle. As for the AFM Web site posting in which Iovine had supposedly alleged an FBI conspiracy, Walden dismissed the claim as typical militia paranoia. There were also reports that a man and woman had escaped from the compound following the raid, but Walden had seen to it that Joan VanderMeer and Marcus Yarborough were left off the list of suspects.

At one point, while Kostigan retreated for a catnap in his private office, Walden had made two quick calls on one of the prepaid cell phones he'd picked up on the way to the capital. The first call was to VanderMeer, who told him that she and Yarborough had split up shortly after fleeing the safehouse located across the mountain from the AFM camp. She was heading back to Washington while Yarborough had taken another car west to carry out his next assassination.

Walden's second call was to Phyllis Dahlgren, a line producer for the nationally televised show *A.M. America.* The senator had a long-standing rapport with the woman and had leaked exclusive information to her many times in the past, so she wasn't surprised when he gave her some insider details on the CIA bombing. In exchange, he asked for a chance to appear on the show later in the morning to present the government's position, preferably as part of a panel discussion that would include a spokesperson for the militia movement.

"We want to deal with this head-on and grab the bull by the horns," he'd said.

Dahlgren had not only risen to the bait but she'd also—as Walden had been expecting—suggested that Jack Foster Stanton speak on behalf of the militias. Walden pretended to have reservations, forcing the producer to badger him before he finally relented, on the condition that Stanton come to Washington so they could debate matters face-to-face on the air. Again Dahlgren unwittingly played into Walden's hands, promising to roust Stanton from bed and have him chauffeured to Washington from his home in Camden, New Jersey. Walden was still waiting to hear if Benjamin Zernial had managed to break into Stanton's house after the man had been picked up.

An *A.M. America* remote crew was due at the office complex in a few minutes. Walden wanted to get some fresh air and collect his thoughts before going on the air. He also had some more private business to attend to. Operation Clean Sweep had become, for him, a mistress even more demanding than his wife. Which was saying a lot, given that Nikki had left a total of eleven messages on his regular cell phone, one reminding him of an appointment with their interior decorator this morning, the others elaborating on the discontent she'd heaped on him during their argument before he'd left the condo the night before. Walden had heard it all before. He looked forward to the day when he wouldn't have to hear it anymore.

The snow had stopped a few hours ago and the temperature had already inched up into the low forties, leaving streets and sidewalks covered with slush. Walden dodged a few puddles on his way to a corner kiosk. As he waited for his coffee, the senator took note of the other pedestrians streaming past him, making far better time than the cars hung up in the snarl of early-morning traffic. By all appearances, it looked to be another routine day on Capitol Hill, with people going on about their normal business, seemingly unaffected by the events that had preoccupied the senator's attention throughout the night. Most likely, Walden thought, there would be a continued sense of complacency even after the next wave of killings. Americans, after all, were notoriously self-absorbed, and Walden suspected that by the time the public realized the nation was in crisis, his plan would be well in motion. By then, he hoped, any mass outcry would be a case of too little, too late.

Walden bought a croissant to go with his coffee and ate as he walked. He'd gone two blocks and was passing John Marshall Park when the last of his prepaid cell phones rang. He veered off the sidewalk, answering the phone as he sat down on a bench overlooking the U.S. Courthouse.

Benjamin Zernial sounded subdued. Yes, he'd heard about Lance Iovine's assassination, which had placed Zernial in charge of the American Freedom Movement, but the machinist was concerned about the extent to which the raid on the Meredith Valley training facility had compromised the organization.

"Take it slow on your end for now," Walden advised. "Lay low while I find out what kind of evidence they got hold of."

"Iovine had a lot of records stored there," Zernial said.

"I know that," Walden said impatiently. "Joan said most of them went through the shredder, but we'll have to see if anything slipped out."

"Understood."

"Now, then," Walden prompted, "what about Stanton? Did you break into his place?"

"Yeah, no problem," Zernial said. "And you're right. He's got a goddamn armory in there. He won't be able to tell there's something missing until it's too late."

"And you planted the rifle where I told you?" Walden asked.

"Piece of cake," Zernial reported. "And, I gotta say, I know I'm not supposed to guess what you've got in mind, but it's pretty obvious."

"Not your concern," Walden told him. "Are we clear on that?"

"Got it," Zernial said. "I don't know anything about it."

"Where are you now?"

"On my way home," Zernial reported. "Gonna open up shop and make like it's business as usual."

"Good idea," Walden said. "Once I have anything more for you, I'll call."

Walden checked the phone. He was about to use up his minutes, so he quickly wrapped up things with Zernial, then made one final call, this one to Marcus Yarborough. The sharpshooter told Walden he was just a few minutes from the stakeout point where he planned to carry out his next assassination.

"Glad to hear it," Walden told Yarborough. "When you're done there, I know the plan was for you to keep moving west and go after McTavish, but something's come up. I need you in Philadelphia instead."

There was a moment of silence on the other line, then Yarborough said, "There's no one on the list in Philadelphia."

"There is now," Walden said.

14

Stony Man Farm, Virginia

"I can't remember the last time I showed up here in a car," Jack Grimaldi said as Mack Bolan drove them past the armed checkpoint leading to Stony Man Farm. "Usually I get the bird's-eye view."

"Same here," Bolan said.

The two men had managed a little sleep after being treated at the Shenandoah National Park medical facility for injuries sustained while tangling with the American Freedom Movement in Meredith Valley. Grimaldi's crash landing of the medevac chopper had left him with a dislocated right shoulder. Bolan had fared a little better, requiring only a few stitches where he'd lacerated his thigh sliding down the mountain ravine after the militia recruit who'd later plunged to his death. Both men were told to limit their activities, but neither was about to pamper himself when there was still work to be done. As for Buck Greene, the security chief had already returned to the Farm along with the surviving blacksuits. The militia compound had been locked down by a replacement force of FBI and BATF agents.

As he approached the house, Bolan saw Buck Greene standing out on the front walk with Barbara Price, who had arrived only a few minutes ahead of Bolan and Grimaldi. Her head was bowed grimly as she listened to Greene's account of the ill-fated raid on the nearby AFM stronghold.

Once Bolan parked the rental car, he and Grimaldi joined the others.

"We lost four men total," Greene was telling Price. He'd taken some painkillers and iced his knee after returning to the Farm. He was still favoring the wounded leg but wasn't about to take any time off work. He finished his debrief, informing Price, "Pete Clary is still in surgery with a slug near his heart. They say it's touch-and-go."

"Let's hope for the best," Price said.

She turned to Bolan and Grimaldi. "What about you two? Neither of you had an easy time of it, from what I hear."

Bolan met the woman's gaze and held it briefly. He and Price had drawn close in the years since she'd been brought on board as the Farm's mission controller, and though they kept their relationship discreet, at times like this it was difficult not to acknowledge the bond between them. Perhaps later they'd have a moment alone, but for now, Bolan knew they would have to make do with an exchanged glance.

"I'm fine," Bolan assured her. "A little fender rash is all."

"Same here," Grimaldi said. Tapping the sling he'd been instructed to wear, he added, "This is for show. Draws chicks like flies."

"Not that you need any help on that front," Price said, managing a tired smile. "Buck and I were just on our way to the Annex. Are you guys up for the walk?"

A thousand-foot-long subterranean passageway linked the main house with the Annex, but after his misadventure in the AFM tunnels a few hours ago, Bolan, for one, was more than willing to stay aboveground, even if it meant foregoing the underground rail car that would have whisked them more quickly across the property.

As they started off, heading past the fruit orchards, Greene told Bolan, "I brought the laptop over earlier. Hopefully they've been able to access the hard drive by now."

"Password problems?" Bolan guessed.

"Yeah," Greene said. "But you know those guys. With them, a password's like tape on a cookie jar. Not gonna keep 'em out."

Bolan nodded. The orchards quickly gave way to endless rows of leafy, fast-growing poplars. The trees were destined for the nearby wood-chipping mill, a venture started up several years ago in conjunction with the building of the Farm's Annex facilities. A dirt trail wound through the trees, and the foursome had to speak up once they came more within range of the mill and its orchestra of chain saws and industrial-sized chippers. Price told the others that Hal Brognola was back in D.C. for an Oval Office meeting with the President and Joint Chiefs of Staff. Topping their agenda was a review of the previous night's events and formulating a response. Priority, of course, was still being given to tracking down Edgar Byrnes. The suspected triggerman in the CIA bombing was still at large, Price reported, as were the man and woman Bolan and Greene had chased through the AFM's network of underground tunnels.

"Did you tell Bear the guy we're looking for worked back at the fantasy camp?" Bolan asked Greene.

"Sure did," the security chief said. "Name's Yarborough, right? Last I checked they'd run into some snags with his background check."

"What kind of snags?" Bolan asked.

"The usual," Greene said. "Bear said most of the dates on the guy's résumé were off. Some of the entries were bogus, too, but once they sort it all out, you can bet they'll find some link between him and the militia. Same with the woman."

"Or maybe not," Bolan cautioned.

"Why would you say that?" Price interjected.

"I found Iovine right after he was shot," Bolan explained. "He took a sniper round to the head. Yarborough's a trained marksman. Add it up."

"You think he popped the guy?" Greene asked.

"It fits," Bolan said. "And don't forget that woman we chased is the same one that helped Yarborough escape from the fantasy camp."

"And then he turned around and returned the favor, getting her out of the tunnels," Greene surmised.

"If you're right," Price told Bolan, "maybe Iovine getting shot had something to do with the haggling over that weapons cache from Aberdeen. After all, if they'd have been able to agree on a price, the stuff might've been moved out of Sykesville earlier."

"Before I blew it all to kingdom come," Bolan said, finishing Price's thought. "As it turned out, they went to all the trouble of stealing that stuff for nothing."

"Not quite," Greene reminded Bolan. "Don't forget it was a rocket launcher from that cache that put a hole in the CIA's fort back in Langley."

"Good point," Bolan said.

"Well, if Bear gets into that computer, hopefully there'll be a file with AFM's chain of command," Price said. "After last night we've got them down for the count. The best way to keep them there is to make sure the survivors don't regroup."

"That's going to be like fighting that Hydra monster," Grimaldi said, "Lop off one head, three more pop up in its place."

The others fell silent, mulling over the pilot's grim pronouncement. Once they'd cleared the poplars, they came to the wood-chipping mill, a mammoth one-story concrete building flanked by two tall storage silos. The silos were outfitted to hold not only wood chips, but also the bulk of the antennas and datalink equipment used by Aaron Kurtzman's cybercrew to exchange information. The Computer Room itself was located, along with the rest of the Annex, inside the main building, one floor down from the chipping facilities.

To access the Annex, Bolan and the others had to pass through two security checkpoints. During the procedures, Bolan and the others passed along their condolences to the blacksuits on duty. The sentries were all somber, and Bolan and the others learned the dark mood was due to more than just a sense of loss over the men's fallen comrades.

"Some clown on TV's painting us as this federal goon squad," one of the blacksuits explained. When the group arrived at the next level, he gestured toward the nearby R&R room. "Go see for yourselves."

The rec room was small; it had been carved out of the adjacent Communications Center. On one side dining chairs were set around a couple tables next to a cramped kitchenette; on the other, two large sofas formed an L facing a large-screen, high-definition television set.

A half-dozen off-duty blacksuits had taken over every available square inch of the two sofas. One of them stood up and offered Price his space, but she waved him off and remained standing alongside Bolan, Greene and Grimaldi. Together, the group trained its collective gaze on the screen.

There, Oscar Venuti—the well-groomed, white-toothed host of *A.M. America*—was seated in the conference room of Gregory Walden's Washington office suite, moderating a discussion of the previous night's events with three guests. One of the guests was Senator Walden himself. Another was Jack Foster Stanton, spokesman for the Citizens Armed Guard.

As Bolan and the others would soon come to realize, Venuti and the third guest were merely window-dressing. Playing out across the nation to more than twenty million viewers was a shrewd bit of media manipulation on the part of Gregory Walden. The senator was, in essence, holding up hoops for Stanton to jump through, and Stanton was unwittingly obliging with the near effortless certainty of a trained seal.

As Bolan watched, he was partly mesmerized, partly sickened. He could barely believe what he was seeing.

Washington, D.C.

THE THIRD GUEST on the televised segment was Judith Prewell, a demure, silver-haired Harvard professor who'd recently written a nonfiction bestseller called *Inside the Militia Mind*. At the urging of *A.M. America* host Oscar Venuti, she was in middiscourse, providing viewers with a textbook profile of the sort of individual likely to join an organization like the American Freedom Movement. With a stilted delivery, and officious voice, she explained that young, alienated loners—usually male—were drawn to such outfits because they offered a sense of structure and belonging that, for whatever reason, was absent from their home or school environment.

"What a load of horsecrap!" Jack Foster Stanton interjected. The head of the Citizens Armed Guard was a squat, bald man with beetling eyebrows as thick and unkempt as his mustache and muttonlike sideburns. Stanton's face flushed red as he leaned forward; it almost looked as if he were about to leap across the conference table and wrap his meaty hands around Dr. Prewell's throat. Seated two chairs to Stanton's right, Senator Walden looked convincingly chagrined by the zealot's outburst.

"If you could watch your tongue, please," Walden scolded, knowing full well that he was fanning the flames of Stanton's temper. "We're trying to have a civilized discourse here."

Stanton pivoted, turning his ire on Walden. "A public brain-washing is more like it!" he retorted.

"Mr. Stanton, could we stay on subject?" Venuti interjected.

"Suit yourself," Stanton retorted. He turned back to Dr. Prewell and taunted, "You must've mixed up your paperwork back at that ivory tower of yours, because what you're describing is the typical recruit for some al Qaeda terrorist sect over in the Middle East. That profile doesn't even come close to matching that of the men who join militias."

"I'm more inclined to believe Dr. Prewell," Walden insisted. "And most of the intelligence briefs that pass my desk support her theory."

"Well, whoever's supplying your intelligence isn't doing their homework," Stanton maintained. "When you talk about militia-men like those members of the American Freedom Movement that were gunned down in that ambush last night, you're talking about patriots! Do you hear me? You're talking about good, decent American folks who are just plain fed up with all the trampling on our constitutional rights!"

"That's the second time you've referred to the events last night in Meredith Valley as an ambush," Walden told Stanton. "That's not what happened and you know it!"

"I'll get back to that," Stanton said, "but first I want to finish up with our Harvard Pollyanna here."

"My name is Dr. Prewell, thank you very much," the author said icily. Stanton was clearly getting to her. "And think what you will, but regrettably there *are* similarities between recruits for al Qaeda and the militia. The disaffected are always the first target of any extremist organization."

"Which, face it, Mr. Stanton," Walden interjected, "is exactly what the American Freedom Movement has to be considered. Same goes for your outfit and every other one like it. You're all extremists, and when you take the law into your own hands, you're no better than the terrorists. Or would you have us believe there is something defensible about staging a rocket attack on a federal building that leaves eight people dead?"

"And how many people were exterminated in that retribution attack on the AFM compound?" Stanton countered, once again focusing his anger on the man seated nearest him. "Answer me that one, Senator!"

"Federal agents showed up at the AFM compound with a legal warrant for the express purpose of gathering evidence," Walden responded calmly. "As I explained earlier, they were the ones attacked and put on the defensive."

"And I'm sure you think if you repeat that enough times it automatically becomes true," Stanton scoffed. "Sorry, not in my book."

"I believe the reports I've read thus far," Walden said.

"Those reports have been cooked and we both know it!" Stanton snarled.

"Cooked?" Oscar Venuti interjected, eager not to lose his fair share of camera time. "What do you mean by that?"

"What I mean is the senator's spin doctors probably burned the midnight oil dancing around the truth," Stanton shot back. "His reports are nothing but a whitewash. Revisionist history, fresh off the press."

"That's a pretty serious accusation, Mr. Stanton," Venuti replied.

"My lawyers would be more likely to call it libel," Walden added. "You're wandering out on the thin ice, there, Jack. You might want to think about tiptoeing back a few steps and trying to save face."

Stanton was silent a moment, but judging from the near-rabid gleam in the other man's eyes, Walden felt he'd finally riled the extremist into taking the bait that had been planted for him on the Internet a few hours earlier by Benjamin Zernial. Stanton paused to sip from the water glass that set before him, then turned to Walden with the look a man about to play a well-concealed trump card.

"Tell me, Senator," he said, for once matching the calm in Walden's voice, "is there anything in that report of yours about government sharpshooters killing the head of the AFM by firing at him through the window of his office? When he was unarmed, I might add."

Dr. Prewell and Senator Walden seemed equally taken aback by Stanton's accusation. Walden, however, was the first to respond.

"I don't know where you get your information," Walden countered, "but all the evidence I've been presented with points to an inside job. Lance Iovine was killed by his own people, not the government."

"That's a lie!" Stanton flared. His eyes bulged and his voice cracked with righteous indignation. "I know the truth! And the truth is that the government has just launched a take-no-prisoners policy when it comes to any organization in this country that attempts to speak up against the growing fascism of Big Brother! By the time they're finished, Ruby Ridge and Waco are going to look like family picnics!"

"This is absurd!" Walden turned to the show's host with a look of helplessness. "This man is clearly delusional."

"And paranoid, as well," Dr. Prewell joined in. "This is exactly the kind of mind-set I warn about in my book. It's all—"

"We aren't here to peddle your goddamn book!" Stanton shot back. "You smug, self-serving—"

The expletive was bleeped out by network censors, and the camera abruptly cut away from Stanton. Oscar Venuti, eager to play the voice of reason, faced the cameras and quickly wrapped up the segment with some generic observation about how trying times often spawned a passionate dialogue. Then, with practiced ease, he dropped the matter and segued to a quick teaser for an upcoming segment on the latest spring fashions.

Walden was only half listening to Venuti. His focus was still on Stanton. The outspoken radical had fallen silent, but there was hatred in his eyes as he glared at Dr. Prewell, then the senator himself. Once the show's director announced that they'd just cut away for a commercial, Dr. Prewell quickly rose to her feet and moved from the table as if fleeing a plague. Stanton stayed put and turned his gaze on Walden. The senator remained seated, as well.

"Try to make me look like a fool, will you?" he said, making no effort to lower his voice.

"I don't think you need anyone's help for that," Walden responded smugly. "You do a fine job on your own."

Stanton suddenly rose to his feet with so much force that he knocked over both his chair and his water glass. In the background, Phyllis Dahlgren, the show's producer, motioned to a couple security guards, who took a few steps closer to the conference table.

Stanton saw them approaching and refrained from making a move toward Walden. His eyes were still filled with rage, however.

"This show may be over," he warned, his hand trembling as he pointed a finger at the senator, "but you and me, we're not finished. Not by a long shot."

"That sounds like a threat," Walden said.

"Call it what you will," Stanton shot back. "No one works me like that and gets away with it!"

Walden stared back at Stanton and smiled thinly. I already have, he thought to himself. I already have.

Stony Man Farm, Virginia

"COULD THEY HAVE PICKED a worse person to give national airtime to?" Barbara Price observed as she followed Bolan out of the rec room. Greene and Grimaldi had remained behind with the blacksuits. "I felt like I was watching *The Jerry Springer Show.*"

"Nothing like a scumbag stirring the pot to crank up your ratings," Bolan observed muttered cynically.

Alone with Bolan for the first time since he'd arrived, Price dropped pretense and allowed herself a look of concern.

"You've been limping this whole time and trying not to show it," she told Bolan. "Are you sure you're all right?"

"Never better," Bolan responded.

"You'd say that if you had two bullets in you and your leg in a bear trap," Price countered with a faint smile.

"No pain, no gain."

"Be that as it may, first break in the action, I'm penciling you in for some TLC," Price said. "I'm thinking a long, hot bath, followed by a full-body massage."

"Make that an order and I just might take you up on it," Bolan said, flashing a rare grin.

"Consider it done," said Price. "Now, back to business."

Bolan led Price into the Computer Room. Aaron "The Bear" Kurtzman and his entire task force were on hand, each at their separate stations, engrossed in their various assignments. Bolan exchanged a quick greeting with the others, then homed in on Kurtzman. The wheelchair-bound guru's ever-cluttered work area was even more congested, as he'd hemmed himself in behind an additional roll cart laden with extra computer gear. There was barely room for Bolan and Price to maneuver to the older man's side.

"What have you guys come up with?" he asked.

"We're in," Kurtzman replied, pointing to the hard drive salvaged from Lance Iovine's laptop. The unit had been placed on the roll cart, where it was linked to two separate mainframe computers.

"We got to try out three passwords at a time before the disk shut down automatically and we had to start all over again," the computer genius explained. "I programmed one computer for quick reboots and had the other on standby with the next three possible passwords. Stop, go, stop, go. It was tedious, but the chips were fast enough to speed up the process until we popped the genie out of the bottle."

"Way too much information," Bolan teased his longtime colleague, "but good job."

"Just remember that when it comes time to hand out Christmas bonuses," Kurtzman wisecracked.

"So, have you turned up anything yet?" Price asked.

"Getting there," Kurtzman said. "They'd apparently just deleted a ton of files, so our priority has been trying to retrieve them, since they probably have all the good stuff. I'm linked up with the others and am farming stuff out as it comes in so we can sort through it all quicker. Anything that gets flagged as useful will go into new files and get broken down by category. Give us an hour or so and we'll be in good shape."

"Fair enough," Bolan said. "Meantime, Buck mentioned something about a few glitches in your background check on Marcus Yarborough."

Kurtzman nodded. "Yeah, he's a mystery man, all right. Nearly every road on him leads to a dead end. You ask me, the guy's made up. Résumé's cobbled from half truths and untraceable sources. Same way we forge your field credentials."

"Well, I can vouch for his being a sharpshooter," Bolan said. "He showed what he can do at the fantasy camp, and you can't fake that."

"That's good to know," Kurtzman said. "I think our best bet would be for you to run a description through some ID software so we can get a composite sketch. We do a fresh search with that and start sniffing around sniper databases, we might come up with something."

"Worth a shot," Bolan said.

"What about membership files?" Barbara asked. "Anything on that front yet?"

"Matter of fact, that's where we're making the most headway," Kurtzman said. "For starters, there were some hard copy mailing addresses in one of the boxes Lance Iovine had packed up before he was shot. Carmen's cross-referencing it with what we've got out of the computer so far."

Kurtzman called Delahunt over and asked for a quick update.

"I've got a pretty good handle on the food chain, I think," the redhead reported. She'd brought along a printout tallying her findings thus far and referred to it as she spelled things out. "We know, of course, that Iovine was top dog before he went down. Second in command was a guy named Chaz Prince. We've got him down as a casualty from that attempted gun heist in Georgetown. Some of the other bigwigs probably went down during the raid, but provided he's still alive, I'm figuring the new guy in charge is a guy named Benjamin Zernial. Vietnam vet. Runs a machine shop in Philly."

"Got an address?" Bolan asked.

"Hey, do I look like an amateur?" Delahunt joked. She pointed at the readout. "Home address is the same as his shop. Probably one of those old two-story brownstones."

"I'll run with it," Bolan said.

Akira Tokaido's station was within earshot of the group and he'd overheard the exchange.

"While you're at it, there's another angle you might want to look into," he called, glancing up from his computer. "The mother of this Edgar Byrnes guy lives in Philadelphia, too. Last I checked, though, no one's been able to track her down for a morgue ID on her boys in D.C."

"They're looking for her, though, right?" Bolan asked.

Tokaido nodded. "FBI's got her place staked out in case Eddie boy tries to make contact."

"What about the father?" Price asked.

"The father's dead," Tokaido said. "His speedboat went down in Chesapeake Bay a couple years ago after some chase with the Coast Guard. He was running guns."

"For who?" Bolan asked. "AFM?"

"Yeah, I think so," Tokaido replied. "Obviously, his sons didn't learn from his mistakes."

"It happens," Kurtzman said.

He turned to Bolan, "In any event, it looks like your next stop is the City of Brotherly Love."

Philadelphia, Pennsylvania

Once she'd stopped for a traffic light two blocks from the Liberty Arms apartment complex listed as the home address for Molly Byrnes, Roberta Williamson sipped the last of the coffee she'd bought back in McLean after filling her car with gas. As if the CIA analyst needed any reminder, one glance in the rearview mirror confirmed that she looked every bit as exhausted as she felt. Williamson had been up all night. Her eyes were bloodshot and her cheeks faintly streaked with mascara from a crying jag surrendered to on the drive to Philadelphia. There was still a faint ringing in her ears from the explosion at Langley that had turned her world asunder. But she was determined to forge on, to do whatever it might take to avenge the death of Felix Garber and the others killed by Molly Byrnes's son.

Hours ago, after the bomb-torn corpses had been bagged and hauled away in paramedic vans, Williamson's colleagues advised her to go home and get some rest, but she refused. Instead, she showered at the Langley gymnasium facilities, then changed into fresh clothes and badgered her way into being allowed access to a computer station three floors down from the bomb site, which had been cordoned off. There, she worked through the night, monitoring all incoming news regarding the bombing and the search for the man who'd pulled the trigger of the AT-4 rocket launcher.

Once it became clear that Edgar Byrnes had eluded capture, Williamson shifted her focus, trying to determine where the militiaman might have fled to. Learning that Edgar Byrnes had two brothers who'd been slain during the night in an altercation with federal agents in Georgetown, Williamson used her Agency credentials to contact an official at the morgue where Wallace and Harlan Byrnes had been taken. She was told that the two young men were still on ice, as no one had yet been able to reach their mother and arrange for her to come in to identify the bodies. It was only after securing Molly's Philadelphia address and phone number that Williamson had finally left the CIA facility. She told her colleagues that she was taking their advice and going home to rest. Rest, however, was the last thing on her mind.

Now, less than an hour later, she was caught up in morning traffic, within three blocks of her destination.

After the light changed, Williamson worked her way over to the right-hand lane, where cars were barely inching their way up Town Crier Road. The slow crawl worked in the woman's favor, allowing her to scrutinize the neighborhood as they came up on the Liberty Arms. Her field instincts kicked in and she had little difficulty spotting the two undercover teams that were staking out the apartment building—one from inside a car parked across the street, the other from the sidewalk. Williamson had tried calling Molly Byrnes several times while on the road. Clearly, the woman wasn't home.

Williamson had no interest in contending with the surveillance crews. Instead, she drove past the apartment complex and continued another five blocks to a twenty-four hour convenience store listed in the computer database as Molly's place of work. Williamson had already called the store and been told that Molly wasn't working that day. The night manager, who'd clearly been questioned several times already, irately told her that he had no idea where the woman might be. Williamson was hoping she'd have better luck with the day shift, which had come on duty only a few minutes ago. It was a long shot, and she knew that if she came up empty-handed her trip would likely have been in vain. Still, it was a chance she felt she'd had to take.

Williamson parked next to the only other car in the parking lot and confirmed that no one was inside. She'd already scanned the surrounding neighborhood and felt reassured that the authorities hadn't bothered to place the store under surveillance. If Williamson came up with a lead, she wouldn't have to share it. Which was the way she wanted it.

The only person out on the floor when Williamson entered the store was a fifty-year-old woman wearing an orange smock as she stocked a shelf with automotive supplies. Williamson had already decided to try a personal approach. Instead of flashing her badge and using intimidation, she summoned the pent-up grief that—except for the crying jag on the highway—she'd reined in for the past seven hours. It was Felix Garber she was mourning, but as she spoke to the worker, Williamson carried on as if her sorrow and anxiety had been brought on by the deaths of Molly Byrne's two sons.

"I'm Molly's cousin," Williamson confided to the other woman, letting tears flood her eyes. "They need someone to come to the morgue in Georgetown to identify her sons' bodies. She's not home and she's not answering her cell phone. I can't get hold of her and it's making me crazy!"

The other woman regarded Williamson, and for a moment the CIA agent thought she may have played her hand too strongly. But then the woman glanced past her at the wall calendar behind the cash counter.

"Seeing how it's Thursday," the woman said, turning back to Roberta, "I have a pretty good idea where she might be."

Schroeder, Pennsylvania

EDGAR BYRNES HAD NEVER been close to his mother, but he knew three things for certain about her: she hated following current events and avoided the news as if it were the plague; she rarely woke up before nine in the morning; and every week on Thursday and Friday she spelled her father-in-law's caregiver at the old family house in Schroeder, a semirural community located twelve miles north of Philadelphia near a bend in the Schuylkill River.

Byrnes drove straight through to Schroeder from Meredith Valley once he realized what day it was. He knew there was a good chance he could make contact with his mother before she learned of the grim way in which her sons had forced themselves into the headlines. It seemed unlikely to Byrnes that the authorities would know about his mother's visiting regimen. If they were looking for her, he suspected they would be haunting her apartment back in Philadelphia. To be safe, however, once Byrnes crossed over the river and drove through one of several newer subdivisions carved out of what only a few years ago had been clover fields, he parked at the Schroeder Little League complex and walked the last quarter mile to Towhee Lane, the isolated two-lane street his grandparents had first moved to nearly a half-century earlier.

Developers had yet to parcel up the old neighborhood, and there were only six houses on the entire block, each sitting on an acre of land. One had a sense that most of the homeowners were on the verge of selling, as only two of the plots were well tended. The others—including the Byrnes property—had been neglected and were overgrown with weeds and wildflowers. Three cars were parked on the street, none of them visibly occupied. Byrnes had a clear view of all three vehicles from the cover he'd taken in the brush at the end of the block, and he kept vigil a few minutes to make certain the cars weren't being used by surveillance teams.

Once convinced the coast was indeed clear, Byrnes broke from cover. There were no sidewalks, so he walked along the gravel shoulder of the road. A dog stared at him from the front porch of a house across the street, but otherwise the neighborhood seemed deserted. The old Byrnes house was a run-down, two-story Victorian structure set well back from the road. The unmowed grass was nearly six inches high and it had been years since pruning shears had been taken to the shrubs that surrounded the house and separated the front yard from the adjacent, weed-choked fields.

Years ago, as a child, Edgar and his brothers had spent many a day playing whiffleball in the side yard, trying to see who could loft the most home runs onto the garage roof situated at the rear of the house. The garage was gone now, having burned to the ground one night fourteen years ago when he and Harlan had been careless and tipped over a kerosene lamp while "camping out." They'd blamed the accident on Dubby, who'd been asleep at the time. Now both Harlan and Dubby were gone. Edgar still couldn't believe it, and halfway up the front walk, he stopped and shuddered as the realization broadsided him, bringing him to tears.

"Get a grip," he chided himself, blinking his eyes.

The front steps creaked under Byrnes's weight as he walked up to the raised porch, which was bare save for a pair of lawn chairs with frayed straps and a small wrought-iron table upon which rested a potted geranium and an ashtray overflowing with cigarette butts. Molly Byrnes always talked about quitting, but Edgar could see that his mother was still going through a pack a day. Not that he blamed her. She'd had a hard life, after all. For a moment, Byrnes began to have second thoughts about having come here to add to the woman's burdens. The moment passed, however. She was going to find out one way or another. He figured it would be best if the news came from him.

Byrnes reached under the geranium pot for a discolored house key. He turned and was approaching the front door when, to his surprise, the knob turned and the door suddenly swung open. One look at his mother's reddened eyes and Byrnes felt his stomach clench.

She already knew.

"I thought it was you," she said, her voice hoarse. She looked Edgar up and down, puzzled. "Your beard. It's gone white, just like your—"

"Mom," Edgar interrupted. "We have to talk."

"It's true, isn't it?" she replied. "Your grandfather had the radio on when I woke up. What they're saying. That bombing. And about Harlan and Dubby."

"I'll try to explain," Edgar said, taking his mother by the arm and guiding her inside. "But first, tell me, has anyone been here? The police? The FBI?"

Molly Byrnes shook her head.

Inside, the house's musty smell brought back a flood of

memories. Edgar tried to shut them out. He knew he had to stay focused. He led his mother into the front sitting room, which was crowded with old furniture and shelves lined with tawdry knick-knacks his grandmother had collected over the years before she'd succumbed to liver cancer. On an end table next to an overstuffed velvet chair facing the front window, steam rose from the cup of coffee Molly had apparently been drinking when she'd seen Edgar come up the walk. Edgar motioned for his mother to sit back down, then he began to pace the cramped room, trying to figure out what to say. Before he could get another word out, he heard his mother sob, a pent-up cry that frightened him because it sounded so much like the outbursts that often accompanied his anxiety attacks.

"What have I done to deserve this?" Molly wailed. She riveted her son with a look that was at once both pleading and accusatory. "Tell me, would you? Please help me to understand."

Edgar stopped his pacing and stared down at his mother paralyzed by shame. He tried to find the words, but his throat constricted. He felt as if he were being strangled. When someone spoke, the voice came not from him, but from a man who'd appeared in the hallway that led from the sitting room to the kitchen.

"What's that, Molly?" rasped Kevin Byrnes, Edgar's seventy-eight-year-old grandfather. The old man navigated his way into the sitting room with the help of an aluminum walker. He was gaunt and frail, wearing a tattered bathrobe and worn pair of slippers. Alzheimer's had set in four years ago, and the ensuing deterioration of the one-time CPA's brain had been slow but certain. When Kevin's gaze fell on his grandson, however, there was a look of recognition in his eyes.

"Mark!" Kevin boomed, his smiling revealing a handful of missing teeth. "What a surprise! Did you bring the boys?"

Edgar turned to his mother. Mark was his father's name. Molly shook her head faintly.

"Don't upset him," she whispered faintly.

Edgar looked back at his grandfather. He drew in a breath.

"Just me, Pops," he replied, playing along as if he were indeed his father. "Can you wait in the kitchen a second? I'll be right here and we can catch up."

"Sure, son," Kevin replied, still smiling. "Sure thing. I'll pour you some coffee."

"That would be great, Pops."

"Just wait at the table," Molly called out to the old man. "I need to make a fresh pot."

"Oh," Kevin said. "Okay, then."

With some difficulty, Edgar's grandfather turned the walker around and fumbled his way back into the kitchen. Watching him, Edgar felt his knees begin to weaken. He took a step toward the sofa and slowly sat down. This was a mistake, he thought to himself. I never should have come.

"He's getting worse," Molly said once the old man was out of the room. "Every day."

"I'm sorry," Edgar managed to say.

"I don't know what to do," his mother said. "I don't know what to do about any of this."

Consumed with guilt, Edgar swallowed hard. He thought he could still taste the metal from the gun he'd shoved in his mouth earlier. He wished now that he'd had the strength to pull the trigger. Anything not to be here. What was I thinking? he thought.

As if she could read her son's mind, Molly said, "Why are you here, Edgar? I don't have enough troubles without you dragging me into yours? And your brothers? How am I going to be able to face anyone after this?"

"I'm sorry," Edgar said again.

"How does that help me?" Molly said. "What good does it do for you to say you're sorry?"

"I need to get away," Edgar said, hating the words even as he was saying them.

Molly stared at him, at a loss.

"You want money?" she said. "Is that it? You think I have some extra money lying around that I can just give you?"

Edgar shook his head. He stared down at his feet and the worn patches in the throw rug on the floor. Just go, he thought to himself. Just get up and leave. The veteran remained seated, however. Finally, he willed himself to lift his gaze and stare back his mother. Somehow he managed to get the words out.

"I need to see Dad," he said.

Molly stared at Edgar as if he were even more deranged than his grandfather.

"What are you talking about?" she said. "Your father's dead."

"No, he isn't," Edgar said. "Mom, I know he's alive. You need to tell me where he is."

16

Destra County, Pennsylvania

Route 9 was an outdated two-lane mountain road winding through the Allegheny foothills between Interstate 80 and the state line. The surrounding land was as rugged as it was isolated. Only a few homesteads could be seen amid the vast sprawl of rolling grasslands, wide blue rivers and heavily forested hillocks. People who lived in this part of the world valued their privacy and, for the most part, they got it.

One local resident, Zeke Ambrose, was about to become an exception.

Roughly three miles south of the Mt. Carruthers Recreation Area, Marcus Yarborough pulled off Route 9 and eased his Ford Focus to a stop at a little-used rest area, ending a cross-state drive that had been interrupted fleetingly for breakfast and a half-hour catnap at a truck stop near Kylertown. As he'd expected, the rest area was deserted, and Yarborough parked behind a stand of conifers that would prevent passing motorists from spotting his car. To further insure that he wouldn't be interrupted, once he got out of his car, Yarborough tracked down a fallen tree branch in the nearby brush and used it to barricade the turnoff.

The previous night's snowstorm had bypassed the area and the early-morning temperature was in the low forties. Once he'd opened the trunk of the Focus, Yarborough took off his heavy jacket and tossed it in the trunk, then removed same M-40 A-1 sniper rifle he'd used to kill Lance Iovine. He quickly assembled the weapon, then closed the trunk and strode away from the parked car.

There were no official trails beyond the curved guardrail encircling the parking lot, but after passing through a flimsy barrier of wild grass and sedge, Yarborough came upon the hint of a path. The trail had been made over the past few weeks by an AFM stakeout team that had made daily treks to the area, compiling the surveillance report whose findings the senator had passed along to Yarborough when assigning him to assassinate Zeke Ambrose. Yarborough followed the path downhill twenty yards to a wide ledge choked with large shrubs. Extending one arm before him, he brushed aside a few branches and made his way to a small clearing. There, the grass had been trampled flat and the ground was dotted with tobacco-juice stains left from earlier stakeouts.

Yarborough sat on a knee-high boulder that allowed him a panoramic view of the surrounding valley, readied his rifle, then turned his full attention to a developed patch of meadowland located a hundred yards downhill from his position. Smoke curled from a two-story stone chimney affixed to the side of a large redwood house. Two cars were parked next to the house—a Lexus mini-SUV and larger Range Rover. There was no one outside, but if the AFM surveillance bore out, that would soon change.

"Okay, shithead," Yarborough murmured, gaze fixed on the rear door of the distant house. "Don't keep me waiting."

ZEKE AMBROSE WAS a retired ACLU attorney who'd wearied of court battles after twenty-seven years in the legal trenches. He'd come to view trials as little more than an obscene form of performance art wherein the pursuit of truth, more often than not, was disregarded in favor of the kind of histrionics juries had come to expect from watching courtroom dramas on television. More times than he cared to remember, Ambrose himself had tap-danced around the facts in order to help acquit clients he knew damn well were guilty and deserving of hard time. Before his conscience had caught up with him, the would-be populist lawyer had had the foresight to take on enough high-profile cases to amass a multimillion-dollar nest egg, much of which had

Homeland Terror 147

gone into buying and developing the isolated tract of Pennsylvania meadowland he now called home.

Ambrose had also made a point to stay in touch with most of the militia members he'd had the occasion to defend in court, and by the time he'd retired, the charismatic attorney had parlayed these connections into the creation of the True Patriots Coalition, a dues-paying organization that, unlike the American Freedom Movement, existed primarily in cyberspace. The TPC was dedicated more to philosophical discussion than saber rattling or combat training, but any members wishing to indulge in such activities were more than welcome to affiliate themselves with other organizations.

Joan VanderMeer had helped Ambrose set up his coalition Web site and recommended a handpicked associate, Corrina Holmes, to serve as the ex-lawyer's consultant. The woman's tech-savvy input, combined with Ambrose's straightforward, hyperbole-free editorial stance, had proved a magnet for radicalized freethinkers who were put off by the cant and pulpit-thumping that had been the trademark of iconoclasts like VanderMeer's father and Jack Foster Stanton. Consequently, TPC's membership had grown by leaps and bounds since its founding, to the point where Ambrose was now receiving annual dues from more than 125,000 kindred spirits.

Ambrose had never been apprised of VanderMeer's association with Gregory Walden, and he'd never had reason to believe the senator even knew of his vast cyberlegion, much less coveted it as a potential recruiting pool. This morning, as Ambrose completed his yoga stretches and prepared to set out for his daily morning jog around the property line of his much loved retreat, the last thing on the advocate's mind was that someone, acting on Walden's orders, might be lying in wait on a nearby mountaintop for a chance to put a bullet through his head.

Corrina Holmes was equally unaware of Joan VanderMeer's ulterior motives. And when Holmes had fallen in love with Ambrose and moved into his mountain home within a few weeks of their first meeting, she'd had no idea that she'd unwittingly played into VanderMeer and Walden's master plan. She'd become a pawn in Operation Clean Sweep. But unlike most pawns, her intended fate was not to be sacrificed as part of some greater strategy. That destiny awaited her lover.

"I'm on my way out," Ambrose called up to the loft office where Holmes was tweaking the layout for the TruePatriot.org's home page.

"Hang on a second, baby," the dreadlock-haired woman called back. She saved the work she'd been doing, then bounded downstairs, embracing the older man when he stood up from tying his jogging shoes.

"I'd go with you," she told him, "but I'm still piecing together all the links on this bombing at the CIA headquarters."

"Terrible business," Ambrose said, tugging at the elastic band that secured the ponytail he wore to compensate for his receding hairline. The ex-lawyer was tanned and clean-shaved, with only the faintest trace of a double chin. He was fourteen years older than Holmes and had taken up jogging to keep his middle-aged paunch at bay. So far it was working.

"Things are really getting stirred up," Corrina said. "You should've seen Stanton beating the war drums on *A.M. America*. It was kinda scary."

"You want to pour gasoline on a fire, Stanton's your man," Ambrose said. He kissed Holmes deeply, then told her, "Not to change the subject, but when I'm back, how about some wheatcakes and strawberries? If it's warm enough out on the terrace we can sit out there and pretend all's right with the world."

"Great idea," Holmes said, brushing a dreadlock from her face. "I'll put the Web site on hold and get things started."

Ambrose smiled at her, then turned and headed out the back door. Holmes watched him bound down the steps and head for the dirt path leading to the meadow. Free Speech, the couple's golden retriever, materialized from under the back porch and began running alongside the lawyer. The sight brought a smile to the woman's face and helped take the edge off the uneasy feeling she'd had since awakening to news of the rocket attack in Langley and the AFM raid during which Lance Iovine had been slain. Her angst had increased after hearing Jack Foster

Stanton's televised claims about a government conspiracy to use snipers to silence dissent in America. She knew Stanton was prone to exaggeration, but, still, his prophecy had given her the creeps. She was glad Ambrose had suggested a leisurely breakfast on the terrace. It sounded like just the thing she needed to put things in perspective and get back on an even keel.

The kitchen was just off to the right of the back hallway. Holmes took some strawberries from the refrigerator, then set a cutting board near the sink and fished through the drawer underneath it for a knife. She quickly rinsed the strawberries and was beginning to slice them when she heard a faint popping sound outside. It sounded like an engine backfiring, something she was used to hearing out on the uphill mountain road that ran past the property. It wasn't until she heard Free Speech begin to yelp with an unfamiliar urgency that she wondered if something was wrong. Leaning over the sink, she peered out the kitchen window.

The retriever was circling through the tall grass just past the driveway. When Holmes looked closer and saw Zeke Ambrose lying facedown in the grass, her heart leaped in her chest. She dropped the knife and it clattered noisily in the sink. Her mind raced back to Jack Foster Stanton's allegations on *A.M. America.* She couldn't remember the exact words, but she could recall Stanton's intimation that government-sanctioned sniper attacks wouldn't stop with Iovine.

"No," she muttered. "Please, no..."

JOGGING BACK to the rest area, Marcus Yarborough felt certain the hit had gone off cleanly. As with Lance Iovine and so many others before him, it took only a single killshot to the head. Now his only concern was leaving the scene before the authorities arrived.

Once Marcus Yarborough reached the parking lot, he quickly cleared away the tree branch blocking the turnout, then returned to his Ford Focus. Instead of putting the rifle in the trunk, he set it across the back seat. He cranked the ignition and switched on the police scanner beneath the dashboard, then pulled out onto Route 9 and headed south. He'd gone nearly two miles before a

dispatcher's voice crackled over the scanner, passing along word
that Zeke Ambrose had just been shot and was presumed dead.
The closest responding police unit was patrolling Route 9 twelve
miles north of the shooting site, meaning they would not cross
paths with Yarborough while racing to investigate. The dispatcher quickly added, however, that she was going to put out
an APB and arrange to have Route 9 roadblocked in both directions.

Yarborough knew he had enough of a lead to reach the interstate ahead of the police, but he still wanted to get rid of the rifle.
It had served its purpose, and Walden had assured him that
another weapon would be waiting for him when he reached
Philadelphia.

As he rounded a bend that ran parallel with the Destra River,
Yarborough checked that there was no other traffic, then veered
into the opposite lane and slowed his Ford to a stop alongside
the far guardrail. Just past the railing, there was a steep drop to
the slow-moving river below. Yarborough grabbed the sniper
rifle and unceremoniously pitched it out the window. The rifle
tumbled end over end, then splashed into the current. The sniper
watched it sink from view, then shifted back into gear and drove
off.

Yarborough wasn't sure how Walden planned to pin
Ambrose's murder on the government, much less why the
senator was so certain the dead man's Web site could be quickly
converted into a propaganda tool for Operation Clean Sweep, but
the sniper wasn't about to waste his time worrying about either
matter. He'd carried out his assignment. It was time to move on.
He still another killing to attend to.

17

Wilgreen Lake, Kentucky

At the same time Zeke Ambrose's daily run was brutally interrupted by a 7.62 mm round from Marcus Yarborough's MA-40
sniper rifle, Kentucky Posse Comitatus founder Darrin Harville
was engaged in his own morning fitness regimen—popping open
a can of Bud Lite out on his back porch and topping it off with
a shot of Wild Turkey bourbon. He jostled the can slightly, giving
the beer and bourbon a chance to get better acquainted, then
tipped his head back and swilled the boilermaker in one long,
protracted gulp. Afterward he belched, a loud, boisterous yawp
that bounded across the glassy waters of Wilgreen Lake like a
skipping stone. Harville's lakefront home was the only one in
sight, and it would be another six weeks before fishing season
brought anglers out onto the water, so the burly Kentuckian
doubted that he was disturbing anyone. Not that he much cared.
Harville often broadcast similar belches at local diners, following the outburst with the proclamation "My compliments to the
chef." Anyone questioning Harville's table manners would be
reminded that it was a free country, and if that didn't settle
matters, the ex-Marine was likely to provoke a full-scale
argument that would invariably end with the other party either
backing down or stepping outside to learn just why Harville had
earned a mantelful of amateur boxing trophies before he'd joined
the service.

Harville's pugilistic career had also been the inspiration for the crude tattoos lettered onto each of his ten knuckles, spelling out Wanna Fight. Even though he'd quit boxing years ago, the anthem remained Harville's battle cry and the motivating force behind his formation of the Kentucky Posse Comitatus. KPC was as physically confrontational as Ambrose's True Patriots were cerebral, and Harville liked nothing better than summoning his minions to emotionally charged rallies and demonstrations guaranteed to end with fists flying, heads cracking and blood flowing in the streets. He usually preferred to clash with civil rights groups or pro-choice advocates, but he had no qualms about raising a ruckus against government officials whenever he felt they were trampling on his constitutional rights and those of his redneck constituency.

As such, Harville had taken a keen interest in this morning's news from back east. When it came to the Langley bombing, he was heartened to learn that somebody'd had the balls to hit the Feds where they hurt. Though he felt it would have made more sense to blow up the FBI's headquarters instead of the CIA's, as he'd told Jack Foster Stanton during their brief phone conversation following the gadfly's appearance on *A.M. America,* the bottom line for him was that nine dead in Langley meant nine fewer government bureaucrats likely to stick their collective nose in militia business.

As for the incident in Meredith Valley, Harville was quick to dismiss any government explanations about "due process" and "executing warrants." Like Stanton, he was convinced the Feds had gone to the AFM compound with the sole intent of retaliating for the CIA bombing. He'd called Stanton specifically to compliment the firebrand for advancing the theory that Lance Iovine had been assassinated by the FBI rather than one of his own men. When Stanton suggested that Harville band his group together with a few others and stage some kind of mass rally at the Kentucky state capital, Harville had been cool to the idea. After all, joining forces with another outfit wasn't his idea of a good time. To Harville, forming alliances always meant wrangling, making compromises and otherwise indulging in some kind of political double-dealing that had turned the U.S. government into the self-serving monolith it had become. No, if Harville was going to react to what had happened in Meredith Valley, he'd do it his own way, on his own schedule and with his own people.

As he sat on his porch pondering his options, Harville belched once more and, fueled by the buzz from his boilermaker, moved on to the next part of his morning workout. He ran a short length of string through the pop tab of the beer can he'd just drained, then leaned back in his rocker and tied the can to a double laundry line extending from the edge of the porch across the back yard to a large woodshed at the edge of his property. The line was rigged to a pulley in the same manner used to hold targets at a shooting range. When Harville pulled on the upper line, the lower line fed outward and the beer can began to float away from him across the backyard.

Once the can was a good twenty yards away, Harville let go of the line and grabbed the Beretta M-9 MM Service Pistol lying on the table beside him. A colleague in the service had spirited the weapon away from the Marine Corps' inventory of eighty-two thousand similar handguns, allowing Harville to possess a facsimile of the weapon he'd used during his stint with the Marines. Judging from all the scraps of bullet-riddled aluminum strewed about the yard, it was clearly the ex-soldier's intent to see how many shots it would take him to blast the beer can off the laundry line.

Once he felt he was ready, Harville raised the gun and lined up the still-dancing beer can in his sights. Before he could pull the trigger, however, a muffled shot echoed across the lake. At nearly the same instant, Harville felt a 7.62 mm slug pound into his left shoulder with so much force it nearly knocked him off his rocker.

"Son of a bitch!" he howled, vaulting from the chair to the raised deck. Blood spilled onto the planks but Harville ignored his wound. He was more concerned about making sure he wasn't brought down by a second shot.

Once a jolt of adrenaline cut through the fog of his inebriation, Harville was quick to assess the situation. The Feds were after him, the same way they'd gone after Lance Iovine. He couldn't believe it.

Harville knew the shot had come from across the lake, barely sixty yards away. The far embankment was edged with tall bullreeds and cattails, and though they provided a semblance of cover, Harville could see someone moving behind the makeshift screen. It was a man, and he looked to be carrying a rifle.

"Mess with me, will ya?" Harville seethed through his clenched teeth as he inched his way to the patio railing. He still had his gun and he took aim through the uprights, rattling off half his 15-round magazine at the distant target.

The fusillade sent a few dozen mallards fluttering up out of the water, and to Harville's right a pair of squirrels bounded crazily from limb to limb in an old plum tree, chattering to each other. Normally his cat would have gone after the squirrels, but the gunshots spooked the animal, as well. It sprang from a nearby chaise longue and quickly disappeared through a pet door leading into the house.

Harville doubted he'd hit the other man, but he figured he'd at least bought himself some time. Staggering to his feet, the posse chief bounded down the porch steps, clutching his wounded shoulder with his left hand. Blood seeped through his fingers, obscuring half the tattooed lettering on his knuckles.

Beer cans clattered through the weeds as Harville lurched to and fro, zigzagging his way to the riverbank. There, a small dock stretched out into the water. Two small boats were moored in the still waters, but Harville knew there was no time to use them. He was already beginning to feel light-headed from the loss of blood. He willed himself to remain conscious, hoping to catch a better glimpse of his would-be assassin.

"You're going down, mutha," he snarled.

HANK TALBOT was furious.

He couldn't remember the last time he'd botched a killshot from such close range. It had been his fault, too. He'd known about Harville's harebrained target-practice regimen and had even positioned himself across the lake so that the ex-Marine would be a clear target once he leaned back in his rocker to fire at the beer can. But at the last possible second—while Harville was peering down the laundry line over the barrel of his raised Beretta—Talbot had sensed that he'd been spotted and that the posse chief was about to turn the gun on him. He'd been wrong. Worse yet, his concern had led him to force his shot. Instead of putting a bullet through the Kentuckian's skull, he'd been lucky to plug Harville in the shoulder. And now he was on the defensive, playing hide-and-seek along the embankment behind some goddamn cattails. He knew that if he didn't finish the job quickly, his wounded prey might well turn the tables and nail him with the next volley from his handgun.

"Asshole," he cursed, directing his anger more at himself than Harville. Crouched low behind the cattails, Talbot could no longer even see his target. To make matters worse, the sniper had just stepped into a small sinkhole, his right leg disappearing into brackish water halfway up his shin. The muck had engulfed his foot, clenching it in a stranglehold, and when he tried to pull himself clear he felt a burning twinge run up his leg. The more Talbot tried to wriggle free, the deeper he felt himself sinking into the quagmire.

Fuming, Talbot squatted lower and plunged his left hand into the cold lakewater, fumbling for his sunken foot. He was still wearing the latex gloves he'd donned to keep his fingerprints off the rifle, however, and it was next to impossible for him to untie the boot. He yanked his hand back out of the water and was prying the glove off when he suddenly stopped, realizing he now had an even more immediate problem to deal with.

Thirty yards behind him, up on the road where he'd parked his Honda Accord, Talbot heard a car door open, then slam shut. Glancing over his shoulder, the assassin spotted a uniformed highway patrol officer circle his vehicle and start to make his way downhill toward the lake. The officer had his service pistol out and was obviously responding to the earlier gunshots. Talbot knew that in a matter of seconds he would be discovered, trapped as surely as a fly stuck in a spiderweb.

CURIOSITY MAY HAVE KILLED the cat, but in the case of Darrin Harville, it was paranoia that proved his undoing.

Leaning for support against one of the wooden posts supporting the far end of his private dock, the wounded ex-Marine ignored the blood drenching his shirt and peered across the tranquil lake, defying his assailant to show himself. When he spied the telltale wide-brimmed hat of a highway patrol officer heading downhill toward the water's edge, he assumed he'd spotted his man. With a malevolent grin, he took quick aim with his Beretta and rattled off six shots. Four of the jacketed 9 mm rounds bored into their unsuspecting target. The lawman went down, pistol dropping from his hand as he keeled into the brush. Harville lost sight of the man but felt sure he'd killed him.

"Last laugh's on you, lawman," the militiaman murmured.

Harville now felt it was safe to turn his attention to his bleeding shoulder. He tore his shirt open and saw that the wound was deep and had obviously nicked an artery. If he didn't get some quick medical attention, he was going to bleed to death. He knew he couldn't dial 911, however. If more cops showed up and realized he'd just killed one of their own, Harville figured they'd lend a hand sending him to his Maker. No, there had to be another way. There was a first-aid kit in the house. He figured if he could patch himself up enough to stop the bleeding, he might be able to call around and get one of his posse members to come lend a hand.

Harville gathered his strength and was about to backtrack to his house when he detected motion out across the river. He turned slightly, just in time to see Hank Talbot drawing a bead on him with his sniper rifle. In an instant, Harville realized he'd gunned down the wrong man. There was no time for him to react. Caught flat-footed, he groaned dully as a second 7.62 mm round thumped into his chest, obliterating his sternum and laying waste to his fast-beating heart.

HANK TALBOT LOWERED his M-40 rifle and stared impassively as Darrin Harville tumbled headlong off the end of the dock and splashed into the lake.

Satisfied the man was dead, Talbot set the rifle aside long

enough to free his leg from the sinkhole, leaving the boot behind, then grabbed the weapon and headed back uphill to his car. As he passed the fallen highway patrol officer, he slowed to a stop. He stared down at the body, then glanced back at the lake, where Harville's corpse now bobbed facedown in the water.

"This is too good to pass up," he told himself.

Crouching beside the slain officer, Talbot carefully placed the man's gun back in his holster, then repositioned his stiffening fingers around the rifle he'd just used to slay Harville. Talbot knew that it wasn't the cleanest of frame-ups—there was, for example, the matter of the spent shell casing and sunken boot he'd left down by the embankment—but given the situation, he felt it was a good idea to throw up some kind of smoke screen. As long as it looked—at first glimpse, at any rate—as if Harville and the patrolman had been the only ones involved in their shootout, there would be no immediate rush to sound the alarm and post any kind of roadblock for other suspects. Talbot would have the time he needed to move on to his next target.

18

Schroeder, Pennsylvania

As she neared the old Byrnes property, Roberta Williamson was even more furtive about her approach than Edgar had been. On the way to Schroeder, she'd stopped at an Internet café long enough to pinpoint the address on a Web site that provided satellite photos of the area. She'd been able to zoom in close enough to see that the property extended back from Towhee Drive to a bend in the Schuylkill River. On the far side of the river was a small park, and there appeared to be a narrow footbridge leading to a hiking trail that ran directly alongside both the river and the old, meandering wooden fence that surrounded the Byrnes estate. Apparently the satellite photo was outdated, however, because when the CIA agent arrived at the park, she saw that the footbridge was no longer standing. From the looks of it, vandals had taken an ax to the posts supporting the park side of the bridge, collapsing it into the river. The current had long since washed away most of the structure, though Williamson could still see a small section dangling over the side of the far embankment like a wooden tongue.

Williamson had come this far, however, and she had no intention of turning back. There were six small rental boats tied to a dock next to a small bait shop servicing the park. The shop had just opened and Williamson was the first customer. She paid the owner twenty dollars up front to rent one of the boats for the day. For that much money she could have had the use of a motorized craft, but Williamson didn't want to make any more noise than necessary. She chose a rowboat instead.

The current pulled her downstream as she paddled her way across the Schuykill, and by the time she reached the other side she was nearly a quarter mile from her destination. She pulled the boat ashore and abandoned it, then took the hiking trail back to the Byrnes property. The wooden fence was more ornamental than protective, and Williamson was soon picking her way through a sea of tall weeds and wild sunflowers leading to the old Victorian house.

Once she could see the roofline, the CIA agent unzipped the fanny pack she'd strapped on back at the car. She'd come prepared. In addition to a can of pepper spray and her registered .45 ACP Para Companion, Williamson had also brought along a Johnson & Guthrie X-32 stun grenade that she'd managed to smuggle out of Langley. For the moment, she decided the Para was her best option. She palmed the handgun and thumbed off the safety before proceeding.

The weeds extended all the way to charred ruins of the old garage, and in a few spots they'd even managed to push their way up through cracks in the slab foundation. Williamson would have preferred more cover, but she took a chance and scrambled her way past the rubble to the rear of the house. Thankfully, a neighbor somewhere down the block had just started a car, providing enough noise to mask her approach. The shades in all the rear windows were drawn, so the CIA agent doubted that anyone had seen her. Still, she had her 8-round Para ready to fire at the first sign of trouble.

Once she'd caught her breath, Williamson edged closer to a back door that led directly into the kitchen. As she drew nearer, she began to hear a man arguing with a woman in the kitchen. Williamson could only make out a portion of what was being said.

"Tell me!" the man kept saying.

The woman claimed she didn't know whatever it was he wanted her to tell him. At one point a third voice joined in briefly, and though Williamson could only make out the pitch and intonation, she was almost positive it was the voice of an older man. That made it almost equally certain, at least in her mind, that the man doing most of the talking was Edgar Byrnes. She'd done it; she'd tracked down Felix Garber's killer.

There was a small, book-sized pet portal set into the bottom half of the kitchen door. Williamson could see a faint gap in the rubberized strips hanging down from the upper framework.

Perfect, she thought to herself.

With her free hand, Williamson reached back into her fanny pack, this time pulling out the stun grenade. She moved a few inches closer, then leaned over, further inspecting the pet door to make sure it wasn't blocked off from the inside. This close to the opening, she could better hear the voices inside the kitchen.

"He just sends cash, Eddie, that's it!" the woman was saying. "No return address, no note. He just sends cash. And not enough of it, if you ask me."

Positive now that she had her man, Williamson drew in a breath, then pulled her arm back slightly. She thumbed the grenade's release pin and heaved the projectile through the pet door.

Williamson had been concerned that the back door might be dead bolted, but when the stun grenade detonated, its 30,000 psi pressure wave rattled the door with so much force it burst open. The CIA agent seized the opportunity and charged through the opening, gun held out before her.

Inside the kitchen, Edgar and Molly Byrnes had been brought to their knees by the explosion. Both were stunned and disoriented, half-blinded by the discharge of aluminum and potassium perchlorate. Kevin, the patriarch, had fallen to the floor next to his toppled walker and was groaning.

"I can't see," he said. "What happened? I can't see!"

Williamson ignored the old man and closed in on Edgar. As the younger man reached for the counter and started to pull himself to his feet, the CIA agent torqued her body and lashed out with a karate kick, catching Edgar square in the solar plexus. He doubled over and once more dropped to his knees. She followed with a blow to the back of Edgar's head with the stainless-steel butt of her pistol, rendering him unconscious. He pitched forward and sprawled across the linoleum, landing a few feet from his grandfather.

By now Molly Byrnes had regained enough of her sight to see Williamson looming over her son. The small Para handgun was aimed at Edgar's head.

"Don't worry, I'm not going to shoot him," Williamson assured Molly. "At least not yet."

19

Philadelphia, Pennsylvania

"Guess there was no time to lay out the red carpet," Jack Grimaldi said as he guided one of Stony Man's Bell commuter choppers down toward a helipad adjacent to the Philadelphia precinct station located closest to Ben Zernial's machine shop. He'd been cleared for landing, and a reception committee of three uniformed officers and a plainclothes detective waited nearby.

"We'll have to make do," Mack Bolan said, readying the Justice Department credentials he and Grimaldi would need to present in order to receive clearance to join the pending SWAT raid on Zernial's building.

The point man for the Philly force was the plainclothes detective. Wes Patterson was tired eyed and burly, with bad skin, ruddy jowls and teeth stained yellow from too much coffee and cigarettes. His thin hair was dyed an unnatural shade of black and combed straight back on his square head. He greeted the new arrivals with a gruff voice, then scowled at the ID claiming Bolan was Justice Department Special Agent Matthew Cooper. Grimaldi's handle this time around was Ike Ferris. Both Stony Man warriors were braced for the usual antagonism local lawmen were inclined to heap on outsiders, but once Patterson handed back the credentials, he took the operatives by surprise.

"Welcome aboard, gentlemen," the detective said, taking his voice down a notch. "We could use some extra manpower on this one."

"We'll do what we can," Bolan replied.

"Lemme cut straight to the chase." Patterson held out an area map and pointed to various areas as he filled Bolan and Grimaldi in on the situation. "Ground zero is right here, halfway down the block. We've got the perimeter pretty well locked up, but there are a couple areas that could use beefing up, especially underground."

Bolan glanced at Grimaldi, then turned back to Patterson. "Are we talking about tunnels?"

"Sewer line, actually," Patterson said. He dragged a stubby finger down the map, indicating Declaration Avenue, the thoroughfare that ran past Zernial's building. "The one here feeds to the subway if you follow it far enough."

"What, you think they're gonna be able to flush themselves down the toilet and wind up on the E-line?" Grimaldi said.

Patterson let the wisecrack pass. "This is an old neighborhood," he went on patiently. "Back during Prohibition, most of the buildings around here doubled as speakeasies."

Bolan could see where this was going. "They used the sewer lines to move booze."

"That, plus it made for a handy escape route if the cops came knocking, like we aim to do any second," Patterson explained. "I can't say for sure Zernial has access to what's down there, but it's a pretty safe bet."

"You want us to cut them off if they make a run for the sewers," Bolan guessed.

Patterson nodded. "I was about to send a couple of men down, but they're already in synch with the game plan up here. If you could oblige, it'd make things go a lot smoother all the way around."

Bolan eyed Grimaldi. He saw skepticism in the pilot's gaze. He had misgivings of his own. Was Patterson glad-handing them in hopes he could stash them down a hole while the raid went down? There was no time for haggling, so Bolan turned his gaze back to the detective, trying to fathom the officer's true intent. Patterson apparently sensed their distrust and sweetened the pot.

"Look, we'll have a com link," he said. "You guys go down and find a way in before we make our move, I'm fine with you leading the charge."

Bolan decided to take a leap of faith.

"We'll do it," he told the detective.

Patterson's expression remained unchanged. "Appreciate it," the cop said, folding the map and stuffing it in his pocket. "Now, let's get cracking."

THERE WERE ZEALOTS in the movement who embraced the militia with every fiber in their being, but Ben Zernial wasn't one of them. Yes, he was dedicated to the American Freedom Movement and all it stood for, but even now, as the new man in charge, Zernial remained first and foremost a blue collar working man. And he was damn proud of it. Pulling sixty-hour work weeks in his grimy shop was something he looked forward to, and few things gave him more pleasure than stripping down a botched engine and re-assembling it so that it purred with the same efficiency as it had when it'd first come off the assembly line. He knew that computers were the way of the future, but he also knew that as long as the world's infrastructure depended in part on machines devoid of microchips or motherboards, there would be work for him and he could feel that he played a valuable role in making that world tick. That feeling was every bit as important to him as touting ideologies or ranting against the abuses of Big Government.

And so it was that, despite the upheaval of the past twelve hours—three hours of which had been spent on his stealth visit to Jack Foster Stanton's home in Camden, New Jersey—Zernial found himself able to start his first day as president of the American Freedom Movement as if it were any other. He'd already wolfed down a healthy breakfast, filled a thermos with fresh coffee, then plodded downstairs from his apartment to the machine shop's back workroom. Now, twenty minutes later, his hands were as caked with grease as his work apron and he was humming a country song as he broke the seal on a rusting winch motor.

He was interrupted by Lyle Jenkins, one of three employees on hand for the day shift. Jenkins, like the others, was also a member of the American Freedom Movement.

"I think we might have a problem," Jenkins told Zernial.

Judging from the other man's expression, Zernial figured the problem was more pressing than that of an irate customer wondering why his lawn blower wasn't ready to be picked up. He grabbed a rag and wiped his hands as he followed Jenkins to the front of the store. Mike Sarnovich, a nerdish-looking recruit in his early twenties, was hunched over a smaller workbench set near the front counter for small repair orders. A fourth man, an ex-SEAL named Reese Calloway, stood near the entrance to the shop, staring out the window into the street.

"What's going on?" Zernial asked him.

"I was just down the block sending off a few packages," Calloway reported. "On the way back, I see all these people being hustled out of the shops on either side of us. There's somebody on the roof across the street, too. I didn't see a rifle, but you know what I'm thinking."

Zernial nodded, absorbing the information. There'd been a part of him that had worried about the Feds trying to make a move on the shop. He was beginning to think maybe he should have gone with his instincts and called off work for the day.

"We're gonna get raided?" Sarnovich called out nervously, peering up from his workbench.

"Looks that way," Zernial said calmly, even as his mind raced, trying to determine their next move. He made a point not to keep any AFM material in the shop or his apartment upstairs, so—with the possible exception of his computer—there was nothing to hide. What concerned him more was the thought that the authorities were looking to haul him and the others in for questioning. He knew he could keep his mouth shut, and he figured he could count on Calloway and Jenkins to do the same. He had his doubts about Sarnovich, however.

"Lock the door and put up the Closed sign," Zernial told Calloway.

"They had to see me come in," Calloway countered. "And if they've been on stakeout, they probably know I'm not here alone."

"I realize that," Zernial snapped. "Still, lock up. It'll buy us some time."

Calloway flipped the dead bolt into place and turned around the plastic sign that hung in the window.

"Okay," he said. "What now?"

"This way," Zernial said, heading back toward the repair room. "All of you."

The others followed. By the time they caught up with Zernial, he'd retrieved a short-barreled Tristar TR-Mag shotgun from under his workbench. Calloway and Jenkins were on the same wavelength and had armed themselves with 9 m Bernardelli P-019s. That left only Sarnovich without a weapon.

"This is nuts, guys," Sarnovich said, his voice trembling at the sight of so much firepower. "If they're after us, there's no way we're going to be able to outshoot them."

"Here." Zernial yanked open a workbench drawer and pulled out a Bersa 45 UC pistol. He tossed the compact pistol to Sarnovich. "Feel better?"

"Not really," the younger man confessed.

"Tough shit," Zernial said. "You come to the ballroom, you better be ready to dance."

Jenkins eyed the short hallway leading to the rear doorway, then told Zernial, "They're gonna have the back covered."

"We're not going out the back," Zernial responded. He unclipped a key chain from his waist and unlocked a cabinet door next to the workbench. "There's another way."

DETECTIVE WES PATTERSON had reached the makeshift SWAT command post a block from the machine shop moments after Calloway had put out the Closed sign. He knew what it meant.

"They're onto us," he told the men assembled around him.

SWAT chief Frank Howell, a squat man wearing the tactical team's trademark black uniform, nodded. "We're set."

"You've cleared out the surrounding shops?" Patterson asked.

"Affirmative," Howell responded, handing Patterson a full-face gas mask. The other SWAT commandos had already pulled similar masks over their heads. "Might've been what tipped 'em off, but that's water under the bridge."

"Then let's get a move on," Patterson said.

Howell brought a walkie-talkie to his lips and started barking commands.

Patterson tried to reach Bolan and Grimaldi, but there was something wrong with the com link.

"You're on your own, guys," Patterson groused, yanking out his service pistol. He broke into a run, following three SWAT members away from the command post. The street had just been cordoned off in both directions, allowing them to beeline diagonally across the street. Eight other commandos broke from their positions and converged with them in front of Zernial's machine shop. Two of them carried pressurized battering rams, long tubes the size of bazookas, each packing as much pounding force as conventional rams twice their size. Patterson knew there was another six-man crew storming the rear exit, and a chopper would soon be hovering above the street to assist snipers situated atop several nearby buildings. Provided the Feds had managed to secure the sewer line, Patterson figured they had the militia boxed in.

The SWAT members poised outside the door had already put on their gas masks. Patterson donned the one Howell had given him, then bellowed through the mouthpiece, "Trick or treat!"

One of the cops slammed the butt of his riot gun against the shop's front window, obliterating the glass. The officer next to him lobbed a tear gas grenade through the opening. Meanwhile, the rams were quickly set in place, one pressed against the dead bolt, the other opposite the uppermost door hinge. The door was reinforced but not enough to withstand concentrated assault of the two rams. Triggered simultaneously, they jolted the door loose on its hinges. Patterson and another cop finished off the job, kicking the door in.

"Police!" he shouted, charging through the haze of tear gas enveloping the cluttered shopfront.

There was no one in sight. The only sound was that of an oscillating fan tucked back in the corner above Sarnovich's workbench. Seconds later, however, Patterson and the others heard the thump of battering rams taking out the rear door. A shouted warning was answered by a blast of gunfire.

"Let's get 'em!" Patterson cried out, the mask muffling his voice as he charged toward the back workroom. He was passing the counter when Sarnovich appeared in the doorway, hacking from the effects of the tear gas, Bersa Ultra Compact barely visible in his raised hand.

Patterson fired first, planting a round in the young recruit's chest. Sarnovich went down, finger on the trigger. His burst missed Patterson but hammered into the Kevlar vest of the SWAT commando directly behind him.

"On your toes!" Patterson yelled to the others as he circled the front counter.

More gunfire sounded in the back room, and by the time the detective had charged through the doorway, Reese Calloway had gone down near the large machine lathe. He'd managed to take out one of Patterson's men, however, with a killshot to the head. Jenkins, meanwhile, had been gunned down in the back hallway and lay dead on the concrete floor. All this Patterson took in with a quick glance before wheeling to his right, having spotted someone duck into a narrow opening between a shelving unit and the far wall.

"Oh, no you don't," he fumed, giving chase to Ben Zernial. By the time he reached the wall, however, a hinged panel had swung back into place, sealing off the AFM honcho's escape route.

Patterson clawed at the panel, then shouted over his shoulder, "Get one of those rams over here, quick! We've got one headed below!"

MACK BOLAN MOVED cautiously through the sewer line that ran beneath Declaration Avenue. There was only a shallow stream of effluent beneath his feet, but the surrounding concrete was slick with algae and the Executioner knew that one false step would likely throw him off balance and into the sludge, which gave off a rank, cloying odor that had both him and Grimaldi fighting nausea.

The Stony Man pilot was two steps behind Bolan, hunched over, sidestepping the condensation that dripped from the above. The only sound besides the dripping and their sloshing footsteps was that made by rats scurrying in flight from the harsh glow of the flashlight clenched in Bolan's left hand.

"Dirty job but somebody's gotta do it, eh, Sarge?" Grimaldi whispered over Bolan's shoulder as he peered at the shadow-den stretch that lay before them. "I tell ya, if it turns out that eefhead sent us down here on a wild-goose chase—"

"Quiet!" Bolan snapped, slowing to a halt, Beretta held out before him.

Grimaldi fell silent and stopped in his tracks. He listened tently. Somewhere above them, they could hear a series of faint umps punctuated by equally muted pops. The acoustics in the wer were such that it was difficult to pinpoint exactly where e sounds were coming from, but both Bolan and Grimaldi ew their meaning.

"It's going down," Bolan murmured.

"So much for getting our cue to join in," Grimaldi murmured.

The men listened further, finally determining that the noise was ming from somewhere up ahead of them. On a hunch, Bolan nt and set the flashlight on the slickened concrete in front of m. The knobbed switch kept the light from rolling into the water aile allowing the beam to flash down the sewer ahead of them.

"Let's back up," he told Grimaldi.

The men retraced their steps a few yards, moving beyond age of the light. Bolan leaned to his left, pressing himself ainst the cool, wet stone wall. Grimaldi did the same. Then y waited.

Seconds passed by, the drips of condensation sounding like ticks of a clock. Then, some twenty yards ahead of them, lan and Grimaldi had a heard a door slam open, followed by sound of footsteps heading down a staircase. Bolan had vered the foregrip on his Beretta and took hold of the weapon th both hands, steadying his aim. Behind him, Grimaldi ught his Government Model Colt into firing position, as well. There was a moment's hesitation as the intruder paused at the ttom of the steps, concealed from view by an apparent recess he sewer wall. Bolan strained his eyes and thought he could the break in the wall where their target was standing. He npsed a flickering shadow within the recess, then saw the inky iouette of a shotgun barrel.

Before the Executioner could fire, the sewer resounded with the deafening roar of Ben Zernial's Tristar shotgun. The shop owner hadn't been aiming at Bolan, however. His target had been the flashlight. Buckshot decimated the light and darkness swept through the passageway as pellets tore through the murky water and glanced off the surrounding walls, caroming past Bolan and Grimaldi.

The Executioner was on the move even as the din echoed in his ears. Lurching into the middle of the sewer, he swung his Beretta to his left and rattled off an autoburst, then quickly dropped to his knees in anticipation of return fire.

There wasn't any.

Bolan heard a metallic clatter as the shotgun fell to the concrete, then there was a fumbling sound as Ben Zernial staggered from the recess and slumped forward, landing face-first in the water.

Bolan and Grimaldi stayed put in the darkness, both men ready to fire at the first indication that their would-be attacker was still alive. Zernial had stopped moving, however. Moments later, the Stony Man commandos heard fresh footsteps heading down the staircase inside the recess. They raised their guns and shifted aim.

"Police!"

Bolan recognized Wes Patterson's muffled voice and called out, "Hold your fire!"

The beams from two different flashlights soon probed their way into the sewer. Three SWAT team members followed Patterson into the cramped passageway. Bolan and Grimaldi froze in place until the lights were trained on them, then slowly moved forward, reaching Zernial's corpse at the same time as Patterson. The detective tugged off his gas mask and quickly inspected the body to confirm that the machinist was dead.

"Good work," the detective said. "I tried reaching you, but couldn't get through."

"Not a problem," Bolan said. "We sort of figured things out."

"There's more stiffs upstairs," Patterson said. "I've got some men checking out the upstairs apartment, but I think we pretty much cleaned them out."

"Be nice if it worked out that way," Grimaldi said.

"What're you talking about?" Patterson countered. "Between his and what went down last night, anybody left in this organization's going to scurry off with their tails between their legs. Trust me, these scumbags are history."

Bolan stared down at Zernial's body, then looked back up at the portly detective. "Like my friend just said, it'd be nice if it worked out that way."

20

Washington, D.C.

It was a short cab drive from Hal Brognola's White House meeting to the Georgetown University Hospital where John Kissinger was still recuperating. After flashing his Justice Department credentials at the front desk, the director of Stony Man Farm was ushered into his wounded colleague's private room. Kissinger was awake, watching the news on a ceiling-mounted television. His face was bruised and swollen and he looked exhausted, but when he saw Brognola he muted the television and managed an upbeat, if tired, grin.

"Hey, boss," he whispered. His voice was ragged due to the breathing tube that had been fed down his throat during surgery.

The men shook hands, then Brognola said, "I hear they really went to town on you in the OR. Luckily all we have to worry about is you not going stir-crazy while you get your strength back."

"Yeah, good luck with that," Kissinger said. "I've been up two hours and already I'm feeling claustrophobic."

"Give it time," Brognola said.

"Got plenty of that," Kissinger responded. He sipped some water, then changed the subject. Gesturing at the television set, he told Brognola, "I've picked up bits and pieces of what's going on. Wanna fill me in on the rest?"

"I'll try."

Brognola pulled up a chair. Much of what had transpired during the meeting with the Joint Chiefs was classified, but

ognola was still able to give Kissinger a passable briefing. He
s halfway through a recap of the altercation with AFM forces
Meredith Valley when Kissinger held up a hand to silence him.

"Hang on," the armorer said, reaching for the remote as he stared
st Brognola's shoulder. "Looks like something just came in."

Brognola turned in his chair and followed Kissinger's gaze to
television set. On the screen was an aerial view of what appeared
be a crime scene, with police and EMTs swarmed around a body
ng in a grassy meadow. An inset photo box showed a middle-
ed man with receding hair and a ponytail. Beneath the photo the
n's name was superimposed in block letters.

"Zeke Ambrose," Kissinger murmured. "Why does that name
g a bell?"

"He's a militia head," Brognola said. "Go ahead and turn up
sound."

Kissinger fingered the volume control. He and Brognola
tened as an offscreen reporter divulged the first, sketchy details
out the shooting of the founder of the True Patriots Coalition.
l that was known so far was that Ambrose had been shot while
gging near his mountain home in central Pennsylvania. After
erviewing the man's live-in lover, Corrina Holmes, authorities
re acting on the theory that the man had been the victim of a
g-range sniper.

"First Iovine, now this," Brognola murmured.

"Same shooter?" Kissinger wondered.

"I'd have to calculate the driving distance," Brognola said,
t, yeah, I think he would have had time to get there."

"It's just what that nutcase was warning about on the morning
ow," Kissinger observed.

Brognola nodded. He hadn't seen Jack Foster Stanton's appear-
ce on *A.M. America* but he'd heard about it from the taxi driver
o'd driven him to the hospital. "You can bet there's going to be
en more finger-pointing as long as that sniper's on the loose."

The newscast switched to some archive footage of Zeke
nbrose addressing a trial jury back in his days as an ACLU
vyer. The reporter was describing the dead man's courtroom
ckground when the image on screen abruptly changed again,

this time to that of the network's top-rated evening news anchor. The man was seated at his studio desk, looking somber as he announced breaking news from Kentucky. Word had just come in about the shooting deaths of Posse Comitatus head Darrin Harville and an officer for the Kentucky Highway Patrol. In this case, the anchorman reported, there were even fewer details available than at the site of the Pennsylvania shooting, although a local sheriff had been quoted as saying there may have been some kind of shootout involving the two victims.

"Unless our guy hopped a Learjet," Kissinger ventured, "there's no way he could've gotten to Kentucky that quick."

"We've got a second shooter," Brognola concluded. "Hell, who knows, maybe even a third."

"This Stanton guy's starting to look like a soothsayer," Kissinger said. "You think he's behind it?"

"I'm not sure," Brognola said, "but it seems too pat for me. You'd think if it was him he wouldn't have gone on the air and tipped his hand."

"Then again," Kissinger countered, "by putting the word out the way he did, he's made it easier for people to jump to the wrong conclusion as far as these shootings go."

"True," Brognola conceded. "In any event, we've got one hell of a mess on our hands now. If the militias think we're after them, how long do you think it'll be until they decide to fight back?"

"They've already done that with that rocket attack at Langley, don't you think?"

"I'm not talking about isolated potshots at public buildings," Brognola responded. "I'm talking about all-out war."

Stony Man Farm, Virginia

BACK AT THE ANNEX Computer Room, Barbara Price and the members of Aaron Kurtzman's cybercrew had also just learned about the assassinations of Zeke Ambrose and Darrin Harville. Like Brognola, they realized that the already grim stakes had just been raised considerably. Or, as Huntington Wethers put it as he ared at one of the cable news feeds playing out on the far wall onitors, "Things are getting out of control."

"It's looking that way, all right," Price murmured. She stood ongside Wethers near the monitors, simultaneously attempting assimilate the news and chart a course of action. It was no easy sk. Things were happening so fast and with so many unantici- ated twists she felt as if she were trying to play chess aboard a unaway train.

"Let's get back to it," she told Wethers.

They crossed the room back to the workstations. Kurtzman d Akira Tokaido were hunched over their computers, plumbing e depths of cyberspace for leads that might help swing the dance back in their favor. Carmen Delahunt was multitasking, cking away at her keyboard while she spoke to someone on a lephone headset.

"How are we doing, people?" Price called out. "I want some od news."

"One sec," Carmen Delahunt called out, raising her index nger. "I've got Mack on the line."

While they waited for Delahunt, Price turned to Tokaido and ked, "Edgar Byrnes? Any sign of him?"

Tokaido shook his head forlornly. Along with sorting through me of the files salvaged from the hard drive to Lance Iovine's ptop, he'd been monitoring four separate hotlines set up by the edia and CIA to take calls from anyone who might have seen yrnes in the hours since the Langley bombing.

"Forty calls in so far," he reported, "and only one has panned t. A rider saw someone matching Byrnes's description on rseback two miles from Langley a few minutes after the ex- osion. They found the horse tranked on sedatives under the 495 verpass. No sign of Byrnes, though."

"What about the other calls?" Price asked.

Tokaido rolled his eyes. "Mostly quacks looking for attention."

"That or a chunk of the reward money," Price guessed.

"What do you expect?" Tokaido said. "Give people a chance a million bucks, they'll convince themselves they just saw vis shooting hoops with Jimmy Hoffa."

"Meanwhile, every wild-goose chase eats into our man power," Kurtzman interjected without looking up from his work. "And then the same people wonder why it's so hard for the au thorities to make headway on anything."

"Well, I don't know if this counts as headway," Carmen Delahunt called out as she clicked off her headset, "but we can now add Ben Zernial to the militia body count." The redhead went on to explain how Bolan had slain the fleeing AFM leader in the sewers beneath his machine shop, concluding, "Three more of their guys were taken down when SWAT stormed the place."

"A couple hours ago I might have considered that good news," Price said. "Now, I'm not so sure."

"I know what you mean," Delahunt responded. "Those other guys—Iovine, Ambrose and Harville—they all got whacked off screen, so to speak. Somebody says the Feds were behind it, there's plenty of room for doubt."

Price understood the point Delahunt was trying to make. "This raid on Zernial's shop was in broad daylight," she said, filling in the blanks. "There had to be hundreds of witnesses. Maybe thou sands."

"News chopper, too, most likely," Delahunt said. "No way do we get to say this one was a frame."

"Not just that," Price said. "It weakens our credibility as fa as the other killings go, too. It's like we're playing right into their hands."

"And we don't even know who 'they' are," Tokaido groaned.

Price turned to Kurtzman, who was still doing the lion's share of the work in terms of sorting through the data on Lance Iovine' laptop hard drive.

"I think that's your cue, Bear," the mission controller said. " know Yarborough and that woman probably aren't calling the shots, but they could sure as hell point us in the right direction."

Kurtzman sat back in his wheelchair and rubbed the kinks in his neck. "I was going to keep my mouth shut until I had some thing more definite," he confided, "but I might be onto some thing. If you want, I'll walk you through it."

"Be right there." Price glanced at the others and told them, "Keep plugging away."

Kurtzman had poured himself another cup of coffee by the time Price had sidled up next to his station, squeezing past the roll cart holding the laptop and the two other computers it was hooked up to.

"I salvaged some deleted files and was able to patch together some meeting notes and a partial membership roll," Kurtzman began. "There's no mention of the Aberdeen heist in the notes and Yarborough's name isn't on the roster, which I was sort of figuring on, seeing how he knew his way around the tunnels."

"He might've been tipped off on that by the woman," Price suggested. "And think back to Sykesville. Mack saw her with Cummings in the same BMW she wound up using to help Yarborough escape. Put it together and I'm thinking she's higher up the pecking order than Yarborough."

Kurtzman nodded. "I'm getting to that," he said, "and the thing is, if this woman was strictly AFM, she'd have been listed high in the chain of command. Definitely above Zernial. No dice, though."

"You think she's an outsider, then?"

"Yes and no," Kurtzman said. He counted off on his fingers as he went on. "To know the tunnels, to know how to set Iovine up to get whacked by a sniper, to know enough to take his computer…all that points to her being familiar with the place and how it's run. By the same token, at this point we're assuming AFM's just a piece of all this, not the whole puzzle. You have to think this woman and whoever she's reporting to are connected somehow with these other organizations. Especially the ones run by the guys who were just killed. They've got to have an eye on the whole picture to be able to orchestrate all these hits."

"Why do I feel like there's a punchline on the way?" Price stared hard at Kurtzman. "You know who she is, don't you?"

"Let me walk you there, okay?" Kurtzman countered. "Ask questions if you're not following everything, because it's a little complicated."

"At this point, I'll take 'complicated' as long as it gets me some answers," Price said.

Kurtzman sipped his coffee as he cleared the window on his computer screen and called up a new file.

"There were a handful of video clips that had been erased from Iovine's computer," the older man began, pointing to the file names listed on the screen. "They're all Web site fodder. Speeches mostly, but a few bits of minicam footage, too. One in particular jumped out at me. It's a clip attached to a long article about what happened in Waco. Correction. An article about what they *say* happened in Waco."

"Conspiracy piece?" Price said.

"The 'real' story," Kurtzman said with thinly veiled sarcasm. He jockeyed his cursor to one of the file icons on the screen and clicked it open, telling Price, "Before I show you the clip, take at look at this. It's a still photo taken outside the compound by a freelancer who wound up siding with the conspiracy buffs."

Price stared at the screen and saw a photo of three men, backs turned to the camera as they stared out at the Branch Davidian compound, some thirty yards in the distance. One of the men stood apart from the others and was taping the siege with a video camera. There was a time print at the bottom of the photo.

"I don't remember the whole chronology," she said, "but this was obviously taken at some point before the fire broke out."

"Right, about twenty minutes before," Kurtzman said. "The two guys on the left are FBI agents. The guy with the camera is Jonathan VanderMeer. Name ring a bell?"

Price sorted through her memory, then nodded. "Conspiracy guy, right? One of the first to take it online."

"That's the guy."

"He died in Waco, didn't he?" Price said. "Some kind of car accident on his way to the airport."

"I guess that depends on who you want to believe," Kurtzman said.

"Meaning what?"

"Coming up. But first, take a good look at the FBI agent on your left. You can see he's wearing a watch and that his socks are white, right?"

"Got it," Barbara said.

"Good." Kurtzman clicked open another file, activating a media player on the screen. "Now here's the vid-clip I was talking about. Check it out."

Price watched, intrigued, as the clip played out. The perspective was from that of an unseen woman shooting handheld video footage of her husband trailing a Geiger counter along a stream-bank in what looked to be remote wilderness. The woman jokingly explained that she and her husband were out for their usual weekend treasure-hunting and usually found some interesting stuff. The husband looked up into the camera and was wisecracking about wishing there would be a rainbow so he could find a pot of gold when, far off in the background, there was the sound of squealing tires, followed by a series of crashing sounds. The camera jostled as both the woman and her husband looked off in the direction of the sound. The husband remarked that it sounded like a car had just gone off the road.

"VanderMeer?" Price whispered as she watched.

"Shh," Kurtzman said. "Stay with me here."

He fast-forwarded through a section of the clip in which the wife followed her husband along the creek toward a cloud of smoke trailing up from the base of a shallow ravine. When he resumed the playback at normal speed, the camera was perhaps fifty yards from the crumpled remains of the smoldering car, which had obviously just tumbled down an embankment leading up to a roadway. The camera jerkily panned up the incline, just in time to see two men emerge from a second car that had pulled off the road.

"They look familiar?" Kurtzman murmured to Price.

"The FBI agents," Price said.

"So it appears," Kurtzman said. "Keep watching."

On Kurtzman's monitor, the men could be seen making their way downhill. As they did so, the husband retreated slightly and waved to the camera for his wife to do the same. The camera backed up a few yards and dropped behind a mesquite brush, all the while continuing to film the men climbing down to the wreckage of the first car. When they reached the vehicle, the men peered inside, then one of them stood watch while the other opened the passenger side door and leaned in. It was hard to tell what he was doing, but moments later he leaned back out of the car and closed the door. As he was showing the other man something that looked like a black book, Kurtzman froze the frame again.

"According to the article that goes with the clip," Kurtzman explained, "what the guy's holding is a cassette from Jonathan VanderMeer's video camera. Supposedly it contains footage of these FBI guys firing incendiary flash grenades into the Branch Davidian compound a few minutes after that photo I showed up front."

"The implication being that the FBI deliberately started the fire," Price concluded.

Kurtzman nodded. "We know the Bureau finally owned up to firing a couple flashers at the structure, but they said it was earlier in the day, hours before the fire."

"VanderMeer's tape proved otherwise," Price said.

"Well, that's if you want to believe the clip here," Kurtzman said. "Me, I don't."

"And you're about to tell me why, I take it," Price said.

Kurtzman nodded and toggled his cursor on some menu options for the media player. On screen, the freeze frame image began to enlarge, as if Kurtzman were zooming in on the man who'd retrieved the videocassette from the car. "Remember what I told you to notice about this guy earlier? White socks and watch? Take a close look."

Once he'd homed in on the agent in question, Kurtzman used the cursor to pan the length of the man's body. Enlarged as it was, the image was grainy, but the details were still clear enough to verify two obvious discrepancies between the man in the picture and the FBI agent photographed back in Waco.

"No watch," Price observed. "And his socks are black."

"Bingo," Kurtzman said. "And according to the timeline in the story here, the FBI followed VanderMeer the moment he left the compound and then forced him off the road so they could get the tape. One continuous piece of action."

"Meaning there was no time for the agent to bother with changing his socks or taking off his watch," Price said.

"Right again," Kurtzman told her. "Now, this is stuff I flagged over the course of, what, a couple hours? Give me a couple days and I'm sure I'd be able to prove that's not the rental car VanderMeer was driving and that the footage wasn't even taken the same day as the Waco fire."

"It's a fake," Price said.

"It's *Capricorn One* all over again," Kurtzman said, referring to the 1978 movie in which a purported NASA Mars landing turned out to be a hoax filmed at a desert film studio.

"Okay, I follow all this," Price said, "but I don't see the connection to this mess we're caught up in."

"Think about it a minute," Kurtzman replied calmly. "Whoever put this clip together obviously went to a hell of a lot of trouble, not to mention expense. The thing you have to ask yourself is why? Was it just to fabricate 'evidence' for anyone who wants to think there was a cover-up at Waco? Or was there another motive, like trying to recruit one particular person to help out with whatever master plan it is we're trying to head off at the pass here?"

Price finally figured it out.

"The woman we're looking for," she said. "Jonathan VanderMeer had a daughter…."

21

Washington, D.C.

Joan VanderMeer awoke to the hornetlike buzzing of the alarm clock set on the nightstand beside her bed. She'd been asleep only a few hours and her first instinct was to press the Snooze button and burrow her way back under the covers. A few seconds later, however, she surfaced and silenced the alarm.

"Get up," she groaned to herself, without a shred of conviction. Her body was equally unresponsive and for a few minutes longer she lay in bed, drained. Her head ached and her stomach was turning on itself, as much with anxiety as hunger. She found herself wishing she were nothing more than an average nine-to-five working girl who could blow the day off and indulge in a well-earned sick day without suffering any consequences. The last thing she felt like was going out into the world to help Gregory Walden spearhead a revolution. After what the senator had told her a few hours ago, VanderMeer wasn't sure she could even face the man again. As she stared up at the ceiling, she recalled Walden's cold pronouncement, and the words weighed on her like some invisible force pinning her to the bed.

"She needs to be taken out."

VanderMeer had been on the phone with Walden when he told her. She was on her way back to Washington after splitting up with Marcus Yarborough and had stopped off for gas, then wound up stuck at a train crossing. For a moment she thought she might have misheard the senator. Surely he hadn't just told her he wanted his wife murdered. She waited until the thundering procession of boxcars passed her, then asked Walden to clarify what he'd just told her.

"I want Nikki dead," he said.

It was for tactical reasons, he explained, saying he was going to have it done in a way that would throw any possible suspicion off him once Operation Clean Sweep shifted into high gear. VanderMeer had been stunned, so much so that it had been all she could do to ask, "When?"

"First thing in the morning," Walden told her.

Now, here it was, nine-thirty. More than likely it had already gone down. As VanderMeer continued to lie in bed.

What the hell have I gotten myself into? she wondered.

With some difficulty, she finally forced herself out of bed and made her way into the kitchen. Once she'd stuffed a slice of bread in the toaster, she started up the coffeemaker, then opened the blinds and grimaced as morning light poured into the apartment. Her cell phone was next to her computer in a work alcove just off the kitchen. Filled with growing apprehension, she turned them both on, then ventured to the living room.

VanderMeer's apartment—which she rented under one of her several aliases—was seven blocks north of Capitol Hill, near Union Station. Looking south through the fourth-story picture window she could see, among the sprawl of other buildings, the upper tip of the Washington Monument, as well as the statue of Freedom poised triumphantly atop the Capitol dome. The early-morning clouds were scattering and it was a beautiful day, but the scenic splendor was lost on VanderMeer. Her mind was elsewhere.

For the better part of ten years, Joan VanderMeer had dedicated nearly every fiber of her being into denouncing the United States government and calling for its overthrow. It had been a tireless and demanding crusade, but she had been unfaltering in her determination. Yet here she was, at long last having crossed the line from plotting schemes to carrying them out, and her resolve had suddenly abandoned her. It made no sense. Why was she faltering like this? Was it the idea that with so much at stake Walden had crossed the line and sidetracked himself with a personal vendetta against his wife? Or was it the fact he'd so lamely attempted to make Nikki's murder sound as if it were an integral part of their plan? Did she feel slighted because he hadn't said he was doing it for her? So they could be together? She didn't know. She, who prided herself in always having the answers, suddenly felt as if she knew nothing.

Her nerves on edge, VanderMeer flinched when her cell phone finally pulled in a signal and bleated to let her know she'd received messages while she was asleep. She moved from the window and cued up the phone log. There'd been four calls the past two hours, all from Gregory Walden. She was about to play the messages back when the toaster coughed up her slice of bread, which she used as an excuse to set the phone aside.

She went back into the kitchen and slathered the bread with butter and jam, then poured some coffee and brought everything back to the alcove. Her home page had come up on the computer screen. As she finished the toast and downed it with coffee, she skimmed the headlines. Nearly every news story had to do with the American Freedom Movement and the assassinations that had just been carried out as part of Operation Clean Sweep. There was no mention, however, of Nikki Walden having been murdered.

VanderMeer stared at her cell phone, then picked it up and cued it to play back Walden's messages. There was no mention of Nikki. He briefly passed along the same news VanderMeer had just read on her computer, but his foremost concern seemed to be her whereabouts. In the first call he'd merely seemed puzzled that she hadn't checked in after returning to Washington, but by the last message his mood had shifted from veiled concern to impatience and outright anger.

"Where the hell are you?" were the last words he'd left her with.

VanderMeer's anxiety came to a sudden head and she flung the phone across the room.

How many years had she been working alongside Walden now? How many thousands of hours of conversations had they shared? Spend that much time with a person and you'd think you would know them. But now, she realized, she really had no idea

ho Gregory Walden was. The realization terrified her. And
ith that terror came a wave of paranoia. Was he trying to track
er down because he'd had second thoughts about confiding in
er about his plans to murder his wife? Did he want her dead
ow, too, so that she couldn't come forward and incriminate
im?

VanderMeer rushed to her door and made sure the dead bolt
as thrown and that the chain lock was secured, as well. Then
e went around the apartment and closed the drapes, shroud-
g herself in darkness. She went to her purse and took out her
andgun, placing it on the alcove table next to her computer.

Trembling, her face flushed, she began to switch from Web
te to Web site, looking for the latest news, hoping somehow
at the more she stayed on top of things, the better her chances
f not being sucked into the black hole of uncertainty that had
pened up around her.

"I'll get through this," she whispered to herself, making the
ords into a mantra. "I'll get through this. I'll get through
is...."

IVE BLOCKS AWAY, in his private office at the Hart Senate
uilding on Pennsylvania Avenue, Gregory Walden was about to
peak to his wife for the first time since he'd decided to have her
urdered.

Nikki had been calling all morning, but the senator had been
 meetings with Huell Kostigan and other members of the In-
lligence Committee. Now that he had a free moment, Walden
ad just directed his secretary to get Nikki on the line. One of
Valden's interns—a pretty, twenty-two-year-old GU political-
cience major named Allie Gantner—had just come by with
ome papers for him to sign, but she offered to step out while
e senator talked to his wife. Walden asked her to stay, motion-
g to a chair set on the far side of his desk. He wanted Allie to
verhear his conversation so that she could corroborate that he
nd Nikki had been on loving terms up to the point of her exe-
ution. Pulling off such a feat might have been difficult a few
ours ago, but Walden had already listened to the last few voice

messages Nikki had left, and she was in a far less combative mood than she'd been in back at the apartment and during the host of calls she'd made immediately afterward. Apparently Nikki had turned on the news at some point and realized the magnitude of the circumstances that had roused Walden from bed and led to his spending the night in Washington. In the last message she'd left, Nikki had said she wanted to apologize for the way she'd talked to him. Lest Walden get the idea she'd undergone a complete personality transformation, his wife had also asked if he planned to make it back home for the morning appointment she'd made with their home decorator. That was the Nikki he knew and had come to detest. The world might be in upheaval, but God forbid that she might have to postpone a chance to look at paint swatches and decide on a new color for the dining room.

Walden controlled the conversation from the moment Nikki got on the line. With Allie eavesdropping, he didn't want to appear as if he had anything to apologize for, so he opted for a friendly tone of voice, hoping he could preempt Nikki from getting bogged down rehashing their argument.

"I just came up for air and wanted to get back to you, sweetie," he told Nikki. "It's been hell here, I'm telling you."

Nikki seemed thrown. She couldn't remember the last time Walden had called her *sweetie* without being sarcastic.

"Did you get my messages?" she asked, flustered.

"Sure did," Walden barreled through, "and I love you, too. I can't make it back this morning like I wanted to, so go ahead with the decorator on your own. I know you'll pick the right color."

"Gregory?" Nikki asked. "Are you all right? What's going on there?"

"I'll tell you all about it over dinner, okay?" Walden said. "How about if we go out? Your choice. Make reservations and I'll do my best to be back in time."

"This is weird, Gregory," Nikki said. "What are you up to?"

"I love you, too, sweetie," Walden said, thankful that Allie could only hear his side of the conversation. "I'm looking forward to it."

Walden blew a kiss into the phone, then smiled across the desk at Allie.

"Okay, now, where were we?" he said, extending his hand.

Allie handed him the paperwork. As she watched him scribble his signature in the appropriate places, she told the senator, "Sounds like you two have something special."

"Yeah, we sure do," Walden said. "I guess I'm one of the lucky ones."

22

Schroeder, Pennsylvania

"I hope this isn't too tight," Roberta Williamson said, stepping back from her handiwork. She just used nearly half a roll of duct tape on Molly Byrnes and her father-in-law, Kevin.

Her two prisoners were seated back-to-back in a pair of kitchen chairs, their wrists taped behind their backs, their ankles tethered to the chairs' front legs. More tape had been used to gag them, so the only way they could respond was by staring back at Williamson as she stepped back from them. Kevin had a look of terror and bewilderment in his eyes and he kept wobbling his knees back and forth as if they were the vestigial wings on some insect unwilling to accept the fact that it couldn't fly. Molly was beyond fear; to her this was but another in a long list of indignities life had chosen to saddle her with. Head bowed with resignation, she stared dully past Williamson's feet at her son. Edgar was still out cold on the linoleum floor. His ankles were taped together, and his wrists, like his mother's and grandfather's, were secured together behind his back.

Williamson felt badly about what she was subjecting Molly and Kevin to, but she saw no way around it. She needed to be able to keep an eye on them until she was finished with Edgar. Their discomfort was, as they were fond of saying in field reports back at Langley, collateral damage.

The CIA agent could see that Edgar was breathing, and when he began to stir, as well, she ventured to the sink long enough to fill a coffee mug with cold water. Crouching over the militiaman, she dashed the water into his face. He came to with a start, kicking outward, his bound feet slamming into the refrigerator door. He blinked his eyes and sputtered, then took in his surroundings and began to writhe on the floor like a fish trying to escape from the bottom of a boat.

"Save your energy," Williamson told him, making sure he got a good look at the Para .45 clutched in her right hand. "You aren't going anywhere. Not until we've talked."

When Edgar spotted his mother and grandfather, a look of anger flashed in his eyes. He turned back to Roberta and demanded, "Who are you?"

She crouched before Edgar and told him, "I'm one of the people you weren't able to kill with that rocket launcher of yours. If you want, though, I'd be happy to tell you about the others. I could tell you how they were going about their business one second, leading lives that included families and loved ones, only to have that taken away in a matter of seconds. Would you like to hear about that?"

When Edgar looked away, Williamson leaned forward, grabbing his chin and turning his head back.

"The lucky ones died instantly," she went on, speaking in an eerily calm voice. "Others lost their arms and legs and bled to death, surrounded by fire. Even the safety sprinklers couldn't put out the fires, did you know that? They couldn't put out the fires and they couldn't take away the smell of burning flesh. Have you ever smelled burning flesh, Edgar?"

It was a point Williamson would have been better off not bringing up. At the mention of burning flesh, Edgar's demeanor swiftly changed. He'd been reminded of the rationale for his actions, given—at least in his mind—some leverage in his showdown with the woman.

"I've smelled my own flesh burning," he retorted coolly, his voice slightly distorted because the CIA agent was still holding on to his jaw. "Shave away my beard and you'll see!"

Williamson let go of Edgar's face but remained crouched before him. She remembered now that she'd read something about Edgar's facial injuries while investigating him on the Langley computers. She'd skimmed over the details at the time but could vaguely recall they'd had something to do with his tour of duty in the Persian Gulf. The related entries documenting Edgar's longstanding dispute with the Veteran's Administration had led her to quickly size him up as a generic disgruntled vet. The unfortunate generalization had derailed her from doing the extra few minutes of research it would have taken to determine that her lover, Felix Garber, had been Edgar's commanding officer. As it was, she'd tracked the militiaman down on the assumption that Garber was just an innocent bystander brought down by Byrnes's need to lash out at the system.

"You think what happened to you justified killing nine people, is that it?" Williamson taunted. "Did you feel proud when it was over? Vindicated?"

"I didn't do it just for me!" Edgar snapped back. He began to draw his legs up toward his chest, like an inchworm about to crawl. "There are hundreds like me! Thousands! Used and then spit out in the gutter!"

"And this is how you choose to deal with it," Williamson said. "Wallowing in self-pity, banding together with a wild pack of other discontents and—"

The woman's voice was suddenly drowned out by two distinct sounds. One was the drone of a helicopter approaching the Byrnes house from the south. The other sound was that of her own name being shouted through a battery-amplified bullhorn.

"Roberta Williamson?"

Startled, the CIA agent turned and glanced through the house in the direction of the front yard, where the other voice was coming from. In all, she took her eye off Edgar Byrnes for barely a second, but it was all the time the veteran needed.

Twisting onto his side, Edgar kicked out with both feet, catching Williamson squarely on the right knee. The woman was still in a crouch and the blow was enough to knock her off balance. She toppled backward, gun falling from her hand as the back of her head glanced off the edge of the kitchen table. Dazed, she fell to the floor.

"Roberta Williamson? Are you in there?" the voice on the bullhorn intoned again.

Edgar moved quickly. Hunched over on the floor, he dragged his taped hands down his lower back and around his buttocks, then wormed his legs through the loop made by his arms until his hands were now in front of him. He leaned forward and pried the tape loose from around his ankles, then grabbed Williamson's gun and staggered to his feet. The whole series of moves had taken him less than ten seconds, and in half that time he'd managed to break the carafe to the coffeemaker and saw his wrists free on the pot's jagged edge. By then the CIA agent had regained her wits and was pulling herself up off the floor. Edgar raced over and grabbed hold of her, twisting her right arm behind her back as he brought her to her feet. She winced in pain as Edgar guided her toward the doorway he'd come in through. The door was still open and out in the backyard he could see a SWAT officer crouched behind the foundation of the old garage, trying to draw a bead on him with a sniper rifle.

"She's a hostage!" Edgar shouted, pressing the barrel of the 45 against the side of Williamson's head. Then, extending his right leg forward, he kicked the door shut and pulled her away, seething in her ear, "Did you hear that? *I'm* calling the shots here now."

23

Philadelphia, Pennsylvania

"Another computer," Mack Bolan murmured sardonically.

The Executioner stood alongside Jack Grimaldi before a cluttered desk in the corner of Benjamin Zernial's second-story apartment. A forensics team roamed about the room behind them, dusting for prints and gathering evidence. Detective Patterson had borrowed a pair of latex gloves from one of the technicians and had booted up the computer.

"At least this one's in better shape than the last one," Grimaldi said.

Once the screen came up, Patterson was prompted to type in a password.

"Son of a bitch!" the detective grumbled.

"I doubt that's it, but you never know," Grimaldi wisecracked.

"Screw it." Patterson turned off the computer and told the forensics team to take it down to the station, then shifted his attention to the mail, paperwork and other items strewed about the desk.

"Don't be shy," he told Bolan and Grimaldi, gesturing at the mess. "Feel free to dive in."

Bolan and Grimaldi exchanged a glance, then pitched in and helped Patterson sift through the slain AFM leader's papers. Grimaldi started in on the mail. Bolan zeroed in on the wastebasket. It turned out to be the right move.

"Here we go," Bolan murmured, unfolding a sheet of paper.

It was a printout from a Web site offering maps and directions. There was a time print across the bottom of the page. "It's from last night."

"Camden, huh?" Patterson muttered. "Who the hell'd want to be there in the middle of the night?"

"Looks like Zernial did," Bolan said.

Patterson leaned back in Zernial's chair and waved the printout at one of his underlings. "Davey!" he called out. "Got an address here. Run it through the reverse directory, would you?"

The other cop took the sheet and started dialing his cell phone as he moved out into the hallway. Patterson, meanwhile, commandeered the wastebasket and pulled out another crumpled sheet of paper resting near the top of the heap.

"Let's see what else the motherlode can cough up for us," he said.

The second sheet was covered on both sides. One side contained printout from the AFM Web site detailing plans for a simulated siege exercise this coming weekend at the Meredith Valley facility. The event was touted playfully, as if it were nothing more than fun-filled family outing. Bolan noted that the article had been posted the previous afternoon, several hours before Langley bombing and the attempted gun-show heist. Clearly, not everyone in the organization had been aware of what lay ahead for the group.

The back of the printout contained a handwritten communiqué. There were numerous corrections, as if it was the first draft of a message that had been later copied elsewhere. In this case, there were clear references to both the bombing and heist incident.

"This stuff sounds familiar," Patterson murmured as he skimmed the document.

"Can I see that a second?" Bolan asked.

Patterson handed him the sheet. Bolan read the first few sentences, then turned to the detective.

"It's a message that was posted on their Web site last night," Bolan said. "Sometime between the bombing and the raid on their place in the mountains."

"Right, right," Patterson said. "But wait. If I remember rightly, that post was made after that Iovine guy wound up dead in that raid."

"Well," Grimaldi interjected, "it looks like either Zernial did some ghostwriting or he's the one who made that post instead of Iovine."

"I'd say Door B," Patterson said. "Looks like Mr. Z here was in cahoots with whoever popped Iovine."

"I'm not sure I follow all the logic," Grimaldi said, pointing at the sheet, "but if we can get word of this out there, it might help the skeptics get over any notion Iovine got whacked by the good guys."

"Yeah, right," Patterson groused. "We tell those morons we found some evidence, all they're going to think is that we planted it."

The detective's colleague returned from the hallway, slipping his cell phone back in his pocket. "That address in Camden?" he called out to Patterson. "Belongs to Jack Foster Stanton."

"Speak of the devil," Patterson said.

"And in case you're wondering why Zernial went there," the other cop went on, "Stanton just filed a robbery report with the Camden police. He says somebody broke in last night and stole one of his high-powered rifles."

ACROSS TOWN, on the west side of the river, Marcus Yarborough rode a decrepit elevator up to the top floor of the old Beaumont Commerce building. He'd thrown on a nondescript long-sleeve shirt over his jeans and found himself a Phillies baseball cap to pull down low over his forehead to obscure his features. He now looked like perhaps any of a hundred thousand middle-aged men living in and around the city of Philadelphia. Anyone giving him a passing glance would not likely have come away with any memorable impression. Asked what he looked like, most would have shrugged and said, "Just some guy."

Once he got off the elevator, Yarborough took an equally run-down staircase up to the roof. The flat roof was crowded with ancient water tanks, air-conditioning equipment and a long-vacant pigeon coop stuffed with debris and rusting machine parts. The sun was out, casting enough shadows to provide Yarborough with cover as he skulked his way to the coop. There, he donned a pair of snug-fitting latex gloves, then creaked open one of the cage doors and rummaged through the trash until he came across an inexpensive gym tote. He wrestled the bag out of the cage and carried it to the roof's edge, which overlooked McNamara Boulevard and, directly across the street, the high-rise where Nikki Walden at that moment was letting the interior decorator into her renovated eighth-floor apartment.

Crouched next to the wooden hoists supporting one of the water tanks, Yarborough unzipped the tote bag and quickly removed a compacted 7.62 mm Galil Sniping Rifle, which Benjamin Zernial had appropriated from Jack Foster Stanton's private collection in Camden. Yarborough thought the Galil, with its two-stage trigger and wobbly receiver-mounted bipod, was a lousy excuse for a rifle, especially in terms of sniping, but he understood the need to use something that could be traced back to the man who'd all but threatened Walden's life on national television. And Yarborough figured to be at a close enough range that the Galil's deficiencies wouldn't come into play.

Yarborough had heard a portion of the senator's clash with Stanton on *A.M. America* over public radio on his way to Phila-delphia after killing Zeke Ambrose. It had been an impressive performance. In another life, Yarborough thought Walden would have made a good matador. Lure the bull into charging, then deftly bring it down.

As he finished assembling the rifle, Yarborough found himself wondering if perhaps Walden was playing him the same way he'd played Stanton. Here he was, preparing to kill the man's wife. Who was to say Walden didn't have some contingency plan in effect whereby Yarborough would be killed next so he couldn't implicate the senator in the murder? It wasn't the first time the matter had crossed Yarborough's mind. And perhaps, under other circumstances, the assassin might have been given more pause. But Yarborough had long ago given up caring much whether he lived or died. He'd been dead inside for longer than he could remember—well before the cancer had been diagnosed. Being put out of his misery, under any pretext, was nothing Yarborough feared. He suspected, too, that it was this lack of fear that had made him so good at what he did.

There was construction going on throughout the neighborhood, and just down the block a work crew was raising a clamor with rivet guns as they erected a new building going up on the site of what had once been a YMCA featured in one of the *Rocky* movies. Yarborough welcomed the noise. No one was likely to notice a gunshot in the midst of so much racket.

Once the rifle was ready, the assassin glanced across the street, counting off the floors a second time to make sure he'd pinpointed the one he was looking for.

He was ready. He steeled his nerves and pressed the stock to his shoulder, then propped the ballcap farther back on his head so that he could better through the Galil's Nimrod scope.

"Okay," he whispered, "C'mon, Nix. It's time for your close-up."

"Oh, I don't know," Nikki Walden said, furrowing her brow as she stared at the samples Jorge Montego had set out on the table before her. "That one there might go well in the other room, but the others just don't work for me. I'm worried they'll clash with the Hockney."

"Not a problem," the interior designer said with the assured calm of someone used to dealing with indecisive clients. "I brought along a few others to choose from."

"I'm thinking more along the lines of something pastel," Nikki said. "A shade of lime, maybe. Or coral."

Montego nodded, fishing through the tooled-leather case he carried his samples in. "I saw your husband on the news this morning," he said, hoping to sidetrack Nikki before she changed her mind yet again on the color scheme she was looking for. "He really went head-to-head with that gun-nut fellow."

"That's Gregory for you," Nikki replied with a shrug. "Always rubbing someone the wrong way." She'd already convinced herself there could be only one reason for her husband's strange behavior on the phone earlier: he'd been trying to show up Huell Kostigan, whose wife of thirty-three years had just left him for a younger man. She would be willing to bet everything she owned that Walden would never make it home for dinner in time, much less remember that he'd asked her to make reservations at a nice restaurant. Those just weren't things he did.

For his part, Jorge Montego made a point never to let himself get caught up in his clients' marital issues, so he quickly steered the subject to more general ground. "I can't say as I'm too crazy about Americans attacking our own buildings," he said. "It's bad enough we have to worry about terrorists."

"Well, you know what they say," Nikki replied. "If we let them interfere with the way we lead our lives, they've won. So I say we forget about bombings and whatnot. Let's see what you have in pastels."

"All right, here's a few that might work for you," Montego said, pulling a swatch book from his case and heading toward the nearby window. "Let's take a good look at them in the light so you'll know what we're dealing with when you get that afternoon sun."

"Absolutely," Nikki said, glad to have things back on the right track. Fretting over CIA bombers and rabble-rousing militiamen—and, for that matter, boorish husbands—could wait for another time. Right now, Nikki had more important things to deal with. She moved into the warm light shining in through the living-room window and stared at the new samples Montego had come up with.

"Yes!" she chirped, beaming as she pointed a finger at a swatch the color of a robin's egg. "That is just the perfect shade of blue."

BY THE TIME he'd lined up Nikki Walden's head in the crosshairs of his rifle scope, Marcus Yarborough was on autopilot. The woman was nothing more than a target to him, and, with resolute calm, he pulled the trigger. The moment the living-room window imploded and he saw Nikki go down, he knew she was dead.

Mission accomplished. The Galil had done the job.

With practiced efficiency, Yarborough disassembled the rifle and stuffed it back in the tote, then made his way back across the roof, pausing long enough to stuff the bag inside the waste-choked pigeon coop. By the time he heard the first cries of alarm out in the street, he'd stuffed the latex gloves in his pocket and was already inside the stairwell leading back down to the elevators. As he waited for the doors to open, Yarborough took a small tube of analgesic balm from his pocket and dabbed some into his left palm, then rubbed his hands together and massaged his neck. Once inside the elevator, he pressed the button for the ground floor, then lowered the brim of his cap and pulled out a real-estate flyer he'd picked up earlier in the building lobby.

The Beaumont had only a twenty percent occupancy and was less than three months away from winding up on the wrong end of a wrecking ball. Even so, the elevator stopped twice on the way down to pick up other passengers. Yarborough greeted each rider nonchalantly, barely glancing up from his flyer, confident the balm had masked any smell of cordite he might have picked up while firing the rifle.

None of the others gave any indication that they were aware a woman had just been shot across the street; they were all caught up in their private worlds, their minds elsewhere. Perhaps at some point down the line they would find themselves questioned by the police, but Yarborough doubted any of them would be able to recall him as a possible suspect in the killing, much less provide anything in the way of an accurate description. And even if they did, by then Yarborough figured he would be half a world away. It was part of his arrangement with Gregory Walden. In exchange for killing the senator's wife, he had a reserved first-class air ticket to Mexico City, where fifty thousand dollars would be waiting for him and where, if need be, he had enough contacts to go underground and disappear until the heat died down or his health gave out. Yarborough knew of several doctors down there who offered alternative treatments to cancer patients. Perhaps if he was stricken with the whimsical notion of trying to prolong his life, he would look one of them up.

Yarborough got off on the third floor and took the rear stairwell down two flights to the parking garage. There, he calmly strode to the Plymouth sedan he'd rented to replace the Ford

Focus he'd abandoned on the outskirts of Philadelphia. He'd transferred the police scanner into the new car, and he turned it on as he exited into the back alley behind the commerce building. He stuck to the back streets, twice passing police cars racing by him in the opposite lane, no doubt bound for Walden's condominium building. To be sure, the assassin fiddled with the controls on the police radio, pulling in their communiqués.

Yes, there had been a call to respond to a shooting in Walden's building. But there was other police activity going on at the moment as well. Yarborough listened impassively to the snippets from dispatches involving the shootout that had just claimed the lives of Benjamin Zernial and four others. He found himself wondering who would replace Zernial as head of the American Freedom Movement. Anyone he knew of with any kind of leadership capabilities was dead. Who did that leave? Would they come to him?

Yarborough was coming up on the Schuylkill Expressway when he intercepted his first dispatch about a hostage situation north of the city in Schroeder. Hearing the town's name, Yarborough felt his heart skip a beat. He pulled over to the curb, wary of driving beyond range of the dispatch he'd just heard. Already, though, the signal was wavering. He did, however, pick up enough words here and there to confirm the situation the police were facing: they'd somehow tracked Edgar Byrnes to his grandparents' home, only to have him take someone prisoner, triggering a standoff.

Yarborough stared out the windshield and could catch a faint glimmer bouncing off the Schuylkill River as it wound alongside the expressway that shared its name. If he took the highway and headed north, he'd soon find himself in Schroeder. If he went south, on the other hand, he would likely reach Philadelphia International Airport in plenty of time to have a drink and a decent meal before the next flight to Mexico City.

It was time for Marcus Yarborough to make some hard decisions.

24

Philadelphia, Pennsylvania

Mack Bolan stood alone outside Benjamin Zernial's machine shop. A team of paramedics had finally spirited the slain militia leader's body up from the sewer, and Bolan watched them wheel the gurney to a medical van parked at the curb. The other fatalities had already been hauled off to the morgue. The rest of the street was congested with cops trying to hold back a growing throng of curiosity-seekers. Several plainclothes officials—some with the local homicide force, others with federal credentials—were scribbling on pads as they took statements from nearby shop owners. Detective Patterson was not among the interrogators; he'd been called away from Bolan's side and stood alongside a patrol car halfway down the block, barking to someone over the cruiser's dispatch microphone.

"Usual circus, eh?" Grimaldi observed as he joined Bolan. The pilot had just gotten off the phone with Carmen Delahunt back at Stony Man headquarters. "Just wait, though. An hour from now, things will be back to normal as if nothing happened."

"Probably," Bolan said. "But hopefully by then we'll have descriptions of some of the people who came by to see Zernial the past few days. If we put together some composite sketches and run them through the databases, maybe we'll find out who was pulling the guy's strings."

"Works for me," Grimaldi said. "Speaking of composite sketches, Carmen says they have some matches on the one you had made up on this Yarborough guy. She's doing a zip-and-send, so all we need to do is track down a computer with a secure line."

"Shouldn't be a problem," Bolan said. Changing the subject, he asked, "What about those notes we found on Zernial? Have they gotten into Iovine's computer to find out if he made that post?"

"Yes, they got in," Grimaldi reported, "and, no, there's no trail from the posting. Which isn't to say one won't turn up, but my money says it's gonna be on Zernial's computer, not Iovine's."

"I think you're right," Bolan said, "in which case we can link Zernial with Yarborough and this mystery woman."

"Actually, we might have something on her." Grimaldi quickly explained how Kurtzman had come across the fabricated video footage attributed to Joan VanderMeer's late father. Since making the discovery, the Farm's cybercrew had cobbled together a Web site devoted exclusively to debunking the legitimacy of the tape.

"Bear just sent out a mass e-mailing to every militia-related Web address he could get his hands on," Grimaldi concluded. "Now we just gotta hope the message winds up in the daughter's mailbox."

"Well, we also have to hope she doesn't just erase it," Bolan cautioned. "We need her to take the bait and go to the Web site, and even then there's a chance she'll think we're just blowing smoke on our end."

"Worth the chance, don't you think?" Grimaldi said. "Besides, even if she doesn't play along, we'll raise enough doubts through the ranks to hopefully keep some army of lemmings from taking to the streets."

The men were distracted when Patterson strode away from the police cruiser and rejoined them, shaking his head.

"They didn't waste much time, I'll give them that much," he said.

"Somebody just got shot with Stanton's rifle," Bolan guessed.

"Give the man a Kewpie doll," Patterson replied. "Just happened, right across the river. Only this time they didn't whack some militia head."

Bolan thought back to the morning-show confrontation he'd watched on *A.M. America*. "Senator Walden?" he said.

"Close," Patterson said. "His wife. Caught a sniper round through her condo window."

"Could be," Patterson ventured. "There was a guy in the condo with her. Interior decorator. Sniper could've thought he was the senator. I'm on my way over to check it out."

"Mind if we come along?" Bolan asked.

"Fine by me, but there's another fish you might want to fry instead," Patterson said. "Hostage situation just north of here. The perp is your buddy Edgar Byrnes."

Washington, D.C.

JOAN VANDERMEER had scarcely moved since sitting down before her computer two hours ago. The woman's entire being remained focused on chasing down headlines and doing all she could to stay on top of breaking news, desperate to track down the one piece of information she well knew she could affirm merely by returning Gregory Walden's phone calls. But she wasn't about to do that: she had not even gotten up to retrieve the cell phone she'd cast across the room earlier, much less turn it on and dial the senator's number. She couldn't bear the thought of talking to the man. As it was, his stentorian voice haunted her, playing over and over in her mind, fueling her need to linger before the computer, searching for the news she hoped she would never find.

I want Nikki dead.

Try as she might, thus far VanderMeer had been unable to find any proof that Walden had acted on his wish. There was no news to the effect that Nikki Walden was dead…or alive, for that matter. All the search engines had coughed up were the woman's name in dated society columns and Capitol Hill tabloid blogs. The most recent entry was dated more than two weeks before—something about Nikki's upcoming appearance in *Architectural Digest.*

At one point it occurred to VanderMeer to call Marcus Yarborough, the man she felt Walden would have approached to kill his wife. It had also crossed her mind, for that matter, that she had Walden's home number on the speed dial of her cell phone; it would have been easy enough to call, then hang up should she hear Nikki's voice. But VanderMeer could not bring herself to get up from her chair and track the phone down; the task seemed insurmountable, plus she was afraid that when she turned the phone on, there would come that telltale bleat informing her that Walden had tried to call her yet again. No, she told herself. She couldn't put herself through that. She had to stay put. She had to keep searching here on the Internet.

All the while she roamed cyberspace for news about Nikki, VanderMeer continued to come across developments involving the CIA bombing and the spate of stories having to do with the American Freedom Movement. She'd read about Zeke Ambrose's assassination and Darrin Harville's, wondering in the latter case how a Kentucky highway patrolman had wound up dead and linked to the killing she knew had been carried out by Hank Talbot. She'd learned about Walden's televised confrontation with Jack Foster Stanton and, while checking various militia sites, she'd seen that a number of militia leaders were echoing Stanton's accusations that the government was out to hunt them down.

It was while skimming through a Web piece presenting the President's first official response to the CIA bombing that VanderMeer finally received confirmation of the news she'd been dreading. Nikki's name had jumped out at her from the headlines on the news ticker scrolling across the top of her screen. Startled, she chased after the headline with her cursor, opening up a screen with the full story. Her spirits, already as low as they'd ever been, sank still further as she read the details, which, at least to her, confirmed that it had indeed been Marcus Yarborough who'd carried out the execution.

"He did it," she whispered to herself numbly. "He did it."

Once she'd read through the first story, VanderMeer toggled to another Web site, which had even more up-to-date information. A rifle had been found on the rooftop across the street from the apartment window where Nikki had been shot. VanderMeer was reading how initial speculation was that the rifle belonged to Jack Foster Stanton when her mail icon suddenly floated up into view on the lower-right-hand corner of her computer screen. When she glanced at the subject line, VanderMeer felt a finger of ice trail down the length of her spine. She couldn't believe what she was reading.

The mail teaser read, "Jonathan VanderMeer's Waco footage was fabricated to mislead his daughter. Web site proof available."

25

"Judging from the vultures up there, we gotta be close," Jack Grimaldi said as he turned right onto Liberty Meadows Road, a two-lane street flanked by open fields and a half-developed housing tract called, appropriately, Liberty Estates.

"About a mile to go," Bolan said, glancing at the map unfolded across his lap. "Next intersection, hang a right."

"Got it."

The "vultures" Grimaldi had been referring to were a half-dozen media helicopters circling above a bend in the Schuylkill River, each vying for an aerial glimpse of the county sheriff's tactical force positioned around the old Byrnes house on Towhee Lane. The pilots had been told the airspace above the neighborhood was off-limits to all aircraft other than a lone SWAT chopper hovering directly above the standoff area. When Bolan and Grimaldi had been forewarned of the stipulation, they'd convinced Detective Patterson to loan them an unmarked Chevy Cavalier for the short drive to Schroeder.

"Wanna bet they're hoping something goes wrong?" Grimaldi said, glancing back up at the news choppers. "Even if they can't get close, some zoom footage of a shootout would be gold for them."

"Let's hope they wind up disappointed," Bolan replied.

Up ahead, a police cruiser, roof lights flashing, had just pulled over a car headed toward the standoff site. The officer had stepped out of his car and was casually approaching the other vehicle, a Plymouth sedan.

"Whaddya think?" Grimaldi said. "Reporter going twenty over trying to chase down a scoop?"

"Could be," Bolan murmured disinterestedly. He was still mulling over the note they'd found in Benjamin Zernial's apartment after the raid on the militia leader's machine shop. Why had Zernial gone to the trouble of forging Lance Iovine's online response to the CIA bombing and what happened in Georgetown? Bolan knew it had something to do with Iovine's subsequent murder, but he couldn't get the pieces to fit and it was driving him crazy. Lost in thought, he barely shot a fleeting glance at the Plymouth as they drove past. He saw the police officer ask the driver for identification, then looked away.

Then, twenty yards farther down the road, it suddenly hit him.

"Pull over!" Bolan snapped, glancing in his mirror. "It's Yarborough!" The map flew from his lap as he reached for the door handle. Even before Grimaldi had slowed to a complete stop, Bolan was halfway out of the Chevy, reaching for the Beretta sheathed in his web holster.

He hadn't heard the gunshot behind him, but when Bolan looked back at the Plymouth, he saw the police officer fall away from the driver's side of the vehicle, gunned down before he'd had a chance to draw his service pistol. Yarborough had already thrown the sedan into gear, and the next thing Bolan knew, his elusive nemesis was racing toward him, accelerator to the floorboard.

There was no time for Bolan to set himself for a shot. He fired quickly, taking out a small chunk of the upper windshield above Yarborough's head. He'd missed his target, though, and even with his visibility reduced and his forehead bleeding from flying glass, Yarborough continued to bear down on Bolan at full speed.

The Executioner thought fast. With Grimaldi parked directly behind him, he was safe for the moment: at some point Yarborough would have to veer to avoid plowing into the Chevy. To Bolan's immediate left, the shoulder quickly gave way to a steep, rock gully, so Yarborough's only real option was to cut back onto the road. The Stony Man commando went with his instincts and took a step backward, dropping to a crouch. Timing would be everything.

As Bolan had predicted, Yarborough was forced to yank hard on the Plymouth's steering wheel well before striking him. As the car lurched hard to the left, tires grabbing at the roadway, Bolan sprang forward, leaping high into the air. With a resounding thud, he landed hard on the hood. The sedan's forward momentum sent him tumbling across the hood and up the steep slant of the car's windshield directly in front of the passenger seat. The glass had been weakened by his earlier shot, but it withstood his weight and quickly passed him on up to the roof. Realizing he was about to skid feetfirst off the flat surface, Bolan let go of his Beretta and threw his arms out before him, clawing at the windshield frame. When his left fingers poked through the gap where the glass had been shot out, he clenched them and held on tight.

Grimaldi, meanwhile, had drawn his Colt and thrown open the driver's door of the Chevy. He was getting out when Yarborough veered around the rear of the car and bore down on him. Grimaldi barely had time to pull himself back inside before the Plymouth barreled past, missing him by inches. The door was still open, however, and the Plymouth snapped it free of the Chevy's chassis and sent it flying through the air.

Overhead, one of the aerial news crews glimpsed the activity and peeled off from the others choppers. Within seconds, the other aircraft followed suit. There were no restrictions on flying over Liberty Meadows Road, and the crews clearly planned to take advantage of it.

By now the Executioner had centered himself on the sedan's roof, curling his right hand over the passenger side near the front door frame for better stability. Directly below Bolan, cold air racing past his face through the punctured section of the windshield, Yarborough spotted Bolan's fingers and reached up to pound at them. When the Chevy's crumpled door suddenly appeared in the road directly ahead of him, however, he was forced to grab the steering wheel with both hands in hopes of avoiding the obstacle.

The Plymouth swerved sharply. Bolan listed to one side atop the roof but continued to hold on. Out on the road before him he could see the drifting shadows of the approaching helicopters. It crossed his mind fleetingly that his dilemma had just eclipsed the hostage situation and was probably being broadcast to half the viewers in Philadelphia County. He could only hope the moment of notoriety wouldn't end with his being thrown from the car and turned into roadkill.

The authorities had caught wind that something was amiss, as well, and well before Yarborough reached the turnoff to Towhee Lane, a pair of police cruisers converged on the intersection, blocking the way. Spotting the roadblock, Yarborough took his foot off the gas and tapped the brakes. Once he'd slowed the Plymouth, he took a sharp left turn into the unfinished entrance to the housing development. The security booth was untended and the drop gate hadn't been installed yet, but Yarborough quickly realized he'd chosen a poor escape route. The unpaved road leading into the development was blocked by a wide-bodied trailer loaded with two mud-encrusted bulldozers. There was no truck pulling the trailer; it wasn't going anywhere.

"Shit!" Yarborough seethed, slamming the brakes.

As the Plymouth screeched to a stop, Bolan was thrown forward off the roof. He bounded off the front hood and rolled clear. With catlike reflexes, he landed on both feet and promptly spun. Yarborough had shifted the sedan into reverse and was looking over his shoulder as he prepared to back up, clearly intent on heading back out to the road.

Before the assailant could pick up speed, Bolan rushed forward and he reached in through the shattered portion of the windshield for Yarborough's left hand, which was resting on the steering wheel. Bolan grabbed the man's wrist and pulled hard. Caught off guard, Yarborough let out a howl and turned, just in time to catch Bolan's right fist with the bridge of his nose.

Dazed, Yarborough lost his grip on the steering wheel. His foot remained on the gas pedal, however, and the Plymouth lurched back toward the street, only to come to a sudden stop when Jack Grimaldi pulled into the driveway and deliberately rammed the vehicle's rear end. Yarborough was now trapped.

Bolan let go of the sharpshooter, but only for the few seconds it took him to tug open the driver's door. Grimaldi, his own door missing, quickly bolted out of the Chevy and reached Bolan in time to help pull Yarborough from the Plymouth. Yarborough started to resist but then thought better of it. He eyed the Colt pistol Grimaldi had trained on his head and told the pilot, "Killing me won't help matters."

"Maybe not, but it might feel nice for a second or two," Grimaldi threatened. "Sometimes that's good enough."

Yarborough, blood trailing from his broken nose, turned to Bolan. For the first time, he recognized his apprehender.

"Schiraldi," he said.

"Not my real name," Bolan told him.

Yarborough started to smile, then his body was rocked by a sudden spasm that doubled him over. Grimaldi kept his Colt trained on the assassin and Bolan helped himself to the sniper's pistol, then aimed it at Yarborough, as well. The older man coughed sharply and spit blood into the muddy ground at his feet. Once the fit passed, he glanced up at Bolan and finished smiling.

"We have something in common, then," the assassin proclaimed, "because my real name's not Yarborough."

26

"I still can't believe he's supposed to be Edgar Byrnes's father," Grimaldi said as he and Bolan watched Marcus Yarborough, a.k.a. Mark Byrnes, being led in handcuffs up the front walk leading to his family's Victorian house on Towhee Lane. Besides the two armed deputies flanking Yarborough, another four officers were poised on either side of the front door, guns at the ready, and four more were positioned in the yard, weapons aimed at the living-room and den windows. The Stony Man operatives had been told more cops were covering the back, and overhead a police sharpshooter leaned out near the open doorway of the hovering SWAT chopper, peering down at the house through his sniper scope.

"The guy's supposed to be dead," Grimaldi went on.

"He's not the first father to bail on his family when the chips are down," Bolan observed. "He was just a little more clever about it than most."

"And this is his idea of making amends?" Grimaldi wondered aloud. "Talking his son into surrendering? What, if he pulls it off we're supposed to overlook how many people he's killed besides that cop back there?"

"I don't think he's looking for favors," Bolan said. "I think for once in his life he thought he might do the right thing."

"Gee, I'm getting all teary-eyed," Grimaldi said.

The two men were standing alongside a black SWAT Hummer parked directly across the street from where the hostage standoff was taking its latest unpredictable turn. Edgar Byrnes had released his mother and grandfather a few minutes before Bolan and Grimaldi had shown up with Yarborough.

Molly and Kevin Byrnes were presently tucked away inside one of the paramedic vans on the scene, being questioned as they were both treated for hyperventilation and chafed limbs from where they'd been taped to the kitchen chairs by Roberta Williamson, who was still being held captive at gunpoint.

When Molly was released, she'd brought out with her a note listing her son's hastily scribbled demands. Edgar wasn't asking for the usual free passage to a safe haven. Instead, he was demanding that the director of the Veterans' Administration come forward with public acknowledgment that American troops during the Gulf War had been routinely—and knowingly—exposed to known carcinogens and that, accordingly, all medical claims made by veterans attributed to this exposure should be immediately approved without question. He was also asking for a public apology and a promise that all veterans in question would be compensated retroactively to their first day of service with the military.

Bolan saw partial merit to Byrnes's grievances, but he knew the veteran's demands would never be met, especially given the circumstances under which they'd been presented.

Marcus Yarborough, who'd overheard the briefing given to Bolan and Grimaldi, felt the same way. It had been his suggestion that he might be able to talk his son into releasing Williamson and surrendering. Yarborough's only stipulation had been that he be allowed to go into the house alone and confront his son one-on-one, man-to-man. The assailant's proposition had been hotly debated, with Grimaldi among the naysayers who suspected a trick, but ultimately the green light had been given.

And now was the moment of truth. As Bolan and Grimaldi watched on, the front door to the old Victorian house was opened by one of the SWAT members. Yarborough's police escort remained on the porch as the sniper headed into the house, alone.

YARBOROUGH'S FIRST WORDS as he entered the house were, "Eddie? It's your father."

Yarborough hesitated in the entryway, overcome by the same

long-forgotten smells his son had experienced when he'd come inside to speak with Molly a short while ago. Having grown up in this house, the sniper had even more memories to contend with than Edgar. And given that some of those memories dated back to his childhood, before everything had started to go wrong, as he stepped farther into the house, the former Mark Byrnes could feel a tightening in his throat, as well as a misting in his eyes. The reaction took him by surprise, and he was struggling with his emotions when his son stepped into view.

Edgar Byrnes was standing in the hallway near the stairwell that led down to the basement. The door behind him was open, and Roberta Williamson was tied to a chair set precariously close to the top step, bound with duct tape the same way she had earlier secured Molly and Kevin to chairs in the kitchen. She was seated with her back turned to Edgar. One nudge from him and she would be sent tumbling down the stairs. Edgar was holding the woman's Para .45 handgun, and the weapon was aimed at his father's chest. He'd caught himself before he'd pulled the trigger.

"Dad?" he said, his voice filled with disbelief. "How did you know I was—?"

"Here?" Yarborough interrupted, "It's not like you haven't drawn attention to yourself the past few hours."

"No," Edgar said, lowering his gun. "I meant, how did you know I was looking for you?"

Instead of answering the question, Yarborough replied, "You don't seem that surprised to see me alive."

"We always had our suspicions," Edgar said, "but we figured, screw it, if that was the way you wanted it, suit yourself. We managed without you."

"And what a great job you all did," Yarborough said. "Your brothers are dead. And you? Look at you. You're the star of this week's *America's Most Wanted*. Three chips off the old block. It never dawned on you that maybe following my example wasn't the brightest idea in the world?"

"We were going to help make changes in this country," Edgar insisted. "We were going to right some wrongs and make this a better place."

"Not gonna happen," Yarborough said. "Who did you think you were kidding? Besides yourselves?"

Staring at his father, Edgar could feel anger rising up inside him. His jaw trembled, then he stammered, "Y-y-you were with them. The militia. You had to believe—"

"I didn't believe squat!" Yarborough snapped. "I screwed up my life and ran out of options. The militia took me on because they could make use of the one thing I was good at. Killing people. None of that lofty-ideals crap or—"

Yarborough was racked with another bout of convulsions. He grimaced, fighting them off, then swallowed the blood he'd coughed up. All the while, Edgar stared at his father, speechless. He continued to tremble.

"What'd you want to see me about, anyway?" Yarborough demanded, wiping his lips with the back of his hand. He started to move closer to his son and the woman hostage. "Fatherly advice? A bump in your allowance? What?"

"Stay back!" Edgar warned, retreating a step from his father's advance. Yarborough kept coming closer, undeterred.

"Tell you what, Eddie," Yarborough responded calmly. "You don't have any answers, then I'll tell you why I'm here. I'm here so we can settle things. Once and for all."

"HE'S TAKING LONG ENOUGH," Grimaldi murmured, glancing at his watch. "Hell, for all we know, they could've slit the woman's throat and escaped out some secret tunnel in the basement. If there's one thing these assholes are big on, its tunnels."

"It's been less than fifteen minutes," Bolan countered. "He's got twenty before we come in."

"Then I guess that leaves me time to check in with the Farm," Grimaldi said, retrieving his cell phone. "I'll tell them not to bother with that file on Yarborough."

Grimaldi headed down the block, passing the paramedics van and a police cruiser, trying to pull in a signal on his phone. Bolan glanced up at the news choppers; they'd dropped back into their holding positions out over the river near where Roberta Williamson had rowed her way to the back end of the Byrnes property. When one of them took it upon themselves to stray into the restricted airspace, Lieutenant Andrew Sandberg, the SWAT team commander standing a few feet away from Bolan, grabbed the Hummer's transceiver microphone and barked, "Tell that goddamn bird to back off, or I'm giving our snipers the green light for target practice!"

As word was being passed along to the offending pilot, there was sudden activity in the front doorway to the Byrnes house. Someone threw open the door open and stumbled out. It was Roberta Williamson, her eyes and mouth taped shut, her hands taped behind her back. Two of the SWAT commandos quickly moved to her side, guiding her away from the door. Once they'd carefully peeled away the tape, they led her down the steps. Bolan and Sandberg moved forward to intercept her.

"I'm fine," Williamson assured the men when asked about her condition. "I feel a little foolish is all. I don't know what I was thinking."

"What's going on in there?" Sandberg asked her.

"The man who came in," Williamson said. "His father? He's the one who let me go. He's pushing the kid's buttons. Egging him on."

"How so?" Bolan asked.

Before Williamson could answer, a single gunshot sounded inside the Byrnes house. It was as if someone had fired a starting pistol. All at once, the entire ground force moved into action, storming the house. The men posted near the front door were about to charge in when there was a second shot.

Bolan and Sandberg joined the charge, rushing up the front walk and taking the porch stairs two at a time. There was no further gunfire. When they entered the house, they found Edgar Byrnes and his father lying dead on the hallway floor near the basement stairwell, each with a bullet wound to the head. Edgar had clearly done the firing, killing his father before turning the gun on himself.

"Maybe we should've seen that coming," Sandberg muttered.

"Yeah," Bolan said, staring down at the bodies. "Maybe so."

Eyes on Yarborough, Sandberg went on, "You said he

wouldn't give up who he was working for, so maybe things are wrapped up here, but the bigger fish are still out on the loose somewhere."

"Maybe not," Grimaldi said. He'd just joined the others after speaking with Barbara Price back at Stony Man Farm. "It's looking like those big fish are about to fry."

27

Washington, D.C.

"Are you really sure you want to do this?" Allie Gantner asked Gregory Walden.

The senator was standing with his intern in the corridor outside his office on Pennsylvania Avenue. Just down the hall, a handful of reporters had gathered, clamoring for Walden's response to the news of his wife's murder. Allie thought Walden might want to bypass the media and take another way out of the building, where a limousine was waiting to take him back to Philadelphia.

"No, it's important that I say something," Walden insisted. "If they send us scurrying, we've lost the fight. I'll be all right."

"I remember you just saying how much she meant to you," Allie said, her voice cracking. Her eyes were red and she looked grief-stricken, even more so than Walden. "I can't believe this is happening."

"We'll deal," Walden assured the younger woman, pressing her arm gently. "We'll deal. Now, excuse me…"

Walden moved away from the intern and drew in a breath, composing himself as he walked the length of the hallway. This would be the first of many performances he would have to put on over the course of the next few days, but he was ready for the challenge. The initial pangs he'd felt when first hearing of Nikki's death had passed, and in their place he felt unburdened, more up to the task of carrying out the intricate maneuverings of Operation Clean Sweep.

The reporters started firing questions even before Walden ad reached the reception area where they were gathered.

"Do you think the sniper meant to kill you instead of your wife?"

"They found Jack Foster Stanton's rifle across the street, but e's saying it was a plant!"

"Do you think we're on the verge of some kind of civil war, enator?"

Walden ignored the questions; he had no intention of reponding to any of them. He'd already prepared a statement in s head. It would touch on all the necessary bases, making him em sufficiently mournful while at the same time morally utraged at the temerity of the sniper who'd taken his wife from m.

The senator waved the reporters quiet, then began, "I appreate your coming here and I'd like to answer all your questions t, as you can understand, this is a hard time for me. So if I ould just make a quick comment, I need to get to Philadelphia attend to my wife's funeral arrangements."

Before Walden could launch into his prepared remarks, a stocky, ey-haired man elbowed his way to the foreground, followed by vo men in plain suits. The senator felt a sinking sensation when e recognized the man who now stood directly before him.

"I'm sorry, Senator," Hal Brognola said, "but it might be adsable for you to hold off on any remarks until you've had the lvice of counsel. You're under arrest for solicitation of murder. nd please rest assured there will be more charges to follow."

A hubbub rose among the reporters as Brognola's pronounceent hung over the room. Walden stared at the Justice Departent official with seeming incomprehension. "There's obviously en a mistake here," he protested.

"I don't think so," Brognola replied calmly. On his signal, his o cohorts moved forward. One had a pair of handcuffs. As he apped them on the senator's wrists, Walden glared at Brognola. en, for the first time, he noticed that a woman had entered the ilding with Brognola and was standing directly behind him.

Joan VanderMeer stepped into view, eyeing her mentor with ld contempt. "It's over," she told him. "All of it."

Epilogue

The next day,
Stony Man Farm, Virginia

"That's it, then, right?" Mack Bolan said, shifting position slightly on Barbara Price's bed in the main house at Stony Man Farm. He was lying on his stomach, with Price straddling his lower back. Neither of them was dressed. Price had been massaging his shoulders when Aaron Kurtzman had called from the Annex to report that Hank Talbot had just been apprehended by the Alabama State Police before he could carry out the execution of Dixie Militia leader Harold Manley. Joan VanderMeer's tip had led to Talbot's capture, and the woman—now a key government witness—was also helping lead officials to other key players in Gregory Walden's ill-fated Operation Clean Sweep. Even if some of the culprits managed to elude capture, VanderMeer had assured the government that without hers and Walden's input, it would be years before the militia movement could pose any sort of orchestrated threat against the U.S. government.

"Things are never totally wrapped up," Price said. "You know that as well as I do."

"True," Bolan said.

"I suppose, though," Price said, "that we might be able to put the world on hold for at least an hour or so. What do you think?"

Bolan glanced over his shoulder and saw that Price had just turned off her cell phone. She smiled mischievously down a

Bolan as she leaned over and set the phone on the nearby dresser, exchanging it for a bottle of massage oil.

"You're the mission controller," Bolan joked. "If you say we need to take a time-out, I guess I'll just have to go along with the program."

"Good," Price told him, pouring some of the lotion into her palm. "Now close your eyes and relax, soldier. This won't hurt a bit...."

JAMES AXLER
DEATH LANDS®
Perdition Valley

Hunted across the southwestern desert, Ryan doesn't know who wants him dead badly enough to slaughter innocents as a way of luring him into the open. But the advanced tech his pursuers are using is unknown in Deathlands, created by the most brilliant minds of twentieth-century America. Now evil is alive and stalking the warrior group. His name is Delphi, and he's prepared to reclaim the one man who understands with brutal certainty how time can be controlled, manipulated, remapped.

Available December 2006, wherever books are sold.

JAKE STRAIT

FRANK RICH
AVENGING ANGEL

In the ruthless, anything-goes world of 2031, enforcer and bounty hunter Jake Strait has his limits—a line he won't cross willingly. But when a rich, pampered couple sets him up, he is drawn into a plot to drench the city with blood. Against his will, Jake Strait becomes the favorite son of a people's revolution—and there's hell to pay.

Available January 2007, wherever books are sold.

GOLD
EAGLE ®

GJS1

The Thibaults

ROGER MARTIN DU GARD

Translated by Stuart Gilbert

New York: The Viking Press

1939

PART

I

J.

A S THEY reached the school-buildings at the corner of the Rue de Vaugirard, M. Thibault, who, throughout the walk, had not spoken a word to his son, suddenly halted.

"No, Antoine, I won't stand it. This time he's gone too far."

The young man made no reply.

It was nine o'clock in the evening and the school was closed. A night porter held the little wicket in the entrance-gate ajar.

"Know where my brother is?" Antoine asked in a peremptory tone.

The porter stared at him with a puzzled air.

M. Thibault stamped his foot angrily. "Go and fetch Abbé Binot," he said.

The porter escorted M. Thibault and his son to the waiting-room, drew a taper from his pocket, and lit the gas.

Some minutes elapsed. M. Thibault, who was out of breath, had settled down heavily into a chair. "Yes, this time we've had enough of it," he muttered through his clenched teeth.

"Excuse me, please." The Abbé Binot had entered without a sound. He was a small, mouse-like man, and now, to put his hand on Antoine's shoulder, had to draw himself up to his full height. "And how is our young doctor today?" he asked, adding at once: "But what's the trouble?"

"Where is my brother?"

"Jacques?"

"Jacques has not been home all day!" M. Thibault exclaimed, rising excitedly from his chair.

"Where can he have been?" the priest inquired, but without much show of surprise.

"Why, here, naturally! He was kept in."

The priest slipped his hands under his girdle. "Jacques was *not* kept in."

"What's that?"

"Jacques did not put in an appearance at school today."

3

Things were getting complicated. Antoine gave the priest a searching look, and with a jerk of his shoulders M. Thibault swung round on the little man his fat, puffy face, in which the eyes were almost hidden by their heavy lids.

"Jacques told us yesterday that he had four hours' detention. He left home this morning at the usual time. Later on, at about eleven, it seems, while we were all at mass, he came back and found everyone out except the cook. He said he wouldn't be back for lunch as he'd been given eight hours' detention instead of four."

"Which was a pure invention," the Abbé put in.

"I had to go out in the latter part of the afternoon," M. Thibault continued, "to hand in my monthly article to the *Revue des Deux Mondes*. It was the editor's reception-day, and I didn't get home till dinner-time. Jacques had not returned. At half-past eight I began to get alarmed. I sent for Antoine, who was on duty at his hospital. So now we have come to you."

The priest pursed his lips, as if in deep reflection. Through his half-parted eyelashes M. Thibault flashed a keen look first at the Abbé, then at his son.

"Well, Antoine, what do you make of it?"

"Obviously, Father," the young man said, "if he's run away on purpose we can discard any theory of an accident—which is so much to the good."

His attitude had a calming effect on M. Thibault, who drew up a chair and sat down again. His nimble mind was exploring several trains of thought, though his face, immobilized by its layers of fat, seemed perfectly expressionless. "Well," he said, "what's to be done?"

Antoine reflected. "This evening, nothing. We can only wait."

That there was no denying. But the impossibility of settling the business off-hand, by some drastic gesture, coupled with the thought of the Congress of Moral Science that was opening at Brussels in two days' time, and the invitation he had received to preside over the French section of it, brought a flood of angry colour to M. Thibault's temples. He stood up.

"I'll have the gendarmes on his track!" he cried. "There is still a police service in France, isn't there? And our criminals are sometimes caught, I suppose!"

His frock-coat flapped on either side of his paunch; the creases of his chin were nipped incessantly between the peaks of his stiff collar as he jerked his jaws forward like a horse chafing at the bridle. "The young ruffian!" he was thinking. "If only he could be run over by a train!" In a vivid flash of imagination he saw every difficulty smoothed out; no more trouble then about his attending the Congress, of which, quite possibly, he might be given the vice-presidency. But then, almost immediately, he visualized the boy brought home on a stretcher, a small corpse laid out on a bed, and a grief-stricken father—himself—beside it, surrounded by his sorrowing friends. And he was ashamed.

He turned to the priest again. "It's a terrible thing—yes, terrible—for a father to have to spend a night of such anxiety, to go through such an ordeal."

He began moving to the door. The Abbé withdrew his hands from his girdle.

"One moment, please," he said, lowering his eyes.

The lamplight fell on a forehead half concealed by a fringe of black hair and a weasel-like face that narrowed sharply down towards the pointed chin. Two pink spots began to show up on his cheeks.

"We have been wondering," he said, "whether we ought to apprise you at once of a most regrettable incident that took place a day or two ago, and which concerns your boy. But, as things are, it might throw some light on . . . Can you spare us a few moments, M. Thibault?"

The Picard accent seemed to emphasize his hesitation. M. Thibault, without answering, went back to his chair and sat down heavily, closing his eyes.

"During the last few days," the priest went on, "we have become aware of certain offences, of a very special character, committed by your son . . . yes, particularly serious misconduct. In fact we had to threaten him with expulsion. Oh, of course, that was only to frighten him. He hasn't said anything to you?"

"Don't you know what a double-dealer the boy is? No, he has kept it to himself—as usual."

"The dear lad," the Abbé protested, "may have his faults, but he isn't bad at heart. No, we believe that on this last occasion it was weakness more than anything; he was led astray. It was the evil influence of another boy, one of those unhappy, perverted youngsters—of whom, alas, there are so many in Paris. . . ."

From the corner of an eye M. Thibault shot an apprehensive glance at the priest.

"These are the facts, M. Thibault, in the order of their happening. Last Thursday . . ." He reflected for a moment, then went on in an almost cheerful tone. "No, I made a mistake, it was Friday, the day before yesterday, Friday morning, during the morning study hour. Just before noon we entered the class-room—abruptly, as we always do. . . ." He gave Antoine a mischievous wink. "We turned the handle noiselessly and flung the door open.

"No sooner had we entered than our eyes fell on our little friend Jacques, whom we had placed just opposite the door on purpose. We went up to his desk and moved aside his dictionary. There it was—a book that had no business there! It was a novel, translated from the Italian, by an author whose name we have forgotten. The book was called *The Maidens of the Rocks.*"

"Disgusting!" M. Thibault exclaimed.

"The boy was so perturbed that we concluded there was more behind it; we are used to that sort of thing. The luncheon bell was due to sound in a few minutes. When it rang we asked the master in charge to take the boys to the refectory. After they had gone we opened Jacques's desk and found two more books there: Rousseau's *Confessions* and something still more objectionable—I hardly like to name it—one of Zola's abominable books, *Abbé Mouret's Transgression.*"

"He's dead to shame."

"We were about to close the desk when it occurred to us to feel behind the row of school-books, and we fished out an exercise-book in a grey linen binding, which at first sight looked innocent enough. But then we opened it and glanced through the first pages." The Abbé paused, his keen, ungentle eyes intent on M. Thibault and his son.

"Well, we read enough then and there to make sure. . . . We carried the book off to a safe place and, during the midday recreation, found time to study it at leisure. The novels (they were in excellent bindings) had the initial 'F' stamped on their backs. The grey exercise-book, the most damning piece of evidence, if I may put it so, contained a series of letters in different writings. There were letters from Jacques, signed 'J,' and others, in a writing we did not recognize, signed 'D.' " He continued in a lower voice. "I am sorry to have to say that the tone, the tenor, of the letters left no doubt as to the nature of the friendship. So much so, M. Thibault, that for a while we took the firm, tall writing for that of girl or, more likely, a somewhat older woman. But, presently, on studying the contents more carefully, we perceived that the unidentified script was that of a fellow-pupil of Jacques—not one of our boys here, thank God! but some boy whom Jacques must have met at the Lycée. To make sure about it, we went that very same day to see the principal, our worthy friend M. Quillard"—he turned towards Antoine as he gave the name—"who is a man of the highest principles and knows only too well what goes on in boarding-schools. He recognized the writing at once. The miscreant who signed the letters with a 'D' is a third-form boy, a friend of Jacques. His name is Fontanin, Daniel de Fontanin."

"Fontanin!" Antoine exclaimed. "That explains it. You know, Father, those people who spend the summer at Maisons-Laffitte; they've a house on the outskirts of the forest. Now that I come to think of it, several times this winter, when I got home, I've found Jacques reading books of poetry lent him by this Fontanin boy."

"What? Borrowed books? Wasn't it your duty to let me know?"

"Oh, I didn't see much harm in them!" Antoine glanced towards the priest as he spoke, as if to show that he was not to be intimidated. And suddenly his thoughtful face lit up with a quick smile that came and went, giving it a singularly boyish look. "It was only Victor Hugo," he explained, "and Lamartine. But I took away his lamp, to prevent him keeping awake till all hours. . . ."

The priest's lips had stiffened. Now he took his revenge.

"But there's worse to come. This Fontanin boy's a Protestant!"

"I knew! I knew it!" There was an accent of despair in M. Thibault's cry.

"Quite a good pupil, however," the priest put in at once, as who should give the devil his due. "I can quote you M. Quillard's exact words. 'He's one of the older boys and we all thought highly of him—in fact he thoroughly hoodwinked all those with whom he came in contact. His mother, too, produced an excellent impression on us.'"

"Oh, his mother!" M. Thibault broke in. "They're impossible people, for all their airs and graces. Why, at Maisons, nobody has anything to do with them; they're scarcely nodded to in the street. Yes, Antoine, your brother can hardly boast of his choice of friends!"

"Dangerous friends!" the Abbé sighed. "Evil communications. . . . Yes, we know only too well what lies beneath the sanctimonious airs of Protestants.

"Be that as it may, when we came back from the Lycée, we knew everything. And we had just decided to set a formal inquiry on foot when yesterday, at the beginning of the study hour, our little friend Jacques burst into our office. Literally burst in. His teeth were clenched and he was very pale. He didn't even say: 'Good morning,' but shouted at us from the threshold: 'Somebody has stolen my books and papers from my desk!' We pointed out to him that it was most unbecoming, bursting in like that. He refused to listen. His eyes, which are usually quite pale, were black with anger. 'It's you who stole my exercise-book!' he shouted. 'It's you, I know it!' He even went so far as to say," the Abbé added with a rather vacuous smile, "that if we dared to read it, he would kill himself. We tried to appeal to his better feelings, but he would not let us speak. 'Where's my exercise-book?' he kept on asking. 'Give it back. If you don't, I shall smash everything here!' Before we could stop him he picked up the crystal paper-weight on our desk—you remember it, Antoine? It was a souvenir some of our old boys had brought us from the Puy-de-Dôme—and threw it with all his might at the marble mantelpiece. Oh, that's a mere trifle," the Abbé added hastily, noticing M. Thibault's embarrassed gesture of regret. "I only mention this small detail to show you the state of excitement your dear boy was in. Next moment he dropped on the floor in a sort of hysterical fit. We managed to secure him and pushed him into a little retiring-room next the study, and locked him in."

"Yes," M. Thibault said, raising his clenched hands dramatically, "there are days you'd think he was 'possessed.' Ask Antoine. How often we have seen him, when he's been crossed over some trifle, fall into such furious fits of temper that we've had to let him have his way! His face turns livid, the veins in his throat stand out, you'd think he was going to suffocate with rage."

"Yes," Antoine remarked, "we Thibaults are a hot-blooded family." He seemed to regret it so little that the priest felt compelled to smile indulgently.

"When we came to let him out an hour later," he continued, "he was sitting at the table, his head between his hands. He gave us a furious look; his eyes were tearless. When we bade him apologize, he did not answer. But he followed us quietly to our study. His hair was ruffled, his eyes were fixed on the ground, and there was a stubborn look on his face. We got him to pick up the fragments of the ill-fated paper-weight, but nothing would make him utter a word. So then we took him to the chapel where we thought it fitting that he should remain for a while in solitary communion with his Maker. After an hour we came and knelt beside him. He looked as if he had been crying, but the chapel was so dark that we couldn't be sure of it. We said a rosary in a low voice, and then we remonstrated with him, picturing to him his father's grief at hearing that an evil companionship had endangered his dear son's purity. He kept his arms folded and held his head high, his eyes fixed on the altar, as if he did not hear us. Seeing that there was nothing to be done with him, we told him to return to the study room. There he stayed till the afternoon was over, at his place, with his arms folded and without opening a book. We thought it best to take no notice of this conduct. At seven o'clock he left as usual, but without coming to say good-night.

"So now you have the whole story, M. Thibault." The priest gave him a glance of eager curiosity. "We had meant not to inform you of these facts till we knew what action has been taken by the vice-principal of the Lycée against that wretched young fellow Fontanin—summary expulsion, we presume. But, seeing you so upset . . ."

"M. l'Abbé," M. Thibault broke in; he was as out of breath as if he had been running upstairs. "M. l'Abbé, I am horrified—but you can guess for yourself what my feelings are. When I think what the future may have in store for us, now that Jacques's evil instincts have shown themselves—yes, I'm horrified," he repeated in a pensive voice, almost in a whisper. He sat unmoving, his head thrust forward, his hands resting on his hips. His eyes were closed and had it not been for the almost imperceptible quivering of his underlip, which shook the short white beard under the grey moustache, he would have seemed asleep.

"The young blackguard!" he burst out suddenly, with a forward jerk of his chin. The vicious glance that shot forth from between the grey eyelashes showed what a mistake it would have been to take his inertia at its face value. Shutting his eyes again, he swung round towards Antoine. But the young man was in a brown study, tugging at his beard, his forehead wrinkled and his eyes fixed on the floor.

"I shall go to the hospital," he said at last, "and tell them not to count on me tomorrow. The first thing in the morning I'll go and see this Fontanin boy and put him through it!"

"The first thing in the morning?" M. Thibault repeated mechanically. He rose from his seat. "Meanwhile, I've a sleepless night before me." Sighing, he moved ponderously towards the door.

The Abbé followed. On the threshold M. Thibault extended to the priest a flabby hand. "It's been a terrible blow," he murmured, without opening his eyes.

"We will pray God to help us in our time of trouble," the priest replied in a polite tone.

Father and son walked a few steps in silence along the empty street. The wind had dropped and the night air was mild. The month of May was beginning.

M. Thibault was thinking of the runaway. "Anyhow, if he's sleeping out, he won't find it too cold." Emotion made his legs go limp under him. He stopped and turned to his son. Antoine's attitude made him feel less unsure of himself, and he felt drawn towards his first-born, and proud of him—especially so tonight, now that his younger son was more antipathetic than ever. Not that he was incapable of love for Jacques; to quicken his affection it would have been enough had Jacques provided some satisfaction for his pride. But the boy's preposterous conduct and wayward impulses always galled him at his most sensitive point, his self-esteem.

"Let's only hope it doesn't cause too much scandal," he muttered. Then he drew nearer to Antoine and his tone changed. "I'm delighted that you were able to get off duty tonight." The feeling he was trying to express made him feel almost bashful. Still more embarrassed than his father, the young man kept silent. "Yes, Antoine, I'm glad to have you with me tonight, dear boy," M. Thibault continued and, for the first time perhaps, linked his arm with his son's.

II

ON THAT Sunday, Mme. de Fontanin, when she came home at about midday, had found a note awaiting her in the hall.

"Daniel tells me he's been kept for lunch by the Bertiers," she told Jenny. "Then you weren't here when he came back?"

"No, I didn't see him," Jenny replied without looking up. She had just dropped on all fours, trying to catch her dog Puce, which was hiding under an arm-chair. It seemed to take her a long time, but at last she caught the dog up in her arms and ran off with it to her room, hugging and petting the little animal.

She did not reappear till lunch-time.

"I'm not a bit hungry," she said, "and I've got a headache. I'd like to go to my room and lie down in the dark."

Her mother put her to bed and drew the curtains. Eagerly Jenny snuggled down between the sheets. But sleep would not come to her. The hours dragged on. Several times in the course of the day Mme. de Fontanin came and laid her cool hand on the little girl's forehead.

Towards evening, in a sudden rush of affection and anxiety, Jenny caught hold of her mother's hand and began fondling it, unable to keep back her tears.

"You're overstrung, darling. I'm afraid you must have a touch of fever."

Seven o'clock struck, then eight. Mme. de Fontanin was waiting for her son before beginning dinner. Never did Daniel miss a meal without telling her in advance; least of all would he have left his mother and sister to dine by themselves on a Sunday. Mme. de Fontanin went out onto the balcony. The evening was mild, but at this hour there were few people about in the Avenue de l'Observatoire. The shadows were deepening between the dark masses of the trees. Several times she fancied she recognized Daniel by his walk, under a street-lamp. There was the roll of a drum in the Luxembourg Gardens. The gates were being shut. Now it was quite dark.

She put on her hat and hurried to the Bertiers' house; they had been in the country since the day before.

So Daniel had lied!

Mme. de Fontanin was not unused to lies of that sort, but that Daniel, her Daniel, should have lied to her was appalling. His first lie. And he was only fourteen!

Jenny had not gone to sleep yet; she was listening intently to every sound. She called to her mother.

"Where's Daniel?"

"He's gone to bed. He thought you were asleep and didn't want to wake you." She tried to speak naturally; there was no point in alarming the child.

After glancing at the clock Mme. de Fontanin settled down in an arm-chair, leaving the door on the corridor ajar, so as to hear the boy when he returned.

So the night passed; a new day came. . . .

Just before seven Puce started growling. The bell had rung. Mme. de Fontanin ran into the hall; she preferred to open the door herself; the less the servants knew, the better. An unknown, bearded young man stood at the door. Had there been an accident?

Antoine gave his name, saying he would like to see Daniel before he left for the Lycée.

"I'm afraid . . . as it so happens, my son can't be seen this morning," she stammered.

Antoine made a gesture of surprise. "Forgive me if I insist, Madame, but my brother, who's a great friend of your son's, has been missing since yesterday. Naturally, we're very anxious."

"Missing?" Her fingers tightened on the fabric of the light veil she had drawn round her hair. She opened the drawing-room door; Antoine followed her in.

"Daniel didn't come home yesterday, either. And I'm feeling worried, too." She had lowered her eyes; she looked up as she added: "All the more so as my husband is away from home just now."

There was a simplicity, a frankness, about her that Antoine had never seen in any other woman. Taken off her guard in this moment of anxiety, after a sleepless night, she made no effort to conceal her feelings from the young man; each successive emotion showed on her features in its natural colours. For a few moments they gazed at each other with all but unseeing eyes. Both were following the vagaries of their own thoughts.

Antoine had sprung out of bed with real detective zest. For he had not taken Jacques's escapade tragically, and only his curiosity was involved. So he had come here to put the other boy, Jacques's accomplice, "through it." But now again it looked as if things would be more complicated than he had foreseen. And that by no means displeased him. Whenever, as now, he came up against the unforeseen, a steely look came into his eyes, and under the square-cut beard his chin, the strong Thibault chin, set like a block of granite.

"What time yesterday morning did your son leave home?" he asked.

"Quite early. But he returned soon after."

"Ah! Was it between half-past ten and eleven?"

"About that."

"Like his friend! Yes, they've run away together." His tone was brisk; he sounded almost cheerful about it.

At that moment the door, which till now had stood ajar, was flung wide open and a child's body, clad only in a chemise, fell forward onto the carpet. Mme. de Fontanin gave a cry. Antoine had already picked up the little girl—she had fainted—and was holding her in his arms. With Mme. de Fontanin showing the way, he carried the child to her room and placed her on the bed.

"Leave her to me, Madame. I'm a doctor. Some cold water, please. Have you any smelling salts?"

After a few minutes Jenny came to. Her mother gave her an affectionate smile, but the child's eyes were unresponsive.

"She's all right now," Antoine said. "All she needs is to have some sleep."

Whispering: "You hear, darling?" Mme. de Fontanin laid her hand on the child's clammy forehead. Presently the hand slipped down over the eyelids and held them closed.

They stood for a while unmoving on either side of the bed. The fumes of sal volatile hovered in the air. Antoine, whose eyes had so far been fixed on the graceful hand and outstretched arm, now discreetly took stock of Mme. de Fontanin. The lace wrapped round her head had come loose and he could see now that her hair was fair, sprinkled with strands of grey. He took her age for about forty, though her manner and the vivacity of her face were those of a much younger woman.

Jenny seemed on the point of sleeping; the hand that rested on her eyes withdrew, lightly as a feather. They went out on tip-toe, leaving the door ajar. Mme. de Fontanin, who was walking in front, turned round.

"Thank you," she said, holding out both hands towards Antoine. The gesture was so spontaneous, so masculine, that Antoine checked his first impulse courteously to press his lips to them.

"She's so nervous, poor child," Mme. de Fontanin explained. "She must have heard Puce bark and thought her brother had come back. She hasn't been at all well since yesterday morning; she's had fever all night."

They sat down. Mme. de Fontanin slipped her hand inside her bodice and produced the note Daniel had written her on the previous day. As Antoine read it, she kept her eyes on him. In her relations with others she always let herself be guided by her first impressions, and from the very first she had felt that she could trust Antoine. "A man with a forehead like that," she thought, "is incapable of an unworthy act." He wore his hair brushed back and his beard came up rather high upon his cheeks; framed in dark auburn hair, the whole expression of his face seemed concentrated in the deep-set eyes and pale expanse of forehead. He folded up the letter and handed it back to her. He appeared to be turning its contents over in his mind; actually he was wondering how to break certain matters to her.

"I think," he began tentatively, "we may infer a connexion between their flight and the fact that their friendship—well, their intimacy—had just been detected by their teachers."

" 'Detected'?"

"Yes. The correspondence they had been keeping up, in a special grey exercise-book, had just been found."

"What correspondence?"

"They used to write letters to each other during lessons. Letters, it seems, of a . . . a very special nature." He looked away from her. "So much so that the two offenders had been threatened with expulsion."

" 'Offenders'? Really, I'm afraid I don't follow. What was wrong about their writing to each other?"

"The tone of their letters was, I gather, so very . . ."

" 'The tone of their letters'?" Obviously she still did not understand. But she was too sensitive not to have noticed Antoine's growing embarrassment. Suddenly she shook her head.

"Anything of that sort is out of the question," she said in a strained voice that shook a little. It was as if a gulf had suddenly opened out between them. She stood up. "That your brother and my son may have planned some sort of schoolboy prank together is quite possible, though Daniel has never uttered in my presence the name of . . ."

"Thibault."

"Thibault!" The name, it seemed, surprised her. "That's curious. My little daughter had a bad dream last night and I distinctly heard her pronounce that name."

"She may have heard her brother speaking of his friend."

"No, I tell you that Daniel never . . ."

"How else could she have learned the name?"

"Oh, these 'supranormal' phenomena are fairly common, really."

"What phenomena?"

"The transmission of thought." There was an intense, almost other-worldly look on her face.

Her explanation and the tone in which she spoke were so new to him that Antoine looked at her curiously. There was more than earnestness on Mme. de Fontanin's face; it was illuminated, and on her lips there flickered the gentle smile of the believer who is used to braving the scepticism of the rest of mankind.

For a while they were silent. Then Antoine was struck by an idea that rekindled his detective enthusiasm.

"May I ask you a question, Mme. de Fontanin? You say your daughter spoke my brother's name. And that all day yesterday she was suffering from an inexplicable attack of fever. Mayn't that be because your son confided in her before going away?"

Mme. de Fontanin smiled indulgently. "You'd realize that such a suspicion is absurd, M. Thibault, if you knew my children and the way they behave with their mother. Never has either of them hidden anything from—" She stopped abruptly, stung by the thought that Daniel's recent conduct gave her the lie. "Still," she went on at once, but with a certain stiffness, moving towards the door, "if Jenny isn't asleep you can ask her about it yourself."

The little girl had her eyes open. Her delicately moulded profile showed against the pillow; her cheeks were flushed. The black muzzle of the little dog peeped comically from between the sheets beside her.

"Jenny, this is M. Thibault—the brother of one of Daniel's friends, you know."

The child cast at the intruder a look that, eager at first, darkened with mistrust.

Antoine went up to the bed, took her wrist and drew out his watch.

"Still too quick," he said. Then he listened to her breathing. He put into each professional gesture a rather self-complacent gravity.

"How old is she?"

"Almost thirteen."

"Really? I wouldn't have thought it. As a matter of principle one can never be too careful about these feverish attacks. Not that there's anything to be alarmed about, of course," he added, looking at the child and smiling. Then, moving from the bedside, he said in a different tone:

"Do you know my brother, Mademoiselle? Jacques Thibault?"

Her forehead wrinkled; she shook her head.

"Really and truly? Your brother has never talked to you about his best friend?"

"Never."

"But, Jenny," Mme. de Fontanin insisted, "don't you remember? When I woke you up last night you were dreaming that Daniel and his friend Thibault were being chased along a road. You said 'Thibault' quite distinctly."

The child seemed to be searching in her memory of the night. Then, "I don't know the name," she said at last.

"By the way," Antoine went on after a short pause, "I've just been asking your mother about a detail she can't remember; we've got to know it if we are to find your brother. How was he dressed?"

"I don't know."

"Then you didn't see him yesterday morning?"

"Yes, I did. Quite early—when he was having his coffee and rolls. But he hadn't dressed then." She turned to her mother. "You've only to go to his wardrobe, and see what clothes are missing."

"There's something else, Mademoiselle, something very important. Was it at nine o'clock, or ten, or eleven that your brother came back to leave the letter? Your mother was out then, so she can't say."

"I don't know."

Antoine caught a hint of annoyance in Jenny's voice.

"What a pity!" He made a gesture of disappointment. "That means we'll have trouble in getting on his track."

"Wait!" Jenny said raising her arm to make him stay. "It was at ten minutes to eleven."

"Exactly? Quite sure about it?"

"Yes."

"You looked at the clock while he was with you, I suppose."

"No. But that was the time when I went to the kitchen to get some bread-crumbs—for my drawing, you know. If he'd come before that, or if he'd come after, I'd have heard the door and gone to see."

"Yes, of course." He pondered for a moment. What use was it to tire her with more questions? He had been mistaken; she knew nothing. "Now," he went on, "you must make yourself comfy, and shut your eyes, and go to sleep." He drew the blankets up over the little bare arm, smiling to the child. "A nice long sleep, and when we wake up we'll be quite well again, and our big brother will be back at home."

She looked at him. Never afterwards could he forget all that he read at that instant in her gaze: an inner life quite out of keeping with her years, such indifference towards all human consolation, and a distress so deep, so desperately lonely, that he could not help being shaken by it and lowered his eyes.

"You were right," he said to Mme. de Fontanin, when they had returned to the drawing-room. "That child is innocence itself. She's suffering terribly, but she knows nothing."

"Yes," she replied in a musing tone, "she is innocence itself; but—*she knows!*"

"You mean . . .?"

"Yes."

"How can you think that? Surely her answers . . .?"

"Her answers?" she repeated in a slow, meditative voice. "But I was near her and I felt it somehow. No, I can't explain it." She sat down, but stood up again at once. Her face was anguished. "She knows, she knows—now I'm certain of it." Then suddenly, in a louder voice: "And I'm certain, too, that she would rather die than betray her secret."

After Antoine had left and before going to see M. Quillard, the principal of the Lycée (as Antoine had advised her to do), Mme. de Fontanin yielded to her curiosity and opened a *Who's Who.*

THIBAULT (Oscar-Marie). Chevalier of the Legion of Honour. Sometime

Member for the Eure. Vice-president of the Child Welfare Society. Founder and President of the Social Defence League. Treasurer of the Joint Committee of Catholic Charities in the Diocese of Paris. Residence: 4A Rue de l'Université, Paris VI.

III

TWO hours later, after her interview with the principal of the Lycée, whom she had left abruptly, without a word, her cheeks aflame, Mme. de Fontanin, not knowing where to turn, decided to go and see M. Thibault. Some secret instinct warned her against the visit, but she overruled it, as she often overruled such premonitions—prompted by a fondness for taking risks and a temperamental wilfulness that she mistook for courage.

At the Thibaults' a regular family council was in session. The Abbé Binot had arrived at the Rue de l'Université at an early hour, but only a few minutes in advance of the Abbé Vécard, private secretary to His Grace the Archbishop of Paris. This priest was M. Thibault's confessor, and a great friend of the family. A telephone-call had secured his attendance.

Seated at his desk, M. Thibault had the air of a presiding judge. He had slept badly and the unhealthy pallor of his cheeks was even more pronounced than usual. M. Chasle, his secretary, a grey-haired, bespectacled little man, was seated on his employer's left. Antoine alone had remained standing, leaning against a bookcase. Mademoiselle, too, had been convoked, though it was the hour when normally she attended to her housekeeping. Her shoulders draped in black merino, she sat perched on the edge of her chair, silently observing the proceedings. Under the coils of grey hair looped round her yellow forehead the fawn-like eyes strayed constantly from one priest to the other. The two reverend gentlemen had been installed on either side of the fireplace, in high-backed chairs.

After laying before them the results of Antoine's inquiries M. Thibault launched into a jeremiad. He liked to feel that he was being approved of by those around him, and the words that came to him, when depicting his anxiety, quickened his emotions. But the presence of his confessor urged him to examine his conscience once again; had he fulfilled all his duties as a father towards the miserable boy? He hardly knew what to answer. Then his thoughts took a new turn: but for that wretched little heretic nothing would have happened.

Rising to his feet, he gave rein to his indignation. "Should not young blackguards like that Fontanin boy be locked up in suitable institutions? Are we to allow our children to be exposed to such contamination?" His hands behind his back, his eyelids lowered, he paced the carpet behind his desk. Though he did not refer to it, the thought of the Congress he was missing rankled bitterly. "For over twenty years I've been devoting myself to the problem of juvenile criminality. For twenty years I've been fighting the good fight, by means of pamphlets, vigilance societies, and detailed reports addressed to various congresses. But I've done more than that!" He turned towards the priests. "Haven't I created in my reformatory at Crouy a special department where depraved children belonging to a different social class from that of the other inmates are given a special course of moral re-education? Well, you'll hardly believe it, but that department is always empty! Is it for me to force parents to incarcerate their erring sons there? I've moved heaven and earth to get the Ministry of Education to take steps about it. But," he concluded, shrugging his shoulders and letting himself sink back into his chair, "what do those fine gentlemen who are ousting religion from our French schools care about public morals?"

At that moment the parlour-maid handed him a visiting-card.

"That woman!" he exclaimed, turning to his son. Then, addressing the maid, he asked: "What does she want?" and, without waiting for an answer, said to his son: "Antoine, you attend to this."

"You can't very well refuse to see her," Antoine pointed out, after glancing at the card.

On the brink of an outburst, M. Thibault mastered his feelings and turned again to the two priests.

"It's Mme. de Fontanin! What's to be done? A certain consideration is due to a woman, whoever she may be, isn't it? And we mustn't forget, this one is a mother."

"What's that? A mother?" M. Chasle murmured, but the remark was only for himself.

M. Thibault came to a decision. "Show the lady in."

When the maid brought the visitor up, he rose and bowed ceremoniously.

Mme. de Fontanin had not expected to find so many people there. She drew back slightly on the threshold, then took a step towards Mademoiselle, who had jumped from her chair and was staring at the Protestant with horrified eyes. The softness had gone out of them and, no longer fawn-like, she looked like an outraged hen.

"Mme. Thibault, I presume?" Mme. de Fontanin said in a low voice.

"No," Antoine hastened to explain. "This lady is Mlle. de Waize, who has been with us for fourteen years—since my mother's death—and brought us up, my brother and myself."

M. Thibault introduced the men to her.

"Excuse me for disturbing you, M. Thibault," Mme. de Fontanin began. All the men's eyes converging on her made her feel uncomfortable, but she kept her self-possession. "I came to see if any news . . . Well, as we are both undergoing the same anxiety, Monsieur, I thought the best thing for us might be to . . . to join forces. Don't you agree?" she added with a faint smile, cordial if a little sad. But her frank gaze, as she watched M. Thibault, found no more response than a blind man's stare.

She tried to catch Antoine's eye; despite the slight estrangement that the last phase of their conversation on the previous day had brought about, she felt drawn towards the young man whose pensive face and forthright manners were so different from the others'. He, too, as soon as she entered, had felt that a sort of alliance existed between them. He went up to her.

"And how is the little invalid now, Madame?"

M. Thibault cut him short. His impatience betrayed itself only in the way he kept on jerking his head to free his chin. Slewing himself round to face Mme. de Fontanin, he began addressing her with studied formality.

"It should be unnecessary for me to tell you, Mme. de Fontanin, that no one understands your natural anxiety better than myself. As I was saying to my friends here, we cannot think about those poor lads without feeling the utmost distress. And yet I would venture to put you a question: would it be wise for us to 'join forces' as you propose? Certainly something must be done, they have got to be found; but would it not be better for us to keep our inquiries separate? What I mean is, we must beware of possible indiscretions on the part of journalists. Don't be surprised if I speak to you as one whose position obliges him to act with a certain caution as regards the press and public opinion. Not for my own sake. Anything but that! I am, thank God, above the calumnies of my adversaries. But might they not try to strike at the activities I stand for, by attacking me personally? And then I have to think of my son. Should I not make sure, at all costs, that another name is not linked with ours in connexion with this unsavoury adventure? Yes, I see it as my duty so to act that no one may be able in the future to throw in his face certain associations—quite casual, I grant you—but of a character that is, if I may say so, eminently . . . prejudicial." He seemed to be addressing the Abbé Vécard especially as, lifting his eyelids for once, he added: "I take it, gentlemen, that you share my opinion?"

During the harangue Mme. de Fontanin had turned pale. Now she looked at each priest in turn; then at Mademoiselle, then at Antoine. Their faces were blank and they said nothing.

"Ah, yes, I understand!" she cried. The words stuck in her throat, and she had difficulty in continuing. "I can see that M. Quillard's suspicions . . ." She paused, then added: "What a wretched creature that man is, a miserable, miserable creature!" A wry smile twisted her lips as she spoke.

M. Thibault's face remained inscrutable. Only his flabby hand rose towards the Abbé Binot, as if calling him to witness, inviting him to speak. With the zest of a mongrel joining in a dog-fight, the Abbé flung himself into the fray.

"We would venture to point out to you, Mme. de Fontanin, that you seem to be dismissing the lamentable conclusions come to by M. Quillard, without even having heard the charges brought against your son."

Mme. de Fontanin cast a quick glance at the priest; then, relying as usual on her intuitions as regards the characters of others, she turned towards the Abbé Vécard, whose eyes met hers with an expression of unruffled suavity. His lethargic face, elongated by the fringe of scanty hair brushed up round his bald patch, gave her the impression of a man in the fifties. Conscious of the heretic's appealing gaze, he hastened to put in an amiable word.

"None of us here, Madame, but realizes how painful this conversation is for you. The trust you have in your son is infinitely touching . . . and laudable," he added as an afterthought. With a gesture that was familiar with him, he raised a finger and held it to his lips while he went on speaking. "But unfortunately, Madame, the facts, ah, yes, the facts . . ."

As if his colleague had given him the cue, the other priest took him up, and went on with greater unction. "Yes, the facts, there's no denying it, are . . . crushing!"

"I beg you," Mme. de Fontanin began, looking away.

But now there was no holding the priest.

"In any case, if you want proof of our assertions, here it is!" Dropping his hat onto the floor, he drew from his girdle a grey, red-edged exercise-book. "Please cast a glance over this, Madame. However cruel it may seem to kill your illusions, we feel it our bounden duty, and we are convinced that you will yield to the evidence."

He moved towards Mme. de Fontanin as if he were going to force the book on her. She got up from her chair.

"I refuse to read a line of it. The idea of prying into the secrets of this child behind his back, in public, without giving him a chance to explain—it's revolting! I have never treated him in such a manner, and I never will."

The Abbé Binot gazed at her, his arm still holding out the book, a sour smile on his thin lips.

"Have it your own way," he said at last, with a derisive intonation. He placed the book on the desk, picked up his hat, and sat down again. Antoine felt a great desire to grasp him by the shoulders and put him out. His disgust was visible in his eyes, which, meeting the Abbé Vécard's eyes, found them in accord.

Meanwhile Mme. de Fontanin's attitude had changed; she raised her head defiantly and walked up to M. Thibault, who had not risen from his chair.

"All this is beside the point, M. Thibault. I came here only to inquire what you propose to do. My husband is away from Paris at the moment and I have to act alone. What I really came for was to tell you that in my opinion it would be a great pity to call in the police."

"The police!" M. Thibault shouted, so exasperated that he rose from his chair. "But, my good woman, don't you realize that the police in every department of France are after them already? I telephoned myself this morning to the private secretary of the Chief of Police, asking that every possible step be taken, with the utmost discretion, of course. I have also had a telegram sent to the Town Council at Maisons-Laffitte, in case the truants have had the idea of hiding in a neighbourhood they both know well. All the railway companies, frontier posts, and ports of embarkation have been advised. And, Madame, if it weren't for the scandal, which I want to avoid at all costs, I'd say it would be a very good thing to give those two young ragamuffins the lesson they need, and have them brought home in handcuffs, escorted by the police—if only to remind them that even in these degenerate days there's still a semblance of justice in France, some deference to parental rights."

Without replying, Mme. de Fontanin bowed and moved towards the door.

M. Thibault regained his self-control.

"Anyhow, Madame, you may rest assured that, if we get any news, my son will communicate with you at once."

She acknowledged the remark with an almost imperceptible nod. Antoine and, after him, M. Thibault escorted her to the door.

"The Huguenot!" Abbé Binot jeered, as soon as she was out of sight. The Abbé Vécard could not repress a gesture of reproach.

"What? A Huguenot?" M. Chasle stammered, and recoiled as if he had just trodden in some revolting offal from Saint Bartholomew's shambles.

IV

ON HER return Mme. de Fontanin found Jenny lying half asleep in bed. Her fever showed no signs of going down. She lifted her head, gave her mother a questioning look, then shut her eyes again.

"Please take Puce away, Mother. The noise hurts me."

As soon as Mme. de Fontanin was back in her room a fit of dizziness came over her; she sank into a chair, without even taking off her gloves. "Am I, too, in for a spell of fever?" she wondered. "Just when I most need to keep my head, to be strong and confident." She bowed her head in prayer. When she raised it, she had settled on her line of action; the principal thing was to find her husband, bring him back.

Crossing the hall, she paused in front of a closed door, then opened it. The room was cool and had evidently not been used for some time; a faint, bitter-sweet tang of verbena and lavender hovered in the air —a scent of perfumed soaps and hair-oils. She drew aside the curtains. A desk occupied the centre of the room; a layer of fine dust covered the blotter. There were no papers lying about, no addresses, no clues. All the keys were in the locks. The man who used the room was certainly of a trusting nature. She pulled out a drawer in the desk and saw a number of letters, a few photographs, a fan, and, in a corner, screwed up in a ball, a shabby black silk glove. Her fingers tightened on the edge of the table. A memory floated up into her mind and, in her day-dream, she seemed to be gazing at a half-forgotten scene.

One summer evening two years before, as she had been going in a tram along the bank of the Seine, she had caught a glimpse of some-thing that made her stiffen up abruptly. Yes, she had recognized her husband Jerome, bending over a girl who was sitting on one of the benches by the riverside. The girl was crying. How often since then her fancy had cruelly enlarged on that brief glimpse, taking a sad pleasure in elaborating the details: the young woman shamelessly parading her grief, with her hat clumsily askew, and hastily extract-ing from her skirt a large, coarse handkerchief! And Jerome's ex-pression, above all! How sure she was of having guessed aright the feelings that possessed him then! A little pity, to be sure, for she knew that he was weak and easily moved; and a good deal of exasperation at being involved in such a scene in public; and, behind it all, cruelty. Yes, in his very attitude as he bent forward solicitously but without real tenderness, she could see only too clearly the shallow compunction of the lover who has "had enough of it," who is perhaps already in quest of new adventure, and who, despite his pity, despite a secret shame, has decided to exploit the woman's tears to make the breach between them absolute. All this had been revealed to her in a flash of insight, and each time the haunting memory returned she felt the faintness she was feeling now.

She left the room hastily and locked the door.

A definite plan had suggested itself: that young maid she had had to dismiss six months ago—yes, she must see Mariette. Mme. de Fon-tanin knew the address of her new place. Mastering her distaste, with-out further hesitation, she went there.

The kitchen opened onto a service-staircase, on the fourth floor. It was the unsavoury hour of washing-up. Mariette opened the door. She was a bright little thing with golden curls and candid eyes—hardly more than a child. When she saw her former mistress, she blushed, but her eyes lit up.

"It's very nice seeing you again, Ma'am. . . . Is Miss Jenny all right?"

Mme. de Fontanin hesitated, an anguished smile on her lips.

"Mariette—please tell me my husband's address."

The girl blushed scarlet; her large, puzzled eyes filled with tears. The address? She shook her head, she didn't know—not where he was *now*. The master hadn't been living at the hotel where . . . No, he had dropped her almost immediately. "Then you don't know, Ma'am?" she added innocently.

But Mme. de Fontanin was moving away towards the door, with lowered eyes; she could not bear hearing any more. There was a short silence. The water in a saucepan was boiling over, hissing as it fell onto the range. Without thinking, Mme. de Fontanin pointed to it.

"Your water's boiling over," she said. Then, still moving towards the door, she added: "Are you happy here, my dear?"

The girl made no reply. When Mme. de Fontanin looked up, it seemed to her that there was something of the animal in the eyes and the keen teeth that showed between the young, parted lips. After a pause that seemed interminable to both, the girl brought herself to speak.

"Couldn't you ask . . . Mme. Petit-Dutreuil?" she stammered.

Mme. de Fontanin did not hear the burst of sobbing that followed. She was hurrying down the stairs as if the house were on fire. That name had cast a sudden light on a number of coincidences she had hardly noticed at the time and had forgotten immediately. Now they all came back, and each fell into place in a chain of damning evidence.

An empty cab was passing; she jumped into it—the sooner she was home, the better. But, on the point of giving her address, an uncontrollable impulse gripped her—she fancied she was obeying a prompting from above.

"Rue de Monceau," she told the driver.

A quarter of an hour later she was ringing at the door of her cousin, Noémie Petit-Dutreuil.

A fair-haired little girl of about fifteen opened the door. Her eyes smiled a greeting to the visitor.

"Good morning, Nicole. Is your mother at home?"

She was conscious of the child's stare of astonishment.

"I'll go and fetch her, Aunt Thérèse."

Mme. de Fontanin waited in the hall. Her heart was beating so rapidly that she pressed her hand to her breast and dared not take it away. She tried to bring her emotions under control. The drawing-room door was open and the sun was bringing out the sheen of the velvet curtains and the colours of the carpet. The room had the careless elegance of a bachelor's "den." "And they said her divorce had left her penniless," Mme. de Fontanin murmured. The thought reminded her that her husband had not sent her any money for two months; how was she to meet this month's bills? And, following it, another thought crossed her mind: could Noémie's unexpected opulence have come from—him?

Nicole did not return. Not a sound could be heard. More and more ill at ease, Mme. de Fontanin entered the drawing-room and sat down. The piano was open; a fashion paper was lying on the sofa; cigarettes lay on a low table; there was a bunch of red carnations in a vase. The more she looked around her, the more disturbed she felt. What could it be?

Because *he* was here, and his presence filled the room. It was he who had pushed the piano at that angle to the window, exactly as in her own home. It was he who had left it open or, if not he, it was for his sake that music lay scattered on it. It was he who had insisted on that wide, low sofa and the cigarette-box within easy reach. And it was he whom she now pictured there, lolling amongst the cushions, spruce and debonair as usual, gay eyes flashing under the long lashes, an arm dangling over the sofa edge, a cigarette between his fingers.

A soft, rustling sound made her start. Noémie had just entered, in a lace-trimmed dressing-gown, her arm resting on her daughter's shoulder. She was a tall, dark, and rather plump woman of thirty-five.

"Good morning, Thérèse; you must excuse me. I've had such a

frightful headache all day, it's laid me out completely. Nicole dear, will you pull down the blind?"

The sparkle of her eyes and the healthy pink cheeks gave her the lie. Her volubility betrayed the embarrassment she felt at Thérèse's visit, an embarrassment that grew to alarm when the latter, turning towards the child, said gently:

"There's something I want to talk to your mother about, darling. Would you leave us alone for a few minutes?"

"Run off to your room, Nicole, and do your lessons there." Noémie turned to her cousin with a high-pitched, unnatural laugh. "Children of that age are so annoying, aren't they?—always wanting to show off in the drawing-room. Is Jenny like that? I'm afraid I was just the same, do you remember? It used to drive poor Mother to despair."

The object of Mme. de Fontanin's visit had been only to get the address she required. But now she was here, Jerome's presence had made itself so strongly felt, the injury done her seemed so flagrant, and the sight of Noémie flaunting her rather vulgar beauty in this room offended her so deeply that once again she gave way to impulse and came to a sudden, desperate decision.

"Do sit down, Thérèse," Noémie said.

Instead of sitting down, Thérèse walked towards her cousin and held out her hand. The gesture was not in the least theatrical; it was too spontaneous, too dignified for that.

"Noémie, give me back my husband!" The words came with a rush. The smile froze on Mme. Petit-Dutreuil's lips. Mme. de Fontanin was still holding her hand. "You needn't answer. I'm not blaming you—I know only too well what he is." She paused for a moment, breathless. Noémie did not take advantage of the moment to defend herself, and Mme. de Fontanin was glad of her silence, not that it was tantamount to a confession but because it showed that she was not so hardened as to be able to parry such a home-thrust on the spur of the moment.

"Listen, Noémie," Mme. de Fontanin continued. "Our children are growing up. Your daughter . . . and my two children as well. Daniel's over fourteen now. You know the terrible effects of bad examples, how contagious evil is. Things can't go on like this any longer—I'm sure you agree. Soon I shan't be the only one to watch him . . . and to suffer." A note of pleading came into her voice. "Yes, give him back to us, Noémie."

"But, Thérèse, I assure you. . . . Why, you must be off your head!" The younger woman was recovering her self-composure, but there was a glint of anger in her eyes, and her lips were set. "Yes, you must be mad, Thérèse, to think of such a thing. It was silly of me to let you go on talking like that, but I couldn't believe my ears. You've been dreaming—or else been listening to a lot of ridiculous gossip. Now I want you to explain."

Mme. de Fontanin gave her cousin a pensive, almost affectionate glance that seemed to say: "Poor stunted soul! Still, your heart is better than your way of living." But then her eyes fell on the smoothly rounded shoulder, the soft voluptuous flesh that seemed fluttering, like a trapped dove, beneath the gauzy lace. And the picture that rose before her eyes was so realistic that she had to close them. A look of hatred, then of grief, flitted across her face. She felt her courage failing, and decided to put an end to the interview.

"Well, perhaps I'm mistaken. But do, please, give me his address. No, not his address. I only ask you, let him know that I have need of him."

Noémie stiffened up. "Let him know? Do you think *I* know where he is?" She had gone very red. "Look here, Thérèse, I've had about enough of your nonsense. I admit Jerome comes to see me now and then. Why not? We make no secret of it. After all, we're cousins. Why shouldn't we?" Instinct gave her the words that would cut deepest. "He'll be *so* tickled when I tell him that you came and made this absurd scene. I wish you could be here then!"

Mme. de Fontanin drew back. "You're talking like a prostitute."

"Very well then, do you want to hear the truth?" Noémie retorted. "When a woman's husband leaves her, it's her own fault. If Jerome had found in your company what he gets elsewhere, you wouldn't have to go running after him, my dear."

Mme. de Fontanin could not help asking herself: Can it be true?

Her nerves were at their breaking-point and she felt inclined to leave at once. But she could not face the prospect of being back at home again, without the address, without any means of getting in touch with Jerome. Her eyes softened once more.

"Noémie, please forget what I said just now and listen to me. Jenny's ill, she's had a temperature for two days, and I'm alone. You are a mother, you must know what it is to watch at the bedside of a child who's starting an illness. For three weeks now Jerome hasn't been home, not once. Where is he? What's he doing? He *must* be told his daughter's ill; he must come back. Do tell him that." Noémie shook her head, wholly unmoved by the appeal. "Oh, Noémie, it's not possible you've grown so heartless! Listen, I'm going to tell you everything; it's true that Jenny's ill and I'm dreadfully worried about her; but that's not the worst." Her voice was humbler yet. "Daniel has left me; he's run away."

"Run away?"

"Yes. Inquiries will have to be made. I simply can't remain alone at such a time—with a sick child on my hands. Surely you understand that? Noémie, do please tell him he must come back."

For a moment Mme. de Fontanin thought the younger woman was about to give way; there was a look of sympathy on her face. But then she turned abruptly away and cried, raising her arms to emphasize the words:

"But, good heavens, what do you expect me to do about it? Didn't I tell you just now I can't help you in any way?" And when Mme. de Fontanin disgustedly refrained from answering, she swung round on her with blazing cheeks. "You don't believe me, Thérèse, eh? So much the worse for you; now you shall know everything. He's let me down again—bolted, I don't know where! Run away with another woman. So now you know! Well, do you believe me?"

All the colour had left Mme. de Fontanin's face. Unthinking, she repeated: "Run away with another woman!"

Noémie had flung herself upon the sofa and buried her head among the cushions.

"Oh, if you only knew how he's made me suffer! I've forgiven him too often, so he thinks I'll go on forgiving him all the time. He's greatly mistaken. Never again! The way he's treated me is positively atrocious. Under my eyes, in my own house, he seduced a little slut of a maid I had here, a wretched brat of nineteen. She decamped, bag and baggage, a fortnight ago without giving notice or anything. And, would you believe it, he was waiting for her at the front door, with a cab!" Her voice grew shrill and she jumped up from the sofa. "In the street where I live, at my own door, in broad daylight, with my own servant. Did you ever hear of such a thing?"

Mme. de Fontanin had gone to the piano and was steadying herself against it; she was feeling on the verge of collapse. A picture was taking form before her, of Mariette as she had seen her a few months earlier, of all the little things she had noticed then, their furtive contacts as they brushed against each other in the hall, her husband's surreptitious expeditions up to the sixth floor, where the maid's bedroom was, until that day when it had become impossible to overlook what was going on, when she had had to dismiss the girl, who, overcome by remorse, had begged her mistress's forgiveness. And she remembered the glimpse she had had of that little shop-girl in black, drying her eyes, beside the river bank. Now, looking up, she saw Noémie in front of her, and she averted her eyes. But her gaze drifted involuntarily back to the handsome woman sprawling across the sofa, the bare shoulder shaken by spasms of sobbing, and the gleam of white flesh under the filmy lace. And the picture that rose before her then was the most horrible of all.

Noémie's voice was reaching her consciousness by fits and starts.

"But it's over now! I'm through with him. He can come back, he can go down on his bended knees, I won't give him a look. I hate and despise him. I've caught him lying time after time without the faintest reason, just to amuse himself, because he's built that way. He can't open his mouth without lying. He doesn't know what it means to tell the truth."

"You're unjust to him, Noémie."

The younger woman sprang up in amazement. "You of all people! *You* defend him!"

But Mme. de Fontanin had regained her self-control; when she spoke again her voice had changed.

"You haven't got the address of that . . . that maid?"

Noémie reflected for a moment, then, bending towards her, answered with a confidential air:

"No. But the concierge, perhaps . . ."

Thérèse cut her short with a quick gesture, and began to move towards the door. To hide her discomfiture Noémie buried her face amongst the cushions and made as if she did not see her going.

In the hall, as Mme. de Fontanin was drawing aside the front-door curtain, she suddenly felt Nicole's arms hugging her passionately; the little girl's face was wet with tears. She had no time to say anything to the child, who kissed her again, almost hysterically, and ran back into the apartment.

The concierge was only too glad to gossip. "Yes, Ma'am, I readdress her letters to the place in the country where she comes from. It's Perros-Guirec, in Brittany; her folks send them on to her, I expect. If you'd like to know the address . . ." She opened a greasy, well-thumbed address-book.

On her way home Mme. de Fontanin entered a post-office, and filled in a telegraph-form.

Victorine Le Gad,
Place de l'Eglise,
Perros-Guirec, Côtes-du-Nord.

Please inform M. de Fontanin that his son Daniel disappeared last Sunday.

Then she asked for a post-card.

Pastor Gregory,
Christian Healers Group,
2A Boulevard Bineau,
Neuilly-sur-Seine.

Dear James,

Daniel left home two days ago without saying where he was going. I have had no news from him and I am terribly worried. To make things worse, Jenny is ill; she has a high temperature, but we don't know yet what's wrong. And I cannot let Jerome know, as I don't know where he is.

I am feeling very lonely, my dear friend. Please come.

Thérèse de Fontanin.

V

TWO days later, Wednesday, at six o'clock in the evening, a
tall, ungainly, grotesquely thin man, whose age it was impossible to
guess, made his appearance at the building in which Mme. de Fontanin's flat was situated.

The concierge shook her head. "The poor young lady's dying,
and the doctors are with her. They won't let you see her."

The pastor climbed the stairs. The door on the landing was open.
The hall seemed full of men's overcoats. A nurse came running up
the hall.

"I am Pastor Gregory," he said to her. "What's wrong? Is
Jenny . . . ?"

The nurse stared at him, murmured: "She's dying," and turned
off into one of the rooms.

He shook all over as if he had been dealt a blow. It seemed to him
the air had suddenly become unbreathable, stifling. Going into the
drawing-room, he opened both windows wide.

Ten minutes passed. People were moving to and fro in the passage,
doors opening and shutting. There was a sound of voices. Mme. de
Fontanin appeared, followed by two elderly men in black. When she
saw Gregory she ran towards him.

"Oh, James! At last you've come! Please, please don't leave me
now."

"I only got back from London today," he explained.

She drew him aside, leaving the two doctors to their consultation. In
the hall Antoine, in his shirt-sleeves, was plying a nail-brush over a
basin the nurse was holding in front of him. Mme. de Fontanin grasped
the pastor's hands. She had changed out of recognition; her cheeks
were pale and haggard, her lips were quivering.

"Please stay beside me, James. Don't leave me alone. Jenny is . . ."

A sound of moaning came from the far end of the flat and, without ending the phrase, she hurried back to the bedroom.

The pastor went up to Antoine; his anxious look voiced an unspoken question.

Antoine shook his head. "I'm afraid there's no hope."

"Come, come! Why talk in that way?" Gregory sounded indignant.

"It's meningitis," Antoine said with a certain emphasis, raising his hand to his forehead. "What a queer bird!" he was thinking, as he looked at the English pastor.

Gregory's face was peaked and sallow; his long black hair, lustreless as a dead man's, straggled over a high, straight forehead. He had a long, pendulous nose flushed an unhealthy red, and the eyes, jetblack, almost without whites, deep-set beneath heavy brows, had an oddly phosphorescent glow. They brought to mind the eyes of certain monkeys; they had the same restlessness, the same melting softness combined with the same obduracy. Yet more unusual was the lower half of his face. He seemed to be perpetually laughing, but with a laugh that expressed no known emotion and twisted his mouth into all sorts of unexpected shapes. The chin was no less odd: it was hairless, and drawn skin-tight over the bones like a wrapper of old parchment.

"Was it sudden?" the pastor asked.

"The fever began on Sunday, but the symptoms became definite only yesterday morning. I arranged for a consultation at once. Everything possible has been done." His face grew earnest. "We shall hear what my colleagues have to say, but in my opinion—well, I'm afraid the poor child is . . ."

"Don't!" the pastor exclaimed in English, in a hoarse, harsh voice. His eyes were fixed on Antoine's; their indignation contrasted quaintly with the laugh that never left his mouth. As though the air were stifling him, he raised an emaciated hand towards his collar, spreading out the fingers stiffly. The hand looked like some hideous spider resting on his throat.

Antoine was studying the pastor with a professional eye. "Remarkably asymmetrical, that face," he was thinking, "what with that silent laugh, that vacant, maniacal grimace, and the rest of it."

Gregory addressed him in a formal tone. "Might I know if Daniel has returned?"

"No, and there's no news of him."

His voice grew tender. "Poor, poor lady!" he murmured.

Just then the two doctors came out of the drawing-room. Antoine went up to them.

"She's dying," the elder of the two said in a nasal voice, placing his hand on Antoine's shoulder. Antoine turned and glanced at the pastor.

The nurse came up and asked in a low voice: "Really, doctor, do you think there's no . . . ?"

Gregory moved away so as to hear no more. The oppression in the air was more than he could endure. Through the half-open door he saw the staircase; he hurried down it into the open air. Crossing the avenue he began to run straight ahead under the trees, his hair fluttering in disorder, his spidery fingers splayed across his chest. Eagerly he inhaled the cool evening air, his mouth still gaping in a preposterous laugh. "Those accursed doctors!"

He was as devoted to the Fontanins as if they had been his own family. When he had landed in Paris, sixteen years before, without a penny in his pocket, it was Pastor Perrier, Thérèse's father, who had befriended him. And he had never forgotten. Later on, during his benefactor's last illness, he had thrown up his work to hasten to his bedside, and the old pastor had died with one hand in his daughter's and the other in that of Gregory—his son, as the old man always called him. It all came back to him so poignantly at that moment that he turned on his heel and strode rapidly to the house. The doctors' carriage was no longer standing in front of it. He ran upstairs.

The front door had been left ajar. A sound of moans guided him to Jenny's room. In the semi-darkness he could hear the child whimpering, gasping for breath. It was all that Mme. de Fontanin, the nurse, and maid could do among them to keep the little body still. It was twisting convulsively like a fish dying on a river bank.

For a few moments Gregory did not speak, but watched them with a surly look on his face, pinching his chin between his fingers. At last he bent towards Mme. de Fontanin.

"They'll kill your child between them!"

"Kill her? What ever do you mean!" she exclaimed, as she clutched at Jenny's arm, which kept on slipping from her grasp.

"If you don't drive them out"—he spoke with deep conviction— "they'll kill Jenny."

"Who will?"

"Every one of them!"

She stared at him blankly—could she believe her ears? His sallow face bending above her looked terrifying.

One of Jenny's hands was fluttering outside the sheets; he gripped it and, stooping over the bed, began talking to her in a low, crooning voice.

"Jenny! Jenny darling! Don't you know me?"

Her distraught eyes, which had been staring up at the ceiling, swung slowly round towards the pastor's. Then, bending still nearer, he let his gaze sink deep into hers, and such was its insistence that the child ceased suddenly to whimper.

"Stop holding her!" he said to the three women, and, as none of them complied, he added, without moving his head, in a voice that admitted no denial: "Give me her other hand. All is well. Now, go!"

They moved away from the bed. Alone at the bedside, he bent over the dying child, mastering her with the hypnotic fixity of his eyes. The child's arms struggled convulsively in his grip for a few moments, then gently sank towards the sheets. For a time the legs went on twitching, then they too relaxed. And, subdued at last, the tired eyes closed. Still bending over her, Gregory signed to Mme. de Fontanin to approach.

"Look," he murmured, "she's quiet now, she's calmer. Drive them away, I tell you, drive away those sons of Belial. Error alone dominates them, and Error had all but killed your child."

He laughed, with the soundless laugh of a mystic who is in sole possession of the eternal verities, for whom the rest of the world is composed of madmen. Without shifting his gaze, still fixed on Jenny's eyes, he went on in a lower voice.

"Woman, I tell you *There is no Evil!* It's you who bring it into being and give it its baneful power—because you fear it, because you admit its existence. Now, for instance, those men have given up hope. They all say: 'She is . . .' And you think the same thing. You all but said it just now. 'Set a watch, O Lord, before my mouth; keep the door of my lips.' Poor little one, when I entered this room, there was nothing round her but the void, nothing but the Negative. . . . But I deny the Negative; I say: *'She is not ill.'*"

The violence with which he spoke was so compelling that the women were carried away by his conviction.

"She is well!" he added. "But leave me alone with her now."

With the dexterity of a conjurer, he gradually relaxed his hold on the child's wrists, finger by finger, then gave a little backward jump, leaving her limbs free. She lay, relaxed and docile, on the bed.

"Life is good!" he chanted. "And all things are good. Good is wisdom, and good is love. All health is in Christ, and Christ is in us all."

He turned to the maid and nurse, who had moved away to the far end of the room. "Please go, and leave me with her."

"Yes, go!" Mme. de Fontanin said. But Gregory had drawn himself up to his full height and his outstretched arm seemed to be hurling an anathema at the table with its medicine bottles and compresses and the bowl of crushed ice. "First take these things away!" he commanded.

The women obeyed.

No sooner was he alone with Mme. de Fontanin than he cried cheerfully: "Now, open the window! Open it as wide as you can, my dear."

Outside in the street a cool breeze was rustling in the tree-tops. Sweeping into the room, it seemed to hurl itself on the polluted air, driving it aloft in eddying flurries and in a final onslaught whirling it outside the window. And then it laid its cool caress on the sick child's burning cheeks. She shivered.

"Won't she catch cold?" Mme. de Fontanin murmured.

A cheerful grin was his first rejoinder. At last he spoke.

"Yes, you can shut it now. Yes, all is well. And now light all your lights, Mme. de Fontanin. We must have brightness round us, we must have joy. And in our hearts too we must have light, and joy abounding. 'The Lord is my light and my salvation; whom shall I fear?' " And, raising his hands, he added: " 'Thou hast granted me to come before the accursed hour.' "

He drew up a chair to the bedside. "Be seated," he said. "You must be calm, perfectly calm. Hold on to the Personal Control. Listen only to the promptings of Our Lord. I say to you it is Christ's will that she shall recover. Let us share His will. Let us invoke the mighty power of Good. Spirit is everything, everything is spirit. The material is dominated by the spiritual. For two days this poor child has been exposed to the influences of the Negative. With what disgust those men and women inspire me! Their minds are bent upon the worst, and they can evoke nothing but the powers of ill. And they think that 'all is over' when they have come to the end of their wretched, puling little 'certainties'!"

The moans set in again and Jenny began tossing about on the bed. Suddenly she threw back her head and her lips parted as if she were about to breathe her last. Mme. de Fontanin flung herself on the bed, her body stretched above the child's and cried out passionately:

"No, no! For pity's sake!"

The pastor advanced on her, as if he held her responsible for the sudden crisis.

"Afraid? So your faith has failed you? Fear is of the body only. In God's presence there is no fear. Put aside your carnal being, it is not truly you. Hear what Jesus Christ says: 'What things soever ye desire, when ye pray, believe that ye receive them, and ye shall have them.' Now, have done with fear and—pray!" She knelt down. "Pray!" he repeated sternly. "Pray first of all for yourself, oh doubting soul! May God restore to you trust and peace. It is in your perfect trust that the child will find salvation. Call on God's Holy Spirit. I unite my heart with yours. Now, let us pray."

He communed with himself for a while, then began the prayer. He was standing up, his feet together, his arms folded, his closed eyes turned heavenward; wisps of hair straggled on his forehead like an aureole of black flames. At first it was only a faint murmuring, but gradually the words became distinct, and, like the deep, rhythmic drone of a church organ, the laboured breathing of the child accompanied the invocation.

"Omnipotent, creative Breath of Life, Thou who art everywhere, in every tiny atom of all Thy creatures, I call upon Thee from the depths of my heart. Fill with Thy peace this sorely afflicted home. Drive far away from this couch all that is not a thought of life. Evil lies only in our weakness. O Lord, cast out of us the Negative.

"Thou alone art Infinite Wisdom, and all Thou doest with us is according to the Law. Therefore this woman commends to Thee her child, on the threshold of death. She makes her daughter over to Thy will; Thy will be done. And if it must be that this young child be snatched from her mother, she bows to Thy decree."

"Oh, James, please don't say that," she moaned. "Not that! Not that!"

Gregory did not move from where he stood, but she felt his hand fall heavily on her shoulder.

"O woman of little faith," he said, "can this be you, you on whose heart the heavenly spirit has breathed so often?"

"Oh, James, these last three days have been more than I could bear. I can't, I can't bear any more!"

He stepped back a pace. "I look at her—and it is no longer she. I can no longer recognize her. She has let Evil enter into her soul, into the holy temple of the Lord. . . . Pray, poor soul, pray!"

The child's limbs were twitching under the bedclothes, racked by violent discharges of pent-up nervous force. Her eyes seemed starting out of their sockets, as they roved round the room, staring at each lamp in turn. But Gregory paid no attention to her. Clasping the little girl tightly in her arms, Mme. de Fontanin did her best to check the convulsions.

"All-Powerful Force," the pastor intoned, "Thou who art the

Truth and the Life, Thou hast said: 'Whosoever will come after me, let him deny himself.' So be it. If this mother is to be bereaved of her child, she bows herself to Thy will."

"No, James, no!"

The pastor bent towards her.

"Renounce! Renunciation is the leaven; as leaven works in dough, so does renunciation with all evil thinking, making the Good rise." He drew himself up. "And so, O Lord, if it is Thy will, take her daughter from her. She yields her child to Thee. And if Thou hast need of her son also . . ."

"No! No!"

". . . and if Thou hast need of her son also, let him, too, be reft from her! May he never cross again his mother's threshold!"

"My Daniel! Oh, for pity's sake!"

"Lord, she yields her son to Thy wisdom, with her free consent. And, if her husband must be taken from her, let him be taken, too!"

"Not Jerome. No. . . ." Her voice was broken with emotion and she had sunk onto her knees.

"May he, too, be taken from her!" the pastor cried, his voice rising in a wild ecstasy. "May he be taken, without cavil, and in obedience to Thy will alone, O Fountainhead of Light, Source of all Good, Spirit Divine!"

For a while he was silent; then, without looking at her, he asked: "Well, have you made the sacrifice?"

"Please have some pity, James. I can't, I can't . . . !"

"Then pray." After some minutes had passed, he spoke again. "Well, have you made the sacrifice, the sacrifice of *all* you love?"

She made no answer but fell forward, fainting, onto the bed. . . .

Nearly an hour had passed. There was no movement from the bed; only the child's swollen head kept tossing to and fro upon the pillow. Her cheeks were red and each intake of breath seemed to rasp her throat. Her unclosing eyes had the blank stare of madness.

Suddenly, though Mme. de Fontanin had not moved or spoken, the pastor gave a start as if she had called his name, then went and knelt beside her. She drew herself up; her features were less strained. For a long while she gazed at the young face lying on the pillow.

Stretching out her arms, she cried: "Not my will, but Thy will be done, O Lord!"

Gregory had never doubted that these words would be spoken, at their due hour. His eyes were closed; with all his fervour he was invoking the grace of God.

The night wore on. At times it seemed as if the child were at her last gasp, that what little life remained to her was flickering out, as intermittently her eyes grew dim. Now and again her body was racked by spasms of pain; each time this happened Gregory took her hand in his and raised his voice in humble prayer.

"We shall gather in our harvest. But prayer is needed. Let us pray."

Towards five o'clock he rose, replaced a blanket that had slipped onto the floor, and flung the window open. The cold night air poured into the room. Mme. de Fontanin, who was still on her knees, made no movement to restrain him.

He went out onto the balcony. There was little sign of dawn as yet. The sky was still a dim metallic grey and the avenue a long tunnel of darkness. But beyond the Luxembourg Gardens there was a faint sheen on the horizon, and wraiths of mist were drifting up the avenue, swathing the black tree-tops in fleecy vapour. To keep himself from shivering, Gregory stiffened his arms and clenched his hands on the balcony rail. Waves of coolness borne on the light breeze bathed his moist forehead and pale cheeks, on which the long vigil and the strain of fervent prayer had left their mark. Gradually the roofs were turning blue, and bright rectangles of Venetian blinds were taking form upon the drab, smoke-grimed walls.

The pastor gazed towards the sunrise. From the sombre depths of shadow a flood of light was surging up towards him, a rosy glow that slowly permeated all the sky. Nature was waking, millions of dancing atoms sparkling in the morning air. And suddenly his chest seemed swelling with a breath of new-born life, a preternatural energy penetrated him, filling him with a sense of incommensurable vastness. In a flash he grew aware of boundless possibilities; his mind controlled the universe, nothing was forbidden him. He could bid that tree: "Tremble!" and it would tremble; say to that child: "Arise!" and, lo, she would rise from the dead. He stretched forth his arm and suddenly, as if in answer to the gesture, the foliage of the avenue began to quiver and a cloud of birds rose twittering with joy into the brightening air.

He went back to the bed and laid his hand on the head of the mother, who was still kneeling at the bedside.

"Now all things have been made clean, let us rejoice, my dear. Hallelujah!"

He moved to Jenny's side.

"The shadows are cast forth. Give me your hands, sweetheart."

For two days the child had hardly understood a word, but now she gave her hands to him.

"Look at me!" he bade her, and the haggard eyes, which had seemed to have lost the faculty of seeing, gazed into his eyes.

" 'For He shall redeem thee from death . . . and the beasts of the field shall be at peace with thee.' You are well, my little one. The shadows all have fled. Glory be to God! Now, pray!"

The light of understanding had come back to the child's eyes, her lips were moving.

"And now, darling, let your eyelids close. Quite softly. That's right. . . . Now sleep, for all your troubles are over. Now you must sleep—for joy!"

Some minutes later—for the first time in fifty hours—Jenny fell asleep. Quiet at last, her head nestled upon the pillow, her eyelashes cast tranquil shadows on her cheeks, and through the parted lips her breath flowed in an even cadence. She was saved.

VI

IT WAS a school exercise-book bound in plain grey cloth which Jacques and Daniel had selected as being least likely to catch the master's attention when they passed it to and fro. The first pages were filled with queries jotted down in haste.

What are the dates of Robert the Pious?
Which is it, *rapsody* or *rhapsody*?
What's the trans. of *eripuit*?

And so forth. Then came some pages filled with notes and corrections, presumably referring to poems Jacques had written—on separate sheets.

Presently, however, the two boys settled down to a steady exchange of letters.

The first letter of any length was written by Jacques:

Paris, Lycée Amyot, Form IIIA, under the suspicious eye of QQ, alias Hogshair. Monday, March 17; the time being 3 hours, 31 minutes, and 15 seconds p.m.

Is your prevailing mood one of indifference, of sensuality, or of love? I rather think it must be number three, which is more natural to you than the others.

Personally, the more I study my feelings, the more I realize that man's a BRUTE, and love alone can rescue him from that state. That is the cry of my stricken heart and my heart speaks true! Without you, best beloved, I should be a hopeless fool, a dunderhead. If there's a spark of understanding in me, I owe it to you alone.

I shall never forget the moments, too few, alas, and too brief, when we are entirely one another's. You are my only love. I shall never love again; for a thousand memories of you would bar the way. Good-bye, I feel feverish, my forehead is throbbing, my eyes are going dim. Nothing shall ever separate us, promise me. Oh, when, when shall we be free? When shall we be able to live together, go abroad together? How I shall enjoy foreign lands! Think of travelling together, gathering our romantic first impressions and transmuting them into poems, while they are still fresh and fiery!

I hate waiting. Write to me as soon as you possibly can. I want you to be sure and answer this before four, if you love me as I love you.

My heart clasps your heart, as Petronius clasped his divine Eunice.

Vale et me ama!

J.

Daniel's reply followed on the next page:

I feel that, were I to live alone beneath another sky, the utterly unique bond that links your soul and mine would somehow make me know what is becoming of you. And it seems to me that the lapse of time means nothing to our mutual affection.

It is impossible to tell you the pleasure your letter gave me. You were my friend already and you've become far more than that—the better part of me. Have I not helped to shape your soul, as you have helped to shape mine? Good God, how real I feel that is when I'm writing to you! I am alive then! And everything in me is alive—body, mind, heart, imagination—thanks to your devotion, which never shall I doubt, my true and only friend.

D.

P.S. I've induced Mother to get rid of my old boneshaker. Good biz! It was falling to pieces.

Tibi,

D.

Another letter from Jacques:

O dilectissime!

How do you manage to be so cheerful at times and so sad at others? Personally, even in my moods of maddest gaiety, time and again I feel myself the prey of sombre thoughts. And I know that never, never again shall I be able to be gay, light-hearted. Always there will rise up before me the spectre of an unattainable ideal.

Ah, sometimes I understand the ecstasy of those pale nuns with bloodless faces who spend their lives remote from this too, too real world! How pitiable to have wings if it is only to break them against prison bars! I am alone in a hostile universe; my father, whom I love, does not understand me. I am not so very old, but already how many fair flowers of hope lie broken, how many dews have turned to floods of rain, how many pleasures have been frustrated, what despairs have embittered my life!

Forgive me, beloved, for being so lugubrious—I suppose my "character is being formed." My brain is in a ferment; my heart even more so, were that possible. Let us remain united for ever. Together we will steer clear of the rocks and reefs, and of the whirlpool men call pleasure.

Everything has turned to ashes in my hands; but there remains the supreme delight of knowing I am yours, and of our SECRET, O chosen of my heart!!

J.

P.S. I end this letter in great haste, as I have my recitation to learn by heart and I don't know a word of it yet, damn it!

O my love, if I didn't have you, I really think I'd kill myself!

J.

Daniel had replied immediately:

So you are suffering?

Why should you, dearest of friends, why should you, who are so young, curse life? It's sacrilege! You say your soul is tethered to the earth. Well, then—work, hope, love, read books!

How can I console you for the sorrow that is preying on your soul? What remedy can I offer for your cries of despair? No, my friend, the Ideal is not incompatible with human nature. No, no, it is not a mere childish fancy, a phantom born of some poet's dream. For me the Ideal (it's hard to explain), for me it's the mingling of what is greatest with the humblest earthly things; it is to bring greatness into all one does; it is the complete development of all those divine faculties that the Creative Breath has instilled in us. Do you understand me? That is the Ideal as I feel it in the depths of my heart.

And then, if you will but trust a friend who is faithful unto death, who has lived much because he has dreamed and suffered so much; if you will trust your friend who has never wished anything but your happiness, let me remind you once again that you don't live for those who cannot understand you, for the outside world that despises you, poor boy, but for someone—that "someone" is I—who never ceases thinking of you, and feeling like you, with you, about all things.

O my friend, may the sweetness of our wonderful love be like a holy balm on your wounds.

D.

Instantly Jacques had scribbled in the margin:

Forgive me! It is the fault of my violent, extravagant, fantastical nature, dearest love!! I pass from the depths of despair to the most futile hopes; one moment I am in the abyss and the next carried aloft into the clouds! Am I then never to love anything continuously? (If it be not you!!) (And my ART!!!) Yes, such is my destiny—let me confess it . . . to you!

I adore you for your generosity, for your flower-like sensitiveness, for the earnestness you impart to all your thoughts, to all your actions, even to the delights of love. All your tender emotions I share with you, at the selfsame moment as you feel them. Let us thank Providence that we love each other and that our lonely, suffering hearts have been able to mingle thus, indissolubly, flesh to flesh!

Never forsake me.

And let us both remember eternally that each has in the other
the passionate object of
His Love

J.

There followed two long pages from Daniel, written in a bold, firm hand.

Tuesday, April 7.

My Friend,

Tomorrow I shall be fourteen. Last year I used to whisper to myself: "Fourteen!" It was like some lovely, impossible dream. Time passes and marks us. But in our depths nothing changes. We are always ourselves. Nothing has changed except that I feel weary and grown old.

Yesterday evening as I was going to bed I took up a volume of Musset. The last time I read it I began to tremble, at the first verse, and sometimes even wept. Yesterday for long sleepless hours I struggled to feel a thrill, but nothing came. I found the phrases well turned, harmonious. . . . Oh, what sacrilege!! Only at the end did the poetic emotion revive in me and, with a torrent of delicious tears, I felt that thrill.

Oh, if only my heart doesn't dry up! I so fear that life may blunt my heart and senses. I am growing old. Already those great ideas of God, the Spirit, Love, are ceasing to make my bosom throb as once they did, and at times I feel Doubt gnawing at my heart. How sad it all is! Why can't we live with all the might of our souls, instead of reasoning? *We think too much!* I envy the vitality of youth which blindly flings itself into every danger without taking thought. How I would love to sacrifice myself, with closed eyes, to a sublime Idea, to an ideal and immaculate Woman, instead of being always thrown back on myself. How dreadful they are, these longings which have no outlet!

You congratulate me on my earnestness. You are wrong; it is my curse, my evil destiny! I am not like the questing bee who goes to suck the honey from flower to flower. I am like the beetle that installs itself in the bosom of a single rose, in which it lives till the petals close about it and it dies suffocated in that last passionate embrace—the embrace of that one flower singled out from all the rest.

My devotion to you, my dear, is like that—faithful till death. You are that tender rose which, in the desolation of the earth, has opened its heart to me. In the depths of your loving heart bury my black despair!

D.

P.S. You can write to my house without danger during the Easter hols. My mother never interferes with my letters (not that they're anything very special!).

I have just finished Zola's *La Débâcle*. I can lend it to you. I haven't yet got over the emotions it produced. It has such wonderful power, such depth! I am going to begin *Werther*. There, my dear, we have at last the book of books. I have also taken Gyp's *Elle et Lui*, but I shall read *Werther* first.

D.

Jacques replied in a severe tone.

For my friend's fourteenth birthday.

In the universe there is a man who by day suffers unspeakable torments and who cannot sleep of nights, who feels in his heart an aching void that sensual pleasure cannot fill and in his head a fearful chaos of his faculties; who in the giddy whirl of pleasure, amongst his gay companions, feels, of a sudden, solitude with dark wings hovering above his heart. In the universe there is a man who hopes for nothing, and fears nothing, who loathes life and has not the strength to leave it; 'tis HE WHO DOES NOT BELIEVE IN GOD!!!

P.S. Keep this. You will read it again when you are utterly forsaken and lift your voice in vain amid the darkness.

J.

"Have you been working during the hols.?" Daniel asked at the top of another page.

Jacques's answer followed:

I have just completed a poem in the same style as my "Harmodius and Aristogeiton." It begins rather neatly:

> *Hail, Cæsar! Lo, the blue-eyed maid from Gaul*
> *Dancing for thee the dance of her dear land,*
> *Like a river-lotus 'neath the snowy flight of swans.*
> *A shudder passes through her swaying form.*
> *Hail, Emperor! . . . See the huge blade flash*
> *In the fierce sword-dance of her far-off home. . . .*

And so on. . . . Here's the end:

> *Cæsar, thou growest pale! Alas, ah, thrice alas!*
> *Her sword's fell point has pierced the lovely throat.*
> *The cup falls from her hand, the blue eyes close,*
> *All her white nakedness is red with blood,*
> *Red in the pale light of the moon. . . .*
> *Beside the great fire flaring on the lakeside*
> *Ended is the dance*
> *Of the white warrior maid at Cæsar's feast.*

I call it "The Crimson Offering" and I have a mimed dance to go with
it. I would like to dedicate it to the divine Loie Fuller, and for her to
dance it at the Olympia. Do you think she'd do it?

Still, some days ago I took an irrevocable decision to return to the regular
metres and rhymed verse of our great classics. (Really, I think I "despised"
them because they are more difficult.) I have begun an ode in rhymed
stanzas on the martyrdom I spoke to you about. This is the beginning:

> *Ode to Father Perboyre, who died a martyr's death in*
> *China, Nov. 20, 1839, and was beatified in January 1889.*
>
> *Hail, holy priest, at whose most cruel fate*
> *All the world shuddered through its length and breadth!*
> *Thee would I sing, to Heaven predestinate,*
> *   And faithful unto death.*

But since yesterday I have come to think that my true vocation will be
to write, not poems, but stories and, if I have patience enough, novels. A
great theme is fermenting in my mind. Listen!

A young girl, the daughter of a great artist, born in a studio and herself
an artist (that's to say, rather unstable in character and finding her ideal
not in family life but in the cult of Beauty), is loved by a sentimental
but bourgeois young man, whom her exotic beauty fascinates. But their
love changes to bitter hatred and they part. He then marries a harmless
little provincial girl, while she, heart-broken for lost love, plunges into
debauchery (or dedicates her genius to God—I don't yet know which).
That's my idea; what does my friend think of it?

The great thing, you know, is to produce nothing that's artificial, but
to follow one's bent. Given the instinct to create, one should regard oneself as having the noblest and finest of missions there can be, a great duty
to fulfil. Yes, sincerity is all that matters. Sincerity in all things, always.
Ah, how cruelly that thought torments me! A thousand times I have
fancied I detected in myself that insincerity of the pseudo-artist, pseudo-

genius, of which Maupassant discourses in *Sur l'Eau*. And my heart grew
sick with disgust. O dearest, how I thank God that He has given you to
me, and how greatly we shall need each other, so as to know ourselves
truly and never fall into illusions about the nature of our genius!

I adore you and I clasp your hand passionately, as we did this morning,
do you remember? With all my being, which is yours, whole-heartedly,
passionately!

Take care! QQ has given us a dirty look. He can't understand that one
may have noble thoughts and pass them on to one's friend—while *he* goes
mumbling on over his Sallust!!

J.

Another letter, almost illegible, seemed to have been dashed down
without a pause:

Amicus amico.

Too full, my heart is overflowing! What I can capture of the flood, I
commit to paper.

Born to suffer, love, and hope, I hope and love and suffer! The tale of
my life can be told in two lines: *What makes me live is love, and I have
but one love, YOU!*

From my early youth I always felt a need to pour the emotions welling
up in my heart into another, into an understanding heart. How many
letters did I write in those days to an imaginary person who matched me
like a brother! But, alas, it was only my own heart, carried away by its
emotion, speaking, or, rather, writing to itself!! Then suddenly God willed
that this Ideal should become Flesh, and it took form in You, my love!
How did it begin? There is no telling; step by step, I lose myself in a
maze of fancies, without ever tracing it to its origin. Could any one ever
imagine anything so voluptuous, so sublime as our love?? I seek in vain
for comparisons. Beside our great secret everything else turns pale! It's a
sun that warms, enlightens our two lives. But no words can describe it.
Written, it is like the photo of a flower.

That's enough!

Perhaps you are in need of help, of hope or consolation, and here I am
sending you not words of affection but the sad effusions of a heart that
lives only for itself. Forgive me, my love! I cannot write to you otherwise!
I am going through a crisis, my heart is more parched than the stones of
a dry watercourse. I am so unsure about everything, unsure of myself;
can crueller suffering be??

Scorn me! Write to me no more! Go, love another!! No longer am I
worthy of the gift you make me of yourself!

What irony is in this implacable destiny that urges me . . . to what goal?
To nothingness!!!

Write to me. If you were lost to me, I should kill myself!

Tibi eximo, carissime.

J.

The Abbé Binot had slipped in between the last pages of the book
a note intercepted by the teacher, on the eve of their flight. It consisted of an almost illegible pencilled note from Jacques.

On all who accuse basely and without proof, on all those persons, shame!
Shame to them! Woe to them!

Their machinations are prompted by vile curiosity, they want to nose
out the secrets of our friendship. What a foul thing to do!

No sordid truckling to them! We must face out the storm together!
Death rather than defeat!

Our love is above calumny and threats!

Let us prove it!

Yours FOR LIFE,

J.

VII

THEY had reached Marseille on Sunday, after midnight. The first
flush of their enthusiasm had waned. They had slept, doubled up, on
the wooden seats of an ill-lighted carriage, and the noise of turn-
tables and the sudden halt had waked them with a start. They had
stepped onto the platform, blinking their eyes, dazed and apprehensive. The glamour had departed.

The first thing was to find somewhere to sleep. Opposite the station
was a white globe of light inscribed "Hotel"; at the uninviting entrance the proprietor was on the watch for custom. Daniel, the more
confident of the two, had boldly asked for two beds for the night.
Mistrustful on principle, the man put them some questions. They
had their story pat. At the Paris station their father had found he

had forgotten a trunk, and had missed the train. He would be arriving in the morning, without a doubt, by the first train. The hotel-keeper hemmed and hawed, eyeing the youngsters. At last he opened a register.

"Write your names there."

He addressed Daniel not only because he seemed the older of the two—he looked sixteen—but even more because there was something distinguished in his looks and general demeanour that compelled a certain respect. On entering the hotel he had taken off his hat, not out of timidity but because he had a way of taking off his hat and letting his arm drop to his side—a gesture that seemed to imply: "It isn't specially for you I'm doing this, but because I believe in observing the customs of polite society." His dark hair came down to a neat point in the exact centre of his forehead, the skin of which was white as a young girl's. But there was nothing girlish in the firmly moulded chin, which, though quietly determined in its poise, had no suggestion of aggressiveness. His eyes had countered, without either weakness or bravado, the hotel-keeper's scrutiny, and he had written without hesitation in the register: "Georges and Maurice Legrand."

"The room will be seven francs. We always expect to be paid in advance. The night train gets in at 5:30. I'll see you're up in time for it."

They did not dare to tell him they were faint with hunger.

The furniture of the room consisted of two beds, a chair, and a basin. As they entered, a like shyness came over them both—they would have to undress in front of each other! All desire for sleep had fled. To postpone the awkward moment, they sat down on the beds and began checking up their resources. Their joint savings came to one hundred and eighty-eight francs, which they shared equally between them. Jacques, on emptying his pockets, produced a little Corsican dagger, an ocarina, a twenty-five-centime edition of Dante, and, last of all, a rather sticky slab of chocolate, half of which he gave to Daniel. Then they sat on, wondering what next to do. To gain time, Daniel unlaced his shoes; Jacques followed his example. A vague feeling of apprehension made them feel still more embarrassed. At last Daniel made a move.

"I'll blow out the candle," he said.

When he had done so, they hastily undressed and climbed into bed, without speaking.

Next morning, before five o'clock, someone started banging loudly on their door. Wraith-like in the pale light of the breaking day, they slipped into their clothes. The proprietor had made some coffee for them, but they refused it for fear of having to talk to him. Hungry and shivering, they visited the station bar.

By noon they had made a thorough exploration of Marseille. With freedom and the broad daylight, their daring had come back to them. Jacques invested in a note-book in which to record his impressions; now and then he stopped to jot down a phrase, the light of inspiration in his eye. They bought some bread and sausages and, going to the harbour, settled down on a coil of rope in front of stolid, stationary liners and dancing yachts and smacks.

A sailor told them to get up; he needed the cable they were sitting on. Jacques risked a question. Where were those boats going?

"That depends. Which of 'em?"

"That big one."

"Her? She's off to Madagascar."

"Really? Shall we see her sail?"

"No, she ain't sailing till Thursday next. But if you want to see a liner going out, you'd best come back here this afternoon. The *La Fayette* there is sailing for Tunis at five."

At last they had the information they wanted.

Daniel, however, pointed out that Tunis was not Algeria.

"Anyhow it's Africa," Jacques said, biting off a mouthful of bread. Squatting against a heap of tarpaulins, with his shock of coarse red hair standing up, like a tuft of autumn grass, from his low forehead; with his angular head and protruding ears, his scraggy neck and queer-shaped little nose that kept on wrinkling, he brought to mind a squirrel nibbling beechnuts.

Daniel had stopped eating. He turned to Jacques.

"I say! Supposing we wrote to *them* from here, before we—!"

The glance the younger boy flashed at him cut him short.

"Are you mad?" he spluttered, his mouth half full of bread. "Just for them to have us arrested the moment we land?"

He scowled furiously at his friend. In the unprepossessing face, which a plentiful crop of freckles did nothing to improve, the blue, harsh, deep-set, imperious eyes had a curiously vivid sheen. Their expression changed so constantly as to make them seem inscrutable. Now earnest, and a moment later gay and mocking; now soft and almost coaxing, they would suddenly go hostile, almost cruel. And then, unexpectedly, they would grow dim with tears; though oftenest they were shrewd and ardent, seemingly incapable of gentleness.

On the brink of a retort Daniel checked himself. His face expressed a meek submission to Jacques's outburst and, as if to excuse his last remark, he smiled. He had a special way of smiling: the small, pursed mouth would suddenly open on the left, showing his teeth, in a quaint, twisted grin that lent a charming air of gaiety to the pensive face.

On such occasions it seemed odd that the tall, mature-minded youngster did not rebel against the ascendancy of his childish friend. His education and experience, the liberty he had enjoyed, gave him an uncontestable advantage over Jacques. Not to mention that at the Lycée where they had met Daniel had proved a good pupil, Jacques a slow-coach. Daniel's nimble wits were always ahead of any demand that was made on them; Jacques, on the other hand, was a poor worker, or rather did not work at all. It was not that his intelligence was at fault. The trouble was that it was directed towards matters that had no connexion with his studies. Some demon of caprice was always prompting him to do the most ridiculous things. He had never been able to resist temptation and seemed quite irresponsible, seemed to follow only the promptings of that inner voice. But the oddest thing was that, though he was at the bottom of his class in most subjects, his fellow-pupils and even the masters could not help feeling a certain interest in him. Among the other youngsters, whose personalities were kept in somnolent abeyance by habit and discipline, among the sedulous masters, whose natural gifts seemed to have gone stale on them, this dunce with the unpromising face but given to outbursts of sudden candour and caprice, who seemed to live in a world of day-dreams created by and for himself alone, who launched without a second thought into the most preposterous adventures—this odd little creature, while he thoroughly dismayed them, compelled their tacit admiration.

Daniel had been among the first to feel the attraction of Jacques's mind, less developed than his own but so fertile, so lavish of surprises, and so remarkably instructive. Moreover, he too had in him a strain of waywardness, a like inclination towards independence and revolt. As for Jacques, a day-boarder in a Catholic school, the offspring of a family in which religious exercises bulked so largely—it had been for the sheer excitement of another evasion from the narrow life at home that he had gone out of his way to attract the Protestant boy's attention; for even then Jacques had guessed that Daniel would reveal to him a world far different from his own. But in a few weeks their their comradeship had blazed up into an all-absorbing passion, and in it both had found a welcome relief from the moral solitude from which the two, unconsciously, had been suffering so long. It was a chaste, almost a mystical love, in which the two young souls fused their common yearnings towards the future, and shared all the extravagant and contradictory feelings that can obsess the mind of a fourteen-year-old boy—from a passion for silkworms or secret codes to the most intimate heart-searchings, even to that feverish desire for Life which seemed to intensify with every day they lived through.

Daniel's silent smile had calmed Jacques, and now he was munching away again at his bread. The lower part of his face was rather gross: he had the characteristic Thibault jaw, and an over-large mouth, with chapped lips. But, though ugly, the mouth was expressive and suggested a strong-willed, sensual nature.

He looked up at his friend. "You'll see, I know the ropes!" he boasted. "Life's easy in Tunis. Anybody who applies is taken on for the rice-fields. You can chew betel—it's delicious. You earn wages right away, and you get all the grub you want—dates and tangerines and so on . . . and, of course, lots of travelling."

"We'll write to them from there," Daniel suggested.

"Perhaps," Jacques corrected, with a toss of his red poll. "Once we've found our feet and they realize we can get on without them."

They fell silent. Daniel had finished his meal and was gazing at the big black hulls, the busy scene on the sunlit wharves, and the luminous horizon glimpsed through a forest of masts. He was struggling against himself, trying to fix his mind on what he saw, so as not to think about his mother.

The main thing was somehow to get on board the *La Fayette* that evening.

A waiter pointed out to them the offices of the Messageries Line. The fares were posted up. Daniel went to the ticket-office window.

"Please, my father has sent me to get two third-class passages to Tunis."

"Your father?" The old clerk went on placidly with his work. All that could be seen of him was the top of his forehead, rising above a pile of papers. He continued writing for a while. Then, without looking up, he said to Daniel: "Very well, go and tell him to come here himself— and to bring his identification papers with him, don't forget!"

They grew aware that the other people in the office were staring at them, and fled without another word. Jacques, who was boiling with rage, thrust his hands deep into his pockets. His imagination was suggesting to him a series of expedients. They might get taken on as cabin-boys, or as cargo—in crates well stocked with food; or hire a row-boat and go by easy stages along the coast to Gibraltar and thence to Morocco, halting each night at a port where they would play the ocarina and pass the hat round on the terraces of the little inns:

Daniel was pondering; that inner voice had once again made itself heard, warning him. He had heard it thus several times since they had run away. But this time he could no longer turn a deaf ear; he had to take heed of it. And there was no mistaking the disapproval manifest in that still small voice.

"Why not lie low in Marseille for a bit?" he suggested.

"We'd be spotted before two days were out," Jacques retorted scornfully. "Oh, yes, you can be sure the hunt is up already; they're on our tracks all right."

Daniel pictured the scene at home: his mother's anxiety as she plied Jenny with questions, and, after that, her visit to the principal to ask if he knew anything about her son.

· "Listen," he said. He was breathing with an effort. Then he noticed a bench near by and made Jacques sit beside him. Taking his courage in both hands, he went on: "Now or never, we've got to think things out. After all, when they've hunted for us high and low for two or three days, don't you think they'll have been punished enough?"

Jacques clenched his fists. "No, I tell you! No!" he shouted. "Have you forgotten everything so soon?" Such was the nervous tension of his body that he was no longer sitting on the bench, but lying propped against it, stiff as a board. His eyes were aflame with rage against the school, the Abbé, the Lycée, the principal, his father, society, the world's injustice. "Anyhow they'll never believe us!" he cried. His voice went hoarse. "They've stolen our grey letter-book. They don't understand and they can't understand! If you'd seen the priest, the way he tried to make me confess things! His Jesuit tricks, of course. Just because you're a Protestant, he said, there's nothing you wouldn't do, nothing . . . !"

Shame made him turn away. Daniel's eyes dropped and a pang of grief shot through his heart at the hideous thought that their foul suspicions might have been imparted to his mother.

"Do you think they'll tell Mother?" he muttered.

But Jacques was not listening.

"No!" he exclaimed again. "No, I won't hear of it. You know what we agreed on. Nothing's changed. We've gone through enough persecution. Good-bye to all that! When we've proved by deeds the stuff we're made of, and that we don't need them, you'll see how they'll respect us. There's only one thing to do, and that's to go abroad and earn our living without them. After that, yes, *then* we can write and say where we are, and state our terms, and tell them we intend to remain friends, and be free, because our friendship is for life and for death!" He stopped, steadied his nerves, and went on in a normal tone. "Otherwise, as I've told you, I shall kill myself."

Daniel gazed at him with a scared expression. The small pale face, mottled with yellow blotches, had a look of deadly earnest, exempt from any bravado.

"I swear to you," Jacques continued, "that I'm quite determined not to fall into their clutches again. Before that happens I'll have shown them what I am. Either we win our freedom or—see that?" Raising the edge of his waistcoat, he let Daniel see the handle of the Corsican dagger that he had filched, on the Sunday morning, from his brother's room. "Or this might be better." He drew from his pocket a small bottle done up in paper. "If you dared to refuse, now, to embark with me, I'd . . . I'd make short work of it. Like this!" He made the gesture of drinking off the bottle. "And I'd drop down dead."

"What . . . what is it?" Daniel murmured, terrified.

"Tincture of iodine," Jacques replied, still watching Daniel's face.

"Look here, Thibault! Do please give me that bottle!" Daniel pleaded.

Horrified though he was, he felt a thrill of love and admiration; once more he was carried away by his friend's extraordinary charm. And again the project of adventure tempted him. Meanwhile Jacques had put the bottle back in his pocket.

"Let's walk," he said, scowling at Daniel. "One can't think properly sitting down."

At four o'clock they were back at the quay. The *La Fayette* was the focus of an animated scene. A steady stream of dock-hands, with crates and boxes on their shoulders—like ants rescuing their eggs— was passing along the gangplanks. The two boys, Jacques in front, followed them. On the freshly scrubbed deck sailors were operating a winch above a yawning gulf, lowering baggage and cargo into the hold. A small, sturdy man with a beaked nose, hairy black hands and cheeks, and a smooth pink skin, was directing operations. He was wearing a blue jacket with gold braid on the sleeves.

At the last moment Jacques backed out.

"Excuse me, sir," Daniel began, slowly removing his hat, "are you the captain?"

"Why do you want to know that?" the man inquired with a laugh.

"I've come with my brother, sir. We'd like to ask you . . ." Even before the end of the phrase Daniel was conscious he had taken a wrong line, that he had bungled it beyond redress. ". . . to—er—take us to Tunis on your ship."

"All alone like that, eh?" the man asked with a sort of leer. There was something in his bloodshot eyes—a glint of unsavoury effrontery, almost maniacal—that suggested more than the words conveyed.

Daniel realized that there was nothing for it but to go on with their preconcerted story.

"We came to Marseille to join our father; he's been given a job in Tunis, on a rice-farm, and—er—he has written to us to join him there. We have the money for our fares." That improvised addition to their story, he realized, once he had made it, sounded as lame as all the rest.

"Right. Who are you staying with at Marseille just now?"

"With . . . with nobody. We've only just come from the station."

"You don't know any one at Marseille?"

"N-no."

"And so you want to come on board today?"

Daniel was on the point of answering no and bolting without more ado. But he answered feebly:

"Well, yes, sir."

"See here, my young beauties," the sailor grinned, "you're mighty lucky the Old Man didn't find you here. He don't have much time for jokers like you, that he don't, and he'd have clapped you into irons and sent you off to the police, just to find out what your little game may be. And, now I think of it, I'm damned if that ain't the best thing to do with little scallawags like you!" he suddenly roared, catching Daniel by the sleeve. "Hi there, Charlot! You nab the little chap, while I . . ."

But Jacques, who had seen his gesture, took a wild leap over the packing-cases, dodged Charlot's outstretched arm with a wriggle, and was at the gangway in three strides. Slipping like a monkey between the dockers coming up it, he jumped onto the quay, turned left, and started bolting for dear life. Then suddenly he remembered Daniel, and looked back. Yes, Daniel was escaping, too. Jacques watched him thread his way between the ant-like file of dock-hands, dash off the gangway, and swerve to the right, while the supposed captain, leaning on the bulwarks, roared with laughter at their panic. Jacques started running again. He and Daniel could meet later; for the moment the thing to do was to hide among the crowd and to get away, to get away at all costs!

A quarter of an hour later, out of breath, in a deserted street on the outskirts of the city, he stopped. At first he felt a cruel glee in fancying Daniel had been caught. If he had been, he deserved it. Wasn't it his fault their plans had come to grief? He hated him now and was half inclined to make off into the country and carry on the escapade alone, without bothering about Daniel. He bought cigarettes and began smoking. However, after making a long detour through a modern quarter of the town, he found himself back at the quayside. The *La Fayette* was still there. From where he was he could just see the three decks lined with people, packed like sardines; the liner was getting under way. He ground his teeth and turned on his heel.

Then he began to look for Daniel, feeling he must vent his anger on somebody. After wandering through various streets, he entered the Cannebière, followed the stream of loiterers for a time, then turned on his tracks. The air was oppressive; a storm was brewing. Jacques was bathed in sweat. How was he to find Daniel among all those people? His desire to get in touch with his companion became more and more insistent, as his hopelessness of doing so increased. His lips, parched by the unaccustomed cigarettes and the fever in his blood, were burning.

Without caring whether he attracted attention, or troubling about a distant growl of thunder, he started running desperately along the streets, peering in all directions till his eyes ached. Then a sudden change came over the city. The façades of the buildings stood out pale against a livid sky and a grey light seemed rising from the cobbles. The storm was rapidly approaching. Great drops of rain began to star the pavement. A violent clap of thunder, close at hand, set him trembling. He was walking past some steps, beneath a pillared entrance which he discovered was the porch of a church. The door was open; he ran in.

His steps echoed under the high roof and a familiar scent assailed his nostrils. Immediately he felt a vast relief, a sense of security. He was no longer alone; the presence of God was round him, sheltering him. But at the same moment a new fear gripped him. Since leaving home he had not once thought of God. And suddenly he felt hovering above him the unseen Eye that sees and penetrates the most secret places of the heart. He knew himself for a miserable sinner whose profanation of this holy place might well bring down on him God's vengeance. Rain gushed down the roof, violent flashes lit up the windows of the apse, the thunder roared incessantly, echoing round him as he cowered in the incense-laden darkness; almost he fancied that the fires of heaven were seeking out the offender! Kneeling at a *prie-dieu,* Jacques humbled himself before the altar, with bowed head, and hastily recited a paternoster and some aves.

At last the crashes began to space out; a spectral light glimmered across the stained-glass windows: the storm was passing. All immediate danger was over. He had a feeling that he had cheated, had eluded just reprisals. Deep down in him the sense of guilt persisted, but tempered by a thrill of perverse arrogance at having escaped the hand of justice. And, though he had qualms about it, it gave him a certain pleasure. Night was closing in. Why was he lingering here? With the passing of his fear a curious apathy had come over him and, staring at the wavering candle-flames upon the altar, he was conscious of a vague feeling of dissatisfaction, almost of resentment, as though the church had been secularized. A sacristan came to close the doors. He fled like a thief, without the merest apology for a prayer, without a genuflexion. He knew well that he was not taking away with him God's pardon.

A brisk wind was drying up the pavements. Few people were about. Jacques began to wonder where Daniel might be. He pictured the mishaps that might have befallen him and his eyes filled with tears, blurring the road ahead. He tried to keep them back by walking more quickly. At that moment had he seen Daniel crossing the street and coming towards him, he would have swooned with joy and affection for his friend.

A clock struck eight. Windows were lighting up. Feeling hungry, he bought some bread, then continued walking straight before him, haunted by his despair, without so much as troubling to scrutinize the people he encountered.

Two hours later, thoroughly fagged out, he noticed a seat under some trees in a deserted avenue. He sat down. From the branches of a plane-tree heavy drops fell on his head. . . . A peremptory hand was shaking his shoulder. He realized he must have fallen asleep. He saw a police-man examining him, and felt like fainting; his legs seemed giving way beneath him.

"Get home now, my lad; and look sharp about it!"

Jacques fled into the darkness. He had ceased wondering about Daniel, had ceased thinking about anything. His feet were sore. Whenever he saw a policeman he slunk out of his sight. He made his way back to the harbour. Midnight was striking. The wind had fallen; coloured lights, two by two, were dancing on the water. The wharf was deserted. He all but fell over the legs of a beggar snoring in a nook between two bales. Stronger than his fears, there came on him an irresistible desire to lie down, to sleep, no matter where, at all costs. He took a few steps, lifted the corner of a big tarpaulin, stumbled over boxes smelling of sodden wood, fell down, and was asleep at once.

Meanwhile Daniel was hunting high and low for Jacques. He had roamed round the station, round the hotel where they had slept and the offices of the shipping company; all in vain. He went back to the harbour. The *La Fayette's* berth was empty, the port seemed dead; the storm was sending the loiterers home.

With lowered head he started back to the centre of town, the rain beating on his shoulders. After buying some food for Jacques and himself he took a seat at the café which they had visited in the morn-ing. It was coming down in torrents in this part of the city. At every window the sun-blinds were being hauled in and the waiters at the café, with napkins on their heads, were rolling up the large awnings above the terraces. Trams sped past, their trolleys flashing vivid sparks along the wires against the leaden sky, their wheels cutting like plough-shares through the torrent on the road and throwing the water up on either side. Daniel's feet were sopping, his temples throbbing. What could have become of Jacques? Even more painful to him than the fact that he had lost touch with the younger boy was the thought of his anxiety and distress, all alone. He told himself that he would catch sight of him just over there, at that corner by the bakery, and watched intently. With his mind's eye he pictured Jacques trudging through the puddles, his face ghastly white and his eyes desperately hunting for his friend in every direction. Time and time again he was on the point of calling out—but it was not Jacques, only an unknown little boy dashing into the baker's and emerging with a loaf tucked under his coat.

Two hours passed. The rain had stopped and darkness was falling. Daniel dared not go; he felt sure Jacques would turn up the moment he left the place where he was waiting. At last he made a move, to-wards the station. The white globe above the door of their hotel was lit up. It was a badly lighted neighbourhood; would they be able to recognize each other, he wondered, if they met in this obscurity?

A voice cried: "Mummy!" He saw a boy of his own age crossing the street and joining a lady, who kissed him. She had opened her umbrella to protect herself from the drips off the roofs. Her son linked his arm with hers; affectionately talking, they disappeared into the darkness. An engine whistled. Daniel felt too exhausted to fight down his depression.

Ah, what a fool he had been to follow Jacques! Only too well he knew it now; indeed, he had been conscious of it all the time, from the very start, since their early morning meeting at the Luxembourg, when they had decided on the mad adventure. No, never for a moment had he been able to shake off the idea that if, instead of running away, he had hastened to explain things to his mother, far from reproaching him she would have shielded him from everything and everybody, and no harm would have come to him. Why had he given way? He simply could not understand what had possessed him to act as he had done.

He saw himself again, that Sunday morning, in the hall. Jenny, hearing his footsteps, had run up to him. On the tray had lain a yellow envelope with the Lycée stamp—announcing his expulsion, he assumed. He had hidden it under the tablecloth. Silently Jenny had gazed at him with her keen eyes; she had guessed that some alarming event had happened, and followed him to his room. She had seen him pick up the wallet in which he kept his savings. Then she had thrown herself on him and clasped him in her arms, kissing him, holding him so tightly that he could hardly breathe. "What's the matter? What are you going to do?" He had confessed that he was running away, that he was in trouble at school, he was falsely accused and all the masters were leagued against him; that it was essential he should disappear for a few days. "Alone?" she had asked. No, he was going with a friend. "Who is it?" Thibault. "Take me with you!" He had drawn her to him as he had used to do when they were little, and had asked in a low voice: "What about Mother?" She had burst into tears. Then he had said: "Don't be afraid, and don't believe anything they may say. In a few days I'll write, and I shall come back. But swear to me, swear that you will never tell Mother, or anyone else—never, never—that I came home and you saw me and you knew I was going away." She had given a quick nod. Then he had tried to kiss her, but she had run off to her bedroom, sobbing bitterly. Her last cry of utter, heart-rending despair still rang in his ears. . . . He stepped out more briskly.

Walking straight ahead, without looking where he was going, he soon found himself at some distance from the city, in the suburbs. The pavements were deep in slush, and street-lamps few and far between. Black gulfs of darkness yawned on either side: the entrances of yards and evil-smelling alleys. Children swarmed in the squalid tenement-houses, and in a sordid tavern a gramophone was grinding away. Turning, he walked for some time in the opposite direction. And now he realized that he was dead-tired. A lighted clock-tower showed up, and he knew that he was back at the station. The hands marked one. A long night lay before him; what was he to do? He looked round for some place where he could stop and take breath. A gas-lamp was burning at the entrance of a blind alley; crossing the tract of light, he crouched down in the darkness. A high factory wall rose on his left; resting his back against it, he closed his eyes.

A woman's voice woke him with a start. "You don't propose sleeping there all night, do you? Where do you live?"

She led him out under the light. He stared at her, tongue-tied.

"I can see," she went on. "You've had a row with your dad, and you daren't go back home. That's it, eh?"

Her voice was gentle. He saw no need to undeceive her.

"Yes, Madame," he said politely, hat in hand.

" 'Yes, Madame'!" She laughed. "That's good! Well, well, you'll have to go back home; there's no two ways about it. I've been through it myself, and I *know*. And, as you'll have to do it, what's the use of waiting? The more you put it off, the worse it is." Puzzled by his silence, she asked in a lower voice: "Are you afraid of getting a hiding from your dad?" Her manner of asking it was that of a fellow-conspirator, friendly but inquisitive.

He still said nothing.

"Ain't he a card!" she laughed. "And that pig-headed he'd rather spend the night out in the street! Oh, well, come along then. There's no one at my place and I can give you a mattress on the floor. I couldn't bring myself to leave a poor kid out all night in the street."

She looked decent enough, but he felt a vast relief at having someone to talk to at last. He would have liked to say: "Thank you, Madame," but he said nothing, and followed her.

They came to a low door. She rang the bell but the door was long in opening. The hall smelt of washing. He stumbled against the bottom step of a flight of stairs.

"I'll lead the way," she said. "Give me your hand."

The lady's hand was gloved and warm. He followed her meekly. The air, too, was warm inside the house. Daniel was glad to be no longer out of doors. They went up several flights of stairs; then she produced a key, opened a door, and lit a lamp. He saw an untidy room, an unmade bed. He remained standing, blinking in the sudden light, worn out and half asleep. Without waiting to take off her hat, she pulled a mattress off the bed and dragged it into another room. Turning, she began laughing again.

"Why, he's half asleep already, poor kid. . . . Look here, you'd better take your shoes off, anyhow."

He complied, with nerveless hands. His project of returning next morning to the station buffet, at exactly five, in the hope that Jacques might have the same idea, was haunting him like an obsession.

"Would you please wake me very early?"

"Don't you worry! I'll see you're up in time," she laughed.

He vaguely felt her helping him to take off his tie and undress. Then he dropped like a log onto the mattress, and lost consciousness at once. . . .

When Daniel opened his eyes, it was already day. He thought at first that he was in his bedroom at home. Then he was struck by the colour of the light filtering through the curtains. A young voice was singing in the next room, the door of which was open. Then he remembered.

Glancing into the room, he saw a little girl (or so she seemed) washing her face over a basin. Turning, she saw him lying on the mattress, propped up on an elbow.

"Ah, so you're awake. Good for you!" she laughed.

Could this be the lady of the night before? In a chemise and short skirt, her arms and legs bare, she looked like a child. Now that she was not wearing a hat he noticed that she had short brown hair, cut like a boy's and brushed vigorously back.

Suddenly a memory of Jacques appalled him.

"Good heavens, and I'd meant to be at the buffet first thing!"

But the warmth of the blankets she had tucked round him while he was asleep made him disinclined to move. And anyhow he did not dare to get up while the door stood open. Just then she came in, carrying a steaming cup and a hunk of buttered bread.

"Look here! Get your teeth into this, and then clear off. I don't want to have your pa coming round and making trouble for me."

He felt embarrassed at being seen by her half dressed, in his shirt and with his collar open, and even more embarrassed at seeing her come towards him, for her neck, too, was bare and so were her shoulders. She bent towards him. Lowering his eyes, he took the cup and, to hide his bashfulness, began to eat the bread and butter. Shuffling her slippers and singing, she moved from one room to the other. He dared not lift his eyes from the cup, but, when she passed close by, he could not help noticing her naked, slender, blue-veined legs almost level with his eyes and, gliding above the deal floor, her reddened heels emerging from the slippers. The bread stuck in his throat. He felt unnerved, incapable of facing this new day, big with unpredictable events. It flashed across his mind that at home, at the breakfast table, his chair was empty.

A sudden burst of sunlight flooded the room; the girl had just thrown the shutters open, and her young voice trilled in the bright air like bird-song.

> *"Ah, si l'amour prenait racine*
> *J'en planterais dans mon jardin!"*

His self-control gave way. The sunshine, her careless joy—at the very moment when he was fighting down his despair! His eyes filled with tears.

"Come along! Hurry up!" she cried gaily, picking up his empty cup. Then she saw he was crying.

"Feeling low?" she asked.

She had a kind, big-sisterly voice; he could not keep back a sob. She sat down on the edge of the mattress, slipped her arm round his neck, and, with a mothering gesture of consolation—the final argument of women all the world over—pillowed his head upon her breast. He dared not make the slightest movement; he could feel, through her chemise, the rise and fall of her breast, and its soft warmth against his cheeks. He felt his breath failing him.

"You silly boy!" Drawing back, she hid her breast with her bare arm. "It's seeing that, is it, that makes you go all funny! Why, I'd never have believed it of you—at your age! By the by, how old are you?"

The lie came out automatically after his practice during the past two days.

"Sixteen."

"Sixteen?" She sounded surprised.

She had taken his hand and was examining it absent-mindedly. Pushing back the sleeve, she uncovered his arm.

"My word, the kid's skin is as white as a girl's," she smiled.

She had raised the boy's wrist and was fondling his hand with her cheek. The smile died from her face. Taking a deep breath, she dropped his hand. Before he realized what she was doing, she had unfastened her skirt.

"I'm cold. Warm me up!" she whispered, slipping between the blankets.

Jacques had slept badly under the tarpaulin stiffened by the cold rain. Before dawn he had crept from his hiding-place and begun to wander aimlessly in the dim light of daybreak. "It's certain," he mused, "that if Daniel's free, he'll have the idea of going to the station buffet as we did yesterday." He was there, himself, before five o'clock. At six he still could not make up his mind where to go.

What was he to think? What should he do? He ascertained where the prison was. Sick at heart, he hardly dared to raise his eyes to the closed entrance-gate: City Jail.

There, perhaps, Daniel . . . He dared not complete the thought. He walked all round the endless wall, stepped back to judge the height of the barred windows; then, seized with sudden fear, he fled.

All that morning he scoured the town. The sun was blazing hot and the bright colours of the linen hanging out to dry made the crowded streets seem gay with bunting. On doorsteps gossips laughed and chattered in acrimonious tones. The sights of the street, its freedom and adventurous possibilities, gave him a brief exhilaration. But at once his thoughts harked back to Daniel. He held the bottle of iodine clutched in his hand, deep down in his pocket; if he did not find Daniel before night, he would kill himself. He swore it, raising his voice a little to bind himself more strongly; inwardly he wondered if he would have the necessary courage.

It was not till nearly eleven, when he was passing for the hundredth time in front of the café where, the evening before, they had asked the way to the shipping office, that—yes, there he was!

Jacques charged down on him between the tables and chairs lining the terrace. Daniel, more self-controlled, had risen.

"Steady there!"

People were staring at them. They shook hands, Daniel paid, and, leaving the café, they turned down the nearest side-street. Then Jacques clutched his friend's arm and, clinging to him, hugged him passionately. Suddenly he began to sob, his forehead pressed to Daniel's shoulder. Daniel was not crying, but he was very pale. He walked steadily on, his gaze untender and focused far ahead, but he was pressing Jacques's small hand to his side. His upper lip, drawn back across his teeth on one side of his mouth, was trembling.

Jacques described his adventures. "Just think, I slept on the quay like a thief, under a tarpaulin! What about you?"

Daniel was embarrassed. His respect for his friend and for their friendship was immense; yet now, for the first time, he was bound to conceal something from Jacques, something of vital importance. The enormity of the secret that had come between them overpowered him. He was on the point of letting himself go, of telling everything; but no, he could not. He remained ill at ease and tongue-tied, unable to expel the haunting memory of all that had befallen him.

"What about you?" Jacques repeated. "Where did you spend the night?"

Daniel made a vague gesture. "On a seat, over there. But most of the time I just mooned about."

After a meal, they talked things over. To stay in Marseille would be imprudent: their movements would be bound to arouse suspicion, sooner or later.

"In that case . . . ?" Daniel murmured tentatively.

"In that case," Jacques replied, "I know what to do. We must go to Toulon. It's only ten or twenty miles from here, over there on the left, along the coast. We'll go on foot; they'll think we're schoolboys out for a walk. At Toulon there are any number of boats, and we'll manage somehow or other to get on board one."

While he spoke, Daniel could not take his eyes off the loved face
that he had found again, the freckled cheeks, the frail, almost trans-
parent ears, and the blue eyes in which seemed to come and go pictures of the things he was describing: Toulon and ships and the vast
horizons of the sea. But, however great his desire to share Jacques's
fine tenacity of purpose, his common sense made him sceptical; he
felt sure they would never set out on that voyage. . . . And yet was
it really so impossible? At times almost he hoped he was wrong, that
dreams might prove truer than common sense.

They bought some food and started for Toulon. Two women of
the town stared at them, and smiled. Daniel blushed; their skirts no
longer hid from him the secrets of their bodies. Fortunately Jacques
was whistling, and noticed nothing. Daniel felt that that experience,
the mere memory of which made his heart beat faster, would be from
now on a barrier between them. Jacques could never now be his
friend in the fullest sense; he was only a "kid."

After passing through the suburbs they reached at last a road ribboning the windings of the coast like a line traced in pink chalk along
the seashore. A light breeze met them, with a tang that had an after-
taste of brine. Their shoulders scorched by the sun, they trudged
through the white dust. The nearness of the sea intoxicated them; they
left the road and ran to it, crying: *"Thalassa! Thalassa!"* and reaching eager hands towards the sparkling blue waves. But the sea proved
less easy of access than they had hoped. At the point where they approached it, the shore did not shelve down to the water's edge along
the reach of golden sand their eagerness had pictured. It overhung a
deep gulf of equal width throughout, in which the sea was breaking
over dark, jagged rocks. Immediately below them a mass of tumbled
boulders projected like a Cyclopean breakwater; waves were charging
furiously against the granite ledges only to slip back in impotent confusion, foam-flecked, along the smooth, steep flanks. They had joined
hands and, bending over the abyss, forgot everything in contemplation
of the seething eddies faceted with broken lights. And in their wordless ecstasy there was a certain awe.

"Look!" Daniel said.

A few hundred yards out a boat, a miracle of dazzling whiteness, was gliding over the dark blue expanse. The hull was painted green beneath the water-line, the bright green of a young leaf, and the boat was moving forward to a strong rhythm of oars that lifted the bows clean out of the water and with each stroke displayed a streaming glint of green, vivid as an electric spark.

"Ah, if only one could describe all that!" Jacques murmured, crushing the note-book in his pocket between his fingers. "But you'll see!" he cried, with a jerk of his shoulders. "Africa is even more lovely! Come along!"

He dashed back, between the rocks, onto the road. Daniel ran beside him, and for the moment his heart was care-free, emptied of regret, all eagerness for adventure.

They came to a place where the road climbed and turned off at a right angle, to reach a group of houses. Just when they came to the bend, a terrific uproar made them stop abruptly; they saw charging down at break-neck speed towards them, zigzagging across the road, what seemed to be a confused mass of horses, wheels, and barrels. Before they could make a movement to get out of the way, it had crashed, fifty yards off, against an iron railing. A large, heavily laden dray, coming down the slope, had not been braked in time. The momentum of its downward rush had swept the four horses drawing it off their feet and, rearing, struggling, tripping over one another, they had fallen at the turn. Wine was gushing out onto the road and a crowd of excited men, shouting and swearing and waving their arms, was gathering round a hideous, inextricable tangle of bleeding nostrils, hoofs, and cruppers floundering in the dust. Suddenly across the thuds of steel-shod hoofs against the iron apron, the clank of chains, jangling bells, the neighing of the other horses, and the imprecations of the drivers, there sounded a hoarse, grating cough that dominated all the other sounds. It was the death-rattle of the leader, a grey horse on which the others were trampling and which, its legs pinned under him, was suffocating, strangled by the harness. A man dashed in amongst the maddened horses, brandishing an axe. They saw him stumble, fall, and rise again; now he was holding the grey horse by an ear and desperately hacking at his collar. But the collar was of iron and he merely dented the edge of his axe upon it. The man drew himself up, his features convulsed with helpless rage, and flung the axe against the wall, while the rattle rose to a strident gasping that grew shriller and shriller, and a stream of blood gushed from the dying horse's nostrils.

Jacques felt the world reeling around him. He tried to grasp Daniel's sleeve, but his fingers went stiff and his nerveless legs gave way under him. People gathered round the boys; Jacques was helped to a seat in a little garden, beside a pump, and a kindly soul began bathing his forehead with cold water. Daniel was as pale as he.

When they returned to the road, the whole village was busy with the barrels. The horses had been extricated. Of the four only one had escaped unscathed; two, their forelegs broken, were kneeling on the road. The fourth was dead and lay sprawling in the ditch into which the wine was flowing, his grey head pressed to the earth, his tongue lolling, his glazed eyes half shut, and his legs neatly doubled up beneath him—as if, before dying, he had tried to make himself as portable as could be for the knacker. The utter stillness of the shaggy grey bulk, smeared with blood and wine and road-dust, was in striking contrast with the heaving flanks of the other horses, standing or kneeling, unheeded, in the middle of the road.

They watched one of the truckmen go up to the dead horse. The old, weathered face with the sweat-matted hair was convulsed with rage yet had a certain gravity ennobling it and proving how much he took to heart the disaster. Jacques could not take his eyes off him. He watched him place between his lips a cigarette he had been holding, then bend over the fallen horse and feel the swollen tongue already black with flies, and insert his finger in the mouth, baring the yellow teeth. He remained for a few moments, stooping, running his fingers over the mottled gums. Then he straightened himself up and sought some friendly eye. His gaze met that of the two boys and, without troubling to wipe his hands, smeared with sticky froth in which flies were crawling, he replaced the cigarette between his lips.

"He wasn't seven, that poor horse," he said with an angry jerk of his shoulders. Then he turned to Jacques. "The best one of the team, he was, the hardest worker of the lot. I'd give two of my fingers, these two, to have him back." He looked away, a wry smile screwing up his lips, and spat.

The boys began to walk away, and now their gaiety had given place to a profound dejection.

"Have you ever seen a real corpse, a human being's, I mean?" Jacques suddenly inquired.

"No."

"You've no idea, Daniel, how strange it looks. . . . I'd been thinking about it for a longish while; then one Sunday, at catechism time, I rushed off there."

"Where?"

"To the Morgue."

"What? By yourself?"

"Of course. You simply can't imagine, Daniel, how pale a corpse can be. Just like wax, or plaster of Paris. There were two corpses there that day. One had its face all gashed about, but the other looked almost alive. . . . Yes, it looked alive," he repeated, "but at the very first glance you couldn't help knowing the man was dead. There was something about him—oh, I don't know what. You saw that horse just now; well, it was just the same thing. . . . One day, when we're free," he added, "some Sunday, you must come there with me, to the Morgue."

Daniel had ceased to listen. They had just passed below the balcony of a house from which there came the tinkle of a piano: a child was playing scales. Jenny! And suddenly there rose before him Jenny's delicately moulded features, the expression of her face when she had cried to him: "What are you going to do?" while the tears welled up in her grey eyes, large with wonder.

"Aren't you sorry you haven't got a sister?" he asked after a while.

"Yes, I am! An elder sister's what I'd like. I have a—a sort of little sister." Seeing Daniel's puzzled look, he added: "Mademoiselle is bringing up at home a little niece of hers, an orphan. Gise is ten. Her name's Gisèle, but we call her Gise for short. She's just like a little sister to me."

Suddenly his eyes grew moist. Then his thoughts took a new turn. "You, of course, were brought up in a quite different way. For one thing, you're an ordinary day-boy, you're almost free, you have much the same life as Antoine. . . . But, then, you're such a sensible chap—that makes all the difference." There was a hint of regret in his tone.

"Meaning—you're *not* a sensible chap?" There was no irony in Daniel's tone.

"I 'sensible'!" Jacques's eyebrows puckered. "Don't I know that I'm . . . unbearable! And there's nothing to be done about it. Sometimes I have fits of rage, you know, when I lose my grip on things completely—I storm about and break things, I shout most horrible words; when I'd be quite capable of jumping out of a window or knocking somebody down. I'd rather you knew everything about me, that's why I'm telling you all this." It was evident that he took a morose pleasure in accusing himself. "I don't know if it's my fault, or not. I rather think that, if I lived with you, I shouldn't be like that. But I'm not so sure.

"At home, when I come back in the evening—if you only could imagine what they're like!" he went on, after a while, staring into the distance. "Father has never taken me seriously. The Abbés tell him I'm a perfect terror at school; that's to suck up to him, of course, to make out they're having no end of trouble bringing up the son of M. Thibault, who has a lot of influence with the Cathedral people. But Papa is kind, you know"—his voice took on a sudden fervour—"awfully kind, really. Only—I don't know how to explain it. He's so wrapped up in his public duties, his committees, in his lectures and religion. And Mademoiselle, too; whenever something goes wrong with me, it's always God who's punishing me for my sins. Do you understand? After dinner Papa always shuts himself up in his study, and Mademoiselle hears my lessons—I never know them!—in Gise's room, while she puts her to bed. She won't even let me stay alone in my room. They've unscrewed my switch—would you believe it?—to prevent me using the electric light."

"What about your brother?" Daniel asked.

"Oh, Antoine, he's an awfully good sort; only he's always out. I rather think, though he's never said anything to me about it, that he, too, doesn't much like being at home. He was quite grown up when Mother died; he's exactly nine years older than I—so Mademoiselle never managed to get much of a hold over him. It's different for me, of course; she's looked after me all my life."

Daniel said nothing.

"You can't imagine what it's like," Jacques repeated. "Your people know how to treat *you;* you've been brought up quite differently. It's the same with books. *You* are allowed to read everything; all the bookshelves are open in your home. But I'm never allowed to read anything except rotten old picture-books, bound in red and gold, Jules Verne, and all that sort of rubbish. They don't even know I write poetry. It's just as well. They'd raise such a row about it, they wouldn't understand. And very likely they'd ask the masters to keep an eye on me and give me a putrid time at school."

There was a rather long silence. Swerving from the sea, the road began to climb towards a grove of cork-trees.

Suddenly Daniel drew nearer Jacques and took his arm.

"Listen," he said, and his voice, which was just breaking, had a low, sonorous emphasis, "I'm thinking of the future. One never can tell. We might be separated from each other some day. There's something I've been wanting to ask you for a long time, something that would . . . would seal our friendship, for always. Promise that you'll dedicate your first book of poems to me. Oh, you needn't put the name. Just, *To My Friend*. Will you, Jacques?"

"I swear it," Jacques said, and it seemed to him that he had suddenly grown taller. . . .

Entering the wood, they sat down under the trees. Over Marseille the sun was setting in a blaze of fire. Feeling his ankles swollen and painful, Jacques took off his shoes and socks and lay down on the grass. Daniel looked at him absent-mindedly; then suddenly he averted his eyes from the small bare feet with the reddened heels.

"Look, there's a lighthouse!" Jacques exclaimed, pointing towards the horizon. Daniel gave a start. Far away, on the coast, an intermittent gleam raked the dusk. Daniel made no comment.

The air was cooler when they started off again. They had intended to sleep out under the trees, but it looked like being a bitterly cold night.

They walked on for half an hour without exchanging a word. Presently they came to a newly white-washed inn, with arbours overlooking the sea.

The lights were on in the main room; it was apparently empty. They eyed each other doubtfully. A woman, who had seen them hesitating near the entrance, opened the door. She held up to their faces a glass lamp, the oil in which gleamed like a topaz. She was a short, elderly person, with two gold pendants dangling from her ears along her scraggy neck.

"Excuse me, Madame," Daniel said; "could you let us have a room with two beds for the night?" Without giving her time to put any questions, he went on. "My brother and I are on our way to meet our father at Toulon; only we left Marseille too late to reach Toulon tonight."

"That's a good one!" the woman laughed. She had merry, surprisingly youthful eyes, and gesticulated freely as she talked. "You were going to Toulon on foot, were you? Tell that to the marines, my boy! Anyhow, it's all the same to me. Yes, you can have a room for two francs—cash down, of course." And, while Daniel was bringing out his wallet, she added: "I've some soup on the fire. Like a couple of platefuls?"

Both said yes.

The room was an attic and there was only one bed, the sheets of which showed signs of having already been used. Prompted by the same unspoken motive, they rapidly took off their shoes and slipped into bed, fully dressed, back to back.

It was long before they fell asleep. The moon shone full through
the window. Rats were scampering about in an adjoining loft.
Jacques saw a hideous-looking spider crawling on the dingy grey wall
and, as he watched it vanish into the darkness, vowed he would
stay awake all night. Daniel's mind was full of pictures of the sensual
pleasure of the morning, and imagination was already adding its
lascivious glamour to his memories. Sweating, thrilled with delight,
disgust, and curiosity, he dared not move.

Next morning, when Jacques was still asleep, Daniel was on the
point of rising, to get some respite from the phantoms of his imagination, when he heard a disturbance in the inn-parlour below. So vivid
had been his nightlong obsessions that his first idea was that the
police were coming to arrest him for his licentious conduct. And, no
sooner did the door open (the bolt had broken off) than it was a
policeman who appeared, accompanied by the proprietress. As he
came in he hit his forehead on the lintel and knocked off his *képi*.

"The youngsters fetched up here last evening, covered with dust."
The woman was still laughing, her ear-drops swaying to and fro.
"They told me all sorts of fancy yarns—that they wanted to walk
all the way to Toulon, and the good Lord knows what else! And
that young scamp"—she extended a long arm jingling with bangles
towards Daniel—"gave me a hundred-franc note to pay the four francs
fifty for their room and supper."

The gendarme was dusting his *képi* with an air of bored indifference.

"Come along, boys, up with you!" he grumbled. "Now then, what's
your names, first names, and the rest of it?"

Daniel hesitated. But Jacques jumped off the bed in his knicker-
bockers and socks, aggressive as a young fighting-cock. For a moment
it looked as if he would try to lay out the tall, stalwart gendarme.

"I'm Maurice Legrand!" he shouted in the man's face. "And this
is Georges, my brother. Our father's at Toulon. And you shan't stop
us going to meet him there. I defy you to!"

A few hours later they were entering Marseille in a farm-cart, with two gendarmes and a miscreant in handcuffs beside them. The lofty prison-gate opened, then clanged to behind them.

"Go in there," a policeman told them, opening the door of a cell. "Now turn out your pockets. Yes, hand it all over. You'll be left together till dinner-time, while we check up on your story."

But long before then a sergeant came and took them to the inspector's office.

"It's no use denying it, my boys; you're nabbed. We've been looking for you since Sunday. You've come from Paris; the big boy's name is Fontanin, and you are Thibault. Fancy boys like you, from decent families, taking to the roads like little tramps!"

Daniel had assumed an air of outraged dignity, but inwardly he felt vastly relieved. Thank goodness, it was over! His mother knew by now that he was alive and safe, and she was awaiting his return. He would beg her forgiveness, and that would blot out everything— yes, everything!—even what he was thinking of with such horror at that moment. *That,* anyhow, he would never dare to confess to any one in the world.

Jacques gritted his teeth and, remembering his bottle of iodine and the dagger, clenched his fists ragefully in his empty pockets. A host of schemes for vengeance or escape flashed through his mind. But just then the officer spoke again.

"Your poor parents are in a terrible state."

Jacques cast a furious glance around him; then suddenly his face seemed to crumple up and he burst into tears. He had pictured his father, Mademoiselle, little Gise. . . . His heart overflowed with affection and regret.

"Now go and have a sleep," the inspector went on. "We'll fix things up for you tomorrow. I'm waiting for instructions."

VIII

For two days Jenny had been in a comatose state; the fever had gone down, leaving her very weak. Standing at the window, Mme. de Fontanin was keenly on the alert for every sound that came from the avenue. Antoine had gone to Marseille to fetch the runaways and was due to bring them home that evening. Nine o'clock had just struck; they should be here by now.

She gave a start. That surely was a cab pulling up in front of the house!

In a flash she was out on the landing outside the entrance of her flat, clasping the banisters. The dog had run out after her and was barking to greet the homecomer. Mme. de Fontanin leaned over the rail. There, suddenly, queerly foreshortened by the height, there he was coming up the stairs! That was his hat, with the brim hiding his face; that was the way he had of moving his shoulders as he walked. He was in front; Antoine followed, holding his brother by the hand.

Looking up, Daniel saw his mother. The landing lamp, just above her head, made her hair snow-white, and plunged her face in shadow, yet it seemed to him he had seen her every feature. With lowered eyes he continued on his way up the stairs, intuitively conscious that she was coming down to meet him. Suddenly he felt incapable of making another step, and, just as he was taking off his hat, still not daring to raise his head and hardly daring to breathe, he found himself clasped in her arms, his forehead on her breast. Yet he felt little of the joy he had expected. He had longed so intensely for this moment that when it came he had no more feeling left, and when at last he freed himself from her embrace, his face was shamefast, tearless. It was Jacques, with his back against the staircase wall, who burst out sobbing.

Mme. de Fontanin took her son's face between her hands, and drew it to her lips. Not a word of reproach; a long kiss. But the

agony of mind she had endured during that terrible week made her
voice tremble when she spoke to Antoine.

"Have the poor children had any dinner?"

Before Antoine could reply, Daniel had murmured: "Jenny? How
is she?"

"She's out of danger now; she's in bed and you shall see her;
she is waiting for you." Daniel freed himself at once and ran into
the flat. She called after him: "Gently, dear! Don't forget she's been
very ill. You mustn't excite her."

Jacques's tears were quickly dried, and now he could not refrain
from casting a curious glance around him. So this was Daniel's
home, this was the staircase he climbed each day when he came back
from school; that was the hall he entered and this the lady he called
"Mother" with that strange tenderness in his voice.

"What about you, Jacques?" she smiled. "Will you kiss me, too?"
"Speak up, Jacques!" Antoine laughed, giving his brother a slight
push.

She extended her arms towards him. Jacques slipped between them,
pillowing his head where Daniel's had lain a little while before. Pensively Mme. de Fontanin stroked the boy's red hair; then, turning
towards the elder brother, she tried to smile. As Antoine remained
standing by the door, evidently anxious to leave, she held out to him,
over the head of the boy whose arms were round her now, both her
hands in token of her gratitude, and said to Jacques:

"Go, my dear; your father, too, must be longing to see you."

Jenny's door stood open.

Kneeling at the bedside on one knee, his head resting on the sheets,
Daniel was pressing his lips to his sister's hands, clasped within his
own. Jenny had been crying; to reach out towards him she had twisted
herself sideways on the pillow, and the strain showed on her face. It
was so emaciated as to seem expressionless, but for the eyes. In their
look there still was something morbid, and a trace of hardness, almost
obstinacy; they were almost the eyes of a grown woman, and they
had a dark inscrutability, wise beyond her years, as if the light-
heartedness of youth had long forsaken her.

Mme. de Fontanin went up to the bed. On the point of bending down and gathering the two children in her arms she remembered that she must take care not to tire Jenny. She made Daniel get up and come with her to her own room.

The room was brightly lit and cheerful. In front of the fireplace Mme. de Fontanin had set out the tea-table, with toast and butter and honey. Kept hot under a napkin was a mound of boiled chestnuts, one of Daniel's favourite dishes. The kettle was purring; the room was very warm and the air so stuffy that Daniel felt almost nauseated. He waved away the plate his mother held out to him. A look of disappointment settled on her face.

"What is it, dear? I hope you're not going to deprive me of the pleasure of a cup of tea with you this evening?"

Daniel gazed at her. Something about her had changed; what was it? She was drinking her tea as she always did, in little scalding sips, and he could see her face with the light behind it smiling through the vapour rising from her cup. Yes, for all its traces of exhaustion, it was the face that he had always known. But there was something in the smile, the lingering gaze—no, he could not bear its too-much-sweetness! Lowering his eyes, he helped himself to buttered toast and, to keep himself in countenance, pretended to be eating it. She smiled all the more, lost in her wordless happiness, and found an out-let for her rush of emotion in gently stroking the head of the little dog, which was nestling in the folds of her dress.

Daniel put down his toast. Without raising his eyes, he asked: "What did they tell you at the Lycée?" His cheeks had gone pale.

"I told them—it wasn't true."

At last Daniel's brows relaxed. Raising his eyes, he met his mother's gaze; there was trust in it but, none the less, a silent question, as if she sought for confirmation of her trust. And happily Daniel's candid eyes confirmed it beyond all manner of doubt. Her face was shining with joy as she went up to him.

"Why," she whispered, "oh, why didn't you come and tell me about it, my big boy, instead of . . . ?"

She left the question unended, and stood up. There was the jingle of a bunch of keys in the hall. She stood unmoving, looking towards the opening door. The dog began wagging its tail and ran, without barking, to meet the old friend who had entered.

It was Jerome.

He was smiling.

Wearing neither overcoat nor hat, he came in so naturally that one could have sworn he had just walked across from his own room. He glanced at Daniel, but went up at once to his wife and kissed her extended hand. A faint perfume of verbena and lavender hovered round him.

"Well, darling, here I am! What's been happening? Really, I've been dreadfully worried."

Daniel went up to him delightedly. Little by little he had come to love his father, though in early childhood he had for many years displayed an exclusive, jealous affection for his mother. Even now he accepted with unconscious satisfaction the fact that his father was so often away and left them to themselves.

"So you're back, Daniel, after all? What's all this they've been telling me about you?" Jerome was holding his son's chin and observing him frowningly.

Mme. de Fontanin had remained standing. "When he returns," she had said to herself, "I shall refuse to let him stay." Her resentment had not weakened, nor her resolve; but he had caught her unawares, had taken everything for granted with such airy unconcern that she was at a loss. She could not take her eyes off him; she would not admit to herself how profoundly she was affected by his presence, how touched she still was by the winning charm of his look, his smile, his gestures; would not admit that he was the one love of her life. The money problem had just crossed her mind, and she fell back on it to justify her weakness. That morning she had had to broach the remnants of her savings, and now was practically at her last penny. Jerome, of course, knew it; probably he was bringing the money needed to tide over the month.

At a loss how to answer, Daniel had turned to his mother, and just then he saw a look flitting across the calm, maternal face, a look of something—he could not have put it into words—something so significant, so intimate, that he turned away with a feeling of bashfulness. At Marseille he had lost even the innocence of the eye.

"Ought I to scold him, sweetheart?" Jerome's lips parted in an insinuating smile that showed his flashing teeth. "Must I play the stern father?"

She did not reply at once. Then, with an undertone of bitterness, of a desire to punish him, she blurted out: "Do you realize that Jenny very nearly died?"

He let go his son and took a step towards her, and such was the consternation on his face that she was ready to forgive him on the spot, if only to wipe out the distress that she had deliberately caused him.

"But she's much better now. The danger's past!" she exclaimed. She forced herself to smile, so as to reassure him the sooner, and the smile was tantamount to a capitulation. She was aware of it. Everything seemed to be conspiring against her dignity.

"Go and see her," she added, noticing that Jerome's hands were shaking. "But please don't wake her."

Some minutes passed. Mme. de Fontanin sat down. Jerome came back on tip-toe, shutting the door very carefully. His face was radiant with affection; no trace of apprehension remained. He was laughing again, and his eyes twinkled.

"Ah, if you'd seen her just now! Charming! She's lying on her side, her cheek resting on her hand." His fingers sketched in air the graceful outlines. "She has grown thinner, but that's almost a good thing, really; it makes her all the prettier, don't you think so?"

She did not answer. He was staring at her with a puzzled air.

"Why, Thérèse, you've gone quite white!"

She rose, and almost ran to the mirror above the mantelpiece. It was true; in those two days of anxiety her hair, which till then had been fair, with a light silver sheen, had turned completely white over the temples. And now Daniel understood what had seemed to him different, inexplicable since his homecoming. Mme. de Fontanin scanned her reflected self, uncertain of her feelings but unable to stifle a regret. Then, in the mirror, she saw Jerome's face smiling towards her and unwittingly she found a consolation in his smile. He seemed amused, and lightly touched a vagrant silver lock that floated in the lamplight.

"Nothing could suit you better, sweetheart; nothing could better set off—what shall I call it?—the youngness of your eyes."

When she answered, the words, seemingly an excuse, served to mask her secret pleasure.

"Oh, Jerome, I've been through some awful days and nights! On Wednesday we'd tried everything, and we'd lost hope. I was all alone. I was so frightened!"

"Poor darling!" he cried impulsively. "I'm dreadfully sorry; I could so easily have come back. I was at Lyon on that business you know about." He spoke with such assurance that for a moment she began to search her memory. "I'd completely forgotten that you hadn't my address. And besides, I'd only gone away for twenty-four hours; I've even wasted my return ticket."

Just then it flashed across his mind that he had given Thérèse no money for a long while. Annoying! He had no money coming in for another three weeks. He reckoned up what he had on him and unthinkingly made a grimace which, however, he promptly explained away.

"And to think that all my trouble was practically wasted—I just couldn't put that deal through! I went on hoping till the last day, but here I am back again, with empty pockets! Those fat Lyon bankers are infernally hard to deal with, an unbelieving lot." He launched into a story of his experiences, letting his fertile imagination run away with him, without a trace of embarrassment; he had the born story-teller's delight in his inventions.

Daniel, as he listened, felt for the first time a sort of shame for his father. Then, for no reason, without any apparent relevance, he thought of the man the woman at Marseille had told him about, her "old boy" as she had called him—a married man, in business, who always came in the afternoon, she had explained, because he never went out in the evening without "his missus." In the face of his mother, who was listening too, there was something that baffled him. Their eyes met. What did the mother read in her son's eyes? Did she see far within, into thoughts to which as yet Daniel himself had given no definite form? When she spoke there was an abruptness in her tone that betrayed her annoyance.

"Now run away to bed, my dear; you're absolutely tired out."

He obeyed. But just as he stooped to kiss her, a picture rose before him of his mother so cruelly forsaken while Jenny was on her death-bed. And his affection was enhanced by a realization of the distress he had caused her. He embraced her tenderly, murmuring in her ear:

"Forgive me."

She had been waiting for those words since his return, and now she could not feel the happiness she would have felt, had he uttered them sooner. Daniel was conscious of this, and inwardly blamed his father for it. Mme. de Fontanin, however, could not help feeling a grievance against her son; why had he not spoken sooner, while they were alone together?

Half in boyish playfulness, half out of mere gluttony, Jerome had gone up to the tray and was examining the "spread" with comically pursed lips.

"My word, and who are all these nice things for?"

His laughter never sounded quite natural; he would throw back his head, slewing round his pupils into the corners of his eyes, and then emit in quick succession three rather theatrical Ha's: "Ha! Ha! Ha!"

He had drawn up a stool to the table and was already busy with the tea-pot.

"Don't drink that tea, it's almost cold," Mme. de Fontanin said, and lit the spirit-lamp under the kettle. When he protested, she added, but unsmilingly: "No—I insist!"

They were alone. To attend to the tea, she had come up to the table, and the bitter-sweet perfume of the lavender and verbena scent he used came to her nostrils. He looked up at her with a half-smile; his look conveyed at once affection and repentance. Keeping his slice of buttered toast in one hand, like a hungry schoolboy, he slipped an arm round his wife's waist with a free-and-easy deftness that showed long experience in the amorous art. Mme. de Fontanin freed herself abruptly; she knew her weakness, and dreaded it. When he withdrew his arm she came back to finish making the tea, then moved away once more.

She wore a look of dignity and sadness, but somehow his complete insouciance had taken the sting out of her resentment. She studied his appearance, surreptitiously, in the mirror. His amber-coloured skin, his almond eyes, the graceful poise of his body, the slightly exotic refinement of his dress, and his languid airs gave him an oriental charm. She remembered having written in her diary, during their engagement: *My Beloved is beautiful as an Indian Prince.* And even tonight she was seeing him through the same eyes as in those far-off days. He was sitting slantwise on a stool that was too low for him, and stretching his legs towards the fire. Daintily his fingers, tipped by well-manicured nails, were taking up slices of toast, one after another, and gilding them with honey. As, bending above the plate, he ate them, his white teeth flashed. When he had finished eating, he drank his tea at a gulp, rose with a dancer's suppleness, and ensconced himself in an arm-chair. He behaved exactly as if nothing had happened and he were living here now just as he had always done. The dog jumped onto his knee and he began patting it. His left ring-finger bore a large sardonyx ring left him by his mother, an ancient cameo on which the milk-white figure of a Ganymede rose from a deep black background. The gold had worn down with the years and the ring kept on slipping to and fro as he moved his hand. His wife watched all his gestures intently.

"Do you mind if I light a cigarette, sweetheart?"

Incorrigible he was—but how charming! He had a way of his own of pronouncing that word "sweetheart," letting the syllables flutter on his lips, like a kiss. His silver cigarette-case shone between his fingers; she recognized so well the little brittle click it made and, yes, he had still that habit of tapping his cigarette on the back of his hand before putting it into his mouth. And how well she knew them, too, those long,

veined hands that the lighted match changed suddenly to two translucent, flame-red shells!

She steeled herself to calmness as she cleared the tea-table. This
last week had broken her, and she realized it just at the moment she
needed all her courage. She sat down. She no longer knew what to
think; she could not clearly discern what the Spirit wished of her.
Was it God's will that she should stay beside this sinner who, even
in his worst lapses, always remained amenable to the promptings of
his kindly heart, so that she might guide him one day towards a
better life? No, her immediate duty was to safeguard the home, the
children. Little by little she was vanquishing her weakness, and it was
a relief to find herself more resolute than she had foreseen. The decision she had come to during Jerome's absence—when, after prayer,
a still small voice within had counselled her—held good.

Jerome had been watching her for some time with meditative
eyes. Now his face took on an expression of intense sincerity. Only
too well she knew that seeming-timid smile, that look of circumspec-
tion; and they dismayed her. For, though she had a knack of deciphering at any moment, almost without conscious effort, what lay behind
her husband's frequent changes of expression, all the same her intuition always ended by being held up at a certain definite point, beyond
which lay a quicksand of uncertainties. How often she had asked
herself: What kind of man is he really, under the surface?

"I see how it is." There was a touch of rather perfunctory regret
in Jerome's voice. "I can see you judge me severely, Thérèse. Oh, I
understand you—only too well. If another man behaved like that,
I'd judge him as you do. I'd think of him as being a scoundrel. Yes,
a scoundrel—why mince words? Ah, how on earth can I make you
understand . . . ?"

"What's the good?" she broke in miserably, casting him a naïvely
beseeching look. Never, alas, could she conceal her feelings!

He was smoking, lying well back in the arm-chair; he had crossed
his legs, and the ankle of the leg he was indolently swinging was
well in evidence.

"Don't worry, Thérèse; I'm not going to argue about it. The facts are there, and the facts condemn me. And yet . . . perhaps there are other explanations for it all than the all too obvious ones." He smiled sadly. He had a weakness for expatiating on his faults, and invoking arguments of a moral order—a procedure which perhaps appeased what was left of his Protestant upbringing. "Often," he said, "a bad deed springs from motives of a different kind. One may seem to be out merely to gratify, quite shamelessly, one's instincts, but sometimes, indeed quite often, one is actually giving way to an emotion that is not a bad one—to pity, for instance. When one causes suffering to someone whom one loves, the reason sometimes is that one's sorry for someone else, someone who's in trouble, or of a lower walk of life—to whom a little kindness might mean salvation."

A picture rose before her of the girl she had seen sobbing by the riverside. And other memories took form, of Mariette, of Noémie. . . . Her eyes were held by the movement of his patent-leather shoe, swinging to and fro, now lit up by the lamplight, now in shadow. She remembered the early days of their marriage—those "business dinners," so urgent and so unforeseen, from which he had come back at dawn, only to shut himself up in his room and sleep till evening. And all the anonymous letters she had glanced through, then torn up, burned, or ground under her heel, but without being able to stamp out their rankling maleficence. She had seen Jerome seduce her maids, and turn the heads of her friends, one by one. He had made a void around her. She remembered the reproaches which at first she had ventured to address to him, and the many occasions on which, without making any "scene," she had spoken to him frankly but with indulgence—only to find herself confronted by a being at the mercy of his every impulse, self-centred and evasive, who began by denying everything with puritanical indignation and, immediately after, vowed smilingly that he would never do it again.

"Yes, indeed," he was saying, "I've treated you abominably. Abominably! Don't let's be afraid of words. And yet I love you, Thérèse, with all my soul; I look up to you and I'm sorry for you. There's been nothing in my life, nothing which at any time, even for a moment, could stand beside my love for you, the only truly deep and permanent love I've ever felt.

"Yes, my way of living is disgusting; I don't defend it, I'm ashamed of it. But really, sweetheart, you're doing me an injustice; yes, for all your sense of justice, you're unfair if you judge me by my acts. I admit my . . . my lapses, but they aren't all of me. Oh, I'm explaining myself badly, I know; I feel you aren't listening to me. It's all so terribly complicated, far more so than I can ever explain, in fact. I only get glimpses of it myself, in flashes. . . ."

He fell silent and leaned forward, his eyes focused on the void, as if he had worn himself out in a vain effort to attain for a moment the uttermost truth about his life. Then he raised his head and Mme. de Fontanin felt his gaze lingering on her face, that careless glance of his, seemingly so light, but endowed with a strange power of fascination for the eyes of others. It was as if his gaze drew their eyes towards it, and held them trapped inescapably for a moment, then released them—like a magnet attracting, lifting, and letting fall a weight too heavy for it. Once again their eyes met and parted. She was thinking: "Yes, you are better than the life you lead." But she merely shrugged her shoulders.

"You don't believe me?" he murmured.

"Oh, I'm quite ready to believe you." She tried to speak in a detached tone. "I've done it so many times before . . . but that isn't the point. Guilty or not, responsible or not, Jerome, you have done wrong, you are doing wrong every day, and will go on doing so. And that state of things can't be allowed to last. Let us part for good."

The fact that she had been thinking it over so assiduously during the past four days imparted to her voice an emphasis and harshness that Jerome could not ignore. Seeing his amazement and distress, she hastened to add:

"It's the children I'm thinking of. So long as they were small, they didn't understand, and I was the only one who . . ." On the point of adding "suffered," a sense of shame prevented her. "The wrong you've done me, Jerome, no longer concerns me only and my . . .

personal feelings. It comes in here with you, it's in the very air of our
home, the air my children breathe. I will not allow this state of things
to go on. Look what Daniel did this week! May God forgive him,
as I've forgiven him for hurting me so cruelly. He is sorry for it;
his heart is still uncorrupted." Her eyes lit with a flash of pride that
was almost a challenge. "But I'm sure it was your example that led
him astray. Would he have gone off so light-heartedly, without a
thought for my anxiety, if he hadn't seen you so often going away
from us . . . on 'business'?" She rose, took an uncertain step towards
the fireplace, and saw in the mirror her white hair; then, bending a
little towards her husband, without looking at him, she went on speaking. "I've been thinking deeply about it, Jerome. I have suffered a great
deal this week and I have prayed and pondered. I've not the least
wish to reproach you. In any case, I'm feeling so dreadfully tired tonight, I don't wish to talk about it. I only ask you to face the facts.
You'll have to admit I'm right, that there's no other way out. Life in
common"—she caught herself up—"what remains to us of our life in
common, little though it is, is still too much. Yes, Jerome, too much."
She drew herself erect, rested her hands on the marble mantelpiece,
and, stressing each word with a movement of her head and shoulders, said gravely: *"I will not bear it any longer."*

Jerome made no answer, but, before she could retreat, he had slipped
to her feet and pressed his face against her knee, like a child pleading
to be forgiven.

"How could I possibly separate from you?" he murmured abjectly.
"How could I live without my children? I'd rather blow my brains
out!"

She felt almost like smiling, so naïvely melodramatic was the gesture
with which he aimed his forefinger at his forehead. Thérèse's arm was
hanging at her side; grasping her wrist, he covered it with kisses.
Gently she freed her hand and listlessly, hardly knowing what she
was doing, began to stroke his forehead with her fingertips. The
gesture, seemingly maternal, was one of utter, unchangeable detachment. He misinterpreted it and raised his head; but a glance at her
face showed him how grievously he was mistaken. She moved away

at once, and pointed to a travelling-clock on the bedside table. "Two o'clock. It's terribly late. No more tonight, please. Tomorrow, perhaps. . . ."

He glanced at the clock and from it to the double bed with its solitary pillow, made ready for the night.

"I'm afraid you'll have trouble in finding a cab," she said.

He made a vague, puzzled movement; obviously the idea of going out again that night had never entered his head. Was it not his home here? His bedroom was, as ever, awaiting him, just across the passage. How often had he returned like this, in the small hours, after a five- or six-day escapade! On such occasions he would appear next morning at the breakfast table in pyjamas, but very spick and span, joking and laughing rather loud, so as to quell his children's unspoken mistrust, which he felt but did not understand.

Used to his ways, Mme. de Fontanin had followed on his face the trend his thoughts had taken; but she did not waver, and opened the door leading into the hall. He walked out, inwardly discomfited, but heroically keeping the appearance of an old friend saying goodbye to his hostess.

While he was putting on his overcoat, it occurred to him again that his wife must be short of money. He would have handed over to her such little money as he had, readily enough—though he was not in a position to put himself in funds again. But the thought that such an incident might create an awkward situation, that, after taking the money, she might no longer feel at liberty to show him out so firmly, offended his sense of delicacy. Worse still, Thérèse might suspect him of an ulterior motive.

"Sweetheart," he said simply, "I have a great deal more to say to you."

A thought flashed through her mind, first of her intention to break with him, then of the money she needed. Hastily she answered: "Tomorrow, Jerome. I'll see you tomorrow, if you'll come here. We'll have a talk."

There was nothing for him but to take his leave, and he did so with good grace, clasping her hand and pressing his lips to it. Even then both hesitated for a moment. But she quickly withdrew her hand and opened the door of the flat.

"Well, *au revoir,* sweetheart. Till tomorrow!"

Her last glimpse of him as he began going down the stairs was his smile and courteous gesture as he raised his hat, bowing towards her.

The door closed. Left to her solitary musings, Mme. de Fontanin leaned her forehead on the door-jamb; the clang of the closing street door jarred the whole building and she could feel the vibration in her cheek. A light-coloured glove was lying on the carpet almost under her eyes. Without thinking, she picked it up and pressed it to her lips. Across the smell of leather and tobacco-smoke she seemed to detect a subtler, familiar perfume. Then, seeing her gesture reflected in a glass, she blushed, let the glove fall again, switched off the lights almost angrily, and, freed from her own reproachful gaze by the kindly darkness, groped her way hastily to the children's rooms, and stayed a little while in each, listening to their tranquil breathing.

IX

ANTOINE and Jacques were back in the cab. The horse's hoofs rattled on the roadway like castanets, but they made slow progress. The streets were in darkness. A smell of musty cloth pervaded the rickety old vehicle. Jacques was crying. Utter weariness and the kiss he had just received from the lady with the mothering smile had at last filled him with contrition. What ever was he going to say to his father? He felt at his wit's end; unable to conceal his anguish, he sought consolation from his brother, pressing himself against his shoulder. Antoine put his arm round him. For the first time the barrier of their mutual shyness was withdrawn.

Antoine wanted to say something, but could not overcome his distaste for effusion, and when he spoke there was a forced heartiness in his voice that made it sound almost gruff.

"Now then, old man! Buck up! There's no need to get into such a stew about it, you know. It's all over now."

For a moment he pressed the boy to him affectionately, without speaking. But he was unable to restrain his curiosity.

"What came over you, Jacques?" His voice was gentler now. "What really happened? Did he persuade you to run away?"

"Oh, no. He didn't want to a bit. It was all my idea."

"Then why . . . ?"

No answer. Antoine fumbled for his words as he continued.

"You know, Jacques, I know all about these school . . . intimacies. You needn't mind telling me. I know how it is; one lets oneself be led on."

"He's my friend, that's all," Jacques whispered, still pressing against his brother's shoulder.

"But," Antoine ventured, "what exactly . . . what do you do together?"

"We talk. He consoles me."

Antoine did not dare to ask more questions. "He consoles me!" Jacques's tone cut him to the heart. He was on the point of saying: "Are you so unhappy, old man?" when Jacques burst out, almost truculently:

"Well, if you want to know 'everything'—he corrects my poems."

"Good for you!" Antoine smiled. "I'm delighted to hear that. Do you know, I'm very glad you're a poet!"

"Honour bright?" the boy asked.

"Yes, honour bright. I knew it anyhow. I've seen some of your poems; you left them lying about, you know, and I had a squint at them. I never spoke about it to you. As a matter of fact, we never do seem to talk together, I can't think why. Some of your poems struck me as damned good, d'you know! You've quite a gift for that sort of thing, and you must make the most of it."

Jacques nestled up to his brother.

"Yes, I'm awfully keen on poetry," he whispered. "There are some poems that I love more than anything else in the world. Fontanin lends me books—but you won't tell anyone, will you? It's thanks to him I've read Laprade and Sully-Prudhomme and Lamartine and Victor Hugo and Musset. Musset's wonderful! Do you know this one, I wonder?

> *"Pâle étoile du soir, messagère lointaine*
> *Dont le front sort brillant des voiles du couchant . . .*

"And this one:

> *"Voilà longtemps que celle avec qui j'ai dormi,*
> *O Seigneur, a quitté ma couche pour la vôtre,*
> *Et nous sommes encor tout mêlés l'un à l'autre,*
> *Elle à demi vivante et moi mort à demi.*

"And Lamartine's 'Le Crucifix,' do you know it?

> *"Toi que j'ai recueilli sur sa bouche expirante,*
> *Avec son dernier souffle et son dernier adieu . . .*

"It's lovely, isn't it? So . . . so wonderfully limpid. Each time I read that, the beauty of it almost hurts me." And now he poured out his heart without reserve. "At home they don't understand a thing; I'm certain I'd be plagued if they knew that I write poems. You're not like them"—he pressed Antoine's arm against his breast—"somehow I've felt you weren't, for ages. Only you never said anything, and, besides, you're not often there. Oh, if you only knew how happy I am! I feel that now I'm going to have two friends instead of one."

Antoine recited, smiling, a line of one of Jacques's own poems:

> "Hail Cæsar! Lo, the blue-eyed maid from Gaul . . ."

Jacques moved away suddenly, exclaiming: "You've read our exercise-book!"

"But, old chap, why ever . . . ?"

"Has Father read it too?" So piteous was the cry that Antoine dared not tell the truth.

"I don't really know. A page or two, perhaps."

Before he could say more Jacques had recoiled to the far corner of the cab; he sat there rocking himself to and fro, his head between his hands.

"It's foul! That Abbé is a Jesuit, a filthy beast! I shall tell him so, I'll shout at him in the middle of the class-room, I'll spit in his beastly face. They can expel me; I don't care a damn, I'll run away again. I'll kill myself!"

His whole body was shaking with fury. Antoine dared not breathe a word. Suddenly the boy stopped shouting and sank back into the corner, pressing his hands to his eyes. His teeth were chattering, and his silence alarmed Antoine even more than his outburst of rage. Fortunately the cab was entering the Rue des Saints-Pères; they were almost home.

Jacques got out first. Antoine, as he paid the cabman, never took his eyes off his brother, fearing he might make a sudden rush into the darkness. But now the boy seemed utterly exhausted; the elfish little face was drawn and haggard with fatigue and disappointment, and the eyes, fixed on the ground, were dry.

"Ring the bell, will you?" Antoine said.

Jacques said nothing and did not move. Antoine gently coaxed him towards the door. Lamb-like, Jacques followed his brother through the hall, without even troubling to think that the curious eyes of the old concierge, Mme. Frühling, were watching him. He had realized his helplessness and had no heart left to resist. The elevator whisked him up, more dead than alive, to face his father's righteous indignation. He was trapped again in the prison-house of the Family, of the social order, inescapably.

And yet, when he stood again on the landing, when he saw all the lamps lit in the hall as on the evenings when his father gave his stag dinner-parties, somehow he could not help finding a certain restfulness in the familiar home-life closing in again around him. When he saw Mademoiselle come limping up the hall, thinner and shakier than ever, he felt his rancour passing and a sudden impulse to throw himself into the embrace of the stumpy black-sleeved arms stretched out towards him. She pressed the boy to her, fondling him affectionately, but all the time scolding him in a shrill, quavering monotone. "Oh, dear! What wickedness! The cruel, heartless boy! Did you want to make us die of grief? Bless and save us, what wickedness! Haven't you any heart at all?" The litany of reproach went on, while large tears brimmed over from her llama-like eyes.

The door of the study opened. Jacques saw his father standing on the threshold, looking down the hall.

His eyes fell at once on Jacques, and he could not check an impulse of affectionate emotion. But then he halted, let his eyelids close; he seemed to be waiting for the culprit to fling himself at his feet, as in the Greuze picture, a copy of which hung in the drawing-room.

Shyness prevented Jacques from moving towards his father.

The study, too, was lit up as if for some festivity, and the two maids had just appeared at the kitchen door. Moreover, M. Thibault was in a frock-coat, though it was the hour when he usually wore a smoking-jacket. The boy felt paralysed by the queerness of it all. He freed himself from Mademoiselle's embrace, shrank back, and stood, with bowed head, waiting for he knew not what, so flustered by a rush of pent-up feeling that he felt an uncontrollable impulse to weep and, in the same breath, burst out laughing.

But M. Thibault's first words seemed to ban him from the family circle. Jacques's attitude, in the presence of witnesses, had effectively dispelled any inclination to indulgence which he might have felt. The better to bring the young rebel to heel, he feigned complete detachment.

"Ah, so you're back!" He addressed the words solely to Antoine. "I was beginning to wonder. Did everything go off all right?" When Antoine nodded, shaking the flabby hand his father held out to him, he continued: "I'm very grateful to you, my dear boy, for sparing me a distasteful task. Most distasteful indeed!"

He paused, still hoping for some gesture of contrition from his younger son. But the boy was staring sullenly at the carpet. M. Thibault glanced first at the culprit, then at the maids. Now he was definitely angry.

"We'll decide tomorrow on the best course to adopt, to prevent the repetition of such scandalous misconduct."

Mademoiselle made a step towards Jacques, to urge him to his father's arms—a movement Jacques was aware of, though he did not raise his eyes. Indeed he had been waiting for it, his last forlorn chance of reconciliation. But M. Thibault stretched out a peremptory arm.

"Let him be! He's a young scoundrel, with a heart of stone. Was he worth all the anxiety we've gone through on his account?" He turned again to Antoine, who was watching for an opportunity to intervene. "Antoine, dear boy, do us the favour of looking after this miserable boy for one night more. Tomorrow, I promise you, you shall be freed from all responsibility for him."

There was still a moment of indecision. Antoine went up to his father; Jacques timidly raised his head. But now M. Thibault was speaking again, in a tone that brooked no controversy.

"Now then, Antoine, you heard what I said? Take him off to his room. This revolting scene has lasted quite long enough. Take him away."

Steering Jacques in front of him, Antoine vanished down the corridor; the maids shrank back against the walls, as if they were watching victims on their way to execution. M. Thibault, his eyes still closed, went back to his study and shut the door behind him.

He went straight across it into the room where he slept. The furniture had come to him from his parents, and the room was exactly like their bedroom as he had known it in his early childhood, in the residence attached to his father's factory near Rouen. After his father's death he had brought the whole lot of it to Paris, where he had come to study law. He had kept everything as it was: the mahogany chest of drawers, the old-fashioned chairs, the blue rep curtains, the bed in which his father and his mother had died. Before the *prie-dieu,* the upholstery of which had been embroidered by Mme. Thibault, hung the crucifix which he himself, at a few months' interval, had placed between their folded, lifeless hands.

Alone now, he could be himself again; he let his shoulders droop, and yet the mask of fatigue seemed to have slipped from the heavy features, leaving them with a simple, almost childish look that recalled the portraits of him as a boy. He went to the *prie-dieu* and, kneeling down, gave himself up to prayer. His puffy hands moved rapidly to and fro—a habit with him when he was by himself; there was something unconstrained, yet curiously clandestine, in all his gestures now he was alone. He raised his expressionless face, and the eyes, under the half-shut lids, went straight to the crucifix.

M. Thibault was committing this new burden laid upon him, his disappointment, to God's mercy, and now that his heart was purged of anger, he prayed fervently and with a father's love for his erring son. From the arm-rest on which he kept his books of devotion he took a rosary which had been given him for his first communion; after forty years' polishing the beads slipped effortlessly between his fingers. He had shut his eyes again, but his head was still lifted, as if he were gazing at the crucifix. That smile coming from the heart and that look of candid happiness were never seen on his face in ordinary life. The words he was murmuring made his heavy cheeks quiver and the little, jerky movements of his head which he made at regular intervals to free his neck from the stiff, tight collar somehow brought to mind a censer swinging before the altar of his God.

Next morning Jacques was left to himself. Sitting on his unmade bed, he wondered what to do with himself this Saturday morning. It wasn't the holidays—quite the contrary—and yet here he was, it seemed, spending the day in his room. He thought of school, the history class, Daniel. The domesic sounds he heard outside his door seemed unfamiliar and vaguely hostile: a broom rasping the carpet, doors creaking in the wind. He was not depressed; exalted, rather; but his inactivity, coupled with the mysterious threat brooding over the house, made him feel almost unbearably ill at ease. What a relief it would have been if he could have found an opportunity for some sacrifice, some heroic and absurd act of devotion, which might have given vent to the pent-up emotions that now were suffocating him! Now and then a gust of self-pity caused him to raise his head and he felt a brief thrill of morbid pleasure, a mingled thrill of frustrated love, of pride and hatred.

The door-handle turned. It was Gisèle. Her hair had just been washed and her black curls were drying on her shoulders; she was wearing a shirt and drawers. Her brown neck, arms, and legs gave her the look of a little Algerian lad—what with her flapping drawers, with her fuzzy mop of hair, her ripe young lips, and melting dog-like eyes.

"What do you want?" Jacques asked in a peevish tone.

"I've come to see you." She looked at him intently.

During the past week little ten-year-old Gisèle had guessed more than her elders suspected. And now her Jacquot had come back! But things at home had not resumed their normal course. Just now her aunt, when doing Gisèle's hair, had suddenly been called away to see M. Thibault, and had left her in her room, her hair "all anyhow," after making her promise to "be good."

"Who was it who rang?" he asked.

"The Abbé."

Jacques frowned. She climbed onto the bed beside him.

"Poor Jacquot!" she whispered.

Her affection did him so much good that, to show his gratitude, he took her on his knees and hugged her. But his ears were on the alert.

"Run! There's someone coming!" He pushed her towards the door.

He had just time enough to jump off the bed and open a grammar-book when he heard the voice of Abbé Vécard behind the door, talking to Gisèle.

"Good morning, my dear. Is Jacquot here?"

Entering, he stopped on the threshold. Jacques looked down. The Abbé came up to him and playfully tweaked his ear.

"Here's a pretty kettle of fish!" he began.

But the stubborn look on the boy's face made him change his tactics. With Jacques he always proceeded warily. He felt for this so often erring member of his flock a particular regard, not unmixed with curiosity and a certain esteem, for he had realized the vigour of the boy's personality.

Sitting down he called Jacques towards him.

"The least thing you could do was to ask your father's forgiveness.

Have you done so?" Of course, he knew perfectly well the state of affairs, and, furious with his deceit, Jacques cast him a furtively indignant look, shaking his head. For a while neither spoke.

Then the priest began in a low, somewhat ill-assured voice. "My child, I won't conceal from you that I have been deeply grieved by what has happened. Till now, for all your unruliness, I've always stood up for you. I have often said to your father: 'Jacques has a good heart, everything will come right, only we must be patient.' But now I hardly know what to say and, worse still, I have learnt things about you which never, never could I have brought myself to suspect. We'll come back to that. And yet, I said to myself: 'He will have had time to reflect, he will return to us repentant, and there is no sin that cannot be atoned for by sincere contrition.' Instead of that I find you with a stubborn face, without a semblance of regret, without a tear. Your poor father, this time, has really lost heart, and I am grieved for his sake too. He asks himself how far you have sunk in perversity, whether your heart is utterly hardened. And, upon my word, I ask myself that question too."

Clenching his fists in his pockets, Jacques pressed his chin hard against his chest so that no sob might escape from his throat, no muscle of his face betray him. He alone knew how bitterly he suffered for not having asked forgiveness, what exquisite tears he would have shed, had he had Daniel's welcome. No! Since it was thus, he would never let anyone see what he felt for his father; that almost animal attachment, tinctured with rancour, seemed to have become even keener, now that there was no hope of its being returned.

The Abbé paused. The studied calm of his features made his silence all the more telling. Then, his eyes fixed on the middle distance, without a word of introduction, he began speaking, or, rather, intoning words that Jacques knew well:

" 'A certain man had two sons. . . . And he divided unto them his living. And not many days after the younger son gathered all together, and took his journey into a far country, and there wasted his substance with riotous living. And when he had spent all . . . and came to himself he said, I will arise and go to my father and will say unto him, Father, I have sinned against heaven, and before thee, and am no more worthy to be called thy son. . . . And he arose, and came to his father. But when he was yet a great way off, his father saw him, and had compassion, and ran, and fell on his neck, and kissed him. And the son said unto him, Father, I have sinned against heaven, and in thy sight, and am no more worthy to be called thy . . .' "

Before the priest could utter the last word, Jacques's self-control broke down and he burst into tears.

The priest continued in a different tone:

"Yes, my child, I felt sure you were not utterly corrupted. This morning I said my mass for you. Well, like the Prodigal Son, arise and go to your father, and he will have compassion. And he, too, will say: 'Let us be merry, for this my son was lost and is found.' "

Then Jacques remembered how the hall had been lit up for his homecoming, how M. Thibault had worn his frock-coat, and it made him still more contrite to think that perhaps he had "let down" their preparations to welcome him.

"There's something else I want to say to you," the priest went on, stroking the boy's hair. "Your father has just come to a grave decision about you." He hesitated and, as he groped for his words, mechanically passed his hand to and fro over Jacques's protruding ears, laying them flat against his cheeks, then letting them spring back. Jacques felt his ears burning, but dared not move his head. "I approve of his decision," the Abbé added, putting his forefinger on his lip and riveting his gaze on the boy's eyes. "He intends to send you, for a while, away from home."

"Where?" The word was a stifled cry.

"He will tell you, my child. But whatever you may think at first, you must accept the punishment with a contrite heart, as a measure taken for your good. At the start, perhaps, it will sometimes be a little hard, when you find yourself alone for hours on end; but remember at those moments that there is no solitude for the true Christian, and that God never forsakes those who put their trust in Him. Come, my boy, come with me and ask your father's forgiveness."

A few minutes later Jacques was back in his room, his face swollen with tears, his cheeks blazing. He walked over to the looking-glass and gave his reflected self a look of concentrated ferocity; it was as if he felt the need of some living human form to act as the target of his malevolence, his imprecations. But just then he heard a step in the passage. Glancing at the door, he saw the key had been removed. He piled a barricade of chairs against it. Then, running to the table, he scribbled a few lines in pencil, pushed the letter into an envelope, wrote the address, stuck on a stamp, and rose. He seemed at his wit's end. To whom could he entrust the letter? Here, everyone was an enemy. He opened the window. The morning was grey, the street deserted. After a while an old lady and a child came slowly past. Jacques dropped the letter; it fluttered slowly down and came to rest on the pavement. When he ventured to look out of the window again, the letter had disappeared, the lady and the child were almost out of sight.

And now he gave way to his despair; with a whimpering cry, the moan of a trapped animal, he flung himself onto the bed, his feet pressing against the boards, his body arched convulsively, his limbs quivering with baffled fury. To stifle his cries, he clenched his teeth on the pillow, for, in the chaos of his mind, one thought was clear: he must not let the others gloat over his despair.

That evening Daniel received the letter:

To you, My Friend, to you, the only person in the world whom I love, the daystar of my life, this is my last will and testament to you.

They are severing me from you, from everything; they are going to put me in a place—I dare not tell you what it is, I dare not tell you where it is. I am ashamed for my father's sake!

I feel that I shall never see you again, you who are all to me, you who alone could make me kind and good.

Good-bye, my dear, good-bye.

If they make me too miserable, too angry with everything, I shall kill myself. Then you must tell them that I killed myself deliberately, because of them. And that yet I loved them.

But my last thought on the threshold of the next world will have been for you! For you, my friend!

Farewell!

PART

II

∎∎

I

D URING the nine months which had elapsed since the day when Antoine brought back the two young truants, he had not gone to see Mme. de Fontanin again. The maid, however, recognized him and, though it was nine o'clock, showed him in immediately.

Mme. de Fontanin was in her room, the two children with her. Sitting very straight under the lamp, in front of the fire, she was reading aloud. Jenny, snugly ensconced in an easy chair, was toying with her plaits and, as she listened to her mother, gazing at the flames. Daniel was sitting a little way off, his legs crossed, a drawing-board on his knee, finishing a charcoal sketch of his mother. As he paused for a moment on the dark threshold of the room, Antoine was uncomfortably conscious that his visit was ill-timed; but it was too late to retreat.

Mme. de Fontanin's greeting was rather chilly, but principally she seemed surprised to see him. Leaving her children to themselves, she led Antoine to the drawing-room. On learning the reason of his visit, however, she went out again to fetch her son.

Daniel looked seventeen now, though actually he was two years younger, and an incipient moustache darkened the curve of his upper lip. A little disconcerted, Antoine looked the youngster full in the face, in the rather blustering way he had; now his look seemed to imply: "There's no shilly-shally about me; I'm one of those fellows who always go straight to the point." As on his previous visit, an unavowed instinct led him to exaggerate this pose of "downrightness," once he was in Mme. de Fontanin's presence.

"This is it," he said. "Our meeting yesterday set me thinking and I've come to talk things over." Daniel looked surprised. "Yes," Antoine went on, "we scarcely exchanged two words—you were in a hurry and so was I; but it struck me—I don't quite know how to put it. Well, for one thing you didn't inquire about Jacques, from which I drew the conclusion that he'd been writing to you. I was right, wasn't I?

What's more, I suspect he tells you things I don't know, and which I ought to know. No, wait, please, and hear what I have to say. Jacques left Paris last June; it's near the beginning of April now, which makes it nine months he's been away. I haven't seen him, he's never written to me, but Father sees him often. He tells me Jacques is fit and working well, that the solitary life and discipline have already done him a world of good. I sometimes wonder if he isn't deceiving himself, or being deceived. Since seeing you yesterday I've been feeling worried about it. I got an idea that perhaps he's unhappy in his present surroundings, but as I'm in the dark about it, there's nothing I can do to help him. And I can't bear to think that. That's why I decided to come and talk it over frankly with you. I appeal to your affection for him. It's not a question of betraying confidences, but I'm sure he tells you what his life is like in that place. You're the only one who can either reassure me, or prompt me to take active measures about it."

Daniel heard him out impassively. His first impulse had been to decline the interview altogether. Holding his head high, he gazed at Antoine, and his very indecision gave a certain aloofness to his look. At a loss, he glanced towards his mother. She had been watching him, wondering what he would do. After some minutes of suspense she smiled to him.

"Tell the truth, my boy," she said, with a decisive gesture. "One never has reason to regret it when one tells the truth."

With a gesture curiously like his mother's, Daniel began to speak. Yes, he had had letters from Thibault, now and then; letters that had become shorter and shorter, less and less communicative. Daniel knew, of course, that his friend was boarding with a tutor somewhere in the country—exactly where he did not know. The postmarks on the envelopes showed that they had been posted on a train, somewhere on the Northern Railway. Was it a sort of cramming school Jacques was at?

It was an effort for Antoine to conceal his amazement at the pains that Jacques had evidently taken to hide the truth from his closest friend. Why had he done it? Perhaps it was the same feeling of shame as that which led M. Thibault to convert, for the benefit of the world at large, the reformatory colony where he had confined his son, into "a religious institution on the banks of the Oise." A suspicion that perhaps his brother had been compelled to write such letters crossed his mind. Perhaps the poor little chap was being terrorized! He remembered the campaign run by a Beauvais newspaper of the scurrilous sort, and the lurid charges it had brought against the Social Defence League. True, M. Thibault had won his libel action against the newspaper, all along the line—yet could one be so sure . . . ?

Antoine felt that, in the last resort, he could rely only on his own judgment.

"Might I see one of the letters?" he asked. Noticing that Daniel was blushing, he excused his abruptness with a belated smile. "Just one letter," he explained. "Whichever you care to show me."

Without answering, without waiting for a lead from his mother, Daniel rose and left the room.

Now that he was alone with Mme. de Fontanin, Antoine was conscious of the same feelings as he had had before: curiosity, a sense of an unfamiliar atmosphere, and a certain attraction. She was looking in front of her and did not seem to be thinking of anything. But her mere presence seemed enough to stimulate Antoine's mental processes and quicken his receptivity. It was as if the air around her were charged with a peculiar conductivity. And, at that moment, unmistakably, Antoine felt an atmosphere of disapproval. He was not far wrong. Though she had nothing definite against M. Thibault, or Antoine—she had no idea what had become of Jacques—the one glimpse she had had of their home-life had left her with a most distasteful impression. Antoine guessed her feelings and was inclined to agree with her. If anyone had ventured to criticize his father's conduct, he would certainly have protested vigorously; but at that moment, in his inmost self, he was on Mme. de Fontanin's side against his father. He had not forgotten how, the year before, after his first experience of the atmosphere of the Fontanins' home, he had for several days found that of his own home almost unbreathable.

Daniel returned. He handed Antoine a cheap-looking envelope.

"That's the first. It's the longest letter, too." He went back to his chair.

My dear Fontanin,

I write to you from my new home. You mustn't try to write to me; it's absolutely forbidden. Apart from that, everything is all right. My tutor is nice, he is kind to me, and I am working hard. And I have met quite a lot of nice fellows here. My father and brother come to see me on Sundays. So you see I'm quite all right. I beg you, my dear Daniel, in the name of our friendship, do not judge my father too harshly; you don't know all the facts. I know he is kind and good, and he has done well to send me away from Paris, where I was wasting my time at the Lycée; I see it myself now, and I'm glad. I don't give you my address—to make sure you won't write, for if you did so it would be terrible for me here.

I will write to you again when I have a chance, my dear Daniel.

                                                        Jacques.

Antoine read the letter twice. Had he not recognized his brother's writing, he would have had difficulty in believing it came from him. Someone else had written the address on the envelope—obviously a more or less illiterate person—and there was something mean and furtive about the handwriting. Form and contents disturbed him equally. Why those lies? About the "nice fellows," for instance. Jacques was living in a cell in the famous "special annex" which M. Thibault had provided for boys of good family, and which was always empty. Jacques, he knew, never spoke to a soul except the servant who brought his meals and took him for walks, and a tutor who came from Compiègne two or three times a week. "My father and brother come to see me"! M. Thibault visited Crouy in his official capacity on the first Monday of each month, to preside over the administrative committee, and it was true that on that day, just before leaving, he always had his son brought to see him for a few minutes in the parlour. As for Antoine, he had proposed going to visit his brother during the summer holidays, but M. Thibault had put his foot down. "It's essential," he had said, "for the course of re-education your brother is undergoing, that he should be kept in absolute isolation."

His elbows propped on his knees, Antoine twiddled the letter between his fingers. His peace of mind was badly shaken and of a sudden he felt so painfully at a loss, so lonely, that he was on the point of telling everything to the enlightened woman who, by some happy chance, had crossed his path. Looking up, he saw her with her hands resting on her lap, and with a thoughtful, somehow expectant look on her face. Her eyes seemed to read his thoughts.

"Do you think we could help in any way?" she smiled. The silken whiteness of her hair made the smile and the features seem those of a still younger woman.

But, just as he was about to make the plunge, he paused, noticing Daniel's shrewd gaze intent on him. Antoine could not bear to seem irresolute, and even more disliked the idea that Mme. de Fontanin might not regard him as the man of rapid measures that he was. But to himself he gave a more congenial reason for his silence—that he could not divulge a secret Jacques was at such pains to hide. Feeling unsure of himself, he cut the awkward situation short. He rose and, as he held out his hand, assumed the impressive look he deliberately cultivated, a look implying: "No questions, please! You see the man I am! We understand each other; that's enough!"

In the street he strode ahead, repeating to himself: "Keep calm, and act with firmness!" Five or six years spent in studying science had given him the habit of casting his thoughts in ostensibly logical form. "Jacques does not complain; therefore Jacques is happy." But, inwardly, he discredited his syllogism. The press campaign against the reformatory haunted his thoughts; notably he recalled an article on "Children's Jails" that had described in detail the physical and moral degradation of the ill-fed, ill-housed boys, the corporal punishments they were subjected to, the callous treatment often meted out to them by the guards. Unconsciously he made a menacing gesture. The role of rescuer appealed to him. Cost what it might, he would get the poor boy out of it! But how? Any idea of telling his father about it or having it out with him could be dismissed; for it was his father, and the institution founded and managed by him, that he was up against. This feeling of revolt against his father was so unprecedented that at first he felt a certain embarrassment, which soon changed to pride.

He remembered what had happened the year before, the day after Jacques's return. At the earliest stage of the proceedings M. Thibault had summoned him to his study. The Abbé Vécard had just come. M. Thibault was bellowing: "The young ruffian! We've got to break his will!" He had stretched out his plump, hairy hand, had spread out the fingers, then slowly closed them, cracking the joints. A self-satisfied smile had lit up his face. "Yes, I think I've found the solution." And, after a pause, raising at last his eyelids, he had uttered the one word: "Crouy."

"What! Do you mean to send Jacques to the reformatory?" Antoine had exclaimed. A heated argument had followed. "We've got to break him in," his father had repeated, cracking his knuckles again. The Abbé had demurred. Then M. Thibault had explained the special discipline Jacques would undergo—a regime which, to hear him, was amiably benevolent, paternal. He had concluded in an unctuous tone, with measured emphasis. "In these conditions, out of reach of evil influences and purged by solitude of his baser instincts, imbued with a taste for work, he will come to his sixteenth year, and I venture to hope it will then be possible for him safely to resume his place in our family life." The priest had acquiesced: "Yes, isolation does effect marvellous cures." Impressed by his father's arguments and the priest's approval, Antoine had finished by thinking they were right. But now he could forgive neither his father nor himself.

He walked rapidly, without looking where he was going. In front of the Lion of Belfort he turned on his heel, then went striding on again, lighting cigarette after cigarette, puffing the smoke into the lamp-lit darkness. Yes, he must make haste to Crouy, strike hard, do justice. . . .

A woman accosted him, murmuring cajoleries. He did not answer, but continued walking down the Boulevard Saint-Michel. "I shall have justice done!" he repeated. "I'll show up the double-dealing of the directors; I'll make a public scandal and bring the boy back."

But somehow the edge of his enthusiasm had been blunted; all the time, his thoughts had been sheering off their first preoccupation, and another impulse kept cutting across his grandiose campaign. He crossed the Seine, well knowing to what place his wayward steps were taking him. After all, why not? With his nerves strung up like this, there was no point in going home to bed. He inhaled deeply, puffed out his chest, and smiled. "One's got to be a man," he thought, "to prove one's strength." As he blithely entered the furtive, ill-lit street, another rush of generous emotion carried him away. In his mind's eye he saw his resolution beaconing him to triumph. Now that he was about to realize one of the two projects that had been vying for his attention during the past quarter of an hour, the other, by the same token, seemed to him all but realized. And as, with the assurance born of habit, he pushed open the glazed door, his plans were cut and dried. "Tomorrow's Saturday—impossible to get away from the hospital. But on Sunday, Sunday morning, I'll visit the reformatory."

II

As THE morning express did not stop at Crouy, Antoine had to get out at Venette, the last station before Compiègne. He alighted from the train in the highest spirits. Next week he had to sit for an examination, but throughout the journey he had been unable to apply his mind to the medical manuals he had brought with him. The decisive moment was near. For the past two days he had been picturing so vividly the triumphant climax of his crusade that he almost fancied he had already effected Jacques's release, and the only problem troubling him was how he was to regain the boy's affection.

He had a mile and a half to walk along a level, sunlit road. For the first time that year after weeks of rain there was a promise of spring in the dewy fragrance of the March morning. He feasted his eyes on the tender verdure already mantling the ploughlands. Wisps of vapour lingered on the bright horizon, and the hills along the Oise glittered in the young sunlight. For a moment he was weak enough to hope he was mistaken, so pure, so calm was the countryside around him. Could this be the setting of a convict prison?

He had to cross the entire village of Crouy before reaching the reformatory. Then, suddenly, as he came round the last houses, he had a shock. Though he had never seen it and distant though it was, he could not be mistaken. There, in the midst of a chalk-white plain, ringed round on all sides, like a new graveyard, by bare, bleak walls, rose the huge building with its tiled roof, its clock-face gleaming in the sun, and endless rows of small, barred windows. It would have been taken for an ordinary prison but for the gold lettering on the cornice over the first story:

THE OSCAR THIBAULT FOUNDATION

He walked up the treeless drive leading to the penitentiary. The little windows seemed watching from afar the visitor's approach. Entering the portico, he pulled the bell-rope; a shrill clang jarred the Sabbath calm. The door opened. A brown watchdog, chained to its kennel, barked furiously. Antoine entered the courtyard, which consisted of a lawn surrounded by gravel paths and curved on the side facing the main ward. He had a feeling of being watched, but no living being was in sight except the dog, which, tugging at its chain, was barking lustily as ever. To the left of the entrance was a little chapel topped by a stone cross; on the right he saw a low building with the notice "Staff," and turned towards it. The closed door opened the moment he set foot on the step. The dog went on barking. He stepped into a hall, with a tiled floor and yellow walls and furnished with new chairs; it reminded him of a convent parlour. The place was overheated. A life-sized plaster bust of M. Thibault, giving an impression of enormous bulk under the low ceiling, adorned the right-hand wall. On the opposite wall a humble black crucifix, garnished with a sprig of box, seemed to be playing second fiddle to it. Antoine remained standing, on the defensive. No, he had not been wrong! The whole place reeked of the prison-house.

At last, in the wall furthest from him, a hatch was opened and a guard put out his head. Antoine threw down his own card and one of

his father's, and curtly told the man he wished to see the superintendent.

Nearly five minutes passed.

Annoyed by the delay, Antoine was just about to start on a round
of exploration, unaccompanied, when a light step sounded in the
corridor and a bespectacled, plump, fair-haired young man ran up to
him with little dancing steps. He was in brown flannel pyjamas and
wearing Turkish slippers. All smiles, he held out both hands in
welcome.

"Good morning, doctor. What a happy surprise! Your brother will
be so delighted, *so* delighted to see you. Of course I know you well;
your father, the Founder, often speaks of his grown-up doctor son.
And besides there's a family resemblance. Oh, yes," he laughed, "I
assure you there's a likeness. But do come to my office, please. And
forgive me for not introducing myself before; I'm Faîsme, the
superintendent here."

He shepherded Antoine towards his office, shuffling his feet and
following close behind with his arms extended and fingers spread, as
if he expected Antoine to slip or stumble and wanted to be sure to
catch him before he fell.

He made Antoine take a seat and himself sat at his desk.

"Is the Founder in good health?" he asked in a high-pitched voice.
"What an extraordinary man he is—he never seems to get older! Such
a pity he couldn't come today as well!"

Antoine cast a mistrustful glance round the room, then scanned
without amenity the young man's face, which for all its pink-and-
white complexion had a Chinese cast: behind the gold-rimmed spectacles the two small slanted eyes seemed twinkling and beaming with
perpetual joy. The voluble welcome had taken him off his guard, and
it upset his calculations to find that the stern prison warden he had
pictured was a smiling young man in pyjamas instead of the grim-
faced martinet—or, at best, the prim pedagogue—he had expected to
confront. It was an effort for him to recover his composure.

"By Jove!" M. Faîsme suddenly exclaimed. "It's just struck me:
you've arrived in the middle of mass. All our youngsters are in chapel,

including your brother, of course. What's to be done?" He consulted
his watch. "There's another twenty minutes, half an hour, perhaps, if
there are many communions—and that's quite possible. The Founder
must have told you; we are particularly fortunate in our confessor:
he's quite a young priest with go-ahead ideas and any amount of tact.
Since he's been here the religious tone of the institution has wonderfully
improved. I'm so sorry to keep you waiting, but really I don't see how
it can be helped."

Mindful of the investigation he proposed to carry out, Antoine made
no show of friendliness.

"As the buildings are empty for the moment," he said, standing up
and fixing his eyes on the little man, "I presume there would be no
objection to my having a look round the institution. I've heard it so
much discussed ever since I was a boy that I'd like to have a nearer
view of it."

"Really?" The superintendent seemed surprised. "Nothing could
be simpler, of course," he added with a smile, but made no sign
of moving. For a moment he seemed lost in thought, the smile
still lingering on his lips. "Really, you know, the buildings aren't
particularly interesting; more like a miniature barracks than anything else. And when I've said that, you know as much about them
as I do."

Antoine remained on his feet.

"Still, it would interest me," he repeated. The superintendent stared
at him, his little slotted eyes twinkling with amused incredulity. "I
mean what I say," Antoine added in a determined voice.

"In that case, doctor, I'll be delighted. . . . Please give me time to
put on a coat and shoes and I'll be with you."

He went out. Antoine heard an electric bell ring. Then a big bell
in the courtyard clanged five times. "Aha!" he thought. "That's the
alarm; the enemy is within the gates!" Unable to bring himself to sit
down, he walked to the window; the glass was frosted. "Steady now!"
he adjured himself. "And keep your eyes open. The first thing's to
make sure. Then to act. That's the line to take."

After a good while M. Faîsme returned.

They went out together.

"You see here our main quadrangle!" he said, turning the pompous nomenclature with a laugh. The watchdog started barking again; he ran up to it and gave it a violent kick in the ribs that sent it slinking back into the kennel.

"Are you anything of a gardener? But of course a doctor must know his way about in botany, eh?" He halted, beaming, in the middle of the little lawn. "Do give me your advice. How'm I to hide that bit of wall? What about ivy? Only it would take years, wouldn't it?"

Ignoring the question, Antoine walked on to the main building. First they visited the ground floor. Antoine went in front; nothing escaped his observant eye, and he made a point of opening every door without exception. The upper half of the walls was white-washed; up to the height of six feet they were tarred black. All the windows, like those in the office, had frosted glass, and here there were bars as well. Antoine tried to open a window, but a special key was necessary; the superintendent produced one from his pocket and turned the latch. Antoine was struck by the dexterity of his short, fat, yellow fingers. He cast a shrewd exploring glance into the inner court, which was quite empty—a large rectangle of dry, well-trodden mud without a single tree and enclosed by high walls topped with broken glass.

M. Faîsme described with gusto the uses of the different rooms: class-rooms and shops for carpentry, metalwork, electricity, and so forth. The rooms were small, clean, and tidy. In the refectory servants were just finishing clearing the deal tables; an acrid smell came from the sinks in the corners.

"Each boy goes to the sink after the meal to wash his bowl, mug, and spoon. They never have knives, of course, nor even forks." When Antoine gave him a puzzled look, he added with a grin: "Nothing with a point, you know!"

On the first floor there were more class-rooms, more workshops, and a shower-bath which did not seem much used, but of which the superintendent was evidently particularly proud. He bustled from room to room, flapping his arms and prattling away. Now and then he would stop to push back a carpenter's bench, pick up a nail from the floor, turn off a dripping tap, set perfect order in each room he entered.

On the second floor were the dormitories. They were of two sorts. The greater number contained ten low bedsteads, spread with grey blankets and arranged in rows; each was fitted with a kit-rack as in French military barracks, which these resembled, except that in the centre of each room was a sort of iron cage enclosed in fine-meshed wire netting.

"Do you shut them up in that?" Antoine inquired.

M. Faîsme flung up his arms in a gesture of comical dismay, then began laughing again.

"Certainly not! That's where the watchman sleeps. It's quite simple; he puts his bed plumb in the middle, at an equal distance from each wall. In that way he can see and hear everything that goes on, in perfect safety. And he has an alarm-bell, too; the wires go under the floor."

The other sort of dormitory consisted of rows of adjoining cells, built of solid stone and barred like the animal-cages in a menagerie. M. Faîsme had stopped on the threshold. Now and then his smile had a pensive, disillusioned air which gave his doll-like features the melancholy that pervades the Buddha's face in certain statues.

"Alas, doctor," he said, "it's in these cells we have to lodge our 'hard cases.' The boys, I mean, who come to us too late to be re-educated; I'm afraid there's little to be said for them. Some boys have vice in the blood—don't you agree? Well, there's nothing for it but to shut them up by themselves at night."

Antoine pressed his face to the bars and peered into the gloom of one of the cells. He could just make out an unmade pallet bed and walls covered with obscene drawings and inscriptions. Instinctively he drew back.

"Don't look, it's too distressing," the superintendent sighed, drawing him away. "Here you have the central corridor where the watchman on duty patrols all night. The light isn't put out here, and he doesn't go to bed. Though they're securely locked up, the little rascals would be quite capable of giving us a lot of trouble, take my word for it!"

He shook his head mournfully, then suddenly started laughing; his slotted eyes grew narrower still and all trace of compunction had left his face. "Yes," he added with an air of naïveté, "it takes all sorts to make a world, you know."

Antoine was so much interested in what he saw that he had forgotten most of the questions he had prepared in advance. One, however, he remembered now.

"How do you punish them? I'd like to see your punishment cells."

M. Faîsme stepped back a pace, his eyes wide open, flapping his hands in consternation.

"Come, come, doctor, what do you take us for? This isn't a convict prison. Punishment cells, indeed! We haven't any, thank God! For one thing, the Founder would never tolerate such methods."

Silenced and baffled, Antoine had to endure the irony that twinkled in the little narrow eyes, whose lashes flickered humorously behind the glasses. He was beginning to find the role he had assumed—of scrutiny and suspicion—rather irksome. Nothing he had seen encouraged him to maintain his attitude of hostility. Moreover, he had a feeling that the superintendent might have guessed the invidious motive that had brought him to Crouy. Still it was hard to know, so genuine seemed the little man's simplicity despite the occasional flashes of mockery that glinted in the corners of his eyes.

He stopped laughing, came up to Antoine, and put his hand on his arm.

"You were joking, weren't you? You know as well as I do what comes of overdoing discipline; it leads to rebellion or, what is still worse, hypocrisy. Our Founder made a fine speech on the subject at the Paris Congress, in the year of the Great Exhibition."

He had lowered his voice and there was a look of special understanding on his face as he gazed at the young man, a look implying that he and Antoine belonged to an élite, capable of discussing such educational problems without falling into the errors of the common herd. Antoine felt flattered, and his favourable impressions grew stronger.

"It's true that in the courtyard, just as in a military barracks, there's a small shed that the architect described on his plan as 'punishment cells.' "

"Yes?"

"But we only use it for storing coal and potatoes. What's the use of punishment cells? You get so much more by persuasion."

"Really?"

With a subtle smile the superintendent placed his hand on Antoine's arm.

"Let's get it clear," he said. "What I call 'persuasion,' I prefer to tell you right away, is the deprivation of certain items of the daily diet. Our young folk are always greedy. That's only natural at their age, isn't it? Dry bread, doctor, has a persuasive power you'd never suspect; only you must know how to use it—it's essential not to isolate the boy whom we're trying to reform. That, by the way, shows you how little the solitary cell enters into our method. No, it's in a corner of the dining-hall that the youngster eats his hunk of stale bread, at noon, when the best meal of the day is served, with the smell of a nice steaming dish of stew in his nostrils and with all the others tucking it away under his eyes. That's our method, and it never fails. At that age they thin down in no time; in a fortnight or three weeks I've broken in even the most stubborn cases. Persuasion—there's nothing like it!" His eyes were round with satisfaction. "And never have I had to take other measures; I've never lifted a finger against any of the young folk in my charge."

His face was shining with pride and benevolence. He really seemed to love his youthful miscreants, even the toughest.

They went down the stairs again. M. Faîsme took out his watch.

"To finish up, let me show you a truly edifying spectacle. You'll tell the Founder, I hope, and I'm sure he'll be pleased to hear about it."

They crossed the garden and entered the chapel. M. Faîsme sprinkled holy water. Antoine saw the backs of some sixty boys in grey overalls, kneeling in strict alinement on the stone floor, motionless. Four of the staff, stalwart figures in blue uniforms with red braid, marched up and down the aisle, keeping their eyes fixed on the boys. Attended by two acolytes, the priest at the altar was just concluding the service.

"Where's Jacques?" Antoine whispered.

The superintendent pointed to the gallery beneath which they were standing and tip-toed back towards the porch.

"That's where your brother always sits," he said as soon as they were outside. "He's alone there; that's to say, only the young man who looks after him is with him. By the way, you might tell your father that a new servant, the man we spoke to him about, has been allotted to Jacques. He took up the post a week ago. Léon, the man whom Jacques had before, was getting too old for the job, and we've detailed him to supervise a workroom. The new man's a young Lorrainer, a very, very decent fellow. He's just ended his military service; used to be the colonel's orderly, and his references were excellent. It'll be less boring for your brother on his walks, don't you think so? Good heavens, here I am chattering away to you and the boys are coming out of the chapel."

The dog began to bark furiously. M. Faîsme reduced it to silence, adjusted his glasses, and took his stand in the centre of the big quadrangle.

Both leaves of the chapel-door had been thrown open and, three by three, with the attendants beside them, the boys were filing out, keeping perfect step, like soldiers on parade. All were bare-headed and wearing rope-soled shoes, which gave them the noiseless step of gymnasts; their overalls were clean and held in at the waist by leather belts, the buckles of which flashed in the sun. The oldest were seventeen or eighteen, the youngest ten or eleven. Most had pale complexions, downcast eyes, and a look of calm quite out of keeping with their age. But Antoine, though he scrutinized them with the utmost attention, could not detect a single questionable glance, not one unsavoury smile, nor even any trace of sullenness. Those boys did not look "hard cases," and, he could but own to himself, they did not look like oppressed victims either.

When the little procession had vanished into the building and the sound of muffled footsteps on the wooden stairs had died away, he turned to M. Faîsme, who seemed to be waiting for his comment on the scene.

"An excellent turn-out," he said.

The little man said nothing, but gently rubbed one plump palm against the other, as if he were soaping them, while his eyes, sparkling with pride behind the glasses, conveyed his silent gratitude.

At last, when the quadrangle was quite empty, Jacques appeared outside the sunlit porch.

At first Antoine wondered if it was really he. He had changed so greatly, grown so much taller, that Antoine all but failed to recognize him. He was not wearing uniform but a lounge suit, a felt hat, and an overcoat thrown over his shoulders. He was followed by a fair-haired, thick-set young man of about twenty, who was not wearing the official uniform. They came down the steps together. Neither seemed to have noticed Antoine and the superintendent. Jacques was walking composedly, his eyes fixed on the ground, and it was not till he was within a few yards of M. Faîsme that, raising his head, he stopped, displayed astonishment, and briskly took off his hat. His demeanour was completely natural, yet Antoine had a suspicion that his surprise was simulated. Jacques's expression remained calm and, though he was smiling, did not seem to convey any real pleasure. Antoine held out his hand; his pleasure, too, was feigned.

"Well, this is a nice surprise, Jacques, isn't it?" the superintendent exclaimed. "But I'm going to scold you, my dear boy. You should put on your overcoat properly. It's chilly up in the gallery and you might catch cold."

Jacques had turned away from his brother as soon as he heard M. Faîsme speak and was looking the superintendent in the face with a respectful, remarkably attentive expression, as if he were trying to grasp some underlying meaning that the words might be intended to convey. Then promptly, without answering, he slipped the overcoat on.

"By Jove!" Antoine sounded almost startled. "It's amazing how you've shot up." He could not take his eyes off his brother, trying to analyse the complete change that had come over the boy's demeanour, face, and general appearance, and his surprise hampered his spontaneity.

"Would you like to stay outside for a bit?" the superintendent amiably suggested. "It's such a nice day, isn't it? Jacques can take you to his room when you've done a few turns round the garden."

Antoine hesitated. His eyes were asking his brother: "What about it?"

Jacques made no sign. Antoine took it to mean that he would rather not stay where he was, in full view of the reformatory windows.

"No," he said, and turned to Jacques again. "We'll be better in your room, won't we?"

"As you like," the superintendent smiled. "But first of all I want to show you one more thing; you really must have a look at *all* our boarders, while you're about it. Come along, Jacques."

Jacques followed M. Faîsme, who, his arms extended, laughing like a schoolboy playing a practical joke, was shepherding Antoine towards a shelter built against the wall of the porter's lodge. There were a dozen little rabbit-hutches. M. Faîsme, it seemed, had a passion for small-stock raising.

"This litter was born last Monday," he explained gleefully, "and look, they're opening their eyes already, dear little things. In this hutch are my buck-rabbits. Have a good look at this one, doctor; he's a real 'hard case.'" He plunged his arm into a hutch and hauled out by the ears a big silver Champagne, kicking violently.

There was a ring of boyish merriment in his laugh; it seemed impossible to think ill of the little man. Then Antoine remembered the dormitory above and its hutches barred with iron.

The plaintive smile of a misunderstood man came to M. Faîsme's face. "Good heavens," he said, "here I am chattering away, and I can see you're only listening out of pure politeness, eh? I'll take you as far as Jacques's door, and leave you. Come, Jacques, show us the way."

Jacques went in front. Antoine overtook him and put a hand on his shoulder. He was trying vainly to conjure up a picture of the small, nervous, weakly, short-legged urchin he had gone to retrieve at Marseille less than a year before.

"Why, you're as tall as I am!"

From the shoulder his hand moved up to the boy's neck. It was as thin and frail as the neck of a bird. Indeed all the boy's limbs seemed to have outgrown their strength, to be extraordinarily fragile. The elongated wrists protruded from the sleeves, the trousers left his ankles almost unclad, and there was a stiffness, an awkwardness in his way of walking, paradoxically combined with a certain adolescent suppleness, that was quite new to Antoine.

The rooms reserved for the special inmates were in an annex to the administrative offices and could be approached only through them. Five identical rooms gave onto a corridor the walls of which were painted yellow. M. Faîsme explained that as Jacques was the only "special" and the other rooms were unoccupied, the young man who looked after him slept in one, while the others were used as storerooms.

"And here's our prisoner's cell," he said, giving Jacques a playful tap with his plump finger; the boy smiled and drew back to let him enter.

Antoine inspected the room with eager curiosity. It might have been a bedroom in some small, unpretentious, but pleasantly appointed hotel. The wall-paper had a floral pattern and there was a fair amount of light, though it came only from above through two fanlights of frosted glass criss-crossed by iron bars. They were immediately beneath the ceiling and, the room being lofty, nearly ten feet above the floor. Sunlight did not enter, but the room was warmed, not to say over-heated, by the heating-plant of the establishment. The furniture consisted of a pitch-pine wardrobe, two cane chairs, and a black table covered with an array of books and dictionaries. The little bed was smooth and trim as a billiard-table, and had been freshly laid with clean sheets. The wash-basin stood on a clean cloth and there were several immaculate towels on the towel-rail.

A minute inspection of the room gave the final blow to Antoine's preconceived ideas about the institution. Everything he had seen during the past hour had been the exact opposite of what he had expected. Jacques was effectively segregated from the other boys and treated with every consideration; the superintendent was a good fellow, as

unlike the warden of a prison as one could well imagine. In fact, all
M. Thibault had said was true. Obstinate though he was, Antoine
was being forced to retract his suspicions one by one.

He caught M. Faîsme's gaze intent on him.

"Well, I must say you're pretty comfortable here," he remarked,
rather abruptly, turning to Jacques.

Jacques made no reply. He was taking off his hat and coat, which
the servant took from him and hung up on the pegs.

"Your brother has just said that you seem comfortable here," the
superintendent repeated.

Jacques swung round, with a polite, good-mannered air his brother
had never seen him assume before. "Yes, sir," he said. "Very comfortable indeed."

"No, don't let us exaggerate," M. Faîsme smiled. "It's all very
primitive really; we only insist it shall be clean. In any case, it's
Arthur we must compliment," he added, turning to the servant.
"That bed does you credit, my lad!"

Arthur's face lit up. Antoine, who was watching him, found himself making a friendly gesture towards the young man. He had a
bullet head, pale eyes, and smooth features, and there was something
frank and forthright in his smile and gaze. He had stayed beside the
door and was tugging at his moustache, which seemed almost colourless against his sun-tanned cheeks.

"So that's the grim guard I had pictured—creeping about with
a dark lantern and a bunch of keys!" Antoine was saying to himself,
and could not help laughing at his mistake. Then he went up to the
books and, still laughing, ran his eyes over them.

"Sallust, I see. Are you making good progress with your Latin?"
he asked, a cheerful smile still lingering on his face.

It was M. Faîsme who answered his question.

"Perhaps I shouldn't say it in front of him," he began with feigned
reluctance and a flutter of his eyelashes in Jacques's direction, "but I
don't see why I shouldn't tell you his tutor is very pleased with his
progress. We work our eight hours a day," he continued in a more
serious tone. He went up to the blackboard and straightened it while

he went on talking. "Still that doesn't prevent us from going every day, whatever the weather—your worthy father attaches much importance to it—for a good long two hours' tramp with Arthur. They've both good legs, and I leave them free to choose the walks they like. With old Léon it was another matter; I suspect they didn't cover much ground, but they made up for it by gathering herbs along the hedgerows. I should tell you old Léon was a pharmacist's assistant in his youth and knows all about plants, not to mention their Latin names. Jacques must have learned quite a lot from him. Still I must say I'd rather see them taking long walks in the country—much better for Jacques's health, isn't it?"

Antoine had turned to his brother several times while M. Faîsme was speaking. Jacques seemed to be listening in a dream; now and then he had to make an effort to follow, and at these moments a look of vague distress crossed his face, his lips parted, and his eyelids quivered.

"There I am again, babbling away, and it's ages since Jacques had a chance of seeing his big brother." M. Faîsme backed towards the door with little, friendly gestures. "Are you going back by the eleven o'clock train?" he asked.

That had not been Antoine's intention, but M. Faîsme's tone implied it was the obvious thing to do, and, moreover, he felt only too glad of the pretext for an early escape. He was conscious that the dreary atmosphere of the place and Jacques's indifference were getting on his nerves. And, in any case, he had learned what he wanted to learn. What was the use of staying on?

"Yes," he replied. "Unfortunately I must get back to Paris early, for my afternoon visits."

"There's nothing to regret; the next train doesn't leave till late in the day. Well, so long, doctor!"

The brothers were alone. For a moment both felt embarrassed.

"Take the chair," Jacques said, and moved towards the bed as if to seat himself on it. Then he noticed the second chair, changed his mind, and, offering it to Antoine, repeated: "Take the chair" in a natural tone, as if he were saying: "Do sit down!"

Nothing of this byplay had escaped Antoine; his suspicions were aroused.

"So you have only one chair as a rule," he observed.

"Yes. But Arthur's lent us his today, as he does when my tutor comes."

Antoine did not press the point.

"Well, they seem to do you pretty well here." He cast another glance around the room. Pointing to the clean sheets and towels, he added: "Do they change the linen often?"

"Sundays."

Antoine had been speaking in the crisp, cheerful tone that was usual with him, but somehow in this echoing room, in the atmosphere created by Jacques's apathy, it sounded incisive, almost aggressive.

"Just think," he said, "I was worried about you, I hardly know why. I was afraid they might be treating you badly here."

Jacques gazed at him with surprise, and smiled. Antoine kept his eyes fixed on his brother's face.

"Well, now, honestly, between ourselves, you've nothing to complain of?"

"Nothing."

"Now that I'm here, isn't there anything I could fix up for you with the superintendent?"

"What sort of thing?"

"How can I tell? Think, now."

Jacques seemed to ponder, smiled again, then shook his head.

"No. As you can see, everything's quite all right."

His voice had changed, like everything else about him; it was a man's voice now, with an agreeable, if rather muffled, resonance, which came as a surprise from one so obviously a mere boy.

Antoine gazed at him again. "Yes, Jacques, how you've changed! No, 'changed' isn't really the word for it; you're no longer the same, not a bit, not in any way."

He still kept his eyes on Jacques, trying to recognize in the unfamiliar face the features he had known. There was still the same reddish hair, a little darker and browner now, but still coarse and growing low on the forehead; there was the same narrow, ill-formed nose, the same cracked lips, shaded now by a faint fringe of down; the same heavy jaw, but more massive than in the past; and the same protuberant ears that seemed tugging at the mouth, keeping it stretched. Yet nothing of it all was really like the youngster of the day before yesterday. "It looks as if his temperament has changed as well," Antoine mused. "He used to be so changeable, always on edge —and now he looks half asleep, as if his face had been ironed out! Yes, he used to be a nervous type, and now he's gone lymphatic."

"Stand up for a moment," he said.

Jacques submitted to the examination with an amiable smile, but there was no warmth in it. The pupils of his eyes seemed misted over.

Antoine felt his arms and legs.

"Goodness, how you've shot up! Sure it isn't telling on your health?"

Jacques shook his head. Antoine was holding the boy in front of him, by the wrists. He was struck by the paleness of the freckled cheeks and the pouches under the eyes.

"None too healthy, your colour," he went on, with a touch of seriousness. He frowned, was on the point of saying something more, but stopped.

Suddenly the sight of Jacques's submissive, expressionless face had revived all the suspicions he had vaguely felt when he first had seen Jacques in the quadrangle.

"I suppose they told you I was waiting for you after mass, didn't they?" he asked abruptly.

Jacques looked at him uncomprehendingly.

"When you came out of the chapel," Antoine persisted, "did you know that I was here?"

"Certainly not. How could I know?" Jacques's smile conveyed candid amazement.

Antoine decided to drop the subject. "Well, I rather thought they had. . . . Can I smoke here?" he asked, to change the subject.

Jacques looked at him anxiously. Antoine held out his cigarette-case.

"Have one?"

"No, thanks." A shadow seemed to settle on his face.

Antoine was at a loss what to say. As usually happens when someone wants to prolong a conversation with a taciturn companion, Antoine racked his brains to think of questions he might put.

"So really and truly," he began, "there's nothing you need. You've got all you want?"

"Yes, thank you."

"Is your bed comfortable? Have you enough blankets?"

"Oh, yes; I'm too warm sometimes."

"What about your tutor? Is he decent to you?"

"Very."

"But doesn't it bore you rather, working like this, all by yourself?"

"No."

"How do you spend the evenings?"

"I go to bed after dinner, at eight o'clock."

"When do you get up?"

"When the bell rings, at half-past six."

"Does the confessor come to see you sometimes?"

"Yes."

"Do you like him?"

Jacques stared blankly at Antoine. He did not understand the question, and made no answer.

"And does the superintendent come as well?"

"Yes, often."

"He looks a good sort. Do the boys like him?"

"I don't know. I expect so."

"You never meet the—the others?"

"Never."

At each question Jacques, whose eyes were constantly lowered, gave a slight shiver, as if it were a strain for him to jump like this from one subject to another.

"How about your poems? Do you still write poetry?" Antoine asked with a smile.

"Oh, no."

"Why not?"

Jacques shrugged his shoulders; a placid smile came to his lips and lingered there for some moments. It was the sort of smile Antoine would have expected had his question been: "Do you still play with a hoop?"

In despair Antoine switched the conversation round to Daniel. Jacques was not prepared for that; he flushed a little.

"How do you expect me to know anything about him?" he said. "We don't get letters here."

"But," Antoine went on, "don't you ever write to him?" He kept his eyes fixed on his brother.

The boy smiled as he had done when Antoine had referred to his poems, and made a faint gesture as if to wave away the topic.

"It's ancient history, all that. Don't let's talk of it any more."

What did he mean by that? If he had said: "No, I've never written to him," Antoine would have bluntly given him the lie, and felt a secret pleasure in doing so, for Jacques's air of apathy was beginning to irritate him. But Jacques had eluded his question, and there had been a melancholy finality in his tone that had silenced Antoine. Just then he fancied he saw Jacques's eyes grow suddenly intent on something behind himself, by the door; and, in his mood of latent irritation, he felt all his suspicions come crowding back. The door had a window in it, no doubt to make it possible to see from outside what was going on in the room, and over the door was a grating through which what was said could be overheard from outside.

"There's someone in the corridor, isn't there?" Antoine asked bluntly, but in a low voice.

Jacques stared at him as if he had gone mad.

"Someone in the corridor? What do you mean? Sometimes people go by. Just now I saw old Léon passing."

There was a knock at the door and Léon came in to be introduced to the big brother. Without more ado he sat down on the edge of the table.

"I hope you find him fit, sir. Ain't he shot up since the autumn?"

He was laughing. He looked a typical old-school French sergeant-major. He had a big, drooping moustache, and tanned cheeks which his jovial belly-laugh suffused with a glow of blood that ramified across them in a network of red veins, spreading into the whites of his eyes and blurring their expression, which normally, it seemed, was one of fatherly good humour with a spice of mischief in it.

"They've packed me off to the workshops," he said to Antoine, with a resigned shrug of his shoulders. "And I'd got so used to this young gentleman! Ah, well," he added, as he moved away, "it's no use crying over spilt milk, as they say. . . . Give my respects to M. Thibault, if it ain't too much trouble, sir. He knows me well, does your old dad."

"What a fine old chap!" Antoine exclaimed when he had gone.

Then he tried to get their talk under way again.

"I could take him a letter from you, if you want to send one," he said. When Jacques stared at him uncomprehendingly, he added: "Wouldn't you like to write a word to Fontanin?"

Yet again he was trying to summon up to the boy's listless face some hint of real feeling, some memory of the past; and again he failed. Jacques merely shook his head, unsmiling.

"No, thanks. I've nothing to say to him. All that's ancient history."

Antoine left it at that. Inwardly he was furious. Moreover, it must be getting late; he took out his watch.

"Half-past ten. In five minutes I must go."

Jacques suddenly looked ill at ease, as if there were something he wanted to say to his brother. He went on to inquire about Antoine's health, the time the train went, his medical examinations. And when Antoine rose he was struck by the tone in which Jacques sighed.

"What? So soon? Do stay a little longer."

He fancied then that the boy might have been put off by his coldness, that the visit might have given him more pleasure than he chose to evince.

"Are you glad I came?" he murmured awkwardly.

But Jacques's thoughts seemed far away. He gave a little start, as if surprised, and answered with a polite smile:

"Yes, of course. Very glad, thank you."

"Righto, I'll try to come again. Good-bye till then." He was feeling really annoyed. He looked at his young brother again, full in the face; all his perceptive powers were on the alert, and his emotions, too, were stirred.

"I often think of you, and I must say I'm feeling worried—that you mayn't be happy here." They were near the door. Antoine grasped Jacques's hand. "You'd tell me if you weren't, wouldn't you?"

Jacques looked embarrassed. He made an impulsive movement, as if at last he were about to confide in Antoine. Then he seemed to come to a quick decision.

"Antoine, I wish you'd give something to Arthur, the servant. He's so obliging, you know." Antoine was so taken aback that he did not answer at once. Jacques went on in a pleading voice: "You'll give him a tip, won't you?"

"But," Antoine replied, "mightn't it lead to . . . complications?"

"No, of course not. When you're going, say good-bye to him nicely and give him a small tip. Please, Antoine!" His attitude was almost imploring.

"Of course I will. But I want to know the truth about you, and I want a straight answer. Are you unhappy here?"

"No, certainly not!" There was a hint of vexation in Jacques's voice. Then he added in a lower tone: "How much will you give him?"

"Haven't an idea. What do you think? How about ten francs? Or would you rather twenty?"

"Oh, yes, twenty!" Jacques seemed delighted, but embarrassed at the same time. "Thank you, Antoine." And he gripped affectionately the hand his brother gave him.

Arthur was going along the corridor as Antoine went out. He took the tip without demur, and his frank, slightly childish face flushed with pleasure. He escorted Antoine to the superintendent's office.

"It's a quarter to eleven," M. Faîsme said. "You've got time enough, but you must start at once."

They crossed the vestibule in which the Founder's bust lorded it superbly. And now, when Antoine saw it again, his sense of irony was quelled. For he realized now how well founded was his father's pride in this institution, which he had built up unaided; and he felt a vicarious pride in being his father's son.

M. Faîsme accompanied him to the gate, begging him to present his respects to M. Thibault. As he spoke, he never ceased laughing, puckering his eyes behind the gold-rimmed spectacles. The hands he pressed almost affectionately round Antoine's hand were plump and yielding as a woman's. At last Antoine managed to free himself. Looking back, he saw the little man standing in the road, bare-headed in the sunlight, still laughing and wagging his head with every sign of amity.

"Really, I'm as silly as a hysterical schoolgirl, letting my imagination run away with me like that!" Antoine was saying to himself as he walked to the station. "That show is excellently run, and Jacques isn't a bit unhappy.

"And the silliest thing," he suddenly thought, "is that I wasted my time cross-examining the boy instead of having a friendly chat with him."

He was almost inclined to believe his brother had been positively glad to see the last of him. "But it's a bit his own fault," he concluded with some exasperation; "he seemed so . . . so callous!" Still he was sorry he had failed to make the first advances.

Antoine did not keep a mistress and was satisfied with casual adventure. But he was twenty-four, and he sometimes felt an almost painful yearning for the nearness of some weaker being on whom he could lavish his compassion, whom he could protect and shield. His affection for Jacques was growing stronger with every step he took away from him. And now—when would he see him again? On the least pretext he would have turned back.

He walked with his eyes to the ground, to escape the glare of the morning sun. When, after a while, he raised them again, he saw he had missed his way. Some children showed him a short cut through the fields. He quickened his pace. "Supposing I missed the train," he thought, "what should I do?" Playing with the idea, he pictured his return to the reformatory; he would spend the day with Jacques, would tell him of his fantastic fears, and this journey he had kept secret from their father. And this time he would play the part of a real confidant, a comrade, and remind the boy of the scene in the cab on their return from Marseille, and how that night he had felt they might become real friends. His desire to miss the train became so urgent that he slackened his pace, though he had not yet come to an actual decision. Suddenly he heard the engine whistle, and a plume of smoke rose on his left, above the clump of trees. Unthinking, he began to run. The station was in sight. He had his ticket in his pocket, had only to jump into a car, running across the rails, if necessary. His head thrown back, his elbows pressed in to his sides like a professional sprinter, he took deep breaths of the keen air. Proud of his athletic fitness, he felt certain he would get there on time.

But he had reckoned without the embankment. To reach the station the road made a bend, passing under a little bridge. Vainly he made a spurt, getting the last ounce out of his muscles; when he came out on the far side of the bridge, the train was already moving out of the station. He had missed it by about a hundred yards.

Such was his pride that he would not admit he had been beaten in the race; he preferred to think he had missed the train on purpose. "I could still jump into the caboose if I wanted to," he thought, "but that would settle things peremptorily; then it would be impossible for me to see Jacques again." He stopped, pleased with his decision.

Immediately all he had been picturing took concrete form; he would lunch at the inn, go back after lunch to the reformatory, and spend the whole day with his brother.

III

ANTOINE was back at the reformatory gate a little before one. M. Faîsme was just going out, and was so taken aback that for a few seconds he seemed like a man of stone, but for the little eyes twinkling as usual behind his glasses. Antoine explained what had happened. Only then did the superintendent burst out laughing and regain his wonted loquacity.

Antoine explained that he would like to take his brother out for the afternoon, for a walk.

The superintendent looked dubious. "That's a bit of a problem. The regulations, you know. . . ."

But Antoine pressed his point with such insistence that the man gave in.

"Only I must ask you to explain the particular circumstances to the Founder. . . . Well, I'll go and fetch Jacques."

"I'll come with you," Antoine said.

He regretted it; they arrived at an unfortunate moment. They had scarcely entered the corridor when Antoine came on his brother squatting, for all the world to see, in the retreat known to the staff as the *vater-closette*. The door was being held open by Arthur, who was leaning against it, smoking a pipe.

Antoine walked quickly past and entered Jacques's room. M. Faîsme was rubbing his hands with an air of jubilation.

"You see!" he said. "The boys we look after are looked after—even there!"

Jacques came to his room. Antoine had expected he would seem embarrassed, but nothing of the sort. Jacques was buttoning up his clothes quite unconcernedly as he entered and his face was expressionless; he did not even seem surprised at Antoine's return. M. Faîsme explained that he would permit Jacques to be out with his brother until six. Jacques watched his face as if he wanted to be sure of understanding exactly what he meant, but made no comment.

"Now I really must fly, if you'll excuse me," M. Faîsme said in his brisk falsetto voice. "There's a meeting of my Municipal Council. Would you believe it, I'm the Mayor here!" He was roaring with laughter, as if he had cracked a joke of the first order, as he vanished through the door. Even Antoine was infected by his merriment.

Jacques dressed composedly. Antoine was struck by Arthur's attentiveness to Jacques as he handed him his clothes. When he volunteered to give his shoes an extra shine, Jacques made no objection.

The room had already lost the well-kept aspect that had so favourably impressed Antoine in the morning. He tried to discover why. The luncheon-tray was still on the table; there were an empty mug, a dirty plate, bread-crumbs. The clean linen had disappeared; a single soiled hand-towel hung on the rail; under the basin was a square of dirty, tattered oilcloth. The white bed-linen had been replaced by rough, unbleached, shabby-looking sheets. And suddenly all his suspicions were reawakened. But now he refrained from asking questions.

They set out onto the high road side by side.

"Where shall we go?" Antoine asked in a cheerful tone. "You don't know Compiègne? It's only about two miles' walk, along the banks of the Oise. Like to have a look at it?"

Jacques agreed. He seemed decided to agree with everything his brother proposed.

Antoine slipped his arm through his brother's and fell into step with him.

"What did you think of the towel trick?" he asked. He looked at Jacques, and laughed.

"The towel trick?" his brother repeated blankly.

"Don't you remember? This morning, while I was being trotted round the place, they took advantage of it to lay your bed with clean sheets and hang nice clean towels by your washstand. Very clever! Unluckily I turned up again, like a bad penny! One in the eye for them!"

Jacques stopped abruptly, a faint, uneasy smile on his lips.

"Really one would think you want to find fault with everything that goes on at the institution," he blurted out, his deep voice quivering a little.

He fell silent for a while and continued walking at his brother's side. A moment later he spoke again, obviously forcing himself to do so, as if it bored him desperately having to enlarge on so futile a topic.

"You don't realize, Antoine. It's quite simple, really. The linen is changed on the first and third Sundays of each month. Arthur, who has been looking after me for the last ten days, had changed the sheets and towels last Sunday, so he thought it was his duty to change them again this morning, as it was a Sunday. The people at the linen-room told him he had made a mistake, so he had to take back the clean linen, which I'm not due to get till next week." Again he fell silent, gazing at the landscape.

A bad start! Antoine applied himself to turn their conversation into another channel, but he was still feeling annoyed at his clumsiness; somehow he could not strike the note of everyday good-fellowship he wanted. Jacques answered briefly, yes or no, to Antoine's questions, and did not show the slightest interest. At last he spoke, of his own accord.

"Please, Antoine, don't mention the business about the towels to the superintendent; it would only get Arthur into trouble over nothing at all."

"All right."

"Nor to Papa, either," Jacques added.

"I'll tell nobody, don't worry. As a matter of fact it had passed out of my mind. Now, look here, Jacques," he went on, "I'm going to tell you the truth. Just imagine, I'd got it into my head, I don't know why, that this was a rotten place, that you were having a bad time here."

Jacques turned a little and examined his brother's face with a serious expression.

"I spent the morning nosing round," Antoine went on. "Finally, I saw I'd been mistaken. Then I pretended to miss my train. You see, I didn't want to go without having had time for a good talk with you."

Jacques made no reply. Did he relish the prospect of a "good talk"? Antoine felt uncertain and, fearing to make a false step, kept silent.

The road fell steeply towards the river, and they began to walk ahead more briskly. Presently they came to a bend of the river, which was converted at this point into a canal and spanned by a narrow iron bridge, crossing a lock. Three empty barges, their fat brown hulls almost entirely above the water-level, were floating on the all but stagnant stream.

"How'd you like the idea of a trip in a barge?" Antoine asked. "It would be fun dropping down through the morning mists, between the poplars on the banks, stopping at the locks now and then— wouldn't it? And, in the evening, at sunset, smoking a cigarette in the bows, thinking of nothing, dangling one's legs over the water. . . . By the way, do you still go in for drawing?"

Jacques gave a very definite start, and Antoine was certain he saw him blush.

"Why . . . ?" he asked in an uneasy voice.

"Oh, I hadn't any special reason for asking." But Antoine's curiosity was aroused. "I was only thinking one could make a rather pretty sketch here, with the barges, the lock, and the little bridge."

The towpath broadened, became a road. They were coming to a wide reach of the Oise, whose swollen waters rolled towards them.

"There's Compiègne," Antoine said.

He had stopped and put his hand to his forehead to shelter his eyes from the sun. On the horizon, above the green mass of the woods, he saw a group of pinnacles around a belfry, the round tower of a church. He was about to tell the names of the churches to his brother —who, like himself, was holding his hand over his eyes and seemed to be gazing towards the horizon—when he noticed that Jacques's eyes were fixed on the ground beside his feet. He seemed to be waiting for Antoine to go on with the walk; without a word, Antoine started forward again.

All Compiègne was out of doors. The brothers joined the crowd streaming across the bridge. There had evidently been a medical examination of recruits that morning, for groups of young men in their Sunday best were buying tricolour ribbons from street venders and lurching down the pavements arm in arm, leaving no room for the ordinary townsfolk, and bawling soldiers' songs. On the Mall, amongst young women in summery attire and booted cavalrymen the local families were strolling, greeting each other affably.

The sight of all these people was making Jacques feel more and more ill at ease and he begged Antoine to come away.

They took a street that turned off from the main thoroughfare; shaded and quiet, it gently rose towards the Palace Square. When they came out into the open again, the sunlight almost blinded them. Jacques blinked his eyes. Halting, they sat down under the trees, neatly set out in alternating rows, shadeless as yet.

"Listen!" he said, putting his hand on Antoine's knee. The bells of Saint-Jacques's were ringing for vespers, and their long vibrations seemed to merge into the sunlight.

Antoine supposed that at last, unwittingly, the boy had responded to the bright enchantment of that first spring Sunday.

"A penny for your thoughts!" He smiled.

But, instead of answering, Jacques rose and began walking towards the park. The majesty of the scene did not seem to evoke the slightest response from him. What he wanted most of all apparently was to get away from places where there were people about. The calm that reigned around the château, on the great walled terraces, drew him towards it. Antoine followed, making conversation about whatever caught his eye: the clipped box borders skirting the green lawns, the ringdoves settling on the statues' shoulders. But the boy's replies were always evasive.

Suddenly Jacques asked: "Have you spoken to him?"

"To whom?"

"Fontanin."

"Yes, I met him the other day in the Latin Quarter. Do you know, he's a day-boy now at the Lycée Louis-le-Grand?"

"Really?" was all Jacques said at first. Then he added, with a faint tremor in his voice that for the first time had something in it of the peremptory tone familiar with him in the past: "You didn't tell him where I was, did you?"

"He didn't ask me. Why? You'd rather he didn't know?"

"No."

"Why?"

"Because . . . !" He did not go on.

"An excellent reason!" Antoine laughed. "But I suppose you've got another, eh?"

Jacques stared blankly at him; evidently he had not realized Antoine was joking. Aloof as ever, he started walking again. Then abruptly he asked another question.

"And Gise? Does she know?"

"Where you are? No, I don't think so. But with children one can never be sure of anything." Now that Jacques himself had started a topic of conversation, Antoine made the most of it. "And Gise is such a quaint little thing. Some days you'd think she was quite grown up; she listens to everything that's said with her eyes full of interest —and pretty eyes they are! And on other days she's just like a baby. Would you believe it, yesterday Mademoiselle was looking for her everywhere, and there she was playing with her dolls under the hall table! And she's going on eleven, you know."

They were going down towards the wistaria arbour; Jacques halted at the bottom of the steps beside a sphinx in mottled pink marble, and began stroking pensively the sleek, cool forehead gleaming in the sunlight. Was he thinking of Gise and Mademoiselle? Had a sudden picture risen before him of the old hall table, with its fringed cloth and silver platter full of visiting-cards? So Antoine thought, and went on cheerfully.

"Heaven only knows where she gets all her ideas from. Our home can't be much fun for a kid, can it? Mademoiselle adores her, but you know what she's like; she's always in a flutter, she won't let the poor child do anything, never leaves her in peace for a moment."

Laughing, he tried to catch his brother's eye, feeling that these little details of their family life were like a secret treasury to which they alone had the key—something unique and irreplaceable, the memories of childhood spent in common. But Jacques vouchsafed only a fleeting, artificial smile.

Antoine, however, was not to be silenced now.

"Meals aren't much fun nowadays, I can tell you. Father doesn't open his mouth, or else serves up to Mademoiselle a sort of rehash of his latest public speeches, or tells her how he spent the day, down to the least detail. By the way, his election for the Institute is going very well, I hear."

"Yes?" A hint of tenderness crept over Jacques's face. After musing for a moment, he smiled. "So much the better!"

"All his friends are putting their backs into it," Antoine went on. "The Abbé's a pillar of strength; he has friends in every camp, you know. The election is in three weeks." He had stopped laughing, and added in a lower voice: "You may say what you like, but to be a member of the Institute means something. And Father really deserves it, don't you agree?"

"Rather!" the boy cried enthusiastically. "He's awfully good, really —a really good man at heart." He stopped; then, obviously eager to continue, could not bring himself to do so. He was blushing.

"I'm waiting till Father's comfortably ensconced beneath that august dome before springing a great surprise on him." Antoine was obviously carried away by his subject. "I'm really awfully cramped in my room at the end of the hall; I've no room for my books, for one thing. Did you know Gise has been put in your old room? I'd like to persuade Father to rent the little flat on the ground floor, where that old chap we called 'the gay old spark' is now; he's leaving on the fifteenth. There are three rooms and I could have a proper study where I could see patients, and perhaps a sort of laboratory—I could fix it up in the kitchen."

Suddenly he realized how tactless he was being in thus depicting the freedom he enjoyed and his preoccupations with his personal comfort, to this unhappy boy cut off from the world. And he realized, too, that he had just spoken of Jacques's room as if he were never to come back to it. He stopped abruptly. Jacques had resumed his air of indifference.

"Well, now," Antoine said, to clear the air, "how about something to eat? What do you say to it? I expect you're feeling peckish."

He had lost all hope of establishing easy fraternal relations between Jacques and himself.

They went back to the town. The streets were still crowded, and buzzing like a beehive. The tea-shops were overflowing with customers. Brought to a full stop by the crowd, Jacques stood unmoving in front of a confectioner's window resplendent with gaudy rows of cakes in sugar icing and exuding cream, the sight of which seemed to fascinate him.

"Right! Let's go in here," Antoine smiled.

Jacques's hands were trembling as he took the plate Antoine handed him. They sat down at the far end of the shop, in front of a pyramid of mixed cakes. Rich wafts of vanilla and warm pastry came up through a service hatch. Unspeaking, slumped in his chair, his eyes swollen as if with unshed tears, Jacques wolfed his food down, stopping after each cake and waiting for Antoine to hand him another, which he began at once to eat voraciously. Antoine ordered two ports. Jacques's fingers were still trembling as he took up his glass. The first sip of the wine seemed to burn him, and he coughed. Antoine drank his wine slowly, feigning not to notice his brother. Taking courage, Jacques gulped down a mouthful, felt it tingling in his gullet like liquid fire; after another gulp he drained his glass to the dregs. When Antoine began to pour him out a second glass, he pretended not to notice and, only when the glass was nearly full, made a vague gesture of refusal. . . .

When they left the shop the sun was nearing the horizon and the temperature had dropped. But Jacques was unconscious of the change. His cheeks were burning and his whole body tingled with a feeling of well-being so unaccustomed that it was almost painful.

"We've got those two miles to cover," Antoine said. "I suppose we'd better start back at once."

Jacques was on the verge of tears. Clenching his fists in his pocket, he set his jaw and bent his head. Antoine, who was secretly watching him, was alarmed by the change that had come over the boy's face.

"Sure the walk hasn't tired you?" he asked.

It seemed to Jacques that there was a new note of affection in his brother's voice. But he could not find a word to say, and the face he turned towards Antoine was grief-stricken, the eyes were full of tears.

Greatly amazed, Antoine followed him in silence. After they had crossed the bridge and left the town behind, and were once more on the towpath, he moved closer to Jacques, and took his arm.

"Not too sorry to have missed your usual walk?" he asked with a smile.

Jacques made no reply. Then suddenly it all came over him with a rush—the after-effect of this first heady taste of freedom, of the strong wine, and now the soft, sad dusk falling from the bright air. His emotions were too strong for him; he burst out sobbing. Antoine put his arm around him, steadying him, then sat down on the embankment and drew his brother to his side. He was no longer bent on prying into the intimacies of his young brother's life. He was conscious only of a vast relief that at last the blank wall of apathy against which he had been coming all day long seemed to be giving way.

They were alone on the deserted river bank, alone with the dark recession of the water, under a misty sky dappled with the fires of sunset. In front of them a punt, chained to the bank, was swaying on the eddies, making the dry reeds rustle.

They had still a good way to go, Antoine was thinking, and they could not stay here for ever. Above all, he wanted to make the boy raise his head.

"What's come over you, Jacques? Why are you crying?"

Jacques pressed tighter against him.

"Was it thinking about your usual walk that made you cry?"

Jacques felt he must say something. "Yes," he answered.

"Why should it? Where do you usually go on Sundays?"

No answer.

"So you don't like going out with Arthur?"

"No."

"Why don't you say so? If you'd rather have old Léon, it's easy to fix up, you know."

"No! No!" The change in his voice from apathy to rage was startling. Jacques had straightened up, and Antoine was dumbfounded by the look of bitter hatred on his face.

It seemed as if Jacques could not bear staying still; he began hurrying along the path, dragging his brother after him.

"So you didn't like going out with Léon, either?"

Jacques went on walking, his eyes wide open, gritting his teeth, and obstinately silent.

"Still, he behaved quite nicely to you, didn't he?" Antoine went on.

Again no answer. He was afraid Jacques was going to shrink back into his shell once more, and tried to take his arm. The boy shook it off, and hurried on. Antoine followed, uncertain how to continue, anxiously wondering how to regain his confidence. Then, unexpectedly, Jacques slowed down, with a sudden sob. Tears were running down his cheeks; he did not look at his brother.

"Antoine, please promise not to tell, never to tell any one. I didn't go walking with Léon, scarcely at all. . . ."

He stopped. Antoine was on the brink of asking a question, but instinct warned him not to utter a sound. And presently Jacques spoke again in a voice that sounded uncertain, a little hoarse.

"On the first days, yes. As a matter of fact it was on our walks that he began to—to tell me things. And he lent me books; I didn't believe such books existed! Afterwards he said he'd post letters for me, if I wanted. It was then I wrote to Daniel. But I hadn't any money for stamps. Then something happened. Léon had noticed I could draw a bit. Then—but you can guess, can't you? It was he who told me what was wanted. Then, in exchange, he paid for the stamp on my letter. In the evening he showed the drawings round to the guards, and they kept on asking for others, more and more elaborate ones. From that moment Léon did just as he liked, he stopped our walks altogether. Instead of going into the country, he used to take me round the back of the buildings, through the village. The children used to run after us. We always went by a side-street to get into the tavern through the back yard. Then he'd go off to drink and play cards or whatever he wanted to do, and while he was at it I was kept hidden in a wash-house, with an old blanket over me."

"What? They kept you in hiding?"

"Yes, I used to have to stay two hours locked up in the wash-house like that."

"But why?"

"I don't know. Well, of course the people who kept the place felt anxious. . . . One day there was some washing to be dried in there, so I was kept in a passage instead. The woman there said—she said . . ." His voice was broken by sobs.

"What did she say?"

"She said: 'One never knows with these beastly little . . .'" He was sobbing so violently that he could not go on.

"'These beastly little . . .'?" Antoine prompted.

"'. . . little jailbirds!'" He brought out the word with an effort, then burst into a storm of weeping.

Antoine waited; just then his keen curiosity blunted the edge of his compassion.

"And what else?" he asked. "Tell me what else they did to you."

"Antoine, Antoine!" he cried. "Swear to me you won't tell anyone. Swear! If ever Papa suspected anything, he'd . . . Papa is so good, you know; it would upset him terribly. It's not his fault if he doesn't see things as we do." His voice grew appealing. "Antoine, please, Antoine—don't leave me now! Please!"

"Of course not, Jacques; I'm here and I'll stand by you. I won't breathe a word, I'll do exactly what you want. Only—tell me the truth." Seeing Jacques could not bring himself to speak, he added: "Did he beat you?"

"Who?"

"Why, Léon."

"Of course not!" Jacques was so surprised that he could not help smiling through his tears.

"They don't beat you there?"

"Never."

"Really and truly, never?"

"Never, Antoine."

"Well—what else?"

Jacques was silent.

"This new man, Arthur? He's not a nice chap, eh?"

Jacques shook his head.

"What's wrong with him? Does he go to the tavern, too?"

"No."

"Ah! So you do go out for real walks with him?"

"Yes."

"Well, what have you got against him? Is he harsh with you?"

"No."

"Then what is it? You don't like him?"

"No."

"Why? There must be some reason. . . ."

"Because . . ." Jacques turned his eyes away.

Antoine was silent for a moment, then he broke out: "But, damn it all, why don't you complain? Why don't you tell the superintendent about it?"

Carried away by nervous excitement, Jacques pressed his body feverishly against his brother's.

"Oh, Antoine," he begged, "you mustn't! You swore you wouldn't tell anyone about it. You know you did."

"Yes, yes, that's understood. But what I'm asking is, why didn't you complain of Léon to M. Faîsme?"

Jacques merely shook his head, without a word.

"Do you suspect that the superintendent knows what's going on, and connives at it?" he suggested.

"Oh, no!"

"What do you think of the superintendent?"

"Nothing."

"Do you think he gives the other boys a bad time?"

"No. Why?"

"Well, he looks decent enough, but now I feel all at sea. Old Léon, too, looked a good chap. Have you heard anything against the super-intendent?"

"No."

"Are the staff afraid of him? Old Léon and Arthur, for instance?"

"Yes, a bit."

"Why?"

"I don't know. Because he's the superintendent."

"How about you? When he's with you have you noticed anything?"

"What do you mean?"

"So you don't dare to speak freely to him?"

"No."

"Supposing you'd told him that Léon went to the tavern instead of taking you for walks, and that you were kept locked up in a wash-house, what do you think he'd have done?"

"He'd have had Léon sent away." Jacques sounded terrified at the thought.

"So something prevented you from telling him. What was it?"

"That, of course!"

Antoine could make nothing of the answer, but he had a feeling that his brother was trapped in a network of complicities. Neverthe-less, at all costs, he was determined to get at the truth.

"Look here! Is it that you don't want to tell me what it really was? Or don't you know, yourself?"

"There were some drawings that—that they forced me to sign." Jacques lowered his eyes. Then, after a moment's hesitation, he added: "But it's not only that. One can't say anything to M. Faîsme, you understand, because—well, because he is the superintendent. You see what I mean, don't you?"

His tone was weary, but sincere, and Antoine did not insist; he mistrusted himself, knowing how apt he was to jump to over-hasty conclusions.

"Anyhow," he said, "are you working well?"

The sluice-gates were in sight; behind the little windows in the barges lamps were already being lit. Jacques walked ahead, his eyes fixed on the ground.

Antoine repeated his question.

"So you're not going ahead with your work, either?"

Jacques shook his head, without looking up.

"But the superintendent told me your tutor was pleased with you."

Jacques seemed to have difficulty in keeping up with his brother's cross-examination.

"Well, you see," he said at last, in a toneless voice, "the tutor is quite old and he doesn't care much whether I work or not. He comes because he's been told to come, that's all. He knows nobody will check what he does. And he prefers having nothing to take home with him to correct. He stays for an hour, and we just chat; he's very friendly with me, he tells me about Compiègne and his other pupils and all sorts of things. He's not very happy, either. He's told me about his daughter who has stomach trouble and quarrels with his wife, because he's married again; and about his son who was a company sergeant-major, but was cashiered because he ran into debt over a woman. We just pretend to be reading, doing lessons, but we don't do anything, really."

He stopped. Antoine found nothing to say. He felt almost intimidated by this youngster who already had such wide experience of life. Besides, he had nothing more to ask. The boy resumed speaking, of his own accord, in a low, monotonous voice; but, in the disconnected flow of phrases, it was impossible to make out the associations between his ideas, or even what, after his previous taciturnity, was impelling him to pour his heart out.

"It's like what I do about the wine and water at the meals—I leave it to them, you see. Léon asked me to at the start, and it's all the same to me, you know; I'd just as soon drink plain water from the jug. What really annoys me is that they're always prowling about in the corridor; with their soft slippers one can't hear them. Sometimes, almost, they frighten me. No, I'm not really frightened; only the dreadful thing is that I can't make a movement without their seeing and hearing me. One's always alone, but never really alone, you understand. Not on my walks, not anywhere at all. It's nothing so very terrible, but in the long run, you know—oh, you've no idea of the effect it has, it makes one feel as if—as if everything was going round. There are days when I'd like to hide under my bed and cry. Not just to cry, you know, but to cry *without being seen*. It's like when you came this morning. They told me in the chapel. The superintendent sent the chief clerk to see what I was wearing and they brought my overcoat and my hat, as I was bare-headed. Oh, don't think they did it to deceive you, Antoine. No, not at all; it's just the custom here. It's like that on Mondays, the first Monday in the month, when Papa comes for the committee meeting, they always do things like that; just little trifles to make Papa pleased. It's the same thing with the bed-linen; what you saw this morning is clean linen that's always kept in my cupboard, to put out in the room if anyone comes. It's not that they leave me with dirty linen; no, they change it quite often enough and, when I ask for an extra towel, they always give it. But it's the custom, you know, to make things look nice when a visitor comes. . . .

"It's wrong of me to tell you all this, Antoine; it'll make you fancy all sorts of things that aren't true. I assure you I've nothing really to complain of, that the discipline isn't at all irksome, they don't try to make things hard for me; not a bit of it. But it's just this—this softness, do you see? And then, having nothing to do all day, tied up like that with nothing, absolutely nothing to do. At first the hours seemed to me so, so long, you've no idea. But one day I broke the mainspring of my watch, and since then it's been better, little by little I've got used to it. But I don't know how to express it, it's as if one had gone asleep deep down in oneself. One doesn't really suffer, because it's like being asleep, but it's disagreeable all the same, you understand."

He was silent for a moment. When he spoke again it was in broken phrases and the words seemed to come with an immense effort.

"And then, Antoine . . . no, I can't tell you everything. But you must know. . . . Left alone like that, one gets to have a whole lot of ideas . . . ideas one shouldn't have. Especially as . . . Well, there are Léon's stories, you know. And the drawings. Well, in a way it helps to pass the time, you know. I make them in the daytime and at night somehow my mind comes back to them. I know it's not right, I oughtn't to. Only . . . When one's alone . . . you understand, don't you? Oh, I'm wrong to tell you all this, I feel I shall regret it. But I'm so tired this evening, I can't hold myself in."

Suddenly he gave way to a flood of tears.

He had a strange feeling of frustration, as if, for all his efforts, he could not help lying, and the more he tried to tell the truth, the worse he succeeded in doing so. Yet nothing of what he had said was actually untrue. But by his tone, by overcolouring his troubles, and by the choice of facts he had described, he was conscious of having given a false impression of his life—and yet he could not do otherwise.

They had been making slow progress and were only half-way back. And it was half-past five. There was plenty of daylight left, but a mist was rising from the river, brimming over into the fields and swathing them in drifting vapour.

Antoine, as he helped the stumbling youngster on his way, was thinking hard. Not of what he must do; on that score his mind was made up: he must get the boy out of it. But he was wondering how to get his consent, and that looked like being difficult. At his first words Jacques clung to his arm, sobbing, reminding him of his promise to say nothing, do nothing.

"But of course, old man; I've sworn it! I'll do nothing you don't want me to do. Only, listen. Do you want to go on like this, frittering your life away in idleness, with no one of your own kind to talk to, in these sordid surroundings? And to think that only this morning I imagined you were happy here!"

"But I *am* happy!" In a moment all he had complained of fled from his mind, and all he now was conscious of was the languid ease of his seclusion, the somnolent routine and absence of control, not to mention his isolation from the family.

"Happy? If you were, I'd be ashamed of you! No, Jacques, I can't believe you really enjoy rotting away in that place. You're degrading yourself, ruining your brains—and it's been going on for far too long. I've promised you not to act without your consent; I'll keep my word, don't worry. But do think seriously about it; let's look the facts squarely in the face, like two friends, you and I—for we're friends now, aren't we?"

"Yes."

"You trust me, don't you?"

"Yes."

"Well, then? What are you afraid of?"

"I don't want to go back to Paris."

"Look here, Jacques, after the picture you've given me of your life here, family life couldn't be worse."

"Yes, it could!"

The bitterness in his voice stunned Antoine into silence, and he began to feel less sure of himself. "Damn it!" he muttered, vainly racking his brain for a solution. Time pressed, and he felt as if he were walking in pitch darkness. Then suddenly he saw light, he had hit on the solution! In a flash the whole plan was outlined in his head. He laughed.

"Jacques!" he cried. "Now listen to me and don't interrupt. Or, rather, answer. Suppose we found ourselves, you and I, alone in the world, wouldn't you like to come and live with me?"

At first the boy failed to understand what Antoine meant.

"But, Antoine," he said at last, "what ever do you mean? There's Papa. . . ."

Menacing, between them and the future, loomed their father's figure. The same idea crossed the minds of both: how easy things would be if he . . . ! Catching its reflection in his brother's gaze, Antoine felt suddenly ashamed and averted his eyes.

"Of course," Jacques was saying, "if I'd lived with you and only you, I'd have turned out quite different. I'd have worked well . . . I would work well; I might become, perhaps, a great poet."

Antoine stopped him with a gesture. "Well, then, listen; if I gave you my word that no one except myself should have anything to do with you, would you agree to leave this place?"

"Ye-es," Jacques murmured doubtfully. It was his craving for affection and his reluctance to offend his brother that led him to agree.

"But would you promise to let me plan out your life and studies, and keep an eye on you generally, just as if you were my son?"

"Yes."

"Right!" For a while Antoine kept silent, thinking things out. His desires were always so imperative that he never questioned their feasibility, and indeed he had never failed so far in bringing off what he had set his heart on, definitely and doggedly. He turned to the youngster, smiling.

"It's not a day-dream, Jacques." His tone was emphatic, though the smile did not leave his lips. "I know what I'm embarking on. Within a fortnight—do you hear?—within a fortnight it shall happen; take my word for it. Now, you've got to go back to your precious institution, looking as innocent as a lamb. Got it? And within two weeks, I swear it, you shall be free."

Though he had hardly heard what his brother was saying, Jacques pressed against Antoine, seized by a sudden longing for affection; he would have liked to take him in his arms and hug him and to stay thus, unmoving, pressed to the comforting warmth of his big brother's chest.

"You can depend on me," Antoine repeated.

He, too, was feeling comforted and uplifted in his own esteem, rejoicing in a welcome sense of power. He compared his life with Jacques's. "Poor devil," he thought, "things are always happening to him that would never happen to anyone else!" He meant: "the sort of things that have never happened to me." He pitied Jacques, but above all he felt a very keen joy at being the man he was, so levelheaded and so well equipped for happiness, for becoming a personality, a great doctor. He felt inclined to quicken his step, to whistle a gay tune. But Jacques seemed tired, and could make only slow progress. Anyhow, they were coming into Crouy.

"Trust me," he murmured once again, tightening his pressure on Jacques's arm.

M. Faîsme was smoking a cigar in front of the entrance-gate. No sooner did he catch sight of them than he came tripping along the road towards them.

"Hallo, my friends! Had a good time, eh? I don't mind betting you've been to have a look at Compiègne." Laughing out of sheer high spirits, he waved his arms in the direction of the town. "You went along the towpath, didn't you? Such a nice walk that is! Really, the country round here is charming, too charming for words!" He took out his watch. "I don't want to hurry you, doctor, but if you don't want to miss your train again . . ."

"I'm off," Antoine said. There was emotion in his voice as he said quietly: "*Au revoir,* Jacques!"

Night was falling. Jacques had his back to the fading light, and Antoine dimly saw a young, submissive face and eyes gazing towards the dark horizon. Again he said:

"*Au revoir!*"

Arthur was waiting in the quadrangle. Jacques would have preferred to take leave of the superintendent politely, but M. Faîsme had turned his back on him. He was bolting the entrance-gate, as he did every evening. The dog was barking loudly and across the noise Jacques made out Arthur's voice.

"Now then! Are you coming?"

He followed Arthur obediently.

He came back to his cell with a feeling of relief. Antoine's chair was still there by the table, and his elder brother's affection seemed still lingering round it. He put on his old suit. His body was tired, but his brain active. There seemed to be within him, beside the everyday Jacques, a second self, an immaterial being, new-born today, who watched the first self going about its tasks, and dominated it.

Somehow he found it impossible to sit still and he began pacing round and round the room. He was in the grip of a new and powerful emotion, which kept him on his feet, a vital force that thrust itself upon his consciousness. He went to the door and stood there, his forehead resting on the glass pane, his eyes fixed on the lamp in the deserted corridor. The stifling atmosphere from the hot pipes increased his fatigue. He was half asleep now. Suddenly on the far side of the glass a shadow loomed up. The double-locked door opened; Arthur was bringing his dinner.

"Come along, get a move on, you little *Schwein!*"

Before starting on the lentils, Jacques removed from the tray the slice of gruyère and the mug of wine and water.

"For me?" the young man asked. Smiling, he took the piece of cheese and moved across to the wardrobe before starting to eat it, so as not to be visible from the door. It was the time when, before beginning his dinner, M. Faîsme made a round of inspection along the corridors. He always wore slippers and oftener than not his visits became known only after his departure, by the reek of cigar-smoke wafted through the grating.

Jacques ate what remained of his bread, dipping the pieces into the lentil juice. No sooner had he finished than Arthur called to him.

"Now, young man, turn in!"

"But it's not eight yet."

"Don't you know it's Sunday and the boys are waiting for me downtown? Get a move on!"

Without answering, Jacques began to undress. Arthur, his hands in his pockets, watched him. There was a touch of unexpected, almost feminine grace in the coarse face and stalwart, stocky figure of the fair-haired young man.

"That brother of yours," he said with a knowing air, "he's a bit of all right; a real gent he is!" Smiling, he made as if to slip a coin into his pocket, then took the empty tray and went out.

When he returned Jacques was in bed.

"Mighty quick you've been tonight." The young man kicked Jacques's shoes under the washstand. "Look here, can't you tidy up your things a bit before turning in?" He came up to the bed. "Hear what I say, you little *Schwein?*" He pressed his hands on Jacques's shoulders and gave a little laugh. The smile on the boy's face grew more and more strained. "Quite sure you aren't hiding anything between the sheets? No books? No candles?"

He slipped his hand between the sheets. But with a movement that Arthur could neither foresee nor forestall, the boy broke free and flung himself away, his back to the wall. His eyes were dark with hatred.

"Aha!" Arthur chuckled. "We're very high and mighty tonight, ain't we? . . . But I could tell some tales, too—and don't you forget it!" He spoke in a low tone, keeping an eye on the door. Then, without paying any more attention to Jacques, he lit the oil-lamp that remained on all night, shut off the electric circuit with his master-key, and went out, whistling.

Jacques heard the key turn twice in the lock and then a sound of receding steps, rope-soled shoes padding away along the corridor. Then he rolled into the middle of the bed, stretched his limbs, and lay on his back. His teeth were chattering. He had lost heart, and when he recalled the events of the day and his confessions, he had an access of fury quickly followed by a mood of utter misery. Glimpses rose before him of Paris, of Antoine and his home, of quarrels and work and parental discipline. Yes, he had made an irremediable blunder, he had made himself over to his enemies! "But what do they want of me? Why can't they leave me alone?" He began to cry. Despairingly he tried to console himself with the thought that Antoine's fantastic idea would come to nothing, that M. Thibault would put his foot down. And now he saw his father as a deliverer. Yes, of course nothing would come of it, they would end by leaving him in peace, by letting him stay here, in this haven of repose, of lethargy and loneliness.

Above his head, on the ceiling, the light from the night-lamp flickered, flickered. . . .

Yes, here was peace, peace and happiness.

IV ·

ON THE ill-lit staircase Antoine met his father's secretary, M. Chasle, coming down, slinking rat-like close along the wall. Seeing Antoine, he pulled up abruptly with a startled look.

"Ah, so it's you?" He had picked up from his employer the trick of opening a conversation with this remark. Then he announced in a

confidential whisper: "There's bad news! The university group are
backing the Dean of the Faculty of Letters for the vacant seat at the Institute; that's fifteen votes lost at least; with those of the law members
that makes twenty-five votes gone. Bad luck, isn't it? Your father will
tell you all about it." He coughed. M. Chasle was always coughing,
out of nervousness, but, believing himself to be a victim of chronic
catarrh, sucked cough-lozenges all day. "I must fly now, or Mother
will be getting anxious," he went on, seeing that Antoine made no
comment. He took out his watch, listened to it before looking at the
time, turned up his collar, and went on down the stairs.

For seven years the little bespectacled man had been coming daily
to work for M. Thibault, yet Antoine hardly knew him better now
than on the first day. He spoke little, and always in a low voice, and
his conversation was a tissue of commonplaces, a thesaurus of catch-
words. He was a creature of trivial habits and a model of punctuality,
and he seemed to have a touching devotion for his mother, with whom
he lived. His shoes always squeaked. His Christian name was Jules, but
M. Thibault, mindful of his own dignity, always addressed his secretary as "M. Chasle." Antoine and Jacques had two nicknames for him:
"Old Gumdrop" and the "Pest."

Antoine went straight to his father's study. He found him setting his
papers in order before going to bed.

"Ah, so it's you? Bad news!"

"I know," Antoine said. "M. Chasle told me about it."

With an irritated jerk of his head M. Thibault freed his chin from
his collar; it always vexed him to find that what he was proposing
to announce was known already. But just now Antoine was not inclined to pay attention to his father's mood; his mind was full of the
object of this interview, and he was unpleasantly conscious that a sort
of paralysis was creeping over him. He decided for a frontal attack,
before it was too late.

"I, too, have some bad news for you, I'm sorry to say. Jacques cannot stay at Crouy." He took a deep breath, then went on at once:
"I've just come back from there. I've seen him. I got him to talk
frankly, and I've learned some abominable things. I want to talk to you

about it. It's up to you to get him out of the place as soon as possible."

For some seconds M. Thibault did not move; his stupefaction was perceptible only in his voice.

"What's that? You've been to Crouy? When? Why did you go there? You must be off your head. I insist on your explaining this conduct."

Relieved though he was to have taken the obstacle in his first stride, Antoine was extremely ill at ease and incapable of speaking. There followed an oppressive silence. M. Thibault had opened his eyes; now they closed again slowly, reluctantly, it seemed. Then he sat down and set his fists on the desk.

"Explain yourself, my dear boy," he said. He spoke each syllable with careful emphasis. "You say you have been to Crouy. When did you go?"

"Today."

"With whom?"

"Alone."

"Did they—let you in?"

"Naturally."

"Did they let you see your brother?"

"I have spent the day with him. Alone with him."

Antoine had a belligerent way of rapping out the last word of every phrase he spoke; it made M. Thibault angrier than ever, but also warned him to go warily with his son.

"You are a child no longer." The way he said this gave the impression he had just inferred Antoine's age from the sound of his voice. "You must understand the unsuitability of acting thus, behind my back. Had you any particular reason for going to Crouy without telling me? Did your brother write to you to come?"

"No. I had suddenly become anxious about him, that's all."

"Anxious? In what way?"

"About everything, about the whole system, about the effects of the life Jacques has been subjected to for nine months."

"Really, my dear fellow, you—you surprise me." He hesitated. The measured terms he was deliberately employing were belied by the large, tightly clenched hands and the furious way he jerked his head forward at each pause. "This mistrust of your father is . . ."

"Anybody can make mistakes," Antoine broke in. "And I can prove what I say."

"Prove it?"

"Listen, Father, it's no use losing your temper. I suppose we both desire the same thing—Jacques's welfare. When you know the state of moral decay I found him in, I'm sure you will be the first to decide that he must leave the reformatory at the earliest possible moment."

"That I will not!"

Antoine tried not to hear the sneering laugh which accompanied the remark.

"You will, Father."

"I tell you I will not!"

"Father, when you've heard . . ."

"Do you, by any chance, take me for a fool? Do you suppose I've had to wait for you to go and look round Crouy to learn how things are done there? I'd have you know that for over ten years I've been making a thorough inspection of the place every month and followed it up by a written report. No new step is taken there without being first discussed by the committee whose president I am. Now are you satisfied?"

"Father, what I saw there . . ."

"That's enough. Your brother may have poisoned your mind with all the lies he pleases; you're easy game. But you'll find I'm not so easy to hoodwink."

"Jacques didn't breathe a word of complaint."

M. Thibault seemed thunderstruck.

"Then, why on earth . . . ?" he asked, raising his voice a little.

"Quite the contrary," Antoine continued, "and that's the alarming thing. He told me he didn't worry; in fact he said he was happy, that he likes being there." Provoked by his father's chuckle of self-satisfaction, Antoine added in a cutting tone: "The poor boy has such memories of family life that even prison life strikes him as more agreeable."

The insult missed its mark.

"Very well," M. Thibault retorted, "then everything's as it should be; we're at one on that. What more do you want?"

As he was feeling less sure now of Jacque's release, Antoine judged it wiser not to repeat to M. Thibault all the boy had told him. He resolved to keep to generalities and withhold his detailed complaints.

"I'm going to tell you the whole truth," he began, gazing intently at his father. "I admit that I'd suspected ill-treatment, privation, solitary confinement, and so forth. Now I know. Happily there is nothing of that sort at Crouy. Jacques is not suffering physically, I grant, but in his mind, his morals—and that's far worse. You're being deceived when they tell you that isolation is doing him good. The remedy is far more dangerous than the disease. His days are passed in the most degrading sloth. As for his tutor, the less said the better; the truth is that Jacques does no work, and it's already obvious that his brain is growing incapable of the least effort. To prolong the treatment, believe me, will be to compromise his future irreparably. He is sinking into such a state of indifference to everything, and his mental flabbiness is such, that in another month or two he'll be too far gone, it will be too late to bring him back to mental health."

Antoine's eyes had never left his father's face as he was speaking. He seemed to be concentrating the utmost impact of his gaze on the stolid face, trying to force from it some gleam of acquiescence. M. Thibault, withdrawn into himself, preserved a massive immobility; he brought to mind one of those pachyderms whose strength remains hidden so long as they are at rest, and he had the elephant's large, flat ears and, now and then, his cunning eye. Antoine's harangue had reassured him. There had been some incipient scandals at the reformatory, certain attendants had had to be dismissed without the reasons for their departure being bruited abroad, and M. Thibault had for a moment feared that Antoine's revelations were of this order. Now he breathed freely again.

"Do you think that's news to me, my dear boy?" he asked with an air of jocular good humour. "All you've been saying does credit to your kindness of heart; but permit me to say that these questions of reformatory treatment are extremely complex, and in this field one does not become an expert overnight. Trust my experience, and the opinions of those who are versed in these subjects. You talk of your brother's—what do you call it?—'mental flabbiness.' But that's all to the good. You know what Jacques was like. Don't you realize that is the only way to crush out such evil propensities as his—by breaking down his will? For by gradually weakening the will-power of a depraved boy, you sap his evil instincts and, in the end, eradicate them. Now, consider the facts. Isn't your brother completely changed? His fits of rage have ceased; he's disciplined, polite to all who come in contact with him. You yourself admit that he has come to like the order and routine of his new life. Well, really, shouldn't we be proud of getting such good results within less than a year?"

He was teasing out the tip of his beard between his puffy fingers as he spoke; when he had finished, he cast a side-glance at his son. That booming voice and majestic delivery lent an appearance of force to his least words, and Antoine was so accustomed to letting himself be impressed by his father that in his heart he weakened. But now his pride led M. Thibault to commit a blunder.

"Now that I come to think of it," he said, "I wonder why I'm taking so much trouble to defend the propriety of a step which is not being, and will not be, reconsidered. I'm doing what I consider I ought to do, after taking careful thought, and I do not have to render an account to anyone. Get that into your head, my boy!"

Antoine made a gesture of indignation.

"That's not the way to silence me, Father! I tell you once more, Jacques must not remain at Crouy."

M. Thibault again emitted a harsh, sarcastic laugh. Antoine made an effort to keep his self-control.

"No, Father, it would be a crime to leave Jacques there. There are sterling qualities in him which must not be allowed to run to seed. And, let me tell you, Father, you've often been mistaken about his character; he irritates you and you don't see his . . ."

"What don't I see? It's only since he's gone that we've had any peace at home. Isn't that true? Very well, when he's reformed, we shall see

about having him back. Not before!" His fist rose as if he were about
to bring it down upon the table with a crash, but he merely opened
his hand and laid his palm flat on the desk. His wrath was still
smouldering. Antoine made no effort to restrain his own.

"I tell you, Father," he shouted, "Jacques shall not stay at Crouy!
I'll see to that!"

"Really now!" M. Thibault sounded frankly amused. "Really! Aren't
you, perhaps, a little inclined to forget that you're not the master here?"

"No, I'm not forgetting it. That's why I ask you—what you intend
to do."

"To do?" M. Thibault repeated the words slowly, with a frosty
smile. For a moment his eyebrows lifted. "There's no doubt about
what I mean to do: to give M. Faîsme a good dressing-down for
admitting you without my authorization, and to forbid you ever again
to set foot in Crouy."

Antoine folded his arms.

"So that's all they mean," he said, "your pamphlets, your speeches,
all your noble sentiments. They come in handy for public meetings,
but when a boy's mind is being wrecked, your own son's mind, it's all
the same to you. All you want is a quiet life at home, with no worries—
and to hell with all the rest!"

"You young ruffian!" M. Thibault shouted, rising to his feet. "Yes.
I'd seen it coming. I've known for quite a while what to expect of you.
Yes, I've noticed them—the remarks you sometimes let fall at table
and the books you read, your favourite newspapers. I've seen your
slackness in performing your religious duties. One thing leads to another; when religious principles go, moral anarchy sets in and, finally,
rebellion against all proper authority."

Antoine made a contemptuous gesture.

"Don't let's confuse the issues. We're talking about the boy, and it's
urgent. Father, promise me that Jacques . . ."

"I forbid you to speak to me again about him. Not another word.
Now have I made myself clear enough?"

Their eyes met, challenging.

"So that's your last word, is it?"

"Get out!"

"Ah, Father, you don't know me!" There was defiance in Antoine's laugh. "I swear to you I'll get Jacques out of that damned jail! And that I'll stop at nothing!"

A bulky, menacing form, M. Thibault advanced towards his son, his under-jaw protruding.

"Get out!"

Antoine had opened the door. Turning on the threshold, he faced his father and said in a low, resolute tone:

"At nothing, do you hear? Even if I have to start a campaign, a new one, in my 'favourite newspapers'!"

V

Eᴀʀʟʏ next morning, after a sleepless night, Antoine was waiting in a vestry of the Archbishop's Palace for the Abbé Vécard to finish his mass. It was essential that the priest should know the whole story, and somehow intervene; that was now Jacques's only chance.

The interview lasted for a long time. The Abbé had had the young man sit beside him, as if for a confession, and listened meditatively to him, in his favourite position, leaning well back in his chair, with his head slightly drooping to the left. He let Antoine have his say without interrupting him. The long-nosed, sallow face was almost expressionless, but now and again he cast a gentle, searching look on his companion, a look that conveyed his wish to read the thoughts behind the spoken words. Though he had seen less of Antoine than of the other members of the Thibault family, he had always treated him with particular esteem; what just now gave a certain piquancy to this attitude was that it was largely due to M. Thibault himself, whose vanity was always agreeably tickled by Antoine's successes, and who was fond of singing his son's praises.

Antoine did not try to win over the Abbé by dint of argument, but gave him an unvarnished account of the day he had spent at Crouy, ending by the scene with his father. For that the Abbé reproved him, not by words but by a deprecating flutter of his hands, which he had a way of holding level with his chest. They were the typical priest's hands, tapering smoothly away from round, plump wrists and capable of manifesting sudden animation without moving from where they were; it was as though nature had accorded them the faculty of expression which she had denied the Abbé's face.

"Jacques's fate is now in your hands, M. l'Abbé," Antoine concluded. "You alone can make Father listen to reason."

The priest did not answer, and the gaze he now gave Antoine was so aloof and sombre that the young man could draw no conclusion from it. It brought home to him his own powerlessness and the appalling difficulties of the task he had undertaken.

"And afterwards?" the Abbé softly questioned.

"What do you mean, sir?"

"Supposing your father brings Jacques back to Paris, what will he do with him afterwards?"

Antoine felt embarrassed. He knew exactly what he wanted to do, but wondered how to put it, for he had the gravest doubts as to whether he could get the Abbé to approve of his plan, involving as it did Jacques's quitting his father's flat and coming to live with his brother on the ground floor of the same building. And dare he tell the priest that he meant to remove the boy almost entirely from parental authority, to take on himself alone the supervision of Jacques's education, indeed the entire control of his brother's life? When he explained this to the priest, the latter smiled, but the smile was perfectly good-humoured.

"You'd be taking on a heavy task, my friend."

"No matter!" Antoine replied impetuously. "You know I'm absolutely convinced that what the boy needs is plenty of freedom, that he'll never develop in an atmosphere of repression. You may laugh at me, sir, but I'm positive that if I took entire responsibility for him . . ."

But he could get nothing more out of the Abbé than another shrug of the shoulders, followed by one of his shrewd, searching glances, that seemed to come from very far away and sink so deep. He felt profoundly disheartened when he left the Abbé. After the furious rebuff from his father, the priest's unenthusiastic reception of his scheme had left him scarcely any hope. He would have been much surprised to learn that the Abbé had resolved to go to see M. Thibault that very day.

He did not need to take that trouble. When he returned, as he did every day after mass, to drink his cup of cold milk in the flat, a few steps from the Archbishop's Palace, where he lived with his sister, he found M. Thibault waiting for him in the dining-room. The big, thick-set man, sunk in a chair with his large hands resting on his legs, was still nursing his resentment. At the Abbé's entrance he rose heavily from the chair.

"So here you are?" he murmured. "I suppose my visit is a surprise to you?"

"Not so much as you suppose," the Abbé answered. Now and again the ghost of a smile and a gleam of mischievous humour lit up the impassive face. "I have an excellent detective service and there's little I'm not informed of. But will you excuse me?" he added, going towards the mug of milk awaiting him on the table.

"What's that? Do you mean you've seen . . . ?"

The Abbé drank his milk in little sips.

"I learned how Astier was, yesterday morning, from the Duchess. But it was only last night that I heard of the withdrawal of your competitor."

"Astier? Do you mean . . . ? I don't follow. I've not been told anything. . . ."

"Well, now, that's amazing!" the Abbé smiled. "Is the pleasure of breaking the good news to you to be my privilege?" He took his time. "Well, then, old Astier's had a fourth stroke; this time the poor man's doomed, and so the Dean, who's no fool, is withdrawing, leaving you as the only candidate for election to the vacant seat at the Institute of Moral Science."

"What!" M. Thibault exclaimed. "The Dean's withdrawing! But why? I don't follow."

"Because, on second thought, he realizes that the post of Registrar would be more suitable for a Dean of the Faculty of Letters, and also because he'd rather wait a few weeks for a seat that isn't contested than risk his chance against you."

"Are you quite sure of it?"

"It's official. I met the permanent secretary at the gathering of the Catholic Association yesterday evening. The Dean had just called in, and he had his letter of withdrawal with him. A candidature that lasted less than twenty-four hours—that's rather unusual, isn't it?"

"But, in that case . . . !" M. Thibault panted. His surprise and delight had taken his breath away. He moved a few steps forward, without looking where he was going, his hands behind his back; then, turning to the priest, he all but embraced him. Actually he only clasped his hands.

"Ah, my dear Abbé, I shall never forget. Thank you. Thank you."

Again delight submerged him, leaving no room for any other feelings, sweeping away his anger; so much so that he had to exercise his memory when the Abbé—having without his noticing it led him to the study—asked in a perfectly natural tone:

"And what can have brought you here so early, my dear friend?"

Then he remembered Antoine, and at once his anger mastered him again. He had come, so he explained, to ask the Abbé's advice as to the attitude he should adopt towards his elder son, who had much changed lately, changed for the worse, towards a mood of unbelief and insubordination. Was he, for instance, conforming with his religious obligations? Did he go to mass? He was growing more and more erratic in his attendance at the family table—giving his patients as an excuse—and, when he did put in an appearance, behaved in a new and disagreeable manner. He contradicted his father and indulged in unthinkable liberties of speech. At the time of the recent municipal elections, the discussion had several times taken so bitter a turn that it had been necessary to tell him to hold his tongue, as if he were a small boy. In short, if Antoine was to be kept in the way he should go, some new line would have to be taken with him; in this respect M. Thibault felt that the assistance and perhaps the active intervention of his good friend the Abbé were indispensable. As an illustration, M. Thibault described the undutiful conduct of which Antoine had been guilty in going to Crouy, the foolish notions he had brought back with him, and the shocking scene that had followed. Yet all the time, the esteem in which he held Antoine and which, without his knowing it, was actually enhanced by the very acts of insubordination with which he was now reproaching him, was always evident; and the Abbé duly noted it.

Sitting listless at his desk, the priest from time to time signified his approval with little fluttering movements of his fingers on each side of the clerical bands that fell across his chest. Only when Jacques's name was mentioned did he raise his head and show signs of extreme interest. By a series of skilful, seemingly disconnected questions, he obtained confirmation from the father of all he had been told by the son.

"But really!" he exclaimed vaguely. He seemed to be talking to himself. He meditated for a few moments. M. Thibault waited, in some surprise. When the Abbé spoke again his voice was firm.

"What you tell me about Antoine's behaviour doesn't worry me as much as it does you, my friend. It was to be expected. The first effect of scientific studies on an inquiring and active mind is always to puff up a young man in his own conceit and cause his faith to waver. A little knowledge leads a man away from God; a great deal brings him back again. Don't be alarmed. Antoine's at the age when a man rushes from one extreme to another. You did well to tell me about it. I'll make a point of seeing him and talking to him oftener. None of that is very serious. Only have patience, and he'll come back to the fold.

"But what you tell me about Jacques's present life makes me feel far more anxious. I had no idea that his seclusion was of so extreme a nature. Why, the life he's leading is that of a convict, and I cannot but believe it has its perils. In fact, my dear friend, I confess I'm very worried about it. Have you given the matter your earnest consideration?"

M. Thibault smiled. "In all honesty, my dear Abbé, I can say to you as I said yesterday to Antoine: don't you realize that we are far better equipped than the common run for dealing with such problems?"

"I don't deny it," the priest agreed good-humouredly. "But the boys you usually have to deal with don't need the special handling that your younger son's peculiar temperament calls for. In any case, I gather, they are treated on a different system, they live together, have recreation hours in common, and are employed on manual work. I was, as you will remember, in favour of inflicting on Jacques a severe punishment, and I believed that a taste of somewhat prison-like surroundings might lead him to reflect and mend his ways. But, good heavens, I never dreamt of its being a real imprisonment; least of all that it would be inflicted on him for so long a period. Just think of it! A boy of scarcely fifteen has been kept alone in a cell for eight months under the supervision of an uneducated guard, as to whose probity of character you have only the assurances of the local officials. He has a few lessons—but what do you really know about this tutor from Compiègne who, in any case, devotes a mere three or four hours a week to teaching the boy? I repeat, what do you really know about him? Then again, one of the points you made was your experience. There let me remind you that I've lived amongst schoolboys for twelve years, that I'm far from ignorant of what a boy of fifteen is like. The state of physical and, worse, of moral decay into which this poor child may have fallen, without its being apparent to you—it makes one shudder!"

"Well, well!" M. Thibault exclaimed. "I'm surprised at that from *you*. I wouldn't have thought you so sentimentally minded," he added with a brief, ironic laugh. "But we aren't concerned with Jacques at present."

"Excuse me," the Abbé broke in, without raising his voice, "Jacques is our first concern just now. After what I've just learned, I consider that the physical and moral health of this child is being exposed to terrible risks." After seeming to ponder, he added with slow emphasis: "And he should not remain one day longer where he is."

"What!"

For a while neither spoke. It was the second time within twelve hours

that M. Thibault had been touched on the raw. He felt his temper
rising but kept it in check.

"We'll talk it over some other day," he said, beginning to rise. His
tone implied that he was making a great concession.

"No, I'm sorry, but that will not do," the priest broke in, with unwonted vivacity. "The least one can say is that you have acted with
an imprudence that is almost inexcusable." He had a way, soft but
emphatic, of letting his voice linger on certain words, though his face
showed no emotion, and at the same time raising his forefinger to his
lips, as if to say: Mark well what I am saying. He made this gesture
as he repeated: "Almost inexcusable!" After a momentary pause he
said: "And now the essential thing is to remedy the evil that's been
done."

"What? What do you want me to do?" M. Thibault had given up
trying to restrain his anger, and faced up to the priest aggressively.
"Am I going to cut short, without any reason, a treatment that has
already produced such excellent results, and take that young scoundrel
back into my house? Just to be once more at the mercy of his disgusting
fads and fancies? No, thank you!" He clenched his fists so fiercely that
the knuckles cracked, and his set teeth gave a guttural harshness to his
voice. "With all due consideration, I say—emphatically—*No!*"

The Abbé's hand made a brief conciliatory gesture, implying: Have
it your own way!

M. Thibault had pulled himself up heavily from his chair. Once
more Jacques's fate hung in the balance.

"My dear Abbé," he went on, "I see there's no prospect of a serious
talk with you this morning, so I'm off. But let me tell you, you're allowing your imagination to run away with you, exactly as Antoine did.
Come now! Do I look like an unnatural father? Haven't I done everything to bring back this child to the right path, by affection and kindness, by good example and the influences of family life? Haven't I endured for years the utmost a father can endure from a son? And can
you deny that all my well-meaning efforts have been wasted? Fortunately I realized in time that my duty lay along different lines and,
painful as it was, I did not hesitate to take stern measures. You agreed

with me then. Moreover, God in His mercy had given me some experience; I've often thought that in inspiring me with the idea of establishing that special department at Crouy, Providence enabled me to prepare in advance the remedy for a personal affliction. Have I not borne this trial with a certain courage? Would many fathers have done as I have done? Have I anything to reproach myself with? God be thanked, I have a quiet conscience." But, as he made the proud assertion, there came into his tone a note of uncertainty, as if some still small voice within were protesting against it. "My wish for every father is that his conscience may be as clear as mine!"

He opened the door, a complacent smile hovering on his face. For his parting shot, his voice had an accent of pawky humour, not without a savour that smacked of his native Norman soil.

"Luckily, my friend, I've a harder head than yours!"

He crossed the hall, followed by the Abbé, who made no reply.

On the landing he turned. "Well, well, good-bye for the present."

As he was proffering his hand, suddenly the priest began speaking in a low voice, almost to himself:

"'Two men went up into the temple to pray; the one a Pharisee, and the other a publican. The Pharisee stood and prayed thus with himself, God I thank Thee, that I am not as other men are. . . . I fast twice in the week, I give tithes of all that I possess. And the publican, standing afar off, would not lift up so much as his eyes unto heaven, but smote upon his breast, saying, God be merciful to me a sinner.'"

M. Thibault's eyelids lifted and he saw his confessor standing in the shadowy hall, with a finger on his lip.

"'I tell you, this man went down to his house justified rather than the other: for everyone that exalteth himself shall be abased; and he that humbleth himself shall be exalted.'"

Without flinching the burly "Pharisee" heard him out; his eyes were closed now and he made no movement. Presently, as the silence continued, he ventured to look up again. Without a sound the priest had closed the door on him. Left to himself, he stared for a moment at the closed door; then, shrugging his shoulders, he turned on his heel and started down the stairs. Half-way down he halted, his hand clutching the balustrade; his breath was coming in short gasps and he was jerking his jaw forward, like a horse chafing at the bit.

"No," he murmured to himself. "No."

Without more hesitation he went on his way downstairs.

All that day he did his best to forget the interview. But in the course of the afternoon, when M. Chasle was slow in handing him a file he wanted, he had an access of rage that he had difficulty in repressing. Antoine was on duty at the hospital. Dinner that night was a silent meal. Without waiting for Gisèle to finish her dessert, M. Thibault folded his napkin and returned to his study.

Eight o'clock struck. "I might go back to him," he thought as he sat down. "It's not too late yet." But he was quite determined to do nothing of the kind. "He'll start talking to me again about Jacques. I have said no, and no it is.

"But what did he mean with the parable of the Pharisee and the publican?" he asked himself for the hundredth time. Suddenly his underlip began quivering. He had always been afraid of death. He stood up and, over the bronzes crowding the mantelpiece, scanned his face in the mirror. His features had lost the look of self-complacency that had stamped itself, indelibly as it had seemed, upon them, the look that never left them even when he was alone, even in prayer. A shudder ran through his body. His shoulders sagged and he dropped back into his chair. He was picturing himself on his deathbed, and a dread came over him that he might have to face his last hour empty-handed. He tried to reassure himself by recalling the high esteem in which the world held him.

"Still, am I not an upright man?" he kept on asking himself, but always with a rankling doubt. Words were not enough to quell his anxiety, for he was in one of those rare moods when a man delves down into himself, letting light into the dark places of his heart. With his hands clenched on the arms of his chair, he looked back on his life and found in it not one act that was wholly pure. In the twilight of his mind harrowing memories flickered into consciousness. One of them, crueller than all the rest, stung him so bitterly that he bowed his head and hid it with his hands. For the first time in his life perhaps, M. Thibault was ashamed. He knew at last that supreme self-disgust, so intolerable that no sacrifice seems too great, if only it sets a man right with his own conscience, buying divine forgiveness and restoring to the stricken heart a feeling of peace and hope of eternal salvation. Ah, to find God again! But first of all he must regain the good opinion of the priest, God's mandatory. No, he could not live an hour longer with this sense of damnable estrangement, under such obloquy.

Once he was in the open air, he felt calmer. To save time he took a cab. The Abbé opened the door; his face, under the lamp held high to see his visitor, betrayed no emotion of any kind.

"It's I," M. Thibault said mechanically, holding out his hand; then in silence he walked to the priest's study. "No, I've not come to talk to you about Jacques," he declared, the moment he was seated. The priest's hands made a vague, conciliatory movement. "There's nothing more to be said on that subject, I assure you; you're on a false scent. But, of course, if you feel you'd like to do so, why not go to Crouy and see for yourself?" With a rather naïve abruptness he continued: "Forgive me for my bad temper this morning. You know how easily roused I am. But really, well, at bottom I'm . . . Look here, you were too hard on me, you know. Much too hard on the 'Pharisee' you take me for! I'm perfectly justified in protesting—perfectly! Why, for thirty years haven't I been giving all my time, all my energies, to good works—not to mention the greater part of my income? And all the thanks I get is to be told by a priest, who is my personal friend, that I'm . . . Come now, own up, it's not fair!"

The Abbé looked at his penitent, and the look implied: "Pride is showing through again, for all you try to mask it, in every word you say."

There was a long silence, broken at last by M. Thibault.

"My dear Abbé," he said in an uneasy tone, "I admit I'm not altogether . . . Well, yes, I admit it; only too often I . . . But that's the way I'm built, if you see what I mean. You know that well enough, don't you?" He seemed to be pleading for the priest's indulgence. "Ah, it's a strait and narrow path indeed—and you're the only one who can guide me, keep me from stumbling. . . ."

Suddenly he murmured in a broken voice: "I'm getting old, I'm afraid. . . ."

The Abbé was touched by the change in his tone. Feeling he had been silent overlong, he drew his chair nearer to M. Thibault's and began to speak.

"It's I who now feel unsure of myself, and, indeed, my dear friend, what should I add, now that the holy words have sunk so deep into your heart?" He mused for a while before continuing. "I know well that God has placed you in a difficult position; the work you do for Him gives you authority over other men, and honours—and that is as it should be. Yet it may possibly incline you sometimes to confound His glory with your own. And might not this lead you, little by little, even to prefer yours to His?"

M. Thibault's eyes were for once wide open, and showed no sign of closing; there was consternation in their pale intensity, and a gleam of almost childish awe.

"And yet remember!" the Abbé went on. "*Ad majorem Dei gloriam.* That alone counts, and nothing else should weigh with us. You, my friend, are one of the strong ones of the earth, and the strong are usually proud. Oh, I know how hard it is to control the driving force of pride, to direct it into its proper channel. How hard it is not to live for onself, not to forget God, even when all one's life is taken up with acts of piety! Not to be amongst those of whom Our Lord once spoke so sadly: 'This people honoureth me with their lips, but their heart is far from me.' "

"Ah, yes," M. Thibault cried excitedly, without lowering his eyes, "indeed it's hard! No one on earth knows as well as I do how terribly hard it is."

In self-humiliation he was finding a delightful anodyne, and he was vaguely conscious, too, that by this attitude he might regain the priest's esteem, without having to make concessions in the matter of Jacques's detention. And a secret force within him urged him to go still further, to prove the depth of his faith by an astounding declaration and the display of an unlooked-for nobility. No price would be too high if he could force the respect of his friend the priest.

"Listen, Abbé!" he exclaimed; for a moment his face had the same resolute expression that was often Antoine's. "Listen! If until now my pride has made of me a miserable sinner, has not God offered me this very day an opportunity to make—to make atonement?" He hesitated, as though engaged in an inner struggle. And indeed at that moment he was struggling against himself. The Abbé saw him trace the sign of the cross rapidly with his thumb across his waistcoat, above his heart. "I am thinking about this election, you understand. That would be a genuine sacrifice, a sacrifice of my pride, since you told me this morning that my election was assured. Well, then, I . . . But wait! There's vanity even in this. Shouldn't I keep silent and do it without telling anyone, even you? But . . . let it be! Very well, then, Abbé, I make a vow to withdraw tomorrow, and for ever, my candidature for the Institute."

The Abbé made a gesture that M. Thibault did not see; he had turned his eyes towards the crucifix hanging on the wall.

"O Lord," he prayed, "have mercy on me, a sinner!"

He put into the prayer a residue of self-satisfaction that he himself did not suspect, for pride is so deep-rooted that, at the very moment of his most fervent repentance, he was savouring his humility with a passionate thrill of pride. The priest gazed at him intently; he could not help wondering how far the man before him was sincere. And yet at that moment there shone on M. Thibault's face the illumination of a mystic who has made the great renunciation; it seemed to obliterate the puffiness and wrinkles, giving the time-worn features the innocence of a child's face. The priest could hardly believe his eyes. He was ashamed of the rather despicable satisfaction he had felt that morning at confounding this gross Pharisee. Their roles were being reversed. He turned his mind's eye on his own life. Was it really for the sole glory of God that he had been so ready to abandon his pupils and canvass his present exalted post, with its pomp and prestige? And was there not something sinful in the pleasure he felt, day after day, in the exercise of that diplomatic adroitness which was his specialty—even if it was exercised in the service of his Church?

"Tell me honestly, do you believe that God will pardon me?"

The tremor of anxiety in M. Thibault's voice recalled the Abbé to his function of spiritual director. Clasping his hands beneath his chin, he bent his head, and forced a smile onto his lips.

"I have not tried to stop you," he said, "and I have let you drain the cup of bitterness to its dregs. And I am very sure that the divine compassion will take into account this moment of your life. But"— he raised his forefinger—"the intention is enough, and your true duty is not to carry out the sacrifice to the end. Do not protest. It is I, your confessor, who free you from your vow. Indeed God's glory will be better served by your election than by this gesture of renunciation. Your family and your wealth impose obligations which you must not ignore. That title 'Member of the Institute' will confer on you, amongst the great republicans of the conservative group, who are the backbone of our country, an added authority, and one which we consider necessary for the advancement of the highest interests of our faith. You have at all times submitted your life to our guidance. That being so, let the Church, speaking through my lips, show you once more the course to take. God declines your sacrifice, my dear friend; hard as it may be, you must bow to His will. *Gloria in excelsis!*"

As he spoke, the priest had been watching M. Thibault's face and had noticed how its traits had gradually changed, readjusting themselves and settling back to their normal composure. At the last words he had lowered his eyelids, and it was impossible to guess what was passing in his mind. The priest, in giving him back his seat in the Institute, an ambition of twenty years' standing, had given him back life. But the effects of the tremendous struggle he had gone through had not yet worn off; he was still in an emotional mood, thrilled with a sense of infinite gratitude. At the same moment both men had the same impulse. Bowing his head, the priest began to offer humble thanks to God, and when he looked up again he saw M. Thibault already on his knees, gazing heavenwards with unseeing eyes, his face lit up with joy. His moist lips were quivering, his hairy hands

—so bloated that they looked as if the fingers had been stung by wasps—were locked in an ecstasy of fervour. Why did this edifying spectacle suddenly strike the priest as unbearable to see—so much so that he could not help stretching out his arm till it all but touched the penitent?

He checked the gesture at once, and laid his hand affectionately on the shoulder of M. Thibault. The latter rose with an effort from his knees.

"Everything has not been settled yet," the priest reminded him, with the inflexible gentleness that was his characteristic. "You must come to a decision about Jacques."

M. Thibault seemed to stiffen up, suddenly, violently.

The Abbé sat down.

"Do not follow the example of those who think they have done all they need do because they have faced some arduous duty, while neglecting the one that is immediate, close at hand. Even if the ordeal you have made this child undergo has not been so injurious as I fear, do not prolong it. Think of the servant who buried the talent his master entrusted to him. Come now, my friend, do not leave this room till you have dealt faithfully by all your responsibilities."

M. Thibault remained standing, shaking his head, but much of the obstinacy had gone out of his expression. The Abbé rose.

"The difficult problem," he murmured, "is how to avoid producing an impression of having given way to Antoine." He saw that he had hit the mark, took a few steps, and suddenly began to speak in a cool, business-like tone. "Do you know what I'd do, my friend, if I were in your place? I'd say to him: 'So you want your brother to leave the reformatory, do you? Yes? And you're still of the same opinion? Very well, then, I take you at your word, go and fetch him—and keep him with you; you want him back, and it's for you to take charge of him.'"

M. Thibault made no response. The priest went on speaking:

"I'd go even further. This is what I'd tell him: 'I don't want Jacques at home at all; arrange things as you please. You always look as if you thought we didn't know how to deal with him. Very

well, have a try yourself!' And I'd saddle him with the full responsibility for Jacques. I'd give them a place where they could live together—near you, of course, so that they could have their meals at
home. But I'd give Antoine entire charge of his brother. Don't say
no, my dear friend," he added, though M. Thibault had made no
movement of any kind. "Wait, let me finish; my idea is not so fantastic as it may seem."

He returned to his desk and sat down, resting his elbows on the
table.

"Firstly: it's quite likely that Jacques will put up with his elder
brother's authority more easily than with yours, and I'm inclined to
believe that if he enjoys greater freedom, he may lose that spirit of
revolt and insubordination which has been so distressing in the past.

"Secondly: as regards Antoine, his level-headedness entitles him to
our entire trust. If you take him at his word, I'm convinced he won't
reject this chance of freeing his brother. And, as to those regrettable
tendencies we were talking of this morning, a small cause can have
great results. In my opinion the fact of being responsible for the
spiritual welfare of another will tend to counteract them, and we shall
find him coming back to a less—a less anarchical conception of society,
and morals, and religion.

"Thirdly: your parental authority, once it is spared the friction of
everyday contacts which wear it down and disperse its efficacy, will
keep its prestige intact; you'll be able to use it for that general supervision of your sons which is its prerogative and—how shall I put it?—
its main function.

"Finally"—his tone grew confidential—"I must confess that, at the
moment of your election, it strikes me as desirable that Jacques shall
have left Crouy, and that the whole unhappy episode should be put
out of mind. Celebrity attracts all sorts of interviews and inquiries,
and you would be a target for the indiscretions of the press. That's
an entirely secondary consideration, I know; yet all the same . . ."

M. Thibault could not restrain a glance betraying his uneasiness.
Though he would not admit it to himself, he knew that it would
salve his conscience if the "prisoner" were released; in fact the plan

suggested by the priest had everything in its favour. It would save his face *vis-à-vis* Antoine and bring Jacques back to normal life without his having to trouble about the boy.

"If I could be sure," he said at last, "that the young rascal after being released wouldn't bring new scandals upon us . . ."

The Abbé knew that he had gained his point. He undertook to exercise a discreet supervision over the two boys, anyhow during the first few months. Then he accepted an invitation to dine on the following day, and to take part in an interview M. Thibault would arrange for with his son.

M. Thibault rose to go. A weight had been lifted off his heart and he felt a new man. Still, just as he was shaking hands with his confessor, he felt a final qualm of conscience.

"May God in His compassion forgive me for being the man I am." There was a note of sadness in his voice.

The priest beamed on him, and recited in a low voice, like a benediction:

"'What man of you, having an hundred sheep, if he lose one of them, doth not leave the ninety and nine in the wilderness, and go after that which is lost, until he find it?'" A sudden smile lit up his face; he raised a finger to emphasize the words. "'I say unto you, that likewise joy shall be in heaven over one sinner that repenteth.'"

VI

ONE morning—it was barely nine—the concierge of the building where Mme. de Fontanin lived asked to have a word with her. A "young person," it seemed, wanted to see her but would neither go up to the flat nor give a name.

"A 'young person'? Do you mean a woman?"

"A little girl."

Mme. de Fontanin's first impulse was to refuse to see her; the visit had probably to do with one of Jerome's love-affairs; or was it blackmail?

"She's quite a child," the concierge remarked.

"I'll see her."

It was indeed a child whom she found hiding in the darkness of the concierge's "lodge," a child who met her eyes reluctantly.

"Why, it's Nicole!" Mme. de Fontanin cried when she recognized Noémie Petit-Dutreuil's daughter. Nicole was on the point of throwing herself into her aunt's arms, but she checked the impulse. All the colour had gone out of her face and she was looking haggard, but she was not crying, and though her eyes seemed unnaturally large and her nerves were obviously on edge, she had complete control of herself.

"I'd like to speak to you, Auntie."

"Come along upstairs."

"No, not in your flat."

"Why?"

"I'd rather not, please."

"But why? I'm all by myself in the flat this morning." She realized Nicole was uncertain what to do. "Daniel's at school and Jenny's gone to her piano lesson. I shall be alone till lunch. Now come along upstairs."

Nicole followed her without a word. Mme. de Fontanin led her to her bedroom.

"What's the matter?" She could not conceal her mistrust. "Who told you to come here? Where have you come from?"

Nicole looked at her without lowering her eyes, but her eyelids were fluttering.

"I've run away."

"Run away!" Mme. de Fontanin looked distressed. Yet, at the same time she felt relieved. "And what made you come to us?"

Nicole made a movement with her shoulders that implied: "Where could I go? There's nobody else."

"Sit down, darling. Now let's see. . . . You're looking dreadfully tired. By the by, are you hungry?"

"Well, a bit," she confessed with a timid smile.

"Why ever didn't you say so at once?" Mme. de Fontanin smiled and led Nicole into the dining-room. When she saw with what appetite the little girl fell on the bread and butter, she went and fetched what remained of some cold meat from the sideboard. Nicole ate without saying a word, ashamed of showing such voracity but unable to conceal her hunger. The colour was coming back to her cheeks. She drank two cups of tea in quick succession.

"How long is it since your last meal?" Mme. de Fontanin asked. She was looking even more upset than the little girl. "Are you feeling cold, dear?"

"No, thank you."

"But you must be. You're shivering."

Nicole made a petulant gesture; she was always angry with herself for not being able to conceal her moments of weakness.

"I travelled all night. I expect that's why I'm feeling a bit cold."

"You travelled all night! Where on earth have you come from?"

"From Brussels."

"Good heavens! All by yourself?"

"Yes," Nicole answered in a level voice, "all by myself." The firmness of her tone showed that she had acted not on caprice but a set purpose. Mme. de Fontanin took her hand.

"You're freezing, child! Come along to my bedroom. Wouldn't you like to lie down and sleep a bit? You can tell me all about it later."

"No, I'd rather tell you now, while we're alone. Besides, I'm not sleepy. Really, I'm quite all right now."

It was one of the first days in April. Mme. de Fontanin wrapped a shawl round the little runaway, lit the fire, and tried to get her to sit in front of it. At first the child resisted, but at last she gave way. She seemed in a highly nervous state, her eyes were shining with a hard, unnatural fixity, and she was staring at the clock on the mantelpiece. Obviously she was eager to speak, but, now she was seated beside her aunt, had suddenly become tongue-tied. Not to increase her embarrassment, Mme. de Fontanin refrained from looking at her.

Minutes passed, and still Nicole did not say anything. Mme. de Fontanin decided to speak first.

"Whatever you've done, dear, no one here will ask you anything about it. Keep your secret, if you'd rather do so. I'm grateful to you for having thought of coming to us. You're like a daughter here, you know."

Nicole stiffened up, startled by the thought that she was being suspected of having done something wrong, something she disliked confessing. She made a sudden movement that let slip the shawl from her shoulders, revealing the curves of a healthy young body, strangely incongruous with her haggard cheeks and the immaturity of her features.

"It's not that at all!" Her eyes were flashing. "And now I'm going to tell you everything." Her voice had an almost aggressive harshness as she began her story.

"You remember, Auntie, the day you came to see us at our flat in the Rue de Monceau . . . ?"

"Yes, indeed!" Mme. de Fontanin sighed, and again a look of anguish crossed her face.

"Well, I heard everything, every word!" The words came with a rush; her eyelids were quivering.

There was a pause.

"I knew it, my dear."

The child stifled a sob and hid her face with her hands as if the tears were flowing from her eyes. But almost at once she took her hands away; her eyes were dry, and her lips tightly set—which changed not only the expression of her face but the quality of her voice.

"Don't think hardly of her, please, Aunt Thérèse. She's so dreadfully unhappy, you know. You do believe me, don't you?"

"Yes." A question was hovering on Mme. de Fontanin's lips, and she looked at the girl with a calm that carried no conviction. "Tell me, is—is your Uncle Jerome at Brussels, too?"

"Yes." For a moment she was silent, then her eyebrows lifted and she added: "Why, it was he who gave me the idea of running away, of coming here."

"What! He told you to run away?"

"Well, no, not exactly that. You see, he'd been coming every morning all last week. He gave me some money to buy myself food, as I'd been left all alone. Then the day before yesterday he said: 'If some kind soul would find room for you, it would be much better for you than staying here.' 'Some kind soul,' he said, and of course I thought of you at once, Aunt Thérèse. And I'm sure he had the same idea. Don't you think so?"

"Very likely," Mme. de Fontanin murmured. And suddenly a feeling of such happiness swept over her that she all but smiled.

Eagerly she asked: "How did you come to be alone? Where ever were you?"

"At home."

"In Brussels?"

"Yes."

"I didn't know your mother had gone to live in Brussels."

"We had to, at the end of November. Everything was sold up at our place in Paris. Mummy never has any luck, she's always in trouble, with bailiffs coming round for money. But now the debts have been paid off, she'll be able to return."

Mme. de Fontanin looked up quickly, on the brink of asking: "*Who is paying them?*" And so obvious was the question in her gaze that she could read its unspoken answer on the little girl's lips. She could not restrain herself from asking:

"And *he*—he left in November, with her, I suppose?"

There was such anguish in her voice that Nicole did not answer for a while. At last she forced herself to speak.

"Auntie, you mustn't be cross with me; I don't want to hide anything from you, but it's so difficult to explain everything, all at once. Do you know M. Arvelde?"

"No. Who is he?"

"He's a wonderful violinist who used to give me lessons here. He's a really great artist, you know; he plays in concerts."

"Well?"

"He lived in Paris, but he's a Belgian really. That's why, when we had to run away, he took us to Belgium. He has a house of his own in Brussels, and we stayed there."

"With him?"

"Yes." She had understood the question and did not shirk it; indeed she seemed to find a certain perverse pleasure in vanquishing her reticence. But for the moment she did not dare to say more.

After a rather long pause Mme. de Fontanin spoke again.

"But where were you living during these last few days, when you were by yourself and Uncle Jerome came to see you?"

"There."

"At that Belgian gentleman's house, you mean?"

"Yes."

"And did your uncle visit you there?"

"Why, of course."

"But how did you come to be alone?" Mme. de Fontanin's voice had lost none of its gentleness.

"Because M. Raoul is on tour just now, in Lucerne and Geneva."

"M. Raoul? Who is that?"

"M. Arvelde."

"So your mother left you alone in Brussels to go to Switzerland with him?" The little girl's gesture was so desperate, so pitiful, that Mme. de Fontanin blushed. "You must forgive me, darling," she added weakly. "Don't let's talk any more about all this. You've come here and that's quite all right, and I hope you'll stay with us."

Nicole shook her head energetically.

"No, no, there's not much more to tell." She took a deep breath, then broke into a voluble explanation. "This is what's happened, Auntie. M. Arvelde has gone to Switzerland. But Mamma didn't go with him. He had got her an engagement at a theatre in Brussels; she's playing in a light opera—because of her voice, you know; he made her work hard at her singing, and she's been awfully successful, really. They talk about her in the papers; I've got the clippings in my bag—would you like to see them?" She stopped suddenly, uncertain of her ground. A curious look came into her eyes as she went on. "So you see it was just because M. Raoul went to Switzerland that Uncle Jerome came, but it was too late. When he arrived Mamma had left the house. One evening she came and kissed me. No, that's not true." Her eyebrows knitted, and she continued in a low, forlorn voice: "She didn't kiss me, she almost beat me, because she didn't know what on earth to do with me." Raising her eyes, she forced a smile to her lips. "Oh, no, she wasn't really angry with me; it wasn't that at all." A sob broke from the smiling lips. "She was so awfully unhappy, Aunt Thérèse; you simply can't imagine. She had to go, as someone was waiting for her downstairs, and she knew Uncle Jerome would be coming soon, because he'd been to see us several times; he even played music with M. Raoul. But, the last time, he said he wouldn't come again while M. Arvelde was there. So, just before she went out, Mamma told me to tell Uncle Jerome that she'd gone away for a long time, that she was leaving me behind and he was to look after me. I'm sure he would have done so, only I didn't dare to say it when I saw the way he looked when he came and found her gone. He was so terribly angry, I was afraid he might go after them, so I had to tell him a lie. I said Mamma was coming back next day; and every day I told him I was expecting her. He kept on hunting for her high and low; he thought she was still in Brussels. But everything was so awful, I felt I simply couldn't stay there any longer—because of M. Raoul's valet especially. He's such a nasty man; I hate him!" She shivered. "Oh, Aunt Thérèse, he has such horrible eyes—I can't bear him! So, the day Uncle Jerome spoke to me about some kind soul, all of a sudden I made up my mind. Yesterday morning, when he gave me a little money, I went out at once so that the servant shouldn't take it from me. I hid in churches until the evening, and I caught the slow night train."

She had told her story hastily, with lowered eyes. When she raised her head and saw the look of profound disgust and indignation on Mme. de Fontanin's face, she clasped her hands imploringly.

"Oh, Aunt Thérèse, please don't think unkindly of Mamma; it really wasn't her fault at all. I'm not always nice and I'm really a dreadful nuisance to her; you understand, don't you? But I'm grown up now, and I don't want to go on with that life any more. I couldn't bear it!" Her mouth set in a look of firm resolve. "I want to work, to earn my living, and not be a drag on anyone. That's why I've come, Aunt Thérèse. There's no one else but you. Please tell me how to set about it, please, Auntie. You won't mind looking after me, will you? Just for a few days."

Mme. de Fontanin was too deeply moved to reply at once. Could she ever have believed this child would one day become so dear to her? There was a world of tenderness in her eyes as she gazed at Nicole, an affection that warmed her own heart, too, and allayed her distress. The little girl was not so pretty as she used to be; those feverish days had left their mark, and an ugly rash blemished the young lips—but her deep blue eyes were lovelier than ever. Just now they seemed dilated, unnaturally large, yet what courage and what steadfastness shone in their limpid depths! . . . At last, smiling, she leaned towards the little girl.

"Darling, I quite understand. I respect your decision and I promise to help you. But for the present you're going to live here, with us; it's rest you need." She said "rest," but her eyes implied "affection." Nicole read their meaning, but she still refused to soften.

"I want to work; I don't want to be a charge on anyone, any longer."

"What if your mother comes back to fetch you?"

Her clear gaze grew misted; then suddenly an unbelievable hardness came over it.

"I'll never go back to her. Never!" Her voice was harsh with bitter resolution.

Mme. de Fontanin made as if she had not heard, and merely said: "I—I'd very much like to keep you with us—for always!"

The girl rose unsteadily, then suddenly sank onto the floor and laid her head on her aunt's knees. As Mme. de Fontanin stroked the child's cheek, her mind was busy with a delicate problem which she felt it her duty to settle once for all.

"My dear, you've seen a great many things that a girl of your age oughtn't to have seen," she began.

Nicole tried to rise, but Mme. de Fontanin prevented her. She did not want the child to see her blushing. As she held the girl's forehead to her knee, unthinkingly she was winding a strand of golden hair round her finger, groping in her mind for the right words to say. "And you must have guessed a number of things, things which, I think, had better remain a secret. You understand me, don't you?" Nicole had moved her head and was looking up at her. A sudden light came into the child's eyes.

"Oh, Aunt Thérèse, you can be sure of that. I won't breathe a word to anyone. They wouldn't understand; they'd say Mamma was to blame."

She was as bent on concealing her mother's weakness as Mme. de Fontanin was on concealing Jerome's. The strange complicity that was springing up between the little girl and Mme. de Fontanin was sealed by Nicole's next remark. She was standing, her face lit up with eagerness.

"Listen, Aunt Thérèse. This is what you must tell them: that Mamma has been obliged to earn her living and has found a situation abroad— in England, let's say. A situation that has prevented her from taking me with her. As French teacher in a school, we might tell them." A childish smile hovered on her lips as she added: "And, as Mamma's away, there'll be nothing surprising if I seem rather sad, will there?"

VII

THE "gay old spark" on the ground floor moved out on the fifteenth of April.

On the next morning Mlle. de Waize, preceded by two maids, by Mme. Frühling the concierge, and a handy man, went to take possession of the little bachelor flat. The reputation of its previous occupant had been anything but savoury and Mademoiselle, drawing her black merino mantle round her shoulders, waited until all the windows had been opened before crossing the threshold. Then only did she risk entering the little hall of the flat and making a thorough inspection of the rooms. Though somewhat reassured by the immaculate bareness of the walls, she directed the rite of cleansing in the spirit of an exorcist.

Much to Antoine's surprise the worthy spinster had agreed almost without protest to the idea of the two brothers' being installed outside the parental walls, though such a project must have run counter to all her notions of home-life as it should be lived, and played havoc with her views of the Family and Education. Antoine accounted for Mademoiselle's attitude by the pleasure she felt at Jacques's return, and the respect in which she held the decisions of M. Thibault, above all when they had the commendation of the Abbé Vécard.

As a matter of fact there was another reason for Mademoiselle's almost enthusiastic acquiescence: the relief she felt at seeing Antoine leave the flat. Ever since she had taken Gise under her wing the poor old lady had lived in constant terror of infectious diseases. One spring she had actually kept Gise imprisoned in her room for six weeks, not daring to let her take the air elsewhere than on the balcony and delaying the departure of the whole family to their summer residence, because little Lisbeth Frühling, the concierge's niece, had whooping-cough and, to leave the house, it would have been necessary to pass in front of the concierge's premises on the ground floor. Naturally Antoine, with his clothes redolent of the hospital, his medical books and instruments, seemed to her a source of daily peril in their midst. She had begged him never to take Gise on his knee. If, on coming home, by some unlucky chance he dropped his overcoat across a chair in the hall instead of taking it to his room, or if he arrived late and came to table without washing his hands—though she knew he did not wear an overcoat when seeing patients, and never left the hospital without first visiting the lavatory—she was too terrified, too obsessed by fears of "germs," to eat, and, the moment dessert came on the table, would sweep Gise away with her to her room and inflict on her a fiercely antiseptic washing of throat and nostrils. To install Antoine on the ground floor meant creating a protective zone of two stories between Gisèle and him, and diminishing to that extent the peril of infection. Thus she displayed particular zest in preparing for the bearer of contagions this remote quarantine. In three days the rooms were scraped clean, washed, carpeted, and equipped with curtains and furniture.

All was ready now for Jacques's return.

Every time she thought of him, her activity redoubled; or else she would indulge in a sentimental breathing-space, conjuring up before her melting eyes the well-loved face. Her affection for Gise had by no means ousted Jacques from his priority in her regard. She had doted on him since he was born; indeed she had loved him even longer than that, for she had loved and brought up, before him, the mother whom he had never known, whose place she had taken from the cradle. It was between her outstretched arms that one evening, tottering along the carpet in the hall, Jacques had taken, towards her, his first step; and for fourteen successive years she had trembled for him as now she trembled for Gisèle. And with boundless love went total incomprehension. The boy, from whom she scarcely ever took her eyes, remained a mystery to her. There were days when she gave up hope—so "inhuman" did she find the child—and then she would weep, recalling Mme. Thibault's childhood, for Jacques's mother had been as meek and mild as an angel out of heaven. She never tried to puzzle out from whom Jacques had inherited his propensity for violence, and could blame only the Devil. And yet there were days when one of those sudden, impulsive gestures in which the child's heart suddenly flowered forth would quicken her emotion, making her weep again, but now with joy.

She had never been able to get used to Jacques's absence nor had she ever been able to understand the reasons for his exile. Now she wanted his return to be a festive occasion and his new room to contain everything he loved. Antoine had to put his foot down or she would have crammed the cupboards full of his old toys. She had brought down from her own room his favourite arm-chair, the chair in which he had always used to sit when a black mood was on him; and, on Antoine's advice, she had replaced Jacques's old bed by a brand-new sofa-bed which, folded up in the day, gave the room the dignity of a study.

Meanwhile Gisèle had been left to her own devices for two days, but with plenty of work to keep her out of mischief. Try as she might, she could not fix her attention on her lesson-books. She was dying of curiosity to see what was happening down below. She knew her Jacquot was going to return, that all this commotion was on his account, and, to calm her nerves, kept pacing up and down the room, which seemed to her a prison-cell.

On the third morning she could bear it no longer, and the temptation was so strong that at noon, noticing that her aunt had not come up again, she ran out of her room without more ado and raced down the stairs, four steps at a time. Antoine was just coming in. She burst out laughing. Antoine had a special way of looking at her—a stolid, concentrated glare he had invented for their mutual amusement—that never failed to send her off into peals of uncontrollable laughter, which lasted as long as Antoine could retain his gravity. Mademoiselle used to scold them both for it. But just now they were alone, and the occasion was too good to miss.

"What are you laughing at?" he said at last, catching hold of her wrists. She struggled, laughing all the more. Suddenly she stopped.

"I really must get out of this habit of laughing. If I don't, you know, nobody will ever want to marry me."

"So you want to get married, do you?"

"Yes," she said, gazing up at him. There was a mildness in her gaze that brought to mind the eyes of a large, sentimental dog. Looking down at her plump little body, with its wild-flower grace, he reflected for the first time that this imp of eleven would one day become a woman, would marry. He let go her wrists.

"Where were you rushing off to like that, by yourself, without even a hat or a shawl on? Don't you know it's lunch-time?"

"I'm looking for Auntie. She's given me a sum I can't make out," she added with a little giggle. Then, blushing, she pointed to the mystery-laden door from which a single ray of light was streaming. Her eyes were shining in the dimness of the vestibule.

"You'd like to have a look at it, eh?"

She made a "yes" with a flutter of her red lips, soundlessly.

"You're in for a scolding, I warn you," Antoine smiled.

She hesitated, eyed him boldly to see if he were joking. Then she made up her mind.

"No, why should I be scolded? It's not a sin."

Antoine laughed; he had recognized Mademoiselle's phraseology for Right and Wrong. He fell to wondering what effect the old maid's influence was having on the child. A glance at Gisèle reassured him; she was a healthy plant which would flourish in any soil and defy the gardener's restraint.

Her eyes were still fixed on the half-opened door.

"Well, why don't you go in and have a look round?" Antoine said.

As she slipped in like a scared mouse, she stifled a cry of joy.

Mademoiselle was alone. She had climbed onto the sofa-bed and, standing tip-toe, was straightening the crucifix she had just hung on the wall; it was the crucifix she had given Jacques for his first communion, and it was still to watch over her dear one's sleep. She seemed gay, happy, young, and was singing as she worked. She had recognized Antoine's step in the entrance-hall, and thought he must have forgotten the time. Meanwhile Gisèle had made an inspection of the other rooms and, unable to restrain her glee, had begun dancing and clapping her hands.

"Good heavens!" Mademoiselle exclaimed, jumping down from the bed. In a mirror she saw her niece, her hair streaming in the breeze from an open window, capering like a young fawn, and screaming at the top of her voice.

"Hurrah for lovely draughts! Hurrah!"

She did not understand, did not try to understand. The idea that an act of wilful disobedience might account for the little girl's presence here never crossed her mind; for sixty-six years she had been in the habit of bowing to the exigencies of fate. She made a dash at the child and, unhooking her cape, wrapped her hastily in its folds, and without a word of reproach hurried her out. And, after making Gisèle run up the stairs even quicker than she had run down them, she did not draw breath till she had put the child in bed under a warm blanket and made her drink a bowl of boiling-hot herb-tea.

It must be admitted her fears were not entirely groundless. Gisèle's mother, a Madagascan whom Major de Waize had married in Tamatave, where he was garrisoned, had died of tuberculosis, less than a year after the birth of the child; two years later the Major himself had succumbed to a slow, never fully diagnosed disease that was thought to have been transmitted to him by his wife. Ever since Mademoiselle, the orphan's only relative, had had her sent home from Madagascar and taken charge of her, the dangers of hereditary disease had constantly obsessed her, though actually the child had never had a serious cold in her life, and the various doctors and specialists who examined her each year had never found the least flaw in her healthy constitution.

The election for the Institute was taking place in a fortnight, and M. Thibault seemed in a hurry to have Jacques back. It was arranged that M. Faîsme should personally escort him to Paris on the following Sunday.

On the previous Saturday evening, Antoine left the hospital at seven o'clock, dined at a neighbouring restaurant so as to escape the family dinner, and, round about eight, alone and in high spirits, took possession of his new domain, where he was to sleep that night for the first time. He found a pleasure in the feel of his private key turning in the lock, in slamming his own door behind him, and, after switching on all the lights, began to walk slowly from room to room, with the zest of a conqueror exploring a new-won kingdom. He had reserved for himself the side looking out on the street: two big rooms and a dressing-room. The first large room had little furniture in it: only a few chairs of various shapes and sizes grouped round a small circular table. This was to serve as the waiting-room, when patients came to consult him. Into the second room, which was the larger of the two, he had moved the furniture belonging to him in his father's flat, his big desk, his bookshelves, his two leather arm-chairs, and all the various accessories of his industrious hours. His bed was in the dressing-room, which also contained a washstand and wardrobe.

His books were stacked on the hall floor alongside his unopened trunks. The heating-apparatus was emitting a gentle warmth, and brand-new electric lamps shed an uncompromising brilliance on everything in the flat. Antoine had the rest of the evening before him to

set his house in order; he made up his mind to have everything unpacked and in its appointed place—a congenial setting for the new life
that was beginning—within the next few hours. He pictured the dinner
in the flat above drawing to its dreary close: Gisèle drowsing over her
dessert; M. Thibault, as usual, perorating. And Antoine relished the
peace around him, and the inestimable boon of solitude.

The glass over the mantelpiece reflected him half length. He drew
near it, not without a certain self-satisfaction. He had a way of his own
with mirrors, and always viewed himself full face, squared his
shoulders, and clenched his jaws, while his eyes seemed boring almost
angrily into their reflected selves. He preferred not to see his lanky
torso, short legs, and somewhat puny arms, for the disproportion
between his rather undersized body and the bulkiness of his head, the
volume of which was increased by the thick beard, was distasteful to
him. But he approved of himself; he regarded himself as a fine figure
of a man, built on exemplary lines. What particularly pleased him
was the look of grim determination on his face, for, by dint of creasing
his forehead as if he felt obliged to concentrate his full attention on
each incident of daily life, a bulge had formed at the level of his
brows, which, overshadowing his eyes, imparted to them a curious
piercingness that pleased him as the outward sign of an indomitable
will.

He decided to begin with his books, and, taking off his coat, started
by giving a vigorous tug to the closed doors of the empty bookcase.
Let's see now, he mused. Lecture note-books at the bottom, dictionaries
within easy reach; medical manual—yes, that's the place for it. Tra
la la! he hummed light-heartedly. Well, well, here I am, I got my way.
The ground-floor flat; Jacques. It all panned out—who'd have believed that possible three weeks ago? He began to speak aloud, in a
high-pitched voice, impersonating an admirer. "That chap Thibault
has an in-dom-i-ta-ble will. Never knows when he's beaten. Indomitable!" Casting a humorous glance at the mirror, he cut a caper, which
all but dislodged the pile of books and pamphlets he was propping
under his chin. Steady now! he adjured himself. That's better. My
shelves are coming to life again. Now for the manuscripts. Oh, for this

evening, let's put the files back into the file-case, as they were before. But one of these days we'll have to sort them out, all those notes and comments. Quite a lot I've got together. The important thing is to have a simple, efficient system for classifying them; with an index, of course, that I keep absolutely up to date. Like Philip's. Yes, a card-index. Of course, all the great doctors . . .

Gaily, with an almost dancing step, he moved to and fro between the hall and the bookcase. Suddenly he emitted a boyish laugh, which came as a surprise. "Dr. Antoine Thibault!" he announced, halting for a moment and straightening his shoulders. "It's Dr. Thibault! Of course you've heard of him; the child specialist!" He side-stepped nimbly, made a rapid bow, then, sobering down, resumed his journeys to and fro between the hall and study. The wicker basket, next. In two years' time I'll annex the Gold Medal. House physician at a clinic. Hospital diploma. So I'm setting up here for three or four years at most. Again he mimicked a high falsetto voice: "Thibault is one of our youngest hospital staff doctors; Philip's right-hand man." I got on the right scent when I specialized at once on children's diseases. When I think of Louiset, Touron, and the rest of them—the damned fools!

Damned fools! he repeated absent-mindedly. His arms were full of all sorts of objects and he was looking round perplexedly for the best place for each. Pity Jacques doesn't want to be a doctor. I could help him, I'd see him through. Two Thibaults as doctors! Why not, after all? It's a career worthy of a Thibault. Hard, I grant you, but how rewarding, when one has a taste for fighting against odds, and a bit of personal pride! Think of all the attention, memory, will-power it demands! And one never gets to the end of it. And consider what it means when one's made good! A great doctor, that's somebody! A Philip, for instance. One has to learn, of course, how to adopt that gentle, assured manner. Very courteous, but distant. Yes, it's pleasant to be someone, to be called in for consultations by the colleagues who're most envious of one!

Personally I've chosen the most difficult branch: children. Yes, they're the trickiest cases; never know how to tell you what's wrong and, when they do, lead you all astray. That's it; with children one can count only on oneself; got to face up to the disease and hit the diagnosis. X-rays luckily . . . A competent doctor today has got to be a radiologist, and know how to use the apparatus himself. Soon as I've taken my M.D., I'll take a course on X-rays. And later on, next door to my consulting-room, there'll be an X-ray room. With a nurse. No, a male assistant's better; in a white coat. On consulting days, for every case that's in the least complicated—zip!—a photo.

"What gives me confidence in Dr. Thibault is that he always begins with an X-ray examination."

He smiled at the sound of his own voice, and winked towards the mirror. Why, yes, I don't deny it, that's Pride, with a capital P! He laughed ironically. The Thibault pride, as Abbé Vécard calls it. My father, too, of course. But I—oh, well, let it go at that! It's pride. Why not? Pride comes in very useful as a driving force. I make good use of it, too. Why shouldn't I? Isn't it up to a man to make the most of his talents? What are my talents, now? He smiled. Easy to answer that. For one thing, I'm quick at getting things, and I'm retentive; what I know sticks. Next, I can work. "That chap Thibault works like a horse!" So much the better; let 'em say it if they want to, they'd all like to be able to do as much. And then, what more? Energy. Definitely that. "An ex-traor-di-nar-y energy!" He said it out loud, syllable by syllable, turning again to the mirror. It's like a battery; well, a charged cell, always on tap for any effort I require of it. But what would all those talents come to, if there wasn't a driving force to actuate them? Tell me that, M. l'Abbé! He was holding in his hand a flat, nickel-plated instrument-case that gleamed under the ceiling light, and was wondering where to put it. Finally he reached up and placed it on the top of the bookcase. "Eh, lad, it's naught to be ashamed of!" he shouted in the jovial, bucolic Norman voice his father sometimes affected. "And there's a lot in pride, saving your respects, M. l'Abbé."

The wicker basket was nearly empty. From its depths Antoine took two little portraits in plush frames and gazed at them musingly. They were photographs of his maternal grandfather and his mother. The former portrait showed a handsome old man standing beside a table piled with books, on which his hand was resting; the other, a young woman with fine features and indefinite, rather gentle eyes. She was wearing an open square-cut bodice and two silky tresses fell upon a shoulder. He was so familiar with this likeness of his mother that it was thus he always pictured her, though the portrait dated from the time of Mme. Thibault's engagement, and he had never known her with her hair like that. He had been nine years old at Jacques's birth, when she had died. He could remember better his grandfather, Couturier the economist and friend of MacMahon, who had just missed being made Prefect of the Seine Department on the fall of M. Thiers, and had been for some years Dean of the Institute. Antoine had never forgotten his pleasant face, his white muslin cravats, and his razors with mother-of-pearl handles, one for every day of the week, in their sharkskin case.

He stood the two portraits on the mantelpiece, amongst his specimens of stones and fossils.

The room was rapidly undergoing a complete transformation. The miscellaneous objects and papers littering his desk had still to be arranged. He set about it with a will and, when everything was in place, surveyed his handiwork with satisfaction. As for my clothes and linen, he decided lazily, that's old Mother Frühling's affair. To make his escape from Mademoiselle's leading-strings still more complete, he had arranged for the concierge to do all the work in the ground-floor flat, without help or interference from above. Lighting a cigarette, he settled luxuriously into one of the leather arm-chairs. It was seldom he had a whole evening to himself like this, without anything definite to do, and he was feeling rather lost. It was too early to go to bed and he wondered what to do with himself. Should he stay where he was, smoking cigarettes, thinking of anything, or nothing? Of course he had letters to write but—no, he didn't feel like letter-writing.

I know, he suddenly thought, rising from the chair and going to the bookcase. I meant to look up what Hémon says about infantile diabetes. Setting the fat, paper-bound volume on his knee, he began glancing through its pages. Yes, I ought to have known that; it's obvious. A frown had settled on his face. Yes, I was completely mistaken; if it hadn't been for Philip that poor child would be done for, and it would be my fault. Well, not exactly my fault. Still . . . He closed the book and slammed it onto the table. Curious how stiff, almost cutting, the chief can be on such occasions. Of course he's awfully vain, likes to act impressive. "My poor good Thibault," that's what he said. "My poor good Thibault, the diet you prescribed was bound to make the child get worse." Yes, he said that in front of the nurses and students; a nasty slap in the eye!

Thrusting his hands into his pockets, he took a few steps in the room. I really ought to have answered him back. I should have said: "For one thing, if you did your own duty . . ." Just that. He'd have said: "M. Thibault, on that score I do not see how anyone . . ." Then I'd have driven home my point. "Excuse me, Chief. If you came to the hospital punctually in the morning, and if you stayed until the end of the consultation hour, instead of dashing off at half-past eleven to visit your paying patients, I wouldn't have to do your work for you, and I wouldn't run the risk of making blunders." Yes! In front of them all! What a sensation! Of course he'd have been sick to death with me for a couple of weeks or so—but what the devil would that matter? Who cares?

A vindictive expression had suddenly come over his face. Then, shrugging his shoulders, he began absent-mindedly winding up the clock. He shivered, put on his coat again, and went back to his chair. His cheerfulness of a short while back had evaporated and he felt a sudden chill at his heart. The damned fool! His lips twisted in a rancorous grin. Crossing his legs impatiently, he lit another cigarette. But even as he murmured: "Damned fool!" he had been thinking of the sureness of eye, the experience, the amazing intuition of Dr. Philip, and at that moment the genius of his chief seemed to him something almost superhuman.

What about me? he thought, and a vague distress seemed to grip his throat. Shall I ever get to understand things in a flash, as he does? Shall I ever have that almost infallible perspicacity which is what really makes the great physician? Shall I? Of course I've a good memory, I'm hard-working, persevering. But those are virtues of the underling. Have I anything more in me? It's not the first time I've boggled over an easy diagnosis—yes, there's no getting over that, it was simplicity itself, a "classical" case, with all the obvious symptoms. Suddenly he flung his arms up. Yes, it's going to be a hard struggle. I've got to work, pile up knowledge day by day. But then his face grew pale. He had remembered Jacques was coming next day. To-morrow evening, he thought, Jacques will be in the room over there, and I . . .

He had jumped up. And now the project he had formed of living with his brother appeared to him in its true light, as the most ir-reparable of follies! He was no longer thinking of the responsibility he had undertaken, he was thinking only of the handicap that was bound from now on, whatever he might do, to retard his progress. What a fool he had been! It was he himself who had hung this mill-stone round his own neck. And now there was no escape.

He crossed the hall unthinkingly, opened the door of the room that had been prepared for Jacques, and stood on the threshold, un-moving, peering into the darkness. He felt profoundly discouraged. "Damn it!" he said aloud. "Is there no way of escape, no place where one can have some peace? Where one could work, and have only oneself to think about? Here one has to give in all the time—to the family, to friends, and now to Jacques! They all conspire to prevent me from working, to make a mess of my life!" The blood had gone to his head; his throat was parched. He ran to the kitchen, drank two glasses of cold water, and returned to his study.

In a mood of black depression he began to undress. All in this room, in which he had not yet got used to his surroundings, in which fa-miliar objects seemed different from their former selves—everything in the room suddenly seemed hostile.

He took an hour to go to bed, and longer still to fall asleep. He was not accustomed to have the noises of the street so near; each passing footfall made him start. His mind was obsessed with trifles; he remembered the trouble he had had in finding a cab, coming home the other night from an evening at Philip's place. And from time to time the thought of Jacques's return came back with harrowing intensity, and he started tossing this side and that in nervous exasperation.

Furiously he adjured himself: I've my own way to make, blast it! Let them look after themselves! I shall let him live here, now that it's all fixed up, and I'll see he does the work he has to do. But there it ends. I've promised to look after him, and that's all. It must not stand in the way of my career. My career! That's the big thing!

Of his affection for the boy not a trace remained that night. Antoine recalled his visit to Crouy. He pictured his brother as he then had seen him: emaciated, with the pale cast of loneliness. Quite possibly, it struck him now, the boy was consumptive. In that case he would persuade his father to pack off Jacques to a good sanatorium, to Auvergne, to the Pyrenees, or, better still, to Switzerland; then he, Antoine, would be alone, his own master, free to work just as he pleased. He even caught himself thinking: I'd take his room and use it as my bedroom.

VIII

ANTOINE woke up in an entirely different mood. In the course of the morning, at the hospital, he frequently consulted his watch with cheerful impatience, all eagerness to go and take over his brother from the hands of M. Faîsme. He was at the station long before the train was due and, while he walked up and down the platform, busied himself memorizing what he intended to say to M. Faîsme about the Foundation. But when the train came in and he saw Jacques's form and the superintendent's glasses amidst the press of passengers, he completely forgot the home-truths he had intended to rub in.

M. Faîsme was all smiles, very spick and span, and accosted Antoine as if he were a bosom friend. He wore light-coloured gloves, and his yellow face, close-shaved to an immaculate smoothness, gave the impression of having been liberally powdered. He seemed little disposed to part company with the brothers and urged them to a café terrace for a drink. Only by promptly hailing a taxi did Antoine manage to escape. M. Faîsme himself lifted Jacques's bag onto the seat, and when the cab moved off, at the risk of having the toes of his patent-leather shoes run over, he thrust his head in through the window and effusively clasped the brothers' hands, bidding Antoine meanwhile convey his profound respects to the eminent Founder.

Jacques was crying.

He had not yet said a word, or made the least response to his brother's cordial welcome. But the state of prostration the boy was evidently in increased Antoine's pity and the new gentleness stirring in his heart. Had anyone ventured to remind him of his rageful feelings of the previous night, he would have disclaimed them indignantly and affirmed in perfect good faith that he had never ceased to feel that the boy's return would give at last a point and purpose to his life, so lamentably empty and futile hitherto.

When he had led his brother into their flat and closed the door behind them, he was as pleasantly elated as a young lover doing the honours of the home he has prepared for her to his first mistress. Indeed that very idea flashed through his mind and made him laugh; perhaps he was being ridiculous, but he was feeling far too cheerful to mind that. And though in vain he tried to catch some gleam of satisfaction on his brother's face, he never doubted for a moment that he was going to make a success of the task he had undertaken.

Jacques's room had been visited at the last moment by Mademoiselle; she had lit the fire to give it a cosier air and placed well to the fore a plateful of the almond cakes dusted with vanilla sugar for which Jacques had had a special fondness in the past. On the bedside table, in a glass, was a little bunch of violets with a streamer cut out of paper attached to it, on which Gisèle had written in chalk of various colours: "For Jacquot."

But Jacques paid no heed to any of these preparations. Almost the moment he entered, while Antoine was taking off his coat, he had sat down near the door, holding his hat.

"Come along, Jacques, and have a look round our estate!" Antoine called out.

The boy went up to him lethargically, cast a listless glance into the other room, and went back to his seat. He seemed to be waiting for, and afraid of, something.

"What do you say to going up and seeing 'them' now?" Antoine suggested. And he guessed from Jacques's shiver that, with all his dread of the impending encounter, he would rather get it over as soon as possible.

"Yes? Well, let's go at once. We'll only stay a minute or two," Antoine added, to give him courage.

M. Thibault was waiting for them in his study. He was in a good humour. The sky was cloudless and spring was in the air. Moreover, that morning when he had gone to mass at the parish church, sitting in his special pew, he had had the pleasure of reminding himself that on the next Sunday there would doubtless be, sitting in that same seat, a new and eminent member of the Institute. He went up to his sons, and kissed the younger. Jacques was sobbing. M. Thibault saw in his tears proof of his remorse and good resolutions; he was more moved than he cared to show. He had the boy sit in one of the high-backed chairs on each side of the fireplace, and stalking up and down the room, his hands behind his back, puffing and blowing as was his wont, he pronounced a brief homily, affectionate yet firm, recalling the terms on which Jacques had been given the privilege of coming home again to his father's house, and bidding him show Antoine as much deference and obedience as if Antoine were his father.

An unexpected caller cut short the peroration; it was a future colleague, and M. Thibault, eager not to keep him cooling his heels in the drawing-room, dismissed his sons. Nevertheless he escorted them up to his study door and, as with one hand he drew back the curtain, placed the other on the head of the repentant boy. Jacques felt his father's hand stroking his hair and patting his neck with an indulgence so unwonted that he could not restrain his emotion and, turning, seized the thick, flabby hand to raise it to his lips. Taken by surprise,

M. Thibault opened a displeased eye, and withdrew his hand with a feeling of embarrassment.

"Tch! Tch!" he muttered gruffly, jerking his neck clear of the collar several times. Jacques's sentimentality seemed to him to augur no good.

They found Mademoiselle dressing Gisèle for vespers. When Mademoiselle, instead of the little imp of mischief she was expecting, saw a tall, pale youth with haggard eyes enter the room, she wrung her hands alarmedly and the ribbon she was tying in the little girl's hair slipped from her fingers. Such was her consternation that it was some little time before she could bring herself to kiss him.

"Bless and save us, Jacques! Is it really you?" was all she managed to say; then flung her arms around him. After hugging him to her bosom, she stepped back to have another look at him, but, though her shining eyes lingered on every feature, they could find no semblance of her dear youngster's face.

Gise was still more startled by the change, and feeling so shy that she kept her eyes fixed on the carpet, she had to bite her lip to restrain herself from bursting into laughter. And Jacques's first smile of the day was for her.

"So you don't recognize me, Gise!" He went up to her and, now that the ice was broken, she threw herself into his arms and then began skipping round him like a young lamb, still clinging to his hand. But she dared not talk to him as yet, not even ask if he had seen her flowers.

They all went down together. Gisèle had not let go Jacques's hand and was nestling against him with the innocent sensuality of a young animal. At the foot of the staircase they parted hands, but in the portico as she was going out she blew him, through the glass door, a big kiss with both hands; he did not see it.

Now they were alone in their new home, Antoine's first glance at Jacques told him a weight had been lifted from the boy's mind by this meeting with the members of the family, and that he was already feeling better.

"You know, I think we'll do very well here, you and I. Nice little flat, isn't it?"

"Yes."

"Well, sit down, Jacques, and make yourself at home. Try that chair over there, it's very comfortable, and tell me what you think of it. Now I'll make some tea. I suppose you're hungry? Go and choose us some cakes at the pastrycook's."

"Thanks. I'm not hungry."

"But *I* am!" Nothing could repress Antoine's geniality. After a laborious, solitary youth, Antoine was now experiencing for the first time the pleasure of loving and protecting someone, sharing his life with another. And for the sheer joy of it he was laughing, carried away by an exhilaration that was making him expansive as he had never been before.

"Have a cigarette then. No? You keep on looking at me. . . . Don't you smoke? You keep on looking at me, I was going to say, as if I was laying a trap for you. Look here, Jacques, let yourself go a bit. Have a little confidence, damn it! You're not in the reformatory now. Can't you trust me even now?"

"Of course I trust you."

"Well, then, what is it? Are you afraid I've let you down, that I've got you back on false pretences and you're not as free as you expected?"

"N-no."

"Then what's worrying you? Are you missing anything?"

"No."

"Then what is it? What's going on behind that stubborn-looking forehead of yours? Out with it!" He went up to the boy, on the point of bending over him, giving him a brotherly kiss, but he refrained. Jacques looked up at his brother with forlorn, hopeless eyes; he realized an answer was expected of him.

"Why do you ask me all those questions?" He shuddered slightly, then added in a very low voice: "What difference can it make?"

There was a short silence. Antoine was gazing at his brother, and

there was such affectionate compassion in his eyes that once more
Jacques felt inclined to cry.

"Yes, Jacques, just now you're like a sick man." All the gaiety had
left Antoine's voice. "But, never fear, you'll get over it. Only let yourself be looked after—and loved!" he added shyly, without looking at
the boy. "We don't yet know one another well. Just think, nine years
between us—it was a regular abyss as long as you were a child. You
were eleven when I was twenty; we couldn't have anything in common. But now it's very different. . . . No, I couldn't say if I had
any affection for you in those days. I didn't ever think about it. You
see I'm being quite frank with you. But now—well, all that, too, is
changed. I'm delighted—yes, damn it—I'm thrilled to have you here
with me. Life will be more pleasant, better in many ways, now that
there are two of us. Don't you think so? For instance, when I'm
coming back from the hospital, I'm sure to hurry now, so as to get
home quickly. And I'll find you here, sitting at your desk, after a
strenuous day's work. Shan't I? And in the evening we'll come down
from dinner early, and each will settle down in his own study, under
a lamp; but we'll leave the doors open so as to see each other and
feel we are together. Or else, some nights, we'll have a good talk,
like two old friends, and it'll be an effort to drag ourselves to bed.
What's up? Why are you crying?"

He went up to Jacques, sat on the arm of his chair, and after a
brief hesitation took his hand. Jacques turned away his tearful face,
but returned the pressure of Antoine's hand, and for some moments
clung to it feverishly with all his might.

"Oh, Antoine!" The cry seemed choking in his throat. "If you only
knew all that's happened inside me, in the last year!"

He was sobbing so violently that Antoine did not dream of putting
any further questions. Placing his arm round Jacques's shoulders,
he pressed the boy tenderly to him. Once before, on that evening
when in the darkness of the cab the barriers between them had fallen,
he had experienced that thrill of vast compassion, that sensation of
a sudden access of strength and will-power—the feeling that he alone
must supply the vital force for both of them. And very often since,

an idea had hovered in the background of his mind, an idea which now was taking clear and definite form. Rising, he began to pace the room.

"Listen!" he began. His voice had an unusual intensity of feeling. "I don't know why I'm speaking to you of this so soon, on our first day. Anyhow, we've plenty of time to return to it. Well, this is what I've been thinking—you and I are brothers. That doesn't sound much of a discovery, does it? And yet the idea is a new one, for me, and one that deeply moves me. We're brothers! Not merely of the same blood, but springing from the same origins since the beginning of time, from the same germ-cells, the same vital impulse. We're not just any two young men, named Antoine and Jacques; we're two Thibaults, we *are* the Thibaults. Do you see what I mean? And what's so alarming in a way is that we both have in us that same vital impulse, that special Thibault temperament. Do you see? For we Thibaults are somehow different from the rest of mankind. I rather suspect we have something in us that others haven't got; just because we *are* Thibaults. Personally, wherever I've been, in college, medical school, or hospital, I've felt myself a man apart; I hardly like to say 'superior to the others'—though, after all, why shouldn't I? Yes, we are superior, we're equipped with an energy others don't possess. What's your opinion? Don't you agree? I know that you passed for a bit of a duffer at school, but didn't you feel it there, too, that 'urge' as they call it, which somehow gave you more—more driving force than the other boys?"

"Yes!" Jacques had stopped crying and was staring at his brother with passionate interest. His face had suddenly an expression of intelligence and maturity that made him seem ten years older.

"It's a long while now since I first noticed it," Antoine went on. "There must be some particular combination in our make-up, of pride and violence and obstinacy—I don't know how to put it. Take Father, for instance. But, of course, you don't know him very well. And it takes a different form with him. Now listen!" He drew up his chair in front of Jacques and leaned forward, his hands resting on his knees: one of M. Thibault's favourite attitudes. "What I wanted to say to you today was that this secret force is always making itself felt in my life; I don't know how to describe it, it's like a wave—one of those sudden swelling waves that buoy you up when you're swimming, and carry you in one tremendous rush a great way forward. But you must know how to turn it to good account. Nothing's impossible, nothing's even difficult, when one has that vital force; and we have it, you and I. Do you understand? In my own case, for example—but I'm not telling you all this just to talk about myself. I want to talk about you. It's up to you now to take stock of this driving force you have in you, to analyse it and apply it rightly. If you make up your mind, you can in one stride catch up on all the time you've wasted. It's a matter of will-power. Some people simply haven't any—as I've discovered only quite recently. I've got it, and you can have it, too. All the Thibaults can have it. And that's why they can make good at anything they turn their hand to. Think of what it means, to forge ahead of others, to make one's value recognized. I tell you, it's our duty to bring this vital energy, which is our heritage, to full fruition. It's in us—in you and in me—that the Thibault stock must come to flower—the full flower of a lineage. Do you see what I mean?" Jacques's eyes had been riveted on Antoine with all but painful fixity. Antoine repeated: "Do you understand all this?"

"Yes, yes, I understand!" he all but shouted. His pale eyes were sparkling, there was an almost vicious edge to his voice, and his lips were curiously twisted. It looked as if he were furious with his brother for shattering his peace of mind by this so unexpected outburst of enthusiasm. A tremor passed through his body, then his features relaxed, and a look of profound weariness settled on his face.

"Oh, let me be!" he suddenly exclaimed, letting his forehead sink between his hands.

Antoine said nothing; he was observing his brother. How much thinner and paler he had grown, in a fortnight! The close-cropped reddish hair made still more apparent the abnormal size of his skull, the scragginess of his neck, and his protruding ears.

"By the way," he suddenly asked, point-blank, "have you turned over a new leaf?"

"In what way?" Jacques murmured, and a mist crept over the brightness of his eyes. He flushed, and, though he managed to keep up an expression of surprise, it was obviously feigned.

Antoine made no reply.

It was getting late. He looked at his watch and rose; he had his second round to make, at five. He pondered if he should tell his brother he was going to leave him alone till dinner; but, much to his surprise, Jacques seemed almost glad to see him go.

And indeed, when he was alone, he felt as if a weight had been lifted from him. He had the idea of making an inspection of the flat, but in the hall in front of the closed doors a vague anxiety came over him and he went back to his own room and shut himself in. At last he noticed the bunch of violets, and the paper streamer. All the events of the day merged together in his memory: his father's welcome, Antoine's conversation. He lay down on the sofa and began crying again, but not with despair; he was weeping above all from exhaustion, but also because of the room, and the violets, and the hand his father had laid on his head, and Antoine's solicitude, and the new life which was beginning for him. He wept because on all sides they seemed to want to love him, because henceforth people were going to take notice of him, and speak to him, and smile towards him, and he would have to respond; because his days of tranquillity were over.

IX

To SOFTEN the transition, Antoine had postponed Jacques's return to the Lycée till October. With the help of some of his old school friends, who were about to enter the university, he had worked out a sort of review course, the object of which was the progressive re-education of the boy's intelligence. Three different tutors shared the task. They were all young, and personal friends. Under those favourable conditions, the youngster worked as and when he pleased, according to the amount of concentration he could bring to his task. And soon Antoine had the pleasure of seeing that his seclusion in the reformatory had not done so much harm to his brother's mental faculties as might have been feared; in certain respects, in fact, his mind seemed to have ripened most remarkably in solitude—so much so that after a rather slow start his progress soon became more rapid than Antoine had dared to hope. Jacques profited, without excess, by the independence he was allowed. Moreover, Antoine, though he did not say so to his father, but with the tacit approval of the Abbé Vécard, felt that no harm could be done by allowing Jacques the utmost freedom. He realized the potentialities of Jacques's mind and believed that there was everything to be gained by letting him develop in his own way, on his own lines.

During the first few days the boy felt a strong distaste for going out of the house. The bustle of the street made him feel dizzy, and Antoine had to exercise his ingenuity in devising errands that took him out into the open air. So gradually Jacques renewed acquaintance with the neighbourhood and after a while came actually to like his walks abroad. The weather kept fine and he found pleasure in walking to Notre Dame along the river bank, and strolling in the Tuileries Gardens. One day he even ventured to enter the Louvre, but he found the air stifling and dusty, and the long lines of pictures so monotonous that he soon went out, and did not return.

At meal-times he was silent; he listened to his father. In any case M. Thibault was so dictatorial and overbearing that all who were constrained to live in his vicinity took refuge in silence and composed their faces into masks of decorous attention. Mademoiselle herself, despite her beatific admiration, always hid her real face from him. M. Thibault enjoyed this deferential silence, which gave free rein to his craving to lay down the law on every topic, and was naïve enough to take it for approval. His attitude to Jacques was studiously reserved, and, faithful to his promise, he never questioned him as to how he spent his time.

There was one point, however, on which M. Thibault had shown himself intractable; he had formally forbidden all intercourse with the Fontanins, and, to make assurance doubly sure, had decided that Jacques should not join the rest of the family that summer at Maisons-Laffitte, where he went every year with Mademoiselle, and where the Fontanins, too, had a little country residence on the outskirts of the forest. It was settled that Jacques should spend the summer in Paris, with Antoine.

The paternal edict against seeing the Fontanins was the subject of a momentous conversation between Antoine and his brother. Jacques's first reaction was a cry of revolt; he felt that the old injustice would never be wiped out, so long as this attitude of suspicion as regards his friend was allowed to persist. The violence of his reaction was far from displeasing Antoine; it proved to him that Jacques, the real Jacques, was being reborn. But when the first blaze of anger had passed, he set himself to reason with the boy. And he had little trouble in extracting a promise that he would not try to see Daniel. As a matter of fact, Jacques was not so set on their meeting as he seemed to be. He was still too shy and too unsociable to desire new contacts; the intimacy with his brother was enough—all the more so as Antoine took pains to live with him on a footing of simple friendship, without anything to indicate the difference in their ages, and still less the authority with which he had been invested.

One afternoon in early June, when he came home, Jacques saw a crowd gathered round the street door. Old Mme. Frühling, the concierge, had had an attack and was lying unconscious on the threshold of her room. She came to in the evening, but her right arm and leg were partly paralysed.

Some days later, when Antoine was about to leave his flat after breakfast, there was a ring at the bell. A young German-looking girl, wearing a pink blouse and black apron, was standing in the doorway. She was blushing, but there was boldness in her smile.

"I've come to do your rooms, sir. Don't you recognize me, M. Antoine? I'm Lisbeth Frühling."

She spoke with an Alsatian accent, the sing-song quality of which was still more emphasized by her childish intonation. Antoine had not forgotten the little girl who was known to all the residents in the block of flats as "old Mme. Frühling's orphan brat," and whom, as he walked past the concierge's lodge, he often used to see playing hopscotch in the courtyard. Lisbeth explained that she had come from Strasbourg to look after her aunt and do her work for her. And forthwith the girl took up her domestic duties in the young men's flat.

She continued to come each morning, bringing their breakfast on a tray and waiting on them as they ate it. Antoine would tease her over her way of blushing in and out of season, and ask her questions about German life. She was nineteen; during the six years since she had left Mme. Frühling, she had been living with her uncle, who kept a hotel-restaurant in the vicinity of the station at Strasbourg. So long as Antoine was present, Jacques put in a word now and then. But whenever he was alone with Lisbeth in the flat he kept studiously out of her way.

All the same, on the mornings when Antoine was on duty early at the hospital, she served the breakfast in Jacques's bedroom. On these occasions he always asked her for news of her aunt, and Lisbeth did not spare him a single detail. The old lady was slowly getting better—she must be, as her appetite was steadily improving. Lisbeth had a great respect for food. She was small and plump, and the suppleness of her body bore witness to her passion for dancing and open-air games. When she laughed, she would look at Jacques without the least constraint. She had a knowing, pretty little face, with a rather short nose, young, pouting lips, china-blue eyes, and clusters of flaxen curls rippling over her forehead.

Each day Lisbeth made the talk last a little longer and gradually Jacques got over his early shyness. He listened to all she said seriously, attentively. He had a way of listening that had at all times won him confidences: the secrets of servants, of schoolmates, sometimes even of his teachers. Lisbeth talked to him more freely than to Antoine, though it was with the elder brother she behaved more childishly.

One morning, noticing that Jacques was looking up a word in his German dictionary, she dropped what little reserve she had so far kept up and asked him to show her what he was translating. It happened to be a *Lied* of Goethe's that she knew by heart and used to sing at home.

> *Fliesse, fliesse, lieber Fluss!*
> *Nimmer werd' ich froh. . . .*

German poetry, it seemed, had a way of going to her head. In a soft voice she sang to him several German love-songs, explaining the meanings of the first lines before she began. The songs she liked best were always sad ones, with a note of childish sentiment.

> Were I a little swallow in the nest
> I would take wing to thee!

But Schiller was her adoration. After thinking hard for a while she recited without a break one of her favourite passages, the lines in *Mary Stuart* in which the young imprisoned queen is given leave to take a few steps in the garden of the keep where she is confined, and runs across the lawns, her eyes half blinded by the sudden light, her heart aflame with youth. Jacques could not understand all the words, so she translated as she went along and, to convey the young queen's delight in that brief spell of freedom, she put such emotion into her voice that Jacques, remembering Crouy, felt profoundly thrilled. Little by little vanquishing his reserve, he began describing his own misfortunes. He was still living so much alone, and spoke so seldom, that the sound of his own voice rapidly went to his head. In his excitement he embroidered on reality and inserted in his narrative all sorts of literary reminiscences; for, during the past two months, a large share of his time and industry had gone to the perusal of the novels on Antoine's shelves. He was keenly aware, moreover, that these romantic travesties were stirring Lisbeth's emotions far more effectively than would have done the plain, unvarnished truth. And when he saw the pretty girl drying her tears, in the graceful attitude of Mignon weeping for her motherland, he felt, almost for the first time, the boundless joy of the creative artist, and such an immense gratitude to Lisbeth for the pleasure she was giving him that, with a thrill of hope, he wondered if this were not love. . . .

Next morning he awaited her impatiently. She guessed his feelings very likely, and had brought with her an album full of picture post-cards, autographs, and dried flowers: a visual record of her young life, of all she had been and done since the age of three. Jacques plied her with questions; he liked being taken by surprise, and was surprised by everything he did not know. Lisbeth's stories of her young days were sprinkled with picturesque details that carried conviction—in fact it was impossible to question her good faith. And yet, when a blush mantled her cheeks and the singing tone of her voice grew more pronounced, somehow she gave the impression of making things up, of lying, that we get from people trying to describe their dreams.

In a flutter of pleasurable excitement she spoke to him of the winter evenings at the *Tanzschule* where the young men and girls of her quarter of the city met. Carrying a tiny violin, the dancing master would follow the couples round, marking the beat, while Madame ground out the latest Viennese waltzes on the player piano. At midnight they all settled down to a meal. Then in merry groups they flocked out into the darkness, and saw each other home from house to house, but never could bring themselves to separate, so soft was the snow underfoot, so clear the wintry sky, so keen the night-wind on their cheeks.

Sometimes non-commissioned officers from the garrison put in an appearance at their dances. One of them she named as Fredi and another Will. Lisbeth took her time before pointing out on a group photograph of men in German uniforms the big doll-like soldier whose Christian name was Will. *"Ach,"* she said, dusting the photograph with her loose sleeve, "he's such a nice boy, Will, so good-hearted and senti-mental!" Evidently she had been to his room, for she told Jacques a long story in which a zither, raspberries, and a bowl of junket figured. In the midst of the tale she caught herself up with a sudden little laugh, and left it unfinished. Sometimes she spoke of Will as her fiancé, and sometimes as if he had passed out of her life. Jacques gathered finally that he had been transferred to a garrison in Prussia after a mysterious, rather comical incident, the memory of which set her shivering at one moment and giggling at another. It seemed that there had been a hotel bedroom at the end of a corridor where the floor squeaked—but at that point the story became quite incomprehensible. One thing seemed clear: the room in question must have been one of those in Frühling's own hotel; otherwise how could her old uncle have been able, in the middle of the night, to rise in anger from his bed, pursue the soldier into the courtyard, and throw him out into the street, in his shirt and socks? By way of explanation Lisbeth added that her uncle thought of marrying her himself, for her to keep house for him. She also informed Jacques that her uncle had a hare-lip, and smoked black cigars that smelt of soot from morn till night. And, at that, suddenly the smile left her lips and she began to cry.

Jacques was sitting at his table, with the album open before him. Lisbeth was perched on the arm of his chair and when she bent down he was conscious of the warm fragrance of her breath and felt her curls lightly brushing his ear. But his senses were not stirred. Perversion he had known, but now another world was opening up before him, a world he fancied he was discovering within himself, but actually was exhuming from an English novel he had recently perused. It was a world of chaste love, happy sentimental satisfactions, and of purity.

All through the day his imagination was busy planning out, down to the last detail, the interview of the next morning. He pictured them alone in the flat; they would, of course, have the whole morning to themselves without fear of interruption. He had made Lisbeth sit on the sofa, on his right; she bent her head forward and, standing, he gazed down, across the ringlets tumbling round her neck, on the smooth curve of her neck, and back under the loose bodice. She did not dare to raise her eyes, and he leaned over her, whispering: "I don't want you to go away again, ever again!" And then at last she raised her head, with a questioning look, and he gave her his answer, a kiss on her forehead, sealing their betrothal. "In five years I'll be twenty. Then I shall tell Papa: 'I'm a child no longer.' If they say:

'She's the concierge's niece,' I . . ." He made a threatening gesture. "So now we're engaged, you and I. You're my fiancée!" The four walls of his room seemed too narrow to contain so much happiness. He went out and walked in the warm summer sunshine, dazed with ecstasy. "She's mine! Mine! My sweetheart!"

Next morning he was sleeping so soundly that he did not even hear her knock and leapt from his bed only when he heard her laugh in Antoine's room. When he went there Antoine had just finished breakfast and was about to leave. He had his hands pressed on Lisbeth's shoulders and was admonishing her in a gruff tone.

"Make no mistake about it! If you let your aunt have any more coffee, you'll have to deal with me!"

Lisbeth was laughing with that characteristic laugh of hers; she refused to believe that coffee served in the good old German manner, with plenty of milk and sugar, and gulped down piping hot, could possibly do any harm to the old woman.

Now, at last, they were alone. On the tray were some pastry twists sprinkled with aniseed; she had made them specially for him. Deferentially she watched him eat his breakfast. Jacques was vexed with himself for being so hungry. Nothing was working out according to plan, and he was at a loss to find a means of linking up reality with the scene he had planned out in fancy, down to its last detail. And, as a crowning misfortune, the bell rang.

It was a surprise visit. Old Mme. Frühling tottered in; she was far from being fully restored to health, but she was feeling better, heaps better, and had come to say good morning to Master Jacques. After that Lisbeth had to help her aunt back to the lodge, and settle her down in her arm-chair. Time passed, and Lisbeth did not come back. Never had Jacques been able to endure the tyranny of circumstance. He stormed up and down his room, in the throes of a baffled fury that resembled the fits of rage that used to come over him in the past. Setting his jaw, he thrust his fists into his pockets. And presently he began to feel a grievance against Lisbeth.

When at last she came back, his mouth was parched and his gaze aggressive; he was so on edge from waiting that his hands were trembling. He pretended to be busy with his books. She hurried through the housework and said *au revoir*. He was still bending over his books. Sick at heart, he let her go without a word. But the moment he was alone, he flung himself back in his chair and his lips set in a smile of such undiluted bitterness that he went to the mirror to enjoy it objectively. For the twentieth time he pictured the scene he had composed in fancy: Lisbeth seated, he standing, her flaxen curls . . . In a rush of bitterness he placed his hand before his eyes and flung himself onto the sofa. But no tears came; all he felt was the throbbing of his nerves, a sense of baffled fury. . . .

When she came next day she had a downcast air and, thinking he was to blame for it, Jacques felt immediately contrite. As a matter of fact, the cause of her dejection was a disagreeable letter she had just received from Strasbourg. The hotel was full, and her uncle wanted her back. Frühling agreed to wait one more week, but no longer. She had thought of showing the letter to Jacques, but the look of timid affection on his face so touched her that she could not bring herself to say anything that would distress him. She sat down, without thinking, on the sofa, and, as chance would have it, at the exact place where, in his day-dream, Jacques had intended her to sit. And now he, too, was standing beside her, just where he had meant to stand. She bent forward and he saw across a mist of flaxen ringlets the smooth curve of her back flowing away under the loosely fitting blouse. Almost mechanically he began to bend towards her, when suddenly she straightened up—a shade too soon. She looked at him with surprise, then, smiling, drew him beside her on the sofa and without the least hesitation pressed her face to Jacques's, her temple resting on his temple, her soft, warm cheek upon his cheek.

"*Chéri . . . Liebling!*"

He felt like swooning with the delight of it, and closed his eyes. Lisbeth's fingers, roughened at the tips by needlework, were fondling his other cheek, and now, very gently, they began to slip down underneath his collar. He felt the button come loose and a delicious tingling ran through his body. Her little hand seemed charged with electricity, as it slipped between the shirt and his skin; at last it settled upon his breast. Taking courage, Jacques moved his own hand towards her blouse, but found the way barred by a brooch. She unfastened the blouse to help him. He held his breath as he felt under his fingers the unfamiliar contact of another's flesh. She made a sudden nervous movement as if he were tickling her, and all at once he realized that the soft warmth of a little breast was nestling in his hand. Blushing, he gave her a clumsy kiss; she returned it, passionately, full on his mouth. He was disconcerted, even a little disgusted, by the clammy moisture lingering on his lips after the warm pressure of the kiss. Once more she rested her cheek on his, unmoving; the silken flutter of her eyelashes lightly brushed his temple. . . .

Henceforth this was their daily ritual. She would start taking off her brooch in the hall and, as she entered, pin it to the door-curtain. Then they would sit on the sofa, cheek to cheek, nestling in their bodies' warmth. Usually they were silent, but sometimes she would begin singing in a low voice a sentimental German ballad, which brought tears to their eyes; and for a while, pressing closely against each other, they would sway from side to side in rhythm with the song, mingling their breath and asking no better joys than that. When Jacques's fingers moved a little under her blouse, or if he changed the position of his head to brush Lisbeth's cheek delicately with his lips, she would gaze at him with eyes that always seemed to hold a mute appeal for gentleness, sighing: "Be loving, *chéri!*"

Once their hands had found the usual resting-place, they did not stray in quest of new delight; by an unspoken pact both young people avoided unrehearsed gestures. They had all the physical nearness they wanted in the long, insistent pressure of cheek on cheek and the fluttering of their breasts, like the ghost of a caress, under each other's hands. For Lisbeth, who often seemed in a half-dream, it was the easiest thing to keep her senses under control; at Jacques's side she was lost in a haze of poetic fancies, of ecstatic purity. As for Jacques, the need for keeping in check any more definite impulse did not make itself felt in any way. Those chaste caresses were an end in themselves, and the idea that they might be a prelude to more ardent

gestures never so much as crossed his mind. If at moments the proximity of the young, warm body had a physical effect upon his senses,
he was hardly conscious of it, and the thought that Lisbeth might
have noticed it would have made him mortally ashamed, disgusted
with himself. No gross desire ever came over him while he was with
her; the gulf between his spiritual and his fleshly self was unbridgeable.
The former belonged to his beloved; the latter had its sordid, solitary
being in another world, the world of night, which Lisbeth never entered. If some nights, unable to go to sleep, he flung himself out of
bed, pulled off his nightshirt and, standing before the glass, fell to
kissing his arms, hugging himself with a sort of desperate frenzy,
never on these occasions did he conjure up Lisbeth's form to join the
phantom rout of his imaginings.

Meanwhile Lisbeth was only too well aware that these idyllic days
were numbered: she was due to leave Paris on the following Sunday,
and she had not had the courage to tell Jacques.

That Sunday, at dinner-time, Antoine, knowing his brother was
upstairs with the family, went to his room, where Lisbeth was awaiting
him.

"Well, what about it?" he asked, with an enigmatic smile.

She shook her head.

"And you're going away this evening, aren't you?"

"Yes."

He made a gesture of annoyance.

"But it's his fault, too," she protested. "He doesn't seem to think
of it."

"You promised to 'think of it' for him."

She gazed at Antoine, despising him a little in her heart of hearts,
for not understanding that, for her, Jacques was "different." Still,
Antoine was good-looking, she liked his imposing manner, and could
forgive him for being like the rest of men.

She had pinned her brooch to the curtain and began to undress in
an absent-minded way; her thoughts were busy with the journey before her. When Antoine took her in his arms she gave a short, nervous

laugh, which seemed to die away deep down in her throat. *"Liebling,"* she whispered, "be extra nice this time—it's our last evening."

Antoine was out all the rest of the evening. Towards eleven Jacques heard him enter and walk at once to his room, as quietly as he could. He was just going to bed, and did not call his brother.

As Jacques got into bed, his knee hit against something hard, a package of some sort—evidently a "surprise" intended for him. It contained some aniseed twists, covered with a sticky coating of burnt sugar and wrapped up in tinfoil, and, inside a silk handkerchief with Jacques's initials on it, a mauve envelope inscribed: "To my beloved."

She had never written to him before. That night it was as if she had come into the room and was bending over his bed. He was laughing for joy as he opened the envelope.

Dear Master Jacques,
When you read this letter I shall be far away from you . . .

The lines grew blurred under his eyes; a cold sweat broke out on his forehead.

. . . I shall be far away from you. I am leaving tonight for Strasbourg by the 10:12 train, from the Gare de l'Est.

"Antoine!"

The cry was so heart-rending that Antoine rushed across to his brother's room, thinking he had had an accident.

Jacques was sitting on his bed, his arms outspread, his lips parted, a look of wild entreaty in his eyes; it seemed as if he were dying and Antoine alone could save him. The letter lay on the counterpane. Antoine glanced through it without surprise; he had just seen Lisbeth off. He bent over his brother, but Jacques pushed him away.

"Don't say a word, Antoine, please. You can't understand, you can't imagine. . . ."

He was using the same words as Lisbeth. A look of obstinacy settled on his face and his eyes had a dark, brooding intensity that brought to mind the boy he used to be. Suddenly his chest began to heave, his lips trembled, and, as if he were trying to take shelter from an enemy, he rolled over and burst into sobs, crushing his face against the bolster. One of his arms was hanging behind him; Antoine gripped the quivering fingers, which instantly closed round his. At a loss for words, Antoine squeezed his brother's hand affectionately, gazing at his bent back racked by sobs. Once more he was struck by the secret fires brooding beneath the crust of seeming apathy and always ready to blaze up in angry flames; and he took stock of the vanity of his educational pretensions.

Half an hour went by; Jacques's hand unclenched; he was no longer sobbing, but his breath still came in gasps. Little by little it became more regular; he was going to sleep. Antoine did not move; he could not bring himself to go. He was thinking with dismay of the boy's future. He waited another half-hour, then went out on tip-toe, leaving the door ajar.

Next morning Jacques was still asleep, or pretending to be, when Antoine left the flat.

They met, for the first time that day, upstairs, at the family table. Jacques's face was tired and drawn, with a scornful twist to the corners of his mouth; he had the expression of children who take pride in thinking themselves misunderstood. Throughout the meal he was careful not to meet Antoine's eye; he did not even want to be pitied. Antoine understood; moreover, he, too, did not particularly want to talk about Lisbeth.

Their life slipped back into its normal rut, as if nothing had happened.

X

ONE evening, just before dinner, Antoine was surprised to find amongst his mail an envelope addressed to him and enclosing a sealed letter for his brother. The writing was unfamiliar, but as Jacques was in the room with him, he did not want to seem to hesitate.

"Here's something for you," he said at once.

Jacques darted towards him, his cheeks flushing an angry red. Antoine, seemingly absorbed in a bookseller's catalogue, handed him the envelope without looking at him. On raising his eyes he saw that Jacques had thrust the letter into his pocket, unread. Their eyes met. Jacques's were aggressive.

"Why are you staring at me like that?" he demanded. "Haven't I the right to get a letter?"

Antoine returned his brother's look without a word, turned his back on him, and left the room.

Throughout dinner he conversed with M. Thibault, studiously ignoring Jacques. As usual after dinner they went down together, but did not exchange a single word. Antoine went straight to his room. He had hardly sat down when Jacques entered without knocking, approached him with a combative air, and flung down the open letter on the table.

"Now that you've taken it on you to censor my correspondence, you'd better have a look at it!"

Antoine refolded the letter without a glance at its contents, and held it out to his brother. As Jacques did not take it, he opened his fingers and let the letter drop onto the carpet. Jacques picked it up and thrust it into his pocket.

"Got the sulks, have you?" he jeered. "Well, they're wasted on me!"

Antoine shrugged his shoulders.

"And, what's more, let me tell you I'm sick and tired of it all." Jacques's voice was shrill with anger. "I'm no longer a child, and I insist—you can't deny I have the right . . ." He left the phrase unfinished. Antoine's air of calm attention maddened him. "I tell you I've had enough of it!" he shouted.

"Enough of what?"

"Of everything." All the finer shades of feeling had left his face; his eyes were smouldering with rage, his ears seemed to be sticking out more than ever, and his mouth gaped. At that moment he looked a boor. His cheeks were growing scarlet. "Anyhow, this letter came here by mistake. My instructions were that I was to be written in care of general delivery. That way at least I can get my letters without interference, without having to render an account to anyone."

Antoine gazed at him steadily without answering. Silence was his trump card, he knew; moreover, it served to mask his embarrassment. Never had the boy spoken to him in that tone before.

"And, to begin with, I mean to start seeing Fontanin again, do you understand? No one shall stop me."

It came back to Antoine in a flash: that was the writing in the grey exercise-book. So Jacques had broken his promise and was writing to Fontanin. Antoine wondered if Mme. de Fontanin was in the secret. Had she authorized the clandestine correspondence?

For the first time Antoine was thinking: "Well, I suppose it's up to me to play the 'stern father'!" He remembered that not so very long ago he might have found himself adopting towards M. Thibault the very attitude Jacques was adopting towards him now. Yes, the tables had been properly turned!

"So you've been writing to Daniel?" he asked with a frown.

Jacques nodded decisively, without the least sign of contrition.

"Without telling me!"

"Well, what about it?" Jacques retorted.

Antoine's first impulse was to give the impertinent youngster a slap on the face. He clenched his fists. The way the argument was going threatened to ruin the very thing on which he set most store.

"Go away," he said in a tone of feigned discouragement. "Tonight you simply don't realize what you are saying."

"I'm saying . . . I'm saying that I've had enough of it!" Jacques stamped his foot. "I'm no longer a child. I insist on being allowed to see whoever I choose. I've had enough of living like this. I want to go and see Fontanin because Fontanin is my friend. That's why I wrote to him. I know what I'm doing. I've asked him to meet me, and you can tell that to—to anyone you like. I'm sick of this life, sick to death of it." He was raging about the room, his mind a chaos of rancour and revolt.

What he did not say, and what Antoine could scarcely be expected to guess, was that ever since Lisbeth had gone away, the unhappy youngster had been feeling such desolation and such heaviness of heart that he had given way to his yearning to confide this first great secret of his young existence to someone of his own age, to share with Daniel the burden that seemed crushing out his life. He had rehearsed the whole scene to himself, carried away by romantic emotion: the climax of their friendship, when he would entreat his friend to love one-half of Lisbeth, and Lisbeth to let Daniel take on himself one-half of their love.

"I've asked you to go," Antoine repeated. He feigned complete detachment and rather enjoyed the feeling of superiority it gave him. "We'll talk it over later, when you've come to your senses."

Maddened by Antoine's imperturbability, Jacques began shouting in his face. "You're a coward! You're just another monitor!" He slammed the door behind him as he went out.

Antoine rose, turned the key in the lock, and dropped into a chair. His face was white with indignation.

"The damned little fool—calling me a monitor! He'll pay for that. If he thinks he can say what he likes to me, he's mistaken. He's spoilt my evening; I shan't be able to do a stroke of work now. Yes, he'll pay for this! And to think I used to have a quiet life. What a mess I've made of things! And all for this stupid little ass. A monitor, indeed! The more one does for them . . . Yes, it's I who've played the fool. For his sake, here I am wasting my time, ruining my work. But now I'm through with him. I have my own life to live, exams to get through. And that little idiot shan't interfere, damn him!" Unable to keep still, he began pacing up and down the room.

Suddenly he visualized himself in Mme. de Fontanin's presence, and a look of stoical disillusionment settled upon his features. "Yes, Madame, I've done everything I possibly could. I've tried kindness and affection, and allowed him the greatest possible freedom. And look at the result! Believe me, Madame, there are some temperaments with which there's nothing to be done. Society can protect itself from them only in one way, and that's by preventing them from doing harm. It may sound pretentious calling a reformatory a 'means of social preservation,' but there's good sense behind it."

A rustling, mouse-like noise made him turn his head. A note had been pushed under the locked door.

"Please forgive me," it ran, "for calling you a monitor. I've got over my temper. Let me come back."

Antoine could not help smiling. Impulsively, in a sudden access of affection, he went to the door and opened it. Jacques was there, his arms dangling by his side. His nerves were still so much on edge that he kept his head bent and had to bite his lip to keep himself from laughing. Assuming a look of vexation and aloofness, Antoine went back to his chair.

"I've work to do." His tone was curt. "You've already made me waste time enough for one evening. What do you want now?"

Jacques raised his eyes, in which the laughter lingered, and looked his brother in the face.

"I want to see Daniel again."

There was a short silence.

"You know that Father's set against it," Antoine began. "What's more, I've taken the trouble to explain to you his reasons. Do you remember? On that day it was settled that you agreed to the arrangement and wouldn't make any attempt to get in touch with the Fontanins. I trusted you. And now, see what's happened! You've let me down; at the first pretext, you've broken our pledge. Well, all that's over now; I'll never be able to trust you again."

Jacques was sobbing.

"Please don't say that, Antoine. It isn't fair. You can't understand. I know I oughtn't to have written without telling you. But that was because there was something else I'd have been obliged to tell you— and I simply couldn't!" In a low voice he added: "Lisbeth . . ."

Antoine cut him short.

"That has nothing to do with it." At all costs he wanted to stave off a confession on that topic. It would have been even more embarrassing to him than to Jacques. To divert the conversation into a new channel, he went on at once: "Well, I'll agree to give you one more chance. You're going to promise me . . ."

"No, Antoine, I can't promise you not to see Daniel again. It's you who are going to promise me to let me see him. Listen to me, Antoine; I swear to you before God that never again will I hide anything from you. But I must see Daniel again—only I don't want to do so without your knowing. Neither does he. I'd written to him asking him to reply in care of general delivery, but he wouldn't. This is what he writes: 'Why general delivery? We have nothing to conceal. Your brother has always been on our side. So I'm addressing this letter to him, and he can give it to you.' At the end he refuses to come and meet me behind the Pantheon as I'd asked him to. Listen! 'I have told Mother about it. The simplest way will be for you to come as soon as you can and spend a Sunday at our place. My mother likes you and your brother very much, and she's told me to invite both of you.' You see what a decent chap he is. Papa has no idea of it and condemns him without knowing a thing about him. I don't feel bitter with Father; but with you, Antoine, it's not the same thing. You've met Daniel, you know what he's like, and you've seen his mother; there's no reason for you to behave like Papa. You should be pleased I have a friend like Daniel. Haven't I had my share of loneliness? Please forgive me; I don't mean that for you, you know I don't. But you must see; it isn't the same thing, Daniel and you. I'm sure you have friends of your own age, haven't you? You must know what it is to have a real friend."

Seeing the look of happiness and affection that lit up Jacques's face as he said the final word, Antoine ruefully admitted to himself that he had no real friend. And suddenly he felt an impulse to go up to his brother and put his arm round him. But there was an obduracy, a challenge in Jacques's eyes that galled his pride and gave him a desire to match his will against it, fight it down. Still, he could not help being shaken by the boy's determination.

Stretching out his legs, he began to turn the problem over in his mind. "Obviously," he mused, "I'm broad-minded enough to admit that Father's veto is absurd. That Fontanin boy can have nothing but a good influence on Jacques. Nothing could be better than the atmosphere of his home life. What's more, it might be of help to me in handling Jacques. Yes, I'm sure she would help me; as a matter of fact, she'd have a better notion of what to do than I, and she'd soon get a great influence over the boy. What a fine woman she is! The devil of it is—supposing Father heard of it! Well, well! I'm not a child. After all, it's I who've taken full responsibility for Jacques— so I've the right to decide things, in the last resort. I consider that, on the face of it, Father's veto is absurd and unjust; well, then, I'll ignore it. For one thing, it will make Jacques more attached to me. He'll think: 'Antoine isn't like Papa.' And then there's Daniel's mother. . . ." He saw himself standing again before Mme. de Fontanin, saw her smile as he explained: "Madame, I've made a point of bringing my brother to you myself."

He rose, took a few steps in the room, then halted in front of Jacques, who stood unmoving, summoning up all his will-power and resolved to fight down Antoine's opposition to the bitter end.

"Well, Jacques," he said, "now that you've forced my hand, I'll have to tell you what my plan has always been about it. I've always intended to override Father's opposition and let you see the Fontanins again. I'd even meant to take you there myself. What do you think of that? Only I preferred to postpone it till you were quite yourself again, anyhow till the beginning of the school term. Your letter to Daniel has precipitated matters. Very well, I'll take the responsibility on myself. Father shall know nothing about it, nor the Abbé either. We'll go there next Sunday, if you like."

He paused a moment, then continued in a tone of affectionate reproach: "I hope you realize now how greatly mistaken you have been, and how wrong not to give me credit for better feelings towards you. Surely I've told you dozens of times, Jacques, that there must be perfect frankness between us, perfect confidence—or it's the end of all we've hoped."

"Next Sunday!" Jacques stammered. This unexpected victory without a struggle had made chaos of his thoughts. He had a vague feeling that he was the dupe of some stratagem too subtle for his comprehension. Then he was ashamed of his suspicion. Antoine was really and truly his best friend. What a pity he was so dreadfully old! But—next Sunday? Why so soon? And he began to wonder if he were really so anxious to see his friend again.

XI

O N THAT Sunday afternoon Daniel was seated beside his mother, sketching, when the little dog started barking. The bell had rung. Mme. de Fontanin put down her book.

"I'll go, Mother," Daniel said, when he saw her beginning to move towards the door. Lack of money had constrained her to dismiss first the maid, then, a month ago, the cook; Nicole and Jenny were helping with the housework.

Mme. de Fontanin had been listening to hear who the caller was; she recognized Pastor Gregory's voice and, smiling, went out into the hall to greet him. She found him holding Daniel by the shoulders and, as he peered into the boy's face, emitting his raucous laugh.

"What do you mean by it, boy, staying indoors on a fine day like this? You should be out taking some exercise. Oh, these Frenchmen, they don't know what sport is—cricket, boating, and the rest of it." The brilliance of his small black eyes, which seemed to have no whites, the pupils filling the entire space between the eyelids, was so overpowering at close quarters that Daniel turned away with an uneasy smile.

"Don't scold him," Mme. de Fontanin said; "he's expecting a friend to call. It's the Thibaults, you know."

Screwing up his face, the pastor groped amongst his memories, then suddenly began rubbing his dry hands together with such demoniac vigour that they seemed to crackle with electric sparks, while his lips parted in an eerie, soundless laugh.

"I've got it!" he said at last. "It's that bearded doctor man. A nice, decent young chap. Do you remember how flabbergasted he looked when he came and found our dear little girl risen from the dead? He wanted to test the resurrection with his thermometer. Poor fellow! By the way, where is she? Is she, too, shut up in her room on this lovely day?"

"No, you needn't trouble about her; Jenny's out with her cousin. They hurried through lunch and went out at once. They're trying a new camera which Jenny was given for her birthday."

Daniel, who had brought a chair for the pastor, raised his head and looked at his mother, whose voice had shaken a little as she spoke.

"What about this Nicole girl?" Gregory asked as he sat down. "Any news?"

Mme. de Fontanin shook her head. She did not want to discuss it in front of her son, who, at the mention of Nicole, had cast a furtive glance at the pastor.

"Now, my boy, tell me," the latter asked abruptly, turning to Daniel, "what about your bearded doctor friend? What time exactly is he going to come and inflict himself on us?"

"I'm not sure. About three, I expect."

Gregory sat up, so as to extract from his clerical waistcoat a silver watch as big as a saucer. "Very well. You've exactly an hour, lazy-bones. Off with your coat and start out at once for a good quick sprint round the Luxembourg Gardens—in record time, mind you! Off you go!"

Daniel exchanged a glance with his mother before rising.

"All right, I'll leave you to yourselves," he said mischievously.

"Cunning little rascal!" Gregory shook his fist playfully at him.

But once he was left alone with Mme. de Fontanin, a glow of kindliness lit up the dry, sallow face, and his eyes grew tender.

"And now," he said, "the time has come when I want to speak to your heart, my dear, and to your heart alone." For a few moments he seemed abstracted from his surroundings, as if in prayer. Then with a nervous gesture he ran his fingers through his straggly black hair, pulled a chair towards him, and sat astride it. "I've seen him." He watched the colour ebbing from Mme. de Fontanin's face. "He asked me to come and see you. He is repentant, and I can't tell you how unhappy." Gregory kept his eyes fixed on hers as if he hoped the joy that glowed in them persistently might alleviate the distress he was imposing on her.

"So he's in Paris?" she murmured, without thinking of what she was saying, for she knew Jerome had come in person, on Jenny's birthday, two days before, to leave the camera with the concierge. Wherever he might be, never had he forgotten the birthday of any member of the family. "So you've seen him?" She spoke in a far-away voice and her face betrayed as yet no definite emotion. For months she had been thinking about him incessantly, but in so vague a manner that, now he was being spoken about, a curious lethargy had crept over her mind.

"Yes, he's so unhappy," the pastor repeated with insistence, "and overwhelmed with remorse. That wretched creature of his is still singing at the theatre, and he is thoroughly disgusted with it all; he wants never to see her again. He says life is impossible for him apart from his wife and children—and I believe he means it. He begs your forgiveness and will make any undertaking you desire, if only he can remain your husband. He implores you to abandon your intention of divorcing him. And I discerned on his face the look of the just man, of one who is fighting the good fight."

She said nothing, but gazed pensively into the middle distance. There was a gentleness about her face, the soft, sensitive lips, full cheeks, and rather heavy chin, that seemed instinct with compassion; and Gregory thought she was in a forgiving mood.

"He tells me you are going to appear, both of you, before the judges," he continued, "for the preliminary attempt at reconciliation and that only if that fails, the actual divorce proceedings will begin. So he now craves your forgiveness, for he has undergone a change of heart; I'm convinced of it. He says he is not the man he seems to be, that he's better at heart than we imagine. And that, too, I believe. And he's quite decided to work now, if he can find work. So, if only you'll consent, he will live here with you; he'll choose the better path, and atone for his misdeeds."

He saw her lips trembling, a nervous tremor convulsing her chin.

Then, with a quick, decisive jerk of her shoulders, she turned to him. "No!"

Her voice was clear, emphatic, and in her gaze there was a sombre dignity, giving the impression that her mind was made up irrevocably. Gregory leaned back and closed his eyes; for a long while he did not speak.

When at last he spoke his voice was remote; all the warmth had gone out of it. "Look here!" he began. "I'm going to tell you a story, if you'll let me, a story that is new to you. It's about a man who was in love. I ask you: listen well. This man, while he was still quite young, was engaged to a poor girl who was so good and beautiful, so truly beloved of God, that he too loved her." His eyes grew dark, intense. "Yes, he loved her with his whole soul. . . ." For a moment he seemed to have lost the thread; with an effort he continued, speaking more quickly: "And then, after their marriage, this is how things went. One day the man discovered that his wife did not love him only; she loved another man, their friend, who was welcome at their house and like a brother to them both. The unhappy husband took his wife away on a long journey, to help her to forget; and then he came to understand that now she would always love that other man, their friend, and himself no more. Thus life became a hell for both of them. He saw his wife suffering adultery in her body, then in her heart, and at last even in her soul, for she was becoming unjust and wicked. Yes," he continued in a slow, sad voice, "they came to a terrible pass, those two poor people; she growing evil because of thwarted love, and he too growing evil because the Negative was rooted in their lives. Well, what did he do then, that man? He prayed. And he thought: 'I love this woman, and I must shield her soul from evil.' And then, with joy in his heart, he summoned his wife and his friend into his study and, setting before them the New Testament, he said: 'In the sight of God I solemnly declare that you twain are joined in holy wedlock.' All three were weeping. But then he said: 'Have no fears; I am leaving you and never shall I return to spoil your happiness.' "

Screening his eyes with his hand, Gregory added in a low voice:

"Ah, my dear, what a noble reward God made that man, in the memory of that great sacrifice, his love-offering!" He raised his head. "And the man did as he had said; he gave away all his money to them, for he had great riches and she was the poorest of the poor. He made a long journey, to the other side of the world, and I know that now, seventeen years later, he is still quite alone and all but penniless, earning his daily bread as I do, as a humble worker for the Christian Healers."

Mme. de Fontanin gazed at him, deeply moved.

"But wait!" His voice grew suddenly shrill, excited. "Let me tell you now the end of the story." His features were working with emotion, his arms were resting on the back of the chair on which he sat astride, with the emaciated fingers feverishly interlocked. "That poor man thought he was bequeathing happiness to those two people, and taking away with him all the evil that had marred their lives. But God moves in a mysterious way and it was of them that Evil took possession. They mocked at him. They betrayed the Spirit. They accepted his sacrifice with crocodile tears, but in their hearts they scoffed. They told lies about him to their mutual friends. They showed his letters round. They even used against him his act of generosity, calling it 'connivance,' and went so far as to say he had left his wife without a penny, deserted her to run away to another woman's arms, in Europe. Yes, they said all that. And they brought a judgment of divorce against him."

He dropped his eyes for a moment, and an odd noise that sounded almost like a chuckle came from his throat. Then he rose and very carefully put back his chair in the place from which he had taken it. All signs of grief had left his face.

"Well," he said, bending over the motionless form of Mme. de Fontanin, "such is love, and so incumbent on us is forgiveness that if at this very instant that dear, faithless woman appeared beside me, saying: 'James, I have come back to live again under your roof. You shall be once more my abject slave, and when I feel inclined, I'll make a mock of you again'—well, even if she said all that, I'd reply: 'Come, take all the little I possess. I thank God for your return.

And I shall strive so ardently to be truly good in your eyes, that you, too, will become good; for Evil does not exist.' Yes, it's the truth, dear, if ever my Dolly comes back to me, asking me to give her shelter, that's how I shall deal by her. But I shan't say: 'Dolly, I forgive you,' but only: 'Christ watch over you!' And so my words will not come back empty, because Good is the power, the only power, capable of holding in check the Negative." Folding his arms, he fell silent, nursing his pointed chin in the hollow of his hand. At last he spoke again, in the sing-song intonation of the professional preacher. "And you, Mme. de Fontanin, should go and do likewise. For you love this man with your heart's love, and Love is Righteousness. Christ has said: 'Except your righteousness shall exceed the righteousness of the scribes and Pharisees, ye shall in no case enter into the kingdom of heaven.'"

She shook her head sadly.

"You don't know him, James," she said in a low voice. "The very air's unbreatheable beside him. Everywhere he brings evil. He would only destroy all our happiness again—and contaminate the children."

"When Christ touched the leper's sore with His hand, the hand of Christ was not infected, but the leper was cleansed."

"You say I love him—no, that isn't true! I know him too well now. I know what his promises are worth. I've forgiven him far too often."

"When Peter asked Our Lord how often he should forgive his brother, saying: 'Till seven times?' Jesus answered: 'I say not unto thee, Until seven times: but, Until seventy times seven.'"

"I tell you, James, you don't know him."

"Who has the right to think: 'I know my brother'? Christ said: 'I judge no man.' And I, Gregory, I say to you: if a man leads a life of sin without being vexed and sore at heart, that is because there is still blindness in his soul. But one who weeps because he has lapsed into a sinful life, verily his eyes are open to the light of truth. I tell you he is stricken with remorse and his face was the face of a just man."

"You don't know everything, James. Ask him what he did when that woman had to run away to Belgium because her creditors were

after her. It was another man that she ran away with, but he left all
to follow them, he threw away every vestige of self-respect. For two
months he worked as a ticket-taker in the theatre where she was singing. The way he behaved was simply revolting. Yes, revolting! She
went on living with her violinist; Jerome put up with everything, he
used to dine with them, to play duets with his mistress's lover! 'The
face of a just man'! No, you've no idea what he's really like. Today
he's in Paris, he's repentant, and tells you he has left that woman,
and doesn't want to see her again. Tell me, why should he be paying
off her debts—if it isn't that he wants to get her to come back to him?
Yes, he's settling with Noémie's creditors one by one, and that's the
reason why he is in Paris now. And the money he's using for it is—
mine and the children's. Listen! Do you know what he did three
weeks ago? He mortgaged our place at Maisons-Laffitte, just to raise
twenty-five thousand francs for one of Noémie's creditors who was
pressing her for payment."

She looked down; there was more to tell, but she left it unsaid.
She was recalling that meeting at the notary's to which she had been
summoned and to which she had gone, suspecting nothing, to find
Jerome waiting for her at the door. He needed her power of attorney
for the mortgage, as the property was hers by inheritance. He had
thrown himself on her mercy, professing to be penniless and on the
brink of suicide; there, in the public street, he had dramatically turned
out his empty pockets. She had given way almost without a struggle,
and had followed him to the lawyer's office, to put an end to the scene
he was making in the street—and also because she, too, was short of
money and he had promised to give her a few thousand francs out
of the proceeds of the mortgage. She had to have the money to tide
over the next six months, pending the settlement that would take
place after the divorce.

"I tell you again, James, you don't know him. He assures you that
everything is changed, and he wants to come back to live with us.
Supposing I tell you that the day before yesterday, when he came here
to leave his birthday present for Jenny, downstairs with the concierge,
he had his cab stop only a few yards from our door, and that there was

someone with him in the cab!" She shuddered; a picture had risen
before her of the little workgirl in black she had seen crying on a
bench beside the Seine. She stood up. "That's the sort of man he is!"
she cried. "He's so dead to every sense of decency that he brings with
him some woman or other, his latest mistress, when he calls to leave
a birthday present for his daughter. And you say I still love him—
that's untrue, absolutely untrue!" She was pale with resentment; at
that moment she seemed genuinely to hate him.

Gregory gazed at her severely.

"The truth is not in you," he said. "Even in thought, should we
return evil for evil? Spirit is everything. The material world is subject to the spiritual. Has not Christ said—?" The barking of the dog
cut him short. "That must be your damned bearded doctor man!"
he muttered, scowling.

He hurried back to his chair and sat down.

The door opened and Antoine entered, followed by Jacques and
Daniel.

Antoine came in with a firm, decided step, now that he had accepted all the consequences this visit might entail. The light from
the open windows fell full on his face; his hair and beard formed
zones of shadow and all the sunlight seemed concentrated on the
pale rectangle of his forehead, lending him an air of high intellec-
tuality. And, though he was of medium height, at that moment he
seemed tall. As Mme. de Fontanin watched him coming towards
her, her instinctive liking for the young man took a new lease of life.
While he was bowing and she was holding out both hands to him in
affectionate welcome, he was annoyed to notice Pastor Gregory in
the background. The pastor, without moving, gave him a curt nod.

Jacques, who was standing at some distance from the others, was
examining with interest Mme. de Fontanin's eccentric-looking visitor,
while Gregory, astride his chair, his chin propped on his folded arms,
his nose as red as ever, and lips set in an uncouth, incomprehensible
grin, watched the young folks good-humouredly. When Mme. de
Fontanin went up to Jacques, there was such affection in her look that
he suddenly recalled that evening when she had held him weeping in

her arms. She, too, was remembering it, as she exclaimed: "Why, he's such a big boy now that I hardly dare to—!" and promptly kissed him, with a laugh that had in it a touch of coquetry. "But of course I'm a mamma, and you're the next thing to a brother to my Daniel." She turned to Gregory, who had just risen and was about to take his leave. "You're not going yet, James, I hope?"

"I'm sorry," he said, "but I've got to go now." He shook hands energetically with the two brothers, then went up to her.

"Just one more word," Mme. de Fontanin said, as they were leaving the room together. "Answer me quite frankly, please. After what I've told you, do you still think that Jerome should be allowed to return to live amongst us?" Her eyes were full of anxious questioning. "Weigh your answer well, James. If you say to me: 'Forgive!' I will forgive."

He was silent. His face was lit up with that look of all-enveloping compassion which is a trait of those who look on themselves as chosen vessels of the Truth. He fancied he detected something like a gleam of hope in Mme. de Fontanin's eyes. It was not that sort of forgiveness Christ desired of her. He turned away his eyes, with a disapproving snort.

Taking him by the arm, she tried to impart a note of affection to their leave-taking.

"Thank you, James, thank you. Please tell him my answer is no."

He was not listening; he was praying for her.

"May Christ reign in your heart," he murmured as he went out, without a backward glance.

When she came back, Antoine was gazing round the drawing-room, his mind full of the last occasion when he had seen it. She had to make an effort to steady her ruffled nerves.

"How nice of you to have come with your brother!" Her voice sounded a little artificial, exaggerating the pleasure she genuinely felt at seeing him again. "Do sit down." She motioned Antoine to the chair beside hers. "Today we'll do better not to count on the young people's company."

While she was speaking, Daniel had slipped his arm through

Jacques's and was taking him off to his own room. They were of the same height now. Daniel had not expected to find his friend so changed. His affection was all the stronger, and his desire to confide in him more urgent. No sooner were they alone than his face grew animated and took on an air of mystery.

"Look here, you'd better know at once—you'll be seeing her presently. She's a cousin of mine, who's living with us. She's absolutely ravishing!" He stopped abruptly, whether it was he noticed a hint of embarrassment in Jacques's attitude, or a belated scruple checked his revelations. "But let's hear about you, Jacques," he went on with a friendly smile. Even with his most intimate friend Daniel maintained a slightly ceremonious courtesy. "Why, it's ages, a whole year, since we saw each other." Jacques made no remark, so he went on: "Oh, there's nothing as yet," and added, bending confidentially towards his friend: "But I've high hopes!"

The insistence of his gaze and the tone in which he spoke were making Jacques feel ill at ease. And then it dawned on him that Daniel was not quite the same as before, though he could not have said exactly where the difference lay. Perhaps the oval face had lengthened out a little, but the features looked much the same; the upper lip formed still the same Cupid's bow, but now its curves were emphasized by the dark line of a moustache, and he had still the trick of smiling with one side only of his face—which marred its symmetry, showing on the left side of his mouth the white flash of his upper teeth. Something perhaps of their former purity had gone out of his eyes, and the tendency of the eyebrows to lift towards the temples was more pronounced, giving an almost feline charm to his gaze. In his voice, too, and manner were traces of a nonchalance which formerly he would not have ventured to display.

Jacques was so busy observing Daniel that he did not think of answering. Then—was it because of that casual manner of his friend, which at once irritated and attracted him?—he suddenly felt a rush of the passionate affection of his schooldays coming over him, and tears rose to his eyes.

"Think of it!" Daniel was exclaiming. "A whole year! Lots of things must have happened to you. Tell me all about them." He had been moving restlessly about the room; now he sat down, so as to fix his attention on his friend.

Daniel's attitude conveyed the sincerest affection, but Jacques thought he discerned in it a conscious effort, and became tongue-tied. Still, feeling he must speak, he began telling about the time he had spent in the reformatory. Once again, without actually intending to do so, he dropped into the same literary clichés that he had tried on Lisbeth; a sort of bashfulness prevented him from giving a bald, unvarnished account of the life he had led there.

"But why did you write to me so seldom?"

Jacques shirked the real reason: his reluctance to expose his father to hostile criticism—which, incidentally, did not prevent him, deep within his heart, from totally disapproving of M. Thibault.

"Being all alone like that changes one, you know," he explained after a pause. The mere fact of recalling it had made his face go apathetic, blank. "You come to feel that nothing really matters. And there's a sort of formless fear that never leaves you. You do things, but without thinking. After a while you hardly know who you are, you hardly know, even, if you exist. In the long run that life would kill one, or else drive one mad." He was staring into vacancy, a bemused look on his face. He shuddered slightly; then, changing his tone, fell to describing Antoine's visit to Crouy.

Daniel listened without interrupting. But once he saw that Jacques's narrative was coming to an end, his face lit up again.

"Why, I've not even told you her name!" he exclaimed. "It's Nicole. Like it?"

"Very much," Jacques said. For the first time he began to think of the charms of such a name as Lisbeth.

"Nicole! It suits her to a T. That's my idea anyhow. Well, you'll be seeing for yourself. She's not pretty-pretty, so to speak. But more than pretty; vivid, full of life, and such eyes!" He paused. "Appetizing, if you see what I mean."

Jacques would not meet his gaze. He, too, would have liked to open his heart to Daniel, tell him of his love; that, indeed, was why he had come here. But, from Daniel's first remark on, he had been feeling ill at ease, and now he listened with downcast eyes, with a sense of constraint, almost of shame.

"This morning," Daniel went on—he could hardly keep his exultation within bounds—"Mother and Jenny went out early, so we had our tea by ourselves, Nicole and I. We were alone in the flat. She hadn't dressed yet. It was simply wonderful! I followed her into Jenny's room; that's where she sleeps. A young girl's bedroom, there's something about it—! Well, I caught her in my arms, just for a second. She struggled, but she was laughing. You've no idea how supple she is. Then she ran out and shut herself in Mother's room, and wouldn't open the door. I can't think why I'm telling you all this—it's too silly for words, really." He tried to smile, but his lips stayed tense.

"Do you want to marry her?" Jacques asked.

"To marry her?"

Jacques felt suddenly hurt, as if he had been insulted. Every minute his friend was growing more and more of a stranger to him. And he felt his heart turn to ice when he saw the expression of Daniel's face—a look of faintly mocking curiosity.

"But what about you?" Daniel asked, coming closer. "In your letter you told me that you, too . . . ?" He left the phrase unfinished.

But, without looking up, Jacques shook his head, as if to say: "No, that's all over; you shan't hear a word from me." In any case, without waiting for an answer, Daniel had just got up. A sound of young voices came to their ears.

"You must tell me about it later on. They've just come. Hurry up!" He glanced at a mirror, threw up his head, and hurried out into the corridor.

"Well, children," Mme. de Fontanin was calling, "aren't you coming for tea?"

The tea was laid in the dining-room.

As Jacques crossed the threshold his heart beat faster; two girls were standing by the table. They had their hats and gloves still on, and their cheeks were glowing after their walk. Jenny ran up to Daniel and clung to his arm. Seeming to ignore her, he steered

Jacques in the direction of Nicole, and introduced him with a breezy unself-consciousness that impressed the boy. He was aware of Nicole's eyes giving him a curious, fleeting glance, of Jenny's lingering on him with more attention. He looked back towards Mme. de Fontanin, who was standing beside Antoine at the drawing-room door, evidently concluding a remark.

". . . to get children to understand," she was saying with a melancholy smile, "that there is nothing more precious than life, and that it is so terribly short."

It was long since Jacques had found himself amongst people he did not know, but he was so keenly interested in observing them that he lost all shyness. Nicole's natural elegance and sparkle were such that, beside her, Jenny struck him as insignificant and almost plain. Just then Nicole was talking to Daniel; she was laughing. Jacques could not hear what they were talking about, but he could see her eyebrows lifting in merriment or wonder. Her grey-blue eyes, if rather shallow, set too far apart, and perhaps a shade too round, made up for these defects by their gaiety and brilliance, which gave the pale, fair features a vitality that seemed unquenchable. And her face, moulded on generous lines, was crowned by a thick, heavy plait of hair tightly coiled above her head. She had a way of holding herself slightly bending forward that gave her an air of always making haste to greet a friend, and lavishing on all who crossed her path the thoughtless vivacity of her smile. As he watched her, Jacques found himself reluctantly applying to her that word "appetizing," which had so profoundly shocked him on Daniel's lips. Just then she realized she was being looked at, exaggerated her spontaneity, and promptly lost it.

It never crossed Jacques's mind to make an effort to conceal the interest other people inspired in him; on such occasions he had the ingenuousness of the child who stares open-mouthed—his face grew rigid, his gaze inert. Formerly, before his return from Crouy, he had not been thus, but used to treat those with whom he came in contact with such indifference that he never recognized anyone. Now, wherever he was, in crowded shop or street, his eyes observed the passers-by. He did not consciously analyse what he discovered in them; his mind worked on them unknowingly. It was enough for him to catch a glimpse of some peculiarity in a face, or in the demeanour of another, for his imagination to attribute to these strangers whom chance had brought his way a host of special traits of character.

Mme. de Fontanin cut short his musings; she had placed her hand on his arm.

"Come and have your tea beside me," she said. "I want *you* to pay me a little visit now." She handed him a cup and plate. "I'm so glad you've come to see us. . . . Jenny, my pet, please bring the cake. . . . Your brother's been telling me about the life you lead in your little flat. I'm so happy about it. It's so pleasant when two brothers understand each other like bosom friends, isn't it? Daniel and Jenny, too, get on very well together, and it's one of my greatest joys. Ah, that makes you smile, my big boy!" She had turned to Daniel, who was coming up with Antoine. "He's always poking fun at his old Mamma! Now, as a punishment, you shall kiss me, in front of everybody."

Daniel laughed, with perhaps a shade of embarrassment, but bent down and touched his mother's forehead lightly with his lips. There was an easy elegance in his least movement.

From the other side of the table Jenny was watching the scene with a smile the charm of which delighted Antoine. Carried away once more by her feelings, she went up to Daniel and linked her arm in his. "There's another," Antoine thought, "who gives more than she gets." When he had seen her for the first time, his interest had been quickened by the way the childish face looked wise beyond its years. He noticed now the graceful way her shoulders moved, as the young bosom gently rose and fell under the light blouse. She was not in the least like her mother, or Daniel either, but that was not surprising, for she seemed destined for a life quite other than the normal.

Mme. de Fontanin was sipping her tea, holding the cup very near her laughing face; through a fragrant mist she was making little amiable gestures towards Jacques. The brightness and the goodness of heart that shone in her eyes seemed to diffuse a gentle glow around her, and the white hair crowned like an incongruous diadem the noticeably youthful forehead. Jacques's eyes strayed from mother to son. At that moment he loved both with such fervour that he wished with all his heart they might perceive it; for, more than most, he felt a craving not to be misunderstood. His interest in the minds of others was so keen that nothing would satisfy him but an intimate communion with their secret thoughts; almost he wished to merge his life into theirs.

Beside the window Nicole and Jenny had embarked on a discussion. Daniel went up to them and joined in. All three bent over the camera to discover whether or not another photograph could be taken on the roll.

"Do! Just to please me!" Daniel suddenly exclaimed in the warm, emotional tone which was something new with him; the gaze he cast at Nicole was at once imperious and caressing. "Yes! Just as you are now, with your hat on, and my friend Thibault beside you."

"Jacques!" he called, then added in a lower tone: "Please do—I'm awfully keen on taking you two together."

Jacques joined their group. Daniel dragged them all into the drawing-room, where the light, so he said, was better.

Antoine stayed on with Mme. de Fontanin in the dining-room. He was bringing to an end the explanation he had thought it best to give her, with the brusqueness which, to his thinking, lent an accent of forthrightness to his manner. "And I'd have you know exactly the circumstances of this visit," he was saying. "If Father knew Jacques was here, he'd take my brother from my keeping, and all the trouble would begin again."

"Poor man," Mme. de Fontanin murmured, in a tone that made Antoine smile.

"Do you really mean you're sorry for him?" he asked.

"Yes, for having failed to win the trust of a son like you."

"It's not his fault, and it's not mine either. My father is what is usually described as an eminent and worthy man. I respect him. But there's no help for it; never, on any question, do we think—I won't say 'alike,' but even on the same lines. Never, whatever the subject we are talking about, can we manage to see it from the same angle."

"There are some who've not yet been touched by the great light."

"If it's religion you're thinking of," Antoine put in at once, "I may as well tell you Father's fanatically religious."

Mme. de Fontanin shook her head. "That's nothing new," she smiled. "Doesn't the apostle Paul tell us that it isn't those who only hearken to the Law who find favour in God's eyes, but rather those who practise it in word and deed?"

For M. Thibault, whom she thought she pitied from the bottom of her heart, she really felt an instinctive, unreasoning aversion. The taboo he had imposed on her son, her household, and herself seemed odious, unjust, and based on the least worthy motives. Not only did the grossness of M. Thibault's appearance revolt her, but she could not forgive him for mistrusting the very things she valued most: her moral standard, her Protestantism. And she felt all the more warmly towards Antoine for having overridden his father's injunction.

"What about you?" she asked with sudden apprehension. "Are you still a practising Catholic?"

When Antoine shook his head, her face lit up with a glow of pleasure.

"As a matter of fact, I kept it up for quite a long time," he began. He found that Mme. de Fontanin's company gave a fillip to his thoughts—and, still more certainly, to his tongue. She had a knack of listening with extreme attention that implied a high esteem of the person speaking to her, and always encouraged him to rise to the occasion, above his normal conversational level. "I kept up my religious observances, but I had no real piety. God was for me a sort of omniscient headmaster, whom it was best to humour by means of certain gestures and a certain line of conduct. I obeyed, but for the most part with a sense of boredom. I was a good pupil, you see, in everything; in religion like the rest. It's hard for me to say now exactly how I came to lose my faith. When I found I'd lost it—that was only four or five years ago—I'd in any case already reached a stage of scientific knowledge that left little room for religious belief. I'm a positivist, you know," he added, with a feeling of self-satisfaction; as a matter of fact he was expressing theories he made up as he went along, for so far he had had scant leisure or occasion to indulge in self-analysis.

"I don't claim," he continued, "that science explains everything, but it tells me what things are, and that's enough for me. I find the *how* of things sufficiently interesting for me to dispense with the vain quest of the *why*. Besides," he added hastily, in a lower voice, "isn't it possible that between these two types of explanation there's only a difference of degree?" He smiled, as if in self-excuse. "As for questions of morality, well, I hardly give them a thought. I hope I'm not shocking you! But you see, I love my work, I love life, I'm energetic, I like getting things done, and my experience has led me to believe that 'Get on with your job!' is a quite adequate rule of life. So far, in any case, I've never felt the slightest hesitation about what it was up to me to do."

Mme. de Fontanin made no reply. She was not in the least vexed with Antoine for being so different from herself. But in her inmost heart she gave thanks all the more fervently to God for His constant presence in her life. To this awareness of divine protection she owed the joyful, never-failing confidence that radiated from her so unmistakably and with such efficacy that, though her life had been a sequence of disaster and her lot was far worse than that of most of those she met, she yet had that peculiar gift of being a source of courage, peace of mind, and contentment for all around her. Antoine at that moment was experiencing it; never in his father's circle had he met anyone who inspired him with such veneration, around whom the atmosphere was so exalting, by reason of its purity. And he wanted to come nearer her, even at the expense of strict veracity.

"I've always felt drawn to Protestantism," he averred, though actually he had never given it a thought till he met the Fontanins. "Your Reformation was a revolution on the religious plane, for it opened the door to ideas of spiritual freedom."

She listened to him with growing appreciation. Young, ardent, chivalrous he seemed to her just now, and she was impressed by the vital energy of his expression, the furrow on his forehead that told of concentrated thought. And when he raised his head she had a childish delight in noting a peculiarity that increased the pensiveness of his expression; the upper eyelids were so narrow that they almost vanished under the heavy brows when he opened his eyes wide; at that moment his eyelashes and his eyebrows were all but indistinguishable.

A man with a forehead like that, she was thinking, could never stoop to an ignoble act. And suddenly it struck her that Antoine was the perfect prototype of a man worthy to be loved. She was still quivering with resentment against her husband. How different would have been a life united with someone of Antoine's calibre! It was the first time she had compared another man with Jerome, the first time a definite regret had crossed her mind and she had been aware of feeling that another might have brought her happiness. It was only a fleeting impulse, strong but secret, that stirred her to the depths of her being; almost immediately she felt ashamed, and she got the better of it quickly enough. But the sense of bitterness that contrition and perhaps regret had left behind them was slower to dissipate.

Just then Jenny and Jacques came in, and their appearance effectively laid the phantoms of her troubled mind. She made a welcoming gesture and called them up to her at once, lest they should think their presence was unwanted. At the first glance she felt that something had happened between them. . . . It had.

Immediately after taking the photograph of Nicole and Jacques, Daniel proposed to find out forthwith whether it had been a success. That morning he had promised Jenny and his cousin to teach them how to develop, and they had made all the necessary preparations in an empty cupboard, at the end of a passage, which Daniel had formerly used as a dark-room. The space in it was so cramped that it was practically impossible for more than two to be in it at the same time. Daniel had adroitly managed to get Nicole to go in first; then, running up to Jenny, had laid a hand trembling with excitement on her shoulder and whispered:

"You stay with Jacques!"

She had cast him a shrewd, disapproving glance. Yet she had obeyed, such was her brother's influence over her, so irresistible his manner of demanding—not only in so many words but by the sheer effrontery of his gaze and the vehemence of his demeanour—that his wishes should be complied with then and there.

While the brief scene between brother and sister was in progress, Jacques had stayed in the background, examining the contents of a glass cabinet in the drawing-room. Jenny persuaded herself, as she went to join him, that he could not have noticed Daniel's manœuvre. With a little pout she asked him:

"How about you? Do you go in for photography?"

"No."

The almost imperceptible embarrassment with which he replied made her realize that she should not have asked the question. It came back to her that he had only recently been released from some sort of institution in which he had been to all intents and purposes a prisoner. Following an association of ideas, and by way of making conversation, she put another question:

"You haven't seen Daniel for quite a long time, have you?"

Jacques lowered his eyes.

"No. Not for a very long time. Not since . . . ! Why, it's over a year."

A shadow flitted across her face. Her second attempt had been hardly more successful than her first. He would think she was trying to remind him of the Marseille episode. So much the worse for him! She had never approved of that adventure, and in her eyes he alone was responsible for it. From the start, unconsciously, she had been disliking Jacques. When she saw him that afternoon, at tea-time, she had been unable to help recalling the injury he had done her family, and from the moment she set eyes on him had felt an unqualified repugnance. For one thing, she found him ugly, vulgar even; his big head and uncouth features, his jaw, chapped lips, protuberant ears, and red hair bunched up over his forehead—all displeased her. She could hardly forgive Daniel his attachment to such a friend, though her jealousy prompted her to be more glad than otherwise to discover that the only being who dared to contest with her the first place in her brother's heart was so unattractive.

She had taken the little dog on her lap and was stroking it absent-mindedly. Jacques was still staring at the floor; he, too, was thinking of the escapade to Marseille, of the memorable night when he first had crossed this threshold.

"Do you find him much changed?" she asked, to break the silence.

"Not at all," he said, then hastily corrected himself. "No, that's wrong; he has changed quite a lot."

His keen regard for truth impressed her, and for a moment she found him less distasteful. Perhaps Jacques was conscious of this fleeting change of mood, for he stopped thinking about Daniel. Looking at Jenny, he began to wonder what she was like. And suddenly he had a brief glimpse into her character, a revelation that he found he could not put into words, though he had guessed the nervous insta-bility, the cross-currents of intense emotion, behind those features seemingly expressive, yet so reticent, and the eyes which, for all their animation, kept their secret. It struck him that he would like to know her better, gain access to that fast-shut heart—even, perhaps, become the friend of this young girl. And for a while his fancy toyed delight-fully with the thought that he might come to love her. All his troubled past was out of mind, and now it seemed to him that never again could he be unhappy.

He let his eyes rove round the room, and linger now and then on Jenny; in his gaze there were both curiosity and a shyness which pre-vented him from noticing how reserved her attitude was, how much she was on the defensive. Suddenly, by an inevitable flash-back of emotion, the picture of Lisbeth rose before him—but a Lisbeth who had dwindled now into a little, insignificant domestic creature, of no account. For the first time he realized the childishness of his romantic scheme of marrying Lisbeth. But—what then? He was appalled at the void that of a sudden loomed up in his life, a void that at all costs he must fill. In Jenny, obviously, he might find the friend he needed, but . . .

Her voice took him from his reverie, with a start.

". . . at a school?"

He caught only the tail-end of the phrase.

"Sorry! I didn't catch . . . What were you saying?"

"I asked if you were going to school just now."

"Not yet." His voice betrayed his discomfiture. "I'm very behind-hand with my studies, you know. I'm working with private coaches, friends of my brother." Then, in all innocence, he added: "And you?"

She was offended by his putting a direct question to her and the too familiar glance that accompanied it.

"I don't go to school," she answered curtly. "I have a governess."

With his next observation he made another blunder.

"Of course, for a girl, it doesn't matter really."

She bridled.

"That's what you think. But it's not Mother's view, or Daniel's."

Now there was no mistaking her hostility. He realized too late his clumsiness and tried to retrieve the situation by a remark which he imagined amiable.

"What I mean is, a girl always knows enough to get along with."

He saw that he was sinking in deeper; he could not control his thoughts or words. That damned reformatory! It had made an idiot of him! He reddened, and the sudden rush of blood to his head seemed to complete his befuddlement. The only issue he could see now was to give vent to his anger. For a moment he groped vainly for some stinging retort; then, throwing discretion to the winds, he blurted out in the vulgar, bantering tone his father often used:

"The principal thing isn't taught in schools; it's character."

She had herself well under control, and did not flinch. But just then the dog yawned noisily and she exclaimed:

"Oh, you nasty little creature! What disgusting manners!" Her voice was trembling with rage. "What disgusting manners!" she re-peated, with a shrill, rancorous insistence. Then she put the dog down, rose, and walked out onto the balcony.

Five slow minutes passed, five minutes of intolerable silence. Jacques had not moved from his chair; he felt as if he were suffocating. From the dining-room came the sound of alternating voices: Mme. de

Fontanin's and Antoine's. Jenny was leaning on the balcony rail, with her back to him, humming one of her piano exercises and beating time with her foot as if to emphasize her truculent contempt. She had made up her mind to tell her brother all about it, and get him to drop this vulgar, ill-bred friend of his. At that moment she hated Jacques. Glancing furtively into the room, she saw him sitting there, flushed but on his dignity. She felt even surer of herself and set her mind to finding some new remark to hurt him.

"Come along, Puce! I'm off!"

Leaving the balcony, she walked past him as if he were not there and calmly proceeded to the dining-room.

Jacques was terrified at the thought that if he stayed behind he would never find a way of getting up and going. So he rose, and followed her at a distance. Mme. de Fontanin's affectionate welcome changed his resentment into melancholy.

"So your brother's deserted you?" she said to her daughter.

"Oh, I asked Daniel to develop my films right away," she explained, but without meeting her mother's eye. "He won't be long now."

She had a shrewd suspicion that Jacques had not been taken in; and this complicity that circumstances had forced on them intensified their mutual dislike. Inexorably Jacques wrote her down a liar, and disapproved of her readiness to shield her brother. She guessed his feelings and her pride was wounded; she carefully refrained from looking in his direction.

Smiling, Mme. de Fontanin motioned them towards the sofa.

"I see my little patient has grown famously," Antoine remarked.

Jacques said nothing, and kept his eyes bent upon the floor. He was foundering in an abyss of hopelessness; never would he recover his former self! Conscious at once of his weakness and his brutality, he felt profoundly sick at heart; every impulse had him at its mercy, he was a puppet in the hands of implacable fatality.

He heard Mme. de Fontanin asking him a question: "Are you fond of music?"

He pretended not to understand, tears were filling his eyes, and he bent quickly down, as if to tie a shoelace. He heard Antoine answering on his behalf. His ears were buzzing and he felt like death. Was Jenny looking? he wondered.

Daniel and Nicole had been together in the dark-room for more than a quarter of an hour. Daniel had shot the bolt the moment he entered, then taken the films out of the camera, and unrolled them.

"Don't meddle with the door," he said. "The least speck of light will fog the whole roll."

Nicole's first impression was one of total obscurity, but after a while she began to see what looked like incandescent shadows moving in the red glow of the lantern close beside her. Gradually they took form, and she saw two long, delicate hands, cut off at the wrists, tilting a long dish. Those two disembodied hands were all she could make out of Daniel, but there was so little space in the dark-room that she was as conscious of his every movement as if he were actually in contact with her. They held their breath, each haunted by a vivid memory of the kiss exchanged that morning in the bedroom.

"Can you see anything?" she whispered.

But he would not answer her at once; the silence had an exquisite suspense that thrilled his senses and, now that darkness was doing away with the restraints of normal life, he had turned towards her and was inhaling eagerly the perfume floating round her.

At last he brought himself to speak. "No, there's nothing yet."

Again there was silence. Then suddenly the dish on which Nicole's eyes were fixed ceased moving. The two spectral hands had left the zone of the lamplight. The moment seemed never-ending. All at once Nicole felt his arms encircling her, closely, passionately. She experienced no surprise, rather a vague sense of relief that the suspense was over. But she drew her shoulders back as far as she could, twisting and turning, to elude the lips whose impact she both dreaded and desired. At last their faces touched. Daniel's burning forehead came in contact with something cold, slippery, and pliant; it was Nicole's hair, the long, glossy plait she wore coiled round her head. He could not help giving a start, and drawing back a little. For a

moment her lips were free, and she had just time to utter a strangled
cry: "Jenny!"

Roughly his hand closed her lips; then, leaning against her with
the full weight of his body, he crushed her against the door. His voice
came in quick gasps through his clenched teeth; there was a note
almost of madness in it.

"Keep quiet! Stop! Nicole darling, dear little girl, I want—I want
to tell you . . ."

She had almost ceased struggling and he thought she was giving
way to him. She had slipped her arm behind her and was feeling
for the latch. The door fell open abruptly, letting in a flood of light.
He released her, and shut the door again at once. But in the sudden
light she had seen his face, and it was unrecognizable, like a livid
Chinese mask, with great blotches of red round the eyes that seemed
to slew them up towards the temples. The pupils, shrunk to pin-
points, were expressionless, and the thin, tight lips of a few minutes
past were puffy now, clumsily agape. A thought of Jerome flashed
through her mind. There was hardly any likeness between Daniel
and his father, yet in that harsh, revealing beam of light, it was
Jerome's face she had seen!

"My congratulations!" His voice was shrill with vexation. "The
whole roll's ruined."

"I'm quite ready to stay," she said composedly. "In fact I want to
talk to you. Only, please unlatch the door."

"No; Jenny will come in."

After a momentary hesitation she said: "Then promise me on your
honour that you won't touch me again."

He felt like flinging himself on her, gagging her with his hand,
ripping up her blouse; but, at the same time, knew that he was beaten.

"All right. I promise."

"Good! Now listen to me, Daniel. I was very silly this morning;
I let you go too far, much too far. But this time I say definitely *no!*
I didn't run away from home just to get involved in this sort of
thing." She spoke the last words hurriedly, to herself. Then she addressed Daniel again: "Yes, I'll trust you with my secret. I ran away

from Mother's place. Oh, there's nothing really to be said against her —only that she's very unhappy . . . and very weak. That's all I can tell you." She paused. That face she loathed above all, Jerome's face, still hovered before her eyes; his son might bring her to the state to which Jerome had brought her mother. Alarmed by Daniel's silence, she went on hastily: "You don't understand me a bit. Of course that's my fault, really; I've not been my real self with you. With Jenny, yes. With you I've gone on in a silly way, and you've imagined all sorts of things. But, underneath, I'm not like that, not in the least. I don't want the sort of life that—that begins that way. What would have been the point of coming to live with someone like Aunt Thérèse? No! I want—you'll laugh at me, but I don't care—I want to be able later on to deserve the respect of a man who'll love me truly, for always; a man who—who takes it seriously."

"But I *do* take it seriously!" From the tone she guessed the smile of naïve self-pity hovering on his lips, and knew at once that she had no more to fear from him.

"No, you don't!" She sounded almost cheerful. "And you mustn't be angry, Daniel, if I tell you straight out—you don't love me."

"Not love you? Oh, Nicole . . . !"

"No, it's not me you love, it's . . . something else. And I don't love you either. Now listen, I'm going to be quite frank; I don't think I could ever love a man like you."

"Like me?"

"I mean, a man like all the rest. It isn't that I don't want to love someone, one day. I do. But it's got to be someone, well, someone who's pure, and who'll have approached me in a very different way, and for . . . for other reasons. Oh, I don't know how to express it! Anyhow, a man quite different from you."

"Thanks very much!"

His desire for her was dead; and all he wanted now was to escape seeming ridiculous.

"Now then," she said, "let's make peace, and forget all about it." She began to open the door; this time he did not try to stop her. "Is it 'friends'?" she asked, holding out her hand. He made no answer.

He was looking at her eyes, her cheeks, the young face that seemed proffered like a ripe fruit. He forced a smile onto his lips; his eyelashes were fluttering. She took his hand and grasped it tightly.

"Don't spoil my life as well!" she murmured in a coaxing voice, and suddenly her eyebrows took a humorous inflexion. "Isn't a roll of films quite enough damage for one day?"

Good-naturedly he laughed. She had not expected that much of him, and felt a little chagrined. Still, all in all, she was well satisfied with her victory and with the opinion he would have of her henceforward.

"Well?" Jenny asked when they appeared together in the dining-room.

"No go," Daniel said gruffly.

Jacques felt a thrill of spiteful satisfaction. Nicole's eyes twinkled as she repeated slowly, emphatically:

"Ab-so-lutely no go!"

Then she noticed that Jenny's cheeks were quivering, her eyes blurred with sudden tears, and, running up to her, she kissed her.

From the moment his friend had come into the room, Jacques had stopped thinking about himself; he could not keep his eyes off Daniel. A change had come over Daniel's features, a change that was painful to observe. It was as if the upper and lower halves of his face no longer matched; the enigmatic, troubled, almost sinister expression of his eyes was out of keeping with the smile that lifted one side of his mouth and screwed the lower portion of his face round to the left.

Their eyes met. Daniel frowned slightly and moved uneasily away.

This indication of mistrust grieved Jacques more than all the rest. All the time, from the very start, Daniel had been obscurely disappointing him; now at last he was consciously aware of it. There had not been a moment of real intimacy between them; why, he had not even been able to tell Lisbeth's name to his friend!

For a while he fancied that the cause of his distress was his disillusionment regarding Daniel. But the real reason, though he had only a vague inkling of it, was that now for the first time he was viewing his love from a critical angle and, by the same token, eliminating it from his system. Like all young people, he lived only for the present; the past lapsed so swiftly into oblivion, and thoughts of the future merely whetted his impatience. And today, the present, every moment of it, seemed to have a bitter savour; as the afternoon drew to a close, he felt more and more hopelessly depressed. When Antoine signed to him to get ready to go, he felt actually relieved.

Daniel had noticed Antoine's gesture. He went up to Jacques at once.

"You're not going yet?"

"Yes, we must."

"So soon?" Then he added in a lower tone: "But we've seen hardly anything of each other."

He, too, had got nothing but disappointment from the day. And now, to make things worse, he began to feel remorseful for the way he had treated Jacques and—what grieved him even more—their friendship.

"Please forgive me," he said suddenly, leading Jacques towards the window-recess. And there was such humility, such genuine solicitude, in his manner that Jacques, forgetting all his disappointments, felt carried away by an access of the old affection. "It's been a rotten day," Daniel continued. "Everything went wrong. When shall I see you again?" His tone grew pressing. "Look here, I've got to see you alone and have a good long talk. We've got out of touch with each other somehow. Of course, there's nothing odd in that—why, we haven't seen each other for a whole year! But we can't let that go on."

He suddenly wondered what future lay before their friendship, which so long had had nothing to thrive on except an almost mystical sentiment of loyalty, the fragility of which had just been shown to them. No, they must not let it wither. True, Jacques struck him now as rather childish; but his affection remained intact and, for all he knew, the keener for his feeling so much older than his friend.

"We're always at home on Sunday," Mme. de Fontanin was saying just then to Antoine. "We shan't leave Paris till after the school prize-day." Her eyes lit up. "Daniel has won several prizes," she said in a low voice, but with evident pride. "Wait!" she added hastily, after making sure her son had his back to her and was not listening. "Before you go, I'd like to show you my treasures." She hastened lightheartedly to her room, Antoine following, and led him to a desk. In one of the drawers, in a neat row, lay twenty laurel crowns in painted cardboard. She shut the drawer almost immediately and began laughing, a little flustered at having yielded to a sentimental impulse.

"Don't tell him," she said. "He hasn't the least idea I keep them all." They returned in silence to the hall.

"Hallo, Jacques!" Antoine called.

"Today doesn't count," Mme. de Fontanin said, holding out both hands to Jacques and giving him a keen glance, as if she had guessed everything. "You're amongst friends here, Jacques dear, and any time you feel like coming you'll always be welcome. And your big brother, too, I needn't say," she added with a graceful gesture for Antoine.

Jacques turned round to see if Jenny was there; but she had gone off with her cousin. Bending over the little dog, he kissed its sleek, smooth forehead. . . .

Mme. de Fontanin went back to the dining-room to clear the table. Daniel followed her pensively, then leaned against the doorway and, without speaking, lit a cigarette. He was turning over in his mind what Nicole had told him. Why had they concealed from him the fact that his cousin had run away from home and come to them for refuge? Refuge against what?

Mme. de Fontanin was moving to and fro with the supple movements that gave her still the easy grace of a much younger woman. She was thinking of what Antoine had said, of all he had told her about himself, his studies, and his plans for the future, and about his father. "What a noble character!" she was saying to herself. "And I do like that forehead of his. It's so"—she groped for an epithet—"yes, so earnest," she added with a little thrill of pleasure.

Then she recalled the idle fancy that had crossed her mind; for an instant had not she, too, sinned in thought? Gregory's words came back to her. And all at once, for no definite reason, she felt her heart full of such abounding joy that she put down the plate she was holding so as to pass her fingers over her face and feel under her hand the imprint of that sudden ecstasy. She went up to her son and startled him from his reverie, gaily clapping her hands on his shoulders. Then she gazed deep into his eyes, kissed him, and, without a word, went quickly out of the room.

She went straight to her desk and began writing in her large, childish, rather wavering hand.

My dear James,

I have behaved too arrogantly towards you. Who of us has the right to judge another? I thank God for having enlightened me once again. Tell Jerome I will not press for a divorce. Tell him . . .

Through her tears the words seemed dancing on the paper.

XII

A FEW days later Antoine was awakened by a sound of hammering on the shutters. The garbage collector had failed to get the street door opened for him, though the bell was in order—he could hear it ringing in the concierge's room—and suspected that something was wrong.

Something was wrong, indeed: old Mme. Frühling was dead. She had had another seizure, a fatal one, in the course of the night, and had dropped dead on the floor.

Jacques came in just as the body was being laid out on the mattress. The old woman's mouth was gaping, showing some yellow teeth. What was it—something horrible—it reminded him of? Yes, that dead grey horse lying on the Toulon road. Then suddenly it struck him very likely Lisbeth would be coming for the funeral.

Two days passed and she did not appear; it seemed she was not coming at all. Jacques caught himself thinking: so much the better! He could not make out his real feelings just now. Even after his visit to the Fontanins, he had gone on tinkering with a poem in which he glorified his heart's beloved and lamented her absence. But somehow he had no real wish to see her again.

None the less he walked past the concierge's room ten times a day, and each time glanced eagerly inside, only to turn away each time, reassured, yet dissatisfied.

On the day before the funeral, as he was coming in after dining alone in the little restaurant where he and Antoine had been having their meals since M. Thibault's departure to Maisons-Laffitte, the first thing to meet his eye was a valise in the entrance-hall, just outside the concierge's door. He felt himself trembling, his forehead damp with sweat. In the light from the candles round the bier he saw a girlish form, swathed in heavy mourning veils, kneeling beside it. He entered the room at once. The two nuns glanced round at him without interest; but Lisbeth did not turn. The night was sultry, and a warm, sickly sweet odour filled the room: the flowers on the coffin were wilting. Jacques remained standing, feeling sorry he had ventured in; the deathbed and everything connected with it had given him a sensation of discomfort that he was unable to vanquish. Lisbeth had passed out of his mind and all he wanted now was a pretext to get away. When a nun rose to snuff a candle, he slipped out of the room.

It seemed as if Lisbeth had intuitively felt his presence, or perhaps she had recognized his step, for she caught him up before he had reached the door of the flat. Hearing her step behind him, Jacques turned. For a few seconds they stood gazing at each other in a dark corner of the entrance-hall. Under the black veil her eyes were clouded with tears, and she did not see the hand he was holding out to her. He would have liked to weep in sympathy, but he was conscious of no emotion, only a vague boredom and a certain shyness.

A door banged on one of the upper landings. Fearing they might be caught outside his door, Jacques took out his keys. But what with his confusion and the darkness, he was unable to find the keyhole.

"Sure it's the right key?" she murmured. He was profoundly moved by the slow cadence of her voice. When at last the door was open, she hesitated. Footsteps could be heard coming down the stairs from one of the upper flats.

"Antoine's on duty at the hospital," Jacques whispered, to persuade her. Then, without the least sign of embarrassment, she crossed the threshold.

As he shut the door and switched on the lights, he saw her walking straight to his room. When she sat down on the sofa, each of her movements reminded him exactly of the past. Through the crape veil he saw her eyes swollen with weeping; grief had perhaps taken away some of the prettiness of her features, but it had added pathos. He noticed that she had a bandaged finger. He did not dare to sit down; he could not take his mind off the bereavement that had led to her return.

"How close it is tonight!" she said. "I'm sure there's going to be a storm."

She moved a little on the sofa; and the movement seemed an invitation to him to take the place beside her, his usual place. Jacques sat down and at once, without a word, without even taking off her veil, but simply drawing it aside, she pressed her cheek against his, exactly as before. The crape veil had an odour of dye and starch, and he found the contact of her moist skin disagreeable. He felt at a loss what to do or say. When he took her hand in his she gave a little cry.

"Have you hurt yourself?"

"*Ach,* it's only a—a whitlow," she sighed.

The sigh seemed to be for all her troubles at once: her sore finger, her bereavement, and the baffled tenderness fretting her heart. Without thinking, she began unwinding the bandage. When the finger was laid bare—livid and misshapen, with the nail displaced by the abscess—Jacques felt his breath stop short and for a moment his senses reeled as if she had suddenly exposed some secret place of her body.

Meanwhile he was beginning to feel, through his clothes, the warmth of the young body touching his. She turned her china-blue eyes towards him, plaintive eyes that always seemed entreating him not to be unkind. And then he had an impulse, stronger than his repugnance, to press his lips on the disfigured finger and make it well again.

She rose and with a dejected air started winding the gauze again round her finger.

"I'll have to be going back now."

She looked so worn out that he made a suggestion.

"Oh, let me make you a cup of tea. Shall I?"

She gave him a curious look, and only afterwards smiled.

"Thank you, I'd like a nice cup of tea. I'll run across and say a little prayer; then I'll come back."

In a few minutes he had the water boiled, the tea made, and was bringing it back to his room. Lisbeth was not yet there. He sat down. Now he was all eagerness for her return. He felt his nerves on edge, but did not try to ascertain the reason. Why was she delaying like this? He could not bring himself to call to her; it would be like an affront to the dead woman. But what could be keeping her all this time? As the minutes passed he kept on going up to the tea-pot, feeling its declining warmth. At last it was stone-cold and, having no pretext for getting up, he stayed unmoving in his chair. His eyes were smarting with staring at the lamp and, with his exasperation, he felt the fever rising in his blood.

A sudden glare of lightning between the slats of the closed shutters jarred his nerves to breaking-point. Was she *never* coming back? He felt half asleep, so weary of everything he would have liked to die.

There was a low rumble, a black crash. That was the tea-pot bursting. Let it burst! The tea was pouring down in rain, lashing the shutters. Lisbeth was soaked through, water was streaming down her cheeks, down the black crape, washing the colour out of it till it was snow-white, white and translucent, a bridal veil.

Jacques gave a violent start. She had just sat down beside him again, pressing her cheek to his.

"Were you asleep, Jacques dear?"

Never before had she called him by his Christian name. She had taken off her veil and, in a half-dream, he seemed to see once more the well-beloved face of the Lisbeth he had known, though now there were dark rings round her eyes and the corners of her lips were drooping. She made a gesture of weary resignation.

"Now," she said, "my uncle will marry me."

Her head was bowed, and Jacques could not see if she was crying.

There had been sadness in her voice, but acquiescence too; perhaps her regret was touched with curiosity about the new life opening before her. But Jacques was not disposed to press such speculations too far. He wanted to believe her unhappy, to revel in the thrill of pitying her. Putting his arms round her, he pressed her body against his with all his might, as if he were trying to merge them into one. Her lips found his, and passionately he gave his mouth to her mouth's kiss. Never in his life had he felt such an ecstasy of emotion. Evidently she had unfastened her blouse before coming in, for suddenly, almost without a movement on his part, the warmth of her young breast was nestling in his hand.

She shifted her position a little so that Jacques's hand could move, untrammelled, under the dress.

"Let's pray together for Mother Frühling," she murmured.

He felt no inclination to smile; almost he believed he was really praying, such was the fervour of his caresses.

Suddenly she gave a little moan, and shuffled free from his embrace. He supposed that he had hurt her finger, or else that she was about to leave him. But she only moved towards the lamp-switch; after turning off the light she came back to the sofa. Close beside his ear he heard her whisper: *"Liebling!"* and then again he felt her soft lips crushed on his, her feverish fingers on his clothes. . . .

Another clap of thunder woke him; rain was hissing on the cobbles in the courtyard. Lisbeth? Where was Lisbeth? All was darkness in the room. He had half a mind to get up, to go and look for her, and even made a tentative effort to rise, propping himself on his elbow; but then a flood of sleep swept over him, and he sank back amongst the cushions.

It was broad daylight when at last he opened his eyes.

First, he saw the tea-pot on the table, then his coat inexplicably sprawling on the floor. Now everything came back to him, and he got up at once. A sudden, urgent craving had come over him to take off what clothes he still had on and wash his limbs in good clean water. The cold bath seemed like a purifying rite, a baptism.

Still dripping, he began to walk about the room, throwing out his chest, testing his muscles, and patting the cool, firm skin; the odious associations of this cult of his own nakedness had been completely blotted from his memory. Reflected in a glass he saw his slim young body and for the first time since a very long while he found that he could gaze at every part of it coolly, with unruffled equanimity. Remembering certain lapses of the past, he merely shrugged his shoulders with an indulgent contempt. "All that was childish silliness!" That chapter of his life, he felt, was definitely closed; it seemed to him that certain energies, after a long spell of incomprehension and deviation from their natural course, had at last found their proper function. Though what had happened during the past twelve hours was only vaguely present in his consciousness, and though he did not even give a thought to Lisbeth, he felt light-hearted, clean, and sound in mind and body. He had not the least impression of having lit on something new; rather, it seemed to him he had recovered a long-lost equilibrium, like a convalescent who, though delighted by his return to health, finds nothing new in it.

Still naked, he moved into the hall, and held the door ajar. He fancied he could make out Lisbeth in the darkened room where the dead body lay, on her knees and swathed in the black veils she had worn the previous night. Men on ladders were festooning the street-entrance with black draperies. He remembered the funeral was fixed for nine, and dressed in eager haste, as if for a holiday. That morning every act was a delight.

He had just finished tidying his room when M. Thibault, who had made a point of returning from Maisons-Laffitte for the funeral, came to fetch him.

He walked beside his father in the cortège. He had a vague sense of almost patronizing superiority as at the church he filed in with the others, amongst all those people who did not know; and without much emotion he clasped Lisbeth's hand.

All that day the concierge's room was empty. Jacques counted the minutes, waiting for Lisbeth's return; but he would not own to himself the reason for his impatience, the desire smouldering in the background of his mood.

At four o'clock the bell rang, but when he ran to open the door, it was his Latin tutor. He had quite forgotten he had a lesson that afternoon.

He was listening to his tutor's explanations of a passage of Horace with an inattentive ear, when the bell rang again. This time it was she. From the threshold she could see the open door of Jacques's room, and the tutor's back bent over the table. For a few moments their eyes met, questioning. Jacques had no idea that she had come to say good-bye, that she was leaving by the six-o'clock train. She did not dare to speak, but a slight tremor ran through her body and her eyelids quivered. Raising her bandaged finger to her mouth, she came quite close to him and, as if she were already in the train that was to carry her away from him for ever, threw him a hasty kiss and fled.

The tutor went on with the interrupted lesson:

"*Purpurarum usus* means the same thing as *purpura quâ utuntur*. But there's a shade of difference. Do you feel it?"

Jacques smiled as if he felt it. He was telling himself Lisbeth would be back quite soon and a picture was hovering before his eyes of Lisbeth's face in the dusk of the hall, and the raised veil, and the kiss she had seemed to snatch with her bandaged finger from her lips, to throw to him.

"Go on translating," the tutor said.

Note. As regards Parts I and II of The Thibaults the present Translator wishes to acknowledge the assistance he has derived from the previous version by Mr. Stephen Haden Guest.

PART

III

PART

III

I

THE two brothers walked along by the Luxembourg railings. The Senate clock had just gone half-past five.

"Your nerves are on edge," Antoine observed. Jacques had been forcing the pace for some time, and his brother was growing tired of it. "Sweltering, isn't it? Looks like a storm brewing."

Jacques slowed down and took off his hat, which was pinching his temples.

"Nerves on edge? Not a bit of it. Quite the contrary. You don't believe me? Well, I'm amazed at my own calmness. Each of the last two nights I've slept like a log; so much so that, on awaking, I felt stiff all over. Cool as a cucumber, I assure you. But you shouldn't have bothered to come with me, you've such heaps of things to do. All the more so as Daniel's going to turn up. Amazing, isn't it? He came all the way from Cabourg this morning just for me. He telephoned a moment ago to know when the results would be posted. Damned thoughtful he is about things like that. Battaincourt promised to come too. So, you see, I shan't be alone." He glanced at his watch. "Well, in half an hour . . ."

Yes, his nerves are on edge, all right, thought Antoine. Mine too, a bit. Still, as Favery swears he's in the list . . . Antoine brushed aside, as in his own case he had always done, all thought of failure. Casting a paternal glance at the youngster beside him, he hummed through closed lips: *In my heart, in my heart* . . . What that girl Olga was singing this morning; can't get it out of my head. By Duparc, I suppose. I only hope she doesn't forget to remind Belin about tapping number seven. *In my heart tra-la-la* . . .

And if I've passed, Jacques mused, shall I be really, really pleased? Not so much as they, anyhow, he added to himself, thinking of Antoine and his father.

A memory flashed across his mind.

"Do you know," he said, "the last time I dined at Maisons-Laffitte—

I'd just got through the orals and my nerves were in rags—when we were at the dinner-table, Father suddenly addressed me, with that special look of his, you know: 'And what shall *we* make of you, if you're not passed?'"

The picture faded and another memory crossed his mind. What a state I'm in this afternoon! he thought and, smiling, took his brother's arm.

"No, Antoine, there was nothing unusual about that, of course. It was next day, the following morning. Look here, I simply must tell you about it. As I had nothing to do, Father told me to attend M. Crespin's funeral in his place. Remember? And it was then that something happened—something quite inexplicable. I got there too soon and, as it was raining, I went into the church. I was thoroughly sick, you know, at having my morning spoiled like that; all the same, as you'll see, that doesn't really explain it. Well, I entered the church and sat down in an empty row, when—what do you think?—a priest came up and took the chair beside me. Mind you, there were any number of empty chairs, yet this priest deliberately planted himself next to me. He was quite young, still at the seminary, no doubt, smooth-shaven and smelling clean, of good mouth-wash—but he had disgusting black gloves and, worst of all, a huge umbrella with a black handle that reeked like a drenched dog. Don't laugh, Antoine; wait and see! I simply couldn't get that priest out of my mind. He had his nose buried in a prayerbook and I could just see his lips moving as he followed the service. So far, so good. But, at the elevation, instead of using the kneeling-desk in front of him—that, of course, I'd have understood—he knelt on the ground, prostrated himself on the bare stone slabs. I, meanwhile, remained standing. When he rose he saw me like that and caught my eye; perhaps my attitude may have struck him as provocative. Anyhow, I caught a look of pious disapproval on his face and he rolled his eyes upwards—it maddened me, his air of smug superiority. To such a pitch that—I can't think what possessed me to do it, it's a mystery to me yet—I drew a visiting-card from my pocket, scrawled a phrase on it, and handed it to him." (As a matter of fact, all this was make-believe; Jacques had merely fancied at the moment that he might act thus. What prompted him to lie?) "He raised his nose from his book, and hesitated; yes, I had positively to force the card into his hand. He glanced at it, stared at me in consternation, and then, slipping his hat under his arm, quickly picked up his umbrella and—ran! You'd have thought he had a lunatic at large beside him. Well, for that matter, I *was* pretty mad at the moment; it was all I could do to keep a hold on myself. I went away without waiting for the service to end."

"But what in the world did you write on the card?"

"Oh, yes, the card. It was so perfectly idiotic I hardly like to tell you. What I wrote was this: *I do NOT believe!* With an exclamation mark. Underlined. On a visiting-card. A monkey-trick, eh? *I do NOT believe!*" His eyes widened, staring ahead. "In the first place, can one ever affirm such a thing—positively?" He stopped speaking for a moment, to watch a smartly dressed young man in mourning who was crossing at the Médicis corner. When he spoke again his voice sounded brittle, as though he were forcing himself to an odious confession. "It's absurd. Do you know what I've been thinking of for the last minute? I was thinking, Antoine, that if you died I'd like to have a close-fitting black suit like the one that fellow there has on. I even, for an instant, longed for your death— impatiently. Now, don't you think I'll end my days in a padded cell?"

Antoine merely shrugged his shoulders.

"It mightn't be such a bad thing, perhaps," Jacques continued. "I might try to analyse myself right up to the final stage of madness. Say, that's an idea! I might write the story of a highly intelligent man who goes mad. Everything he did would be insane, yet he would act only after the most scrupulous deliberation and behave, on his own estimate, with perfect logic. Do you see? I'd install myself in the very centre of his mind, and I'd . . ."

Antoine kept silence. That was another pose he had essayed and it had become second nature with him. But there was such awareness in his silences that his companions' thoughts, far from being paralysed, were stimulated by them.

"Oh, if only I had the time to work, to try out my ideas!" Jacques sighed. "One exam after another! And I'm twenty already; it's ghastly!"

He lifted his hand to his neck, where the collar-edge chafed the tip of a pimple. Another boil in the making, he mused dolefully; the iodine hasn't stopped it.

He turned to his brother again.

"Listen, Antoine! When you were twenty, you weren't childish, were you? I remember you quite well. But I'm different, I never change. Really, I feel exactly the same as I was ten years ago. Don't you agree?"

"No."

All the same, Antoine reflected, he's right about that. Consciousness of continuity; or, better, the continuity of consciousness. Like the old fellow who says: "Personally, I was very keen on leapfrog." Same feet, same hands, same old duffer. I, too, that night I had such a fright at Cotterets, that colic attack. Didn't dare leave my room. Dr. Thibault it was, yes, the doctor himself and no other—our house-physician, a first-rate man, he added complacently, as though he overheard one of his subordinates describing him.

"Am I boring you?" asked Jacques, lifting his hat to mop his forehead.

"Why do you ask?"

"That's what it looks like. You hardly answer a word, and listen to me as if I were a fever case."

"Oh, no, I don't."

If, Antoine mused, the ear-douche doesn't bring the temperature down . . . He was thinking of the boy they had brought to the hospital that morning, the look of agony on his face. *In my heart . . . In my heart tra-la-la.*

"You think I'm feeling nervous," Jacques went on. "I tell you again, you're mistaken. I may as well make a clean breast of it: there are moments when I'd almost rather hear I'd failed the entrance!"

"Why on earth—?"

"To escape."

"To escape? Escape what?"

"Everything. The whole show. You, them, the whole bunch!"

Instead of uttering the comment that rose to his lips—"You're talking nonsense"—Antoine turned to his brother and examined him thoughtfully.

"To burn my boats," Jacques continued, "and go away. Oh, if only I could go right away, all by myself, anywhere on earth! Somewhere far away, where I'd have some peace and settle down to work." Well knowing that he would never go, he yielded to his day-dream with all the greater zest. He paused for a moment, then, with a wry smile, turned to his brother again.

"And there, there perhaps, but nowhere else, I might bring myself to forgive them."

Antoine stopped short.

"Still harping on that, eh?"

"On what?"

"Forgive them, you say. Forgive whom, for what? The reformatory?"

Jacques cast a hostile glance at him, shrugged his shoulders, and walked on. A lot his stay at Crouy had to do with it! But what was the good of explanations? Antoine would never understand.

And, anyhow, what did this idea of "forgiveness" amount to? Jacques himself could not explain it satisfactorily, though he was always finding himself at grips with a dilemma: to forgive or, alternatively, to cultivate his rancour. To take things as they came, get his degree, become a cogwheel in the machine; or—the other way out—to give full rein to the destructive forces that surged within him and launch himself with the full impetus of his resentment against—against what, he could hardly say; against morality, the cut and dried life, the family, society. An ancient grievance, that, and harking back to childhood; a vague awareness that none had known him for what he was, a boy who needed to be properly treated, but, time and again, everyone had failed him. Yes, he was sure of it; had escape been feasible, he would have found that peace of mind which he accused "the others" of frustrating.

"Once I got there, Antoine, I'd work."

"'Got there.' *Where,* exactly?"

"There you are—asking me 'where?'! No, Antoine, you can't understand. You've always felt in harmony with other people. You were always satisfied with the path of life you'd chosen."

Jacques fell to summing up his grown-up brother in terms which usually he held taboo. He saw him as a diligent, contented man. He had energy, all right, but what about his brains? The brains of a zoologist. An intellect so positive and so realistic that it had found its natural field in scientific research. An intellect that based its theory of life on the one concept of activity, and with that was satisfied. And—this struck even deeper—an intellect which stripped things of their secret virtue, of all, in a word, that gave significance and beauty to the universe.

"I'm not a bit like you," he burst out passionately and, swerving a little from his brother's side, walked silently aloof along the kerb.

I'm stifled here, he mused; everything they make me do is loathsome, sickening. The tutors, my fellow-students—all alike! And the things they rave about, their favourite books! Their "great modern authors"! Oh, if only someone in the world could guess what I am, my real self—and what I'm out to do. No, no one has a notion of it, not even Daniel.

His raging mood had passed. He did not listen to Antoine's reply. To forget all that has been written up to now! he adjured himself. To get out of the rut and, looking inside oneself, say *everything!* No one's ever had the nerve to say everything, as yet. But someone might; *I* might. . . .

It was hard going up the Rue Soufflot incline in such a temperature, and they slackened speed. Antoine talked on; Jacques was silent. Noticing the contrast, Jacques smiled to himself. After all, he thought, I can never argue with Antoine; either I stand up to him and lose my temper, or else I dig myself in before the arguments he methodically marches up, and hold my tongue. Now, for instance. It's a

sort of low cunning, really; I know that Antoine takes my silence
for assent. But it's not so. Far otherwise. I stick to my guns, my
ideas. I don't care if other people find them muddled; I'm sure,
myself, of their soundness and I've only got to develop the knack
of proving this to others—a matter of getting down to it one day,
that's all. Arguments—they're easily found. But Antoine rattles on
and on, never stops to wonder if there's any sense in my ideas. All
the same, how lonely I feel! . . . And once again the desire to go
away flamed up in him. Wonderful it would be to give up everything, all at once. *Rooms left behind! Wonders of setting forth!* He
smiled again and, throwing a teasing glance at his brother, began
to declaim:

"'Families, I hate you! Closed circles round the hearth! Fast shut
doors. . . .'"*

"Who's that by?"

"'Nathanael, look at everything as you pass by and stop nowhere. . . .'"

"By whom?"

"Oh," Jacques exclaimed—the smile had left his lips and he was
walking faster—"that comes from a book that's blamed for everything, a book in which Daniel has found every sort of excuse—far
worse, a panegyric!—for his—his ruthlessness. He's got it off by
heart, while I. . . . No"—his voice trembled—"no, I can't say I loathe
it, but—don't you see, Antoine?—it's a book that burns your fingers
while you read, and somehow I can never feel at ease with it, so
dangerous do I think it." With grudging appreciation he repeated:
"'Rooms left behind! Wonders of setting forth!'" When, after a
moment's silence, he spoke again, his voice was changed, had suddenly grown harsh, staccato. "I may talk about it—going away. But
it's too late. I shall never be able to get *really* away."

"You talk about 'going away,'" Antoine replied, "as if it meant
leaving home for good. And that, obviously, is easier said than done.

* *For this and for the other passages from Gide's* Les Nourritures Terrestres
*cited in this chapter, I have used the authorized translation by Mrs. Dorothy
Bussy. Translator.*

But why not travel a bit? If you've passed the entrance exam, Father will be quite agreeable to your going away during the summer."

Jacques shook his head.

"Too late."

What did he mean by that?

"Surely you don't propose to spend the two months' holidays at Maisons-Laffitte, with only Father and Mademoiselle?"

"I do."

He made an evasive gesture and, now they had crossed the Place du Panthéon and entered the Rue d'Ulm, he pointed to the groups collecting outside the Ecole Normale. His face darkened.

"What a queer character he has!" Antoine reflected. He had often made the same observation—indulgently and with unconscious pride. Much as he hated the unforeseen, and despite Jacques's habit of constantly springing surprises on him, he was for ever trying to make his brother out. Round and about the incoherent phrases Jacques let fall, Antoine's nimble wits were busy with intellectual gymnastics which not only amused him but enabled him (so he imagined) to read the riddle of the boy's personality. Unfortunately, no sooner did Antoine see himself adding the crowning touch to his diagnosis of the boy's mind, than Jacques would utter some new remark that upset all his inferences. A fresh start had to be made, leading him more often than not towards entirely different conclusions. The result was that, for Antoine, every conversation with his brother involved a sequence of improvised and incompatible deductions, the last of which he always took to be decisive.

The grim façade of the Ecole Normale was looming above them, and Antoine, turning to Jacques, cast a long, meditative look at him. Reading between the lines, he reassured himself: you can see the youngster appreciates family life far better than he imagines.

The gate was open now, and the quadrangle crowded. At the vestibule entrance Daniel de Fontanin was talking to a blond young man.

"If it's Daniel who spots us first," Jacques murmured to himself, "that means I've passed." But Fontanin and Battaincourt turned simultaneously when Antoine hailed them.

"Not too nervous?" Daniel inquired.

"Not in the least."

(If, thought Jacques, he mentions Jenny's name, it means I've passed.)

"This quarter of an hour's suspense before the results are posted," Antoine observed, "is simply damnable."

"I wonder now!" Daniel demurred. He took a childish delight in contradicting Antoine, whom he addressed as "doctor" and whose precocious gravity amused him. "There's always a spice of pleasure in suspense."

Antoine shrugged his shoulders and turned towards his brother.

"Hear what he says? . . . Personally," he continued, "I've been through this sort of suspense fourteen or fifteen times, but I've never managed to get used to it. What's more, I've noticed that the fellows who put on an air of stoicism on such occasions are nearly always the second-raters, weaklings."

"The joys of hope deferred are not for everyone," Daniel oracled. When he addressed the doctor there was a glint of mockery in his eyes that softened to tenderness as they turned to Jacques.

Antoine insisted.

"I'm speaking in earnest. A strong man finds uncertainty intolerable. True courage isn't just a matter of facing events with coolness; it's going out to meet them half-way, so as to take their bearings at the earliest moment, and act accordingly. Isn't that so, Jacques?"

"No, I'm more inclined to agree with Daniel," Jacques replied, though he had not been listening. And, as Daniel went on talking to Antoine, he slipped in a leading question, aware that he was cheating destiny.

"Are your mother and sister still at Maisons-Laffitte?"

Daniel did not hear, and, in the act of dinning the thought, "I failed," into his head, Jacques realized how solid was his faith in his success. Father'll be delighted, he thought, and, smiling at the prospect, bestowed the smile on Battaincourt.

"Very decent of you to come today, Simon."

Battaincourt glanced towards him affectionately; he made no secret
of his fervent cult of Daniel's friend, an adoration which sometimes
irritated Jacques, since he could not respond to it with a friendship
of equal warmth. . . .

The hubbub in the quadrangle ceased abruptly. A roll of white
paper had flashed into view at one of the windows. Jacques had a
vague impression of being swept off his feet, borne by a wave towards
the fateful scroll.

A buzzing in his ears; then Antoine's voice:

"Passed! Third on the list!"

Warm, vibrant with life, the voice rang for a moment in his ears,
but he did not grasp the meaning of the words till, looking timidly
round, he saw the jubilation on his brother's face. Then, lifting a
clammy hand, he fumbled with his hat; sweat was pouring down his
forehead. Daniel and Battaincourt were edging round the crowd towards him. Daniel's eyes were on him and, scanning his friend as
he approached, Jacques noticed how his raised upper lip bared his
teeth, though no other feature showed the least trace of a smile.

A murmur grew, filling the place with sound; and life went on
its way again. Jacques drew a deep breath, and the blood once more
flowed freely through his limbs. He had a sudden vision of dangers
ahead, a pitfall. "Trapped!" he murmured. Then other thoughts welled
up. He seemed to live again some seconds of his Greek oral, the crucial
moment when he made that slip; the tablecloth rose green before
his eyes, with the examiner's thumb splayed flat on the *Choephoroi*,
his bulging nail flaked like a shred of horn.

"Who is first?"

He did not hear the name that Battaincourt announced. I'd have
been first, he thought, if I'd tumbled to *asylum, shrine. Wardens
of the domestic shrine*. Then, again and again, he struggled to reconstruct the train of thoughts which had misled him to that appalling blunder.

"Wake up, doctor! Try to look pleased!"

Daniel clapped Antoine on the shoulder and Antoine deigned to smile. For that was Antoine's way; pleasure for him almost always involved a feeling of constraint, for the gravity of his demeanour precluded any show of gaiety. It was different with Daniel: his gaiety was untrammelled. He seemed to find an almost sensual pleasure in poring on the faces of his friends, his neighbours, and, above all, the women present, mothers or sisters, whose artless affection frankly betrayed itself in every accent, every gesture.

Glancing at his watch, Antoine turned to his brother.

"Well? Anything more to do here?"

Jacques gave a start.

"What? Oh, no, nothing at all!" He looked dejected; he had just realized that inadvertently—at the moment when the results were posted, most likely—he had made the pimple on his lip (which for a week past had spoilt his appearance) start bleeding again.

"Then let's be off," Antoine proposed. "I've a patient to see before dinner."

As they left the quadrangle, they saw Favery hurrying up to greet them. He was jubilant.

"There you are! I told you I'd heard your French composition was a fine piece of work."

Favery had left the Ecole Normale a year previously and, eschewing provincial posts, had got himself nominated to a temporary vacancy at the Lycée Saint-Louis. He did coaching in his off-hours by day so that by night he might enjoy the life of Paris. Teaching did not appeal to him; his preferences went to journalism, with a secret hankering after politics.

It came to Jacques's mind that Favery was fairly intimate with the examiner in Greek, and again a picture of the green tablecloth and the examiner's finger flashed across his mind; he felt his cheeks reddening with shame. That he'd nevertheless passed had not yet dawned on him; he experienced no sense of relief, rather a mood of listlessness, with occasional bursts of rage whenever he recalled his blunder or the pimple on his lip.

Daniel and Battaincourt linked their arms in his and swung him along, to a dancing lilt, towards the Pantheon. Antoine and Favery followed behind.

"My alarm goes off at six-thirty," Favery explained, "standing in a saucer poised precariously upon a tumbler." His voice was loud, his laugh complacent. "I curse a bit, open an eye, switch on the light; then I move on the hand to seven o'clock and go to sleep again, clasping the infernal machine against my chest. Presently the house, the whole neighbourhood, is rocked by an earthquake; I damn its eyes, but disobey. I give myself till five past, then ten, then a quarter past, and, when it's two minutes over the quarter, I allow myself till twenty past—to make it a round figure. At long last I scramble out of bed. All my things are spread out ready—like a fireman's kit—on three chairs. At seven-twenty-eight I'm in the street; naturally I've had no time for breakfast or a wash. Just four minutes remain to catch my subway. At eight o'clock I'm standing at my desk and the cramming process begins. You know when I get away. I have to find time for a bath, for dressing, and looking up friends. How the devil am I to do any work?"

Antoine listened with half an ear, while his eyes roved in quest of a taxi. He turned to his brother.

"Dining with me, Jacques?"

"Jacques is having dinner with us," Daniel protested.

"No, no!" Jacques exclaimed. "I'm dining with Antoine tonight." And to himself he added with impatience: "Won't they ever leave me in peace, confound it! For one thing, I've got to put some more iodine on my boil."

Favery put in a suggestion:

"Let's all have dinner together."

"Where?"

"Any old place. How about Packmell's?"

Jacques demurred:

"No. Not tonight. I'm tired."

"Tiresome old thing!" murmured Daniel, slipping his arm in Jacques's. "Doctor, you'll join us at Packmell's, won't you?"

Antoine had secured a taxi. He turned towards them, obviously in two minds.

"What sort of a place is Packmell's?"

Favery drew a bow at a venture.

"Not by any means what *you* think. . . ."

Antoine looked at Daniel questioningly.

"Packmell's?" Daniel said. "Hard to classify, isn't it, Batt, old boy? Quite out of the ordinary run of cabarets. More like a well-conducted boarding-house. Certainly the bar functions from five to eight, but at eight-thirty the bar-flies flit with one accord, leaving the field to the 'regulars.' The tables are run together and we all dine off a vast and highly decorous tablecloth, with Mother Packmell in the seat of honour. A good band; pretty girls. What more can you want? So that's that. You will meet us at Packmell's?"

Antoine rarely went out at night; he led laborious days and reserved his evenings for examination work. Today, however, he did not feel in the mood for hæmatology. Tomorrow would be Sunday; Monday, the daily round began again. Occasionally he took a Saturday evening off and plotted out a night's amusement. Packmell's appealed to him. Pretty girls . . .

"Have it your own way!" His voice was studiously indifferent. "Where is it, by the way?"

"Rue Monsigny. We'll look out for you up to half-past eight."

"I'll be there long before that," said Antoine, slamming the taxi door.

Jacques made no protest; his brother's assent had changed his outlook and, moreover, he always took a secret pleasure in giving in to Daniel's caprices.

"Shall we walk there?" Battaincourt asked.

"Personally, I'm taking the subway," said Favery, stroking his chin. "I'll change in a jiffy and meet you there."

Paris was stifling in a sultry heat presaging storm, the heat-wave which so often ends July, when at each nightfall the air grows drab and dense—with dust or mist, indistinguishably.

They had a good half-hour's walk before them. Battaincourt came up to Jacques's side.

"So now you've started on the path of glory!" There was no irony in his voice.

Jacques made a petulant gesture; Daniel smiled. Though Battaincourt was five years older than himself, Daniel regarded him as a mere child, and the very quality which so irritated Jacques—his incorrigible naïveté—endeared him to Daniel. He recalled the days when they used to ask Battaincourt to recite, and the latter, planted on the hearthrug, would declaim:

"O sleek-haired Corsican, how fair thy France
Under the sun of Messidor . . . !"

The would-be Napoleonic gesture that accompanied this exordium always set them loudly laughing, but their hilarity never shook Battaincourt's simple faith.

In those days Simon de Battaincourt, a new-comer to Paris from the city in Northern France where his father, a Colonel, lived, used to wear a black, close-fitting coat, which he had had specially made to order, as being most seemly for a student at the Paris School of Divinity. The budding clergyman was at that period a frequent visitor at Mme. de Fontanin's house; she made a point of encouraging his visits, as Colonel de Battaincourt's wife had been one of her childhood friends.

"I can't stand this Latin Quarter of yours!" exclaimed the ex-divinity student, who now lived near the Etoile, wore light suits, and had quarrelled with his people over the fantastic marriage on which his heart was set. He was now employed, at a salary of four hundred francs a month, cataloguing prints in the Ludwigson Art Gallery, where Daniel had found him a post.

Raising his eyes, Jacques looked about him. His gaze fell on an ancient flower-vender squatting behind her basket of roses; he had passed her earlier in the day, when he was with Antoine, but then he had observed her with brooding eyes, aloof from all distractions of things seen. Recalling their walk together up the Rue Soufflot, he suddenly felt that he missed something, as if some familiar thing

were lacking, like a ring that he had always worn. The feeling of
unrest which had haunted him for the past three weeks, and, less
than an hour since, weighed on his every step, had vanished, leaving
behind a void that was almost pain. For the first time since the
results were out, he took the measure of his success; but it left him
dazed and broken, as though he had fallen from a height.

"Anyhow, you had some sea-bathing, I suppose," Battaincourt
was saying to Daniel.

Jacques turned to his friend.

"Yes, by Jove!" he exclaimed, and his eyes grew tender. "To
think that you came back all on my account! Had a good time
down there?"

"Far better than I'd any reason to expect," Daniel replied.

Jacques smiled ruefully.

"As usual!"

The look that passed between them was the aftermath of a long-
standing controversy.

Jacques's affection for Daniel had an astringent quality, far different from the easy-going friendship Daniel accorded him. "You're far
more exacting where I'm concerned," Daniel once remarked, "than
for yourself. You've never fallen in with the life I lead." "No," Jacques
had answered, "I've nothing against your way of living; what I
cannot bear is the attitude you have adopted towards life." And therein
lay the source of many a quarrel in the past.

After Daniel had taken his degree, he had refused to follow any
beaten track. His father was away and did not trouble about him.
His mother left him free to choose his path; she respected strength
of will in any form and was fortified by her mystical faith that all
was for the best where her children—and, in general, the family—
were concerned. Above all she wished her son to feel free and
under no obligation of earning money to better the fortunes of his
family. Nevertheless, Daniel could not ignore this duty. His inability
to help his mother had preyed upon his mind for two consecutive
years and he had anxiously cast about for ways and means of reconciling duty to his kin with other and more urgent needs that shaped

his conduct. Scruples whose complexity even Jacques was far from appreciating. The truth was that—judging by the haphazard way in which Daniel had set about learning his art, unaided, taking instinct (mere caprice, it often seemed) as his only guide, painting so little, drawing little more, sometimes shutting himself up all day with a model, only to cover half the pages of an album with outline sketches, and then not touching a pencil again for weeks on end—the truth was that few indeed would have suspected the sublime faith he felt in his talent, and in his future. A tacit self-esteem untainted by conceit: he waited for the day when, in the long process of unalterable law, all that was best in him would find a medium of expression; for he was certain of his destiny—that of a first-rate painter. When and by what path would he win to that high estate? He had no notion and, judging by his conduct, did not greatly care. "We must let life take charge," he proclaimed, and followed his precept to the letter. Not without twinges of remorse, however; but his timorous reversions to his mother's moral code had been short-lived and never restrained him effectively from following his bent. "Even when in the past two years my conscience pricked me most acutely," he once wrote to Jacques (he was eighteen at the time), "I can swear I never reached the point of being genuinely ashamed of myself. What is more, when in those hours of doubt I blamed myself for yielding to temptation, I actually felt far less angry with myself than later on, when life had taken charge again, and I recalled my puerile gestures of self-restraint and abnegation."

Soon after this letter was written, Daniel happened to share a compartment in a suburban train with another passenger (known to them thereafter as "the man in the train") who can assuredly have had no inkling of the repercussions that brief encounter was to have upon the early life of two young people.

Daniel was returning from the Versailles Park, where he had lounged away a fine October afternoon under the shadows of the trees. He jumped aboard a car just as the train was leaving. As chance would have it, the face of the elderly man sitting opposite him was not entirely unfamiliar; their paths had crossed that afternoon in the Trianon shrubberies and Daniel had observed him with some interest. He welcomed the chance of examining the man at his leisure. A near view of the traveller gave the impression of a much younger man: though his hair was white, he could be little more than fifty. A short white beard set off effectively the oval of a face whose symmetry enhanced its gentle charm. His complexion, hands, and bearing, the cut of the summer suit he wore, the exotic shade of his tie, and, above all, the clear blue gaze, vibrant with life and light, that he cast on all about him—all gave the impression of a quite young man. The book whose leaves he was turning with a practised hand was bound in flimsy leather like a guide-book, and the cover bore no title. Between Suresnes and Saint-Cloud he rose and, going into the corridor, leaned forth to contemplate the panorama of Paris, all flecked with gold under the fires of sunset. Then, drawing back, he leaned against the inner window, behind which Daniel sat. The hands that held the cryptic book were level now with Daniel's eyes, only the pane of glass intervened; plastic hands, emotional yet listless—a thinker's hands. The fingers moved, half opening the book, and on a page flattened against the glass Daniel could read a few phrases:

> Nathanael, I will teach you fervour . . .
> A throbbing, lawless life. . . .
> A harrowing existence, Nathanael, rather than tranquillity.

The book slipped aside, but not before Daniel had caught a glimpse of the title heading the page: *Les Nourritures Terrestres.*

What could this be: *Fruits of the Earth?* He visited a series of booksellers that evening, only to find that they knew nothing of the book. Would "the man in the train" keep his secret to himself? *A harrowing existence,* Daniel repeated to himself, *rather than tranquillity.* Next morning he hastened to examine all the catalogues available in the arcades of the Odéon and, a few hours later, shut himself up in his room with his new acquisition.

The whole afternoon went to its perusal and he read it at one sitting. He left the house at nightfall. Never had his mind been in such ferment, uplifted by such splendid visions. He walked on and

on, taking long strides—a conqueror's progress. Night came on. He
had been following the bank of the Seine and was very far from
home. He dined off a roll and returned; the book lay on his table,
awaiting him. Should he, or should he not . . . ? Daniel dared not
open it again. Finally he went to bed, but not to sleep. At last he
capitulated and, wrapping a dressing-gown around him, slowly read
the book once more, from beginning to end. He well knew that
this was a momentous hour for him, that at the deepest levels of his
consciousness a slow, mysterious process of gestation was at work.
When with the dawn he turned, for the second time, the final page,
he found that now he looked on life with new eyes.

"I have boldly laid my hands everywhere, and believed I had a
right to every object of my desire. . . .

"Desires are profitable, and profitable the surfeiting of desires—for
so they are increased."

He realized how in a flash the burden that his upbringing had
laid on him—the obsession of moral standards—had been lifted; the
word "sin" had changed its meaning.

"We must act without considering whether the action is right or
wrong; love, without troubling whether what we love is good or evil."

Feelings to which hitherto he had yielded grudgingly, if at all,
suddenly broke free and beckoned him on; in the brief period of a
night the scale of moral values which from his earliest days had
seemed immutable went up in flames. Next day he felt a man bap-
tized anew. As, stage by stage, he repudiated everything he had
hitherto held true beyond all question, a miracle of peace allayed the
forces that, until now, had grappled with his soul.

Daniel spoke of his great discovery to none but Jacques, and to
Jacques only after a long while. It was one of the bosom secrets
of the friends; they thought of it as all but a religious mystery and
alluded to it only in veiled terms. Nevertheless, for all Daniel's zealotry,
Jacques obstinately refused to be inoculated with his friend's cult.
And, in refusing to quench his thirst at this too heady spring, he
saw himself making a stand against his instincts and gaining thus
in strength and personal integrity. But he well knew the book gave

Daniel the *regime,* the·"fruits of the earth," that suited him, and Jacques's resistance was accompanied by feelings of envy and despair.

"So you look on Ludwigson as one of nature's freaks, eh?" Battaincourt was saying.

"Ludwigson, my dear Batt—" Daniel began explaining.

Jacques shrugged his shoulders and fell back behind his friends. The Ludwigson of whom they spoke—Daniel had just come back from a short stay at his place—had earned the reputation in the various centres where he had established himself of being one of the "smoothest" art-dealers in Europe, and had been for some time past a bone of contention between Jacques and his friend. Jacques could never stomach the notion that Daniel should, directly or indirectly—even to earn his living—take part in the schemes promoted by this dealer. But no one, not even Jacques, could ever boast of having dissuaded Daniel from any venture on which his heart was set. In the case of Ludwigson, the man's intelligence and tireless activity (carried to a pitch that made insomnia a habit with him), the contempt for luxury and, up to a point, of money, too, evinced by this merchant-prince who found his life's interest in adventuring and winning, the efficiency of this big business-man whose career evoked the picture of a fiery brand, shaken by the wind, smoky yet dazzling, too—everything about the man seemed wildly interesting to Daniel. In fact it was curiosity more than necessity that led him to agree to work for this modern buccaneer.

Jacques remembered the day when Daniel first confronted Ludwigson; two races, two cultures, met face to face. He had chanced to drop in at the studio which Daniel was sharing with some friends as impecunious as himself. Ludwigson entered without knocking, and countered Daniel's indignant outburst with a smile; then brusquely, without making himself known or taking a chair, he drew a wallet from his pocket, with the gesture of a high-comedy actor tossing his purse to an underling, and offered "the gentleman present whose name is Fontanin" a salary of six hundred francs a month as from that day, for the next three years, provided that he, Ludwigson, proprietor of the Ludwigson Art Gallery and manager of Messrs. Ludwigson & Co., Art-Dealers, should have sole rights in all the works of art produced by M. Fontanin during this period, the said works to be signed in the artist's hand and dated. Daniel, least industrious of artists, who had never exhibited or sold a single sketch, had never understood how Ludwigson had come to form so flattering an opinion of his talents as to justify the offer. In any case he was resolved to be sole arbiter of his output and well aware that, had he closed with the offer, he would have taken Ludwigson's money only on furnishing month by month a sufficiency of pictures, ample to cover the salary proposed. But it was one of his pet theories that work should be performed joyfully, without constraint. So, to the stupefaction of his fellow-artists, he had shown Ludwigson the door with icy politeness, and, giving him no time to collect his wits, had made the dealer beat a retreat onto the landing as quickly as he had come.

But that was not the end of it. Ludwigson returned to the attack, but with more tactful strategy, and some months later a business connexion had been established between the dealer and Daniel— somewhat to the latter's amusement. Ludwigson was the editor of a sumptuous art magazine appearing in three languages; he asked Daniel to select the French articles for publication. The young man's character had pleased him from the start and he was impressed by the excellence of Daniel's taste. The work was far from boring and Daniel devoted his spare time to it. Very soon he had complete charge of the French section of the magazine. Ludwigson, always lavish in his personal expenditures, made a point of engaging few but carefully selected associates, giving them a free hand, and paying for their work on a generous scale. Daniel, though he had laid no claim to it, was soon being paid the same salary as the English and German collaborators. As he had to earn his living, he preferred an avocation wholly independent of his artistic career. Moreover, some of his drawings (Ludwigson arranged a private show for him) had already made good with certain connoisseurs. The advantages he derived from his association with the picture-dealer enabled him not only to contribute to the welfare of his mother and sister, but to lead the easy life he liked, without being tied down to any rigid task or encroaching on the hours of freedom essential to his true calling.

Jacques caught up his friends at the Boulevard Saint-Germain crossing.

". . . the priceless experience," Daniel was saying, "of being introduced to the dowager Mme. Ludwigson."

"Why, I never dreamt that Ludwigson of yours had ever had a mother!" Jacques observed, by way of joining in the conversation.

"Nor did I," Daniel concurred. "And what a mother! Try and imagine—no, only a sketch would do her justice. I've done several, but not from life, worse luck! Imagine a mummy tricked out by some clown to do a circus turn. An old Egyptian Jew, at least a hundred years old, bloated with gout and natural fat, reeking of fried onions, who wears mittens, has pet names for her footmen, calls her son *bambino,* lives on bread soused in red wine, and passes the unwary visitor a tobacco-jar——"

"So the old lady fancies a pipe?" Battaincourt broke in.

"No, it contains—snuff! The old creature's always dribbling black powder on the mass of diamonds with which Ludwigson's thought fit—why, God alone knows—to plaster her dewlaps." A quaint analogy struck him and he paused to find words for it. "Like the lanterns they post round a house that's being pulled down."

Jacques grinned; he was always taken by Daniel's flow of spirits.

"And what did he want to get out of you when he revealed the skeleton in his cupboard?"

"You've guessed it! He has a new scheme up his sleeve. Wonderful chap he is!"

"Wonderful, yes; because he's so damned rich. If he were poor he'd be no better than a——"

Daniel cut him short.

"Leave it at that, if you don't mind. I like him. And he's hit on a sound idea: a series of monographs, *Great Masters in Their Paintings.* That's his long suit: lavishly illustrated handbooks at astounding prices."

Jacques listened no longer; he felt peevish, out of spirits. Over-tired, perhaps, after the day's emotions. Or was it vexation at having

been let in for this evening's jaunt, when he so longed for solitude?
Or just the chafing of the collar on his neck?

Battaincourt slipped between the two friends. He was waiting for
a chance of asking them to act as witnesses at his wedding. For
months past, by night and by day, that event had loomed large in
his thoughts and under the fever of his desire his bloodless features
were visibly wasting away. Now, at last, he had not long to wait. The
period set by law to the parental veto had just run out and, that very
morning, the date of his wedding had been fixed. In two weeks'
time . . . The thought of it brought the blood to his cheeks; he
turned away to hide his blush, took off his hat, and mopped his
forehead.

"Don't move!" cried Daniel. "It's fantastic how, in profile, you're
the living image of a deer—*d*, double *e*, *r*, of course!" And indeed
Battaincourt had a long nose which almost joined his lip, arched
nostrils, round eyes, and, just then, a wisp of towy hair, matted
with sweat, that curled up into a little tapering horn above his
forehead.

Battaincourt replaced his hat mournfully and let his eyes roam
across the Place du Carrousel and Trajan's Arch towards the Tuileries
Gardens, where the dust glowed red.

Poor little belling deer, Daniel mused. Who'd have believed him
capable of such a passion? There he goes, a traitor to all his principles,
quarrelling with his people, and all for that woman! A widow, fourteen years his senior, a shop-soiled widow—attractive, I grant, but
shop-soiled. He smiled inwardly, remembering the afternoon last
autumn when Simon had badgered him into meeting the fascinating
widow—and the sequel of their meeting, a week later. . . . Well,
anyhow, he could honestly say he had done his utmost to restrain
Battaincourt from that act of folly. But he was at grips with blind
instinct and, since he deferred to passion wherever he encountered it,
he had confined himself to steering clear of the lady in question and
watching the developments of his friend's matrimonial venture from
a safe distance.

"For a conquering hero you look pretty glum," observed Battaincourt, who, aggrieved by Daniel's mockery, hoped for amends from Jacques.

"Don't you realize that he wanted to fail?" Daniel suggested. He was surprised by the pensive look in Jacques's eyes and, approaching him, laid his hand on his shoulder, murmuring with a smile: ". . . 'for each thing has a special and a different value.'"

The words sufficed to bring back the whole passage—Daniel used often to repeat it—to Jacques's mind:

"Woe betide you if you say your happiness is dead because you had not dreamt it would take that shape! . . . Your dream of tomorrow is a delight—but tomorrow has a delight of its own—and nothing, fortunately, is like the dream we have dreamt of it, for each thing has a special and a different value."

Jacques smiled.

"Give me a cigarette."

He tried to shake off his lethargy, for Daniel's sake. *Your dream of tomorrow is a delight.* . . . And indeed he seemed to feel delight, as yet evasive, hovering round him. Tomorrow? Ah, to awake and see, across his open window, the sun rise level with the tree-tops! To-morrow: Maisons-Laffitte, and the cool shadows of the woods!

II

NOTHING in the sleepy street near the Paris Opera, nothing except a file of cars drawn up along the kerb called the attention of passers-by to an anonymous cabaret with close-drawn blinds. A page swung round the revolving-doors to let them through and Daniel made way for Jacques and Battaincourt to pass, as though he were receiving them at his own house.

Some discreet exclamations greeted Daniel's arrival. Few of the patrons of the place knew his real name; to everyone he was the "Prophet." Just now the cabaret was rather empty. Behind the bar, in the alcove whence a slender spiral staircase, painted white and edged with gold to match the panelling of the room, led up to Mme. Packmell's quarters on the next floor, a piano, violin, and 'cello were playing the hits of the season. The tables had been pushed back against the grey plush settles that flanked the walls and a few couples were dancing a boston on the purple carpet under the last gleams of the sunset filtering through the lace curtains. Close under the ceiling fan-blades droned monotonously, fluttering the pendants of the chandeliers, green foliage of palms, and lifting trailing clouds of muslin about the dancing couples.

Jacques, always swept off his feet by a first glimpse of new surroundings, meekly followed Daniel to a table from which the two rooms could be observed in vista. A group of girls in the further room had pounced on Battaincourt and he had already begun to dance.

"You always need screwing up to the point," Daniel said. "Now that you are here, I'm sure you'll like it. Now, own up, isn't it a homy, cheery little dive?"

"Order a cocktail for me," Jacques broke in on his encomium. "You know the sort—with milk, red-currant juice, and lemon-peel in it."

Young women in white dresses served the customers; they were known as the "nurses."

"Shall I give you a little 'Who's Who' of some of these people?" Daniel asked, changing his seat and coming to sit by Jacques. "That fair woman over there, in blue, to begin with—she's the boss. 'Mother Packmell,' we call her, though, as you see, she's still quite a fetching wench! She's here, there, and everywhere all night long, with the same old smile on her face, amongst her bright young things—rather like a fashionable dressmaker showing off her mannequins. See that dark chap over there who's saying 'How do you do?' to her? Now he's talking to a pale little kid, the girl who was dancing with Battaincourt just now—no, nearer us; that's Paule, the fair young girl who looks like an angel—a slightly, ever so slightly tarnished angel. Look, what's that queer-looking dope she's swilling now? Might be green curaçao. The chap who's standing, talking to her, is Nivolsky, the painter, quite a fine fellow in his way; a knave and a liar, but for all that chivalrous as a knight of old! Whenever he turns up late for an appointment he says he's just been fighting a duel, and, for the moment, genuinely believes it. He borrows money right and left and is always broke, but he has talent; he pays his bills with pictures. This is his system, in a nutshell: he spends the summer in the country and paints a strip of road on a canvas fifty yards long—complete with trees, farm-carts, cyclists, a sunset and so on; then, in the winter he retails his road in driblets proportioned to the money owed and his creditor's standing. He says he's Russian and owner of heaven knows how many 'souls.' So, you see, during the Russo-Japanese war, every-one was pulling his leg for staying in Montmartre and indulging in tap-room patriotism. Know what he did? He cleared out, vanished for a year, and returned only after the fall of Port Arthur, bringing with him a sheaf of war-photos; his pockets bulged with them. 'Just observe, old man,' he'd say, 'this battery in action. Do you see that big rock at the back? And just behind the rock the business end of a rifle? Well, old man, I was behind that rifle.' The trouble was that he brought back several crates of sketches, too, and during the next two years he always paid his debts with landscapes of Sicily. Hallo! He's caught on that I'm talking about him; he's flattered. Watch, and you'll see him go through his paces!"

Jacques, resting his elbow on the table, kept silence. In such moods his face seemed emptied of intelligence; with his dull eyes and slightly parted lips he had the look of an animal, brooding and lethargic. Listening to his friend's chatter, he watched Nivolsky and the girl Paule. She had a vanity-box in her hand and, pouting her lips, dabbed them with a lipstick, to which her fingers gave a brisk little twirl, as though she meant to bore a hole with it. As the painter watched her, he kept swinging her bag round and round his finger. It was obvious that theirs was merely a cabaret acquaintanceship; neverthe-less, she touched his hands and knee, and set his tie straight. Once, when he leaned towards her confidentially, she pressed her little white hand against his face and teasingly pushed him away. Jacques's senses tingled.

Not far from her a dark woman was sitting by herself, huddled up at the far end of the settle, her black satin cloak drawn tightly round her as though she feared the cold; her ardent gaze was riveted on Paule, who showed no sign of being aware of it.

Jacques's brooding eyes rested on all these folk; was he studying them, or building fancies round them? He had only to watch any one of them for a while to surmise in him or her a maelstrom of emotions. Moreover, he did not seek to analyse the feelings he read into each and could not have put his intuitions into words; he was far too taken by the spectacle before his eyes to double his personality and register his impressions. But, anyhow, this sense of communion, real or illusive, with other beings gave him unbounded pleasure.

"Who is that tall woman talking to the barman?" he asked.

"In peacock-blue, with a necklace down to her knees?"

"Yes. What a cruel face!"

"That's Marie-Josèphe; a name that would become an empress. Fine-looking woman, eh? There's a funny history to those pearls of hers. Are you listening?" With a smile Daniel turned to his friend. "She was kept by Reyvil, the perfume-king's son. Now, Reyvil had a lawful, if unfaithful, spouse at home, who was Josse the banker's mistress. . . . Look here, are you listening?"

"Yes, yes—with all my ears."

"Well, you look half asleep. Josse is immensely rich and one day he was moved to make a present of some pearls to his mistress, Mme. Reyvil. The problem was how to do so without angering her husband. But Josse is as cute as you make 'em! He faked up a lottery in aid of the White Slaves' Rescue League, persuaded M. Reyvil, the husband, to take ten tickets at a franc each, and saw to it that Reyvil won the necklace intended for Mme. Reyvil. But then the trouble began. Reyvil wrote to Josse to thank him, but added a postscript asking him not to breathe a word about the lottery to Mme. Reyvil as he had just given the pearls to his mistress, Marie-Josèphe. But there's more to come—the end of the story goes one better. Josse saw red; his one idea was to have the necklace back or, failing that, to have the lady who was wearing it. And, three months later, he'd dropped Mme.

Reyvil and cut out his dear friend Reyvil with Marie-Josèphe—exchanged the pearlless wife for the pearl-decked mistress. So now the worthy Reyvil, who has completely forgotten that the necklace only cost him ten paltry francs, declaims in season and out of season against the unspeakableness of the demi-rep! Hallo, Werff!" He paused to shake hands with a handsome youth who had just come in, greeted from the far end of the room with cries of "Apricot! Hi, Apricot!"

"You know each other, don't you?" Daniel asked Jacques, who held out his hand somewhat ungraciously to the new-comer. "Good morrow, fair lady!" Daniel continued, as Paule, the Russian painter's anæmic companion, walked past; and stooped to kiss her hand. "May I introduce my friend Thibault?" he added. Jacques rose. The girl's neurotic eyes just glanced at Jacques's and lingered more intently on Daniel's face; she seemed about to address him, then changed her mind and walked away.

"Do you come here often?" Jacques inquired.

"No. Well . . . yes; several times a week. A habit. And yet, as a rule, I get tired of seeing the same people, the same place, pretty quickly. I like to feel that life is moving on. . . ."

Suddenly Jacques remembered: "I've passed!" and drew a deep breath. An idea flashed through his mind.

"Do you know when the Maisons-Laffitte telegraph-office shuts down?"

"It's closed by now. But, if you send a wire at once, your father will get it first thing in the morning."

Jacques beckoned to a page.

"Telegraph-blank, please."

He scribbled the telegram in such feverish haste, and this belated eagerness to announce his success was so like Jacques, that Daniel smiled and leaned over his friend's shoulder; but only to draw back hastily, surprised and even annoyed by his unwitting tactlessness. He had read, not M. Thibault's address, but: "Mme. de Fontanin, Chemin de la Forêt, Maisons-Laffitte."

A buzz of curiosity had greeted the appearance of an elderly dame, a familiar figure at the cabaret, who had just come in accompanied by a pretty, dark girl whose observant air, though in no wise timid, gave the impression that this was her first visit to the place.

"Hallo, something new!" Daniel murmured under his breath.

Werff, who happened to be passing, smiled.

"Don't you know? Ma Juju's launching a 'deb.'"

"Damned pretty little thing, anyhow," commented Daniel after taking a good look at her.

Jacques turned. Yes, she was really charming, with her bright eyes, natural complexion, and general air of not "belonging" here. Her gauzy dress was of the palest pink; she wore no ornaments, no jewels. Beside her even the youngest women present looked tawdry.

Daniel had returned to his seat beside Jacques.

"You should get a close-up view of Ma Juju," he suggested. "I know her well; she's quite a character. Nowadays she enjoys a social standing of sorts; she has quite a nice flat and an at-home day, indulges in evening parties, and gives young girls their start in life. Her peculiarity was that she would never let a man keep her; she was just a nice little prostitute and never tried to 'better' herself. For thirty years she figured on the police register and plied her trade between the Madeleine and the Rue Drouot. But her life fell into two compartments: from nine a.m. till five p.m. she went as Mme. Barbin and led a quiet middle-class existence in a ground-floor flat in the Rue Richer, with a hanging lamp, a housemaid, and all the household cares of that walk of life—accounts to keep, the stock-markets to be watched with an eye to her investments, servant troubles, family ties, nephews and nieces, birthdays, and, to crown all, a children's party round the Christmas tree. It's gospel truth. Then at five each evening, wet or fine, she doffed her flannel camisole for a smart tailor-made coat and skirt and sallied forth, without the least compunction, on her beat; Mme. Barbin had changed to Juju, pretty lady, a keen worker, ever cheerful, never glum, and a familiar, well-liked client of all the accommodating hotels along the boulevards."

Jacques could not take his eyes off Ma Juju. With her laughing, energetic, rather cunning face, she had the genial aspect of a country parish priest; her bobbed hair showed snow-white beneath a wide-awake hat.

"Without the least compunction . . ." Jacques repeated pensively.

"Of course," said Daniel. There was a touch of raillery, almost of aggressiveness in his manner as, glancing towards Jacques, he murmured Whitman's lines:

"You prostitutes flaunting over the trottoirs or obscene in your rooms,
Who am I that I should call you more obscene than myself?"

Daniel knew he was administering a shock to Jacques's modesty and he did it deliberately, for it irritated him to see how easily Jacques, for months on end—was it by way of a reaction against his friend's loose living?—endured a life of all but perfect chastity. Daniel was simple-minded enough, in fact, to be greatly upset about it and he knew that Jacques too was sometimes rather uneasy about the insidious lethargy gaining on a temperament which in early youth showed promise of more ardent ways. Once in the course of the past winter they had broached that delicate topic; it was on their way home from the theatre, as they threaded their way along the boulevards dense with a seething crowd of lovers. Daniel had expressed amazement at his companion's apathy. "Still," Jacques answered, "I'm fit as a fiddle. At my army medical I noticed that they put me in the top class physically." But Daniel had remarked a quaver of anxiety in his friend's voice.

His musings were cut short by the arrival of Favery, who had appeared in the offing and was looking in their direction; with studied nonchalance he committed hat, stick, and gloves to the cloak-room attendant. He hailed Jacques with a grin.

"Hasn't your brother come yet?"

In the evening Favery always wore collars that were a trifle too high, new suits that looked as if they were someone else's, and he stuck out his smooth-shaven chin with a jaunty air that prompted Werff to sneer: "See the conquering proctor comes!"

"I've passed!" thought Jacques, with half a mind to take French leave and catch an evening train to Maisons-Laffitte. Only the thought that Antoine had promised to meet him here and might turn up at any moment held him back. If not tonight, he consoled himself, then tomorrow morning very early. And at the thought the cabaret faded out and, drenched in coolness, he was watching the new-risen sun drinking up the dew along the avenues.

A blinding flash as all the lights went on together startled him out of his day-dream. I—have—passed! The thought seemed to restore at once his contact with reality. He looked round for his friend and espied Daniel talking confidentially to Ma Juju in a corner of the room. Daniel was perched sideways on a swivel-chair and his vivacious gestures as he rattled on brought out the graceful poise of his head, the bright awareness of his eyes and smile, the shapeliness of his hands poised in mid-air—hands, look, and smile spoke no less than his lips. Jacques could not take his eyes off him. How handsome he looks! was his unformulated thought. How fine that one so young, so splendidly alive, should sink himself so utterly in the Now, the Here! And do it all so naturally! He doesn't know I'm watching him, or give it a thought; he has no notion of being under scrutiny. Curious, to catch a fellow unawares like that, to pry into his inmost secrets! How can anyone manage to be so oblivious of his surroundings, when in public? When he talks, he is whole-heartedly in what he says. I'm different; I can't be "natural." I could never give myself away like that—except in a closed room, safe from prying eyes. And even then . . . ! He gave his musings pause. Daniel's not so very observant, he resumed, that's why he's not absorbed, as I am, by environment; he can remain himself. Jacques pondered again; then, as he rose from his seat, he summed the matter up: But I am always an easy prey to the world around me. . . .

"No, my charming Prophet," Ma Juju was admonishing Daniel at that moment, "it's no use begging; that little girl is not for you." The suppressed fury in Daniel's eyes made her burst into laughter. "Well, upon my word! Have a nice sit-down, dearie, and you'll get over it!"

This Parthian shot was one of a batch of pointless gags—others

were: "That's nobody's business," "Be my mascot, baby!" "That ain't
nothing so long as you keep fit"—one of the second-hand phrases, re-
stocked from time to time, wherewith the Packmell "crowd" were
wont to interlard their conversation in and out of season, smiling
the while masonically.

"But how did you get to know her?" Daniel insisted; his eyes were
obdurate.

"No, my dear. Nothing doing in that quarter. She's one in a thousand, that kid, a nice little thing and no nonsense about her. A top-
notcher!"

"Tell me how you got to know her."

"Will you leave her alone?"

"Yes, I promise."

"Well, it was when I had the pleurisy—remember? She heard about
it and turned up one day, all out of her own head. And, don't forget,
I hardly knew the girl—I'd helped her a bit once or twice, but only
in a small way. You see the kid had had a deal of trouble, a rotten
time of it. She'd fallen in love with a society man, as far as I can
make out, and there was a child (wouldn't think it, now, would you?)
who died almost at once, with the result that one can't mention the
word 'baby' without her starting to howl! Anyhow, when I had
my attack, she came and settled in at my place, like a trained nurse,
and, day and night for six weeks and more, she looked after me better
than if she'd been my own daughter. Why, there were days she put
as many as a hundred cupping-glasses on my chest. Yes, my dear,
she saved my life, and that's gospel truth. And didn't spend a sou.
One in a thousand! So I swore I'd see her fixed up all right. These
young folk, they're always running after whims and fancies. But my
job's to see her launched, properly launched, you know. . . . By the
way, you might lend me a hand there—I'll explain presently. . . .
She hasn't been out of my sight for three months now. First I had
to find a name for her. Her real name is Victorine—Victorine Le
Gad. 'Le Gad,' a double-barrelled name, might pass. But 'Victorine'—I
ask you! So I changed it to 'Rinette.' Not bad, eh? And the rest to
match. Colin's given her elocution lessons; she had a Breton accent

you could cut with a knife; well, she's kept just the right dash of it, a bit of a foreign twang—might be English—delicious anyhow. She learnt the boston in a fortnight; she's light as a feather. What's more, she's no fool. She sings in tune; a real rich voice she has, with a tang of the gutter in it; that's how I like 'em! So there she is, ship-shape, ready to be launched. The one thing now is to give her a good send-off. No, don't laugh; that's where *you* come in. I've talked to Ludwigson about her; since Bertha gave him the air, he's all at a loose end. He's promised to come tonight to meet the child. Put in a word saying you like her and he'll be as keen as mustard. Ludwigson, you see, is exactly the man to suit her. She has only one idea: to collect a little nest-egg and go back to Brittany, where her home is. Damned silly, but there you are! All Bretonnes are like that. A cottage near the village pump, the usual white streamers, and plenty of proces-sions—just Brittany, in a word! She's not asking for the moon; if she keeps straight and listens to reason, she'll get what she wants in no time. I hope she'll have twenty thousand francs put away by the New Year and I know just how I'm going to invest them for her. . . . Look here, do you know anything about the Rand market?"

Hungry voices vociferated: "Dinner! Take your seats!"

Daniel returned to Jacques.

"Hasn't your brother come yet? Anyhow let's pick our seats."

The long table was laid for twenty people; there was some hesitation as they chose their places. Daniel so manœuvred that Jacques was placed beside Rinette, on her left; Ma Juju, who clung to her like a leech, sat on her right, as close as she could squeeze beside her. But just when everyone had picked his place and Jacques was about to take his own, Daniel forestalled him.

"Change with me!"

Without more ado he pulled Jacques to one side, gripping his arm so roughly that Jacques felt his fingers nipping his wrist and all but gave a squeal of pain.

Daniel was too preoccupied to think of excusing himself. He turned to Ma Juju.

"Isn't it up to you, Ma Juju, to introduce me to my neighbour?"

"Ah, there you are!" muttered the old lady, who had just noticed Daniel's ruse. Then she apostrophized the company at large:

"May I introduce Mlle. Rinette to you all?" and added in menacing tones: "She's under my wing."

"Introduce us!" voices clamoured on all sides. "Introduce us to her!"

"Save us, what a to-do they're making!" sighed Ma Juju, and with a bad grace she removed her hat and tossed it to one of the "nurses" waiting at table. She pointed to Daniel first of all.

"This is the Prophet," she announced, "and a real bad egg!"

"How do you do?" said the girl amiably. Daniel took her hand and kissed it.

"Next, please!"

"His friend—I don't know his name." Ma Juju's finger indicated Jacques.

"How do you do?" said Rinette.

"Next: Paule, Sylvia, Mme. Dolores—also a child unknown; the Wonder-Child, no doubt. Then Werff, *alias* 'Apricot,' and Gaby. The Chump."

"Thanks," a sarcastic voice broke in; "I prefer the name of my forefathers. Favery, Mademoiselle, and one of your most ardent admirers."

"Be my mascot, baby!" someone chirped ironically.

"Lily and Harmonica, or the Inseparables," Ma Juju went on, steeled against interrupters. "The Colonel. Maud, Queen of the Garden. A gentleman I don't know and with him two ladies whom I know very well, though I can't recall their names. An empty chair. Ditto another. Then Battaincourt, otherwise 'Little Batt.' Marie-Josèphe, *plus* the pearls. Madame Packmell." Then, with a bow, she added: "And Ma Juju, your humble servant."

"How do you do? How do you do?" Rinette echoed herself in silvery cadences, smiling without a shadow of constraint.

"Rinette's no sort of name for her," Favery observed. "What about Miss Howd'youdo?"

"Why not?" the girl replied.

"Three cheers for Miss Howd'youdo!"

Smiling still, she seemed delighted by their noisy acclamations.

"And now, the soup!" The suggestion came from Mme. Packmell.

Jacques nudged Daniel with his elbow and showed him the bruise on his wrist.

"What ever came over you just now?"

His friend threw him a quizzing glance, without the least sign of contrition, a glance that was ardent to the point of fierceness.

" 'I am he that aches with amorous love,' " he quoted in English, lowering his voice.

Jacques leaned forward to examine Rinette, who happened to be looking towards him; he met her cool eyes, green-glistening like Marennes oysters.

Daniel continued in the same low voice:

" 'Does the earth gravitate? Does not all matter aching attract all matter?

" 'So the body of me to all I meet and know.' "

Jacques frowned slightly. This was not the first time he had chanced to witness one of these paroxysms of passion which carried Daniel off his feet in quest of pleasure, beyond all possibility of restraint. And each of them made a rift in Jacques's affection despite his efforts to keep it whole. A comic detail shifted the trend of his thoughts; he had suddenly noticed that the inner surface of Daniel's nose was lined with jet-black down, making his nostrils like the vent-holes of a mask. Then his eyes fell on the "Prophet's" hands, fine, tapering hands, shaded too with dusky down. *Vir pilosus,* he thought, repressing a smile.

Daniel leaned towards him again and continued in the same low tone, as though finishing the quotation from Whitman.

"Fill up your neighbour's glass, my dear."

"Mme. Packmell, the menu ith quite illegible thith. evening," lisped a voice from the far end of the table.

"Two black marks against Mme. Packmell!" declared Favery severely.

"That ain't nothing so long as you keep fit," the comely blonde riposted philosophically.

Jacques was sitting next to Paule, the slightly tarnished angel with the snow-white skin. Beyond her sat a big-breasted girl who never spoke and applied her napkin to her lips after each spoonful. Further on, almost facing Jacques, beside a dark woman whose forehead rippled with tiny curls—Dolores, as Ma Juju called her—sat a little boy, seven or eight years old, dressed in rather shabby black; his eyes followed every movement of the others and, now and again, a smile lit up his face.

Jacques addressed the girl beside him:

"Why, they've forgotten your soup."

"Thanks, I'm not taking any."

She kept her eyes lowered and only raised them to look in Daniel's direction. She had tried her best to get a seat beside him but at the last minute had seen him exchanging chairs with his friend; Jacques was to blame for this, she thought. Where had this fellow with the spotty face and a boil on his neck sprung from? Her pet aversion was redheads, and there was something in Jacques's looks and in his auburn hair that put him in this category. Only to see the disorderly mat over his forehead, his jowl and loose-set ears, you knew him for a bit of a brute!

Mme. Dolores's shrill voice broke in:

"Well, what's come over you? Why don't you put your napkin on?" She jerked the youngster to and fro, tucking the starched linen, which half submerged him in its folds, into his collar.

"When a woman owns to a certain age," Favery was laying down the law to Marie-Josèphe, "it means she's past it. She got into the Conservatoire, I tell you, at the extreme age-limit exactly forty-five years ago, by producing her younger sister's birth-certificate—which made her two years under her true age. So it comes to this . . ."

"That's nobody's business," Ma Juju declared in a loud stage-whisper.

"Favery is one of those excellent folk who can never engage in a conversation without premising that the rate of velocity for falling bodies is 32 feet, 2 inches per second at Paris," observed Werff, who once had crammed for the Polytechnic. He owed the nickname of Apricot to the hue of his skin; it had been burnt to a dull gold, spangled with freckles, by his practice of open-air sports. He cut a handsome figure, with his supple shoulders, strongly moulded face, and full, red lips; by night his sunburnt cheeks and blue eyes radiated hale well-being, a muscular gusto regaled by the day's athletics.

"Nobody knows what he died of," someone remarked, eliciting a jesting repartee. "The real mystery was what he lived on!"

"Hurry up now!" Mme. Dolores admonished the boy. "They serve dessert here, you know—but you shan't have any."

"Why?" the lad pleaded, turning his shining eyes towards her.

"Because you shan't if I say no! Now do as you're told, hurry up!" She saw that Jacques was watching and sped him a confidential smile. "He's a fussy kid, you see. He shies off anything he's not used to. Salmis of pigeon—you won't see that every day, my pet! Gammon and greens came his way oftener than pigeon, I should say. He's been spoilt. Fussed over, petted, like all only children. Especially as his mother was an invalid for so long. That's what he is"—she stroked the child's round, close-cropped head—"a spoilt child. A naughty, spoilt child. But, now his aunt's in charge of him, there'll be a change. Our young gentleman wanted to keep his lovelocks, like a little girl, eh? We'll hear no more about those fads of his; no more pampering for him. Eat your dinner now. The gentleman's looking. Be quick!" Delighted to have an audience, she cast another smile in the direction of Jacques and Paule. "He's a little orphan," she announced complacently. "He lost his mother only this week; she was married to my brother. She died in her village down in Lorraine—of consumption. Poor little kid," she added, "it's lucky for him that I am willing to look after him. He has no one in the world now except me. But I shall have my hands full!"

The little boy had ceased eating and was staring at his aunt. Did he understand? There was a curious intonation in his voice as he questioned her.

"Was it my mummy who died?"

"Don't bother with questions. Eat your dinner!"

"Don't want to now."

"There you are! That's how he is," Mme. Dolores lamented. "Well, if you must know, it *was* your mummy who died. Now do as you're told and go on eating, or you won't have any ice-cream."

Paule averted her eyes just then and, as their looks crossed, Jacques saw the image of his own distress. Her neck was slim and lithe and very pale, still paler than her cheeks; its slender grace invited thoughts of dalliance. As his gaze rested on her fine-grained skin, shaded with a slight down, a faint savour of sweetness rose to his lips. He groped for something to say, found nothing, and smiled. Watching him from the corner of an eye, she found him less uncouth. But a sudden twinge at her heart brought a deathly pallor to her face; resting her hands on the table edge, she let her head sink back a little, biting her tongue to save herself from fainting.

Seeing her thus, Jacques pictured a bird alighted on the tablecloth, there to die.

"What is it?" he whispered.

Her eyes were swimming and a line of white showed between her half-shut eyelids. Without moving she forced out two words:

"Say nothing!"

A lump had risen to his throat and, even had he wished, he could not have called out. In any case the others paid no heed to them. He looked at Paule's hands; her rigid fingers, diaphanous like tiny tapers, had grown so livid that the nails showed up as patches of dark violet.

"My alarm goes off at six-thirty," Favery was explaining to the girl beside him, with chuckles of self-satisfaction, "standing in a saucer poised precariously on a tumbler . . ."

Meanwhile Paule's colour had returned a little and she opened her eyes again; turning, she weakly smiled her thanks to Jacques for his silence.

"It's over," she murmured breathlessly. "I'm liable to these attacks— my heart, you know." Then she added ruefully, with lips that quivered still: "Have a nice sit-down, dearie, and you'll get over it!"

He had an impulse to catch her in his arms and carry her far, far away from all this sordidness; in a day-dream he devoted all his life to her and made her well. So potent was the love he felt within him

for any weaker being who might claim, or merely accept, the refuge
of his strength! He had half a mind to tell Daniel of his fantastic
scheme, but Daniel's thoughts were otherwise occupied.

Daniel was chatting with Ma Juju, across Rinette; a pretext for
watching the girl beside him and feeling her warm nearness. Though
all through the meal he had diplomatically refrained from addressing
her in any but the briefest phrases, while paying court to her with
delicate attentions, she obviously filled his thoughts. On several occasions she had noticed his eyes fixed on her and on each occasion,
though she could not analyse the cause, his look, far from attracting
her, evoked a feeling of estrangement; she was not blind to the virile
charm of Daniel's face, but it annoyed her.

Meanwhile a heated discussion was in progress at the far end of the
table.

"Conceited ass!" Apricot apostrophized Favery, who pleaded guilty.

"That's what I often say to myself!"

"But not loudly enough, I fear."

Amidst the general laughter Werff kept the upper hand.

"My dear Favery," he declared, deliberately raising his voice, "allow
me to tell you something: what you've just said *about* women proves
that you don't know what to say *to* them."

Daniel glanced at Favery. The young pedagogue was laughing and
Daniel fancied he saw him glance towards Rinette, as though she
had been the theme of the discussion. There was a certain effrontery,
a lewdness, in Favery's look which gave a fillip to Daniel's antipathy
for him. He knew stories about Favery which did him little credit,
and felt a brutal impulse to retail them in Rinette's hearing. And he
never could resist impulses of that order. Lowering his voice so as
to be heard by the two women only, he bent towards Ma Juju in such
a way as to include Rinette in the conversation, and asked in a casual
voice:

"Do you know that one about Favery and the woman taken in
adultery?"

The old woman snapped at the bait.

"No, let's hear it! And chuck us a cigarette! This dinner seems likely to last all night."

"One fine day—she'd been his mistress for a good spell then—the woman rolled up at his place with a valise in her hand. 'I've had enough of it. I want to live with you,' and the usual stuff. 'But how about your husband?' 'Him? I've just written him this letter: "Dear Eugene, I have come to a turning-point in my life," and so on . . . "I want, as I have the right, to bestow my affection on a heart that understands," and so on and so forth. . . . "That heart—I have found it, and so I leave you."'"

"And what a heart—I ask you!"

"That was her lookout. But guess what happened next! Old Favery was in the devil of a stew. A woman on his hands and, what was worse, a woman who'd soon be divorced and free to insist on his marrying her. Then he brought off what he claims to be a stroke of genius. He sent this letter to the woman's husband: 'Dear Sir, I hereby inform you that your wife has left her home with the intention of coming to live with me. Faithfully yours . . .'"

"Very decent of him," Rinette remarked.

"So you think!" A malicious smile flitted across Daniel's face. "But wait a bit! Favery's astute; he was simply taking his precautions for the future. Her husband, he knew, would produce the letter in court. And the marriage of an unfaithful wife with her lover is forbidden by law. So Favery winds up his story with the maxim: Heaven helps those who know the Civil Code."

Rinette pondered a while; then it dawned on her.

"A dirty trick!"

Daniel, as he bent towards her, felt her breath hover on his face and lips, and he took a deep breath, almost closing his eyes.

"So he let her drop, eh?" the old woman inquired.

Daniel did not reply. Rinette looked towards him. He kept his eyes lowered now, for he felt powerless to hide their frenzy of desire. Close to her eyes she saw the smoothness of his skin, the savage line of his mouth, his quivering lashes, and, as though she long had known and tested their dark treacheries, something within her, urgent as an instinct, turned her suddenly against him.

"But what became of the woman?" Ma Juju asked again.

"They say she killed herself. His version is that she was consumptive." With a forced smile he passed his fingers across his forehead.

Rinette drew herself up, shrinking against the back of her chair, so as to keep as far apart as possible from Daniel. What was the cause of this revulsion that had come over her so suddenly? His face, his smile, his expression—all about this handsome youth repelled her; his way of leaning forward, the grace of his gestures, and most of all, his long, sensitive hands. Never had she dreamt there slumbered in her heart, biding their time but so far held in leash, such potencies of loathing for a total stranger.

"So, in other words, I'm a flirt!" exclaimed Marie-Josèphe, calling the company to witness.

Battaincourt smiled ingenuously.

"Am I to blame if our language has no other word to describe that most charming of traits: the desire to fascinate?"

"Oh, how disgusting!" Mme. Dolores's shrill voice broke in.

All eyes turned in her direction, only to find that the little boy had spilt a spoonful of cream on his black coat and was being hauled away by his aunt towards the lavatory.

Jacques profited by her eclipse to question Paule, glad of this chance of breaking the ice.

"You know her?"

"Slightly."

Paule's impulse was to stop there; she was naturally reserved, and felt depressed. But, as Jacques had been so nice to her just now, she continued. "She's not a bad sort, you know. And she's well off. She was once, for quite a long while, the mistress of a fellow who writes plays. Then she married a pharmacist. He's dead now and his patent medicines bring her in a tidy income still—the 'Dolores Corn-Cure,' you must have heard of it. No? Better tell her so, she always carries samples in her bag. A striking woman, you'll see; quite a character.

She keeps a dozen cats picked up here, there, and everywhere, and a large aquarium of fishes in her bedroom. She loves animals."

"But not children."

Paule shook her head.

"That's the sort she is," she concluded.

Jacques noticed that after speaking she breathed with difficulty. All the same he wanted to prolong their talk. The reminder that she had heart-disease brought to his lips, somewhat inaptly, a familiar phrase: "The heart has its reasons which reason does not know."

She reflected a moment, then, strumming on the table with her fingers, corrected him:

"It should be: 'The heart its reasons has . . .' The first way it didn't sound like poetry."

His longing for her persisted, but he now felt less disposed to devote his life to her. No sooner, he thought, am I allowed the smallest glimpse into another's soul than I am half in love already! He recalled the first occasion when he noticed this habit of his: one day during the previous summer he had gone for a walk with some of Antoine's friends in the Viroflay woods; a Swedish girl, studying medicine at Paris, had leaned on his arm and chattered to him of her childhood. . . .

Suddenly he realized that it was half-past nine and Antoine had not yet come. A panic fear came over him and, forgetting everything else, he clutched Daniel's arm and shook it.

"I'm positive something's happened to him!"

"What . . . ?"

"To Antoine."

Dinner had just ended and people were leaving their seats. Jacques rose to his feet. Daniel was standing too and, while manœuvring to keep in touch with Rinette, tried to reassure his friend.

"Don't be an ass, Jacques! He's a doctor. An urgent call . . ."

But Jacques was already out of earshot. Unable to collect his wits or master his forebodings, he had hurried off to the cloak-room. Without saying good-bye to anyone or giving a thought to Paule, he ran outside. "It's my fault," horror-stricken, he admonished himself. "I've brought Antoine bad luck. My fault! My fault! And all to have a black suit, like that fellow at the Médicis crossing!"

The three-piece band had just struck up a waltz and a few couples had started dancing near the bar. Daniel saw Favery's chin uptilted, as if he sniffed the air, his twinkling eyes fixed on Rinette, and, by a quick move, forestalled him.

"Shall we . . . ?"

She had noticed his approach and met it with a hostile look. She gave him time enough to bend a little towards her before replying.

"No."

He masked his surprise with a smile.

" 'No.' Why 'no'?" he said, mimicking her intonation. So sure was he of getting his way that he took a step towards her. "Come along!" The touch of over-confidence in his gesture clinched her distaste.

"No, not with you," she said pointedly.

"No?" he repeated; but there was a challenging gleam in his dark eyes that seemed to say: "My time will come!"

She turned away and, noticing Favery's hesitant approach, went up to him as if he had already asked her for the dance. They danced together in silence.

Ludwigson had just arrived. Wearing a dinner-jacket and an incongruous straw hat, he stood beside the bar, chatting with Mother Packmell and Marie-Josèphe, whose necklace he was fingering complacently. But stealthily his slow eyes, slotted between reptilian lids, would alight, like a blow from a loaded cane, on something or someone present, summing up the company.

Ma Juju steered a course between the dancers in quest of Rinette. When she had found the girl, she nudged her with her elbow.

"Hurry up! And remember what I said!"

Paule had buttonholed Daniel in a corner of the room and he was listening to her with a far-away smile. He watched Ma Juju proceeding with the most natural air in the world to join Marie-Josèphe's group, while Rinette, ceasing to dance, went and sat down alone at a distant table in the far room. A moment later Ludwigson and Ma

Juju crossed both rooms and joined her there. Ludwigson always—
and especially when he knew he was being looked at—stiffened his
back, like an old-time cabby, as he walked. He knew only too well
that nature had cursed him with a houri's hind parts and that whenever he moved fast his hips were apt to sway from side to side; so he
stepped delicately. He pressed his thick lips on Rinette's proffered
hand. As he made the gesture Daniel noted his somewhat receding
skull, plastered with black and skilfully dekinked hair. "The fellow's
got a distinction of his own all the same," he said to himself. "There's
a touch of the coolie in our Levantine mountebank—but something
of the Grand Turk, too."

As Ludwigson slowly drew off his gloves his expert, appraising
gaze was sizing up Rinette. He sat down facing her, Ma Juju beside
him. Drinks were served at once, though Ludwigson had given no
order; they knew his ways. He never drank champagne, but always
Asti—a still variety—not iced or even cool, but slightly warmed.
"Tepid," he explained, "like the yuice of frucht in sunshine."

Daniel left Paule and, lighting a cigarette, strolled round the bar,
greeting his friends; then he returned and settled down in the further
room. Ludwigson and Ma Juju had their backs to him, but he was
directly opposite Rinette, though the full width of the room lay between them. A breezy conversation had sprung up all at once around
the glasses of Asti. Rinette was smiling at Ludwigson's sallies; leaning towards her, he made no secret of his admiration and spared no
pains to please her. When she saw Daniel watching she put on an even
gayer air.

The two rooms adjoined, and dancing couples kept coming and
going through the opening between them. A little rosy-cheeked "professional," who might have stepped out of a Lawrence canvas, had
perched herself on the first step of the tiny white staircase behind the
bar, and, with both hands on the banisters and standing on one leg,
she swung the other to and fro in time with the music, and yelled,
her face uptilted, a meaningless refrain that everyone that summer
knew by heart:

"*Timmyloo, lammyloo, pan, pan, timmylah!*"

Daniel, a cigarette between his lips, rested his head on his hands; his eyes were riveted on Rinette. He had ceased smiling; his features had grown rigid, his lips pinched. "Where have I seen him before?" the girl asked herself. She laughed over-noisily, studiously evading Daniel's gaze. But evasion grew more and more difficult; oftener and oftener, like a lark lured towards a mirror, she found her attention caught and held by his unswerving eyes. Shadowed yet clear, they seemed precisely focused on a point in space far beyond Rinette; keen, burning eyes and never faltering; twin magnets from whose pull she managed to break free each time, but each time found it harder.

Suddenly Daniel felt something moving almost at his side. Such was the tension of his nerves that he could not help starting. It was the little orphan who had gone to sleep on the settle, curled up in Dolores's silky mantle, one finger near his mouth, and eyelashes still moist with half-dried tears.

The band had ceased playing while the violinist went his round in quest of tips. When he came to Daniel the latter slipped a banknote under the napkin.

"The next boston—make it last a quarter of an hour, non-stop," he whispered. The musician's dusky eyelashes fluttered in assent.

Daniel felt that Rinette was watching him and, raising his eyes, he took possession of her gaze. And now he knew that it was in his thrall; once or twice—to amuse himself—he played at cat-and-mouse, pouncing on it and letting it go, to test his power. And then . . . he let it go no more.

Ludwigson, greatly smitten, waxed more and more insistent in his wooing, while the attention Rinette paid him grew more and more perfunctory and vacillating. When the violin struck up another waltz, from the first touch of the bow upon the strings, she knew by the thrill his tense features gave her that things were coming to a head. Yes, there was Daniel getting up! Coolly, with eyes fixed on his prey, he crossed the room, came straight up to her. It flashed across him that he was risking his post with Ludwigson and the thought was like a rowel to his passion. Rinette watched him come, and in her glassy stare there was something so abnormal that Ludwigson and

Ma Juju both swung round at once. Ludwigson, imagining that Daniel meant to greet him, made a tentative gesture in his direction. But Daniel did not seem even to know him. As he leaned forward his look bored into the girl's sea-green eyes, bright with mingled terror and consent. Subdued, she rose. Without a word he slipped his arm around her, drew her close, and disappeared with her into the further room where the band was playing.

For a second or two Ludwigson and Ma Juju sat in stony silence, blankly staring at their retreating backs. Then their eyes met.

"Well, of all the damned cheek . . . !" Ma Juju could heardly speak and her double chin quivered with fury.

Ludwigson's eyebrows lifted, but he did not answer. He was naturally so pale that he could not grow paler. The nails of his huge fingers glowed darkly like cornelians as he reached for his glass and raised the Asti to his lips.

Ma Juju was panting like a winded sprinter. "Anyhow," she ventured, with the dry chuckle of a woman getting her revenge, "that means the sack for the young scallawag, I guess, as far as you're concerned."

Ludwigson looked surprised.

"M. de Fontanin? But why should you think that?"

His smile implied that a man of breeding does not stoop to such acts of petty spite. Cool and collected, he drew on his gloves. Perhaps, indeed, he was genuinely tickled at the situation. Taking a note from his pocket-book, he tossed it onto the table and rose with a courteous gesture of farewell to Ma Juju. Then he went to the room where dancing was in progress and halted on the threshold till the couple came round to where he stood. Daniel caught his drowsy gaze, in which a spice of malice mingled with jealousy and admiration; then he saw him sidling past the settles towards the exit and vanish through the swinging-door, which seemed to swish him round in its wake, into the outer darkness.

Daniel waltzed slowly; his body did not seem to move, and he held his head erect. There was a certain coolness in his deportment, partly ease and partly stiffness; he danced on the tips of his toes and his feet never left the ground. Rinette, lost to her surroundings—whether spellbound or outraged, she could not decide—followed so perfectly Daniel's least movements that it was as if they had always danced together. After ten minutes they were the last couple left in; the others, whose energy had failed them long before, formed a circle round them. Five more minutes passed and left them dancing still. Then, after a last repeat, the band cried quarter. They danced on till the final chord—the girl half swooning on his shoulder, Daniel self-possessed, veiling with closed eyelids the burning gaze which now and again he let fall on her, thrilling her by turns with loathing and desire.

To the accompaniment of clapping hands Daniel led Rinette back to Ludwigson's table, quite composedly took the vacant chair, asked for another glass, and, filling it with Asti, gaily lifted it to Ma Juju and drained it at a draught.

"Faugh!" he exclaimed. "What syrup!"

Rinette broke into a nervous laugh and her eyes filled with tears.

Ma Juju stared at Daniel, big-eyed with wonder; her anger had evaporated. She rose and, shrugging her shoulders, sighed comically.

"Well, that ain't nothing so long as you keep fit!"

Half an hour later Daniel and Rinette left Packmell's together. Rain had fallen.

"A taxi?" the page inquired.

"Let's walk a bit first," Rinette proposed. There was a soft fall in her voice that Daniel found charming.

Despite the rain, the air was still sultry. The ill-lit streets were empty. They went slowly on along the rain-bright sidewalk.

An infantryman passed by; he held two women by the waist and was laughingly teaching them how to change step. "Left, right! Not like that. Hop on your left foot! Left, right!" Laughter rang receding, long echoing along the silent house-fronts.

When they left the cabaret she thought he would slip his arm through hers at once. But Daniel so keenly relished joys deferred that he would postpone them almost to the breaking-point. She made the first move, startled by a distant flash of lightning.

"The storm's not over yet. It'll rain again."

"And that will be delightful." His voice was like a caress, charged with hidden meanings, rather too subtle for the girl, whom his aloofness disconcerted.

"You know, I can't get it out of my head that I've seen you somewhere before."

He smiled in the shadow, thankful that she kept to commonplace remarks. He was far from suspecting that she really thought she had met him before, and all but answered: "Nor can I," by way of joining in the game; then, of course, they would fall to guessing when it had happened. But it amused him more to go on mystifying her by keeping silence.

"Why do they call you 'Prophet'?" she asked, after a pause.

"Because my name is Daniel."

"Daniel what . . . ?"

He hesitated, reluctant to drop the defensive, even on a minor point. Still Rinette's curiosity was so patently ingenuous that he felt it unfair to dupe her with a false name.

"Daniel de Fontanin."

She did not reply, but gave a start of astonishment. She's stumbled, he thought, and made as if to come to her aid; but she eluded him. That was enough to make him eager to coerce her and, going up to her, he tried to take her arm. Swerving nimbly aside, she kept beyond his reach; then suddenly she turned away, making for a side-street. Playing a game with me, he thought; well, I'll join in! But it looked as if she were trying to escape him in earnest; she quickened her step till he could hardly keep his distance without breaking into a run. Their point-to-point along the deserted streets amused him. But, when she dived into a darker street that would have brought them back, by a roundabout way, to their starting-point, feeling rather tired, he made a third attempt to grasp her arm. She eluded him again.

"Don't be so silly!" he cried angrily. "Stop now!"

But she fled all the faster, darting into patches of shadow and constantly swerving from one sidewalk to the other, as if she really meant to shake off his pursuit. All at once she broke into a run. With a few strides he drew level and brought her to bay before a door-porch. Then on her face he caught a look of terror that could not have been feigned.

"What's the matter?"

She crouched in the dripping doorway, panting, staring up at him with haggard eyes. He thought for a moment. It was clear to him, though he could make nothing of it, that she had had some serious shock. He tried to draw her towards him; she recoiled in such panic haste that a flounce of her dress was torn.

"What on earth is the matter?" he asked again, moving back a pace. "Are you afraid of me? Or do you feel ill?"

A nervous shudder passed through her body; she could not utter a sound and never took her eyes off him.

It was all as much a mystery as ever, but now he took pity on her.

"Would you rather I left you?"

She nodded. Feeling slightly ridiculous, he repeated his question: "You mean it? You'd rather I went away?" He might have been soothing a lost child, such was the gentleness he put into his voice.

"Yes." Her tone was almost brutal.

Obviously, he decided, this was no acting. He realized that any more insistence on his part would be unmannerly and, suddenly resigned to losing her, determined to take it like a sport.

"Have it your own way," he said. "Only I can't leave you stranded here in the middle of the night, in this doorway. We'll hunt round for a taxi first, and then I'll leave you. . . . Right?"

The lights of the Avenue de l'Opéra were visible in the distance and they walked silently towards them. Quite soon an empty taxi came their way and, at a sign from Daniel, drew up beside the kerb. Rinette kept her eyes fixed on the ground. Daniel opened the door. Only when her foot was on the step did she turn towards him and look him in the face; it was as if something compelled her to survey him once again. With a forced smile he stood before her, bare-headed, doing his best to keep up the appearance of a friend who is bidding a casual good-bye. Once she was sure he would not try to accompany her, her features relaxed. She told the driver where to go. Then, turning to Daniel, she whispered an apology.

"I'm sorry, but tonight, M. Daniel, you must leave me. I'll explain tomorrow."

"Tomorrow, then," he said, with a bow. "But—where?"

"Oh, yes. . . . Where?" she repeated innocently. "At Mme. Juju's, if you like. Yes, at her place. Three o'clock."

"Right!"

He took her extended hand in his, and his lips lightly brushed the tips of her gloved fingers.

The taxi started.

Then suddenly a gust of anger swept over Daniel. He was just mastering it when he observed the girl's white shoulders leaning from the window and saw her bid the driver stop.

In a few strides he had caught up the taxi, the door of which Rinette had opened. He saw her huddled together at the far end of the seat, her eyes staring into the darkness. He read their meaning and sprang in beside her; when he took her in his arms, she crushed her lips to his and now he knew it was no fear or weakness that moved her to surrender, but that she freely gave herself. She was sobbing, sobbing desperately, and murmured broken phrases:

"I want . . . I want . . ."

Daniel was dumbfounded by the words that followed:

"I want . . . to have . . . a child by you!"

"Same address, sir?" the taxi-driver inquired.

III

AFTER leaving Jacques and his friends Antoine had the taxi take him to Passy, where he had "a pneumonia case" to visit; thence to his father's residence in the Rue de l'Université, where for the past five years he and his brother had shared the ground-floor flat between them. Lolling in the car that took him homewards, a cigarette between his lips, he decided that his little patient was certainly on the mend, that his day's work was over, and that he was feeling in excellent spirits.

Yesterday, he mused, I wasn't too pleased with myself. As a rule, when expectoration ceases so abruptly . . . *Pulsus bonus, urina bona, sed æger moritur*. The essential now is to prevent endocarditis. His mother's still a pretty woman. Paris is looking pretty, too, this evening.

As the car sped by, his eyes searched the green shadows of the Trocadero and he swung round to follow with his gaze a couple turning up a lonely pathway. The Eiffel Tower, the statues on the bridges and the Seine were flushed with rosy light. *In my heart tra-la-la* . . . The engine purred a ground-bass to his voice. *In my heart* . . . *sleeps,* he suddenly added. Got it! *In my heart sleeps la-la-la.* Provoking not to be able to remember the words. Now what the devil sleeps in anybody's heart? The beast in all of us, he thought, smiling to himself. And again his wandering thoughts veered to the prospect of a festive evening at Packmell's. Some girl, perhaps . . . ? He felt glad to be alive, borne on an undercurrent of desire. Throwing away the cigarette, he crossed his legs and drew a deep breath of air, to which the rapid motion of the taxi lent an illusive coolness. Let's hope Belin didn't forget the cupping-glasses for that child. We'll save the poor kid—what's more, without an operation. I'd love to see the look on Loiselle's face. Those surgeons! They're all the rage but—what are they? Mere acrobats. As old man Black used to say: "If I had three sons, I'd say to the least gifted one: 'Go in for midwifery!'; to the most sporting: 'The lancet for you, my boy!'; but, to the cleverest, I'd say: 'Be a general practitioner, treat lots of patients, and try to better your knowledge every day.'" A joyous mood swept over him again; he felt each sinew tense with deep-set joy. "I've played my cards well," he murmured under his breath.

When he reached home, the open door of Jacques's room reminded him that his brother had passed his examination, a success that crowned his five years' vigilance and careful handling of the boy. How well I remember, he mused, the evening when I met Favery in the Rue des Ecoles and the idea of urging Jacques to join the Ecole Normale first came to me! The Square Monge was white with snow. A bit cooler than this! he sighed. Zestfully he foresaw his body under the cool, clear water, and tossed his garments hither and thither with childish impatience.

He felt a new man when he turned off the shower and, thinking of Packmell's, whistled merrily. He accorded but a minor role in his life to "the girls," as he called them; and none to sentimental love. Easy come, easy go, was his method, and he prided himself on its matter-of-factness. Moreover, certain nights excepted, he held aloof from "that sort of thing"—not for discipline's sake or through physical indifference, but because "that sort of thing" belonged to a scheme of life in which the line he had decided once for all to take had no part. He had a feeling that such preoccupations were fit for weaklings, whereas he was a "strong man."

There was a ring at the bell. He glanced at the clock; if it came to that, he would have time to visit a patient before joining the others at Packmell's.

"Who's there?" he called through the door.

"It's I, M. Antoine."

He recognized M. Chasle's voice and opened the door. During M. Thibault's absence at Maisons-Laffitte his secretary continued to work in the Rue de l'Université.

"Ah, there you are!" murmured M. Chasle vaguely. Abashed by the vision of Antoine in his shorts, he looked aside, muttering: "What?" with an interrogative grimace. "I see you're dressing," he added almost immediately, one finger uplifted, as though he had just solved an enigma. "I hope I'm not intruding."

"I have to be off in twenty-five minutes," Antoine made haste to inform him.

"That's more than enough. Look here, doctor." He put down his hat and, taking off his glasses, opened his eyes wide. "Don't you see anything?"

"Where?"

"In my eye?"

"Which eye?"

"This one."

"Keep still. No, I can't see anything at all. You got it in a draught, perhaps?"

"Yes, it must be that. Thank you. I'd opened both windows." He coughed shortly and replaced his spectacles. "Thanks. You've set my mind at rest. That was all; a draught. An airy nothing. Hee! Hee!" He tittered to himself before continuing. "You see, I haven't taken up much of your time." But, instead of reaching for his hat, he perched himself on the arm of a chair and mopped his forehead.

"It's hot," Antoine observed.

"Terribly." M. Chasle knitted his brows with a knowing air. "Thunder about, that's sure. It's hard on people who're bound to keep moving, people who have got steps to take. . . ."

Antoine, who was lacing up his shoes, glanced at him inquiringly.

" 'Steps to take'?"

"Well, in heat like this! In offices, in police-stations, why, it's stifling! So one just puts it off to another day." He wagged his head with an air of kindly commiseration.

Antoine could make nothing of the rigmarole.

"By the way," said M. Chasle, "I have often wanted to ask you about it; do you know the Superannuates' Home?"

" 'Superannuates' . . . ?"

"Yes. For old people; not incurables. A rest-home at Point-du-Jour; the best air in France. By the by, while we're on that topic, there's something else I'd like your opinion about, M. Antoine. You've never chanced to find a five-franc piece which had been forgotten?"

" 'Forgotten'? How? In a pocket?"

"No. In a garden. In the street, so to say."

Antoine stood up, trousers in hand, and stared at M. Chasle. One can't be a moment with the old blighter, he said to himself, without beginning to feel like a mental case. With an effort he pulled his wits together.

"I don't quite follow your question." He spoke with careful gravity.

"It's like this. Suppose somebody happens to lose something. Well, someone else may happen to find it, the thing that was lost, I mean, eh?"

"Quite."

"Now supposing it happened to be you who found the thing, what would you do with it?"

"I'd try to discover the owner."

"Yes, of course. But supposing the party wasn't there any more?"

"Where?"

"In the garden, in the street, for instance."

"Well, I'd take the—the thing to the police-station."

M. Chasle smiled knowingly.

"But, if it was money? What then? A five-franc piece? We all know what would become of it at the police-station."

"Do you imagine the police would keep the money?"

"To be sure!"

"Not a bit of it, M. Chasle. To begin with, there are the formalities, papers to sign. Look here! Once when I was with a friend in a cab I found a baby's rattle, quite a pretty little thing really, ivory and silver-gilt. Well, at the police-station they took our names—my friend's name, the cabby's, our addresses, and the cab number; we had to sign a form and they gave us an official receipt. That's news to you, eh? What's more, my friend was notified a year later that, as no one had appeared to claim the rattle, he could come and get it."

"Why?"

"That's the law; if lost property is not claimed, the finder is entitled to keep it, after a year and a day."

"A year and a day? The finder?"

"That's so."

M. Chasle shrugged his shoulders.

"A rattle, maybe. But supposing it were a note—a fifty-franc note, for instance?"

"Exactly the same thing."

"I don't believe it, M. Antoine."

"But I'm positive, M. Chasle."

The grey-haired dwarf perched on the chair stared at the young man over his spectacles. Then, averting his eyes, he coughed behind his hand.

"I asked you that—it's about my mother."

"Has your mother found some money?"

"What?" ejaculated M. Chasle, wriggling on the chair-arm. His cheeks were crimson and for a moment his face betrayed an agony of doubt. But almost immediately a subtle smile crept over his lips. "Of course not. I was speaking of the Home." Then, as Antoine began to slip on his coat, he leapt down from the chair to help him pass his arms through the sleeves. "A passage of arms," he tittered. Then, taking advantage of his position at Antoine's back, he continued quickly, speaking into his ear: "The dreadful thing, you see, is that they want nine thousand francs. With the extras, ten thousand francs all told. And *payable in advance,* what's more; it's written down. And then, if anyone wants to leave, eh?"

"To leave?" Antoine faced round, uncomfortably aware that he was losing the thread yet again.

"Good heavens, she won't stay there three weeks! Is it really worth it, do you think? She's getting on for seventy-seven, you see. And it's odds on she won't have time to spend all that at home, ten thousand francs. What do you think?"

"Seventy-seven," Antoine echoed, involuntarily working out the dismal reckoning.

He had lost track of the time. The moment you deflect your attention to other people, he had observed, you find a "case." Despite his professional training, his attention always centred so instinctively on himself that, whenever he directed it to others, he had a feeling of its being deflected. This fool is certainly a case, he said to himself; "the Chasle case." He remembered the time when he first met M. Chasle; on a recommendation from the priests at the boys' school, M. Thibault had engaged him for the holidays as the children's tutor. After their return to Paris, enchanted by the tutor's punctuality, he had given him the post of secretary. For eighteen years, Antoine mused, I've seen the little man day after day and yet I know nothing about him!

"My mother is a splendid woman," M. Chasle continued, avoiding his eyes. "You must not think, M. Antoine, that as a family we're nobodies. I may be one—but Mother, not she! She was born to be a great lady, not to the humble life we lead. Still, as the gentlemen at

Saint-Roch so often say, and they've been true friends to us, not forgetting the Curé, who knows M. Thibault by name quite well— 'Every life has its cross,' they say, and it's quite true. It isn't as if I didn't want to do it. I do. If only one could be sure. . . . Ten thousand francs! . . . And then I'd have a quiet little life, as I like it! But, there, she wouldn't stay! And they wouldn't give me back the money. They see to that all right. When you go there they make you sign a long rigmarole, with an official stamp on it, a sort of affidavit. Like at your police-station. But they're cannier than your policemen: they don't write to you after a year, they give nothing back. Not a sou," he repeated with a harsh guffaw. Then, in the same tone, he continued: "And your friend—what did he do? Did he go and get it?"

"The ivory rattle? No, he didn't."

M. Chasle seemed to ponder deeply.

"A child's rattle, well, yes. . . . But money, that's another story. People who lose money in the street are off like a flash to claim it at every police-station in Paris. Shouldn't wonder if some people put in for more than they lost. But what about proving it, eh?"

Antoine did not reply. M. Chasle fixed him with an inquisitorial eye and chuckled. "How about proving it, I'm asking."

"Proving it?" Antoine sounded annoyed. "What about all the particulars they have to specify—how the money was lost, if it was in notes or coin, if——"

"No, not that," M. Chasle broke in excitedly. "They surely wouldn't ask if it was in notes or coin. Details, I grant you. But, anyhow, not that one!" He murmured bemusedly. "No, not that one, most certainly not!"

Antoine glanced at the clock.

"Look here, I don't want to hurry you away but I really must be going."

M. Chasle seemed to waken from a trance and slipped off the chair-arm.

"Many thanks, doctor, for the consultation. I'll go home and put a bandage on . . . and a wad of cotton-wool in my ear. It'll pass off, I'm sure."

Antoine could not help smiling as he watched the little man hopping warily across the polished hall floor. M. Chasle's shoes always creaked, and this was one of the "crosses" of his life. He had consulted a host of bootmakers, tried every shape of click and upper, every kind of sole—leather, felt, and rubber; he had visited pedicures and even (on the advice of a floor-polisher who, on occasion, acted as a waiter) taken his chance with the inventor of an elastic shoe, known as the "Sleuth," specially built for waiters and domestics. But all in vain. Thus he had acquired a habit of walking on tip-toe and, with his beady eyes set in a tiny head and coat-tails flapping on his hips, looked like a wing-clipped magpie.

"There now, I was forgetting!" he exclaimed as he reached the door. "All the shops are shut. Have you any change?"

"For . . . ?"

"For a thousand francs."

"Might have," said Antoine, opening a drawer.

"I don't care to carry such big notes on me," M. Chasle explained. "And, as you happened to speak of people losing money . . . Could you give me ten hundred-franc notes? Or twenty fifties? The fatter the wad is, the safer, so to speak."

"No, I've only two five-hundreds," Antoine said, making as if to close the drawer.

"Better than nothing," said M. Chasle, approaching him. "Quite different, anyhow." He handed Antoine the note which he had just extracted from the lining of his coat, and was about to slip the other two into the same recess when the door-bell rang so stridently that both men jumped and M. Chasle, who had not yet inserted the money in his cache, stammered: "Wait! Wait a bit!"

His features twitched convulsively when he knew the voice for that of his concierge; the man was hammering on the door and shouting:

"Is M. Chasle there?"

Antoine hastily opened to him.

"Is he there?" the man panted. "It's urgent. An accident. The little girl's been run over."

M. Chasle, who had heard the man's words, staggered, and Antoine returned to the room just in time to catch him as he fell. Laying him on the floor, he fanned his face with a wet towel. The old man opened his eyes and tried to stand up.

"Do come quickly, M. Jules," said the man at the door. "I've a taxi waiting."

"Is she dead?" Antoine asked, without pausing to wonder who the little girl might be.

"As near as may be," the man replied under his breath.

Antoine took from a shelf the first-aid kit which he had handy for such emergencies and, suddenly remembering that he had lent Jacques his bottle of iodine, ran to his brother's room, shouting to the concierge:

"Get him into the taxi! Wait for me! I'll come with you."

When the taxi pulled up near the Tuileries in front of the house in the Rue d'Alger where the Chasles lived, Antoine had pieced together, from the concierge's flustered explanations, an outline of the accident. The victim was a little girl who used to meet "M. Jules" each evening on his way back. Had she tried to cross the Rue de Rivoli on this occasion, as M. Jules was late in coming home? A delivery tri-car had knocked her down and passed over her body. A crowd had gathered and a newspaper-vender who was present had recognized the child by her plaited hair, and furnished her address. She had been carried unconscious to the flat.

M. Chasle, crouching in a corner of the taxi, shed no tears, but each new detail drew from him a racking sob, half muffled by the hand he pressed against his mouth.

A crowd still lingered round the doorway. They made way for M. Chasle, who had to be helped up the stairs as far as the top landing by his two companions. A door stood open at the end of a corridor, down which M. Chasle made his way on stumbling feet. The concierge stood back to let Antoine pass, and touched him on the arm.

"My wife, who's got a head on her shoulders, ran off to fetch the young doctor who dines at the restaurant next door. I hope she found him there."

Antoine nodded approval and followed M. Chasle. They crossed a sort of anteroom, redolent of musty cupboards, then two low rooms with tiled floors; the light was dim and the atmosphere stifling despite the open windows giving on a courtyard. In the further room Antoine had to edge round a circular table where a meal for four was laid on a strip of dingy oilcloth. M. Chasle opened a door and, entering a brightly lit room, stumbled forward with a piteous cry:

"Dédette! Dédette!"

"Now, Jules!" a raucous voice protested.

The first thing Antoine noticed was the lamp which a woman in a pink dressing-gown was lifting with both hands; her ruddy hair, her throat and forehead were flooded with the lamplight. Then he observed the bed on which the light fell, and shadowy forms bending above it. Dregs of the sunset, filtering through the window, merged in the halo of the lamp, and the room was bathed in a half-light where all things took the semblance of a dream. Antoine helped M. Chasle to a chair and approached the bed. A young man wearing pince-nez, with his hat still on, was bending forward and slitting up with a pair of scissors the blood-stained garments of the little girl. Her face, ringed with matted hair, lay buried in the bolster. An old woman on her knees was helping the doctor.

"Is she alive?" Antoine asked.

The doctor turned, looked at him, and hesitated; then mopped his forehead.

"Yes." His tone lacked assurance.

"I was with M. Chasle when he was sent for," Antoine explained, "and I've brought my first-aid kit. I'm Dr. Thibault," he added in a whisper, "house-physician at the Children's Hospital."

The young doctor rose and was about to make way for Antoine.

"Carry on! Carry on!" Antoine drew back a step. "Pulse?"

"Almost imperceptible," the doctor replied, intent once more on his task.

Antoine raised his eyes towards the red-haired young woman, saw the anxiety in her face, and made a suggestion.

"Wouldn't it be best to telephone for an ambulance and have your child taken at once to my hospital?"

"No!" an imperious voice answered him.

Then Antoine descried an old woman standing at the head of the bed—was it the child's grandmother?—and scanning him intently with eyes limpid as water, a peasant's eyes. Her pointed nose and resolute features were half submerged in a vast sea of fat that heaved in billowy folds upon her neck.

"I know we look like paupers," she continued in a resigned tone, "but, believe me, even folk like us would rather die at home in our own beds. Dédette shan't go to the hospital."

"But why not, Madame?" Antoine protested.

She straightened up her back, thrust out her chin, and sadly but sternly rebuked him.

"We prefer not," was all she said.

Antoine tried to catch the eye of the younger woman, but she was busy brushing off the flies that obstinately settled on her glowing cheeks, and seemed of no opinion. He decided to appeal to M. Chasle. The old fellow had fallen on his knees in front of the chair to which Antoine had led him; his head was buried on his folded arms as though to shut out all sights from his eyes, and, from his ears, all sounds. The old lady, who was keenly watching Antoine's movements, guessed his intention and forestalled him.

"Isn't that so, Jules?"

M. Chasle started.

"Yes, Mother."

She looked at him approvingly and her voice grew mothering.

"Don't stay there, Jules. You'd be much better in your room."

A pallid forehead rose into view, eyes tremulous behind their spectacles; then, without a protest, the poor old fellow stood up and tip-toed from the room.

Antoine bit his lips. Meanwhile, pending an occasion further to insist, he took off his coat and rolled up his sleeves above the elbows, Then he knelt at the bedside. He seldom took thought without at the same time beginning to take action—such was his incapacity for long deliberation on any issue raised, and such his keenness to be up and doing. The avoidance of mistakes counted less with him than bold decision and prompt activity. Thought, as he used it, was merely the lever that set an act in motion—premature though it might be.

Aided by the doctor and the old woman's trembling hands, he had soon stripped off the child's clothing; pale, almost grey, her body lay beneath their eyes in its frail nakedness. The impact of the car must have been very violent, for she was covered with bruises, and a black streak crossed her thigh transversely from hip to knee.

"It's the right leg," Antoine's colleague observed. Her right foot was twisted, bent inwards, and the whole leg was spattered with blood and deformed, shorter than the other one.

"Fracture of the femur?" suggested the doctor.

Antoine did not answer. He was thinking. "That's not all," he said to himself; "the shock is too great for that. But what can it be?" He tapped her knee-cap, then ran his fingers slowly up her thigh; suddenly there spurted through an almost imperceptible lesion on the inner side of the thigh, some inches above the knee, a jet of blood.

"That's it," he said.

"The femoral artery!" the other exclaimed.

Antoine rose quickly to his feet. The need to make, unaided, a decision gave him a new access of energy and, as ever when others were present, his sense of power intensified. A surgeon? he speculated. No, we'd never get her alive to the hospital. Then who? I? Why not? And, anyhow, there's no alternative.

"Will you try a ligature?" asked the doctor, piqued by Antoine's silence.

But Antoine did not heed his question. It must be done, he was thinking, and without a moment's delay; it may be too late already, who knows? He threw a quick glance round him. A ligature. What can be used? Let's see. The red-headed girl hasn't a belt; no loops on the curtains. Something elastic. Ah, I have it! In a twinkling he had thrown off his waistcoat and unfastened his braces. Snapping them with a jerk, he knelt down again, made with them a tourniquet, and clamped it tightly round the child's groin.

"Good! Two minutes' breathing-time," he said as he rose. Sweat was pouring down his cheeks. He knew that every eye was fixed on him.

"Only an immediate operation," he said decisively, "can save her life. Let's try!"

The others moved away at once from the bed—even the woman with the lamp, even the young doctor, whose face had paled.

Antoine clenched his teeth, his eyes narrowed and grew hard, he seemed to peer into himself. Must keep calm, he mused. A table? That round table I saw, coming in.

"Bring the lamp!" he cried to the young woman, then turned to the doctor. "You there—come with me!" He strode quickly into the next room. Good, he said to himself; here's our operating-theatre. With a quick gesture he cleared the table, stacked the plates in a pile. "That's for my lamp." Like a general in charge of a campaign, he allotted each thing its place. "Now for our little patient." He went back to the bedroom. The doctor and the young woman hung on his every gesture and followed close behind him. Addressing the doctor, he pointed to the child:

"I'll carry her. She's light as a feather. Hold up her leg, you."

As he slipped his arms under the child's back and carried her to the table, she moaned faintly. He took the lamp from the red-haired woman and, removing the shade, stood it on the pile of plates. As he surveyed the scene, a thought came suddenly and went: "I'm a wonderful fellow!" The lamp gleamed like a brazier, reddening the ambient shadow, where only the young woman's glowing cheeks and the doctor's pince-nez showed up as high-lights; its rays fell harshly on the little body, which twitched spasmodically. The swarming flies seemed worked up to frenzy by the oncoming storm. Heat and anxiety brought beads of sweat to Antoine's brow. Would she live through it? he wondered, but some dark force he did not analyse buoyed up his faith; never had he felt so sure of himself.

He seized his bag and, taking out a bottle of chloroform and some gauze, handed the former to the doctor.

"Open it somewhere. On the sideboard. Take off the sewing-machine. Get everything out."

As he turned, holding the bottle, he noticed two dim figures in the dark doorway, the two old women like statues posted there. One,

M. Chasle's mother, had great, staring eyes, an owl's eyes; the other was pressing her breast with her clasped hands.

"Go away!" he commanded. They retreated some steps into the shadows of the bedroom, but he pointed to the other end of the flat. "No. Out of the room. That way." They obeyed, crossed the room, vanished without a word.

"Not you!" he cried angrily to the red-haired woman, who was about to follow them.

She turned on her heel and, for a moment, he took stock of her. She had a handsome, rather fleshy face, touched with a certain dignity, it seemed, by grief; an air of calm maturity that pleased him. Poor woman! he could not help thinking. . . . But I need her!

"You're the child's mother?" he asked.

"No." She shook her head.

"All the better."

As he spoke he had been soaking the gauze and now he swiftly stretched it over the child's nose. "Stand there, and keep this." He handed her the bottle. "When I give the signal, you'll pour some more of it on."

The air grew heavy with the reek of chloroform. The little girl groaned, drew a deep breath or two, grew still.

A last look round. The field was clear; the rest lay with the surgeon's skill. Now that the crucial moment had come, Antoine's anxieties vanished as if by magic. He went to the sideboard where the doctor, holding the bag, was laying on a napkin the last of its contents. "Let's see," he murmured, as though to gain a few seconds' respite. "There's the instrument-box; good. The scalpel, the artery-forceps. A packet of gauze, cotton-wool, that'll do. Alcohol. Caffeine. Tincture of iodine. And so forth. . . . All's ready. Let's begin." And yet again there came to him that sense of buoyancy, of boundless confidence, of vital energies tautened to breaking-point, and, crowning all, a proud awareness of being lifted high above his workaday self.

Raising his head, he looked his junior for a moment in the eyes. "Have you the nerve?" his eyes seemed to inquire. "It's going to be a tough job. Now for it!"

The young man did not flinch. And now he hung on Antoine's gestures with servile assiduity. Well he knew that in this operation lay their only hope, but never would he have dared to take the risk, alone. With Antoine, however, nothing seemed impossible.

He's not so bad, this young chap, thought Antoine. Lucky for me! Let's see. A basin? No matter—this will do as well. Grasping the bottle of iodine he sluiced his arms up to the elbow with the liquid.

"Your turn!" He passed the bottle to the doctor, who was feverishly polishing the lenses of his pince-nez.

A vivid lightning flash, closely followed by a deafening clap of thunder, lit up the window.

"A bit previous, the applause," Antoine said to himself. "I hadn't even taken up my lancet. The young woman didn't turn a hair. It'll cool things down; good for our nerves. Must be pretty nearly a hundred degrees in this room."

He had laid out a series of compresses round the injured limb, delimiting the operative field. Now he turned towards the young woman.

"A whiff of chloroform. That'll do. Right!"

She obeys orders, he mused, like a soldier under fire. Women! Then, fixing his eyes on the swollen little thigh, he swallowed his saliva and raised the scalpel.

"Here goes!"

With one neat stroke he cut the skin.

"Swab!" he commanded the doctor bending beside him. "What a thin child!" he said to himself. "Well, we'll be there all the sooner. Hallo, there's little Dédette starting snoring! Good! Better be quick about it. Now for the retractors."

"Now, you," he said aloud, and the other let fall the blood-stained swabs of cotton-wool and, grasping the retractors, held the wound open.

Antoine paused a moment. "Good!" he murmured. "My probe? Here it is. In Hunter's canal. The classical ligation; all's well. Zip! Another flash! Must have landed pretty near. On the Louvre. Perhaps on the 'gentlemen at Saint-Roch.' " He felt quite calm—no more anxiety for the child, none for death's imminence—and cheerfully repeated under his breath: "The ligature of the femoral artery in Hunter's canal."

Zip! There goes another! Hardly any rain, either. It's stifling. Artery injured at the site of the fracture; the end of the bone tore it open. Simple as anything. Still she hadn't much blood to spare. He glanced at the little girl's face. Hallo! Better hurry up. Simple as anything—but could be fatal, too. A forceps; right! Another; that will do. Zip! These flashes are getting a bore; cheap effect! I've only plaited silk; must make the best of it. Breaking a tube, he pulled out the skein and made a ligature beside each forceps. Splendid! Almost finished now. The collateral circulation will be quite enough, especially at that age. I'm really wonderful! Can I have missed my vocation? I've all the makings of a surgeon, sure enough; a great surgeon. In the silent interval between two thunder-claps dying into the distance, the sharp metallic click of scissors snipping the loose ends of the silk was audible. Yes; quickness of eye, coolness, energy, dexterity. Suddenly he picked up his ears and his cheeks paled.

"The devil!" he muttered under his breath.

The child had ceased to breathe.

Brushing aside the woman, he tore away the gauze from the unconscious child's face and pressed his ear above her heart. Doctor and young woman waited in suspense, their eyes fixed on Antoine.

"No!" he murmured. "She's breathing still."

He took the child's wrist, but her pulse was so rapid that he did not attempt to count it. "Ouf!" He drew a deep breath, the lines of anxiety deepened on his forehead. The two others felt his gaze pass across their faces, but he did not see them.

He rapped out a brief command.

"You, doctor, remove the forceps, put on a dressing, and then undo the tourniquet. Quickly. You, Madame, get me some note-paper—no, you needn't; I've my note-book." He wiped his hands feverishly with a wad of cotton-wool. "What's the time? Not nine yet. The pharmacist's open. You'll have to hurry."

She stood before him, waiting; her tentative gesture—to wrap the dressing-gown more closely round her body—told him of her reluctance at going thus, half dressed, into the streets, and for the fraction of a second a picture of the opulent form under the garment held his imagination. He scribbled a prescription, signed it. "A two-pint am-poule. As quickly as you can."

"And if—?" she stammered.

"If the pharmacist's shut, ring, and keep on hammering on the door till they open. Be quick!"

She was gone. He followed her with his eyes to make sure she was running, then addressed the doctor.

"We'll try the saline. Not subcutaneously; that's hopeless now. Intra-venously. Our last hope." He took two small phials from the sideboard. "You've removed the tourniquet? Right. Give her an injection of camphor to begin with, then the caffeine—only half of it for her, poor kid! Only, for God's sake, be quick about it!"

He went back to the child and took her thin wrist between his fingers; now he could feel nothing more than a vague, restless fluttering. "It's got past counting," he said to himself. And suddenly a feeling of im-potence, of sheer despair, swept over him.

"God damn it!" he broke out. "To think it went off perfectly—and it was all no use!"

The child's face became more livid with every second. She was dying. Antoine observed, beside the parted lips, two slender strands of curling hair, lighter than gossamer, that rose and fell; anyhow, she was breath-ing still.

He watched the doctor giving the injections. Neat with his fingers, he thought, considering his short sight. But we can't save her. Vexation rather than grief possessed him. He had the callousness common to doctors, for whom the sufferings of others count only as so much new experience, or profit, or professional advantage; men to whose fortunes death and pain are frequent ministers.

But then he thought he heard a banging door and ran towards the sound. It was the young woman coming back with quick, lithe steps, trying to conceal her breathlessness. He snatched the parcel from her hands.

"Bring some hot water." He did not even pause to thank her.

"Boiled?"

"No. To warm the solution. Be quick!"

He had hardly opened the parcel when she returned, bringing a steaming saucepan.

"Good! Excellent!" he murmured, but did not look towards her.

No time to lose. In a few seconds he had nipped off the tips of the ampoule and slipped on the rubber tubing. A Swiss barometer in carved wood hung on the wall. With one hand he unhooked it, while with the other he hung the ampoule on the nail. Then he took the saucepan of hot water, hesitated for the fraction of a second, and looped the rubber tubing round the bottom of it. That'll heat the saline as it flows through, he said to himself. Smart idea, that! He glanced towards the other doctor to see if he had noticed what he had done. At last he came back to the child, lifted her inert arm, and sponged it with iodine. Then, with a stroke of his scalpel, he laid bare the vein, slipped his probe beneath it and inserted the needle.

"It's flowing in all right," he cried. "Take her pulse. I'll stay where I am."

The ten minutes that followed seemed an eternity. No one moved or spoke.

Streaming with sweat, breathing rapidly, with knitted brows, Antoine waited, his gaze riveted on the needle. After a while he glanced up at the ampoule.

"How much gone?"

"Nearly a pint."

"The pulse?"

The doctor silently shook his head.

Five more minutes passed, five minutes more of sickening suspense. Antoine looked up again.

"How much left?"

"Just over half a pint."

"And the pulse?"

The doctor hesitated.

"I'm not sure. I almost think . . . it's beginning to come back a little."

"Can you count it?"

A pause.

"No."

If only the pulse came back! sighed Antoine. He would have given ten years of his own life to restore life to this little corpse. Wonder what age she is. Seven? And, if I save her, she'll fall a victim to consumption within the next ten years, living in this hovel. But shall I save her? It's touch and go; her life hangs on a thread. Still—damn it!—I've done all I could. The saline's flowing well. But it's too late. There's nothing more to be done, nothing else to try. We can only wait. . . . That red-haired girl did her bit. A good-looker. She's not the child's mother; who can she be then? Chasle never breathed a word about all these people. Not his daughter, I imagine. Can't make head or tail of it! And that old woman, putting on airs. . . . Anyhow, they made themselves scarce, good riddance! Curious how one suddenly gets them in hand. They all knew the sort of man they had to deal with. The strong hand of a masterful man. But it was up to me to bring it off. Shall I now? No, she lost too much blood on the way here. No signs of improvement so far, worse luck! Oh, damn it all!

His gaze fell on the child's pale lips and the two strands of golden hair, rising and falling still. The breathing struck him as a little better. Was he mistaken? Half a minute passed. Her chest seemed to flutter with a faint sigh which slowly died into the air, as though a fragment of her life were passing with it. For a moment Antoine stared at her in perplexity. No, she was breathing still. Nothing to be done but to wait, and keep on waiting.

A minute later she sighed again, more plainly now.

"How much left?"

"The ampoule's almost empty."

"And the pulse? Coming back?"

"Yes."

Antoine drew a deep breath.

"Can you count it?"

The doctor took out his watch, settled his pince-nez, and, after a minute's silence, announced:

"A hundred and forty. A hundred and fifty, perhaps."

"Better than nothing!" The exclamation was involuntary, for An-

toine was straining every nerve to withstand the flood of huge relief
that surged across his mind. Yet it was not imagination; the improvement was not to be gainsaid. Her breathing was steadier. It was all he
could do to stay where he was; he had a childish longing to sing or
whistle. *Better than nothing tra-la-la*—he tried to fit the words to the
tune that had been haunting him all day. *In my heart tra-la-la. In my
heart sleeps* . . . Sleeps—sleeps *what?* Got it. *The pale moonlight.*

> In my heart sleeps the pale moonlight
> Of a lovely summer night . . .

The cloud of doubt lifted, gave place to radiant joy.

"The child's saved," he murmured. "She's *got to be* saved!"

> . . . a lovely summer night!

"The ampoule's empty," the doctor announced.

"Capital!"

Just then the child, whom his eyes had never left, gave a slight
shudder. Antoine turned almost gaily to the young woman, who,
leaning against the sideboard, had been watching the scene with steady
eyes for the past quarter of an hour.

"Well, Madame!" he cried with affected gruffness. "Gone to sleep,
have we? And how about the hot-water bottle?" He almost smiled at
her amazement. "But, my dear lady, nothing could be more obvious.
A bottle, piping hot, to warm her little toes!"

A flash of joy lit up her eyes as she hastened from the room.

Then Antoine, with redoubled care and gentleness, bent down and
drew out the needle, and with the tips of his fingers applied a compress
to the tiny wound. He ran his fingers along the arm from which the
hand still hung limp.

"Another injection of camphor, old man, just to make sure; and
then we'll have played our last card. Shouldn't wonder," he added
under his breath, "if we've pulled it off." Once more that sense of
power that was half joy elated him.

The woman came back carrying a jar in her arms. She hesitated,
then, as he said nothing, came and stood by the child's feet.

"Not like that!" said Antoine, with the same brusque cheerfulness.

"You'll burn her. Give it here. Just imagine my having to show you how to wrap up a hot-water bottle!"

Smiling now, he snatched up a rolled napkin that caught his eye and, flinging the ring onto the sideboard, wrapped the jar in it and pressed it to the child's feet. The red-haired woman watched him, taken aback by the boyish smile that made his face seem so much younger.

"Then she's—saved?" she ventured to ask.

He dared not affirm it as yet.

"I'll tell you in an hour's time." His voice was gruff, but she took his meaning and cast on him a bold, admiring look.

For the third time Antoine asked himself what this handsome girl could be doing in the Chasle household. Then he pointed to the door.

"What about the others?"

A smile hovered on her lips.

"They're waiting."

"Hearten them up a bit. Tell them to go to bed. You too, Madame, you'd better take some rest."

"Oh, as far as I'm concerned . . ." she murmured, turning to go.

"Let's get the child back to bed," Antoine suggested to his colleague. "The same way as before. Hold up her leg. Take the bolster away; we'd better keep her head down. The next thing is to rig up some sort of a gadget. . . . That napkin, please, and the string from the parcel. Some sort of extension, you see. Slip the string between the rails; handy things these iron bedsteads. Now for a weight. Anything will do. How about this saucepan? No, the flat-iron there will be better. We've all we need here. Yes, hand it over. Tomorrow we'll improve on it. Meanwhile it will do if we stretch the leg a bit, don't you think so?"

The young doctor did not reply. He gazed at Antoine with spellbound awe—the look that Martha may have given the Saviour when Lazarus rose from the tomb. His lips worked and he stammered timidly:

"May I . . . shall I arrange your instruments?" The faltered words breathed such a zeal for service and for devotion that Antoine thrilled with the exultation of an acknowledged chief. They were alone. Antoine went up to the younger man and looked him in the eyes.

"You've been splendid, my dear fellow."

The young man gasped. Antoine, who felt even more embarrassed than his colleague, gave him no time to put in a word.

"Now you'd better be off home; it's late. There's no need for two of us here." He hesitated. "We may take it that she's saved, I think. That's my opinion. However, for safety's safe, I'll stay here for the night, if you'll permit me." The doctor made a vague gesture. "If you permit me, I repeat. For I don't forget that she's your patient. Obviously. I only gave a hand, as there was nothing else for it. That's so, eh? But from tomorrow on I leave her in your hands. They're competent hands and I have no anxiety." As he spoke he led the doctor towards the door. "Will you look in again towards noon? I'll come back when I'm done at the hospital and we will decide on the treatment to follow."

"Sir, it's . . . it's been a privilege for me to . . . to . . ."

Never before had Antoine been "sirred" by a colleague, never before been treated with such deference. It went to his head, like generous wine, and unthinkingly he held out both hands towards the young man. But in the nick of time he regained his self-control.

"You've got a wrong impression," he said in a subdued tone. "I'm only a learner, a novice—like you. Like so many others. Like everyone. Groping our way. We do our best—and that's all there is to it!"

Antoine had looked forward to the young man's exit with something like impatience. To be alone, perhaps. Yet, when he heard approaching footsteps, the young woman's, his face lit up.

"Look here, don't you intend to go to bed?"

"No, doctor."

He did not press her further.

The little girl moaned, was shaken by a hiccup, expectorated.

"Good girl, Dédette," he said. "That's a good girl." He took her pulse. "A hundred and twenty. Steady improvement." He looked at the woman, unsmiling. "I think I can say now that we're out of the wood."

She did not reply, but he felt she had faith in him. He wanted to talk to her and cast about for an opening.

"You were very plucky," he said. Then—as was his wont when he felt shy—he went directly to the point. "What are you here, exactly?"

"I? Nothing. I'm not even a friend of theirs. It's only that I live on the fifth floor, just below."

"But who is the child's mother then? I can't make head or tail of it."

"Her mother is dead, I think. She was Aline's sister."

"Aline?"

"The servant."

"The old thing with the shaky hands?"

"Yes."

"So the child's not in any way related to the Chasles?"

"No. Aline's bringing up her little niece here—M. Jules pays, of course."

They spoke in undertones, bending a little towards each other, and Antoine had a nearer view of her lips and cheeks, and the pale beauty of her skin, touched with a curious glamour by fatigue. He felt over-tired and restless, at the mercy of every impulse.

The child stirred in her sleep. As they approached the bed together her eyelids fluttered, then closed again.

"Perhaps the light worries her," the young woman suggested, taking the lamp and placing it further from the bed. Then, returning to the bedside, she wiped the beads of perspiration from the child's forehead. Antoine followed her movements with his eyes and, as she stooped, he felt a sudden thrill; outlined as in a shadow-play under the flimsy dressing-gown, the young woman's body was silhouetted, frankly pro-vocative as if she stood naked before him. He held his breath; a dark fire seemed to sear his eyes, watching through misty shadows the lan-guid rise and fall of her bosom, rhythmed to her breath. Antoine's hands grew suddenly cold as ice, contracted as in a spasm. Never before with such an urgency of passion had he desired another human being.

"Mlle. Rachel," a voice whispered.

She drew herself up.

"It's Aline; she wants to come and see the child."

Smiling, she seemed to plead the servant's cause and, though vexed
by the intrusion, he dared not deny her.

"So your name's Rachel," he stammered. "Yes, let her come."

He hardly noticed the old woman kneeling beside the bed. He went
to an open window; his temples were throbbing. No cooling breeze
came from without; far above the housetops the distant glimmer of a
star or two spangled the darkness. Now at length he realized his weariness; he had been on his feet for three or four hours on end. He
looked round for a seat. Between the windows two small mattresses
resting on the tiled floor formed a sort of couch. Here, no doubt, Dédette usually slept; the room was evidently Aline's bedroom. He sank
onto the pallet, propping his back against the wall, and again an uncontrollable desire swept over him—to see once again, half veiled beneath
the tenuous fabric, Rachel's firm breasts, their rhythmic rise and fall.
But she was no longer standing in the light.

"Didn't the child move her leg?" he inquired without rising. As she
walked towards the bed, her body lithely swayed beneath the wrap.

"No."

Antoine's lips were parched and he still felt a burning at the sockets
of his eyes. How could he lure Rachel out into the lamplight?

"Is she still as pale as she was?"

"A little less."

"Move her head straight, will you? Quite flat and straight."

Now she stepped into the zone of light, but only for a moment, as
she passed between the lamp and Antoine. The moment sufficed, however, to quicken his desire anew. He had to shut his eyes, jam his back
against the wall and thus remain, clenching his teeth, struggling to keep
his eyelids closed upon their secret vision. The stench of cities in the
summer, a mingled reek of horse-dung, smoke, and dusty asphalt,
stifled the air. Flies pattered on the lampshade, hovered on Antoine's
damp cheeks. Now and again thunder rumbled still, above the remoter
suburbs.

Little by little, fever, heat and the very urgency of his emotion sapped
his powers of resistance. He was unconscious of the slow tide of

lethargy advancing; his muscles relaxed, his shoulders settled down against the wall, he fell asleep. . . .

It was as if a summons, gently insistent, were calling him from sleep and, still on the verge of dreams, he was vaguely aware of a pleasurable feeling. For a long while he hovered in an ecstatic limbo, unable to discover by what channel and at what point on the surface of his body the warm tide of well-being was seeping in. Presently he traced it to his leg and, at the same moment, grew conscious that someone was seated at his side; that the warmth along his thigh emanated from a living body; that this warmth and the body were Rachel's and the sensation was really one of sensual pleasure, enhanced now that he knew its origin. Her body must have slipped towards him as she slept. He had self-control enough to sit quite still. . . . Now he was wide-awake. All the feelings of his body were centred in a little space, no wider than a hand's breadth, where, across the thin covering of their garments, thigh touched thigh. He stayed thus, motionless, breathing rapidly yet fully lucid, finding in the mingling of his body's warmth with hers a thrill more potent than the subtlest of caresses.

Suddenly Rachel awoke and stretched her arms; drawing away from him, but without haste, she sat up. He made as if he, too, were just awaking, roused by her movement.

"I dozed off," she confessed with a smile.

"So did I."

"It's almost daylight," she murmured as she raised her arms to settle her hair.

Antoine glanced at his watch; it was just on four.

The child lay all but motionless. Aline's hands were clasped, as if in prayer. Antoine went to the bed and drew aside the blankets.

"Not a drop of blood—that's good."

While his eyes followed Rachel's movements, he took the child's pulse; a hundred and ten.

How warm her leg was! he was thinking.

Rachel was examining her reflection in a strip of looking-glass,

tacked with three nails to the wall, and smiling. With her shock of
red hair, open collar, strong bare arms, and her bold, free-and-easy,
slightly scornful air, she might have stood for a heroine of the Revolution, a Marseillaise on the barricades.

"I'm a fine sight!" She pouted at her reflected self, though well aware
that the young bloom of her cheeks lost, even in the acid test of
waking, nothing of its charm. This was plain to read on Antoine's face
as, moving to her side, he peered into the mirror. She noticed that the
young man's gaze fastened not on her eyes, but on her lips.

But then Antoine took stock of his own appearance—sleeves rolled
up, arms burnt with iodine, his shirt crumpled and stained with blood.

"And to think I was due to dine at Packmell's!" he exclaimed.

A curious smile flickered on Rachel's face.

"Say! So you go to Packmell's sometimes?"

Their eyes were smiling, and Antoine's heart leapt with joy. He knew
little of women other than those of easy virtue. Now suddenly Rachel
seemed to become less inaccessible to his desire.

"I'll go downstairs to my flat," she said and turned to Aline, who was
watching them. "If I can be of any help, don't hesitate to call me."

Then, without bidding Antoine good-bye, she drew the flaps of her
dressing-gown together and discreetly made her exit.

No sooner had she gone than he too felt a wish to leave. "A breath of
fresh air," he murmured, glancing over the housetops towards the
morning sky. "Must go home too, and explain to Jacques. I can return
when I've done with the hospital. Washed, presentable. Might have
them send for her to help with the dressing. Or shall I look in on my
way up? But I don't even know if she's living by herself."

He explained to Aline what to do, should the child wake before his
return. Then, just as he was leaving, a scruple held him back; how
about M. Chasle?

"His room opens into the hall alongside the stove," the servant
explained.

Antoine discovered a cupboard door beside the stove, answering to
her description. Opening it, he saw a triangular recess, lit from the far

end by a makeshift window let into the party-wall of the staircase. This
was the so-called bedroom. M. Chasle lay fully dressed on an iron
bedstead, his mouth wide open, placidly snoring.

"Sure enough, the old loon's plugged his ears with cotton-wool!"
Antoine exclaimed.

He decided to wait a minute or two, hoping the old fellow would
decide to open his eyes. Pious pictures on coloured cardboard mounts
lined the walls. Books—devotional, too—filled a whatnot, on whose
topmost shelf stood a terrestrial globe, flanked by two rows of empty
scent-bottles.

"The Chasle case!" I've a mania for seeing "cases" everywhere,
Antoine reflected. Nothing complex about him, really; a second-hand
face and a fool's life! Whenever I try to see into people, I distort,
exaggerate. Bad habit! That servant-girl at Toulouse, for instance. Now
why should I think of her? Because her bedroom window opened onto
a staircase, too? No; must be the stale smell of toilet-soap. Funny
things, associations of ideas! . . . He was conscious of a vivid sense
of pleasure in recalling that juvenile experience; the chambermaid with
whom, when travelling with his father to attend a congress, he had
passed a night in an attic room at a hotel. And, at this very minute, he
would have given much to possess the buxom maid as he had known
her then between the rough sheets of her bed.

M. Chasle went on snoring. Antoine decided not to wait, and returned to the hall.

No sooner had he begun to descend the stairs than he remembered
that Rachel occupied the floor below. Coming round the bend of the
stairs, he glanced down towards her door; it was open! No other door
was visible, so it must be hers. Why was it open?

No time to hesitate; it would seem odd if he halted on the way down.
Soon he was on her landing.

Rachel was in the hall of her flat and, hearing footsteps outside,
glanced round. Her hair was tidy, she looked neat and cool. The pink
dressing-gown had given place to a white kimono. Above its silken
whiteness her red hair glowed like the flame upon an altar candle.

He addressed her first:

"*Au revoir!*"

She came to the door. "Won't you come in, doctor, and have something before going out? I've just made some chocolate."

"No, really, thanks—I'm too filthy to come in. *Au revoir!*"

He held out his hand. A smile hovered on her lips, but she did not imitate his gesture.

"*Au revoir!*" he repeated. Smiling still, she still refrained from taking his proffered hand, to his surprise. "You won't shake hands with me then?"

He saw the smile freeze on her lips, her eyes grow set. Then she held out her hand. But, before Antoine could touch it, she had grasped him firmly and, with a brusqué movement, drawn him over the threshold. She slammed the door behind them. They stood in the hall facing each other. She had ceased to smile, but her lips were parted still; he saw the white gleam of her teeth. The perfume of her hair drifted towards him and he remembered a naked breast, the warm contact of her limbs. Deliberately, he brought his face near to Rachel's, his eyes bored into hers, grown large in nearness. She did not flinch; he felt, or seemed to feel, her wavering in his embrace and it was she who raised her lips to his mouth's kiss. Then with an effort she drew back from Antoine and stood with lowered head, smiling again.

"A night like that works you up . . . !" she murmured.

Through an open door at the far end of the passage he had a glimpse of a bed and, all about it, the glimmer of pink silk; under the waxing light the alcove, distant and so near, seemed the great calyx of a flower aglow there in the dawn.

IV

ON THE same morning, at about half-past eleven, Rachel knocked at the Chasles' door.

"Come in!" a shrill voice answered.

Mme. Chasle was at her wonted place beside the open window of the dining-room. She sat stiffly erect, her feet resting on a hassock, her hands, as usual, unemployed. "I'm ashamed of doing nothing," she sometimes explained, "but there comes a time of life when one can't go on slaving oneself to death for others."

"How is the little girl?" Rachel inquired.

"She woke up, had something to drink, and went to sleep again."

"Is M. Jules in?"

"No, he's out," Mme. Chasle replied with a shrug of resignation.

Rachel felt chagrined.

"All the morning," the old woman lamented, "he's been going on like—like a mosquito! Sunday's such a dreadful day with a man about the place. I hoped this accident would teach him to treat us better. No such luck! The first thing this morning I could see he had something else on his mind, the Lord knows what! Nosing around, and don't I know that way of his? These fifty years now I've had to put up with it anyhow. He left for high mass more than an hour too early. Now that's a queer thing, and no mistake. And he's not back yet. Look there!" Her lips set tight. "There he comes! Talk of the devil . . . Really, please, Jules," she continued, craning her neck towards her son, who had just tip-toed in, "don't bang the doors like that! Not only because of my heart trouble; there's Dédette as well to think of now—you'll be the death of her."

But M. Chasle showed no contrition; he looked worried and absent-minded.

"Let's go and see how she is," Rachel suggested. No sooner were they at the bedside of the sleeping child than she put a question to him. "Have you known him long—Dr. Thibault, I mean?"

"What?" M. Chasle exclaimed with a look of consternation. Then he began to smile knowingly and, "What?" he murmured again, like an echo. After a pause he brusquely turned towards her as though he had a secret to impart.

"Look here, Mlle. Rachel, you've been so kind about Dédette that I'm going to ask a small favour of you. I was so put out by that business that I seem to have lost my head this morning; honestly I must go back there. At once. But it's—it's awkward going back a second time to that office of theirs all by myself. Don't say no!" he implored. "I give you my word of honour that it won't last more than ten minutes."

Smiling, she assented, though she had no notion what he might mean. She foresaw amusement in humouring the old man's foibles and meant to seize the opportunity of putting further questions concerning Antoine. But all the way he was deaf to her inquiries and did not open his mouth once.

It was well after noon when they reached the police-station. The inspector had just left. M. Chasle seemed so upset by his absence that the police clerk was nettled.

"I can do it for you just as well, you know. What exactly do you want?"

M. Chasle cast a furtive glance towards him and, lacking the courage to draw back, embarked on explanations.

"It's because I've been thinking things over. I want to add something to my statement."

"What statement?"

"I came here this morning—I reported at the other end of the counter, over there."

"What name? I'll turn up the file."

Her curiosity aroused, Rachel came and stood beside M. Chasle. The clerk returned in a moment with some papers; he gave the old man a shrewd look.

"Chasle? Jules-Auguste? That your name? Well, what do you want?"

"It's like this. I fear the inspector didn't quite gather where I found the money."

"In the Rue de Rivoli," the clerk replied, after perusing the record.

M. Chasle smiled as though he had just won a wager.

"You see! No, that's not quite right. I revisited the spot and some details came back which might be helpful, you know; one's got to be quite honest, eh?" He coughed into his hand. "It's this. I can't be quite sure that it was in the street; more likely in the Tuileries. Yes. I was in the garden, you see. I was sitting on a stone bench—the second from the news-stand on the way from the Concorde to the Louvre. I was sitting there with my stick in my hand. You'll see why I lay stress on this point. I saw a gentleman and lady passing in front of me, with a child following. They were talking. I remember saying to myself: 'Well, there's a couple that have managed to set up a family . . . a child and so forth.' You see, I'm telling you everything. Then, just when he was passing my bench, the child fell down and started crying. I'm not used to handling these delicate situations, so I didn't budge. The child's mother ran up. And then, when they were just in front, almost at my feet—not my fault, was it?—she knelt down to wipe the child's face and took a handkerchief or something of the kind from the little bag she was carrying. I remained seated. Well"—he raised his index finger—"it was after they had gone that, poking about in the sand with my stick, with the ferrule, you know, I happened to see the money. It all came back to me afterwards. I've always kept straight, as people say. This young lady will tell you so. Fifty-two years old and nothing on my conscience; and that's what *tells,* eh? So there's no need to beat about the bush. I've come to think that perhaps the lady with the little bag may have some connexion or other with this business of the money; and I tell you honestly what I think."

"Couldn't you have run after them?" Rachel asked.

"They had gone too far."

The police clerk looked up from his papers.

"Well, can you describe their appearance?"

"I'm not sure about the gentleman. The lady, I know, wore dark clothes; looked thirty or thereabouts. The baby had a steam-engine. Yes, I'm sure about that detail—a little locomotive. Well, when I say 'little' I mean about *that* size. He was dragging it behind him. You're taking it all down?"

"That's all right. Anything more?"

"No."

"Thank you."

Rachel was already near the door. But M. Chasle did not follow her. Leaning on the counter, he stared at the clerk.

"There's another little detail." A deep blush came over his face. "I rather think I made a slight mistake when I handed in the money this morning. Yes." He paused and wiped his brow. "I rather think I made over two notes, didn't I? Yes, yes. I'm sure of it now. That was a little mistake—an oversight, I should say. Because . . . well, you know . . . the money I found wasn't exactly that. It was a single note, a thousand-franc note, do you see?" His face was pouring with sweat and once again he passed his handkerchief over his brow. "Make a note of that, now that I remember it—though, in a way, it comes to the same thing, really."

"It doesn't come to the same thing by any means," the clerk replied. "On the contrary, it's an important point. The gentleman who lost a thousand-franc note might have come to us a dozen times but we shouldn't have given him back the two five-hundreds." He stared at M. Chasle disapprovingly. "Look here, have you your identification papers with you?"

M. Chasle fumbled in his pockets.

"No."

"This won't do at all. I regret it, but under the circumstances I cannot let the matter drop. An officer will go with you to your residence and your concierge will have to certify that the name and address you gave are not fictitious."

A mood of resignation seemed to have come over M. Chasle, for, though he continued to mop his face, his expression was serene, almost cheerful.

"Just as you please," he said politely.

Rachel burst out laughing. M. Chasle cast a mournful glance at her; then, after a moment's hesitation, he nerved himself to approach her and address her haltingly.

"Sometimes, Mademoiselle, there lies beneath the plain coat of a mere nobody a nobler heart—and when I say 'nobler' I mean 'more honest,' too—than under the silk lapels of one of the great ones of the earth, for all his name and titles." His underlip quivered; no sooner had he spoken than he regretted the outburst. "I don't mean that for you, Mademoiselle, nor for you, officer," he added, turning without the least timidity towards the policeman who had just entered.

Rachel left M. Chasle and the policeman to their explanations in the concierge's room and went up to her flat.

Antoine was waiting for her on the landing.

She was far from expecting to meet him there and, when she saw him, a sudden thrill of pleasure made her half close her eyes, but hardly showed at all upon her face.

"I rang and rang. I'd almost given up hope," he confessed.

Gaily their glances met and their lips smiled a mutual avowal.

"What are your plans for this morning?" he asked. He was delighted to find her so smart in her summery tailor-made and flower-trimmed hat.

"This morning! But it's after one. And I haven't had lunch yet."

"Nor have I." He came to a sudden decision. "Will you have lunch with me? Say yes!" She smiled, charmed by his eagerness, as of a greedy child who has not learned self-control.

"Say yes!"

"All right then . . . yes!"

"Good!" he exclaimed. He took a deep breath. She opened the door of her flat.

"Just a moment; I must let my charwoman know, and pack her off home."

As he waited alone outside her door, his emotion of that morning when she had moved towards him came back in all its intensity. "Ah, how she gave me her lips!" he murmured, and was so carried away that he steadied himself with his hand against the wall.

Rachel returned.

"Come along! I'm ravenous!" she cried, with a smile of almost animal eagerness.

"Would you rather go down by yourself?" he ventured awkwardly. "I can join you in the street."

She burst out laughing.

"By myself? Why? I'm quite free and make no secret of anything I do."

They entered the Rue de Rivoli. Once again Antoine observed the easy rhythm of her steps; she seemed to dance along rather than walk.

"Where would you like to go?" he inquired.

"Why not try that place over there? It's getting late, you know." She indicated with her parasol a small restaurant at the street corner.

The room on the mezzanine was empty; small tables were alined in a semicircle beside the windows that opened onto a covered-in arcade and, extending downwards to the sidewalk level, lighted the room from an unusual angle. Here the air was cool, the twilight never varied. They sat down facing each other with the air of two children starting to play a game.

"Why, I don't even know your name!" Antoine suddenly exclaimed.

"Rachel Goepfert. Age: twenty-six. Chin: oval. Nose: medium . . ."

"And all her teeth?"

"See for yourself!" she laughed, falling upon the sliced sausage in the hors d'œuvre dish.

"Better be careful. I suspect garlic in it."

"What about it?" she laughed again. "I'm all for anything that's low!"

Goepfert . . . A Jewess, very likely; and, with the thought, a dusty residue of his upbringing stirred in Antoine's mind, adding a spice of the exotic, a piquant independence to the adventure.

"My father was a Jew," she announced as if she had read the young man's thought.

A white-cuffed waitress brought the menu.

"A mixed grill?" Antoine suggested.

A most unexpected smile, which obviously she was unable to control, lit up Rachel's face.

"What are you smiling at? It's jolly good. A lot of tasty things from the grill—kidneys, bacon, sausages, cutlets . . ."

"With water-cress and puffed potatoes," the waitress put in as a garnish.

"I know. That'll do for me." The merriment which she had momentarily repressed seemed once again to sparkle in her enigmatic eyes.

"What will you drink?"

"Beer, please."

"So will I. Off the ice."

He watched her nibble the leaves of a tiny raw artichoke.

"I love things with a taste of vinegar," she confessed.

"So do I."

He wanted to resemble her and could hardly refrain from breaking in with a "So do I!" after each remark she made. In all she said and did she was the woman of his dreams. She dressed exactly as he had always wished a woman to dress. A necklace of old amber was round her neck, and the heavy beads hung in long translucent ovals like pulpy fruit, huge Malaga grapes or golden plums aglow with sunlight. Behind the amber her skin took on a milk-white sheen that stirred his senses. Gazing at her, Antoine felt like a starved jungle creature whose raging hunger nothing, nothing could ever quiet. As he recalled their kiss, the pressure of her lips on his, his pulses raced. And here she was, under his eyes—the selfsame Rachel!

Two mugs of foaming beer were set before them. He and she were equally impatient to taste it. Antoine amused himself by timing his gestures with hers, never taking his eyes off her; at the same moment as he felt the soapy, pungent brew lapping his tongue and thawing on it, an icy draught flowed cool on Rachel's tongue—and it was as if their mouths were mingled once again. The emotion left him dazed with pleasure and a minute passed before he caught what she was saying.

". . . and those women treat him like a menial."

He pulled himself together.

"What women?"

"His mother and the servant." He realized that Rachel was speaking of the Chasles. "The old woman always addresses him as 'Woolly Head'!"

"Well, you must admit that she's not far out."

"No sooner is he back than she starts badgering him about. Each morning he has to clean their shoes—even the child's shoes—on the landing."

"What, the old boy?" Antoine smiled as he recalled another picture: the worthy Chasle writing to M. Thibault's dictation or solemnly receiving in his employer's stead some colleague from the Institute of Moral Science.

"And they join forces to bleed him dry; why, they even filch the money from his pockets, pretending they're brushing his coat before he leaves. Last year the old woman signed I.O.U.'s for three or four thousand francs, forging her son's signature. The old man nearly fell ill with the shock of it."

"What did he do?"

"Why, he forked up of course. In six months, by instalments. He dared not give his mother away."

"And to think we see him every day, yet nothing of that sort ever entered our heads!"

"You've never been to his place before?"

"Never."

"Nowadays their home looks poverty-stricken. But you should have seen how the little flat looked even two years ago; with the tiled floor, the panelling and cupboards, you'd think you were back in the time of Voltaire. Inlaid furniture, family portraits, even some fine old silver plate."

"What's become of it?"

"The two women disposed of it behind his back. One evening when the old man came home the Louis XVI davenport had decamped; another day it was the tapestry, the easy chairs, the miniatures. They even sold the portrait of his grandfather—a fine figure of a man in uniform, with a cocked hat on his head and a map open in front of him."

"A distinguished soldier, perhaps?"

"Yes, he'd made a name for himself. He saw service under La-fayette in America."

He noticed that she was voluble, but had the knack of expressing herself well. The details she gave had local colour. Obviously she had brains, but, above all, a mental outlook, a gift for noting and re-membering facts, that pleased him.

"He never breathes a word of complaint," Antoine remarked, "when he's with us at home."

"No doubt—yet I've come across him time and time again when he'd crept out onto the stairs to hide his tears."

"Well, I'd never have believed it!" he exclaimed, and there was such vivacity in his look and smile that her thoughts veered from her narra-tive towards the young man himself.

"Are they really so terribly hard up?" he asked.

"Not a bit of it! The two old women are hoarding all the money; they've hidden it away somewhere. And, I assure you, they're lavish enough where they themselves are concerned; but they read him a curtain-lecture if he dares to buy a few gumdrops. The stories I could tell you of what goes on in that flat! Aline wanted—guess what!— to get the old fellow to marry her. Don't laugh! She nearly brought it off, too. The old woman was backing her up. But, luckily enough, one day they fell out."

"And Chasle, did he agree?"

"Oh, he'd have ended by giving in, because of Dédette. That child is all the world to him. When they want to squeeze something out of him they threaten to send her away to Aline's home in Savoie; then he starts crying, and gives way all along the line."

He hardly heard what Rachel was saying; he watched the move-ments of the mouth that he had kissed—a well-shaped mouth, fleshy at its centre and clean-cut as an incision at the edges. When in repose, the corners of her lips lifted a little, poised in a smile that was not mocking but serene and gay.

So far were his thoughts from the sorrows of M. Chasle that he murmured under his breath: "I'm a lucky chap, you know!" and blushed.

She burst out laughing. Last night beside the operating-table, she had gauged this man's true worth, and now she was enchanted to discover that he was half a child; it brought him nearer to her.

"Since when?" she asked him.

He equivocated.

"Since this morning."

Yet it was true enough. He recalled his feelings when he left Rachel's place and plunged into the sunlight of the streets; never had he felt in such fine fettle. In front of the Font-Royal, he remembered, the traffic had been dense, but he had launched himself athwart it with amazing coolness, murmuring to himself as he threaded his way through the moving maze of vehicles: "How sure of myself I am, how well I have my energies in hand! And some people tell you there's no free will!"

"Let me help you to a fried mushroom," he suggested.

She answered him in English.

"With pleasure."

"So you speak English?"

"Rather! *Si son vedute cose più straordinarie.*"

"Italian, too. How about German?"

"*Aber nicht sehr gut.*"

He reflected for a moment. "So you've travelled?"

She repressed a smile. "A bit." There was an enigmatic quality in her voice that made him scan her face intently.

"What was I saying . . . ?" he murmured vaguely.

But their words little mattered—there was a strange telepathy at work, in every look and smile, in their least gestures and their voices.

After a long look at him she exclaimed:

"How different you are today from the man I watched last night!"

"I assure you it's one and the same man." He raised his hands still stained with iodine. "But just now I can show off my surgical abilities on nothing better than a cutlet."

"I had a good look at you last night, you know."

"And what was your impression?"

She was silent.

"Was it the first time you'd witnessed a performance of that kind?"
She stared at him, hesitated, then began to laugh.

"The first time?" she echoed, and her voice implied: I've seen a
good many things in my time! But she turned the question adroitly.

"And do *you* have operations like that every day?"

"Never. I don't go in for surgery. I'm a physician, a child-specialist."

"But why aren't you a surgeon? With your ability . . ."

"I suppose it wasn't my vocation."

They were silent for a moment; her words had conjured up a vague
regret.

"Pshaw! A doctor or a surgeon!" he exclaimed. "People have a lot
of false ideas about 'vocations.' Men always imagine they have chosen
their vocation. But it's circumstances . . ." She saw his face masked
for a moment by the resolute look which had so deeply moved her
at the child's bedside. "What's the good," he continued, "of raking
up the ashes? The path we have chosen is always the best one, provided it enables us to go ahead." Then suddenly his thoughts returned
to the handsome girl seated in front of him and the place that in a
few brief hours she had made for herself in his life. A shade of apprehension crossed his face. That's all very fine, he thought, but first of
all I must make sure this business won't handicap my work, my
future. . . .

She saw the shadow on his brow.

"You're terribly headstrong, I should say."

He smiled.

"Look here, don't laugh at what I'm going to tell you. For many
years my motto was a Latin word, *Stabo:* I will stand firm. I had it
stamped on my note-paper and the first pages of my books." He drew
forth his watch-chain. "I even had it engraved on this old seal which
I still wear."

She examined the pendant he showed her.

"It's very pretty."

"Really? You like it?"

She caught his meaning and handed it back to him.

"No."

But he had already undone the clasp.

"Do, please. . . ."

"But what's come over you?"

"Rachel. To remind you . . ."

"Of what?"

"Of everything."

"Everything?" she repeated, her eyes still fixed on his, and laughing heartily.

Adorable she looks just now, he thought. It's charming too, that unrestrained smile of hers, that almost boyish smile. She was as different from the "professionals" he had known as from the girls or married women who had crossed his path in society functions or at holiday resorts, and whom he always found intimidating, seldom attractive. Rachel did not intimidate him; he met her upon an equal footing. She had the pagan charm and even a little of the frankness one finds in harlots who like their calling; but in Rachel that charm had nothing furtive or vulgar about it. How delightful she is! he thought, and saw in her more than an ideal playmate; for the first time in his life he had encountered a woman who might be a friend, a comrade, to him.

The idea had been simmering in his mind all the morning and he had built a castle in the air, a new design of life, in which Rachel had her place. One thing only was lacking: the consent of the other party to the contract. And now he was burning with childish impatience to take her hands and say: "You are the woman I have waited for. I want to have done with casual adventures. But, as I loathe uncertainty, I'd like our mutual relations settled once for all. You shall be my mistress. Let's fix things up accordingly." Now and again he had conveyed a hint of such designs and let fall a word or two touching their future, but always she had seemed to miss his meaning. Knowing her non-committal attitude was deliberate, he hesitated to let her into his plans.

"This is a nice place, isn't it?" she observed, nibbling at a cluster of crystallized red-currants which stained her lips with carmine.

"Yes, it's worth making a note of. In Paris you can find everything, even the atmosphere of a country town." He pointed to the empty tables. "And no risk of meeting anyone."

"Don't you want to be seen with me?"

"Oh, come now! I was thinking about you, of course."

She shrugged her shoulders.

"About me?" That he should find her so mysterious delighted her and she was in no hurry to make things clearer. But his unspoken anxiety was writ so large upon his face that she could not but confess: "As I told you, I'm absolutely on my own. I have enough to live on in a simple way and want nothing more. I am quite free."

His anxious, drawn expression relaxed with frank relief. She guessed the meaning he read into her words: I am yours for the asking. It would have revolted her in any other man, but she had a genuine liking for Antoine. The pleasure of feeling that he desired her outweighed whatever irritation she might feel at his complete misjudgment of her.

Coffee was served. She was silent, lost in thought. For she, too, had not failed to weigh the chances of an understanding between them; indeed she had caught herself thinking only a moment earlier: "I'll get him to shave off that beard!" All the same, he was a stranger to her and, after all, if she felt drawn towards him now, so she had felt to others in the past. He must, she thought, make no mistake about it, must not go on looking at her as he now did with as much complacency as hunger in his eyes.

"A cigarette?"

"No, thanks. I have my own—they're milder."

He held a match to her cigarette. She puffed a cloud of smoke towards him.

"Thanks."

Yes, she mused, the big thing was to avoid all misunderstanding, from the start. She could speak all the more freely because she knew she ran no risk. She moved her cup forward a little, rested her elbows on the tablecloth, her chin on her locked fingers. Her eyelids, puckered with the smoke, almost completely veiled her eyes.

"I say that I am free." She weighed her words. "But that doesn't mean I'm—in the market! You see the point?"

Antoine was wearing his tragic air.

"I must tell you that I've been through the mill, I haven't always had my independence; two years ago I hadn't it. But now I've got it —and I mean to keep it." (She believed she spoke sincerely.) "I set so much store by my freedom that for nothing in the world would I abandon it. Do you follow me?"

"Yes."

Now they were silent. He watched her intently. Her eyes were averted; there was the ghost of a smile on her lips as she stirred her coffee.

"What's more—to speak quite frankly—it's not in me to be a real friend to a man, or even his trusted mistress. I like to indulge all my whims—every one of them. And for that you have to be free. . . . You see what I mean?" With an air of unconcern she raised her cup and drank the coffee in little, scalding sips.

For a moment Antoine felt quite desperate. The bitter end! . . . But no, there she was still in front of him; the battle was not lost, far from it! To give up anything on which his heart was set was quite beyond him; he had no precedents for failure. Anyhow there was no mistaking how things lay, and that was better than mirage. When one has all the facts, action can be taken. Never for an instant did it cross his mind that she might possibly slip through his fingers or meet his projects for their future with a blank refusal. That was Antoine's way: he never doubted he would gain his end.

The main thing was to get to know her better, to rend the veils that still enveloped her.

"So two years ago you were not free?" His tone was frankly inquisitive. "And are you really free now, now and for the future?"

Rachel looked him all over as if he were a child, while a shade of irony hovered on her face, as though she said: "If I answer, it's only because I choose to do so."

"The man with whom I used to live," she explained, "has settled in the Sudan. He will never return to France." She ended her explanation with a faint, soundless laugh and averted her eyes. Then, as though to close the subject once for all, she rose from her seat.

"Let's go!"

When they were outside she took a street leading to the Rue d'Alger. Antoine walked beside her saying nothing, wondering what to do. He could not bring himself to leave her so soon.

When they had reached the street door, Rachel came to the rescue. "Will you have a look at Dédette?" she asked. Then, taking herself up, she added: "But what am I thinking of? Very likely you've somewhere else to go."

As a matter of fact Antoine had promised to return to Passy in the afternoon to visit the sick child there. Moreover, he had to go over the proofs of a report that his chief had sent him that morning, asking him to check the references. More important still, he was due to dine that evening at Maisons-Laffitte and meant to keep the appointment; he had firmly resolved to arrive there early so as to have a chat with Jacques before dinner. But all those good resolves went up in smoke, the moment he saw a possibility of staying in Rachel's company.

"I'm free all day," he boldly lied, making way for her to enter.

Qualms for the duties left undone, the upset to his scheme of life, glanced lightly off his conscience. So much the worse for them! . . . So much the better for me! he all but thought.

They climbed the stairs in silence.

At the door of her flat, as she put her key in the lock, she turned towards him. His features were aglow with candid, undisguised desire; desire untrammelled, jubilant, and not to be frustrated.

V

JACQUES had rushed home from Packmell's at headlong speed. When his concierge informed him that M. Antoine had been called away for an accident, his superstitious fears vanished into air, leaving him vexed with his credulity—that he had thought a passing fancy for a mourning suit could have brought about his brother's death. The absence of the bottle of iodine which he needed for his boil was the last straw; he undressed in the mood of vague but fierce resentment which he knew only too well and always bitterly regretted as unworthy of him. For a long time he could not sleep; he got no joy of his success.

Next morning Antoine met Jacques at the street door, when the latter was just setting out for Maisons-Laffitte, having decided not to await his brother's return. Antoine gave him a rapid account of the past night's happenings, but did not breathe a word about Rachel. His eyes were bright and there was a combative expression on his face which his brother put down to the strain of the operation.

The church-bells were ringing full peal when Jacques left the Maisons-Laffitte station. There was no need to hurry: M. Thibault never missed high mass, nor did Gisèle and Mlle. de Waize. He had ample time for a stroll before going to the house. The warm shadows in the park were an invitation to saunter. The avenues were empty. He sat down on a bench. No sounds broke the stillness but the hum of insects in the grass, and the sudden whir of sparrows as, one by one, they left the branches above his head. He sat unmoving, a smile on his lips, thinking of nothing in particular, glad simply to be there.

The ancient domain of Maisons, bordering the forest of Saint-Germain-en-Laye, was bought under the Restoration by Laffitte, who sold off the fifteen hundred acres of the park in parcels, reserving only the château for his use. But the financier saw to it that the dispersion of the estate did not impair the grandiose vistas that radiated from the château, and that damage to the standing timber should be reduced to a minimum. Thanks to his foresight, Maisons remained a vast seigniorial domain; its avenues of lime-trees hundreds of years old offered magnificent approaches to a whole colony of small estates, unwalled and nestling in the woods.

M. Thibault's summer residence lay north-east of the château in a grassy clearing, ringed with white palings and the shade of immemorial trees; in the middle of the greensward a round pond gleamed, set off by shrubberies of box.

Jacques made his way slowly towards this green retreat. As the house came into view in the far distance, he discerned a white dress pressed against the garden gate: Gisèle was looking out for him. Her eyes were fixed on the station road and she did not see him coming. Thrilled with sudden joy, he began to run. Then she saw him and, making a speaking-trumpet of her hands, called to him.

"Passed?"

Though she had turned sixteen, she did not dare to go outside the garden without leave from Mademoiselle.

To tease her, he did not answer. But she read the good news in his eyes and began capering like a child. Then she flung herself into his arms.

"Don't be a silly kid," he growled, more out of habit than anything else. She drew away laughing, but a moment later threw herself once again into his arms, quivering with excitement. He saw her gleeful smile, tears flashing in her eyes; touched and grateful, he held her for a moment closely to his heart.

Laughing still, she lowered her voice.

"I had to make up such a yarn to get Auntie to go with me to low mass; I thought you'd be here at ten, you see. Father isn't back yet. Come along!" She led him towards the house.

Mademoiselle's diminutive figure came into view at the far end of the hall; her back was hunched a little with the years. She hurried forward, her head shaking slightly with excitement. She halted at the edge of the terrace and, as soon as Jacques was near, stretched out her doll-like arms, nearly losing her balance as she kissed him.

"You've passed? Yes?" she mumbled as if she had something in her mouth.

"Whoa!" he gaily implored. "Do mind my boil. It's terribly painful."

"Turn round! Good heavens!" Jacques's small infirmity evidently lay more within her province than examinations at the Ecole Normale, for she asked no more about his success, but led him off to have his neck bathed with boiled water and a soothing compress applied.

The minor operation was just ending in Mademoiselle's room when the gate-bell tinkled. M. Thibault had returned.

"Jacquot's passed!" Gisèle shouted from the window, while Jacques went down to meet his father.

"Ah, there you are! What place?" M. Thibault asked, a quick flush of satisfaction colouring his pasty cheeks.

"Third."

M. Thibault's approval grew even more pronounced. His eyelids did not rise, but the muscles of his nose began to quiver, his glasses dropped to the end of their tether, and he held out his hand.

"Well, well! Not too bad!" he muttered, pressing Jacques's hand between his flabby fingers. He paused a moment, frowning. Then, "How hot it is!" he murmured. He drew his son to him and kissed him. Jacques's heart beat faster. He raised his eyes towards his father, but M. Thibault had already turned away and was hurriedly ascending the terrace steps. He went to his study, dropped his prayerbook on the table, and, taking out his handkerchief, mopped his face.

Lunch was on the table. Gisèle had placed a bunch of marshmallows at Jacques's place and the family table wore a festive air. So blithe was her heart that she could not restrain her laughter. The life she led with the two old people was hard upon her youth, but, such was her vitality, it never weighed on her; with hopes of happiness to come, why not be happy now?

M. Thibault came in, rubbing his hands.

"Well, Jacques," he said, unfolding his napkin and planting his fists on either side of his plate, "now you mustn't rest on your laurels. We're no fools in the family and, as you've entered third, what's to stop you, if you work hard enough, from coming out first in the finals?" Half closing an eye, he perked up his beard with a knowing air. "For may we not assume that in every competitive examination *someone* must be first?"

Jacques greeted his father's sally with an evasive smile. He was so used to play-acting at the family table that it cost him little effort to carry through his part; occasionally, however, he blamed himself for the habit as lacking dignity.

"To take a first place," M. Thibault continued, "in the finals of such an Alma Mater as the Ecole Normale—your brother will bear me out—stamps a man for life; he is sure of being looked up to in whatever career he chooses. How is your brother?"

"He said he was coming after lunch."

The idea of telling his father that there had been an accident in M. Chasle's household never for an instant crossed Jacques's mind. All who came in contact with M. Thibault were involved in a conspiracy of silence; they had learned how rash it was to give him any kind of information, for there was no knowing what conclusions that burly busybody would draw from even the smallest piece of news, or what steps he might not take, whether by interviews or correspondence, in the exercise of what he deemed his right of meddling in—and muddling—other people's business.

"Have you seen that the morning papers confirm the failure of our Villebeau Co-operative Society?" he inquired of Mademoiselle, though he knew she never opened a newspaper. She answered, nevertheless, with an emphatic nod. M. Thibault emitted a short, brittle laugh; thereafter, till the meal ended, he said no more and seemed indifferent to the others' conversation. Daily he grew more hard of hearing, more isolated from his family. Sometimes throughout a meal he stayed thus—devouring in silence the huge helpings that an appetite worthy of a boxer demanded, and lost in thought. At such moments he was pondering on some complicated scheme, and his inertia was that of a sedulous spider; he was waiting till the tireless workings of his mind had ravelled out some social or administrative problem. Thus, indeed, he had always worked—with eyes half shut, only his brain active, calm as a man of stone. Never had this great worker taken a note, or mapped out the sequence of a speech; everything took form, and was indelibly recorded down to the least detail, behind that brooding forehead.

Mademoiselle sat in front of him, keeping a sharp eye on the servants. Her hands lay folded on the tablecloth, diminutive and comely hands which she kept in condition (a secret, as she thought) with a lotion made of milk of cucumber. She had almost given up eating. For dessert she took a mug of milk and a biscuit only; out of coquetry she never dipped the biscuit in the milk but nibbled it dry with her well-preserved, mouse-like teeth. She was convinced that everyone ate too much, and kept close watch on her niece's plate. Today, however, in honour of Jacques, she waived her principles so far as to suggest, when the meal ended:

"Jacquot, will you try the jam I've been making?"

" 'Delicious flavour, perfectly digestible,' " Jacques murmured, winking at Gisèle, and this standing joke of theirs, calling up a certain packet of bull's-eyes and their screams of laughter as children, set them off laughing as in the past, till the tears came to their eyes.

M. Thibault had not heard the remark, but smiled benevolently.

"You're a bold young scamp!" Mademoiselle protested. "But just look how well they've set." On the dumbwaiter a squad of fifty jam-pots, filled with ruby jelly and protected by a strip of muslin against the flies' offensive, glowed in anticipation of their caps of rum-soaked parchment.

The French windows opened from the dining-room onto a veranda bright with flower-boxes; and sunbeams, slipping past the blinds, streaked the floor with dazzling light. A wasp buzzed round the jar of greengages and, droning under the caress of noonday, set the whole house ahum. Jacques was destined to recall this meal as the only moment when his success in the examination gave him a fleeting thrill of pleasure.

Gisèle was wildly happy and, though habit kept her silent, exchanged clandestine glances with him, as if to share some unspoken secret. At everything Jacques said she broke into a peal of merry laughter.

"Oh, Gise, that mouth of yours!" Mademoiselle twittered; never could she get over the enormity of Gisèle's mouth and her thick lips. No better could she abide the dusky warmth that glowed in the girl's fair skin, her flattish nose, and black, slightly fuzzy hair—all that reminded her only too well of Gisèle's mother, the half-caste, whom Major de Waize had married during his stay in Madagascar. She never missed a pretext for alluding to her niece's forebears on her father's side. "When I was younger," she used to say, "my grandmother—the one with the Scotch shawl, you know—used to make me repeat 'prunes and prisms, prunes and prisms' a hundred times a day, to make my mouth smaller." While she talked she was flicking her napkin at the wasp, trying to catch it, and laughing every time she missed it. There was nothing of the kill-joy about the worthy old creature; her life had been a hard one, but her contagious laugh rang blithe as ever. "Grandmother," she continued, "danced at Toulon with Count de Villèle, the cabinet-minister. She'd be dreadfully unhappy if she had to live in these present times, for she couldn't bear the sight of big mouths or big feet." Mademoiselle was very vain of her feet, shaped like a new-born babe's, and always wore blunt-ended cloth shoes to keep her toes from losing their shape.

At three, the hour of vespers, the house became empty. Jacques, left to himself, went up to his bedroom. It was an attic on the top floor, but a large, cool room, gay with a floral wall-paper; the view was restricted, but agreeably so, by the high branches of two chestnut-trees whose feathery leaves formed an attractive foreground.

Dictionaries, a textbook of philology, and the like, still littered the table; he bundled them all away into the bottom of a cupboard, and came back to his desk.

Am I still a child or am I a man? he suddenly wondered. Daniel . . . but that's another matter altogether. But I—what am I really? He felt a world in himself, a world of warring impulses; a chaos, but a chaos of abundance. Pleased with his private universe, he set his gaze roaming over the expanse of smooth mahogany. Why had he cleared the table? Well, anyhow, he was not short of plans. For how many months had he not been repressing an impulse to set about doing something? "Wait till you've passed," he had admonished himself. And now that liberty deferred was here at last, he could see nothing worthy of his undertaking—not *The Story of Two Young Men,* not *Fires,* nor yet *The Startled Secret.*

He rose from the desk, took a few steps, and glanced towards the shelf where he had been hoarding books (some of them acquired the year before) against the day that set him free. Which of them should be his first choice? he wondered; then, in a fit of petulance, flung himself on the bed, empty-handed.

"Damn all these books and arguments and phrases!" he exclaimed. " 'Words, words, words!' " He stretched his arms out towards some phantom of his mind, intangible; and all but wept. May I now begin to—live? he asked himself perplexedly. And again: Am I a child still, or a man?

His breath came and went in painful gasps; he felt crushed and broken. He could not have said what it was he asked of fate.

"To live!" he repeated. "To *act!*"

Then, "To love," he added, and closed his eyes. . . .

He rose an hour later. Had he been in a day-dream or asleep? His head was heavy and his neck smarted. Deep exhaustion, due at once to a vague boredom and excess of energy, put any mode of action out of reach and dulled his thoughts. He cast a glance round the room. Must he vegetate for two months in this house? Yet he felt some enigmatic destiny chained him here for the summer, and that elsewhere his plight would be still worse.

Going to the window, he rested his elbows on the sill. And suddenly his anguish lifted. Gisèle's dress gleamed white across the lower branches of the chestnuts and now he knew her nearness would give him back the zest of youth and life.

He had meant to take her unawares, but her ears were on the alert, or else her book had little interest for her, for she swung round at once, hearing Jacques's footstep behind her.

"No luck that time!"

"What's this you're reading?"

She refused to answer and hugged the book to her breast in her folded arms. Their eyes challenged each other with a sudden thrust of pleasure.

"One, two, three . . ."

He rocked the chair to and fro till she slipped off onto the grass. But she would not let go of her book and he had to grapple with her lithe, warm body for a strenuous minute before he could secure his booty.

"*Le Petit Savoyard,* Vol. I. My word! Are there many more of this?"

"Three volumes."

"Congrats. Is it exciting, anyhow?"

She laughed.

"Why, I can't even get through the first volume!"

"Why do you read trash like that?"

"I've no choice, you see."

(After several experiences of the kind Mademoiselle had given her verdict: "Gisèle doesn't care for reading.")

"I'll lend you some books instead," Jacques proposed, pioneer as usual of disobedience and revolt.

But Gisèle did not seem to hear him.

"Don't hurry away," she begged, stretching herself on the grass. "Take my chair. Or lie down here if you like."

He lay down beside her. The sun beat remorselessly on the villa some sixty yards away and on the sanded terrace round it, set with orange-trees in tubs; but here, under cover of the chestnut-trees, the grass was cool.

"So, Jacquot, now you're free." Then in a voice that vainly tried to sound detached, she added: "And what are you going to do next?" She bent in his direction, with eager, parted lips.

"What do you mean?"

"I mean, where will you go now that you have two months to do as you like?"

"Nowhere."

"What? You're going to stay here with us for a bit?" She looked up at him; her eyes were round and glowing with dog-like devotion.

"Yes. I'm going to Touraine on the tenth, for a friend's wedding."

"And then?"

"I'm not sure." He averted his eyes. "I'm thinking of staying at Maisons during my whole vacation."

"Really and truly?" She leaned forward to study Jacques's expression.

He smiled, rejoicing in her joy, and now he viewed with few or no misgivings the prospect of spending two months in the company of this simple, affectionate child whom he loved like a sister—far more than a sister. His presence here had always seemed unwanted and he had never dreamt his coming could bring such radiant happiness to her life; the revelation made him feel so grateful to her that he took the hand lying listless on the grass and stroked it.

"What a nice skin you have, Gisèle! Do you use cucumber lotion, too?"

She laughed and Jacques was impressed by her suppleness as lithely she snuggled up to him. She had the natural, playful sensuality of a young animal and in her full-throated laugh, when it had not a ring of childish glee, sounded an amorous, dove-like cooing. But there was peace between the virgin soul and the ripe, young body, thrilled though it might be by countless vague desires whose meaning she could not guess.

"Auntie still won't let me join the tennis-club this season." She made grimace. "You'll be going there, I suppose?"

"Certainly not."

"Will you go for bicycle rides?"

"Perhaps I will."

"How lovely!" she exclaimed, and her look implied: Wonders will never cease. "You know, Auntie's promised to let me go for rides with you. Would you like that?"

For a moment he peered into the dark pools of her eyes.

"You have pretty eyes, Gisèle."

It seemed to him that they grew darker yet, ruffled by a strange unrest. Smiling still, she turned away. That blithe and laughing charm of hers, the first thing people usually noticed, showed not only in the sparkle of her eyes and the little dimples that played incessantly about the corners of her lips, but also in her ripely moulded cheeks, the blunt tip of her nose, the roguish roundness of her chin—it lit up all her small, plump face, vivid with health and cheerfulness.

She grew uneasy at his evasion of the question she had asked.

"Jacques, you will—won't you?"

"Will what . . . ?"

"Why, take me for bike rides in the woods, or to Marly, like last summer."

She was so delighted to see him smile a vague assent that she wriggled still closer, and kissed him. They lay on their backs, side by side, their eyes exploring the green depths above.

Sounds reached their ears, the tinkle of a fountain, a chuckling chorus of frogs around the pond, and, now and again, voices of passers-by beyond the garden fence. The scent of petunias whose gummy whorls had toasted daylong in the sun slowly drifted from the flower-boxes on the veranda, lingering on the warm air.

"You *are* funny, Jacques. Always thinking! What ever do you think about?"

Propping himself on his elbow, he looked at Gisèle and saw the wonder on her parted, glistening lips.

"I was thinking what pretty teeth you have."

She did not blush, but gave a little shrug.

"No, Jacques, I'm being serious."

Her tone of childish gravity set Jacques laughing.

A bumble-bee, drenched in amber light, hovered round them, blundering like a tiny woolly ball against Jacques's cheek; then, veering earthwards, it dived into a hole in the turf, humming like a threshing-machine.

"I was also thinking, Gise, that you remind me of that bee there."

"I do?"

"Yes."

"Why?"

"I don't know." He stretched himself out again on his back. "It's round and black like you and, what's more, its buzz is rather like the noise you make when you laugh."

He made the announcement in such a serious tone that the words seemed to set Gisèle deeply pondering. Both were silent now. The slanting shadows lengthened on the sun-scorched lawn and a level ray caught Gisèle's face. Spangles of gold played on her cheeks, fretting her eyes across the lids; the tickling on her face started her laughing again. . . .

A chime of the gate-bell announced Antoine's arrival and when Jacques saw his brother at the end of the drive he rose promptly, as though it were all thought out beforehand, and hurried to meet him.

"You're going back this evening?"

"Yes, by the ten-twenty."

Jacques was impressed once again, not by the weariness so evident on Antoine's features, but by their brightness, that gave him an unwonted, almost defiant, air.

He lowered his voice.

"Won't you come with me after dinner to Mme. de Fontanin's?" He knew his brother would demur and, averting his eyes, he added hastily: "I simply must call on them and I'd hate to have to go there alone tomorrow."

"Will Daniel be there?"

Jacques knew for a fact that he would not.

"Of course," he said.

M. Thibault appeared at a window of the drawing-room, holding an open newspaper, and they ceased speaking.

"Ah, there you are!" he called to Antoine. "I am glad you were able to come." He always spoke to Antoine with studied courtesy. "Stay where you are; I'll join you."

"That's fixed up then?" Jacques whispered. "We can say we're going for a stroll after dinner."

M. Thibault had never withdrawn the veto he had pronounced long ago against any revival of Jacques's relations with the Fontanins.

For safety's sake the hated name was never mentioned in his hearing. Was he unaware that for some time past his injunction had been disregarded? Impossible to be sure. So blind was his paternal pride, it well might be that the notion his orders were being persistently disobeyed never crossed his mind.

"Well, he's passed," said M. Thibault, descending with heavy tread the terrace steps, "so now we need feel no more anxiety about his future." Then, as an afterthought: "Shall we take a stroll round the lawn before dinner?" The unusual proposal called for explanation. "I want to have a talk with you both. But, first of all"—he turned towards Antoine—"have you seen the evening papers? What do they say of the Villebeau bankruptcy? Have you seen anything about it?"

"Your Workmen's Co-operative Society?"

"Yes, my dear boy. An absolute disaster—with a scandal behind it, too! Quick work, eh?" He emitted a short laugh that sounded like a cough.

Ah, how she gave me her lips! Antoine was thinking, and a picture of the restaurant rose before his eyes: Rachel sitting opposite him, the light welling up from below—as on a stage—from windows that extended to the sidewalk. . . . I wonder why she laughed like that when I suggested a mixed grill!

He tried his best to be interested in his father's conversation. Moreover, it puzzled him that M. Thibault should take this "disaster" so calmly, for the philanthropist was a member of the group that had supplied the Villebeau button-makers with funds when, after the last stroke, they had founded a co-operative workers' union to demonstrate that they could do without their employers.

M. Thibault had reached his peroration.

"In my opinion the money was not spent in vain. We have no reason to regret our conduct; we took the workers' utopian projects seriously and volunteered to assist them with our capital. With this result: the enterprise went bankrupt in less than eighteen months. As it happens, the middleman between the workmen's delegates and ourselves did his work well. He's an old acquaintance of yours, by the by." He halted and turned to Jacques. "It's Faîsme, who was at Crouy in your time."

Jacques made no comment.

"He has a hold on all the men's leaders, thanks to the letters those noble souls addressed us, asking for funds—letters penned during the worst phase of the strike. So none of them can think of climbing down." He emitted another little cough of self-satisfaction. "But that is not what I wish to consult you about," he added, moving forward again.

He walked with heavy steps and flagging breath, trailing his feet in the sand, with his body bent forward and hands behind his back; his unbuttoned coat flapped loosely round him. His two sons walked beside him. Jacques recalled a sentence he had read, though he could not place it: "Whenever I meet two men walking side by side and finding nothing to say to each other, I know them for father and son."

"It's this," said M. Thibault. "I want your opinion on a plan I have in mind—on your behalf." They heard a note of sadness, and a ring of sincerity in his voice, quite other than his usual tone. "You will find out, my sons, when you attain my age, that a man cannot but look back and ask himself: What will remain of my life's work? I know very well—Abbé Vécard has often told me so—that all our efforts spent on doing good work together to the same end are cumulative. Still—is it not cruel to think that all the strivings of a life may be utterly obliterated in the nameless jetsam each generation leaves behind? May not a father legitimately desire that his own children will keep some personal memory of him? . . . If only by way of an example to others?" He sighed. "I can honestly say that I have your interests at heart, rather than mine. It has struck me that in future years you, as my sons, will prefer not to be confounded with all the other Thibaults in France. We have two centuries behind us—as commoners, if you like; but we can prove who we are. That, anyhow, is something. And I believe that, to the best of my ability, I have added to this worthy heritage, and have the right—this will be my reward —to hope there may be no misunderstanding as to your parentage, and to desire that you may bear my name in its entirety and transmit it intact to those who will be born of my blood. It lies with the Heralds' College to deal with such requests. So, some months ago, I took the requisite steps to have a formal alteration of your names recorded; I expect very shortly to receive the deed-polls, which I shall ask you to sign. And, by the end of the vacation, I trust—in any case, not later than Christmas—each of you will have the legal right to call himself no longer just plain 'Thibault,' but 'Oscar-Thibault' with a hyphen; 'Dr. Antoine Oscar-Thibault,' for example." Bringing his hands in front of him, he rubbed them together. "That is what I wanted to tell you. No thanks, if you please; we will not mention it again. And now to dinner; I see Mademoiselle beckoning." He laid a patriarchal arm around the shoulder of each of his sons. "If it so happens that this distinction helps you on in life, so much the better, my sons. Surely, in all conscience, it is only justice that a man whose heart was never set on worldly gain should endow his heirs with such prestige as he has himself acquired."

There was a tremor in his voice and, to hide his emotion, he swerved from the path along which they were walking and hurried on by himself, stumbling over the hummocks, towards the house. Never before had Antoine and Jacques seen their father so profoundly moved.

"Well, that beats everything!" Antoine chuckled.

"Oh, don't, Antoine!" It seemed to Jacques that dirty hands, his brother's, were pawing at his heart. Jacques rarely spoke of his father without a certain deference; he declined to judge him, and deplored his own clear-sightedness when (oftener than he would have wished) his father was its target. And tonight the agony of doubt that lay behind his father's longing for survival had touched him deeply, for even Jacques, though only twenty, could never think of death without a sinking of the heart.

Why ever did I get Antoine to come? Jacques asked himself as, an hour later, he accompanied his brother down the green avenue, flanked by centenarian lime-trees, that led from the château to the forest. His neck was smarting; Mademoiselle had insisted on having the boil inspected by Antoine, who had thought fit to lance it, despite his victim's protest—for the idea of paying a visit with a bandage on his neck did not at all appeal to him.

Antoine was tired but talkative; his thoughts were all for Rachel. Yesterday at this hour he did not know her yet, and now she filled every moment of his life.

His exuberance contrasted with his brother's mood; Jacques had passed a restful day and now, as he walked on, his thoughts were busy with a visit whose prospect stirred in him a fugitive emotion, sometimes akin to hope. He felt dissatisfied and mistrustful as he walked at Antoine's side. Some cautionary instinct warned him against his brother, setting a wall of silence between them, though their conversation was cordial as ever. But in reality each was building up a screen of words and smiles, like hostile forces tossing up clods of earth to make a barrier against attack. Neither was hoodwinked by the other's strategy. The tie of blood linked them so intimately that nothing of importance could remain a secret between them. The very tone of Antoine's voice as he praised the fragrance of a late-flowering lime—it had called up a secret memory of Rachel's scented hair—if it did not tell Jacques everything, was all but tantamount to a confession. So he was little surprised when Antoine, yielding to his obsession, caught his arm and, setting a faster pace, launched forth into an account of his eventful night, and of its aftermath. Antoine's tone, his grown-up air, taken with certain broad details little in keeping with his normal, elder-brotherly reserve, made Jacques feel strangely ill at ease. He put a good face on it, smiled and nodded his approval —but he was distressed. He was angry with his brother for causing this distress, and even for the sentiment of disapproval which accompanied it. The more his brother hinted at the state of rapture in which he had been living for the past twelve hours, the more Jacques shrank back into his shell of cold disdain and felt the thirst for chastity grow strong within him. When Antoine, describing his afternoon, ventured to use the words "a day of love," Jacques was profoundly shocked, and showed it.

"No, Antoine," he protested, "no, and no again! 'Love'—that's something quite different."

A rather self-complacent smile hovered on Antoine's lips; but he was taken aback for all that, and said no more.

The Fontanins were living in an old house, left them by Mme. de Fontanin's mother, at the far end of the park on the outskirts of the forest. The house abutted on the old park wall. A road, lined with acacias and so seldom used that patches of rank grass were growing on it, led from the main avenue to a postern gate let into the garden wall.

Night was falling when they arrived, and lights shone in some of the windows. A bell tinkled and, at the bottom of the garden beside the house, Puce, Jenny's dog, began to bark. Antoine and Jacques knew where to find them. After meals the Fontanins resorted to the far side of the house where, shaded by two plane-trees, a natural terrace overhung the ancient fosse. A car had pulled up in the drive and they had to grope their way around it.

"Visitors!" Jacques murmured, and suddenly regretted he had come. But Mme. de Fontanin was already on her way to meet them.

"I knew it was you!" she exclaimed as soon as she saw their faces. She hastened towards them with brisk, glad steps, holding out her hands and smiling her greetings. "We were ever so pleased this morning when Daniel's wire came." Jacques did not flinch. "But I *knew* you would pass," she continued, looking earnestly at Jacques. "Something told me so that Sunday in June when you came here with Daniel. Dear Daniel, how delighted, how proud he must feel! Jenny was delighted, too."

"So Daniel isn't here tonight?" Antoine remarked.

As they neared the circle of chairs, they heard a sound of gay voices. Jacques singled out at once a certain voice with a distinctive quality of its own, vibrant yet subdued: Jenny's voice. She was seated beside another girl, her cousin Nicole, and a man some thirty years of age towards whom Antoine advanced with an air of surprise—a young surgeon who had been his colleague at the Necker Hospital. The two men shook hands cordially.

Mme. de Fontanin beamed. "So you know each other. Antoine and Jacques Thibault are great friends of Daniel's," she explained to Dr. Héquet. "So you won't mind letting them into the secret, will you?" She turned to Antoine. "I'm sure my little Nicole will let me tell you about her engagement—won't you, darling? It's not really quite official yet, but, as you see, Nicole's already brought her fiancé here to meet her aunt, and you need only look at them to guess their secret."

Jenny had not gone to meet the brothers and did not rise till they were actually standing before her; she shook hands with them coldly.

"Nico dear, come and see my pigeons," she said to Nicole before they had time to sit down again. "I've eight baby pigeons who are . . ."

"Still on the bottle," Jacques broke in; his voice, which he meant to sound insolent, was merely ill-mannered and out of place. This he realized at once, and clenched his teeth.

Jenny did not seem to hear.

". . . who are just learning to fly," she continued smoothly.

"But they're all in bed by now," Mme. de Fontanin protested, to keep her from going.

"So much the better. You can't get near them in the daytime. Will you come too, Felix?"

Dr. Héquet, who was talking to Antoine, hastened to follow the two girls.

As soon as the engaged couple was out of earshot Mme. de Fontanin bent towards Antoine and Jacques.

"It's a most fascinating little match, you know. Our little Nicole has no means of her own and she was quite set against being on anyone's hands. So for three years she's been earning her living as a nurse. And now, just see how she has been rewarded! Dr. Héquet met her at the bedside of a patient and was so impressed by her devotion and intelligence, and the plucky way she was facing life, that he fell in love with her. There's the whole story. Now don't you think it's perfectly charming?"

The romantic glamour of her tale, where virtue triumphed and every sentiment was lofty, enchanted her simple soul, and the light of faith shone in her eyes. Most of her remarks were addressed to Antoine and she spoke to him in a cordial manner that seemed to imply they saw eye to eye in everything. She liked his forehead and keen gaze, never reflecting that he was sixteen years her junior; that she might, or almost might, have been his mother. She was overjoyed when he assured her Felix Héquet was a first-rate surgeon with a great future before him.

Jacques took no part in the conversation. "On the bottle"! He was furious with himself. Everything, even Mme. de Fontanin's effusive amiability, had been ruffling his nerves ever since he came. He had not been able to hear her congratulations out, but turned away, feeling ashamed on her account—that she should seem to attach any importance to his success, the news of which, however, he had been at pains to telegraph to her. "Jenny at least spared me her compliments," he murmured to himself. "Did she realize that I am capable of better things? I wonder. No. Just indifference. Better things! 'Still on the bottle'! I wonder if she even knows what the Ecole Normale means. Anyhow, what does she care about my future? She hardly said 'Good evening' to me. But how about me? Why did I make that idiotic remark?" He blushed, gritting his teeth again. "And while she said 'Good evening' she went on listening to her cousin. Her eyes—inscrutable, they are. The rest of her face is almost childish, but her eyes . . . !" At every moment painful twinges were reminding him of his boil, but he resented still more the bandage that all of them— not only Mademoiselle but Gisèle too—had foisted on him. A hideous sight he must be looking!

Antoine was talking cheerfully, paying no heed to Jacques.

". . . and from the moral point of view . . ." he was saying.

When Antoine talks, Jacques thought, there's no room for anybody else. Then suddenly his brother's easy manners in society and that "moral point of view," following as it did avowals of a very different order, disgusted him as a piece of unforgivable hypocrisy. How different from him his brother was! Rushing to extremes, Jacques decided that he had not a single thing in common with Antoine. Sooner or later their ways would part, inevitably; their different bents were incompatible and had no point of contact. A mood of utter hopelessness came over him; even their five years of close communion, he realized, had failed to make them proof against this coming estrangement, could not prevent them from growing indifferent to each other, strangers, or even enemies! He all but rose, snatching at any pretext for escape. Ah, could he but wander away alone into the darkness, out into the forest, anywhere! One human being had smiled her way into his heart: little Gisèle. Yesterday's success—how gladly would he forgo it, could he but be with her again at this very moment, lying on the grass, watching her face and eyes—so unmysterious, hers!—and hear her cry: "You will, won't you?" with that cooing laugh of hers! Now that he thought of it, never had he seen Jenny laugh; even her smile seemed disillusioned. What ever has come over me? he wondered and tried to pull himself together. But the dark mood was stronger than his will, a bitter nausea filling him with loathing for everything and everybody, for Mme. de Fontanin's remarks, Antoine's degradation, people in general, his own wasted youth, the world at large—yes, and for Jenny too, who seemed so much at home in a world of futility.

"What are your plans for the vacation?" Mme. de Fontanin inquired. "Couldn't you induce Daniel to spend a few weeks away from Paris? It would be so nice for you both and would benefit you in other ways." She was discovering with some dismay that the brilliant career on which she had hoped to see her son embark was slow to shape itself and, for all her reluctance to linger on such thoughts, she was sometimes worried by the life he led; it was too free, too easy-going and—though she shirked the thought—too dissipated.

When Jacques told her that he intended to stay at Maisons, she was delighted.

"That's splendid! I hope you'll persuade Daniel to go out a bit; he never will take a holiday and I'm so afraid he will make himself ill. Jenny!" She had noticed the girl returning with her friends. "Good news! Jacques will be here all summer. That will mean some good tennis, won't it? Jenny's simply mad about tennis this summer; she spends all her mornings at the club. Our local tennis-club is quite famous in its way," she explained to Dr. Héquet, who had taken the chair beside her. "Such nice young people! They all turn up there every morning. The courts are excellent and they're always arranging matches, tournaments, and that sort of thing. I don't know much about it," she added with a smile, "but it's terribly exciting, they tell me. And they're always grumbling about the shortage of men. Are you still a member, Jacques?"

"Yes."

"That's good. Nicole, you must bring Dr. Héquet and stay a week or ten days with us this summer. That will be nice, won't it, Jenny? I'm sure Dr. Héquet is a good player, too."

Jacques turned towards Héquet. The drawing-room lamp shone through the open window, showing up the young surgeon's lean, austere face, his close-cropped brown beard and temples prematurely streaked with silver. He certainly looked ten years older than Nicole. The lamplight, glinting on his glasses, masked the expression of his eyes, but his thoughtful air was decidely engaging. Yes, thought Jacques, *there* is a man—and I am only a child! A man who can inspire love. Whereas I . . .

Antoine had risen from his chair. He felt tired and did not want to miss his train. Jacques cast him an angry look. Though a few minutes before he himself had been in half a mind to snatch at any pretext for departure, now he could not bring himself to end the evening thus. Still, he would have to leave at the same time as his brother.

He moved towards Jenny.

"Whom are you playing tennis with at the club this summer?"

She looked at him, and the slender line of her eyebrows knitted a little.

"With anyone who happens to be there," she replied.

"Meaning the two Casins, and Fauquet, and the Périgault crowd?"

"Naturally."

"They're just the same, I suppose, and as witty as ever?"

"What about it? We can't all be shining lights at the Ecole Normale!"

"Yes, I dare say one has to be a bit of a fool to play tennis properly."

"Very likely." She threw him an aggressive look. "Anyhow, *you* should know about that; you used to be pretty good at tennis once." Then, ostentatiously breaking off their conversation, she turned to her cousin. "You're not going yet, Nicole darling, I hope."

"Ask Felix."

"What's this you're to ask Felix?" said Dr. Héquet, who had approached the two girls.

Antoine's eyes were fixed on Nicole; yes, he mused, the girl certainly has a dazzling complexion. But, beside Rachel's . . . ! And suddenly his heart beat faster.

"So, Jacques, we'll be seeing you again quite soon?" said Mme. de Fontanin. "Are you going to play tomorrow, Jenny?"

"I don't know, Mamma—I hardly think so."

"Well, if it isn't tomorrow, you're bound to meet there one morning," Mme. de Fontanin continued in a conciliatory tone. And, despite Antoine's protest, she insisted on escorting the two young men to the gate.

"I must say, darling, you weren't very nice to your friends!" Nicole exclaimed as soon as the Thibaults were out of earshot.

"To begin with, they're not my friends," Jenny replied.

"I've worked with Thibault," Héquet observed. "He's a first-rate man and has already made his mark. I've no ideas about his brother but"—behind the glasses his grey eyes twinkled quizzingly, for he had overheard the short passage between Jacques and Jenny—"it's rather rare for a duffer to get through the Normale exam at his first shot, and take a high place, too."

A deep blush mantled Jenny's cheeks, and Nicole came to her rescue. She had lived with the Fontanins long enough to learn the kinks in Jenny's character, one of which was her shyness always at issue with her pride, and sometimes lapsing into a morbid readiness to take offence.

"The poor boy had a boil on his neck," she put in good-naturedly, "and that doesn't help a man to be his social best."

Jenny made no comment, and Héquet did not insist. He turned to Nicole.

"We must be getting ready now, dear." His tone was that of a man who always runs his life by clockwork.

Mme. de Fontanin's return was the signal for a general move. Jenny went with her cousin to the bedroom where she had left her coat. Some minutes passed before she spoke.

"So there's my summer spoilt, absolutely ruined!"

Seated before the mirror, Nicole was tidying her hair for the sole benefit of her fiancé. She felt that she was looking her best, wondered what he was saying to her aunt downstairs, and pictured the long drive home in her lover's car across the silent night. So she paid little heed to Jenny's ill-humour. Noticing the sullen look on her friend's face, she merely smiled.

"What an infant you are!"

She did not see the look that Jenny flung her.

A motor-horn sounded and Nicole swung round gaily and darted towards her cousin to embrace her, with the mixture of affection, innocence, and coquetry that made her so attractive. But Jenny, uttering an involuntary cry, swerved out of her reach. She shrank from being touched by anybody and had always refused to learn to dance, so physically repugnant to her was the contact of another's arm. Once, in early childhood, she had sprained her ankle in the Luxembourg and had to be taken home in a carriage; she had preferred to climb the stairs, trailing an injured limb, to letting the concierge carry her in his arms up to their landing.

"What a touch-me-not you are!" laughed Nicole. Then, with a cheerful glance at her cousin, she changed the subject, returning to their conversation before dinner in the rose-alley. "I'm ever so glad to have had my talk with you, darling. Some days I'm positively oppressed by my happiness. With you of course I'm always perfectly sincere—just myself, my real self, exactly as I am. Oh, how I hope, darling, it won't be long before you, too . . ."

Under the headlights the garden had the glamour of a stage, set for a gala night. Héquet had raised the hood of his car and was tightening a plug with the measured gestures of a skilled surgeon. Nicole suggested keeping her coat folded on her knees, but he insisted on her wearing it. He treated her like a little girl for whom he was responsible. Did he treat all women thus—like children? But Nicole gave in with a good grace that startled Jenny and roused in her a vague resentment towards the engaged couple. "No," she said to herself, with a shake of her head; "that sort of happiness . . . not for me, thanks!"

For a long while her eyes followed the flail of light that swept the trees before the receding car. Leaning against the garden wall, with Puce clasped in her arms, she felt such hopeless hope, such bitterness against she knew not what, that, lifting her eyes towards the starstrewn spaces, she wished for an instant or two that she might die thus, before attempting life's adventure.

VI

GISÈLE was wondering why for some days past the daylight hours had seemed so short, summer so glorious, and why each morning as she dressed before her open window she could not help singing, smiling at everything—her mirror, the cloudless sky, the garden, the sweet peas she watered on her window-sill, the orange-trees on the terrace, which seemed to be curling themselves into balls, like hedgehogs, the better to screen themselves from the far-darting sun.

M. Thibault rarely spent more than two or three days at Maisons-Laffitte without making a business trip to Paris, where he stayed overnight. When he was away a brisker air seemed to pervade the house. Meals came and went like games, and Jacques and Gisèle once more gave free vent to their bursts of childish glee. Mademoiselle, in gayer mood, pattered from pantry to linen-closet, from kitchen to drying-room, lilting antiquated hymns that sounded like bygone music-hall refrains. On such occasions Jacques felt unconstrained, his brain alert and full of warring projects, and gave himself whole-heartedly to his vocation. He spent the afternoons in a corner of the garden, getting up, sitting down again, scribbling in his note-book. Gisèle, too, infected by a desire to turn her leisure hours to good account, posted herself on a landing whence she could watch Jacques coming and going beneath the trees and, immersed in Dickens's *Great Expectations*— Mademoiselle, on Jacques's suggestion, had sanctioned its perusal as being "good for Gisèle's English"—wept ecstatically for having guessed from the outset that Pip would give poor Biddy up for the exotic charms of cruel Miss Estella.

Jacques's brief absence in the second week of August to attend Battaincourt's wedding in Touraine—he had not dared to stand out against his friend's request—sufficed to break the spell.

The day after his return to Maisons he awoke too early after a restless night; shaving warily, he noticed that his cheeks were innocent of rash and the boil had given place to an invisible scar, and now the prospect of resuming this too uniform existence seemed so exasperating that he suddenly stopped dressing and threw himself upon his bed. The weeks are passing, passing, he thought. Could this be the vacation to which he had looked forward so? He sprang up from the bed. "Exercise is what I need," he murmured in a cool voice that assorted ill with his fevered gestures. He took a tennis-shirt from the wardrobe, saw that his white shoes and racket were in order, and a few minutes later jumped on his bicycle and was off post-haste to the tennis-club.

Two courts were in play; Jenny was one of the players. She did not seem to notice Jacques's arrival and he made no haste to greet her. A new toss-up brought them into the same four; first against each other, then as partners. As players, there was little to choose between them.

No sooner were they together than they dropped back into their old-time unmannerliness. True, Jacques paid ample attention to Jenny, but always in an irritating, not to say offensive way; he jeered at her

bad shots and obviously enjoyed contradicting her. Jenny gave him
tit for tat, in a shrill voice that was quite unlike her. She could easily
have replaced him by a less churlish partner, but apparently did not
want to do so; on the contrary she seemed set on having the last
word. When it was lunch-time and the players began to disperse she
challenged Jacques in a voice that had lost nothing of its hostility:

"Play four up with me!"

The energy she put into her play was so intense, so combative, that
she beat Jacques four–love.

The victory made her generous.

"There's nothing in it, you know; you're out of training. One of
these days you'll have your revenge."

Her voice had once again the soft, brooding tone that was natural
to her. We're just two kids, Jacques thought. It pleased him that they
shared a failing and he seemed to see a gleam of hope. A wave of
shame traversed his mind when he recalled his attitude to Jenny,
but when he asked himself what other to adopt he found no answer.
There was no one with whom he longed so keenly to be natural; yet
in her company he found it utterly impossible.

Noon was striking when they left the club together, wheeling their
bicycles.

"*Au revoir,*" she said. "Don't wait for me. I'm so hot that I might
catch a chill if I started riding now."

Without replying, he continued walking at her side.

Jenny disliked the clinging type of person; to be unable to dislodge
a companion at the moment of her choice always annoyed her. Jacques
had no idea of this; he meant to return for another game next day
and cast about for a pretext to justify this sudden assiduity.

"Now that I'm back from Touraine . . ." he began awkwardly.
The tone of mockery had left his voice. Last year she had noticed the
same thing; when they were alone, he dropped his teasing ways.

"So you were in Touraine," she repeated, for want of anything
better to say.

"Yes. A friend's wedding. But of course you know him; I met him
at your place—Battaincourt."

"Simon de Battaincourt?" Her tone implied that she was piecing together her memories of him. She summed them up bluntly. "Ah, yes—I didn't like him."

"Why not?"

She resented being cross-examined in this fashion.

"You're too hard on him," Jacques continued, seeing she would not answer. "He's a good sort." Then he thought better of it. "No, you're right, really; there's nothing much in him." She vouchsafed an approving nod which delighted him.

"I didn't know you were so attached to him," she observed.

"Hardly that," Jacques smiled. "He attached himself to me. It happened on our way back from some show or other. It was very late and Daniel had deserted us. Without a word of warning, Battaincourt launched out into a plenary confession. The way he unloaded his life-story on me made me think of a fellow handing his money over to a banker: 'Look after my capital; I put myself in your hands!' "

Jacques's description interested her up to a point and, for the moment, she ceased wishing to shake him off.

"Do many people confide in you?"

"No. Why should they? . . . Well, perhaps they do." He smiled. "Yes, as a matter of fact, quite often. Does that surprise you?" There was a note of defiance in his voice.

He was touched to hear her answer quickly:

"No, not at all."

Gusts of warm wind wafted towards them the fragrance of the gardens beside the road, a fume of freshly watered mould, and the thick pungency of marigolds and heliotropes. Jacques found nothing more to say and it was she who broke the silence first.

"And by dint of all those confessions, you brought off the marriage?"

"Certainly not, quite the opposite. I tried my best to prevent him from doing anything so silly. Think of it! A widow, fourteen years older than he, with a child, what's more! And now his people have dropped him completely. But there was no holding him." He remembered that he had often used the word "possessed"—in its theological sense—when speaking of his friend and it had struck him as felicitous. "Battaincourt is positively possessed by that woman."

"Is she pretty?" Jenny asked, disregarding the strong term he had used.

He pondered so deeply that she pursed her lips.

"I'd no notion I was setting you such a poser!"

But he remained, unsmiling, in a brown study.

"Pretty? Well, hardly that. She's sinister. I can't find any other word for it." He paused again. "Oh, it's a queer world!" he exclaimed. He caught the look of surprise on Jenny's face. "Yes, I mean it. Every one's so queer. Even quite uninteresting people. Have you ever noticed, whenever you speak of a person you know to others who know him too, how many small points that are really suggestive and revealing seem to have escaped them? That's why people misunderstand each other so often."

He looked at her again and felt that she had been listening attentively and was repeating to herself what he had just said. And suddenly the cloud of mistrust which hung over his relations with Jenny seemed to lift, giving place to radiant understanding. To make the most of her attention, so rarely given him, and rouse her interest further, he fell to describing certain incidents at the wedding which were still fresh in his mind.

"Where was I?" he murmured hazily. "Oh, I'd love to write that woman's life one day—from the little I learned of her! She was once a shop-girl in one of the big stores, they say. That woman's a ruthless climber" (he quoted a tag he had jotted down in his note-book), "a Julien Sorel in petticoats! Do you like *Le Rouge et le Noir?*"

"No, not a bit."

"Really? Yes, I see what you mean." After a pensive moment he smiled and spoke again. "But, if I switch off onto side-issues, I'll never get to the end of it. Sure I'm not taking up too much of your time?"

She answered without thinking, reluctant to betray her desire to hear more.

"Oh, no; we won't lunch till half-past twelve today, on Daniel's account."

"So Daniel's at home?"

She had to fall back on a downright lie.

"He said he might come," she replied with a blush. "But how about you?"

"I needn't hurry, as Father's in Paris. Shall we take the shady side? What I really want to tell you about is the wedding breakfast. Nothing much happened, yet, I assure you, it was a very poignant experience. Let's see! The setting, to begin with: an Old World château of sorts, with a dungeon restored by Goupillot. Goupillot was her first husband, a remarkable fellow too; he started as a haberdasher in a small way, but he had big business in the blood, and died a multimillionaire after providing every French provincial town with its 'Goupillot's Store.' You must have come across them. The widow, by the way, is enormously wealthy. I'd never met her before. How shall I describe her? A thin, lithe, ultra-smart woman, with rather shrewish features and a haughty profile; pale eyes that showed up against a rather muddy complexion—eyes of a moleskin grey, with a sort of gloss upon them, like stagnant ooze. Does that give you an idea of her? She has the manners of a spoilt child—far too youthful for her looks. She has a shrill voice and laughs a lot. Now and again—how shall I describe it?—you catch a flicker of grey fire between her eyelids, along the lashes, and, all of a sudden, the childish small-talk she reels off seems to have something macabre behind it and you can't help recalling what people said soon after Goupillot's death, that she had poisoned him by inches."

"She gives me the shivers!" Jenny exclaimed, no longer trying to repress the interest Jacques's narrative roused in her. He felt the change and was pleasantly elated by it.

"Yes, you're right; she's rather terrifying. That was just what I felt when we took our seats and I saw her standing with that mask of steel upon her face behind the white flowers on the table."

"Was she in white?"

"Almost. It wasn't absolutely a wedding-dress; more of a garden-party costume, rather theatrical, a rich, creamy white. Breakfast was served at separate tables. She went on asking people right and left to sit at her table, quite regardless of the number of places at it. Battaincourt, who was near her, looked worried. 'You're muddling everything up, my dear,' he protested. You should have seen the look that passed between them—a curious look! It struck me that all that was young and vital had died out of their relations; they were living on the past."

Perhaps, thought Jenny, perhaps he is not so spoiled as I imagined, not so callous and . . . In a flash it dawned on her that she had always known Jacques to be sensitive and gentle. The discovery thrilled her and now, as she listened to his narrative, she found herself snatching at each phrase that might confirm her new and kindlier judgment of him.

"Simon had made me sit on his left. I was the only one of his friends to turn up. Daniel had promised, but backed out of it. Not a single member of Simon's family was present, not even the cousin with whom he had been brought up, and whom he had been counting on till the last train had gone. One felt sorry for the poor devil! He's a sensitive, rather nice-minded fellow, really; I know a lot of decent things about him. He looked at the people round him—strangers all! He thought of his family. 'I never dreamt,' he told me, 'that they'd be so terribly unrelenting. They *must* have it in for me!' He came back to it during the meal. 'Not a word from them, not even a wire! It looks as if they'd blotted me out of their lives. What do you think?' I didn't know what to reply. 'But,' he made haste to add, 'I don't mention this so much on my account—I don't care a damn! It's Anne I'm thinking of.' As luck would have it, the sinister Anne was opening a telegram that had just been delivered, when he spoke. Battaincourt went quite pale. But the telegram was really for her, from a friend. That was the last straw; regardless of all the people watching, even of Anne with her impassive face and steely eyes intent on him, he burst into tears. She was furious, and he realized it soon enough. He was sitting next to her, of course. Putting his hand on her arm, he stammered out excuses like a naughty child: 'Do forgive me!' It was dreadful to hear him. She never turned a hair. And then— it was even more painful to witness than his fit of weeping—he began

talking cheerfully, cracking jokes, and sometimes, while he was saying something or other in a tone of forced gaiety, you could see the
tears come to his eyes and, still talking away, he brushed them off
with the back of his hand."

Jacques's emotion made it all so vivid that Jenny too was carried
away.

"How horrible!"

Now, for the first time in his life, perhaps, he knew the thrills of
authorship. An ecstasy. But he masked it disingenuously and made
as if he had not heard her cry.

"Sure I'm not boring you?" He paused, then hurried on with his
story. "That's not all. When dessert was served, they started shouting
at the other tables: 'The bride and groom!' Battaincourt and his wife
had to stand up, smile, and go the round of the room, lifting their
glasses of champagne. Just then I observed a little incident that was
touching in its way. On their tour round the tables they overlooked her
daughter by husband number one—a little girl eight or nine years
old. The kid ran after them. They'd got back to their seats by then.
Anne embraced the little girl rather roughly, rumpling the child's
collar. Then she pushed her daughter towards Battaincourt. But after
that melancholy, unfriended tour of the room, his eyes were swimming with tears; he noticed nothing. Finally they had to put the
little girl on his knee; then, with a ghastly, forced smile, he bent
towards the other man's child. The kid held her cheek towards him;
sad eyes she had—I shall never forget them. At last he kissed her
and, as she stayed where she was, he started tickling her chin in a
silly sort of way, like this, with one finger—do you see what I mean?
It was painful to watch, I assure you; but it makes a good story,
doesn't it?"

She turned towards Jacques, struck by the tone in which he had
said "a good story." And now she noticed that the brooding, almost
bestial look that so displeased her had left his face; the pupils of his
eyes showed crystal-clear, sparkling with emotion and vivacity. Oh,
why isn't he always like that? she thought.

Jacques began to smile. Painful as the experience had been, its poignancy weighed little beside the interest he took in other people's lives, in any display of human thoughts and feelings. Jenny shared his taste and, perhaps in her case just as in his, the pleasure was now enhanced by the knowledge that she was not alone.

They had reached the end of the avenue and the outskirts of the forest were in sight. Under the sun the grass shone like a burnished mirror. Jacques halted.

"I've been boring you with all this talk."

She made no protest.

But, instead of bidding her good-bye, he ventured a suggestion. "As I've come so far, I'd like to have a word with your brother."

The reminder of the lie she had told was decidedly ill-timed, and she was the more annoyed that he had so readily believed it. She did not answer him, and Jacques took her silence to mean that she had had enough of his company.

He felt chagrined, but could not bring himself to leave her thus, with an unfavourable impression of him—now, least of all, when it seemed to him that something new had come into their relations, something after which, for months, perhaps for years, he had been yearning unawares.

They walked in silence between the acacias lining the road that led to the garden gate. Jacques, who was a little behind Jenny, could see the pensive, graceful outline of her cheek.

The further he advanced, the less excuse he had for leaving her; minute linked minute in a chain. Now they were at the gate. Jenny opened it; he followed her across the garden. The terrace was deserted, the drawing-room empty.

"Mother!" Jenny called.

No one answered. She went to the kitchen window and, bound by her lie, inquired:

"Has my brother come?"

"No, Miss. But a telegram has just been brought."

"Don't disturb your mother," Jacques said at last. "I'm off."

Jenny remained stiffly erect, an obdurate look on her face.

"*Au revoir,*" Jacques murmured. "See you tomorrow, perhaps?"

"*Au revoir,*" she said, making no move to see him to the gate.

The moment Jacques had turned to go she entered the hall, slammed her racket into the press, and flung it upon a wooden chest, venting her ill-humour in a display of needless violence.

"No, not tomorrow!" she exclaimed. "Certainly not tomorrow!"

Mme. de Fontanin, who was in her bedroom, had not failed to hear her daughter calling, and had recognized Jacques's voice, but she was too upset to feign an air of calmness. The telegram she had just opened came from her husband. Jerome announced that he was at Amsterdam, penniless and friendless, with Noémie, who had fallen ill. Mme. de Fontanin had come to a speedy decision: she would go to Paris that very day, draw out all the money in her account, and send it to the address given by Jerome.

When her daughter entered the room, she was dressing. Jenny was shocked by the anguish on her mother's face and the sight of the telegram lying on the table.

"What ever is the matter?" she exclaimed, while the thought flashed through her mind: Something's happened and I wasn't there. It's all Jacques's fault!

"Nothing serious, darling," Mme. de Fontanin replied. "Your father . . . your father's short of money, that's all." Then, ashamed of her own weakness and, most of all, thus to disclose a father's failings to his child, she blushed and hid her face between her hands.

VII

BEHIND the misted windows dawn was rising. Huddled in a corner of the railway-car, Mme. de Fontanin watched with unseeing eyes the green plains of Holland slipping past.

She had gone to Paris on the previous day and found another telegram from Jerome awaiting her at home: "Doctor given Noémie up. Cannot stay here alone. Implore you come. Bring money if possible."

She had not been able to get in touch with Daniel before the night train left, and had scribbled a note telling him she was leaving and he must look after Jenny.

The train stopped. Voices were crying: "Haarlem!"

It was the last stop before Amsterdam. The lights were switched off. The sun, invisible as yet, sheeted the sky with a pearly lustre, mottled with rainbow gleams. Her fellow-travellers awoke, stretched their limbs, and bundled up their things. Mme. de Fontanin remained unmoving, trying to prolong the apathy which spared her still, to some extent, from realizing what she had undertaken. So Noémie was dying. She tried to peer into her mind. Was she jealous? No. For jealousy—that meant the fiery gusts of feeling that had seared her heart during their early years of married life, when she still kept open house to doubt and blinded herself to reality, fighting back a hateful horde of visual obsessions. For many years past not jealousy had rankled, but a sense of the injustice done her. And had it really rankled, truth to tell? Her trials had been of a quite different order. Had she in fact been at any stage a jealous woman? Her real grief had always been to discover—ever too late—that she had been duped; her feeling towards Jerome's mistresses was oftener than not a rather distant pity, sometimes touched with fellow-feeling, as towards sisters in distress.

Her fingers were trembling when it was time to fasten up her luggage. She was the last to leave the compartment. The rapid, startled glance she cast about her did not meet the look whose impact she expected. Surely he had got her wire? It might be that his eyes were fixed on her, and at the thought she pulled herself together and followed the outgoing stream of passengers.

Someone touched her arm. Jerome stood before her, looking diffident but delighted. As, with bared head, he bowed towards her, despite his care-worn features and the slight stoop he had developed, he had still the exotic charm of some eastern potentate. They were caught in the rush of travellers before he could shape a phrase of welcome for Thérèse, but he took her bag from her hands with tender solicitude.

So *she* is not dead, Mme. de Fontanin reflected, and shuddered at the thought that she might have to watch her die.

They entered the station yard in silence and M. de Fontanin hailed a cab. Suddenly, as she was stepping into it, a wave of emotion that was almost joy flooded her senses: she had heard Jerome's voice. While he was talking to the cabman in Dutch, telling him where to go, she paused a moment on the step in vibrant immobility, then, opening her eyes again, she sank onto the seat.

No sooner was he seated in the open carriage than he turned in her direction; once again she looked into the darkly glowing eyes she knew so well and felt their ardency envelop her like a caress. He seemed about to take her hand, to touch her arm; the gesture was so ill assorted with the courteous reticence of his demeanour that she felt almost shocked, as if he had offered her an insult, yet thrilled by the intimation of a living love, all hope of which had died.

She was the first to break the silence. "How is . . . ?" Stumbling at the name, she hastily went on: "Is she in pain?"

"No, no. That's all over now."

Though she would not meet his eyes, the way he spoke convinced her that Noémie was much better; it seemed to her that he was feeling some embarrassment at having summoned his wife to the bedside of a sick mistress. A pang of regret shot through her heart. Now she could not imagine what evil genius had prompted her to take this ill-considered step. What business had she here—now that Noémie would recover, and life go on its way again, unchanged? She decided to leave at once.

"Thank you, Thérèse," Jerome murmured. "Thank you."

There was a note of affection in his voice, of diffidence and respect. She noticed that Jerome's hand, resting on his knee, was thinner, and evidently trembling a little; the massive signet-ring hung slack upon his finger. She would not raise her eyes, but fixed them on his gloveless hand, and now she could not bring herself to regret the impulse that had brought her here. Why go away? She had acted spontaneously, prayer had inspired the impulse, surely no harm could come of it! Now that she could fall back on her faith, as bidding her reject all thoughts of drawing back, her confidence revived. Never had her heavenly guide left her for long the prey of doubts.

They were entering a vast and spacious city, laid out in endless vistas. At this early hour the shutters were still drawn across the shop-fronts, but the sidewalks were loud with workmen hastening to their tasks. The cab turned into a narrower street where short stretches of causeway alternated with hump-backed bridges spanning a sequence of parallel canals. Tall, slender houses lined the water-front, and the red façades, bare of ornaments but studded with white windows, were mirrored in the almost stagnant water between the branches of elms that drooped beside the quays. Mme. de Fontanin realized that France was very far away.

"How are the children?" Jerome inquired.

She had noticed his hesitation in putting the question; he was moved, and for once made no attempt to hide his emotion.

"Quite well."

"What's Daniel doing?"

"He's at Paris, working. He comes to Maisons whenever he is free."

"So you're at Maisons?"

"Yes."

He was silent; the park, the house beside the forest that he knew so well, rose up before his eyes.

"And . . . Jenny?"

"She is quite well." An unspoken question hovered in his eyes. "Jenny's grown much taller," she went on; "very much changed, in fact."

Jerome's eyelids quivered and his voice was shaken by emotion when he answered her.

"Yes, I suppose that's so. She must have changed a lot." Looking away, he relapsed into silence. Then, passing his hand over his forehead, he exclaimed in a sombre voice: "How ghastly it all is!" And, almost in the same breath, added: "I have practically no money left, Thérèse."

"I've brought some," she answered impulsively.

She had heard such agony in Jerome's cry that, with the knowledge she could set his fears at rest, her immediate feeling was one of thankfulness. But close upon it came another thought that stung her: the report of Noémie's illness had, quite likely, been exaggerated—it was for the money, only for that, they had lured her here! And she felt sick with disgust when, after a slight hesitation, in a voice thickened by shame, Jerome blurted out the question:

"How much?"

She fought back a brief temptation to understate the sum.

"All I could scrape together," she replied. "A little over three thousand francs."

"Thank you, thank you," he stammered. "Ah, Thérèse, if you only knew . . . ! The chief thing is to settle the doctor's bill: five hundred florins."

The cab had crossed a stone bridge spanning what looked like a wide river, crowded with shipping; now, after traversing some narrow suburban streets, it entered a small square and pulled up in front of a flight of steps abutting on a chapel. Jerome alighted, paid the cabman, and lifted out his wife's bag. Then, without more ado, he helped Thérèse down from the vehicle, walked up the steps, and held the door ajar. It seemed to be neither a Catholic nor a Protestant church; a synagogue, perhaps.

"I must ask you to excuse me," he whispered, "but I don't want to drive up to the house. They keep a sharp lookout on strangers—I'll explain later." Then with a quick change of tone he became the man-about-town, making an affable suggestion. "Isn't the air delicious this morning? I'm sure you won't mind a short walk. I'll lead the way, shall I?"

She followed him without comment. The cab was out of sight. Jerome took her along a vaulted passage leading down a flight of stone steps to the solitary quay of a canal; on the other side the houses came down straight to the edge of the water which lapped the basements. Sunlight played on brick walls and flashing window-panes; the sills were gay with nasturtiums and geraniums. The quay was crowded with people, trestle-tables, and baskets; an open-air market was being set up and, amidst the oddments and old junk, small craft were unlading boatloads of flowers whose perfumes mingled with the musty reek of stagnant water.

Jerome turned towards his wife.

"Not too tired, sweetheart?"

He gave a singing lilt to the word—"sweet-heart"—just as in the old days. She dropped her eyes and did not answer him.

Without an inkling of the emotions he had conjured up he pointed to a house with low eaves, to which a footbridge gave access.

"There it is," he said. "Yes, it's not much of a place. You must forgive me for this poor welcome."

As he said, the house had a humble appearance, but the fresh coat of brown stucco and the white woodwork reminded her of a well-kept yacht. The flame-coloured blinds of the second floor were down, and on them she could read in unassuming letters:

Pension Roosje-Mathilda.

So Jerome was living in some sort of hotel, a nondescript abode where the sensation that they were her hosts would not weigh too heavily; that, anyhow, was a relief.

They stepped onto the footbridge. There was a movement at one of the blinds. Was Noémie on the watch? Mme. de Fontanin drew herself erect. It was only then she noticed, between two ground-floor windows, a crudely painted metal sign depicting a stork beside its nest, whence a naked baby was emerging.

They went along a corridor, then up a staircase redolent of beeswax. Jerome halted on the landing and knocked twice. She could hear whispers behind the door, a peephole shutter was drawn aside, and presently the door was opened cautiously, just enough to let Jerome in.

"Will you allow me . . . ?" he murmured. "I'll just let them know."

Mme. de Fontanin heard a brief colloquy in Dutch, and almost immediately Jerome opened the door wide. The others had gone. She

followed him along an interminable, winding passage with a bees-
waxed floor. Mme. de Fontanin felt ill at ease; the thought that she
might encounter Noémie at any moment unnerved her and she had
to summon up all her courage to preserve her calm demeanour. But
there was no one in the room they entered; it was clean and cheerful,
and gave onto the canal.

"Here, sweetheart," said Jerome, "you are—at home!"

An unuttered question rose to her lips: "And what about Noémie?"
He read her thought.

"I must leave you for a moment," he said. "I'll just go and see if I'm
needed."

But, before leaving, he went towards his wife and took her hand.

"Oh, Thérèse, I must, I must tell you. . . . If you only knew what
a terrible time I've been having! But, now you are here. . . ." His
lips and cheek caressed Mme. de Fontanin's hand. She shrank from
his touch; he made no effort to coerce her. "I'll come back for you in
a moment. . . . You're sure you don't mind—seeing her again?" He
began to move away.

Yes, she would see Noémie once again; she had come to this place
of her own accord, and she would see it through. But after that,
without wasting a moment, she would go away, whatever came of it.
She made a gesture of assent, and, oblivious of Jerome's stammered
thanks, bent over her valise, pretending to hunt for something in
it, till he had left the room.

Alone now with her thoughts, she felt less sure of herself. Taking
off her hat, she glanced into the mirror and noticed her tired face.
She passed her hand over her forehead. What could have induced
her to come here? She felt ashamed.

A knock at the door cut short her mood of weakness. She had no
time to say "Come in" before it opened. The woman in a red dressing-
gown who entered was obviously past her prime, despite her jet-
black hair and made-up complexion. She put some questions in a
tongue that Mme. de Fontanin did not understand, made an impatient
gesture, and called in another woman who evidently had been waiting in the corridor. The new-comer was younger and she, too, wore

a dressing-gown; hers was sky-blue. She greeted Mme. de Fontanin in a guttural voice:

"*Dag,* Madame. Good morning."

The Dutchwomen held a brief colloquy, the older explaining what the other was to say. The younger woman paused a moment, then, turning amiably towards Mme. de Fontanin, addressed her, halting between each sentence:

"The lady says you shall take off the sick lady. You must pay the bill and move to one other house. *Verstaat U?* Understand you what I say?"

Mme. de Fontanin made an evasive gesture—all this was no concern of hers. The older woman broke in again; she seemed worried and determined to have her way.

"The lady says," the young woman interpreted, "even if you pay not the bill at once, you must move, go away, take the sick lady to a room in an hotel somewhere else. *Verstaat U?* That is better for the *Politie.*"

The door was flung open and Jerome appeared. Going up to the woman in red, he began scolding her in Dutch, propelling her meanwhile over the threshold. The woman in blue said nothing; her bold eyes wandered from Jerome's face to Mme. de Fontanin's, and back again. The older woman was obviously in a blazing temper; raising an arm that jangled a full peal of bracelets like a gipsy's, she spluttered incoherent phrases in which certain words recurred like a refrain:

"*Morgen . . . Morgen . . . Politie . . .*"

At last Jerome managed to ged rid of them, and turned the key.

"Really, I'm dreadfully sorry." His face showed his vexation as he turned towards his wife.

Thérèse realized now that, instead of going to Noémie, he had adjourned to his room, to complete his toilet; he had just shaved, there was a touch of powder on his cheek, and he looked younger. And I, she thought, what a sight I must be, after travelling all night!

"I should have told you to lock yourself in," he explained. "The old dame who runs the place is a decent soul in her way, but she talks too much and has no manners."

"What did she want of me?" Thérèse inquired absent-mindedly. The odour of lavender that always floated round Jerome when he had just finished dressing had evoked the past, leaving her pensive for some moments, with parted lips and brooding eyes.

"I haven't a notion what she was jabbering about," he replied. "She probably mistook you for someone else who's staying here."

"The woman in blue told me several times to pay the bill and go elsewhere."

Jerome laughed. She seemed to hear an echo from the past—that rather artificial, self-satisfied way he had of laughing, with his head flung back.

"Ha! Ha! Ha! Too absurd for words!" he guffawed. "Perhaps the old hag thought I wouldn't pay her." He seemed to consider it unthinkable that he should ever be at a loss to pay his debts. Then suddenly his face fell. "Am I to blame? I tried my best, but no hotel would hear of taking us in."

"But I gathered from her it had to do with the police."

He seemed astounded.

"What? She mentioned the police?"

"Yes, I think so." Once more she caught on Jerome's face that look of dubious innocence which she associated with the darkest moments of her life; it gave her a sudden nausea, as though the air in the room were plague-infected.

"An old wives' tale, all that! Why should there be a police inquiry? Just because there happens to be a consulting-room on the ground floor? No. The only thing that matters is to be able to pay that doctor fellow his five hundred florins."

Mme. de Fontanin was as mystified as ever and this distressed her, for she always liked things made clear. But what grieved her most was to find that once again Jerome had let himself become entangled in a network of intrigues of which she hardly liked to think.

"How long have you been staying here?" she asked, hoping to get something definite out of him.

"Two weeks. No, not so long; ten or twelve days, more likely. I've lost track of things. . . ."

"And . . . her illness?" The tone was so insistent that he dared not evade her question.

"That's just what the trouble's about." The reply came pat enough. "With these foreign doctors it's so hard to make out what is really the matter. It's a local disease of sorts, one of those—er—Dutch fevers, you know—something to do with the miasma from the canals." He pondered for a moment. "This city reeks with malaria, you know; the air is full of infections the doctors don't know much about."

She listened to him perfunctorily, but could not help noticing that, whenever Noémie was in question, Jerome's attitude—the way he shrugged his shoulders, his casual air when speaking of her illness— was hardly that of a devoted lover. But she forbade herself to see in this an avowal of estrangement.

He did not observe the searching glance she cast on him; he had gone to the window, and, though he had not moved the blind, his eyes were fixed intently on the quay. When he came back to her, his face had assumed the earnest and sincere yet disillusioned air she knew so well and so much dreaded.

"Thank you, dear, you're very good to me!" he suddenly exclaimed. "I've wounded you again and again—and yet you have come to me. Thérèse . . . Sweetheart . . ."

Shrinking away, she would not meet his eyes. But, such was her insight into others' feelings—into Jerome's most of all—she could not question the sincerity of his emotion and his gratitude at this moment. Yet she could not bring herself to answer, or prolong the conversation.

"Please take me . . . there," she said.

After a brief hesitation, he gave way.

"Come."

The moment she dreaded was at hand. "I must be brave," she murmured as she followed him down the long dark corridor. "Is she still in bed . . . convalescent? What shall I say to her?" It struck her once more how worn out she must look after her journey, and she wished she had at least put on her hat again.

Jerome halted at a closed door. With a trembling hand Mme. de

Fontanin settled her white hair. "She'll find me looking terribly old," she all but said aloud, and all her self-confidence oozed away.

Jerome opened the door noiselessly. So she's in bed, Mme. de Fontanin decided.

Chintz curtains patterned with blue flowers were drawn across the window and a subdued light filled the room. Two women, whom she had not seen before, rose as she came in. One of them, who wore an apron and was busy knitting, was presumably a servant or an attendant; the other, a buxom matron some fifty years old, had a violet bandanna round her head and looked like an Italian peasant. As Mme. de Fontanin entered, the older woman began to beat a retreat, whispering something in Jerome's ear as she went out.

Thérèse did not notice the woman's departure, or the disorder of the room, the basin and the dirty towels littering the sheets. Her gaze was riveted on the sick woman stretched flat upon the pillowless bed. Would Noémie turn in her direction? She was snoring, seemingly asleep. A craven impulse urged Mme. de Fontanin to leave her to her rest, and go; but then Jerome signed to her to come to the foot of the bed and she dared not refuse. Then she saw that Noémie's eyes were open and the stertorous breathing came in gasps from her wide-open mouth. As she grew used to the half-light she saw a bloodless face and ice-blue eyes, their pupils set in the glassy stare of butchered animals. In a flash it came to her that she was standing by a deathbed and in her consternation she turned quickly with a cry for help upon her lips. But Jerome was at her side, gazing at the dying woman; his grief was plain to read upon his face and she saw at once that he had nothing to learn from her.

"Since her last hæmorrhage—it was the fourth attack," he whispered, "she has never regained consciousness. She has been like that all night." Tears gathered slowly at the edges of his eyelids, hung for a moment on the lashes, rolled down his sallow cheeks.

Mme. de Fontanin tried in vain to pull herself together; she could hardly bring herself to admit the evidence of her eyes.

Yes, Noémie was dying and would pass out of their lives; Noémie, whom only a moment ago she had pictured as triumphing over her!

She dared not take her eyes off the dying woman's face where even now all movement was arrested—the rigid nostrils, dulled eyes, and bloodless lips through which the rattling breath, coming, it seemed, from very far away, rose and ebbed, and feebly rose again. She lingered on each feature, turn by turn, with curiosity (which was half terror) still unsated. Could that be Noémie—that shape of ashen, bloodless flesh, with a wisp of brown hair plastered across a dry, white-gleaming forehead? Drained of colour and expression, the face seemed wholly unfamiliar. How long was it since she last saw Noémie? Then it came back to her, the day five or six years ago when she had rushed to Noémie's house to cry in vain: "Give me back my husband!" Her cousin's shrill laugh seemed echoing in her ears, and she remembered with a shudder the handsome woman lolling on the sofa, and her glimpse of a plump shoulder stirring beneath the lace. That was the day when Nicole had run up to her in the hall and . . .

"What about Nicole?" she asked abruptly.

"Nicole?"

"Have you let her know?"

"No."

How was it she did not think of this herself, when leaving Paris? She drew Jerome aside.

"You *must,* Jerome. She's Nicole's mother."

The look of entreaty on his face gave her the measure of his weakness, and her resolution faltered too. To think of Nicole coming to this hateful house, entering such a room, confronting Jerome by this bedside! But she insisted, though her tone was less assured.

"You *must!*"

The curious earth-brown hue which darkened Jerome's dusky skin still more whenever he was thwarted came to his cheeks; his narrow lips set in a harsh grimace, baring his teeth.

"Jerome, Nicole must be sent for," she repeated gently.

His slender eyebrows drew together, drooped, and for a while he still held out. At last, raising his hard eyes to hers, he yielded.

"What is her address?"

When he had left to send the telegram she returned to the bed; somehow she could not tear herself away from it. She stood beside it with drooping arms, her fingers locked. What had possessed her to imagine Noémie out of danger? And why did Jerome not seem more distressed? What were his plans? Would he come back to live with her? Certainly no such suggestion would cross her lips; yet she would not deny him shelter, if he asked it.

A grateful mood of peace, almost of happiness, crept over her; the feeling shamed her and she sought to banish it. To pray. To pray for this departing soul that was returning to the Universal Soul. Poor soul, she thought, that takes so little with her on her way! Yet, in the ineluctable ascent of all towards a higher plane, through the vast sequence of our earthly incarnations, does not each upward effort, however feeble, tell in favour of the one who makes it? Does not each trial mean a step forward on the pathway of perfection? That Noémie had suffered, Thérèse could not doubt. Despite the specious glamour of her life, surely there had rankled in the poor woman's heart a deep unrest, the dull ache of a conscience that, for all its unconcern, trembled in secret at its degradation. And now that suffering would be accounted to the poor soul's credit in another, better life; and her love, too, despite its guilt and the evil it had done. This, in her present mood, Thérèse could readily forgive. Still, she reflected, such forgiveness did her little honour. For, there was no denying it, she could not persuade herself that Noémie's death would be a great misfortune. For anyone. Her feelings were evolving with remorseless speed; she, like Jerome, was growing used to the notion that Noémie was to pass out of their lives. Less than an hour had gone since first she *knew*—and, already, almost her only feeling was one of resignation.

When, two days later, Nicole stepped down from the Paris express, her mother had been dead for thirty-six hours; the funeral was to take place on the following morning.

Everyone concerned seemed eager to have done with it—the proprietress of the pension, Jerome, and, most of all, the young doctor, recipient of the five hundred florins, who had signed the death-certificate without even coming upstairs to view the body, after a brief parley in one of the ground-floor rooms.

Harrowing though the task would have been, Thérèse expressed a desire to help in laying out the body; she wished to be able to tell Nicole that she had carried out this pious duty in her stead. But, at the last moment and on trivial grounds, they had refused her access to the room; the midwife had insisted on attending to the laying out—"After all, she's used to it," Jerome had observed—in the presence of the nurse alone.

Nicole's arrival brought a welcome change. Hour by hour Mme. de Fontanin had been finding her encounters in the corridor, with pension-keeper, doctor, and the nurse, more and more unbearable; indeed, from the moment she had come, the atmosphere she was breathing in this house seemed to suffocate her. Nicole's open face, her youth and health, brought a breath of fresh, cleansing air into the place. The violence of her grief, however—Jerome was so unnerved by it that he took refuge in another room—struck Mme. de Fontanin as disproportioned to the girl's true feelings towards a mother she had cast out of her life. The childish extravagance of her outburst bore out the older woman's view of her niece's mentality; a warm-hearted girl, she thought, but lacking real depth of character.

Nicole wanted to bring her mother's body back to France; as she declined to have anything to do with Jerome, whom she still held responsible for her mother's lapse, her aunt volunteered to sound him on the matter. Jerome met the proposal with an emphatic veto. He expatiated on the exorbitant railway charges in such cases, the endless formalities involved, and, finally, the inquest on which, needless though it was, the local police would certainly insist; they delighted, Jerome averred, in putting foreigners to inconvenience. So Nicole's plan had to be dropped.

Exhausted though she was by her emotions and the journey, Nicole insisted on keeping vigil beside the coffin. The three of them passed the night, in silence and alone, in Noémie's room. The coffin, spread with flowers, rested on two chairs. So heady was the perfume of jessamine and roses that they had to keep the window wide open. The night was hot, and bright as day with dazzling moonlight. Now and again they heard low sounds of water lapping round the piles which supported the house. Near at hand the passing hours chimed from a clock-tower. A moonbeam, gliding across the floor, crept every minute nearer to an over-blown white rose fallen beside the coffin's foot, making it seem translucent, almost blue. Nicole's indignant eyes took in the squalor of the room; here her mother had lived, perhaps; assuredly had suffered. She was counting up, perhaps, the printed flowers on yonder curtain when first she heard death's summons and, in a tragic pageant, the follies of her wasted life had passed before her dying eyes. Had she given her daughter then a last, belated thought?

The funeral took place very early next day. Neither midwife nor pension-keeper put in an appearance. Thérèse walked between Jerome and Nicole, and the only other mourner was an old clergyman whom Mme. de Fontanin had sent for to attend the funeral and read the burial service.

To spare Nicole another visit to the odious house beside the canal, Mme. de Fontanin decided to take the girl directly to the station on leaving the graveyard. Jerome would follow up with the luggage. Moreover, Nicole refused to take over any object whatsoever associated with her mother's life abroad; the decision to leave Noémie's trunks behind made the final settlement with the proprietress a much simpler matter.

When all the bills had been paid and Jerome was on his way to the station, he found he had a good deal of time on his hands before the train was due to leave; yielding to a sudden impulse, he directed the cabman to take another road, and revisited the graveyard for the last time.

He lost his way several times before finding the grave again. When he sighted in the distance a mound of newly turned earth, he took off his hat and walked towards it with measured steps. Here lay all that remained of their six years of life in common, of quarrels, jealousy, and reconcilements; six years of memories and secrets shared—all to end in the final, most tragic secret whose upshot lay before his eyes.

"After all, things might have turned out worse; I do not seem to feel it much," he consoled himself, though his careworn forehead and blinding tears appeared to belie the thought. Was he to blame if rejoicing over his wife's return outweighed his grief? Surely there had been one love only in his life—Thérèse! But would she ever understand that? Would she ever forgo her cold austerity and realize that, appearances notwithstanding, she alone fulfilled the life of this too wayward lover, who yet had loved with all his soul one woman only? Would it ever come to her that, beside the whole-hearted devotion he bestowed on her, no other love of his was more than a passing fancy? Surely this very moment bore him out—Noémie's death had left him neither lost nor lonely. So long as Thérèse lived, though she were even more aloof from him, though she might fancy every bond between them severed, he was not alone. For an instant he tried to picture Thérèse lying there under the flower-strewn turf; but found the thought unbearable. He hardly blamed himself at all for any of the sufferings he had brought on his wife, so firm was his conviction at this solemn moment that he had deprived her of nothing which really mattered, but had devoted to her all that was best and most enduring in his heart—so sure was he that he had never for a moment been unfaithful to her. What are her plans for me? he asked himself, but with no anxiety. Surely she would want him to come back to her and to the children. His head was bowed, his cheeks were wet with tears—but in his heart hope glowed insidiously.

If it weren't for Nicole, all would be for the best! he thought. He recalled the girl's hostile silence and her steely eyes. He saw her again bending above the grave, and heard again the dry, racking sob she had not been able to keep back.

Yes, the thought of Nicole was a torment to him. Was it not on his account that, angered beyond bearing, she had fled her mother's house? A passage from the Gospels echoed in his memory: "Woe to that man by whom the offence cometh!" How shall I make amends?

he wondered. He could not endure the thought that anyone disapproved of him. . . . Suddenly he had an inspiration. Why not adopt her as his daughter?

Yes, that settled everything! In his mind's eye he pictured it—the little flat that he would share with Nicole; she would, of course, arrange it to her liking, keep house for him, help him to entertain. How everybody would admire his gesture of contrition! Thérèse, too, would approve.

He put on his hat again and, turning his back on the grave, walked briskly to the cab.

The train had been in for some time when he reached the station. The two women had already taken their seats. Mme. de Fontanin was perturbed by her husband's delay in coming. Had some complication arisen at the pension? Almost anything seemed possible. Would Jerome be prevented from leaving? Was her dream of bringing him back to Maisons, of smoothing the way for his return to her and, it well might be, for his repentance—was her fond dream so soon to vanish like a mirage? Her apprehension grew to panic when she saw him approaching with rapid strides and an anxious air.

"Where is Nicole?"

"Why, over there, in the corridor," Mme. de Fontanin replied with some surprise.

The window was half down and Nicole stood beside it, idly gazing at the gleaming network of rails. She felt sad, but weary most of all; sad, yet happy too, for today's sorrow could not even for an instant quell her secret joy. Her mother was dead—but was not the man she loved awaiting her? And once again she tried to ban the thought, as something impious, from her mind, that her mother's death could not but prove, for her lover anyhow, a relief—a lifting of the one and only shadow that hitherto had dimmed their future.

She did not hear Jerome's step behind her.

"Nicole, I implore you—for your mother's sake—forgive me!"

She started and turned round. He stood before her, hat in hand, his eyes aglow with humble entreaty. And now his face, ravaged by sorrow and remorse, no longer disgusted her; she was touched by pity. She could almost fancy that this opportunity for kindliness was of her seeking; yes, she would forgive him.

Without answering, impulsively, she held out her little black-gloved hand, and he pressed it with unfeigned emotion.

"Thank you," he murmured. Then he moved away.

Some minutes passed. Nicole did not move. Things were better so, she thought, if only for her aunt's sake; and then, of course, there would be Felix to tell about this touching little incident. People were bustling along the corridor, jostling her with their luggage. At last the train began to pull out. The sudden stresses helped to dispel her lethargy, and she returned to the compartment. Late-comers occupied the seats which only a moment earlier were empty. At the far end, ensconced in the corner-seat facing Mme. de Fontanin, one arm lolling in a leather window-strap and eyes fixed on the landscape, her uncle Jerome, she observed, was munching a ham sandwich.

VIII

JACQUES spent the evening trying to reconstruct, word for word, his talk with Jenny. He made no attempt to analyse what exactly it was that drew his thoughts so urgently towards that conversation, yet it obsessed his mind. He woke up several times in the course of the night and harked back each time to the same theme with unabated eagerness. So, naturally enough, he was bitterly disappointed when he went to the tennis-club next morning only to find that Jenny had not turned up.

He was asked to join in a set and thought it better to comply, but he played badly, for his eyes strayed all the time towards the entrance-gate. The morning passed and soon it was too late to hope that Jenny would come. He made his escape the moment he could decently do so. His hope had failed him, but he was not hopeless yet.

Then he saw Daniel coming towards him.

"Where's Jenny?" he asked at once. Daniel's presence at this hour was unexpected, but he made no comment on it.

"She's not playing this morning. Are you leaving now? Then I'll come along with you. I've been at Maisons since yesterday evening." As soon as they had left the club grounds he explained: "Mother's been called away, you see; she asked me to sleep at home so that Jenny wouldn't be alone at night—our house is such miles from anywhere. It's another of my father's little games and Mother, poor thing, can never say no to him." A shadow flitted across his face, but soon was vanquished by a resolute smile, for Daniel had a short way with disagreeable thoughts. "And how are you getting on?" His eyes conveyed affectionate concern. "I've been thinking quite a lot about your *Startled Secret;* I like it as much as ever, you know. And the more I think about it the better I like it. Psychologically it's in a class by itself—a trifle brutal, perhaps, and a bit obscure in places. But you've hit on a fine idea and your two heroes are very life-like and, what's more, original."

"No, Daniel," Jacques broke in, unable to master his annoyance. "You mustn't judge me by that. To begin with, the style's abominable. Flatulent, lumpy, long-winded!" And to himself he added, raging inwardly: "Heredity, no doubt!"

"The theme, too," Jacques continued, "is still far too conventional, too made-to-order. A man's mental underworld. . . . Oh, I see quite well what's wanted, only . . ." He broke off abruptly.

"What are you working at now? Have you started on something else?"

"Yes." Jacques felt a blush rising to his cheeks, though he knew no reason for it. "But I'm mostly resting; I was more run down than I suspected, after a year's cramming. And then I've only just come back from attending poor old Battaincourt's wedding—that's one for you, you slacker!"

"Yes, Jenny told me about it."

Jacques blushed again. At first he felt a brief annoyance—that yesterday's talk had ceased to be a secret shared by Jenny and himself alone; but then he was agreeably thrilled to learn that she set store by what he said and it had so impressed her that she had spoken of it that very evening to her brother.

"Shall we take a stroll as far as the bank of the Seine?" he suggested, linking his arm in Daniel's. "We can talk on the way."

"Can't be done, old man. I'm off to Paris by the 1:20. I'm prepared to play the watchdog at night, you see; but in the daytime—" His smile conveyed the nature of the appointment that called him back to Paris; Jacques was displeased by it, and withdrew his arm.

"Look here," Daniel hastily suggested, anxious to ease the tension, "you'd better lunch with us. Jenny'll be delighted."

Jacques lowered his eyes to hide a new emotion and feigned some indecision. As his father was not back, there would be no bother about his missing a meal. He was dumbfounded by the rapture that swept over him, but mastered it enough to answer his friend.

"Thanks very much. I'll just drop in to warn them at home. You go on ahead. I'll meet you in the Castle Square."

Some minutes later he rejoined his friend, who was waiting for him, lying on the grass in front of the Château.

"Isn't it fine here!" Daniel exclaimed, stretching his legs out in the sunshine. "The park's at its best this morning. You're a lucky fellow to live in such surroundings."

"And so could you," Jacques observed, "if you chose to."

Daniel stood up.

"Yes, no doubt I could," he admitted musingly but with a twinkle in his eye. "But I—well, it's not my style! Look here, old man!" He moved towards Jacques and a change came over his voice. "I think I'm in for a perfectly marvellous adventure."

"The green-eyed girl?"

"Green-eyed? I don't . . ."

"At Packmell's, you know."

Daniel stopped short and stared for a few seconds at the grass. Then a curious smile crossed his face.

"Ah, Rinette, you mean. No, someone new—miles ahead of her."

He paused a while, lost in thought, before he spoke again. "Rinette! Yes, that was a queer girl, all right! Just imagine, it was she who dropped me after a day or two!" He laughed—the laugh of one whose way such an experience had never come before. "As a novelist, you'd have thought her thrilling, very likely. Personally, I found her boring. I've never known a woman one could make so little of. Why, even now I've no idea whether she was ever keen on me for ten consecutive minutes; but, when the loving mood was on her, well . . . ! A bit queer, I should say. She must have had a pretty shady past and couldn't shake it off. I shouldn't be in the least surprised to learn that she belonged to some secret society or other."

"So you've quite lost touch with her?"

"Absolutely. I don't even know what's become of her; she never showed up at Packmell's again. Sometimes I rather miss her," he added after a pause. "Anyhow it would have had to end pretty soon; I couldn't have stood her very long. You've no idea how tactless she could be. Always asking questions about my private life, yes—damn it!—about my family, my mother and sister . . . my father, even!"

He walked on in silence.

"Still, when all's said and done, I'm indebted to her for a priceless experience—that evening at Packmell's when I handed one to Ludwigson right in the eye."

"And, with the same shot, brought down your prospects, I suppose?"

"Meaning, I got the sack?" Daniel's eyes twinkled and a wide grin displayed his teeth. "I'd never had such an opportunity of taking friend Ludwigson's measure; well, he pretended not to remember a thing about it. You may think what you like about him; what I say is, he's a great boy in his own way."

Jenny had stayed at home all morning. When Daniel proposed escorting her to the tennis-club she had emphatically declined, professing to be busy. But she felt listless, at a loose end, and the time hung heavy on her hands.

When, from her window, she saw the two young men crossing the garden, her first feeling was one of vexation. She had looked forward to having her brother to herself, and here was Jacques spoiling everything! Still her ill-humour was not proof against Daniel's exuberance, as he cried to her through the half-open window:

"Guess whom I've brought back to lunch!"

I've time to change my dress, she thought.

Jacques was strolling to and fro in the garden; never as today had he appreciated the quiet beauty of Jenny's home. After the park, studded with villas, it had all the charm of an old-world farmhouse secluded on the margin of the forest. The central portion with its tall windows had evidently been a hunting-lodge, many times restored; more or less incongruous annexes had been built onto it at different periods. A flight of wooden steps, like the open ladders clamped to barns, led under a penthouse to the more lofty of the two wings. Jenny's pigeons scudded to and fro along the shelving tiles and the walls were rough-coated with a bright pink distemper which drank up the sunlight like an Italian stucco. A tangled conclave of tall fir-trees cast dry, cool shadows on the house and sun-burnt grass, and the air beneath them had a brisk tang of resin.

Daniel was in great form at lunch and his gaiety was contagious; he had had an exhilarating morning and the afternoon promised well. He congratulated Jenny on her blue frock and pinned a white rose in her blouse, calling her "sister mine." He was amused by everyone and everything, even his own high spirits.

He insisted on being escorted to the station and seen into his train by Jacques and Jenny.

"Will you be back for dinner?" she inquired. Sometimes, Jacques noticed with a vague distress, a jarring undertone—which certainly was not intentional—crept into Jenny's voice, contrasting with her gentle, unassuming ways.

"It's quite in the cards," Daniel replied. "Anyhow I'll do my level best to catch the seven-o'clock train. In any case I shall be back before dark, as I promised Mamma in my letter." The small-boyish voice in which Daniel spoke the last words and his mature appearance were so charmingly incongruous that Jacques could not help laughing and even Jenny, as she stooped to clip the leash on her little dog's collar, looked up with a smile of amusement.

When the train came in Daniel noticed that the front cars were empty and ran towards them; from where they stood they saw him leaning out of the window and waving with his handkerchief a frivolous farewell.

Now they were alone, and the situation found them unprepared to deal with it; Daniel's high spirits had carried them off their feet. They managed, however, to keep up a tone of easy intimacy, as if Daniel still were serving as a link between them; and this new truce was such a relief to both that they were careful not to break its amity.

Rather depressed to see her brother leave, Jenny recalled his all too frequent absences from home.

"Couldn't you get Daniel to stop spending his vacation running backwards and forwards like this? He doesn't realize how sad it makes Mother, seeing so little of him this summer. But, of course, you'll stick up for him," she added, though without the least aggressiveness.

"No, I've not the least wish to do so," he replied. "Do you imagine I approve of the life he's leading?"

"Well, do you let him know that, anyhow?"

"Of course I do."

"And he won't listen to you?"

"He listens all right. But it goes deeper than that. I rather think he doesn't understand me."

"You mean, that he has *ceased* to understand you?"

"Very likely. . . . Yes."

From the outset their conversation had taken a serious turn. With Daniel as their theme there was a mutual understanding between them, which since yesterday was no new thing, but it had never before been given such free play. And, when they were about to turn into the park, it was from her that the suggestion came:

"How about going by the highroad? Then you could see me home through the forest. It's quite early, and such a lovely day!"

He made no effort to conceal the happiness that flooded his heart, but dared not let it master him. Fearing to snap the golden thread of sympathy between them, he hastily reverted to their common interest.

"Daniel has such a zest for living."

"Yes," she said, "I know it only too well. For living without control. But a life that's uncontrolled is very—very dangerous." Averting her eyes, she added: "And . . . impure."

"Impure," he repeated gravely. "Yes, I agree with you, Jenny."

Impurity! A word he little cared to use, yet one which very often rose to his lips, and now on hers he heard it with a sudden thrill. Yes, all Daniel's "affairs" were sullied by "impurity," and so was Antoine's passion. All carnal lusts were tainted in the same way. One thing, one only, in the world was pure—the nameless feeling which had been growing up within him for months and months and since yesterday unfolding, in gradual beauty, like a flower.

Steadying his voice, he continued:

"Sometimes I'm furious with him for the attitude he has taken up towards life, a sort of——"

"Perverseness," she added ingenuously; it was a word that often crossed her thoughts, her name for all that seemed obnoxious to her innocence.

"Personally, I'd rather call it cynicism," he amended, using in his turn an incorrect expression which he had twisted to his uses. But no sooner had he spoken than he felt he was not being wholly loyal to himself. "Don't imagine," he exclaimed hastily, "that I approve of a nature that is always fighting against itself. I prefer——" He paused, and Jenny hung on his words, eager to take his meaning—as though what he had just said were of exceptional importance in her eyes. "I prefer people who make a point of living according to their natures. All the same, they shouldn't——" He broke off. Several instances he did not think fit for Jenny's ears had crossed his mind.

"Yes," she agreed. "And I'm so afraid that Daniel may end by losing—what should I call it?—the sense of sin. Do you see what I mean?"

He nodded approval and now he could not refrain, either, from gazing at her intently, for the earnestness of her look added significance to her words. How she betrayed herself unwittingly, he mused, in that last remark!

She had her features well under control, but her set lips and laboured breathing vouched for the effort she was making to fight down one of those gusts of wild emotion which so often swept across her, emotion which she always did her utmost to conceal.

What can it be, Jacques wondered, that makes her face so apt to wear that hard, aloof expression? Is it because the line of her eyebrows is rather narrow, too precise? No, I fancy it must be the two dark cavities her pupils form in the grey-blue of the iris, when they contract. And, from this moment on he forgot about Daniel; his thoughts were all for Jenny.

For some minutes they walked on without speaking, and to them the silent interval, though it lasted quite a while, seemed very short. But, when they wanted to pick up the fallen strand of conversation, they found their thoughts had wandered far afield, almost, it seemed, in opposite directions. Neither could find a word to break the silence.

It so happened that they were passing a garage; the road was lined with cars under repair and the noise of running engines gave little scope for conversation.

A decrepit, mangy old dog shambled across the grease-stains on the road towards Puce, and began to show an interest in her; Jenny picked up her little dog in her arms. No sooner had they passed the workshop entrance than they heard cries behind them. A skeleton chassis, driven by a youngster of fifteen, had clattered out of the repair-shop and swung round so sharply that, despite the lad's belated cry of warning, the old dog had no time to get out of the way. Jacques and Jenny, who had turned round at the cry, saw the chassis catch the unfortunate animal in the side and two wheels pass over his body in quick succession.

Jenny gave a scream of horror:

"Oh, he's killed! He's killed!"

"No. He's got up again."

The dog had struggled up and fled in a blind panic, yelping and covered with blood. His shattered hindquarters trailed on the ground, making him move in zigzags, collapsing every few yards.

Jenny's face was twitching and she went on crying monotonously: "He's killed! Oh, he's killed!"

The dog turned into a courtyard, its cries grew less frequent, then ceased altogether. The garage hands, glad of an excuse for knocking off work, followed up the trail of blood. One of them went as far as the house with the courtyard and shouted:

"He's dead! Not a kick left!"

With a gesture of relief, Jenny let her dog slip from her arms, and they set off again towards the forest. The emotion they had shared brought them still nearer to each other.

"I shall never forget," said Jacques, "your face and your voice when you called out just now."

"One loses one's head—it's silly. What did I say?"

" 'He's killed!' That's an interesting point, isn't it? You'd seen the dog run over by the car, pounded into a shapeless, bleeding mass— that was the really sickening part of it. And yet the real tragedy began only at the moment, the dreadful moment, when the poor beast who'd been alive a second earlier had to lie down and die. Don't you agree? The most moving thing of all is the unknowable transition, the head-long fall from life into nothingness. It haunts us all, the terror of that moment; it's a sort of—of mystical awe, always waiting on the threshold of our thoughts. Do you often think of death?"

"Yes. Well, I mean . . . not so very often. Do you?"

"Personally, I'm almost always thinking about it. Most of my thoughts bring me back to the idea of death. But"—he sounded dis-couraged—"however often one comes back to it, it's only a notion of the mind. . . ." And there he left it. For the moment he looked almost handsome, his face aglow with fervour, a zest for life mingled with dread of death.

They walked a little way before she broke the silence.

"I can't think what's brought it into my head—really it has nothing to do with what you were saying," she began in a hesitating voice.

"But I've just remembered something . . . the first time I saw the sea. But perhaps Daniel's told you already?"

"No. Tell me about it."

"It's ancient history, you know—when I was fourteen or fifteen. It was near the end of the holidays and Mamma and I were going to join Daniel at Tréport. He'd asked us to get out at some station or other on the way, and met us there with a farm-cart. As he didn't want to spoil my first impression of the sea by casual glimpses at the bends of the road, he blindfolded me—a silly idea, wasn't it? After a while he told me to get down and led me by the hand. I followed him, stumbling at every step. A terrific gale lashed my face and there was a perfectly fiendish din roaring and shrieking in my ears. I was scared to death and begged him not to take me any further. At last we came to the summit of the cliff, and Daniel slipped behind me and untied the handkerchief. Before my eyes lay the open sea and far beneath, where the cliff fell sheer, the waves were breaking on the rocks. On every side was sea, sea everywhere as far as eye could reach. I stopped breathing and collapsed into Daniel's arms. It took me some minutes to come to, and then I started sobbing, sobbing. They had to take me home and put me to bed; I had a temperature. Mamma was terribly upset. But now—do you know?—I don't regret it one bit; I feel I really know the sea."

Jacques had never seen her thus; no trace of melancholy on her face, her look unclouded, almost ecstatic. Then, suddenly, the fervour died from her face.

Little by little Jacques was discovering an unknown Jenny. Her abrupt changes of mood, from reticence to sudden outbursts, brought to his mind a choked but copious spring, which flowed only in sudden gushes. Here lay, he guessed, the secret of that innate sadness which gave her face its contemplative air and lent such charm to her rare, transient smiles. And suddenly the thought appalled him, that such a walk as this must have an end.

"No need to hurry, is there?" he tentatively suggested, now they had passed beneath the arch of the old forest gate. "Let's take the long way round. I'll bet you've never tried that lane."

A sandy track, soft underfoot, led down into the darkness of a glen. Flanked at first by wide strips of grass, it narrowed as it went on. Here the trees thrived ill; their meagre leafage let the sunlight through on every side.

They walked on, not in the least troubled by their silence.

What's come over me? Jenny was wondering. He's so different from what I thought. Yes, he's . . . he's . . . But she could not find the word she wanted. How alike we are! she thought, with a strange thrill of certitude and joy. But then she grew anxious. What thoughts were in his mind?

But Jacques's mind was empty, lulled by a bliss devoid of thoughts. He walked beside her and asked nothing more of life.

"I'm afraid I'm taking you into one of the ugliest parts of the forest," he murmured at last.

She started at the sound of his voice and the same thought flashed across the minds of both: that their brief silence had been of crucial import for the vague dream that haunted both alike.

"Yes, I agree with you," she replied.

"Why, it isn't even real grass!" Jacques prodded the ground with his toecap. "It's a sort of dog-grass."

"Well, Puce certainly seems to take to it—just look!"

They spoke at random; common words seemed to have completely changed their sense and value for them.

That's a charming blue, thought Jacques, looking at her dress. How is it that a soft, greyish blue is so exactly *her* colour? Then his thoughts flew off at a tangent.

"I want to tell you something!" he exclaimed. "What makes me so dense is that I never can switch my attention off what's going on in my mind."

"I'm just the same." Jenny fancied she was capping his remark. "I'm nearly always day-dreaming. I like it awfully; so do you, don't you? The things I dream are quite my own and I like to feel I needn't share them with anyone. Do you see what I mean?"

"Yes, absolutely!"

A sweet-brier grew beside the lane; some branches were in flower and on one the tiny hips were forming. Jacques was in half a mind to proffer them to her and quote: "I bring thee flowers and fruit and leafy boughs. And with them all . . . my heart!" Then he would pause, observing her. But his courage failed him. When they had passed the bush, he said to himself: "What a *littérateur* I am!"

"Do you like Verlaine?" he asked.

"Yes. *Sagesse,* which Daniel used to like so much, is my favourite."

He murmured:

> *"Beauté des femmes, leur faiblesse, et ces mains pâles*
> *Qui font souvent le bien et peuvent tout le mal . . .*

"And how about Mallarmé?" he continued, after a pause. "I've quite a decent anthology of modern poets. Would you like me to bring it?"

"Yes."

"Do you care for Baudelaire?"

"Not so much. He's rather like Whitman. Anyhow, I don't know much of Baudelaire."

"Have you read Whitman?"

"Daniel read me some of his poems last winter. I can quite understand Whitman's appeal for him. But, as for me—" Again the word "impurity," which they had used a little while ago, rose to their minds. How like me she is! Jacques thought.

"As for you," he went on, "that's just the reason why you don't like Whitman so much as he does, isn't it?"

She nodded, grateful to him for uttering her unsaid thought.

The pathway, wider now, debouched into a clearing where a bench was set between two oak-trees stripped of their foliage by caterpillars. Jenny threw her wide-brimmed hat of supple straw onto the grass, and sat down.

"There are times," she exclaimed impulsively, as though she were thinking aloud, "when I almost wonder how it is you're such a bosom friend of Daniel's!"

"Why?" He smiled. "Do I strike you as being so very different from him?"

"Very different indeed—today."

He lay down on a grassy bank a little way from her.

"My bosom friend . . ." he repeated musingly. "Does he ever talk to you about me?"

"No. I mean, yes. Now and then."

She blushed; but he was not looking her way.

"Yes," he continued, nibbling a blade of grass, "nowadays there's a solid bond of affection between us; it's calm and tolerant. But we weren't always like that." Pausing, he pointed to a snail, translucent as an agate, which, clinging to a grass-haulm, timidly probed the sunlight with its viscid horns. "When I was working for the exam, you know," he added inconsequently, "I often used to think for weeks on end that I was going off my head; my brain was seething with such a ferment of ideas. And then—I was so lonely!"

"But you were living with your brother, weren't you?"

"Yes, luckily enough. And I was quite free—that, too, was a stroke of luck. Otherwise I think I'd have gone mad, really mad. Or else run away."

For the first time in her life she recalled the Marseille escapade with something like indulgence.

"I felt misunderstood." His voice grew sombre. "Misunderstood by everyone, even by my brother; often enough even by Daniel, too."

Just as I did! was her unspoken comment.

"When I was in those moods I couldn't summon up the faintest interest in my studies. I doped myself with reading—everything in Antoine's library, all the books Daniel could supply. I must have sampled nearly every modern novelist, French, English, and Russian. You simply can't imagine the thrills I got from books! And, afterwards, everything else seemed so deadly dull—my tutors, all their pedantic fumbling with texts, their precious cult of respectability. No, most decidedly that wasn't in my line at all!" He talked about himself without a trace of self-conceit; like all young people he was full of himself and could imagine no keener pleasure than to dissect his personality under attentive eyes; and his pleasure was infectious. "Those were the days," he continued, "when I used to write Daniel thirty-page letters that I'd spent all night concocting. Letters where I poured out all my day's enthusiasms and, most of all, disgusts. I suppose I ought to laugh at all that, now. But, no, I can't." He pressed his hand against his forehead. "The life I led in those days made me suffer far too intensely for me to make my peace with it, as yet. I had Daniel give me back my letters and I read them over again! They read like the confessions of a madman in his lucid intervals. Sometimes there were several days between them, sometimes only a few hours. Each was a sort of volcanic outburst, the eruption of a mental crisis, and, often as not, in flat contradiction with the one that went before it. A religious crisis, really, for I'd just been soaking myself in the Gospels or the Old Testament—or else in Comte and positivism. What a letter I wrote just after reading Emerson! I'd been through all the usual maladies of youth; a galloping 'Baudelairitis,' a sharp attack of Vinci. But none of them was chronic; they came and went! One day I rose a classicist and went to bed romantic, and made a secret holocaust of my Boileau and Malherbe in Antoine's laboratory. I performed the rite in solitude, laughing like a fiend. Next day everything that had to do with literature seemed to me utterly stale and unprofitable. I started delving into geometry, from the primers on; I'd set my heart on unearthing new laws that would turn all previous theories inside out. Then I had a spell of poetizing. I wrote odes for Daniel, Horatian epistles of two hundred lines, dashed off with hardly one erasure. The oddest thing of all"—his voice had suddenly grown calm—"was a pamphlet I composed in English, yes entirely in English, and entitled 'The Emancipation of the Individual in Relation to Society.' I gave it a preface, a short one, I grant, in—would you believe it?—modern Greek!" (The last detail was untrue; he remembered merely his intention to compose such a preface.) He burst out laughing. "No, I'm not really so mad as I seem!" he exclaimed after a pause. Then he fell silent again and, half laughingly, but without the least trace of vanity, declared: "Anyhow, I was quite different from the rest of them."

Jenny was in a brown study, stroking her little dog. How often in the past had she pictured Jacques as a disturbing, almost a dangerous personality! Now, however, she could not but admit her views had changed; he had ceased to be alarming.

Jacques was stretched out on the grass, staring in front of him, glad to have unburdened his heart so freely.

"Isn't it pleasant here under the trees?" he murmured lazily.

"Yes. What's the time?"

Neither of them had a watch. Anyhow, they were at the confines of the park and need not hurry. From the bench Jenny could see the tops of two familiar chestnut-trees and, further on, the cedar beside the forester's lodge, a tracery of palm-like foliage etched in black against the blue.

She bent towards the dog, which was crouching against her skirt, and took care not to look in Jacques's direction when next she spoke.

"Daniel has read me some of your poems."

His silence was so portentous that now she could not help stealing a glance at him. A blush had mounted from cheeks to brow, to the peak-point of his hair, and he was glaring angrily about him. She, too, began to blush.

"Oh, I shouldn't have told you that!" she exclaimed.

But already Jacques regretted his annoyance and was trying to overcome it; yet he could not bear to think that someone—and that someone, Jenny—should choose to judge him by his fumbling first attempts; he was all the more touchy on this count because he knew only too well that he had never done himself justice—a thought that never ceased to rankle in his mind.

"My poetry, why, it's—rubbish!" he exclaimed brutally. She did not protest or stir a finger; he was grateful for her reticence. "You must have a very poor opinion of me, if you . . . If anyone . . ." He broke off, then passionately exclaimed: "Oh, if anyone could guess the things I mean to do!" The all-absorbing topic, the woodland peace, Jenny's proximity, stirred him to such emotion that his voice faltered and his eyes began to smart as if he were on the brink of tears. "Take, for instance," he went on after a pause, "take the people who congratulate me on getting into the Ecole Normale. You can't imagine how I feel about all that! I'm ashamed of it. Yes, positively ashamed. Not merely ashamed of having got in at all, but of having bowed to . . . to the opinions of all those . . . If you knew what they really are, those people! All shaped in the same mould, by the same books. Books and books and books! And to think I had to cringe to them! I! That I gave in to their . . . Just imagine it!" Words failed him yet again. He fully realized that he had given no plausible motive for his aversion; the true and valid arguments for it had sunk their roots too deeply into his being to be dragged forth to order and paraded on the surface. "Yes, I despise the whole crowd of them!" he exclaimed. "And myself still more for having had any truck with them. No, I shall never, never—yes, it's unforgivable, all that!"

She kept her self-control the better for seeing him so uncontrolled. Though she had no clear insight into Jacques's mind, she had noticed that he often gave vent to a vague rancour of this sort, and his reluctance to forgive. How he must have suffered! Yet—and this was the difference between them—his faith in the future and happiness in store was unmistakable. A ceaseless undertone of hope and confidence pervaded his invectives; boundless as his ambition might seem, it was untouched by doubt. Hitherto Jenny had never speculated on Jacques's future, yet she was not surprised to learn that he aimed high, very high indeed; even in the days when she had thought of Jacques as a brutal, oafish schoolboy, she never failed to recognize that his was a force to be reckoned with. Today his feverish outburst and her glimpse of the dark fires that preyed upon his heart made her feel dizzy; it was as if she too were being drawn against her will into a maelstrom of emotions. So vivid was the sense of insecurity it gave her that she stood up to go.

"I'm awfully sorry," Jacques stammered nervously; "only, you see, I take these things so dreadfully to heart."

Taking a path that closely followed, like a sentinel's beat, each zigzag of the old-time fosse, they came to the further gate between the forest and the park; its iron grille bristled with spikes and the lock creaked like a dungeon bolt.

The sun was high, and it was only four o'clock; there was no necessity to end their walk so soon. What prompted them to choose a path that brought them home at once?

There were people strolling in the park and, though Jacques and Jenny had walked along the selfsame avenue on the previous day without the least self-consciousness, they both felt bashful now at the thought of being seen walking together by themselves.

"Listen," Jacques ventured when they came to a crossroads, "hadn't I better leave you now? What do you think?"

Her answer came promptly. "Oh, yes. I'm practically home now."

He stood before her, feeling—though he ignored the reason for it —rather ill at ease, forgetting even to raise his hat. Embarrassment brought back to his face the sullen, uncouth look that he so often wore but, during their walk, she had not once observed. He did not hold out his hand to her, but tried to smile and, just as he was turning away, ventured a timid glance in her direction.

"Oh, why," he murmured in a voice shaken by emotion, "why can't I always be . . . like this . . . with you?"

Jenny did not seem to hear, but walked straight on, without one look behind, across the grass. That last remark of his—was it not almost word for word what, since yesterday, she had been saying to herself time and time again? But suddenly a surmise that she hardly dared put into words flashed into thought; supposing Jacques had meant: "Why shouldn't I spend all my life with you beside me, as you've been today?" and the thought seared her mind like wildfire. She quickened her pace and fled for refuge to her bedroom; her limbs were trembling, her cheeks aflame, and she forbade herself to think.

The rest of her afternoon was spent in feverish bursts of energy; she reorganized her bedroom, changing the position of the furniture, tidied out the linen-cupboard on the landing, and replenished the flower-vases throughout the house. Now and again she picked up her little dog, hugged it to her breast and lavished caresses on it. When for the last time she glanced at the clock and it was certain Daniel would not be back for dinner, a mood of despair came over her. Unable to face the empty dining-room, she dined off a plate of strawberries on the terrace and, to escape the tedious agony of the dying day, took refuge in the drawing-room, where she lit all the lamps. She picked up a Beethoven album but, changing her mind, set it back on the shelf and ran to the piano with Chopin's *Etudes* under her arm. . . .

That evening daylight seemed exceptionally long in dying, for the moon had risen unseen behind the trees and, little by little, moonlight had effaced the last gleams of the sunset.

Without any definite plan in mind, Jacques slipped into his pocket the book of modern poems he had mentioned to Jenny. On such a night as this the tedium of the domestic scene was past endurance and he went out for a stroll into the park. He could not keep his wandering wits on any subject. In less than half an hour he found himself hurrying along the path between the acacias, with only one thought in his mind: Let's hope the gate hasn't been locked for the night!

It was not locked. When the bell tinkled he started like a trespasser caught red-handed. A warm, resinous fragrance, mingled with the acrid fume of anthills, drifted towards him from the shadow of the firs. Only the muted throb of a piano ruffled the stillness of the garden with faint sounds of life. Jenny and Daniel, he supposed, were having a musical evening together. The drawing-room lay on the far side of the house; all the windows facing Jacques were closed and the house seemed asleep. But, to his surprise, the roof was flooded with a ghostly light. Looking round, he saw the moon had risen above the tree-tops, spreading the tiles with a pale sheen and striking white fire from the dormer-windows. His heart beat faster as he neared the house; the thought of coming on them unawares abashed him, and he was relieved when Puce rushed up to him, barking. But there was no pause in the music; the sound of the piano must have drowned Puce's noisy greeting. Stooping, he took the little dog in his arms and lightly touched her silken forehead with his lips. Walking round a wing of the house, he reached the terrace onto which the tall French windows of the drawing-room opened. He moved towards the light, trying to recognize the piece that Jenny was playing. The melody seemed to hesitate, poised in mid-air between smiles and tears, to soar at last into an empyrean where joy and pain alike were meaningless.

When he reached the threshold it seemed as though the room were empty. At first he could see only the Persian shawl that draped the piano, and the knick-knacks standing on it. Then, in the gap between two vases, he made out a face, wraithlike in the misty candlelight—Jenny's face convulsed by the stresses of her inward vision. Her expression was so unstudied, so bare of all disguise, that he recoiled instinctively; it was as if he had surprised her naked.

Pressing the little dog to his shoulder and trembling like a thief, he waited outside the house under cover of the shadows till she had finished playing. Then he called loudly to Puce to make it seem that he had just entered the garden.

Jenny started when she recognized his voice and stood up hurriedly. Her face still bore traces of the emotion felt in solitude, and her startled eyes parried Jacques's gaze, as though to keep inviolate their secret.

"I hope I didn't startle you," he said.

She frowned, but could not utter a word.

"Isn't Daniel back yet?" he asked, adding, after a pause: "Here's the anthology I spoke about this afternoon."

He fumbled in his pocket and produced the book. Taking it, she fluttered the pages mechanically, without sitting down or asking him to do so. Jacques realized that he had better go, and retreated to the terrace. Jenny followed.

"Please don't bother to see me to the gate," he stammered nervously.

But she persisted in accompanying him, for she fancied this the quickest way to have done with it, and somehow did not dare hold out her hand and break off then and there. Once they were clear of the trees the moonlight was so bright that, when he turned to Jenny, he could see her eyelashes fluttering. The blue dress seemed unreal, spectral pale.

They crossed the garden in silence. Jacques opened the postern gate and stepped outside. Jenny followed him unthinkingly and stood in the middle of the narrow road, haloed with moonlight. Then, on the whitely gleaming wall, he saw a graceful shadow, Jenny's profile, neck, and chin, her plaited hair, even the set of her lips—like a silhouette cut in black velvet, exact in every detail. He pointed to it. Suddenly a fantastic notion stirred in his mind and, without giving himself time to reflect, ardent with the temerity that visits only timid natures, he bent towards the wall and kissed the shadow of the beloved face.

Jenny stepped back hastily, as though to wrest her shadow from his lips, and vanished through the doorway. The moonlit vista of the garden faded as the gate swung to. Jacques listened to her flying steps along the· gravelled path and then he too launched himself into the darkness.

He was laughing.

Jenny ran and ran as though all the phantoms, black and white, haunting the eerie silence of the garden, were at her heels. She ·fled into the house, ran upstairs to her room, flung herself on the bed. She was shivering, in a cold sweat, there was a pain at her heart, and she pressed her trembling hands against her bosom, crushing her forehead against the pillow. Her whole will was bent on one aim only: to forget. A sense of shame oppressed her, checking her rising tears. A feeling till then unknown had mastered her: fear of herself.

Downstairs Puce was barking; Daniel had come home.

Jenny heard him climb the stairs, humming a tune, and pause a moment at her door. No light showed through the chinks; thinking his sister was asleep, he dared not knock. But then—why were the drawing-room lamps alight? Jenny did not move; she wanted to be left alone, in the darkness. But, when she heard her brother's steps recede, an anguish gripped her heart and she jumped down from the bed.

"Daniel!"

The light of the lamp he was holding revealed her haggard face and staring eyes. It struck him that his late return must have alarmed his sister and he fumbled for excuses. She cut him short.

"No. I'm all nerves tonight." Her voice was shrill. "That friend of yours! I couldn't get rid of him, he kept following me, he stuck to me like a leech." White with rage, she rapped out every syllable. Then a sudden flush spread on her cheeks and she began to sob. Worn out by her emotion, she sank onto the edge of the bed. "Daniel, I beg you, tell him . . . ! Send him away! I can't, no, I simply can't . . . !"

He stared at her perplexedly, struggling to guess what might have passed between them.

"But—what is it?" he murmured. A suspicion flitted across his mind, but he hardly dared give words to it. He screwed his lips into a forced smile. "Poor old Jacques!" he suggested tentatively. "Why, I shouldn't wonder if he's . . ."

He had no need to end the sentence; the tone conveyed his meaning well enough. To his surprise, Jenny betrayed no emotion; her eyes were lowered and she seemed indifferent. She was pulling herself together. When her silence had lasted so long that he had ceased to expect an answer, she spoke.

"Possibly." Her voice had regained its usual intonation.

So she's in love with him! Daniel thought, and so amazing was the discovery that it left him speechless, dumbfounded. But at that moment Jenny's eyes met his and read his thought. It spurred her to revolt; an angry light flashed into her blue eyes, her look grew challenging. She did not raise her voice, but her eyes bored into Daniel's and she shook her head peremptorily.

"Never! Never! Never!"

Daniel seemed unconvinced, and his face wore a look of affection and elder-brotherly concern that stung her like an insult; she went up to him, settled a vagrant lock of hair upon his forehead, and patted his cheek.

"Anyhow tell me, you old silly, have you had dinner yet?"

IX

STANDING in front of the fireplace, in pyjamas, Antoine was chopping up a slab of plum-cake with a Malayan creese.

Rachel yawned.

"A thick one for me, Toine dear," she murmured lazily. She was lying on the bed, naked, her hands behind her head.

The window stood wide open but, mellowed by the drawn blind, the light inside the room was golden, like the warm twilight of a tent under the sun. Paris was sweltering in the blaze of an August Sunday. No sound came from the streets below and the house, too, was silent, empty perhaps but for the flat above; there, no doubt, Aline was reading the newspaper aloud for the benefit of Mme. Chasle and the little invalid who, though convalescent, had to lie flat for some weeks yet.

"I'm starving!" Rachel murmured, exhibiting an open mouth, pink as a cat's.

"The water can't have boiled yet."

"Doesn't matter. Give me one!"

He tipped a thick slice of cake onto the plate and placed it on the edge of the bed. Slowly, without rising, she slewed her head and shoulders round and, leaning on her elbow, with her head thrown back, began to eat, rolling pellets of cake between her fingers and letting them drop into her open mouth.

"How about you, dear?"

"Oh, I'll wait till the tea's ready," he replied, sinking among the cushions on the easy chair.

"Tired?"

He answered her with a smile.

The bed was low and open on all sides, and the alcove hung with curtains of pink silk, setting off Rachel's nakedness in all its splendour;

she might have been some fabled daughter of the sea, ensconced within a glimmering shell.

"If I were a painter . . ." Antoine murmured.

"That settles it; you *must* be tired." A smile came and went on Rachel's face. "When you start being artistic, it always means you're tired."

She flung her head back, and her face, framed in the fiery halo of her hair, was lost in shadows. A pearly lustre emanated from her body. Her right leg lay in an easy, flowing curve upon the mattress, sinking a· little into it; the other, flexed and drawn up· in the opposite direction, displayed the graceful outline of her thigh, lifting an ivory knee towards the sunlight.

"I'm hungry," she whimpered. But, when he went to the bed to fetch her empty plate, she flung her strong arms round his neck and drew his face towards her.

"Oh, that beard of yours!" she exclaimed, but did not let him go. "When shall we abate the nuisance?"

He stood up, cast an anxious look at the glass, and brought her another slice of cake.

"Yes, it's just that I like so much in you," he declared, watching her teeth close on an ample mouthful.

"My appetite?"

"No, your fitness. Your body with its splendid circulation. You're bracing, like a tonic. . . . I'm pretty well built, too," he added, and, turning to the mirror, viewed his reflected self. Squaring his shoulders, he straightened up his chest and puffed it out, but failed to realize how undersized his limbs appeared in proportion to his head; he always persuaded himself that his physique as a whole had the same look of vigour as the facial expression he had cultivated. During the past two weeks his sense of power and plenitude had been stimulated beyond all measure by the emotions love engendered. "Do you know," he concluded, "you and I are built to see a century through?"

"Together?" she whispered, with half-shut, tender eyes. And then a passing shadow dimmed her happiness: the dread that one day his appeal for her, the source of so much present joy, might lose its power.

Opening her eyes, she lightly stroked her legs, running her palms over the lissom skin.

"Personally," she declared, "if no one murders me, I'm certain to die old. Father was seventy-two when I lost him and he was hale as a man of fifty. He died quite by accident, really—the after-effects of a sunstroke. As a matter of fact it runs in our family, death by misadventure, I mean. My brother was drowned. I shan't die in my bed, either; a revolver-shot will be the end of me, I feel it in my bones."

"How about your mother?"

"Mother? She's very much alive. Every time I see her she looks younger. No wonder, of course, considering the life she leads." Her voice had a curious inflexion as she added: "She's shut up—at Saint Anne's."

"The asylum?"

"Hadn't I told you?" Her smile seemed almost apologetic and she made haste to satisfy his curiosity. "She's been there for seventeen years. I can hardly remember what she was like—before. When one's only nine, you know . . . Anyhow she's cheerful, doesn't seem to worry in the least, always singing. Yes, as a family, we're a tough lot! Look, the water's boiling!"

He hurried to the gas-ring and, while the tea was brewing, surveyed himself in the dressing-table glass, covering his beard with his hand to see how he would look clean-shaven. No. It suited him, that dark mass at the bottom of his face; it emphasized so well the pale rectangle of his forehead, the curve of his eyebrows, and his eyes. Moreover, some instinct made him chary of unmasking his mouth—almost as if it were a secret better kept concealed.

Rachel sat up to drink her tea, then lit a cigarette, and stretched herself again on the bed.

"Come near me. What are you up to, mooning about over there?"

Gaily he slipped beside her and bent above her face. In the warm alcove the perfume of her loosened hair enveloped him, honey-sweet

yet piquant, clinging and almost cloying; sometimes he ached for it
and sometimes turned away, for, if he inhaled it too long, it left his
throat and lungs filmed with a bitter-sweet aroma.

"What are you after now?" she asked.

"I'm looking at you."

"Toine darling!"

When their lips parted he bent over her again, gazing down at her
with insatiable eyes.

"What on earth are you staring at like that?"

"I'm trying to make out your pupils."

"Are they so hard to find?"

"Yes; it's because of your eyelashes. They form a sort of golden
haze in front of your eyes. That's what makes you look so . . ."

"So what?"

"So sphinx-like."

She gave a little shrug.

"My pupils are blue, if you want to know."

"So you say."

"Silvery blue."

"Not a bit of it!" He set his lips to Rachel's, then teasingly withdrew them. "Sometimes they look grey, and sometimes mauve. A
muzzy sort of colour . . . blurred."

"Thanks very much!" Laughing, she rolled her eyes from side to
side.

He gazed at her musingly. "Only a fortnight," he said to himself,
"but it seems like months. Yet I couldn't have described the colour
of her eyes. And her life—what do I know of it? Twenty-six years
she's lived without me, in a world so different from mine. Years
crowded with a host of things, adventurous years. Mysteries, too, that
I'm beginning to discover, bit by bit." He would not admit the
pleasure each discovery afforded him; still less give her an inkling
of his pleasure. He never asked her anything, but she was always
ready to talk about herself. He listened, ruminated, set facts and
dates together, trying to understand, but above all amazed, taken
aback at every turn. He was at pains to hide his wonder, but it was

not chicanery that prompted him to do so. For years now his pose had been that of the man who understands everything; the only people he had learned to question were his patients. Surprise and curiosity were feelings that his pride had taught him to conceal, as best he might, under a mask of quiet interest and knowingness.

"One would think you'd never seen me before, the way you're staring at me today," she said. "That's enough, drop it now for goodness' sake!"

Under his scrutiny she was growing restive and, to escape it, shut her eyes. He began prising her lids apart with his fingers.

"Look here! That's quite enough of it! I won't have your eyes prying into mine like that." She crooked her arm over her eyes.

"So you want to keep me in the dark, little sphinx?" He sprinkled kisses on the shining, shapely arm, from shoulder to wrist.

Secretive, is she? he asked himself. No, a trifle reserved, but not secretive. Quite the contrary; she likes chattering about herself. In fact she gets more talkative every day. And that's because she loves me, he thought delightedly. Because she loves me. . . .

Putting her arm round his neck, she drew his face beside hers once more. When she spoke again, there was a graver note in her voice.

"That's a fact, you know; one has no idea how one can give oneself away in a mere look." She paused. He heard, deep down in her throat, the silent little laugh which so often preceded her evocations of the past. "That reminds me. . . . It was by his look, just the look on his face, that I hit upon the secret of a man with whom I'd been living for months. At a table, in a Bordeaux restaurant. We were facing each other, talking. Our eyes were going to and fro, from the plates to each other's face, or glancing round the room. Suddenly— I'll never forget it—for the fraction of a second I caught his eyes fixed on a point behind me, with an expression . . . I was so startled that I couldn't help turning in my chair to see."

"Well?"

"Well, that just shows," she continued in a changed voice, "that one should mind the look in one's eyes."

"And what did you find out?" The question was on the tip of

Antoine's tongue, but he dared not utter it. He had a morbid dread of making himself ridiculous by putting futile questions. Once or twice already he had ventured to ask for explanations at such moments and Rachel had looked at him with surprise, followed by amusement, laughing with an air of gentle mockery that deeply galled him.

So he held his tongue and it was she who broke the silence.

"All those old memories give me the blues. Kiss me. Again. Better than that." But evidently the subject had not left her thoughts, for she added: "As a matter of fact, I shouldn't have said 'his secret,' but 'one of his secrets.' You could never get to the bottom of that man's mind."

Then, to break away from the past and, perhaps, to elude Antoine's unspoken query, she rolled right over on the bed, with a slow, lithe, snake-like wriggle of all her body.

"How supple you are!" He stroked her body appreciatively, like a fancier stroking a thoroughbred.

"Yes? Did you know I'd had ten years' training at the Opera School of Dancing?"

"What? At Paris?"

"Yes, my boy! What's more, when I left I was a leading ballerina!"

"Was that long ago?"

"Six years."

"Why did you give it up?"

"My legs." Her face darkened for a moment. "After that, I almost joined a circus—as a trick-rider," she continued quickly. "Are you surprised?"

"Not a bit," he replied coolly. "What circus was it?"

"Oh, not a French one. A big international show that Hirsch was touring all over the world at the time. Hirsch, you know—that's the fellow I told you about, who's settled in the Sudan. He wanted to exploit my talent, but I wasn't taking any!" While she spoke, she amused herself crooking and straightening out each leg in turn with the effortless agility of a trained gymnast. "What gave him the idea was that he'd persuaded me to try my hand at trick-riding some time before that, at Neuilly. I loved it. We had a fine stable then, and we made the most of it, you may be sure!"

"Were you living at Neuilly?"

"No; but he was. He owned the Neuilly riding-school in those days; he was always keen on horses. So was I. Are you?"

"I ride a bit," he replied, straightening his back. "But I haven't had many opportunities for getting on a horse—or the time for it."

"Well, I had opportunities all right. And to spare. Why, we were once on horseback for twenty-two days on end!"

"Where was that?"

"At the back of beyond. In Morocco."

"So you've been to Morocco?"

"Twice. Hirsch was selling obsolete Gras rifles to the tribes in the south, and an exciting job it was! Once there was a regular pitched battle round our camp. We were under fire for twenty-four hours; no, all night and the following morning. They don't often make night-attacks. It was a terrifying business; we couldn't see a thing. They killed seventeen of our bearers and wounded over thirty of them. I threw myself between the crates of rifles at each volley. But they got me all right!"

"What? You were wounded?"

"Yes." She laughed. "Only a scratch it was." She pointed to a silky scar on the line of her waist, just under the ribs.

"Why did you tell me you'd had a carriage-accident?" Antoine inquired unsmilingly.

"Oh," she exclaimed with a little shrug, "that was our first day together! You'd have thought I was trying to show off."

They were silent. So she's capable of lying to me, Antoine thought.

Rachel's eyes grew darkly pensive, then suddenly brightened again—but with a glint of hatred that quickly came and went.

"He'd got it into his head that I'd follow him anywhere and always. Well, he was wrong."

Antoine felt an uneasy satisfaction every time she cast such rancorous glances at her former life. "Stay with me—always!" he felt inclined to say. Pressing his cheek against the little scar, he waited. His ear, true to its professional training, followed the languid vascular flux and reflux murmuring deep down in her chest, and heard, remote yet clear, the full-toned throbbing of her heart. His nostrils quivered. On the warm bed all Rachel's body breathed the perfume of her hair, but subtler, more subdued; a faint yet maddening odour with a tang of spices in it, a humid fragrance redolent of a curious range of scents—hazel-leaves, fresh butter, pitchpine, and vanilla candy; less of a perfume, truth to tell, than a fine vapour, almost a flavour, leaving an after-taste of spices on the lips.

"Let's drop the subject," she said. "Give me a cigarette. No, the ones on the little table. They're made by a girl I know; she puts a dash of green tea in with the Virginia leaf. They smell of burning leaves, camp-fires, and—yes, that's it—shooting-parties in September; the smell of gunpowder, you know, when you shoot the coverts and the smoke hangs in the mist."

He stretched himself out beside her under the smoke-rings, and his hands caressed the almost phosphorescent whiteness, hardly pink at all, of Rachel's belly, ample as a vase turned on the potter's wheel. She had acquired, probably in the course of her travels, the habit of eastern unguents and, in its maturity, her skin still kept the fresh and flawless smoothness of a young child's body.

"*Umbilicus sicut crater eburneus,*" he murmured, recalling as best he could the sonorous Latin of the Vulgate which had so thrilled him in his sixteenth year. "*Venter tuus sicut*—like a what?—*sicut cupa.*"

"What on earth does it mean?" She sat up on the bed. "Wait a bit! I'll try and guess. *Culpa;* I know that word. *Mea culpa,* that's it; a fault, a sin. 'Thy belly is a sin,' eh?"

He burst out laughing. Since she had come into his life, he no longer kept a hold on his high spirits.

"No, *cupa.* 'Thy belly is like a goblet,' " he amended, leaning his head on Rachel's hip, and proceeded with his slightly garbled versions of the Song of Solomon. "*Quam pulchræ sunt mammæ tuæ, soror mea!* 'How beautiful are thy two breasts, my sister!' *Sicut duo* (what's the Latin for them?) *gemelli qui pascuntur in liliis.* 'Like two young roes that are twins, which feed among the lilies.' "

Delicately she held them up, first one and then the other, with a tender little smile for each, as if they were two friendly little animals.

"They're awfully rare, you know, pink tips like that—really pink, like the buds on apple-trees," she declared with almost judicial gravity. "As a doctor, you must have noticed that."

"Yes, I believe you're right. A skin without pigmental granulation. White on white, with pink shadows." Shutting his eyes, he crushed himself against her. "Soft, soft shoulders . . ." he murmured sleepily. "I can't bear flappers with their skimpy little shoulders."

"Sure?"

"I love your delicious plumpness, every curve's so smooth and firm; its texture's like . . . like soap! Don't move; I'm so comfortable."

Suddenly a galling memory crossed his mind. "Like soap!" . . . A few days after Dédette's accident he had travelled with Daniel from Maisons to Paris. They were alone in the compartment. Antoine's mind was full of Rachel and the thought that now at last he could regale this expert amorist with an adventure of his own had proved too tempting; he could not contain himself, but launched into an account that lasted out the journey, of his dramatic night, the operation *in extremis,* the anxious vigil at the child's bedside, and his sudden passion for the handsome red-haired girl dozing beside him on the couch. Then he had used those very words, "delicious plumpness," "texture like soap." But he had not dared to tell Daniel of what followed; describing how, as he went down the stairs, he noticed Rachel's open door, he had added (less from motives of discretion than an absurd anxiety to prove his strength of will): "Did she expect me? Should I take the opportunity? Anyhow, I sized things up, pretended not to see, and passed the door. What would you have done in my place?" Then Daniel, who so far had heard him out in silence, looked him up and down, and rapped out: "Why, I'd have acted just as you did—you humbug!"

Daniel's exclamation echoed in his ears, sceptical, ironic, almost cutting, but with just the touch of geniality it needed not to be effective. Whenever he recalled it, it stung him to the quick. A humbug! Well, of course he was apt to lie upon occasion; or, more accurately, to catch himself out lying. . . .

Meanwhile, that "delicious plumpness" had made Rachel think too.

"I'll grow into a fat old dame, quite likely," she said. "Jews, you know. . . . Still, my mother wasn't fat and I'm only half Yiddish. But you should have seen me sixteen years ago when I joined the beginners' class. A regular little pink mouse I looked!"

She slipped off the bed before he had a chance of stopping her.

"What's up?"

"I've got an idea. . . ."

"Anyhow you might give a fellow some warning."

"Least said, soonest mended." Laughing, she eluded his outstretched arm.

"Lulu dear . . . come back and sleep a bit," he murmured lazily.

"No more bye-bye today! Closing time!" She slipped into her wrap.

She ran to her desk, unlocked it, and pulled out a drawer full of photographs. Then she came back and sat on the edge of the bed, resting the drawer on her knees.

"I love looking over old photos. Some nights I take the whole collection to bed with me and spend hour after hour turning them over, thinking. Don't move! Have a look at them too, if it won't bore you."

Antoine, who had been lying curled up on the bed behind her, sat up at once; his interest was aroused and, resting his arms on the mattress, he settled into a comfortable position. As Rachel pored over her photographs he saw her in profile; her face had grown earnest and her drooping lashes showed like a faint filigree in pale gamboge along her slotted eyes. She had hastily put up her hair; against the light it shone like a chain-helmet woven of fine-spun silk, and almost orange-red; at every movement sparks seemed to flicker round her neck and at the corners of her temples.

"Here's the one I was hunting for. See that little ballet-girl? It's me! I got a rare telling-off that day, as a matter of fact, for spoiling the flounces of my ballet-skirt, crushing them against the wall like that. Aren't I weird with my elbows like pin-points, my hair all

over my shoulders, and that flat, high-cut bodice? I don't look over-
cheerful, do I? Look here, that's me in my third year; my calves were
filling out a bit. Here's the dancing-class, the bunch of us lined up
along the practice-bar. Can you spot me amongst them? Yes, that's
me. That's Louise over there—the name doesn't mean anything to
you, eh? Well, you're looking at the famous Phytie Bella; we went
through the school together and in those days she was just plain
Louise to us. Louis, for short. We ran neck and neck for the first
place. Yes, I might have been their star dancer today, only for my
phlebitis. . . . Like to have a look at Hirsch? Ah, now you're interested, I can see. Here he is. What do you think of him? I'm sure
you didn't guess he was so old. But, for all that he's fifty, there's lots
of kick in the old dog yet, you may take my word for it. Loathsome
creature! Look at that neck, that bull's neck of his wedged between
his shoulders; when he turns his head all the rest goes round with
it. At first sight you might take him for almost anything—a horse-
trader, or a trainer, perhaps—don't you think so? His daughter was
always saying to him: 'Your Royal Highness reminds me of a slave-
dealer!' That used to start him laughing every time, with that fat
belly-laugh of his. But they're worth looking at—his skull and that
hook nose like a hawk's, the curve of his lips. Ugly, I grant you, but
he's got *style*, all right. Just look at his eyes; he'd seem even more
of a brute if it wasn't for that—well, the kind of eyes he has; I don't
know how to describe them. And doesn't he look self-confident, a
real tough customer, hot-tempered, too? What? Hot-tempered and
sensual as they're made. How that man loves life! For all my loathing of him I can't help saying what one says of some kinds of bulldog:
'He's so ugly that he's a beauty!' Don't you agree? Look, that's Papa!
Papa with his work-girls round him. That's how he always was: in
his shirt-sleeves, with his little white beard and scissors dangling.
He'd build you a fancy dress with a couple of dish-rags and half a
dozen pins. That was taken in the work-room. Do you see the draped
manikins at the end of the room, and the designs on the walls? He'd
been appointed costumier at the Opera and given up working for
private customers. Just go and ask the Opera people what they thought

of old man Goepfert in those days! When my mother had to be put away and he and I were left alone, he wanted to take me on as his partner, poor old fellow; he meant to leave the business to me. A good paying business it was; it's thanks to it that I can get along now without working. But you know how it would affect a kid—seeing actresses about the place all day. I had only one ambition: to be a dancer. He let me have my way; what's more, he got old Mme. Staub to take me under her wing, and it was a real joy to him to see me getting on so well at it. He was always harping on my career. Well, it's a good thing the poor old boy can't see how I've gone downhill since those days. I cried, you know, when I had to give up dancing. Women as a rule haven't much ambition; they take things as they come. But on the stage we're at it all the time—struggling to make good; and one soon gets to enjoy the struggle as much as one's actual successes. So it seems the end of the world when one has to say good-bye to all that and live a humdrum life with nothing to look forward to. Look, here are my travel photos! All in a jumble, of course! There we're having lunch; I'm not sure where—in the Carpathians, I think. Hirsch was on a shooting-trip. He sported a long, drooping moustache in those days; rather like a Sultan, isn't he? The Prince always addressed him as 'Mahomed.' Do you see that sunburnt fellow standing behind me? It's Prince Peter, who became King of Servia. He gave me the two white whippets lying down in front; see the way they're curled up—just like you! That man there who's laughing, don't you think he's very like me? Look hard! No? Well, it's my brother all the same. He was dark, like Papa, while I take after Mother—fair; well, it's auburn, if you like. Don't be so absurd! Oh, well, have it your own way; carroty! But I've inherited my father's character, and my brother took after Mother. Look, he comes out better in this one. . . . I've no photo of Mother, not one; Papa destroyed the lot. He never spoke of her to me, or took me to Saint Anne's. But all the same he used to go and see her there, himself, twice a week; year in, year out, he never missed a visit. The attendants told me about it later. He used to sit there in front of her for an hour—sometimes longer. Quite futile it was, as she didn't recognize him or anyone else. But he simply adored her. He was much older than she. He never got over the worry she gave him. One evening, I remember it so well, Papa was sent for, at the workroom, as Mother'd been arrested. She had been caught stealing from a counter at the Louvre Stores. What a to-do! Mme. Goepfert, the costume-maker at the Opera—just think! They found a child's jersey and a pair of socks in her muff. She was released at once; a fit of kleptomania, they said. You know all about that of course. That was the beginning of her breakdown. Well, my brother took after her in many ways. He got into dreadful trouble with a bank. Hirsch helped him out. But he'd have gone Mother's way sooner or later, if there hadn't been that accident. No, leave that one alone! Drop it, there's a good man! I tell you, it's not a photo of me; it's . . . it's a little godchild, who died. Look at this one instead. It's . . . it was taken . . . just outside Tangiers. No, don't take any notice, Toine dear, it's over now; I've stopped crying, can't you see I've stopped? The Bubana plain, our camp by the Si Guebbas caravanserai. That's me; beside the Marabout of Sidi-Bel-Abbès. Do you see Marrakesh in the background? What do you think of this one? It was taken near Missum-Missum, or it might be Dongo; I can't remember. Those are two Dzem chiefs, and a rare job I had taking 'em! They're cannibals; oh, yes, they still exist, all right! Now that's a ghastly one! Look, don't you see? Just there, that little heap of stones. Got it? Well, there's a woman beneath that heap. Stoned to death. Horrible, isn't it? Try to imagine it—a decentish sort of woman whom her husband had deserted for no earthly reason three years before. He'd vanished and, as she thought he was dead, she'd married again. Two years later he came back. Bigamy in those tribes is reckoned the crime of crimes. So they stoned her. Hirsch made me come to Meched just to see it, but I took to my heels and stayed half a mile away. I'd seen the woman dragged through the village the morning before the execution, and that was sickening enough, I assure you. But he saw it out; yes, he pushed his way to the front. Listen! It seems they dug a hole, a very deep hole, and led the woman to it. She lay down in it of her own accord, without saying a word. Would you believe it? She didn't utter a sound, but the crowd were yelling for her death so loudly that I could hear them, even at that distance away. Their high priest gave the lead. First of all he read out the sentence. Then he picked up a huge boulder and hurled it with all his force into the hole. Hirsch told me she didn't utter a cry. That started the crowd off. They'd big piles of stones stacked up ready, and each of them took what he wanted there and flung his quota into the hole. Hirsch swore to me that, for his part, he didn't throw any. When the hole was full— brimming over, as you can see—they stamped it down, yelling all the time, and then they all decamped. Hirsch insisted on my coming back to take a snapshot, as it was I who had the camera. I had to give in. Why, even now the mere thought of it sets my heart palpitating —don't you feel it? There she lay, under those stones. Dead, most likely. . . . No, not that one! Hands off!"

Antoine, craning his neck over Rachel's shoulder, had just time to catch a glimpse of tangled, naked limbs before Rachel deftly clapped her hands over his eyes. The warmth of her palms upon his eyelids brought back to him, with less of feverish insistence but in all else the same, her gesture at the climax of her ecstasy, to veil from her lover's eyes the passion on her face. He made a playful effort to free himself. Suddenly she sprang down from the bed, pressing to her dressing-gown a sheaf of photographs tied up together. Laughing, she ran to the desk, slipped the package into a drawer, and turned the key.

"For one thing," she explained, "they aren't mine. I've no rights over them at all."

"Whose are they?"

"They belong to Hirsch."

She returned and sat at Antoine's side.

"Now will you promise to be sensible? I'll carry on, then. Sure you're not bored? Look here; that's another travel picture of sorts. A donkey-ride in the Saint-Cloud woods. As you can see, those kimono sleeves were just coming in. That was a fetching little dress I had on, wasn't it now?"

X

ALWAYS, Mme. de Fontanin mused, I am lying to myself; were I to face the facts, I'd give up hope.

Standing at a window of the drawing-room, she observed across the silk-net curtain the trio in the garden—Jerome, Daniel, and Jenny—pacing to and fro.

"How easily even the most honest of us can make themselves at home in a world of lies!" she murmured. But, just as she so often failed to hold in check a rising smile, so now she could not stem the tide of happiness that, wave on wave, came surging through her heart.

Leaving the window she went out to the terrace. It was the hour when eyes grow tired of trying to discern the forms of things; on an iridescent sky some pale and early stars were glimmering. Mme. de Fontanin sat down, letting her eyes linger for a moment on the familiar scene. Then she sighed. Only too well she knew Jerome would not continue living at her side as for the past fortnight he had done; that this renewal of their home-life would prove short-lived as ever. For did she not discern, with mingled joy and apprehension, in his whole attitude towards her, yes, even in his sedulous affection, the selfsame Jerome whom she had always known? Did it not prove that he had never changed and soon would leave her once again? Already the crestfallen, ageing Jerome whom she had brought back home with her from Holland, the husband who had clung to her for succour like a drowning man, was changed out of recognition. Even now, though in her presence he might affect the manner of a contrite child, and despite the seemly sighs of resignation that escaped him when he remembered his bereavement—even now he had unpacked a summer suit, and (though he was unaware of it) was looking vastly younger. "Why not call for Jenny at the club this morning? That will give you a nice walk," she had suggested. True, he had feigned indifference; yet he had risen without demur, and presently she had seen him walking briskly away, in white flannel trousers and a light coat, holding himself erect. Yes, she had even caught him picking a sprig of jessamine for his buttonhole!

Just then Daniel, who had noticed that his mother was alone, came up to her. Since Jerome's return Mme. de Fontanin had felt rather ill at ease in her relations with her son. Daniel had noticed this and, as a result, was coming oftener to Maisons and doing his utmost to show himself more attentive than ever to his mother. He wished to make it clear to her that he quite grasped the situation, and blamed her not at all.

Stretching himself full length in a low deck-chair, his favourite seat, he lit a cigarette and smiled towards his mother. . . . How like his father's are his hands and gestures! she thought.

"Will you be leaving us again tonight, dear boy?"

"Yes, Mother, I must. I've an appointment early tomorrow morning."

He fell to talking of his work—a thing he rarely did; he was preparing for the autumn season a special number of *Progressive Art,* devoted to the newest schools of European painting, and found the choice of the abundant illustrations that would accompany the text a thrilling task. But the theme was soon talked out.

The silence was murmurous with the vague sounds of evening, and the shrill chorus of the crickets in the forest fosse below the terrace dominated all the rest. Now and again a vagrant breeze wafted towards them from the firs a tang of toasted spices, rustled the fibrous plane-leaves and shreds of bark across the sand. Swiftly, on flaccid wings, a bat swooped down and lightly brushed Mme. de Fontanin's hair; she could not repress a cry of alarm.

"Will you be here on Sunday?" she asked.

"Yes, I'll come back tomorrow and stay two days."

"You should ask your friend to lunch. I met him, by the by, in the village, yesterday." And, partly because she really thought it, partly because she credited Jacques with all the qualities she thought to see in Antoine, and—last, but not least—wishing to please her son, she added: "What a sincere, noble-minded fellow he is! We had quite a long walk together."

Daniel's face fell, for he remembered Jenny's outburst the evening after her walk with Jacques across the forest.

What an ill-developed, ill-starred, ill-balanced mind Jenny has! he mused regretfully; old beyond her years with thought and solitude and reading! Yet she knows nothing, nothing at all of life. But what can I do? She doesn't trust me now, as she used to. If only she had a solid constitution! But she's all nerves, like a little girl. And full of romantic ideas! She refuses to explain herself, prefers to fancy she's "misunderstood." A sort of uncommunicative pride it is, that's poisoning her life; or is it only a hang-over from the awkward age?

He rose from his chair and moved to his mother's side, feeling it his duty to let her know.

"Tell me, Mother, have you noticed anything special in Jacques's attitude towards you . . . and towards Jenny?"

"Towards Jenny?" Mme. de Fontanin echoed Daniel's words and, as they sank into her consciousness, they seemed to crystallize around a dim, unformulated fear. Less than a fear, perhaps—one of the transient impressions whose purport her keenly sensitive mind had noted, but without putting it into words. A spasm of anguish gripped her heart; and at once her faith took wing towards the Spirit. "Forsake us not!" she prayed.

The others came up to them.

"Hadn't you better cover yourself up a bit more, sweetheart?" Jerome exclaimed. "You must be careful; it's turned much cooler than usual this evening."

He went to the hall and fetched a scarf, which he wrapped round his wife's shoulders. It happened that the long wicker chair in which, on the doctor's orders, Jenny rested after meals had been left under the plane-trees. No sooner did Jerome catch sight of her, dragging it across the sand, than he hurried to her aid and helped her to settle down in it.

But he had found it a none too easy task to tame her wild bird's nature. The bond uniting Jenny with her mother had been so close throughout her early years that, even as a mere child, she had always judged her father without lenience. Jerome, however, delighted with his new-found daughter just ripening into womanhood, had been all attention, cajoled her with his subtlest methods of approach, and with so good a grace, such tact, that Jenny had been touched. Today, indeed, father and daughter had talked without reserve, like bosom friends, and Jerome was still tingling with the emotion he had felt.

"The air is fragrant with your roses this evening, sweetheart," he said, as he dropped languidly into a rocking-chair and set it swaying. "The Gloire de Dijon round the dovecot's a blaze of flowers."

Daniel stood up.

"Time to be off," he said and, going up to his mother, kissed her forehead.

She took the young man's face between her hands and for a moment scanned it closely, murmuring:

"My own big boy!"

"D'you know, I think I'll go with you as far as the station," Jerome suggested. The morning's escapade had whetted his appetite for brief evasions from the garden where, for a fortnight now, he had been leading a cloistered life. "Won't you come too, Jenny?"

"I'll stay with Mamma."

"Got a cigarette?" asked Jerome, taking Daniel's arm. Since his return he had eschewed tobacco rather than go out and buy it.

Mme. de Fontanin watched the two men's receding figures; Jerome's voice came wafted back to her.

"Do you think I can get Turkish tobacco at the station?" Then they disappeared behind the fir-trees.

Jerome pressed to his side the arm of this good-looking youth, his son. Any young creature had an intense appeal for him; intense, yet barbed with keen regret. Each day he spent at Maisons quickened his distress; time and again the sight of Jenny evoked—how cruelly!—his own lost youth. And, at the tennis-club, with what self-pity had he watched them—young men and girls, bright-eyed, their hair in disorder, their collars open and their clothes "all anyhow," yet for all that flaunting the glorious panoply of youth! Lithe bodies, steeped in sunlight, whose very sweat was wholesome, redolent of health. In ten brief minutes he had realized in all its bitterness the handicap of his declining years. He was shamed and sickened by the thought that henceforth, day in day out, he must wage war against himself, against decrepitude and dirt, the noisesomeness of age; against the premonitions of that ultimate decay which had already set its mark upon his body. The contrast between his heavy gait, shortness of breath, and struggles to keep brisk, and his son's limber strides appalled him; releasing Daniel's arm, he gave vent to an envious cry.

"What wouldn't I give to be your age, my boy!"

Mme. de Fontanin had made no protest when Jenny volunteered to keep her company.

"You're looking fagged out, darling," she said when they were alone. "Perhaps you'd rather go up to bed at once?"

"Oh, no!" Jenny replied. "The nights are quite long enough as it is."

"Aren't you sleeping well just now?"

"Not too well."

"But why not, darling?"

The tone of Mme. de Fontanin's voice conveyed more than a casual question. Jenny looked at her mother in surprise, and it dawned on her that something lay behind the words, an explanation was being asked of her. Instinctively she decided to elude it; though not secretive, she shrank from any effort to draw her out.

Mme. de Fontanin had not the art of subterfuge and the look she now cast on her daughter in the dying light was plain to read. If only the affection in her eyes might break the barrier of reticence that Jenny had set up between them!

"As for once in a way we're alone," she began—there was a hint of emphasis in her tone, as though she begged the girl's forgiveness for the inroads Jerome's return had made upon their intimacy—"there's something I'd like to speak to you about, darling. I'm thinking of the Thibault boy, whom I met yesterday. . . ." She paused; after this frontal attack on her subject, she was puzzled how to proceed. But her anxious air as she bent towards the girl spoke for the unspoken words, pointed a tacit question.

Jenny said nothing and Mme. de Fontanin slowly drew herself up, fixing her eyes upon the darkening garden.

Five minutes passed. The breeze freshened and Mme. de Fontanin imagined she saw Jenny shiver.

"You're catching cold. Let's go in."

Her voice had regained its normal intonation. A new idea had come to her: what was the use of insisting? Glad she had spoken out and sure she had been understood, she faced the future confidently.

Mother and daughter rose and crossed the hall without a word, then climbed the stairs in almost total darkness. Mme. de Fontanin, who was in front, waited on the landing at Jenny's door to kiss her goodnight as usual. Though she could not see the girl's face, she felt her body, as she kissed her, stiffening with revolt, and for a moment held the young cheek pressed to hers, in a movement of compassion which made Jenny recoil instinctively. Mme. de Fontanin gently released her, then moved away towards her own bedroom. But then she noticed that, instead of opening the door and entering her room, Jenny was following; just as she was about to turn she heard the girl's excited voice behind her, exclaiming passionately, in one breath:

"You've only got to treat him a bit more stiffly, Mamma, if you think he comes here too often."

"Treat whom?" Mme. de Fontanin stared at her daughter. "Jacques? If he comes too often? But he hasn't shown up for a fortnight or more!"

(Jacques's non-appearance was deliberate; learning from Daniel of M. de Fontanin's return and the disturbing factor it had proved in their home-life, he had thought it more tactful to keep away altogether for the present. Jenny, too, went far less often to the club and, when she did so, avoided Jacques as much as possible, waiting till he was playing in a set to slip away before he had a chance of saying more than a casual word to her. The result was that the two young people had seen very little of each other during the past fortnight.)

Jenny deliberately entered her mother's bedroom; shutting the door, she stood there, unspeaking, in an attitude of resolute courage. Mme. de Fontanin's heart thrilled with pity; her one thought was to make it easy for Jenny to speak out.

"I assure you, darling, I really can't see what you mean."

"Why did Daniel ever bring those Thibaults to our place?" Jenny broke out passionately. "Nothing would have happened if Daniel hadn't, for some fantastic reason, taken such a liking for those people."

"But what *has* happened, darling?" Mme. de Fontanin's heart beat quicker.

Jenny flared up.

"Nothing! Nothing has happened! That's not what I meant. But, if Daniel and you, too, Mamma, hadn't always been pressing those Thibaults to come here, I, I wouldn't . . ." Her voice gave way.

Mme. de Fontanin summoned up all her courage.

"Please, Jenny dear, tell me about it. Do you think you've noticed that . . . that . . . well, that he feels in a special way towards . . . ?" She did not need to end her question, for Jenny had lowered her head in a gesture of mute assent. Once again the moonlit garden, the little door, her profile on the wall, and Jacques's outrageous gesture rose before Jenny's eyes; but she was firmly resolved to breathe no word about the dreadful incident whose memory still haunted her nights and days. It was as though, by keeping the secret locked in her breast, she reserved to herself the choice of treating it as a source of horror, or simply of emotion.

Mme. de Fontanin knew that the crucial moment had come; she must not let Jenny build up once again a wall of silence between them. Resting a trembling hand on the table behind her to steady herself, the poor woman bent towards Jenny, whose face she could just barely discern in the faint glimmer coming from the open window.

"Darling," she said, "there's no need to take it to heart unless you, too . . . unless you are . . ."

An emphatic gesture of denial, repeated several times, was her answer. Now that the agony of doubt was past, Mme. de Fontanin heaved a sigh of relief.

"I've always loathed the Thibaults!" Jenny suddenly exclaimed in a tone her mother had never heard from her before. "The elder one's no better than a conceited lout, and the other . . ."

"That's not true," Mme. de Fontanin cut in, and in the darkness her cheeks glowed fiery red.

"And the other one has always been Daniel's evil genius," Jenny added, harking back to an early grievance which even she had long ago discarded as unjust. "No, Mamma, please don't stick up for them. You *can't* like them—they're so utterly different from you. They are—I don't know what! Even when they seem to think like us, we shouldn't let ourselves be taken in; they always think differently, and from different motives. As a family, they're . . ." She groped for an epithet. Then, "They're loathsome!" she exclaimed. "Loathsome!" Her mind was in a turmoil which now she made no effort to control. "No, Mamma," she continued in the same breath, "I don't want to hide anything from you. Nothing! Well, when I was quite little, I think I had a nasty sort of feeling towards Jacques, a sort of jealousy. It upset me to see Daniel making such a fuss over him. 'He's not good enough for my brother,' I used to think. 'He's vain and selfish. A sulky, jeering, ill-bred schoolboy! Only to look at him—that mouth of this, the shape of his jaws!' I tried to keep him out of my thoughts. But I couldn't; he'd always let fly some cutting remark that made me furious, that rankled! Then he was always coming to our place—it looked as if he made a point of hanging round me. But that's all ancient history. I can't think why I'm always coming back to it. Since those days I've observed him more closely. This year, especially—this last month. I've come to see him in another way. I try to be fair. I'm not blind to his good points, such as they are. There's something I must tell you, Mamma; sometimes I've imagined, yes, it's struck me sometimes that I, too—without realizing it—I felt somehow . . . drawn towards him. No, that's impossible! It isn't true a bit! I loathe everything about him . . . almost everything."

"About Jacques," Mme. de Fontanin admitted, "I can't be sure. You've had more opportunities than I of judging what he is. But, as far as Antoine's concerned, I can assure you——"

"No," the girl broke in impulsively. "I never said that Jacques was . . . I mean, I've never denied that he's got very fine qualities too." Little by little her voice had changed and she now spoke calmly. "To begin with, you can tell that he's extremely clever by everything he says. I admit that. I'll go even further; his nature isn't warped, he can be not merely sincere, but generous, noble-minded. So you see, Mamma, I'm not at all biased against him. What's more, I firmly believe"—she spoke with such deep conviction that Mme. de Fontanin was taken aback and gazed at her intently—"I believe that a great future awaits him, perhaps a very great one indeed. So now you can't say that I'm unjust to him. Why, I'm almost convinced that the driving force behind him is nothing less than what is known as 'genius'; yes, just that, genius!" The word, as she repeated it, rang like a challenge, though her mother had shown no sign of contradicting her.

Then suddenly she cried out in a paroxysm of despair:

"But all that doesn't change anything! He has a Thibault's character—he *is* a Thibault! And I hate them all!"

Mme. de Fontanin was stupefied, bereft of speech.

"But . . . Jenny . . . !" at last she murmured.

Jenny perceived behind her mother's exclamation the selfsame meaning as that which she had read so clearly on Daniel's face. With childish impetuosity she darted forward and put her hand over her mother's mouth.

"No! No! It isn't that. I tell you it isn't that!"

Then as her mother clasped her to her breast, safe in the shelter of her mother's arms, Jenny felt suddenly the stranglehold of sorrow loosening at her throat; now at last she could sob her heart out, repeating over and over again, in the small voice of her childhood when something had upset her:

"Mummy dear . . . oh, Mummy!"

And Mme. de Fontanin soothed her like a child upon her breast, murmuring vague consolations.

"Darling . . . don't be frightened. . . . Don't cry. . . . There's nothing to worry about. No one's going to force you to . . . Everything's quite all right, so long as you don't . . ." For a memory had flashed through her mind of the occasion when she had met M. Thibault, the morning after the two boys had run away from home; she seemed to see him again, big and burly, with the two priests on either side of him. And now she pictured him refusing to countenance Jacques's love and desecrating Jenny's with cruel scorn. "Oh, I'm so glad there's nothing in it. And you mustn't blame yourself the least little bit. I'll talk to him myself; I'll see the boy and make him understand. Don't cry, darling. You'll forget all about it. There, there, it's all over. . . . Don't cry any more."

But Jenny sobbed more and more violently; each of her mother's words dealt a new stab at her heart. For a long while they stayed thus in the darkness, closely enfolded; the girl nursing her sorrow in her mother's arms, the mother murmuring cruel consolations, with staring, panic-stricken eyes. For, with her wonted prescience, she foresaw the path of destiny that Jenny must follow ineluctably; no fears of hers, not love, not even prayer could avert its menace from her child. For, as the whole creation moves on its slow upward progress to the spiritual plane—the thought appalled her!—each of us must make his way alone, from trial to trial—often enough from error to error— along the path which has been appointed him from all eternity.

At last the sound of the front-door closing and Jerome's steps in the tiled hall startled them into movement. Jenny hurriedly let fall her arms and fled to her room, stumbling as though a load of grief were laid on her frail shoulders, a burden no one in the world could ever lighten.

XI

A GIGANTIC poster, flaunted on the boulevard, brought passers-by to a full stop before the picture-house.

IN DARKEST AFRICA

TRAVELS AMONGST THE SAVAGE TRIBES OF THE INTERIOR

"It doesn't begin till half-past eight," Rachel sighed.

"I told you so."

Not without regret had Antoine forgone the privacy of the pink bedroom, and now, to console himself with an illusive isolation, he booked one of the shut-in boxes at the back of the amphitheatre.

While he was doing so, Rachel came back to him.

"I say, I've just spotted a real beauty!" she cried, and led him to the lobby, where stills from the film were being exhibited. "Look there!"

Antoine read the caption first: "A Mundang girl winnowing millet on the banks of the Mayo Kebbi." Then his eyes rose to a bronzed body, stark naked but for a ribbon of plaited straw knotted round the loins. Intent upon her task, the girl, resting her weight on her right leg, her bust strained upwards, her right arm rising in a sweeping curve above her head, had the poised beauty of a statuette. In her right hand she held a tilted calabash filled with grain that she was pouring in a thin trickle, from as high as she could reach, into a wooden bowl below, clasped in her left hand at the level of her knee. Nothing was studied in her attitude; the poise of her head, flung back a little, the balanced harmony of her curving arms, the upward surge of the torso, tip-tilting the firm young breasts, the flexure of her waist and tension of her hip, the forward swing of the unweighted limb that lightly spurned the soil at its extremity—all breathed harmonious beauty, adjusted to the rhythms of toil, an artless counterpoint of movements.

"Look, what do you think of that?" She pointed to a file of ten young Negroes bearing on their shoulders a tapering pirogue. "Isn't that little fellow lovely? He's a Wolof, you know. That's a *grigri* he has round his neck, and he's wearing a blue *boubou* and a tarboosh." Her voice was vibrant with unwonted excitement that evening and, when she smiled, her lips all but refused to part, as though the muscles of her face had stiffened unawares. Her eyes moved restlessly between the narrowed lids, fever-bright and lit with silvery gleams; never had Antoine seen them thus before.

"Let's go in," she suggested.

"But there's a good quarter of an hour before it starts."

"That doesn't matter!" she insisted, like an impatient child. "Let's go in now."

The house was empty. In the orchestra pit some musicians were tuning up. As Antoine began to raise the lattice-window in front of the box Rachel pressed herself to his side.

"Do loosen your tie!" she pleaded laughingly. "You always look as if you'd just been trying to throttle yourself and dashed off with the rope round your neck." Letting the window fall, Antoine made a vague gesture of petulance. "Yes," she murmured in the same breath, "I'm ever so glad you're with me to see this show." Prisoning Antoine's face between her hands, she drew it to her lips. "You've no idea how much I love you now that beard of yours is gone!"

She took off her hat, gloves, and cloak, and they sat down. Across the lattice which screened them from the public, they saw the theatre coming to life under their eyes; from a mute, dingy cavern, bathed in dim red light, whence here and there emerged a speck of human flotsam, it became a seething mass of life, a busy aviary whose twitterings were sometimes drowned by a chromatic scale from some wind instrument. The summer had been exceptionally hot, but the latter half of September had brought many Parisians home again perforce, and even now the Paris of high summer, which Rachel delighted in exploring like a new-found city year by year, had ceased to be.

"Listen!" she said. The orchestra had begun to play the spring-song from the *Walküre*. Antoine was sitting very close beside her, and her head drooped on his shoulder; from Rachel's lips, through her closed lips, there came to him an echo as it were of the melody the violins were playing.

"Have you ever heard Zucco, the tenor?" she inquired casually.

"Yes. Why?"

Lost in a day-dream, she did not reply at once; at last she whispered under her breath, as if a belated scruple forbade her keeping him in the dark:

"He was my lover once."

Though in no way jealous, Antoine was keenly curious about Rachel's past. He realized exactly what she meant by her remark: "My body has no memory." All the same—that fellow Zucco! What a figure of fun he'd looked in his white satin doublet, perched on a sort of wooden crate, in the third act of the *Meistersinger;* a fat and stocky oaf who, for all his yellow wig, looked like a gipsy and, in the love-duets, splayed his fat fingers against his heart. Antoine was rather vexed that Rachel should have stooped so low as that!

"Have you heard him sing it?" she asked, while her fingers traced in air the sinuous curves of melody. "I never told you about Zucco, did I?"

"No."

He was pressing Rachel's hand against his breast and need only look down to observe her face. She had not the lively air habitual with her when she evoked the past; her eyebrows were a little knitted, her eyelids all but closed, and the corners of her mouth were drooping. "How well the cast of grief would fit her face!" he said to himself. Then, struck by her silence, and anxious once again to prove he took no umbrage at her past, he put a leading question:

"Well, what about your Signor Zucco?"

She started.

"Zucco?" she repeated with a faint smile. "Well, you know, there's little enough to tell, really. He was number one, that's all."

"And where do I come on the list?" The question cost him a slight effort.

"Why, number three, of course," she replied coolly.

A threesome, Antoine mused: Zucco, Hirsch, and I. *Only* a three-some?

She seemed to wake up suddenly.

"You want to hear more? But there's nothing in it, really. It was just after Papa's death; my brother had a job at Hamburg. I was busy at the Opera all day and every day, but the nights I wasn't dancing I felt rather lonely—you know how one is at eighteen. Zucco had been after me for ages. I didn't think much of him; he was inclined to put on airs." She hesitated. "A bit of an ass, really. Yes, I rather think that even then I found him rather maudlin. But I never guessed he was a brute as well!" she suddenly burst out.

The lights had just gone down; she glanced round the theatre.

"What comes first?"

"News-reels."

"Then?"

"A Wild West film—rotten, I expect."

"And Africa?"

"Last of all."

"Oh, well," she murmured, resting again her fragrant hair on Antoine's shoulder, "you can tell me if there's anything worth watching. . . . Sure I don't tire you, Toine dear, like that? I'm ever so comfy."

He saw her glistening, parted lips, and pressed his mouth to her mouth's kiss.

But, when he mentioned Zucco's name again, to his surprise the smile died from her face.

"Now I look back on it," she said, "I can't imagine how I ever stood the way he treated me—worse than a brutal drover treats his cattle! He'd been a muleteer, as 'it happens, in Oran. All the other girls were sorry for me; no one could make out why I put up with him; in fact I can't understand it myself. Of course, so they say, some women like being knocked about. . . ." She was silent for a while, then added: "No; it must have been because I so dreaded being alone again."

Never before within his memory had Antoine heard such sadness in

Rachel's voice. He drew his arms more closely round her, as if to
shelter her from the rough world. But then his embrace grew weaker;
he was thinking of his over-readiness to pity—a facet, doubtless, of
his pride, and, perhaps, the secret of his devotion to his young
brother. Indeed he had sometimes wondered—before Rachel crossed
his path—if he were capable of any other form of love.

"And then?"

"Then it was he who dropped me. . . . Needless to say," she
added, without a trace of bitterness.

After an interval she continued in a lower voice, as though she
wanted the avowal to pass in silence:

"I was going to have a baby."

Antoine was dumbfounded. Rachel had been a mother! Impossible!
Was it credible that he, a doctor, should have failed to note the
signs . . . ? Preposterous!

His eyes strayed, fretful and bemused, towards the captions reeling
out before him:

THE ARMY MANŒUVRES
M. Fallières converses with the German Military Attaché.
THE INTELLIGENCE SERVICE OF THE FUTURE
*Latham lands in his monoplane with important dispatches for the
Commander-in-Chief.*
The intrepid airman is greeted by the President of the Republic.

"Oh, that wasn't his only reason for dropping me," Rachel explained. "If I'd gone on paying his bills . . ."

Antoine suddenly remembered the photograph of a baby which he
had seen at her place, and her words as she snatched it away from
him: "It's a little godchild, who died."

He was less astonished by Rachel's revelation than aggrieved at
it, piqued in his professional self-esteem.

"Is that really so?" he murmured. "You had a child?" Then quickly
added with a knowledgeable smile: "Of course I had guessed as
much, some time ago."

"Still, it doesn't show a lot, does it? I took no end of trouble about
myself—because of my job at the theatre."

"But a doctor's eyes, you know!" He gave a slight shrug.

She smiled. Antoine's perspicacity made her still prouder of him. For some moments she was silent and when she spoke again her voice had the same languorous tone.

"When I think of those days, you know, Toine dear, I feel that the best of my life lies behind me. How proud I was about it! And when I was getting a bit ungainly and had to ask them at the Opera for a holiday, guess where I went! To Normandy. A little village at the back of beyond, where an old woman who'd been our nurse, my brother's and mine, was living. What a fuss they made over me down there! I wouldn't have minded settling there for good and all; and that's what I should have done. Only the stage, you know, when once one's got it in the blood . . . I acted for the best, as I thought, and left the kid there with the wet-nurse; I felt quite safe. Then, eight months later . . . Meanwhile I'd fallen ill, too," she sighed after a moment's pause. "The confinement had wrecked my health. I had to leave the Opera, say good-bye to everything. And there I was again— alone in the world!"

He scanned her face. She was not weeping; her eyes were wide open, staring up at the ceiling. But slowly, very slowly, tears were welling up beneath her eyelids. Abashed by her emotion, he dared not kiss her. He was thinking out what she had told him. Each day he fancied he had found a stable vantage-point whence to survey her life in its entirety and judge it whole; but the very next day some reminiscence or avowal, even a casual hint, sufficed to open unsuspected vistas which once again he could not get in focus.

Suddenly she drew herself up, raising an arm to set her hair straight; but, as abruptly, stayed the gesture.

"Look! Oh, look!" she cried, pointing to the screen.

Involuntarily, across a mist of tears, she gazed wide-eyed at a girl on horseback flying from pursuit, with a furious pack of Redskins at her heels. The fearless maiden and her steed whisked up a rocky slope, posed for a second statue-like upon the summit, then scudded down a dizzy gradient. Intrepidly she plunged into a torrent, and thirty horsemen splashed in after her, vanishing in clouds of spray.

Now she was on the further bank, spurring her horse, galloping ahead. Vain hope! The kidnappers rode hell-for-leather on her track, closed in around their quarry. Lassos whipped the air above her, snaked round her head. An iron bridge hove into sight, beneath it an express in full career. In a flash she slipped from the saddle, vaulted the parapet, leapt into the void.

The audience gasped.

Brief panic. Now they saw her standing on the roof of a car, borne past at headlong speed, her hair awry, with flying skirts and arms akimbo, while, from the bridge, the Redskins discharged thirty guns at her in vain.

"Were you watching?" Her voice thrilled with delight. "I love it!"

He drew her towards him again, this time onto his knees, and rocked her like a child. He wanted to console her, make her forget everything, everything but their love. But he said nothing of it and began toying with her necklace. Inset between the honey-golden beads were little balls of leaden-hued ambergris which, as he fingered them, grew warm and fragrant; so clinging was the perfume that some-times, two days later, he would catch a sudden tang of it in the hollow of his hands. Unfastening her blouse, he pressed his cheek upon her breast; she did not try to stop him. Then:

"Come in!" she cried.

A young attendant appeared; she had opened the door of their box by mistake and quickly closed it, but not before casting an interested glance at the half-undressed girl in Antoine's arms. Antoine released Rachel in haste, but not in time—much to her amusement.

"How silly you are! Perhaps she wanted to . . . Anyway she looks nice. . . ."

The words and the way she said them were so astonishing that he tried to catch the look on her face, but she had buried her forehead on his shoulder and all he noticed was her laugh—an almost soundless, enigmatic chuckle that always made him ill at ease.

The element of mystery in Rachel that still was apt to baffle him always gave Antoine the impression of a yawning gulf between them. It roused in him a feeling of unrest, tinctured with curiosity, subtly obnoxious to his self-esteem. For hitherto it had been he who, as a man of science, by veiled allusions, sceptic smiles, set others in a quandary. Rachel had turned the tables on him; beside her Antoine felt atrociously small-boyish and (loath though he was to own to it) rather at sea where certain subjects were concerned. Once, to redress the balance, he had ventured to garnish his professional reminiscences with echoes from the students' mess and even invented for her benefit a far-fetched amorous adventure in which, so he alleged, he had played a leading part. But she had shut him up with a burst of affectionate laughter.

"Drop it, my dear! Whom do you take me for? Don't I love you just as you are?"

He had reddened with annoyance; and he had learned his lesson.

Neither had felt inclined to speak during the interval which was just ending. The film of Africa was announced and the lights went down. The band struck up a Negro melody. Rachel moved to a seat in front of the box.

"Let's hope they've made a good job of it."

Landscapes began to flicker across the screen. A stagnant river under enormous trees tethered to the soil by a network of lianas. A hippo's back, like the corpse of a drowned bull, bulged on the surface of the water. Little black monkeys, white-bearded, like ancient mariners, frolicked on the sand. Then came a village: an empty space of beaten soil fissured by the heat, and, in the background, rows of stockaded huts. Next, a compound where some young Peuhl girls, naked to the waist, the muscles of their hips working beneath the loin-cloths, were busily pounding grain in high wooden mortars, surrounded by pickaninnies sprawling in the sun. Then more women, carrying large baskets; then a group of spinners, squatting cross-legged on the ground; each grasped a distaff in her right hand, while the left twirled inside a wooden trough the bobbin, shaped like a peg-top, which took the yarn.

Leaning well forward, Rachel gazed intently at the screen, her elbow resting on her crossed knees, her chin cupped in her hand.

Antoine could hear the rapid intake of her breath. Sometimes, without turning, she spoke to him in a hushed whisper.

"Toine dear! Look! Just look!"

The film ended with a barbaric dance to the sound of tomtoms in a clearing ringed with palm-trees. Night was falling and a crowd of Negroes, their faces tense, their bodies squirming with delight, had formed a circle round a couple of their fellow-tribesmen. The dancers, two jet-black but extremely handsome males, were almost naked; their bodies shone with sweat. They flew at each other, collided, bounded back, and crashed together again, gnashing their teeth, or, now and again, circled in the love-chase, rubbing their bodies together, varying the rhythms of their frenzy as they portrayed the rage of battle or the spasms of sensual desire. Panting, capering with excitement, the dark crowd closed in round the frenzied couple; faster and faster they clapped their hands and faster drummed upon the tomtoms, goading the dancers on and on towards a climax of delirium. The picture-house band had stopped playing; a clapping of hands in the wings kept time with the gestures of the Negroes, restoring a fantastic semblance of life to the dark figures and infecting the audience with something of the fierce pleasure, strung to the pitch of pain, that convulsed the savage faces on the screen. . . .

The show was over, the audience filing out. Attendants were beginning to sheet the empty seats.

Silent and exhausted, Rachel could hardly bring herself to move. When Antoine, who was already on his feet, held up her evening-cloak she rose and pressed her lips to his. They were the last to go; neither of them spoke. As they left the cinema they found themselves caught in a crowd of people flocking out together from all the amusement places on the boulevards. The warm, soft darkness shimmered with twinkling lights and already some autumn leaves were slowly spinning down. Antoine took her arm, whispering in her ear: "Let's go back to your place now."

"Oh, not yet, please," she protested. "Let's go somewhere first. I'm thirsty." Then the posters outside the theatre caught her eye and she swerved aside to examine once more the photograph of the young Negro. "It's extraordinary," she remarked, "how he's like a boy who once came down the Casamance with us. A Wolof boy: Mamadou Dieng."

"Where shall we go?" he asked, concealing his disappointment.

"Oh, any old place! The Britannic? No, what about Packmell's? Let's walk there. That's it: an iced chartreuse at Packmell's, and then we'll go home." She nestled up to him with a sudden tenderness that seemed like an earnest of better things to come.

"It's upset me a bit, you know, thinking of poor little Mamadou this evening, just after seeing that film. You remember the photo I showed you, with Hirsch sitting in the stern of the jolly-boat? You said he looked like a Buddha in a sola topee. Well, the boy on whom he's leaning, a real blackamoor in a little white shift—do you remember?—that's Mamadou."

"And how do you know it wasn't he in the film?" he asked, to humour her.

After a moment's silence she shuddered slightly.

"Poor kid, I saw him eaten alive under my eyes, some days later. He was bathing in a stream. No, it was really Hirsch who . . . You see, Hirsch bet Mamadou he wouldn't swim a tributary of the river to get an egret that I'd just brought down—and how often I've wished I'd missed it! The boy said he'd have a try, and dived in. We watched him swimming across, when suddenly—! Oh, it was like a nightmare! It all happened in a flash, you know. We saw him suddenly standing up out of the water; he'd been nipped below the waist, you see. I shall never forget his scream. Hirsch always rose to the occasion at such moments. He knew at once that the boy was a goner, and would endure agonies. He brought his gun to his shoulder and— bang!—the child's head crumpled up like a calabash. The best way out, wasn't it? But I felt like being sick."

She paused and pressed herself to Antoine's shoulder.

"Next day I went to take a snapshot of the place. The water was calm, so calm, you'd never have dreamt . . ."

Her voice shook. There was a longer pause before she spoke again.

"With Hirsch, you see, one life more or less simply doesn't count. Still, he liked that boy of his. Well, he didn't turn a hair. That's how he was. Even after the accident, he stuck to his idea; he promised an alarm-clock to anyone who'd retrieve my egret. I tried to stop him, but he shut me up. He always insisted on being obeyed. Well, in the end I got it. One of the porters fetched it; he had better luck than the boy." She was smiling now. "I've got it still. I wore it last winter on a little brown velvet toque; a dinky little hat it was, too!"

Antoine made no comment.

"Oh, you old stay-at-home!" she burst out, and petulantly drew away from him. "A trip to Africa'd have been the making of you!"

Then, in swift contrition, she came back and took his arm again.

"Don't take any notice of me, Toine dear; a show like tonight's works me up till I'm positively ill. I'm sure I've got a touch of fever— haven't I? One stifles here in France. It's only over there one can really live. You can't imagine what it means—the white man's freedom among all those blacks. Not a soul on this side has the faintest notion how far it goes. No laws, nothing to tie you down! You needn't even bother what other people think of you. See what I mean? Can you even imagine what it's like? You have the right to be yourself every-where and all the time. You're just as free amongst those black folk as you are at home with only your dog to watch you. And, what's more, they're really charming people to live among. You'd never believe how tactful, how quick to understand, they can be. Just fancy having only cheerful, smiling faces round you, and keen young eyes that can read your least desire. Why, I remember . . . Sure I'm not boring you, dear? I remember one day when we pitched camp out in the desert and Hirsch was chatting with a headman near the spring where the women used to draw water; it was getting dark—that's the time they always come—and we saw two darling little girls come up, carrying a huge oxhide waterskin between them. 'They my girls,' the Cadi explained to us. That was all. But the old fellow had guessed. . . . That night when I was with Hirsch in the *dar,* the mat slid up without a sound, and lo and behold our two little girls, smiling all over their faces!" She walked a few paces in silence before continuing. "As I said . . . your least desire. And . . . yes, I remember, another time—it's such a relief to have someone to tell about it! At Lomé, it was. At the pictures, too, as it happens; everybody there goes to the pictures in the evening. It's just a café terrace, very brightly lit, with evergreens in tubs all round it. Suddenly the lights go out and the show begins. You sip iced drinks while you watch it—see the idea? The Europeans, dressed up in their white ducks, sit in front, with the light reflected from the screen falling on their faces; behind them it's pitch-dark, no, blue-dark—you'd never believe how blue—and I've never seen the stars so bright anywhere else. That's where the natives sit and watch, youngsters and girls. You can hardly see their faces for shadows, but their eyes glow like the eyes of cats—such lovely eyes! Well, you needn't even make a sign. Your eyes just linger on one of the smooth, dark faces, meet his eyes for a second—and that's all. But it's enough. A few minutes later you get up and go, without a glance behind, to your hotel; all the doors are left open on purpose. I had a room on the second floor. I'd hardly had time to undress when I heard someone scratching at the shutter. I put out the light and opened the window. There he was! He'd slithered up the wall like a lizard. Without a word he let his one and only garment slide off his little body. I shall never forget it. His mouth was moist and cool . . . so cool!"

"Good God!" Antoine could not help exclaiming to himself. "A nigger—and not even vetted beforehand to make sure!"

"They've such wonderful skins," Rachel went on. "Fine-grained like the rind of a fruit. None of you over here have an idea of what it's really like. It's smooth as satin, their skin; dry and sleek as if it had just been dusted with talcum powder, without a single blemish or trace of unevenness or moisture, but hot as fire under the surface; hot, like a feverish arm across a muslin sleeve—see what I mean?— or a bird's body underneath the feathers. And when you look at it under the glaring African sun and the light's splashing all over their shoulders, that gold-brown skin of theirs looks like shot silk, speckled with blue flashes—oh, I simply can't describe it!—like little specks of powdered steel, or a shower of broken moonbeams. Such eyes they have, too! Surely you've noticed how their glance hovers over you like a caress; it's the white of their eyes, you know, a trifle browned, with the pupils swimming about in it, never quite at rest. Then—I can hardly explain it—love-making in those parts isn't a bit like yours, over here. It's all done without words—like a sacrament, but the most natural thing in the world. There's not an atom of thought goes into it. Over here people are bound to keep it more or less dark when they're out for pleasures of that kind, but there—why, it's as normal as life itself, and just as sacred as life and love. Do you see what I mean, Toine dear? 'In Europe,' Hirsch always said, 'you have what you deserve. Happily there are other countries for people like our-selves, free-minded people.' He simply adores the black man." She started laughing. "Do you know how I first discovered that about him? Surely I've told you? No? It was at a restaurant, in Bordeaux. He was sitting opposite me and we were talking. Suddenly I noticed him staring hard at something behind me; it only lasted a second, but there was a curious glitter in his eyes. . . . It was so striking that I swung round at once. I saw a little Negro, a lad of about fifteen, near a side-table, carrying a bowl of oranges." In a soft, brooding voice, she added: "It was that day, most likely, I too began to hanker after going over there."

They took some steps in silence.

"My ambition," she suddenly exclaimed, "my dream for when I'm old is to—to run a brothel. Don't look so shocked! There are brothels and brothels, and naturally I'd keep a high-class one. I'd loathe grow-ing old amongst old people. I'd like to be sure of having young folk round me, fine young bodies; free, sensual bodies. Can't you under-stand that, dear?"

They were almost at Packmell's, and Antoine had not answered her. What, indeed, could he have found to say? Rachel was an un-charted land for him, where he encountered nothing but surprises. He felt so alien from her, rooted to the soil of France by his middle-class upbringing, by his work and his ambitions, by the career he had so carefully mapped out. He saw the bonds that held him and had not the faintest wish to break them; but for all that Rachel liked, that alien world of hers, he had the antipathy of a domesticated animal for the prowling denizens of the wild that are a menace to the home.

Nothing in the placid frontage of the carbaret, except the streaks of garish light that filtered past the edges of the crimson curtains, gave any inkling of the cheerful scene behind them. The revolving-door swung round with a groan, launching a gust of purer air into the atmosphere within, fetid with dust and heat and the stale fumes of alcohol.

The place was crowded and dancing was in progress.

Rachel headed for a vacant table near the cloak-room and did not wait to let her cloak drop from her shoulders before ordering a green chartreuse with crushed ice. When the drink appeared she propped her elbows on the table and sat before it motionless, with the twin straws between her lips.

"In the dumps?" Antoine inquired.

Her eyelids flickered and, drinking still, she threw him as gay a smile as she could muster up.

Near them a dark woman was flaunting shamelessly upon the tablecloth a biceps worthy of a boxer, which a Japanese, his childish face belied by an array of small but rusted teeth, squeezed with polite disdain.

"I'd like another drink, please; the same as before." Rachel pointed to her empty glass.

Antoine felt a light tap on his shoulder.

"I wondered for a moment if it was you," a cordial voice addressed him. "So you've shed your beard!"

Daniel stood before them. The lamplight fell harshly on the fault-less oval of his face as he stood there, slim and willowy, twiddling an advertisement-fan between his ungloved hands; bending it into a circle, then letting it spring back, with a provocative smile upon his lips, he called to mind the stripling David, testing his sling.

While Antoine was introducing him to Rachel, Daniel's taunt came back to him. "I'd have acted just as you did—you humbug!" But now it seemed to him the taunt had lost its sting, and it was with a thrill of pleasure he observed the look the young man, after stooping to kiss Rachel's hand, cast on her face, lifted towards him, and on her arms and neck, gleaming snow-white against the blush-pink bodice.

Daniel took another look at Antoine, then smiled towards the girl, as though congratulating her on her handiwork.

"Yes, by Jove!" he exclaimed. "It's a vast improvement."

"Yes, I dare say it is, as long as one's alive!" Antoine affected the tone of a facetious medical student. "But if you'd seen as many 'stiffs' as I have . . . ! After two days—!"

Rachel rapped on the table to make him stop. She often forgot that Antoine was a doctor. Turning to him, she scanned him for a moment, then murmured tenderly:

"My medicine-man!"

Could it be possible this face she knew so well was the same face as that which she had watched during the operation under the garish lamplight—a hero's face and terrible in beauty, superbly inaccessible? How well she knew it—better than ever, now she saw it unconcealed, with all its contours, its smallest details visible! The razor had exposed a slight hollow in the cheeks—a certain slackness of the tissues—giving them a milder air that somewhat redeemed the sternness of the jaw. She had learned by touch, as blind men learn their world, under the nightly pressure of her palms, the squareness of his jawbones, the squat curve of his chin, so oddly flattened on its under surface that she had exclaimed: "Why, your under-jaw's almost exactly like a snake's!" But now his beard had gone, what she found most perplexing in his face was the long, sinuous line of his mouth—so rigid was it, yet so plastic; its corners hardly ever lifted and seldom drooped—cut short abruptly on either side by a straight line, a trait of more than human will-power, such as is sometimes found on the faces of ancient statues. "Is his will *really* so strong as that?" she asked herself. Bending forward, she scrutinized him rather mischievously from the corner of an eye, and a brief glint of gold flickered along her eyelashes.

Antoine suffered her scrutiny with the pleased smile of a man who knows himself beloved. Since shaving off his beard, he had come to take a rather different view of himself; he set less store by his hypnotic gaze, for he detected in himself new possibilities, new and eminently agreeable ones. Moreover, for some weeks past, he had felt a thorough-going change coming over him; so drastic was it that the events in his life which preceded his meeting with Rachel were falling away into obscurity—they had taken place *before*. Before what? Before his transformation. A vicious circle; but he let it go at that. Yes, his temperament had changed, had grown more supple; more mature and, at the same time, younger. He liked to tell himself that he had also gained in strength of mind, and he was not far wrong. True, less reflection lay behind his forcefulness; but its very spontaneity made it more telling, more authentic in its exercise. The change that had come over him had affected even his life's work; at first his love-affair had tended to divert it from its course, but, of a sudden, it had gathered strength, till his life brimmed over with it, like a river in spate.

"Don't take so much interest in my appearance," Antoine protested, waving Daniel into a chair. "We've just come from the movies. *In Darkest Africa;* do you know it?"

"Have you ever been outside Europe?" Rachel suddenly inquired. The resonance of her voice took Daniel by surprise.

"No, never."

"Well," she said, drawing towards her the glass that had just arrived, and greedily plunging two fresh straws into the cold, green depths, "it's a film you should see. That view, for instance, of a string of porters on the trek at sunset. Don't you think so, Antoine? And the kids playing in the sand while the women are unloading the canoes."

"Certainly I'll go and see it," Daniel replied, his eyes intent on her. Then, after a short pause, he added: "Do you know Anita?"

She shook her head.

"She's a coloured girl from America, who is usually to be seen at the bar. Yes, there she is, you can see her now, just behind Marie-Josèphe—the tall woman, you know, with all the pearls."

Drawing herself up, Rachel discerned, across the throng of dancers, a fawn-coloured face half hidden in the shadow of a massive hat.

"That's not a Negress!" Rachel made no attempt to hide her disappointment. "She's only a Creole."

Daniel smiled faintly.

"So sorry!" he murmured, then turned to Antoine. "Do you come here often?"

Antoine was about to answer yes, but Rachel's presence checked the impulse.

"Hardly ever."

Rachel's eyes were following Anita, who now was dancing with Marie-Josèphe. The supple body of the American girl showed to advantage in a close-fitting white satin dress, lustrous as a bird's plumage and glittering at every movement of her long, lithe limbs, with gleams of pearly light.

"Will you be going to Maisons tomorrow?" Antoine asked.

"I've only just come from there," Daniel replied. He was about to speak of Jacques when his eyes fell on a Spanish-looking girl, with a saffron shawl draped round her, who seemed to be hunting for someone. "Excuse me," he murmured hastily and made off. Slipping a practised arm beneath the shawl, he danced the girl away, to the strains of a boston, towards the corner where the band was playing.

Anita had stopped dancing and Rachel watched her breasting the flood of dancers with a swan's easy grace, steering a course, as chance would have it, towards the table where she and Antoine sat. The Creole brushed against the young man's chair and, coming to the settle where Rachel was seated, took out of her bag an object which she kept hidden in the hollow of her hand, then, thinking herself unobserved—indifferent, perhaps, to being seen—placed her foot on the settle and, whisking up her skirt, punctured her thigh. Rachel caught a fleeting glimpse of chocolate skin showing between two waves of silken whiteness, and her eyelids twitched involuntarily. Letting her skirt drop back, Anita drew herself erect with a slow, languid movement that set the crystal, dangling from a pearl in her earlobe, sparkling with sudden fires. Then she went back to her friend.

Rachel rested her elbows on the table, her eyes half closed, and slowly drew into her mouth the iced liqueur. The violins' caress, the passionate insistence of their throbbing strings, worked on her mood of sensuous languor till it was almost unendurable.

Antoine looked at her.

"Lulu . . . !" he murmured.

Raising her eyes to his, she drew away the last faint tinge of green from the crushed ice in her glass. The look she gave him came as a surprise; a laughing, almost saucy look.

"You, I suppose, you've never . . . seen a black woman?"

"No," Antoine unblushingly confessed.

She made no comment. A cryptic smile flickered on her lips.

"Come along then!" she suddenly commanded.

Rising at once, she wrapped her coat of shining black about her as if it were a domino for some nocturnal masquerade. As she went out by the revolving-door with Antoine at her heels, he heard once more, behind her close-set lips, the husky little laugh that always so dismayed him.

XII

IN THE days when Jerome was still living in Paris, his concierge in the Avenue de l'Observatoire had standing orders to keep his mail for him, and he called periodically to collect his letters. Then his visits had abruptly ceased. He had left no address and for two consecutive years a mass of correspondence had been accumulating. Now that the concierge had heard of M. de Fontanin's return to Maisons-Laffitte, he requested Daniel to deliver it in person to its rightful owner.

Buried in a pile of circulars, two letters came as a surprise to Jerome.

One of them, eight months old, announced that an ill-starred enterprise from which he had long ceased to expect returns had been wound up, and his share of the assets—six thousand francs and some odd hundreds—was lying to his credit. His face brightened. The remittance was a godsend; now at last he could shake off the vague discomfort which had been oppressing him ever since he had settled down at Maisons—a feeling due not only to his presence in a home where he now felt out of place but also to a lack of ready money, which piqued his pride.

(Five years previously his share of the family fortunes had passed out of his hands. Without applying for a divorce Mme. de Fontanin had sequestrated the modest inheritance left her by her father, the clergyman. This sum, though by no means intact at the time of their separation, had enabled her to live so far in some degree of comfort, and to keep up her flat without stinting her outlay on the children's education. Jerome had not yet squandered all the money left him by his parents and still kept up his business activities; even when, dancing attendance on Noémie, he had settled down in Holland or in Belgium, he had dabbled in the stock-markets, speculated, and promoted new inventions. For all his lack of ballast, he was quick to see an opening, and this ability, coupled with his fondness for taking risks, enabled him, now and again, to back a winning venture. Fat years and lean, he had lived them through, oftener than not upon a lavish scale; sometimes indeed, for conscience' sake, he had even contrived to remit a thousand francs or so to his wife's account, by way of contribution to the children's maintenance. But, during the last few months of his sojourn abroad, things had taken a turn for the worse and, for the moment, he had no means of drawing on his capital. He could see no way of refunding the money Thérèse had brought to Amsterdam and, worse still, he was now obliged to live at his wife's expense. This was bitter enough; but bitterer still was the thought that she might misinterpret his motives, might imagine it was lack of money that had brought the wanderer home.)

Thanks to this windfall, then, Jerome felt his dignity slightly restored. He would be able now to discharge his obligations.

So eager was he to impart the news to his wife that he began to move towards the door, opening as he went the other envelope, inscribed in an illiterate hand, which conveyed nothing to him. Suddenly he stopped, aghast.

Dear Sir,

I take up my pen to tell you something has happened to me which I am not put out about at all not in the least in fact I am quite happy about it as I have been so awfull lonely, but I have been dismissed from my place because of it and I dont know what to do, but I am sure you will not go on leaving me without any money at such a time because this is it I cant get another place people can see it to much, and I have only 30 francs fifty and nothing more to keep the baby after and I do so want to feed it myself as everybody ought to.

I dont blame you one bit only I hope that when you get this you will do the right thing by me, you must bring me the needfull tomorrow or the day after or thursday at the latest as I dont know what will become of me if you dont.

With all my true love

V. Le Gad.

At first he could make nothing of it. "Le Gad—who's that?" Then suddenly he remembered. "Victorine! Why, it's Cricri!"

Retracing his steps, he sat down, rolling the sheet of note-paper between his fingers. "Tomorrow or the day after." He could just decipher the date on the postmark; the letter had been awaiting him for two whole years! Poor Cricri! What had become of her? What meaning had she read into his silence? And—the child? No genuine emotion touched him as he asked himself these questions; the commiserating air that unawares he had put on was a tribute to convention. Yet, all the while, a young, shy, tremulous body, two ingenuous eyes, a girlish mouth, were taking shape in his memory and stirring his senses more and more definitely.

Cricri? Where had he come across her? Ah, yes, at Noémie's place; Noémie had brought the girl back with her from Brittany. And after that? His memories of the suburban hotel where he had kept her hidden for a fortnight were rather blurred. Why had he left her then? Much clearer was the picture of another meeting two years after, during one of Noémie's escapades. Every detail of the servant's attic bedroom which he used to toil up to at nightfall came back to him clearly, and then the furnished rooms somewhere in the Rue de Richepanse where he had set her up later, during that second lease of passion which had lasted two or three months—or was it longer?

He read the letter again, noted the date. A familiar warmth flooded his brain and clouded his eyes. Rising, he drank a glass of water, slipped Cricri's note into his pocket, and, with the business letter in his hand, went out to find his wife.

An hour later he was stepping into the Paris train.

It was striking ten o'clock when, in a delightful state of excitement, he left the Saint-Lazare station under a genial September sun. He drove to his bank and, simmering with impatience, waited at the counter; only when he had signed the receipt, had slipped the notes into his pocket-book and flung himself triumphantly into the waiting taxi—only then he felt that the shadow which had darkened his life for all these recent weeks had lifted; he had risen from the dead!

The arduous quest on which he now embarked took him all over Paris, from one concierge to another; indeed it promised to be fruitless till at about two in the afternoon—he had forgone luncheon—it led him to the home of a certain Mme. Barbin, *alias* Mme. Juju. The mistress of the house was out, but the maid, who was youthful and loquacious, informed him that she knew the young lady, Mlle. Le Gad—"Rinette, they all call her"—quite well.

"Only," she went on, "she never goes to her room at the hotel except Wednesdays; that's her day off."

Jerome blushed; but with a flash of understanding.

"Yes, of course." His smile conveyed that he was in the know. "But, you see, it's her other address I'm after."

By this time they were on the best of terms. "A nice little thing," Jerome suddenly said to himself. But he was quite decided to keep his mind exclusively on Cricri.

"It's in the Rue de Stockholm," the maid at last informed him with a smile.

Jerome had the taxi take him there, alighted, and was not long in finding the house described by the maid. An insidious melancholy which he would not avow—though for some time he had been trying to shake it off—was ousting his high spirits of the early hours.

The swift transition from the sunlit streets to the meretricious twilight of the establishment he now entered made him feel uneasier than ever. He was shown into the "Japanese" room, where the sole touch of local colour was a cheap Japanese fan pinned to the wall above the bed. He waited, hat in hand, affecting an unembarrassed air; but, wherever he turned his eyes, a mocking mirror presented him with his reflected self, till he could endure it no longer and seated himself at the extreme end of the sofa.

At last the door was flung open; a young prostitute, draped in a mauve tunic, bustled in and as abruptly halted, facing him.

"Oh!" she gasped; he supposed she had entered the room by mistake. But then, as she recoiled towards the door which she had closed instinctively on entering, she stammered out one word:

"You!"

Even now he was far from sure that it was she.

"Is it you, Cricri?"

Keeping her eyes fixed on Jerome, almost as if she half expected him to whip out a revolver from his pocket, Rinette reached towards the bed, pulled off the bedspread, and wrapped herself up in it.

"What's happened?" she asked. "Did someone send you?"

Vainly he tried to discover the childish Cricri he had known, behind the painted features of this showy harlot, with her bobbed hair and rather puffy cheeks. Even her country accent, her clear, young voice, had left her.

"What do you want of me?" she asked.

"I've come to see you, Cricri."

For a moment she misconstrued the gentleness in his voice; he puzzled her. Then, averting her eyes, she decided, or so it seemed, to let things take their course.

"Please yourself," she said.

She went to the sofa and sat down, keeping the bedspread wrapped round her body, but letting it fall a little from her neck and arms.

"Who told you to come here?" she repeated with lowered eyes.

The question nonplussed him. Standing awkwardly before her, he began explaining that he had come back to France after a long stay abroad and had only just received her letter.

"What letter?" she asked, raising her eyes.

Once again he saw the grey-green lustre of her pupils; they, any-how, looked innocent as ever. He handed her the envelope; she stared at it bemusedly.

"Well, upon my word!" she exclaimed, casting a venomous look at him. Holding the letter she nodded emphatically several times. "Of all the low-down tricks! To think you didn't even bother to answer it!"

"But, I tell you, Cricri, I only opened it this morning."

"That's neither here nor there; you might at least have answered me," she persisted with an obstinate toss of her head.

"I did better than that; I came here myself right away," he patiently explained. Then, unable to control himself, he asked: "And—the child?"

Her lips tightened, she gulped down her saliva and tried to speak, but the words would not come. Her eyes filled with tears.

At last she managed to speak.

"Dead. It was born too soon."

Jerome sighed—but it sounded like a sigh of relief. Under Rinette's vindictive stare, he felt cowed, humiliated, bereft of speech.

"To think it's all your fault!" she continued in a voice that was less hostile than her eyes. "I wasn't one of them fast ones, and very well you knew it. Twice I believed what you had promised me, twice over I gave up everything to live with you. Oh, how I cried when you left me again, for the second time!" She held him with a down-ward look, her shoulders hunched and mouth a little twisted; her eyes were shining greener than ever through her tears. He felt at once aggrieved and sick at heart; uncertain what line to take, he forced his lips into a smile. . . . How like Daniel he was with that crooked smile of his!

She dried her eyes and, unexpectedly, addressed him in a steady voice.

"And how is the mistress?"

Jerome realized at once that she meant Noémie. On his way he had decided not to allude to Mme. Petit-Dutreuil's death, lest the news should prey on Cricri's feelings, calling up sentiments or scruples which might thwart the plans he had in mind. So, without further thought, he kept to the story he had decided on.

"She's on the stage, abroad." It cost him an effort to go on. "She's quite well, I believe."

"On the stage!" Rinette echoed the words respectfully.

Now they were silent. She turned towards him with an expectant air. Smiling, she let the drapery fall a little lower on her neck and shoulders.

"But all that—it isn't only for that you've come to see me," she said.

At the least sign from him, Jerome was well aware, Cricri would be in his arms. But nothing, alas, survived of all the wild desire which had sped him all the day, like a hound in cry, hot-foot on her trail, tracking his quarry to her lair from end to end of Paris.

"That," he replied, "is the only reason why I've come."

Rinette looked surprised, almost offended.

"Well, let me tell you, here we're not supposed to see . . . ordinary visitors."

Jerome made haste to change the subject.

"Why have you cut your hair?"

"They prefer it short."

He concealed his discomfiture with a smile, and could think of nothing else to say. And yet he could not make up his mind to leave. A secret discontent gnawed at his heart, compelling him to stay. It was as if something important remained to do. But what? . . . Poor Cricri! Well, the damage had been done; there was no way of mending it. . . . No way at all?

Somewhat abashed by his silence, she stole a furtive glance at Jerome, a look more curious than hostile. Why had he come back? Could he be still just a little in love with her? The fancy stirred her with faint longings and suddenly a wild idea flashed through her mind: couldn't she have another child by him? All her frustrated hopes flamed up again. Jerome's son, Daniel's little brother, a child of her own, and for her only! She all but cast herself at Jerome's feet and clasped his knees, murmuring with a look of fond entreaty:

"I want to have a child by you!" No! That would shatter, for a mere caprice, all the future which, inch by hard-won inch, she was now rebuilding. A brief emotion thrilled her body, and for a moment her eyes brooded on an elusive dream; but then she murmured through tight-set lips: "No, it can't be done."

"How's Daniel?" she suddenly inquired.

"Who? My son?" Then in a constrained voice he added: "Do you know him?"

Rinette, though why she hardly knew, had hoped that Daniel had something to do with Jerome's return. Now she was sorry that his name had crossed her lips, and decided to say nothing more about him; neither father nor son must ever guess her secret, the strange dilemma of her love.

She turned the question.

"Do I know him? Why, everyone in Paris knows him! Yes, I've met him."

Jerome's anxiety deepened, but he dared not put the question: "Was it here?"

"Where did you meet him?" he asked.

"Oh, all over the place. In cabarets."

"Yes," he observed, "I thought as much. I've told him more than once what I think of the life he's leading."

"Oh, that was ages ago," she made haste to add. "I don't know if he still goes to such places. Perhaps he's turned over a new leaf— like me!"

He gazed at her in silence, sincerely grieving over the depravity of the younger generation, the collapse of moral codes—and, most of all, over this brothel, and this fellow-creature abandoned to the powers of evil.

Such is life, he mused, but why must it be so? And suddenly he felt crestfallen, conscience-stricken.

Rinette, lost once again in roseate visions of the future, the goal towards which henceforth all her efforts would be directed, gave utterance to her day-dream, clicking her garter against her thigh.

"Yes, I've straightened things out at last—that's why I've not got my knife into you any more. If I stick to my job and don't play the fool, in another three years it's good-bye to Paris for me! That god-forsaken old Paris of yours!"

"Why in three years?"

"Why, it's simple as shelling peas. I've been here just under a month now and I'm making fifty or sixty francs clear, day in, day out. Four hundred a week. That means, in three years—sooner, with any luck—I'll have scraped together thirty thousand francs. When that day comes you'll hear no more of Cricri, Rinette, and the bunch of 'em; Miss Victorine will hop into the Lannion train with all her bags and baggage, and a wad of banknotes in her pocket. Good-bye to the whole lot of you!"

She chuckled.

"No," Jerome reassured himself with desperate insistence, "surely I'm not so depraved as my acts would make me. No, the problem's not so simple as all that; I'm better than the life I lead. Yet, only for me, this girl . . . Only for me!" And from the depths of memory the words came back to him once more: "Woe to that man by whom the offence cometh!"

"Are your parents alive?" he asked.

A notion, imprecise as yet, though even now he was at pains to keep it under, was slowly taking form within his mind.

"My old dad, he died last year, on Saint Yves' day." She paused, doubtful if she should cross herself or not; she decided against it. "I've only Auntie left. She has a little house on the market-square, just behind the church. You don't know Perros-Guirec, do you? As it so happens, I'm the old dame's only heir. 'Tisn't that she's so mighty well-to-do, but the house is hers, that's something. She lives on a pension, a thousand francs a year. She was in service with titled folk for years and years. She lets out the chairs in church, too, and that brings in a bit. Well"—she paused a moment, then her face bright-ened—"with thirty thousand francs' capital Mme. Juju swears that I can have the same income, or as near as may be. I'll find some-thing to do to make up the difference, sure enough. And then we'll keep house together. We always hit it off, her and I. . . . And down there," she added, watching her toes twisting and turning in the tiny satin slippers, "down there nobody knows a mortal thing about me; it'll all be done with, for good and all."

Jerome had risen. His plan was taking definite shape, obsessing his mind. For a moment or two he paced to and fro. An act of generosity . . . to make amends!

He halted in front of Rinette.

"You're really fond of your home—of Brittany, aren't you, Victorine?"

So taken aback was she by his punctilious "Victorine" that she could not reply at once.

Then, "I should say so!" she rejoined.

"Well, you're going back there. Yes, you are. Now listen!"

Again he fell to his restless pacing to and fro, eager to have his way, like a spoilt child. "It's now or never," he reflected. "Otherwise I won't be answerable for the consequences."

"Listen!" He jerked out the words. "You're going back there." Then, looking her boldly in the eyes, he added peremptorily: "This very night."

She laughed.

"Am I?"

"Yes."

"Tonight?"

"Yes."

"To Perros?"

"To Perros."

Now she had ceased to laugh; with malevolent eyes and lowered brows she looked him up and down. What business had he to play the fool with her? Was it a subject to make jokes about?

"If you had a thousand francs a year like your aunt . . ." he began.

His smile convinced her that he meant her well. But what could he be after with his "thousand francs a year"? She worked it out composedly: twelve into a thousand.

The smile had left his lips.

"Is there a notary in your village? What's his name?"

"A notary? Who do you mean? M. Benic?"

Jerome puffed his chest out.

"Well, Cricri, I give you my word of honour that every year, on the first of September, M. Benic will hand you a thousand francs on my behalf. Here's the money for this year." He pulled out his pocketbook. "And here's another thousand to pay your expenses settling in." He held out the money.

She opened her eyes wide and bit her lip without replying. There the money lay, within her reach; she had only to stretch out her hand. So simple-minded was she still, in spite of all, that the proposal left her wonder-struck, but not incredulous. Patiently Jerome held out the notes and at last she took them; after folding and refolding them as small as possible she slipped them inside her stocking and stared at Jerome, tongue-tied. It never entered her head that she might kiss him; she had forgotten not only what she now was but what they had been to each other. He was once more M. Jerome, Mme. Petit-Dutreuil's friend, and she was as shy of him now as the first time she had set eyes on him.

"But," he added, "it's on one condition—that you leave this place at once."

She was not prepared for that.

"What? At once? This afternoon? No, I can't manage that, sir; really, it's impossible."

But rather than retard the issue of his good intentions even for a day, he would have preferred to drop them altogether.

"This afternoon without fail, my dear, and, what's more, I'll see you off."

Now there was no mistaking his determination, she flew into a temper. At once? What nonsense! For one thing, this was just the time she started work. Then, what about her things at the hotel? And the girl friend who shared the room with her? And Mme. Juju? And all her washing at the laundry? And anyhow the people here wouldn't hear of her going off like that. She fussed and fluttered like a netted bird.

"I'll go and fetch Mme. Rose!" she exclaimed at last, with tears
in her eyes, when all her protests proved of no avail. "Then you'll
see it simply can't be done. And, what's more, I don't want to do it!"

"Fetch her at once!"

Jerome foresaw a heated argument and was prepared to take a firm
line with the lady. Mme. Rose's amiable smile came as a surprise.

"Of course she can. Why not?" she replied, for she had scented a
police trap from the start. "All our young ladies are quite free; they
can leave when they like." Turning to Rinette, she addressed her in
a peremptory tone, rubbing her plump hands together. "Run along,
my dear, and get dressed. Can't you see the gentleman's waiting?"

Rinette, clasping her hands, stared at her "madame" and at Jerome,
turn by turn, in blank bewilderment. Big tears were sluicing down
her make-up. Her mind was in a ferment of conflicting emotions,
of mingled helplessness and rage and consternation. At that moment
she hated Jerome. Moreover, she was reluctant to leave the room before conveying to him that he must not breathe a word about the
money hidden in her stocking. Mme. Rose ended by flying into a
towering passion and, grasping Rinette's arm, she ejected her forcibly.
"Will you do as you're told, you!" she shouted at the girl, then hissed
under her breath: "And never show your dirty, spying face here
again!"

Half an hour later a taxi set Jerome and Rinette down at the hotel
where the latter had a room. Rinette had ceased crying and, as she
had no personal initiative to take, was coming to accept, though still
reluctantly, the over-hastiness of the proceedings. But now and then
a protest rose to her lips, like a refrain.

"In three years, I don't say no. But not now, please, not at once!"

Jerome made no answer, but patted her hand. "Today," he was
repeating under his breath. "This very evening, without fail!" Just
now he felt that he had strength enough to break down all resistance,
but already he could see, only too clearly, the limit of his power; no
time must be lost.

He had the hotel bill brought him, with a time-table. The train
left at 7:15 p.m.

Rinette asked him to help her drag from underneath a wardrobe a battered wooden trunk containing a bundle of garments.

"My uniform when I was in service," she explained.

A memory of Noémie's dresses which Nicole had handed over to the pension-keeper at Amsterdam flashed across Jerome's mind. He sat down, drew Rinette onto his knee, and calmly, yet with real fervour throbbing in the cadence of each phrase, exhorted her to leave her finery behind, cast off the harlot's stock-in-trade, and begged her to go back, for good and all, to the simple ways, the purity of her former life.

She listened to him earnestly. His words were like an echo of some long-forgotten voice within herself. "And then," she could not help reflecting, "imagine me wearing those things at home! At high mass, for instance! What would they think of me?" She could never have brought herself to throw away, even to give away, the lace-trimmed underlinen and showy dresses on which so much of her savings had been spent. But she owed the girl with whom she shared the room two hundred francs and, now she was leaving Paris, the debt loomed large in her mind. Why not settle it by leaving the clothes to her friend, and keep intact the round sum Jerome had provided? An excellent way out!

At the idea of putting on once more her shabby black serge dress she clapped her hands with glee, as if she were preparing for a fancy ball. She slipped off Jerome's knee with a burst of hysterical laughter that racked her body like a fit of sobbing.

Jerome had averted his eyes so as not to embarrass her while she dressed. He walked to the window and stared, in a brown study, at the courtyard wall in front. Surely, he mused, I'm worth more than people think! To his mind, this act of merit redeemed the error of the past, responsibility for which, however, he had never frankly taken on himself.

One thing more was needed to set his mind at rest. Without turning his head, he addressed the girl impulsively:

"Tell me that you're not angry with me any more."

"Not a bit!"

"No, but say the words.' Say: 'I forgive you.' " Her courage failed her and, still gazing out of the window, he implored: "Be generous. Say just those three words!"

She obeyed him.

"Of course . . . of course, I forgive you, sir."

"Thank you."

Tears came to his eyes. He was an exile returning to his place in the scheme of things, regaining, after years of deprivation, a tranquil heart! At a window of the lower story a canary was in full song. "There is a soul of goodness in me," Jerome reflected. "People judge me over-harshly; they don't understand. As a man I'm better than the way I live." His heart overflowed with compassion, indiscriminate benevolence.

"Poor Cricri!" he murmured.

When he turned he saw Rinette fastening the last buttons of her black woollen bodice. She had drawn her hair back and, after a wash, her cheeks had regained their bloom; once more she looked the timid, rather mulish little servant-girl whom Noémie had brought back with her six years earlier from Brittany.

Unable to contain his feelings, Jerome went up to her and slipped his arm round her waist. "I'm good at heart," he kept on repeating to himself like a refrain. "Far better than anyone supposes." Instinctively his fingers unhooked her skirt while his lips rested on the girl's forehead in a paternal kiss.

Rinette shrank away—almost she seemed the shy, reluctant little girl of former days. He pressed her closely to him.

"Ah," she sighed, "so you still use the same scent—you know what I mean, the one that smells like lemonade." Smiling now, she lifted a responsive mouth to his, closing her eyes.

Was it not, indeed, the only token of gratitude that she could offer? And for Jerome, too, was it not the one gesture adequate in his present mood of mystic fervour to express in its entirety the devout compassion abounding in his heart?

When they reached the Montparnasse station her train was in. Now, for the first time, when she saw the car labelled "Lannion," Rinette woke to a sense of realities. No, there was no catch in it; the dream that she had cherished for so many years was coming true at last. Why then, she wondered, should she feel so sad?

Jerome found a seat for her and they paced up and down the platform in front of her car, in silence. Rinette was thinking of something, of someone. . . . But she found no words to break the silence. Something, it seemed, was preying on Jerome's mind as well, for several times he turned to her, as if about to speak, then looked away. At last, shunning her eyes, he blurted it out:

"I didn't tell you the truth, Cricri. Mme. Petit-Dutreuil is dead."

She asked for no details, but began to cry, and in her silent grief Jerome took heart of grace, thinking with flattering unction: "What kindness there is in all of us!"

No more words passed between them till the train was due to leave. Had she dared to do so, Rinette would have snatched at any pretext to hand back the money and return to Mme. Rose, begging to be taken back. The delay was getting on Jerome's nerves as well; the thought that he had achieved the rescue of this girl had lost its zest.

Only when the train was pulling out did Rinette pluck up her courage.

"Will you be so kind, sir, as to give my respects to M. Daniel?"

But the noise of the train drowned her voice. She saw he had not heard her; her lips began to quiver, her fingers tightened upon her breast. Jerome, all smiles, delighted to see her go, waved her good-bye with a courteous sweep of his hat.

A new thought had waylaid him and set him tingling with impatience; he would take the first train back to Maisons-Laffitte and, throwing himself at his wife's feet, confess everything—well, nearly everything.

"And then," he murmured to himself as he lit a cigarette and moved away from the station with brisk steps, "about the yearly allowance—I'd better explain matters to Thérèse; she's got a head on her shoulders and will see it's properly attended to."

XIII

ANTOINE had formed the habit of calling several times a week at Rachel's place to take her out to dinner.

One evening as Rachel was on her way towards the mirror, preparatory to going out, and taking her powder-box out of her bag, she let a scrap of folded paper drop to the floor. Antoine picked it up and held it out to her.

"Eh? Oh, thanks!"

He thought he had detected an uneasy tremor in Rachel's voice; she read his thought at once.

"Well?" she said, trying to pass it off with a joke. "What's all the fuss about? It's only a time-table."

He said nothing and she replaced the paper in her bag. A moment later he blurted out the question:

"Are you going away?"

And now the flutter of her lashes, her twisted smile, were not to be mistaken.

"Well, Rachel . . . ?"

Her smile had gone; a spasm of anguish gripped him. No, he thought; no, I mustn't let her. . . . I couldn't do without her, even for a day or two!

He went up to her and touched her arm; sobbing, she sank onto his breast.

"But what . . . what ever . . . ?" he stammered.

She replied at once in brief, staccato sentences.

"No, it's nothing, nothing at all. Just my nerves. I'll tell you; then you'll see it's nothing much really. It's on account of baby's grave; at Gué-la-Rozière, you know. I haven't been to visit it for ages and ages; I really shall have to go there soon. You understand, don't you?

Imagine my frightening you like that! I'm sorry. So you'd be dread-fully cut up—would you?—if . . . if one day——"

"Don't go on!" he begged in a low voice. Now for the first time he realized the place that Rachel had come to occupy in his life, and it appalled him. "How long will you be away?" he faltered.

Loosening her embrace, she ran off, with a forced laugh, to the wash-stand, to sponge her eyes.

"Isn't it silly, starting crying like that!" she exclaimed. "Do you know, the news came one evening—exactly like tonight—when I just going out to dinner. I was at my place with some friends—people you don't know. There was a ring at the bell; a wire. 'Baby dan-gerously ill. Come.' I knew what it meant. I rushed off to the station just as I was, in a light tulle hat and evening shoes, and caught the first train out. What a journey that was! I was all alone and almost off my head. It's a wonder I wasn't quite crazy by the time I got there." She turned towards Antoine. "Wait just a bit longer! I'm let-ting them dry off; that's the best way." Her face lit up suddenly. "Antoine, do you want to do something very, very nice? Then you'll come along there with me. It would only take two days, you know —Saturday and Sunday. We could stay the night at Rouen or Caude-bec and go on next day to the Gué-la-Rozière cemetery. Wouldn't it be great—to go off like that together, all on our own! Don't you think so?"

They left on the last Saturday in September. The afternoon was fine, the train almost empty, and they had the car to themselves. Antoine was delighted with his two days' holiday in Rachel's com-pany; a weight seemed lifted from his shoulders and he looked younger. Like a schoolboy, he seemed unable to keep still, he laughed at everything and twitted Rachel about her luggage deployed along the rack. The better to feast his eyes upon her face, he refused to sit beside her.

"That'll do!" she protested when he got up again, this time to lower the blind. "I'm not going to melt."

"Perhaps not. But, when the sun's on your face, I'm positively blinded." And, indeed, when the light fell full on her cheeks and set her hair ablaze, his eyes grew dazzled if he looked long at her. "This is the first time we've travelled together," he presently remarked. "Has that struck you?"

She could not bring herself to smile. Her mouth was a little drawn, tense with resolve and contained emotion. He bent towards her.

"What's the matter?"

"It's nothing. Only the journey."

He was silent, aware that selfishly he had forgotten the object of their pilgrimage. But then she explained what she meant.

"Travelling always sets my nerves on edge. The landscape flying past. And always at a journey's end . . . the unknown!" Her eyes dwelt for a moment on the transient horizon. "And I've travelled in so many of them, trains and boats." Her look grew sombre.

Antoine slipped across to her side and, stretching himself full length on the seat, laid his head on her lap.

" 'Thy navel is like a round goblet . . . set about with lilies,' " he murmured. Then, after a moment's silence, realizing that Rachel's thoughts were far away, he asked her: "What are you thinking about?"

"Nothing." She tried to speak lightly. "About your head-masterish tie, perhaps!" She slipped a finger under the silk. "To think that even when you travel you can't manage to knot it a trifle looser, let it out a bit!" She stretched herself and smiled. "A stroke of luck—isn't it?— having the car to ourselves. Now it's up to you to talk. Tell me about things that have happened to you."

He laughed.

"That's more in your line—things that happen! I've only my 'cases,' examinations, and so forth. How on earth could I have anything to yarn about? I've always lived like a mole, underground; it's you who've pulled me up to the surface and taught me to look at the world."

Never before had he confessed as much to her. Bending above the head she loved so well, pillowed on her knees, she took it between her hands, gazing into his eyes.

"You mean that? You really mean it?"

"Next year, you know," he went on, without changing his position, "we won't stay in Paris all the summer."

"No?"

"I haven't taken any leave this year; I'll fix things up to get a fortnight off at least."

"Yes."

"Three weeks, perhaps."

"Yes."

"We'll go abroad together, somewhere or other. Like the idea?"

"Yes."

"To the mountains, if you like. The Vosges, or Switzerland. Or we might go further afield."

There was a far-away look on Rachel's face.

"What are you thinking about now?" he asked.

"About what you're saying. Switzerland—rather!"

"Or the Italian lakes, perhaps."

"No."

Lying on his back, lulled by the rhythms of the swaying train, he drowsily agreed.

"All right then, we'll go somewhere else." After a moment's silence he added lazily: "What have you got against the Italian lakes?"

With the tips of her fingers she stroked Antoine's forehead, his eyelids, and his temples, slightly sunken like his cheeks, and did not answer. His eyes were closed, but the question he had put still simmered in his brain.

"Why won't you tell me what you have against the Italian lakes?"

She made a slight movement of impatience.

"Because, if you must know, that's where my brother died. My brother Aaron. At Pallanza."

He regretted his insistence, but did not drop the subject.

"Had he settled in Italy, then?"

"Oh, no, he was travelling. On his honeymoon." Her eyebrows frowned; then, after a moment, as if she had read Antoine's thought, she murmured: "No, there's no denying it, I've had my share of queer experiences in my time!"

"You don't hit it off with your sister-in-law, I suppose?" he suggested. "Anyhow you never speak of her."

The train was stopping; getting up, she looked out of the window. But she had heard Antoine's question, for she turned round towards him.

"Eh? What sister-in-law? Clara?"

"The one who married your brother; he died, you said, on his honeymoon."

"She died at the same time. Didn't I tell you about it? No?" She was still looking out of the window. "They were drowned in the lake. Nobody ever knew how it happened." She hesitated. "Nobody, except, perhaps . . . Hirsch."

"Hirsch!" he exclaimed, propping himself on his elbow. "Hirsch was with them, was he? Then—weren't you there, too?"

"Please don't let's talk about it today," she begged, returning to her seat. "Hand me my bag, please. Feeling hungry?" She unwrapped a bar of chocolate and, holding one end between her teeth, proffered the other end to Antoine, who gaily joined in the game.

"It tastes better that way," she observed with a greedy flicker of her eyelashes. Then a sudden, almost startling change came over her voice. "Clara was Hirsch's daughter. Got it straight, now? I came to know Hirsch through his daughter. Haven't I told you about it?"

He shook his head, but refrained from putting further questions; he was trying to make these latest details tally with what he had already gleaned from her. Anyhow it was not long before Rachel launched forth again—as she never failed to do when he ceased questioning her.

"You've never seen Clara's photo, have you? I'll hunt it up for you. She was a great pal of mine; I got to know her in the beginners' class. But she only stayed a year at the Opera; didn't have the stamina for it. And I suppose Hirsch preferred keeping her at home; that's more than likely, in fact. She and I were thick as thieves, and

I used to go to see her every Sunday at the Neuilly riding-school. That's how I started learning riding, along with her. We got into the way of going out for rides together, the three of us, and kept it up afterwards."

"Whom do you mean by 'the three of us'?"

"Why, Clara, Hirsch, and I, of course. From Easter on I used to join them at six o'clock sharp, three mornings a week. I had to be back at eight sharp at the Opera. We had the Bois de Boulogne to ourselves at that hour—and it was heavenly!" She paused a moment, and he gazed up at her, propping his elbows on the seat, and stayed thus without moving. Rachel harked back to her memories of the past. "A queer girl and no mistake! Full of grit and good-hearted as you make 'em. Lots of charm—with a spice of the gutter in it, and now and then you'd catch that terrifying expression of her father's on her face. Yes, Clara was the best friend I had in those days. Aaron had been keen on her for years; that was all he worked for, really —to marry her some day. But she wouldn't consent; no more would Hirsch, needless to say. Then one day she made up her mind all of a sudden; at the time I couldn't think why she did it. Why, even when the engagement was announced, I had no idea what was at the back of her mind. When I knew—it was too late to say anything." She paused again. "Then, three weeks after their marriage, Hirsch wired to me to come to Pallanza. I didn't know that he had gone off to join them, and the moment I heard he was there I knew something dreadful had happened. . . . Anyhow, there's no secret about it; everyone could see the bruises round Clara's neck. He must have strangled her."

"'He'? Whom do you mean?"

"Aaron. Her husband. He had engaged a boat that evening for a trip on the lake—all by himself. Hirsch didn't try to stop him, it suited his book too well. He knew what he was about, I suppose, and guessed that Aaron meant to kill himself. Only Clara had an inkling of it, too; she picked a moment when Hirsch wasn't watching her and sprang into the boat, just as Aaron was starting to row away. Anyhow that's how I've pieced it together, bit by bit, for Hirsch . . ."

She shuddered, then continued: "You never know what Hirsch has in his head."

Antoine broke the silence that ensued.

"But why should he have killed himself?"

"Aaron was always talking about suicide. He had it on the brain, even as a child. That's just why I didn't dare say anything to him, and let the marriage take place. Oh," she exclaimed in a tone of deep distress, "how I've reproached myself for it, since! Perhaps if I'd spoken out in time—" She gazed at Antoine, as though it lay with him to justify her to her conscience. "I'd found out their secret, you see. But was that a reason for letting Aaron know about it? What could I do? He had told me several times that he'd kill himself if Clara didn't marry him. And it's sure he'd have done it, if I'd told him what I had discovered—quite by accident, too. Don't you think so?"

Antoine could not answer; he repeated her words.

"By accident?"

"Yes, quite by accident. I'd gone to join Clara and Hirsch for a morning ride. I went straight upstairs to Clara's room; when I was near it I heard a scuffle going on and started to run. The door was ajar. Clara had no blouse on, her arms were bare and her riding skirt hampered her movements; then, just as I flung the door wide open, I saw her snatch up her riding-whip from a chair and slash him across the face with it as hard as she could. Hirsch felt it all right!"

"What? Her own father . . . ?"

"Yes, my dear. That was a scene if you like—I often think of it!" She chuckled with vindictive glee. "The sight he was that morning, I shan't forget it in a hurry! His face went yellow, while the weal grew darker and darker. He was pretty free with his fists, himself, and, when he was at it, he hit hard. But that time it was his turn to get a cut across the face, for a change!"

"But . . . I don't follow."

"Well, I never knew exactly what had happened that morning. It struck me at once that, now she was engaged, Clara must have told him to . . . well, to leave her alone. Various details I'd already noticed, things that had puzzled me at the time, came back to me. In a flash I *understood*. . . . Hirsch marched out of the room with a high and mighty air, without saying a word to me. He seemed quite confident that I'd hold my tongue, and, as you know, he wasn't far wrong there. I ferreted the whole story out of Clara. But she swore to me—I'm sure she meant it, too—all that was over and done with, and she was marrying just to get away from it. To get away from Hirsch? Or did she mean from her own infatuation? That's what I should have asked myself that morning. I ought to have guessed it wasn't done with, not by any means, if only from the way she talked of Hirsch." After a pause, she went on in a brooding voice: "When you hear a woman say she hates a man as much as that, you may be sure she's hankering after him all the time."

Again she seemed lost in her musings and stayed a minute thus, with lowered forehead, eyes downcast. At last she spoke again:

"Yes, and it only shows how true that is, what I've just said; it was Clara herself, right in the middle of their honeymoon—would you ever believe it?—who asked Hirsch to come to Italy. I don't know exactly what happened after that. Anyhow, Aaron must have caught them together; otherwise he wouldn't have wanted to drown himself. The one thing I've never quite made out is just what Clara was after. Why did she jump into the boat alongside her husband? To stop him from killing himself? Or did she intend to die with him? Either theory would fit. Think of that last talk of theirs together, out on the lake in the middle of the night! What passed between them there? Over and over again I've put myself the question. Did she blurt out the whole truth in that cynical way she had? She was quite capable of doing so. Did Aaron decide to do away with her, just to make sure *that* could never happen again after he was dead? Their boat was recovered next day, empty; the bodies were found together several days later. But the queerest thing of all to my mind is that Hirsch should have sent for me to come quite early that evening, before the telegraph-office closed and before even the search party had gone out to look for them. . . . Anyhow," she continued after some pensive moments, "you must have seen all about it in the papers—only you didn't pay much attention, I suppose. The Italian police held an inquiry, and the French police took a hand in it too. They had searches made at my place and Aaron's, but they never solved the mystery; I know more about it than they do."

"And they never got on the tracks of your friend Hirsch?"

She drew herself up abruptly.

"No," she coolly replied, "they did *not* get on the tracks of my friend Hirsch."

There was a hint of truculence in her voice and in the glance she flung at Antoine, but he took no notice, for often, when she talked of her experiences, she affected a rather provocative tone; it seemed as if she took a delight in startling the man who, on the evening when first they met, had impressed her so profoundly.

"No, they didn't get on his track," she repeated with a chuckle, "but he thought it wiser not to come back to France that year."

"Are you really quite sure it was she, his daughter, in the middle of her honeymoon, who . . . ?"

"Pretty sure," she replied, then, flinging her arms about him with the passion she always manifested when their conversation turned on Hirsch, she sealed his lips with an imperious kiss. "Ah," she sighed, nestling to his breast, "you're so different from everyone else. You're generous and kind. You're straight. Oh, how I love you, Toine dear!" When Antoine, his mind still haunted by her story, showed signs of questioning her further, she was firm in her refusal. "No, that's enough on the subject. It works me up too much; I'd rather forget, forget everything—for as long as I can. Hold me tight, darling, and be nice to me . . . yes, hug me, like that . . . closer, still closer— and help me to forget!"

He clasped her in his arms; but then, from the depths of his unconscious self, a craving for adventure, like a new instinct, flared into sudden life. Ah, could he only swerve from the rut of a too orderly existence, make a new start, live dangerously and divert to free, spontaneous acts the energies which it had been his pride to lavish on laborious ends!

"Supposing we went right away, just you and I? Listen, why

shouldn't we start life together, far away from Paris? You've no idea what a success I'd make of it!"

"What? You!" she laughed, lifting her lips to his.

He sobered down at once and smiled, to make believe he had not been in earnest.

"How I love you!" she murmured, poring on his face with a look of anguish he was destined to recall in after-days.

Antoine knew Rouen well; his father's family came of Norman stock, and some more or less near relatives of M. Thibault were still living there. Moreover, some eight years earlier, Antoine had been posted to Rouen for his military service.

He insisted on Rachel's coming with him before dinner across the bridges to an outlying suburb, swarming with troops, and led her along beside a never-ending barrack wall.

"There's the sick-ward!" Antoine announced delightedly, pointing to some lighted windows. "Do you see the second window there? That's the medical office. What days and days I've wasted in that room with damn near nothing to do—why, I couldn't even read a book!—except keep an eye on a couple of malingerers and a few youngsters with a dose!" He laughed without a trace of rancour, then joyfully exclaimed: "What a change! Why, I'm the happiest man in the world today!"

She made no reply and slipped hastily in front of him; he did not notice she was on the brink of tears.

A picture-house announced *In Darkest Africa*. Antoine drew Rachel's attention to the poster, but she shook her head and hurried him back to their hotel.

While they dined, all his efforts to make her laugh were unavailing and, remembering why they had come here, he felt a little ashamed of his high spirits.

But the moment they were in the bedroom, she flung her arms round his neck.

"Don't be angry with me," she pleaded.

"Angry? What for?"

"For spoiling our trip like this."

He was going to protest when she embraced him again.

"Oh, how I love you!" she repeated, almost as if she were talking to herself.

Early next morning they arrived at Caudebec. The heat was more oppressive than ever; a veil of scintillating mist hung over the wide river. A small hotel announced conveyances for hire and Antoine carried their luggage to it. The carriage they had ordered drew up, well before the appointed time, in front of the window near which they were breakfasting. Rachel hurried through the dessert and, refusing Antoine's aid, piled all her parcels into the hood, then, after explaining to the driver the route she wanted him to take, sprang gaily into the ancient victoria.

The nearer came the melancholy climax of their expedition, the more her spirits seemed to rise. She grew ecstatic over the countryside, each hill and each declivity, the crosses by the roadside, each village market-place. Everything came as a surprise to her; she might have never roamed beyond the suburbs of some great city.

"Look at those hens! And that palsied old crone over there, toasting in the sun! And that grade-crossing barrier with a great chunk of stone to weigh it down. Aren't they back numbers, the folk in these parts! Well, I warned you you were coming to the back of beyond, didn't I? And I wasn't far wrong."

When she caught sight of the roofs down in the valley, clustering round the spire of the little church of Gué-la-Rozière, she stood up in the carriage and her face lit up as if she were a wanderer returning to her native land.

"The graveyard's over on the left, a long way from the town. Behind those poplars. You'll see it in a minute. . . . Keep your horse at a trot through the village, please," she told the driver, as they came to the first houses of Gué.

Half hidden at the far end of grassy orchards, white house-fronts, striped with black and trimly capped with thatch, flashed back the sunlight through the apple-trees; the windows all were shuttered. They passed a slate-tiled building flanked by two sentinel yews.

"That's the town hall," Rachel cried delightedly. "Not a single thing has changed. That's where they fixed up the certificates and so forth. See that house over there? That's where baby's nurse used to live. Nice folk they were. They've gone away, or else I'd look them up and give the old girl a kiss. Hallo, that's where I stayed once. When I came, I put up where there happened to be a spare bed. I took my meals there; how I used to laugh at the funny way they talked! And they gaped at me as if I'd escaped from a menagerie. The old girls used to come and inspect me in bed—my pyjamas, you know. You'd never believe what back numbers they are in these parts. Nice people, for all that. They were terribly kind to me when baby died. After that I sent them heaps and heaps of things: candied fruit, ribbons for their bonnets, liqueurs for the curé." She stood up again. "The graveyard's there, just beyond that ridge. If you look well you'll see the graves, down in the hollow. Put your hand there—do you know why my heart's fluttering like that? I'm always in terror I shan't be able to find her again, poor little thing. We didn't care to take out a permanent lease, you see; everyone assured us that wasn't the custom hereabouts. And, every time I come, I can't help thinking to myself: 'Suppose they've bundled her out of it!' They'd have the right, you know, if they did so. . . . Pull up in front of the pathway, driver; we'll walk to the gate. . . . Come along, be quick!"

Jumping down, she ran to the iron gate, opened it, and vanished round a wall. Almost immediately she came into sight again and called to Antoine.

"It's still there."

Sunlight fell full upon her face, where only joy was manifest. She vanished again and this time Antoine followed her. He found her standing, arms akimbo, gazing at a patch of weeds wedged in the angle between two walls; some vestiges of masonry showed through the nettles.

"It's there all right, but what a state it's in! Yes, poor kid, your grave could do with a brush-up—and, just think, I pay them twenty francs a year to look after it!"

She turned to Antoine, and now her voice sounded almost diffident, as though she craved his indulgence for a caprice.

"Toine dear, would you mind very much taking off your hat?"

Blushing, Antoine removed his hat.

"Poor little darling!" she suddenly exclaimed, and rested her hand on Antoine's shoulder, while her eyes filled with tears. "To think I wasn't even with her when she died! I came too late. She was such a sweet little thing, just like a little angel, and so pale. . . ." Then, in a sudden change of mood, she wiped her eyes and smiled. "Well, it's a queer sort of expedition I've brought you on, isn't it? Of course it's ancient history in a way, but one can't help feeling it all the same. It's just as well we have work before us—it takes one's mind off things. Come along!"

She insisted on going back to the carriage and, refusing the driver's help, carried her packages to the graveyard. There, waving Antoine aside, she unfastened them herself, kneeling on the ground. On an adjoining tombstone she alined methodically a bill-hook, a shovel, and a mallet; last of all a big cardboard box containing a wreath woven of strings of white beads.

"Now I know why it was so heavy," said Antoine smiling.

She drew herself up gaily.

"Look here, stop ragging and lend us a hand for a change. Off with your coat! Here, take this pruning-hook! We've got to root up, or hack away somehow, all those damned weeds which have overgrown everything. See those bricks there, underneath? That's the grave. She had such a mite of a coffin, and it didn't weigh much either, poor darling! Pass me that, please. It's all that's left of a wreath; a pretty old one, that. 'In memory of our darling daughter.' Zucco brought it. I'd had nothing to do with him for a year, but I thought I ought to let him know about it all the same—you understand, don't you? Anyhow he did the right thing; he put in an appearance, in mourning, too. What's more, I was really glad he'd come; I didn't feel so lonely at the funeral. Silly of me, but there you are! Hallo, that's the cross. Set it up straight, please; we can bank it up with earth afterwards."

As he drew aside a wisp of grass, Antoine had a shock; a first glimpse had not revealed the entire inscription: "Roxane Rachel Goepfert." The "Roxane" had been hidden, and he had only seen *her* name. For some seconds he stood there, lost in thought.

"Now then," Rachel admonished him. "Let's get down to it! We'll begin here."

Antoine "got down to it" with a will; he was no believer in half-measures. In his shirt-sleeves, brandishing pruning-hook and shovel, he very soon was sweating like a ditch-digger.

"Now for the wreaths," she said. "Pass them to me and I'll clean them one by one. Hallo, there's one missing! Can't you find it? It's Hirsch's, the best of the lot. In china flowers, it was. Well, I must say, that's a bit thick!"

Antoine watched her with amusement; hatless, the red tangle of her hair burning in the sunlight, lips curling with scorn and indignation, her skirts tucked up and sleeves rolled to her elbows, she raged about the churchyard, from first to final grave, muttering imprecations.

"Someone's gone and lifted it, the dirty thief—damn him!"

When she came back she seemed disheartened.

"And I was so fond of it! They've chopped it up into trinkets, I suppose. Yes, they're a primitive lot, all right! Still"—her anger evaporated as if by magic—"I've spotted some yellow sand over there which will brighten things up no end."

With the passing minutes the little grave was taking on a new aspect; the cross, trued up again and hammered into the ground, rose high above a brick rectangle, meticulously cleared of weeds; a narrow border of sand, laid all around it, added the finishing touch to a neat, well-kept grave.

They had not noticed the horizon clouding up, and some premonitory raindrops took them by surprise. A storm was gathering above the valley. Under the leaden sky the tombstones seemed to grow whiter yet, the grass more green.

"Hurry up!" Rachel cried. She cast a mothering glance towards the tiny grave. "Yes, we've made a good job of it. Why, it might be a little cottage garden!"

Antoine had espied in a corner of the graveyard two saffron-hearted roses on a drooping branch, tossing in the breeze. He thought of laying them in token of farewell on little Roxane's grave, but could not bring himself to make the romantic gesture, which would come so much better from the child's mother. He picked the roses and handed them to Rachel.

Taking them from his hand, she thrust the stems hastily into her blouse.

"Thanks," she said, "but we must hurry or my hat will be ruined."

Without looking back, she ran to the carriage, holding up her skirts under the downpour.

The driver had taken out his horse, and man and beast were sheltering in a hollow of the hedge. Antoine and Rachel took cover under the hood, spreading on their knees the heavy apron reeking of musty leather. She was laughing, amused at the trick the elements had played on them, and rejoicing, too, in a sense of duty done.

It was only a summer shower. Soon the rain abated, the clouds sheered off towards the east. Across the clear, pellucid air the setting sun shone out again in blinding splendour. The driver began to harness his horse, and some children came along the road, driving before them a flock of rain-drenched geese. A little boy of nine or ten climbed onto the step and hailed them in a shrill, childish voice:

"It's nice to be in love, ain't it, mister?"

He jumped off again; they heard his clogs clattering down the road. Rachel burst out laughing.

"Back numbers?" Antoine chuckled. "The rising generation strikes me as being very much up-to-date."

At last the vehicle was ready to take the road. It was too late to catch the train at Caudebec and they had to drive directly to the nearest main-line station. As Antoine had not arranged for a substitute at the hospital on Monday morning, he was bound to return to Paris that night.

The driver persuaded them to halt at Saint-Ouen-la-Noue for supper. The inn was thronged with the usual Sunday night crowd of topers. The new-comers were allotted one of the back rooms.

They ate in silence. Rachel's joviality had spent itself and she was musing on the past—that evening when at this very hour, after the funeral, she had driven to this inn in a similar, perhaps the same, conveyance; but then the famous tenor had been her companion. Most vivid memory of all was the dispute that had flared up between them almost at once. Zucco had grown violent and dealt her a blow —just there it had happened, in front of that corn-bin. But that very night she had given herself to him again in one of the bedrooms overhead, and for the next four months she had once more put up with his brutal ways, his boorishness. Still, she bore him little malice; there was even a certain sensual thrill in her memories of the man and of the blow he had inflicted. But she took good care not to tell Antoine the story; she had never confessed to him in so many words that the singer used to beat her. . . . Then another and more poignant memory loomed through the darkness of her thoughts, and now she realized that she had dallied all this time with other fancies only to shake off its obsession.

She rose.

"Shall we walk to the station?" she suggested. "The train's not due till eleven. The driver can bring along the luggage."

"What? A five-mile tramp along these muddy roads, in the middle of the night?"

"Why not?"

"I never heard of such an idea!"

"Oh," she sighed, "then I'd have got there fagged out and that would have done me no end of good!" But, without further protest, she followed him to the waiting carriage.

The night was pitch-dark, the air refreshed by rain. No sooner was she seated than she prodded the driver's back with her parasol.

"Drive slowly, please; as slowly as you like. We've heaps of time." Then she snuggled up to Antoine, murmuring: "It's such a lovely night; I'm so comfy, like this."

But when, a moment later, he lightly stroked the cheek that nestled against his shoulder, he felt it wet with tears.

"My nerves are all upset," she exclaimed, and moved her face away. Then suddenly she flung herself into his arms. "Oh, my darling, keep me, hold me close, close in your arms!"

They were silent now, locked in each other's arms. Trees and houses, briefly lit up by the carriage-lamps, flickered into phantom life and died into the darkness. A host of stars spangled the zenith. Rachel's drooping head swayed to and fro on Antoine's shoulder with each lurch of the ramshackle conveyance; now and again she drew herself up and her arms tightened round his shoulders.

"Oh, how I love you!"

They were the only passengers awaiting the Paris train on the platform of the little junction. They took shelter under a shed. Rachel, still in silent mood, held Antoine's arm.

Porters were bustling hither and thither in the darkness, swinging their lanterns over the rain-drenched platform and lighting it with evanescent gleams.

"Stand back for the express!"

With a rattle and a roar the express hurtled past, a black fire-eyed mastodon, whirling aloft whatever might take wing, draining away the very air behind it. The tumult passed; silence closed in again. Suddenly above their heads the thin, exasperating buzzing of an electric bell announced the coming of their train.

There was only half a minute's halt and they had barely time to scramble into a compartment, no time to choose one. Three other passengers were in their carriage, sound asleep; visored in blue, the roof-lamp glimmered wanly. Rachel took off her hat and sank into the only remaining corner-seat. Antoine sat down at her side, but, instead of leaning towards him, she pressed her forehead against the window.

In the half-light her hair, which glowed in sunshine orange-yellow, almost pink, had lost its normal hue, changed to a white-hot, molten fluorescence, like spun glass or a metallic floss. Her cheeks were bathed in a phosphorescent sheen which made the skin seem insubstantial, wraithlike. Antoine clasped Rachel's hand, which lay drooping on the cushions. Thinking he had seen her shiver, he questioned her in a low voice; her only response was a febrile pressure of his hand; she did not turn in his direction. He had no inkling of what might be passing in her mind. He remembered her demeanour in the graveyard, her nervous attack at the inn; could the errand which had brought them there account for it? Yet she had seen it through cheerfully enough. He could make nothing of her present mood.

When they reached Paris, and their fellow-travellers, struggling to their feet, unmasked the lamp, he noticed that her eyes were fixed on the ground. He followed her in silence through the crowd and only when they were in the taxi did he venture a question.

"What is the matter?"

"Nothing."

"Tell me what it is, Rachel."

"Leave me in peace! Can't you see it's over now?"

"No, I won't leave you in peace. I've the right . . . Now do tell me what it is."

Raising her tear-stained face, she gazed at him with a look of utter despair.

"No, I can't tell you what it is." But then her self-control broke down and she flung herself into his arms. "I'll never have strength enough, my darling; never, never, never . . . !"

In a flash he knew his happiness was drawing to an end; Rachel would leave him, pass from his life—and there was nothing, nothing at all, that he could do against it. He realized the bitter truth without a word from her and long before he guessed what lay behind it, even before the sorrow of it touched his life; it was as if he had always, from the first, been prepared for this to happen.

In silence they climbed the stairs and entered Rachel's flat. She left him to himself for a few moments in the pink room. He stood there, bereft of thought, gazing vacantly at the bed, the dressing-table, the alcove—at all that had become a second home to him. She had taken off her cloak when she came back to the room. He watched her enter, shut the door, come near him, her eyes veiled by the golden lashes, her lips close-set and enigmatic.

His courage gave way, and he stumbled towards her, stammering: "But you can't mean it, surely you can't? You're not really going to leave me?"

Then she sat down and in a weary, broken voice asked him to face it calmly; she had a long journey before her, a business trip to the Belgian Congo. She launched into explanations. Her father's estate, every sou he had, had been invested by Hirsch in an oil-refinery which hitherto had done very well indeed and paid good dividends. But recently one of the managers had died, and now she had learned that the other manager, who was running the factory at present, was hand in glove with some wealthy business-men from Brussels who had just established at Kinchassa—in close proximity, that was—a rival factory, and the Belgians were doing their utmost to ruin the concern in which she, Rachel, was interested. (As she went on, her voice grew rather more assured.) The situation was complicated, moreover, by political intrigues. The Müller group was backed by the Belgian government. There was no one she could trust on the spot. Her entire fortune was in jeopardy, her material welfare and her future. She had thought things over, tried to find some other way out. Hirsch was living in Egypt and quite out of touch with the Congo at present. The only solution was to go there herself and set the business on its feet again, or dispose of it to the Müller group at a suitable price.

Vanquished by her coolness, Antoine heard her out, pale-faced, with tight-set lips.

"But"—he ventured at last to intervene—"surely it won't take you so very long?"

"That depends."

"How long? A month? More than that . . . two months?" There was a tremor in his voice. "Or three months?"

"Yes."

"Less, perhaps."

"Hardly less. Why, it takes a month to get there!"

"Supposing we could find someone to send instead? Someone you could depend on?"

She shrugged her shoulders.

"How could I rely on anyone during the month or so he'd be out of my control? With my rivals over there only too ready to grease his palm!"

There was no arguing against the logic of it. As a matter of fact, a word had been hovering on his lips ever since she began her explanation—the query: when? All other questions could bide their time. He made a timid move towards her, and murmured in a humble voice which curiously belied the masterful set of his features:

"Lulu dear, you're not thinking of leaving me at once, are you? Do please tell me."

"No, not at once. But quite soon."

He mustered up all his courage.

"When?"

"When I've got everything ready. I can't say exactly."

Their fixity of purpose wavered in the ensuing silence. Antoine could read on Rachel's haggard face that she was near her breaking-point, and he too felt his will-power ebbing. He went up to her, pleaded with her again.

"You don't really mean it, do you? You're not going to . . . go away?"

She strained him to her breast and drew him stumblingly towards the bed; they fell across it, locked in each other's arms.

"Don't speak," she whispered. "Don't ask me anything. Say nothing more about it . . . nothing at all—or I shall go away at once, without a word of warning!"

Desolate and defeated, he kept silence, and now, in his turn, fell to weeping, crushing his face upon her loosened hair.

XIV

RACHEL kept her word, and for a whole month turned a deaf ear to any further questions. Whenever she detected a certain flicker of anxiety in Antoine's eyes, she looked away. It was a terrible month; life went on its usual way, and yet no act, no thought, but had its repercussion on their suffering.

On the day after she broke the news to him, Antoine had summoned up all his strength of mind to see him through, but it had failed him; he was appalled to find his grief so poignant, ashamed of having it so little under control. A disturbing suspicion had crossed his mind: "Can it be that I'm . . . ?" and, close on its heels, another thought: "Anyhow, I mustn't let others see it." It was as well for him the duties of his calling gave him no respite, and daily, as he crossed the precincts of the hospital, professional instinct got the upper hand again and saw him through the day; at each bedside his thoughts were only for the patient. But in his spells of leisure—between two visits, or at the family table (for M. Thibault was back in Paris and, since the beginning of October, their domestic life followed the old routine)—the mood of irremediable gloom, for ever brooding in the background of his mind, bore down on him, and he grew inattentive, quick to take offence; it seemed that all the energy on which he used to pride himself could find its only outlet now in fits of temper.

He spent his evenings and every night with Rachel; joyless evenings, joyless nights. All that they said, even their silences, were poisoned by unuttered thoughts, and their embraces quickly wore them out, yet never slaked their almost hostile craving each for each.

One evening at the beginning of November when he was about to enter Rachel's flat, Antoine found the door wide open. Bare walls. A carpetless floor. The whole aspect of the hall had changed. He rushed into the flat. His footsteps echoed emptiness, and in the pink bedroom the alcove gaped, a meaningless recess.

He heard sounds in the kitchen and ran there, panic-stricken. He saw the concierge on her knees, fumbling with a pile of discarded garments. Antoine snatched from her hand the letter she held up to him. His heart began to beat again once he had read the first few lines; no, Rachel had not left Paris yet, she was waiting for him in a neighbouring hotel and would not be leaving for Le Havre till the following night. At once he fell to planning a campaign of lies that would enable him to take the night and morning off, and see Rachel on board her boat.

He spent most of the following day in unsuccessful attempts to arrange this, and it was not till six o'clock that everything had been settled, a substitute provided, and he was free to go.

He joined Rachel at the station, where she was busy registering a pile of brand-new trunks. She looked pale, much older, and wore a tailor-made costume that he had not seen before.

It was not till the following morning, at the Havre hotel, when he was trying to steady down his throbbing nerves in a boiling hot bath, that something he had vaguely noticed yesterday flashed through his mind, vivid as lightning and as startling: Rachel's luggage was marked "R.H."

He sprang out of the water, flung open the bathroom door.

"You . . . you're going back to Hirsch!"

To his utter bewilderment Rachel's face lit up with a tender smile.

"Yes," she whispered, but so faintly that he caught only a far-off sibilance; then he saw her eyelids flutter an avowal, and she nodded twice.

He sank into a chair. Some minutes passed. No word of reproach rose to his lips, and it was not grief or jealousy that bowed his shoulders now, only a sense of his own powerlessness, the crushing load of life; they were puppets in the hands of fate.

A shivering fit reminded him that he was wet and naked.

"You'll catch cold," she said. So far no word had passed between them.

Hardly aware what he was doing, Antoine dried himself and began to dress. She remained standing there, as she had been when he burst in, leaning against the radiator, a nail-file in her hand. For all their sorrow, both of them, he hardly less than she, were conscious of a vague relief. How often during the past month had Antoine felt that something was being kept back from him! Now, at least, the truth in all its stark reality lay bare before his eyes. And Rachel, shaking off the irksome trammels of her lie, could feel her sense of dignity return, and be herself again.

At last she broke the silence.

"Perhaps I shouldn't have told a lie!" Love shone on her face, and pity, unshadowed by the least remorse. "What a lot of silly notions one has about jealousy—false, conventional ideas! Anyhow, I assure you, it was only for your sake—to spare you—that I lied; personally, it only made me more miserable than ever. But now I'm glad I haven't got to go away with a lie between us."

He made no comment, but stopped dressing and sat down.

"Yes," she went on, "Hirsch has asked me to return, and I am going back to him."

She paused again and, now she understood his silence was deliberate, all the thoughts she had kept back so long clamoured for utterance.

"It's sweet of you, Toine dear, not to say anything—thank you! For, oh, my darling, don't I know all that might be said? I've been arguing it out with myself for weeks and weeks. It's pure madness, what I'm doing—but nothing could stop me from doing it. I suppose you think it's Africa that tempts me, the call of the wild, as they say. Well, there's something in that, of course; sometimes that call's so urgent that I'm positively sick with longing. But that, by itself, wouldn't have been enough. Or perhaps you think I'm acting from mercenary motives. There's some truth in that, too. Hirsch is going to marry me; he's immensely rich and at my age—you may say what you like—marriage has its importance; it's pretty hard spending all one's days on the outside edge of things. But there's more in it than that. I really think that I'm a bit above such considerations, so far as anyone who's a Jew, or half a Jew, can be above them. Here's a proof of it: you're a rich man, or will be one; well, you might ask me to marry you tomorrow, but I wouldn't give up my plan of going away.

"I know I'm hurting you, Toine darling, but do be brave and hear me out; it does me good to tell you everything. For your sake, too—it's better for you to know all. . . . I thought of killing myself. Morphine gives you a quick death, with no fuss, no pain. I even bought the bottle; I threw it away yesterday before leaving Paris. I want to live, you see; I never really, really wished to die. You never seemed jealous when I spoke of him—and you were right. It's he, as you very well know, who should be jealous of you. I love you, dear, I love you as I've never loved anyone before; and—I hate *him!* Why shouldn't I own to it? I hate him. He's not a man, he's a . . . I don't know what. I hate him and he terrifies me. Time after time he's beaten me. And he'll beat me again—kill me, who knows? He, any-how, is jealousy itself. Once on the Ivory Coast he bribed one of our porters to strangle me. Do you know why? Because he imagined his boy had come to my hut one night, to see me. No, he'd stop at nothing!

"At nothing!" she repeated in a brooding voice. "But one can't stand up against him. Listen to this—I've never dared to tell you about it before. You remember when I went to Pallanza after the tragedy—when he sent for me? Well, that's when it all began. Yet I'd guessed the truth and I was scared to death of him. One day I didn't dare to drink a cup of tea he'd made for me, because of the queer smile on his face when he brought it. And yet, in spite of that, in spite of all . . . Do you understand? No, you simply can't con-ceive the curious fascination of that man!"

Antoine shivered again. Rachel wrapped a dressing-gown round his shoulders and went on in a cool, unemotional voice:

"Don't imagine he had to use threats, or force. He had only to bide his time; that was all and he knew it, he knew his power. Why, it was I who went and knocked at his door! And it as only on the second night that he opened it to me. Then I gave up everything to go away with him; I didn't return to France. I followed him everywhere, like a dog, like his shadow. For two, nearly three, years I put up with everything—blows, exhaustion, ill-treatment, prison . . . everything! For three years I couldn't look a day ahead without being terrified of what might happen. Sometimes we had to stay in hiding for weeks on end, without daring to go out of doors. At Salonika there was a terrible scandal, we had all the Turkish police hunting us down; we had to change our names five times before we could make the frontier. Always the same story, trouble over his . . . propensities. In one of the London suburbs he managed to buy up a whole family—a prostitute from the slums, her two sisters, and her little brother; his 'mixed grill,' he called it. One day the police surrounded the house and nabbed us. We had three months in the lock-up over that. But he managed to get us off in the end. Oh, if I started telling you everything . . . ! The things I've seen, the things I've been through!

"I can see you saying to yourself: 'Now I know why she left him.' Well, you're wrong; it wasn't I who left him. I told you a lie. I could never have done it. It was he who told me to go. He roared with laughter. 'Clear out!' he said. 'When I want you, you'll come back right enough!' I spat in his face. Now, do you want to hear the truth? Since I came back, I've never been able to stop thinking of him. I've been waiting, waiting. And now at last he has told me to return. Now do you understand why I'm going?"

She went to Antoine and knelt before him, resting her head on his knee, sobbing. He gazed down at her shoulders, shaken with sobs. He, too, was trembling.

"How I love you, my darling!" she murmured, closing her eyes.

All day, as though they had made a pact of silence, they spoke no more of all these things. What good would it have been? At lunch they had to sit face to face, and now and again his eyes and hers, haunted by a like obsession, drew together, then resolutely turned aside. What good would it have been?

She had some small purchases to make and lingered over them as long as possible, feigning to be interested. Rain-squalls, sweeping in-

land from the sea, sluiced down the streets and hissed along the house-
fronts. Antoine followed her meekly from shop to shop till it was
dinner-time. She did not even need to book a berth in the mail-
steamer, as she was travelling by the *Romania,* a freighter which
carried some passengers, and put in at Le Havre on her way from
Ostende at about five a.m., sailing an hour later. Hirsch was to meet
her at Casablanca. There had not been a word of truth in her story
about the Congo oil-refinery.

They spun the dinner out as long as possible; the prospect of re-
tiring to their bedroom and being alone together for this final night
made cowards of them both. The café into which they drifted consisted of one huge, crowded room, noisy and brightly lit; drinking-
hall, billiard-room, and dance-floor were combined in one and, in a
blue haze of tobacco-smoke, the click of billiard-balls fretted the
languid throb of waltzes. When it was nearly ten a troupe of strolling
Italians made a sudden entry; there were a dozen of them, red-shirted,
white-trousered fellows, flaunting Neapolitan fishing-caps whose tassels
dangled on their shoulders. They jigged and capered with demoniac
glee, yelling at the top of their voices, and playing, as they danced,
on violins and castanets, guitars and tambourines. Antoine and Rachel
watched them gratefully, glad of this foolish respite from the bane
of thought; but, when the merry-makers had sung their last and
passed the hat round, their grief flared up with new intensity. They
rose and, shivering in the downpour, walked back to the hotel.

It was midnight. Rachel was to be called at three a.m. Flurries of
wild November rain beat on the iron balcony, and, huddled side by
side like two forlorn, lost children, they spent their last, brief night
together, without a word . . . without desire.

Once only Antoine spoke.

"Are you cold?"

She was trembling violently.

"No," she replied, and nestled up against him, as though even now
he still might rescue her, might save her from herself. "No, I'm
frightened."

He let it pass, for he was almost tired of trying, always in vain, to understand her.

There was a knock at the door and, springing from the bed, she cut short their last embrace. He was grateful to her, for each depended on the other's fortitude to see it through.

They dressed in silence, with studied calmness, giving each other now and then a helping hand, keeping up to the bitter end the habits of their life in common. He helped her to close a recalcitrant suit-case, kneeling on it with all his weight while, squatting on the floor, she turned the key. When at last everything was ready and the time past for commonplace remarks, when she had strapped her rugs together, put on her hat, pinned her veil, slipped on her gloves, and buttoned up the cover of her dressing-case, there were still some minutes to go before the cab arrived. She sank into a low chair near the door. A shivering fit came on her and, setting her jaws to stop her teeth from chattering, she crouched there, her hands clasped round her knees. Equally at a loss for anything to say or do, Antoine perched himself on a pile of trunks, with dangling arms, not daring to approach her. The moments dragged by in an agonizing silence, dark with forebodings, each moment charged with suffering so keen that, under its strain, they must have broken down, had they not known that in a few more seconds the end would come. A memory flashed through Rachel's mind—the custom of certain Slav tribes who, when someone they love is setting forth on a long journey, form a circle and sit around the pilgrim for a while, in silent meditation. She all but spoke her thought aloud, but feared her voice might fail her.

When she heard, outside the door, the footsteps of the men coming to take her luggage, she suddenly raised her head and swung her body round towards him. Such love shone in her eyes, such sheer despair and terror, that he flung out his arms towards her.

"My dearest!"

The door opened and the men streamed into the room. Rachel rose. She had waited for others to be present before she said good-bye. She moved towards Antoine, stood beside him. He dared not put his arms around her lest he should never let her go. For the last time, the last, he felt under his lips the warm, soft pressure of her trembling mouth. He heard, or seemed to hear, a whisper:

"Good-bye, good-bye . . . my darling."

With a swift movement she drew away, vanished without a look behind into the passage. He stared towards the open door, twisting his hands together, and his only feeling was a dull amazement.

She had made him promise not to escort her to the steamer, but it was understood between them that he would go to the far end of the northern jetty and, standing at the foot of the lighthouse, watch the *Romania* putting out to sea. The moment he heard the cab drive away, he rang and gave instructions for his luggage to be carried to the cloak-room; he did not wish to have to see this room again. Then he flung out into the darkness.

Shrouded in dripping mist, the town looked like a city of the dead. Overhead an angry wrack of storm still lowered, while another cloud-bank rose on the horizon, and, as the masses drew together, the zone of limpid sky between them seemed to melt away.

After walking blindly ahead for a while, Antoine halted under a street-lamp and, struggling against the serried impact of wind and rain, unfolded a map of the city. Fog blinded his eyes, but the sound of breakers and a distant wail of sirens gave him his direction. At last, groping his way across an expanse of slippery mud, in the teeth of a sea-wind that slapped his overcoat against his legs, he reached a rough-hewn quay and struggled on along it.

The breakwater narrowed as it advanced into the waves. On his right the open sea thundered in massive cadences; leftwards he heard the waters of the harbour lapping in restless undertones. Louder and louder in his ears, though he could not locate the sound, a fog-horn bellowed through the darkness. Hoo! Hoo! Hoo!

After he had tramped ahead for ten minutes without meeting a soul on the way, Antoine suddenly perceived almost above his head the beam of the lighthouse, which till now the fog had veiled. He had come to the end of the breakwater.

He halted at the foot of the steps leading up to the platform and tried to take his bearings, cut off from the world in a wild turmoil of wind and waves. Just before his eyes a streak of livid light proclaimed the east, where over other lands a wintry dawn was rising. At his feet a flight of steps, hewn in the granite, descended to the water's edge, but, though he peered into the dark abyss, he could not see the waves fretting against the sea-wall; he could only hear their measured breathing, almost at his feet, a long-drawn sigh, ending in a muted sob.

The minutes passed, but he was unaware of their passing. Little by little the canopy of vapour that screened him from the world of living men grew less opaque. Now he could perceive an intermittent glow upon the southern jetty, and dared not lift his eyes from the pale void between him and the further lighthouse, for there it was, along that silvery expanse between the harbour-lights, that she would pass.

Suddenly, to the left of where his eyes were fixed, a dark mass hove into sight, framed in the aureole of golden haze heralding the dawn. Tall and slender, slowly taking form against the white effulgence, it became a ship, a huge and hueless hull stippled with lights and drawing in its wake a low, dark ribbon of smoke.

The *Romania* was swinging round to make the fairway.

His hands clenched on the iron rail, his cheeks lashed by the rain, Antoine, unknowing what he did, began to count the decks and masts and funnels. . . . Suddenly he awakened from his trance. Rachel— Rachel was there, only a few hundred yards away, straining towards him as now he strained towards her, watching him with unseeing eyes, blinded with tears; and all their ruined love that urged them for the last time each to each was powerless to grant that final consolation, a gesture of farewell. Only the shaft of light, veering in radiant circles over Antoine's head, touched with a fugitive caress the blind, dark mass that was passing, out of the mist into the mist, bearing hence its secret, this last precarious meeting of their eyes.

For a long time Antoine stood there with no mind to go, tearless and void of thoughts. His ears had grown accustomed to the fog-horn and no longer heard its piercing blasts. At last he glanced at his watch, and started back to the town. Hardly knowing what he was doing, he splashed his way ahead through pools of water, without seeing them. The dockyards on the sea-front were ablaze with violet light and the thudding of hammers set up dull vibrations in the fog-bound air. Beyond the beach, on which a flood-tide beat, the city glimmered like the fabric of a dream. Long trains of trucks clattered across the gravel to an accompaniment of shouts and cracking whips. It was a relief to Antoine to regain the world of human sounds, and he paused to listen to the iron rims grinding upon the stones.

Suddenly it occurred to him that his train did not leave till ten; not once so far had he bethought himself of the three hours of wait-ing. Rachel's departure had meant the beginning and the end of his preoccupations. What was to be done about it? The hateful prospect of those three empty hours was the last straw; he yielded to his grief and, leaning against the paling beside him, broke down and wept.

Unconsciously he started on again, walking straight ahead. Life was returning to the streets, and hordes of draggled children were wrangling for first turn at the street-fountains. Huge vans, spanning the roadway, thundered down towards the docks. Presently he grew aware that it was broad daylight and he was standing amongst the flower-stalls in the market-square facing their hotel; here it was that yesterday, just before dinner, he had been on the point of buying a sheaf of chrysanthemums for Rachel. But then the same motive had deterred him as that which had led them to refrain, till it was time to part, from any gesture, any word, that might weaken their fixed resolve, open the flood-gates of a grief they strove their hardest to repress.

He suddenly remembered that he had his cloak-room ticket to pick up at the office of the hotel, and he was seized by a desire once more to see their room. But it was no longer free; two women had just engaged it.

In a mood of blank despair he walked down the steps and drifted aimlessly across another square; then, recognizing a street in which they had walked together, he retraced his steps to the café where the Neapolitans had given their performance. An impulse to enter it came over him.

He tried to discover the table where they had dined, the waiter who had served them; but somehow everything seemed changed. A garish light flowed in through the glazed roof, transforming the scene of nightly revelry into a place of squalor, like a bleak, abandoned warehouse. Chairs were stacked upon the tables and, with its prostrate music-stands, a 'cello cribbed in its black coffin, the piano draped in oilcloth like the scaly hide of some dead pachyderm, the bandsmen's platform might have been a raft piled high with corpses, adrift on a sea of dust.

"By your leave, sir!"

A waiter was preparing to sweep the floor under the table. Antoine swung his legs up onto the seat and idly watched the busy broom at work. A cork, two matches, a scrap of orange-peel—no, a tangerine, more likely. A gust of wind drove through the room, fanning the dusty litter into movement. The waiter coughed. Antoine woke from his trance; had he missed the train? He sprang from his seat, spied out a clock; no, he had been here only seven miserable minutes.

He decided against sitting down again, and went out. Haunted by the notion that, were he once seated in the train, his grief would be allayed, he jumped into a cab and set out for the station, as to a haven of refuge.

But, when he had booked his luggage through, he still had time and to spare. Over an hour to go! He set to walking up and down the platform with hurried strides, as though an enemy were at his heels. "What the hell do *you* want with me?" he muttered, glaring at an engineer who was eyeing him from the running-board of his locomotive. Turning round, he noticed a group of railway hands observing him curiously.

Then, stiffening his back, he retraced his steps, opened the door of the waiting-room, and sank into a chair. The room was bleak and gloomy; he had it to himself. Outside an old woman was squatting against the glass door with her back to him; he could see her grey hair bobbing up and down as she dandled a child in her arms, crooning in a toneless, yet almost girlish voice the old song with its sickly-sweet refrain that Mademoiselle so often sang to Gisèle in the past:

"We'll go no more a-fishing,
A-fishing in the sea . . ."

His eyes filled with tears. Ah, if only he could never hear another sound, see nothing, nothing more for ever!

He buried his face between his palms. And, in a flash, Rachel was in his arms again! Last night his hands had toyed with her necklace and its fragrance clung about them still. He could feel the smooth curve of her shoulder against his chest; under his lips the warm, soft texture of her skin. So violent was the shock it gave him that he jerked his head back, tautening every sinew; his fingers stiffened round the chair-arms and he thrust his head back violently into the thick upholstery. Something Rachel had said came back to him. "I thought of killing myself." Yes, to have done with it all! Suicide: for such despair as this, the one way out. An unpremeditated, almost involuntary death; simply to make an end, no matter how, of this intolerable spasm of anguish that gripped him like a vice, tightening across his temples—to cut it short before its unbearable climax!

Suddenly he started up from his seat; someone had approached him unawares and tapped him on the arm. He all but yielded to a blind impulse to lash out at the intruder, hurl him away.

"Here! Watcher gettin' at?" It proved to be a venerable ticket-collector, going his rounds.

"The . . . the Paris train?" Antoine stammered.

"Platform Number 3."

Antoine stared blindly at him, like a sleep-walker, then moved away unsteadily towards the platform.

"There ain't no hurry," the old man shouted after him. "Train's not in yet." His eyes followed Antoine as he left the waiting-room, observed him stagger, colliding with the door.

"And these young 'uns think they're somebody!" he muttered under his breath, shrugging his shoulders disdainfully.

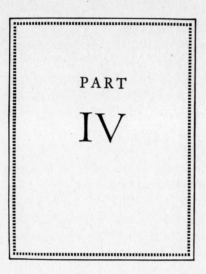

PART

IV

I

THE clocks were striking the half-hour after noon when the taxi halted in the Rue de l'Université. Antoine sprang out and plunged below the portico. "It's Monday," he reminded himself; "my consulting-day."

"Morning, sir!"

He swung round; in a corner of the lobby two little boys had taken shelter, apparently, from the wind, and the bigger of the two, cap in hand, perked up to Antoine a little bird-like face, round and restless as a sparrow's, but without a trace of shyness. Antoine halted.

"It's like this, sir; we want to know if you'll give some medicine to this kid here, what's ill."

Antoine went up to the "kid," who was hovering in the background.

"What's the trouble, my boy?"

A gust of wind, lifting the little boy's cape, revealed an arm in a sling.

"It isn't much," the older boy asserted confidently. "Not even an accident at his job, though he did get that ugly lump on his arm at the printing plant. It gives him twinges right up to his shoulder."

Antoine was pressed for time.

"Has he a temperature?"

"A what, sir?"

"Fever. Has he any fever?"

"Yes, that's what it must be," the elder boy agreed, wagging his head gravely and watching Antoine's face with an anxious eye.

"You'd better tell your parents to take him to the Charité at two and have him seen to—the big hospital over there on the left, you know."

A twitching of the little bird-like face, quickly controlled, betrayed the youngster's disappointment; then his lips half parted in a coaxing smile.

"I thought maybe you'd be nice enough . . ."

But he checked himself at once and went on in the tone of one who long has learned to bow to the inevitable:

"That's all right, sir. We'll fix it up somehow. Thank you, sir. Come along, Eddie!"

With a frank, good-humoured smile and a flick of his cap to Antoine, he began to move away towards the street.

Antoine's curiosity was aroused; he hesitated for a moment.

"Were you waiting for me?"

"Yes, sir."

"Who told you . . . ?" He opened the door leading to the staircase. "Come in anyhow; don't stay out in the draught. Who told you to come here?"

"No one." The child's face lit up. "Of course I know you very well. Why, I'm the office boy at the lawyer's—at the bottom of the courtyard, you know."

Unthinkingly Antoine had clasped the hand of the little invalid beside him, and somehow he could never help being moved by the contact of a clammy palm or fevered wrist.

"Where do your parents live, my boy?"

The younger boy raised his lack-lustre eyes towards his companion.

"Robbie!"

Robert came to the rescue.

"We haven't any, sir," he said; then added after a short pause: "We're living in the Rue de Verneuil."

"Neither father nor mother?"

"No."

"Grandparents, perhaps?"

"No, sir."

The boy's composed expression, his candid eyes, made it evident he had no wish to play on Antoine's sympathy, or even curiosity; nor did he seem the least dejected. Indeed, it was Antoine, rather, whose amazement struck a puerile note.

"How old are you?"

"Fifteen."

"And—his age?"

"Thirteen and a half."

Confound them! Antoine thought. Why, it's a quarter to one already! I must telephone to Philip; lunch; see them upstairs; then go back to the Faubourg Saint-Honoré before my consultations. Today of all days!

"Come along!" he suddenly exclaimed. "Let's have a look at it!"

Robert's face lit up with joy, though he did not seem at all surprised; to avoid meeting his happy eyes, Antoine stepped hastily in front of him, pulled out his latch-key, and opened the door of his flat. Then he shepherded the boys into his consulting-room.

Léon appeared at the kitchen door.

"Luncheon will have to wait a bit, Léon. . . . Now then, my boy"— he turned to the child—"hurry up and get your things off. Your brother will help you. . . . Gently does it. . . . Right, come here!"

A puny arm, swathed in a bandage that was almost clean. Just above the wrist a superficial boil, clearly defined, seemed to have come to a head. Antoine, no longer mindful of the passing minutes, laid his forefinger on the pustule while, with two fingers of the other hand, he gently pressed another aspect of the swelling. Good! He could distinctly feel the liquid shifting under his forefinger.

"Does it hurt there as well?" He ran his hand along the swollen forearm, then up along the upper arm as far as the dilated glands of the axilla.

"Only a little bit," the child whispered. He was holding himself stiffly, his eyes fixed on the other boy.

"No, it hurts a lot," Antoine corrected him gruffly. "But I can see you're a plucky little fellow." He fixed his gaze full on the child's eyes and, as the contact was established, a spark of sudden confidence flickered in their misted depths, then boldly leapt out towards him. When at last Antoine's lips relaxed into a smile, the little boy dropped his eyes at once. Antoine patted his cheek and gently lifted the boy's chin, which seemed to yield reluctantly.

"Look here! We'll make a tiny puncture just there and in half an hour it'll hardly hurt at all. Now then, come along with me!"

The child, duly impressed, advanced bravely enough for a few steps, but, as soon as Antoine's eyes were turned, his courage faltered, and he looked imploringly at his brother.

"Robbie! You come with me, too!"

The adjoining room, with its tiled floor, linoleum, sterilizer, and white-enamelled table placed under a powerful lamp, served on occasion for minor operations. In earlier days a bathroom, it had become what Léon styled "The Surgery." The ground-floor flat under M. Thibault's which Antoine and his brother used to share had proved quite inadequate, even after Antoine had become its only occupant. He had jumped at an opportunity which had recently presented itself of renting a four-room flat, also on the ground floor, in an adjoining house, and had shifted his consulting-room and bedroom to his new quarters, where he had had the "surgery" installed as well. His whilom consulting-room had been converted into the patients' waiting-room. A passage had been opened in the party-wall between the two flats, which were thus merged in one.

A few minutes later he was neatly puncturing the abscess with his scalpel.

"Keep a stiff upper lip, my boy. . . . Here goes! . . . Once more now. There, it's over!" Antoine stepped back a pace and the child, pale and half fainting, sank into his brother's waiting arms.

"Hi there, Léon!" Antoine shouted cheerfully. "A spot of brandy for these young hopefuls!" He dipped two lumps of sugar in a finger's depth of cognac. "Here, get your teeth into that! You, too!" He bent towards the little patient. "Not too strong for you?"

"It's nice," the child whispered, with a wan smile.

"Show me your arm. Don't be frightened. I told you it was over. Washing and bandaging—that doesn't hurt a bit."

A ring at the telephone; Léon's voice in the hall. "No, Madame, the doctor is engaged. Not this afternoon, it's the doctor's consulting-day. Oh, hardly before dinner-time. Very good, Madame, thank you."

"Yes, a gauze drain, to make sure," Antoine murmured. "Right. And the bandage pretty firm, that's essential. . . . Now you, big boy, listen to what I say. You'll take your brother home at once and see that he's put to bed, to be sure he doesn't move his arm. Whom do you live with? Surely there's someone who looks after your little brother?"

"*I* do."

There was a glow of honest self-assurance in his eyes, and in his look such dignity that it was quite impossible to smile at the emphatic declaration. Antoine glanced at the clock and once more had to repress his curiosity.

"What number in the Rue de Verneuil?"

"37B."

"Robert what?"

"Robert Bonnard."

When he had jotted down the address Antoine looked up and saw the two boys side by side, gazing at him with candid eyes in which he read no trace of gratitude, but only self-surrender, illimitable confidence.

"Now then, young men, off you go! I'm in a hurry. I'll look in some time between six and eight to change the drain. Got that?"

"Yes, sir," replied the elder boy, who seemed to take it quite as a matter of course. "It's the top floor, room 3, opposite the stairs."

No sooner were the children gone than Antoine told Léon to serve luncheon. Then he went to the telephone.

"Hallo, Elysées 0132." On the hall table, beside the telephone, his engagement-book lay open. Holding the receiver to his ear, Antoine bent over it and read the entries: *1913. October 13. Monday. 2:30 p.m., Mme. de Battaincourt.* I shan't be back; she can wait. *3:30. Rumelles,* yes, *Lioutin,* right! *Mme. Ernst,* don't know her. *Vianzoni . . . de Fayelles. . . .* Right! Hallo, 0132? Is Professor Philip back yet? Dr. Thibault speaking." There was a pause. "Hallo! Good morning, Chief. Hope I'm not taking you from your lunch. It's about a consultation. Very urgent. Héquet's child. Yes, Héquet, the surgeon. . . . In a very bad way, I fear, hopeless; an otitis that's been neglected, all sorts of complications. I'll explain. . . . A bad business. . . . No, Chief, it's you he wants, he's set on seeing you. You surely can't refuse him that. . . . Of course, as soon as possible, immediately. I'm in the same boat, Monday's my consulting-day. . . . Right, that's settled then; I call for you at a quarter to. Thanks, Chief."

Hanging up the receiver, he went over the day's appointments once again. "Whew! What a day!" But the sigh was mere convention and his contented look belied it.

Léon stood before him, a rather fatuous grin rippling his clean-shaven cheeks.

"Do you know, sir, the cat had her kittens this morning?"

"Really?"

Smiling, Antoine followed his servant to the kitchen. Snug in a cosy nest of rags, the cat lay on her side amid a writhing mass of small black lumps of sticky fur which she was scrubbing vigorously with her rasp-like tongue.

"How many are there?"

"Seven. My sister-in-law would like one kept for her."

Léon was the concierge's brother. For the two years and more that he had been in Antoine's service he had performed his duties with ritual assiduity. He was a man of few words and uncertain age; his skin was colourless and on his elongated head straggled a scanty growth of pale, downy hair; his over-long, drooping nose and his trick of lowering his eyelids gave him an air of sheepishness, which his smile accentuated. But all this was only a convenient mask, even, perhaps, a studied pose; behind it lay a keen intelligence, shrewd common sense, and a natural gift of humour.

"How about the other six?" Antoine asked. "You'll drown them all, of course."

"Well, sir," Léon placidly replied, "do you wish me to keep them?"

Antoine smiled, turned on his heel, and hastened to the room which once was occupied by Jacques and now served as a dining-room.

His meal was all laid out ready on the table: an omelet, veal cutlets on spinach, and fruit; for Antoine could not endure waiting between courses. The omelet smelt deliciously of melted butter and the frying-pan. . . . Brief interlude of fifteen restful minutes between a morning at the hospital and the afternoon's engagements.

"No message from upstairs?"

"No, sir."

"Did Mme. Franklin telephone?"

"Yes, sir. She made an appointment for Friday. It's down in the book."

There was a ring at the telephone. "No, Madame," Léon answered, "he will not be free at five-thirty. Nor at six. Thank you, Madame."

"Who?"

"Mme. Stockney." He made bold to shrug his shoulders slightly. "About a friend's little boy. She will write."

"Who is this Mme. Ernst, at five?" Without waiting for an answer, he went on. "Will you ask Mme. de Battaincourt to excuse me? I shall be at least twenty minutes late. The newspapers, please. Thank you." He glanced at the clock. "They should have finished upstairs, eh? Give them a ring, please. Ask for Mlle. Gisèle and bring the receiver here. At once, along with the coffee."

As he picked up the receiver his features relaxed and he smiled towards an unseen face, almost as though he had taken wings and been transported to the other end of the wire.

"Hallo! Yes, it's I. Yes, I've almost done. . . ." He began laughing. "No, grapes; a present from a patient, and very good they are! . . . And how are things upstairs?" As he spoke a shadow fell upon his face. "What? Before or after the injection? Anyhow the main thing is to convince him that it's quite normal." Another pause, and now his face brightened up again. "I say, Gise, are you by yourself at the phone? Look here, I must see you today. I've something to say to you. Something important. Why, here, of course. Any time you like after half-past three. Léon will see you don't have to wait. . . . Good. I'll just finish my coffee and come upstairs."

II

ANTOINE had the key of his father's flat; he entered without ringing, and went directly to the linen-room.

"The master has been taken to the study," Adrienne informed him.

He made his way on tip-toe down a passage reeking like a pharmacy, to M. Thibault's dressing-room. "Curious the sort of oppression I always feel the moment I set foot inside this flat," he said to himself. "For a doctor, you'd think . . . But here, of course, it isn't the same for me as in other people's houses."

His eyes went straight to the temperature-chart pinned to the wall. The dressing-room looked like a laboratory; table and whatnot were littered with phials, china recipients, and packets of cotton-wool. "Let's have a look at the bottle," he said to himself. "Yes, it's as I thought; kidneys . . . the analysis will bring that out. And the morphine—how much is gone?" He opened the box of ampoules whose labels he had camouflaged to keep the patient from suspecting anything. "Half a grain in twenty-four hours. Already! Let's see, where's the sister put—ah, here it is—the graduate."

With brisk, almost light-hearted gestures he set about the analysis; just as he was heating a test-tube over the alcohol-lamp the door creaked on its hinges; the sound made his heart beat faster and he turned hastily to see who had come in. But it was not Gise. It was Mademoiselle, bent double, like an old witch, who was ambling towards him; nowadays her stoop was so pronounced that, even when she craned her neck, she could hardly lift her eyes (which still shone bright as ever behind the smoked-glass spectacles) to the level of Antoine's hands. Were she in the least upset or frightened, her tiny forehead, yellow as old ivory between the snowy bandeaux, started swaying like a pendulum.

"Ah, so you've come, Antoine," she sighed and, in a voice that quavered with each wobble of her head, plunged into her subject: "Really, since yesterday, things have been going from bad to worse. Sister Céline took it into her head to waste two jars of broth and a quart of milk quite needlessly. She's always peeling bananas for him to eat—they cost a pretty penny, too—and then he won't touch them. And the things he leaves can't be used, because of the microbes. Oh, I've nothing against her, or anyone; she's a good, religious young woman. But do speak to her, Antoine, do tell her to stop! What's the good of pressing food on an invalid? Much better wait till he asks for it. But she's always trying to foist things on him. This morning it was an ice—just think! Imagine offering him an ice—why, the chill of it might make his heart stop! And where's Clotilde to find the time to go running round to the ice-man, with all the household to cook for? Tell me that!"

Antoine was patiently completing the test, giving her only non-committal grunts by way of answer. "She's had to put up with the old fellow's harangues," he said to himself, "for a quarter of a century without saying a word, and now she's getting even!"

"Do you know," the old lady went on, "how many mouths I have to feed—how many they come to with the nursing sister and Gise as well? Three in the kitchen, three of us, and then your father. Work it out for yourself! And really, considering I've turned seventy-five, and the state of my——"

She drew aside abruptly; Antoine had stepped back from the table and was on his way to the basin. She was still as terrified as ever of infection and disease; for a year past she had been obliged to live in the shadow of a serious illness, to rub shoulders with doctors and nurses and breathe a sick-room atmosphere; the experience had affected her like a slow poison taken in daily doses, and was hastening the general decline that had set in three years before. Moreover, she was not wholly unaware of her decrepitude. "Since it was His will," she would lament, "to take Jacques out of my life, I'm only the ghost of what I used to be."

When Antoine showed no sign of moving and went on lathering his hands above the basin, she took a timid step towards him.

"Talk to the sister, Antoine, do please give her a talking-to. She'll listen to *you,* anyhow."

He humoured her with a compliant "yes" and, paying no more attention to her, left the room. Her eyes glowed with affection as they followed his receding limbs, for (as she proclaimed) she had come to see in Antoine, since he so rarely answered her and never contradicted, "the light of her life."

He went out into the passage so as to enter his father's study from the hall, and seem to have just arrived.

M. Thibault was alone with the sister. "So Gise is in her bedroom," Antoine murmured; "she must have heard me go by. She's avoiding me."

"Good afternoon, Father," he said in the breezy manner that now he always assumed at his father's bedside. "Afternoon, Sister."

M. Thibault's eyelids lifted.

"Ah, there you are."

He was in his big arm-chair, upholstered in tapestry, which had been dragged beside the window. His head seemed to have become too heavy for his shoulders, his chin was squeezed against the napkin the sister had tucked round his neck, and the two black crutches, propped against the chair on either hand, seemed tall out of proportion with his hunched-up body. A stained-glass pseudo-Renaissance window lit with rainbow gleams the fluttering white wings of Sister Céline's headdress, casting wine-red stains upon the tablecloth and a soup-plate of steaming milk and tapioca.

"Come along now!" the sister wheedled, and, lifting a spoonful of the liquid, drained off the drops along the edge of the plate; then, with a cheerful "Ups-a-daisy!" as if she were coaxing a child to take his pap, she tilted the spoon between the old man's lips, and emptied it down before he had time to turn away. His fingers, splayed upon his knees, twitched with annoyance. It galled his self-respect to seem so helpless, unable to feed himself. He lunged forward to grasp the spoon the sister was holding, but his fingers, stiffened with the years and swollen now with dropsy, refused their service. The spoon slipped from his hand, clattered onto the floor. With an angry sweep of his arm he thrust them all aside—table, plate, and nurse.

"Not hungry. Won't be forced to eat!" he cried, turning towards his son, as though to call for his protection. Antoine's silence gave him heart, it seemed, for he cast a furious glance at the nurse. "Take all that mess away!" Unprotesting, the sister beat a hasty retreat out of the old man's eyeshot.

He coughed. At frequent intervals he emitted a short, dry cough which, mechanical though it was and unaccompanied by loss of breath, made him clench his fists and pucker his tightly shut eyelids.

"Let me tell you"—M. Thibault spoke with asperity, as though to voice a rankling grievance—"last night and this morning again I've been having fits of vomiting."

Antoine felt himself being stealthily observed, and assumed a detached air.

"Really?"

"That doesn't surprise you, eh?"

"Well, to tell the truth, I half expected it," Antoine rejoined smilingly. He had little trouble in playing his part. Never had he treated any other patient with such long-suffering compassion; he came every day, often twice a day, and at each visit, indefatigably—as though he were renewing the dressing on a wound—racked his brains to conjure up new arguments, logical, if insincere, and repeated in the same tone of certitude the selfsame words of comfort. "What can you expect, Father? Your digestive organs aren't what they were when you were a young man, and they've been pestered for at least eight months with drugs and medicines. We may count ourselves lucky they didn't show signs of revolt very much sooner."

M. Thibault was silent, thinking it over. Already Antoine's words had taken effect and given him new heart; moreover, it was a relief to be able to fix the blame on something or someone.

"Yes," he said, clapping his large palms noiselessly together, "those idiots with their drugs, why, they've . . . Ow, my leg! . . . Yes, they've—they've ruined my digestion. Ow!"

The twinge was so acute and sudden that for a moment his features were convulsed. He let his body slip to one side; then, resting his weight on Antoine's and the sister's arms, he managed to stretch out his leg, halting the stream of liquid fire that was shooting down the limb.

"You told me that . . . that Thérivier's injections would . . . do my sciatica good!" he shouted. "Well, now, out with the truth! Is it any better?"

"It is," said Antoine coolly.

M. Thibault cast a bewildered look at his son.

"M. Thibault himself told me that he'd been having much less pain since Tuesday last," the sister put in shrilly; she had formed a habit of pitching her voice as high as she could, to make herself heard. Seizing the auspicious moment, she slipped a spoonful of tapioca into her patient's mouth.

"Since Tuesday?" the old man spluttered, making a valiant effort to remember. Then he held his peace.

In silent distress Antoine observed the symptoms of disease upon his father's face; every mental effort loosened the muscles of his jaw and made his eyelids rise, his lashes flutter. The poor old man was only too eager to believe that he was getting better, and indeed, till now, had never doubted it. Once more, taken by surprise, he let himself be spoon-fed; then, in desperate disgust, he pushed the sister away so angrily that she thought better of it and began undoing the napkin round his neck.

"They've ru-ruined my digestion," he mumbled, as the woman wiped his chin.

No sooner had she left the room with the tray than M. Thibault, who had, it seemed, been waiting for this chance of a heart-to-heart talk with Antoine, slewed himself round and, with a confidential smile, motioned him to come and sit beside him.

"Sister Céline," he began in a tone of deep emotion, "is an excellent creature, yes, Antoine, a really saintly soul. We can never be too . . . too grateful to her. But there's the convent to consider, and . . . Oh, I know that the Mother Superior is under obligations to me. And that's just the point! I have scruples about it; I'm loath to take advantage of her devotion when there are more pressing calls, sick and suffering folk who need her help. Don't you agree?"

Forestalling Antoine's protest, he silenced him with a gesture; then, his chin thrust forward with an air of meek entreaty, he went on in phrases broken by fits of coughing.

"Needless to say, it isn't today I'm thinking of, nor yet tomorrow. But . . . don't you think that . . . that quite soon . . . well, as soon as I'm really on the mend . . . this excellent woman could be released from her duties here? You can't imagine, my dear boy, how disagreeable it is always to have someone at one's elbow. As soon as possible, then, do let's . . . get rid of her."

Antoine, lacking the heart to answer, made feeble gestures of approval. So that inflexible authority, against which all his youth had vainly struggled, had come to—this! In earlier days the old autocrat would have dismissed the offending nurse without a word of explanation; now he was growing weak, defenceless. At such moments his father's physical decline struck Antoine as even more apparent than when he gauged, under his fingers, the wastage of the inner organs.

"What? Are you going already?" M. Thibault murmured, seeing Antoine rise. There was a note of protest in his voice, of pleading and regret; almost of tenderness. Antoine was touched.

"I've no choice," he said with a smile. "My whole afternoon's taken up with appointments. But I'll try to look in again this evening."

He went up to his father to kiss him, a habit he had recently formed. But the old man turned away his head.

"All right then, off you go, my boy! Have it your own way!"

Antoine went out without replying.

In the hall, perched on a chair, Mademoiselle was in wait for him. "I've got to speak to you, Antoine. It's about the sister. . . ."

But he could bear no more. He picked up his coat and hat, and closed the front-door behind him. On the landing he suddenly felt depressed; struggling into his overcoat, he was reminded of the jerk he used to give his shoulders in his soldiering days, to hoist the pack into position before he set out on the march again.

Out in the street the tides of traffic and the passers-by, struggling against an autumn gale, restored his spirits, and he hastened forward in quest of a taxi.

III

"JUST twenty to," Antoine observed as the taxi passed the Madeleine clock. "Pretty close. The chief's so infernally punctual—I'll bet he's getting ready for me now!"

As Antoine surmised, Dr. Philip was standing waiting for him at the door of his consulting-room.

"Afternoon, Thibault," he rapped out. He always spoke in a curious Punch-and-Judyish staccato, with what sounded like an undertone of irony. "Exactly quarter to. Let's be off."

"Right, Chief," Antoine cheerfully assented.

Antoine welcomed every occasion that placed him once again in Dr. Philip's tutelage. For two consecutive years he had worked as his resident assistant and lived in constant intimacy with his senior. Though, after that, he had been transferred to another branch, he had never lost contact with his former teacher, and, in the years that followed, Dr. Philip, to the exclusion of all others, had remained for him the "chief." Antoine was known as "Thibault, Philip's pupil," but he was more than that; he was his senior's right-hand man, his spiritual son. Yet, often enough, his adversary, too—in the clash of youth with riper age, of adventurousness and a proclivity for taking risks, with prudence. The bond that had grown up between them during their seven years' friendship and professional co-operation was proof against all rupture. No sooner was Antoine in Philip's company than, insensibly, his personality underwent a change, dwindled, as it were, in bulk; the self-contained world-in-himself that he had been a moment before lapsed automatically into a satellite. But this circumstance, far from displeasing him, flattered his self-esteem

and deepened his affection for his chief; for the professor's unques-
tioned eminence, coupled with his reputation for being hard to satisfy
where colleagues were concerned, conferred a special value on his
attachment for Antoine. Whenever master and pupil were together,
good humour was the order of the day; both were convinced that
the common run of mortals consisted of numskulls and incapables;
they themselves were lofty exceptions to the general rule. The manner in which the chief, so reticent by habit, spoke to Antoine, his
confident expansiveness, the meaning smiles and winks which accompanied certain remarks, even the terms he used—comprehensible only
to a few initiates—all seemed to prove that Antoine was the only
person with whom Philip could talk freely, by whom he was assured
of being precisely understood. On the occasions when they disagreed,
the subject of dispute was always of the same order: Antoine accused Philip of hoodwinking himself and taking the brilliant sallies
of his sceptical mind for reasoned conclusions. Or, it might be, after
threshing out a problem with his junior and finding their views
concur, Philip would suddenly sheer off on the opposite tack and
ridicule all they had just been saying: "Viewed from another angle,
you know, those ideas of ours are buncombe"—which was tantamount
to saying: "It's a waste of time pondering over things; one 'truth'
is as true as another!" Antoine's blood boiled; he could not stomach
such an attitude, and it galled him like a physical infirmity. On such
occasions he would bid his chief a prompt but courteous farewell
and, flinging himself into his work, redress his mental balance in a
wholesome burst of energy.

On the landing they met Thérivier who had come to seek urgent
counsel from the chief. Thérivier, too, had worked under Philip; an
older man than Antoine, he was now a general practitioner. M. Thibault was one of his patients.

The professor halted. Slightly stooping, motionless, with dangling
arms, his garments floating round his tall, slight form, he looked like
a gaunt marionette dangling from its unpulled strings. The man who
was addressing him, plump and stocky, fidgeting and smiling, struck
a comical contrast with him. They stood in the full light of the landing

window and Antoine, posted in the background, amused himself watching his chief; he always relished such sudden glimpses from an unwonted angle of people he knew well. Just now Philip was observing Thérivier with his keen, pale eyes, truculent as ever under the beetling eyebrows, which had kept their blackness despite the grey streaks in his beard—a goat's beard, almost too unsightly to be natural, and looking like an absurd fringe of straggling hair tacked onto his chin. Everything, indeed, about the man was disconcerting, not to say repellent: his general untidiness, his off-hand manner, and certain personal idiosyncrasies—a red and over-prominent nose, the hissing intake of his breath, his caustic grin and pendulous, moist lips whence a nasal drawl seemed to trickle out laboriously, rising now and then to a shrill falsetto when he let fly a shaft of satire or a scathing comment. At such moments his simian eyes twinkled behind their bushy thickets with a glint of secret exultation that asked no reciprocity.

But only novices and nonentities were estranged from Philip by their unfavourable first impression. As a matter of fact, as Antoine had observed, no other doctor was more popular with patients, no teacher more esteemed by his colleagues, more ardently sought after by the unruly youngsters training in the hospitals. His bitterest gibes were aimed at human folly, life's absurdities; and only fools resented them. None could watch him at his professional task without admiring, not merely the bright activity of a master-mind devoid of pettiness or any real scorn, but, what was more, a sensitive, warm-hearted being who was genuinely distressed by his daily intercourse with suffering. It was obvious at such moments that that acid wit of his was only Philip's way of fighting down depression, only another facet of his clear-visioned sympathy; obvious, too, that the cutting remarks which turned so many fools against him were, in the last analysis, part and parcel of his philosophy.

Antoine paid little attention to what the two doctors were saying. They were talking about one of Thérivier's patients whom the chief had visited on the previous day. A serious case, it seemed. Thérivier stuck to his guns.

"No, my boy," Philip declared, "one c.c. is the most I'd care to give. Better still, the half of that. And in two doses, if you please." And, when the younger man grew restive, obviously hostile to such half-measures, Philip, laying a moderating hand upon his shoulder, continued in a nasal drawl: "Look here, Thérivier, when a patient's come to that pass, there are just two forces fighting it out over his body: nature and disease. Up comes the doctor and deals a blow at a venture. Heads or tails. If his blow lands on the malady, it's heads. But, should he knock nature out, it's tails, and the patient's *moriturus*. That's how it works out, my lad. So, when a man has reached my age, he walks warily and takes care not to hit too hard." For some seconds he stood motionless, swallowing his saliva with little hissing noises. With a twinkle in his eye he was studying Thérivier's face. Then he dropped his hand and, with a humorous glance at Antoine, started to go down the stairs.

Antoine and Thérivier followed behind.

"How's your father?" Thérivier inquired.

"He's been having vomiting attacks since yesterday."

"Is that so?" Thérivier frowned and pursed his lips. After a short silence he went on: "Have you examined his legs recently?"

"No."

"They seemed a trifle more swollen the day before yesterday."

"Albumin?"

"Phlebitis setting in, more likely. I'll give him a visit between four and five. Will you be there?"

Philip's car was waiting at the door. Thérivier said good-bye and hopped briskly away. Considering what I spend in taxis nowadays, Antoine reflected, it would pay me to invest in a small car.

"Where are we going, Thibault?"

"Faubourg Saint-Honoré."

Philip, who seemed to feel the cold, crouched in a corner; before the driver slipped in the gear, he put a question to Antoine.

"Give me an outline of the case, my boy. Really hopeless, is it?"

"Quite hopeless, Chief. It's a little girl, two years old, a premature child and malformed from birth, poor little thing; hare-lip and congenital cleft palate. Héquet himself operated last spring. Functional debility of the heart as well. Got it? Right. To make things worse, there was a sudden and acute attack of otitis; it developed when she was in the country. She's their only child, by the way."

Philip, who was gazing into the distance along the transient vista of the streets, made sympathetic noises in his throat.

"Unfortunately Mme. Héquet's seven months pregnant, and it's a hard pregnancy. She doesn't take the least care of herself, I imagine; anyhow, to avoid another accident of the kind, Héquet had his wife leave Paris and stay at Maisons-Laffitte, where an aunt of hers lent them a house—as a matter of fact I know these people; they were friends of my brother. It was at Maisons that the otitis set in."

"What day?"

"We can't be sure. The nurse can't say; most likely it escaped her notice. The child's mother has to stay in bed; at first she didn't notice anything, then she put it down to toothache. Not till Saturday evening . . ."

"The day before yesterday?"

"Yes. Héquet went to Maisons to spend Sunday there as usual; he saw at once that the child was in danger. He arranged for an ambulance and rushed his wife and child to Paris that night. He rang me up first thing when he arrived and I saw the child early Sunday morning. I'd arranged for Lanquetot, the ear specialist, to be present. We found every possible complication: mastoiditis, of course, infection of the lateral sinus, and so on. Since yesterday we've tried all sorts of treatments, but none of them helped. She's going from bad to worse. This morning there were meningeal symptoms."

"Operation?"

"Impossible, so it seems. Péchot, whom Héquet called in last night, was firm on the point; the heart condition rules out an operation. And we can't do anything to allay the pain—it's terrible—except applying ice."

Philip, his eyes still fixed on some far-off point, grunted again.

"Well, that's how things are," Antoine concluded in an anxious voice. "Now it's up to you, Chief." After a pause he added: "Personally, I confess, my only hope is that we've come too late and—all is over."

"Héquet has no illusions about it, eh?"

"None."

Philip was silent for a moment; then he laid his hand on Antoine's arm.

"Don't you be so sure about it, Thibault. As a doctor, of course, poor Héquet must *know* there's no hope left. But, as a father . . . The worse things are, the more a man's inclined to throw dust in his own eyes." A disillusioned smile flickered on his face as he added in a high-pitched drawl: "And it's just as well, isn't it? Just as well."

IV

HÉQUET'S flat was on the third floor. The front-door opened at the sound of the ascending elevator; they were expected. A fat man in a white coat, with a black beard that emphasized his Semitic cast of features, shook Antoine's hand. Antoine introduced him.

"Isaac Studler."

Studler had once been a medical student and, though he had given up medicine, was a familiar figure in medical circles. On Héquet, a former fellow-student, he lavished a blind affection, a dog-like devotion. A telephone-call had apprised him of his friend's abrupt return and, cancelling all engagements, he had hastened to the sick child's bedside.

All the doors stood open and the flat had a lugubrious aspect; things had been left just as they were when it was vacated in the spring. There were no curtains up, the blinds were drawn and lamps lit everywhere. Under the garish light the pyramids of furniture stacked in the middle of each room and covered with white sheets looked like so many children's catafalques. The floor of the study where Studler left the two doctors when he went to summon Héquet was strewn with a medley of objects, scattered round a partly unpacked trunk.

A door was flung open and a half-dressed young woman burst in, her face convulsed with grief and her bright golden hair disordered. She hastened towards them as quickly as her cumbered gait permitted, one hand steadying her abdomen, the other holding up her dressing-gown so as not to trip over it. Her breath came in gasps and she could not speak; her lips were quivering. She went straight up to Philip and gazed at him with tear-dimmed eyes and a look of silent entreaty so heart-rending that he did not think of greeting her but held out both hands towards her in an instinctive gesture of reassurance and profound sympathy.

Héquet entered suddenly from the hall.

"Nicole!"

His voice shook with indignation. Pale, his features twitching, he sprang towards his wife and, paying no heed to Philip, caught her up and swung her off her feet into his arms with an access of energy that took the others by surprise. Sobbing, she offered no resistance.

"Open the door!" he gasped, turning towards Antoine, who darted forward to his aid.

Antoine went with them, supporting Nicole's drooping head. A desolate lament broke from her lips and Antoine caught the broken phrases. "You'll never forgive me. I'm to blame for everything, everything. It's my fault she was born a cripple. You've been angry with me so long! Now it's my fault again. If only I'd understood, if I'd looked after her at once . . . !" As they entered the bedroom Antoine caught sight of a large, gaping bed, and it struck him she had been listening for the doctors' coming and risen in haste despite her husband's orders.

Seizing Antoine's hand, she clung to it with the frenzy of despair. "I beg you, doctor . . . Felix would never forgive me. I'd lose all hope of being forgiven, if . . . Try everything you possibly can. Oh, I implore you, doctor, save her!"

Her husband had gently laid her in the bed and was drawing back the quilt. She let go Antoine's hand and ceased speaking.

Héquet stooped over her and Antoine caught the expression in the eyes of each: in hers a look of forlorn hopelessness; in his, exasperation.

"I forbid you to get up, do you hear?"

She shut her eyes. Bending more closely over her, he touched her hair with his lips, then pressed a kiss on her closed eyelids that seemed to seal a pact between them, almost as if he promised her his pardon, come what might. Then he led Antoine from the room.

Studler had taken the chief to the child's bedside and when they joined him there Philip had already taken off his coat and put on a white apron. Calmly, impassively, as though he and the child inhabited a world apart, he was proceeding with a minute, methodical examination of his patient, though he had realized from the first that nothing could be done to save her.

Héquet's eyes were fixed on his face; his hands were trembling and he did not speak.

The examination lasted ten minutes.

When it was ended Philip raised his head and turned his eyes on Héquet. Héquet had changed out of recognition; his face was sombre, and between the eyelids, red and shrivelled as though a dusty wind had parched them up, his eyes were deathly still—a frozen calm that masked the inner tragedy. From the quick glance he cast at Héquet, Philip knew there was no need to beat about the bush and said nothing of the treatment which, out of pity, he had intended to prescribe. He took off the apron and quickly washed his hands. The nurse handed him his coat, he put it on, and, without another glance at the little bed, went out of the room. Héquet, then Antoine, followed him.

Standing in the hall, the three men gazed at each other.

"Anyhow, it was very kind of you to come," Héquet murmured.

Philip gave a slight shrug and his lips smacked with a little watery hiss. Focused on his across the glasses, Héquet's eyes grew hard, then scornful, almost malevolent; but all at once their angry light died out and he stammered in an apologetic voice:

"Somehow, one can't help hoping for the impossible."

Philip made a vague, ambiguous gesture and placidly reached for his hat. But, instead of opening the door, he turned back to Héquet and, after a brief hesitation, laid his hand awkwardly on Héquet's arm. There was another silence; then Philip seemed to collect himself, gave a slight cough, and at last went out.

Antoine went up to Héquet.

"It's my consulting-day, but I'll look in tonight, at about nine."

Héquet stood stock-still, staring blindly towards the open door through which, with Philip's going, his last hope had vanished; he moved his head to show that he had understood.

Followed by Antoine, Philip went quickly down the two flights of stairs without speaking. Suddenly he halted, sucked back his saliva with a little hissing sound, like the lisp of running water, and, when he spoke, his drawl seemed more pronounced than ever.

"I suppose it was up to me to prescribe something, eh? *Ut aliquid fieri videatur*. But, upon my word, I didn't dare." He went down a few steps in silence, then muttered, without looking towards Antoine:

"Personally I'm not so optimistic as you are. It may well drag on for another day or two."

When they came to the foot of the staircase, they met two ladies who were just entering.

"M. Thibault!"

Antoine recognized Mme. de Fontanin.

"Well?" she asked in a level voice from which she studiously excluded any sound of apprehension. "We are just on our way to make inquiries."

Antoine's only response was a slow movement of his head from side to side.

"No, no! Can one ever be sure?" Mme. de Fontanin exclaimed with a shade of reprobation, as though Antoine's demeanour constrained her to avert, as quickly as she could, an evil omen. "Let's have confidence, doctor, confidence! No, *that's* out of the question, it would be too horrible! Don't you think so, Jenny?"

Only then did Antoine notice the girl standing in the background. He made haste to apologize. She seemed ill at ease, irresolute; at last she held out her hand to him. Antoine saw her look of utter dejection, the nervous flutter of her eyelids, but, knowing Jenny's affection for her cousin Nicole, was not surprised.

Yet he could not help murmuring to himself, as he followed up the chief: "How changed she is!" And memory lit up a picture of the past, already so remote: a summer evening in a garden, a young girl in a light, bright dress. The chance encounter stirred the embers of a latent grief. "Poor old Jacques!" he thought. "He wouldn't have recognized her, that's sure."

Philip was crouching morosely in a corner of his car.

"I'm off to the School of Medicine," he said. "I can drop you at your place."

He did not utter three words all the way. Only when they were at the corner of the Rue de l'Université and Antoine was about to say good-bye did he seem to shake off his lethargy.

"By the way, Thibault, you've specialized a bit in cases of defective speech. I sent someone to you the other day, a Mme. Ernst."

"I've an appointment with her today."

"She will bring her little boy; he's five or six years old, but talks in monosyllables, like a baby. What's more, there are some sounds he seems unable to form at all. But, if you ask him to say his prayers, he goes on his knees and rattles off 'Our Father' from beginning to end, and articulates almost perfectly. Seems an intelligent child, too. You'll find it quite an interesting case, I imagine."

V

Léon came forward as soon as he heard his master's key turn in the lock.

"Mlle. de Battaincourt has come." Then, with his usual air of diffidence, he volunteered the information: "There's a governess, I think, come with her."

"She's not a Battaincourt, really," Antoine amended, *sotto voce*. "She's Goupillot's daughter—Goupillot of 'Goupillot's Stores.'"

He stepped into the bedroom to change his coat and collar, for he set store by his appearance and dressed with sedulous good taste. Then he went to the consulting-room, glanced round to see that all was spick and span, and, exhilarated by the prospect of the strenuous after-noon before him, briskly drew aside a curtain and opened the door of the waiting-room.

A slim young woman rose when he entered. (He recognized her as an English girl who had accompanied Mme. de Battaincourt and her daughter in the previous spring, and at once a freak of memory brought back to him a little detail which had struck him at the time. When the visit had ended, as he was writing out the prescription at his desk, he had chanced to look up and his eyes fell on Mme. de Battaincourt. She and the English governess, in summery frocks, were standing close together at the bay-window and he had caught a curious gleam—it haunted his memory yet—in the fair Anne's eyes as she stroked back into place a vagrant lock on the younger woman's smooth, fair forehead, with fondling, gloveless fingers.)

The English girl, with a casual nod for Antoine, motioned to the child to enter first. As Antoine drew aside to let them pass, the subtle fragrance of two young, delicately nurtured bodies was wafted to-wards him. Both girls had fair hair and glowing cheeks, were tall and slim.

Huguette was carrying her coat slung over her arm; though barely thirteen, she was so tall that it came as a surprise to see her in so juvenile a frock; short and sleeveless, it showed to full advantage her childish skin, gloriously burnished by the summer sun. Her hair, a rich, warm gold, tumbled in wanton ringlets round her cheeks; its look of youthful gaiety was oddly out of keeping with the listless eyes that gave an impression of profound melancholy, and her nervous smile.

The English girl turned to Antoine. The bloom on her cheeks grew rosier still as she set about explaining in her French, melodious as bird-song, that her employer was lunching out, had asked her to be sure and send back the car, and would be coming presently.

Antoine had gone up to Huguette and, tapping her lightly on the shoulder, made her turn towards the light.

"And how do we feel today?" he inquired vaguely.

Huguette's only answer was a wan smile and a shake of the head.

Meanwhile Antoine was summarily examining the coloration of lips and gums, and of the conjunctivæ; but his deeper thoughts had taken another trend. Just now in the waiting-room he had noticed the awkward way in which the girl, for all the natural grace which obviously was hers, had risen from the chair, and a hint of stiffness in her walk as she approached him. After that, too, when he had tapped her on the shoulder, a slight wince and an almost imperceptible grimace had not escaped his vigilant attention.

This was only his second time of seeing the child; he was not the family doctor. It was no doubt Simon de Battaincourt, an old friend of Jacques, who had persuaded his wife to pay a surprise visit to Antoine during the spring, and take his opinion on the general health of her daughter, who, she said, had outgrown her strength. On that occasion Antoine had not discovered any trace of lesion, though her general condition had impressed him unfavourably. He had prescribed a strict regimen and told the mother to bring the child to see him every month. She had never come again.

"Now will you take your things off, please?" he said.

Huguette turned to the governess.

"Please come, Miss Mary."

Seated at his desk, Antoine read through the diagnosis he had made in June, with studied impassivity. Though so far he had failed to detect any definite symptom, he had his suspicions. Often enough such first impressions had led him to put his finger on diseases still in the latent state; nevertheless, he refused on principle to accept their verdict over-hastily. He spread out on the table the X-ray photograph that had been taken in the spring and examined it carefully. Then he rose.

Perched on the arm of a chair in the middle of the room, Huguette was indolently letting herself be undressed. Whenever she tried to help her governess to undo a ribbon or a hook, she set about it so clumsily that the Englishwoman pushed her hand aside. At one moment her irritation was so great that she rapped the child smartly over the knuckles. The fretful gesture and a hint of sullenness that flawed the madonna-like purity of Mary's features convinced Antoine that the pretty governess had little liking for the child. Moreover, Huguette seemed afraid of her.

"Thanks, that will do," he said, going up to the girl.

The young girl raised her eyes to his—beautiful blue eyes, clear and luminous, for, though she could not say why, she had taken a liking to this "big doctor-man." (Indeed, for all his opinionated air and the unrelaxing tension of his features, Antoine seldom gave his patients the impression of being really stern. Even the youngest and least observant were rarely led astray; the line across his forehead, his deep-set, insistent eyes, his strong jaw and firmly cut mouth impressed them, rather, as the outward signs of forcefulness and wisdom. "The only thing patients really want," the chief had once remarked with a sardonic grin, "is—to be taken seriously.")

Antoine began by a systematic examination. The lungs: nothing wrong there. Like Philip, he proceeded step by step. The heart's in order, too. But, "Pott's disease," something was whispering in his ear. "What about Pott's disease?"

"Bend forward," he suddenly commanded. "No, wait a bit! Pick something up—your shoe, for instance."

To avoid flexing her back, she bent her knees. A bad sign, that. He still hoped he was wrong, but the thing was to make certain.

"Hold yourself straight. Cross your arms. Like that. Now lean forward, please. Bend . . . more than that!"

As she straightened herself again, her lips slowly parted, with a languid grace, and smiled towards him coaxingly.

"That hurt!" Her voice was soft, apologetic.

"Right!" said Antoine. He considered her a moment covertly. Then he met her eyes and smiled. She was a quaint little thing, desirable too, as she stood there in her young nakedness, with her shoe in her hand and the wondering, tender gaze of her big eyes fixed on Antoine. She had already grown tired of standing up and was leaning now on the back of a chair. The mellow glow of a ripe apricot coloured her shoulders, her arms, her rounded thighs, and made them look almost dark in contrast with the gleaming whiteness of her torso.

"Lie down there!" he told her, spreading a sheet upon the couch. Once more a feeling of deep concern had mastered him, and the smile died from his face. "Lie on your face. Quite flat, please."

The decisive moment had come. Antoine knelt down, resting the weight of his body on his heels, and thrust his arms out to free his wrists from the cuffs. For a couple of seconds he seemed lost in thought and did not move; his brooding eyes roamed over the firm, muscular skin of the back from the shoulder-blades to the shadowed flexure of the loins. Then, placing his hand on the warm neck that flinched a little under its touch, he laid two exploring fingertips upon the spinal column, and, palpating each segment with an even pressure, told one by one the beads of living tissue, like a rosary. . . . Suddenly the child's body twitched, winced from his touch, and Antoine hastily withdrew his hand. A laughing, but emphatic voice, half stifled in the cushions, protested.

"Now you're hurting me, doctor!"

"Really? Where exactly?" To divert her attention, he touched some other parts of her skin.

"Here?"

"No."

"And here?"

"No."

Then, to make assurance the more sure, he briskly tapped the affected vertebra with his forefinger.

"And here?"

The girl uttered a little cry that quickly changed to a forced laugh. There was a silence.

"Turn over, please," said Antoine with a fresh, unwonted gentleness in his voice.

He ran his fingers over her neck, her chest and arm-pits. Huguette braced herself up, determined not to cry out again. But, when he pressed the groin-glands, she could not keep back a little moan of pain.

Antoine stood up; his face was impassive, but he eluded the child's inquiring eyes.

"Well, I'm through with you!" he grumbled, making believe he was scolding her. "I never saw such a cry-baby!"

There was a knock at the door. Before the girl could answer, it swung open and the fair Anne made a tempestuous entrance.

"Here I am, doctor!" There was a warm resonance in her voice. "You must forgive me for being so shockingly late. But really, doctor, you live at the back of beyond!" She laughed. "Anyhow, I hope you didn't wait for me," she added, eyeing her daughter. "Mind you don't catch cold!" There was no tenderness in her tone. Then a sudden change came over her voice; losing its overtone of harshness, it sank to a deep, sensuous contralto. "Mary dear, will you be very sweet and put something round her shoulders?"

She moved towards Antoine. There was a frank appeal in her lithe body, but beneath her lively gestures there lay a vein of hardness, a ruthless obstinacy, mellowed and disciplined though it was by years of practice in the game of seduction, with femininity as her trump-card. A pungent perfume, too heavy, as it seemed, to rise, hung about her. With an airy gesture she held out a white-gloved hand, tinkling with bangles.

"How do you do?"

Greyly her eyes bored into Antoine's. On her temples, below the waved brown hair, an imperceptible tracery of tiny lines gave the skin round her eyelids a look of great fragility. He turned away his eyes.

"Well, doctor, are you satisfied?" she asked. "How far have you got with your examination?"

"As a matter of fact it's just over for today," Antoine replied with a constrained smile; then he turned to the English girl. "You can dress her now."

"Anyhow, you can't deny she's ever so much better," Mme. de Battaincourt gaily exclaimed, seating herself, as was her habit, with her back to the light. "Did she tell you that we spent . . ."

Antoine, who had gone to the basin, turned his head politely in her direction, as he began to wash his hands.

". . . two months at Ostende, and all on her account? You can see the effects; brown as a berry, isn't she? But you should have seen her six weeks ago! Shouldn't he, Mary?"

Antoine was thinking things out. Doubt was no longer possible about the presence of tuberculosis; it was undermining the foundations of the child's body and already deeply rooted in the spine. He tried to persuade himself that the lesions were curable, but he did not really think so. Despite appearances, her general condition was alarming. The whole glandular system was inflamed. Huguette was old Goupillot's daughter and the shadow of an evil heredity menaced her future, even her life.

"Did she tell you she got the third prize in the sun-tan contest at the Palace Hotel? And a consolation prize at the Casino?"

She had a very slight lisp, just enough to lend a reassuring touch of childishness to her rather formidable charms. The grey eyes seemed curiously out of place in her dark complexion and at times, for no apparent reason, a rapid, disconcerting gleam would flash out from their pupils. She had taken a vague dislike to Antoine at first sight. Anne de Battaincourt liked to feel she exercised a physical attraction on men and women and, though with the years she turned it less often to account, the more her pleasure in it tended to remain platonic, the greater seemed her eagerness to be assured on every possible occasion of her sensual charm. Antoine's attitude vexed her, just because the attentive, if slightly quizzing, way in which he looked at her showed he was not wholly insensitive to her appeal; yet, as she saw only too well, he had not the slightest difficulty in controlling his feelings, and would remain coolly critical in every circumstance.

"You must excuse me," she remarked with a low-pitched laugh, "but I'm simply stifling in this coat." Remaining seated in the chair and keeping her eyes fixed on the young man, with a lithe movement that set her trinkets jingling, she slipped out of her furs and let them sink onto the seat behind her. Her bosom heaved more freely, and the opening of her blouse revealed a willowy neck, almost a young girl's neck, that had a quaintly authoritative air—so proudly did it flaunt the little helmeted head with the clean-cut, hawk-like profile.

Leaning forward to dry his hands, Antoine listened to her with half an ear; he was moodily picturing to himself the progressive inflammation of the bony structures, the gradual softening and ultimate collapse of the carious spine. There was just one chance of saving her, and it must be tried at once. She must be immobilized in a plaster cast for months, perhaps for years; a living death!

"We had a very gay season at Ostende last summer," Mme. de Battaincourt went on, raising her voice so as to compel Antoine's attention. "The place was simply packed—rather too much so for my liking. A regular omnium gatherum!" She laughed. Then, seeing she could not catch the doctor's ear, she gradually lowered her voice and ceased speaking, casting an approving glance at Mary, who was helping Huguette into her frock. But she could not bear to play the part of a mere onlooker for long; somehow she had to make her presence felt. Rising abruptly, she smoothed out a crease in Huguette's collar and settled her blouse with an emphatic little tug. Then, bending familiarly towards the English girl, she began to talk to her in undertones.

"You know, Mary, I like that chemisette from Hudson's much better; we must get Suzy to copy it. Stand up!" she angrily addressed her daughter. "Always sitting down! How are we to know if you've got your dress on straight?" Then with a sinuous movement of her body she turned to Antoine. "You can't imagine, doctor, what a lazybones she is, this great gawk of a girl of mine. It's maddening for anyone like me who wants to be always up and about."

Antoine's eyes met Huguette's look of vague interrogation and he could not withhold a little conspiratorial twinkle, which started the child smiling too.

"Let's see"—he hastily thought out a programme—"it's Monday

today. She must be put in plaster by Friday or Saturday. After that, we'll see."

After that? As he stood there, lost in thought, a picture formed before his eyes: the terrace of a sanatorium at Berck-sur-Mer and, in the row of beds like open coffins tilted towards the sea-breeze, one bed, a trifle longer than its neighbours, and, prone on the pillowless mattress, the cripple's upturned face, blue eyes roaming the low horizon of the dunes.

Meanwhile Mme. de Battaincourt continued airing her grievances against her daughter's laziness.

"Just imagine! When we were at Ostende there was a dancing-class each morning at the Casino and of course I took her there. Well, after each dance, our young lady used to collapse onto the sofa and start whimpering, trying to look interesting, I suppose." She shrugged her shoulders. "Personally, I loathe the pathetic touch!" Such was her vehemence, and so ruthless the steely look she flashed at Antoine, that he suddenly remembered certain rumours he once had heard—that Goupillot, turned jealous in old age, had conveniently succumbed to poison. There was a vicious edge to her voice as she added: "In fact she made herself so ridiculous that I had to let her have her way."

Antoine gave her an unamiable look. He had come to a swift decision. Any serious conversation with this woman was out of the question; he would get rid of her at once and send an urgent summons to her husband. True, Huguette was not Battaincourt's daughter, but Antoine remembered Jacques's description of the man: "Deficient in grey matter, but a heart of gold."

"Is your husband in Paris?" he asked.

At last, thought Mme. de Battaincourt, he means the interview to take a more sociable turn. About time, too! She had a favour to ask of Antoine and, to that end, wanted to be in his good books. She burst out laughing and called the English girl to witness.

"Did you hear what he said, Mary? No, my dear doctor, there's no escaping Touraine till February—the shooting keeps us there. It was all I could do to get away this week, between two house-parties. On Saturday I'm expecting another houseful."

Antoine made no comment; his silence gave the final touch to her vexation. Really there was nothing to be done with such a boor! How ridiculous he looked with that absent-minded air of his; ill-mannered, too!

She crossed the room to get her coat.

"Yes," Antoine was saying to himself. "I'll wire to Battaincourt at once; I've got his address. . . . He'll be in Paris tomorrow or the day after at the latest. X-ray examination on Thursday. And, to make sure, a consultation with the chief. We'll have her in plaster by Saturday."

Huguette, seated in a chair, was demurely putting on her gloves while her mother, resplendent in a vast fur-coat, settled her little casque of golden pheasant's plumage, shaped like a Valkyrie's helmet. There was an undertone of rancour in her voice when she spoke again.

"Well, doctor, what about it? So there's no prescription? What's your advice for her this time? Anyhow, I suppose you won't say no to her attending some meets with Mary, in the dog-cart? . . ."

VI

AFTER seeing Mme. de Battaincourt off, Antoine returned to the consulting-room and once again opened the curtained door. Rumelles entered with the brisk alacrity of a man who has never a minute to spare.

"I fear I kept you waiting," Antoine suggested politely.

With an urbane gesture the visitor waved the apology aside and cordially held out his hand, as though to imply: "Here I am merely one of the common herd of patients."

"Hallo!" Antoine exclaimed quizzingly. "You look as if you'd just been visiting the President of the Republic, to say the least!"

Rumelles gave a self-satisfied laugh. He was wearing a silk-lined frock-coat and there was a top-hat in his hand. A well-set-up man, he carried the habit of officialdom with no mean success.

"Not quite that, my dear fellow. But I've just been at the Servian Embassy, where there was a luncheon in honour of the Janilozsky mission, who are visiting Paris this week. And I shall be on duty again presently; the minister has deputed me to receive Queen Elisabeth, who has had the lamentable notion of announcing that she will visit the Chrysanthemum Show at five-thirty. Luckily I know her; she's quite simple, really, a delightful woman. She adores flowers as much as she detests ceremony, so I shall confine myself to a few quite informal words of welcome."

He smiled to himself, and it struck Antoine that he was thinking out a neat conclusion for his speech, something gallant and respectful, with a spice of wit in it.

Rumelles was a man in the early forties, with a lion's mane of shaggy, yellowish hair brushed back from his temples, the rather heavy features of a Roman emperor, a truculent, upcurled moustache, and clear blue eyes on which he studiously imposed a keen, alert expression. "But for the moustache," Antoine sometimes reflected, "our lion would have the profile of a sheep."

"And what a lunch it was, my dear fellow!" He paused, his eyes half closed, wagging his head in feigned dismay. "Twenty or twenty-five of us sat down to table, functionaries and front-rankers all; yet, with the best of good will, you couldn't point to more than two or three intelligent men amongst them. Shocking, isn't it? Still, I fancy I made rather a useful move. Happily the minister has no idea of it; whenever he gets onto anything, he's like a dog with a bone, and he'd be sure to botch it." His emphatic delivery and the subtle smile which rounded off his simplest phrases gave a distinct, if uniform, incisiveness to all he said.

"Excuse me a moment." Antoine went to his desk. "I've an urgent telegram to write. . . . But I'm listening just the same. How are you feeling after your Servian beanfeast?"

But Rumelles, seeming to ignore the question, continued beating the air with words. Once he starts speechifying, thought Antoine, you'd never think him pressed for time. As he scribbled the telegram to Battaincourt, some scattered phrases caught his inattentive ear.

"Now that Germany is on the war-path . . . The Leipzig demonstrations at the unveiling of the memorial . . . They jump at any pretext . . . The hundredth anniversary of 1813 . . . It's coming, my dear fellow, it's coming like a house on fire. Just wait another two or three years, and you'll see!"

"What's coming?" Antoine asked, looking up with an amused glance at Rumelles. "A war, do you mean?"

"Yes, war." Rumelles's voice was earnest. "We're heading straight for it."

He had always had a harmless mania for predicting an impending European war. It sometimes looked as if he positively banked on it—a view which his next words bore out. "And that will be the moment for a man to show the stuff he's made of." An ambiguous remark, which might have meant: "to go on active service," but Antoine had no doubt about his meaning: "to scramble into power."

Rumelles, going up to the desk, leaned towards Antoine and instinctively lowered his voice.

"You've been following what's going on in Austria?"

"Well . . . yes—like anyone else who's not in the know."

"Tisza is putting himself forward as Berchtold's successor. Well, I had a close-up view of Tisza in 1910—he's the deadliest of fire-eaters; he made that clear enough when he was President of the Hungarian Chamber. Did you read that speech of his in which he addressed an open threat to Russia?"

Antoine had finished writing and had risen from his chair.

"No," he replied. "But ever since I've been old enough to read the papers, I've always seen Austria referred to as the danger-spot of Europe. Still, so far, that hasn't led to much harm."

"Because Germany was putting the brake on. But just at present, owing to the change which has come over Germany in the past month or so, the Austrian attitude is becoming definitely alarming. And of that change the general public has not the least idea."

"Tell me about it." Antoine could not repress his interest.

Rumelles glanced at the clock, then drew himself erect.

"I need hardly tell you that, in spite of the ostensible alliance and the fine speeches of the two emperors, relations between Germany and Austria during the last six or seven years——"

"Well," Antoine broke in, "and if they're strained, doesn't that mean a guarantee of peace, so far as we're concerned?"

"The best of guarantees. Indeed it *was* the only one."

"'*Was*,' you say. Then . . . ?"

"All that, my dear fellow, has gone to pot." He looked at Antoine and, as though he were wondering how far he dare commit himself, muttered between his teeth: "And it's our fault, perhaps."

"Our fault?"

"Yes, I'm afraid so. But that's another story. Supposing I were to tell you that the most clear-sighted people in Europe are convinced that we have bellicose projects at the back of our minds?"

"We? What nonsense!"

"The Frenchman doesn't travel. The Frenchman, my dear fellow, has no conception how his flag-waving propensities may strike outsiders. Anyhow, the understanding which has been growing up between France, England, and Russia, their latest military pacts, all the diplomatic wire-pulling that has been going on for the last two years, are, rightly or wrongly, beginning seriously to alarm Berlin. Confronted with what she describes in quite good faith as the 'menace' of the Triple Entente powers, Germany is waking up to the possibility that she may find herself isolated. She knows that Italy is only in theory a member of the Triple Alliance. So she has only Austria to fall back on, and that is why in the last few weeks Germany has made it her business to tighten up the bond of amity between them. What was the price she paid—was it the offer of important concessions, or a deviation from her former line of policy? You catch the point? From that to a quick reshuffle of the cards, an acquiescence in, not to say the active championship of, Austria's Balkan policy, it was only a step; and, so they say, that step has been taken. What makes it all the more serious is that Austria, seeing how the wind lies, has seized the occasion, as you have observed, to force the pace. So now we have Germany deliberately backing the wildcat ambitions of the Austrians, and heaven alone knows where those ambitions, backed by Germany, may land us at any moment! It can only mean that Europe will be drawn, drawn ineluctably, into the Balkan imbroglio. Now do you see why one can't help being pessimistic, or, at the least, uneasy, if one is even a little in the know?"

Antoine maintained a sceptical silence. He knew from experience that experts in foreign politics have a way of predicting "inevitable" wars. He had rung for Léon and, standing near the door, waited for him to appear; after that, he would divert his visitor's attention to serious topics. Meanwhile he watched Rumelles with an uncharitable eye as he paced to and fro before the fireplace, oblivious of the time, all for his verbiage, and obviously delighted with himself.

The late Senator Rumelles, his father, had been a friend of M. Thibault, and had died just in time to miss his son's elevation to high official rank. Antoine had come across the younger Rumelles now and then in the past, but till a week ago had not seen much of him. His opinion of the man, never a favourable one, had gained in definition with each visit. He had observed that Rumelles's incessant flow of talk, his premature adoption of a statesman-like urbanity, and his interest in world-problems always disclosed, sooner or later, a streak of meanness, a crude concern with personal advancement. Indeed, ambition seemed the only strong emotion known to Rumelles, an ambition aiming somewhat higher than his mental equipment (Antoine thought little of it) warranted. He was far from being well educated, timid though by no means modest, and unstable as water; but these defects were artfully concealed under the semblance of a "rising man."

Meanwhile Léon had come and gone. "That's enough of politics— and psychology," Antoine said to himself, and stemmed the spate of words.

"Well, then? No improvement?"

Rumelles's face fell.

One evening during the previous week—it was nearly nine o'clock

—Rumelles had entered Antoine's consulting-room, white with emotion. Two days previously he had discovered that he was suffering from a disease which he dared not disclose to his family doctor, still less to a total stranger. "You see, my dear fellow," he explained, "I'm a married man, and something of a public figure too; for both these reasons I can't afford to fall into the hands of a babbler, or a blackmailer." He had remembered that old Thibault's son was a doctor, and now begged Antoine to treat his case. After trying without success to induce him to consult a specialist, Antoine had consented; he was always ready to practise his art, and curious to see what kind of man this politician was.

"Really no improvement at all?"

Rumelles's only answer was a tragic shake of the head. For all his loquacity he could not bring himself to talk about his ailment, or admit that at times he endured the tortures of the damned, and that just now, after the official lunch, he had been obliged to break off an important conversation and beat a hasty retreat from the smoking-room, so violent had been the spasms of pain.

Antoine thought it over.

"Then," he announced in a firm voice, "we shall have to try the silver nitrate treatment."

He opened the "surgery" door for Rumelles, whose flow of words had quite dried up, to enter. Then, turning his back on him, he prepared the solution and charged a syringe with cocaine. When he returned, his victim had doffed the ceremonial frock-coat; collarless and trouserless, he looked like any poor afflicted mortal—a suffering, uneasy, shamefaced man, removing his soiled underlinen with awkward gestures.

But he would not own himself beaten yet. When Antoine came up he raised his head a little and forced his lips into a would-be casual smile. He suffered none the less, and in a myriad ways. Even his spiritual loneliness was preying on his mind. For, in his present plight, it was an added tragedy that he could never wholly lay aside the mask, could not impart to anyone his loathing for this grotesque misadventure, which galled not only his body, but his pride. For—

in whom could he confide? Not in a friend, for he had none. For ten years his political career had forced him to lead a life apart, behind a barrage of feigned and dubious good-fellowship. He had not a single genuine affection to fall back on. Yes, there was one: his wife's. She was, in fact, his only friend, the one person in the world who knew and loved him for what he really was, the only being to whom he could have unburdened his heart—and she, she was the one person in the world from whom, above all and at all costs, he must conceal this damnable mishap!

A stab of physical pain cut across his musings; the nitrate was beginning to take effect. Rumelles stifled his first cries of agony, but presently, despite the action of the sedative, he clenched his fists and teeth in vain, and could restrain himself no longer. Deep in his body coursed a stream of liquid fire, and he groaned like a woman in labour, while big tears rose and glistened in his blue eyes.

Antoine felt sorry for him.

"Bear up, old man; it's over now. Painful, of course, but there was nothing else for it and it won't last. Keep quite still; I'll give you some more cocaine."

But Rumelles was not listening. Stretched out on the table under the harsh light, he was jerking his legs spasmodically, like a frog on the dissecting-table.

At last Antoine managed to bring down the pain.

"It's a quarter past," he said. "When have you to be off?"

"Not . . . not till . . . till five o'clock," his victim stammered. "I've my car . . . wait—waiting."

Antoine bade him take heart with a good-natured smile, but there was a touch of irony behind it; he could not help picturing the dapper chauffeur with his tricolour cockade awaiting, statue-like upon his seat, His Excellency's delegate. And then—at this very moment, perhaps, they were unfurling under the marquee of the Flower Show the roll of carpet along which, only an hour hence, friend Rumelles, who now lay there wriggling and writhing like a new-born babe, would advance in solitary state with measured steps, resplendent in his frock-coat, his cat-like moustache uptilted in a smile, to greet the little queen. But, on the instant, the vision faded; now under the doctor's eyes there lay merely a patient—less than that, a "case"; less still, a chemical process, the action of a caustic on a mucous membrane, an action which he had deliberately provoked, for which he was responsible, and whose latent but inevitable operation he was now observing with his mind's eye.

Léon's three discreet taps on the door deflected his attention to the outside world. "Gise has come," he said to himself as he slapped his instruments into the tray of the sterilizer. Eager though he was to see the last of Rumelles, it was against his principles to palter with the duties of his calling, and he waited patiently till the painful effects of the nitrate had eased off.

"Make yourself at home and rest a bit," he said as he went out. "I shan't be needing this room. I'll come and tell you when it's ten to the hour."

VII

"WILL you be so good as to wait there, Miss?" Léon had said to Gise.

By "there" he meant Jacques's old room, which now was darkening with the nightfall, sombre and silent as a crypt. Her heart-beats quickened as she crossed the threshold and the effort she had to make to master her distress took, as usual, the form of a prayer, a brief appeal to Him who never leaves His children unconsoled. Instinctively she went towards the bed-sofa where, at so many different periods of her life, she had sat and talked the happy hours away with "Jacquot." Gise could hear—was it in the street or in the waiting-room?—a child's tempestuous sobs. She always found it difficult to control her feelings. Nowadays, for nothing at all, her eyes would brim with tears. A good thing she was alone just now. Yes, she would have to see a doctor. Not Antoine, however. She was out of sorts, losing weight—her insomnia, most likely. Anyhow it wasn't normal for a girl of nineteen. . . . For a minute or two she let her mind dwell on the curious sequence of those nineteen years, her never-ending childhood passed in the company of two old people; then—in her sixteenth year—heavy with cruel mystery, the blow had fallen!

Léon came in and turned on the light; Gise did not dare to tell him she would rather have been left in semi-darkness. Now, under the lamplight, she knew each object in the room for a familiar friend. Obviously enough, out of devotion to his brother's memory, Antoine had made a point of not disturbing anything; and yet, by slow degrees, once he had started using the room for meals, each object had been shifted from its place or changed its function till everything looked different—the table, for instance, planted with its leaves outspread plumb in the middle of the room, and the tea-service lording it on the disused desk between the bread-basket and a bowl of fruit. Even the bookcase. . . . Yes, those green curtains behind the glazed doors used not to be like that. One of them was gaping a little and, when Gise stooped to look at it, she caught the glint of glass and silver. Léon had piled up all the books on the top shelf. If poor Jacques could have seen his bookcase transformed into a sideboard . . . !

Jacques! Gise refused to think of him in terms of death; not merely would it not have startled her in the least, suddenly to see him standing there on the threshold, but she was always expecting him to reappear at any moment. And for the past three years her fanatic expectancy had kept her in a day-dream, ecstatic—yet depressing.

Here, in these familiar surroundings, phantoms of the past flocked round her. She could not move and hardly dared to breathe, lest the faint movement of the air should desecrate the silence. There was a photograph of Antoine on the mantelpiece and, as her eyes fell on it, she remembered the day when Antoine had given that copy to Jacques; he had presented Mademoiselle with another like it, which she still had upstairs. It brought back to her an Antoine of earlier days, the Antoine who had been her stand-by in the three dark years that followed. How often since Jacques had left them had she come downstairs to talk to him about the fugitive, how often all but shared with him her secret! But now—everything had changed. Why? What had come between them? She could not fix on anything definite; the only thing she could recall was that brief scene last June, just before she left for London. The imminence of her departure, of whose secret motive he had no inkling, had seemed to throw him off his balance. What exactly had he said to her? She had gathered that his love for her was no longer a mere elder-brotherly regard, but he felt towards her in "quite another way." Surely she was mistaken, she must have dreamt it! Yet, no; even the letters he had written to her—how puzzling they had seemed, too tenderly effusive and, for all that, so reticent!—no longer conveyed the tranquil affection of former years. And so, ever since her return to France, she had instinctively kept out of his way, and during the past fortnight avoided being alone with him at any moment. And now today—what did he want of her?

She started at a sound; rapid yet measured footsteps: Antoine's steps. He entered the room and stood before her, smiling. He looked rather tired, but his brow was calm, his eyes were gay and sparkling. Gise, who had been feeling herself adrift, pulled herself together at once; Antoine's presence always had that effect on others, it seemed to emanate a vibrant energy.

"Hallo, Blackie!" he hailed her with a smile. ("Blackie" was a nickname which M. Thibault, in a burst of good humour, had bestowed on her. It dated from those far-off days when circumstances had compelled Mlle. de Waize to adopt her little orphan niece and, taking the child under her wing, had introduced into the staid Thibault household what at the time had seemed to them an untamed little savage.)

"I suppose you have a crowd of patients this afternoon," Gise remarked, to make conversation.

"All in the day's work," he cheerfully replied. "Will you come to the consulting-room? Or shall we stay here?" Without waiting for her answer he sat down beside her. "How are you getting on? We hardly ever seem to see each other nowadays. That's a pretty shawl. . . . Give me your hand." He took the little, unresisting hand without more ado, laid it flat upon his fist, and held it up to his eyes. "Not so plump as it used to be, your little hand." Gise smiled good-humouredly and Antoine saw two little dimples form in her brown cheeks. She made no effort to withdraw her arm, but Antoine felt that she was on her guard, ready to shrink from him. He all but murmured: "You're not so nice as you used to be before you went away," but thought better of it, and lapsed into a moody silence.

"Your father insisted on going back to bed, on account of his leg," she said evasively.

Antoine made no comment. What an age it was since he was last alone with Gise! He riveted his gaze on the small, dark hand, and his eyes followed the blue tracery of veins along the slender, well-knit wrist; then, examining the fingers one by one, he tried to laugh it off. "Do you know what they remind me of? Dainty little half-coronas!" But all the while, across a shimmering haze that seemed to rise before them, his eyes were lingering in an insidious caress on all the sinuous curves of her lithe, bent body, from the soft round-ness of her shoulder to the angle of her knee under the silk shawl. It made his senses tingle, that languid grace of hers, so naïve . . . and so near. Sudden and catastrophic, like a rush of blood to the head or a pent-up torrent chafing at the flood-gates, came a flood of desire. He almost yielded to an impulse to slip an arm around her, draw the young, lithe body closely to his side. But then . . . he only bowed his head and lightly pressed his cheek against the little hand. "How soft your skin is, Blackie!" he murmured. He lifted his eyes slowly towards her face and when she saw the look in them, a look of famished, almost insensate craving, instinctively Gise turned aside, withdrew her hand.

"What did you want to tell me?" she asked in a level tone.

Antoine pulled himself together.

"I've some terrible news to give you, my dear."

Terrible news? A dreadful fear leapt into her mind. Suppos-ing . . . ? Was this the bitter end of all her hopes? Her terror-stricken eyes swept round the room, lingering for an agonizing moment on each familiar landmark of her love.

"Father is dangerously ill, you know," Antoine went on.

At first it seemed she had not heard him; her thoughts had been so far away.

Then, "Dangerously ill?" she repeated and, as she spoke, grew suddenly aware that she had known it all the time. Her brows lifted and her eyes showed an anxiety that was partly feigned.

"Do you mean that he will . . . ?"

Antoine nodded. When he spoke again his tone implied that he had long foreseen that it would come to this.

"The operation last winter, the excision of the right kidney, served only one purpose, really: it prevented us from nursing any more illusions as to the nature of the tumour. The other kidney became infected almost immediately after. But since then the disease has taken a new turn, it's become generalized, and that's just as well, in a way. It helps us to keep the truth from the patient; he has no suspicions, no idea that it's a hopeless case."

There was a brief silence before Gise spoke again.

"How long do you think . . . ?"

He observed her with satisfaction. She would make a good wife for a doctor. She knew how to face the inevitable; she had not shed a single tear. Those months she passed abroad had formed her character. And he regretted his habit of always regarding her as more of a child than she really was.

"Two or three months at the most," he replied in the same tone. Then added, rather hastily: "Very much less, perhaps."

Though inclined to be slow in the uptake, Gise guessed that Antoine's last remark had some special application to her, and was relieved when he went on to explain himself at once.

"Look here, Gise, now that you know the truth, can you really leave me all by myself? Must you go away again?"

She did not reply, but gazed sedately at the wall in front with bright and steady eyes. Her round little face seemed quite composed but for a tiny wrinkle that came and went incessantly between her brows, the only outward sign of her inward struggle. Her first response had been a thrill of affection; his appeal had touched her. It had come as a surprise that anyone should appeal to her for support

—Antoine most of all, whom the whole family looked up to as a tower of strength.

No! She had seen through his ruse, guessed why he wanted to detain her at Paris; and all her being rebelled against it. Only by going to England could she carry out her great project, the one thing in the world for which she lived. If only she could have told Antoine all about it! No, that would be a betrayal of her heart's secret; more, a betrayal of it to the last person on earth to welcome such a confidence! Later on, perhaps . . . in a letter. But not now.

Her eyes remained obdurately focused on the middle distance. A bad sign, Antoine thought, but nevertheless persisted.

"Why won't you answer?"

A tremor shook her body, but her look was as determined as ever.

"But surely, Antoine, it's just the other way round. There's all the more reason for me to hurry up and get my English certificate. I shall have to start earning my living much sooner than I expected."

Antoine cut her short with a gesture of annoyance. On her tight mouth and in her eyes he was surprised to see what seemed the shadow of a despondency past all redress, and, at the same time, a rapture, a passion of wild, unreasoning hope. Obviously, there was no place for him in such feelings as those. In a spasm of vexation he tossed back his head. Vexation or despair? Rather despair; a lump rose in his throat, tears to his eyes. For once he did not try to check them or conceal them; they might help him yet to break down her incomprehensible resistance.

Gise was deeply touched; she had never seen Antoine cry, had never even dreamt he could do so. She avoided looking at him. Her affection for him was tender and profound, and she never thought of him without a quickening of the heart, a thrill of enthusiasm. For three years he had been her only comforter, a tried and stalwart comrade whose nearness was the one bright spot in her life. And now—why should he seem to want of her more than her trust, her loyal admiration? Why must she now conceal her sisterly regard?

A bell tinkled in the hall. Instinctively Antoine pricked up his ears. A sound of closing doors; then, once again, silence.

They sat there side by side, unmoving, unspeaking, while their thoughts raced on and on along divergent paths. . . .

At last the telephone rang. There was a footstep in the hall, and Léon appeared at the door.

"It's a call from upstairs, Miss. Dr. Thérivier has come to see M. Thibault."

Gise got up at once. Antoine called Léon back and asked in a weary voice:

"How many people in the waiting-room?"

"Four, sir."

Then he, too, rose; life took charge again. "And there's Rumelles expecting me at ten minutes to the hour!" he said to himself.

"I must go upstairs at once," she said, without coming near him. "Good-bye, Antoine."

He gave a slight shrug and his lips parted in a forced smile.

"All right, then, off you go . . . Blackie!" In the sound of his own voice he seemed to hear an echo of his father's "All right then, off you go, my boy!" earlier in the day—and the reminder galled him. He added in a different tone: "Please tell Thérivier that I can't get away just now. If he has anything to say he can drop in here on his way out. Got it?"

She nodded and opened the door; then, as if she had come to a sudden decision, she turned back to Antoine. No, it was useless. What could she say to him? Since she couldn't tell him everything, what would be the good? Wrapping her shawl more closely round her, she went out, her eyes still fixed on the ground.

"The elevator's just coming down," Léon pointed out. "Won't you wait for it, Miss?"

Shaking her head, she began to walk up the stairs, slowly, broodingly. All her will was bent on that one obsession: London! Yes, she must leave at the earliest moment, must not even wait till the end of her holiday. Oh, if only Antoine could guess all that it meant to her—to be over there, across the Channel!

It had happened two years ago, ten months after Jacques's disappearance. One morning in September Gise had chanced to meet the postman coming up the garden-path at Maisons-Laffitte, and he had handed her a hamper bearing the label of a London flower-shop and addressed to her. Puzzled, but with a sudden intuition that somehow it concerned her deeply, she contrived to reach her room without being seen, cut the string, tore off the lid, and all but fainted with emotion when she saw, lying on a bed of damp moss, a simple bunch of roses. Her thoughts flew to Jacques. *Their* roses! Crimson roses with tiny dusky hearts; exactly, yes, exactly the same. And September: the anniversary! The meaning of the nameless gift was as clear to her as a code-telegram, worded in a familiar code. Jacques was not dead, M. Thibault was wrong, Jacques was living in England, and—*Jacques loved her!* Her first impulse was to open the door wide, call out for all to hear: "Jacques is alive!" Just in time, she pulled herself together. Fortunately. How could she have explained just why it was these crimson roses conveyed so wonderful a meaning? They would badger her with questions and—anything, anything rather than betray her secret! Closing the door, she prayed to God for strength to hold her peace, till the evening, anyhow; for she knew that Antoine was expected back at Maisons for dinner.

That evening she led him aside and spoke to him of a mysterious present, a box of flowers sent her from London, where she knew no one; mightn't it be Jacques? In any case the clue should be followed up without delay. Antoine's interest was aroused, though a series of failures during the past year had made him sceptical, and lost no time in setting an inquiry on foot in London. The florist supplied a detailed description of the customer who had sent the flowers, but the man in question was not in the least like Jacques. So this line of inquiry also had been dropped.

But not by Gise. She alone had certain knowledge. But she said no more about it. With a power of self-control extraordinary for her seventeen years, she kept her secret. But she was determined to go to England and, cost what it might, to follow up Jacques's trail herself. The plan seemed doomed to fail. But, for two long years, with the subtle, silent assiduity of the dark jungle-folk from whom she sprang, she had paved the way for her departure, and plotted it out, step by step. And what a struggle it had been! She recalled each gradual advance. She had needed all her patience, every artifice, to instil certain ideas into her aunt's reluctant mind. First, she had needed to convince her that a penniless young girl, even though she came of a good family, should be able to earn her living; then she had had to bring her round to the idea that her niece, like herself, had a vocation for educating young children, and furthermore that, considering the keen competition for such posts, it was essential nowadays for any would-be teacher to have a good command of English. Next, she had to inveigle her aunt into meeting a local woman-teacher who had just finished a course at an English training-school, established in the neighbourhood of London by a group of Catholic nuns. As good luck would have it, M. Thibault was moved to make inquiries and received a favourable report on the institution. In the previous spring, after a thousand and one delays, Mlle. de Waize had at last been won over to her niece's view, and Gise had spent the summer in England. But those four months had not given the results she hoped for; she had been victimized by shady detective-agencies, and nothing but disappointment had come of her attempts. Now at last she would be able to take action and pull the necessary strings. She had just sold some jewellery and collected her savings. Moreover, she had at last got into touch with honest agencies. Best of all, she had managed to interest the daughter of the Metropolitan Police Commissioner in her romantic quest; she had been invited to lunch with the Commissioner on her return to England, and he well might prove a very useful friend in need. How then could she do otherwise than hope?

Gise had to ring at the door of the Thibaults' flat; her aunt had never let her have a latch-key.

"Yes, how can I do otherwise than hope?" she asked herself, and suddenly the certainty that she would find Jacques again came back with overwhelming force, sweeping all doubt before it. Antoine had said "it" might last three months. "Three months?" she murmured. "Why, in less than that I shall have succeeded!"

Meanwhile, downstairs, Antoine was standing where she had left him in Jacques's room, facing the closed door with a steadfast gaze that seemed to beat in vain against its dark, impenetrable barrier. He felt his life had reached a turning-point. Often in the past he had pitted his will against the most formidable difficulties, and overcome them, but never had he vainly grappled with a sheer impossibility. And, just now, something was being wrenched from his existence; it was not Antoine's way to persevere in a hopeless struggle.

He took two hesitating steps, glanced into the mirror, then, leaning on the mantelpiece, with his face thrust forward, gazed intently for some seconds at his reflected self. "And supposing she'd said it, like that: 'Yes, marry me'?" A thrill of retrospective apprehension ran through his body. "Playing with fire—a fool's game!" He turned on his heel. "Good Lord! It's five o'clock! And . . . how about Queen Elisabeth?"

As he hurried to the surgery Léon met him, his lips impassive as ever, a whimsical smile flickering on his lips.

"M. Rumelles has left. He's made an appointment for the same time tomorrow."

"Good," said Antoine, much relieved. And for the moment this small relief sufficed to blunt the edge of his chagrin.

He went back to the consulting-room, crossed it diagonally, and, slipping back the curtain with the familiar gesture which, every time he made it, gave him a vague satisfaction, opened the door of the waiting-room.

"Hallo!" he exclaimed, with a friendly pinch of the cheek for a pale-faced little boy who came towards him, looking thoroughly scared. "So you've come all by yourself, like a big boy! How are your father and mother?"

Taking the child's arm, he led him to the window and, seated on a stool with his back to the light, pressed back the docile little head gently but firmly, so as to have a clear view of the throat. "Well, well," he murmured without raising his eyes, "there's no mistaking them this time, those tonsils of yours!" His voice had automatically regained the brisk and sonorous, almost astringent, quality which acted like a tonic on his patients.

As he bent forwards, gazing intently at the little boy, a sudden twinge of wounded pride fretted his mind and he could not repress the thought: "Anyhow, if I think fit, we can always wire for her to come back."

<h1 style="text-align:center">VIII</h1>

As HE was seeing the boy off, Antoine was not a little surprised to discover Mary, the English girl with the peach-bloom complexion, sitting in the hall. When he went up to her she rose and bestowed on him a leisurely, bewitching smile; then, silently but with a resolute air, she handed him a pale blue envelope.

Her present attitude, so changed from her aloofness of two hours ago, and her bold, if enigmatic, look convinced Antoine—though he could have given no reason for his belief—that there was something abnormal about her errand.

Much mystified, he remained standing in the hall and was hastily opening the envelope, when he observed the English girl deliberately making for the consulting-room, the door of which stood open. He followed her, unfolding the letter as he went.

My Dear Doctor,
   I have two small requests to make of you and, to ensure they won't be frowned on, I send them by the least forbidding messenger I can find.
   Firstly, my scatter-brained little Mary was silly enough to wait till she had left your place before telling me that she'd been feeling out of sorts for some days past, and couldn't sleep for coughing the last few nights. Would you be so good as to give her a thorough going-over, and also your advice?
   Nextly, we have an old fellow, a retired keeper, living on the estate, who suffers most terribly from arthritis; the poor old chap goes through agonies at this time of the year. Simon has taken compassion on him and gives him injections to ease the pain. We usually keep some morphine in the house, but his last attacks have quite used up our little reserve and Simon has asked me to be sure and bring some back—which I can't do without a doctor's prescription. I quite forgot to tell you about it this

afternoon. Now will you be terribly nice and give the charming bearer of this note a prescription—one which can be used again, if possible—so that I can get five or six dozen tubes at once?

Thanks in advance for attending to my little "nextly." As to my request number one, which of us, my dear Doctor, should be the grateful one? I feel sure you often have much less attractive patients to examine!

Very sincerely yours,
Anne-Marie S. de Battaincourt.

P.S. You may think it odd that Simon shouldn't ask our local doctor to fix it up. Well, he's a narrow-minded, fanatical old curmudgeon who always votes against us and has his knife into the "château people"— meaning us—for refusing to call him in. Otherwise, of course, I wouldn't have troubled you. A.

Though Antoine had read the last word he did not raise his eyes from the page. His first feeling was one of indignation—what did they take him for? Then the whole business struck him as rather comic; why not laugh over it instead?

There were two mirrors in the consulting-room and Antoine, who had once been caught that way himself, had learned a trick that could be played with them. From where he stood, resting his elbow on the mantelpiece, he had only to change the angle of his gaze under his lowered eyelids to study the English girl without her seeing it. He did so. Mary was sitting a little way behind him. She had unfastened her cape, freeing her neck and throat, and, while she pulled off her gloves, kept her eyes fixed, with a show of absent-mindedness, on her toe-cap, toying with a fringe of the carpet. She looked perturbed, but on her mettle. Thinking he could not see her without moving from where he was, with a sudden lift of her long eyelashes, she sped a quick glance at him, blue as lightning and as vivid.

Her indiscretion did away with any doubts that lingered still in Antoine's mind. He began to laugh and, with bent head, perused the fair tempter's letter for the last time; then slowly refolded it. Smiling still, he drew himself up and looked Mary in the face; each experienced a sudden shock, sharp as a blow, as eye met eye.

For a moment the English girl seemed in a quandary. He did not say a word but, dropping his eyelids, shook his head slowly from one side to the other several times, to signify an unequivocal "no." He still was smiling, but his expression made his meaning so clear that Mary could not be mistaken. It was exactly as if he were saying in so many words, with cool effrontery: "No, my dear young lady, there's nothing doing; it simply won't work. Don't imagine I'm shocked. I'm too old a hand at the game, you see, to be anything but amused. Only I must regretfully inform you that, even on the terms you offer, you'll get nothing out of me!"

She rose, speechless, her cheeks aflame with vexation, and, stumbling over the carpet, backed out into the hall. He escorted her out as calmly as if her hurried exit were not in the least unusual, but chuckling inwardly. Tongue-tied, her eyes fixed on the ground, she continued to retreat, trying to button up her collar with feverish, ungloved fingers that showed deathly pale against her blazing cheeks.

In the hall, when he moved to her side to open the door, she made as if to bow. He was just about to return her greeting when, with a brusque movement, she snatched the letter from his fingers and darted through the doorway; a professional pickpocket could not have done it more neatly.

Antoine could but pay grudging tribute to the girl's adroitness and presence of mind.

When he returned to his room he tried to picture their faces when the three of them—the fair Anne, Mary, and himself—would have their next encounter (in a few days, presumably) and, at the prospect, smiled again. A glove lay on the carpet; he picked it up and sniffed it before flinging it light-heartedly into the waste-paper basket. . . .

Those English girls . . . a queer lot! And Huguette, he wondered —what sort of life would she have, poor little thing, with those two women in charge of her?

Night was falling; Léon came in to close the shutters.

"Has Mme. Ernst come?" Antoine asked, after a glance at his engagement-book.

"Yes, sir, she's been here quite a time. There's a whole family of them: the mother, father, and a little boy."

"Good!" said Antoine cheerfully, as he swung back the curtain.

IX

A LITTLE man, in the sixties, came forward to meet him.

"Would you be so very kind, doctor, as to see me first?" He spoke in a thick, somewhat drawling voice; his manner was that of a well-bred, rather timid man. "There are some things I should like to tell you."

Antoine carefully closed the door and pointed to a chair.

"My name is Ernst. Dr. Philip has told you, I presume. . . . Thank you," he murmured, settling down into the chair.

M. Ernst impressed Antoine favourably. He had deep-set eyes and a gaze that, for all its melancholy and wistfulness, glowed with youthful fervour. Not so his face, an old man's face; furrowed and worn, dried up yet fleshy, it was all in pits and ridges, without a level inch on it; chin, cheeks, and forehead, all seemed gouged and modelled out by some sculptor's rough thumb. A short, stiff, iron-grey moustache seemed to cut his face in two; his hair was sparse and drab, like the rank grass that sprouts on sand-dunes. It was impossible to tell if he was conscious of Antoine's tactful scrutiny.

"Anyone might take us for our little boy's grandparents," he observed sadly. "We married late in life. . . . I am a graduate of the Paris University and German teacher at the Lycée Charlemagne."

"Ernst," said Antoine to himself, "and that accent of his. An Alsatian, most likely."

"I don't want to trespass on your time, doctor, but as you have kindly consented to take up our child's case it is my bounden duty, as I see it, to inform you of certain matters, *confidential* matters. . . ." He looked up, and a shadow fell across his eyes as he went on. "Matters, I mean to say, of which my wife knows nothing."

Antoine's nod conveyed his understanding of the secrecy required of him.

"Well, then, to begin. . . ." He seemed to be nerving himself for the plunge. Doubtless he had thought out all he was to say, for he now began to talk, his eyes fixed on the wall in front, in the easy, measured rhythm of one versed in the use of words. Antoine had a feeling that Ernst would rather not be looked at while he spoke.

"In 1896, doctor, I was forty-one and a master at the Versailles Lycée." His voice lost something of its assurance. "I was engaged." He pronounced the word in three syllables, giving them a curious lilt, like three notes of a major chord, played in *arpeggio*. "I was, moreover," he continued in a more emphatic tone, "a fervent champion of the cause of Captain Dreyfus. You are too young, doctor, to realize all it meant, the moral drama of the Dreyfus case"—"tramma," he pronounced it, with a deep-pitched, solemn resonance—"still, you are doubtless aware how dangerous it was then for a man to be at once a government servant and a militant Dreyfusite. I was one of those who . . . who took that risk." His tone was calm, devoid of any bravado, but its firmness gave Antoine a good idea of what, some fifteen years before, had been the faith, the enterprise and rashness of this sedate old fellow with the gnarled forehead, obstinate chin, and eyes still darkly glowing with enthusiasm.

"I tell you this," M. Ernst went on, "to explain why it was that after the summer of '96 I was exiled to the Lycée at Algiers. Meanwhile"—his voice grew gentler—"my engagement had been broken off; my brother-in-law to be, a naval officer (in the merchant marine, as it happens—but that made no difference), did not see eye to eye with me, you understand." Obviously he was doing his utmost to present the facts impartially.

"Four months after I landed in Africa," he continued in a lower voice, "I found that I was . . . ill." His voice faltered once more, but he mastered his weakness. "Why be afraid of words? I had developed syphilis."

So that's it, Antoine thought. The little boy . . . That explains everything.

"I lost no time in consulting several doctors attached to the Faculty of Medicine at Algiers, and on their advice put myself in the hands of the best local specialist." He seemed reluctant to give the name. "It was Dr. Lohr; you know his work, very likely," he said at last, without looking towards Antoine. "The disease was taken at its first stage; only the primary lesion had developed. I was the type of man who obeys his doctor's orders, however irksome, to the letter. That is what I did. When four years later the excitement of the Dreyfus case had died down and I was recalled to Paris, Dr. Lohr assured me that, for a year past, he had considered me completely cured. I believed him. Anyhow, since then I have not detected any indications, not the slightest symptom, of a relapse."

He turned calmly towards Antoine and looked him full in the eyes. Antoine's gesture indicated that he was listening attentively.

But he was not merely listening; he was observing the man himself. Both the look and the demeanour of the little schoolmaster told Antoine of a life of faithful, unremitting service. He had met others of his kind before, but in this case he deemed the man superior to his calling. Obviously, too, his attitude of reserve had long since become second nature with him; he had cultivated the fastidious aloofness that, for certain finer natures, is their only refuge from the struggle for existence, a life of thankless toil which, for all its scant rewards, is accepted with a loyal, steadfast heart. The tone in which he had alluded to the broken engagement expressed better than any words how much that thwarted love had counted in his lonely life, and the veiled emotion that sometimes lit his eyes was poignant evidence that the grey-haired pedagogue was no less keenly sensitive than a youngster in his teens.

"Six years after my return to France," he went on, "my fiancée lost her brother." He groped for words, then added simply: "So I could see her again."

His feelings overpowered him, he could not continue. Antoine kept his eyes lowered and observed a tactful silence. He was almost startled by the sudden outburst of emotion that ensued.

"Doctor, I don't know what opinion you may have of a man who acts as I did then. My illness—why, it was ancient history, ten years had elapsed! Past and done with. I was over fifty. . . ." He sighed. "And my loneliness had been weighing on me all those years. . . .

But I'm afraid it's a muddled sort of story I'm telling you, doctor!"

Antoine looked up, but, even before he saw the face of the man before him, he had understood everything. That he had begotten a mentally defective son would in itself be a bitter enough trial in all conscience for a man of erudition. But what was that beside the agony of a father who, racked by remorse, aware that the responsibility was his alone, could only watch the progress of a nemesis that he had set in action, and could not avert?

"All the same I wasn't easy in my mind about it," Ernst continued in a weary voice. "I intended to consult a doctor and nearly did so. No, that's not true. One mustn't burke the truth. I convinced myself that it was needless. I reminded myself of Lohr's opinion, and tried to find some easier way out. One day I met a doctor at a friend's house and steered the conversation towards that topic, just to have him confirm Lohr's opinion—that the disease can be *permanently* cured. That was all I needed to set my mind at rest."

He paused again.

"And then, I said to myself, a woman of her age—there's . . . there can't be any danger of her having a . . . a child."

His voice failed in a sob, but he still kept his head high, and as he sat there, unmoving, his fingers tightly clenched, such was the nervous tension of all his body that Antoine could see the muscles throbbing in his neck, while across a film of unshed tears his eyes glowed still more deeply. He made an effort to go on speaking, but his voice broke in a strangled cry of grief.

"Doctor . . . I'm so sorry for . . . for the poor little fellow!"

Antoine was deeply moved. Happily for him such violent emotions were apt to key him up to a pitch of feverish excitement, an almost frenzied urgency to make a prompt decision, and act upon it.

He did not hesitate for a second.

"Eh? What's that?" he exclaimed in a tone of feigned bewilderment. He stood up, knitting his brows; it seemed that he had only the haziest idea of what his visitor was driving at, and hesitated to believe his ears. "What possible connexion can there be between that . . . that little misfortune of yours, which was taken in hand at once and com-plete-ly cured, and your little boy's infirmity—which very likely will pass away quite soon?"

Ernst stared at him, dumbfounded.

Antoine's face lit up with a genial smile.

"If I've grasped your meaning, my dear sir, your scruples do you credit. But, speaking as a professional man, let me tell you quite frankly: from the scientific point of view they're simply . . . ludicrous!"

M. Ernst rose, as though some sudden impulse drew him towards Antoine. But then he stood stock-still, his eyes distraught with emotion. He was one of those beings whose mental life is deep-set, all of one piece, and who, when once a noxious thought begins to fester in their minds, unable to restrict its influence, surrender to it heart and soul. For years it had been rankling in his heart, that infinite remorse whose secret he had never dared to share even with his companion in distress; this was his first moment of respite, his first hope of deliverance.

Antoine had diagnosed his feelings. But, fearing to be pressed with questions and driven back on detailed and complicated lies, he deliberately changed the subject. . . . And, anyhow, why waste more time on such futile and depressing fancies?

"Was the child born before term?"

M. Ernst blinked at Antoine; the question took him by surprise.

"What? Before term? . . . No."

"Was it a difficult labour?"

"Very much so."

"Forceps used?"

"Yes."

"Ah," Antoine murmured as though it threw a flood of light on the problem. "That, I should say, explains quite a lot." Then, to cut things short, he added: "Well, let's have a look at our little patient," and began to move towards the waiting-room.

But then the child's father stepped quickly forward and clutched Antoine's arm.

"Is that true, doctor? Is it really true? You're not saying it just

to . . . ? Oh, doctor, will you give me your word for it? Your word
of honour?"

Antoine swung round towards him and saw a look of entreaty, of
famished hunger to believe, mingled with boundless gratitude. The
joy that surged across him was that which follows only on successful
effort, on a good deed well done. The child? Well, he would see what
he could do. Meanwhile, where the man before him was concerned,
his duty was plain; at all costs he must lift the load of anguish from
that tormented soul.

He let his gaze sink into the other's eyes, and answered in a deep,
emphatic voice:

"I give you my word of honour!"

After a moment's silence he opened the door.

In the other room he saw an elderly lady in black and a playful
little scamp with curly brown hair whom she was trying to keep
quiet, penning him between her knees. Antoine's first glance was for
the child who, at the sound of the opening door, had stopped playing,
to gaze with big, dark, intelligent-looking eyes at the stranger. He
smiled; then, scared by his own smile, turned sulkily away.

Antoine shifted his gaze towards the child's mother. There was
a sad and gentle beauty in her careworn features that went straight
to Antoine's heart. "Courage!" he said to himself. "It's only a matter
of putting one's will into it. It's *always* possible to get results."

"Would you mind coming this way?"

Raising the curtain to let her pass, followed by the child, he gave
the poor woman a reassuring smile—that crumb of comfort, anyhow,
he could bestow on her at once. He could hear the laboured breathing of the man behind him as, patiently holding back the curtain,
he watched mother and child coming towards him, and a wave of
elation swept over his mind. "What a fine profession it is!" he murmured to himself. "Yes, by God, the finest in the world!"

X

NIGHT had come before the steady stream of patients ceased, but Antoine was oblivious both of the time and of his own exhaustion; as often as he raised the curtain, his energy revived without an effort to meet the new occasion. When he had seen out the last caller, a handsome young woman hugging a strapping baby that was threatened, he feared, with almost total blindness, he was amazed to discover it was eight o'clock. "Too late for the kid with the boil," he said to himself. "I'll look in on my way back from Héquet's, later in the evening."

He went back to the consulting-room, opened the window to change the air, and, standing at a low table piled with books, hunted for one to read while he was dining. "Ah, yes," he reminded himself, "I've got to check that reference—the Ernst child's case." He fluttered the pages of some back numbers of the *Neurological Review*, trying to trace the epoch-making symposium on aphasia that took place in 1908. "A really typical case, that Ernst boy; I must tell Treuillard about it."

A smile of amusement flickered on his face as he remembered Treuillard's eccentric ways, a byword in the profession. He called to mind the year he had spent as the nerve-specialist's assistant. "What the devil possessed me to do it?" he asked himself. "Looks as if I've always had a hankering after that branch of medicine. Perhaps I'd have done better to devote myself to nervous and mental diseases. That's a field where much remains still to be discovered." Suddenly a picture formed before his eyes . . . of Rachel. Now what association of ideas had brought her into his mind? She'd had no medical or scientific training, of course; yet psychological problems of every kind had always appealed to her very strongly. Yes, there was no doubt she had played a part in developing the keen interest he now

felt in other people's lives. In any case—he had noticed it time and
time again—she had changed him in a thousand different ways.

A far-away look, a shade of melancholy, dimmed his eyes as he stood
beside the table, his shoulders bowed with weariness, swinging the
medical journal to and fro between his thumb and forefinger. Rachel!
He never could recall without a rush of bitterness the enigmatic girl
who had flashed across his life. Never had he received a line of news
from her. And, indeed, this did not surprise him; that somewhere
in the world Rachel was still alive seemed most improbable. She
had succumbed, more likely, to the climate, or malaria, or the
tsetse. Or, perhaps, she had come to a violent end, been drowned,
or, quite possibly, strangled. Dead she was—of that he was convinced.

He drew himself up and, slipping the journal under his arm, went
out into the hall and told Léon to bring his dinner. One of the chief's
sallies came back to his mind. Philip had been away and, on his
return, Antoine had given him a brief account of the new patients
who had come for treatment; laying his hand on Antoine's arm,
the chief had observed in a tone of affectionate irony: "Better look
out, my boy! You're getting more and more interested in your patients'
mentalities, and less and less in their complaints!"

As Antoine settled down into his chair before the steaming soup-
tureen, he realized how tired he was. "Still, it's a fine profession!"
he consoled himself.

His talk with Gise came back to him and, to dispel the memory,
he made haste to open the bulky review. In vain; the very air of
the room, where something of her presence lingered, seemed still
charged with cruel evidences of his failure. He recalled certain obsessions of the past few months. How was it he had dallied a whole
summer long with so impossible a project? Now he could look upon
his shattered dream as on the wreckage of some flimsy palace on a
stage, crumbled into a heap of insubstantial dust. He suffered little
or not at all. Only his vanity was wounded. And now it seemed to
him that there had been something shoddy about the whole affair,
something puerile and beneath him.

A timid ring at the door-bell came as a welcome interruption. He put down his napkin and pricked up his ears, his hand resting on the tablecloth, ready to rise from his seat at a moment's notice.

He heard a palaver in the hall, and women whispering. Then the door opened and, to his surprise, Léon showed two women into the room without more ado. They proved to be M. Thibault's maids. At first, in the dim light, Antoine failed to recognize them; then it suddenly struck him that they had come to fetch him, and he jumped up so hastily that his chair toppled over behind him.

"No, sir, no!" they cried in the utmost confusion. "Please excuse us, sir. We thought we'd give less trouble if we came at this time."

"Yes, I thought Father had died," Antoine said to himself so calmly that he realized how well prepared he was for that to happen. The possibility that the phlebitis might have caused an embolism had crossed his mind immediately. When he thought of the lingering agony that such a development would have averted, he could not help feeling almost disappointed.

"Sit down," he said. "I'll go ahead with my dinner, as I've some more visits to make this evening."

The two women remained standing.

Jeanne, their mother, had been M. Thibault's cook for a quarter of a century. She was now past work, her legs were raddled with varicose veins, and she herself admitted that her place was "on the shelf." Now the old woman's working days were done, her daughters installed her daily in an arm-chair facing the kitchen range, and there she spent her days, wielding an ineffectual poker. She still enjoyed a feeble illusion of responsibility, for she had a finger in every pie, occasionally whipped the mayonnaise, and plagued her daughters (both women in the thirties) with good advice from morn till night. Clotilde, the elder of the two, was a sturdy wench, devoted if somewhat disobliging, a chatterbox but a hard worker. She had been employed on a farm for many years and had retained a rough-and-ready manner and a racy vocabulary like her mother's; she did the cooking. Adrienne, who had had a convent education and always

THE THIBAULTS   569

been in service in town, was more refined than her elder sister; she had a weakness for dainty lingerie, sentimental ballads, a nosegay on her work-table, and "pretty services" on church-days.

Clotilde, as usual, did the talking.

"It's on account of Mother we've come to see you, M. Antoine. It's been hurting her something awful for the last few days, poor thing, and no mistake! There's a big lump she has in front, on her right side. She can't sleep of nights and when she goes to the bathroom, poor old soul, you can hear her whimpering like a child. But she's plucky, Mother is; she never says a word. You might have a look at her, sir, without letting on what you're about—eh, Adrienne?— and then you're sure to see the great bulge she has there, under her apron."

"Right you are!" said Antoine, taking out his note-book. "I'll find some excuse for visiting the kitchen tomorrow."

While her sister talked, Adrienne busied herself changing Antoine's plate, moving the bread within his reach, and making herself generally useful at table—by force of habit. She had said nothing so far, but now she put a question in an unsteady voice.

"Do you think, sir, that it's . . . it's likely to be dangerous?"

A tumour which develops so quickly . . . Antoine reflected. And, an operation at her time of life—much too risky! He visualized with pitiless precision the course a case like the old woman's might take: the huge proliferation of the neoplasm, its fatal progress, the gradual constriction of the organs, and—most horrible of all—the body's slow decomposition; a death in life.

Lacking courage to meet her anxious gaze, which he could not have brought himself to answer with a lie, he looked askance, with knitted brows and lips set sulkily. Making an evasive gesture, he pushed his plate away from him. But just then fat Clotilde, who never could let a pause elapse without putting in a word, came opportunely to his rescue.

"Of course there's no knowing it right away like that; M. Antoine must have a look at her first. But there's one thing I can tell you: my poor husband's mother, well, she died of a cold on her chest

after going about for fifteen years and more with a lump just like
that one in her stomach!"

XI

A QUARTER of an hour later Antoine had made his way to
B37 Rue de Verneuil and was entering a dark courtyard surrounded
by a block of antiquated buildings. Room 3 was on the sixth story, the
first door in a passage that reeked of gas.

Robert opened the door; he had a lamp in his hand.

"How's your brother?"

"Quite well now, sir."

The lamplight fell full on the boy's eyes, cheerful and candid eyes,
but with a glint of hardness in them, wise before their time; a childish
face, tense with precocious energy.

Antoine smiled.

"Let's have a look at him."

Taking the lamp from the boy's hand, Antoine held it aloft to
get a better view of his surroundings. A round table spread with
oil-cloth took up most of the room. Robert had evidently been writing; a bulky ledger lay open between an uncorked ink-bottle and a
pile of plates, on top of which reposed a hunk of bread and a couple
of apples: a humble still-life. The room was tidy, almost comfortable.
A kettle was singing on a little stove in front of the fireplace.

Antoine went up to the high-pitched mahogany bedstead at the
far end of the room.

"Asleep, were you?"

"Oh, no, sir!"

The little boy, who had obviously wakened with a start, was propping himself on his unbandaged arm, wide-eyed and smiling fear-
lessly.

His pulse was regular. Antoine placed on the bedside table the box of gauze which he had brought, and began to take off the bandage.

"What's that you're boiling on the stove?"

"Just water." Robert laughed. "We were going to have something hot to drink; the concierge gave me some lime-flowers to flavour it." Suddenly his eyelashes began to quiver. "Won't you have some, sir? With sugar. Do try it, sir! It's awfully nice like that!"

"No, thanks, really." Antoine was amused by the boy's eagerness. "What I want is a little boiled water for washing his arm. Just pour some into a clean plate. Right. Now we must wait for it to cool off." He sat down and looked at the children, who were beaming at him as if they had known him all their lives. Yes, he thought, they look decent little lads—but can one ever be really sure? He turned to the older boy.

"How is it that two kids like you come to be living here on your own?"

The boy's eyelashes fluttered and he made a vague gesture, as if to say: "Beggars can't be choosers!"

"What about your father and mother?"

"Oh, they . . . !" Robert's tone implied that such a question really harked back much too far into the past. "We used to live with Auntie." He pointed to the big bed with a meditative air. "She died there in the middle of the night; on the tenth of August it was, over a year ago. And an awfully bad time we had after that, eh, Eddie? Luckily we were on the soft side of the concierge and she didn't say anything to the old landlord, so we didn't have to leave."

"How about the rent?"

"It's paid."

"Who pays it?"

"We do."

"Where does the money come from?"

"Why, what d'you think? We earn it. *I* do, that is to say. He, you see—well, that's where the shoe pinches. Got to find him another job. He's at Brault's—do you know the shop?—in Grenelle; he's their errand-boy. Forty francs a month, all told. Rotten pay, isn't it? Why, you've only got to figure out what he costs in shoe-leather!"

He paused, all eyes for Antoine, who had just removed the bandage. The abscess showed little suppuration, the swelling of the arm had gone down, and the wound looked healthy.

"And how about you?" asked Antoine, as he dipped the dressing in the water.

"Me?"

"Well, you earn your living somehow, don't you?"

"Me . . . ?" Robert repeated in a dawdling voice that suddenly slapped out like a flag in the wind. "You bet I do! I know a trick or two, what's more!"

Antoine glanced up in some surprise and his eyes met a look, keen as a razor-blade, a rather disconcerting look, on the high-strung, resolute little face.

The boy asked nothing better than to talk. How to earn one's living—that was the theme of themes, the only one that counted, the dominant of all his thoughts since ever he began to think. He started with a rush, eager to pour out everything, to unload all his secrets.

"When Auntie died I was only making sixty francs a month as a copyist. Now that I attend the courts as well, my pay's a hundred and twenty francs. Then M. Lamy, the head clerk, fired the office-cleaner—the man who shines the floor each morning—and gave me his job. A lazy old fellow he was, too; never cleaned the floor except there'd been a rainy day, and then only in front of the window where the mud shows. They did well out of the change, you bet! I get another ninety-five francs for that, and it's fine sport polishing the floor every morning, just like roller-skating!" He gave a little whistle. "But that's not all. I've got some other little grafts."

He paused, waiting for Antoine to look again in his direction; then, at a glance, he seemed to sum his man up once for all. Favourable though the judgment was, he evidently thought it best to lead off with a word of warning.

"I don't mind telling you, as I know it's safe with you. But you mustn't ever let on you know about it, eh?" He began to speak more loudly, warming up to his subject as he went on. "You know Mme. Jollin, the concierge at No. 3 in front of your place? Well—but mum's the word, don't forget!—well, the old dame makes cigarettes on the q.t. Say, I wonder if you'd care to . . . ? No? They're A1 smokes, you know—mild and not too tight-packed. Dirt cheap, too. I'll bring you some to sample. Anyhow, it seems it's a hell of a business if you get copped making cigarettes to sell like that. So she needs someone to take round the packages and collect the cash, someone who knows his way around. That's my job; after office-hours, from six to eight, I go my rounds, looking as if butter wouldn't melt in my mouth. She gives me lunch every day except Sundays for my trouble. And a mighty good cook she is, I'll say that for her. Just think what I save! Not to mention that the customers—they're all of them real sports—nearly always slip a nice little tip into my hand, a franc or fifty centimes, it's a matter of luck. Anyhow every little helps, as they say, and we don't do too badly."

He paused. From his tone Antoine could guess the look of pride that sparkled in his eyes, but he purposely refrained from looking up.

Robert, now he was started, rattled on cheerfully.

"When the kid comes back in the evening, he's dog-tired, so we have our grub here; soup, or eggs, or a hunk of cheese, it don't take long anyhow. That's much better than going round the lunch-counters, eh, Eddie? Now and then, like tonight, I spend the evening writing up headings for the cashier. They're nice—aren't they?—big, fat round-hand titles like that; why, I could write 'em just for the fun of it. At the office they . . ."

"Hand me the safety-pins, will you?" Antoine broke in, feigning indifference to the boy's chatter; he was afraid of giving the youngster a taste for showing off. Inwardly, however, he said to himself: "These kids are worth keeping an eye on!"

The dressing had been renewed, the arm was back in its sling. Antoine glanced at his watch.

"I'll look in once again tomorrow, about noon. After that you can come to my place. You'll be fit to go back to work on Friday or Saturday, I guess."

After a moment's silence the little boy stammered: "Th . . . thank you, sir." His voice was just breaking and he jerked the words out with such incongruous emphasis, they cut so quaintly through the silence, that Robert burst out laughing. There was an unnatural shrillness in his laugh, which gave a sudden indication of the state of nervous tension in which the high-strung little fellow always lived.

Antoine took twenty francs from his purse.

"To help you through the week, young fellows."

Robert recoiled as if he had been stung; frowning, he looked up at Antoine.

"No, sir, no! We couldn't think of it. Didn't I tell you we have all we need?" Then, to convince Antoine, who, in haste to be off, was beginning to insist, he launched his Parthian shot: "'Do you know how much we've saved, just us two? A nice little nest-egg— guess! Seventeen hundred of the best! Yes, sir. Haven't we, Eddie?" Then suddenly his voice dropped to a whisper like the villain's in a melodrama. "Not to mention a heap more that will be rollin' in, if my little scheme comes off!"

Such eagerness was in his eyes that Antoine's curiosity was whetted and he halted on the threshold.

"Yes, quite a new dodge. It's like this. . . . Bassou—he's a clerk in our office—has a brother who is a salesman for wine, olive-oil and so forth. Here's the idea! On my way back from the courts in the afternoon—that's nobody's business, eh?—I drop in at all the taverns, grocers', wine-merchants', and show them my stuff. I haven't got the patter off yet—but that'll come with practice. Anyhow, I've placed quite a lot of kegs this last week. Forty-four francs' rake-off. And Bassou says that, if I'm fly . . ."

Antoine chuckled as he hurried down the six flights of stairs. Yes, they'd quite won his heart, the youngsters, and he'd do anything for them. "All the same," he added to himself, "I'd better watch out and see they don't become *too* 'fly'!"

XII

I T WAS raining; Antoine took a taxi. As he neared the Faubourg Saint-Honoré his cheerfulness evaporated and a frown settled on his brows.

"If only it were all over!" he said to himself as, for the third time that day, he gloomily climbed the three flights of stairs. When he reached the door of the Héquets' flat he fancied for a moment that his wish had been fulfilled. The maid who opened the door looked at him in a peculiar manner and stepped forward hastily to whisper something in his ear. But it was only a private message from Mme. Héquet that she imparted; her mistress wanted Antoine to see her first, before going to the child.

There was no eluding it. The light was on in Nicole's room; the door stood open. As he entered he saw her head lying on the pillow. He walked up to the bedside. She did not stir. She had obviously dozed off, and it would have been brutal to disturb her. In repose she looked much younger, care-free, now that sleep had smoothed away the lines of grief and weariness. Antoine gazed at her, holding his breath, afraid to move; it startled him to read upon those features, whence sorrow had withdrawn itself only so short a while ago, this all so sudden ecstasy, so keen a longing for oblivion and happiness. The pearly lustre of her closed eyelids, fringed with fine-spun, tenuous strands of gold, her languid grace and air of uncon-cern—all the naked, self-revealing beauty of the face before him made his senses tingle. How fascinating, too, the drooping curve of her mouth and the half-parted lips that now in their repose seemed to express only relief and hopefulness! "Why," Antoine asked himself, "why should the face of any young being seen asleep appeal to us so strongly? What instinct lies behind the thrill, the almost sensual thrill of pity it evokes in every one of us?"

Turning away, he tip-toed soundlessly from the room. Though the doors were shut the child's hoarse, incessant wailing come to his ears as he proceeded down the passage. With an effort he nerved himself to turn the handle, cross the threshold, and renew contact with the dark powers at work within.

The child's cradle had been placed in the middle of the room and Héquet was seated beside it, his hands resting on the edge, rocking it slowly, intently, to and fro. On the far side of the cradle the night-nurse, her hands pressed tight against her apron, her veiled grey forehead bent above the child, sat waiting like an effigy of disciplined, indomitable patience. Isaac Studler, ungainly as ever in his white linen coat, was leaning against the mantelpiece, with folded arms, stroking his jet-black beard.

The nurse rose as the doctor came in. But Héquet, his eyes fixed on the child, did not seem to notice anything. Not till Antoine went up to the cradle did Héquet raise his head towards him, with a sigh. Antoine had hastily grasped the burning little hand that fluttered on the coverlet, and, as he did so, the child's body seemed to shrink away, like some tiny insect trying to wriggle back into its hole. The child's face was red and mottled, almost the colour of the ice-bag placed behind her ear; her curls, as fair as Nicole's, clammy with sweat or wetted by the compresses, were smeared across her cheeks and forehead. Her eyes were half shut and between the eyelids the swimming pupils had a dull metallic lustre, like the eyes of butchered animals. The movement of the cradle rocked her head slowly to and fro, giving a rhythmic cadence to the moans that issued from the little parched throat.

The nurse made as if to fetch the stethoscope, but Antoine signed to her he did not need it.

"It's an idea of Nicole's," Héquet suddenly remarked in an unnatural, almost high-pitched tone. Then, seeing Antoine's puzzled look, he explained in a studiously level voice: "The cradle. Yes. It's Nicole's idea." He smiled uncertainly; across the twilight of his mind such details seemed to loom out in preternatural relief. "Yes," he added almost in the same breath, "we went and fetched it from the attic. Covered with dust. It's the only thing that calms her a bit, you see, being rocked like that."

Antoine gazed at him compassionately and, as he did so, realized how very far his pity, for all its deep sincerity, fell short of such a sorrow. He placed his hand on Héquet's arm.

"You're utterly fagged out, old man. You'd much better go and lie down for a while. What's the use of wearing yourself out?"

Studler put in a word.

"Yes, it's the third night you haven't slept."

"Do be reasonable now," Antoine insisted, bending towards his friend. "You'll be needing all the strength you have—very soon." He felt an almost physical impulsion to drag the unhappy man away from contact with the cradle, to plunge as soon as might be all that unavailing anguish in the anodynes of sleep.

Héquet did not answer, but went on rocking the cradle. His shoulders sagged more and more, as though Antoine's "very soon" had laid on them a burden not to be endured. Then, of his own accord, he rose, beckoned to the nurse to take his place beside the cradle, and, without waiting to dry his tear-stained cheeks, moved his head slowly round as if in search of something. At last he went up to Antoine and tried to look him in the face. Antoine was struck by the changed expression of his near-sighted eyes; their look of keen alertness had lost its edge, they seemed to move stiffly in their sockets, tending to settle down into a heavy, torpid stare.

Héquet gazed at Antoine and his lips moved before the words came out.

"Something—something *must* be done," he murmured. "She's in great pain, you know that. Why let her go on suffering? Don't . . . don't you agree? We must have the courage to . . . to do something." He paused, seeming to look to Studler for support; then once again his heavy gaze rested on Antoine. "Look here, Thibault, you *must* do something." Then, as though to elude Antoine's answer, he let his head fall, shambled across the room, and left the two men to themselves.

For some moments Antoine seemed incapable of movement; a

sudden blush darkened his cheeks. His mind was a ferment of conflicting thoughts.

Studler tapped him on the shoulder.

"Well?" he asked in a low tone, watching Antoine's face. Studler's eyes resembled those of certain horses—over-large and elongated eyes, with languid pupils slackly floating in pools of watery whiteness. Just now, however, his look, like Héquet's, was searching, masterful.

"Well, what are you going to do about it?" he whispered.

In the brief silence that ensued each felt the impact of the other's thought.

"What will I do?" Antoine echoed evasively. But he knew that Studler would not let him off without an explanation. "Damn it!" he broke out. "Of course I realize. . . . But when he says 'do something' one daren't even appear to understand!"

"Hush!" Studler whispered, glancing towards the nurse; then he led Antoine into the passage and closed the door.

"You're convinced, aren't you, that nothing can be done?" he asked.

"Quite convinced."

"And that there's not the least, not the very faintest hope?"

"Not the faintest."

"Well, then?"

Antoine felt a mood of tense excitement gaining on him, and took refuge in an acrimonious silence.

"Well, then?" Studler insisted. "There's no use beating about the bush; the sooner it's ended, the better."

"And I assure you I want it to end quite as much as you do."

"Wanting's not enough."

Antoine raised his head and answered resolutely:

"That, unfortunately, is all that can be done."

"No!"

"Yes!"

The dialogue had grown so vehement that Studler kept silence for some seconds.

"Those injections," he presently observed. "I wonder now. . . . Supposing the doses were doubled? . . ."

Antoine cut him short.

"Hold your tongue, damn it!"

His mind was seething with exasperation. Studler watched him without speaking. Antoine's eyebrows stood out like an iron bar, in an almost straight line across his forehead, the muscles of his face twitched uncontrollably, dragging his mouth awry, and now and then a little stream of ripples fretted the tight-drawn skin, as though the nervous system just below the surface were in a state of violent commotion.

A minute passed.

"Hold your tongue!" Antoine repeated, but less harshly, stammering a little with excitement. "I know what you feel. We've all f-felt like that, wanted to cut things short; but that's just a beg-beginner's weakness. Only one consideration counts: the sanctity of human life. Yes. The sanctity of life. If you'd gone on with medicine, you'd see things in the same light as every other doctor. The necessity for certain fixed principles. A limit to our powers. Otherwise . . ."

"A limit? If a man's a man at all, the only limit is—his conscience."

"Exactly! His conscience; his professional conscience. But just think, man! Supposing doctors were to claim the right to . . . Anyhow, Isaac, there isn't one who would, not one. . . ."

"In that case—" Studler hissed the words out. Antoine cut him short.

"Héquet has dealt with cases every bit as hopeless, as pit-pitiful as this one, dozens of times. But he's never once deliberately . . . Never. Nor has Philip, nor Rigaud, nor Treuillard. No doctor worthy of the name would dream of it, do you hear me? Never!"

"In that case," Studler broke out, "you doctors may set up to be the high priests of the world today, but to my mind you're just a pack of scrimshankers!"

As he moved back a step the light from the hanging lamp fell on his face. Its look conveyed more than his words had said; not only scorn and indignation but a sort of challenge, almost a threat—a secret will to *act*.

"That being so," Antoine said to himself, "I'll stay here till eleven and make the injection myself." He said no more but, with a shrug of his shoulders, went back to the bedroom and sat down.

The rain drummed on the shutters an endless monotone, and drippings from the eaves pattered incessantly upon the sill while, in the room, the swaying cradle timed the moaning of the dying child to its slow rhythm; and, across the hush of night, tense with death's immanence, all the sounds blended in a sad, persistent counterpoint.

"I stammered once or twice just now," Antoine, whose nerves were still on edge, muttered to himself. He was not often taken that way; it happened only when he had to keep up a distasteful pose—when, for example, he was forced to tell a complicated lie to some over-perspicacious patient, or when in conversation he was led to bolster up some conventional idea regarding which he had so far no personal convictions. "It's all the Caliph's fault!" With the corner of his eye he saw the "Caliph" back at his old place, leaning against the mantel-piece. He remembered Isaac Studler in his student days, when he had met him for the first time, ten years ago, in the neighbourhood of the School of Medicine. Bearded like a Persian king, with his silky voice and Rabelaisian laugh, the Caliph had been a familiar figure in the Latin Quarter of those days; then, too, there had been a truculent, subversive, and fanatical side to his character; half-measures were not the Caliph's way. An exceptionally brilliant future was predicted for him. Then one day the news went round that he had dropped his studies and set to earning his living; it was said that he had taken under his wing the wife and children of one of his brothers who had just killed himself after embezzling money from the bank where he was employed.

A shriller cry from the child cut short his musings. Antoine fixed his eyes for a moment on the writhing little body, trying to estimate the frequency of certain spasms, but there was nothing to be made of them; the movements were as incalculable as the palpitations of a chicken that is being bled. Then suddenly the feeling of unrest against which Antoine had been struggling ever since his passage of words with Studler grew to an acute distress. Ready though he always was to take the utmost risks when a patient's life was in danger, it was more than he could bear thus to come up against a hopeless situation, to feel so utterly at a loss for any form of action, condemned to watch the unseen enemy's triumphant progress with folded hands. And to-night the child's interminable struggle, her inarticulate cries, were working on Antoine's nerves with a peculiar urgency. Yet the sight of suffering, even the agony of little children, was nothing new to him. How was it that tonight he could not hold his feelings in? Confronted with the element of mystery and horror that attends a death-agony, he found himself tonight as impotent to curb his anguish as if he were the veriest novice. He was stirred to the depths of his being; his self-confidence was shaken—and, with it, his confidence in science, in activity, in life itself. Like a great wave, despair broke over him, dragging him down into the depths. In a ghastly pageant they streamed before his eyes, all the patients he had written down as "hopeless cases." Why, taking only those whom he had seen on this one day, the list was formidable in all conscience! Four or five hospital patients, Huguette, the Ernst boy, the blind baby, and now the child before him. And, doubtless, others too. Yes, his father; an old man with thick, milk-sodden lips, prisoned in an arm-chair. In a few weeks, after some days and nights of pain, the robust old veteran, too, would go their way. The way they all must go, one following the other. And in all this world-wide suffering there was no sense, no meaning. . . . "No, life's absurd, a beastly thing!" he adjured himself furiously, as though to argue down some quite incorrigible optimist; and who was that confirmed, pig-headed optimist if not—himself, his normal self?

The nurse rose soundlessly. Antoine glanced at his watch; it was time for the injection. The pretext for moving, doing something, came as a vast relief; he felt almost cheerful, too, at the prospect of being able to get away from this room in a few minutes.

The nurse brought all he needed on a tray. Clipping off the tip of the ampoule, he plunged the needle in, filled the syringe to the pre-scribed level, then tipped out the contents of the ampoule (still three-quarters full) into the slop-pail. He could feel Studler's gaze intent on him.

After making the injection he sat down again; it seemed to have eased the pain a little. He bent over the child, took her pulse once more—it was terribly weak—and whispered some instructions to the nurse. Then he rose without haste, washed at the basin, shook Studler's hand without a word, and left the room.

He made his way out on tip-toe. The lights were on but no one was visible; Nicole's door was shut. As he moved away the sound of wailing seemed to grow fainter. He opened and shut the hall-door noiselessly. Outside, on the landing, he paused and listened. Not a sound. With a deep sigh of relief he sped briskly down the stairs.

Out in the street he could not refrain from gazing up towards the dark façade cut by a string of lighted windows as though a party were being given in the Héquets' flat.

The rain had just stopped and the pavements were streaming after the downpour. As far as eye could reach the empty streets shimmered with liquid light.

Antoine felt a sudden chill; turning up the collar of his coat, he quickened his steps.

XIII

A SOUND of water dripping; rain-drenched pavements. Suddenly the picture rose before him of a face streaming with tears, of Héquet standing there, Héquet's insistent gaze. "Look here, Thibault, you *must* do something!" For all his efforts to dispel it, the harrowing vision held his eyes a while. "A father's love," he mused; "yes, that's a feeling utterly unknown to me, however much I try to picture it." Suddenly the thought of Gise leapt to his mind. "A home. Children." An idle dream, all that, and, happily, unrealizable. That idea of marriage, why, now it struck him as more than premature; grotesque! "Am I an egoist?" he wondered. "Or is it simply cowardice?" His thoughts turned a new corner. "Anyhow, there's someone damns

me for a coward just now, and that's the Caliph!" He remembered
disgustedly the way Studler had cornered him in the passage, the
man's hot, vulgar face and stubborn eyes. He struggled to brush
away the swarm of ideas which ever since that moment had been
buzzing in his brain. "A coward?" Rather an obnoxious word, that!
"Over-cautious," perhaps. "Studler thought me over-cautious. The
damned fool!"

He had reached the Elysée. A patrol of military police had just
completed their circuit of the Palace. There was a clatter of rifle-
butts on the sidewalk. Before he could avert their onset a horde of
wild imaginings, like the protean pageant of a dream, streamed through
his mind. He pictured Studler sending the nurse out of the room,
taking a syringe from his pocket. Presently the nurse came back
and passed her fingers over the little corpse. Then . . . ugly rumours;
a report of the police; burial refused; an autopsy. The coroner; the
police. "I'll take the blame." He was passing a sentry-box just then,
and glared defiantly at the sentry within. "No," he heard himself
affirming boldly to a phantom coroner, "no injections were made by
anyone except myself. I administered an over-dose—deliberately. It
was a hopeless case, and I take upon myself all the . . ." Shrugging
his shoulders, he smiled and quickened his step. "What drivel I'm
thinking!" But well he knew he had not laid the spectres of his
mind. "If I'm so ready to take the blame for a fatal dose administered by another man, why did I so emphatically refuse to administer
it myself?"

Whenever a brief but strenuous mental effort failed, if not to clarify
a problem, at least to throw some light on it, he always felt intensely
irritated. He recalled the passage of words with Studler, when he
had lost his temper, stammered. He did not regret it in the least;
yet he was unpleasantly aware that he had played a part and voiced
opinions which were somehow out of keeping with his personality
as a whole, disloyal to his truest self. He had, moreover, a vague
but galling presentiment of a day to come when his outlook and conduct might well belie his attitude and words on this occasion. His
sense of self-disapproval must have been keen indeed for Antoine

now to feel so impotent to shake it off; as a rule he firmly refused to pass judgment on any of his acts; the feeling of remorse was wholly foreign to his nature. True, he enjoyed studying himself; of recent years, indeed, he had made a veritable hobby of self-analysis—but always from a strictly scientific point of view. Nothing could be more alien to his character than to sit in moral judgment on himself.

Another question shaped itself in his mind, adding to his perplexity. "Would it not have needed greater strength of mind to consent, than to refuse, to act?" Whenever he had to choose between two alternatives and when, all things considered, one seemed as cogent as the other, he usually chose the line of action involving the greater exercise of will-power; experience had taught him, so he averred, that this was almost always the better one to follow. But tonight he had to admit that he had chosen the line of least resistance, followed the beaten track.

Some of his own remarks still echoed in his ears. He had prated to Studler of "the sanctity of life." A ready-made phrase, and treacherous like all its kind. We "reverence" life, we say—or do we make a fetish of it?

He recalled an incident which had struck his imagination at the time—the case of the bicephalous child at Tréguineuc. Some fifteen years earlier, at the Breton seaport where the Thibaults were passing the summer holidays, a fisherman's wife had given birth to a freak of nature, with two separate, perfectly formed heads. Father and mother had begged the local doctor to put an end to the little monstrosity, and, when he refused to do so, the father, a notorious drunkard, had flung himself on the new-born child and attempted to strangle it. It had been necessary to secure him, lock him up. There was great excitement in the village and it was a burning topic at the dinner-tables of the summer visitors. Antoine, who was sixteen or seventeen at the time, had embarked on a heated discussion with his father (it was one of the first occasions on which father and son came into violent conflict), Antoine insisting, with the naïve intractability of youth, that the doctor should be permitted to cut short a life, doomed from the outset, without more ado.

It startled him to find how little his point of view regarding such a case had changed. "What view would Philip take?" he asked himself. The answer was not in doubt; Antoine could but admit that the idea of ending the child's life would never have crossed Philip's mind. What was more, did any dangerous malady develop, Philip would have strained every nerve to save its miserable life. Rigaud would have done the same thing. Terrignier, too. And Loiselle. So would every doctor. Wherever the least spark of life remains, the doctor's duty is imperative. Saviours of life, like trusty Saint Bernards! Philip's nasal voice droned in his ears: "You've no choice, my boy; you haven't the right . . . !"

Antoine rebelled. " 'The right'? Look here, you know as well as I do what they amount to, those ideas of 'right' and duty. The laws of nature are the only laws that count; they, I admit, are ineluctable. But all those so-called moral laws, what are they really? A complex of habits, foisted upon us by the past. Just that. Long ago they may have served their purpose, as furthering man's social progress. But what of today? Can you, as a thinking man, assign to all those antiquated rules of hygiene and public welfare a sort of divine right, the status of a categorical imperative?" And, as no answer was forthcoming from the chief, Antoine shrugged his shoulders and, thrusting his hands deeper into his overcoat pockets, crossed to the opposite sidewalk.

He walked blindly ahead, debating still—but only with himself. "One thing's sure: for me, morality simply doesn't exist! 'Ought' and 'ought not,' 'right' and 'wrong,' are meaningless to me—just words I use, like everyone else, as the small change of conversation; but in my heart I've always known they have no application to reality. Yes, I've *always* thought like that. No, that's going too far. I've thought like that since . . ." Rachel's face rose suddenly before his eyes. "Well, for quite a long time, anyhow." For a while he made a conscientious effort to sort out the principles governing his daily life. He could find none. "A kind of sincerity?" he ventured tentatively. He thought again and found a better definition. "Isn't it rather a kind of clear-sightedness?" His mind was still unsettled, but he was fairly satisfied with his discovery. "Yes. Obviously it doesn't amount to much. But, when I look into myself, my impulse to think clearly—well, it's about the only sure and solid thing I can find. Very likely I've made of it—unconsciously, no doubt—a kind of moral principle, my private creed. 'Complete freedom, provided I see clearly.' That sums it up, I imagine. Rather a risky principle, when you look into it. But it works out pretty well. The way one sees things, that's the only thing that matters. To profit by one's scientific training and examine oneself under the microscope coolly, impartially. To see oneself as one is; and, as a corollary, to accept oneself as one is. And then? Then I could almost say: Nothing is forbidden me! Nothing, provided I don't dupe myself; I know what I am doing and, as far as possible, why I am doing it."

But, almost at once, a wry smile pursed his lips. "The queerest thing is that, if I look into it carefully—my life, I mean, with its famous gospel of 'complete freedom' that does away with good and evil—the queer thing is, my life is almost entirely devoted to 'doing good,' as people call it! What has it brought me to, my precious emancipation? To acting not merely just like everybody else, but, oddly enough, in the very way which according to the present code of morals sets me among the best of men! The way I behaved just now is a case in point. Can it be that, for all practical purposes and despite myself, I've come to kotow to the cut-and-dried morality of those around me? Philip would smile. . . . No, I can't allow that our human obligation to behave as social animals should overrule our impulses as individuals. How then explain the line I took just now? It's fantastic how little the way we think fits in with, or even influences, the way we act. For, in my heart of hearts—why quibble over it?—I think Studler's right. The platitudes that I hurled at him carried no weight at all. It's he that has logic on his side; that poor child's sufferings are so much needless agony, the issue of her fight with death is a foregone conclusion, foregone and imminent, too. Well, then—the least reflection tells me that if her death can be accelerated, it's so much the better on every count. Not only for the child, but for her mother; it's obvious that in her present condition the sight of the baby's lingering agony may well prove dangerous to her—as Héquet, no doubt, is well aware. And there are no two ways about it; on a purely logical view the soundness of such arguments is as plain as daylight. But isn't it odd how mere logic seldom or never really satisfies us? I don't say that just to condone an act of cowardice; indeed, I know quite well that what drove me to act as I did this evening, or, rather, to refuse to act, was not mere cowardice. No, it was something as urgent, as imperative as a law of nature. But what it was, that urgency—that's what passes me." He ran over in his mind some possible explanations. Was it one of those inchoate ideas (he was convinced that such exist) that seem to sleep below the level of our lucid thoughts, but sometimes come awake and, rising to the surface, take control of us, impel us to an act— only to sink back once more, inexplicably, into the limbo of our un- known selves? Or—to take a simpler view—why not admit that a law of herd-morality exists and it is practically impossible for a man to act as if he were an isolated unit?

He seemed to be turning in a circle, his eyes blindfolded. He tried to recall the wording of Nietzsche's well-known dictum: that a man should not be a problem, but the solution of a problem. A self-evident axiom, he used to think, but one with which, year after year, he had found it ever harder to conform. He had already had occasion to observe that some of his decisions—the most spontaneous, as a rule; often the most important ones he made—clashed with his reasoned scheme of life; so much so, indeed, that he had sometimes wondered: "Can I be really the man I think I am?" The mere suspicion left him dazed and startled; it came like a lightning-flash that slits the shadows, leaving them the darker for its passing. But he was always quick to brush the thought aside, and now again he flouted it.

Chance befriended him. As he came into the Rue Royale a whiff of baking bread, warm as a living creature's breath, came to his nostrils from the vent-hole of a bakery, and started off his thoughts on a new tack. Yawning, he looked about him for an open tavern; then he was suddenly impelled to go and have something to eat at Zemm's, a little café near the Comédie Française which stayed open till dawn and where he sometimes dropped in at night before proceeding homewards across the river.

"Yes, it's a queer thing," he admitted to himself after a moment of no thoughts. "We can doubt, destroy, make a clean sweep of all our beliefs, but, whether we like it or not, there remains a solid kernel proof against every doubt, the human instinct to trust our reason. A truism of which I've been the living proof for the last hour or so!"

He felt tired, disconsolate, and hunted for a reassuring formula apt to restore his peace of mind. He fell back on an easy compromise. "Conflict is the common rule, and so it has always been. What is happening in my mind just now is going on throughout the universe: the clash of life with life."

For a while he walked on mechanically, thinking of nothing in particular. He was nearing the serried tumult of the boulevards and questing women here and there pressed on him their companionable charms; he shook them off good-humouredly.

But all the time his brain was unconsciously at work, his thoughts were crystallizing round an idea.

"I am a living being; in other words I am always choosing between alternatives and acting accordingly. So far so good. But there my quandary begins. What is the guiding principle on which I choose and act? I've no idea. Is it the clear-sightedness I was thinking of just now? No, hardly that. That's theory, not practice. My zeal for clarity has never really guided me to a decision or an act. It's only *after* I have acted that my lucidity comes into play—to justify to me what I have done. And yet, ever since I've been a sentient being, I've felt myself directed by a kind of instinct, a driving force that leads me almost all the time to choose this and not that, to act in this way, not in another. But—most puzzling thing of all!—I notice that all my acts follow precisely the same lines; everything takes place as if I were being controlled by an unalterable law. Exactly. But what law? I haven't a notion! Whenever at some critical moment of my life that driving force inside me leads me to take a certain course and act in consequence, I ask myself in vain: What was the principle that guided me? It's like running up against a wall of darkness! I feel sure of my ground, intensely alive, lawful in my occasions, so to speak—yet I'm outside the law. Lawful and lawless! Neither in the teaching of the past nor in any modern philosophy, not even in myself, can I find any satisfactory answer. I see clearly enough all the laws which I can't endorse, but I see none to which I could submit; not one of all the standard moral codes has ever seemed to me even approximately to fit my case, or to throw any light upon the way in which I act. Yet, all the same, I forge ahead, and at a good pace, too, without the least hesitation, and, what's more, keeping a pretty straight course. Yes, it's extraordinary! Driving full-steam ahead like a fast liner whose steersman's scrapped the compass! It almost looks as if I were acting under orders. Yes, that's exactly what I feel; my way of life is ordered. Under orders, yes; but *whose* orders? . . . Meanwhile I don't complain; I'm happy. I've not the least wish to change; only I'd like to know why I am as I am. It's more than simple curiosity; there's a touch of apprehension in it. Has every man alive his mystery? I wonder. And shall I ever find the key to mine? Shall I know one day what it is: my guiding principle?"

He quickened his steps. Beyond the cross-roads a flashing shop-sign, Zemm's, had caught his eye, and hunger drove out thought.

So quickly did he dive into the entrance of the café that he stumbled over a pile of oyster-baskets that filled the passage with the sour smell of brine. The restaurant was in the basement, to which a narrow spiral staircase, picturesque and vaguely conspiratorial in appearance, gave access. At this late hour the room was full of night-birds taking their ease in a warm bath of vapour, thick with the fumes of alcohol, cigar-smoke, and odours from the kitchen, all churned up together by the whizzing fans. With its polished mahogany and green leather seats the long, low, windowless tavern had the aspect of a liner's smoking-room.

Antoine made for a corner of the room, deposited his overcoat beside him, and sat down. He felt a mood of calm well-being gaining on him. Then all at once there rose before his eyes a very different scene: the nursery, the little body bathed in sweat and vainly struggling against its unseen foe. He seemed to hear the rhythmic cadence of the swaying cradle, like a tragic footfall marking time. A spasm of horror gripped him and he shrank together.

"Supper, sir?"

"Yes. Roast beef and black bread. And some whisky in a big tumbler; iced water, please, not soda."

"Will you have some of our cheese-soup, sir?"

"Very well."

On each table stood a generous bowl of potato-chips, spangled with salt-flakes, brittle and thin as "honesty" pods, infallible thirst-producers. The zest with which he crunched the chips gave Antoine the measure of his hunger as he waited for the gruyère-soup to come; simmering and cheese-scummed, stringy and crisped with shreds of onion, it was one of Zemm's specialties.

At the cloak-room near his corner some people were calling for their coats. One of the noisy group, a girl, glanced covertly at Antoine and, as their eyes met, gave him a faint smile. Where was it he had seen that smooth, sleek face that brought to mind a Japanese print, with its etched-in eyebrows and tiny, slightly oblique eyes? He was amused by the clever way in which she had signalled to him without being noticed by the others. Why, of course, she was a model he had seen several times at Daniel de Fontanin's place—his old studio in the Rue Mazarine. It all came back to him now quite clearly: the sweltering summer afternoon, the model on her "throne"; why, he could remember even the hour it was, the lighting of the room, the model's pose—and then the emotion which had made him linger on, though he was pressed for time. His eyes followed her as she went out. What was it Daniel called her? Some name that sounded like a brand of tea. She looked back at him from the door. Yes, now he remembered how he had then been struck by the flatness of her body; an athlete's body, clean-limbed and sinewy.

While, during the last few months, he fancied himself in love with Gise, other women had hardly counted in his life. In fact, since he had broken off with Mme. Javenne—the liaison had lasted two months and all but ended in a catastrophe—he had dispensed with mistresses.

Now, for a few seconds, he bitterly regretted it. He took a few sips of the whisky which had just been brought; then, lifting the lid of the soup-tureen, relished its appetizing fumes.

Just then the page-boy brought him a crumpled fragment of a music-hall programme, folded envelope-wise, in the corner of which some words were scrawled in pencil:

Zemm's tomorrow, 10 p.m.???

"Anybody waiting for an answer?" he asked with interest, but in some perplexity.

"No, sir. The lady's gone."

Antoine was determined to take no action on the assignation; all the same he slipped the note into his pocket before beginning his meal.

"What a damned fine thing life is!" he suddenly reflected as an unexpected rout of cheerful thoughts danced through his brain. "Yes, I'm in love with life!" He took a moment's thought. "And, in reality, I don't depend on anyone at all." Once more a memory of Gise flitted across his mind. Now he was sure that life itself, even if love were lacking, sufficed to make him happy. He honestly admitted to himself that when Gise had been away in England he had not felt her absence in the least. Truth to tell, had any woman ever held a large place in his life or in his happiness? Rachel? Yes. But what would have been the outcome, had not Rachel gone away? Anyhow, he had said good-bye to passions of that order once and for all. No, as he saw things now, he would no longer dare to describe his feeling towards Gise as "love." He tried to find another, apter word. "An attachment?" For a few moments yet Gise held the foreground of his thoughts and he resolved to clarify his feelings of the past few months. One thing was sure: he had imagined an ideal Gise, the mirror of his dreams, quite other than the flesh-and-blood Gise who, only this afternoon . . . But he declined to work out the comparison.

He took a pull of his whisky and water, tackled the roast beef, and told himself once more he was in love with life.

Life, as he saw it, was a vast, open arena into which the man of action has but to launch himself enthusiastically. By "love of life" he really meant self-love, self-confidence. Still, when he visualized his own life in particular, it presented itself as something far more definite than a wide field of action placed by some miracle at his disposal and offering an infinity of possible achievements; he saw it, rather, as a clean-cut track, a long, straight road leading infallibly towards a certain goal.

There was a familiar ring about the phrases he had just employed, but their sound was always welcome to his ears. "Thibault?" the inner voice went on. "He's thirty-two: the very age when great careers begin. What of his body? Remarkably fit; he's always in fine fettle, and strong as a cart-horse. And his mind? Quick in perception, adventurous, a pioneering intellect. His capacity for work? All but unlimited. . . . And comfortably off, into the bargain. All that a man can want, in fact! No vices, no bad habits, nothing to trammel his vocation. . . . On the crest of the wave!"

He stretched his limbs and lit a cigarette.

His vocation. . . . Since he was fifteen all things medical had always had a singular appeal for him. Even now it was his firm conviction that in the science of medicine we may see the fine flower of all man's intellectual efforts in the past, the most signal reward of twenty centuries' research in every branch of knowledge, and the richest field available for human genius. It knew no limits on the speculative side, yet it was founded on the very bedrock of reality and kept in close and constant contact with humanity itself. He had a special leaning towards its human aspect. Never would he have consented to shut himself up in a laboratory and glue his eyes upon a microscopic field; no, what most delighted him was the doctor's never-ending tussle with proteiform reality.

"What is needed," the inner voice resumed, "is that Thibault should work more on his own account and not, like Terrignier or Boistelot, let himself be hamstrung by his practice. He should find time to organize and follow up experiments, collate results, and thus evolve the outlines of a *system*." For Antoine pictured for himself a career akin to those of the great masters of his profession; before he was fifty he would have a host of new discoveries to his credit and, above all, he would have laid the foundations of a system of his own, glimpses of which, vague though they were as yet, he seemed to have at certain moments. "Yes, soon, quite soon. . . ."

Leaping an interval of darkness, his father's death, his thoughts came out again into the cheerful sunlight of the near future. Between two puffs at his cigarette he contemplated his father's death from a new angle, without the least misgiving or distress. Rather, he saw it now as a prime condition of his long-awaited freedom, opening new horizons and favouring the swift ascension of his star. His brain teemed with new projects. "I'll have to thin out my practice at once so as to get some spare time for myself. Then I shall need an assistant for my research-work, or a secretary, why not? Not a collaborator; no, quite a youngster, someone open to ideas whom I could train, who'd do the spade-work for me. Then I could really get down to it, put everything I've got into it! And make discoveries. Yes, one day, that's certain, I'll bring off something *big!*" The ghost of a smile hovered on his lips, an upcrop of the optimistic mood that buoyed him.

He threw his cigarette away, struck by a sudden thought. "That's a queer thing, now that I think of it! The moral sense that I've cast out of my life, from which I felt only an hour ago that I'd escaped for good and all—why, here it is, all of a sudden, back again in its old place! Not skulking furtively in a dark byway of my awareness; no, on the contrary, solid and serene, and very much in evidence, standing up like a rock square in the centre of my active life—the nucleus of my professional career! No, it's no use beating about the bush; as a doctor and a scientist I've an absolutely rigid code of right and wrong and, what's more, I'm pretty certain I'll stand by it, come what may. But then—how the devil is one to fit that in with . . . ? Oh, after all," he consoled himself, "why want to make every blessed thing 'fit in'?" And very soon he gave up the attempt, letting his thoughts grow blurred, and indolently yielding to a mood of vague well-being mingled with fatigue, a comfortable lethargy.

Two motorists had just come in and settled down at a neighbouring table, depositing their bulky overcoats on the seat beside them. The man looked about twenty-five, the girl a year or two younger. A handsome couple, slim and athletic, dark-haired both, with forthright eyes, large mouths set with an array of valiant teeth, cheeks ruddied by the cold; a perfect match in age and health, in natural elegance and social standing, they shared, presumably, the same tastes. In any case their appetites ran neck and neck, for side by side and at exactly the same speed they munched their way through a pair of sandwiches as like as like could be; then, with the selfsame gesture, drained their beer-mugs, donned their fur-coats, and, keeping step together, moved springily away. Antoine watched them with interest, so typical they seemed of the ideal couple, of cordial entente.

Just then he noticed that the room was almost empty. His eyes lit on the dial of a clock above his head, reflected in a distant mirror. "Ten past ten. No, the wrong way on. Eh? Nearly two."

Shaking off his lethargy, he rose. "A fine state I'll be in tomorrow morning!" he ruefully bethought himself.

As he went up the narrow staircase, passing the page-boy drowsing on a step, a cheerful thought flashed through his mind; so realistic was the picture it evoked that he smiled furtively. "Tomorrow, 10 p.m."

He hailed a taxi, and was home five minutes later.

On the hall-table where the evening mail awaited him a slip of paper was laid out, well in view. He recognized Léon's writing:

They rang up from Dr. Héquet's about 1 a.m. The little girl is dead.

He held up the sheet between his hands for some moments, then read it over again. "One a.m.? Very soon after I left. . . . Studler? With the nurse looking on? No. Most decidedly, no. What then? My injection? Possibly. A minimal dose, however. Still, the pulse was so weak. . . ."

Once the shock had spent itself, his feeling was one of relief. Hard though the blow must be for Héquet and his wife, at least it had cut short their horrible suspense. He remembered Nicole's face in sleep. Quite soon another little one would fill the absent place between them. So life is served, and every wound heals up at last. "Still, I'm sorry for them," he thought with a tightening of the heart. "I'll look them up on my way to the hospital."

In the kitchen the cat was mewing plaintively. "She'll keep me from sleeping, damn her!" Antoine grumbled. Then suddenly he remembered her kittens and opened the door. The cat flung herself across his legs and rubbed herself against him in a frenzy of caresses, with desperate importunity. Antoine stooped over her basket; it was empty.

"You'll drown them all, of course." Yes, those had been his words. Yet that too was life—why make a distinction? By what right—?

Shrugging his shoulders, he glanced at the clock, and yawned.

"Four hours' sleep. No time for dawdling!"

Léon's note was still in his hand; he rolled it into a ball and tossed it cheerfully onto the dresser.

"And now for a good cold shower. The Thibault system: Sluice away your tiredness before you go to bed!"

PART

V

PART

V

"A NSWER: 'No!'" M. Thibault said peremptorily, without opening his eyes. He cleared his throat with the dry, rasping sound that members of the household called his "asthma cough"; his head, sunk in the pillow, hardly moved at all.

Instilled in a high chair beside a folding table, M. Chasle was just opening the morning mail, though it was well after two.

That day the one kidney which still was functioning had worked so badly and the pain had been so continuous that, throughout the forenoon, M. Thibault had not been able to receive his secretary. This had gone on till twelve o'clock, when Sister Céline had thought it best to find an excuse for making the hypodermic injection which she ordinarily deferred till much later in the day. The pain had subsided almost at once, but M. Thibault, whose sense of time was greatly impaired, had fumed and fretted at being obliged to wait till M. Chasle came back from lunch, to have his letters read to him.

"What next?" he said.

M. Chasle skimmed the contents of another letter.

"Aubry (Félicien), ex-sergeant in a Zouave regiment applies for a post as guard at the Crouy Penitentiary."

"'Penitentiary'? Why not say 'prison' right away? Put it in the wastepaper basket. Next."

"Eh? 'Why not say "prison"?'" M. Chasle repeated *sotto voce* in a puzzled tone. Then, giving up hope of understanding the remark, he settled his glasses on his nose and hastily opened another envelope.

"From the Villeneuve-Joubin Vicarage. Profound gratitude . . . thanks for the improvement in a boy's character. There's nothing in it."

"Nothing in it? Read it, M. Chasle."

"Dear Sir,
"My sacred calling gives me the opportunity of fulfilling a very welcome task. I am requested by one of my parishioners, Mme. Beslier, to express her profound gratitude . . ."

"Louder!" M. Thibault commanded.

". . . her profound gratitude for the beneficial effects his stay at Crouy has had on young Alexis. When you were so good as to allow him to enter the Oscar Thibault Institution four years ago, we had all but given up hope of making anything of the unfortunate lad. His depraved instincts, evil ways, and propensity for violence boded ill for his future. But within three years a miracle, which we owe to you, has taken place. Alexis has now been back at home nine months. His mother, sisters, neighbours, and myself, as well as M. Jules Binot, the local carpenter, who employs him as an apprentice, can all speak highly of the lad's docility, keenness for his work, and zeal in performing his religious duties.

"I pray Almighty God to grant His blessings to an institution which is capable of bringing about such moral reformations, and I would express my deep respect for its illustrious Founder, in whom the spirit of charity and generous vision of a Saint Vincent de Paul are once more incarnate in our midst.

"J. Rumel, P.P."

M. Thibault's eyes were still closed, but the tip of his short, pointed beard was quivering; the old man was in such a weak state that the least emotion had an overwhelming effect.

"A very fine letter, M. Chasle," he said, once he had mastered his feelings. "Don't you agree it's well worth printing in our next year's *Bulletin?* Please be good enough to refresh my memory, when the time comes. Next."

"A letter from the Ministry of Home Affairs. The Prisons Department."

"What's that . . . ?"

"No," M. Chasle amended. "It's only a circular of some kind or other. Incomprehensible."

The door opened slightly; Sister Céline sidled in.

"Must get the letters finished first," M. Thibault said gruffly.

The nurse made no protest but went to the fireplace and added another log. (She always kept a log-fire burning to counteract the odour in the sick-room, which, as she sometimes put it, making a wry face, "smelled like a hospital.") After a moment she went out.

"What next, M. Chasle?"

"The Institute of France. A meeting on the twenty-seventh."

"Speak louder. Next?"

"The Diocesan Charities. Governing Committee meetings on November 23 and 30. In December, on . . ."

"Send a card to the Abbé Baufremont, asking him to excuse my absence on the twenty-third. And on the thirtieth as well," he added after a moment's thought. "Note the December meetings in the engagement-book. Next."

"That's all, sir. That's to say, only a subscription form from the Parish Relief Fund. And some visiting-cards; the callers yesterday were Father Nussey, M. Ludovic Roye, Secretary of the *Revue des Deux Mondes,* and General Kerigan. This morning the Vice-President of the Senate called to inquire for you. And some circulars. Parish magazines. Newspapers."

The door opened again, this time inexorably. Sister Céline entered, and now she carried a steaming poultice laid out on a plate.

M. Chasle lowered his eyes and left the room—on tip-toe, to prevent his boots from squeaking.

The nurse had already begun turning back the blankets. Fomentations were her latest fad. As a matter of fact, though they reduced the pain, they had none of the hoped-for effect on the sluggish organs. Indeed, so ineffectual were they that now, notwithstanding M. Thibault's repugnance, she had no choice but to use a sound again.

Once the operation was over, he felt some physical relief, but the nurse's activities had left him in a despondent mood. It had just struck half-past three; the close of the afternoon threatened to be a gloomy one. The effects of the morphine were beginning to wear off; the five o'clock enema was not due for more than an hour. To keep her patient's mind off his troubles, the nun took it upon herself to call M. Chasle back.

The little man entered discreetly and took his seat again by the window.

He was feeling worried. When, a moment before, he met fat Clotilde in the corridor, she had whispered in his ear: "This last week the master's been going downhill fast, there's no denying it." And while M. Chasle gazed at her with startled eyes, she had added: "No, that disease he has don't let no one off."

M. Thibault lay quiet in bed, though now and then he gave a little gasp, or groaned—from sheer force of habit, for the pain had not come back yet. In fact just now he was feeling comfortable, at ease. But, always fearing that the twinges might return, he wanted to doze off, and his secretary's presence fretted him.

Lifting an eyelid, he cast a melancholy glance towards the window.

"Don't waste your time waiting here, M. Chasle. Any more work is out of the question for me today. Look at me!" He tried to raise his arm. "Yes, I'm at the end of my tether."

M. Chasle made no attempt to hide his feelings. "Already!" he exclaimed, in a tone of consternation.

Surprised, M. Thibault turned his head; there was a glint of humour in his half-closed eyes.

"Can't you see my strength is failing day by day?" he sighed. "What's the good of nursing false hopes? If one's got to die, the sooner it's over the better."

"What's that? To die!" M. Chasle wrung his hands emotionally.

M. Thibault was amusing himself.

"Yes, to die," he repeated in a gruff tone, opened both eyes suddenly, and closed them again.

Speechless with horror, M. Chasle stared at the puffy, inert face, which seemed already corpse-like. Had Clotilde been right? In that case, what about himself? The prospect of a penniless old age loomed up before him.

M. Chasle began trembling as he always did when he had to screw up his courage; soundlessly he slipped off his chair.

"There comes an hour," M. Thibault went on in a low voice—he was already on the brink of sleep—"there comes an hour when rest is all one yearns for. Death should have no terrors for a Christian."

With closed eyes he listened to the echoes of the words he had just uttered buzzing in his head. He gave a start on hearing M. Chasle's voice almost in his ear.

"That's so. Death should have no terrors." The little man was scared by his own temerity. He stammered: "Yes, indeed, for me, M—Mother's death . . ." He stopped short, as if his breath had failed him.

A set of false teeth, which he had only recently begun wearing, gave him difficulty in speaking. It was a prize he had won in a puzzle competition promoted by a dental institute in the South of France, the specialty of which was treatment by correspondence and the supply of dentures built to fit the wax impressions sent by their clients. As a matter of fact M. Chasle found his false teeth quite satisfactory, provided he took them out for meals and when he had a good deal to say. He had developed a technique of jerking them out of his mouth and catching them in his handkerchief, while pretending to sneeze. He did so now.

Freed from his incubus, he spoke more briskly.

"For me, too, my mother's death—would you believe it?—has no terrors. Why should I be afraid of it? Still, it's a quiet time for us just now with her away in the Home; and a quiet time, that's what makes the charm of life, even in childhood."

He paused again, trying to link up what he had said with what he had in mind.

"I don't live by myself, you know; that's why I said 'for us.' Perhaps you know it, sir? Aline has stayed on with me; she used to be Mother's servant. And Dédette, her niece, the little girl M. Antoine operated on, that famous night. Yes," he added with a smile that lit up his face with a sudden glow of tenderest affection, "the little girl's living with us; why, she even calls me 'Uncle Jules'—it's a way she's got into. What makes it so funny is that I'm not really her uncle."

The smile died from his lips and a shadow crossed his face. Then he blurted out in a rather harsh voice:

"Three mouths to feed, my word, that takes a lot of money!"

With an unwonted familiarity he had edged up quite near the bed, as if he had some pressing information to convey, but he was careful not to look M. Thibault in the face.

Taken by surprise, the invalid had not yet quite closed his eyes, and now was scrutinizing M. Chasle. The little man's remarks, for all their incoherence, seemed to be hovering round some unstated project; there was something unusual, not to say disquieting, about it all that vanquished M. Thibault's desire to be left to sleep.

Suddenly M. Chasle stepped back and fell to pacing up and down the room. His shoes were squeaking, but now he paid no heed to this. When he spoke again there was a certain bitterness in his voice.

"What's more, the thought of my own death doesn't scare me, either. When all is said and done, that's my Maker's concern, not mine. But life's a different story. Ah, yes, I'm afraid of life, and I don't deny it. Growing old, you know." He turned on his heel and murmured: "Eh?" in a puzzled voice, before continuing. "I'd saved up ten thousand francs. I brought them one evening to the Superannuates' Home. 'Here's my mother and here's ten thousand francs. Take them!' That was the fee they charged. Things like that oughtn't to be allowed. It meant a quiet life, that's sure—but ten thousand francs . . . I ask you! All my savings. What about Dédette? Nothing in hand, nothing coming in. Less than nothing, as Aline's advanced me two thousand francs, her own money. For our living expenses, just to keep us afloat. Now suppose we reckon it out; the four hundred francs a month I'm getting here isn't such a great deal. Not for the three of us. The little girl, you see, she needs her bread and butter too. She's only an apprentice and doesn't earn anything as yet, so she costs money. But I ask you to believe me, sir, on my Bible oath—we're thrifty folk. Thrifty about everything, even the newspapers; nowadays we read the old ones that we'd put by." There was a quaver in his voice. "I hope you'll excuse me, sir, if I'm lowering myself by telling you about the newspapers. But such things oughtn't to be allowed, no, they shouldn't indeed, after twenty centuries of our Christian era, not to mention all they say about our civilization."

There was a slight flutter of M. Thibault's hands, but M. Chasle could not bring himself to look towards the bed. He began speaking again.

"Suppose I stopped getting those four hundred francs, what would become of us?" Turning away towards the window, he cocked his ear as if hoping to hear "voices." Then abruptly, as though a sudden light had come to him, he exclaimed: "Why, of course! A legacy!" Almost at once he frowned. "Heaven knows, four thousand eight hundred francs, that's the very least the three of us can do on. Well, if God is just and merciful to us, He'll provide a bit of capital to yield that much. Yes, sir, He'll send us a—a little nest-egg."

He took out his pocket-handkerchief and mopped his forehead, as if he had just put forth a herculean effort.

" 'Have confidence, M. Chasle!' That's what they're always saying —the gentlemen at Saint Roch's, for instance. 'It isn't as if you didn't have a protector. *You* have nothing to fear.' Well, I'm not denying it; it's not as if I hadn't a protector. And, as for confidence, I'd be only too glad to have that too. Only I'd like to have that bit of capital first, that nest-egg."

He had halted at the bedside, but still refrained from looking towards M. Thibault. "It'd be easier to have confidence," he murmured, "if one could be *sure*. Yes, indeed, sir!"

Little by little his gaze, like a bird that is getting over its first panic, was hovering nearer the old man; lightly it skimmed the face upon the pillows, sped back and settled on the quiet brows, fluttered away again, again alighted, and finally came to rest for good, as if it had been snared, on the closed eyes. The light was failing now. When at last M. Thibault's eyelids lifted, he saw across the dusk M. Chasle's eyes riveted on his.

The surprise finally dispelled his lethargy. For a long time past he had regarded it as his duty to provide for his secretary's future by a legacy; indeed the bequest was explicitly included in his will. But it seemed to him essential that the beneficiary should be unaware of this until the will was read. M. Thibault, who thought he understood human nature, mistrusted everyone. He believed that if M. Chasle got wind of the bequest, he would cease being a punctual employee—and his generosity would defeat itself. "I think I get your meaning, M. Chasle." His tone was amiable.

A sudden flush rose to the secretary's cheeks, and he looked away. M. Thibault pondered for some moments before continuing.

"But—how shall I put it?—isn't there more courage, in certain cases, in rejecting a suggestion such as yours, on the strength of well-established principles, than in yielding to it, without consideration, out of blindness or a false sentiment of charity—out of weakness, in a word?"

Standing at the bedside, M. Chasle nodded meekly. The tone of self-assurance in his employer's harangues always had such a compelling effect on him, and he was so used to falling in with all M. Thibault's opinions, that now as usual he was quite unable to stand up against them. Only later did it strike him that, by thus agreeing with what had just been said, he was approving the frustration of his hopes. He resigned himself at once. He was used to disappointments. How often had he made the most legitimate petitions in his prayers—and they had not been granted! But he did not rebel, for that, against Divine Providence. And M. Thibault, likewise, had come to be credited by his secretary with supreme, impenetrable wisdom, to which, as a matter of course, he bowed.

He had resigned himself to silence and assent with such finality that he decided to put back his artificial teeth. He thrust his hand into his pocket. His cheeks went scarlet. The plate was no longer there.

Meanwhile M. Thibault was placidly continuing his homily. "Don't you realize, M. Chasle, that when you handed over your savings, the fruits of honest toil, to a secular and questionable institution like that Home, you were the victim of sharp practice? For we could easily have found some religious institution where old folk are looked after free of charge, provided the applicant is penniless and backed by somebody of influence? Were I to fall in with what you seem to be requesting, and include you in the provisions of my will, isn't it obvious that, when I'm gone, you'd fall again into the clutches of some swindler who would drain you of the last sou of my bequest?"

But M. Chasle had stopped listening. He could remember having taken out his handkerchief; then, presumably, the set of false teeth had dropped on the carpet. He had a horrid vision of this all-too-revealing—possibly malodorous—appliance, in the rude hands of strangers. Craning his neck, his eyes starting out of his head, he was peering under each piece of furniture, flustered and fluttering about like a scared hen.

M. Thibault noticed him, and now was stirred to compassion. "I might increase that legacy," he thought.

Thinking it would calm his secretary's ruffled feelings, he went on in a genial tone.

"And after all, M. Chasle, isn't it a mistake we often make, comparing penury with poverty? Penury, of course, is deplorable; it's an evil counsellor, for one thing. But poverty—isn't it often a manifestation, in a disguised form, of God's grace?"

His employer's voice came in vague, fitful gusts to M. Chasle's ears, which were buzzing like those of a drowning man. He made an effort to collect his scattered wits, patted the pockets of his coat and waistcoat, thrust a despairing hand under his coat-tails. Suddenly a cry of joy all but escaped his lips. There they were, the false teeth, entangled in his bunch of keys!

M. Thibault was still discoursing on the same topic. "For a Christian, has poverty ever been incompatible with happiness? And is not the inequality of worldly goods a prime condition of social equilibrium?"

"Rather!" M. Chasle exclaimed, with a little gleeful chuckle and rubbing his hands. Then he added absent-mindedly: "That's just what makes the charm of it."

M. Thibault's energy was flagging, but he turned his eyes towards the little man, touched to find him displaying such proper sentiments, and pleased to feel himself approved of. He made a special effort to be agreeable.

"Yes, M. Chasle, I've instilled sound methods into you, and, with your careful, painstaking habits, I don't doubt that you'll always find employment." After a pause he added: "Even if I left this world before you."

The calmness with which M. Thibault contemplated the misfortunes of such as would outlive him had a sedative effect that was contagious. Moreover, the vast relief that M. Chasle was feeling had for the time being allayed all his worries for the future. His eyes were twinkling with joy behind the glasses as he exclaimed:

"Yes, sir, as far as that's concerned, you can die in peace! I can always keep my head above water, that's sure! I've got several strings to my bow, I have. Useful inventions, gadgets, as they call them, and so forth," he added with a laugh. "I have it all worked out already, my little plan. A business I'm going to start—when you're gone."

The invalid opened one eye wide; M. Chasle's involuntary thrust had struck home. "When you're gone"! What exactly did the old fool mean by that?

Just as M. Thibault was about to put a question, the nurse entered and turned on the switches, flooding the room with sudden light. Like a schoolboy when the bell rings to announce the end of lessons, M. Chasle deftly swept his papers together and with little gestures of farewell slipped out.

II

IT WAS time for M. Thibault's enema. The nurse had already whisked back the sheets and now was bustling round the bed, making the ritual gestures. M. Thibault was brooding. His mind was haunted by M. Chasle's last remark and, above all, by the tone in which he had made it. "When you're gone." In so natural, so matter-of-fact a tone! Obviously for M. Chasle it was a foregone conclusion that his employer was to "go" in the very near future. "The graceless fool!" M. Thibault muttered irritably. He was only too glad to give way to his vexation; it took his thoughts off the question hovering in the back of his mind.

The nurse had rolled up her sleeves. "Up with you!" she called out briskly.

She had no easy task. A thick layer of towels had to be built in beneath the invalid. M. Thibault was heavy and gave no assistance, merely letting himself be rolled this way and that, like a dead body. But each movement cost him a stab of pain along his legs and in the hollow of his back, and the physical pain was worsened by mental distress. Each phase of this daily ordeal was another outrage to his pride and sense of decency.

Sister Céline had developed a tactless habit of seating herself at the foot of the bed during the period, more prolonged each day, while they waited for her ministrations to take effect. At first her nearness at such a moment had infuriated the invalid. Now he put up with it; perhaps, indeed, he preferred not being left to himself.

His eyes shut, with wrinkled brows, M. Thibault was turning over and over in his mind that nerve-racking question: Am I really in such a bad way? He opened his eyes, which by chance alighted on the bed-pan that the nurse had placed within easy reach and well in view on the chest of drawers. Huge, absurd, it loomed before him with an air of insolent expectancy. He looked away.

The nurse turned the brief respite to account by telling her beads.

"Pray for me, Sister," M. Thibault suddenly remarked in a tense whisper, more solicitous and earnest than his usual tone.

She finished the last ave, then replied: "I do, sir, indeed; several times a day."

There was a short silence, broken abruptly by M. Thibault.

"I am very ill, Sister, as you know. Very, very ill." The words caught in his throat; he sounded on the brink of tears.

She protested, with a rather forced smile. "Very ill! What an idea!"

But M. Thibault was not to be convinced. "Everyone shirks telling me the truth. But I can feel it in my bones; I shall never get well again." Noticing she did not interrupt, he added with a certain challenge in his tone: "Yes, I know that I have only a little while to live."

He was watching her. Shaking her head, she went on with the prayer.

M. Thibault became alarmed.

"I wish the Abbé Vécard to come at once," he said in a hoarse voice.

The nun merely protested: "Oh, you received Holy Communion last Saturday! There can be nothing on your conscience now."

M. Thibault made no reply. His forehead was beaded with sweat, his jaws were chattering. The enema was beginning to take effect—seconded by his fears.

"The bed-pan!" he gasped.

A minute later, in the pause between two spasms of colic, two groans, he shot an angry glance at the nun.

"I'm getting weaker," he panted, "every day. I've got to see—to see the Abbé."

She was too busy pouring hot water into the basin to notice the desperate anxiety with which he was watching her expression.

"As you like," she said evasively, then put back the kettle and tested the water with her finger. Without raising her eyes, she went on mumbling over the basin.

". . . can never be too careful," was all that M. Thibault caught.

His head dropped over his breast; he gritted his teeth.

A few minutes later, after a wash and change of nightshirt, he was lying in cool, clean sheets—with nothing to do but to nurse his pain.

Sister Céline was back in her chair, still toying with her beads. The ceiling light had been put out, and the room was lit only by a low table-lamp. There was nothing to take the sufferer's mind off his apprehensions, or the neuralgic, lancinating pains which grew sharper and sharper, shooting along the posterior surface of his thighs and radiating in every direction, then becoming suddenly localized, as sharp, stabbing twinges, in definite spots on his loin, knee-caps, and ankle-joints. During the momentary lulls when the pain sank to a dull ache, the irritation of the bed-sores left him no peace.

M. Thibault opened his eyes, and stared into vacancy, while his all-too-lucid thoughts turned in the same sad circle: "What do they all really think? Can one be in danger without knowing it? How find out the truth?"

Noticing that her patient was suffering more and more pain, the nurse decided to make the nightly injection of a half-dose of morphine at an earlier hour.

M. Thibault did not see her going out. Suddenly he found he was alone, left helpless before the malignant influences hovering in the silent, darkened room, and a wild panic came over him. He tried to cry out, but just then the pain came back with unwonted violence; he tugged frantically at the bell.

It was Adrienne who rushed into the room.

He was unable to speak; only hoarse, meaningless sounds broke from his writhing lips. The sudden effort he made to draw himself up into a sitting position seemed to be tearing his body in two. He sank back, groaning, onto the pillow.

At last he managed to speak. "What do they mean by leaving me to die, all by myself? Where's the sister? Send for the Abbé. No, fetch Antoine. Quickly!"

Panic-stricken, the maid stared at the old man; the consternation in her eyes was the last straw.

"Go away! Fetch M. Antoine. D'you hear me? Immediately!"

The sister came back with the hypodermic syringe ready. She saw the maid rush past her out of the room, but had no idea what could have occurred. Sprawled half across the bolster, M. Thibault was paying the penalty of his excitement with a new bout of pain. As it happened, he was in a good position for the injection.

"Don't move," the sister said, uncovering his shoulder; and without more ado she pressed the needle home.

Antoine was stepping forth into the street when Adrienne caught up with him.

He ran up the stairs at once.

As he entered, M. Thibault turned his head. Antoine's presence, which in his panic he had invoked with no great hope that it could prove forthcoming, was an immediate solace. He murmured mechanically:

"Ah, so there you are!"

The injection was already beginning to take effect: he felt better. Propped on two cushions, with his arms stretched out, he was inhaling a few drops of ether which the sister had sprinkled on a handkerchief. Through the opening of the nightshirt Antoine could see the old man's emaciated neck, and his Adam's apple jutting between two stringy muscles. The nerveless immobility of the forehead was in striking contrast with the constant tremor of the heavy under-jaw. The huge cranium, the ears, and large, flat temples had something of the pachyderm about them.

"Well, Father, what is it?" Antoine smiled.

M. Thibault made no reply, but for some moments stared at his son; then he closed his eyes. He would have liked to cry: "Tell me the truth. Is everybody hoodwinking me? Am I really going to die? Speak out, Antoine—and save me!" But he was tongue-tied by the steadily increasing deference he felt towards his son, and by a super-stitious dread that if he put his apprehensions into words he would suddenly give them an inexorable reality.

Antoine's eyes met the sister's gaze, which led them towards the table where the thermometer was lying. He went up to it and saw it read 102. The sudden rise puzzled him; till now there had been practically no fever. Going back to the bed, he took his father's pulse, more to tranquillize the patient than for any diagnostic reason.

"The pulse is good," he said almost at once. "What's wrong?"

"What's wrong? I'm suffering the torments of the damned!" M. Thibault exclaimed. "I've been in pain all day. I—I nearly died. Isn't that so?" He shot an imperious glance at the nurse. Then his tone changed and a look of fear came into his eyes. "You mustn't leave me, Antoine. I'm so nervous, you know. I'm afraid it may start again."

Antoine's compassion was aroused. As it happened, there was no urgent reason for him to go out. He promised to stay with his father till dinner-time.

"I had an appointment," he said, "but I'll ring up and call it off."

Sister Céline followed him to the study, where the telephone was installed.

"What sort of day did he have?"

"Not too good. I had to make the first injection at noon, and I've just given him another. A half-dose," she added. "But the real trouble's his state of mind. He has such terrible ideas. 'Everyone's lying to

me,' he says. 'I want to see the Abbé, I'm going to die,' and heaven
knows what else."

Antoine's troubled eyes seemed asking a specific question: "Do you
think it possible that he suspects . . . ?" The nun, no longer daring
to say no, merely nodded.

Antoine thought it over. That was not enough to explain the temperature, in his opinion.

"What we've got to do"—he made an emphatic gesture—"is to root
out immediately the least trace of suspicion from his mind." There
flashed across his mind a method, fantastically rash, but drastic; he
kept it to himself. "The first thing," he continued, "is to make sure
that he has a calm evening. Please have another eighth of a grain of
morphine ready to give him when I tell you."

He re-entered the bedroom with a cheerful exclamation. "I've fixed
it! I'm free till seven." His voice had its incisive ring, and his face the
tense, determined look he wore at the hospital. Now, however, he
was smiling.

"There was the devil to pay! When I rang up the house where the
little girl is ill, her grandmother answered. The poor old thing was
dreadfully upset. She kept on wailing down the phone: 'What?
You can't mean it, doctor? Won't you be coming this evening?'"
He suddenly assumed an air of consternation. "'I'm so sorry,
but I've just been called to the bedside of my father, who is dangerously ill.'" (M. Thibault's face grew tense.) "But a woman isn't
put off so easily. She said: 'I had no idea! What's he suffering
from?'"

Carried away by his temerity, Antoine scarcely hesitated a moment
before taking the last, fantastic plunge.

"What was I to say? Guess! I said to her, cool as a cucumber: 'My
father, Madame, if you want to know, has a . . . a prostatic cancer!'"
He added with a nervous laugh: "After all, why not? While I was
about it."

He saw the nurse's arm (she was pouring water into a tumbler)
go rigid. And suddenly he realized that he was playing with fire;
almost he lost his nerve. But it was too late to draw back now.

He burst out laughing.

"But that lie, Father, I set down to your account, you know."

On the bed M. Thibault seemed to be listening with every fibre of his being. His body was taut; only the hand on the counterpane was trembling. Never could the most precise denials have swept away his fears so utterly. Antoine's diabolical audacity had, with òne deft stroke, laid low the phantoms of his mind, and brought the sick man back to hope and confidence. Opening both eyes, he looked at his son, and could not bring himself, it seemed, to drop the lids again. A new emotion, a warm glow of affection, was quickening in the old man's heart. He tried to speak, but a sort of dizziness came over him, and at last, after a brief smile of which the young man caught a fleeting glimpse, he shut his eyes once more.

Any man other than Antoine in a like case would have mopped his brow, murmuring perhaps: "Ouf! That was a close shave!" But Antoine, only a trifle paler than before and well pleased with himself, was thinking merely: "The main thing for stunts like that is to make up one's mind, definitely, to bring them off."

Some minutes passed. Antoine would not meet the sister's eyes. M. Thibault's arm moved; then he spoke, as if continuing a discussion.

"In that case, will you explain why I've more and more pain? It looks almost as if the drugs you're pumping into me made it more acute, instead of . . ."

"Of course," Antoine broke in. "Of course they make it more acute; that's what shows they're taking effect."

"Really?"

M. Thibault asked nothing better than to let himself be convinced. And, as in point of fact the afternoon had not been quite so trying as he made out, he felt almost sorry that his sufferings had not lasted longer.

"What do you feel just now?" Antoine asked. The rise in his father's temperature worried him.

If M. Thibault had been frank, he would have replied: "I'm feeling extremely comfortable." Instead he muttered: "I've a pain in my legs, and a dull ache in the small of my back."

"I passed a sound at three," Sister Céline put in.

"And a sort of weight, a feeling of oppression, here . . ."

Antoine nodded. "Yes, it's rather curious," he began, turning to the sister. He had no idea this time what new story he was going to concoct. "I'm thinking of certain—certain phenomena I've observed in connexion with changes of treatment. Thus in skin diseases, we often get unlooked-for results by using different treatments alternately. I dare say Thérivier and I were wrong in deciding to use so continuously this serum, Number—er—17.

"Most certainly you were wrong." M. Thibault spoke with firm conviction.

Good-humouredly Antoine broke in. "But that's your fault, Father. You're in such a hurry to get well. We've been forcing the pace, that's it." Turning to the sister, he addressed her with the utmost gravity. "Where did you put the ampoules I brought yesterday—the D 92, you know?"

She made an awkward gesture; not because she had the least objection to mystifying a patient, but because she had some difficulty in finding her way about amongst all the new "serums" Antoine kept on inventing whenever the occasion arose.

"Please make an injection immediately with D 92. I want it made before the effects of Number 17 have worn off. I'd like to see how the mixture affects the blood."

M. Thibault had noticed the nurse's hesitant air, and his glance in her direction had not escaped Antoine. To cut short any suspicion that might have been aroused, he added:

"I'm afraid you'll find this injection a bit more painful, Father. D 92 is less fluid than the others. But that's only a moment's discomfort. Unless I'm greatly mistaken, you'll feel very much relieved tonight."

Antoine said to himself: "I'm getting smarter at this sort of thing every day," and noted it with satisfaction, as a sign of his professional progress. Moreover, in the macabre game he was playing, there was not only a constant element of difficulty but a spice of risk, which, Antoine had to own, appealed to him.

The sister came back.

M. Thibault submitted to the injection with a certain nervousness; before the needle had even touched his skin, he began to whimper.

"Most painful, this new stuff of yours," he muttered, when it was over. "Much thicker than the other. Like liquid fire under the skin. And it has a smell—don't you notice? The other, anyhow, was scentless."

Antoine had sat down. He made no reply. There was not the faintest difference between this last injection and the one before it; the ampoules came out of the same box, the needle and the hand that used it were identical. Only—it was supposed to have a different label. Yes, he thought, one has only to set the mind off on a wrong track, and all the senses "play up" to the delusion. What feeble instruments, those senses of ours, which we fancy infallible! And what of that childish craving we all have, to humour our intellect at all costs? Even for a sick man the tragedy of tragedies is not to "understand." Once we have managed to give a name to what is happening and assign to it a plausible cause, once our poor brain contrives to link up two ideas with a show of logic, we're pleased as Punch. "And yet," Antoine murmured, "surely intelligence is the one fixed point in the eternal flux. Without it, where'd we be?"

M. Thibault had closed his eyes again.

Antoine signed to Sister Céline to leave the room. They had noticed that the patient was apt to be more fretful when they were together at his bedside.

Though Antoine had been seeing his father daily, he was struck now by the change in his appearance. The skin had an amber translucence, and a peculiar gloss that augured ill. The face was puffier than ever, and flabby pouches had formed under the eyes. The nose, however, had shrunk to a long, lean ridge, which oddly changed the whole expression of the face.

The old man made a movement. Little by little his features were growing animated, losing their moroseness. And between the eyelids, which parted more and more frequently, the dilated pupils had an unwonted brilliance.

"The double injection is taking effect," Antoine thought. "In a few moments he'll be getting talkative!"

M. Thibault was experiencing a sort of general relaxation and a desire for repose, all the more agreeable for being unaccompanied by any sense of weariness. Nevertheless, his thoughts still turned on his death; only, now that he no longer believed in it, he found it possible, not to say pleasant, to discourse about it. What with the added stimulus of the morphine, he was unable to resist the temptation of staging, for his own benefit and his son's, the edifying spectacle of a Christian deathbed.

"Listen to me, Antoine!" he said abruptly, in a solemn tone. Then, without more preamble, he began: "In the will that you find after my death . . ." He made a slight pause, like an actor waiting for his cue.

Good-humouredly Antoine played his part. "Really, Father," he exclaimed, "I didn't know you were in such a hurry to see the last of us!" He laughed. "Why, only a moment ago I was pointing out how eager you were to get back into harness again."

Satisfied, the old man raised a monitory hand.

"Let me speak, my boy. It is possible that, on the strictly scientific view, my life is not in danger. But within myself I know . . . I have a feeling that . . . In any case, death . . . The good—alas, so little!—that I have tried to do in this world will be set down to my account. And, if the day has come when . . ." He cast a fleeting glance at Antoine to make sure the incredulous smile was still on his lips. "Well, we must not lose heart. God's mercy is infinite."

Antoine listened in silence.

"But that's not what I wanted to talk to you about. At the end of my will, you'll find a list of bequests. Old servants. I'd specially like to draw your attention to that codicil, my boy. It's several years old now. Perhaps I haven't been quite . . . quite generous enough. I'm thinking of M. Chasle. That worthy man owes much to me, I grant you. Indeed he owes everything to me. But that's no reason why his . . . his devotion should not be rewarded, even if the reward's . . . superfluous."

His remarks were frequently interrupted by coughing, which obliged him to stop and take breath. "It looks as if the disease is rapidly becoming generalized," Antoine thought. "That cough is getting worse, so is the nausea. The tumour must be invading other parts of the body. The lungs and stomach are involved. His vitality's at the mercy of the first complication that may arise."

"I have always," continued M. Thibault, whom the drug was rendering at once more lucid and more incoherent, "I have always been proud of belonging to that prosperous middle class which in all ages has been the mainstay of my country and my Church. But, my boy, that relative affluence imposes certain duties." Again his thoughts took a new turn. "You, Antoine, have a most regrettable tendency; you're much too self-centred." He spoke abruptly, casting an angry look at his son. "But you'll change when you grow up." He corrected himself. "When you're older and, like me, have founded a family. A family," he repeated. The word "family," which he always spoke with a certain emphasis, called forth a host of vagrant echoes in his mind, fragments of speeches he had made in former days. Once more he dropped the thread of his thoughts. His voice grew orotund. "Undoubtedly, my boy, once we grant that the family must be regarded as the germ-cell of the social organism, is not its proper function to build up that . . . that plebeian aristocracy from which the leaders of the nation will henceforth be recruited? Ah, the Family! I ask you, are we not the pivot on which turn the middle-class democracies of today?"

"Why, of course, Father; I quite agree with you," Antoine said gently.

The old man seemed not to hear him. Gradually his tone was becoming less pompous, and his real meaning easier to grasp.

"You'll grow out of it, my boy. I'm positive of that, and so's the Abbé. You'll get over certain views of life, and my prayer is that the change of heart may come quite soon. Ah, Antoine, how I wish that change had come already! When I am about to leave this world, isn't it a bitter thought that my son . . . ? Brought up as you were, living under this roof, should you not have . . . ? Some religious zeal, in short. A faith that's more robust, more loyal to its duties."

Antoine was thinking: "If he had the least idea of what my 'faith' amounts to!"

"Who knows," M. Thibault sighed, "if God will not set it down against me? Ah, if only that dear, departed saint, your mother, had not been taken from us so soon, had been spared to help me in that Christian duty!"

Tears were welling up between his eyelids; Antoine watched them brim over and trickle down the old cheeks. He had not expected this, and could not help being stirred by emotion, which increased when he heard his father's next remark. M. Thibault began speaking in a confidential, almost urgent undertone that Antoine had not heard before; and he now was perfectly coherent.

"I have other accounts to render to my Maker. For Jacques's death. Poor lad! Did I do all I should have done for the boy? I wanted to be firm; I was hard. Yes, I accuse myself before the judgment seat of having been hard towards my son. I never managed to win his trust. Nor yours, Antoine. No, don't protest; that's the truth. It was God's will to withhold from me my children's trust. My two sons! They've respected me, feared me; but from their youth up, they've kept aloof from me. Pride! Mine, and theirs. . . . And yet, did I not do my whole duty by them? Didn't I make them over to the Church from their early years? Didn't I take the utmost care of their education? Ingratitude! O Father in heaven, judge if the fault was mine. Jacques was always up in arms against me. And yet . . . ! How could I possibly give my consent to that . . . to such a thing? How could I?"

He was silent for a moment, then suddenly exclaimed: "Go away, shameless son!"

Antoine stared at his father in bewilderment. The words were obviously not addressed to him. Was the old man getting delirious? His jaws were set, his forehead clammy with sweat; he was waving his arms as if bereft of reason.

"Go away!" he said again. "Have you forgotten all you owe to your father, to his name and rank? Are they nothing to you—the family honour, your soul's salvation? There are certain acts which— which take effect beyond ourselves, which imperil all traditions. I'll— I'll break you! Go away!" Fits of coughing cut across the phrases. He took a deep breath. His voice sank lower still. "O Lord, I am not assured of Thy forgiveness. . . . 'What did you make of your son?'"

Antoine broke in. "Father . . . !"

"Alas, I failed to shield him. Evil influences. The plotting of those Huguenots. . . ."

Antoine thought: "Ah, the Huguenots again!" No one had ever discovered the origin of the old man's fixed idea about the "Huguenots." Antoine's theory was that shortly after Jacques's disappearance, while the inquiries were still in progress, thanks to some indiscretion, M. Thibault had discovered that throughout the previous summer Jacques had been seeing a great deal of the Fontanins, at Maisons-Laffitte. From that moment there had been no way of shaking the old Catholic's obsession; blinded by his aversion for all Protestants, harking back presumably to memories of Jacques's escapade to Marseille in Daniel's company, and perhaps confounding the present with the past, he had never ceased to hold the Fontanins wholly responsible for his son's disappearance.

"Where are you going?" he shouted, trying to raise himself on the pillow.

Then he opened his eyes, and seemed to take heart when, through his tears, he saw Antoine beside him.

"Poor lad!" he murmured brokenly. "Those Huguenots lured him away. Yes, they stole him from us, my boy. It's all their fault. They drove him to suicide."

"Oh, come, Father!" Antoine exclaimed. "Why do you persist in imagining that he . . . ?"

"He killed himself. He went away; he went off and killed himself." Antoine seemed to hear a faint whisper, "My curse"; but the words were meaningless; he concluded he had been mistaken. The rest of the phrase was stifled by weak, heart-rending sobs, which gave place to a fit of coughing that died down almost at once.

Antoine had an impression that his father was falling asleep, and was careful not to make a sound.

Some silent minutes passed.

"Antoine!"

Antoine gave a start.

"That boy, Aunt Marie's son—do you remember Aunt Marie who lived at Quillebœuf? No, of course you can't have known her. Well, he—he did the same thing. I was a youngster when it happened. With his shotgun one evening; he'd been out shooting. They never learned . . ."

In a half-dream, his mind adrift on a flood of memories, M. Thibault was smiling to himself.

"How she used to rile Mamma with her songs—she was always singing! What was that song now? About the 'pretty pony,' 'clinkety-clankety' something. During the summer vacation, at Quillebœuf. You didn't know old Niqueux's rickety wagon, of course. Ha! Ha! Ha! That time the servants' luggage tumbled off it. Ha! Ha! Ha!"

Antoine rose abruptly; his father's merriment was even more painful than his sobs. During the past few weeks M. Thibault had often shown a tendency, especially after the injections, to hark back to trivial details of bygone days. In the old brain, half emptied now of memories, these details took on an amplitude, like murmurs in a hollow shell. Then for days on end he would con them over and over, laughing to himself like a baby.

Turning cheerfully to Antoine, he began singing in a soft, almost childish voice:

> "I have a pretty pony,
> And her name is . . . something trot,
> And I wouldn't give my pony
> For all the—yes—all the gold you've got.
> So clinkety and clankety . . ."

"There!" he exclaimed petulantly. "I've gone and forgotten the rest. Mademoiselle knows that song, too, quite well. She used to sing it when Gise was little."

He had ceased thinking of Jacques's death, and of his own. And indefatigably, till Antoine left, he delved into his memories of Quille-bœuf, trying to piece together the old nursery song.

III

ALONE now with Sister Céline, M. Thibault had recovered his solemnity. He bade her bring his soup, and submitted, without a word, to being spoon-fed. After they had said the evening prayer together, he had her turn off the ceiling light.

"Sister, will you be kind enough to ask Mademoiselle to come? And send for the servants, please; I wish to speak to them."

Though put out at being disturbed at such an hour, Mlle. de Waize hobbled across to the bedroom at once and halted, out of breath, just inside the door. In vain she tried to raise her eyes towards the bed; her bent back made it impossible for her to see above the chair-legs and, in the zone of lamplight, the mended places in the carpet. When the nun brought up a chair for her, Mademoiselle recoiled in horror. She would rather have stayed like a water-fowl perched on one leg for ten consecutive hours than let her skirts come in contact with that germ-infested chair.

Ill at ease, the two maids kept as near each other as they could, two dark forms lit up, now and again, by the flickering firelight.

M. Thibault meditated for some moments. His conversation with Antoine had not been enough; he was torn by an irresistible desire to round off the evening with another dramatic scene.

"I feel"—he gave a slight cough—"I feel that my last hour is rapidly approaching, and I desire to take advantage of a brief respite from my pain, the cruel sufferings that are imposed on me, to bid you farewell."

The sister, who was busy folding towels, stopped short in amazement; Mademoiselle and the two servants were too startled to say a word. For a moment M. Thibault fancied that the announcement of his death came as a surprise to no one, and a hideous fear gripped his heart. Fortunately, the sister had more presence of mind than the others, and exclaimed: "But, M. Thibault, you're getting better every day! How can you talk about dying? What would the doctor say if he heard?"

At once M. Thibault felt his moral courage revive; and, frowning, made a feeble gesture, to impose silence on the babbler.

Then like a man reciting a set speech, he continued.

"On the eve of my appearance before the judgment seat of Heaven, I ask to be forgiven, forgiven by all. Too often I have lacked indulgence for others; I have been harsh, and perhaps wounded the feelings of my . . . of those who live under my roof. Now I acknowledge my . . . my debts . . . the debts I owe to all of you. To you, Clotilde and Adrienne, and, above all, to your good mother who is now confined to a bed of suffering, as I am. And lastly, to you, Mademoiselle, you who gave up . . ."

At this point Adrienne burst into tears so copious that M. Thibault all but broke down himself. He gulped a sob down, hiccuped; then, recovering his self-control, proceeded:

". . . you who abandoned a quiet, unpretentious existence, to come and take your place in our bereaved home and . . . and tend the sacred flame, the flame of our family life. Who was there better qualified than you to . . . to look after the children, whose dear mother you had brought up from her earliest days?"

Whenever he halted to take breath, the women's sobs could be heard in the dark background. The little spinster's back was more hunched than ever, her head bobbed up and down, and in the pauses a faint sucking sound came from her quivering lips.

"We owe it to you, and to your constant care, that the family has been enabled to follow its appointed course, under the eye of Heaven. For this I thank you, Mademoiselle, in public; and it is to you, Mademoiselle, that I address a final request. When that last, dread moment comes . . ." The effect of the words was so devastating that to master his brief panic M. Thibault paused and took stock of his present state, the comfortable afterglow of the morphine injection, before continuing. "When the dread moment comes, I would ask you, Mademoiselle, to say aloud that noble prayer—you know the one I mean—the 'Litany for a Happy Death,' which I read with you at the deathbed of my . . . my poor wife, in this same room—do you remember?—under that crucifix."

His dim eyes strove to pierce the shadows. Of the bedroom furniture, mahogany upholstered in blue rep, nothing had been changed. In this selfsame setting years ago, at Rouen, he had seen his parents die. Then, in his youth, he had brought it with him to Paris, and later, it had furnished the bedroom he had shared with his wife. In this bed Antoine had been born one cold March night, and nine years later, on another winter's night, his wife had died in it, bringing Jacques into the world. A picture formed before his eyes of the white, wasted form laid out on the huge, violet-strewn bed.

His voice shook with emotion as he went on:

"And I trust that my dearly loved wife, that saintly soul, will befriend me when I meet my Maker . . . will inspire me with her courage, her resignation . . . yes, the courage she displayed in her last hour." He closed his eyes, and with an awkward effort folded his hands. He seemed asleep.

Sister Céline signed to the maids to leave the room as quietly as possible. Before leaving their master, they gazed earnestly at his face, as if already taking their last leave of a body laid out for burial. The sound of Adrienne's sobs and Clotilde's subdued, flustered chatter —she had given the old lady an arm—receded down the corridor. At a loss where to turn, the three women with one accord took refuge in the kitchen, round the table. All were weeping. Clotilde decreed that none of them must go to bed, so as to be ready to go and fetch a priest at a moment's notice. No sooner had she spoken than she began grinding coffee.

The nun was alone in knowing how things really were; she was used to such scenes. In her view, the serenity of a dying man was always a proof that deep within his heart he believed—often enough quite wrongly—that his life was in no immediate danger. So now, after tidying the room and banking up the fire, she opened the folding bed on which she slept. Ten minutes later, without having exchanged a word with her patient, the nurse slipped tranquilly from prayer to sleep, as she did each night.

M. Thibault, however, had not fallen asleep. The double dose of morphine, while continuing its anodyne effect, was keeping him awake, in a voluptuous lethargy peopled with a host of schemes and fancies. The act of spreading panic around him seemed to have definitively cast out of his mind his own alarms. True, the heavy breathing of the sleeping nurse was rather irritating, but he consoled himself by picturing the day when he would dismiss her with a word of thanks —and a handsome donation to her Order. How much? Well, that could be settled afterwards . . . very soon. He was fretting with impatience for a return to active life. What was becoming of his charitable societies now he could not attend to them?

A log collapsed into the embers, and he half opened a sleepy eye. A little, vacillating flame set the shadows dancing on the ceiling. And suddenly with his mind's eye he saw himself, a lighted candle in his hand, groping his way along the corridor of Aunt Marie's house at Quillebœuf, that musty old corridor which smelt year in year out of apples and saltpetre. There, too, great shadows had suddenly loomed before him and gone dancing up across the ceiling. And he remembered the terrifying black spiders that always lurked at night in the dark corners of the closet. In his mind just now there was so little difference between the timorous boy of many years ago and the old man of today that it cost him an effort to distinguish between them.

The clock struck ten. Then the half-hour . . . Quillebœuf. The rickety old wagon. The poultry-yard. Léontine . . .

All this jetsam of the past, which a chance play of light had stirred in the abyss of memory, kept floating up to the surface of his mind, refused to be thrust down again into the depths. And like a desultory burden to these evocations of his childhood, the tune of the old nursery song ran in his head. He could as yet recall hardly any of the words, except the first few lines, which he had gradually pieced together, and part of the refrain which had unexpectedly flashed up across the twilight of his thoughts.

"I have a little pony
And her name is Trilbytrot,
And I would not give my pony
For all the gold you've got.
So clinkety and clankety
Along the lanes we go . . ."

The clock struck eleven.

"I have a little pony
And her name is Trilbytrot . . ."

IV

AT ABOUT four on the following day, it happened that the journey from one professional call to another took Antoine so near home that he dropped in to hear the latest news. That morning his father had seemed to him considerably weaker; the fever showed no sign of abating. He wondered if some new complication was setting in; or was it merely symptomatic of the general progress of the disease?

Antoine did not want to be seen by the invalid, who might have been alarmed by this unexpected visit, and therefore entered the dressing-room directly from the hall.

There he found Sister Céline, who reassured him in an undertone. So far the patient had had a fairly good day. For the moment M. Thibault was under the influence of a morphine injection. These repeated doses of the drug were becoming imperative, to enable him to bear the pain.

The door leading into the bedroom was not completely closed and a vague murmur, a sound of singing, could be heard. Antoine listened. The nurse shrugged her shoulders.

"He went on at me till I had to go and fetch Mademoiselle; he wanted her to sing him some old song or other. It's been running in his head all day; he can't talk of anything else."

Antoine tip-toed to the door. The little old lady's quavering voice floated to him across the silence.

> "I have a pretty pony
> And her name is Trilbytrot,
> And I would not give my pony
> For all the gold you've got,
> When clinkety and clankety
> Along the lanes we go
> To where my lovely Lola
> Is waiting for me now."

Then Antoine heard his father's voice like a wheezy bagpipe taking up the refrain.

> "When clinkety and clankety
> Along the lanes we go . . ."

The quavering soprano broke in again.

> "I'll cull me yonder floweret
> While Trilby browses near,
> The fairest, rarest floweret
> To deck my dark-eyed dear."

"That's it!" M. Thibault broke in triumphantly. "We have it! Aunt Marie could never get that right. She used to sing: 'La-la-la-la, my dear!' No words. 'La-la-la-la!' "

They joined in the chorus together.

> "Then clinkety and clankety
> Along the lanes we'll go
> To where my lovely Lola
> Is waiting for me now."

"Anyhow, he doesn't complain while he's at it," the sister whispered. Sad at heart, Antoine left the room.

As he was going out into the street, the concierge called to him from her doorstep. The postman had just delivered some letters for him. Antoine took them absent-mindedly. His thoughts were still on what was happening upstairs.

> "Then clinkety and clankety
> Along the lanes we go . . ."

He was amazed to find himself so distressed by his father's illness. When, a year earlier, he had realized that there was no hope of saving the old man, he had detected in himself a puzzling but indubitable affection for the father whom, as he had thought till now, he had never loved. It came to him then as a new-born impulse, and yet it somehow had the semblance of a very old, latent affection, which the approach of the irreparable had merely fanned to sudden flame. Moreover, as the malady dragged its course, natural emotion had been implemented by professional instinct; he felt a special interest in this patient, of whose death-sentence he alone was aware and whose last months it was his task to make as bearable as could be.

Antoine had begun walking down the street when his eyes fell on one of the letters in his hand. He stopped short.

M. Jacques Thibault
4A Rue de l'Université

Now and again a stray pamphlet or bookseller's catalogue addressed to Jacques still came in; a letter was quite another matter. . . . The envelope was pale blue, the address was written in a tall, flowing, faintly supercilious hand, whether a man's or a woman's was hard to say. Antoine turned back. This needed thinking over. He shut himself up in his office. But before even sitting down, he had boldly, unhesitatingly, opened the envelope.

The very first words came as a shock.

1A Place du Panthéon,
November 25, 1913.

Dear Sir,
    I have read your short story . . .

"A short story! So Jacques is a writer?" he murmured. Then, triumphantly: "He's alive. This proves it!" The words danced before his eyes. Feverishly he ran his eyes down the page, looking for the signature—"Jalicourt."

    I have read your short story with the keenest interest. Of course you do not expect an elderly "don" like myself . . .

Jalicourt! Antoine thought. Yes, it's Valdieu de Jalicourt, the professor, Member of the Academy and so forth. Antoine knew him well, by repute; in fact he had two or three books by Jalicourt on his shelves.

. . . to give it an unqualified approval; obviously the classical traditions in which my mind is moulded, not to say most of my personal preferences, run counter to the romantic technique you employ. I cannot wholeheartedly commend either the manner or the matter of your tale. But I must own that, even in its extravagances, this work is stamped by the creative impulse and a knowledge of human nature. Reading your story, I was several times reminded of a remark made by a great composer, a friend of mine, to whom a young musician—one, I imagine, of your clan—showed an experimental work of the most provocative audacity: "Take it away at once, sir; I might get to like it!"

Jalicourt.

Antoine was trembling with excitement. He sat down, unable to take his eyes off the letter lying open before him on the desk. Not that it came as any great surprise to learn his brother was alive; he had seen no reason to suppose Jacques had killed himself. The first effect the coming of this letter had had on him was to arouse his hunting instinct; three years earlier he had played the sleuth for months on end, following up each clue that seemed to lead towards the fugitive. And now, with the revival of his detective zeal, came a rush of such affection and so intense a longing to see Jacques again that he felt almost dizzy. Often lately—indeed, that very morning—he had had to fight down a feeling of resentment at being left alone to bear the brunt of his father's illness; so crushing was the burden that he could not help feeling aggrieved with the runaway brother who was deserting his post at such an hour.

This letter changed everything. Now it looked as if he could get in touch with Jacques, tell him what was happening, bring him back—and no longer stand alone.

He glanced at the address on the letter, then at the clock, then at his engagement-book.

"Right!" he murmured. "I've three more appointments this afternoon. Can't miss that one at half-past four, in the Avenue de Saxe; it's urgent. Must look up, too, those people in the Rue d'Artois, that scarlet fever case just starting; no time fixed, however. Number three: the child's

getting better; that can wait." He rose. "Yes, I'll go to the Avenue de
Saxe first, and see Jalicourt immediately after."

Antoine was in the Place du Panthéon soon after five. It was an old
house without an elevator. Anyway, he was feeling too impatient just
then to waste time with elevators. He raced up the stairs.

"M. Jalicourt is out. It's Wednesday. He has his lecture at the Ecole
Normale from five to six."

"Keep cool now!" Antoine admonished himself as he went down the
stairs. "There's just time to see that scarlet fever case."

At exactly six he alighted briskly from his taxi, outside the Ecole
Normale.

He recalled his visit to the principal just after his brother's disappearance; then, that already distant summer day when he had come
to this same grim-looking building with Jacques and Daniel, to learn
the results of the entrance examination.

"The lecture isn't over yet. You'd better go up to the second floor.
You'll see the students coming out."

An incessant draught whistled through the courtyards, up the stair-
cases, along the corridors. Few and far between, the electric lights had
the dull glow of oil-lamps. Flagstones, arcades, and banging doors, an
enormous, dark, dilapidated staircase along which, on the dingy walls,
tattered notices flapped in the autumn wind—the whole place with its
air of general decay, its silence and solemnity, gave the impression of
some provincial bishop's-palace left mouldering for eternity.

Some minutes slowly passed, while Antoine waited outside the lecture-room. Soft footsteps sounded on the flags; a hirsute, down-at-heel
student carrying a bottle of wine came down the corridor, giving Antoine a keen glance as he moved by in slippers. Silence again. Then
a confused buzz which, when the door of the lecture-room was flung
open, rose to the hullabaloo of a parliamentary session. Laughing,
shouting to each other, the students came flocking out and rapidly
dispersed along the corridors.

Antoine waited. Presumably the professor would be the last to leave.
Only when the hive seemed to have disgorged its last inmate, did he
enter. The room was large and badly lighted, panelled with wood and

flanked with busts. At the far end, he saw a tall, drooping figure; an elderly white-haired man was lethargically arranging sheets of foolscap on a table. Obviously Professor Jalicourt.

Jalicourt had fancied himself alone; on hearing Antoine's footsteps he looked up with a frown. To see in front of him he had to turn his head to one side; he was blind in one eye and on the other wore a monocle thick as a magnifying glass. When he saw he had a visitor, he moved forward a little and with a courteous gesture signed to Antoine to approach.

Antoine had expected to encounter a venerable don of the old school. This well-set-up man in a light suit, who looked more as if he had just dismounted from a horse than stepped down from a lecture platform, took him by surprise.

He introduced himself. "I'm the son of Oscar Thibault, your colleague at the Institute, and the brother of Jacques Thibault, to whom you wrote yesterday." As Jalicourt made no sign and continued observing him, affable but aloof, with lifted eyebrows, Antoine went straight to the point. "Can you give me any news, sir, of my brother Jacques? Where is he now?"

Jalicourt made no answer, but his forehead puckered, as if he had taken offence.

"I must explain, sir," Antoine hastened to add. "I took the liberty of opening your letter. My brother has disappeared."

"Disappeared?"

"Yes, he left home three years ago."

Jalicourt thrust his head forward abruptly and with his keen, short-sighted eye scrutinized the young man at close range. Antoine felt his breath fanning his cheek.

"Yes, three years ago," he repeated. "He gave no reason for leaving us. Since then he hasn't communicated with his father or myself. Nor with anyone—except with you, professor. So you'll understand why I've rushed to see you like this. We didn't even know if he was still alive."

"Alive he certainly is—as he has just had this story published."

"When? Where?"

Jalicourt did not reply. His clean-shaven, pointed chin, cleft by a deep furrow, jutted with a certain arrogance between the high peaks of his collar. The slender fingers were toying with the drooping tips of his long, silky, snow-white moustache. When he spoke, his voice was low, evasive.

"After all, I can't be sure. The story wasn't signed 'Thibault'; but with a pen name—which I believed I could identify as his."

The disappointment was a cruel blow to Antoine. "What was the pen name?" he asked in an unsteady tone.

Jalicourt, his one eye still intent on Antoine, seemed somewhat touched by his anxiety.

"But, M. Thibault," he said firmly, "I do not think I was mistaken."

He was obviously on the defensive; not from any exaggerated fear of taking responsibility, but because he had an instinctive aversion to meddling in the private affairs of others, to anything resembling an indiscretion. Realizing that he had to overcome a certain mistrust, Antoine hastened to explain the situation.

"What makes it so urgent is that my father has been suffering from an incurable disease for a year, and his state is getting rapidly worse. The end will come in a few weeks. Jacques and I are the only children. So you understand, don't you, why I opened your letter? I know Jacques well enough to be sure that if he is alive and I can get at him, and tell him what is happening, he'll come home."

Jalicourt pondered for a moment. His face was twitching. Then, with a quick, impulsive gesture he held out his hand.

"That puts a new complexion on it," he said. "In that case I'll be only too glad to help you." He seemed to hesitate, and glanced round the lecture-room. "We can't talk here. Would you mind coming with me to my place, M. Thibault?"

Quickly, without a word, they made their way across the huge, draughty building. When they came out into the quiet Rue d'Ulm, Jalicourt began speaking, in a friendly tone.

"Yes, I'll be glad to help. The pen name struck me as pretty obvious: 'Jack Baulthy.' Don't you agree? I recognized the writing, too;

your brother had written to me once before. I'll tell you the little I know. But tell me first, why did he run away like that?"

"Why, indeed? I've never been able to find a plausible reason for it. My brother has an impulsive, ill-balanced nature; there's something of the mystic in him. All his acts are more or less erratic. Sometimes one fancies one has got to know him; then the next day he's quite different from what he was the day before. I may as well tell you, M. de Jalicourt, that Jacques ran away from home once before, when he was fourteen. He induced a school-friend to go with him; they were found three days later on the Toulon road. To the medical profession—I'm a doctor, by the way—this type of escapade has long been familiar; it has a morbid origin and its characteristics have been diagnosed. It's just possible that Jacques's first escapade was of a pathological order. But how can we account for an absence lasting three years? We've not found anything in his life that could justify such an act. He seemed happy, he had had a quiet summer vacation with his family. He had done brilliantly in the exam for the Ecole Normale, and was due to enter it at the beginning of November. The act can't have been premeditated; he took hardly any of his things with him, little or no money, only some manuscripts. He hadn't let any of his friends know of his project. But he sent a letter to the principal, resigning from the Ecole; I've seen the letter, it bears the date on which he left us. Just then I happened to be away from home for a couple of days; Jacques left during my absence."

"But—hadn't your brother some reluctance about entering the Ecole?" Jalicourt suggested.

"Do you think so?"

Jalicourt did not continue, and Antoine put no further question.

Never could he recall that dramatic period of his life, without emotion. The absence of which he had just spoken was the occasion of his journey to Le Havre . . . Rachel, the *Romania,* that last farewell. And no sooner had he come back to Paris, still in the throes of his emotion, than he had found the household in turmoil: his brother vanished on the previous day, and the police called in by his father, who, it seemed, had lost his head completely, and was obstinately repeating: "He's gone and killed himself!" without deigning to give the least explanation. The domestic catastrophe had come on top of the raw wound left by the tragic ending of his love, and, now he came to think of it, he felt the shock had been a salutary one. That fixed idea of tracking down the runaway had taken his mind off his personal obsession. What little time was left over from his duties at the hospital had been spent in hurried visits to the police-stations, to the Morgue, and to detective-agencies. He had borne the brunt of everything: his father's morbid, blundering agitation, and the anxieties caused by Gise's breakdown, which for a time had endangered her life; letters that must be answered, the importunities of callers, the endless investigations carried on by private detectives abroad as well as in France, constantly raising hopes that came to nothing. When all was said and done, the strenuous life imposed on him at that time had saved him from himself. And when, after some months of vain endeavour, he had been forced little by little to give up his inquiries, he found he was inured to living without Rachel.

They were walking fast, but this did not check Jalicourt's flow of conversation; his sense of the amenities precluded silence. He chatted of one thing and another with easy-going affability. But the more affable he seemed, the more he gave an impression that his thoughts were elsewhere.

They came to the Place du Panthéon. Jalicourt took the four flights of stairs without slackening pace. On his landing, the elderly gentleman drew himself erect, removed his hat, and, standing aside, threw open the door of his flat, with the gesture of one ushering a visitor into the Hall of Mirrors at Versailles.

The foyer was redolent of all the vegetables known to the French cuisine. Without lingering in it, Jalicourt ceremoniously showed his guest into a drawing-room that opened into his study. The little flat was crowded up with richly inlaid furniture, chairs upholstered in tapestry, ancient portraits, and knick-knacks of all sorts. The study was dark, and gave the impression of being a very small, low-ceiled room, the reason being that the back wall was entirely covered by a gaudy tapestry depicting the Queen of Sheba paying an official visit to King Solomon, and out of all proportion with the height of the room. It had been necessary to fold back the top and bottom edges, with the result that the figures, which were larger than life-size, touched the cornice with their diadems and had their legs cut short.

M. de Jalicourt motioned Antoine to a seat, then he himself sat on the flattened, faded cushions piled on a grandfather's chair that stood in front of the mahogany desk, littered with books and papers, at which he worked. Against the background of olive-green velvet, between the projecting wings of the old chair, his gaunt features, the large aquiline nose, slanting forehead, and the white curls that looked like a powdered wig, gave him the air of an old eighteenth-century dandy.

"Let's see now," he began, fiddling with the signet-ring that kept slipping down his thin finger, "I must set my memories in order. The first relations I had with your brother were by letter. At that time— it must be four or five years ago—your brother was, I believe, studying for his entrance examination. If my memory serves me right, he wrote to me about a certain book I brought out in that bygone era."

"Yes," Antoine put in. *"The Dawn of a Century."*

"I think I've kept his letter. I was struck by its tone, and I answered it. In fact I asked him to come and see me. He did not do so, however; not just then. He waited till he had passed the entrance examination before visiting me. That began the second phase of our acquaintance; a brief phase—an hour's conversation. Your brother dropped in quite unexpectedly, rather late in the evening, three years ago—a little before term began, in the first week of November."

"Just before he went away."

"I let him in; my door is always open to young folk who want to see me. I haven't forgotten the determined, passionate, almost feverish expression of his face that evening." (As a matter of fact, Jacques had struck him as over-excited and rather conceited.) "He was torn between two projects, and came to ask my advice. Should he join the Ecole and complete his general education there in the usual way, or should he take another line altogether? He didn't seem to have a clear notion of exactly what it should be, that 'other line.' But I gathered he meant to turn his back on the examinations, and start working as the spirit moved him—writing."

"I had no idea," Antoine murmured. His mind was full of memories of what his own life had been during that last month preceding Rachel's departure. And he reproached himself for having left Jacques so completely to himself.

"I must confess," Jalicourt went on with a touch of affectation that became him charmingly, "that I can't remember very well what advice I gave him. Obviously I must have told him not to think of dropping the Ecole. For young men of his calibre, our curriculum is really quite harmless; they pick and choose by instinct, they have—how shall I put it?—a healthy intolerance of constraint, and refuse to be kept in leading-strings. The Ecole can damage only the timid, over-scrupulous type of mind. In any case it struck me that your brother had come to ask my advice merely as a matter of form; he had already made up his mind. And that's the surest proof that a youngster has a real vocation—has it in the blood. Don't you agree? He showed a rather—rather callow violence, when speaking to me of the 'university mentality,' of the discipline, of certain tutors—even, if I remember rightly, of his family life and social milieu. Does that surprise you? I have much affection for young people—they prevent me from ageing too quickly. They have an inkling that under the professor of literature I officially am there lurks an incorrigible old poet to whom they can open their hearts. Your brother, if my memory serves me, did not fail to do so. I must say that the intolerance of the young appeals to me. It's a good sign when a youngster is temperamentally in revolt against the world in general. All those amongst my pupils who have gone far were natural rebels, born, as my teacher Renan puts it, 'with an imprecation on their lips.'

"But let's get back to your brother. I can't recall exactly what our last words together were. All I know is that some days later—yes, a day or two later, I should say—I got a communication from him. I have it still. The instinct of the literary collector!"

Rising, he opened a cupboard and came back with a sheaf of papers, which he laid on the table.

"It's not a letter; just the copy of a poem by Walt Whitman. No signature. But your brother writes the sort of hand that one never forgets. Fine handwriting, isn't it?"

As he spoke, he was glancing over the sheet before him. He passed it to Antoine, who felt his heart beating faster as his eyes fell on it. Yes, that was Jacques's writing, emotional and simplified to excess, yet level, sinewy, rough-hewn.

"I'm afraid," Jalicourt was saying, "I must have thrown away the envelope. I wonder from what place he sent it. Anyhow, it's only today I realize exactly what he was driving at when he sent that poem."

"My English isn't up to understanding it right off, I fear," Antoine confessed with a smile.

Jalicourt picked up the sheet, brought it near his eyeglass, and began reading the poem, translating it line by line:

"Afoot and light-hearted I take to the open road,
    Healthy, free, the world before me,
    The long brown path before me leading wherever I choose.

"Henceforth I ask not good-fortune, I myself am good-fortune,
    Henceforth I whimper no more, postpone no more, need nothing,
    Done with indoor complaints, libraries, querulous criticisms,
    Strong and content I travel the open road."

When he had finished, Antoine gave a sigh. A short silence followed, which he was the first to break.

"And the short story?"

Jalicourt extracted from the file a foreign magazine.

"Here it is. It appeared in the September issue of *Calliope*, a 'modernist' review, brim-full of new ideas, which is published at Geneva."

Antoine had reached forward at once and was turning the pages excitedly. Suddenly once again he was startled by the sight of his brother's writing. Over the title of the story, *"La Sorellina,"* Jacques had written in his own hand:

Did you not say to me, on that famous November evening: "Everything is subject to the influence of two poles; the truth is always double-faced"? So, sometimes, is love.

Jack Baulthy.

"Meaning . . . ?" Antoine asked himself. Oh, well, that could wait. A Swiss magazine; did that mean Jacques was in Switzerland? *Calliope, 161 Rue du Rhône, Geneva.* Yes, it would be damnably bad luck if he could not trace Jacques now! All impatience, he rose from his seat.

"I received this magazine," Jalicourt explained, "at the end of the vacation. I found no time to acknowledge it till yesterday. I nearly sent my letter to *Calliope,* as a matter of fact. Then it struck me that publishing in a Swiss magazine doesn't necessarily mean the author has left Paris." (He omitted to mention that his choice had been influenced as well by the cost of the postage-stamp.)

But Antoine was not listening. His eagerness to *know* had outrun his patience, his cheeks were flushed, and he was mechanically turning over the pages that were a token of Jacques's return to life, catching here and there a baffling, enigmatic phrase. He was in such haste to be alone—as though the story were to give him some amazing revelation—that he took his leave rather curtly.

To an accompaniment of amiable phrases, Jalicourt escorted him to the door; all his remarks and gestures seemed part of a set ritual. In the hall he stopped and pointed with his forefinger at *"La Sorellina,"* which Antoine had tucked under his arm.

"You'll see," he said. "I fully recognize that quite a deal of talent has gone into that. But, personally, I must confess . . . No! I'm too old." When Antoine made a politely deprecating gesture, he added: "Yes, I am. It's no use burking the truth: I've lost the power of understanding the ultra-modern. Yes, one fossilizes. Music's another story; there I've had the luck of being able to keep in step. After having been a fanatical Wagnerite, I managed to understand Debussy. But only in the nick of time; I very nearly missed Debussy! Well, M. Thibault, I'm certain that I'd miss a Debussy—in modern literature."

He had straightened his shoulders again. Looking at him, Antoine could not withhold his admiration. There was no doubt about it; the old professor cut a stately figure. As he stood below the hanging lamp, his white hair gleamed silver, and the craggy brows beetled above two gulfs of shadow, one of which the heavy lens lit up at moments with a golden glow, like a window touched by the setting sun.

Antoine made a last effort to express his gratitude. But Jalicourt seemed determined to regard polite amenities as his own prerogative. He cut the young man short, and, raising his arm, proffered a nonchalant, wide-open hand.

"Please give my best wishes for his recovery to M. Thibault. And I hope you'll be good enough to let me know what news you have of your brother."

V

THE wind had fallen and a drizzle had set in; the street-lamps showed as blurs of light across the misty air. It was too late to think of taking any active steps, and Antoine's only idea was to get home as soon as possible.

There were no taxis at the stand. He had to make his way on foot down the Rue Soufflot, hugging the magazine to his side. But his patience was flagging with every step, and he soon felt he could wait no longer. At a corner of the boulevard the lights of the Grande Brasserie offered, if not isolation, at least a convenient shelter. Antoine decided for it.

As he moved through the revolving door, he passed two beardless youths coming out, arm in arm, laughing and chattering—of their love-affairs, he surmised. Then he heard one of them remark: "No, old man, if the human mind could envisage a relation between those two concepts . . ." and realized he was in the heart of the Latin Quarter.

On the ground floor all the tables were occupied and he walked to the staircase through a haze of tepid smoke. The upper floor was set apart for games of various sorts. Round the billiard-tables young men were laughing, shouting, quarrelling. "13, 14, 15." "No luck!" "Miscued again, damn it!" "Eugène, hurry up with that pint!" "Eugène, a Byrrh!" Light-hearted clamour fretted by the staccato, Morse-like click of billiard-balls. Everywhere youth in its first flush: pink cheeks glowing under the fledgeling down, bright eyes behind pince-nez, callow exuberance, eager smiles—everything told of the joy of breaking from the chrysalis, of hopes untrammelled, life for life's sake.

Antoine threaded his way between the tables, looking for a quiet corner. The noisy gaiety of the youngsters round him took his mind for a moment off his own preoccupation; for the first time he felt his thirty-odd years of life weighing on him.

"The youth of 1913," he mused. "An excellent vintage. Healthier and perhaps even more go-ahead than mine, their seniors by ten years."

He had travelled little, and rarely thought about his country; that night he was conscious of a new feeling towards France and her future as a nation—a feeling of confidence and pride. But then a shadow fell on his mood; Jacques might have been one of these promising young men. Where was Jacques? What was he doing at this moment?

Antoine noticed at the far end of the room some unoccupied tables which had been used as a rack for overcoats and hats. There was a bracket-lamp above them, and it struck him that he might do worse than settle down there, behind the rampart of piled-up garments. The only people in that part of the room were a quiet-looking couple: a youngster, pipe in mouth, reading L'Humanité and oblivious of the girl beside him, who was sipping a glass of hot milk. She was whiling away the time by counting her small change, polishing her nails, and examining her teeth in a pocket-mirror, while watching from the corner of an eye the people coming in. An elderly, worried-looking student held her interest for a moment, till, without waiting to order a drink, he opened a book and became absorbed in it.

Antoine had started reading, too, but somehow could not fix his attention on the words before him. Absent-mindedly, he felt his pulse; it was too fast—rarely had he been so little master of his emotions. In any case the first lines he read were baffling enough.

The hottest hour. Odours of parched soil: dust. The path drives upwards. Sparks flash from the rock under the horse-hoofs. Sybil rides in front. Ten o'clock striking at San Paolo. A tattered foreshore ribboning the garish blue: gold and azure. On the right, endlessly, Golfo di Napoli. To the left a speck of solid gold, poised on liquid gold: Isola di Capri.

So Jacques was in Italy? Impatiently Antoine skipped some pages. What an odd jerky style of writing!

His father. Giuseppe's feelings for his father. That secret corner of his heart, a prickly cactus, ingrowing spines. Years of unconscious, frantic, restive adulation. Every impulse of affection rebuffed. Twenty years before he brought himself to hate. Twenty years before realizing hatred was incumbent on him. Whole-hearted hatred.

Antoine stopped short. He felt ill at ease. Who was this Giuseppe? He turned back to the opening pages, bidding himself keep cool.

The first scene described the two young people riding out together: Giuseppe, who seemed like Jacques, and Sybil, presumably an English girl, judging by her remarks.

"In England we do with tentative arrangements, when they're called for. That gives us time to choose our line and act on it. You Italians want everything cut-and-dried from the start." She was thinking: In this respect, anyhow, I'm Italian already; but no need for him to know it.

On the summit Sybil and Giuseppe dismount, to rest.

She alights before Giuseppe, flicks the scorched grass with her hunting-crop to drive the lizards away, sits down. On the furnace-hot soil.
"In the sun, Sybil?"
Giuseppe stretches himself on the fringe of shade along the wall. And rests his head on the warm bricks, watching her, thinking: All her movements cry out to be graceful, but never will she yield to herself.

Antoine was so carried away by his eagerness that he jumped from one paragraph to another, trying to understand before he had read the phrases out. His eye lit on a sentence.

She is English, Protestant.

He read the whole passage.

For him all in her is new and strange. Adorable and hateful. That charm of hers, to have been born, to have lived, to be living still in a world of which he knows almost nothing. Her sadness. Her purity. Her friendliness. Her smile. No, Sybil smiles with her eyes, never with her lips. And his feelings for her—harsh, intense, embittered. She wounds him. Wishing, it seems, to think him of a lower breed, and suffering by it. "You Italians," she says. "You Southerners." She is English, Protestant.

Presumably, Sybil was some girl whom Jacques had met and loved. Perhaps he was living with her now.

Down they ride through vineyards, lemon-groves. The beach. A herd driven by a bambino, sombre-eyed, bare shoulders peeping through the rags. He whistles, calling two white dogs to heel. The bell on the leader, clanging, clanging. Infinite space. Sunlight. Their steps leave water-holes in the sand.

Wearied by the descriptive passages, Antoine skipped two pages. His eyes fell on an account of Sybil's home.

Villa Lunadoro. A ramshackle old house, rose-beleaguered. A double garden, riotous with flowers.

Literature! Antoine turned the page; a sentence caught his attention.

The rose-garden, crimson drifts of blossom, low cloisters coved with roses, a fragrance so intense under the fires of noon that it is hardly to be borne—fragrance that seeps through the pores and permeates the blood, blurring the eyes, slowing or speeding up the heart-beats.

That rose-garden, of what did it remind him? Yes, it led straight to the cote where "white pigeons fluttered." Maisons-Laffitte. And Sybil, the Protestant, could she be—? Wait, here was more about her!

In her riding-habit Sybil sinks onto a garden-seat, arms outspread, lips tight, eyes hard. Now she is alone, everything is clear again: life has been given her to one end only—to make Giuseppe happy. But it's when he isn't here I love him. On the days when I have waited most desperately for him to come, I'm certain to make him suffer. What futile, shameful cruelty! Ah, women who can cry are the lucky ones! My heart is frozen, indurated.

At "indurated" Antoine smiled. "A medical term, that. He must have picked it up from me."

Can he read my feelings? Ah, how I wish he could! And the moment he seems to understand me, I cannot, cannot bear it; I shrink away, I lie, I do anything, anything to elude him!

There followed a description of Sybil's mother.

Mrs. Powell is coming down the terrace steps. Her hair is silver in the light. Shielding her eyes with her hand, she smiles before she speaks, before she has seen Sybil. "A letter from William," she announces. "Such a nice letter. He's just begun two sketches. He intends to stay some weeks more at Pæstum."
Sybil bites her lips. Despair. Should she await her brother's return to solve the riddle of her heart, to understand herself?

Now Antoine had no doubts left. These were Mme. de Fontanin, Daniel, Jenny—figures mustered from the past. He turned hurriedly over to the next chapter, eager to find again the portrait of the father, Seregno.

Yes, here it was. . . . No, this was the Palazzo Seregno, an ancient mansion on the shore of the Bay.

. . . tall, arched windows set in frescoed foliage.

Descriptions followed of Vesuvius and the Bay.
Antoine skipped some pages, sampling a passage here and there, so as not to lose the thread.

Giuseppe was staying, it appeared, at his father's country house, by himself except for the servants. Annetta, his "little sister," was abroad. His mother was dead—naturally. His father, Judge Seregno, had to remain in Naples, where the court was in session, and came only on Sundays or, occasionally, on week-days, for a night. "Just as Father did at Maisons," Antoine observed to himself.

He landed from the boat at dinner-time. After dinner, the digestive process. A cigar, a stroll up and down the courtyard. Rose early to admonish stable-boys and gardeners. Taciturn as ever, caught the first morning boat.

Then, the father's character-sketch. Antoine felt a qualm of apprehension as he broached it.

Judge Seregno. A worldly success. Everything about him interlocks, fits in. Social standing, family, wealth, professional acumen, genius for organization. The majesty of office, consecrated, truculent. Adamantine probity. The steeliest virtues. And a physical appearance in keeping. Massive self-assurance. Violence at full pressure, always menacing, always under control. . . . A mighty caricature that inspires respect in all, and awe. Spiritual son of the Church, and model citizen. At the Vatican, as on the bench, in office and at home—everywhere lucid, commanding, exemplary, complacent, imperturbable. A force, or, rather, a dead weight to reckon with; the might of an inertia that does not move yet crushes. A well-built unity, four-square. A monument. And, ah, that small, secret, bitter laugh of his . . . !

For a moment the page grew blurred under Antoine's eyes. How had Jacques ever dared to write such words? The ruthlessness of the boy's revenge appalled him when he pictured the old man's pitiful decline.

> Then clinkety and clankety
> Along the lanes we'll go . . .

And suddenly the gulf between his brother and himself seemed to yawn wider.

Ah, that small, secret, bitter laugh of his, following a sneering silence! For twenty years Giuseppe has endured that laugh, those silences. Fostering vengeance.

Giuseppe's youth, a forcing-bed of hatred and revolt. When he thinks of his boyhood, a thirst for revenge sears his throat. From his earliest days all his instincts, as they took form, urged him against his father. All, without exception. Idleness, disrespect, disorderliness, flaunted by way of reprisal. A wilful dunce, and heartily ashamed of it. But these were his best weapons of revolt against the hated system. An insatiable craving for the worst. Each act of disobedience with a sweet savour of revenge.

A heartless child, they said. Heartless he, whom the moan of a hurt animal, a street-musician's fiddle, the smile of a signora met in a church porch, sent sobbing to his sleep of nights! A wasteland, loneliness, childhood of frustration. Giuseppe came to man's estate without once having heard a gentle word spoken to him but by his little sister.

"What about me?" Antoine thought. A note of tenderness crept into the story when it spoke of the "little sister."

Annetta, Annetta, *sorellina*. A miracle that such a flower could grow in that dry land! Sister of his childish despairs, revolts. Sole gleam of light, cool spring in a waste of arid gloom.

"What about me?" Ah, a little further on was something about an elder brother, Umberto.

Sometimes Giuseppe seemed to catch in his brother's eyes a faint gleam of affection . . .

A faint gleam! What ingratitude!

. . . of affection, tainted with condescension. But between them lay nine years, an abyss of time. Umberto hid his true self from Giuseppe, who lied to Umberto.

Antoine stopped reading. His disagreeable first impression had passed; what did it matter if the subject of these pages touched him so nearly? After all, what real importance had Jacques's opinions about people? For that matter, what he said about Umberto was substantially correct. What amazed him was the bitterness behind it all. After three years' separation, three years by himself without news of the family—yes, Jacques must have loathed his past with a vengeance to write such words! One thing worried him: though he might find his brother again, could he find the way back to his brother's heart?

He skimmed the remaining pages to see if there was more about Umberto, and found he was hardly mentioned. With a secret disappointment. . . .

Then his eyes lit on a passage, the tone of which whetted his curiosity.

Without friends, curled up into a ball against the blows of circumstance, watching his life fall to pieces . . .

That was Giuseppe's life, alone in Rome; had that been Jacques's life in some foreign city?

Some evenings. The air in his room unbreathable. The book falls. He blows out the lamp, goes forth into the night, like a young wolf. Messalina's Rome, squalid districts, everywhere death-traps, lures. Furtive gleams between the provocatively drawn curtains. Crowded darkness, shadows offering themselves, cajoling: lasciviousness. He slips past walls honeycombed with lust. Is he fleeing from himself? What can quench the thirst consuming him? For hours, his mind a chaos of wild deeds undone, he drifts on, unheeding. His eyes are burning, hands fever-hot, throat parched. As foreign to himself as if he had bartered body and soul. Sweating with fear and lust, he moves in a circle. Slinks down alleys, skirting the same pitfalls again and again. Hour after hour.

Too late. The lights are dying out behind the furtive curtains. Streets grow empty. He is alone now with his evil genius. Ripe for any lapse. Too late. Impotent, drained dry by the riot of imaginative lust.

Night is ending. Belated purity of silence, lonely hush of daybreak. Too late. Sick at heart, dead beat, unsatisfied, degraded, he drags himself to his room, slips between the sheets. Without remorse. Bewildered. And lies there till the sky pales, chewing the cud of bitterness; bitterness of not having dared. . . .

Why did Antoine find this such painful reading? It gave him no surprise that his young brother had taken his fill of life, had stooped to sordid adventures; indeed, he was quite prepared to laugh it off with a genial "Why not?" or even: "So much the better!" And yet . . .

Hastily he turned over some more pages. He could not bring himself to read methodically, and merely guessed, with more or less success, at the development of the story.

The Powells' villa, on the shore of the Bay, was near the Palazzo Seregno. Thus Giuseppe and Sybil were neighbours during vacations. They went out for rides together, and boating in the Bay.

Giuseppe went daily to the Villa Lunadoro. Sybil never refused to see him. The mystery of Sybil. Giuseppe dangled round her, joylessly.

Antoine was getting bored by the descriptions of this love-affair; it held up the story. Still, he brought himself to read a portion of a rather long scene, following a seeming estrangement of the two young people.

Sundown. Giuseppe comes to the villa. Sybil. Drunk with the perfumes of sun-steeped flowers, the garden is sobering down as night comes on. Like a prince in the *Arabian Nights,* Giuseppe walks between two walls of flame, the pomegranates in flower fired by the sunset. Sybil! Sybil! No one answers. Closed windows, drawn blinds. He stops. Round him the swallows weave shrill, dizzying circles in the air. No one. Is she under the pergola, behind the house? With an effort he keeps from running.

At the corner of the house, an eddy of soft sounds. Sybil playing the piano. The bay-window is open. What is she playing? A murmur of heart-rending sighs, a sad, unanswered plea rising on the calm evening air. An almost human tone, a phrase spoken yet incomprehensible, beyond translation into words. Listening, he comes nearer, steps onto the threshold. Sybil has not heard him. Her face, shamelessly naked. Fluttering eyelids, parted lips—all reticence gone. Shining through that face, the soul; no, her soul, her love, is there incarnate. In solitude revealed, a startled secret, love's offering, stolen, ravished. She is playing; tendrils of light sound float up, entwining in a supreme ecstasy. A sob abruptly stifled, then a sad arpeggio that rises up and up, attenuated, rarefied, mysteriously hovering on the silence, before taking wing into the blue, like a sudden flight of birds.

Sybil has lifted her fingers from the keys. The piano is throbbing still; a hand pressed on the lid would feel the tumult of a pulsing heart. She thinks she is alone. She turns her head. With a slowness, a grace unknown to him. And then . . .

Antoine was exasperated by this mania for short, jerky phrases. "Literature" run wild! Still—had Jacques really fallen in love with Jenny?

But his imagination was running ahead of the story; he came back to the text.

Again his eye was caught by the name Umberto. The passage described a brief scene at the Palazzo Seregno; one evening the Judge came back unexpectedly to dinner, accompanied by his elder son.

The vast dining-room. Three vaulted windows, opening on a pink sky ribboned by the smoke from Vesuvius. Stucco walls, green pilasters supporting a false dome painted on the ceiling.
Benedicite. The Judge's thick lips flutter. He crosses himself. The gesture sweeps across the room. Umberto follows suit, for appearance' sake. Giuseppe obstinately refrains. They take their seats. Immaculate, austere, the huge white tablecloth. Three places laid, too far apart. Filippo, felt-shod, with the silver dishes . . .

Antoine skipped some paragraphs. Then:

In the father's presence the Powells' name is never uttered. He refused to know William. That foreigner. A painter, too. Poor Italy, the happy-hunting-ground of every vagabond! A year ago, he had put his foot down. "I forbid you to see those heretics."
Does he suspect he is being disobeyed?

Impatiently Antoine turned some pages, and came on another reference to the elder brother.

Umberto puts in some innocent remarks. Then silence closes in again.

A handsome forehead, Umberto's. Proud, thoughtful eyes. Elsewhere, most likely, he is young, expansive. He has studied. A brilliant career lies before him. Giuseppe loves his brother. Not as a brother. Like an uncle who might become a friend. Were they together long enough, Giuseppe would speak out perhaps. But their talks are brief, are few and only on set occasions. No, intimacy with Umberto is ruled out.

"Obviously," Antoine murmured, remembering the summer of 1910. "That was because of Rachel. My fault, of course."

He stopped reading for a moment and let his head sink dejectedly against the chair-back. He was disappointed; all this high-flown verbiage led nowhere, left unsolved the mystery of Jacques's disappearance.

The orchestra was playing the refrain of a Viennese waltz; people in the café were humming it in undertones, with here and there an unseen whistler joining in. The quiet couple near him had not moved. The woman had drunk her milk and now was smoking, with a bored expression. Now and again, resting her bare arm on her companion's shoulder—he had just unfolded *The Rights of Man*—she absent-mindedly stroked the lobe of his ear, while yawning like a cat.

"Not many women here," Antoine observed. "The ones there are, are mostly youngish. And relegated to a secondary plane; merely bedmates."

A discussion had sprung up between two groups of students, who were hurling the firebrand names of Jaurès and Péguy from one table to the other with noisy truculence.

A young, blue-jowled Jew had sat down between the youth reading *The Rights of Man* and the yawning girl; she no longer seemed bored.

With an effort Antoine started reading again. He had lost his place. Turning the pages, he lit on the closing lines of *"La Sorellina."*

Here life and love are impossible. Good-bye.
Lure of the unknown, lure of a wholly new tomorrow, ecstasy. The past forgotten, take to the open road.
The first train to Rome. Rome, the first train to Genoa. Genoa, the first liner. . . .

No more was needed to rekindle Antoine's interest. "Slowly now!" he adjured himself. "Jacques's secret is hidden somewhere in these pages, and I've got to find it." He must go right through the story, paragraph by paragraph, carefully, composedly.

He turned back and, propping his forehead on his hands, settled down to work.

He began with the homecoming of Annetta, Giuseppe's foster-sister, from the Swiss convent where she was completing her education.

A little changed, Annetta. Before, the servants used to boast of her. *E una vera napoletana.* Plump shoulders. Dusky skin. Fleshy lips. Eyes that flashed into laughter on the least pretext.

Why had he dragged Gise into this story? Moreover, from the first scene between brother and foster-sister, Antoine began to feel a certain discomfort.

Giuseppe had gone to meet Annetta; they were driving back to the Palazzo Seregno.

The sun has dipped behind the summits. The antiquated barouche rocks under the shaky hood. Shadows. Sudden coolth.

Annetta, chatterbox Annetta. She slips her arm through Giuseppe's. And prattles away. He laughs. How alone he was—till just now! Sybil does not dispel his loneliness. Sybil, a dark, deep, ever-translucent lake, blinding depths of purity.

The landscape tightens round the old barouche. Dusk closing in. Nightfall.

Annetta snuggles up, as in the past. A hurried kiss. Warm, supple, dust-roughened lips. As in the past. In the convent, too, laughter, chatter, kisses. In love with Sybil, what warm, sweet comfort he finds in the *sorellina's* caresses! He gives her kiss for kiss. Anywhere, on her eyes, on her hair. Noisy, brotherly kisses. The driver laughs. She prattles on. At the convent, you know . . . oh, those exams! Giuseppe, too; of anything and everything: their father, next autumn, plans for the future. But keeps one thing to himself; not a word about the Powells. Annetta is religious. In her bedroom, six candles burn at the Madonna's shrine. The Jews crucified Christ; they did not know He was the Son of God. But the heretics knew. They denied the Truth wilfully, through pride.

During their father's absence, the two young people settle down together at the Palazzo Seregno. Some passages were painful reading for Antoine from the first word to the last.

Next morning Annetta runs in while Giuseppe is still in bed. Yes, now he notices, she has changed a little. Her eyes are still as large and pure as in the past, and full of a vague wonder, but a new glow is in them; the least thing might blur their serenity for ever. Warm, yielding flesh. She has come straight from her bed. Her hair all rumpled; a child she is, no coquetry. As in the past. Already she has fished out of her boxes her "souvenirs" of Switzerland. "Just look at this—and this!" Gleams of white, well-formed teeth behind the fluttering lips. Telling about her fall, out skiing. A spike of rock pierced her knee. Look, the mark's not gone! Under the dressing-gown, the smooth curve of her leg, her thigh; warm naked flesh. She strokes the scar, a white patch on the warm brown skin. Absent-mindedly. She loves fondling herself; dotes on her mirror every morning, every night, smiling to her body. Now she is chattering again. All sorts of memories. Riding-lessons. "I'd like to go out riding with you—in my riding costume; we'd have gallops along the beach." Still stroking her leg. Crooking, straightening her knee; ripple of silken skin. Giuseppe's eyelids flutter, he lies back in bed. At last the dressing-gown falls back. She runs to the window. Sunbeams romping on the Bay. "Lazybones, it's nine! Let's go for a swim!"

For several days they see each other thus, each morning. Giuseppe shares his time between his *sorellina* and the sphinx-like English girl.

Antoine skimmed the pages rapidly. Then one day when Giuseppe has come to take Sybil for a boating expedition in the Bay, a scene, seemingly decisive, takes place between them. Overcoming his distaste for the insufferable lushness of the writing, Antoine read almost every word of it.

Sybil under the pergola, on the edge of the sunlight. Lost in dreams. Her hand resting on a white pillar, in the light. Waiting for him? "I expected you yesterday." "I stayed with Annetta." "Why don't you bring her here?" Her tone displeased Giuseppe.

A few lines further on.

Giuseppe stops rowing. Round them the air grows still. Winged silence. The bay is all quicksilver. Sheen. Water-music. Ripples lapping against the boat. "What are you thinking about?" "And you?" Silence. A change in their voices. "I'm thinking of you, Sybil." "And I am thinking of you, Giuseppe." He is trembling. "For all our lives, Sybil?" Yes, her head droops. He sees her lips part with a painful effort, her hand clasp the gunwale. A silent pledge, almost a regret. The sea ablaze in the flaming noon. Dazzling effulgence. Heat. Immobility. Time and life halted, in suspense. Unbearable oppression. Then a sudden flight of gulls brings life back to the listless air. They soar and dive and skim the sea, dip their beaks, and soar again. Gleams of sun-bright wings, clash of swords. "We are thinking about the same things, Sybil."

Actually Jacques had seen a great deal of the Fontanins that summer. Antoine began to wonder if the explanation of his flight might not be the failure of his love-affair with Jenny.

Some pages further on, the action began, it seemed, to move more quickly.

Among descriptions of everyday events that recalled to Antoine the life Jacques and Gise had led at Maisons, he followed the disturbing trend of the affection between Giuseppe and Annetta. Did the young people realize the nature of their intimacy? As for Annetta, all she knew was that the whole set of her being drew her towards Giuseppe; but so simple was her faith, so entire her innocence, that she lent her feelings the colour of a harmless, sisterly devotion. For Giuseppe, the love he confessedly had for Sybil seemed at first to absorb his thoughts, blinding him to the nature of the physical attraction Annetta exercised on him. The question was, how long would he be able to keep up this self-deception?

Late one afternoon Giuseppe made a suggestion to the *sorellina*.

"What do you say to a stroll, now it's getting cooler, then dinner at a country inn, and a good long tramp afterwards, till it's dark?" She claps her hands. "Oh, Beppino, I do love you so when you're cheerful!"

Had Giuseppe laid his plans in advance? After a makeshift meal in a fishing village, he led the girl along paths she did not know.

He is walking quickly. Along the stony paths between the lemon-groves which he had trod a hundred times with Sybil. Annetta grows anxious. "Sure you know the road?" He turns left. The path slopes down. An old well, a low, curved gateway. Giuseppe stops. "Now come and see," he laughs. She moves forward, unsuspecting. He pushes the door open, a bell tinkles. "What on earth are you doing?" Laughing, he draws her into the black garden. Under the firs. She is frightened, puzzled.

She steps into Villa Lunadoro.

That low, curved gateway, the tinkling bell, the fir-grove; Antoine recognized each detail, unmistakably.

Mrs. Powell and Sybil are in the pergola. "May I introduce my sister Annetta?" They give her a seat, question her, make much of her. Annetta fancies she is dreaming. The white-haired lady's welcome, her smile. "Come with me, my dear; I want to give you some of our roses." Vaulted shadows of the rose-garden, drenching the air with heady fragrance.

Sybil and Giuseppe are alone now. Should he take her hand? She would only shrink away. That steely reserve of hers is stronger than her will, than her love. He thinks: How hard it is for her to let herself be loved!

Mrs. Powell has picked the roses for Annetta. Small, close-set crimson roses, without spines; crimson petals with black hearts. "You must come again, dear; Sybil has so few friends, you know." Annetta fancies she is dreaming. Are these people the "gang of heretics"? Is it possible she once feared them like the plague?

Antoine skipped a page and came to the description of Annetta and Giuseppe's walk home.

The moon is veiled. The darkness deeper. Annetta feels light, buoyed on wings. She lets the full weight of her young body hang on Giuseppe's arm; Giuseppe guides her through the darkness, his head high, heart far away, lost in a dream. Shall he tell her his secret? Why not? He bends over her. "It's not only for Will's sake, you know, that I go to see them."

His face is hidden in shadows, but she hears the low intensity of his tone. "Not only for Will's sake!" Wildfire racing through her veins. She had never dreamt . . . Sybil, then? Sybil and Giuseppe . . . ? Choking, she breaks loose, tries to escape, stricken, barbed death in her flanks. No strength. A few steps more. Her teeth are chattering. She goes limp, stumbles, drops back onto the grass under the tall lime-trees.

Uncomprehending, he kneels beside her. What is wrong? But then her arms shoot up like tentacles. And now—he understands. She winds her arms around him, clings desperately, sobs. "Giuseppe! Oh, Giuseppe!"

The love-cry. He has never heard it. Never before. Sybil, cloistered in her secrecy. Her alien blood. And pressed to him now a young, sensuous body, aching with regret, yielding, yearning. Thoughts dance through his brain, memories of childhood, the love they bore each other, the trust and tenderness; how can he not love her? She is of his own kind; he must comfort her, make her well. Flowing round him, clinging, the soft warmth of a living body, fluent limbs. Then a sudden wave sweeping all before it, drowning consciousness. In his nostrils a new, yet familiar fragrance of loosened hair; under his lips a tear-drenched face, throbbing mouth. All love's accomplices: darkness, perfumes, ungovernable ecstasy, a fever of the blood. On the moist lips he presses his mouth's kiss; on the half-parted lips, awaiting they know not what, a lover's kiss. She gives herself to his caress, does not return it yet, but only yields, surrenders, offers her mouth again and again. Floods of longing surge up from their hearts, meet and clash as the wet lips cling together. Bitter yearning . . . sweetness. Mingled breaths, limbs, desires. Overhead the green darkness eddies, the stars go out. Clothes scattered, disarrayed, all resistance gone, all barriers falling, close, closer, flesh to flesh surrendering, a thrill of sweet pain, consummate, ah, consummate joy. . . .

Ah! A single sigh, and time stands still.

The silence throbs with echoes, blurred sounds. Elemental fear. Arrested movement. The man's face, panting, pillowed on the young breast; thud of racing heart-beats, two separate rhythms, unconsonant, irreconcilable.

Then suddenly a questing moonray, a prying, callous eye, flicks them like a whiplash, tears them apart.

Abruptly they stand up. Bewildered, lost. Tormented lips. Shuddering, but not with shame; with joy, with joy and wonder. With joy and new desire. In a little grassy hollow the bunch of crimson roses sheds its petals under the moon. Annetta makes a romantic gesture, picks up the roses, shakes them. A cloud of petals flutters down over the crushed grass, which bears the imprint of a single body.

Antoine was profoundly shocked, quivering with disgust. Unthinkable that Gise should have acted thus!

And yet—! Everything rang so precisely true—not only such details as the old wall, the rose-garden, the gate-bell. At the moment when they sank onto the grass, locked in an embrace, the mask of fiction fell. That was no stony path in Italy, nor were the shadows those of lemon-trees. No, that was unmistakably the rank grass of Maisons, which Antoine was recalling now only too clearly; and the trees were the centenarian lime-trees of the green avenue. Yes, Jacques must have taken Gisèle to the Fontanins', and on such a summer night, on the way back . . . Simpleton—to have lived beside them, so close to Gisèle, and to have guessed nothing of it all! . . . And yet—no, Antoine did not believe; in his inmost heart he could not bring himself to admit that that chaste, elusive little Gise could shelter such a secret.

Still, there were so many pointers, the crimson roses for instance.

Now he understood Gisèle's emotion when she received that anonymous box from a London florist and why, on the strength of what seemed so slender a clue, she had pressed him to have inquiries made immediately in England. Obviously she alone had read the message of those crimson roses sent a year, to the very day perhaps, after the love-scene under the lime-trees.

So Jacques must have stayed in London. Perhaps in Italy, too. And Switzerland. Could he be still in England? He might very easily contribute to a Genevan review, while living there.

Then, of a sudden, other facts that had baffled him grew clear, as if screening shadows were withdrawing from a nucleus of light. Gisèle's departure, her insistence on being sent to that English convent. Obviously it had been in order to trace Jacques. And now Antoine reproached himself for not having followed up, after his first failure, the clue provided by the London florist.

He tried to set his data in order, but in vain; too many theories— too many memories, as well—kept cropping up. He was coming to see the whole past in a new light. How easy now it was to understand Gise's despair when Jacques disappeared! He had never suspected all the implications of her grief, though he had done his best to allay it. He remembered how sorry he had been for her then; indeed it was out of his sympathy that another feeling for her had been born.

In those days he had found it impossible to talk about Jacques to his father, who obstinately clung to his theory of the boy's suicide; or to Mademoiselle, immersed day in, day out, in her prayers and religious exercises. But Gise had been different; her fervour for the quest had brought her very near him. Daily after dinner she had come down to hear the latest news. He had enjoyed imparting to her his hopes, and the steps he was taking. And it was in the course of those long, intimate talks that he had began to feel drawn towards the high-strung little girl, whose secret love was the keynote of her existence. Unknowingly, perhaps, he had yielded to the heady lure of the young body already bespoken to another. He recalled her sudden outbursts of affection, the little coaxing ways that reminded him of a suffering child's. Annetta! Yes, she had tricked him well! Of course, in his utter sentimental isolation after Rachel's eclipse, he had been only too ready to imagine—things. He shrugged his shoulders angrily. Damned fool! He had been taken with Gise, only because his emotions had been at a loose end. And he had fancied Gise was drawn to him, merely because, in the throes of her frustrated passion, she had clung to him as the one person capable of finding her lost lover.

Distasteful ideas! Antoine tried to brush them aside. He reminded himself that he had found nothing so far to explain Jacques's hasty flight from home.

With an effort he turned back to *"La Sorellina."*

Leaving the roses scattered on the grass, the young people walked back to the Palazzo.

Homewards. Giuseppe helps Annetta on her way. What lies before them? That brief ecstasy can have been but a prelude. The long night towards which they are walking, their night together in the big, lonely house— what will it bring?

Antoine could hardly bear to read further. Again he felt the blood rising to his cheeks.

Yet of moral disapproval there was little in his mood. When confronted with a passion running its course, he gave short shrift to moral codes. But he was unable to repress a feeling of outraged surprise, touched with rancour; he could not forget the day when Gise had so indignantly repulsed his timid advances. Almost *"La Sorellina"* rekindled his desire for her—a purely physical, unequivocal craving. So much so that, to fix his attention on what he was reading, he had deliberately to banish from his mind the haunting picture of a young, lithe, nut-brown body.

. . . that night together in the big, lonely house—what will it bring? Love bows them to its yoke. Silent, possessed, in an enchanted dream, they walk, escorted by the intermittent moon. Moonlight is playing on the Palazzo, picking out of the shadow the stuccoed pillars. They cross the first terrace. As they walk, cheek brushes cheek. Annetta's cheeks are burning. Already, in that childish body, what natural hardihood for sin! Abruptly they draw apart. A shadow has loomed up between the pillars. The father is there. Awaiting them. He has returned unexpectedly. "Where can the children be?" He has dined alone in the great hall; ever since then paced to and fro on the marble terrace. "Where can the children be?"

His voice jars the silence.

"Where have you been?"

No time to think out a lie. A brief flash of revolt. Giuseppe cries: "With the Powells."

Antoine gave a start. Then had his father known . . . ?

"With the Powells."

Annetta slips away between the pillars, crosses the vestibule, runs up the stairs to her bedroom, locks herself in, and flings herself, in the dark, upon her narrow, virginal bed.

Downstairs, for the first time, the son confronts his father. And—strangest thing of all—for the sheer joy of bravado he affirms that other, wraithlike love in which he believes no more. "I took Annetta to see Mrs. Powell." He pauses, then adds in a clear, emphatic tone: "I am engaged to Sybil."

The father bursts out laughing. A terrifying laugh. Extended by the shadow that prolongs it, the massive form looks more imposing still, of more than human stature, a Titan haloed with moonlight. Laughing. Giuseppe wrings his hands. The laugh ends. Silence. "You shall come back with me to Naples, both of you, tomorrow." "No!" "Giuseppe!" "I do not belong to you. I am engaged to Sybil Powell."

Never yet has the father met a resistance that he has not crushed. He feigns calmness. "Be silent, boy! They come here to eat our bread, to buy our land. To take our sons as well—that's too much. Did you imagine a heretic could ever bear our name?" "My name." "Fool! Never. A Huguenot intrigue . . . The salvation of a soul . . . Honour of the Seregnos. But they reckoned without me. I can defend my own." "Father!" "I'll break your will. I'll cut you off. I'll have you enlisted in the Piedmont regiment." "Father!" "Yes, I'll break you. Go to your room. You shall leave this place tomorrow."

Giuseppe clenches his fists. He wants his father to . . .

Antoine drew a deep breath.

. . . to die.

Somehow he brings himself to laugh: the last affront. "You're comic!"

He walks past his father. His head high, mouth twisted in a mocking laugh, he goes down the steps.

"Where are you going?"

The boy stops. What poisoned barb shall he launch before he disappears for ever? Instinct gives him the words that will tell most. "I am going to kill myself."

With a quick movement he is down the steps. The father has raised his arm. "Go away, you shameless son." For the last time the father's voice is heard, shouting in imprecation. "My curse on you!"

Giuseppe runs across the terrace, out into the night.

Antoine had half a mind to pause again, and ponder; but only a few pages remained and impatience got the better of him.

Giuseppe runs blindly forward. Then stops, breathless, perplexed, all at sea. In the distance a thin, plaintive melody rising, falling; mandolins on some hotel veranda. Melting languor. How blissful death, veins opened, in the soft warmth of a bath!

Sybil does not like the music of Neapolitan mandolins. Sybil, a foreigner. Remote, unreal as the heroine one has loved madly—in a book.

Annetta. The memory of a bare arm nestling in his hand, enough! A buzzing in the ears. Dry lips.

Giuseppe has planned it all. He will come back at daybreak, carry off Annetta, flee with her. He will steal into her room; she will jump out of bed, bare-limbed, welcoming. Ah, sweetness of her embrace, smooth, yielding sinews, the warm fragrance of her body! Almost he feels her now, straining to him, with lightly parted lips, moist lips, Annetta!

Giuseppe plunges into a side-path. His heart beats wildly. At a bound he crosses a ridge of rock. Bracing airs, the countryside under the moon.

At the edge of a thicket he lies on his back, arms outspread. Passes his fingers through his open shirt-neck, strokes his heaving breast. Overhead, a milk-white sky, star-spangled. Peace, purity.

And Sybil?

Giuseppe jumps up. Strides hotfoot down the hillside. Sybil. For the last time; before daybreak.

Lunadoro. The wall, the curving gateway. On that newly whitewashed wall, the exact place of his shadow-kiss. His first avowal, here. On such a night, moon-enchanted. Sybil had come to see him off. Her shadow clean-cut on the white wall. He had taken courage, bent and kissed the shadow of her face. She had run away. On such a night as this.

Why have I come back to the little gate, Annetta? Sybil's pale face, wilful, unyielding. Remote? No, near, and real, yet still all unknown. Can he give Sybil up? No, rather unlock that fast-shut heart, with love the key. Release her stifled soul. What is the secret sealing it? Ah, dream of purity, unsoiled by instinct, real love! His love of Sybil, real love.

Why those meek eyes and too submissive lips, Annetta! No flame leaps in your all-too-docile flesh. Short-lived desire. Love without mystery, depth, horizons. With no tomorrow.

Annetta, let us forget those kisses, lightly given, lightly taken; let's be children again. Dear Annetta, little, lovely girl. Little sister!

Submissive lips, yes, but eager, too; moist, melting, clinging lips. Ah, fatal, criminal desire, who shall deliver us from this body of desire?

Annetta, Sybil. Love rent in twain. Which? Why have to choose? I meant no wrong. Dual attraction; necessary, hallowed equilibrium. Twin impulses, equally legitimate, for they spring from the depth of my being. Why, in reality, irreconcilable? How pure it might be, under the free, broad light of day! Why this ban, if in my heart all is harmony?

Only one solution: one of the three must drop out. Which?

Sybil? Ah, vision unbearable! Sybil in pain; not Sybil. Annetta, then? Annetta, *sorellina,* forgive me.

Not one without the other; well, then—neither! Renunciation, oblivion, death. No, not death; death's likeness. Eclipse. Here a curse lies on all, an interdiction; the prison-house.

Here life and love are impossible. Good-bye.

Lure of the unknown, lure of a wholly new tomorrow, ecstasy. The past forgotten, take to the open road.

Turn away. Hurry to the station. The first train to Rome. Rome, the first train to Genoa. Genoa, the first liner. To America, or to Australia.

Suddenly he laughs.

A woman, women? No, it's life I love. Forward!

Jack Baulthy.

Antoine closed the magazine with a bang, crammed it into his pocket, and stood up. For a moment, dizzily, he blinked at the lights; then, feeling his head spinning, he sat down again.

While he was reading, the room had gradually emptied; the band had stopped, the billiard-players gone off to dinner. Alone in their corner, the Jew and the youth who had been reading *The Rights of Man* were finishing off a game of backgammon, under the pert eyes of the girl beside them. Her friend was puffing at a dead pipe, and each time he threw the dice the minx rubbed her head against the Jew's shoulder with a little provocative giggle.

Antoine stretched his legs, lit a cigarette, and tried to set his thoughts in order. But for some minutes his mind kept wandering, like his gaze; there was no steadying it. The picture of Jacques and Gise kept rising before him; at last he thrust it aside, and regained some measure of calm.

The crucial problem was to draw a sharp dividing line between facts and fiction. That stormy interview between father and son, he was convinced, had actually taken place as Jacques described it. Some of the phrases used by the old judge, Seregno, rang obviously true: "Huguenot intrigues"; "I'll break you"; "I'll cut you off"; "I'll have you enlisted." And the remark about a heretic "bearing our name." Antoine could almost hear the angry voice of his father as he stood there raging on the terrace, hurling his curse into the darkness. And true, undoubtedly, was Giuseppe's threat: "I am going to kill myself"— which at last explained M. Thibault's fixed idea. From the very start, he had always refused to believe that Jacques was still alive, and he had telephoned four times a day to the Morgue. That too explained his remorse, his half-disclosed admission that he had been to blame for Jacques's disappearance. Quite conceivably this rankling self-reproach might have some connexion with the attack of albuminuria the old man had had just before the operation. In the light of these facts many events of the past three years took on a new complexion.

Antoine picked up the magazine and read again the dedication written in Jacques's hand.

Did you not say to me, on that famous November evening: "Everything is subject to the influence of two poles; the truth is always double-faced"? So, sometimes, is love.

Jack Baulthy.

Evidently, he mused, that would account for many things—the tangle Jacques had got into with those two love-affairs. If Gise was Jacques's mistress and, at the same time, he was so desperately in love with Jenny, life must have been infernally difficult for him. And yet . . .

Antoine could not help feeling that there remained something elusive and obscure which he so far had failed to grasp. Try as he might, he could not bring himself to think that Jacques's departure was accounted for merely by what he had just learned of the boy's emotional dilemma. That desperate resolve must have been enforced by other circumstances as well, some sudden impact of imponderable factors.

Then all at once it struck him that these problems could very well wait. The important thing now was to make the most of the clues he had just lit on, and to get on his brother's track as soon as possible.

It would be an obvious blunder to write directly to the office of the review. That Jacques had given no sign of life proved that he was still determined to lie low. To risk letting him guess that his retreat had been detected involved the danger that he might be prompted to move on again, and be lost sight of irretrievably. Yes, Antoine mused, there was only one way to a successful issue and that was to launch a surprise attack, and in person—for he had no real confidence in anyone except himself.

Promptly he pictured himself alighting from the train at Geneva. But what would he do, once there? Jacques might be living in London. No, the best thing would be first of all to send a detective to Switzerland, to ascertain Jacques's whereabouts. "And then," he murmured, rising from the table, "I'll go and dig him out, wherever he is. If only I can take him by surprise, we'll see if he escapes me!"

That evening he gave his instructions to a detective-bureau.

Four days later he received the following document:

Private and Confidential

M. Jack Baulthy is, as you surmised, resident in Switzerland. He is not living at Geneva, however, but at Lausanne, where, we learn, he has had several successive residences. Since April last he has been staying at the Pension Kammerzinn, 10 Rue des Escarliers-du-Marché.

We have not yet been able to verify the date on which he entered Swiss territory. Meanwhile, however, we have taken steps to discover his position as regards the military authorities.

From information elicited by private inquiries at the French Consulate we learn that M. Baulthy presented himself in January 1912, at the military bureau of the said consulate, bringing various identification and other papers in the name of Jacques Jean Paul Oscar-Thibault, of French nationality, born in Paris in 1890. We were unable to procure a copy of his description on the military registration form (this description is, however, identical with that already cited), but we would inform you that the said form shows that M. Baulthy was granted a provisional exemption from military service on the ground of functional disorder of the heart, in 1910, under an order of the Board of Military Examiners, in Paris; and an extension of the said exemption, in 1911, by virtue of a medical certificate submitted in

1911 to the French Consul at Vienna. He underwent another medical examination at Lausanne in February 1912; the decision of the Board was transmitted through the proper channels to the Recruiting Bureau of the Seine Department. A third extension was granted by the Bureau, and as a result he has nothing to apprehend from the French Authorities as regards the question of his military service.

We gather that M. Baulthy is leading a respectable life, and his friends are for the most part journalists and students. He is a registered member of the Swiss Press Club. The literary work he does for several daily papers and periodicals assures him an honest livelihood. We are told that M. Baulthy writes under several names besides his own, which we shall be pleased to ascertain if further advices are received from you to that effect.

The report was marked *Urgent,* and was brought to Antoine on a Sunday at 10 p.m. by a special messenger from the detective-bureau.

It was quite impossible for Antoine to leave the following morning, but M. Thibault's condition was such that he dared not delay. After consulting his engagement-book and the time-table, he decided to take the Lausanne express on Monday evening. All that night he did not sleep a wink.

VI

THAT Monday was already a particularly heavy day for appointments, but somehow Antoine, owing to his departure, had to fit into it several extra visits. He left for the hospital at an early hour and spent the rest of the day rushing to and fro in Paris, without even finding time to snatch a lunch at home. He did not get back till after seven in the evening. The train left at eight-thirty.

While Léon packed his suitcase, Antoine ran up to see his father, whom he had not visited since the previous day. There had been, he noticed, a definite change for the worse. M. Thibault had been unable to take food; he was in a very weak state and in constant pain.

It was an effort for Antoine to greet him as usual with that cheery

"Hallo, Father!" which acted on the old man as a never-failing tonic. He sat down in his usual chair and began putting the daily series of questions, eschewing like a pitfall the least interval of silence. Though outwardly he looked cheerful as ever, a thought kept running in his mind insistently: "He is very near his end."

Several times he was struck by the brooding gaze his father cast on him, dark with unuttered questions.

Antoine wondered how far the dying man guessed the truth as to his actual condition. M. Thibault often spoke with resignation and solemnity of his approaching end. But what did he really think deep within his heart?

For some minutes father and son, each absorbed in his unspoken thoughts—the same thoughts, very likely—exchanged trivial remarks about symptoms and the latest treatments. Then Antoine rose, remarking that he had an urgent case to visit before dinner. M. Thibault, who was in pain, made no effort to detain him.

So far Antoine had let no one into the secret of his departure. His intention had been to tell no one but the nurse that he would be away for the next thirty-six hours. Unfortunately, when he was leaving the sick-room, she was busy with the invalid.

There was no time to lose. He waited some moments in the corridor; then, when she failed to appear, he looked in on Mlle. de Waize, who was writing a letter in her room.

"I'm so glad you've come, Antoine," she began at once. "You must lend me a hand! Do you know, a basket of vegetables has somehow gone astray!"

He had immense difficulty in making her understand that he had been summoned to the country that night for an urgent case, that he would probably not be back next day, but that there was no need for anxiety; Dr. Thérivier had been informed of his departure and would come immediately, if necessary.

It was after eight; Antoine had not a minute to lose. He told the taxi-driver to make haste, and, to the accelerated tempo of an adventure film, the Place du Carrousel, the sleek, black bridges and deserted quaysides scudded past the windows. For Antoine, who rarely travelled, there was a thrill in speeding thus across the darkness; the sense of sudden crisis, the myriad thoughts fermenting in his brain, and, most of all, the element of risk in his rash quest, had plunged him into an exciting world of high adventure.

The car in which his seat had been reserved was nearly full. In vain he tried to sleep. His nerves on edge, he began counting the stops. Towards the end of the night, when he was just dropping off, the engine emitted a long, lugubrious shriek; the train was slowing down for the Vallorbe station. After the customs formalities, after standing in line in bleak, cold passages, and gulping down a cup of strong Swiss coffee, he abandoned hope of getting to sleep again.

The visible world was slowly taking form in the tardy December dawn. The train was following the bed of a valley, and dim hillsides loomed on either hand. No colour anywhere; in the harsh grey light the landscape showed like a charcoal sketch, all in blacks and whites.

Antoine's gaze registered the scene impassively. Snow crowned the hill-tops, and sprawled in slabs of melting whiteness along pitch-black ravines. Sudden shadows of tall fir-trees etched the grey slopes. Then all grew blurred: the train was passing through a cloud. Presently he had a glimpse of open country studded everywhere with pin-point yellow lights glimmering through the mist, tokens of a thickly populated countryside and early-rising folk. Already clusters of houses were becoming visible and, as the tide of darkness ebbed, fewer lights shone in the buildings.

Gradually the blackness of the soil was fading into green, and soon the whole plain showed as a bright expanse of luxuriant meadows, streaked with white bands marking each fold of the ground, each watercourse and furrow. In the low farmhouses squatting on their crofts like broody hens, all the little window-shutters were swinging open. The sun had risen.

Gazing vaguely across the trembling pane, Antoine felt the melancholy of this foreign landscape colouring his mood. A sense of hopelessness came over him, and now the difficulties of his project seemed insuperable. Moreover, he was alarmingly conscious that after his sleepless night he was in the worst possible form to face them.

Meanwhile Lausanne was drawing near; the train was already passing through the suburbs. He gazed at the still sleep-bound housefronts; tiered with balconies, four-square and standing on its own ground, each block of flats looked like a miniature skyscraper. Quite possibly behind one of those light-hued Venetian blinds, Jacques was getting up at this very moment.

The train stopped. An icy wind was sweeping the platform. Antoine shivered. The passengers were flocking down a subway. Dog-tired, his nerves in rags, his mind and will for once completely out of hand, he followed the crowd, wearily dragging his bag along, uncertain what step to take next. A notice, "Wash and Brush-up, Baths, Showers," caught his eye. Just the thing! A warm bath first to relax his muscles, followed by an invigorating shower. He could shave, too, and change his shirt. His last chance of getting in trim again.

His ablutions proved a wonder-working tonic; he left the bathroom feeling a new man. Hastening to the cloak-room, he deposited his bag there, and set out determinedly on his quest.

Rain was coming down in torrents. He jumped into a street car bound citywards. It was barely eight, but the shops were already open, and many people up and about, silently going their busy ways, in raincoats and rubbers. Though there was no wheeled traffic in the street these people took care, he noticed, to keep to the pavements, which were crowded. "An industrious, level-headed folk," he observed to himself. Antoine was fond of quick generalizations. Helped by his map of Lausanne, he found his way to the little square beside the town hall. When he peered up at the belfry, it was striking half-past eight. The street where Jacques lived was at the far end of the square.

The Rue des Escaliers-du-Marché seemed to be one of the oldest streets in Lausanne. It was less a street, in fact, than a truncated alley, consisting of a steep ascent with houses only on the left. The little street climbed tier by tier; facing the houses rose a wall ribboned by an ancient wooden staircase, which was roofed over with medieval timberwork painted a purplish red. This sheltered staircase offered a convenient observation-post, of which Antoine took advantage. The few houses in the alley followed an irregular alinement; they were small and tumbledown, and the lower stories gave the impression of having served as small shops perhaps as far back as the sixteenth century. A low doorway, overweighted by its lavishly carved lintel, gave access to Number 10. On one of the panels was a weather-worn inscription: "Pension J. H. Kammerzinn." So that was where Jacques lived.

After those three weary years without news, after feeling that the whole world lay between him and his brother, the thought that in a few minutes he would see Jacques again came with an unexpected thrill. But Antoine had the knack of mastering emotion—his profession had schooled him well—and as he summoned up his energy, his thoughts grew lucid, untouched by feeling. "Half-past eight," he said to himself. "He's at home presumably. Half-past eight—why, it's the usual time for police arrests! If he's in, I'll say I've an appointment and go straight into his room, unannounced." Screening his face with his umbrella, he crossed the street with a determined tread and climbed the two steps leading to the street-door.

A paved hall led up to an old-fashioned staircase, flanked by banisters; it was wide and well kept, but dark. There were no doors. Antoine began going up the stairs. Presently he heard a vague murmur of voices. When his head was above the level of the landing he saw, through the glass door of a dining-room, some ten or twelve boarders seated round a table. "Lucky the stairs are so dark," he thought. "They can't see me." Then: "The boarders are having their breakfast. *He* isn't there yet. He'll be coming down." And suddenly—yes, it was Jacques, his voice and intonation. He had just spoken. Jacques was there, living, large as life!

Antoine tottered and, gripped by a sudden panic, hastily retreated a few paces. His breath came in gasps; surging up from the depths, that rush of affection seemed flooding his lungs, suffocating him. A nuisance, all those strangers! What was he to do? Go away for a bit? No. He pulled himself together; as usual, difficulty was a spur to his energies. There must be no delay; he must act promptly. He could see Jacques's profile only now and then because of the people round him.

A little old man with a white beard was sitting at the head of the table; five or six men of various ages were in the other seats. Opposite the old man was a good-looking, fair-haired woman, still young, with a little girl on each side of her. Jacques was bending forward, speaking in quick, eager tones. He seemed at ease amongst these people. Antoine, whose presence hovered like an impending threat over his brother's peace of mind, was struck by the unawareness of what the next instant is to bring, the insouciance, that attends the most critical moments of a lifetime. The others seemed interested in the discussion, the old man was laughing; Jacques appeared to be holding his own against two youths sitting opposite him. Twice, to emphasize a remark, he made that commanding gesture with his right hand which Antoine had forgotten. Unexpectedly, after a swift exchange of repartee, he smiled. Jacques's smile!

Then, without more ado, Antoine went up the steps again, walked to the glazed door and softly opened it, taking off his hat.

Ten faces swung round towards his, but he did not see them. He did not see the little old man rising from his chair to put a startled question. Gay and resolute, his eyes were fixed on Jacques, and Jacques returned his brother's gaze, his pupils large with wonder, his lips half parted. Cut short in the midst of a remark, he still had on his frozen features the look of merriment that had accompanied it, changed to an odd grimace. The deadlock lasted only a few seconds; Jacques rose to his feet, with one idea in his head—above all, to pass it off and to avoid any appearance of a "scene."

With hurried steps, with a clumsy effusiveness meant to give the impression that his caller was expected, he walked straight up to Antoine, who, playing his part, moved back towards the landing. Jacques joined him there, then closed the door behind him. Neither was conscious of shaking hands, though they must have done so, automatically. Neither could utter a word.

Jacques seemed to hesitate, made an awkward gesture, as if inviting Antoine to follow, and began walking upstairs.

VII

TWO, three flights of stairs. Jacques walked heavily up, clinging to the banisters, without looking back. Behind him, Antoine was feeling perfectly calm and collected; so much so that he was surprised at being so little moved. Indeed, there had been occasions in his life when he had asked himself not without a qualm: "What's one to make of a composure so easily come by? Is it presence of mind, or just absence of emotion, callousness?"

On the fourth floor there was one door only; Jacques opened it. Once they were in the room he turned the key, and for the first time looked his brother in the eyes.

"What do you want of me?" he asked in a low, grating voice.

But the truculence of his gaze could not stand up against Antoine's affectionate smile; under his geniality, Antoine was shrewdly biding his time, willing to temporize, but prepared to hold his own. Jacques lowered his eyes.

"What do you want of me?" he repeated. The tone was bitterly indignant, but tremulous with apprehension, almost plaintive. Antoine was surprised at feeling so little stirred by it. He had to feign emotion.

"Jacques!" he murmured, drawing nearer. While he played his part, he was studying his brother with keen, observant eyes. Jacques's commanding presence surprised him, as did his general aspect and expression, all so changed from what they once had been, from what he had imagined.

Jacques's eyebrows contracted. Vainly he tried to control his feelings; it was all he could do to keep his lips closed on the sobs that welled up from his heart. Then suddenly his ill-temper passed out in a deep sigh, he seemed to give up the struggle, and, yielding to his weakness, let his forehead sink on Antoine's shoulder.

"Oh, Antoine," he cried again, "what do they want of me? Tell me!"

Antoine had an intuition that he must answer at once, and strike hard.

"Father is in a very bad way. He is dying." After a pause he added: "That's why I've come to fetch you, old man."

Jacques had not flinched. So his father was dying? But why suppose that, in this new life he had carved out for himself, his father's death could affect him, draw him forth from his retreat, or change one jot of the circumstances that had compelled him to leave home. Nothing in what Antoine had just said had deeply moved him; nothing except the last two words, "old man!" What years since he had heard them!

The silence was so embarrassing that Antoine hastened to continue: "I'm all by myself." Then he had a sudden inspiration. "Mademoiselle doesn't count, of course, and Gise is away in England."

Jacques looked up. "In England?"

"Yes, she's at a convent near London, studying for a diploma, and can't get away. I'm all alone, and I want your help."

Though he was unaware of it, Jacques's dogged resistance had been shaken and, while as yet unformulated in his mind, the notion of a possible return had lost something of its sting. He drew away, took some faltering steps; then as if he preferred to let his mood of black despondency engulf him, he sank into the chair in front of his desk, burying his head in his hands, and broke into a storm of sobs. He did not feel the hand that Antoine laid on his shoulder. He was picturing this place of refuge he had so laboriously built up—in pride and solitude, stone by stone, during the past three years—falling in ruin. In the twilight of his thoughts there was enough clear vision left to confront the inevitable, to see that any resistance on his part was bound to fail, that sooner or later he would have to go home, and his glorious isolation, if not his freedom, had come to an end; that the wisest course was to come to terms with what must be. But his inability to resist made him choke with rankling despite.

Antoine had remained standing, keeping his eyes on his brother, in a thoughtful attitude, as though his affection were for the moment in abeyance. The sight of the bent back shaken with sobs brought to his mind Jacques's fits of despair in early youth; meanwhile, however, he was coolly weighing his chances. The longer the fit lasted, the better chance there was that Jacques would bring himself to yield. He had withdrawn his hand and, while he took stock of his surroundings, his brain was busy with a host of thoughts. The room, he noticed, was not merely clean, but also cosy. Though the low ceiling showed that it was a converted attic, it was well lit, spacious, and the colour-effect of limpid yellow was agreeable to the eye. Wax-hued and highly polished, the floor emitted faint crackling sounds, no doubt due to the heat from the little white porcelain stove in which a log-fire roared cheerfully. There were two easy chairs covered with a gay cretonne, and several tables strewn with newspapers and documents. Some books, not more than fifty in all, stood on a shelf above the still unmade bed. Not a single photograph, nothing to recall the past. Antoine's disapproval was tempered with a spice of envy.

He noticed that Jacques was growing calmer, and wondered if it meant that he had yielded, would come back to Paris. Actually, Antoine had always been certain he would carry out his project. And now that the flood-gates were open, a great wave of affection swept over him, an overpowering rush of love and pity; he would have liked to strain his unhappy young brother to his breast. Bending over the bowed back he whispered:

"Jacques!"

With a brusque movement Jacques swung himself erect. Furiously he dried his eyes and glared at his brother.

"Are you angry with me?" Antoine asked.

No reply.

"Father's dying, you know," he continued, as though to excuse himself.

Jacques looked away.

"When?" His tone was curt, almost indifferent, but his eyes were haggard. He realized what he had just said, when he caught Antoine's look.

"When," he murmured, staring at the floor, "when . . . do you want to start?"

"As soon as possible. His condition is alarming."

"Tomorrow?"

Antoine hesitated. "This evening, if it can be managed."

Their eyes met for a moment. Then Jacques shrugged his shoulders; tonight, tomorrow, what did it matter now?

"The night express then," he agreed in a toneless voice.

Antoine understood that *their* departure had been settled. But he was still awaiting what he had desired with all his heart; actually he felt neither pleasure nor surprise.

Both were standing now, in the centre of the room. No sound came from the street; they might have been in the heart of the country. Rain was streaming down the steep-pitched roof, and sudden gusts of wind came whistling under the loose tiles. And every moment the tension between them was increasing.

Antoine had a feeling that Jacques wished to be alone.

"I expect you've plenty to do," he said. "I'll go out for a bit."

Jacques flushed. "Plenty to do? No; why should I?" Hastily he sat down again.

"Quite sure?"

Jacques shook his head.

"In that case," Antoine remarked with a cordiality that rang false, "I'll sit down too. We've lots to say to each other."

What he really wanted was to ask questions, but his courage failed him. To gain time he launched out into a detailed and, despite himself, technical account of the various phases of their father's illness. These details did not merely recall to his mind a hopeless case; they summoned up the sick-room, the bed, and the dying, swollen, pain-racked body on it, the convulsed features and the piteous cries wrung from an agony which it was almost impossible to subdue. And it was Antoine's voice now that trembled with emotion, while Jacques, hunched up in his chair, stared at the stove with a look of stubborn aloofness, as if to say: "Father is dying, and you've come to drag me away—well and good, I'll go. But ask no more of me." At one moment Antoine fancied he saw Jacques unbend a little from his impassibility. It was when he described how he had heard through the door the sick man and Mademoiselle singing together the old nursery song. Jacques remembered the "pretty pony" and, while his eyes remained fixed on the stove, a slow smile formed on his lips. A wan, far-away smile—exactly the smile he used to have as a little boy.

But, almost immediately after, when Antoine said in conclusion: "After all the suffering he's been through, it will be a happy release," Jacques, who till then had not said a word, remarked in a harsh, incisive voice:

"For us, undoubtedly."

Antoine was too profoundly shocked to answer. In Jacques's callous attitude there was, he realized, a good deal of bravado, but behind it was only too apparent an animosity that would not be disarmed, and this hatred for a sorely afflicted, dying man was more than Antoine could stomach. To his mind it was unjust and, to say the least of it, quite ill-timed, as things were now. He remembered the evening when M. Thibault had shed tears, accusing himself of being responsible for his son's suicide. Nor could he forget the effect Jacques's disappearance had had on the old man's health. Grief and remorse might well have played a part in bringing on the nervous depression which had enabled the malady to take root, and but for which the present complications would perhaps not have developed so rapidly.

Then, as if he had been waiting impatiently for his brother to finish speaking, Jacques stood up abruptly and burst out with the question:

"How did you find out where I was?"

Evasion was impossible.

"Oh, through—through Jalicourt."

"Jalicourt!" It seemed as if this was the last name he had expected. He repeated it syllable by syllable, incredulously: "Ja-li-court?"

Antoine, who had taken out his pocket-book, quietly handed to his brother the letter from Jalicourt which he had opened. This seemed the simplest course; no verbal explanations would be needed.

Jacques took the letter and glanced over its contents; then, going to the window, he perused it carefully, his eyes half hidden by the lids, and his lips tight-set, inscrutable.

Antoine was observing him. Surely Jacques's face, which three years earlier had still the undecided features of an adolescent, should not, clean-shaven as it was, now seem so very different? He scanned it with interest, puzzled to define exactly how it had changed. He found in it more energy, less pride, and less unrest as well; less obstinacy and more self-reliance. Jacques had certainly lost his charm, but he had gained in physique. His build was almost stocky; his shoulders had widened, and his head, which had grown larger, seemed set too low between them. Jacques had a way of holding his head well back—giving an impression of pugnacity, not to say of arrogance. His under-jaw was formidable, and, for all their melancholy droop, the lines of his mouth were firm and forceful. What particularly struck Antoine was the changed expression of Jacques's mouth. His complexion was as pale as ever, with a few freckles over the cheek-bones. Jacques's hair had changed colour—its auburn tint had darkened into brown—and, growing in a thick, unruly mop, it made the resolute features seem more massive still. A lock of hair, dark brown with glints of gold, which Jacques was always pushing back impatiently, kept falling over his forehead, shadowing a portion of it.

Antoine saw the forehead twitching; two deep furrows had formed between Jacques's brows. He realized what a shock there must be for Jacques in all the thoughts that letter was evoking, nor was he in the least surprised when, letting the hand that held the letter drop to his side, his brother turned to him and muttered:

"I suppose you . . . you, too, have read my story?"

Antoine's only answer was a flutter of the eyelashes. The affection in his gaze—he was smiling less with his lips than with his eyes—gradually got the better of his brother's vexation. When Jacques spoke again it was in a less aggressive tone.

"And who . . . who else has read it?"

"No one."

Jacques looked incredulous.

"No one else, I assure you," Antoine said emphatically.

Jacques thrust his hands into his pockets, and said nothing. As a matter of fact, he was rapidly getting used to the thought that his brother had read "*La Sorellina,*" and would even have liked to hear his opinion of it. Personally, he was severe in his judgment of this work, written in a mood of fiery exaltation, but a year and a half earlier. He believed he had made vast strides since that period, and he now found unbearable its experimentalism and lyrical effusion, its juvenile exuberance. The oddest thing was that he did not give a thought to its theme, so far as that theme was linked up with his own life. Once he had transmuted past experience into terms of art, he felt that he had got it definitely out of his system. Nowadays, whenever he chanced to think of those troublous times, it was to tell himself at once: "I've got over all that, thank goodness!"

Thus, when Antoine had said: "I've come to fetch you," his first response had been to reassure himself: "Anyhow, I've got over all that," following it up with: "What's more, Gise is away, in England." For, if need be, he could bear with being reminded of Gise, and hearing her name; only of the faintest allusion to Jenny was he fanatically intolerant.

For a moment he stood unmoving, silent, in front of the window, gazing into the distance. Then he turned again.

"Who knows that you've come here?"

"No one."

This time he insisted. "What about Father?"

"I tell you, he knows nothing."

"And Gise?"

"No. Nobody knows." To reassure his brother still further, Antoine added: "After what happened, and as Gise is in London, it's best for her to know nothing, for the present."

Jacques was watching his brother; the glint of an unspoken question flickered in his eyes, died out.

Again there was a silence—Antoine had come to dread these silences;

unfortunately, the greater his desire to break the tension, the more an opening eluded him. Obviously a host of questions suggested themselves, but he dared not voice them. He kept on groping for some harmless, neutral topic which might pave the way for greater intimacy; no such theme presented itself.

The tension was growing strained to breaking-point when suddenly Jacques threw the window open, then stepped back from it. A superb Siamese tom-cat, with dusky muzzle and thick, cream-brown coat, sprang lithely down to the floor.

"Ah, a visitor!" Antoine exclaimed with relief.

Jacques smiled. "A friend. And the nicest kind of friend, an intermittent one."

"Where does he come from?"

"I've not been able to find out. From some distance, I imagine. No one in our street knows anything about him."

The handsome cat made a lordly circuit of the room, purring like a musical top.

"Your friend is soaked through," Antoine observed; he felt that dreaded silence on the point of closing in again.

"Yes," Jacques said, "he usually honours me with a visit when it's raining. Sometimes as late as midnight. He scratches on the pane, jumps in, and gives himself a cleaning in front of the stove. Once he's done, he asks to be let out. I've never persuaded him to let me stroke him, still less to feed him."

After his inspection of the room, the cat went back towards the window, which was still ajar.

"Look!" Jacques said almost cheerfully. "He didn't expect to find you here; he's off again."

The cat sprang lightly onto the zinc windowsill and, without a look behind, was off along the tiles.

"Your protégé is rather tactless," Antoine remarked half in earnest, "rubbing it into me like that, that I'm an intruder."

Jacques went up to the window and shut it; a pretext for not replying. But when he turned round, his cheeks were scarlet. He fell to pacing slowly up and down the room.

Silence again, uneasy, hostile silence.

As a last resort, presumably in the hope of changing Jacques's attitude, and because his mind was haunted by thoughts of the dying man, Antoine began speaking again of his father. He laid stress on the changes that had come over M. Thibault's character since the operation, and went so far as to observe:

"You'd judge him differently, perhaps, if you'd seen how he has aged, as I have, during these last three years."

"Perhaps," Jacques replied evasively.

But Antoine was not to be discouraged so easily.

"In any case," he went on, "I've often wondered if you and I ever really understood what sort of man he is, at bottom." It struck him that, while on this subject, he might describe to Jacques a little incident which had happened to him quite recently. "You remember that hairdresser, Faubois, don't you, in front of our place, next door to the cabinet-maker's, just before you turn into the Rue du Pré-aux-Clercs?"

Jacques, who was walking to and fro with lowered eyes, stopped short. Faubois . . . that little side-street! It was like the sudden, blinding inrush of a world he had fancied out of mind for ever, into the dark seclusion he had deliberately sought. How vividly it all came back, down to the smallest detail: each slab of the sidewalk, every shop-front, the old cabinet-maker with his fingers stained walnut-brown, the gaunt-faced man and his daughter who kept the curiosity shop, and then "our place" (as Antoine called it), with its carriage entrance always kept ajar, and the concierge's quarters on the ground floor, and Lisbeth, and, further back in time, all the childhood he had abjured: Lisbeth, his first experience. In Vienna he had known another Lisbeth, whose husband had killed himself out of jealousy. Suddenly he remembered he must warn Sophia, old Kammerzinn's daughter, that he was leaving.

Antoine was going on with his anecdote.

One day, Jacques gathered, being pressed for time, his brother had dropped in at Faubois's shop for a shave. The brothers had always refused to give their patronage to Faubois, because this hairdresser had for twenty years had their father's custom, trimming his beard each Saturday. The old man, who knew Antoine well by sight, had at once begun talking to him about M. Thibault. And, little by little, Antoine, as he listened absent-mindedly, a towel round his neck, found, to his amazement, the old barber's gossip blocking out a portrait of his father far different from any he had anticipated. "For instance," Antoine said, "he was always talking about us to Faubois. About you, especially. Faubois well remembers the day when 'M. Thibault's boy'—that's you—passed his 'matric.' As he was going by, Father pushed the shop-door open and announced: 'M. Faubois, my boy's got through his exam.' 'Pleased as Punch, your old dad was that day; it did one good to see it!' That's how Faubois put it. Surprising, isn't it? But what staggers me most is what's been happening—the change—in these last three years."

A slight frown had settled on Jacques's face; Antoine wondered if he were not blundering. Still, he had gone too far to stop.

"Yes. Ever since you left. I discovered finally that Father had never let the truth leak out, that he'd made up a whole yarn to hoodwink everybody. Here's the sort of thing Faubois said to me that day: 'There's nothing like foreign travel. Your father did well to send his young son abroad, seeing he had the money to pay for it. Why, with the mails, there ain't no trouble nowadays getting letters from anywhere on earth, and your father, he told me he got a letter each week from his boy, regular as clockwork.'"

Antoine refrained from looking at Jacques, and decided to sheer off these memories that touched him too nearly.

"Father used to talk to him about me, too. 'My elder boy will be a professor at the Medical School one of these days.' About Mademoiselle, too, and the maids. Faubois knows all about the household. About Gise, as well. By the way, that's a curious thing; it seems that Father talked quite a lot about Gise. I gathered that Faubois used to have a daughter of about the same age; I believe she's dead. He would say to Father: 'My girl does so and so,' and Father'd cap it with: 'My girl does so and so.' Would you believe it? Faubois reminded me of a great many things I'd forgotten and Father'd told him of—childish pranks, things Gise said when she was little. And there's something else. I can quote the exact words Faubois used: 'Your dad was always sorry he hadn't had a daughter. "But," he says to me, "this little girl she's just like a daughter to me."' Exactly that! Well, I tell you I was simply staggered! Yes, under all his gruffness Father had a heart—shy, perhaps, and over-sensitive—that no one ever dreamt of."

Without a word, without once looking up, Jacques was still walking to and fro; though he rarely glanced in his brother's direction, none of Antoine's movements escaped him. He was not stirred emotionally, but he was torn by violent, contradictory impulses. What was most painful to him by far was the feeling that the past was breaking into his life inevitably, whether by force or with his free consent.

Confronted by Jacques's silence, Antoine was losing heart; it seemed quite futile trying to get a conversation under way. He kept a close watch on his brother's face, hoping against hope to catch some gleam of a responsive thought. But all he saw was gloomy, stubborn indifference. And yet he could not bring himself to feel resentful. Even with its aloofness from him, for all its dourness, that was the face he loved more than all other faces, his brother's. And once again, though he dared not betray it by word or gesture, a wave of deep affection swept over him.

But now silence had set in again, oppressive, ineluctable. The only sounds were the ripple of water in the gutters, the crackling of the fire, and now and then the creak of a loose board as Jacques stepped on it.

Going up to the stove, he opened it and put in two logs; as he crouched before it, almost on his knees, he turned to his brother, who was following him with his eyes, and muttered in a surly tone:

"You judge me harshly. But I don't care; you're wrong."

"But I don't judge you, Jacques," Antoine hastened to put in.

"I've a perfect right to be happy in my own way," Jacques went on.

He drew himself up with a quick jerk, was silent for a moment, then added through his clenched teeth: "And here I've been completely happy."

Antoine bent forward. "Do you really mean that?"

"Yes. Completely."

After each remark they gazed intently at each other for a moment. In their eyes was curiosity, but behind it loyalty, the deeper for its reticence.

"I believe you," Antoine said. "In any case, your leaving home . . . Still, there are so many things that I . . . well, that puzzle me." He made haste to add: "Don't think I want to blame you in the least, my dear Jacques. . . ."

Then for the first time Jacques noticed his brother's smile. The Antoine he remembered had been so painfully strenuous, so aggressively the man of action, that the charm of the changed smile came as a surprise. Perhaps fearing to yield to his emotion, he clenched his fists and made a gesture of annoyance.

"Oh, Antoine, stop it! Don't talk about that any more!" Then, as if to qualify his outburst, added: "For the present." A look of real distress passed over his face; turning towards a dark corner of the room, he said in a low, veiled voice: "You don't, you can't possibly understand. . . ."

They were silent again, but the oppressiveness had lifted from the air.

Antoine rose and, in a casual tone which he was none the less careful not to overdo, inquired: "Don't you smoke? I'm dying for a cigarette, if you don't mind." He felt it necessary to keep the situation on an undramatic level; gradually, by cordiality and easy manners, to wean his brother from his churlishness.

He took a few puffs at his cigarette, then went to the window. Below him he saw the roofs of old Lausanne cataracting down towards the lake in an inextricable tangle of black humps and ridges, the outlines of which blurred into the vapour steaming off them. Coated with lichen, the tiled roofs looked sodden as rain-drenched felt. A range of mountains with the light behind them fretted the far horizon, their snow-caps gleaming white against the drab grey sky, and long pale streaks trailing down the leaden-hued slopes. It was as if a range of black volcanoes had erupted milk, depositing a creamy lava.

Jacques went up to him.

"Those are the Dents d'Oche," he said, pointing towards the snow-caps.

Falling away in tiers, the city masked the nearer bank, and against the light the further shore loomed through the veil of rain like a sheer cliff of darkness.

"So much for your charming lake!" Antoine remarked. "Today it looks more like the Channel in a squall."

Jacques vouchsafed a fleeting smile. He stayed at the window, unmoving, unable to take his eyes off the far bank; lost in a day-dream, he was picturing its green woods and villages, the fleets of little boats moored along the piers, the winding paths leading to rustic inns perched on the mountainside. There he had wandered, lived adventurously, and now he was to leave it all—for how long? he wondered.

Antoine tried to divert his attention. "I'm sure you've heaps to do this morning. Especially if . . ." He was going to say: ". . . if we're to leave tonight," but thought better of it.

Jacques shook his head pettishly. "No, I've nothing to do. I tell you I'm quite independent. Everything's as simple as daylight when one lives alone, when one keeps . . . free." The word seemed to linger on the air after he had spoken it. Then the cheerfulness went out of his voice; gazing fixedly at his brother, he sighed: "But of course you can't understand."

Antoine wondered what sort of life Jacques might be leading at Lausanne. "There's his writing, obviously. But what does he live on?" He made some guesses at it, then by way of giving expression to his thoughts, remarked in a careless tone:

"Really, now that you've come of age, you might have claimed your share of what Mother left us."

A gleam of amusement lit Jacques's eyes. He all but put a question. For a moment he felt a slight regret; yes, on occasion, there'd been jobs he would have gladly forgone! At the Tunis docks, in the Adriatica basement at Trieste, in the Deutsche Buchdruckerei at Innsbruck. But the feeling passed at once, and the thought that M. Thibault's death would make him definitely well off did not even cross his mind. No! He did not need them, or their money. He could stand on his own feet.

"How do you manage?" Antoine ventured to ask. "Have you any trouble in earning enough to live on?"

Jacques cast a glance round the room. "You can see for yourself," he said.

Antoine could not refrain from asking a direct question: "But what exactly do you do?"

The stubborn, secretive look came back to Jacques's face. His brows knitted, then grew smooth again.

"Don't imagine," Antoine hastened to explain, "that I'm trying to poke my nose into your affairs. There's only one thing I want, old man, and that's for you to make the most of your life, to be happy."

"Happy!" Jacques sounded almost startled. It was as if he had said: "I—happy? What an idea!" Then hastily he added in an exasperated tone: "Oh, please drop it, Antoine. You'd never really understand." He tried to smile, took a few uncertain steps, then went back to the window and stared vaguely out across the lake. Seemingly unconscious that it contradicted his exclamation of a moment past, he murmured: "I've been completely happy here. Completely!"

He glanced at his watch and, without giving Antoine time to put in another word, remarked:

"I'd better introduce you to old Kammerzinn. And to his daughter, if she's in. Then we'll go and have lunch. Not here; somewhere outside." He had opened the stove again and was replenishing it as he spoke. "He used to be a tailor. Now he's a town-councillor. A keen trade-unionist too. He has started a weekly paper, which he runs almost single-handed. A very decent old fellow, you'll see."

They found Kammerzinn sitting in his overheated office. He was in his shirt-sleeves, busy correcting proofs. The old man wore curious rectangular glasses with gold stems, supple as hairs, coiling round

his small, fleshy ears. Sharp-witted for all his air of guilelessness, inclined to rant, but with a redeeming twinkle in his eye, he had a
way of looking his interlocutor full in the face, above the gold-rimmed
lenses, chuckling to himself the while. He sent for beer at once. He
started by addressing Antoine as "My dear sir"; a moment later it
was "My dear boy."

Jacques informed him briefly that his father's health obliged him
to absent himself "for some time"; he was leaving that night, but
would keep his room, paying the month's rent in advance, and would
leave "all his things" in it. Antoine heard without moving a muscle.

Waving in the air the sheets he was correcting, old Kammerzinn
launched into a voluble harangue about a project for co-operative
printing of the various party newspapers. Jacques seemed interested
and put in suggestions. Antoine listened. It looked as if Jacques were
in no hurry to be alone with him again. Or was he waiting for someone who did not appear?

At last he made a move.

VIII

OUT in the street a bitter wind was blowing, driving before it
flurries of melting snow.

"It's turned to sleet," Jacques said.

He was trying to be less taciturn. As they walked down a flight
of wide stone steps flanking a public building, he volunteered the
information that this was the university. His tone implied a certain
pride in the city of his choice. Antoine duly admired. But the alternating blasts of icy rain and snow made them little inclined to linger
out of doors.

At the junction of two narrow streets, thronged with pedestrians
and cyclists, Jacques made straight for a row of large windows along

the sidewalk; the only indication of the nature of the premises was an inscription on the glass entrance-door in white capitals:

GASTRONOMICA.

Panelled in old oak, the interior gleamed everywhere with bees-wax. The proprietor—a fat, active, red-faced man, puffing and blow-ing but obviously well pleased with himself, his health, his staff and cheer—was fussing round his customers, treating them all like un-expected guests. The walls were covered with gothic letter inscrip-tions such as *Our motto: Honest Food, not Chemicals,* and *At Gas-tronomica, no dry Mustard on the Rims of Mustard-Pots.*

Jacques, who since the interview with Kammerzinn and his walk in the rain had been seeming less on edge, smiled amiably at his brother's amused interest. It was quite a surprise to him to find Antoine so eager to observe the world around him, taking stock so zestfully of every little touch of "local colour," so avid of peculiarities.

In earlier days, when the brothers happened to dine together in the restaurants of the Latin Quarter, Antoine had never noticed any-thing; the first thing he had always done was to prop some medical journal against the water bottle on the table.

Antoine was conscious that Jacques was watching him.

"Do you find me changed?" he asked.

Jacques made an evasive gesture. As a matter of fact Antoine seemed to him greatly changed. But how? Most likely during the past three years he had forgotten many of his brother's traits; now he was re-discovering them one by one. The way Antoine squared his shoulders, spread his fingers out when he was making an explanation, the flicker of his eyelids—each little movement suddenly came back to him; it was like coming on a once familiar picture the memory of which had vanished with the years. But there were other characteristics that baffled him, for they did not fit in with anything remembered: the general expression of his face, his attitude, his calmness and concilia-tory disposition, the absence of hardness and impatience in his eyes. All that was new to Jacques. He tried to explain it in a few stumbling phrases. Antoine smiled. That was Rachel's doing. For several months

that passionate adventure had stamped his face—till now inapt for
any show of happiness—with a kind of gay self-confidence, even, perhaps, the complacence of the favoured lover; and those months had
left their trace for good.

The food was excellent, the beer light and well iced, the atmosphere congenial. Antoine displayed a cheerful interest in the local
characteristics; he had noticed that his uncommunicative brother un-
bent more readily when talking on such subjects. All the same, whenever Jacques opened his mouth he seemed to be flinging himself, desperately, into the conversation. The words came with an obvious effort,
in jerks; then, on occasion, for no apparent reason, they would pour
out in a torrent, cut by sudden silences. And all the time his eyes were
boring into Antoine's.

"No, Antoine!" he exclaimed. His brother had just made a humorous comment. "You're quite wrong if you think . . . I mean it's
not fair to say the Swiss are like that. I've seen a lot of other countries, and I can assure you . . ."

The involuntary look of curiosity on Antoine's face cut him short.
Presently, perhaps regretting the access of ill-humour, he went on, of
his own accord.

"That fellow over there, on our right, is far more typical, really. I
mean the one who's talking to the proprietor. A pretty good specimen
of the Swiss man in the street. His look, his way of behaving, his
voice . . ."

"Which sounds," Antoine put in, "as if he had a cold in the head."

"No!" Jacques expostulated with a slight frown. "It's a rather slow,
drawling voice, the voice of someone who thinks deeply. But what's
most striking is his look of being sufficient unto himself, always mind-
ing his own business. That's thoroughly Swiss. Also that air of feeling
secure, always and everywhere."

"He has intelligent eyes," Antoine conceded, "but, oh, what a lack
of any sort of animation!"

"Well, at Lausanne there are thousands and thousands like him;
from morn till night, without wasting a second, without fluster, doing
what they have to do. They may run up against other modes of life,

but they take no part in them. They rarely cross their frontiers; at every instant of their lives they are wholly taken up with what they're doing or will do a moment later."

Antoine listened without interrupting; his attentiveness rather intimidated Jacques, but encouraged him too. And it gave him a secret feeling of importance which made him more loquacious.

"You talked of animation just now," he said. "People think the Swiss are 'heavy.' That's easily said, but false. They've a different mentality from—from yours. More compact, perhaps. Almost as supple, when in action. Not heavy—but *stable*. Which is a very different thing."

"What surprises me," Antoine said, taking a cigarette from his case, "is to see you of all people so much at home in this hive of industry."

"Why shouldn't I be?" Jacques moved aside the empty cup he had just missed upsetting. "I've lived everywhere, you know; in Italy, Germany, Austria . . ."

Antoine, his eyes fixed on his match, ventured to add, without looking up:

"And in England?"

"No. Why in England?"

For a moment, in silence, each tried to read the other's thoughts. Antoine was still looking down. Puzzled though he was, Jacques went on:

"Well, I'm sure I'd never have been able to settle down in any of those countries. It's impossible to work in them. One's always at fever-heat. This is the only place where I've found my equilibrium."

Indeed, just then he seemed to have achieved a certain poise. He was sitting aslant, in what seemed to be a frequent attitude of his, with his head bent to one side, the side on which was the unruly lock—as if his brows were overburdened by the mass of hair. His right shoulder was thrust forward. All the upper portion of his body seemed buttressed by his right arm, with its hand solidly planted on his thigh. His left elbow rested lightly on the table and the fingers of the left hand were toying with the bread-crumbs on the cloth. It was a man's hand now, sinewy, expressive.

He was thinking over what he had just said. "Yes, these people are restful." There was a note of gratitude in his voice. "Obviously, that stolidity of theirs is only on the surface. There are passions in the air here, as in other countries. But, you see, emotions which, day in, day out, are so well kept in hand aren't very dangerous. Not so contagious, I mean." Suddenly he flushed, and added in a low voice: "For in these last three years, you know . . ."

He paused, flicked back the lock of hair with a quick gesture, and shifted his position.

Antoine did not stir, but swept his eyes over his brother's downcast face. In his look there was a tacit invitation; at last, perhaps, Jacques was going to say something about himself.

Deliberately Jacques changed the subject, rising from the table.

"It's still pouring," he said. "But we'd better be getting back, hadn't we?"

As they were leaving the restaurant, a passing cyclist jumped off his machine and ran up to Jacques.

"Have you seen anyone from over there?" he panted, without a word of greeting. The mountaineer's cape which he was wresting from the wind, with his arms locked tightly over his chest, was drenched.

"No," Jacques replied, without betraying any sign of surprise. "Let's go in there," he added, pointing to a building, the street-door of which stood open. Antoine, out of discretion, lingered behind; Jacques, however, turned and called to him. Still, when they were together in the doorway, he made no introductions.

With a toss of his head the cyclist jerked back the hood covering his eyes. He was a man in the thirties and, despite the somewhat abrupt way in which he had accosted them, his expression was mild, almost over-affable. His face was reddened by the biting wind, and across it ran a streak of livid white, the trace of an old scar that, half closing his right eye, slanted up across the eyebrow and disappeared under his hat-brim.

"They're always falling foul of me," he said in an excited tone, paying no heed to Antoine's presence. "And I don't deserve that, do I now?" He seemed to attach particular importance to Jacques's verdict. Jacques made a calming gesture. "Why do they go on like that? They say it was done by paid agents. Why blame me? Anyhow, now they've cleared out, they know they won't be informed against."

"Their scheme can't work out," Jacques said decisively, after a moment's thought. "It's a choice of two things, either . . ."

"Yes, yes," the man broke in, with a fervour, a thankfulness, that came as a surprise. "Yes, that's exactly it! Only we must mind the political papers don't upset the apple cart before we're ready."

"Sabakin will be off the moment he scents trouble," Jacques replied, lowering his voice. "So will Bisson, you'll see."

"Bisson? Well, possibly."

"But—how about those revolvers?"

"Oh, that's easily accounted for. Her former lover bought them at Basel, when a gunsmith's shop was sold out after the owner's death."

"Look here, Rayer," Jacques said. "You mustn't count on me for the present; I can't do any writing from here for some time to come. Go and see Richardley. Get him to hand over the papers to you. Tell him you're acting for me. If he needs a signature, he can ring up MacLair. Got it?"

Rayer clasped Jacques's hand without replying.

"What about Loute?" Jacques asked, still holding Rayer's hand.

Rayer dropped his eyes. "I can't do anything about it," he replied with a timid laugh. Then, looking up, he muttered ragefully: "No, I can't do a thing. I love her."

Jacques dropped Rayer's hand, was silent for a moment, then said gruffly: "And where's it all going to land you, the two of you?"

Rayer sighed. "It was such a terribly hard birth, she'll never get over it; anyhow, never well enough to do any work."

"Do you know what she said to me?" Jacques broke in. "'If I had an ounce of pluck, there'd be a way out, sure enough.'"

"There you are! That's how it is, and I can't do a thing, not a thing about it!"

"What about Schneebach?"

The man made an angry gesture, and a gleam of hatred kindled in his eyes.

Jacques's fingers closed tightly on Rayer's arm.

"Where will all that land you, Rayer?" he repeated sternly.

The other man gave an impatient jerk of his shoulders. Jacques withdrew his hand. There was a pause, then Rayer raised his right arm with a certain solemnity.

"For us, as for them, death is waiting round the corner—and that's all there is to it," he said in a low voice. Then added with a little soundless laugh, as if what he was going to say was childishly self-evident: "Otherwise the living would be the dead, and the dead alive!"

Gripping his bicycle by the seat, he swung it up with one arm. The scar across his face turned an angry red. Then he drew the hood of his cape over his face, like a cowl, and held out his hand.

"Thanks. I'll see Richardley. You're damned decent, Baulthy, one of the best." He sounded cheerful, sure of himself again. "Yes, just meeting you almost reconciles me with the world—with men and books, even the newspapers. *Au revoir.*"

Though he had not the least idea what it was all about, Antoine had not missed a word of the conversation. From the start he had been struck by the attitude of the man who had just left them. He was obviously a good deal older than Jacques, yet treated him with the affectionate deference usually shown to seniors. But what had most impressed, indeed dumbfounded, him during the interview was the change in Jacques's appearance; not only had the wrinkles left his forehead, not only was no trace of sulkiness left, but he gave an impression of ripened wisdom and even authority. For Antoine it was a revelation. For some minutes he had had a glimpse of an entirely unknown Jacques, of whose existence he had never had an inkling—yet this undoubtedly was the real Jacques for all the world, the Jacques of today.

Rayer had mounted his bicycle, and, without troubling to bid Antoine good-bye, rode off between two sudden spurts of mud.

IX

THE two brothers moved on; Jacques did not volunteer the slightest comment on this meeting. In any case, the wind which forced its way under their clothes and seemed bent especially on playing havoc with Antoine's umbrella, made any attempt at conversation almost hopeless.

Just when things were at their worst, however, as they came out into the Place de la Riponne—a spacious esplanade where all the winds of heaven seemed to be running riot—Jacques, impervious to the pelting rain, suddenly slackened his pace and asked:

"Tell me, when we were at the restaurant just now, what led you to mention England?"

Antoine was conscious of an aggressive intent behind the question. Ill at ease, he mumbled a few vague words which were swept away by the wind.

"What did you say . . . ?" Jacques had not caught a single word. He had drawn closer and was walking crab-wise, thrusting his shoulder forward like a prow breasting the wind-stream. The questioning look he bent upon his brother was so insistent that Antoine, brought to bay, scrupled to tell a lie.

"Well—er—on account of the red roses, you know," he confessed.

The tone in which he spoke was rougher than he had intended it to be. Again the memory of Giuseppe and Annetta's passion had forced itself upon his thoughts; he seemed to see her stumbling, falling upon the grass, and the attendant horde of visions, only too familiar now, yet unbearable as ever, surged through his imagination. Annoyed and irritable, raging against each gust of wind that buffeted him, he swore aloud and angrily shut his umbrella.

Dumbfounded, Jacques had come to a sudden halt; he was evidently far from expecting such an answer. Then, biting his lips, he took a few steps without saying a word. . . . How often had he not already lamented that moment of incredible sentimentality, and regretted the sending of that basket of roses, bought abroad through an obliging friend—an incriminating message, proclaiming to all and sundry: "I am alive and my thoughts are with you"—at the very time when he wished to be looked upon as dead and buried, by all his family! But it had at least been possible for him, until now, to believe that his rash act had been kept a profound secret. Such indiscreetness on the part of Gise, unexpected and incomprehensible as it was for him, provoked him beyond measure. Nor could he now restrain his bitterness.

"You've missed your calling," he sneered. "You were born to be a detective!"

Annoyed by the tone in which he was addressed, Antoine flared up.

"Look here," he replied; "when a man's so keen on keeping his private life a secret, he should not flaunt it publicly in the pages of a magazine."

Stung to the quick, Jacques shouted in his face:

"Really! Do you mean to say it was my story that informed you of my sending those flowers?"

Antoine was no longer master of himself.

"No," he replied, with feigned composure, and added in a biting voice, spacing the syllables: "But, anyhow, it did enable me to appreciate the full meaning of the gift."

Having launched this retort, he forged ahead in the teeth of the wind.

But, immediately, the feeling of having blundered past recall came over him so overpoweringly that it took his breath away. Just a few words too many and everything was in jeopardy: he would now lose Jacques once for all. . . . Why had he suddenly lost control of himself, given way to that outburst of temper? Because Gise was concerned, most likely. And what was to be done now? Have it out with Jacques, apologize to him? Probably it was too late. Well, he could only try; he was prepared to make all possible amends.

He was about to turn to his brother and as affectionately as possible admit he was in the wrong, when suddenly he felt Jacques lay hold of his arm and cling to him with all his might: an impassioned, utterly unexpected hug, a rough, brotherly embrace, doing away in one second not only with the acid remarks that had passed between them, but also with the whole of the three long silent years they had spent apart from each other. Then a broken voice faltered, close to Antoine's ear.

"Why, Antoine, what can you have imagined? Did you really suppose that Gise . . . that I . . . ? You thought *that* possible? You must be dreaming!"

They gazed deep into each other's eyes. Jacques's were sorrowful now, and younger-looking; and over his cheeks offended modesty sent a wave of indignation to mingle with his sorrow. To Antoine it came as an all-healing revelation. Joyfully he pressed his brother's arm against his side. Had he really suspected the two young people? He could no longer tell. He thought of Gise with intense emotion; and a sense of relief, of deliverance, of splendid happiness, came over him. At last he had found his long-lost brother.

Jacques remained silent. A flood of painful memories had come back to him: that evening at Maisons-Laffitte, when he had discovered both the love of Gise and the unconquerable physical attraction she awoke in him—that brief, shrinking kiss, snatched in the dark under the lime-trees, the girl's romantic gesture as she strewed rose-petals over the spot where that shy token of love had passed between them.

Antoine, too, was silent. He would have liked to say something, but he felt tongue-tied and self-conscious. He did, however, attempt by a pressure of his arm to convey to Jacques some such message as: "Yes, I've been a damned fool—and how glad it makes me!" His brother reciprocated the pressure. And they understood each other better, that way, than by the spoken word.

They walked on, arm in arm, under the rain. The over-affectionate, unduly prolonged contact was making both of them uncomfortable, but neither dared to be the first to break away. Then, as they came under cover of a wall that screened them from the wind, Antoine put up his umbrella again; thus it seemed as though they had drawn together for the shelter it afforded.

They reached the boarding-house without having spoken another word. But just outside the door, Antoine stopped short, unlinked his arm, and observed in a natural voice:

"Jacques, you surely have lots of things to attend to here. I'd better leave you, hadn't I? I'll take a stroll round the town."

"In this sort of weather?" Jacques asked. He was smiling, but Antoine had caught a fleeting hesitation. As a matter of fact, both dreaded spending the long afternoon together. "No," he added, "I've two or three letters to write, a twenty minutes' job, and perhaps a business call to pay before five. That's all." The prospect seemed to cast a gloom upon his features. With an effort he drew himself up. "Till then I'm quite free. Let's go upstairs."

While they were away, the room had been tidied up. There was a roaring fire in the stove. They helped each other off with their overcoats, hung them up to dry before the fire.

One of the windows had remained open. Antoine stepped over to it. Among the multitude of roofs sloping down to the lake a pinnacled tower rose high aloft, its tall spire coated with verdigris and gleaming under the rain. He pointed to it.

"That's Saint Francis's Church," Jacques said. "Can you make out the time?"

On one side of the steeple glowed a red-and-gold clock-face.

"A quarter past two."

"Lucky fellow! My eyesight's grown very bad. And I simply can't get used to wearing glasses, on account of my headaches."

"Your headaches!" Antoine exclaimed, closing the window. He turned round abruptly. His look of professional interrogation made Jacques smile.

"Why, yes, doctor. I had a spell of fearful headaches and I haven't quite got over them."

"What kind of headaches?"

"A throbbing there."

"Is it always on the left side?"

"No."

"Any dizziness? Any trouble with your eyes?"

"It's nothing, really." Jacques was beginning to be embarrassed by his brother's questions. "I'm much better, now."

"Better, be damned!" Antoine was not to be put off so easily. "Look here, I'll have to give you a thorough going-over. . . . Your digestion, for one thing, how's it working?"

Though he had obviously no intention of starting the going-over at once, he unconsciously came a step nearer Jacques, who could not help drawing back slightly. He was no longer used to having people fuss over him. The slightest attention seemed an encroachment on his independence. Almost at once, however, he began to remonstrate with himself. Indeed, his brother's concern had left behind it a comforting sensation, as though a gentle warmth had been breathed upon some secret fibre of his being that had long lain atrophied, inert.

"You never used to have any trouble of that kind in the old days," Antoine remarked. "How did it start?"

Jacques, who was sorry to have shrunk back as he had, did his best to answer, to explain things more clearly. But dare he tell the truth?

"It came on after some kind of illness; quite a sudden attack, it was—perhaps it was the flu, or it may have been a touch of malaria. . . . I was in the hospital about four weeks."

"In the hospital? Where?"

"At . . . Gabès."

"At Gabès? That's in Tunisia, isn't it?"

"Yes, I was delirious, it appears. For months afterwards I had frightful pains in my head."

Antoine made no reply, but he was obviously saying to himself: "What an idea, when one has a comfortable home of one's own in Paris, and is the brother of a doctor, to run the risk of dying like a dog in an African hospital!"

"What saved me," Jacques went on, hoping to turn the conversation into a different channel, "was fear. The fear of dying in that furnace-heat. I thought of Italy the way a shipwrecked sailor, on his raft, must think of land, of wells and running streams. . . . I had only one idea in my head: dead or alive to get on board the steamer, to escape to Naples."

Naples. . . . Antoine's thoughts reverted to Lunadoro, to Sybil, to Giuseppe's boating-trips in the Bay.

"Why Naples?" he ventured to ask.

Jacques flushed. He seemed to be struggling to say something by way of explanation; then his steel-blue eyes grew hard.

Antoine hastened to break the silence.

"What you needed, to my mind, was just rest, but in some bracing climate."

"To Naples, first," Jacques repeated. Obviously he had not been listening. "I had a letter of introduction to a man in the Consulate. You see, it's easier to get a postponement of one's military service when one is abroad." He straightened his shoulders. "And, besides, I'd rather have been reported as a deserter than go back to France to be cooped up in their barracks!"

Antoine gave no sign of disapproval. He changed the subject.

"But had you—had you the money for your fares?"

"What a question! That's you all over!"

He started walking up and down the room with his hands in his pockets.

"I was never very long without money, just enough to get along on, I mean. At first, of course, out there, I had to turn my hand to anything that cropped up."

He flushed again, and looked away. "Oh, that was for only a few days. You manage pretty soon, you know."

"But what on earth did you do?"

"Well, for instance, I used to give French lessons in an industrial training school. Then proofreading, at night, for the *Courrier Tunisien* and the *Paris-Tunis*. It often came in handy, my being able to write Italian as fluently as French. Fairly soon they began to publish articles of mine. Then I was given the press summary to do for a weekly, and the news items, all the odd jobs, in fact. And after that, as soon as I was able to manage it, I got a reporter's job." His eyes sparkled. "That was something like a job, and if only my health had held up, I'd still be at it. What a life! I remember, one day, at Viterbo . . . Look here, please sit down. No, personally I'd rather go on walking. I was sent to Viterbo, as no one else dared to go there, for that fantastic Camorra case—you remember that, I suppose? In March 1911, it was. What an experience! I put up with some Neapolitans. A regular den of thieves, I must say. During the night of the thirteenth they all decamped. When the police turned up, I was sound asleep, alone in the house. I had to . . ."

He broke off in the middle of the sentence, in spite of Antoine's sustained attention—on account of it, perhaps. How could mere words convey even a faint idea of the breathless life he had led for months on end? Though his brother's questioning eyes urged him to go on, he dropped the thread of his reminiscences.

"How far away it all seems! Oh, let it go! Let's talk of something else. . . ."

He was conscious that these evocations of the past were laying their spell on him and, to break it, he forced himself to go on speaking. He continued in a calm, detached voice:

"What were you asking me about? Ah, yes, those pains in my head. Well, you see, Italy in the spring never agreed with me. As soon as I was able, the moment I was free . . ." He stopped, frowning; once again, it seemed, he had come up against distressing memories. "As soon as I was able to get away from it all," he went on, with a violent swing of his arm, "I travelled north."

He had come to a stop, looking down at the stove, with his hands in his pockets.

"To Northern Italy?" his brother asked.

"No!" Jacques exclaimed. A tremor ran through his body. "Vienna, Budapest; then Saxony, Dresden. And after that, Munich."

His face suddenly became overcast; this time he darted a sharp glance at his brother and seemed to be really on the verge of speaking out; his lips moved slightly. But after a few seconds he made a wry face and, clenching his teeth so tightly that the last words were almost inaudible, muttered merely:

"Ah, Munich! Munich, too, is a dreadful place, simply appalling." Antoine cut him short hastily.

"Anyhow, you should . . . Until we've ascertained the cause . . . Headache isn't a disease, of course, but only a symptom."

But Jacques was not listening and Antoine fell silent. Several times before, the same thing had happened; one could have sworn that Jacques suddenly felt the need to unbosom himself of some rankling secret, and then, all of a sudden, it seemed as if the words stuck in his throat, and he stopped short. And each time Antoine, inhibited by some absurd apprehension, instead of helping his brother over the jump, shied off the topic, turning away stupidly on a sidetrack.

He was wondering how he could best bring back Jacques into the main track, when a patter of light footsteps sounded on the staircase. There was a knock. The door half opened almost immediately, and Antoine had a glimpse of an untidy mop of hair and a boyish face.

"Oh, I beg your pardon! Am I in the way?"

"Come in," Jacques said, walking across the room.

On a better view, the caller proved to be not a boy, but an undersized clean-shaven man of no definite age, with a creamy-white complexion and tousled, tow-coloured hair. He hung back for a moment in the doorway, and seemed to dart a timorous glance towards Antoine, but the pale lashes fringing his eyes were so thick that the movements of the pupils were hidden.

"Come over to the stove," Jacques said, and helped the visitor off with his dripping overcoat.

Again he seemed set upon not introducing his brother. Still, he wore an entirely unconstrained smile, and appeared to be by no means put out by Antoine's presence.

"I came to tell you that Mithoerg has arrived. He is bringing a letter," the new-comer explained. He had a jerky, sibilant voice, but spoke now in a low, almost apprehensive tone.

"A letter?"

"From Vladimir Kniabrovski."

"From Kniabrovski!" Jacques exclaimed, his features lighting up.

"Sit down, you look tired. Will you have a glass of beer? Or a cup of tea?"

"No, thank you, nothing at all. Mithoerg arrived during the night. He has come from over there. . . . So what am I to do? What do you advise me to do? Shall I have a try?"

Jacques thought it over for some little time before answering.

"Yes. It's the only way of finding out now."

The other man grew excited.

"Great! I thought as much. Ignace advised me not to, and so did Chenavon. But you know better. Good work!"

He stood facing Jacques, his little face radiant with trustfulness.

"Only—watch out!" Jacques put in severely, lifting an admonitory finger.

The albino nodded assent.

"By kindness, that's the way," he declared solemnly. And iron determination was discernible in that frail body.

Jacques was observing him intently.

"You haven't been ill, have you, Vanheede?"

"No, no. Just a bit run down. I feel so uncomfortable, you know, in that big shanty of theirs!" he added with a wry smile.

"Is Prezel still here?"

"Yes."

"And Quilleuf? Tell Quilleuf from me that he talks too much. Just that, eh? He'll understand."

"Oh, Quilleuf! I told him straight: 'You behave, the lot of you, just as if you were the scum of the earth.' He tore up Rosengaard's proclamation without so much as reading it! Everything's putrid in that group. Yes, everything's putrid," he repeated in a hollow, indignant voice, while at the same time an indulgent, angelic smile lit up the girlish lips.

In a high-pitched sibilant tone he went on: "Saffrio! Tursey! Paterson! Every one of them. And even Suzanne! They stink of rottenness!"

Jacques shook his head.

"Josepha, perhaps, but not Suzanne. Josepha, mind you, is a despicable creature. She'll set you all by the ears."

Vanheede had been watching him silently, sliding his doll-like hands over his diminutive knees, bringing into view fantastically pale and fragile wrists.

"I know. But what is to be done about it? We can hardly consign her to the gutter at this time of day. Would *you* do that, tell me, now? Is that a reason? She's a human being, when all's said and done, and one who isn't bad through and through. And she has put herself under our protection, after all. Something can be done, surely. By kindness, perhaps, by kindness. How many such creatures haven't I met in the course of my life!" he added with a sigh. "There's rottenness everywhere."

Again he sighed, shot a veiled glance at Antoine, then, going up to Jacques, he burst out excitedly:

"That letter of Vladimir Kniabrovski's is a damn fine letter, let me tell you!"

"Tell me," Jacques inquired, "what exactly are his plans for the present?"

"He's looking after his health. He has gone back to his wife, to his mother, to his kids. Getting in trim for a new lease of life."

Vanheede was pacing up and down in front of the stove; now and then he locked his hands in a sudden access of excitement. As though talking to himself, he added with a rapt expression:

"One of the pure in heart, that's what old Kniabrovski is!"

"Yes, indeed—one of the pure in heart," Jacques echoed immediately, in the same tone of voice, adding after a pause: "When does he expect to bring out his book?"

"He doesn't say."

"Ruskinoff tells me it's a simply amazing work."

"How could it be otherwise? A book he wrote from beginning to end in a prison cell!" He took a few steps. "I haven't brought you his letter today. I've lent it to Olga to take to the club. I'll have it back this evening." Without looking at Jacques, like a dancing will-o'-the-wisp he flitted about the room, his eyes uplifted, beatifically smiling. "Vladimir tells me he has never been so completely himself as he was in that prison. Alone with his loneliness." The singing quality in his voice grew more pronounced, though he spoke in a lower tone. "He says that his cell was nice and light, right at the top of the building, and that he used to stand on the boards of his bed, so as to bring his forehead level with the edge of the barred window. He says he used to stand there for hours, thinking, watching the snow-flakes swirling above. He says he could see nothing else, not a roof, not a tree, never anything at all. But as soon as the spring came round and all through the summer, late in the afternoon a ray of sunlight would fall across his face. He says he used to wait for that moment all day long. You'll read his letter. He says he once heard a little child crying in the distance. Another time he heard the report of a gun." Vanheede glanced across at Antoine, who was listening to what he said and could not help following his movements interestedly with his eyes. "But I'll bring you the letter itself, tomorrow," he added, returning to his seat.

"Not tomorrow," Jacques said; "I shan't be here tomorrow." Vanheede showed no surprise. But he looked round at Antoine again and rose to his feet after a short pause.

"Please excuse me. I'm afraid I've been intruding; I only wanted to let you know about Vladimir."

Jacques, too, had risen.

"You're working a bit too hard just now, Vanheede. You should take care of yourself."

"Oh, no."

"Still at Schomberg and Rieth's?"

"Why, yes." He smiled mischievously. "I do the typing. I say: 'Yes, sir,' from morn to night and pound the typewriter. What harm can that do? When the day's over, I am my own self again. Then, I'm free to think: 'No, sir,' all night long if I choose—till the next morning."

As he spoke, little Vanheede was holding his small head very high and his tousled flaxen forelock gave him the air of drawing himself up still further. He turned slightly, as though addressing Antoine for the first time.

"I starved and starved for ten years, gentlemen, for the sake of my ideals, and I'm not going to give them up."

Then he moved back to Jacques, held out his hand, and a note of distress came into the high-pitched, reedy voice.

"You are leaving us, perhaps? That's a shame! It always did me a lot of good, coming here, you know."

Deeply moved, Jacques made no answer, but placed his hand affectionately on the albino's arm. Antoine remembered the man with the scar. Him, too, Jacques had greeted in the same friendly, encouraging, and rather patronizing manner. He seemed really to hold a place of his own in these queer groups of people. They consulted him, sought his approval, and feared his censure; obviously, too, it did their hearts good to be in his company.

"He's a regular Thibault!" Antoine thought with satisfaction. But, immediately after, a feeling of sadness came over him. "Jacques will never remain in Paris," he mused; "he'll come and live in Switzerland again—that much is quite certain." In vain did he say to himself: "We'll write to each other, I'll come and see him, it won't be the same now as these last three years." That sense of disappointment rankled. "But what will he turn his hand to, what sort of life will he lead amongst these people? What use will he make of his talents? Ah, it will be very different from the wonderful career I'd mapped out for him in my dreams!"

Jacques had caught hold of his friend's arm and was steering him discreetly towards the door. There Vanheede turned round, took leave of Antoine with a shy nod, and disappeared onto the landing, followed by Jacques.

Once more, and for the last time, Antoine heard the small indignant voice.

"Everything's gone so rotten. They won't have anyone about them but fawning toadies."

X

O N HIS return, Jacques volunteered no more information about this visitor than he had given about the hooded cyclist they had met in the street. He had poured out a glass of water and was sipping it slowly.

Antoine, to keep himself in countenance, lit a cigarette, and got up to throw the match into the stove; after a glance out of the window, he returned to his seat.

The silence lasted a few minutes. Jacques was again pacing up and down the room.

"Look here, Antoine!" he said abruptly, still walking to and fro. "Do try to understand me a bit! How could I possibly have given three whole years, three years of my life, to that Ecole Normale of theirs?"

Antoine was startled, but at once assumed an attentive, studiously indulgent air.

"It would only have been my school-life all over again," Jacques went on, "with a thin veneer of freedom. Lectures, and lessons, and everlasting essays! And 'proper feelings' of respect for all authority. And then the promiscuousness of it all! Every idea peddled round, and torn to tatters by that half-baked mob in the poky dens they call their 'digs.' Why, even the jargon they use—'freshies' and 'profs' and 'grinds'—it's all in keeping! No, I could never have put up with life under such conditions.

"Don't misunderstand me, Antoine. I don't mean . . . Of course I have a high opinion of them. The teacher's job is one that can only be carried on in an honourable way, as an act of faith. There's something attractive, I grant you, in their self-respect, the mental efforts they put forth, and the faithful service they give for so beggarly a reward. Yes, but . . .

"No, you can't really understand," he muttered after a pause. "It wasn't only to escape that barrack-like existence, nor from a distaste for all that machine-made education—that wasn't it. But, just think of the footling life, Antoine!" He broke off, then repeated the word "footling," with his eyes stubbornly fixed on the floor.

"When you went to see Jalicourt," Antoine asked, "I suppose you'd already made up your mind to . . . ?"

"Certainly not!" Jacques remained standing where he was, with his brows raised, staring at the floor; he was making a genuine attempt to reconstruct the past. "Oh, that month of October! I'd come back from Maisons-Laffitte in a really dreadful state!" He hunched his shoulders as if a heavy load weighed on them, murmuring: "There were too many things that wouldn't fit together."

"Ah, yes, I remember that October." Antoine was thinking of Rachel.

"Then, on the last day before the beginning of the term, with that crowning misfortune, the threat of the Ecole looming just ahead, a sort of panic came over me. Just think how strange it all is! At the present moment I realize quite clearly that till my call on Jalicourt, I'd had only a deep-seated fear of what was coming, nothing more. Of course, I'd often felt heartily sick of the whole business and thought of giving up the Ecole, even of running away. But all that was no more than a vague dream. It was only after that evening with Jalicourt that it all took definite shape. You can hardly believe me, eh?" he said, looking up at last and noticing his brother's bewilderment. "Very well, you shall read the very words I jotted down in my diary that night, on reaching home; it so happens I came across them only the other day."

Again he fell to pacing gloomily up and down; the memory of that visit seemed still to upset him, even after so long an interval.

"When I think of it all . . ." he began, shaking his head. "But tell me, how did you get in touch with him? Did you write to each other? You went to see him, of course. How did he strike you?"

Antoine merely made an evasive gesture.

"Yes," Jacques said, supposing his brother's impression of the professor to have been unfavourable, "you can hardly realize what he meant to youngsters of my generation!" And, with a sudden change of mood, he came and sat down opposite Antoine, in an arm-chair beside the stove. "Oh, that Jalicourt!" he exclaimed with an unexpected smile. His voice had softened. He stretched out his legs luxuriously towards the fire. "For years, Antoine, we'd been saying to one another: 'When I am a pupil of Jalicourt.' By 'pupil' we really meant 'disciple.' And whenever some misgiving came over me, as regards the Ecole, I'd comfort myself by thinking: 'Yes, but there's always Jalicourt.' He was the only one whom we thought worth while, you see. We knew all his poems by heart. We retailed all we could pick up about him and his ways, we quoted his witticisms. His colleagues were jealous of him, so we were told. He'd not only succeeded in making the university put up with his lectures—long extempore effusions, full of bold views, digressions, sudden confidences, and broad jokes—but with eccentricities, his dandified get-up, his eyeglass, and even that jaunty soft hat of his. A curious character, whimsical, enthusiastic, a bit of a crank in his way—but what a mind, so well stocked and generous! What was so fine about him was his feeling for the modern world; he was the one man, for us, who had managed to lay his finger on its pulse. I had corresponded with him. I had five letters from him—my most valued treasures. Think of it, five letters, three of which, if not four, are, I still believe, simply masterpieces!

"Now listen to this. One spring morning at about eleven o'clock, we met him, I and a friend, in the street. How could one ever forget such a thing? He was walking up the Rue Soufflot, with long, springy steps. I can still see him with his coat-tails ballooning behind him, his grey spats, the white hair peeping out under the wide brim of his hat. Very upright, his monocle screwed into position, his Roman nose jutting out like a tall ship's prow, and the drooping white moustache that brought to mind a Gallic chieftain's. The profile of an old eagle, ready to strike. A bird of prey, with the spindle-shanks of a heron. And something of an old-school English nobleman, as well. Unforgettable, he was!"

"Yes, I can see him!" Antoine exclaimed.

"We shadowed him up to his door. We were spell-bound. We visited a dozen shops, trying to get a photo of him!" Jacques jerked back his legs under him with sudden violence. "And now that I think of it, I loathe him!"

"I'm pretty sure he's never had the faintest idea of that!" Antoine grinned.

But Jacques was not listening. Facing the fire, a pensive smile on his lips, he went on speaking in a far-away voice.

"Shall I tell you all about it? Well, it was after dinner, one night, I suddenly made up my mind to go and call on him. To explain, well, everything to him. So off I went, on the spur of the moment, without giving the matter a second thought. By nine o'clock I was ringing his bell, in the Place du Panthéon. You know the house, don't you? A dark entrance-hall, a stupid-looking Breton maid, the dining-room, the rustle of a vanishing skirt. The table had been cleared, but there was a work-basket left behind, with clothes to be darned in it. A smell of food, of pipe smoke, a stuffy heat. The door opened. There was Jalicourt. Not a thing to remind one of the old eagle of the Rue Soufflot, or of the writer of those marvellous letters. Nothing of the poet, or the lofty thinker! Or any Jalicourt we knew. Nothing whatever. A round-shouldered Jalicourt, minus the eyeglass, an old pea-jacket mottled with dandruff, a dead pipe, a peevish mouth. He must have been quietly snoring, digesting his boiled cabbage, with his big nose nodding over a stove. I certainly shouldn't have been admitted, if the maid had known her job. Well, he'd been caught napping, taken off his guard, and had to see it through. He showed me into his study.

"I was too excited to think. I just blurted out what I had come to say. 'I've come to ask you, sir,' and so forth. He pulled himself together, came to life, more or less, and I got a glimpse of the old eagle again. He put up his eyeglass and motioned me to a seat. There was a touch of the old peer in his manner. 'So you want my advice?' he asked in a surprised tone. As if he meant: 'Have you no one else to apply to?' True enough. I'd never thought of that. You see, Antoine, it's not your fault, but it was very seldom I could bring myself to follow your advice—or anyone else's, for that matter. I preferred to steer my own course; I'm built that way. My answer to Jalicourt was to that effect. His attentiveness led me on. I told him straight out: 'I want to be a novelist, a great novelist!' I had to tell him; no use beating about the bush. He never turned a hair. I went on pouring my heart out, I explained to him, well, everything, in fact. That I was conscious of a store of energy within me, of a deep-seated, vital impulse that was my very own, personal, unique! That for years past every step forward that I made in 'culture' had always been made at the expense of what was best in me, that vital force. That I had developed an intense dislike for study, for schools, and learning, for pedantry and idle chatter, and that this aversion had all the violence of an instinct of self-defence, of self-preservation! Yes, I'd taken the bit between my teeth! I said to him: 'All that is weighing on me, sir; it's stifling me, and it's warping all my natural impulses!' "

As he spoke Jacques's expression was constantly changing; at one moment his eyes were obdurate, smouldering with passion, then suddenly the hardness would go out of them; they grew tender, wistful, almost appealing.

"Antoine!" he cried. "It's true, every word of it, you know."

"I quite realize that, old man."

"But don't imagine that there's pride behind it," Jacques went on. "I've no wish to be above the rest, not a trace of what most people call ambition. You've only got to look at the way I'm living. And yet, Antoine, believe me, I've been perfectly happy here!"

After a few seconds, Antoine spoke again.

"Well, what happened next? What was his answer?"

"Wait a bit. He made no answer, so far as I can remember. Ah, yes, in the end, I came out with some lines from a poem I'd begun. It was called 'The Spring.' A sort of prose-poem, it was. Awful nonsense, really!" he added, with a blush. "I'd written that I aspired 'to bend above myself as one bends over a flowing spring,' and so forth. 'To draw aside the tall grass and peer unhindered into the crystal depths.' There he stopped me. 'A pretty conceit.' That's all he had to say! The crabbed old pedant! I tried to catch his eye. But he would not look at me; he kept on fiddling with his signet-ring."

"I can quite picture him!" Antoine said.

"Then he embarked on a regular lecture. 'It doesn't do to be too scornful of the beaten track. The advantages, indeed the mental agility, one derives from being subjected to discipline,' and so forth. Oh, he was just like the rest of them. He hadn't understood a thing, not a thing! All he could do was to offer a few well-worn platitudes. I was furious with myself for coming, for having laid bare my heart to him! He kept on for some time in the same strain. The one thing he seemed concerned with was to pigeonhole me neatly. He'd say, for instance: 'You are the type of person who . . . Young fellows of your age . . . You might be classed among those characters whom . . .' Finally, I lost my temper. 'I loathe classifications and I hate the people who make them. Under the pretext of classifying you, they maim you, whittle you down. By the time you're out of their clutches you're no more than a mutilated fragment of yourself—a cripple.' He kept on smiling; he seemed quite ready to take any amount of punishment! Then I began to shout at him. 'Yes, sir, I hate professors! That's the reason I came to see you, and none of the others.' He was still smiling, as though I'd flattered him. To make himself agreeable, he asked me a few questions. Maddening questions! He wanted to know what I had done. 'Nothing!' What I intended to do. 'Everything!' The old humbug hadn't even the pluck to laugh me down. He was much too frightened of being sized up by one of the rising generation. For that was his obsession: what the coming generation thought of him. From the time I'd crossed his threshold, the only thought at the back of his mind was for the book he was writing, *My Experiences*. (It must have been published, by now, but I shall never read it.) He was in a blue funk at the idea his book wouldn't be up to the mark, and, whenever a youngster like myself crossed his path, he would hark back to that anxiety of his: 'I wonder what this young fellow will think of my work?' "

"Poor devil!" Antoine exclaimed.

"Oh, yes, I don't deny it; he was really to be pitied. Still, I hadn't come there just to have a view of his anxieties. I was still hankering after the Jalicourt of my dreams. Under any of his avatars: the poet, the philosopher, and so on—any of them except the one he was showing me just then. Finally I got up to leave. It was a grotesque performance. He followed me out, keeping up his patter. 'So difficult to advise the younger generation . . . No hard-and-fast rules of life . . . Every man must blaze his own trail,' and so forth. I walked in front, without saying a word; my nerves were on edge, as you may well imagine! The drawing-room, then the dining-room, then the hall. I opened the door myself, in the dark, stumbling over his rubbishy antiques; I hardly left him time to find the electric switches."

Antoine could not help smiling; well did he recall the arrangement of the flat—the "period" furniture, the upholstered chairs, the bric-à-brac. But Jacques had not finished yet; a look of something like alarm came over his face.

"Then—wait a bit!—I can't quite remember how it happened. Perhaps it dawned on him why I was bolting like that. I heard his raucous voice behind me in the hall. 'What more do you want me to say? Can't you see I'm played out, done for?' I turned round, couldn't believe my ears. What a pitiful figure he cut just then! He kept on repeating: 'Played out . . . done for! And my whole life wasted!' I began to protest. Yes, I meant it; I'd stopped being annoyed with him. But he wouldn't give in. 'I've done nothing,' he said. 'Nothing at all. And I'm the only one who knows that.' And as I went on protesting, rather clumsily, he flew into a sort of rage. 'What on earth is it that fools you all? My books? Zero for them! I've put nothing into them, not a scrap of what I might have. Well, then, what's left? My degrees? My lectures? The Academy? What's left, I ask you? This thing?' He caught hold of the lapel of his coat, with the Legion of Honour rosette on it, and was shaking it pettishly. 'This thing, I ask you? This "riband to stick in my coat"?' "

Carried away by his reminiscences, Jacques had risen from his seat, and was acting out the scene with ever-increasing vehemence. And Antoine was put in mind of the Jalicourt he had had a glimpse of, in the same setting, holding himself erect, preening himself, in his brightly lit room.

"All of a sudden he calmed down," Jacques went on. "I fancy he was afraid of being overheard. He opened a door and showed me into a sort of pantry that smelled of oranges and beeswax. His lips were drawn back in a derisive grin, but his expression was hard and bitter, and his eye bloodshot behind the monocle. He was leaning against a shelf on which were some glasses and a fruit-dish. It was a marvel how he managed not to knock anything over. All that happened three years ago, but the tone of his voice and his words are still ringing in my ears.

"He began talking, endlessly, in a low, monotonous voice. 'Listen! I'm going to tell you the whole truth, nothing but the truth. At your age, I too . . . I was a trifle older, perhaps; I'd just graduated from the Ecole. And I too felt myself called to be a novelist. I too had that vital energy which needs freedom if it is to realize its full potentialities. And I too felt intuitively that I was taking the wrong road. Just for a moment. And I too had the notion of asking an older man's advice. Only I applied to a novelist. Guess who it was! No, you'd never understand, you can't conceive what that man stood for in the minds of the younger generation, in 1880. I called on him at his house, he let me ramble on, watching me with his gimlet eyes, and fumbling with his beard. He was in a hurry—he always was in a hurry—and he got up without hearing me out. Oh, there was no hesitation, in his case! He said to me, with that peculiar lisp he had that turned the *s*'s into *f*'s: "There'f only one royal road for the would-be novelift, and that'f journalifm!" Yes that's what he told me. Well, I left, no wiser than I'd come, my young friend—like the fool I was! I went back to my manuals, to my tutors, to my fellow-students, to the examination-rooms, the "advanced" reviews, the debating-societies, and all the rest of it. With a fine future before me. A fine future, indeed!' Bang! Jalicourt's hand crashed on my shoulder. Never shall I forget his eye, that Cyclops eye blazing behind the monocle. He had drawn himself up to his full height, he spluttered in my face. 'What's it you want of me, my boy? A piece of advice?

Well, here it is, but beware of it! Drop your books, and follow your instincts! Here's a home-truth for you, my friend; if there's a spark of genius in your make-up, your only way of making something of yourself is from within, under the stress of your natural impulses. Perhaps, in your case, it's still not too late. Waste no time about it. Go out and live. Anywhere, anyhow! You're a boy of twenty, you have eyes and legs, haven't you? Trust Jalicourt. Join the staff of a newspaper. Keep on the lookout for "stories." Do you hear me? I know what I'm talking about. "Stories." The plunge into the pauper's grave! Nothing else will rub the cobwebs off you. Go at it, with all you've got, morning, noon, and night; mind you don't miss a single accident, a single suicide, or scandal in high life, or murder in a brothel! Keep your eyes wide open; notice everything that the tide of civilization sweeps along with it—the good, the bad, the unsuspected, the unimagined! And after that, perhaps, you may venture to say something about men, about society, about yourself!'

"Believe me, Antoine, at that moment I wasn't just looking at him, I was devouring him with my eyes, thrilled through and through. Only, a moment later, all was over. Without saying a word, he opened the door and good as pushed me out, across the entrance-hall, onto the landing. I've never been able to make out why he did it. Had he checked himself deliberately? Was he sorry he had let himself go like that? Was he afraid I might tell people about it? I can still see that lanky jaw of his quivering with emotion. He kept on mumbling in a low voice: 'Go away! Go away! Go back to your libraries, sir!'

"The door was slammed in my face. A fat lot I cared! Ah, you should have seen me racing down the four flights of stairs and out into the street, kicking up my heels in the darkness, like a colt just turned out to grass!"

Emotion had taken away his breath; he poured out another glass of water and drank it at a gulp. As he set down the glass with an unsteady hand, it jarred against the water-jug. In the long silence, the thin, crystalline sound seemed to linger on interminably.

Hardly less overwrought than his brother, Antoine was trying to piece together the events that had led up to Jacques's flight. There were many gaps still to be filled in. He would have liked to elicit a few confidences as regards Giuseppe's emotional dilemma. But that was a delicate subject. "Too many irreconcilable things," Jacques had said just now, with a sigh. That was all he had to go on; but Jacques's stubborn reticence showed how large a part those sentimental entanglements had played in his decision to run away. Antoine wondered how far, at the present time, his heart was still preoccupied with them.

He endeavoured roughly to muster the facts. In October, then, Jacques had come back from Maisons. At that moment, of what nature were his relations with Gise, his meetings with Jenny? Had he tried to break off? Or entered into commitments impossible to fulfil? Antoine pictured his brother in Paris, lacking a clearly defined course of study, alone and far too free, turning the unsolvable problem over and over in his mind. He must have been living in a precarious state of mingled rapture and depression; with nothing to look forward to but the beginning of the term and the cloistered routine of the Ecole Normale, the mere thought of which must have sickened him. Then, suddenly, his visit to Jalicourt had shown him a way out of it all, a bright rift in the drab horizon of his future. How he must have exulted in that prospect of escape from an impossible situation and of a new, adventurous existence, living his own life! Yes, Antoine mused, that accounts for the fact not only that Jacques left us, but that for three whole years he persisted in that silence of the tomb. He was embarking on a new life and, to achieve this, to blot out the past entirely, he needed to be forgotten, dead to his family and friends.

But he could not help remembering how Jacques had taken advantage of his trip to Le Havre, had not waited even one day to see him and talk things over. His resentment was stirring again, but he fought it down, subdued his grievances, and made an effort to renew the conversation, to lead his brother to the sequel.

"So that was it," he remarked. "And it was the next day that you . . . ?" He paused.

Jacques had sat down again by the stove, resting his elbows on his knees, his shoulders hunched and his head bent low; he was whistling.

Now he looked up.

"Yes, the next day." Then, in a reluctant tone he added: "Immediately after the scene with . . ."

The scene with their father, of course, the scene at the Palazzo Seregno! Antoine had forgotten that.

"Father never breathed a word of it to me," he added quickly.

Jacques looked surprised. Nevertheless, he averted his gaze, making a vague gesture as if to imply: "Oh, let it go! I haven't the heart to speak of that again."

Antoine was thinking: "Of course that accounts for his not waiting till I came back from Le Havre," and felt a certain consolation in the thought.

Jacques had resumed his meditative attitude, and started whistling to himself again. His eyebrows twitched nervously. Despite his efforts to blot it out, that tragic scene had flashed across his memory once more. Father and son had been left alone together in the dining-room, just after lunch; M. Thibault had asked some question about the beginning of the term at the Ecole Normale, and Jacques had bluntly told his father he had decided not to enter. An altercation had followed, of ever-increasing violence. M. Thibault had pounded on the table with his fist. At last Jacques had thrown discretion to the winds and in an unaccountable fit of madness had blurted out Jenny's name—as a direct challenge to his father. By now he had lost his head completely, answering threats with counter-threats and launching out into a series of irrevocable declarations. And then had come that tragic climax when, now he had burned his boats and rendered all compromise impossible, he had uttered that last cry of rebellion and despair, had rushed out of the room, shouting: "I'll go and kill myself!"

The picture evoked was so clear-cut, so poignant, that he jumped up as if he had been stung. Antoine had just time to catch a glint of madness in his brother's eyes; but Jacques quickly pulled himself together.

"It's past four," he said; "I must be off, if I'm to attend to that business of mine." He was already putting on his overcoat; he seemed impatient to get away. "You'll stay here, won't you? I shall be back before five. My bag won't take long to pack. We can dine at the station restaurant; that will be simplest." He had laid on the table some files stuffed with papers of various shapes and sizes. "Here," he said, "dip into these, if you feel inclined to. They're magazine articles, short stories. The least worthless of the things I've written these last few years."

He was already outside the door when, turning round awkwardly, he threw out in a detached manner: "By the way, you haven't told me anything about—about Daniel?"

Antoine had the impression his brother had been going to say: "about the Fontanins."

"Daniel? Why, just think, we've become great friends! After you went away, I found him so loyal, so devoted, so affectionate!"

To cover up his confusion, Jacques feigned extreme astonishment; Antoine made as if he were taken in by it.

"That's a surprise now, isn't it!" he laughed. "Of course he and I are pretty different, but I've come to accept his attitude to life; it may very well be justifiable in so gifted an artist. You know, his success exceeds all our expectations! His private show at Ludwigson's in 1911 brought him right into the limelight. He could sell any number of pictures if he chose; only he paints so few. We are very unlike each other—or, rather, we *were* unlike," he amended, pleased to grasp an opportunity for putting in a few words about himself, and showing Jacques that the portrait of Umberto's character no longer fitted him. "I've become much less rigid in my way of looking at things, you see. I'm inclined to think that one needn't . . ."

"Is he in Paris?" Jacques cut in rudely. "Does he know that . . . ?"
Antoine had some difficulty in keeping his temper.

"Why, no; he's doing his military service, as a sergeant, at Lunéville. He's there for another ten months or so, till October '14. I've hardly come across him at all for a whole year."

He stopped speaking, chilled by the gloomy, far-away look in his brother's eyes.

Once Jacques felt sure that his voice would no longer betray his agitation, he said:

"Don't let the fire go out in the stove, Antoine." And with these words he was gone.

XI

LEFT to his own devices, Antoine went over to the table and untied the files lying there. His interest was aroused.

All sorts of documents were contained in them. First, a selection of articles on topical events, cut out from newspapers and signed "Jacques the Fatalist." Then a number of poems, rhapsodies on mountain scenery, which had appeared in a Belgian magazine over the pseudonym "J. Mühlenberg." Lastly a series of short stories with a general title, *Leaves from the Black Book;* they were in the nature of sketches more than stories, by-products, it seemed, of Jacques's experiences as a reporter, and signed "Jack Baulthy." Antoine read some of these: "The Octogenarians," "The Child Who Killed Himself," "A Blind Man's Jealousy," "A Fit of Rage." The characters were drawn from everyday life and, though etched only in outline, all seemed to stand out in bold relief. Jacques used the graphic, choppy style of "*La Sorellina,*" but divested these sketches of all poetic verbiage—which imparted to them a faithfulness to life that gripped the reader's interest.

Yet, despite the interest of these literary efforts, Antoine's attention wandered. There had been too many unexpected happenings that morning. And, above all, now that he was left to himself, his thoughts kept drifting back to the sick-bed he had left the day before; what terrible events might be in progress there at this very moment! Had he done wrong to leave? No, certainly not, since he was bringing Jacques home.

A gentle, though determined, tap at the door roused him from his musings.

"Come in," he said.

He was surprised to see a woman's form outlined against the dark background of the staircase. He seemed to recognize the girl he had caught sight of at breakfast-time, that morning. She was carrying some logs of firewood in a basket, of which he hastened to relieve her.

"My brother's just gone out," he said.

She nodded, as though to say: "I know that"; perhaps indeed: "That's why I've come upstairs." She was taking stock of Antoine with undisguised curiosity, but there was nothing in the least pert in her attitude; on the contrary, it seemed that she had carefully thought out the bold step she was taking now, and had compelling reasons for it. Antoine gathered the impression that she had been crying a very short time before. Presently her eyelashes began to quiver; then brusquely, in a bitterly reproachful voice, she asked him:

"Are you going to take him away?"

"Yes. My father is very ill."

She seemed not to have heard.

"Why?" She stamped her foot angrily. "I don't want you to!"

"I tell you, my father is on the verge of death," Antoine replied.

But explanations were obviously lost on her. Slowly her eyes filled with tears. She swung round towards the window, folded her hands and wrung them. Then she let her arms fall limply.

"He'll never come back!" she murmured in a broken voice.

She was tall, broad-shouldered, and rather plump; febrile in her movements, and listless when in repose. Two sleek, heavy braids of flaxen hair encircled her low brow, and were twisted into a knot at the back of her head. Under this diadem, her regular, if somewhat coarse, features had an almost queenly air, which was enhanced by the classical mould of her full, sinuous, yet determined lips, that ended unexpectedly on either side in two attractive dimples.

She turned round to face Antoine.

"Promise me," she said, "swear to me by Jesus Christ that you will not prevent him from coming back."

"Of course I won't! Why should I?" he said, with a conciliatory smile.

She did not smile in return, but stared fixedly at the young man across a mist of shining tears. Under the close-fitting fabric, her bosom heaved convulsively. She gave herself quite shamelessly to Antoine's interested scrutiny. From between her breasts she took out a tiny handkerchief, screwed up into a ball, and applied it to her eyes and then, with a sniff, to her nostrils. The slumberous pupils, slotted between the half-closed lids, had a velvety, voluptuous appeal. They brought to mind deep, stagnant pools; now and again there would well up in them an eddy of inscrutable thoughts. At such moments, she would bend down or turn away her head.

"Did he speak to you of me? Of Sophia?"

"No."

A steely-blue flash shot from between her eyelids.

"You won't let him know I told you all this, will you?"

Antoine smiled again. "But you haven't told me anything!"

"Oh, yes, I have," she retorted, throwing back her head and half closing her lids again.

She looked round for a chair, then drew it up near Antoine's and sat down in feverish haste, as though she had not a minute to lose. "Listen," she remarked, "you've something to do with the stage, haven't you?" He shook his head. "Yes, you have. I've a picture post-card of someone just like you. He's a stage-star in Paris." She was smiling now. A sentimental, almost sensual smile.

"So you're very keen on the theatre?" he asked; it was too much bother trying to undeceive her.

"On the movies—yes! And real dramas. I adore them!"

Now and then a brief, unlooked-for change came over the girl's features, ruffling their composure. At such moments her mouth, which she opened wide for the least remark, opened still wider, disclosing her broad white teeth and coral-pink gums.

He maintained a reserved attitude.

"I suppose you have quite good companies here, haven't you?"

She drew closer still. "Have you ever been at Lausanne before?" Her whole attitude, as she bent towards him, even her way of speaking in low, fluttering undertones, seemed to suggest that she was expecting and prepared to reciprocate advances.

"Never," he replied.

"Do you think you'll come back?"

"Quite likely."

Her eyes hardened for a second, as her gaze sank into his. Then, shaking her head emphatically, "No, you won't," she said.

She opened the door of the stove to put fresh fuel in.

"Oh, come now!" Antoine protested. "It's too hot in here already."

"That's so." She put the back of her hand to her cheek. None the less she picked up a log and dropped it onto the glowing embers, then a second one and a third. "Jack likes it better that way," she said defiantly.

She remained on her knees, her back towards him, her eyes bent upon the blazing fire, which was toasting her cheeks. Night was falling. Antoine's gaze wandered over the rippling curve of her shoulders, the nape of her neck, her thick, plaited hair haloed by the glow. What was she waiting for? Obviously she was conscious that his eyes were fixed on her. He seemed to glimpse a smile hovering on what little he could see of her averted features. But then, with a supple twist of her body, she rose to her feet. After shutting the stove-door with her foot, she took a few steps across the room, caught sight of a sugar-bowl on a side-table, dipped her fingers greedily into it, and began crunching a lump of sugar. Fishing out another, she held it towards him, from a distance.

"No, thanks," he laughed.

"Bad luck if you don't!" she exclaimed, tossing the lump of sugar towards him; he deftly caught it.

They observed each other shrewdly. Sophia's eyes seemed to be asking: "Who are you?" even: "What's it to be, between you and me?" Her indolent, insatiate eyes, flecked with motes of gold by the long translucent lashes, had the pale lustre of a sandy beach just before a summer storm breaks. Yet they were heavy with listlessness rather than with desire. "One of those minxes," Antoine was thinking, "who yield at the first touch. And bite you as they kiss you! And hate you ever after. And give you no peace till they've played some dirty trick on you—by way of vengeance."

As if she had guessed his thoughts, she moved away and began staring out of the window at the grey downpour that was hastening the close of day.

The silence was so prolonged that Antoine began to feel uncomfortable.

"What are you thinking about?" he asked.

"Oh! I don't often think," she confessed, without moving from the window.

"But when you do think, what is it about?"

"Nothing!"

Hearing him laugh, she left the window and gave him an engaging smile. Her movements now did not seem in the least hurried. She walked vaguely towards the door, her arms dangling. When she came beside it, her hand happened to brush against the key.

Antoine had an impression that she was turning it in the lock; the blood rose to his cheeks.

"Good-bye," she whispered without looking up.

She had opened the door.

Surprised and obscurely disappointed, Antoine leaned forward, hoping to catch her eye. Like an echo, half playfully, in a soft, almost appealing tone, he murmured:

"Good-bye."

But the door closed. She had vanished, without turning back.

He heard the rustle of her skirt against the banisters, and the song she was forcing herself to sing as she went downstairs.

XII

LITTLE by little darkness was filling the room, but Antoine, lost in a maze of thoughts, could not find the energy to get up and turn on the lamps. More than an hour and a half had passed since Jacques had gone out. And, try as he might to repress it, a reluctant suspicion kept hovering at the back of Antoine's mind. As the minutes passed he felt his anxiety steadily increasing; then all at once it vanished— he had recognized his brother's footstep outside the door.

Jacques entered without a word, and did not even seem to notice that the room was in darkness. He sank wearily into a chair beside the door, his face just visible in the faint glow from the stove. His hat was down over his eyes, his overcoat still across his arm.

He gave a sudden little sigh.

"Oh, Antoine, don't take me away. Go to Paris by yourself and leave me here. You know, I very nearly didn't come back just now!" Then, before Antoine had time to put in a word, he cried out: "No, don't speak, don't say anything! I *know*. I'll come with you."

Rising, he turned on the light.

Antoine carefully refrained from looking in his direction; to tide over the awkward moment he pretended to go on reading the clippings on the table.

Jacques began moving lethargically about the room. After tossing various articles onto the bed, he opened a suitcase and began packing his clothes and other personal effects in it. Now and then he whistled under his breath—always the same tune. Looking up, Antoine saw him drop a bundle of letters into the stove, and stow away in a closet all the loose papers lying about the room. Then he locked the closet, putting the key in his pocket. Presently he sat down in a corner, his head sunk between his shoulders, his back bent, and began scribbling post-cards on his knee, nervously pushing back his long hair from his forehead as he wrote.

Antoine's heart softened. Had Jacques said to him just then: "Please go away without me," he would have embraced his brother and gone back alone, without another word.

It was Jacques who broke the silence. After changing his shoes and closing the suitcase, he went up to his brother.

"It's seven o'clock, you know. We'd better be off."

Without replying, Antoine stood up at once. After putting on his overcoat, he turned to Jacques.

"Can I give you a hand?"

"Thanks. Don't bother."

They spoke in lower tones than they had used during the day.

"Let me take your suitcase."

"It's not heavy; thanks. You go in front!"

They crossed the room almost without a sound. Antoine went out first. He heard Jacques switching off the light behind him and closing the door gently.

They snatched a hasty meal at the station restaurant. Jacques did not speak a word, and ate hardly anything. Antoine, whose mind was as heavy as his brother's, respected his desire for silence and made no pretence of cheerfulness.

The train was in; they walked up and down the platform till it was time to start. From the underground passage a never-ending stream of passengers came pouring up.

"Looks as if the train will be crowded," Antoine remarked.

Jacques made no reply. Then suddenly, unexpectedly, he volunteered a confidence.

"You know, I've been here for two and a half years."

"At Lausanne?"

"Not only at Lausanne. In Switzerland, I meant." After a few steps along the platform he murmured: "Ah, what a wonderful time that was for me, the spring of 1911!"

Once more they walked the full length of the train without speaking. Jacques's thoughts were evidently following the same trend as before, for suddenly he launched into an explanation.

"I'd been having such dreadful headaches in Germany that I put by every penny I could so as to be able to escape, to go to Switzerland and live an open-air life. I got here at the end of May, when the spring was at its height. I lived in the mountains, at Mühlenberg in the Canton of Lucerne."

"Ah, Mühlenberg—that explains."

"Yes. That's where I wrote nearly all the poems which I signed 'Mühlenberg.' I was working very hard at that period."

"Did you stay there long?"

"Six months. In a farmhouse. Only the two old people, the farmer and his wife; no children. I'll never forget that spring, or that summer. The day I arrived, and for the first time looked out of my window—the beauty of it all! A spacious, rolling countryside, all in simple outlines—nature at her noblest! I was out of doors from dawn to dusk. The meadows were full of flowers and wild bees, and the huge pastures billowed up to the skyline, with cows grazing everywhere, and little wooden bridges over the mountain streams. I'd walk for miles and miles, working as I walked. I'd tramp all day, and sometimes I went out at night as well. Ah, those nights at Mühlenberg!" His arm rose slowly, described a wide circle, slowly sank again.

"What about your headaches?"

"Oh, I began to feel ever so much better almost from the day I got there. Yes, Mühlenberg cured me outright. In fact, I've never felt in better form, or my mind so untroubled." His face lit up at the memory of it. "Untroubled, without a worry in the world—and all the time full of thoughts and projects, the maddest fancies! I almost think the seeds of everything I'll write in my lifetime were sown during that wonderful summer, in that bright air. I can remember days when I was so carried away—oh, I knew then what it means to be drunk with happiness. Why—I hardly dare to talk about it—there were times when I started jumping in the air and scampering up hill and down dale as if I'd gone off my head! Then I'd fling myself on my face into the grass, and start sobbing, crying my heart out for the ecstasy of it all. Can you believe that? Well, it's true; yes, so true that I remember some days when I had been crying like that and had to come back by a roundabout path, so as to bathe my eyes at a little spring I'd discovered on the mountainside." He lowered his eyes, walked some steps in silence, then, without looking up, repeated: "Yes, but all that was two and a half years ago—ancient history!"

He did not speak again before they left.

The train drew out without a whistle, with the obdurate insistence and docile force of machines that function like clockwork. Dry-eyed, Jacques watched the empty platform recede and, as the speed accelerated, the myriad lights of the suburbs dance past the pane. Then all was darkness, and now he pictured himself being pitched headlong and defenceless into the black night.

Cooped up amongst all these strangers, he looked round for Antoine, and saw him standing a few yards away, in the corridor. His back was half turned and he, too, seemed to be lost in thought, staring out into the darkness. Jacques felt a sudden wish for closer contact with him and, once again, an irresistible yearning to unburden his heart.

He edged his way to his brother's side and tapped him briskly on the shoulder.

Wedged between other passengers standing in the corridor and a pile of luggage, Antoine supposed that Jacques had merely a word to say to him and, without shifting his position, turned his head and leaned a little to one side. In the crowded corridor where they were penned like cattle, across the roar and rattle of the train, Jacques brought his mouth near Antoine's ear and began speaking in a hurried whisper.

"Look here, Antoine, you've got to know. . . . To start with, I led . . ."

He had intended to say: "I led an unspeakable life. I sank lower and lower. I was an interpreter, a guide, lived by my wits. I got in with Achmet—worse, with the whole underworld, the Rue aux Juifs. My friends were down-and-outers: old Krüger, Celadonio, Carolina, and their bunch. One night, on the quays, they clubbed me on the head; that was when my headaches started. Then I was in Naples. In Germany I lived with Rupprecht and 'little Rosa'—what a pair they were, those two!—and at Munich, because of Wilfried, I was held by the police." But the more fluently such avowals rose to his lips, and the more copiously the turbid flood of memories came pouring from the depths, the more he realized that the "unspeakable" life he had led was quite literally unspeakable; no words could cope with it.

Losing heart, he merely said to his brother in a low voice: "Antoine, I led an unspeakable life. Yes, unspeakable." He tried to put into the flat, ungainly epithet all the indignities, the foulness of the world. "Unspeakable!" he said again, with an accent of despair, and gradually the repetition of the word acted as an anodyne, as efficacious as a full confession.

Antoine had turned round and was facing him, decidedly ill at ease and worried by the nearness of so many strangers. Still, despite his fear that Jacques might raise his voice, and apprehensive of what he might be going to say, Antoine did his best to put a good face on it.

But Jacques, who was leaning against a panel of the corridor, did not seem inclined to embark on further explanations.

Presently the passengers began to file out of the corridor to their seats in the crowded car, and soon Antoine and Jacques were sufficiently isolated to be able to talk without being overheard.

Jacques, who till now had been in a silent mood, seemingly reluctant to go on with the conversation, suddenly turned to his brother again.

"You know, Antoine, the really appalling thing is not feeling sure of what is . . . normal. No, not 'normal'—that's a stupid word. How shall I put it? Not knowing if one's feelings, or, rather, instincts are . . . But you're a doctor, of course; you must know." His brows were knitted and his eyes fixed on the darkness. He spoke in a low tone, hesitating over his words. "Listen! There are things that work up one's feelings; one gets a sort of sudden impulse towards this or that, an impulse that rushes up from what lies deepest in one. Isn't that true? Well, it's impossible to know if other people have similar feelings, similar impulses; or if one's just a—a freak of nature. Do you see what I mean? You, Antoine, you've had to deal with so many people, so many cases, that I suppose you know what is—how shall I put it?—ordinary, and what is exceptional. But for the rest of us, who don't know—well, you can guess how agonizing it can be. Let me give you an example. There are all sorts of inexplicable desires that crop up all of a sudden when a boy's thirteen or fourteen— vague, incoherent thoughts that get hold of his mind, and he can't shake them off. But he feels ashamed of them; they seem like festering sores and he tries to hide them from the world at all costs. Then one day he discovers that nothing's more natural; why, they have even a beauty of their own! And that everyone, without exception, has the same desires. Do you see what I mean? Well, there are other dark impulses, things of the same sort, instincts that well up in one, and about which—even when one's grown up, Antoine, even at my age—one wonders, one can't be sure. . . ."

Suddenly his face grew tense, exasperated; a disturbing thought had flashed across his mind. He had just realized how quickly, how easily, the old allegiance to his brother had come back, linking him up, through Antoine, with his past and all its implications. Only yes- terday that chasm had seemed unbridgeable. And now—a few hours together had been enough to . . . ! He clenched his fists, lowered his eyes, fell silent.

A few minutes later, without once having raised his head or opened his lips again, he went back to his seat.

When, surprised by Jacques's abrupt departure, Antoine decided to follow, he found his brother settled down for the night, it seemed, in the dimly lit compartment; his eyelids shut upon his tears, Jacques was feigning sleep.

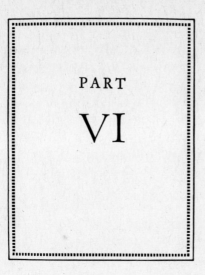

PART

VI

I

WHEN, at eight in the evening, just before taking the train to Lausanne, Antoine had looked in on Mlle. de Waize, to tell her he would be away for twenty-four hours, his remarks had failed to take immediate effect on the old lady. For nearly an hour she had been seated at her desk struggling to concoct a letter to the railway company, complaining that a basket of vegetables had gone astray between Maisons-Laffitte and Paris; and exasperation had prevented her from thinking of anything else. It was only later on, when she had disposed of the letter more or less to her liking, had undressed for bed, and was saying her prayers, that one of Antoine's remarks flashed back into her mind: "Please tell Sister Céline that Dr. Thérivier has been warned and will come, if needed, at a moment's notice." At once, all eagerness to shift her responsibility then and there, without troubling about the hour, without even finishing the prayer, she hurried across the flat to transmit the message to the nurse.

It was nearly ten o'clock. The lights were off, and M. Thibault's room was in darkness but for the fitful glow from the log-fire, kept constantly burning to purify the air. Every day the need for ventilation made itself more acutely felt, and this expedient was proving inadequate to carry off the pungent vapour from the poultices, the smell of the menthol in the liniments, and, worst of all, the odours emanating from the old man's person.

For the moment the pain had abated; the old man lay in an uneasy doze, snoring and groaning in the darkness. For many months he had not enjoyed the deep oblivion of real sleep. Going to sleep, for him, had ceased to mean the loss of consciousness; it meant only that for a brief spell he lost track of the slow lapse of time, minute by minute, and let his limbs sink into a partial torpor. But never for an instant did his brain stop working, calling up a stream of pictures, like an incoherent film in which fragments of his past life were flashed upon the screen; and though this pageant of the past might hold his interest, it was as exhausting as a nightmare.

That night M. Thibault's torpor was not profound enough to free him from a haunting dread, which, mingling with his hallucinations and growing stronger every moment, set him running before an invisible pursuer, across the buildings of his old school, along the dormitory, down the corridors, through the chapel, and out into the playground. There, outside the gymnasium door, in front of the statue of Saint Joseph, he crumpled up, his head buried in his arms. And then, suddenly, from a coign of darkness, that terrifying, nameless Thing, which had been on his track night after night, leapt forth upon him. Just as it was about to crush his life out, he awoke with a start.

Behind the screen, an unwonted candle was lighting up a corner usually left in darkness; two shadows wavered on the wall, cornice-high. He heard whispering: Mademoiselle's voice. Once before she had come like that, by night, to call him; Jacques was having convulsions. One of the children ill? What time was it?

Then Sister Céline's voice recalled him to the present. He could not quite catch what they were saying; holding his breath, he listened hard.

A few words came clear: "Antoine told me the doctor had been warned . . . will come at once . . ."

Someone ill? Of course—*he* was ill. But—why the doctor?

Again that nameless form of fear was prowling in the shadows. Was he worse? What had happened? Had he slept? He had not noticed any change for the worse in his condition. Still, the doctor had been called in. In the middle of the night. He was dying. No hope left.

Then all he had said—without believing it—announcing that his last hour was near, came back to his mind. A cold sweat broke out on his body.

He tried to shout: "Help! Antoine!" But all that passed his lips was a wordless cry—so agonizing, however, that Sister Céline, thrusting aside the screen, rushed to the bed and turned on the light.

Her first notion was that he was having some sort of fit. The old man's face, usually a sickly yellow, had turned scarlet; his eyes were wide open, his lips working inarticulately.

M. Thibault, meanwhile, paid no attention to what was happening round him. Centred on its fixed idea, his brain was functioning with ruthless clarity. In a few seconds he had reviewed the whole course of his illness: the operation, the months of respite, the relapse, and then the gradual decline of his strength, the way his pain was growing more and more recalcitrant to treatment. It all linked up together, everything grew clear. And all at once a bottomless abyss yawned where a few minutes ago there had been that bedrock of security, lacking which it is impossible to live. So sudden was the glimpse of the abyss that his whole balance was thrown out; his mind went limp, incapable of thought. Human reason is so vitally bound up with the future that once all likelihood of a tomorrow is ruled out, and every prospect seems converging on the blind alley that is death, the faculty of thinking falls to pieces.

The old man's hands clutched at the sheets in blind, desperate panic. He tried to cry out, but in vain. The world was toppling over, dissolving into chaos, and he was being swept under, foundering in floods of darkness. Then fear forced a way across his strangled throat in a hoarse gasp that rose and fell, choked out at once.

Unable to straighten up her bent back so as to look at the bed, Mademoiselle began screaming.

"Bless and save us! What is it? What's happening, Sister?"

The nurse did not answer. The old woman fled from the room. Somebody must be sent for—but who? Antoine was away. Then she remembered the priest, Abbé Vécard.

The servants were still in the kitchen; they had heard nothing. At Mademoiselle's first words Adrienne crossed herself, while Clotilde, pinning her shawl round her shoulders and picking up her purse and keys, made for the door.

II

THE ABBÉ VÉCARD lived in the Rue de Grenelle, near the administrative offices of the Archbishopric, where he was now in charge of the Department of Diocesan Charities. When Clotilde came he was still up, working at his desk. She had kept her taxi and, a few minutes later, they were at M. Thibault's door.

Perched on one of the hall chairs, Mademoiselle was waiting for them. At first the priest failed to recognize her, so different she seemed without the braids encircling her forehead; tightly drawn back, her hair fell squirming down her dressing-jacket in corkscrew wisps.

"Please, M. l'Abbé," she pleaded, "oh, please go to him at once, to make him less afraid."

Nodding to her, without stopping, he went to the sick-room.

M. Thibault had flung away the counterpane; to get away from this bed, from this accursed house, was now his one idea—anywhere to escape the Thing hounding him down. He had got back his voice and was hurling abuse at the women.

"Filthy strumpets! Bitches! Ah, I know all about you and your beastliness!"

Suddenly his eyes fell on the priest standing in the doorway, lit up by the hall lamp. He showed no surprise, and merely paused a moment before crying:

"Not you! I want Antoine. Where's Antoine?"

Dropping his hat on a chair, the priest moved quickly forward. Impassive as ever, his features did not reveal how deeply he was moved; only the slightly raised arms, the half-opened hands, conveyed his longing to help his old friend. Going up to the bed, without a word, in all simplicity, he made the sign of benediction.

Then his voice rose through the silence, saying the Lord's Prayer:

"Pater noster, qui es in cœlis, sanctificetur nomen tuum.
"Fiat voluntas tua sicut in cœlo et in terra."

M. Thibault had ceased tossing to and fro and was gazing up at the Abbé. His lips began quivering and a wry look settled on his face, the look of a child who is on the brink of tears. His head swayed slowly this side and that, then sank onto the pillow. Gradually the sobs, which sounded like suppressed guffaws, grew fewer, ceased altogether.

Meanwhile the Abbé had gone up to the nun.

"Is he in much pain just now?" he asked in a low voice.

"Not much. I've just made an injection. Usually the pain doesn't come back till after midnight."

"Good. Leave us alone now. But please ring up the doctor," he added with a gesture that seemed to imply: "I can't work miracles!"

Quietly Sister Céline and Adrienne left the room.

M. Thibault seemed almost unconscious. Before the priest had come he had sunk thus several times into a sort of coma. But these welcome lapses never lasted long; abruptly he came back to the surface, where panic lay in wait for him, and once more with a new lease of strength began the desperate struggle.

The priest guessed that the lull would be brief; he must make the most of it while it lasted. He felt the blood coming to his head; of all the duties of his calling, ministration to the dying was the one he dreaded most.

He went up to the bed.

"You are suffering, my friend. You are going through an hour of bitter trial. Do not try to fall back on yourself, but open your heart to God."

M. Thibault turned towards his confessor, and there was such anguish in his look that the priest's gaze faltered. For a moment the sick man's eyes darkened with anger and malevolent contempt. Only for a moment. The look of dreadful fear came back almost immediately. And now it was so terrible in its intensity that the priest could not face it, and turned away.

The dying man's teeth were chattering; he was muttering feebly: "Oh, dear me! Oh, dear me! I'm so frightened."

The priest pulled himself together.

"I have come to help you," he said in a gentle voice. "First, let us pray. Let us invoke God's presence in ourselves. Now, my friend, we will pray together."

M. Thibault cut him short. "But . . . . but . . . ! Don't you see? I'm . . . I'm at the point . . ." He dared not affront death by naming it.

Frantically his eye ranged the dark corners of the room. Was there no help, none anywhere in all the world? The shadows were deepening, deepening round him. From his lips came a scream that jarred the silence, and to the priest was almost a relief. Then, with all his might, he shouted:

"Antoine! Where's Antoine?" The Abbé made a vague gesture. "No, I don't want you. Antoine!"

The priest changed his methods. Drawing himself up, he gazed sadly down at the furious face on the pillow, and with a sweeping gesture, as if he were exorcizing a man possessed, blessed him a second time.

His calmness was the last straw for M. Thibault. Propping himself on an elbow, despite the agony the effort cost him, he shook his fist. "Ah, the swine! The ruffians! And now you and your claptrap—I've had enough of it." Then a despairing sob broke from his lips. "I'm . . . I'm dying, dying, I tell you! Will no one help me?"

The Abbé gazed down, and did not contradict him; convinced though the old man was already that his end was near, the priest's silence came as a final blow. Shaking from head to foot, feeling what little strength remained ebbing away, unable even to keep back the saliva dribbling down his chin, he kept on repeating in a tone of pitiful entreaty, as though perhaps the priest had not heard him, or had failed to understand:

"I'm dying. I'm dy-ing."

The Abbé sighed, but made no gesture of denial. It is not always the truest charity, he thought, to lavish vain illusions on the dying; when the last hour is actually at hand, the only remedy against the terrors that invest it is not to deny its onset—against which the body, warned by instinct, is already up in arms—but to look death in the eyes, and be resigned to meet it.

He let some seconds pass, then, mustering his courage, said in clear, even tones:

"And supposing it is so, my friend. Is that a reason to be so terribly afraid?"

The old man fell back onto the pillow, as if he had been struck in the face.

"Oh, dear me!" he whimpered. "Oh, dear me!"

All was lost now; the storm had broken, sweeping him from his last foothold; there was no refuge anywhere, he was sinking, sinking . . . ! And the last gleam of consciousness served only to reveal the black gulf of non-being. For other people death was a vague notion that did not touch them personally, one more counter in the common coin of words. For him it was the Now and Here, the one thing real—himself! Dazed and dilated, his eyes peered into the sheer abyss; then very far away, on the other side of nothingness, he saw the priest's face, the face of a living man, denizen of another world. He was alone, cut off from the world of men. Alone with his fear, plunged in the nethermost depth of loneliness.

Through the stillness came a voice, the priest's.

"Reflect! It was not God's will that death should steal on you unawares, *sicut latro,* like a thief in the night. Surely then, you should prove yourself worthy of this grace—for a grace it is, and the greatest God can bestow on us, miserable sinners—that on the threshold of eternal life a warning should be granted."

From an infinite distance M. Thibault listened to the words that, like weak waves fretting a rock, beat on the brain that fear had turned to stone, and for a moment, by mere force of habit, his mind sought refuge in them, in the idea of God. But the impulse died still-born. Eternal Life, Grace, God—the words had lost all meaning, dwindled to futile sounds that had no relevance to the terrible reality.

"Let us thank God," the Abbé continued. "Blessed are those whom He snatches from their earthbound cravings; blessed are those who die in the Lord. Let us pray, my friend. Let us pray together, with all our hearts, and God will help you in your time of trouble."

M. Thibault swung his head round. Under his terror a vestige of rage was seething still. Had he been able, how gladly he would now have crashed his fist into the priest's face! Blasphemies rose to his lips.

"God? What's that? What help? It's sheer nonsense when you come to think of it. Isn't it He, precisely, whose will it is that I . . . ?" The words choked in his throat. "What help can I expect of Him, tell me!" he shouted furiously.

His taste for controversy had come back to him so strongly that he forgot that his agony of mind had made him deny God just a moment before. "Ah, why should God treat me thus?" he groaned.

The Abbé shook his head. "Remember the words of the *Imitation of Christ:* 'In the hour when thou deemest thyself very far from Me, then it is often I am nearest thee.' "

M. Thibault pondered. After some moments' silence he turned to his confessor; and now he made a gesture of distress.

"Abbé, Abbé!" he pleaded, "Do something—pray—anything at all! Surely it can't be possible that I . . . ? Save me, oh, save me!"

The Abbé drew up a chair to the bed, sat down, and clasped the swollen hand, the least pressure on which left a pale imprint.

"Ah," the old man cried, "you'll see what it's like, my friend, one day—when your turn comes!"

The priest sighed. "No one can say: 'I shall be spared temptation,' but I pray God to send me, in the hour of death, a friend who will help me to overcome my weakness while there is yet time."

M. Thibault shut his eyes. The movements he had been making had irritated the bed-sores in the small of his back, and they were smarting like fire. He stretched himself out in the bed; now and again a feeble groan escaped his clenched lips: "Oh, dear me! Oh, dear me!"

"Consider now!" the priest began in his measured, melancholy tones. "You, as a Christian, knew well this life on earth must end. *'Pulvis es . . .'* Had you forgotten that this mortal life does not belong to us? You are protesting now; as if you were being robbed of something that was yours in your own right. Yet you knew our lives are only lent us by our Maker. It may be that the hour has come when you shall be required to pay your debt; how ungrateful it would be, my friend, to haggle!"

Through his half-opened eyelids M. Thibault shot a malevolent glance at the priest. Then, very slowly, his gaze roamed round the room, pausing on all the things he recognized so easily despite the feeble light, things that were his, that he had seen—seen and possessed—so many and many a day.

"To leave all that?" he murmured. "No, I don't want to." A sudden tremor shook the old body. "I'm afraid."

Compassionately the priest bent towards him.

"Our Divine Master, too, endured the agony and bloody sweat. And He, too, for a brief moment, doubted His Father's love, and cried, saying: *'Eli, Eli, lama sabachthani?* My God, my God, why hast Thou forsaken me?'* Think, my friend; is there not a remarkable analogy between your sufferings and those of our Divine Master? But Jesus in His hour of trial took new strength in prayer. With all the fervour of His love he cried: 'O my Father, here am I. Father, I trust in Thee. Father, I yield to Thee. Not as I will be done, but as Thou wilt.'"

The Abbé felt the swollen fingers quiver. After a pause, he continued in the same tone.

"Have you reflected that for centuries, nay, for thousands of centuries, our poor human race has been working out its destiny on earth?" Then, realizing that such arguments were too vague to serve his end, he fell back on precise examples. "Only think of your own family, your father, your grandfather, and your ancestors—of all those men who went before you, lived and struggled, hoped and suffered like you; and all of them irrevocably, one following the other, at the hour appointed from the beginning, returned whence they came. *'Reverti unde veneris, quid grave est?'* Is it not a comforting thought that all creation, every one of us, returns to the bosom of the Heavenly Father?"

"Yes," M. Thibault groaned. "Only . . . not yet!"

"How can you complain? Only think—how many of those men I spoke of enjoyed your advantages? You have had the privilege of reaching an age denied to many. God has shown you mercy in granting you so long a life in which to work out your salvation."

M. Thibault shuddered. "That's just what is so terrible!"

"Terrible, yes. But you have less right than many another to feel fear."

Roughly the old man withdrew his hand.

"No!" he exclaimed.

"Indeed you have." The Abbé's voice was gentle, consoling. "I've watched you at work, my friend. Always, with all your heart, you have aimed at something higher than worldly gain. You have loved your neighbour, fought the good fight against poverty and sin. You have lived the life of an upright man, and death should have no terrors at the close of such a life."

"No," the dying man repeated hoarsely.

When the Abbé tried to clasp his hand again, he freed himself angrily. The priest's remarks had touched him to the quick. No, he had not aimed at something higher than worldly success. On that score he had deceived everybody, including the priest—and himself, too, almost always. In reality he had spared no effort to shine in the eyes of men. All his motives had been vile, wholly vile—under the surface. Selfishness and vanity. A thirst for riches, for ordering others about. A display of generosity, to win honours, to play a specious part. Sins of the flesh, hypocrisy, a whited sepulchre—ah, the falsehood of it all! If only he could wipe the slate clean, make a fresh start! That "life of an upright man"—he was heartily ashamed of it. He saw it now as it had really been. Too late. The day of reckoning had come.

"A Christian like you . . ."

M. Thibault could not contain himself. "Keep quiet, you! I, a Christian? I'm no Christian. All my life I've—I've aimed at . . . what? 'Love of my neighbour'? Nonsense! I've never known what it is to love—anybody, anybody in the world."

"My poor friend!" the Abbé murmured. He was expecting M. Thibault to accuse himself once more of having driven Jacques to suicide. But no, not once in these latter days had the father thought of his missing son. All he could conjure up at present was much remoter phases of his past: his youth consumed with ambition, his start in life, his early struggles, first distinctions—sometimes, too, the honours he had earned in middle age. The last ten years had already faded out into the mists of oblivion.

Despite the twinge it cost him, M. Thibault raised an arm.

"It's all your fault!" he burst out passionately. "Why didn't you warn me, while there still was time?"

Then anger yielded to despair, and he burst into tears. Like ghastly laughter, sobs convulsed his body.

The Abbé bent towards him.

"In every human life there comes a day, an hour, a fleeting moment, when suddenly God deigns to reveal Himself as a real presence and extends His hand to us. Sometimes that moment comes after a life of sin, and sometimes at the close of a long life which has passed for Christian. Who can say? Perhaps it is tonight that God, for the first time, holds out His hand to you."

M. Thibault's eyelids lifted. In the twilight of his mind a certain confusion had grown up between God's hand and the human hand, the priest's, beside him. He put forth his hand to grasp it.

"What must I do?" he panted. "Tell me what to do!"

His tone had changed; the panic terror at death's advent had gone out of it. He spoke as one who asks a question that can be answered; already tempered with contrition, the fear that still persisted in his voice could be dispelled by absolution.

God's hour was approaching.

But, for the priest, this was of all hours the hardest. He communed with himself for a while, as he did in the pulpit before beginning a sermon. Though he had given no sign of it, M. Thibault's reproach had stung him to the quick. For many years he had had spiritual charge of this proud nature; how far had his influence been effective?

How had he fulfilled his task? Well, there was still time to make good the lapses—on both sides. He must lay hold of this poor, wavering soul, and guide it back to the Redeemer's feet.

Then his knowledge of the man suggested a pious expedient.

"What we must deplore," he said, "is not that your earthly life is drawing to a close, but that it was not as it should have been. Still, even if your past life has not always been a source of edification, let the leaving of it, at least, furnish a fine example of a truly Christian end. Let your bearing, when that moment comes, be a pattern for all who have known you, a pattern to observe and to imitate!"

The dying man made a movement and freed his hand. The priest's words were sinking in. Yes, let it be said that Oscar Thibault had had a noble end, worthy of a saint. He locked his fingers awkwardly, and closed his eyes; his under-jaw, the priest observed, was trembling. He was praying God to grant him the grace of an edifying death.

Now fear was giving way to a vague dejection, a sense of feebleness; he was a small, pathetic atom amongst myriads of others, all ephemeral like him. But after those cataclysms of terror, there was some relief in this self-pity.

The Abbé raised his head.

"The Apostle Paul has bidden us not to be sorry, as men without hope. You, my poor friend, are amongst those men. How sad that, at this crucial hour, your faith should have forsaken you! You have forgotten that God is your Father before He is your Judge, and you do your Father grievous wrong to doubt His mercy."

The old man gazed at him with troubled eyes, and sighed.

"Come now, take heart!" the priest continued. "Be assured of the divine compassion, and remember that, granted sincere and thorough-going repentance, a pardon given in the extremity of death will cancel the sins of a lifetime. You are one of God's creatures; does He not know, better than we do, the clay in which He has shaped us? For, mind you, He loves us as we are; and this assurance should be the cornerstone of our courage and our confidence. Yes, *confidence;* for in that word lies the whole secret of a Christian death. '*In te, Domine.*

speravi.' The Christian trusts in God, in His goodness and infinite compassion."

The Abbé had a manner of his own, placid yet weighty, of emphasizing certain words; whenever he used them, his hand would rise with a slight gesture that added to their force. Yet there was little warmth in his monotonous delivery, any more than in the long-nosed, impassive face. And it was proof of the essential virtue of these hallowed words, it showed how centuries of usage had formed them to the exact requirements of the deathbed, that their effect was so immediate on such panic and revolt as M. Thibault's.

His head had sunk, and his beard was brushing his chest. Stealthily a new emotion was permeating him, an emotion less sterile than self-pity and despair. Tears were rolling down his cheeks again, but tears of joy; and all his spirit yearned towards the Omnipotent Consoler. Now his one desire was to lay down the burden, yield his life to Him who gave it.

But then he clenched his teeth; the pain had come on again, shooting through his leg, from the thigh downwards. He ceased listening, stiffened. After a moment the pain died down.

". . . like the climber," the priest was saying, "who has reached the summit and looks back to see the path that he has travelled. And what a sorry retrospect is a man's life! A series of struggles, never ending, unavailing, in a preposterously narrow field of action. Vain activities, tawdry pleasures, an undying thirst for happiness that nothing, nothing in the world can quench. Am I exaggerating? Such was your life, my friend; such, indeed, is the lot of every man on earth. How can a being created by God be content with a life like that? Has it anything worthy of an iota of regret? Very well! To what, I ask you, is it that you cling so much? Is it to your suffering body, this weak, miserable body, that always plays you false, that shirks its proper functions, that nothing can safeguard from pain and decay? Ah, let us face the facts! It is a blessing that after being so long enslaved to our vile bodies, held prisoner by them, we can at last discard them, slough our mortal skins, cast them away, and leave them like a beggar's rags upon the wayside."

For the dying man the words had such immediate cogency that all at once the prospect of escape seemed utterly delightful. And yet —what was this new-found solace but once more the life-impulse, the stubborn hope of survival under a new disguise? And it struck the priest, whose insight had not failed him, that the prospect of another life, of living for eternity in God's presence, is as necessary in the hour of death, as in life the certainty of living the next moment.

After a brief silence the Abbé spoke again.

"Turn your eyes Heavenwards now, my friend. Now you have judged how little it is, what you are leaving, see what awaits you! An end of all the pettiness of life, its harshness and injustice. And ended, too, its trials and responsibilities. Ended, those daily acts of sin, with their after-taste of remorse. Ended, that anguish of the sinner torn between good and evil. There, in the Kingdom of Heaven, you will find peace and plenitude, and the rule of divine order. You are leaving behind the things that are corruptible, to enter into the realm of things everlasting. Do you understand, my friend? *'Dimitte transitoria, et quære æterna.'* You were afraid of dying; your imagination pictured some vague horror of great darkness. But a Christian death is just the opposite of that; it opens out a vista of unfading light. It brings us peace, the peace that passes understanding, rest eternal. What am I saying? It does more than that. It brings Life to its perfection, consummates the union of human and divine. 'I am the Resurrection and the Life.' Not merely an escape, a sleep, or a forgetting; but an awakening, the opening of a flower. To die is to be born again. Death is a resurrection to a new life, in the fullness of understanding, in the communion of the saints. Death, my friend, is not merely the rest that nightfall brings when the labourer's task is done; it is a progress upward and onward into the light of an eternal dawn."

While the priest was speaking, M. Thibault had nodded several times, approvingly. Now a smile was hovering on his face. The shadows had lifted, a dazzling effulgence was kindling facets of the past. With his mind's eye he saw himself a little boy kneeling at the foot of his mother's bed, this very bed on which he now was lying; his mother was clasping his childish fingers while in the radiant light of a summer morning he repeated one of the prayers which first had opened heaven to him: 'Gentle Jesus, who art in Paradise . . ." He saw himself at his first communion, trembling with awe before the Host, for the first time vouchsafed to him. And then he saw himself as a young man, one Whit-Sunday after mass, walking with his fiancée up the garden path at Darnetal, between the peonies. Back with those sunny memories, he had forgotten his old, dying body; he was smiling.

Not merely had all fear of death departed, but what troubled him just now was that he had still to live, if only for a little while. The air of this world had become unbreathable. "A little patience," he thought, "and I'll have done with it all." It seemed to him that he had discovered his true centre of gravity, had reached the vital core of his being; he had found himself at last. And this gave him happiness such as he had never known before. True, his energies seemed broken up, dispersed, lying as it were in havoc round him. What matter? He had ceased to belong to them; they were the rags and tatters of an earth-bound being, with whom he felt that he had broken for good and all; and the prospect of a still more complete disruption, very near at hand, gave him an intense delight—the only joy of which he now was capable.

The Holy Spirit was hovering in the room. The Abbé had risen, full of thankfulness to God. And with his humble gratitude mingled a very human self-satisfaction—like that of a lawyer who has won his suit. No sooner was he conscious of this feeling, than he upbraided himself for it. But this was no time for self-analysis. A sinner was about to appear before his Maker.

Bowing his head, he folded his hands under his chin and prayed aloud:

"O Lord, the hour has come. Father of mercies and God of all comfort, I beseech Thee to vouchsafe this last grace, and grant me to die in peace and in Thy love. *De profundis,* out of the darkness, from the deep pit where I lay trembling with dread, *clamavi ad te,*

Domine, have I called to Thee, O Lord; Lord, hear my voice. The hour has come; I am on the brink of Thy eternity, when at last I shall see Thee face to face, Almighty God. Consider my contrition, accept my prayer, and let me not be outcast in my unworthiness. Let Thy gaze fall upon me, pardoning my sins. *In te, Domine, commendo.* Father, into Thy hands I commend my spirit. My hour has come. Father, O Father, forsake me not."

The dying man's voice came like an echo: "Forsake me not."

There was a long silence. Then the Abbé bent over the bed.

"Tomorrow morning I will bring the holy oil. Meanwhile, my friend, make your confession, so that I may give you absolution."

M. Thibault's swollen lips began to move; with a fervour he had never shown before, he stammered a few phrases, in which the confession of his sins had less place than a passionate avowal of repentance. Then, raising his hand, the priest murmured the words that wash all sins away.

" '*Ego te absolvo a peccatis tuis. In nomine Patris, et Filii, et Spiritus Sancti.*' "

The man on the bed was silent. His eyes were wide open—open as if they were never to close again—and in his gaze there was as yet only the faintest hint of questioning or wonder. The bland innocence of the eyes made the dying old man look strangely like the pastel portrait of Jacques, hanging on the wall above the lamp.

He felt the last threads linking his soul to the world of men strained almost to the point of snapping; but their tenuity, their brittleness, filled him with abounding joy. He was no more now than a frail flame gently flickering out. Life was flowing on without him, as a river goes on flowing after the swimmer has made the further shore. And he felt not only beyond life, but beyond death as well. He was rising, floating up into a zenith, bathed, as is sometimes a midsummernight sky, with supernatural light.

There was a knock at the door. The Abbé ceased his prayer, crossed himself, and went towards it. The doctor had just come; Sister Céline was with him.

"Please continue, M. l'Abbé," Thérivier said, when he saw the priest.

The Abbé caught the nun's eye, and discreetly moved aside.

"Come in, doctor," he said in a low voice. "I've finished."

Thérivier went up to the bed, rubbing his hands. He thought it best to assume a hearty, hopeful tone—his bedside manner. "Well, well? What's the trouble tonight? A touch of fever, eh? That's the new injection doing its job, of course." Stroking his beard, he glanced at the nun, as if calling her to witness. "Antoine will be back any moment. Meanwhile, there's no need to worry. I'll put you right. That new serum, you know . . ."

Without saying a word, M. Thibault watched this man lying to him. He could see through it all now—the doctor's cheerfulness-to-order, his professional play-acting. He was no longer taken in, as he had been too often and too readily, by these infantile "explanations." The make-up had worn thin; he knew them all for what they were: mummers in a macabre comedy that they had been playing for his benefit, for months. Was Antoine really coming back? Could anything they said be trusted? In any case, it was all the same to him. Nothing mattered; nothing whatever mattered now.

It did not even surprise him to read so clearly other people's minds. . . . The universe was a closed system, something apart, remote, in which he, the dying man, had no place. He stood outside it all. Facing the great mystery alone. Alone with his Creator. So utterly alone that even God's nearness left him still alone.

Unwittingly he had let his eyelids fall. He had ceased caring to distinguish vision from reality. A great peace, murmurous with music, had descended on him. He submitted to the doctor's tedious examination without a murmur; inert, aloof, indifferent—in another world.

III

IN THE night train that was taking them back to Paris, the two brothers had long given up any idea of sleep; but each, lying back in his corner seat, half stupefied by the stuffy air in the dimly lit compartment, persisted in feigning slumber, so as to be left alone to his own devices as long as might be.

Antoine's anxiety was keeping him awake. Now that he had started on the return journey, the alarming state in which he had left his father had come back vividly to his mind and, through the long hours of semi-darkness loud with the roaring wheels, his imagination ran riot, picturing the worst. But steadily, as the train came nearer Paris, his fears diminished; once he was on the spot, he could attend to the situation, take charge again. Then another complication crossed his mind. How should he announce to M. Thibault the fugitive's return? How let Gise know? The letter he proposed to send immediately to London was not an easy one to write; he would have to inform Gise not only that Jacques was safe and sound and had been traced, but that he had returned to Paris; nevertheless, somehow she must be prevented from rushing home at once.

Someone uncovered the ceiling-light; the passengers in the car began to stretch their limbs. Jacques and Antoine opened their eyes, looked at each other. The expression on Jacques's face, resigned yet hag-ridden, was so poignant that Antoine felt a swift compassion.

He tapped his brother's knee. "Slept badly, eh?"

Jacques made no attempt to smile; with a vague gesture of indifference he turned towards the window and relapsed into a silent lethargy which, it seemed, he had neither the power nor the will to shake off. The train sped through the suburbs, still in darkness. A hasty cup of coffee in the dining-car—grinding brakes—the platform in the grey chill before dawn—a few steps in Antoine's wake as he hunted for a taxi—there was a curious unreality about it all; each successive act seemed blurred in the dank, fog-bound air, yet guided by some dark necessity that spared him conscious acquiescence.

Antoine said little, just enough to tide over the difficult moment, making only casual remarks which Jacques did not have to answer. Indeed, he managed to give such a matter-of-fact air to the whole proceedings that Jacques's homecoming took the aspect of a perfectly ordinary event. Jacques found himself alighting on the pavement, then standing in the entrance-hall, without having any clear idea of what was happening, even of his own supineness. And when Léon, hearing the door open, stepped out of the kitchen, it was with perfect self-possession, though without meeting his servant's startled gaze, that Antoine bent above the pile of letters on his hall-table, and remarked in a completely casual tone:

"Good morning, Léon. M. Jacques has come back with me. You'd better . . ."

Léon cut him short.

"Haven't you heard, sir? Haven't you been upstairs yet?"

Antoine stiffened up; his face was white.

"M. Thibault's been taken worse, sir. Dr. Thérivier's spent the night here. I hear from the maids that . . ."

But Antoine had already rushed out of the flat. Jacques remained standing in the hall; the impression that he was living in a dream, a nightmare, grew stronger. After a brief hesitation, he darted forward, and followed his brother.

The staircase was in darkness.

"Quickly!" Antoine panted as he pushed Jacques into the elevator.

The metallic clang as the outer door sprang to, the brittle click of the glazed doors closing, the drone of the motor as the cage began to rise—all those well-remembered sounds, following immutably in the same order and now, after what seemed like centuries, echoing in the past, one after another, carried Jacques back to his youth. And suddenly came a vivid, galling memory: that bygone day when he had been pent in this selfsame cage with Antoine, trapped and tamed, after being brought back from Marseille and his escapade with Daniel.

"Wait on the landing," Antoine whispered.

Chance outwitted his precautions. Mademoiselle, who was fluttering distractedly to and fro about the flat, heard the elevator stop. Antoine —at last! She ran to the door as fast as her bent back permitted, saw four feet, stopped in amazement, and recognized Jacques only when he bent to kiss her.

"Bless and save us!" she exclaimed, but without much real wonder. For the past twenty-four hours she had been living in a state of such immense bewilderment that no new surprise could take effect on her.

All the lights were on in the flat, all the doors open. From the study a flabbergasted face peered out, M. Chasle's; blinking, he launched his usual "Ah, so it's you!"

And suitably enough, for once, Antoine could not help thinking. Paying no attention to his brother, he hurried off to the bedroom.

There all was darkness, silence. The door stood ajar; as he threw it open, he saw at first only the faint glow of a bedside lamp; then, on the pillow, his father's face. Despite the shut eyes and the immobility, the old man was unmistakably alive.

Antoine went in. No sooner had he crossed the threshold than he saw grouped round the bed, as if something had just happened, Sister Céline, Adrienne, and a second nun, an elderly woman whom he did not know.

Thérivier emerged from the shadows, buttonholed Antoine, and led him into the dressing-room.

"I was afraid you wouldn't get back in time," he said hurriedly. "Look here, Antoine, his kidney is blocked up. No longer secreting. Not a drop. And I'm sorry to say the uræmia has reached the convulsive stage. I've spent the whole night here, so as not to leave the women by themselves; if you hadn't come, I was going to send out for a male nurse. He's had three acute attacks since midnight—the last of them a very bad one."

"When did the kidney stop working?"

"Twenty-four hours ago, it seems, from what the sister tells me. Since yesterday morning. Naturally she's stopped the injections."

"Naturally," Antoine repeated, but with an air of hesitation.

Their eyes met; Thérivier read Antoine's thoughts easily enough. "When for two months on end we've been deliberately injecting poison into a sick man who has only one kidney working, it's perhaps rather late in the day to develop scruples . . ."

Thérivier craned forward, an arm extended in expostulation. "All the same, old man, we aren't murderers. One can't go on pumping morphine into him in the middle of an attack of uræmia."

Obviously. Antoine nodded, but said nothing.

"Well, I'm off now," Thérivier said. "I'll ring you up some time before twelve." Then suddenly he added: "By the way, how about your brother?"

Antoine half closed his eyes, then, as he opened them again, a sudden gleam lit up the golden-yellow irises.

"I've found him," he said with a quick smile. "What's more, I've brought him back. He's here."

Thérivier thrust his plump hand into his beard, and his shrewd, merry eyes scanned Antoine's face. But it was not the place or time for questions. Sister Céline had come in, bringing Antoine's white coat. Thérivier glanced at the nun, then at his friend.

"Well, then, I'm off!" And added bluntly: "You've a hard day before you."

Antoine frowned and turned to the sister. "He's in terrible pain, isn't he, without the morphine?"

"I'm applying very hot fomentations. Mustard-plasters." Seeing Antoine's sceptical expression, she added: "It relieves the pain a bit, you know."

"Anyhow, I hope you put some laudanum on the fomentations. No?" He knew only too well that, without morphine . . . But never would he acknowledge he was beaten. "I've all that's needed downstairs," he said to the nurse. "I'll be back right away." Then he turned to Thérivier. "Come on, we'll go down together."

Crossing the flat, he wondered what Jacques was up to; but he had no time to give to his brother now.

The two doctors went down the stairs in silence. At the bottom step Thérivier held out his hand. As Antoine took it he asked abruptly:

"Tell me, Thérivier—frankly, what's your prognosis? Surely the end is bound to come pretty quickly, eh?"

"Bound to, if we can't stop the uræmia."

Antoine's only answer was to grip his friend's hand warmly. He felt confident in himself, he would see it through. It was only a matter of hours now. And Jacques had been found. . . .

Upstairs, in the bedroom, Adrienne and the second nun, who were watching at the old man's bedside, had failed to notice that another attack was coming on. When his gasps attracted their attention, his fists were already clenched and his neck stiffening, dragging the head back.

Adrienne rushed out into the corridor.

"Sister!"

No one. She ran into the hall.

"Sister Céline! M. Antoine! Come quick!"

Jacques had stayed in the study with M. Chasle. Hearing the cries, he ran without thinking to the bedroom.

The door stood open. He tripped over a chair. At first he could see nothing, only indistinct figures moving against the glow of the bedside lamp. At last he made out a dark mass sprawling across the bed, arms threshing the air. The old man had slipped sideways, over the edge of the mattress; Adrienne and the nurse were vainly trying to lift him back. Jacques ran up, grasped his father with both arms, and, propping a knee on the bed-frame, managed to shore up the old man's shoulders, and thrust them back into the centre of the bed. As he crouched above the sheets, holding down the huge body racked by spasms, he felt a warm chest heaving violently against his; saw, under his gaze, a mask-like face, with only the whites of the eyes showing—a face that he could hardly recognize.

Gradually the paroxysms began to lose their violence, and the blood to circulate. The pupils of the eyes came back, wavering at first, then growing fixed; it seemed as if the eyes had come to life again and were discovering the young face bent above him. Did the old man recognize his lost son? And, if so, was he still able in that flash of lucidity to distinguish between realities and the vague phantasms of his wandering mind? His lips moved, the pupils dilated. And suddenly those lustreless eyes brought back to Jacques a definite memory; it was just that expression of dim attention, that far-away look, that used to come into his father's eyes whenever he was trying to recall a forgotten name or date.

Jacques felt a tightening at his throat; propping himself on his fists, he stammered unthinkingly:

"Well, Father? How are you feeling, Father?"

Slowly M. Thibault's eyelids closed; his underlip and the tip of his beard were faintly quivering. Then his chest and shoulders began to heave with increasing violence; his face became convulsed; he burst into sobs. Sounds came from the flaccid lips like the gurgles of an empty bottle plunged in water. The old nun reached forward to wipe his chin with a wad of cotton-wool. Blinded by tears, not daring to move, Jacques stood bending over the sob-racked body, repeating mechanically, idiotically:

"Well, Father? Tell me, how are you feeling now?"

Antoine, who was coming in followed by Sister Céline, stopped short when he saw his brother. He could not imagine what had happened; in any case, he did not pause to find out. He was carrying a half-filled graduate. The nun had a basin and towels.

Jacques straightened up. The others thrust him aside, grasped the sick man, and began turning back the sheets.

He retreated to the far end of the room. No one took any notice of him. What was the point of staying there, hearing his father's groans, watching his agony? None. He moved to the door and crossed the threshold with a sense of deliverance.

The passage was dark. Where was he to go? There was the study, but he had had his fill of the company of M. Chasle, who was self-installed there, riveted to his chair, his shoulders rounded, hands splayed on his knees, and smiling the angelic smile of a martyr *in extremis*. Mademoiselle was even more maddening; bent double, with her nose to the ground, she went sniffing her way from room to room like a lost dog, trailing after everyone who crossed her line of vision. Small as she was, and large as was the flat, she made it seem overcrowded.

There was only one room unoccupied, Gise's room. As she was away in England, why not take refuge there? Jacques tip-toed in, and locked the door.

Immediately he felt a vast relief; at last he was alone after a day and a night of continuous strain. The room was cold and the lights would not come on. The shutters were closed and the belated half-light of a December morning was glimmering across the slats. For a while he could not associate this darkened room with any memory of Gise. He stumbled against a chair, sat down. Folding his arms for warmth, he stayed there, huddled up, his mind a blank.

When he came out of his doze, daylight was filtering through the curtains, and suddenly he recognized their blue floral pattern. While he was asleep a whole forgotten world had come back to life around him. Paris . . . Gise . . . Each object he set eyes on had been touched at some time by his hands—in a former existence. What had become of the photograph of himself? There was a light patch on the wall-paper where it used to hang beside Antoine's. So Gise had taken it down. Offended with him? No; of course, she had carried it off with her to England. And that meant—all the trouble would begin again. Savagely he lunged forward like an animal trapped in a net, whose every struggle makes it worse entangled. Anyhow, Gise was in England. Thank goodness! And suddenly he heard himself cursing her under his breath. Yes, it was always the same thing when he thought of her; he felt degraded, humiliated.

Anything to lay those spectres of the past! He sprang up from the chair, to escape the memory-haunted room. But he had forgotten about his father, the deathbed. Here at least he had only a phantom to contend with: it was the nearest thing to solitude. He came back to the centre of the room and sat down at the table. On the blotting-pad were imprints in violet ink—her ink. With a faint stirring of emotion he tried for a moment to puzzle out the inverted writing. Then he pushed the pad aside. Again his eyes grew blurred with tears. Ah, if he could sleep, forget! He folded his arms on the table and let his head droop on them—thinking of Lausanne, his friends, his loneliness. Yes, at the first opportunity he must escape! Leave this place again, for ever! . . .

He was roused from his half-sleep by someone trying to open the door. Antoine was hunting for him. It was long past twelve, and for the moment all was quiet in the sick-room; this opportunity for a hasty meal must not be missed.

Two places were laid in the dining-room. Mademoiselle had packed M. Chasle off to his own place for lunch. As for her—bless and save us, no, she couldn't dream of eating, what with all the things she had to attend to!

Jacques had little appetite. Antoine gulped his food down, in silence. They shunned each other's eyes. What an eternity since they last had sat at that table, facing each other! But events were moving too precipitately to allow them time for sentiment.

"Did he recognize you?" Antoine asked.

"I don't know."

After another silence Jacques pushed back his plate and looked up.

"Tell me, Antoine . . . just how do things stand? What do you expect to happen?"

"Well, for the last thirty-six hours the kidneys have failed to secrete. You understand what that means?"

"Yes. And in that case . . . ?"

"In that case, if something doesn't stop the poisoning that has ensued . . . well, it's hard to be definite, but I should say tomorrow, perhaps even tonight . . ."

With an effort Jacques repressed a sigh of relief.

"And what about the pain?"

"Ah . . . that's the difficulty." A look of gloom settled on Antoine's face.

He stopped, as Mademoiselle herself was coming in with the coffee. When she was beside Jacques and about to fill his cup, the coffee-pot began to tremble so violently that Jacques reached out his hand to take it. The sight of those ivory-yellow, skinny fingers, which were associated with so many of his childish memories, suddenly brought a lump to his throat. He wanted to smile towards the little old woman but, even when he stooped, could not manage to meet her eyes. She had accepted without demur her dear "Jacquot's" return, but for three years she had been weeping over him as dead and, now he had come back, could not bring herself to look this phantom frankly in the face.

"I'm afraid," Antoine continued, when she had left them, "that the pain will probably become more and more acute. Usually uræmia gives rise to an increasing amount of anæsthesia, so that the end is practically painless. But when it takes this convulsive form . . ."

"In that case," Jacques said, "why have the morphine injections been stopped?"

"Because the kidneys have ceased secreting. A morphine injection would kill him as he is now."

The door was flung violently open. A terrified face, the maid's, looked in, then vanished. She had tried to say something, but could not get out a word.

Antoine ran out after her. An involuntary hope, of which he was frankly conscious, spurred him on.

Jacques, too, had risen, moved by the same hope. After a moment's hesitation he followed his brother out.

No, it was not the end; only another attack, but a sudden and very acute one.

The dying man's jaws were clenched so tightly that, from the door, Jacques could hear the grinding teeth. The face had turned a purplish crimson and the whites of the eyes showed between the slotted lids. His breathing was uneven and occasionally ceased altogether; the stoppages seemed never ending and, while they lasted, Jacques felt his own heart stop and, himself unable to draw breath, turned desperately towards his brother. The bodily spasm was already such that only the back of the old man's head and his heels touched the bed; yet every moment his body grew more steeply arched. Only when the muscular tension had reached its maximum intensity did it become stabilized in a vibrant equilibrium which, more than any movement, conveyed the tremendous strain to which the body was subjected.

"A whiff of ether," Antoine said. The calmness of his voice struck Jacques with wonder.

The attack was running its course. At intervals hoarse, roaring grunts, louder and louder, issued from the twisted lips. Then the head began lolling from side to side; a confused tremor set in along the limbs.

"Grasp his arm," Antoine whispered, while he seized the other wrist and the nuns struggled to hold down the legs, which now were threshing to and fro, tearing off the sheets.

The struggle went on for several minutes. Then the violence of the spasms diminished and the epileptiform convulsions grew less frequent. The head ceased rolling from side to side, the limbs relaxed, and at last the exhausted body lay flat and still upon the bed.

Then the moans began again. "Ah! Aah! Aaah! . . . Ah! Aah! Aaah!"

Jacques laid back on the bed the arm that he was holding. He noticed that his fingers had left their marks on it. The sleeve of the nightshirt was torn and one of the collar buttons had snapped. Jacques could not take his eyes off the wet, swollen lips incessantly moaning that dreadful "Ah! Aah! Aaah!" And suddenly everything seemed to take effect at once: his emotion, the interrupted lunch, the fumes of ether. He felt himself retching, his cheeks turning green. With a great effort he brought himself to turn away, stumble hastily out of the bedroom.

As Sister Céline, helped by the old nun, was about to tuck in the sheets, she suddenly turned to Antoine. Holding up the top sheet, she pointed to a large moist patch, at the place where the old man had been struggling.

Antoine betrayed no feeling. But, after a moment, he moved away from the bed and leaned against the mantelpiece. Now that the functions of the kidney had been temporarily restored, the effects of the poisoning were staved off—for how long, it was impossible to say. Antoine knew very well that nothing could avert the fatal issue; it had merely been postponed. Two or three days' reprieve, perhaps. He pulled himself together; he did not believe in brooding over distasteful facts. Well, the fight would last longer than foreseen; there was no getting around it. And the longer it was to last, the greater the need for good staff-work. The energies of his helpers must be husbanded.

He decided to organize two shifts of nurses, with fixed periods on and off duty. Léon could be enlisted. He, Antoine, would be on duty in both shifts; he was determined not to quit the sick-room. Fortunately, before leaving for Switzerland, he had cancelled his engagements for some days ahead. If some emergency call came in from any of his patients, he would send Thérivier. What else was there? Ah, yes; warn Philip. And ring up the hospital. What else? He was conscious of forgetting something important. ("A symptom of fatigue. Have some cold tea on tap," he noted.) Why, of course! Gise must be told. He must write to her this afternoon. Lucky that old Mademoiselle hadn't yet spoken of sending for her niece!

He was standing in front of the fire, his hands resting on the marble mantelpiece, mechanically stretching first one foot, then the other, towards the warmth. For him planning was the equivalent of action; he had recovered his poise.

At the other end of the room, M. Thibault's groans were growing louder; the pain was setting in again, fiercely as ever. The two nuns were seated. A chance, this, not to be missed of putting through some telephone-calls. But when Antoine reached the door, something made him walk back to the bed for a closer view of the dying man. It looked as if, already, another attack was coming on; M. Thibault's face was becoming more and more darkly flushed, his breath was failing. . . . Where had Jacques gone?

Then he heard voices in the corridor. The door opened and, followed by Jacques, the Abbé Vécard entered. Antoine noticed his brother's sullen expression; but the priest's eyes were sparkling, though his face was impassive as ever. M. Thibault's groans were coming faster; suddenly he jerked his arm forward and the finger-joints contracted with the brittle sound of cracking nuts.

"Jacques!" Antoine called, as he reached towards the ether.

The priest hesitated, then, after crossing himself discreetly, retired without a word.

IV

ALL that afternoon, all night, and throughout the following morning the two shifts organized by Antoine took turns every three hours at M. Thibault's bedside. The first group consisted of Jacques, the maid, and the older nun; the second of Sister Céline, Léon, and Clotilde, the cook. Antoine so far had not taken a moment's rest.

The attacks were growing more and more frequent, and so terrific was their vehemence that, after each, those who had been holding down the sufferer were as worn out as he was, and fell back, gasping for breath, onto their chairs. After that they had to watch him suffer, with folded hands; there was nothing to be done. In the intervals between attacks the neuralgic pains returned with increased violence, distributed over almost every portion of the body; the ears of the watchers had not a moment's respite from the groans and screams of agony. The old man's brain was too exhausted now to grasp what was happening; sometimes, indeed, he passed into a state of raving delirium. But his nervous responses were cruelly intact and he kept on indicating by gestures each place where he felt pain. Antoine was dumbfounded by the strength that remained in the old body, bedridden for so many months. And so were the two nuns, though long experience had inured them to the vagaries of disease. They were so convinced that the uræmic intoxication could not but get the better of this extraordinary resistance that they inspected the bed several times an hour to see if it was still dry, and the kidney had not resumed its functions.

On the first day the concierge had come to ask that, if possible, the shutters as well as the windows might be closed, so as to deaden the groans, which echoed across the courtyard and spread consternation in the building. The tenant of the flat above, a young woman with child, whose bedroom was just over M. Thibault's, had been so upset as to be obliged to leave the house in the middle of the night and take shelter with her parents. So all the windows had to be kept shut. The only light was the small bedside lamp. Despite the wood-fire kept constantly burning to carry off the noxious odours, the atmosphere in the room was unpleasant to a degree. The emotions of the past three days had taxed Jacques severely, and now under the stupefying effects of the foul air and semi-darkness, he kept on dropping off to sleep for a few seconds at a time, standing, his arm in air, then waking up with a start, and completing the unfinished gesture.

Whenever he was off duty in the sick-room, Jacques went downstairs to Antoine's flat, the key of which he had got back; there he was sure of being alone. He hurried at once to his old room and flung himself fully dressed onto the sofa-bed. But rest eluded him. Across the flimsy window-curtains he saw the snow-flakes eddying, blurring the outlines of the houses and deadening all the noises of the street. And then pictures rose before him of Lausanne, the Pension Kammerzinn, Sophia, his friends. All grew confounded in his thoughts, the present and the past, snows of Paris and Swiss winters, the warmth of the room where he was now and that of his little stove, the smell of ether clinging to his clothes and the tang of resin from his pitch-pine floor. He got up to try a change of atmosphere, dragged himself across to Antoine's study, and, dizzy with exhaustion, sank into an easy chair. He felt sick of everything, as if he had been kept in suspense eternally and to no purpose, torn by sterile longings that nothing could assuage, and haunted by the feeling that nowhere, nowhere on earth, was there a place where he could feel at home.

From noon onwards there were virtually no intervals between the attacks, and it was obvious that M. Thibault's condition had taken a turn for the worse. When Jacques came with his shift for his spell of duty at the bedside, he was horrified by the changes that had taken place since the forenoon. The ceaseless convulsions of the facial muscles and, most of all, the swelling caused by the toxic condition had blotted out the features. The face of the dying man had become almost unrecognizable.

Jacques would have liked to put some questions to his brother, but their several tasks gave them no respite. Besides, he was far too exhausted, too weary in mind and body, to make the effort of framing intelligible phrases to express his thoughts. Sometimes, between two attacks, racked by compassion for this never-ending agony, he would gaze at his brother with haggard, questioning eyes; but always Antoine gritted his teeth and looked away.

After a series of convulsions that seized the old man with increasing violence, Jacques's nerves gave way, and a fit of blind rage came over him. His forehead dripping with sweat, he strode towards his brother, gripped his arm, and dragged him to the far end of the room.

"Look here, Antoine! This has got to stop, you can't let it go on." His voice was vibrant with reproach.

Antoine turned his head, with a slight shrug signifying helplessness.

"But, *do* something!" Jacques shook his brother's arm. "Find some way of stopping the pain. There must be something that can be done. Do it!"

Antoine's eyebrows lifted a shade contemptuously; then he gazed towards the bed, whence long-drawn, agonizing screams of pain were rising. Perhaps a hot bath might be tried; obviously that idea had crossed his mind several times already. Was it feasible? The bathroom was at the other end of the flat, next to the kitchen; the last door in a corridor which had a right-angled turn. A difficult undertaking. Still . . .

In a few seconds he had weighed the pros and cons, formed his decision, and was mapping out a plan of campaign. He must take advantage of one of those periods of prostration, lasting two or three minutes, which usually followed each attack. To bring it off, everything must be made ready in advance. He looked towards the nurse.

"Sister, stop what you're doing now, please, and fetch Léon. Sister Céline, too. Tell her to bring me two sheets. *Two,* you understand. Adrienne, will you go to the bathroom and turn on the hot water. Get the water to a hundred degrees and see it stays at that temperature till we come. Then tell Clotilde to warm some towels in the oven. And to fill the warming-pan with charcoal. Be quick, please."

Sister Céline and Léon, who had been resting, entered just in time to take Adrienne's place at the bedside. An attack was just beginning; it was violent, but brief.

When it was over, and a rapid but calmer respiration had followed the stertorous breathing that now accompanied the periods of convulsion, Antoine cast a rapid glance over the helpers he had mustered.

"Now's the time," he said, and added, turning to Jacques: "No hurrying, please—but there's not a second to lose."

The nuns had already begun untucking the bed; a cloud of powder rose from the sheets, and an odour of mortifying flesh filled the room.

"Get off his nightshirt quickly," Antoine commanded; then turned to Léon. "Two more logs on the fire, in readiness."

There was a feeble moaning from the bed. "Ah! Aah! Aaah!" Daily the bed-sores spread and deepened; the shoulder-blades, buttocks, and heels were an angry mass of sores which, though powdered with talc and bandaged, stuck to the sheets.

"Wait," Antoine said. With his penknife he slit the nightshirt from end to end. As the blade hissed through the cloth Jacques could not repress a slight shudder.

The whole body lay before him, naked. Huge, flaccid, sickly white, it gave the impression of being at once enormously distended, and emaciated. The swollen hands hung like boxing-gloves on the wizened arms. The queerly elongated legs had the look of bones coated with hair. A patch of coarse grey stubble mantled the chest. . . .

Jacques looked away. Many a time in after years he was to recall that moment, and the strange thoughts that crowded in on his brain, as for the first time he looked on the nakedness of the man who had begotten him. Then, in a flash, he saw himself back in Tunisia, reporter's note-book in hand, looking at another body, naked like this, and like this bloated, blotched with grey—the body of an old Italian, a huge, obscene monster of a man who had just hanged himself. It had been lying in the street out in the sun, and a motley horde of brats from neighbouring streets was scampering and squalling round it. And Jacques had seen the dead man's daughter, little more than a child, rush across the courtyard weeping bitterly, drive away the children with kicks and cuffs, then sprinkle handfuls of dry grass over the corpse. Out of modesty, perhaps—or because of the flies?

"Now, Jacques!" Antoine whispered.

He would have to slip his hand under the body to catch an end of the sheet which Antoine and the sister had worked underneath the hips.

Jacques obeyed. And suddenly the contact of the clammy flesh produced an extraordinary, quite unforeseen effect on him—a starkly physical emotion, far more potent than any gust of pity or affection: the self-regarding love of man for man.

"Get him in the middle of the sheet," Antoine ordered. "Right. Not so much that way, Léon; give a tug at this end. Now take away the pillow. You, Sister, lift his legs. A bit more. Mind the bed-sores! Jacques, take your corner of the sheet, beside his head; I'll take the other. Sister Céline and Léon will hold the lower ends. Got it? Right. Let's lift him now, just to try. One, two, three—hoist!"

Hauled energetically by the four corners, the sheet bellied and rose clear of the mattress; but the weight was almost too much for them.

"Good work!" Antoine sounded almost cheerful. All of them were just then feeling the joy of action.

Antoine turned to the older nun.

"Sister, put the blanket over him. And please go in front, to open the doors for us. . . . Everyone ready? . . . Go!"

Staggering, they filed out and entered the narrow corridor. M. Thibault was screaming. For a moment M. Chasle's face showed, peeping from the kitchen-door.

"A little lower, please, at his feet," Antoine panted. "That's better. Shall we stop a bit? No? Then, carry on. Mind that closet key, you'll get caught on it. Stick it out, we're almost there. Mind the turning now." He had a glimpse of Mademoiselle and the two servants crowding up the bathroom. "Out of it, all of you!" he yelled. "There's barely room for the five of us. Adrienne, Clotilde! Now's the time to go and make the bed. Heat it with the warming-pan. Steady, now! We've got to turn, for the door. That's right. No, damn it, don't put him on the floor. Raise him! Up! More than that! We must get him over the bathtub first. Then we'll lower him gently. In the sheet, of course. One more effort! Easy does it. Lower a little. More. Yes, like that. She's filled it too full, confound her! We'll be deluged. Now lower away, everyone!"

As the bulky mass, slung within the sheet, gently descended into the bath, the water it displaced splashed over on all sides, drenching everyone and flooding the whole floor.

"Well, that's that!" Antoine panted. "Ten minutes' breathing space, thank goodness!"

For a moment M. Thibault's screams had ceased—an effect, doubtless, of the shock of the hot water; but now they started again, and shriller than ever. He began struggling convulsively; fortunately the folds of the sheet hampered the movements of his arms and legs.

In any case his restlessness gradually declined; the screams sank to a low, whimpered "Ah! Aah! Aaah!" and soon he ceased to whimper. It was obvious that he was feeling a vast relief. The little "Ah's!" sounded like grunts of satisfaction.

The five of them stood round the bath, their feet in water, thinking with dismay of the task that still lay before them.

Suddenly M. Thibault opened his eyes and began speaking.

"Ah, so it's you? No, not today . . ." His eyes wandered round the room, but obviously he had no idea where he was. "Let me be," he added. (These were the first intelligible words he had uttered for forty-eight hours.) Then he fell silent, but his lips went on moving as if he were saying a prayer. Now and again a weak sound issued from them. Bending his ear, Antoine caught a word here and there. "Saint Joseph . . . friend of the dying." And a moment later: "Miserable sinner."

The eyelids had dropped again. The face was calm, the breathing rapid but regular. It was an incredible relief to them all not to hear those screams of agony any more.

Suddenly the old man gave a little laugh, like a child's laugh, strangely crystalline. Antoine and Jacques stared at each other. What thought was stirring in the dying brain? The eyes were still closed.

Then in a voice roughened by days of screaming, yet fairly clear, he sang once more the refrain of the old song, the words of which he had learned again from Mademoiselle:

> "Then clinkety and clankety
> Along the lanes we go
> To where my lovely Lola
> Is waiting for me now."

Like an echo he muttered: "Clankety . . . clinkety and clankety . . ." Then the voice ceased.

Antoine dared not meet his brother's eyes. "My lovely Lola!" It distressed him to hear such words at such a moment on his father's lips. What must Jacques be thinking?

Jacques had exactly the same feeling; his discomfort came not from what he had heard but from the fact that he had not been alone to hear it. Each of them felt embarrassed, not for himself but for the other. . . .

The ten minutes were up.

While watching the bath, Antoine had been planning the return journey.

"It's out of the question shifting him in that wet sheet," he said in an undertone. "Léon, fetch the mattress belonging to the folding bed. And ask Clotilde to bring the towels she has in the oven."

They laid the mattress on the wet tiles of the floor. Then, under Antoine's directions, they grasped the four corners of the sheet, heaved the heavy body out of the bath and lowered it, dripping, onto the mattress.

"Sponge him—quickly!" Antoine said. "Right. Now wrap him up in the blanket and slip the dry sheet under. Hurry up, or he'll catch cold!"

No sooner spoken than he thought: "And what matter if he does catch cold?"

He glanced round the bathroom. There was not a dry spot anywhere; mattress, sheets, and towels sprawled in pools of water. In a corner a chair lay upside-down. The little room looked as if a free-for-all had taken place in it during a flood.

"Back to your places now, and—hoist!" he ordered.

The dry sheet bulged, and the body swayed for a moment as if suspended in a hammock; then staggering, floundering through pools of water, the little procession started on its way, and slowly receded round the corner of the passage, leaving in its wake a trail of sodden footprints.

Some minutes later M. Thibault was lying pale and motionless in his new-made bed, his head in the centre of the pillow, his arms stretched limp upon the counterpane. For the first time in many days he seemed not to be in pain.

The respite was short-lived. It was striking four and Jacques had just left the bedroom, intending to go down to the ground-floor flat and snatch a few hours' rest, when Antoine caught him up in the hall.

"Quick! He's suffocating. Ring up Coutrot. Fleurus 5402. Coutrot, Rue de Sèvres. Tell him to send some oxygen at once, three or four containers. Fleurus 5402. Got it?"

"Hadn't I better take a taxi?"

"No, they've a delivery car. Hurry up. I need your help."

The telephone was in M. Thibault's study. Jacques dashed into it with such haste that M. Chasle jumped from his chair.

"Father is suffocating!" Jacques cried to him as he unhooked the receiver.

"Hallo! Are you Coutrot the pharmacist? What? Isn't this Fleurus 5402? . . . *Hallo!* Please connect me at once; it's urgent, a dying man. Fleurus 5402. . . . That Coutrot's? Hallo. Dr. Thibault speaking. Yes. Please send . . ."

Bending above the shelf on which the telephone stood, he had his back to the room. As he spoke, he looked up vaguely at the mirror on the wall. Reflected in it was an open door and, framed in the doorway, Gise stood gazing at him, mute with wonder.

V

THE day before, in London, Gise had received the cablegram which Clotilde, with Mademoiselle's approval, had taken on herself to dispatch while Antoine was away at Lausanne. She had travelled by the early boat-train and arrived in Paris without warning anyone of her coming, had driven directly to the house, and, not daring to question the concierge, had gone, with a wildly beating heart, straight up to the flat.

Léon had opened the door. Alarmed at seeing him on this floor, she had murmured:

"And . . . how is . . . ?"

"Not yet, Mademoiselle."

Someone was shouting into the telephone in the next room. "What? Isn't this Fleurus 5402?"

A tremor ran through her body. Had her ears deceived her?

"*Hallo!* Please connect me at once; it's urgent."

The valise dropped from her hand. Her limbs seemed giving way under her. Not knowing what she did, she stumbled across the hall and with both hands pushed open the study door.

Leaning on the shelf, Jacques had his back to her. Dimly she saw, or seemed to see, the outlines of his face, the half-closed eyes, wraithlike in the green depths of the tarnished mirror. So Jacques had been found again—she had never believed him dead—and he had come back to his dying father.

"Hallo! Dr. Thibault speaking. Yes. Please send . . ."

Slowly her gaze fastened on his, his eyes sank into hers. Then Jacques swung quickly round, still holding the receiver, from which came a drone of words.

"Please send . . ." he repeated. His throat was choked. With a violent effort he gulped back saliva; all he would get out was a strangled cry: "Hallo!" He had lost all notion of where he was, why he was telephoning. It cost him a prodigious struggle to reconstruct it all—Antoine, the deathbed, oxygen. "Father's suffocating," he told himself. Shrill reverberations were jarring in his brain.

"Go on! I'm listening!" An impatient voice at the other end.

Suddenly he felt a blind rage sweep over him, rage against the intruder. What was she after? What did she want of him? Why remind him of her existence? Wasn't everything over, dead and done with?

Gisèle had not moved. In the brown face, the big black melting eyes, luminous with dog-like devotion, had a tender glow, intensified by wonder. She had grown much thinner. An impression crossed Jacques's mind—so fleeting that he hardly noticed it—that she had become quite pretty.

Into the silence burst M. Chasle's voice, like a belated bomb.

"Ah, so it's you," he said with a half-witted grin.

Jacques was pressing the receiver nervously to his cheek. He could not bring himself to take his eyes off the charming figure in the doorway, but they had gone blank and betrayed nothing of his seething rage. He stammered into the telephone:

"Please send me at—at once some oxygen. Yes, by a—a delivery car. What? In rubber containers, of course. For a patient who's suffocating."

Rooted to the spot, Gise watched him, without a flicker of her eyelids. She had pictured to herself a hundred times this moment—the moment when, after the years of waiting, she would see him again, let herself sink into his arms. Well, she was living out that moment here and now. He was there, only a few yards away, but taken up by others; not hers—a stranger. And in Jacques's eyes her eyes had met a hardness, a presage of rebuff. The reality confronting her, so different from her dreams, had given her an intuition—though she was hardly conscious of it yet—that she was still to suffer by him.

He, too, while speaking, had his eyes fixed on her all the time; they seemed linked together by that mutual, unfaltering gaze. Meanwhile

Jacques had straightened up; his voice became assured again, over-assured.

"Yes, three or four containers. *At once!*"

Higher-pitched than usual, his voice had an unwonted vibrancy, almost a nasal twang, a bluffness that was unlike him. "Ah, yes, so sorry, the address! Dr. Thibault, 4A Rue de l'Université. No. 4*A*, I said. Come straight up to the third floor. And be quick, please; it's extremely urgent."

Without haste but with an unsteady hand he hung up the receiver. Neither he nor Gise felt able to make a move.

"Hallo, Gise!" he said at last.

A tremor ran through her body. Her lips half parted in an answering smile. Then as if he had suddenly awakened to reality, Jacques moved abruptly forward.

"Antoine's waiting for me," he explained, as he hurried across the room. "M. Chasle will tell you all about it. *He* . . . he's suffocating. You've come at the worst possible moment. . . ."

"Yes," she said, drawing aside as he passed close in front of her. "Go at once, at once!"

Her eyes filled with tears. She had no clear thought, no definite regret; only an aching sense of weakness and disheartenment. Her eyes followed Jacques along the hall. Now that she saw him moving he seemed more alive, more as he used to be. When he was out of sight she clasped her hands impulsively, murmuring: "Jacquot!"

Stolid as a piece of furniture, M. Chasle had watched the whole scene and had noticed nothing. Left by himself with Gise, he felt called on to make conversation.

"Well, Mlle. Gise, here I am, such as I am, at my post." He patted the chair on which he was perched. Gise turned her head, to hide her tears. After a moment he added: "We're waiting to begin."

His tone was so impressive that Gise was taken aback.

"Begin what?" she inquired.

The little man's eyes flickered behind the glasses; he pursed his lips confidentially.

"Why, Mlle. Gise—the prayer!"

This time Jacques had fled to his father's room as to a place of refuge.

The ceiling-lamp was on. M. Thibault, who was being propped up in the sitting position, was a terrifying sight; his head flung back, his mouth agape, he seemed to have lost consciousness. The wide-open eyes, starting out of their sockets, were glazing. Leaning over the bed, Antoine was holding his father in his arms while Sister Céline was shoring up his back with cushions the older nun was passing to her.

"Open the window!" Antoine shouted when he saw his brother. Cold air poured in, bathing the trance-bound face. And now the nostrils began to flutter; a little air was penetrating to the lungs. The inhalations were feeble and jerky, the expirations interminably protracted; it seemed with each slow sigh that it must be the last.

Jacques had gone up to Antoine. He whispered in his ear: "Gise has just come."

Only a slight lift of the eyebrows betrayed Antoine's surprise. Not for a second would he let his attention be diverted from the duel he was fighting with death. The least inadvertence, and that feeble breath might fail for ever. Like a boxer with his eyes riveted on his opponent, brain alert and every muscle set for action, he kept watch. Not for a moment did he pause to think that for the past two days he would have welcomed as a deliverer that last enemy whose onset he was now resisting with all his might. He had even forgotten, or all but forgotten, that the life in peril was his father's.

"The oxygen's on its way," he was thinking. "We can hold out five minutes more, perhaps ten. Once it's here . . . But I'll have to have my arms free, so will the sister."

He called to his brother. "Jacques, go and fetch someone else. Adrienne, Clotilde—anyone. Two will be enough to hold him up."

There was no one in the kitchen. Jacques ran to the linen-room. Only Gise was there, with her aunt. He hesitated for a moment. There was no time to lose. . . .

Why not? Yes. "Come, Gise!" He steered the old lady out into the hall. "Wait on the landing. Some oxygen gas-bags will be coming. Bring them to us at once."

When they entered the bedroom M. Thibault was sinking into a coma. His face had turned a purplish blue, and a brown sordes was drooling from the corners of his lips.

"Quickly!" Antoine said. "Stand here!"

Jacques took his brother's place; Gise, that of Sister Céline.

Antoine turned to the sister. "Pull his tongue forward. . . . No, with a towel. With a towel."

Gise had always shown a certain aptitude for nursing and had been attending first-aid classes in London. While preventing the old man from slipping sideways, she grasped his wrist, and after glancing at Antoine to see if he approved, began performing artificial respirations, keeping time with the nurse, who was pulling at his tongue. Jacques took the other arm and copied her movements. But M. Thibault's face was growing darkly suffused with blood, as if he was being strangled.

"One, two. One, two," Antoine repeated, keeping them in rhythm. The door opened.

Adrienne ran in with one of the containers in her arms.

Antoine snatched it from her and without a moment's delay turned on the tap and applied it to the old man's mouth.

The following minute seemed interminable. But before it was over there had been a visible improvement. Gradually the breathing became stronger, more regular. And soon, unmistakably, the face was getting less blue; the circulation of the blood was coming back.

At a signal from Antoine, who, keeping his eyes fixed on his father, was gently pressing the gas-bag to his side, Jacques and Gise ceased raising and lowering the arms.

Gise could not have gone on; she was at the end of her endurance. The whole room seemed spinning round her. The smell from the bed was more than she could bear. She moved away and clung to the back of a chair to prevent herself from collapsing.

The two brothers remained bending over the bed.

Propped on the cushions, his lips kept open by the mouthpiece of the gas-bag, M. Thibault was breathing easily, his features calm. Immediate danger was over, though it was necessary to keep him in the sitting position and watch his breathing with attention.

Handing the container to the sister, Antoine seated himself on the edge of the mattress to take his father's pulse. He too was suddenly conscious of his utter weariness. The pulse was irregular and very slow. "Ah," he thought, "if only he could pass away as he now is, peacefully!" It did not strike him yet, the inconsistency between this wish and the desperate fight he had just been putting up against the onset of asphyxiation.

Looking up, he caught Gise's eye, and smiled. A moment past he had been using her as a convenient assistant, without a thought for who she was; now suddenly he felt a thrill of joy at seeing her there. Then his gaze swung back towards the dying man. And now at last he could not withhold the thought: "If only the oxygen had come five minutes later, by now all would be over."

VI

THE fit of choking had deprived M. Thibault of the temporary relief which the hot bath might otherwise have given him. Very soon another attack of convulsions came on, and what strength the dying man had drawn from his brief repose served only to enable him to suffer more.

There was an interval of more than half an hour between the first and second attacks. But evidently the visceral pain and neuralgia had set in again with extreme intensity, for all the time he continued groaning and tossing on the bed. The third attack came on a quarter of an hour after the second, and, after that, attacks of varying violence followed in quick succession, at only a few minutes' interval.

Dr. Thérivier had looked in that morning and telephoned several times during the afternoon. When he came again, a little before nine, the paroxysms were of such violence that those who held the patient down were losing control, and the doctor hurried up to help them. But the leg he had grasped wrenched itself free, dealing him a kick that almost knocked him over. How the old man still had such reserves of strength passed their understanding.

When the convulsions had subsided, Antoine led his friend to the far end of the room. He tried to speak, and indeed managed to get out a few words—which the screams coming from the bed prevented Thérivier from hearing—then suddenly stopped short. His lips were quivering, and Thérivier was shocked by the change that had come over his face. With an effort Antoine pulled himself together, and stammered a few phrases in his friend's ear:

"Look here, old man, you can see—see for yourself. It can't go on like—this this. I can't—stand any more." There was an affectionate insistence in his gaze, as if he were appealing to his friend for some miraculous intervention.

Thérivier dropped his eyes. "Now let's keep calm!" he murmured, adding after a pause: "And let's review the facts. The pulse is weak. No micturition for thirty hours. The uræmic intoxication is getting worse, and the symptoms are becoming masked. I quite understand how you're feeling. But, be patient—the end is near."

His shoulders bent, his eyes fixed vaguely on the bed, Antoine made no reply. The expression of his face had changed completely. He seemed half asleep. "The end is near!" After all, it might be true!

Jacques came in, followed by Adrienne and the old nun. It was the change of shift.

Thérivier went up to Jacques. "I'll spend the night here, so that your brother can get a bit of rest."

Antoine had heard. The temptation of escaping for a while from the sick-room, of rest and silence, of being able to lie down, to sleep perhaps, and to forget, was so strong that he was on the point of accepting Thérivier's offer. But almost at once he pulled himself together.

"No, old man." His voice was firm. "Thanks—but I'd rather not."

Something within him had told him—though he could not have accounted for it—that it was his duty to refuse. He must face his responsibility alone; confront fatality alone. When his friend seemed
about to protest, he added: "Don't insist. I've made up my mind.
Tonight we're in full force and fairly fit. Later on, perhaps, I'll call
on you."

Thérivier shrugged his shoulders. Still, as he suspected the present
state of things might last another day or two, and as in any case he
had the habit of always giving in to Antoine, he now made no
protest.

"Very well. But tomorrow night, whether you agree or not . . ."

Antoine did not flinch. "Tomorrow night?" Would they still be
going on—these paroxysms and screams of pain? Obviously that was
possible. And the next day, too. Why not? His eyes met his brother's.
Jacques alone guessed his anguish, and shared it.

Hoarse cries were coming from the bed, announcing another attack.
They had to go back to their posts. Antoine held out his hand to
Thérivier, who clasped it warmly, on the point of whispering: "Courage,
old man!"; but he dared not, and left without a word. Antoine
watched his receding back. How often had he, too, when leaving the
bedside of a patient on the brink of death—after he had shaken a
husband's hand, forcing his mouth into an optimistic smile, or shunned
a mother's eyes—how often had he, too, once he had turned his back
on them, hurried from the room with the same sense of relief that
Thérivier's brisk step betrayed!

At ten that night the attacks, which were now proceeding without intermission, seemed to reach a climax.

Antoine felt that the energies of his helpers were flagging, their
endurance weakening; they were getting slower and less careful in
their movements. As a general rule such lapses would have spurred
him on to greater personal efforts. But he had reached the stage
when his morale could no longer cope with bodily fatigue. It was
his fourth night without sleep since leaving for Lausanne. He had
given up eating; with an effort he had forced himself to drink a
glass of milk earlier in the day, but he had been living most of the

time on cold tea, gulping down a cupful every few hours. His nerves were getting steadily worse, though their tension gave him a semblance—but no more—of energy. For what a situation like the present one called for—never-ending patience, coupled with bursts of spurious activity sapped by the knowledge of its impotence—was something against which his whole character rebelled. His endurance was being taxed to the breaking-point; yet he must keep on, wear himself out in never-ending efforts, without an instant's respite.

Towards eleven, when an attack was just ending, and the four of them were stooping over the bed, watching its last paroxysms, Antoine suddenly straightened up, with a movement of annoyance. Another patch of moisture was spreading on the sheet; the kidney had begun working again, copiously.

Dropping his father's arm, Jacques made a rageful gesture. This was the last straw! The only thing keeping him on his feet had been the thought that, owing to the spread of the toxæmia, the end was imminent. What would happen now? Impossible to know. It was as if, during these past two days, death had been persistently setting his trap, and each time the spring was drawn tight, the teeth about to close, the catch had slipped—and all had to begin again.

After that, he did not even try to conceal his mortification. Between the attacks, he flung himself angrily into the nearest chair, and dozed for a few minutes, his elbows on his knees and his fists against his eyes. When a new attack developed, he had to be called, tapped on the shoulder, shaken into wakefulness.

Shortly before midnight, things had come to such a pass that it looked as if the struggle could no longer be kept up. Three exceptionally violent attacks had followed in quick succession, and there were signs of a fourth under way.

It promised to be catastrophic; all the usual symptoms were present, but in a hideously intensified form. The breathing had nearly stopped, the face was congested, the eyes were starting from their sockets, the forearms tensely contracted and flexed so sharply that the hands were hidden and the wrists, folded beneath the beard, had the look of amputated stumps. All the limbs were quivering with the formidable tension, and the sinews seemed on the point of snapping under the strain. Never before had the phase of rigidity lasted so long; the seconds went by and it showed no sign of easing. Antoine fully believed the end had come.

Then a feeble, gasping breath issued from the mouth, while a frothy saliva formed on the lips. The arms relaxed suddenly, and he passed into the convulsive state. From the very start the paroxysms had a maniacal violence that nothing less than a strait-jacket could have restrained. Helped by Adrienne and the older nun, Antoine and Jacques clung to the old man's arms and legs. He was flinging himself about like a madman, and the four of them were dragged this way and that, hurled against each other, their arms half wrenched from their sockets. Adrienne was the first to let go, and after that, try as she might, could not recapture the leg she had been holding. Then, swept almost off her feet, the nun lost her balance and the other ankle broke free. Out of all constraint, the two legs beat the air; blood spurted from the heels drumming on the frame of the bed. Panting, streaming with sweat, Antoine and Jacques braced themselves to prevent the huge heaving mass from rolling off the bed.

Then, as suddenly as they had begun, the frenzied paroxysms ceased. After settling his father in the middle of the bed, Antoine stepped back some paces. His nerves were frayed to such a point that his teeth were chattering; he was shivering with cold. Going towards the fire to warm himself, he suddenly caught sight of his reflected self, lit by the firelight, in the mirror. His face was haggard, his hair in disorder, there was blind fury in his eyes. He swung round, dropped into a chair, and, letting his forehead sink between his hands, broke into sobs. No, he could bear no more. . . . What little capacity for reaction yet remained to him centred in a wild desire for it all to end—anything rather than to have another night, another day, and perhaps a second night to pass watching this hellish agony, for which he could do nothing, nothing . . . !

Jacques went up to him. At any other moment he would have flung himself into his brother's arms; but, like his energies, his feelings had been blunted, and the sight of Antoine's prostration, instead of quickening his emotion, numbed it. As he gazed down wonderingly on the twisted, tear-stained cheeks, suddenly it seemed to him he was discovering a picture from the past, the tearful face of a little boy whom he had never known.

Then a thought which had several times already crossed his mind came back.

"Look here, Antoine! Supposing you called someone else in, for a consultation . . . ?"

Antoine merely shrugged his shoulders. Obviously he would have been the first to call in all his colleagues if the case had presented any difficulties. He muttered some impatient remark that his brother could not hear; the screams of pain had started again, indicating that an attack would soon be coming on.

Jacques lost his temper. "But, damn it, Antoine—think of something! There must be *something* you can do."

Antoine clenched his jaws. When he raised his eyes towards his brother, they were tearless, hard.

"Yes. There's always *one* thing can be done."

Jacques understood. He did not flinch.

Antoine threw him a questioning look; then murmured:

"And you, Jacques, haven't you ever thought of that?"

Jacques gave an almost imperceptible nod. As his gaze sank deep into his brother's, he had a fleeting impression that at that moment they must be looking very much alike—with the same crease between the eyebrows, the same expression of reckless despair, the same ruthlessness.

They were in shadow, near the fire, Jacques standing, Antoine seated. The screaming was so loud that the two women kneeling beside the bed, half stunned by fatigue, could not overhear what they were saying.

After a short pause Antoine spoke again:

"What about you, Jacques? Would *you* do it?"

For all the blunt directness of the tone, there was a faint, almost imperceptible quaver in Antoine's voice. Jacques would not meet his brother's eyes. At last he brought himself to mutter:

"Really I don't know. Perhaps not . . ."

Antoine broke at once. "Well *I* would . . . and I will!"

He had sprung hastily from the chair. But now he halted and, making an uncertain gesture, bent towards his brother.

"Do you disapprove, Jacques?"

Quietly, without hesitation, Jacques answered: "No, Antoine."

Again their eyes met, and for the first time since their return from Switzerland they had a feeling that was almost joy.

Antoine went back to the fire. Extending his arms, he gripped the marble mantelpiece with both hands. He bent forward and stared into the flames.

His mind was made up. The only problem was that of ways and means, of when and how. No one except Jacques must be in the room. It was getting on towards midnight. Sister Céline's and Léon's shift would be returning to duty at one. It must be done before they came. Nothing could be simpler. A blood-letting to begin with; it would weaken the patient and induce a state of torpor—a pretext for sending off Adrienne and the old nun to take a rest before their time was up. Once he was alone with Jacques . . .

Patting the inner pocket of his white coat, he felt the little botttle of morphine he had had there since—since when? Since the morning of his return. Yes, he remembered now. When he had gone downstairs with Thérivier to get the laudanum, he had slipped the little bottle under his coat, on the off chance . . . The chance of what? It seemed as if he had had the whole programme mapped out in his mind—all he had now to do was to carry out the details of a long-thought-out plan.

A new attack was coming on. He would have to wait till it was over. Jacques, full of zeal once more, had hastened to his post. "The last attack," Antoine was thinking and, as he went up to the bed and saw Jacques's eyes fixed on his, he seemed to read the same thought in his brother's gaze.

It happened that the period of rigidity was shorter than usual, but the paroxysms were no less severe.

The suffering man was tossing wildly on the bed, foaming at the mouth. Antoine turned to the nurse.

"It might ease him if we let some blood. When he's calm again, please bring me my instrument-case."

The effects were almost instantaneous. Weakened by the loss of blood, M. Thibault seemed to fall asleep.

The women were so worn out that they were only too glad to go off duty before the next shift came; no sooner had Antoine made the suggestion than they hastened away to snatch a little extra rest.

Antoine and Jacques were alone.

Both were at some distance from the bed; Antoine had just gone to shut the door that Adrienne had left ajar, and Jacques, without knowing why he did so, had moved away to the fireplace.

Antoine paid no attention to his brother. Just now he had not the least desire to feel an affectionate presence at his side, and he had no need of an accomplice.

He felt in his pocket for the little nickel box. He allowed himself two seconds' grace. Not that he wished once more to weigh the pros and cons; it was a principle with him, when the time came for action, never to rehearse the arguments that had led up to it. But as his eyes lingered on his father's face reposing on the whiteness of the pillow—the face that the long course of the malady had rendered day by day yet more familiar—he yielded for a moment to the melancholy thrill of a last impulse of compassion.

The two seconds were up.

"It would be less distasteful," he reflected as he walked quickly towards the bed, "to do it during an attack."

He took the bottle from his pocket, shook it, and fitted the needle into the syringe. While he did so, his eyes roved round the room. Then he shrugged his shoulders, ironically; from force of habit he had been looking for the alcohol-lamp on which to sterilize the needle.

Jacques saw nothing from where he stood. His brother's bent back hid the bed from him. So much the better! Then, "No!" he muttered, and took some steps aside. . . .

His father seemed asleep. Antoine had unbuttoned a sleeve of the nightshirt and was rolling it up.

"The right arm, yes, for the injection," Antoine murmured. "It was the left I bled."

Nipping a fold of flesh between his fingers, he raised the hypodermic syringe.

Jacques shuddered, and pressed his hand to his mouth.

A whimper came from the sleeping man, his shoulder twitched. In the silence, Antoine's voice:

"Don't move, Father. It's to ease your pain."

"The last words," Jacques thought, "that any voice will say to him."

The process of expelling the contents of the glass syringe seemed interminably slow. Supposing somebody came in! Finished now? No. Leaving the needle sticking in the skin, with a deft movement Antoine detached the syringe and refilled it. The level of the liquid went down more and more slowly. Supposing somebody came in . . . ! Another eighth of a grain. What a time it took! Only a few drops more.

Quickly Antoine withdrew the needle, then wiped clean the tiny scar from which a small pink drop was oozing. He buttoned up the nightshirt and drew back the counterpane. Surely, had he been alone, he would have bent over the pale forehead; for the first time in twenty years he found himself wanting to kiss his father. But then he straightened up, stepped back, slipped his instruments into an inner pocket, and took a look round to see that all was in order. At last he turned towards his brother; stoically calm, his eyes seemed to be saying simply: "It's done."

Jacques had an impulse to go up to Antoine, grasp his hand, convey his feelings by an affectionate gesture. But Antoine had already turned away; drawing up Sister Céline's chair, he seated himself beside the bed.

The dying man's arm lay outside the bedclothes; the hand was almost as white as the sheets and faintly quivering, like a magnetic needle. As the drug gradually took effect, the features were relaxing, the marks of many days of agony being smoothed away, and the mortal lethargy now settling on the tranquil face might have been the calm of a refreshing sleep.

Unable to fix his mind on any definite thought, Antoine had taken his father's wrist; the pulse was weak and rapid. All his attention was absorbed in counting the beats mechanically: forty-six, forty-seven, forty-eight.

His consciousness of what had just taken place was growing more and more blurred, his notions of reality lapsing into a dark bewilderment. Fifty-nine, sixty, sixty-one. The fingers on the wrist relaxed. He felt himself slipping away into a blissful nonchalance, a backwater of dreams where nothing mattered. Then came a great flood of darkness; oblivion.

Jacques dared not sit down, for fear of waking his brother. Stiff with fatigue, he kept his eyes fixed on the lips of the dying man. They were growing paler and paler, and had all but ceased to flutter with the failing breath.

A sudden fear came over Jacques; he made an abrupt movement. Waking with a start, Antoine saw the bed, his father; gently he clasped the wrist again.

"Fetch Sister Céline," he said after a short silence.

When Jacques returned, followed by the sister and the cook, the breathing had become a little stronger and more regular, but accompanied by a peculiar rumbling in the throat.

Antoine stood with folded arms. He had lit the ceiling-lamp.

"The pulse is imperceptible," he said when Sister Céline came up to him.

But it was the nun's opinion that the last moments of a life are outside the competence of doctors; experience is needed. Without replying, she sat down on the low chair, felt the pulse, and for a while contemplated the tranquil face. Then, turning, she made a sign of affirmation to Clotilde, who slipped out of the room.

The gasping intensified, with a rattling, nerve-racking undertone; Jacques's face grew convulsed with horror and distress. Antoine, who had noticed this, was going up to him, to say: "You needn't be anxious.

He can't feel anything now," when the door opened. There was a sound of whispers and Mademoiselle appeared in her dressing-jacket, leaning on Clotilde's arm, her back bent more than ever. Adrienne followed, and after her came M. Chasle on tip-toe.

Vexed by this intrusion, Antoine signed to them to stand back in the doorway, but already all four were kneeling just inside the door. And suddenly Mademoiselle's piercing voice broke the silence, drowning the gasps of the dying man.

"O Lord Jesus, I draw nigh to Thee with a con-trite and hum-ble heart. . ."

Jacques sprang up and ran to his brother. "Stop her! For mercy's sake!" he panted hysterically.

But Antoine's calm, melancholy gaze sobered him at once. "Let her be," he whispered in Jacques's ear. "It's almost over. He can't hear anything." It had come back to him, that evening when M. Thibault had solemnly charged Mademoiselle to recite, as he breathed his last, the "Litany for a Happy Death"; and the memory touched him.

The two nuns were kneeling now, one on either side of the bed. Sister Céline's hand still rested on the dying man's wrist.

"When my lips, pale and trem-bling, shall utter for the last time Thine adorable name, gentle Jesus, have mercy on me."

The poor old creature had mustered up what little will-power still remained to her after twenty years of servitude to redeem the promise she had made.

"When my face, pale and wan, shall inspire the beholders with pity and dismay, gentle Jesus, have mercy on me.

"When my hair, bathed in the sweat of death and stiffening on my head . . ."

Antoine and Jacques kept their eyes bent on their father. The jaws were opening. The eyelids slowly drew apart, showing the glazing eyes set in a blank stare. Was it the end? Sister Céline, who was still holding the wrist and watching the face, made no sign. Mademoiselle's voice, wheezy as a punctured concertina, squeaked on indefatigably, syllable by syllable.

"When my im-ag-i-na-tion, beset by hor-rid spectres, shall be sunk in an abyss of an-guish, gentle Jesus, have mercy on me.

"When my poor heart, oppressed with suf-fer-ing . . ."

The mouth was still opening. A gold tooth glinted. Half a minute passed. Sister Céline did not move. At last she let go the wrist and looked up at Antoine. The mouth was still gaping. Antoine bent forward at once; the heart had ceased to beat. Then he laid his hand on the tranquil forehead and very gently, with the ball of his thumb, pressed shut the unresisting eyelids, one after the other. Without removing his hand—it was as though he wished its loving pressure to befriend his father on the threshold of eternal rest—he turned to the sister and said in a voice that was almost loud:

"The handkerchief, please."

The two maids burst into tears.

Kneeling beside M. Chasle, her hands resting on the carpet so that she seemed to be crouching on all fours, with her pigtail dangling on the white dressing-jacket, Mademoiselle, unaware of what had taken place, proceeded with her litany:

"When my soul, trembling on my lips, shall bid farewell to the world . . ."

They had to help her to her feet, and lead her away. Only when she had turned her back to the bed did she seem to realize what had happened; and she began sobbing like a child.

M. Chasle, too, was weeping; clawing Jacques's arm, he kept on saying, wagging his head to and fro like a Chinese doll:

"Things like that, M. Jacques, they shouldn't be allowed."

As Antoine shepherded them all out of the room, he was wondering what had become of Gise.

Before leaving the room he gave it a final look round. At last, after so many weeks, silence had returned to it.

And suddenly, grown larger than life, it seemed, propped up on the pillows under the glare of the lamp, with the ends of the handkerchief that swathed his chin standing up in two quaint horns above his head, M. Thibault had taken on the weird, enigmatic aspect of a personage in some fantastic folk-tale.

VII

A<small>S HE</small> left the flat Antoine found Jacques standing outside the entrance door, and they went down together. The whole house was asleep; the stair-carpet muffled the sound of footsteps. They did not speak; their minds were void of thoughts, and their hearts light, for there was no withstanding the sense of purely physical well-being that had come over them.

Léon, who had gone down earlier, had lit the lamps in the ground-floor flat and, on his own initiative, laid a cold supper in Antoine's study. Then, discreetly, he had retired from view.

Under the bright light, the little table, with the white cloth and the two places laid opposite each other, had quite a festive air—though neither would acknowledge it. They sat down without a word, each abashed at feeling so hearty an appetite, and trying to keep up an appearance of dejection. The white wine was well iced; the cold meat, bread, and butter rapidly disappeared. At one moment their hands went simultaneously towards the cheese-plate.

"Help yourself."

"No, after you."

Antoine cut in half what remained of the gruyère, and helped Jacques to his share.

"It's really in excellent condition, this cheese," he said, as if in self-excuse.

These were the first remarks they had exchanged. Their eyes met.

"Shall we . . . ?" Jacques raised his finger, pointing to the up-stairs flat.

"No," Antoine replied. "We'll go to bed now. There's nothing to be done upstairs before morning."

As they were bidding each other good night at the door of Jacques's room, suddenly a pensive look came over Jacques's face.

"Did you notice, Antoine," he murmured, "how, at the end, the mouth keeps on opening wider and wider?"

They gazed at each other in silence. The eyes of both were filled with tears. . . .

At six o'clock Antoine, feeling somewhat rested, returned to his father's flat.

To stretch his legs he went upstairs on foot. "Got to send out the usual notices," he was thinking. "That's obviously right up M. Chasle's street. Then the report at the Registrar's; not before nine, however. Let's see, who exactly should be written to? Not many in the family, luckily. The Jeannereaus will look after our relations on my mother's side; Aunt Casimir will see to the rest. For the cousins at Rouen, a wire. An obituary notice in tomorrow's papers, of course. Must send a line to old Dupré; to Jean, too. Daniel de Fontanin's at Lunéville; I'll write to him this afternoon; his mother and sister are staying on the Riviera—just as well they can't come. Anyhow, I doubt if Jacques will feel like going to the service. Léon can ring up the charitable societies; I'll give him a list. I'll look in at the hospital. Philip. Good Lord, I was forgetting the Institute!"

Adrienne came up. "There's two men been round, sir, from the undertaker's. They're coming back at seven. Oh, and did you know, sir," she added rather awkwardly, "Mlle. Gisèle has been taken ill?"

They knocked at Gise's door. She was in bed; her cheeks were flushed and her eyes fever-bright. It was nothing serious, however. Clotilde's cablegram, coming at a moment when she was already rather out of sorts, had been the first shock; after that, the scramble for the train, and particularly the thrill of seeing Jacques again, had thrown her off her balance. The cumulative effect of these emotions on her young, unstable constitution had been so overwhelming that immediately after leaving the sick-room on the previous night, she had had an attack of violent internal pains and flung herself onto the bed. She had suffered all night, listening to every sound and guessing what was happening, but unable to move.

Her answers to Antoine's questions were so reticent that he desisted. "Thérivier's coming this morning. I'll send him to you."

Gise gave a little jerk of her head in the direction of M. Thibault's room; she felt little grief, and was at a loss for words.

"Then . . . it's over?" she asked timidly.

His only answer was a nod; then suddenly the thought came to him, stark, clean-cut: "And it was I who killed him!"

He turned to Adrienne. "Bring her a hot-water bottle and a poultice to start with." Then, with a smile to Gise, he went out.

He repeated to himself: "Yes, it was I who killed him." For the first time he stood back from his act, viewed it in the round. At once he added: "And I did right." His mind was working swiftly, lucidly. "No humbug now; there was an element of cowardice in it—I couldn't face that nightmare experience any longer. But because I had a personal interest in his death, was that a reason for staying my hand? Certainly not." He did not shirk the terrible responsibility. "Obviously it would be dangerous to authorize doctors to . . . However absurd and inhuman a rule like that may be, theoretically it's got to be obeyed to the letter." And the more he recognized the cogency and soundness of the principle as such, the more he approved of himself for having knowingly infringed it. "It's a question for one's conscience to decide. I don't want to generalize. All I say is: in this particular case, what I did was right."

He had come to the death-chamber. He opened the door softly, as he had always done, not to disturb the invalid. And as his eyes fell on the quiet face, his heart missed a beat. There was something so startling, so incongruous in having to associate the mental picture he had of his father with the notion of a corpse, familiar though this was to him. He paused a moment at the door, holding his breath. That dead thing had been his father! That body with the hands serenely folded on the breast, ennobled, calm, so grandly calm. All the chairs had been pushed back against the walls, leaving the deathbed in the centre to make its full theatrical effect. In attitudes of grief, like two mourning dark-robed figures on an ancient vase, the nuns were stationed on either hand of the dead man, whose statue-like repose lent a real grandeur to the scene, for all its artifice. That man had been Oscar Thibault, a master of men. Now that proud voice was stilled, all that power reduced to impotence. Antoine hardly dared to make a gesture, break the silence. Then again he told himself it was his work; and, as his eyes lingered tenderly on the familiar face which he had so well reconciled with silence and repose, he all but smiled.

Entering the room, he was surprised to observe Jacques, who he had thought was still in bed, sitting with M. Chasle in a corner of the room.

The moment he saw Antoine, the little secretary sprang from his chair and tip-toed towards him. Behind the tear-dimmed glasses his eyes were fluttering. He grasped both Antoine's hands and, at a loss for better words to voice his regard for the dead man, he spluttered out: "A charming—charming—charming fellow!" perking his chin towards the bed at every "charming."

"Of course one had to know him," he went on; there was a note of petulance in his tone as if he were arguing down a possible detractor. "A bit crushing at times, that's so. But so just, so very just!" He stretched forth an arm, like a witness making affirmation. "An upright judge, indeed!" Then he tip-toed back to his chair.

Antoine sat down.

A sediment of memory, settled at the deepest levels of his consciousness, was being stirred up by the odours drifting in the air. Across the reek of stale chemicals—an aftermath of recent days—and the new warm fumes of the wax candles, he could make out the musty smell of the old blue rep upholstery that dated from his grandparents' time—an odour of dry wool, to which the polish, applied to the mahogany every day over half a century, had added a faint tang of resin. He recalled the cool fragrance of clean linen that would issue from the wardrobe, were its doors opened, and the odours of varnished wood and old newspapers, mingling with a clinging pungency of camphor, that came from the chest of drawers. And he knew, too— how often had he inhaled it closely, as a little boy, when it was the only seat low enough for his small legs!—the dusty smell of the tapestry-upholstered *prie-dieu* which two generations of obeisant knees had worn to the thread.

All was still; not a breath stirred the candle-flames.

Like all the others in the room, Antoine was gazing at the corpse, fixedly, in a sort of trance. In his tired brain dim wraiths of thought were struggling to take form.

"That something which made Father a being like myself, the life that still was in him yesterday—what has become of it? Lost for ever? Or does it still exist—somehow, somewhere? In what form, then?" He pulled himself up disgustedly. "That sort of thing leads straight to muddled thinking. Really, one would think I'd never seen a corpse before! I know that idea of something 'blotted out,' of 'nothingness,' is totally unsuitable. The continuity of lives—life germinating life *ad infinitum*—that's the right way to look at it.

"Yes, I've said that to myself often enough. And yet, gazing at that dead man, I don't feel so sure. That idea of 'nothingness' forces itself on me, it seems almost defensible. When all is said and done, death is the only reality; it refutes everything, baffles all argument . . . preposterously."

Then, "No!" he said, with an angry shake of his shoulders. "That's morbid nonsense. When one's on the spot with *that* right under one's nose, suggestions filter in. That shouldn't count. It doesn't count."

With an effort he pulled himself together, sprang briskly up from his chair. And at once an emotion, urgent, warm, and comforting, came over him.

Signing to Jacques to follow, he went out into the passage.

"Before settling anything we must find out Father's last wishes. Come with me."

They went together to M. Thibault's study. Antoine turned on all the lights—ceiling-lamp and wall-lamps—and the sudden glare seemed like an outrage on this room where hitherto the only light had come from the green-shaded desk-lamp. As Antoine went up to the desk, the bunch of keys he had taken from his pocket jingled merrily.

Jacques kept in the background. Unconsciously he had moved near the telephone, was standing at the place where yesterday . . . Could it have been only yesterday, fifteen hours ago, that Gise had appeared behind him, at the door?

He cast a hostile glance round this room which for so long he had regarded as an inviolable sanctuary, where of a sudden nothing remained to guard it from intrusion. The sight of his brother kneeling like a burglar in front of the gaping drawers made him feel embarrassed. What did his father's last wishes, all those old papers, matter to him?

Without a word he stole away from the room.

He went back to the death-chamber, which had a morbid fascination for him, and in which he had passed the greater part of the night, in a calm limbo midway between dreams and waking. He foresaw that very soon he would be driven from it by a stream of plaguy intruders, and he did not wish to lose a moment of this tragic confrontation with his youth. For nothing could ever conjure up the past to him so vividly as the mortal remains of that omnipotent being whose hand had ever barred the way of his ambitions, and whose authority had now passed away, wholly and abruptly, like a tale that is told. Walking on tip-toe, he softly opened the door, entered, and sat down. Jarred for a moment, the silence of the room closed in again, and once more Jacques could plunge himself, with a mournful ecstasy, into the contemplation of his dead father.

Immobility.

That brain which day and night, for almost three-quarters of a century, had never ceased one moment to link thought to thought, impression to impression, had run down for ever. So had the heart. But the cessation of thought was what touched Jacques most nearly; how often had he bewailed, as if it were a bodily disease, the never-ceasing activity of his own mind! Even at night he felt his brain, when sleep had let the gears out, racing like a motor out of control, rumbling and roaring in his head, churning together the kaleidoscopic visions that he called dreams, when memory had retained some fleeting atoms from their endless flux. One day, fortunately, all that furious activity would stop. One day he too would be freed from the torment of thinking. Then at last silence would come; and, with the great silence, rest. He remembered that river-bank at Munich, on which he had dallied a whole night long with alluring thoughts of

suicide. And suddenly, like the memory of a phrase of music, some
words he once had heard came echoing through his brain: "We shall
have rest." It was the closing sentence of a Russian play he had seen
at Geneva. He still could hear the voice of the actress, a Russian with
a childish face and candid, fanatic eyes. Swaying her little head from
side to side, she had repeated: "We shall have rest." In her voice
there had been a dream-like quality, with elfin, bell-like overtones;
and her eyes had been a little weary, with less hope in them than
resignation. "You have had no joy in life . . . but patience, Uncle
Vanya, patience! We shall have rest . . . we shall have rest."

VIII

THE influx of visitors began a little before noon; first the tenants
of the other flats and various neighbours to whom M. Thibault had
done kindness came to declare their sympathy. Jacques made off before
any of the family appeared. Antoine, too, was out, attending to urgent
calls. Each of the charity societies to which M. Thibault had belonged
included some of his personal friends on its committee. The stream
of callers did not cease till nightfall.

M. Chasle had transported to the death-chamber the chair which
he called his office stool; it was the chair on which he had sat as he
worked day after day for many years. Throughout the day he refused to leave "the deceased." He ended up by seeming as much part
of the funeral appointments as the wax candles, the sprig of consecrated box, and the kneeling nuns. Each time a caller entered, M.
Chasle would slip from his seat, proffer a mournful greeting to the
new arrival, then hop back onto his perch.

Mademoiselle had made several attempts to shift him—out of
jealousy, most likely; it vexed her to see him cutting so fine a figure
of posthumous devotion. She was suffering—probably she was the

only person in the household to feel genuine grief—but her sorrow took a different form: she was unable to keep still. The poor old creature who all her life had lived in others' homes, and had never possessed anything of her very own, was for the first time, perhaps, feeling the possessive instinct, and feeling it intensely: M. Thibault was *her* corpse. At every moment she would go up to the bed (which the curvature of her spine did not permit her to see in its entirety) and pull a sheet straight or smooth out a crease, murmuring the while a fragmentary prayer. Then, shaking her head and locking her thin fingers, she would exclaim as if it were something quite unbelievable: "He has entered into rest—*before me!*"

Her heart had grown so parsimonious, so sparing of emotion, that neither Jacques's return nor the presence of Gise seemed to have stirred it to any deep response. The two young people had been so long absent from the family circle that she had lost the habit of thinking about them. Only Antoine counted, and the maids. And just now she seemed to have a curious animosity towards Antoine. In fact, she embarked on a downright wrangle with the young man when the day and hour for coffining the body had to be fixed. Antoine wanted this to take place as soon as possible; once a coffin had replaced the corpse visible in their midst, the nerves of all would be better for it. Mademoiselle protested as violently as if she were being robbed of all that remained to her on earth: the mortal remains of the master of the house, the last sad token of his physical existence. She seemed obsessed with the idea that M. Thibault's disappearance was a finale only for her and for the dead man. For the others, and most of all for Antoine, it stood for a beginning, the dawn of a new era. But before her lay no future; the past had fallen to pieces, and with it her world had come to an end.

Towards the close of the afternoon, when Antoine had walked home, exhilarated by the keen, raw air that stung his eyes and braced his sinews, he found Felix Héquet, in full mourning, standing at his door.

"No, I won't come in," the surgeon said; "I only wanted to express my sympathy with you today."

Tourier, Nolant, and Buccard had already left cards. Loiselle had telephoned. The manifestations of sympathy from his colleagues had produced such an effect on him that, when Dr. Philip called in person during the morning, and Antoine heard his "chief's" expressions of condolence, he at last realized something he had been forgetting till now: not only was M. Thibault dead, but he, Dr. Antoine Thibault, had just lost his father.

"Yes, old man, I'm terribly sorry for you," Héquet sighed discreetly. "As doctors we may be always rubbing shoulders with death, but when it visits someone near and dear to us—why, it's as if we'd never seen a death before! . . . I know what it is," he added. Then, straightening up, he held out his black-gloved hand.

Antoine saw him to his car.

It was the first time the parallelism of the cases crossed his mind. For the present he had no time to think "that problem" out all over again, but he now perceived that there was no denying it—the issue was a graver one than he had thought it on that previous occasion. He understood that the decisive act he had carried out on the previous day in cold blood—an act which he still whole-heartedly commended—was something which he must now assimilate, as it were, with his personality, fit into his scheme of things. It was one of those crucial experiences which have a far-reaching influence on the shaping of a man's character; and he felt that his mental centre of gravity would have to be readjusted to meet the stress of this new increment.

He returned to his flat in a brown study.

A youngster—hatless, with a muffler round his neck and cold-nipped ears—was sitting waiting for him in the hall. When Antoine came in, he stood up, blushing to the roots of his hair. It was the office-boy from the lawyer's office, and Antoine, when he recognized him, felt a qualm of compunction for never having gone to see the two boys again.

"Hallo, Robert! Come this way. Well, what's wrong?"

The boy's lips moved, he was obviously struggling to say something but too shy to get the words out. Then from under his cape, he fished out a bunch of violets and held them towards Antoine, who understood at once.

"Thanks, my boy. Thanks very much. I'll take your flowers upstairs. It was very nice of you to think of bringing them."

"Oh, that was Eddie's idea," the boy put in at once.

Antoine smiled. "And how is Eddie getting on? What about you—still as smart as ever?"

"Sure!" Robert replied briskly. His shyness had passed off at once when Antoine smiled—he had not expected him to smile on such a doleful day. Now he was all eagerness to chatter—but that evening Antoine had no time to spare.

"Look here!" he said. "Come along with Eddie and see me some day soon. How about a Sunday?" He felt a genuine affection for these two children, whom he hardly knew. "Is it a promise?" he smiled.

Robert's face grew suddenly earnest. "It's a promise, sir."

While Antoine was seeing the boy out into the hall, he heard M. Chasle's voice in the kitchen.

"Someone else who wants to talk to me," he muttered testily. "Oh, damn it! Better get it over!" He bade the little secretary enter his study.

M. Chasle trotted across the room, and perched himself on the furthest chair; a knowing smile flickered on his lips, though his eyes held a profound distress.

"What have you to say to me, M. Chasle?" Antoine inquired. His tone was friendly, but he remained standing, and began opening his letters.

"What have I to say?" M. Chasle looked startled.

Antoine folded the letter he had been reading. "Yes," he murmured to himself, "I'll try and get there tomorrow morning, after the hospital."

M. Chasle was staring at his dangling feet. In a solemn voice he declared:

"Things like that, M. Antoine, shouldn't be allowed."

"What?" Antoine was opening another envelope.

"What?" M. Chasle parroted.

"What," Antoine asked in exasperation, "what is it that shouldn't be allowed?"

"Death."

Somewhat startled by the answer, Antoine looked up and saw M. Chasle's eyes blurred with tears. The little man took off his glasses, unfolded his handkerchief, and wiped his eyes.

"I've been to see the gentlemen at Saint Roch's," he began, pausing to sigh between each phrase. "I've asked them to say masses—to satisfy my conscience, M. Antoine, no more than that. Because, speaking for myself, till further . . . further evidence is forthcoming . . ." His tears continued flowing, but sparingly, in little spurts; now and again he carefully wiped his eyes, then spread his handkerchief on his knees, folded it up along the creases, and slipped it flat into an inner pocket, like a wallet.

Abruptly he swerved to a new subject. "I'd saved up ten thousand francs . . ."

"Aha!" Antoine smiled to himself. "Now we're coming to it!" Then he said aloud: "I don't know, M. Chasle, if my father had time to make provision for you in his will, but have no anxiety; my brother and myself will guarantee to you, for the rest of your days, the monthly salary you were drawing here."

This was the first time Antoine had been called upon to settle a money matter in the capacity of his father's heir. It seemed to him that, all things considered, he was dealing generously with M. Chasle in pledging himself thus to support him till his death. And it was pleasant to feel himself in a position to make such generous gestures. Despite himself, his thoughts strayed to the financial aspect of the situation: what would his father's estate amount to, and what would be his share? But he had nothing definite to go on.

M. Chasle had gone scarlet. To keep himself in countenance, presumably, he had produced a penknife and begun trimming his nails.

"Not an annuity!" He spoke with an effort, emphatically, his eyes still fixed on his nails. In the same tone he added: "A lump sum, yes; not an annuity." His voice grew sentimental. "Because of Dédette, M. Antoine; the little girl you operated on. You remember her, don't you? You see, it's just the same as if I had a daughter of my own. So an annuity's no earthly use; there wouldn't be a sou for me to leave the little pet."

It all came back to Antoine: Dédette, the operation, Rachel, the sunlit bedroom, her body glowing golden in the shadowy alcove, the perfume of the amber necklace. With a far-away smile on his lips— he had dropped his letters on the table—he listened vaguely to the old man rambling on, following his movements with a casual eye. Suddenly he spun round on his heel; M. Chasle had nicked his pen-knife into his thumb-nail and calmly, like a man tapering off a cork, was slicing off at one stroke a crescent-shaped shred that rasped along the blade.

"Oh, stop it, M. Chasle!" Antoine exclaimed, his teeth on edge.

M. Chasle hopped off his chair.

"Yes, yes. . . . I'm wasting your time, of course. So sorry!"

But the issue at stake was so vitally important to him that he ventured on a last offensive.

"A little lump sum, M. Antoine, that's the thing. What I need is capital. I've had a little scheme in mind for quite a while, you know. I'll tell you about it," he murmured in a far-away voice, "some other time. Later on." Then, with a blank stare in the direction of the door, he added in a quite different tone: "Yes, it's right and proper to say masses for him, I don't deny it. But, if you ask my opinion, the deceased doesn't need any help from us. A man like that leaves nothing to chance. No, in my opinion, it's all fixed up. At this moment, M. Antoine, at this very moment . . ." With little rabbit-like skips he scurried to the door, nodding his grey head and repeating with an air of firm conviction: "At this very moment he—he has settled in already, in his Paradise."

Hardly had M. Chasle left when Antoine had to face the tailor, to try on his mourning suit. His weariness had come back and this tiresome parade before the looking-glass was the last straw.

He had just decided for an hour's rest when, as he was showing the tailor out, he found Mme. de Battaincourt at his door, her finger on the bell. She had rung up previously to make an appointment, and learned the sad news. So she had cancelled an engagement to come and see him.

Antoine greeted her politely, but did not invite her in. She squeezed his hand effusively, expressing her sympathy for his bereavement in a high-pitched voice and with a certain gusto. She showed no sign of leaving, and it seemed difficult to keep her standing there; the more so as she had contrived to make Antoine move back a step, and was now inside the flat.

Jacques had stayed the whole afternoon in his bedroom, the door of which was near by. It struck Antoine that his brother would hear this woman's voice, recognize it, perhaps; and the notion was displeasing to him, though why, he could not have explained. Putting a good face on necessity, he opened his study door and slipped on his coat. He had been in his shirt-sleeves and the fact of having been caught thus unawares added to his annoyance.

During the past few weeks something of a change had come over his relations with his attractive patient. She had been coming to see him oftener, on the pretext of bringing news of her invalid daughter, who was spending the winter on the north coast, with her step-father and the English nurse. For Simon de Battaincourt had cheerfully abandoned his country home and shooting, to settle down at Berck with the young girl and his wife—whereas the latter was always "having to run up" to Paris, on one pretext or another, and staying away several days each week.

She refused to sit down; bending lithely towards Antoine, her breast heaving with little sympathetic sighs, her eyes half closed, she was biding her time to squeeze his hand again. When looking at a man, she always kept her eyes fixed on his lips. Now, through her long lashes, she could see his gaze, too, hovering persistently upon her mouth—and her senses tingled. That evening Antoine struck her as downright handsome; there was more virility in his expression—it was as if the series of decisions he had had to make during the past few days had stamped his face with a look of self-reliance.

"You must be feeling it dreadfully, poor man!" She gave him a commiserating glance.

Antoine found nothing to reply. Ever since she had come, he had been keeping up a vaguely solemn air which, though it helped him through the interview, involved a certain strain. He continued watching her furtively; and suddenly, when his eyes fell on the breasts rising and falling under the light tissue, swift fire coursed through his veins. Looking up, he caught a glimpse of little, dancing lights flickering in her eyes; a project, tempting for all its rashness, was taking form behind the pretty forehead—but she was careful not to betray it.

"The hardest time," she said in a soft, sentimental voice, "is—afterwards. When one's caught up again by life, and finds nothing but emptiness everywhere. I hope you'll let me come and see you sometimes—may I?"

He looked her up and down. Then with a sudden rush of hatred, he flung out brutally, his lips twisted in a mirthless smile:

"Your sympathy is wasted, Madame. I did not love my father."

At once he bit his lip remorsefully. He was more shocked at having thought such a thing than at having said it. "And," he reflected bitterly, "who knows if it wasn't the truth she wrung from me then, the minx!"

For the moment Mme. de Battaincourt was too taken aback to reply; not so much startled by the words as cut to the quick by Antoine's tone. She moved back a step, to collect her wits.

Then, "In that case . . . !" she exclaimed, and began laughing. After all the make-believe, that strident laugh at last rang true.

While she slipped on her gloves her lips were working oddly, whether with suppressed rage or an incipient smile it was impossible to tell. With truculent eyes Antoine watched the enigmatic, fluttering mouth, prolonged by a slim streak of colour vivid as a scratch. At that moment, had she indulged in a frankly brazen smile, very likely he would have been unable to keep himself from throwing her out, then and there.

Reluctantly he found himself inhaling the scent with which her lingerie was liberally sprinkled, and once more his eyes lingered on the amply moulded bosom heaving beneath the flimsy blouse. And as he crudely, unashamedly pictured her nakedness, a thrill ran through his body.

After buttoning her fur-coat she moved further away, and faced him coolly, with an air of asking: "Are you afraid?"

They confronted each other with the same cold fury, the same rancour—yet with more than these; with perhaps the same sense of disappointment, the vague impression of a lost opportunity. Then, as he still said nothing, she turned her back, opened the door for herself, and went out, paying no further heed to him.

The front door slammed behind her.

Antoine turned on his heel. But instead of re-entering his study, he stayed thus for a moment, unable to move. His hands were clammy, and his ears buzzing with the tumult of his blood; greedily he inhaled the insidious perfume that lingered like a living presence in the hall, playing havoc with his thoughts. For a brief moment only the notion flicked his mind like a whiplash, that, after so brutally wounding that ungovernable nature, it was going to be a perilous feat trying to win her back. His eyes fell on his hat and overcoat hanging on the wall; he snatched them off the hook and, with a furtive glance in the direction of Jacques's room, hurried outside.

IX

GISE had not left her bed. Her body ached all over and the least movement hurt her. From where she lay half asleep, she could hear a muffled sound of footsteps in the passage on the far side of the wall, just behind her head—the steady stream of callers entering and leaving the flat. One thought shone bright and steadfast in the twilight of her mind: "He has come back. He's here, quite close; at any moment I may see him. He's sure to come." She listened for his footstep. But all Friday, then all Saturday went by, and he did not come.

Not that Jacques had put Gise out of mind; the truth was that he was haunted, harassed by thoughts of her. But he dreaded this interview too much to go out of his way to bring it on; he was biding his time. Moreover, he had deliberately dug himself in, in the ground-floor flat, hardly going out at all, lest he should be recognized and spoken to. Only at nightfall had he gone upstairs, crept into the flat like a thief, and settled down again in a corner of the death-chamber, where he had stayed till dawn.

On Saturday evening, however, when Antoine casually asked him if he had seen Gise again, he brought himself, after dinner, to go and knock at her door.

Gise was recovering. Her temperature was almost normal, and Thérivier had told her she could get up next day. She was just dozing off when Jacques knocked.

"Well, how are you feeling?" he asked in a cheerful tone. "I must say you're looking remarkably fit." In the soft, golden light of the little bedside lamp her eyes shone large and lustrous, and indeed she looked the picture of health.

He had halted at some distance from the bed. After an embarrassed moment it was she who held out her hand. The loose sleeve fell back and he saw her bare arm glowing in the lamplight. Taking her hand, he played at being the doctor, and instead of clasping it, patted the soft skin; it was burning hot.

"Still a touch of fever?"

"No, it's gone down."

She glanced towards the door, which he had left open as if to show that he had dropped in only for a moment.

"Feeling cold?" he asked. "Shall I shut it?"

"No. Well . . . if you don't mind. . . ."

He acquiesced good-naturedly. Now, with the door closed, they were safe from intrusion.

She thanked him with a smile, then let her head sink back; her hair made a patch of velvety blackness upon the pillow. The rather low-cut nightdress yielded a glimpse of the young curve of her breast; she put her hand up to the collar to keep it closed. Jacques was struck by the graceful outline of the wrist and the colour of her dusky skin, which, against the whiteness, had the hue of moistened sand.

"What have you been doing all day?" she asked.

"Doing? Nothing at all. I've been lying low, dodging the callers."

Then she remembered M. Thibault's death, Jacques's bereavement. She was vexed with herself for feeling so little grief. Was Jacques feeling sad? she wondered. She could not find the words of affection that perhaps she ought to have addressed to him. Her only thought was that, now the father was no more, the son was completely free. In that case, she reflected, there'll be no need for him to leave home again.

"You should go out a bit, you know," she said.

"Yes? Well, as a matter of fact today, as I was feeling rather muzzy, I took a stroll." He hesitated, then added: "Just to buy some papers."

It had not been so simple, however, as he put it; at four, chafing against these empty hours of waiting, and prompted by obscure motives of which he was not aware till later, he had gone out to buy some Swiss newspapers, and then, without fully realizing where he was going . . .

"I suppose you were out of doors a lot over there, weren't you?" she asked after another silence.

"Yes."

Her "over there" had taken him by surprise and involuntarily he had answered in an ungracious, almost cutting tone—which he instantly regretted. And it struck him now that ever since he had set foot in this place everything he did and said, even his thoughts, rang false.

His eyes kept straying back to the bed on which the shaded lamp cast a pale lure of light, bringing out, under the white coverlet, every graceful line of the young body: the long lithe limbs, the full curve of the flanks, and the two small round knolls of the slightly parted knees. He was feeling more and more ill at ease, and in vain tried to assume a natural air and speak in casual tones.

She wanted to say: "Do sit down!" but could not catch his eye, and dared not speak.

To keep himself in countenance, he was examining the furniture, the tiny altar faceted with glints of gold, the little decorative objects in the room. He remembered the morning of his homecoming, when he had taken refuge in it.

"What a pretty room this is!" he said pleasantly. "You didn't use to have that arm-chair, did you?"

"Your father gave it to me, for my eighteenth birthday. Don't you remember it? It used to be on the top landing at Maisons-Laffitte, under the cuckoo-clock."

Maisons! Suddenly it came back to him, that third-floor landing, the sunlight flooding through the dormer window, the flies that swarmed there all the summer and, when the sun was setting, filled the air with the buzz of a hive of angry bees. He remembered the cuckoo-clock with its dangling chains; he heard again along the silent staircase the little wooden bird cooing the quarter-hours. So, all the time he had been away, life for them had gone on just the same. And now he thought of it, was not he too "just the same," or nearly so? Ever since he was back, had he not at every instant, in each spontaneous gesture, been acting as his old self would have acted? The special way he had of rubbing his shoes on the doormat, for instance, then shutting the hall-door with a bang; his trick of hanging his overcoat on the same two pegs before switching on the light. And, when he walked up and down his room, was not each movement little more than a latent memory revived in action?

Meanwhile Gise was quietly taking stock of his appearance: his stubborn jaw, his sturdy neck, his hands, and his expression of alert unrest.

"How big and strong you've got!" she murmured.

He turned to her, smiling. Inwardly he was all the prouder of his robustness because, throughout childhood, his puniness had galled him. Suddenly, unthinkingly—yet another reflex!—to his own surprise he solemnly declaimed:

" 'Major Van der Cuyp was a man of exceptional strength.' "

Gise's face lit up. How often had she and Jacques read those magic words together, poring over the picture underneath which they were printed! It was in their favourite adventure-book, a tale of the Sumatra jungle, and the picture showed a Dutch officer laying out, with the utmost ease, an immense gorilla.

" 'Major Van der Cuyp had been rash enough to go to sleep under the baobab-tree,' " she capped him merrily. Then throwing her head back, she closed her eyes and opened her mouth wide—for in the picture the rash Major was shown thus, snoring lustily.

Laughing, they watched each other laugh—forgetting all the present, as they delved in that quaint treasury of old memories, to which they alone had access.

"Do you remember the picture of the tiger?" she smiled. "And how you tore it up one day, when you were in a temper?"

"Yes . . . why was I?"

"Oh, because we'd had a laughing fit when Abbé Vécard was there."

"What a memory you have, Gise!"

"I wanted later on, like the man in the book, to have a baby tiger of my own. When I went to sleep at night I used to fancy I was nursing it in my arms."

There was a pause. Both were smiling at their childish fancies. Gise was the first to come back to seriousness.

"Still," she said, "when I think of those days, almost all I seem to remember is dreary, never-ending boredom. What about you?"

Fever and fatigue, and now these memories of the past, had given her a look of melancholy languor that went well with her melting eyes and the warm, exotic colour of her skin.

"Yes," she went on, noticing that Jacques merely knitted his brows without replying, "it's terrible being bored with life when one's a child. And then, when I was fourteen or fifteen, quite suddenly, it came to an end. I can't think why. Something changed inside me. Nowadays I've never got the blues. Even when" (she was thinking: "Even when *you* make me unhappy") "even when things go badly."

His hands thrust into his pockets, his eyes fixed on the carpet,

Jacques kept silent. Such evocations of the past sent waves of fury racing through him. Nothing in his earlier life found favour in his eyes. Nowhere, at no stage of his career, had he felt at home, settled down for good in his vocation—as Antoine felt. Always, everywhere, a misfit. In Africa, and Italy, and Germany. At Lausanne, even, almost as much as elsewhere. And not merely homeless, but at bay—hounded down by society, by family and friends, by the very conditions of life, and also by something else, something he could not define, which seemed to come from within himself.

" 'Major Van der Cuyp . . .' " Gise began. She was lingering on these echoes of their childhood because she dared not breathe a word of the more recent memories haunting her mind. But she did not continue; she had learned her lesson: nothing now could fan those dead ashes into flame.

Silently watching Jacques, she tried in vain to solve the dark enigma. Why had he gone away, despite what had passed between them? Some vague remarks Antoine had let fall had disturbed her without explaining anything. What could have been the message the red roses sent from London were meant to convey?

Suddenly she thought: "How different he is from my 'Jacquot' of the past!"

With an emotion that now she could not hide she said aloud:

"How you've changed, Jacquot!"

From the evasive smile, the brief glance Jacques cast her, she guessed that her emotion had displeased him. With a quick change of tone and expression, she launched forth gaily into a description of her experiences in the English convent.

"It's so nice, the healthy, well-regulated life one leads. You simply can't imagine how fit one feels for work after gymnastics in the open air and a hearty English breakfast."

She did not say that, while she was in London, the one thing that had buoyed her up was the hope of finding him again. She did not tell him how that early-morning energy evaporated hour by hour, of the sombre moods that settled on her nightly in the dormitory bed.

"English life's so different from ours, and so fascinating." A commonplace, but to have hit on it was a relief, and to stave off the menace of another silence she kept to the theme. "In England everybody laughs, on purpose, on the least pretext. They simply won't hear of life being treated as 'a vale of tears.' So, you see, they think as little as possible; they play. They make a game of everything—beginning with life!"

Jacques listened to her chatter, without interrupting. He too would go to England. To Russia and America. He had all his future before him—for travelling, for seeking . . . He smiled approvingly, nodding assent now and then. Gise was no fool, and those three years seemed to have ripened her wits considerably. Made her prettier, too, and daintier. His eyes roved back over the counterpane to the slim, frail body which seemed, as it were, relaxed in its own warmth. And suddenly, crudely, it all came back—that gust of passion, their embrace under the great trees in the park. A chaste embrace; and yet even after all those years, after all he had gone through since, he still could feel that vibrant body swaying in his arms; under his mouth's kiss those inexperienced lips. And in a flash all thoughts of prudence, self-restraint, were dust before a fiery wind. . . . Why not? He went so far as to ask himself again, as in his maddest moments: "Why not marry her, make her mine?" But no sooner thought than he came up against some dark, dimly apprehended obstacle sundering him from her; somewhere in his inmost being lay an invincible impediment.

Then, as his gaze rested once more on the lithe, living form before him on the bed, his imagination, already rich with so many memories, cast across the screen the picture of another bed, and such another glimpse of slim, rounded flanks outlined under the bedclothes; and the desire that had just thrilled him melted into remembered pity. He saw again, laid out on her small iron bedstead, that little prostitute at Reichenhall, a girl of seventeen, who had been so stubbornly resolved to die, that she had been discovered squatting on the floor, strangled by a noose tied to the cupboard lock. Jacques had been one of the first to enter the room; he still remembered the smell of sizzling fat that pervaded it, but, clearest of all, the flat, enigmatic face of the woman, still fairly young, who stood breaking eggs over a frying-pan in a corner of the room. A mark or two had loosened her tongue and she even gave some curious details. And on Jacques's asking her if she had known the dead girl well, she had exclaimed with a look of unforgettable sincerity: *"Ach, nein! Ich bin die Mutter!"*

Strange answer! "Oh, no! I'm her mother!" He was on the point of telling Gise the story, but thought better of it. To mention his life "over there" would open the door to questions.

Snug in her bed, with half-closed eyes, Gise was observing him hungrily. She was feeling desperate, on the brink of blurting out: "Speak to me, Jacques! What's become of you? What of me? Have you forgotten—everything?"

He was pacing the room, bringing his weight down on one foot then upon the other, in a brown study. Whenever his eyes met hers, he grew aware how hopelessly their minds worked at cross purposes, and at once feigned an extreme aloofness. There was not the faintest hint of his real feelings—how thrilled he was by her childish charm, and the innocence he glimpsed in her, as naïve as the young throat shyly revealed between folds of filmy whiteness. He felt all the affection of an elder brother for this suffering little girl. But what a horde of impure memories kept forcing their unwelcome way between them! Bitterly he regretted feeling so old, so worn out . . . so soiled. . . .

"I guess you're awfully good at tennis now, aren't you?" he asked evasively; he had just noticed a racket on the top of the wardrobe.

Her moods changed quickly; now she could not repress a smile of childish triumph.

"You'll see for yourself!"

At once she felt dismayed. When would he see—and where? What a silly reply to make!

But Jacques did not seem to have noticed. His thoughts were far from Gise. The tennis-courts at Maisons-Laffitte, a white dress . . . that brisk way she had of jumping off her bicycle at the club entrance. What was the meaning of the closed shutters of their flat in the Avenue de l'Observatoire? (For that afternoon when he had taken a stroll, uncertain where to go, he had walked on to the Luxembourg

Gardens, and down their street. The sun was just setting. He had
walked rapidly, with his collar up. He always made haste to yield to
a temptation, so as to be through with it the sooner. Then suddenly
he had halted, looked up. All the windows were shuttered. Of course
Antoine had told him Daniel was at Lunéville, doing his military
service. But what of *them?* It was not late enough to account for the
closed shutters. . . . What did it matter anyhow? What could it
matter? He had turned on his heel, and walked home by the shortest
way.)

Perhaps she realized how far from her Jacques's thoughts had
drifted. Unconsciously she stretched out an arm, as though to touch
him, clasp him, draw him back.

"What a wind!" His voice was cheerful; he did not seem to have
noticed her gesture. "Gise, doesn't it worry you, that rattle in your
fireplace? Wait a bit!"

He went down on his knees and wedged an old newspaper between the loose iron slats of the fire-screen. Worn out by emotions,
by thoughts she dared not utter, Gise watched him at work.

"That's better!" he exclaimed as he got up. Then he sighed and,
for the first time, spoke without much weighing his words. "Yes, this
fierce wind—how it makes one wish the winter was over, and spring
returning!"

Obviously his mind was busy with the springtimes he had spent
abroad. And she could guess what he was thinking: "Next May I'll
be doing this, I'll be going there . . ."

"And in this coming spring," she mused, "what place does he allow
for me?"

A clock had just struck.

"Why, it's nine!" Jacques said. His tone suggested it was time to go.

Gise, too, had heard the clock strike. "How many nights," she
thought, "have I spent here, with this lamp beside me, waiting, hoping! Hearing that hour strike as it struck now—and Jacques far away,
lost. Now he is here, beside me. He is with me tonight. Hearing, with
me, the clock strike. . . ."

Jacques had come back to the bed.

"Well, well," he said, "it's high time I let you go to sleep."

"He is with me!" she was repeating to herself, her eyes half closed to watch him better. "And yet life, the outside world, everything round us is going on exactly as if nothing had happened, nothing changed." And she had an impression, bitter as remorse, that, truth to tell, she had not changed either—had not changed enough.

Not wishing to seem in too much haste to leave her, Jacques had remained standing at the bedside. Without the least flicker of emotion he lightly clasped the small brown hand lying on the counterpane. He could smell the odour of the cretonne curtains, mingled tonight with a faint acid tang, which he rather disliked so long as he attributed it to her fever, but cheerfully inhaled when he saw a sliced lemon in a saucer on the bedside table.

Gise did not move. Her eyes, wide open, were brimming with the bright tears that she was keeping back.

He made as if he noticed nothing.

"Good night, then! Tomorrow you'll be quite well."

"Quite well? Oh, I'm not so keen about it, really!" she sighed, with a wan smile.

She hardly knew why she had spoken thus. Her indifference about recovering expressed her lassitude, her lack of courage to face life again—and, most of all, her sadness for the ending of this long-awaited hour, so disappointing, yet so sweet. Tense with emotion, her lips would hardly move, but somehow she managed to cry gaily:

"Thank you for having come to see me, Jacquot."

Once more she was on the point of holding out her hand to him; but he had reached the door. Turning, he nodded to her cheerfully and went out.

She turned off the light and snuggled down between the sheets. Her heart was thudding violently. She crossed her arms, hugging her sorrow to her breast, as long ago she used to hug the "baby tiger." Mechanically she murmured: "Holy Virgin, my guide and sovereign Queen, into thy dear hands I commend my hopes and comforts, my griefs and sorrows. . . ." She prayed in fervent haste, trying to lull her brain to rest with the sing-song cadences. Never did she feel so happy as when she was praying, praying her heart out, in a limbo of no thought. Her arms were tightly locked upon her breast. Everything was growing vague, merging into an insubstantial dream-world, till presently it seemed to her that she was clasping to her heart's warmth a real baby, hers and hers alone; and, bending a little forward so as to enfold this phantom gift of love in a soft, safe nest, she strained him to her bosom, weeping over him, as she fell asleep.

X

ANTOINE was waiting for his brother to leave Gise's room and come downstairs to bed; he proposed that night to sort out in a rough-and-ready way the personal papers left by M. Thibault, and he preferred to be alone when doing this. Not that he wished to keep Jacques in the dark with regard to any of his father's affairs, but on the day following the old man's death, when he was rummaging for the will, his eyes had chanced to fall on a sheet of paper headed "Jacques," and though he had then lacked time to give it more than a brief glance, he had seen enough to realize it would make painful reading for his brother. Very likely there were other documents of the same order; it was undesirable for Jacques to light on them—for the present, anyhow.

Before going to the study, Antoine crossed the dining-room to see what progress M. Chasle was making with his task. The table had all its extra leaves in, and on it were stacked some thousands of envelopes and the printed notices of M. Thibault's death to be sent out to friends and acquaintances. Instead of getting on with his job of addressing the envelopes, M. Chasle seemed absorbed in checking up the packets of notices which he was ripping open one after the other.

Puzzled by the sight, Antoine approached him.

"Ah, there's a lot of dishonest folk in the world," the old fellow grumbled, peering up at Antoine. "Each package ought to contain five hundred. Well, here's one with five hundred and three in it, and another with five hundred and one." As he spoke, he was tearing up the notices in excess of the round five hundred. "Of course, it's nothing very serious," he allowed indulgently, "but all the same, if we kept them, we'd soon be snowed under by these notices over and above . . ."

"Over and above . . . what?" Antoine was completely flabbergasted.

M. Chasle raised a monitory finger, with a little knowing cackle of laughter.

"Exactly. That's the point."

Antoine turned on his heel, leaving it at that. He was smiling to himself. "The oddest thing is that when one talks to that old loon, one always gets the impression, for a moment, that one's even loonier than he!"

Once in the study, he turned on all the lights, drew the curtains, and closed the door.

M. Thibault's papers were arranged methodically. "Charities" had a cupboard to themselves. In the safe were a few stock certificates, but mostly old ledgers and documents relating to the administration of the Thibault property. As for the desk, the left-hand drawers contained deeds, contracts, and business papers; those on the right—the ones in which Antoine was interested just now—seemed reserved for personal and private matters. In one of them he had found the will and, under the same cover, the paper relative to Jacques.

He knew where he had replaced it. It turned out to be merely an excerpt from the Bible. Deuteronomy xxi, 18–21.

If a man have a stubborn and rebellious son, which will not obey the voice of his father, or the voice of his mother . . .

Then shall his father and his mother lay hold on him, and bring him out unto the elders of his city, and unto the gate of his place;

And they shall say unto the elders of his city, This our son is stubborn and rebellious . . .

And all the men of his city shall stone him with stones, that he die: so shalt thou put evil away from among you; and all Israel shall hear, and fear.

The sheet was headed "Jacques," and underneath was written: "*Stubborn and rebellious.*"

Antoine read it with emotion. There were signs it had been written fairly recently. The verses had been carefully copied; each letter was neatly rounded off. The whole document seemed to breathe an atmosphere of moral certitude, of ripe reflection, and tenacity of purpose. And yet did not the very existence of this sheet of paper which the old man had (deliberately, Antoine felt quite sure) placed in the envelope that contained his will—did it not testify to certain qualms of conscience, a desire to justify himself?

Antoine picked up his father's will again. It was a huge affair, with numbered pages, divided into chapters, subdivided into clauses, like an official report, and boxed in boards. It was dated July 1912. So M. Thibault had made his will at the start of his illness, shortly before the operation. No reference was made to Jacques; the testator spoke throughout of "my son," "my heir," in the singular.

On the previous day Antoine had only glanced through the chapter headed "Instructions for the Obsequies." Now he studied it in detail.

I desire that, after a low mass has been said at Saint Thomas Aquinas's Church, my remains shall be taken to Crouy. I desire that my obsequies shall be solemnized in the Chapel of the Institution in the presence of the assembled children. I desire that, unlike the funeral service at Saint Thomas Aquinas's Church, the ceremonies at Crouy shall be performed with all the dignity the Committee may deem fitting to accord my mortal remains. I wish to be carried to my last resting-place by representatives of the charitable societies which for many years have availed themselves of my whole-hearted service; and also by a delegation from the Institute of France, whose reception of myself into their midst was the proudest moment of my life. Further, in view of my rank in the Order of the Legion of Honour, I desire, provided the regulations admit of it, that military honours may be accorded me by our army, whose cause I have defended my life long in all I have said and written, and by my vote as an elector. Lastly, I wish that those who may express a wish to say a few words of farewell beside my grave may be permitted to do so without hindrance.

Let there be no mistake: in writing thus, I have no illusions as to the vanity of posthumous encomiums. I tremble at the thought that one day I shall stand before the Judgment Seat. But, after seeking heavenly guidance in prayer and meditation, I am led to believe that my true duty is to shun the counsels of an unprofitable humility, and to take steps that, when death befalls me, my light may, God willing, for the last time so shine before men that other Christians who belong to our great French middle class may be encouraged to devote themselves likewise to the service of the Faith and Catholic Charity.

A clause followed, headed: "Detailed Instructions." M. Thibault had gone to the trouble of arranging the whole ceremony step by step, and Antoine had no say in the matter. Up to the last moment the head of the family was exercising his authority; and, indeed, Antoine found a certain grandeur in the old man's determination to play his patriarchal part up to the very end.

M. Thibault had even drawn up the notice of his death for circulation to his friends, and Antoine had sent it on, as it stood, to the printer's. M. Thibault's numerous distinctions were set forth in an order that had evidently been meticulously worked out, and took up a full dozen lines of print. MEMBER OF THE INSTITUTE was in capital letters. Following this came not only such descriptions as *Doctor of Laws* and *Sometime Member for the Eure Department,* but also *Honorary President of the Joint Committee of Catholic Charities in the Diocese of Paris, Founder and President of the Social Defence League, Chairman of the Governing Board of the Child Welfare Society, Sometime Treasurer of the French Branch of the United Catholic Defence League, President of the Church Council in the Parish of Saint Thomas Aquinas.* Antoine could make little of certain descriptions, such as *Corresponding Member of the Brotherhood of Saint John Lateran.* The imposing catalogue concluded with a list of Orders, that of the Legion of Honour coming after the Orders of Saint Gregory and Saint Isabella, even after that of the Southern Cross. The insignia of all these Orders were to be pinned above the coffin.

The greater part of the will consisted of a long list of legacies to various charities and individuals, many of whom were unknown to Antoine.

Then his eye was caught by Gise's name. M. Thibault bequeathed, in the form of a dowry, a large sum of money to "Mlle. Gisèle de Waize," whom he had "brought up and regarded almost as a daughter." She was charged to provide, from this sum, for "the declining years of her good aunt." Thus the girl's future was comfortably secured.

Antoine stopped reading for a moment, to savour the enjoyable surprise of finding the self-centred old man capable of such kindness, such open-handedness. He blushed with pleasure, and he felt a thrill of gratitude and respect, fully justified by what he learned from the succeeding pages. M. Thibault seemed to have spared no pains to ensure the welfare of those around him: his servants, the concierge, the gardener at Maisons-Laffitte—not one was forgotten.

The last sheet dealt with various endowments, all of which were to bear Oscar Thibault's name. Antoine dipped at random into the lengthy list. There was an "Oscar Thibault Bequest" to the French Academy: a prize for moral excellence. Naturally! Antoine smiled. An "Oscar Thibault Prize," to be awarded quinquennially by the Institute of Moral Science for the best literary work "serving to further the fight against prostitution, and to combat the tolerance that the present Government of the French Republic"—obviously!—"shows towards the social evil." Antoine smiled again. Gise's legacy inclined him to indulgence. Moreover, in this constantly expressed desire of the testator to promote the spiritual well-being of mankind, Antoine could discern—not without emotion—an obscure craving, from which he himself, for all his maturity of mind, was not wholly immune: the craving to outlive his death in the temporal world.

The least foreseeable, most naïve, of the bequests was the granting of a fairly large sum to the Bishop of Beauvais, for the annual publication of an *Oscar Thibault Annual.* As many copies as possible were to be printed, and sold at a low price at all the stationers' and bookshops in the diocese. Described as a "mine of daily information for gardeners and agriculturists," it was to include "an entertaining section of edifying stories for recreation on Sundays and winter evenings," and steps were to be taken to see it found its way into every Catholic home.

Antoine folded up the will. He was anxious to get on with his task. As he slipped the bulky document back into its case, he caught himself thinking, not without satisfaction: "If he could be so lavish in his bequests, it means he's leaving us a pretty handsome sum."

The first drawer contained a large leather portfolio, inscribed "Lucie," Mme. Thibault's given name.

As he undid the strap Antoine had a vague feeling of discomfort— quite unjustified, he reminded himself.

Miscellaneous objects, to begin with. An embroidered handkerchief; a small box with a little girl's earrings in it; a white satin purse ribbed with ivory and containing a confession note folded in four, with some writing in ink that had become illegible. Some faded photographs that Antoine had never seen before showed his mother as a child, and in her teens. Antoine was surprised that a man so unsentimental as his father should have preserved these tender relics, especially in the drawer which stood nearest to his hand. His heart warmed towards the merry, winsome girl shown in the photographs, though as he scanned them he was thinking more of himself than of his mother. When Mme. Thibault died, at Jacques's birth, he had been nine. A serious-minded, stubborn, rather priggish little boy, with —he had to admit it—not much natural affection. Without lingering over these distasteful memories, he investigated the other pocket of the portfolio.

He found two bundles of letters of equal size labelled: "Lucie's Letters," "Oscar's Letters." The latter packet was tied with a silk ribbon, and inscribed in a sloping, school-girlish handwriting. Probably M. Thibault had piously preserved it exactly as he had found it, after his wife's death, in her escritoire.

Antoine hesitated about opening it; he could come back to it later. But it happened that the ribbon was loose and, as he pushed the packet away, his eye was caught by some phrases which stood out, words instinct with reality that called up from the shadows a past of which he had never dreamt, still less had a glimpse.

I shall write to you again from Orléans, before the Congress opens. But, my darling, I want to tell you tonight that my heart beats for you alone, to beg you to have patience, and to try to help you through this first day of our week of separation. Happily Saturday is not so very far off. Good night, my love. Why not keep the baby with you in your room, so as not to feel so lonely?

Before continuing reading Antoine got up and locked the door.

I love you with all my heart and soul, my best beloved. To be separated from you has for me a sharper sting than the bitter frosts of this foreign land. I shan't wait at Brussels for W. P. to come. Before next Sunday I shall press you in my arms again, my darling Lulu. No one can ever guess what our hearts know; no two people have ever loved as we two love each other. . . .

That his father should have penned such phrases was to Antoine so amazing that he could not bring himself to slip the ribbon round the packet and lay it aside. All the letters, however, had not the same fervour.

Something you wrote in your last letter has, I must own, displeased me. I beg you, Lucie, do not take advantage of my absence to waste time practising the piano. Mark well my words; the sort of ecstasy that music induces is apt to have a pernicious effect on the temperaments of young persons; it accustoms them to idleness, to letting their imagination run away with them, and may even lure a woman from her proper duties.

Sometimes a note of actual bitterness crept in.

You don't understand me, and I now realize that you have *never* understood me. You accuse me of egoism—me of all people, whose whole life is spent in serving others! Ask Abbé Noyel (if you dare to) what he has to say on that subject! You would thank God for, and be proud of, the life of self-abnegation that I lead, could you but grasp its inner meaning, the high moral purpose and spiritual fervour that inform it. Instead of that, you give way to sordid jealousy, and all you can think of is how best to hinder, for your own selfish ends, the claims of these philanthropic societies which so greatly need my guidance.

This, however, was an exception. Most of the letters were couched in a deeply affectionate tone.

Not a line from you yesterday, not a line today. I want you so badly that

I hunger for a letter from you each morning in the most absurd way; it's my daily ration, and when I wake and find it missing I have no heart for the day's work. Well, today I consoled myself by rereading that exquisite letter you sent on Thursday—breathing of true love, and purity, and noble feelings. Surely you, my dear one, are the guardian angel God has posted at my side. I am vexed with myself for not loving you as you deserve. True, you have never complained; but that, my love, I know is because you make it a rule not to complain. But how base of me it would be, were I to feign to ignore my shortcomings, and to hide from you my remorse!

Our delegation has had a very fine reception here, and I have been given a flattering place in it. Yesterday there was a dinner for thirty, with toasts to us and all the rest of it. I gather that the speech I made in acknowledgment was much appreciated. But don't think that such success in public makes me forgetful; between sessions, all my thoughts are for you, my best beloved, and for our little one.

Antoine was greatly moved. His hands were trembling a little as he put the packet back in the drawer. M. Thibault had always referred to the "dear departed saint" with a special kind of sigh and a glance ceilingwards, when recalling some past incident in which his wife had been concerned. But this brief insight into an unsuspected period of his parents' younger days had told Antoine more about them than all the allusions made by his father over twenty years.

The second drawer likewise contained bundles of letters: "Letters from the Children," "Reformatory Boys." "The rest of his family," Antoine thought.

He was more at home with that phase of the past—but no less surprised. Who would have dreamed that M. Thibault thus preserved all Antoine's letters, and all Jacques's, even the few letters Gise had sent, and kept them in a special dossier, "Letters from the Children"?

On the top of the pile lay an undated, but very early note; a few words awkwardly pencilled by a little boy, whose hand his mother must have guided.

My dear Papa,
I kiss you lovingly and wish you many happy returns of the day.
Antoine.

For a moment he lingered pensively over this ancient relic, then passed on.

The "reformatory" group of letters seemed comparatively dull.

Honoured Sir,
    We are being transferred this evening to the Ile de Ré. Before leaving the prison, I would like to express my gratitude for all your kindnesses . . .

To My Kind Benefactor

Sir,
    He who writes to you and signs this letter is one who has returned to the fold of honesty so I make bold to ask you for your kind testimonial and enclose a letter from my Father asking you kindly not to pay to much attention to the gramma. My two little girls pray every night for Fathers Godfather as they call your honored self. . . .

Sir,
    I have now been 26 days in custody and am at my wit's end because the investigating Magistrate has come to see me only once in all that time, in spite of the petition I submitted showing cause . . .

A stained sheet of paper, headed "Montravel Prison Camp, New Caledonia"—the ink was yellow with age—ended as follows:

    . . . hoping always for better days, I beg to remain, honoured sir,
                        Most gratefully yours,
                                    Convict No. 4843.

Antoine could not help feeling moved by these expressions of trust and gratitude, all these pathetic evocations of his father's helping hand.

"I must get Jacques to have a look at these letters," he said to himself.

At the bottom of the drawer was a little package without any inscription; it contained three amateur photographs, dog-eared at the corners. The largest showed a woman some thirty years of age, standing at the edge of a pine forest on a mountainside. Antoine held it near the lamp; the woman's face was totally unknown to him. In any case the style of dress—ribboned bonnet, muslin collaret, and leg-of-mutton sleeves—showed that the photograph must be a very old one. The second, a smaller picture, showed the same woman sitting bare-headed in a public square, or possibly the garden of a hotel; under the bench on which she sat a white poodle crouched sphinx-like. In the third the dog had been taken alone, perched on a table, its muzzle pointing upwards and a bow-knot of ribbon on its head. In the box was also an envelope containing the negative of the large photograph, the mountain scene. No name, no date. On a closer view, Antoine judged that, though her figure had not lost its slimness, the woman might be older than he had thought at first—forty, perhaps, or more. She gave an impression of warm vitality and, despite the gaily smiling lips, of thoughtfulness; Antoine, who found the face attractive, pored over it for a while, unable to bring himself to put the photograph back into the box. Most puzzling of all—or was it only autosuggestion?—he was getting less sure that he had never seen this woman before.

The third drawer, otherwise almost empty, contained an old ledger, which Antoine all but failed to open. It was bound in morocco leather stamped with M. Thibault's initials, and, as a matter of fact, had never been used as an account-book.

On the front end-paper Antoine read: "A Present from Lucie for the First Anniversary of Our Wedding. Feb. 12, 1880."

In the middle of the next page M. Thibault had inscribed, likewise in red ink:

NOTES
for a
HISTORY OF PARENTAL AUTHORITY
from the Earliest to Modern Times.

But this title had been struck out. Evidently the project had been dropped. "A quaint hobby, that," Antoine smiled to himself, "for a man who'd been married a year, and whose first child was yet unborn."

After skimming through some pages, his curiosity was whetted. Few were blank. The changes in the handwriting showed that the ledger had served as a note-book for many years. It was not, however, a diary, as Antoine had begun by thinking—and hoping—but a collection of quotations presumably jotted down in the course of reading.

Still, Antoine reflected, the choice of the quotations might well be enlightening, and he studied the first pages with an inquisitive eye.

Few things are more to be feared than making the least change in established order. (Plato.)

Buffon on the sage: Content with his lot, his one wish is to remain as he has always been, to go on living as he has lived; sufficient unto himself, he has small need of others.

Some of the excerpts were rather unexpected.

There are sour, bitter, and naturally churlish hearts which render likewise sour and bitter all that enters into them. (Saint Francis of Sales.)

There is no soul in the world that cherishes more warmly, more tenderly and passionately than mine; nay, I even exceed somewhat in lovingkindness. (Saint Francis of Sales.)

Prayer may have been accorded man to permit him to utter a daily cry of love for which he need not blush.

The last aphorism was written in a fluent hand, and no source was given. Antoine assumed that his father was its author.

Thereafter, indeed, M. Thibault seemed to have got into the way of inserting the fruits of his own musings between his gleanings from the works of others. And, as Antoine turned the pages, he discovered, with keen satisfaction, that the commonplace-book seemed very soon to have diverted from its original usage and become almost entirely a record of its owner's personal meditations.

At the outset most of these apophthegms had a political or social trend. It looked as if M. Thibault had from time to time jotted down such general ideas as might come in handy for his public speeches. There were quite a number of those phrases opening as a query cast in the negative form—"Is it not obvious that . . . ?." "Must there not be . . . ?" and so forth—which had been so characteristic of the old man's thought and conversation.

The authority of the head of a business is amply justified by the efficiency that lies behind it. But is there not more in it than that? For industry to achieve its maximum output must there not be loyal co-operation among all those contributing to that output? And nowadays is not the management the only organization which can ensure that spirit of co-operation among the workers?

The proletariat is up in arms against the inequalities of life, and stigmatizes as "injustice" the marvellous *variety* ordained by God.

Do we not tend to forget nowadays that what a man is "worth," on the material plane, almost invariably determines also his worth as a good citizen?

Antoine skipped two or three years. Opinions on topics of general interest were gradually giving place, it seemed, to meditations of a more personal order.

Is not what gives the Christian his wonderful sense of security the fact that the Church of Christ is *also* a temporal power?

Antoine smiled. "These high-principled folk," he mused, "given zeal and courage, can be more dangerous than real scoundrels. They impress everyone—especially the better class of people, and they're so convinced they have the Truth (with a capital 'T') in their pockets that they stick at nothing to ensure the triumph of their principles. At nothing! Yes, I've seen Father at work; for the good of his party, for the success of one of his charities—well, there were times he did some rather curious things! Things he'd never have dreamed of doing for his own sake, to make money, or for his personal advancement."

His eyes roamed the pages, settling now and then upon a phrase.

Is there not a proper, nay, beneficent form of egoism—or, rather, a way of putting egoism to the service of virtuous ends: for example, using it to buttress our religious zeal, not to say our faith?

Some of the aphorisms might have struck a reader ignorant of M. Thibault's personality and life as positively cynical.

Charities. The grandeur and, above all, the inestimable social service rendered by our Catholic institutions (benevolent societies, the Saint Vincent de Paul Sisterhood, etc.) lies in the fact that the relief they distribute rarely finds its way to other than deserving folk, such as accept their lot; they run no risk of encouraging discontented, rebellious spirits who are always chafing at their humble station and prating of "social injustice" and their "rights."

True charity does not aim at the happiness of others. May God give us the strength to deal harshly by those whom it is our duty to save from themselves!

The same ideas seemed still to preoccupy him several months later.

One must be ruthless with oneself—to have the right to be severe with others.

Among the virtues unrecognized as such, should we not set in the first rank, considering the hard schooling it requires, what, in my prayers, I have so long called "case-hardening"?

In the midst of an otherwise blank page stood this injunction, peremptory as a trumpet-call:

We must compel respect by dint of virtue.

"Case-hardening!" Antoine mused. He was learning that his father had been not only rigid but—deliberately—case-hardened. Yet he would not shut his eyes to a certain sombre grandeur in such self-repression—even though it led to sheer inhumanity. He pictured it as almost a wilful deadening of every natural sentiment. Sometimes, indeed, it seemed that, being the man he was, the merit he had acquired at such cost made M. Thibault suffer.

Respect does not necessarily preclude friendship, but rarely, it would seem, invites it. To admire is not to love and, if virtue wins esteem, it does not open hearts.

A rankling regret, which led him so far as to write, a few pages later:

The just man has no friends; God compensates him with recipients of his benevolence.

Here and there, if rarely, a truly human note was struck—so out of tune with the rest that Antoine was dumbfounded.

If to do good does not come natural to us, let us do good out of despair —or, at least, so as to refrain from doing evil.

"There's something of Jacques in all that," Antoine murmured. But it was hard to lay a finger on it. There was the same emotional tension, the same harshness, the same dark ferment of the instincts. He even wondered if his father's aversion for Jacques's adventurous disposition had not been sometimes implemented by a secret similarity of temperament.

A good many of the aphorisms were headed: *"A Lure of the Tempter."*

A Lure of the Tempter: fetish-worship of the Truth. Sometimes is it not harder, and more courageous, to be loyal to oneself and persevere in a belief, even if it be undermined, than presumptuously to shake the pillars and risk bringing down the whole edifice?

Is not the cult of consistency higher than the cult of truth?

A Lure of the Tempter. To mask one's pride is not to be modest. It is far better to flaunt the failings one has not been able to overcome, and to convert them into energy, than to lie, and weaken oneself by hiding them.

"Pride," "modesty," and "vanity" were words that cropped up on each page.

A Lure of the Tempter. Self-belittlement, speaking humbly of oneself— is not that a stratagem of Pride? The right course is to keep silent about oneself. But that is impossible for any man, unless he feels assured that others, anyhow, will speak well of him.

Antoine smiled once more, but with an irony that soon froze on his lips. What melancholy there was even in a commonplace like this, when written by the pen of M. Thibault:

Are there any lives, even those of saints, in which falsehood does not play a daily part?

Moreover—and this was far from fitting in with Antoine's impression of the last phase of his father's life—it seemed that, crusted though it was with certainties, the old man's peace of mind had steadily diminished with the years.

The output of a man's career, the scope and value of his activities, are determined, more than one would fancy, by the natural affections. Some there are who have missed achieving a life's work worthy of their talents, for lack of a beloved presence at their side.

Occasionally there were intimations of a secret frailty of the flesh.

Can a sin that has not been committed warp a man's character, and cause as much havoc in his spiritual life as an actual misdeed? Its effect is similar, and the sting of remorse as keen.

A Lure of the Tempter. We must not confound with love of our neighbour the emotion that we sometimes experience at the sight of, or contact with . . .

The rest of the line had been struck out; but, holding the page up to the light, Antoine made out the missing words:

. . . young people, even mere children.

There was a pencilled note in the margin: "July 2, July 25, August 6, August 8, August 9."
A few pages further on a new note was struck.

O God, Thou knowest my unworthiness and my affliction. I have no right to Thy pardon, for I have not broken, I cannot break, with my sin. Fortify my resolve that I may shun the Tempter's lure.

Antoine suddenly remembered certain obscene words which had escaped his father's lips when he was delirious, on two separate occasions. M. Thibault's self-examinings were interspersed with appeals to the Creator's mercy.

O Lord, behold, he whom Thou lovest is sick.
Keep watch over me, O Lord, for if Thou leavest me alone I shall betray Thee.

Antoine turned some more pages. A date added in pencil in the margin, "August '95," caught his eye.

A charming token of love. He had left his book lying on the table; his place marked with the wrapper of a newspaper. Who can have been up and about so early this morning? A cornflower, surely from that corsage she was wearing yesterday evening, now replaced the strip of paper.

August 1895. Completely baffled, Antoine searched his memory. In 1895 he had been fourteen. That year M. Thibault had taken the family to a place near Chamonix. Someone he had met at the hotel? His mind went back at once to the lady with the poodle. Perhaps the following pages might clear the matter up. No, there was not another word about the lady of the cornflowers.

Still, a little further on, he found a flat, dry, faded flower—the very flower, perhaps—between two pages, on one of which was a quotation from La Bruyère.

She has the makings of a perfect friend; and, with it, something that might lead one beyond friendship.

In the same year, dated December 31, as if by way of conclusion, came an entry recalling M. Thibault's schooling with the Jesuits:

Sæpe venit magno fœnore tardus amor.

But vainly Antoine racked his brain for memories of the summer vacation of '95—the leg-of-mutton sleeves and the white poodle. . . .

It was impossible to read the whole book at a sitting, and anyhow the entries gradually fell off during the last ten or twelve years. M. Thibault had become a leading light in the world of charities, and his duties in connexion with them left him little spare time. Except during the vacations he rarely wrote in the ledger, and excerpts from religious literature once more bulked large. Not a line had been written since Jacques's departure, or during the old man's illness.

One of the last entries, written in a less firm hand, conveyed a mood of disillusionment.

When a man achieves distinction, he has already ceased to merit it. But may it not be that God in His mercy grants him this eminence in the world's esteem to enable him to bear the disesteem in which he holds himself, and which first poisons, then dries up, the well-springs of all happiness, nay, even of all charity?

The last pages of the book were blank.

At the end was a small pocket in the silk lining of the leather cover; it contained odds and ends: two amusing photographs of Gise as a small child, a calendar for 1902 in which the Sundays were nicked off, and a letter on mauve paper:

April 7, 1906.

Dear W.X. 99,

I could echo word for word all you tell me about yourself. Yes, I cannot now conceive what prompted me to put such an advertisement in the paper, considering how I was brought up; and I am quite as shocked at my having done so as you can be at having studied the Matrimonial Column in your newspaper and yielded to the temptation of writing to a total stranger whose identity was concealed by two mysterious initials.

For I, like you, am a fervent Catholic, and most attentive to my Religious Duties; indeed I have never neglected them even for a single day; in fact it's all so wonderfully romantic, don't you agree, that one would think a Sign had been given us, and God wished you and me to have that moment of weakness when I put in the advertisement,•and you read it and cut it out. I should tell you that I have been seven years a widow and am feeling more and more the sadness of a loveless life; what makes it harder is that I have no children, and so that consolation is denied me. Still, it can't be always such a consolation, as you, who have two grown-up sons, in fact a real Home, and as far as I can make out a very strenuous business life, you too complain of loneliness and lovelessness. Yes, indeed, I agree that this urge for Love we feel must come from God, and in my prayers to Him morning and night I always ask it may be granted me to know once more the joys of having someone tender and true always at my side, joined in the bonds of Holy Wedlock. And to this man, sent me by Heaven, I too will bring a faithful, loving heart, and a youthfulness of the emotions, which surely is a Pledge of Happiness. But though I hate to think I may be giving you pain, I can't send you what you ask, though I quite understand your desire. You do not know the kind of woman I am, or who my dear Parents were, now dead but always living for me in my prayers—or my place in Society. Once more I beg you not to judge me by that momentary weakness when I put that notice in the paper, and please understand that, feeling as I do, I can't bring myself to send you a photo, even a flattering one. But what I will gladly do is to ask my Confessor, who since last Christmas has been Senior Curate in one of the Paris parishes, to get in touch with the Abbé V. of whom you spoke in your second letter; my Confessor will give all the information required. As for my personal appearance—I might go myself and call on the Abbé V., in whom you have confidence; he will then be able . . .

The fourth page ended with these words. Antoine hunted for the next one in the silk flap; it was not there.

He could not doubt the letter had been meant for his father; the references to the "Abbé V." and the two sons proved it. Should he tackle the Abbé Vécard? But the priest, even if he had played a part in this matrimonial project, would certainly refuse to speak about it.

Could it be the lady with the poodle? Antoine wondered. No, this letter was dated 1906—not very long ago. The year when he had been working under Philip at the hospital, and Jacques was in the reformatory. The bonnet, wasp-waist, and leg-of-mutton sleeves wouldn't fit in with any date so recent as 1906. Well, there was no finding out now; he would never know the truth.

He put back the ledger, locked the drawer, and looked at the clock; half-past midnight. He rose from his seat. "The rags and tatters of a man's life!" he murmured. "And yet what a full life it was, a life like Father's! There's always far more to a human life than anyone imagines."

As if to wrest a secret from it, he stared for some moments at the leather-upholstered mahogany chair from which he had just risen, the chair in which, over so many years, solidly planted and leaning a little forward, M. Thibault, turn by turn ironical or cutting or portentous, had pronounced his dooms.

"What did I really know of him?" he mused. "Only one side of him, the patriarchal side—the authority which by divine right he exercised over me, over us all, for thirty years; but I must say this for him, always conscientiously. Stern and ruthless, but always just according to his lights; devoted to us, as to his duties. And, of course, I knew him too as the social despot all looked up to and feared. But the real man, the man he was in solitude, communing with himself, what was that man? I haven't a notion. Never once did he drop the mask and utter in my presence a thought or sentiment in which I could detect anything genuinely personal, anything which came from deep down in his heart."

Now that Antoine had dipped into these papers, lifted a corner of the veil, and had a glimpse into his father's privacy, he realized with a thrill that was almost pain that, for all the pomp and circumstance, the man now in his coffin had been a man like others, and pitiable perhaps as they; and of this man who was his father, he, Antoine, had known absolutely nothing.

And suddenly he asked himself: "And what did he know of me? Still less. Less than nothing! A schoolmate who had lost sight of me for fifteen years would know more about me. Was that his fault? Wasn't it, rather, mine? Here was a well-read old man whom many eminent people regarded as shrewd and level-headed, one whose advice was well worth taking—and I, his son, never asked him his opinion except as a matter of form, after I'd consulted others and already made up my mind. Surely, when we were alone together, two men like us, of the same blood and the same type of character, might have exchanged ideas—and yet between us, father and son, there was no common language, no possibility of communication; we were strangers."

He took a few steps up and down the room. "Yet—no!" he murmured. "I'm wrong. We weren't strangers to each other. That's the terrible thing. There was a bond between us, a very real one—the bond that links father with son and son with father—absurd though it seems, considering our relations with each other, to think of such a thing. That unique, instinctive sense of kinship—it existed, sure enough, deep down in our hearts, in his and in mine. In fact that's why I'm feeling so bowled over just now; for the first time since I was born I've had a glimpse of something that lay behind our life-long estrangement, something I never could have guessed—a possibility, a quite exceptional possibility, of mutual understanding. And I'm now convinced that despite appearances, and though there was never the least glimmer of an entente between us, there has not been and there will never be in the whole world another person—not even Jacques—so well fitted to be understood by me as to the real man he was under the surface, or so well qualified to penetrate, almost at a glance, the secret places of my personality. Because he was my father, because I am his son!"

He was standing by the study door. His fingers settled on the key. "High time to go to bed." But before switching off the light, he turned about and gazed again at the familiar room, once tenanted by a busy mind, and empty now as an abandoned shell.

"Too late," he thought. "There's nothing to be done—for ever."

Light was filtering beneath the dining-room door.

Antoine threw it open. "Hurry up, M. Chasle! It's time for you to be going."

His bowed head flanked by two tall piles of announcements, M. Chasle was addressing envelopes.

"Ah, so it's you. Glad you've come. Have you a minute to spare?" he mumbled, without looking up.

Supposing that the little man needed his help for an address, Antoine went up to him unsuspectingly.

"Only a minute," M. Chasle repeated, still writing. "Eh? Yes, I'd like to make quite clear what I was saying just now, about that little nest-egg."

Without waiting for a reply, he laid down his pen, whisked out his false teeth, and began staring at Antoine with a disarming twinkle in his eye.

"Don't you want to go to bed, M. Chasle?"

"Oh, no! My mind's too busy with ideas for that." He perked his little bird-like head and shoulders towards Antoine. "I'm writing addresses, yes, but all the time, M. Antoine"—he chuckled with the knowing smile of a conjurer who is about to explain one of his tricks —"my brain is teeming, fairly buzzing with ideas, *ad lib.*"

Before Antoine could create a diversion, he went on.

"Well, with that little nest-egg you spoke to me about, M. Antoine, I'll be able to bring off one of my ideas. Yes, one of my pet ideas. The 'Mart.' That's the name I'd thought of—a clever little name, eh? A sort of office, you see. Well, a shop, really. Yes, a shop to start with. In a busy street somewhere hereabouts. But the shop, that's only what meets the eye; there's the idea behind it. . . ."

When, as now, M. Chasle took his theme to heart, he spoke breathlessly, in little spasmodic sentences, his body swaying like a pendulum, his fingers spread and interlocked. The breathing-space after each phrase enabled him to muster ideas for the next remark; once that was ready, it was as if a trigger had been pulled, shooting his shoulders forward and the words out simultaneously. Then he would pause again, as if incapable of secreting more than a thimbleful of thought at one time.

Antoine wondered if M. Chasle's wits were not even more addled than usual, after the alarms of the past few days and several sleepless nights.

"Latoche would explain all that much better than I can," the little man went on. "I've known him for quite a while now, and from what I hear of his past, he has a very good record, has Latoche. A master mind. Bursting with ideas. Like mine. And he shares the credit, you know, of that great idea I mentioned, the 'Mart.' The Mart of Modern Discoveries. Do you see what I mean?"

"Well—I can't say I do."

"It's like this. There's a lot of little inventions nowadays, useful in the home—gadgets, as they call them. And lots of small inventors who think up something and don't know how to handle it. Well, we shall make a sort of clearing-house, Latoche and I. We'll put advertisements in the local papers."

"What locality?"

M. Chasle stared at Antoine as if he did not understand the question. After a pause he went on.

"In the lifetime of the deceased, I'd have blushed for very shame to talk about such things. But now it's different. I've been turning it over in my mind for thirteen years, M. Antoine. Ever since the Exposition. What's more, I've thought up, all on my own, some A-1 little gadgets. Oh, yes, indeed! A patent heel that records the steps you take. An automatic, ever-ready stamp-moistener." Jumping down from his chair, he went up to Antoine. "But my masterpiece, if I may say so, is an egg. The square egg. The trouble's in discovering the right solution, but I'm in touch with researchers about that. The country priests, I've great hopes about them; on winter evenings, after the Angelus, they've heaps of time on their hands for tinkering with inventions, haven't they? I've set them all off on the track of my solution. But that's child's play, hitting on the solution. The idea— that was the difficult thing to hit on."

Antoine gazed at him open-eyed.

"And when you've got your solution . . . ?"

"Why, then I steep the eggs in it, just long enough to soften the shell without spoiling the egg. You see what I mean?"

"No."

"Then I put them to set in moulds."

"Square moulds?"

"Naturally."

M. Chasle was squirming like a sliced worm; Antoine had never seen him in such a state.

"Hundreds, thousands at once. A square-egg factory. No more egg-cups. My egg stands four-square on its base! And the shells come in handy in the home. For match-boxes, or mustard-pots. Square eggs can be packed side by side in ordinary boxes; no more trouble about shipment, don't you see?"

He began climbing back on his office stool, but jumped away at once, as if he had been stung. His cheeks were crimson.

"Excuse me, sir, I'll be back in a moment. Bladder trouble. Nerves, you know. Once I get talking of my egg . . . !"

XI

ON THE next day, a Sunday, Gise woke to find her temperature definitely back to normal; her limbs no longer ached, and she now felt resolute, eager to be up and doing. She was, however, still too weak to go to church, and spent the morning in her room in prayer and meditation. It was annoying to find she could not come to any satisfactory conclusion as to the changes Jacques's return might bring about in her life. She had nothing clear to go on; daylight filled the room, she was alone, and still she racked her brain in vain to find some adequate reason for the after-taste of disappointment, almost of despair, Jacques's visit on the previous evening had left behind it. Yes, they must have an explanation, do away with every misunderstanding. Then, all would become plain.

But the morning passed and Jacques did not appear. Even Antoine had not shown up since the body had been placed in its coffin. Aunt and niece had a solitary lunch, after which the girl retired to her bedroom.

The hours crept slowly through an afternoon of bleak, soul-deadening gloom. At a loose end, tormented by thoughts she was unable to shake off, Gise felt the strain on her nerves becoming so unbearable that at four o'clock, while her aunt was still in church, she slipped on a coat, ran downstairs to the ground-floor flat, and asked Léon to show her into Jacques's room.

He was sitting at the window, reading a newspaper.

Clean-cut against the grey light of the street, the outline of his head and shoulders showed in profile; Gise was struck by his robustness. Once he was no longer near her, she forgot the man he had become and could recall only her "Jacquot," the boy with the almost childish features, who had strained her to his breast under the trees at Maisons three years before.

At her first glance she noticed, though she did not pause to analyse her impressions, the way he was sitting, uncomfortably perched on the corner of a light chair, and the general untidiness of the room— a suitcase gaping on the floor, a hat hung on the unwound clock, the unused desk, two pairs of shoes sprawling beside the bookcase—it all suggested a casual halting-place, a bivouac where there is no point in acquiring habits before the traveller moves on.

Rising, Jacques moved towards her. When she felt the blue sheen of his eyes, in which she caught a flicker of surprise, hovering like a caress upon her face, she grew so flustered that the reasons she had planned to give in accounting for this visit passed clean out of her mind. Only the real reason—her passionate desire to clear things up —persisted. Casting discretion to the winds, pale, determined, she halted in the middle of the room.

"Jacques, we've got to have a talk, you and I."

In the gaze lingering on her with an affectionate insistence she glimpsed a sudden steely flash, veiled almost at once by a flutter of the eyelids.

Jacques laughed. "Good heavens, how serious that sounds!" His voice was a little shrill.

The jesting tone chilled her, but she contrived to smile, a small, woebegone smile that ended in a wince of pain. Her eyes were brimming with tears. Looking away, she took a few steps to the side and sat down on the sofa-bed. The tears were rolling down her cheeks now and, as she dabbed them with her handkerchief, she murmured in a reproachful tone to which she tried to lend a certain playfulness:

"Look, you've made me cry—already! It's silly of me."

Jacques felt a rush of hatred stirring within him. Thus he had always been; even in childhood there had always smouldered deep in his heart a secret fire of anger—like the molten core, he pictured it, that seethes in the bowels of the earth—and now and again from that fiery underworld of rancour there would surge a jet of red-hot lava that nothing could hold back.

"Very well! Have it your own way!" he shouted furiously. "Say what you have to say. Yes, I too would rather get it over!"

She was so unprepared for such brutality, and the question she had meant to put was so completely answered by his outburst, that she sank back onto the cushions, with parted, quivering lips, as if he had actually struck her. With a weak gesture of self-defence she held her hand before her face, murmuring: "Oh, Jacquot!" in so heart-broken a voice that Jacques swung round at once.

Dazed, forgetting in a flash all he had been feeling, he made an abrupt transition from the cruellest malevolence to a sudden, impulsive, yet self-deceptive mood of tenderness. Running to the sofa, he seated himself at Gise's side, and strained the sob-racked body to his breast, murmuring in a broken voice: "Poor little girl! My poor little Gise!" Close under his eyes he saw the velvety texture of her skin; the dark, translucent rings round the tear-stained eyes made them seem sadder, gentler still. But suddenly, overwhelmingly, keener indeed than ever, his lucidity returned and even as he bent above her, breathing in the fragrance of her hair, he perceived as clearly as if he were looking at a stranger, the pitfalls of this purely physical attraction.

Thus far—and no further! Once already, on the treacherous descent of pity, he had saved them both from disaster by putting on the brakes in time—and leaving home. And, now he came to think of it, did not the mere fact that at such a moment he could take so detached a view, so clearly see the miserable risks they ran—did this not prove the superficiality of his feelings for her? And, also, did it not expose the hollowness of the self-deception which might play havoc with their lives?

No great heroism was needed on his part to fight down his emotion and resist the brief temptation to kiss the forehead that his lips were brushing. He contented himself with pressing affectionately to his shoulder, and gently stroking with his fingertips, the warm, silken cheek still moist with tears.

With a wildly thudding heart Gise nestled in his arms, eagerly proffering her cheek and neck to his caress. She made no movement, but she was on the brink of letting herself sink to the floor, clasping Jacques's knees in humble ecstasy.

But he was conscious of his pulses steadily slowing down to normal as he regained an equanimity that almost shocked him. For a moment he actually felt annoyed with Gise for rousing in him such sordid, commonplace lust, and even despised her a little for it. Suddenly like a blaze of lightning, dazzling and dying down at once, the picture of Jenny flashed across his mind, jarring it into renewed activity. Then, with another breathless shift of mood, he began feeling ashamed of himself. How far, far better was Gise than he! That staunch devotion, like a steady flame, which after three years' absence still burned bright as ever; that reckless self-abandonment to the dictates of her love, to the tragic destiny which she accepted, cost what it might, unflinchingly—these assuredly were stronger and purer emotions than any he could muster. . . . And now he found he could review it all with a sort of detachment, a frozen calm enabling him at last, without the slightest risk, to lavish tenderness on Gise.

While his mind drifted thus from thought to thought, Gise was stubbornly intent on one thing, and one only. Set wholly on her love, her mind was so keyed up, so sensitive to everything that emanated from him, that suddenly, though Jacques had not said a word, and though he was still caressing the little cheek that nestled against his hand, she *knew*. If only by the casual, vaguely affectionate way his fingers strayed from her lips to her forehead and back again, intuitively she had guessed all—that the link between them was snapped for ever, that for him she . . . did not count!

Desperately, like one who verifies something proved to the hilt "just to make sure," finally, indubitably—she slipped abruptly from his arms and gazed into his eyes. Taken unawares, he had no time to veil their hardness; and now everything was clear to her, clear beyond question. All was over, irremediably.

None the less, she felt a childish dread of hearing it said aloud. The truth was horrible enough; that it should crystallize into cruel words, words they would be fated never to forget, was more than she could bear. She summoned up what little strength remained to her, so that Jacques should not suspect the havoc of her hopes. She even found the courage to move further away from him, to smile, to murmur with a weak little flutter of her hand:

"What an age it is since I last came to this room!"

Actually she had a clear memory of the last time she had sat where she was now, on the sofa—beside Antoine. That day she had fancied she knew what sorrow was; had thought that Jacques's absence and her heart-racking anxiety about him were trials hardly to be borne. Yet what were they compared with what she now must bear? In those days all that was needed was for her to close her eyes—and there was Jacques, responsive to her call, exactly as her heart would have him be. And now—now, when he had come back, she was learning for the first time what it really meant to have to live without him. "How is it possible?" she asked herself. "How can this have happened?" And her anguish grew so urgent that she had to keep her eyes closed for some moments.

Jacques had got up, to turn on the light. After going to the window to draw the curtains, he did not come back to the sofa.

"Sure you haven't caught cold here?" he asked, noticing that she was shivering.

"Well, it isn't very warm in this room." She snatched at the pretext. "I think I'd better go upstairs."

The sound of their voices, breaking the silence, roused her a little and steadied her nerves.

The staying power she got from the pretence of easy conversation was precarious, yet her need to keep the truth at bay was so pressing that she went on talking by fits and starts, throwing out phrases as the cuttlefish projects its ink-cloud. And Jacques played up to her pretence, with an approving smile, secretly pleased, perhaps, that to-night again he could evade an explanation.

With an effort she had risen, and they stood gazing at each other. They were of almost the same height. "Never, never will I be able to live without him," she was thinking. That was a way to avoid confronting another thought, the cruellest of all: "*He* is so strong; how easily he can live without me!" Then suddenly it dawned on her that Jacques, with the callous unconcern of a man, was choosing the way of life he wanted, whereas she, she had no power to choose, or to give the least deflection to her own course.

She blurted out a question, trying to adopt a casual tone:

"When are you going away again?"

He kept hold on himself, took a few paces absent-mindedly, then half turned towards her.

"How about you—when are *you* going?"

How could he have made it clearer that he intended to leave, and assumed that Gise, too, would not be staying in France?

With a faint shrug of her shoulders, for the last time she forced a weak smile to her lips—she was becoming quite adept at it!—then opened the door and walked out.

He made no effort to keep her, but as his eyes followed her receding form, they had a sudden gleam of pure affection. If only, without risk, he could have taken her into his arms, and shielded her! Against what? Against herself, against himself. Against the pain he was causing her (though he was only vaguely aware of it), and the pain he was yet to bring upon her—that he could not do otherwise than bring on her.

His hands thrust in his pockets, his feet planted well apart, he remained standing in the centre of the untidy room. Flaunting its motley labels, the suitcase gaped up at him, and he pictured himself back at Ancona, or perhaps Trieste, in the dimly lit steerage of a mail-steamer, jostled by emigrants cursing one another in unfamiliar tongues. Then an infernal din broke out at the bows, the sound of metal rasping upon metal drowned the angry voices; the anchor was coming up. The swaying increased and everywhere there was a sudden hush, as the ship began to forge ahead into the black night.

Jacques felt his breast heave; that almost morbid craving for some undetermined struggle, some gesture of creation and fulfilment of his being, was balked by everything about him: this house, the dead man upstairs, Gise—all the past with its snares and shackles.

His jaws clenched stubbornly. "I must get away from all this," he muttered. "I must clear out."

Entering the elevator, Gise sank onto the seat. She wondered if she would have the strength to reach her room.

Yes, all was over now; that explanation on which, in spite of all, she had set such hope, had been attained, accomplished. "Jacques, we've got to have a talk," and his retort, "Yes, I too would rather get it over." Then the two questions, both unanswered: "When are you going away again?" and: "How about you?" Four little phrases, echoing in her baffled brain . . . and now . . . what was she to do?

As she re-entered the huge, silent flat where in the background two nuns kept vigil at a bier, where nothing now was left of the fond dreams she had been dreaming in it half an hour before, a spasm of such distress shot through her heart that the dread of being alone proved more insistent even than her weakness and desire for rest. Instead of hastening to her own room, she entered her aunt's.

Mademoiselle had returned and was sitting at her usual place, in front of her desk littered with bills and samples, pamphlets and medicine-bottles. Recognizing Gise's footstep, she turned stiffly round.

"Ah, there you are? As a matter of fact . . ."

Gise stumbled towards her, kissed the ivory-yellow forehead between the snowy braids and, too big now to shelter in the little old lady's arms, dropped at her knees, like a disconsolate child.

"As a matter of fact, Gise, I meant to ask you: haven't they told you anything about the house-cleaning, disinfecting the flat, you know? No? But there's a law on the subject. Yes, ask Clotilde. I wish you'd speak to Antoine about it. The first thing is to call in the Health Department. Then, to make quite sure, we'll get some fumigator from the druggist's. Clotilde knows how; you have to stop up the doors and windows. You must give us a hand that day."

"But, Auntie," Gise murmured, her eyes filling again with tears, "I'll have to be going back. They're expecting me—over there."

"Over there? After what's happened? You're going to leave me by myself?" The words came out in jerks, timed to the spasmodic shaking of her head. "Can't you see the state I'm in? I'm seventy-five, Gise."

Yes, Gise was thinking, I shall go away. Jacques too. All will be as it was before—but with no hope left. Without a single ray of hope. . . . Her temples were throbbing, her thoughts in turmoil. Jacques had become incomprehensible to her; and it was the keenest pang of all that he, whom she had thought she understood so well all the time he was away, should now be a sealed book to her. How had it come about?

What should she do? she wondered. Enter a convent? There she would have peace, the rest that Jesus gives the heavy-laden. But first she must renounce the world. Could she make that great renunciation?

Giving way at last, she burst into tears and, drawing herself up, clasped her aunt tightly in her arms.

"Oh, it isn't fair," she sobbed. "It's not fair, Auntie—all that!"

Alarmed and somewhat vexed, Mademoiselle began to remonstrate. "What isn't fair? I don't follow. . . . What on earth are you talking about, Gise?"

Gise sank back to the floor, helplessly. Now and again, groping for some support, a friendly presence, she rubbed her cheek on the rough fabric under which jutted the sharp knees of Mademoiselle, whose voice went droning on indignantly, while the old head wagged this way and that.

"Imagine being left alone at seventy-five! Really, considering the state I'm in . . . !"

XII

THE little chapel at the Crouy reformatory was full to overflowing. Raw though the weather was, the doors stood wide open, and in the courtyard, where the snow had been trampled by the crowd into a morass of slime, the two hundred and eighty-six young inmates stood, bare-headed and unmoving, in serried files. The brass badges on their belts gleamed above their brand-new dungarees, and round them were stationed the guards in full uniform with revolver-holsters dangling at their hips.

The mass had been said by the Abbé Vécard; but the Bishop of Beauvais, who had a sepulchral bass voice, was in attendance to pronounce the final intercession.

The responses floated up and hovered for a moment in the throbbing silence of the little nave.

"*Pater noster . . .*"

"*Requiem æternam dona ei, Domine.*"

"*Requiescat in pace.*"

"*Amen.*"

Then the instrumental sextet posted on the dais struck up the closing voluntary.

From the start Antoine had been following the ceremony with keen interest. "It's odd," he thought, "the mania they have for playing Chopin's 'Funeral March' on these occasions; there's very little that's funereal about it. The sadness doesn't last; at once it strays off into a mood of joy—that craving for illusion, I suppose. Like the way consumptives have of thinking about their death light-heartedly." He remembered the last days of a young fellow named Derny—a composer, too—whom he had seen at the hospital. "Most people sentimentalize it; they fancy they're watching the ecstasy of a dying man who sees heaven opening to him. We, of course, know better; it's

just a characteristic of the disease, almost a symptom of the lesions—
like the high temperature."

In any case he had to admit that a mood of tragic grief would have
been out of keeping with the present funeral, which was invested
with the utmost pomp and circumstance procurable. He was—with
the exception of M. Chasle, who, the moment he arrived, had slipped
away into the crowd—the only member of the household present. Having attended the service in Paris, the cousins and distant relatives did
not deem it necessary to make the pilgrimage to Crouy in such glacial
weather. The congregation consisted exclusively of the dead man's
colleagues, and delegates from benevolent societies. "Deputies," Antoine smiled, "like me; I'm deputizing for the family." And he added
to himself, with a touch of melancholy: "Not a single friend." What
he meant was: "No one who's a personal friend of *mine*. And for a
very good reason." Since his father's death he had come to realize
that he had no personal friends. With the possible exception of
Daniel, he had had only colleagues or companions. It was his own
fault; he had lived so long without a thought for others. Indeed, till
quite recently he had been inclined to pride himself on his detachment. Now, he discovered, it was beginning to pall on him.

He watched with interest the movements of the officiating priests.
"What next?" he wondered when he saw them retreat into the sacristy.

They were waiting for the undertaker's men to shift the bier onto
the catafalque erected at the entrance to the chapel. Then once more
the master of ceremonies came and bowed to Antoine with the prim
elegance of a rather jaded ballet-master, ringing on the flags his ebony
wand. The cortège formed again, moved down the aisle, and halted
in the chapel porch, to listen to the speeches. Dignified, holding himself erect, Antoine complied with the requirements of the ceremonial
willingly enough; his consciousness of being the focus of many eyes
stimulated him to play his part. The mourners massed on either side
strained forward to see, following Oscar Thibault's son, the Subprefect,
the Mayor of Compiègne, the Crouy Town Council in full force and
frock-coats, a young bishop *in partibus* "deputizing" for His Grace the
Archbishop of Paris, and, amongst other eminent figures whose names

were whispered round, some members of the Institute who had come unofficially to render homage to their dead colleague.

A powerful voice subdued the whispers of the crowd:

"Gentlemen, in the name of the Institute of France, I have the melancholy honour . . ."

The orator was Loudun-Costard, the jurist, a fat, bald-headed man, in a tight-fitting fur-lined coat with a fur collar. On him devolved the duty of sketching the dead man's career.

"With unflagging zeal he pursued his studies at Rouen College, near his father's factory. . . ."

Antoine remembered the photograph of a schoolboy, his arm resting on a pile of prizes. "So that was Father's boyhood," he mused. "Who on earth could have foreseen then . . . ? No, one never gets to understand a man till he is dead. While he's alive, the sum of the things he still may do is a wholly unknown factor, and it throws out every estimate. At last death comes and fixes every aspect once for all; it's as if the real man came clear at last of the vague cloud of might-have-beens. You can see him in the round, take a back view, form a general opinion. That, by the way, is what I've always said," he added, with an inward smile; "you can never make an absolutely certain diagnosis till you have your patient on the post-mortem table."

He was well aware that he had not yet done with musing on his father's life and character; and that, for a long while yet, he was to derive from such musings interesting and instructive sidelights on his own psychology.

"When he was invited to bear a part in the labours of our eminent fraternity, it was not only his loftiness of purpose, his philanthropic zeal, and his vast energy that we invoked; nor was it only that fine, unswerving probity, which made him an outstanding figure of our generation . . ."

"Yet another 'deputy,'" Antoine smiled to himself, as he listened to the flood of eulogy. But he was not insensitive to it; indeed he felt inclined to think that he had habitually underrated his father's true worth.

". . . and, gentlemen, let us bow our heads in homage to that noble heart, which to its last beat throbbed ever and alone for just and generous causes."

The "immortal" had finished. He folded his sheaf of notes, hastily thrust his hands back into the fur-lined pockets, and modestly retreated to his place amongst his fellow-delegates.

"The President of the Joint Committee of Catholic Charities in the Diocese of Paris," the ballet-master announced in a discreet voice.

A venerable old man, armed with an ear-trumpet and supported by a footman nearly as ancient and infirm as his master, tottered up to the catafalque. The sole survivor of a group of young men from Rouen who had come in the same year as M. Thibault to study law in Paris, not only was he the dead man's successor to the presidency of the charity organization, but he had been his lifelong friend. He was stone-deaf and had been thus afflicted for very many years; indeed since earliest childhood Antoine and Jacques had always referred to him as "Old Door-Nail."

"Gentlemen, in the feelings which unite us here today, there should be something more than grief for our great loss," the old man piped. The high-pitched, quavering voice brought back to Antoine's memory Old Door-Nail's visit, two days previously, to the death-chamber. Then, too, he had tottered forward on the same servant's feeble arm. "Orestes," he had squeaked, on entering the room, "wishes to give Pylades a last token of his friendship." He had been led up to the corpse and his bleary, red-rimmed eyes had pored over it for a long while; then, straightening up, he had gulped down a sob and yelled at Antoine as if they had been thirty yards apart: "Ah, if you only knew what a handsome lad he was, at twenty!" At the time Antoine had been genuinely moved by the old man's remark. "How quickly one's mood changes!" he thought. Recalling it today, he felt merely amused.

"What was the secret of his forcefulness?" the old man declaimed. "To what did Oscar Thibault owe his unfailingly well-balanced judgment, his unruffled optimism, that self-confidence of his which made child's play of every obstacle and assured his triumph in the most arduous undertakings? . . . Is it not, gentlemen, one of the undying glories of the Catholic faith that it gives the world such men as he was and such lives as his?"

"The old man's right," Antoine had to admit to himself. "His faith was a tremendous asset for Father. Thanks to it he never knew what it can mean to be held up by scruples or an exaggerated sense of responsibility, or mistrust of oneself, and all the rest of it. A man with faith can always drive straight ahead." He even fell to wondering if people like his father and Old Door-Nail had not chosen, when all was said and done, one of the securest paths a man may follow from the cradle to the grave. "From the social point of view," Antoine reflected, "they are amongst the few who best succeed in reconciling their lives as individuals with the life of the community. I suppose they are obeying a human species of the instinct that brings about the ant-hill and the hive. And that is no small thing. Even those characteristics which I found so detestable in my father—his pride, his thirst for honours, his love of playing the despot—it's thanks to them, I must admit, that he got far more out of himself, as a social value, than if he'd been humble, easy-going, and considerate. . . ."

"Gentlemen, for this glorious fighter in the good cause our tributes are superfluous today." The old man's voice was growing hoarse. "Never have the times been so critical. Let us not linger burying our dead, but let us replenish our strength at the same holy fountainhead, and waste no time. . . ." Carried away by the sincerity of his emotion, he tried to take a step forward, swayed, and had to clutch his servant's wavering arm. But this did not prevent him from ending his speech with a shrill: "Let us waste no time, gentlemen, in returning to our posts, to fight the good fight side by side!"

"The Chairman of the Child Welfare Society," announced the ballet-master.

The little man with the small white beard who now moved uncomfortably forward seemed literally frozen to the marrow. His teeth were chattering, his face was blue with cold. He cut a pathetic figure, congealed and wizened by the glacial air.

"I am gripped—am gripped"—he seemed to be making superhuman efforts to part his frost-bound lips—"by a profound and melancholy emotion."

"Those children there will catch their death of cold," Antoine grumbled to himself. He was getting impatient; he too felt the cold creeping up his limbs, and his stiff shirt-front like a slab of ice under his overcoat.

"He went his way among us doing good. Well might that be his glorious epitaph: *Pertransiit benefaciendo*.

"He leaves us, gentlemen, laden with tokens of our high esteem."

"Esteem!" Antoine reflected. "He's said it! But whose esteem?" He reviewed with an indulgent eye the phalanx of old gentlemen— all decrepit, shivering in their shoes, eyes watering with the cold, each putting his best ear forward to hear the speaker and greeting every panegyric with demonstrations of approval. Not one of them but was thinking of his own funeral, envious of these "tokens of esteem" which they were lavishing today so copiously on their late lamented colleague.

The little man with the beard was short-winded; very soon he made way for his successor.

The new speaker was a handsome old man with pale, remote, steely eyes; a retired vice-admiral, who had taken to philanthropy. His exordium roused Antoine's dissent.

"Oscar Thibault was gifted with a shrewd, clear-sighted judgment which always enabled him, in the lamentable controversies of our troubled times, to see which side was in the right, and to play his part in building up the future."

Antoine registered a tacit protest. "No, that's untrue. Father wore blinkers, and went through life without ever seeing more of it than the hedgerows of the narrow path that he had chosen. One might almost call him an incarnation of the partisan mentality. From his schooldays up, he never made an attempt to think for himself, to take an independent view, to discover, to understand. Always he followed the beaten track. He had donned a livery, and wore it till the end."

"Could anyone desire a finer career?" the vice-admiral continued. "Was not a life like his, gentlemen, the model . . . ?"

"Yes, a livery." Once again Antoine reviewed the attentive audience with a keen glance. "In fact, they're all exactly alike. Interchangeable. Describe one, and you've hit them all off. Shivering, doddering, myopic old men, who're scared of everything: scared of thinking, scared of progress, of whatever might take arms against their stronghold . . . Steady, now! I'm getting eloquent! Still, 'stronghold' hits it off quite well. They've the mentality of a beleaguered garrison who're always checking up their numbers, to make sure they're in full force behind their ramparts."

He was feeling more and more ill at ease, and had ceased listening to the orator. However, the sweeping gesture that accompanied the peroration caught his eye.

"Farewell, beloved President. A last farewell. So long as those who saw you at your noble task shall walk the earth . . ."

The superintendent of the reformatory stepped forth from the group of speakers. He was the last, and he, at least, seemed to have had a fairly close view of the man whose funeral oration he was going to pronounce.

"Our lamented Founder had not the habit of the specious, flattering phrase, when voicing an opinion. No; always eager to get down to acts, he had the courage to disdain those polite subterfuges that lead nowhere. . . ."

Antoine pricked up his ears; this sounded promising.

"A blunt, forthright manner disguised his natural kindliness, and perhaps added to its efficacy. His uncompromising stands at our council meetings were an expression of his energy, his steadfastness in well-doing, and the high standard he set himself as our President. For him all was a struggle, a struggle that quickly ended in a victory. Everything he said struck home at once; the word, for him, was a keen sword; sometimes, in fact, a sledge-hammer!"

It flashed on Antoine that his father had been a force, and he was surprised to find himself thinking with already well-assured conviction: "Yes, Father might easily have been something more—might have been a really great man."

The superintendent was pointing now towards the rows of boys alined between their guards. All eyes turned to the young criminals, · standing there motionless, blue with cold.

"These juvenile delinquents, doomed from the cradle to fall on evil ways, these lads to whom Oscar Thibault stretched out a helping hand, these unhappy victims of an, alas, very far from perfect social order, are here today, gentlemen, to bear witness to their undying gratitude, and to mourn with us the benefactor who has been taken from them."

"Yes, indeed, Father had all the making of greatness; what might he not have been?" Behind Antoine's insistence lurked a vague hope; an agreeable thought was hovering in the background of his mind. If nature had failed, in his father's case, to endow the robust Thibault stock with its great man . . . ! Why not? With a thrill he pictured the future opening up before him. . . .

The pall-bearers were shouldering the coffin. Everyone was eager to be gone. The master of ceremonies bowed again, clanging his black wand on the flagstones. Bare-headed, impassive, but inwardly exultant, Antoine took his place at the head of the procession bringing the earthly remains of Oscar Thibault to the grave. *Quia pulvis es, et in pulverem reverteris.* . . .

XIII

JACQUES had spent the whole of that morning in his room and, though he had the ground-floor flat to himself—Léon having naturally enough desired to attend the funeral—had double-locked his door. As a precaution against himself, to make sure that when the mourners were filing out he would not peep to see if certain well-remembered figures were amongst them, he had kept the shutters tightly closed. Stretched on his bed, his hands in his pockets, his eyes fixed vaguely on the pale glow of the ceiling-lamp, he was whistling under his breath.

Towards one o'clock, feeling bored and hungry, he decided to get up. The funeral service in the reformatory chapel must by now, he judged, be well under way. Upstairs, Mademoiselle and Gise must have been back some time from the mass at Saint Thomas Aquinas's, and had presumably begun lunch without him. In any case he was quite decided not to see anyone all day. He would find something to eat, no doubt, in the pantry.

As he crossed the hall on his way to the kitchen, his eyes fell on the newspapers and letters that had been slipped under the front door. And suddenly his heart missed a beat, he bent forward. Yes, that was Daniel's writing: "M. Jacques Thibault."

His hands were trembling so violently that he could hardly open the envelope.

My dear Jacques,
Antoine's letter reached me yesterday evening . . .

Across his mood of black depression the friendly greeting struck like a sword-thrust at his heart and he savagely crumpled the letter tighter and tighter, crushing it in his clenched fist. Then angrily he flung back into his room and locked the door again, without the faintest memory of why he had gone out. After some aimless steps he halted under the lamp, unfolded the crumpled sheet and gazed at it with unsteady eyes, making no effort to read the words till the name he was looking for flashed across his vision.

. . . during these last years, Jenny has found the winters in Paris rather trying; both of them left for the South of France a month ago.

Again, as feverishly as before, he screwed up the letter into a ball and this time thrust it into his pocket.

For a while he felt shaken, dazed; then, of a sudden, infinitely relieved.

A minute later—as though the perusal of those lines had changed his decision—he ran to Antoine's desk and opened the time-table. Ever since he had got up, his mind had been on Crouy. If he started at once he could catch the two o'clock express. He would reach Crouy by daylight, but after the funeral was over and all the mourners had

left by the return train; there would be no risk of running across
anyone he knew. He could go straight to the graveyard and return
at once. "Both of them left for the South of France a month ago."

But he had not foreseen the effort of the journey on his already
frayed nerves. He found it impossible to sit still. Luckily the train
was empty; not only was he alone in the compartment, but in the
whole car there was only one other passenger, an elderly lady in
black. Jacques fell to walking up and down the corridor, like a wild
beast pacing its cage. At first he did not realize that his curious behaviour had attracted the notice of his fellow-traveller, perhaps somewhat alarmed her. Furtively he examined her; never could he encounter anyone the least exceptional in look or manner without
pausing a moment to take stock of the specimen of humanity that
chance had thrown across his path.

It struck him that the woman had an attractive face. The cheeks
were pale and ravaged by the years, but in her eyes there glowed a
warm vitality, clouded now with grief, as if her mind were brooding
on the past. A look of gentle candour and repose, finely set off by her
snow-white hair. She was tastefully dressed in black. Jacques pictured her as an old lady of the provincial middle class, who lived by
herself, in quiet, dignified surroundings, and was now on her way
back to her home, at Compiègne, perhaps, or at Saint-Quentin. She
had no luggage. On the seat beside her lay a large bunch of Parma
violets, the stems of which were sheathed in tissue-paper.

Jacques's heart was thudding as he alighted on the Crouy platform. It was deserted. The frosty air was crystal clear.

As he left the station and saw the countryside, a spasm of remem-
brance gripped his heart. Scorning the short-cut and the highroad
alike, he took the road that led by the Calvary—a detour of nearly
two miles.

Fierce gusts of wind came roaring up from all four quarters turn
by turn, scouring the snow-bound waste with sudden, icy blasts.
Somewhere behind the dank, grey cloudwrack a hidden sun was
sinking. Jacques walked on rapidly. Though he had eaten nothing

since the early morning, he was no longer feeling hungry; the eager air was going to his head. He recognized every turning, every hillock, every thicket. In the distance, at the junction of three roads, the great cross loomed up, ringed by its clump of leafless trees. That track yonder led to Vaumesnil, and this roadmenders' cabin—how often during his daily walks with his attendant he had sheltered in it from the rain! On two or three occasions with Léon; once at least in Arthur's time. How well he recalled Arthur's blunt features and pale eyes, the typical face of a decent Lorraine peasant, one would have thought, till suddenly that evil leer traversed it!

Crueler even than the glacial wind that flayed his cheeks and numbed his fingertips, memory lashed his mind. He had altogether ceased thinking about his father.

Greyly the brief winter day was hastening to its close, but there was still some light left.

On reaching Crouy, he all but took, as in the past, the turning that led off into an obscure back-street—as if he were still afraid of being pointed at by the village children. Yet who would recognize him now, after eight years? Anyway, there was no one in the street, and all the doors were shut. The life of the village seemed congealed by the cold, though smoke was pouring up from every chimney against the greyness of the sky. The inn came into view flanked by its flight of steps, its signboard creaking in the wind.

Nothing had changed—not even the snow melting upon the chalky road into a grey slush—almost he fancied he was trudging through it still in his heavy "regulation" shoes. That was the inn where, to cut short their walk, old Léon used to imprison him in an empty wash-house, so as to be free to play cards with his cronies in the tap-room. Emerging from the side-street, a beshawled girl in galoshes slip-slopped up the steps. A new servant? he wondered. Or perhaps she was the proprietor's daughter, the child who always used to run away at the sight of the "little jailbird." Before entering the inn the girl cast a furtive glance at the young man walking by. Jacques quickened his pace.

Now he was at the end of the village. Once he had left the last houses behind him, he saw, ringed round by its lofty walls, alone, aloof, in the midst of the grey plain, the huge, familiar building, snow-capped, pocked with rows of black-barred windows. He quivered in every limb. Nothing had changed. Nothing. The treeless avenue leading to the entrance-gate was now a river of mud. Probably in the wintry twilight a stranger to the place might have had trouble in deciphering the gold inscription on the front. But for Jacques the proud device on which his eyes were fixed was plain to read:

The Oscar Thibault Foundation

Then only he remembered that the illustrious founder was no more, that the ruts in the drive had been made by the carriages of the funeral procession, that it was for his father's sake he had made the pilgrimage to this place. With a sense of relief at being able to turn his back on these forbidding precincts, he turned and walked in the direction of the two big evergreens flanking the cemetery gate. Usually closed, tonight the iron gate stood open. Wheel-marks showed the path to take. Jacques moved mechanically towards a mound of wreaths wilting in the cold and looking more like a refuse dump than a spread of flowers.

In front of the grave a large bunch of Parma violets, their stems wrapped in tissue-paper, lay all alone upon the snow; presumably it had been placed there after the other flowers.

"That's curious!" Jacques mused, but gave no further thought to the coincidence.

And suddenly, bending above the fresh-turned soil, he had a vision of the dead body lying beneath the sodden turf—exactly as he had seen it at that tragic, ludicrous instant when the undertaker, after a courteous gesture for the family, had drawn the winding-sheet over the face that death had changed already.

" 'Then clinkety and clankety, Along the lanes we'll go!' " Like a bright gash of pain, the foolish jingle rang across his mind; a lump came to his throat.

Ever since he had left Lausanne, he had let himself be hustled blindly on, hour after hour, by the sheer force of events. Now, suddenly, there welled up in his heart a long-forgotten, puerile, inordinate affection, as irrational as irrefutable, bitter with a sense of self-reproach and shame. Now at last he understood why he had come here. He remembered his fits of anger, the moods of scorn and hatred, and the lust for vengeance that had slowly poisoned all his youth. Trivial details that had passed out of memory sped back, like boomerangs, to wound him on the raw. And, for a while, all grievances discarded, restored to filial instinct, he wept on his father's grave. For a brief while he was one of the two persons, unknown to each other, who on natural impulse, keeping aloof from the official rites, had felt a need to come that day and pay the dead the tribute of their grief; one of the only two beings on earth who had sincerely wept for M. Thibault.

But he was too well schooled in facing facts squarely not to see almost at once that such sorrow and grief were overdone. He was perfectly aware that, could his father come back to life, he would loathe and shun him as before. And yet he lingered beside the grave, yielding to a mood of vague sentimentality. He regretted—he knew not what; perhaps what might have been. He even let his imagination picture for a moment an affectionate, generous, understanding father, so as to have the thrill of regretting that he had not been the devoted son such a father merited.

Then, with a shrug of his shoulders, he turned and left the graveyard.

The village seemed a little more animated now. Windows were lighting up. The peasants were coming back, their day's work over.

To avoid passing the houses, he took the road going to Moulin-Neuf, instead of that which led directly to the station, and was almost at once in open country.

He was no longer alone. Something persistent and insidious as an odour had dogged his steps and clung about him, creeping into his each successive thought. It moved beside him in the silence of the plain, across the haze of broken lights that glimmered on the snow and the air grown milder in a brief lull of the gale. Unresisting, he surrendered himself to death's obsession; indeed there was an almost sensual thrill in the vividness with which he now perceived the vanity of life, the futility of all endeavour. What was the use of striving? What was there to hope for? All life is vain, unprofitable. For once we realize death's meaning, nothing, nothing whatever is worth the effort.

He felt that what lay deepest in him was being undermined. Gone was all ambition, all desire to be a leader, to achieve an aim in life. And now it seemed to him that never could he shake off that haunting presence, never regain any sort of peace of mind. He had lost even the impulse to believe that, short as is life's span, a man may yet find time to put something of himself out of the destroyer's reach; that sometimes it is given him to raise a fragment of his dream above the flood that sweeps him down, so that something authentically his may remain floating on the waters that have closed over his head.

He walked straight ahead with rapid, jerky strides like a fugitive hugging to his breast some fragile last possession. Ah, to escape from everything! Not only from the hydra-headed social organism; not only from family and friends and love; not only from himself and from the tyrannies of atavism and habit—but to be rid of something latent and inherent in himself, that absurd vital instinct which makes the sorriest wrecks of humanity still cling to life. Once again, as the supreme and logical solution, the idea of a voluntary eclipse, this time for good and all—of suicide—hovered in his mind. And suddenly there rose before him the serene beauty of his dead father's face.

"We shall have rest, Uncle Vanya, We shall have rest."

Then his attention was caught, involuntarily, by the rumble of farm-carts coming towards him; he could see their lamps swaying as they jolted on the ruts, and hear the shouts and laughter of the drivers. He could not face the thought of meeting people. Without a moment's hesitation he jumped the snow-filled ditch bordering the road, stumbled across a ploughed field frozen hard as iron, came on a little wood, and plunged into its darkness. Viciously the thorny undergrowth lashed his face; frozen leaves crackled underfoot. He had deliberately thrust his hands into his pockets, finding a curious relish in the stinging blows across his cheeks, as in a frenzy of escape he forced his way through the dense underbrush. He had no notion where he was going; his one idea was to escape from men, from their ways and highways—from everything.

There was no more than a narrow strip of woodland and he was soon across it. Again he saw in front of him the white plain, ribboned by a road, glimmering under the black sky and, straight ahead, looming upon the skyline, the reformatory, with a row of lighted windows along the floors reserved for class-rooms and the workshops. As he gazed at it a fantastic day-dream, vivid as a cinema film, took form in his imagination: he saw himself climbing the low wall of the shed, scrambling up the roof to the storeroom window, breaking the pane, and flinging in a wisp of blazing straw. The pile of spare beds and bedding flared up like a torch; in a trice the fire had spread through the office building to his old cell, devouring everything in it —his bed, table, blackboard, chair, all went up in flames.

He ran his fingers over his scratched cheeks. With a rush of bitterness he realized his impotence—the folly of such dreams.

Resolutely he turned his back on the reformatory, on the graveyard, on his past, and began walking rapidly towards the station.

He had missed the five-forty by a few minutes. There was nothing for it but to wait for the slow train at seven. The waiting-room was like an ice-box and smelled intolerably musty.

For a long while he paced the empty platform, with his cheeks smarting. In his pocket he gripped the crumpled letter from Daniel; he had vowed to himself not to look at it again.

A lamp with a reflector faced the station clock; he went up to it, and, leaning against the wall, fished the crumpled sheets out of his pocket.

My dear Jacques,

Antoine's letter reached me yesterday evening, and I couldn't sleep a wink. If somehow I could have managed to make a dash to you last night, and see you for just five minutes large as life, I wouldn't have hesitated to take the risk and climb the barrack wall; yes, I'd have done anything to see my oldest, dearest friend again. In these N.C.O.'s lodgings which I share with two other snoring stalwarts, all through the night I stared up at the whitewashed ceiling green with moonlight, and I watched a pageant of our boyhood streaming past—all those wonderful hours we spent together, you and I, at school, and afterwards. You're like a second self to me, Jacques, old pal; I can't imagine how I got on all these years without my second self! And you can be sure—never for a moment did I doubt your friendship. I've just got back from morning drill, and I'm writing to you at once, though I've only Antoine's little note to go on, without even stopping to wonder how you'll take this letter from me, without yet knowing for what earthly reason you maintained for those long years that silence of the grave. How I missed you during those years, and how I miss you now! Most of all, perhaps, I missed you before I was called up for service, when I was at home. Have you any idea of what you meant to me? I wonder. That energy you inspired in me, all the fine things that were latent in me as possibilities only—and which you brought out. Without you, without your friendship, I could never have . . .

Jacques's hands were trembling as he held the crumpled pages near his eyes; in the dim light, across a mist of tears, he could hardly decipher the affectionate words.

Just above his head an electric bell, piercing as an auger, was shrilling incessantly.

That's something I don't suppose you ever suspected; in those days I was too vain to admit it, especially to you. And then, when I learned you'd vanished, I simply couldn't imagine what had happened, couldn't believe my ears. I was terribly distressed—most of all by the mystery surrounding it all. Perhaps some day I'll understand. But in my worst moments of anxiety—even of resentment—never once did the idea enter my head, that (assuming you were alive) your feelings for me had changed. And now too, as you see, I don't feel any doubt about them. . . .

Had to stop. Some tiresome routine work came along. I've taken refuge in a corner of the canteen, though it's out of bounds at this hour. I don't suppose you've the faintest notion what it's like, this world of barracks and parades I was pitchforked into thirteen months ago. . . . But I'm not writing to you to describe a conscript's life!

The appalling thing, you know, is this feeling that one's lost touch; I don't know how or what to write to you. Of course you can guess the swarm of questions at the tip of my pen! . . . But what's the use? Still, I do hope you won't mind answering one of them, because it's something I have so terribly at heart. It's this: Am I going to see you again? Is the nightmare over, and have you really come back to us? Or—will you be taking wing again? Look here, Jacques, as I'm pretty sure you'll read this letter anyhow, and as it may be the only chance I'll have of getting in touch with you, please listen to this appeal! I'm prepared to understand and to put up with everything you choose, but I beg you, whatever your future plans may be, don't vanish again so utterly from my life. I need you. If you only knew how proud I am of you, the great things I expect of you, and all that my pride in you can mean to me! Yes, I'm ready to accept all your terms. If you insist on my not knowing your address, on there being no exchange between us, on my never writing—even if you tell me not to pass on to anybody, not even to poor old Antoine, the news I get from you—well, I agree to everything, I pledge myself blindly to obey. Only, please do send me a line now and then, just to show you are alive and sometimes think of me. I'm sorry for those last words—take them as struck out—for I know, I'm certain that you think of me. (That, too, I've never doubted. Never did it cross my mind that, were you alive, you had ceased thinking about me, about our friendship.)

I can't get my ideas straight; I just jot down whatever comes into my head. But that doesn't matter; just to write to you is such a relief after that appalling silence!

I ought to tell you about myself, so that, when you think of me, you can think of me as I am now, and not only as I was when you left us. Perhaps Antoine will tell you. He knows me quite well; we saw a lot of each other after you went away. But I don't know where to begin. There's so much slack to take up, you see; it seems almost hopeless. And then— after all, you know the way I'm built; I keep moving, I live for the *here* and *now*, I can't look back. This military service cut across my work just when it seemed that I was getting a glimpse of really vital things about myself and about my art—the very things I'd been groping for all my life. Still, I don't regret anything; this experience of army life is something new and very thrilling. It's a great test and a great experience, especially now that I've men under my command. But it's idiotic talking to you about that today.

The one thing that really worries me is having been away from Mother for a year. Especially as I know this separation weighs terribly on both of them. I'm sorry to have to tell you Jenny's health is not all it might be; in fact, we've been quite alarmed about it on several occasions. By "we" I mean, really, *I*, for you know how Mother is, she never will believe that things can turn out badly. Still, even Mother has had to recognize that, during these last years, Jenny has found the winters in Paris rather trying; both of them left for the South of France a month ago. They're staying in a sort of convalescent home where, if it can be fixed up, Jenny will be under treatment till the spring. Poor things, they have more than their share of troubles and anxieties! My father hasn't changed—the less said about him the better. He's in Austria now, but as usual up to his neck in complications.

Dear old pal, it's suddenly come back to me—about *your* father. I'd meant to start this letter with a reference to his death. But somehow I hardly know how to talk to you about your bereavement. Still, when I think of what your feelings must have been, I sympathize most sincerely. For I'm almost certain it must have given you a terrible shock.

I've got to stop now. It's late, and I want to get this letter to the officer in charge of mail. I hope it reaches you safely, and promptly. Now there's one thing more. I've got to write it to you, old pal—on the off chance! Personally I can't get to Paris; I'm tied up here, with not a hope of getting leave. But Lunéville's only five hours away from Paris. I'm in their good graces here; the Colonel's set me to doing some decorative panels in the office—naturally! So I'm pretty free. They'll give me the day off, if you . . . No, I don't even want to dream of such a thing! As I said, I'm ready to accept and to understand *everything,* with no less love for my one true friend, my friend for life.

Daniel.

Jacques had read the eight sheets through without a break. He remained standing under the lamp, trembling, bewildered, deeply moved, his thoughts in a tumult. He was experiencing more than a swift renewal of his friendship—though this was strong enough to make him feel like taking the first train to Lunéville right off; there was something deeper, too: a brooding anguish rankling in a dark, acutely sensitive region of his emotions, on which he neither could nor would let in a ray of light.

He took a few steps, shivering less with the cold than with the fever of his ruffled nerves. He was still holding the letter. Moving back under the hideous stridence of the electric buzzer, he set to reading the letter again, as calmly as he could, from beginning to end. . . .

Half-past eight had just struck when he left the Gare du Nord. The air was keen and pure, the water in the gutters frozen, the sidewalks dry.

He was faint with hunger. A café in the Rue Lafayette caught his eye and, turning in, he sank heavily onto a seat. Without taking off his hat or even troubling to turn down the collar of his overcoat, he dispatched three hard-boiled eggs, a plateful of sauerkraut, and half a loaf of bread.

After satisfying his hunger, he drank two glasses of beer in quick succession, and glanced round the room. It was almost empty. Facing him, at a table on the other side, a woman, dark, broad-shouldered, and still young, was seated in front of an empty glass. The discreet, sympathetic glance she cast in his direction vaguely stirred him. She seemed too quietly dressed to be one of the professionals who prowl about the Paris railway stations. A beginner, perhaps. Their glances met. He looked away; at the least encouragement she would have come and joined him at his table. There was a look of sad experience on her face, yet with it a certain innocence, that had its charm. For a moment he was tempted, in two minds. She seemed a simple soul, very close to nature; and he was utterly unknown to her. It might soothe his nerves. . . . Now she was gazing at him boldly, perhaps guessing his quandary. He, however, took care not to catch her eye.

At last he made a move, paid the waiter, and went out quickly, without looking her way.

Out in the street the cold gripped him. Should he walk home? No, he was too tired. He went to the edge of the sidewalk, watched the traffic, and hailed the first empty taxi.

As it drew up beside the kerb, he felt a light touch on his elbow. The girl had followed him.

"Come to my place, if you feel like it," she murmured awkwardly. "It's in the Rue Lamartine."

Good-naturedly he shook his head, and opened the taxi door.

"Anyhow, please give me a lift, to 97 Rue Lamartine," she pleaded, as if she had some special reason for wanting to keep with him.

Grinning, the driver looked interrogatively at Jacques.

"Well, sir, is it 97 Rue Lamartine?"

She thought, or made as if she thought, that Jacques had consented, and jumped into the taxi.

"All right," Jacques said. "Make it Rue Lamartine."

The taxi began moving.

"Look here, what's the good of trying to snub me like that?" There was a warm resonance in the voice that went well with her appearance. Then, bending towards him, she added in a tender, soothing tone: "Why, boy, anyone can see you've had a hard knock!"

Gently she pressed him in her arms, and the soft warmth of her caress melted Jacques's reserve.

Yielding to the lure of being consoled, he half stifled a sigh, without replying. Then as if his silence and the sigh were a surrender, she hugged him tighter and, taking off his hat, drew his head onto her breast. He let her have her way. Then a wave of misery came over him and, without knowing why, he burst into tears.

"In trouble with the cops, ain't you?" she whispered. Her voice was trembling.

He was too dumbfounded to protest. But then it struck him that with his scratched cheeks and his trouser-legs caked in mud, he might well pass for a fugitive criminal in this dry, frost-bound Paris. He closed his eyes; that this woman of the streets should take him for a criminal gave him an exquisite thrill.

As before she read assent into his silence, and pressed his face passionately against her bosom.

Her voice changed yet again; grew alert, conspiratorial.

"Like to lie low for a while at my place?"

"No," he replied, without moving.

It seemed she was schooled to obey, even when she could not understand. After a moment's hesitation, she whispered:

"If you're short of cash, I can help you out."

This time he opened his eyes, sat up.

"What?"

"I've got three hundred and forty francs in there." She patted her little bag. "Like to have them?" In the vulgar voice there was a rather gruff, big-sisterly affection.

Jacques was so touched that he could not reply at once.

"Thanks," he murmured at last, shaking his head. "I don't need it."

The cab slowed down, and drew up in front of a low doorway in an ill-lit, deserted street. Probably, Jacques thought, she would ask him to come in with her. In that case—what?

The problem was quickly solved. She got up and, resting a knee on the seat, hugged Jacques for the last time.

"Poor kid!" she sighed.

Her lips groped for his mouth and pressed it fiercely as if to wrest its secret, taste the savour of a crime; then quickly she released him.

"Anyhow, don't go and get yourself copped, like a damn fool!"

She jumped out of the cab and slammed the door. Then she handed five francs to the driver.

"Take the Rue Saint-Lazare. The gentleman will tell you where to stop."

The car moved off. Jacques had just time to see the girl vanish down a lightless passage, without once looking back.

He was feeling dazed. He passed his hand over his forehead, let down the window. Cold, clean air fanned his cheeks; he drew a deep breath. Then, smiling, he bent forward to the driver.

"Take me to 4A Rue de l'Université, please," he called out gaily.

XIV

NO SOONER had the last mourners filed out of the graveyard than Antoine took a car to Compiègne on the pretext that he had orders to give the monument-mason. In reality he wished to avoid the crowd returning by the first train back. The five-thirty express would get him to Paris in time for dinner, and, with luck, he would travel back alone.

Luck was against him.

When, some minutes before the train was due, he stepped onto the platform, to his surprise he at once ran into the Abbé Vécard. It was all Antoine could do to conceal his vexation. The priest explained. "The Bishop was kind enough to bring me here in his car; he wanted to have a chat." Then he noticed Antoine's look of weariness and gloom. "I'm afraid, my dear Antoine, you must be quite worn out. Such a crowd and all those speeches! Yet, later on, you'll look back on this day as a very memorable occasion. What a pity Jacques wasn't present!"

Antoine was beginning to explain how, in the present circumstances, his brother's absence seemed to him natural enough, when the priest broke in.

"Yes, yes, I quite follow you. It was wiser he should stay away. But I do hope you'll let him know how—er—edifying the ceremony was. You'll do that, won't you?"

Antoine could not refrain from querying the term the priest had used.

" 'Edifying'? Well, for others, perhaps. But not for me. I assure you that all that pomp, all that eloquence-to-order . . .".

His eyes, meeting the priest's, found in them an understanding twinkle. Obviously he shared Antoine's views of the speeches they had heard that afternoon.

The train was coming in.

Noticing an empty car, they entered it, even though it was ill-lit.

"May I propose a cigarette, Abbé?"

Gravely the priest raised his forefinger to his lips.

"Tempter!" he smiled, taking a cigarette. Puckering his eyelids he lit it, puffed, withdrew it from his lips, and examined it with gusto as he blew the smoke out through his nostrils.

"In a ceremony of that kind," he continued good-humouredly, "there's always bound to be a side that is—as your friend Nietzsche would put it—human, all-too-human. And yet, when all that is discounted, the fact remains that such collective manifestations of the religious and moral sentiments have something that stirs our hearts, to which we can't help responding. Isn't that so?"

Antoine did not reply at once. Then, "I wonder!" he murmured dubiously. Again he fell silent, gazing pensively at the man in front of him.

For twenty years he had been familiar with the Abbé's placid countenance, the shrewd insistence of his gentle eyes, his confidential tone, the air of constant meditation given him by the poise of his head always drooping a little to the left, and the way he had of fluttering his hands at the level of his chest. But tonight he found that something had changed in their relations. Hitherto he had always thought of the Abbé Vécard in terms of M. Thibault—as his father's spiritual mentor. Now death had struck out the middle term. The reasons which formerly had led him to adopt a wise reserve in dealing with the priest had lost their cogency; now he could treat the Abbé as man to man.

After his trying day, he found it harder than usual to tone down the expression of his thoughts, and it was a relief for him to declare bluntly:

"Well, I must own that sentiments of that kind mean nothing, nothing whatever, to me."

The priest assumed a slightly bantering tone.

"Still, unless I'm greatly mistaken, the religious emotion has its place amongst human emotions, and indeed is recognized as fairly widespread in mankind. What's your opinion, my friend?"

Antoine was in no mood for trifling.

"I've never forgotten something Abbé Leclerc, my tutor when I was reading for my philosophy degree, once said to me. 'There are some quite intelligent people who have no feeling for art. You, I suspect, have no feeling for religion.' The worthy man was merely indulging in an epigram. But I've always thought that the remark was absolutely true."

"Supposing it were so," the Abbé replied, in the same tone of affectionate irony, "you'd be greatly to be pitied, I'm afraid! You'd be cut off from half of life. Yes, there are hardly any major problems of life of which it isn't true to say that a man who's unable to bring a religious sentiment to bear on them is doomed to see only a paltry

fraction. That's what makes the beauty of our religion. . . . Why do
you smile?"

Antoine could not think why he had smiled. Perhaps it was merely
a trick of the nerves, natural enough after the emotions of the past
week and the trying day he had been through.

"Come now!" The priest, in his turn, smiled. "Can you deny there's
beauty in our faith?"

"Of course not," Antoine cheerfully asserted. "I'll allow it all the
'beauty' you like," he added teasingly. "But, all the same . . ."

"Well?"

"All the same, beauty's not enough. It should be rational as well."
The Abbé's hands fluttered in amiable deprecation.

" 'Rational'!" The soft brooding tone suggested that the word conjured up a host of problems which, for the moment, he was not disposed to tackle, but to which he had the key. After some reflection
he went on in a more pugnacious tone:

"Perhaps you are one of those who fancy religion is losing ground
in the modern mind?"

"Frankly, I haven't a notion." Antoine's moderation surprised the
Abbé. "Very likely not. It's even possible that the activities of the
most modern minds—I'm thinking of the very men who are furthest
from dogmatic faith—tend indirectly towards assembling the elements
of a religion. Towards—how shall I put it?—bringing together concepts that, taken as a whole, would constitute an entity not so very
different from many Christians' idea of God."

The priest nodded. "How could it be otherwise, human nature
being what it is? Only in religion can a man find a compensation for
the lower instincts he discovers in himself. It is his only dignity. And it
is also the only solace for his griefs, his only source of resignation."

"You're right there!" There was a ring of irony in Antoine's voice.
"Men who set a higher value on the truth than on their peace of mind
are pretty rare. And religion is the supreme purveyor of peace of
mind. But you must forgive me, Abbé, if I remind you there are
others, in whom the desire to understand is more imperative than
the craving to believe. And such people . . ."

"Such people," the priest broke in, "cling to the cramped, precarious assurances of reasoning and the intellect; and never get beyond them. Well, we can only pity them—we whose faith lives and moves on another, infinitely vaster plane, the plane of feeling and volition. Don't you agree?"

Antoine's smile was non-committal. The light in the compartment was too dim for the priest to see it, but the fact that he proceeded to enlarge upon the theme showed he was not altogether dupe of the "we" he had just used.

"People think they're very enlightened nowadays because they insist on 'understanding' things. But believing is understanding. No, it would be better to say that there's no common ground between understanding and believing. Some today refuse to accept as true what their intellect, inadequately trained or warped by a subversive education, is unable to prove to its satisfaction. The explanation's simple: they are the victims of their limitations. It's perfectly feasible to understand God's existence, and to prove it logically. From Aristotle on— and we mustn't forget he was the master of Saint Thomas Aquinas— logical proof has never been lacking. . . ."

So far Antoine had refrained from any overt protest, but now the gaze he cast on the priest was frankly sceptical.

His companion's silence was making the Abbé ill at ease, and he hastened to continue. "Our religious philosophy, when dealing with these subjects, furnishes the most closely reasoned arguments. . . ."

"Excuse me," Antoine broke in at last, genially enough, "but are you sure you've the right to talk about 'religious philosophy' or 'closely reasoned arguments' in such a connexion?"

"What's that?" The priest sounded positively shocked. "Why shouldn't I have the right . . . ?"

"Well, for one thing, strictly speaking, religious 'thought' is usually a misnomer, for behind all thinking there lies doubt. . . ."

"Steady there, my young friend!" the Abbé cried. "Where's that theory going to lead us?"

"Oh, I know, the Church doesn't worry over trifles like that. But all the ingenious devices the Church has been applying, for a hundred years and more, to reconcile faith with modern science and philosophy are—if you'll forgive me the expression—more or less faked. Obviously so, since what keeps faith alive and is its object—the quality which appeals so strongly to the religious mind—is precisely that supernatural element which is denied by science and philosophy."

The Abbé was beginning to fidget in his seat; it was dawning on him that this was a serious argument. A note of petulance crept into his voice.

"You seem to overlook the fact that it's by dint of using their brains, by philosophical reasoning, that most of the younger generation nowadays come by faith."

"I wonder!"

"Your reasons, please!"

"Well, I must admit that I can't picture faith as anything other than a blind, intuitive acceptance. And when it claims to be founded on logic . . . !"

"Have you the old-fashioned notion that science and philosophy deny the supernatural? That's a mistake, my dear fellow—a glaring mistake. Science leaves it out, and that's a very different thing. As for philosophy, every philosophy worthy of the name . . ."

" 'Worthy of the name'! Excellent! That way all dangerous opponents are put out of court."

Ignoring Antoine's irony, the priest went on: "Every philosophy worthy of the name leads us inevitably to the supernatural. But let's go further; let's suppose your modern scientists contrive to show that there's a fundamental opposition between the 'laws' they have discovered and the teachings of the Church—an absurd, not to say Machiavellian hypothesis in the present state of our Christian apologetics—what would that prove, I ask you?"

"Ask me another!" Antoine smiled.

"Nothing at all!" the priest exclaimed with gusto. "It would merely show that the human intellect is incapable of co-ordinating its data, and that its progress is a blundering one at best; a fact," he added with a friendly chuckle, "which is no news to a good many of us.

"Come, Antoine, we're not living in Voltaire's time. Need I remind you that the victories which the so-called reason vaunted by your atheist philosophers scored over religion were but short-lived, illusive victories? Is there a single article of faith regarding which the Church has ever been convicted of defective logic?"

"Not one, I grant you willingly," Antoine broke in with a laugh. "The Church has always had the knack of holding its own in a tight corner. Your theologians are past masters in the art of inventing subtle, seemingly logical arguments that save them from being badgered very long by rationalist appeals to reason. Especially of recent years, I've noticed, they have been displaying a skill at the logic-chopping game that's positively staggering! Still, all that takes in only those who start off by wanting to be taken in."

"No, my friend. You may be sure that if the logic of the Church has always the last word that is because it's . . ."

"Shrewder, more persistent. . . ."

"No. More profound than yours. Perhaps you'll agree with me that the human intellect, left to its own devices, can achieve nothing better than elaborate structures of mere words, which leave the heart, the emotions, unsatisfied. Why should that be? It isn't only that there's a whole order of verities which seems to lie outside the field of normal argument, nor yet because the idea of God seems to transcend the possibilities of normal understanding. Above all—please mark well my words—it's because our reasoning faculty left to itself fails us here, can get no grip on these subtle problems. In other words, a real, lively faith has every right to insist on such explanations as may wholly satisfy the intellect; but our intellect itself must first submit to be schooled by Grace—for Grace enlightens the faculty of reason. The true believer does not merely set out, using his intellect to the utmost, in quest of God; he must also humbly offer himself to God, who is in quest of him. And when by dint of reasoning he has made his upward way into God's presence, he should divest himself of thought, and—how shall I put it?—lay himself open to receive within him the recompense of his quest, the God that he has sought."

After a pregnant silence Antoine rejoined: "Which is tantamount to saying that reasoned thought is not enough to guide us to the truth; we also need what you call Grace. That, I must say, is a very damaging admission."

His tone was such that the priest could not help exclaiming:

"Ah, I'm sorry for you indeed, Antoine! You're one of the victims of our times—a rationalist!"

"I'm . . . well, it's always hard to say just what one is. Still I admit I stand by the satisfactions of the intellect."

The priest's hands fluttered. "And by the blandishments of doubt, as well. It's a survival of the romantic era; that sense of glorious audacity—and Byronic anguish—tickles the vanity, of course."

"No," Antoine cried, "you're absolutely wrong there! I haven't the least sense of audacity or anguish, and I've no use for those muzzy states of mind you're thinking of. Nobody could be less romantic than I. And I don't suffer from 'soul-searchings,' as they call them." No sooner had he made the statement than he realized it was no longer strictly true. Doubtless he had no soul-searchings such as the Abbé Vécard had in mind—on the score of religion. But during the past three or four years he too had been apt to ponder, not without anguish, on the problem of man's place and function in the universe. After a while he added: "What's more, it would be wrong to say I've lost my faith; I rather think I never had it."

"Oh, come now!" the Abbé exclaimed. "Have you forgotten, Antoine, what a religious little boy you used to be?"

"Religious? No. Docile; serious and obedient, nothing more. I was naturally amenable to discipline, and I performed my religious duties like the good little boy I was! That's all."

"No, no! You're deliberately understating your faith in early years."

"It wasn't faith, but a religious upbringing, which is a very different thing."

Antoine was trying less to startle the Abbé than to be sincere. His weariness had given place to a mild exhilaration, which urged him to hold his own in the argument. And now he launched out into a sort of stock-taking, such as he had rarely made before, of his early life.

"Yes, it's a question of upbringing. And, Abbé, just consider how neatly it all links up together. From when he's four, his mother, his nurse, all the grown-ups on whom a child relies, keep dinning into his ears, on every pretext: 'God is in heaven; God made you, and He watches you; God loves you, sees you, judges you; God will punish you if you're naughty, reward you if you're good.' What next? When he's eight he's taken to mass and sees all the grown-up people round him bowing and kneeling; a beautiful gold monstrance is pointed out to him, gleaming amongst flowers and lights, across a haze of incense and music—and it's the same God who's present there, in the white Host. Right! What next? When he's eleven he is told about the Holy Trinity, the Incarnation, Redemption, Resurrection, Immaculate Conception, and all the rest of it—in a tone that carries conviction, from the august eminence of a pulpit. He listens, and believes all he is told. How should he not believe? How could he feel the least doubt about beliefs publicly avowed by his parents, school-fellows, masters, and by all the congregation in the church? How could a little boy like him question these holy mysteries? From the day he was born he's been coming up against equally bewildering phenomena; he is a small, lost waif in a mysterious universe. That, sir, in my opinion is a point of vital importance; in fact, it's the key to the whole problem. For a child everything is equally incomprehensible. The earth, which looks so flat, is round; it doesn't seem to move, yet it's spinning like a top. The sun makes seeds germinate; a live chick comes out of an egg. The Son of God came down from heaven, and died on the cross to redeem us from our sins. Why not? God was the Word, and the Word was made flesh. . . . It may mean something, or it may not. No matter! The trick has worked."

The train had just stopped. A voice in the darkness bawled the name of a station. Supposing the car empty, somebody opened the door hastily and slammed it to again, with a curse. A blast of icy wind buffeted their faces.

Antoine turned again towards the Abbé, but the light had grown still feebler and he could make little of his expression.

As the priest made no remark, Antoine continued, in a calmer tone:

"Well, can that childish credulity be described as 'faith'? Certainly not. Faith is something that comes later. It springs from different roots. And, personally, I can assure you I have never had it."

"It would be truer to say that, though the soil was well prepared for it, you never gave it a chance of springing up in your soul." The Abbé's voice was vibrant with indignation. "Faith is a gift from God— like the faculty of memory; and like memory, like all God's gifts, it requires cultivation. But you—you, like so many others, yielded to pride, to the spirit of contradiction, to the lures of 'free thinking,' to the temptation of rebelling against established order."

No sooner made, than the priest regretted his outburst, justified though it was. He was firmly resolved not to be drawn into a prolonged discussion of religion.

Moreover, the Abbé misinterpreted Antoine's tone. Struck by its incisiveness, its ardour, and the gay truculence which gave the young man's words an air of rather forced bravado, he preferred to question the speaker's absolute sincerity. He still entertained the utmost respect for Antoine, and behind it lurked a hope—more than a hope, a firm conviction—that M. Thibault's elder son would not long persist in such lamentable, indefensible opinions.

Antoine was pondering.

"No," he said composedly. "You're wrong there. It came about quite naturally; neither pride nor a rebellious spirit played any part. Why, I didn't even have to give it a thought. As far as I remember, I began, at the time of my first communion, to have a vague feeling that there was—how shall I put it?—that there was a catch somewhere in what we were taught about religion; a sort of murkiness, not only for us but for everyone, for the grown-ups as well. Even for our priests!"

The Abbé could not withhold a flutter of his hands.

"Don't imagine," Antoine explained, "that I doubted then, or have the least doubt now, as to the sincerity of the priests I've known, or their zeal—perhaps I should say, their need for zeal. But they certainly gave me the impression of men uneasily groping in the dark, uncertain of their bearings, and turning round and round those abstruse doctrines I've mentioned with an unconscious diffidence. They made assertions, yes. But what did they assert? What had been asserted to them. Of course, they had no actual doubts about those doctrines of which they were the mouthpiece. But deep down in their hearts did they feel quite so sure as their dogmatic tone implied? Well, somehow I couldn't convince myself they were so sure as all that. Do I shock you? We had, you see, another set of men to match them with—our masters. Those laymen, I confess, seemed to me much more at ease in their special field of learning, much more sure of their ground. Whether they expounded history, grammar, or geometry, they always gave us the impression that they knew their subjects from A to Z!"

The Abbé pursed his lips. "Before making a comparison, one must be sure the things compared are comparable."

"Oh, I'm not thinking of the subject-matter of their teaching; I have in mind only the angle from which those specialists approached their subjects. There was never anything evasive about their attitude, even when their knowledge happened to fall short; they made no secret of their doubts, or even of the blind spots in their learning. And that, believe me, inspired confidence; it ruled out the least suspicion of . . . of humbug. No, humbug isn't what I meant. Still I must admit that, in the next phase of my education, the more I came in contact with the priests at the Ecole, the less they inspired in me the feeling of security I had got from my lay teachers."

"If the priests under whom you studied had been true theologians, you'd have got an impression of perfect security from your intercourse with them." The Abbé was thinking of the professors of his seminary, of his studious youth unruffled by the faintest doubt.

Antoine did not seem to hear him. "Just think," he exclaimed, "what it means to a youngster, when he's turned loose, by gradual stages, on mathematics, physics, chemistry! Suddenly he discovers that he has all space, the universe, for his playground. And after that, religion strikes him as not only cramped, but false, illogical. Untrustworthy."

This time the Abbé drew back and stretched forth his arm. "Illogical? Can you seriously apply that term to it: illogical?"

"Yes!" Antoine retorted vehemently. "And I've just hit on something I hadn't realized before. You upholders of religion start out with a firm belief, and to shore up that belief you call in logic; whereas people like myself begin with doubt, indifference, and we take reason for our guide, not knowing where it will lead us.

"Of course," he went on at once with a smile, before the priest had time to put in a retort, "if you set to arguing it out with me, it will be child's play for you to prove I don't know the first word on the subject. I admit that right away. I've given very little thought to such matters; perhaps never so much as tonight. So you see I'm not trying to set up as a thorough-going rationalist. I'm only trying to explain why a Catholic upbringing has not prevented me from coming to my present state—a state of total unbelief."

"My dear fellow," the Abbé put in, with a slightly forced geniality, "your plain speaking doesn't shock me in the least. For I'm sure you're very far from being so black as you paint yourself! But go on; I'm listening."

"Well, I continued—like so many others—observing my religious duties all the same. With an indifference which I wouldn't acknowledge even to myself; a polite indifference. Even in later years I never settled down to a serious stock-taking of my beliefs. Most likely because at bottom I didn't attach enough importance to them. Yes, I was very far from the state of mind of one of my fellow-students who was taking the Applied Arts course; he said to me one day, after he'd been through a phase of soul-searching: 'I've given the whole bag of tricks a thorough look-over; take my word for it, boy, there's far too many loose ends, it doesn't hang together.' At that time I was just starting my medical course, and the break—or, rather, estrangement—had already come about. I hadn't waited for the semi-scientific studies of my first year to discover that one can't believe without evidence . . ."

"Without evidence!"

". . . and that we must dispense with any notion of immutable truth, since nothing should be considered 'true' except conditionally, until the contrary is proved. Yes, I continue to shock you! But, if you'll allow me to say so (in fact it's what I've been driving at all the time), I'm that unusual thing—that freak of nature, if you like—a natural, congenital sceptic. Yes, I'm built that way. I'm in sound health and, so far as I can judge, pretty level-headed. I've an active mind, and I've always got on perfectly well without a spark of mysticism. Nothing of what I know, nothing I've observed, warrants my believing that my childhood's God exists; and so far, I must confess, I've found I can do admirably without Him.

"My atheism and my mind developed side by side, so I've never had any allegiance to renounce. No, don't imagine for a moment that I'm one of those believers who have lost their faith, and in their hearts are always craving after God; one of those uneasy souls who make desperate gestures towards the heaven they have found empty. No, desperate gestures aren't in my line at all! There's nothing about a godless world that disturbs me; indeed, as you see, I'm perfectly at home in it."

The Abbé's hand waved a mild disclaimer.

Antoine repeated: "Perfectly at home. And that's been so for fifteen years."

He expected the priest's indignation to blaze up at once. But the Abbé said nothing for some moments, and merely shook his head composedly. At last he spoke.

"But, my dear man, that's pure materialism. Are you still at that stage? To listen to you, one would think you believe only in your body. It's as if you believed in only half—and what a half!—of your self. Happily, all that is merely on the surface; an outer shell, so to speak. You yourself don't realize that deep down in you is something vital and enduring, the influence of your Christian education. You may deny that influence; but it's the directive force of your existence."

"What can I reply? I can only answer you that I owe nothing to the Church. My temperament, ambitions, intellect, took form outside the pale of religion—I might even say in opposition to it. I feel as remote from Catholic mythology as from pagan mythology. I make no distinction between religion and superstition. To speak quite candidly, what remains to me of my Christian education is precisely— *nil!*"

"What blindness!" the Abbé exclaimed, with a quick uplift of his arms. "Can't you see that your whole scheme of life—your conscientiousness, your sense of duty, your devotion to the service of your fellow-men—gives your materialism the lie direct? Few lives imply more clearly the existence of God. No one has more strongly than you the feeling of a mission to fulfil. No one has a better sense than you of his responsibilities in this world. Well, isn't all that a tacit admission that you're under orders from above? To whom, if not to God, can you feel yourself responsible?"

Antoine did not reply at once, and for a moment the Abbé could think his argument had told. In point of fact, on Antoine's view, it was the merest moonshine. His scrupulous performance of his work did not necessarily imply the existence of God, or the value of Christian teachings, or any metaphysical truth. Was he not the living proof of it? Nevertheless he could not help recognizing, yet once again, that there was a baffling incompatibility between the extreme conscientiousness that inspired his conduct and his repudiation of any moral code. A man must love his work. Why that "must"? he wondered. Because man is a social animal, and it's up to him to do his best for the smooth running of society, for progress. "Up to him!" A gratuitous assumption, that; a question-begging postulate. Again there rose in his mind the query which he had put to himself so often, to which he had never found a satisfactory answer: What, then, is this authority that I obey?

"Oh, well," he murmured, "shall we call it conscience? The hallmark left on every one of us by nineteen centuries of Christendom. Perhaps I was over-hasty just now when I set down at *nil* the factor of my upbringing, or, rather, my heredity."

"No, my friend, what has survived in you is the holy leaven to which I was referring. Some day it will become active once more— till the whole is leavened! And then your moral life, which now is following its own course more or less against your wish, will find its proper sphere, its true meaning. No man can understand God when he is rejecting Him, or even while he is searching for Him. You'll see! One day you'll discover that, without wanting it, you've entered port. And then at last you'll know that it's enough to believe in God for everything to become clear, everything to fall into place."

"I grant you that," Antoine smiled, "readily enough. I'm aware that, oftener than not, our ailments create their own remedies; and I'm quite prepared to agree that the majority of people have such an instinctive, urgent craving to believe that they don't give much thought to whether what they believe deserves belief. They label 'truth' whatever their need for faith impels them to accept. In any case," he added in the tone of an aside, "I'm not easily to be convinced that most intelligent Catholics, and particularly priests who are men of learning, aren't pragmatists more or less, without their knowing it. What I find unacceptable in Christian dogma should be equally unacceptable to other cultivated men who think on modern lines. The trouble is, believers cling to their faith and, to avoid imperilling it, refrain from thinking things out. They take their stand on the emotional and ethical aspects of religion. And of course they've had it drummed into their heads so effectively that the Church has given an answer once for all to every possible objection, that they never think of looking into it for themselves. But excuse me—that's only by the way. What I wanted to say was that, however universal the craving to believe may be, that's not a sufficient justification for the Christian faith, cluttered up as it is with ancient myths and abstrusities. . . ."

"When one is aware of God," the priest said, "there's no need to 'justify' Him." For the first time his tone brooked no reply. Then leaning towards Antoine, with a friendly gesture, he went on: "The amazing thing is that it should be you, Antoine Thibault, of all people, who speak thus. In many Christian homes, alas, the children see their parents behaving, life going on, almost as if the God about whom they hear so much did not exist. But you—why, from your earliest childhood you could feel God's presence in your home, at every instant! You saw your late lamented father guided by God in everything he did."

There was a pause. Antoine gazed at the Abbé fixedly, as if he were trying to keep himself from speech. At last, through close-set lips, he muttered:

"Yes. And that's the trouble. I've never seen God except through the medium of my father." His attitude and tone expressed what he had left unsaid. Then, to cut short, he added: "But this is no day to dwell on that subject."

He pressed his forehead to the pane. "We're coming into Creil," he said.

The train slowed down, stopped. The lamp in the car came on brighter. Antoine hoped some passenger would enter; his presence would break off their conversation. But the platform seemed quite empty.

The train drew out.

After a longish silence, during which each man seemed lost in his private meditations, Antoine turned again towards the Abbé.

"The truth is there are at least two things that will always prevent me from returning to the Catholic fold. One is the matter of sin; I'm incapable, it seems, of feeling any horror of sin. The other is the question of Providence; I shall never be able to accept the notion of a personal God."

The Abbé said nothing.

"Yes," Antoine went on, "all that you Catholics call sin is, on my view, precisely all that is strong and vital—instinctive and . . . instructive! It's what enables us (how shall I put it?) to lay our hands on things. And to go ahead. No progress—oh, I'm not unduly hypnotized by that blessed word 'progress,' but it comes in handy—no progress would have been feasible had men always, in blind obedience, kept from sin. But that subject would lead us too far afield," he added, countering the priest's deprecatory gesture with an ironic smile. "As for the theory of a Divine Providence—no, I can't swallow it! If there's one theory that strikes me as absolutely indefeasible, it's that of the utter indifference of the universe."

The priest gave a start. "But surely even that science of yours, whether it wants to or not, has to take its stand on universal order.

(I deliberately avoid using the more correct term: a Divine Purpose.) Don't you see that if we ventured to deny that higher Intelligence which controls phenomena and whose signature is visible on all things here below; if we refused to admit that everything in nature has its purpose and all has been created to fit into a harmonious whole—don't you see it would be impossible to make sense of anything at all?"

"Well, why not admit it? The universe is incomprehensible for us. I accept that as a premiss."

"That 'incomprehensible,' my friend, is God."

"Not as I see it. I haven't yet succumbed to the temptation of labelling all I can't understand as 'God.' "

He smiled and fell silent for some moments. The Abbé watched his face, on the defensive. Still smiling, Antoine spoke again:

"In any case, for the majority of Catholics, their idea of the Divine resolves itself into the rather puerile conception of a paternal God, a small private deity who has his eye on each of us, who follows with sympathetic interest each flicker of the tiny flame of individual conscience, and whom each of us can perpetually consult in prayers beginning: 'Enlighten me, O Lord,' or: 'Merciful God, grant me Thy aid,' and the like.

"Please don't mistake me. I haven't the least wish to wound your feelings by cheap sneers at religion. But I can't bring myself to imagine how anyone can seriously think there is the slightest mental intercourse, the least exchange of question and answer, between any given man—a tiny by-product of universal life—or even this Earth of ours, a speck of dust amid how many myriad others, and the great Whole, the Scheme of Things. How can we ascribe to it such anthropomorphic emotions as paternal love and kindliness of heart? How can we take seriously the functions of the sacraments, the rosary, and—only think of it!—a mass paid for and celebrated for the special benefit of a soul provisionally interned in Purgatory? When you come to think of it, there's little real difference between these rites, these practices of Catholicism, and those of any primitive religion, the sacrifices and the offerings made by savages to their gods."

The Abbé was on the point of replying that there certainly existed a *natural* religion common to mankind; a fact which, as it happened, was an article of faith. But once more he held his peace. Huddled in his corner, his arms folded, his fingers tucked inside his sleeves, he was a figure of sage, mildly ironic patience, as he waited for the young man to conclude his tirade.

Moreover, they were approaching Paris; the train was already swaying upon the switches of the suburban lines. Across the misted panes the darkness glittered with pin-point lights.

Antoine, who had still something to say, made haste to continue: "By the way, sir, I hope you won't misconstrue certain terms I employed. I admit that I'm a mere amateur in metaphysics and I'm not in the least qualified to discuss such matters; still, I'd rather speak my mind out frankly. I talked just now about Universal Order and a Scheme of Things; but that was merely to talk like everyone else. Actually it seems to me that we've as many reasons to question the existence of a Scheme of Things as to take it for granted. From his actual viewpoint the human animal I am observes an immense tangle of conflicting forces. But do these forces obey a universal law outside themselves, distinct from them? Or do they, rather, obey—so to speak—internal laws, each atom being a law unto itself, that compels it to work out a kind of 'personal' destiny? I see these forces obeying laws which do not control them from outside, but join up with them, which do nothing more than in some way stimulate them. . . . And anyhow, what a jumble it is, the course of natural phenomena! I'd just as soon believe that causes spring from each other *ad infinitum,* each cause being the effect of another cause, and each effect the cause of other effects. Why should one want to assume at all costs a Scheme of Things? It's only another bait for our logic-ridden minds. Why try to find a common 'purpose' in the movements of atoms endlessly clashing and glancing off each other? Personally, I've often told myself that everything happens just as if nothing led to anything, as if nothing had a meaning."

The priest looked silently at Antoine, then lowered his eyes and remarked with an icy smile:

"That said, I doubt if it's possible for a man to sink lower."

Rising, he began to button his overcoat.

Antoine was feeling genuinely remorseful. "I hope you'll forgive me, sir, for telling you all this. This sort of conversation never leads to anything, and I can't think what came over me this evening."

They were standing side by side. The Abbé gazed sadly at the young man.

"You've spoken to me frankly, as a man speaks to his friend. For that, at least, I'm grateful."

He seemed on the brink of adding something. But the train was stopping.

"May I take you to your place?" Antoine suggested in a different tone.

"Thanks, that would be kind of you."

In the taxi Antoine said little; his mind was once again engrossed by the difficult problems of the immediate future. And his companion, who seemed in a brown study, was equally taciturn. When, however, they had crossed the Seine, the priest bent towards Antoine.

"You're—how old exactly? Thirty?"

"Nearly thirty-three."

"You are still a young man. Wait and see! Others have ended by understanding. Your turn will come. There are hours in every life when a man can't dispense with God; one hour especially, the most terrible of all, the last. . . ."

"Yes," Antoine mused. "That dread of death, how heavily it weighs on every civilized European! So much so that it more or less ruins his zest for life."

The priest had been on the point of alluding to M. Thibault's death, but checked the impulse.

"Can you imagine what it's like," he continued, "coming to the brink of eternity without faith in God, without discerning, on the further shore, an almighty, merciful Father stretching out His arms in welcome? Do you realize what it means, dying in utter darkness, without a single gleam of hope?"

"All that," Antoine put in briskly, "I know as well as you do." He too had been thinking of his father's death. After a momentary hesitation, he went on: "My profession, like yours, takes me to the bedside of the dying. I, perhaps, have seen more unbelievers die than you have, and I've such hideous recollections of those deathbeds, that I wish I could give my patients *in extremis* an injection of belief. I'm not one of those who feel a mystical veneration for the stoic's way of facing death. And, quite sincerely, I wish for myself that, at that moment, I may be open to all the consolations faith can give. I dread a death without hope as much as a death-agony without morphine."

He felt the priest's hand touch his; it was trembling a little. Probably the Abbé was trying to construe this frank admission as a hopeful sign.

"How right you are!" The priest squeezed Antoine's arm with a warmth that seemed almost akin to gratitude. "Well, take my advice, don't seal up every way of approach to this Consoler whose help you'll need, like all of us, one day. What I mean is: don't give up prayer."

"Prayer?" Antoine shook his head. "That blind appeal—to what? To that problematic Scheme of Things! To a deaf and dumb abstraction, that takes no heed of us!"

"Call it what you will, but that 'blind appeal,' believe me, *tells*. Yes, Antoine, whatever may be the name which for the moment you assign to it, whatever form this notion of an Immanent Will behind phenomena, a Law of which you have brief glimpses, may now take in your mind, you should, however much it goes against the grain, turn towards it—and pray. Ah, do anything, I implore you, anything rather than immure yourself in blank aloofness. Keep in touch with the Infinite, address it in whatever terms you can, even if for the moment there's no reciprocity, if you seem to hear no answering voice. Call it what you like—inscrutable mystery, impersonal force, immeasurable darkness—but pray to it. Pray to the Unknowable. Only pray! Don't disdain that 'blind appeal,' for to that appeal, as one day you will know, there answers suddenly a still small voice, a miraculous consolation."

Antoine said nothing. "Our minds," he thought, "are in water-tight compartments." But, realizing the priest was deeply moved, he decided to say nothing further that might wound his feelings. In any case, they had reached his house and the car was slowing up.

The Abbé Vécard took Antoine's proffered hand and clasped it. Before stepping out, he leaned forward in the darkness and murmured in a tone Antoine had not yet heard him use:

"The Catholic religion, my friend, is very different from what you think; believe me, it means far, far more than what you've been given to see of it up till now."